A POIROT
QUINTET

A POIROT QUINTET

including
THE MURDER OF ROGER ACKROYD
THE MYSTERY OF THE BLUE TRAIN
DUMB WITNESS
AFTER THE FUNERAL
DEATH ON THE NILE

by

Agatha Christie

COLLINS
St James's Place, London
1977

William Collins Sons & Co Ltd
London · Glasgow · Sydney · Auckland
Toronto · Johannesburg

First published 1977
© Agatha Christie 1926, 1928, 1937, 1937, 1953

ISBN 0 00 231645/5

Set in Baskerville
Made and Printed in Great Britain
by Richard Clay (The Chaucer Press) Ltd,
Bungay, Suffolk

CONTENTS

From Agatha Christie's Autobiography:

HOW POIROT CAME TO BE

It was while I was working in the dispensary that I first conceived the idea of writing a detective story. The idea had remained in my mind since my sister Madge's earlier challenge – and my present work seemed to offer a favourable opportunity. Unlike nursing, where there always was something to do, dispensing consisted of slack or busy periods. Sometimes I would be on duty alone in the afternoon with hardly anything to do but sit about. Having seen that the stock bottles were full and attended to, one was at liberty to do anything one pleased except leave the dispensary.

I began considering what kind of a detective story I could write. Since I was surrounded by poisons, perhaps it was natural that death by poisoning should be the method I selected. I settled on one fact which seemed to me to have possibilities. I toyed with the idea, liked it, and finally accepted it. Then I went on to the dramatis personae. Who should be poisoned? Who would poison him or her? Who? Where? How? Why? And all the rest of it. There would naturally have to be a detective. At that date I was well steeped in the Sherlock Holmes tradition. So I considered detectives. Not like Sherlock Holmes, of course: I must invent one of my own, and he would also have a friend as a kind of butt or stooge – that would not be too difficult . . .

I left it to develop, and turned my attention to the detective. Who could I have as a detective? I reviewed such detectives as I had met and admired in books. There was Sherlock Holmes, the one and only – I should never be able to emulate *him*. There was Arsène Lupin – was he a criminal or a detective? Anyway, not my kind. There was the young journalist Rouletabille in *The Mystery of the Yellow Room* – that was the *sort* of person whom I would like to invent: someone who hadn't been used before. Who could I have? A schoolboy? Rather difficult. A scientist? What did I know of scientists? Then I remembered our Belgian refugees. We had quite a colony of Belgian refugees living in the parish of Tor . . .

Why not make my detective a Belgian? I thought. There were all types of refugees. How about a refugee police officer? A retired police officer. Not too young a one. What a mistake I made there. The result is that my fictional detective must really be well over a hundred by now.

Anyway, I settled on a Belgian detective. I allowed him slowly to grow into his part. He should have been an inspector, so that he would have a certain knowledge of crime. He would be meticulous, very tidy, I thought to myself, as I cleared away a good many untidy odds and ends in my own bedroom. A tidy little man. I could see him as a tidy little man, always arranging things, liking things in pairs, liking things square instead of round. And he should be very brainy – he should have little grey cells of the mind – that was a good phrase: I must remember that – yes, he would have little grey cells. He would have rather a grand name – one of those names that Sherlock Holmes and his family had. Who was it his brother had been? Mycroft Holmes.

How about calling my little man Hercules? He would be a small man – Hercules: a good name. His last name was more difficult. I don't know why I settled on the name Poirot, whether it just came into my head or whether I saw it in some newspaper or written on something – anyway, it came. It went well not with Hercules but Hercule – Poirot. That was all right – settled, thank goodness . . .

THE
MURDER
OF
ROGER
ACKROYD

I

DR SHEPPARD AT THE BREAKFAST TABLE

Mrs Ferrars died on the night of the 16th-17th September – a Thursday. I was sent for at eight o'clock on the morning of Friday the 17th. There was nothing to be done. She had been dead some hours.

It was just a few minutes after nine when I reached home once more. I opened the front door with my latchkey, and purposely delayed a few moments in the hall, hanging up my hat and the light overcoat that I had deemed a wise precaution against the chill of an early autumn morning. To tell the truth, I was considerably upset and worried. I am not going to pretend that at that moment I foresaw the events of the next few weeks. I emphatically did not do so. But my instinct told me that there were stirring times ahead.

From the dining-room on my left there came the rattle of tea-cups and the short, dry cough of my sister Caroline.

'Is that you, James?' she called.

An unnecessary question, since who else could it be? To tell the truth, it was precisely my sister Caroline who was the cause of my few minutes' delay. The motto of the mongoose family, so Mr Kipling tells us, is: 'Go and find out.' If Caroline ever adopts a crest, I should certainly suggest a mongoose rampant. One might omit the first part of the motto. Caroline can do any amount of finding out by sitting placidly at home. I don't know how she manages it, but there it is. I suspect that the servants and the tradesmen constitute her Intelligence Corps. When she goes out, it is not to gather in information, but to spread it. At that, too, she is amazingly expert.

It was really this last named trait of hers which was causing me these pangs of indecision. Whatever I told Caroline now concerning the demise of Mrs Ferrars would be common knowledge all over the village within the space of an hour and a half. As a professional man, I naturally aim at discretion. Therefore I have got into the habit of continually withholding all information possible from my sister. She usually finds out just the same, but I have the moral satisfaction of knowing that I am in no way to blame.

Mrs Ferrars's husband died just over a year ago, and Caroline has constantly asserted, without the least foundation for the assertion, that his wife poisoned him.

She scorns my invariable rejoinder that Mr Ferrars died of acute gastritis, helped on by habitual overindulgence in alcoholic beverages. The symptoms of gastritis and arsenical poisoning are not, I agree, unlike, but Caroline bases her accusation on quite different lines.

'You've only got to look at her,' I have heard her say.

Mrs Ferrars, though not in her first youth, was a very attractive woman, and her clothes, though simple, always seemed to fit her very well, but all the same, lots of women buy their clothes in Paris, and have not, on that account, necessarily poisoned their husbands.

As I stood hesitating in the hall, with all this passing through my mind, Caroline's voice came again, with a sharper note in it.

'What on earth are you doing out there, James? Why don't you come and get your breakfast?'

'Just coming, my dear,' I said hastily. 'I've been hanging up my overcoat.'

'You could have hung up half a dozen overcoats in this time.'

She was quite right. I could have.

I walked into the dining-room, gave Caroline the accustomed peck on the cheek, and sat down to eggs and bacon. The bacon was rather cold.

'You've had an early call,' remarked Caroline.

'Yes,' I said. 'King's Paddock. Mrs Ferrars.'

'I know,' said my sister.

'How did you know?'

'Annie told me.'

Annie is the house parlourmaid. A nice girl, but an inveterate talker.

There was a pause. I continued to eat eggs and bacon. My sister's nose, which is long and thin, quivered a little at the tip, as it always does when she is interested or excited over anything.

'Well?' she demanded.

'A bad business. Nothing to be done. Must have died in her sleep.'

'I know,' said my sister again.

This time I was annoyed.

'You can't know,' I snapped. 'I didn't know myself until I got there, and haven't mentioned it to a soul yet. If that girl Annie knows, she must be a clairvoyant.'

'It wasn't Annie who told me. It was the milkman. He had it from the Ferrarses' cook.'

As I say, there is no need for Caroline to go out to get information. She sits at home and it comes to her.

My sister continued:

'What did she die of? Heart failure?'

'Didn't the milkman tell you that?' I enquired sarcastically.

Sarcasm is wasted on Caroline. She takes it seriously and answers accordingly.

'He didn't know,' she explained.

After all, Caroline was bound to hear sooner or later. She might as well hear from me.

'She died of an overdose of veronal. She's been taking it lately for sleeplessness. Must have taken too much.'

'Nonsense,' said Caroline immediately. 'She took it on purpose. Don't tell me!'

It is odd now, when you have a secret belief of your own which you do not wish to acknowledge, the voicing of it by someone else will rouse you to a fury of denial. I burst immediately into indignant speech.

'There you go again,' I said. 'Rushing along without rhyme or reason. Why on earth should Mrs Ferrars wish to commit suicide? A widow, fairly young still, very well off, good health, and nothing to do but enjoy life. It's absurd.'

'Not at all. Even you must have noticed how different she has been looking lately. It's been coming on for the last six months. She's looked positively hag-ridden. And you have just admitted that she hasn't been able to sleep.'

'What is your diagnosis?' I demanded coldly. 'An unfortunate love affair, I suppose?'

My sister shook her head.

'*Remorse*,' she said, with great gusto.

'Remorse?'

'Yes. You never would believe me when I told you she poisoned her husband. I'm more than ever convinced of it now.'

'I don't think you're very logical,' I objected. Surely if a woman committed a crime like murder, she'd be sufficiently cold-blooded to enjoy the fruits of it without any weak-minded sentimentality such as repentance.'

Caroline shook her head.

'There probably are women like that – but Mrs Ferrars wasn't one of them. She was a mass of nerves. An over-mastering impulse drove her on to get rid of her husband because she was the sort of person who simply can't endure suffering of any kind, and there's no doubt that the wife of a man like Ashley Ferrars must have had to suffer a good deal—'

I nodded.

'And ever since she's been haunted by what she did. I can't help feeling sorry for her.'

I don't think Caroline ever felt sorry for Mrs Ferrars whilst she was alive. Now that she has gone where (presumably) Paris frocks can no longer be worn, Caroline is prepared to indulge in the softer emotions of pity and comprehension.

I told her firmly that her whole idea was nonsense. I was all the more firm because I secretly agreed with some part, at least, of what she had said. But it is all wrong that Caroline should arrive at the truth simply by a kind of inspired guess-work. I wasn't going to encourage that sort of thing. She will go round the village airing her views, and everyone will think that she is doing so on medical data supplied by me. Life is very trying.

'Nonsense,' said Caroline, in reply to my strictures. 'You'll see. Ten to one she's left a letter confessing everything.'

'She didn't leave a letter of any kind,' I said sharply, and not seeing where the admission was going to land me.

'Oh!' said Caroline. 'So you *did* inquire about that, did you? I believe, James, that in your heart of hearts, you think very much as I do. You're a precious old humbug.'

'One always has to take the possibility of suicide into consideration,' I said impressively.

'Will there be an inquest?'

'There may be. It all depends. If I am able to declare myself absolutely satisfied that the overdose was taken accidentally, an inquest might be dispensed with.'

'And are you absolutely satisfied?' asked my sister shrewdly.

I did not answer, but got up from table.

2

WHO'S WHO IN KING'S ABBOT

Before I proceed further with what I said to Caroline and what Caroline said to me, it might be as well to give some idea of what I should describe as our local geography. Our village, King's Abbot, is, I imagine, very much like any other village. Our big town is Cranchester, nine miles away. We have a large railway station, a small post office, and two rival 'General Stores.' Able-bodied men are apt to leave the place early in life, but we are rich in unmarried ladies and retired military officers. Our hobbies and recreations can be summed up in the one word, gossip.'

There are only two houses of any importance in King's Abbot. One is King's Paddock, left to Mrs Ferrars by her late husband. The other, Fernly Park, is owned by Roger Ackroyd. Ackroyd has always interested me by being a man more impossibly like a country squire than any country squire could really be. He reminds one of the red-faced sportsmen who always appeared early in the first act of an old-fashioned musical comedy, the setting being the village green. They usually sang a song about going up to London. Nowadays we have revues, and the country squire has died out of musical fashion.

Of course, Ackroyd is not really a country squire. He is an immensely successful manufacturer of (I think) wagon wheels. He is a man of nearly fifty years of age, rubicund of face and genial of manner. He is hand and glove with the vicar, subscribes liberally to parish funds (though rumour has it that he is extremely mean in personal expenditure), encourages cricket matches, Lads' Clubs, and Disabled Soldiers' Institutes. He is, in fact, the life and soul of our peaceful village of King's Abbot.

Now when Roger Ackroyd was a lad of twenty-one, he fell in love with, and married, a beautiful woman some five or six years his senior. Her name was Paton, and she was a widow with one child. The history of the marriage was short and painful. To put it bluntly, Mrs Ackroyd was a dipsomaniac. She succeeded in drinking herself into her grave four years after her marriage.

In the years that followed, Ackroyd showed no disposition to make a second matrimonial adventure. His wife's child by her first marriage was only seven years old when his mother died. He is now twenty-five. Ackroyd has always regarded him as his own son, and has brought him up accordingly, but he has been a wild lad and a continual source of worry and trouble to his stepfather. Nevertheless we are all very fond of Ralph Paton in King's Abbot. He is such a good-looking youngster for one thing.

As I said before, we are ready enough to gossip in our village. Everybody noticed from the first that Ackroyd and Mrs Ferrars got on very well together. After her husband's death, the intimacy became more marked. They were always seen about together, and it was freely conjectured that at the end of her period of mourning, Mrs Ferrars would become Mrs Roger Ackroyd. It was felt, indeed, that there was a certain fitness in the thing. Roger Ackroyd's wife had admittedly died of drink. Ashley Ferrars had been a drunkard for many years before his death. It was only fitting that these two victims of alcoholic excess should make up to each other for all that they had previously endured at the hands of their former spouses.

The Ferrars only came to live here just over a year ago, but a halo of gossip has surrounded Ackroyd for many years past. All the time that Ralph Paton was growing up to manhood a series of lady housekeepers presided over Ackroyd's establishment, and each in turn was regarded with lively suspicion by Caroline and her cronies. It is not too much to say that for at least fifteen years the whole village has confidently expected Ackroyd to marry one of his housekeepers. The last of them, a redoubtable lady called Miss Russell, has reigned undisputed for five years, twice as long as any of her predecessors. It is felt that but for the advent of Mrs Ferrars, Ackroyd could hardly have escaped. That – and one other factor – the unexpected arrival of a widowed sister-in-law with her daughter from Canada. Mrs Cecil Ackroyd, widow of Ackroyd's ne'er-do-well younger brother, has taken up her residence at Fernly Park, and has succeeded, according to Caroline, in putting Miss Russell in her proper place.

I don't know exactly what a 'proper place' constitutes – it sounds chilly and unpleasant – but I know that Miss Russell goes about with pinched lips, and what I can only describe as an acid smile, and that she professes the utmost sympathy for 'poor Mrs Ackroyd – dependent on the charity of her husband's brother. The bread of charity is so bitter, is it not? *I* should be quite miserable if I did not work for my living.'

I don't know what Mrs Cecil Ackroyd thought of the Ferrars affair when it came on the tapis. It was clearly to her advantage that Ackroyd should remain unmarried. She was always very charming – not to say gushing – to Mrs Ferrars when they met. Caroline says that proves less than nothing.

Such have been our preoccupations in King's Abbot for the last few years. We have discussed Ackroyd and his affairs from every standpoint. Mrs Ferrars has fitted into her place in the scheme.

Now there has been a rearrangement of the kaleidoscope. From a mild discussion of probable wedding presents, we have been jerked into the midst of tragedy.

Revolving these and sundry other matters in my mind, I went mechanically on my round. I had no cases of special interest to attend, which was, perhaps, as well, for my thoughts returned again and again to the mystery of Mrs Ferrars's death. Had she taken her own life? Surely, if she had done so, she would have left some word behind to say what she contemplated doing? Women, in my experience, if they once reach the determination to commit suicide, usually wish to reveal the state of mind that led to the fatal action. They covet the limelight.

When had I last seen her? Not for over a week. Her manner then had been normal enough considering – well – considering everything.

Then I suddenly remembered that I had seen her, though not to speak to, only yesterday. She had been walking with Ralph Paton, and I had been surprised because I had had no idea that he was likely to be in King's Abbot. I thought, indeed, that he had quarrelled finally with his stepfather. Nothing had been seen of him down here for nearly six months. They had been walking along, side by side, their heads close together, and she had been talking very earnestly.

I think I can safely say that it was at this moment that a foreboding of the future first swept over me. Nothing tangible as yet – but a vague premonition of the way things were setting. That earnest *tête-à-tête* between Ralph Paton and Mrs Ferrars the day before struck me disagreeably.

I was still thinking of it when I came face to face with Roger Ackroyd.

'Sheppard!' he exclaimed. 'Just the man I wanted to get hold of. This is a terrible business.'

'You've heard then?'

He nodded. He had felt the blow keenly, I could see. His big red cheeks seemed to have fallen in, and he looked a positive wreck of his usual jolly, healthy self.

'It's worse than you know,' he said quietly. 'Look here, Sheppard, I've got to talk to you. Can you come back with me now?'

'Hardly. I've got three patients to see still, and I must be back by twelve to see my surgery patients.'

'Then this afternoon – no, better still, dine to-night. At 7.30. Will that suit you?'

'Yes, I can manage that all right. What's wrong? Is it Ralph?'

I hardly knew why I said that – except, perhaps, that it had so often been Ralph.

Ackroyd stared blankly at me as though he hardly understood. I began to realise that there must be something very wrong indeed somewhere. I had never seen Ackroyd so upset before.

'Ralph?' he said vaguely. 'Oh! no, it's not Ralph. Ralph's in London— Damn! Here's old Miss Gannett coming. I don't want to have to talk to her about this ghastly business. See you to-night, Sheppard. Seven-thirty.'

I nodded, and he hurried away, leaving me wondering. Ralph in London? But he had certainly been in King's Abbot the preceding afternoon. He must have gone back to town last night or early this morning, and yet Ackroyd's manner had conveyed quite a different impression. He had spoken as though Ralph had not been near the place for months.

I had no time to puzzle the matter out further. Miss Gannett was upon me, thirsting for information. Miss Gannett has all the characteristics of my sister Caroline, but she lacks that unerring aim in jumping to conclusions which lends a touch of greatness to Caroline's manœuvres. Miss Gannett was breathless and interrogatory.

Wasn't it sad about poor dear Mrs Ferrars? A lot of people were saying she had been a confirmed drug-taker for years. So wicked the way people went about saying things. And yet, the worst of it was, there was usually a grain of truth somewhere in these wild statements. No smoke without fire! They were saying too that Mr Ackroyd had found out about it, and had broken off the engagement – because there *was* an engagement. She, Miss Gannett, had proof positive of that.

Of course *I* must know all about it – doctors always did – but they never tell?

And all this with a sharp beady eye on me to see how I reacted to these suggestions. Fortunately, long association with Caroline has led me to preserve an impassive countenance, and to be ready with small non-committal remarks.

On this occasion I congratulated Miss Gannet on not joining in illnatured gossip. Rather a neat counter-attack, I thought. It left her in difficulties, and before she could pull herself together, I had passed on.

I went home thoughtful, to find several patients waiting for me in the surgery.

I had dismissed the last of them, as I thought, and was just contemplating a few minutes in the garden before lunch when I perceived one more patient waiting for me. She rose and came towards me as I stood somewhat surprised.

I don't know why I should have been, except that there is a suggestion of cast iron about Miss Russell, a something that is above the ills of the flesh.

Ackroyd's housekeeper is a tall woman, handsome but forbidding in appearance. She has a stern eye, and lips that shut tightly, and I feel that if I were an under housemaid or a kitchenmaid I should run for my life whenever I heard her coming.

'Good-morning, Dr Sheppard,' said Miss Russell. 'I should be much obliged if you would take a look at my knee.'

I took a look, but, truth to tell, I was very little wiser when I had done so. Miss Russell's account of vague pains was so unconvincing that with a woman of less integrity of character I should have suspected a trumped-up tale. It did cross my mind for one moment that Miss Russell might have deliberately invented this affection of the knee in order to pump me on the subject of Mrs Ferrars's death, but I soon saw that there, at least, I had misjudged her. She made a brief reference to the tragedy, nothing more. Yet she certainly seemed disposed to linger and chat.

'Well, thank you very much for this bottle of liniment, doctor,' she said at last. 'Not that I believe it will do the least good.'

I didn't think it would either, but I protested in duty bound. After all, it couldn't do any harm, and one must stick up for the tools of one's trade.

'I don't believe in all these drugs,' said Miss Russell, her eyes sweeping over my array of bottles disparagingly. 'Drugs do a lot of harm. Look at the cocaine habit.'

'Well, as far as that goes—'

'It's very prevalent in high society.'

I'm sure Miss Russell knows far more about high society than I do. I didn't attempt to argue with her.

'Just tell me this, doctor,' said Miss Russell. 'Suppose you are really a slave of the drug habit, is there any cure?'

One cannot answer a question like that off-hand. I gave her a short lecture on the subject, and she listened with close attention. I still suspected her of seeking information about Mrs Ferrars.

'Now, veronal, for instance—' I proceeded.

But, strangely enough, she didn't seem interested in veronal. Instead she changed the subject, and asked me if it was true that there were certain poisons so rare as to baffle detection.

'Ah!' I said. 'You've been reading detective stories.'

She admitted that she had.

'The essence of a detective story,' I said, 'is to have a rare poison – if possible something from South America, that nobody has ever heard of – something that one obscure tribe of savages use to poison their arrows with. Death is instantaneous, and Western science is powerless to detect it. Is that the kind of thing you mean?'

'Yes. Is there really such a thing?'

I shook my head regretfully.

'I'm afraid there isn't. There's *curare*, of course.'

I told her a good deal about curare, but she seemed to have lost interest once more. She asked me if I had any in my poison cupboard, and when I replied in the negative I fancy I fell in her estimation.

She said she must be getting back, and I saw her out at the surgery door just as the luncheon gong went.

I should never have suspected Miss Russell of a fondness for detective stories. It pleases me very much to think of her stepping out of the housekeeper's room to rebuke a delinquent housemaid, and then returning to a comfortable perusal of *The Mystery of the Seventh Death*, or something of the kind.

3

THE MAN WHO GREW VEGETABLE MARROWS

I told Caroline at lunch that I should be dining at Fernly. She expressed no objection – on the contrary.

'Excellent,' she said. 'You'll hear all about it. By the way, what is the trouble with Ralph?'

'With Ralph?' I said, surprised; 'there isn't any.'

'Then why is he staying at the Three Boars instead of at Fernly Park?'

I did not for a minute question Caroline's statement that Ralph Paton was staying at the local inn. That Caroline said so was enough for me.

'Ackroyd told me he was in London,' I said. In the surprise of the moment I departed from my valuable rule of never parting with information.

'Oh!' said Caroline. I could see her nose twitching as she worked on this.

'He arrived at the Three Boars yesterday morning,' she said. 'And he's still there. Last night he was out with a girl.'

That did not surprise me in the least. Ralph, I should say, is out with a girl most nights of his life. But I did rather wonder that he chose to indulge in the pastime in King's Abbot instead of in the gay Metropolis.

'One of the barmaids?' I asked.

'No. That's just it. He went out to meet her. I don't know who she is.'

(Bitter for Caroline to have to admit such a thing.)

'But I can guess,' continued my indefatigable sister.

I waited patiently.

'His cousin.'

'Flora Ackroyd?' I exclaimed in surprise.

Flora Ackroyd is, of course, no relation whatever really to Ralph Paton, but Ralph has been looked upon for so long as practically Ackroyd's own son, that cousinship is taken for granted.

'Flora Ackroyd,' said my sister.

'But why not go to Fernly if he wanted to see her?'

'Secretly engaged,' said Caroline, with immense enjoyment. 'Old Ackroyd won't hear of it, and they have to meet this way.'

I saw a good many flaws in Caroline's theory, but I forbore to point them out to her. An innocent remark about our new neighbour created a diversion.

The house next door, The Larches, has recently been taken by a stranger. To Caroline's extreme annoyance, she has not been able to find out anything about him, except that he is a foreigner. The Intelligence Corps has proved a broken reed. Presumably the man has milk and vegetables and joints of meat and occasional whitings just like everybody else, but none of the people who make it their business to supply these things seem to have acquired any information. His name, apparently, is Mr Porrott – a name which conveys an odd feeling of unreality. The one thing we do know about him is that he is interested in the growing of vegetable marrows.

But that is certainly not the sort of information that Caroline is after. She wants to know where he comes from, what he does, whether he is married, what his wife was, or is, like, whether he has children, what his mother's maiden name was – and so on. Somebody very like Caroline must have invented the questions on passports, I think.

'My dear Caroline,' I said. 'There's no doubt at all about what the man's profession has been. He's a retired hairdresser. Look at that moustache of his.'

Caroline dissented. She said that if the man was a hairdresser, he would have wavy hair – not straight. All hairdressers did.

I cited several hairdressers personally known to me who had straight hair, but Caroline refused to be convinced.

'I can't make him out at all,' she said in an aggrieved voice. 'I borrowed some garden tools the other day, and he was most polite, but I couldn't get anything out of him. I asked him point blank at last whether he was a Frenchman, and he said he wasn't – and, somehow, I didn't like to ask him any more.'

I began to be more interested in our mysterious neighbour. A man who is capable of shutting up Caroline and sending her, like the Queen of Sheba, empty away, must be something of a personality.

'I believe,' said Caroline, 'that he's got one of those new vacuum cleaners—'

I saw a meditated loan and the opportunity of further questioning gleaming from her eye. I saw the chance to escape into the garden. I am rather fond of gardening. I was busily exterminating dandelion roots when a shout of warning sounded from close by and a heavy body whizzed by my ears and fell at my feet with a repellent squelch. It was a vegetable marrow!

I looked up angrily. Over the wall, to my left, there appeared a face. An egg-shaped head, partially covered with suspiciously black hair, two immense moustaches, and a pair of watchful eyes. It was our mysterious neighbour, Mr. Porrott.

He broke at once into fluent apologies.

'I demand of you a thousand pardons, monsieur. I am without defence. For some months now I cultivate the marrows. This morning suddenly I enrage myself with these marrows. I send them to promenade themselves – alas! not only mentally but physically. I seize the biggest. I hurl him over the wall. Monsieur, I am ashamed. I prostrate myself.'

Before such profuse apologies, my anger was forced to melt. After all, the wretched vegetable hadn't hit me. But I sincerely hoped that throwing large vegetables over walls was not our new friend's hobby. Such a habit could hardly endear him to us as a neighbour.

The strange little man seemed to read my thoughts.

'Ah! no,' he exclaimed. 'Do not disquiet yourself. It is not with me a habit. But can you figure to yourself, monsieur, that a man may work towards a certain object, may labour and toil to attain a certain kind of leisure and occupation, and then find that, after all, he yearns for the old busy days, and the old occupations that he thought himself so glad to leave?'

'Yes,' I said slowly. 'I fancy that that is a common enough occurrence. I myself am perhaps an instance. A year ago I came into a legacy – enough to enable me to realise a dream. I have always wanted to travel, to see the world. Well, that was a year ago, as I said, and – I am still here.'

My little neighbour nodded.

'The chains of habit. We work to attain an object, and the object gained, we find that what we miss is the daily toil. And mark you, monsieur, my work was interesting work. The most interesting work there is in the world.'

'Yes?' I said encouragingly. For the moment the spirit of Caroline was strong within me.

'The study of human nature, monsieur!'

'Just so,' I said kindly.

Clearly a retired hairdresser. Who knows the secrets of human nature better than a hairdresser?

'Also, I had a friend – a friend who for many years never left my side. Occasionally of an imbecility to make one afraid, nevertheless he was very dear to me. Figure to yourself that I miss even his stupidity. His *naïveté*, his honest outlook, the pleasure of delighting and surprising him by my superior gifts – all these I miss more than I can tell you.'

'He died?' I asked sympathetically.

'Not so. He lives and flourishes – but on the other side of the world. He is now in the Argentine.'

'In the Argentine,' I said enviously.

I have always wanted to go to South America. I sighed, and then looked up to find Mr Porrott eyeing me sympathetically. He seemed an understanding little man.

'You will go there, yes?' he asked.

I shook my head with a sigh.

'I could have gone,' I said. 'A year ago. But I was foolish – and worse than foolish – greedy. I risked the substance for the shadow.'

'I comprehend,' said Mr Porrott. 'You speculated?'

I nodded mournfully, but in spite of myself I felt secretly entertained. This ridiculous little man was so portentously solemn.

'Not the Porcupine Oilfields?' he asked suddenly.

I stared.

'I thought of them, as a matter of fact, but in the end I plumped for a gold mine in Western Australia.'

My neighbour was regarding me with a strange expression which I could not fathom.

'It is Fate,' he said at last.

'What is Fate?' I asked irritably.

'That I should live next to a man who seriously considers Porcupine Oilfields, and also West Australian Gold Mines. Tell me, have you also a penchant for auburn hair?'

I stared at him open-mouthed, and he burst out laughing.

'No, no, it is not the insanity that I suffer from. Make your mind easy. It was a foolish question that I put to you there, for, you see, my friend of whom I spoke was a young man, a man who thought all women good, and most of them beautiful. But you are a man of middle age, a doctor, a man who knows the folly and the vanity of most things in this life of ours. Well, well, we are neighbours. I beg of you to accept and present to your excellent sister my best marrow.'

He stooped, and with a flourish produced an immense specimen of the tribe, which I duly accepted in the spirit in which it was offered.

'Indeed,' said the little man cheerfully, 'this has not been a wasted morning. I have made the acquaintance of a man who in some ways resembles my far-off friend. By the way, I should like to ask you a question. You doubtless know every-one in this tiny village. Who is the young man with the very dark hair and eyes, and the handsome face. He walks with his head flung back, and an easy smile on his lips?'

The description left me in no doubt.

'That must be Captain Ralph Paton,' I said slowly.

'I have not seen him about here before?'

'No, he has not been here for some time. But he is the son – adopted son, rather – of Mr Ackroyd of Fernly Park.'

My neighbour made a slight gesture of impatience.

'Of course, I should have guessed. Mr Ackroyd spoke of him many times.'

'You know Mr Ackroyd?' I said, slightly surprised.

'Mr Ackroyd knew me in London – when I was at work there. I have asked him to say nothing of my profession down here.'

'I see,' I said, rather amused by this patent snobbery, as I thought it.

But the little man went on with an almost grandiloquent smirk.

'One prefers to remain incognito. I am not anxious for notoriety. I have not even troubled to correct the local version of my name.'

'Indeed,' I said, not knowing quite what to say.

'Captain Ralph Paton,' mused Mr Porrott. 'And so he is engaged to Mr Ackroyd's niece, the charming Miss Flora.'

'Who told you so?' I asked, very much surprised.

'Mr Ackroyd. About a week ago. He is very pleased about it – has long desired that such a thing should come to pass, or so I understood from him. I even believe that he brought some pressure to bear upon the young man. That is never wise. A young man should marry to please himself – not to please a stepfather from whom he has expectations.'

My ideas were completely upset. I could not see Ackroyd taking a hairdresser into his confidence, and discussing the marriage of his niece and stepson with him. Ackroyd extends a genial patronage to the lower orders, but he has a very great sense of his own dignity. I began to think that Porrott couldn't be a hairdresser after all.

To hide my confusion, I said the first thing that came into my head.

'What made you notice Ralph Paton? His good looks?'

'No, not that alone – though he is unusually good-looking

for an Englishman – what your lady novelists would call a Greek God. No, there was something about that young man that I did not understand.'

He said the last sentence in a musing tone of voice which made an indefinable impression upon me. It was as though he was summing up the boy by the light of some inner knowledge that I did not share. It was that impression that was left with me, for at that moment my sister's voice called me from the house.

I went in. Caroline had her hat on, and had evidently just come in from the village. She began without preamble.

'I met Mr Ackroyd.'

'Yes?' I said.

'I stopped him, of course, but he seemed in a great hurry, and anxious to get away.'

I had no doubt but that that was the case. He would feel towards Caroline much as he had felt towards Miss Gannett earlier in the day – perhaps more so. Caroline is less easy to shake off.

'I asked him at once about Ralph. He was absolutely astonished. Had no idea the boy was down here. He actually said he thought I must have made a mistake. I! A mistake!'

'Ridiculous,' I said. 'He ought to have known you better.'

'Then he went on to tell me that Ralph and Flora are engaged.'

'I knew that too,' I interrupted, with modest pride.

'Who told you?'

'Our new neighbour.'

Caroline visibly wavered for a second or two, much as if a roulette ball might coyly hover between two numbers. Then she declined the tempting red herring.

'I told Mr Ackroyd that Ralph was staying at the Three Boars.'

'Caroline,' I said, 'do you never reflect that you might do a lot of harm with this habit of yours of repeating everything indiscriminately?'

'Nonsense,' said my sister. 'People ought to know things. I consider it my duty to tell them. Mr Ackroyd was very grateful to me.'

'Well,' I said, for there was clearly more to come.

'I think he went straight off to the Three Boars, but if so he didn't find Ralph there.'

'No?'

'No. Because as I was coming back through the wood—'

26

'Coming back through the wood?' I interrupted.

Caroline had the grace to blush.

'It was such a lovely day,' she exclaimed. 'I thought I would make a little round. The woods with their autumnal tints are so perfect at this time of year.'

Caroline does not care a hang for woods at any time of year. Normally she regards them as places where you get your feet damp, and where all kinds of unpleasant things may drop on your head. No, it was good sound mongoose instinct which took her to our local wood. It is the only place adjacent to the village of King's Abbot where you can talk with a young woman unseen by the whole of the village. It adjoins the Park of Fernly.

'Well,' I said, 'go on.'

'As I say, I was just coming back through the wood when I heard voices.'

Caroline paused.

'Yes?'

'One was Ralph Paton's – I knew it at once. The other was a girl's. Of course I didn't mean to listen—'

'Of course not,' I interjected, with patent sarcasm – which was, however, wasted on Caroline.

'But I simply couldn't help overhearing. The girl said something – I didn't quite catch what it was, and Ralph answered. He sounded very angry. "My dear girl," he said. "Don't you realise that it is quite on the cards the old man will cut me off with a shilling? He's been pretty fed up with me for the last few years. A little more would do it. And we need the dibs, my dear. I shall be a very rich man when the old fellow pops off. He's mean as they make 'em, but he's rolling in money really. I don't want him to go altering his will. You leave it to me, and don't worry." Those were his exact words. I remember them perfectly. Unfortunately, just then I stepped on a dry twig or something, and they lowered their voices and moved away. I couldn't, of course, go rushing after them, so wasn't able to see who the girl was.'

'That must have been most vexing,' I said. 'I suppose, though, you hurried on to the Three Boars, felt faint, and went into the bar for a glass of brandy, and so were able to see if both the barmaids were on duty?'

'It wasn't a barmaid,' said Caroline unhesitatingly. 'In fact, I'm almost sure that it was Flora Ackroyd, only—'

'Only it doesn't seem to make sense,' I agreed.

'But if it wasn't Flora, who could it have been?'

Rapidly my sister ran over a list of maidens living in the neighbourhood, with profuse reasons for and against.

When she paused for breath, I murmured something about a patient, and slipped out.

I proposed to make my way to the Three Boars. It seemed likely that Ralph Paton would have returned there by now.

I knew Ralph very well — better, perhaps, than anyone else in King's Abbot, for I had known his mother before him, and therefore I understood much in him that puzzled others. He was, to a certain extent, the victim of heredity. He had not inherited his mother's fatal propensity for drink, but nevertheless he had in him a strain of weakness. As my new friend of this morning had declared, he was extraordinarily handsome. Just on six feet, perfectly proportioned, with the easy grace of an athlete, he was dark, like his mother, with a handsome, sunburnt face always ready to break into a smile. Ralph Paton was of those born to charm easily and without effort. He was self-indulgent and extravagant, with no veneration for anything on earth, but he was lovable nevertheless, and his friends were all devoted to him.

Could I do anything with the boy? I thought I could.

On inquiry at the Three Boars I found that Captain Paton had just come in. I went up to his room and entered unannounced.

For a moment, remembering what I had heard and seen, I was doubtful of my reception, but I need have had no misgivings.

'Why, it's Sheppard! Glad to see you.'

He came forward to meet me, hand outstretched, a sunny smile lighting up his face.

'The one person I am glad to see in this infernal place.'

I raised my eyebrows.

'What's the place been doing?'

He gave a vexed laugh.

'It's a long story. Things haven't been going well with me, doctor. But have a drink, won't you?'

'Thanks,' I said, 'I will.'

He pressed the bell, then coming back threw himself into a chair.

'Not to mince matters,' he said gloomily, 'I'm in the devil of a mess. In fact, I haven't the least idea what to do next.'

'What's the matter?' I asked sympathetically.

'It's my confounded stepfather.'

'What has he done?'

'It isn't what he's done yet, but what he's likely to do.'

The bell was answered, and Ralph ordered the drinks. When the man had gone again, he sat hunched in the armchair, frowning to himself.

'Is it really – serious?' I asked.

He nodded.

'I'm fairly up against it this time,' he said soberly.

The unusual ring of gravity in his voice told me that he spoke the truth. It took a good deal to make Ralph grave.

'In fact,' he continued, 'I can't see my way ahead . . . I'm damned if I can.'

'If I could help—' I suggested diffidently.

But he shook his head very decidedly.

'Good of you, doctor. But I can't let you in on this. I've got to play a lone hand.'

He was silent a minute and then repeated in a slightly different tone of voice:

'Yes – I've got to play a lone hand. . . .'

—— 4 ——

DINNER AT FERNLY

It was just a few minutes before half-past seven when I rang the front-door bell of Fernly Park. The door was opened with admirable promptitude by Parker, the butler.

The night was such a fine one that I had preferred to come on foot. I stepped into the big square hall and Parker relieved me of my overcoat. Just then Ackroyd's secretary, a pleasant young fellow by the name of Raymond, passed through the hall on his way to Ackroyd's study, his hands full of papers.

'Good-evening, doctor. Coming to dine? Or is this a professional call?'

The last was in allusion to my black bag which I had laid down on the oak chest.

I explained that I expected a summons to a confinement case at any moment, and so had come out prepared for an emergency call. Raymond nodded, and went on his way, calling over his shoulder:

'Go into the drawing-room. You know the way. The ladies

will be down in a minute. I must just take these papers to Mr Ackroyd, and I'll tell him you're here.'

On Raymond's appearance Parker had withdrawn, so I was alone in the hall. I settled my tie, glanced in a large mirror which hung there, and crossed to the door directly facing me, which was, as I knew, the door of the drawing-room.

I noticed, just as I was turning the handle, a sound from within – the shutting down of a window, I took it to be. I noted it, I may say, quite mechanically, without attaching any importance to it at the time.

I opened the door and walked in. As I did so I almost collided with Miss Russell who was just coming out. We both apologised.

For the first time I found myself appraising the housekeeper and thinking what a handsome woman she must once have been – indeed, as far as that goes, still was. Her dark hair was unstreaked with grey, and when she had a colour, as she had at this minute, the stern quality of her looks was not so apparent.

Quite subconsciously I wondered whether she had been out, for she was breathing hard, as though she had been running.

'I'm afraid I'm a few minutes early,' I said.

'Oh! I don't think so. It's gone half-past seven, Dr Sheppard.' She paused a minute before saying, 'I – didn't know you were expected to dinner tonight. Mr Ackroyd didn't mention it.'

I received a vague impression that my dining there displeased her in some way, but I couldn't imagine why.

'How's the knee?' I inquired.

'Much the same, thank you, doctor. I must be going now. Mrs Ackroyd will be down in a moment. I – I only came in here to see if the flowers were all right.'

She passed quickly out of the room. I strolled to the window, wondering at her evident desire to justify her presence in the room. As I did so, I saw what, of course, I might have known all the time had I troubled to give my mind to it, namely, that the windows were long french ones opening on the terrace. The sound I had heard, therefore, could not have been that of a window being shut down.

Quite idly, and more to distract my mind from painful thoughts than for any other reason, I amused myself by trying to guess what could have caused the sound in question.

Coals on the fire? No, that was not the kind of noise at all. A drawer of a bureau pushed in? No, not that.

Then my eye was caught by what, I believe, is called a silver table, the lid of which lifts, and through the glass of which you can see the contents. I crossed over to it, studying the contents. There were one or two pieces of old silver, a baby shoe belonging to King Charles the First, some Chinese jade figures, and quite a number of African implements and curios. Wanting to examine one of the jade figures more closely, I lifted the lid. It slipped through my fingers and fell.

At once I recognised the sound I had heard. It was this same table lid being shut down gently and carefully. I repeated the action once or twice for my own satisfaction. Then I lifted the lid to scrutinise the contents more closely.

I was still bending over the open silver table when Flora Ackroyd came into the room.

Quite a lot of people do not like Flora Ackroyd, but nobody can help admiring her. And to her friends she can be very charming. The first thing that strikes you about her is her extraordinary fairness. She has the real Scandinavian pale gold hair. Her eyes are blue – blue as the waters of a Norwegian fiord, and her skin is cream and roses. She has square, boyish shoulders and slight hips. And to a jaded medical man it is very refreshing to come across such perfect health.

A simple straightforward English girl – I may be old-fashioned, but I think the genuine article takes a lot of beating.

Flora joined me by the silver table, and expressed heretical doubts as to King Charles I ever having worn the baby shoe.

'And anyway,' continued Miss Flora, 'all this making a fuss about things because someone wore or used them seems to me all nonsense. They're not wearing or using them now. That pen that George Eliot wrote *The Mill on the Floss* with – that sort of thing – well, it's only just a pen after all. If you're really keen on George Eliot, why not get *The Mill on the Floss* in a cheap edition and read it.'

'I suppose you never read such old out-of-date stuff, Miss Flora?'

'You're wrong, Dr Sheppard. I love *The Mill on the Floss.*'

I was rather pleased to hear it. The things young women read nowadays and profess to enjoy positively frighten me.

'You haven't congratulated me yet, Dr Sheppard,' said Flora. 'Haven't you heard?'

She held out her left hand. On the third finger of it was an exquisitely set single pearl.

'I'm going to marry Ralph, you know,' she went on. 'Uncle is very pleased. It keeps me in the family, you see.'

I took both her hands in mine.

'My dear,' I said, 'I hope you'll be very happy.'

'We've been engaged for about a month,' continued Flora in her cool voice, 'but it was only announced yesterday. Uncle is going to do up Cross-stones, and give it to us to live in, and we're going to pretend to farm. Really, we shall hunt all the winter, town for the season, and then go yachting. I love the sea. And, of course, I shall take a great interest in the parish affairs, and attend all the Mothers' Meetings.'

Just then Mrs Ackroyd rustled in, full of apologies for being late.

I am sorry to say I detest Mrs Ackroyd. She is all chains and teeth and bones. A most unpleasant woman. She has small pale flinty blue eyes, and however gushing her words may be, those eyes of hers always remain coldly speculative.

I went across to her, leaving Flora by the window. She gave me a handful of assorted knuckles and rings to squeeze, and began talking volubly.

Had I heard about Flora's engagement? So suitable in every way. The dear young things had fallen in love at first sight. Such a perfect pair, he so dark and she so fair.

'I can't tell you, my dear Dr Sheppard, the relief to a mother's heart.'

Mrs Ackroyd sighed – a tribute to her mother's heart, whilst her eyes remained shrewdly observant of me.

'I was wondering. You are such an old friend of dear Roger's. We know how much he trusts to your judgment. So difficult for me – in my position as poor Cecil's widow. But there are so many tiresome things – settlements, you know – all that. I fully believe that Roger intends to make settlements upon dear Flora, but, as you know, he is just a *leetle* peculiar about money. Very usual, I've heard, amongst men who are captains of industry. I wondered, you know, if you could just *sound* him on the subject? Flora is so fond of you. We feel you are quite an old friend, although we have only really known you just over two years.'

Mrs Ackroyd's eloquence was cut short as the drawing-room door opened once more. I was pleased at the interruption. I hate interfering in other people's affairs, and I had not the least intention of tackling Ackroyd on the subject of Flora's settlements. In another moment I should have been forced to tell Mrs Ackroyd as much.

'You know Major Blunt, don't you, doctor?'

'Yes, indeed,' I said.

A lot of people know Hector Blunt – at least by repute. He has shot more wild animals in unlikely places than any man living, I suppose. When you mention him, people say: 'Blunt – you don't mean the big game man, do you?'

His friendship with Ackroyd has always puzzled me a little. The two men are so totally dissimilar. Hector Blunt is perhaps five years Ackroyd's junior. They made friends early in life, and though their ways have diverged, the friendship still holds. About once in two years Blunt spends a fortnight at Fernly, and an immense animal's head, with an amazing number of horns which fixes you with a glazed stare as soon as you come inside the front door, is a permanent reminder of the friendship.

Blunt had entered the room now with his own peculiar, deliberate, yet soft-footed tread. He is a man of medium height, sturdily and rather stockily built. His face is almost mahogany coloured, and is peculiarly expressionless. He has grey eyes that give the impression of always watching something that is happening very far away. He talks little, and what he does say is said jerkily, as though the words were forced out of him unwillingly.

He said now: 'How are you, Sheppard?' in his usual abrupt fashion, and then stood squarely in front of the fireplace looking over our heads as though he saw something very interesting happening in Timbuctoo.

'Major Blunt,' said Flora, 'I wish you'd tell me about these African things. I'm sure you know what they all are.'

I have heard Hector Blunt described as a woman hater, but I noticed that he joined Flora at the silver table with what might be described as alacrity. They bent over it together.

I was afraid Mrs Ackroyd would begin talking about settlements again, so I made a few hurried remarks about the new sweet pea. I knew there was a new sweet pea because the *Daily Mail* had told me so that morning. Mrs Ackroyd knows nothing about horticulture, but she is the kind of woman who likes to appear well-informed about the topics of the day, and she, too, reads the *Daily Mail*. We were able to converse quite intelligently until Ackroyd and his secretary joined us, and immediately afterwards Parker announced dinner.

My place at table was between Mrs Ackroyd and Flora. Blunt was on Mrs Ackroyd's other side, and Geoffrey Raymond next to him.

Dinner was not a cheerful affair. Ackroyd was visibly preoccupied. He looked wretched, and ate next to nothing. Mrs Ackroyd, Raymond, and I kept the conversation going. Flora seemed affected by her uncle's depression, and Blunt relapsed into his usual taciturnity.

Immediately after dinner Ackroyd slipped his arm through mine and led me off to his study.

'Once we've had coffee, we shan't be disturbed again,' he explained. 'I told Raymond to see to it that we shouldn't be interrupted.'

I studied him quietly without appearing to do so. He was clearly under the influence of some strong excitement. For a minute or two he paced up and down the room, then, as Parker entered with the coffee tray, he sank into an arm-chair in front of the fire.

The study was a comfortable apartment. Book-shelves lined one wall of it. The chairs were big and covered in dark blue leather. A large desk stood by the window and was covered with papers neatly docketed and filed. On a round table were various magazines and sporting papers.

'I've had a return of that pain after food lately,' remarked Ackroyd calmly, as he helped himself to coffee. 'You must give me some more of those tablets of yours.'

It struck me that he was anxious to convey the impression that our conference was a medical one. I played up accordingly.

'I thought as much. I brought some up with me.'

'Good man. Hand them over now.'

'They're in my bag in the hall. I'll get them.'

Ackroyd arrested me.

'Don't you trouble. Parker will get them. Bring in the doctor's bag, will you, Parker?'

'Very good, sir.'

Parker withdrew. As I was about to speak, Ackroyd threw up his hand.

'Not yet. Wait. Don't you see I'm in such a state of nerves that I can hardly contain myself?'

I saw that plainly enough. And I was very uneasy. All sorts of forebodings assailed me.

Ackroyd spoke again almost immediately.

'Make certain that window's closed, will you?' he asked.

Somewhat surprised, I got up and went to it. It was not a french window, but one of the ordinary sash type. The heavy blue velvet curtains were drawn in front of it, but the window itself was open at the top.

Parker re-entered the room with my bag while I was still at the window.

'That's all right,' I said, emerging again into the room.

'You've put the latch across?'

'Yes, yes. What's the matter with you, Ackroyd?'

The door had just closed behind Parker, or I would not have put the question.

Ackroyd waited just a minute before replying.

'I'm in hell,' he said slowly, after a minute. 'No, don't bother with those damned tablets. I only said that for Parker. Servants are so curious. Come here and sit down. The door's closed too, isn't it?'

'Yes. Nobody can overhear; don't be uneasy.'

'Sheppard, nobody knows what I've gone through in the last twenty-four hours. If a man's house ever fell in ruins about him, mine has about me. This business of Ralph's is the last straw. But we won't talk about that now. It's the other – the other—! I don't know what to do about it. And I've got to make up my mind soon.'

'What's the trouble?'

Ackroyd remained silent for a minute or two. He seemed curiously averse to begin. When he did speak, the question he asked came as a complete surprise. It was the last thing I expected.

'Sheppard, you attended Ashley Ferrars in his last illness, didn't you?'

'Yes, I did.'

He seemed to find even greater difficulty in framing his next question.

'Did you never suspect – did it ever enter your head – that – well, that he might have been poisoned?'

I was silent for a minute or two. Then I made up my mind what to say. Roger Ackroyd was not Caroline.

'I'll tell you the truth,' I said. 'At the time I had no suspicion whatever, but since – well, it was mere idle talk on my sister's part that first put the idea into my head. Since then I haven't been able to get it out again. But, mind you, I've no foundation whatever for that suspicion.'

'He *was* poisoned,' said Ackroyd.

He spoke in a dull heavy voice.

'Who by?' I asked sharply.

'His wife.'

'How do you know that?'

'She told me so herself.'

'When?'

'Yesterday! My God! yesterday! It seems ten years ago.'

I waited a minute, and then he went on.

'You understand, Sheppard, I'm telling you this in confidence. It's to go no further. I want your advice – I can't carry the whole weight by myself. As I said just now, I don't know what to do.'

'Can you tell me the whole story?' I said. 'I'm still in the dark. How did Mrs Ferrars come to make this confession to you?'

'It's like this. Three months ago I asked Mrs Ferrars to marry me. She refused. I asked her again and she consented, but she refused to allow me to make the engagement public until her year of mourning was up. Yesterday I called upon her, pointed out that a year and three weeks had now elapsed since her husband's death, and that there could be no further objection to making the engagement public property. I had noticed that she had been very strange in her manner for some days. Now, suddenly, without the least warning, she broke down completely. She – she told me everything. Her hatred of her brute of a husband, her growing love for me, and the – the dreadful means she had taken. Poison! My God! It was murder in cold blood.'

I saw the repulsion, the horror, in Ackroyd's face. So Mrs Ferrars must have seen it. Ackroyd's is not the type of the great lover who can forgive all for love's sake. He is fundamentally a good citizen. All that was sound and wholesome and law-abiding in him must have turned from her utterly in that moment of revelation.

'Yes,' he went on, in a low, monotonous voice, 'she confessed everything. It seems that there is one person who has known all along – who has been blackmailing her for huge sums. It was the strain of that that drove her nearly mad.'

'Who was the man?'

Suddenly before my eyes there arose the picture of Ralph Paton and Mrs Ferrars side by side. Their heads so close together. I felt a momentary throb of anxiety. Supposing – oh! but surely that was impossible. I remembered the frankness of Ralph's greeting that very afternoon. Absurd!

'She wouldn't tell me his name,' said Ackroyd slowly. 'As a matter of fact, she didn't actually say that it was a man. But of course—'

'Of course,' I agreed. 'It must have been a man. And you've no suspicion at all?'

For answer Ackroyd groaned and dropped his head into his hands.

'It can't be,' he said. 'I'm mad even to think of such a thing. No, I won't even admit to you the wild suspicion that crossed my mind. I'll tell you this much, though. Something she said made me think that the person in question might be actually among my household – and that can't be so. I must have misunderstood her.'

'What did you say to her?' I asked.

'What could I say? She saw, of course, the awful shock it had been to me. And then there was the question, what was my duty in the matter? She had made me, you see, an accessory after the fact. She saw all that, I think, quicker than I did. I was stunned, you know. She asked me for twenty-four hours – made me promise to do nothing till the end of that time. And she steadfastly refused to give me the name of the scoundrel who had been blackmailing her. I suppose she was afraid that I might go straight off and hammer him, and then the fat would have been in the fire as far as she was concerned. She told me that I should hear from her before twenty-four hours had passed. My God! I swear to you, Sheppard, that it never entered my head what she meant to do. Suicide! And I drove her to it.'

'No, no,' I said. 'Don't take an exaggerated view of things. The responsibility for her death doesn't lie at your door.'

'The question is, what am I to do now? The poor lady is dead. Why rake up past trouble?'

'I rather agree with you,' I said.

'But there's another point. How am I to get hold of that scoundrel who drove her to death as surely as if he'd killed her. He knew of the first crime, and he fastened on to it like some obscene vulture. She's paid the penalty. Is he to go scot free?'

'I see,' I said slowly. 'You want to hunt him down? It will mean a lot of publicity, you know.'

'Yes, I've thought of that. I've zigzagged to and fro in my mind.'

'I agree with you that the villain ought to be punished, but the cost has got to be reckoned.'

Ackroyd rose and walked up and down. Presently he sank into the chair again.

'Look here, Sheppard, suppose we leave it like this. If no word comes from her, we'll let the dead things lie.'

'What do you mean by word coming from her?' I asked curiously.

'I have the strongest impression that somewhere or somehow she must have left a message for me – before she went. I can't argue about it, but there it is.'

I shook my head.

'She left no letter or word of any kind?' I asked.

'Sheppard, I'm convinced that she did. And more, I've a feeling that by deliberately choosing death, she wanted the whole thing to come out, if only to be revenged on the man who drove her to desperation. I believe that I could have seen her then, she would have told me his name and bid me go for him for all I was worth.'

He looked at me.

'You don't believe in impressions?'

'Oh, yes, I do, in a sense. If, as you put it, word should come from her—'

I broke off. The door opened noiselessly and Parker entered with a salver on which were some letters.

'The evening post, sir,' he said, handing the salver to Ackroyd.

Then he collected the coffee cups, and withdrew.

My attention, diverted for a moment, came back to Ackroyd. He was staring like a man turned to stone at a long blue envelope. The other letters he had let drop to the ground.

'*Her writing*,' he said in a whisper. 'She must have gone out and posted it last night, just before – before—'

He ripped open the envelope and drew out a thick enclosure. Then he looked up sharply.

'You're sure you shut the window?' he said.

'Quite sure,' I said, surprised. 'Why?'

'All this evening I've had a queer feeling of being watched, spied upon. What's that—?'

He turned sharply. So did I. We both had the impression of hearing the latch of the door give ever so slightly. I went across to it and opened it. There was no one there.

'Nerves,' murmured Ackroyd to himself.

He unfolded the thick sheets of paper, and read aloud in a low voice.

'*My dear, my very dear Roger, – A life calls for a life. I see that – I saw it in your face this afternoon. So I am*

38

taking the only road open to me. I leave to you the punish-
ment of the person who has made my life a hell upon earth
for the last year. I would not tell you the name, this after-
noon, but I propose to write it to you now. I have no
children or near relations to be spared, so do not fear
publicity. If you can, Roger, my very dear Roger, forgive me
the wrong I meant to do you, since when the time came, I
could not do it after all....'

Ackroyd, his finger on the sheet to turn it over, paused.

'Sheppard, forgive me, but I must read this alone,' he said
unsteadily. 'It was meant for my eyes, and my eyes only.'

He put the letter in the envelope and laid it on the table.
'Later, when I am alone.'

'No,' I cried impulsively, 'read it now.'

Ackroyd stared at me in some surprise.

'I beg your pardon,' I said, reddening. 'I do not mean read
it aloud to me. But read it through whilst I am still here.'

Ackroyd shook his head.

'No, I'd rather wait.'

But for some reason, obscure to myself, I continued to urge
him.

'At least, read the name of the man,' I said.

Now Ackroyd is essentially pig-headed. The more you urge
him to do a thing, the more determined he is not to do it. All
my arguments were in vain.

The letter had been brought in at twenty minutes to nine. It
was just on ten minutes to nine when I left him, the letter
still unread. I hesitated with my hand on the door handle,
looking back and wondering if there was anything I had left
undone. I could think of nothing. With a shake of the head I
passed out and closed the door behind me.

I was startled by seeing the figure of Parker close at hand.
He looked embarrassed, and it occurred to me that he might
have been listening at the door.

What a fat, smug, oily face the man had, and surely there
was something decidedly shifty in his eye.

'Mr Ackroyd particularly does not want to be disturbed,'
I said coldly. 'He told me to tell you so.'

'Quite so, sir. I – I fancied I heard the bell ring.'

This was such a palpable untruth that I did not trouble to
reply. Preceding me to the hall, Parker helped me on with my
overcoat, and I stepped out into the night. The moon was
overcast and everything seemed very dark and still.

The village church clock chimed nine o'clock as I passed through the lodge gates. I turned to the left towards the village, and almost cannoned into a man coming in the opposite direction.

'This the way to Fernly Park, mister?' asked the stranger in a hoarse voice.

I looked at him. He was wearing a hat pulled down over his eyes, and his coat collar turned up. I could see little or nothing of his face, but he seemed a young fellow. The voice was rough and uneducated.

'These are the lodge gates here,' I said.

'Thank you, mister.' He paused, and then added, quite unnecessarily, 'I'm a stranger in these parts, you see.'

He went on, passing through the gates as I turned to look after him.

The odd thing was that his voice reminded me of someone's voice that I knew, but whose it was I could not think.

Ten minutes later I was at home once more. Caroline was full of curiosity to know why I had returned so early. I had to make up a slightly fictitious account of the evening in order to satisfy her, and I had an uneasy feeling that she saw through the transparent device.

At ten o'clock I rose, yawned, and suggested bed. Caroline acquiesced.

It was Friday night, and on Friday night I wind the clocks. I did it as usual, whilst Caroline satisfied herself that the servants had locked up the kitchen properly.

It was a quarter past ten as we went up the stair. I had just reached the top when the telephone rang in the hall below.

'Mrs Bates,' said Caroline immediately.

'I'm afraid so,' I said ruefully.

I ran down the stairs and took up the receiver.

'What?' I said. '*What?* Certainly, I'll come at once.'

I ran upstairs, caught up my bag, and stuffed a few extra dressings into it.

'Parker telephoning,' I shouted to Caroline, 'from Fernly. They've just found Roger Ackroyd murdered.'

5

MURDER

I got out the car in next to no time, and drove rapidly to Fernly. Jumping out, I pulled the bell impatiently. There was some delay in answering, and I rang again.

Then I heard the rattle of the chain and Parker, his impassivity of countenance quite unmoved, stood in the open doorway.

I pushed past him into the hall.

'Where is he?' I demanded sharply.

'I beg your pardon, sir?'

'Your master. Mr Ackroyd. Don't stand there staring at me, man. Have you notified the police?'

'The police, sir? Did you say the police?' Parker stared at me as though I were a ghost.

'What's the matter with you, Parker? If, as you say, your master has been murdered—'

A gasp broke from Parker.

'The master? Murdered? Impossible, sir!'

It was my turn to stare.

'Didn't you telephone to me, not five minutes ago, and tell me that Mr Ackroyd had been found murdered?'

'Me, sir? Oh! no indeed, sir. I wouldn't dream of doing such a thing.'

'Do you mean to say it's all a hoax? That there's nothing the matter with Mr Ackroyd?'

'Excuse me, sir, did the person telephoning use my name?'

'I'll give you the exact words I heard. *"Is that Dr Sheppard? Parker, the butler at Fernly, speaking. Will you please come at once, sir. Mr Ackroyd has been murdered."* '

Parker and I stared at each other blankly.

'A very wicked joke to play, sir,' he said at last, in a shocked tone. 'Fancy saying a thing like that.'

'Where is Mr Ackroyd?' I asked suddenly.

'Still in the study, I fancy, sir. The ladies have gone to bed, and Major Blunt and Mr Raymond are in the billiard room.'

'I think I'll just look in and see him for a minute,' I said. 'I know he didn't want to be disturbed again, but this odd practical joke has made me uneasy. I'd just like to satisfy myself that he's all right.'

'Quite so, sir. It makes me feel quite uneasy myself. If you don't object to my accompanying you as far as the door, sir—?'

'Not at all,' I said. 'Come along.'

I passed through the door on the right, Parker on my heels, traversed the little lobby where a small flight of stairs led upstairs to Ackroyd's bedroom, and tapped on the study door.

There was no answer. I turned the handle, but the door was locked.

'Allow me, sir,' said Parker.

Very nimbly, for a man of his build, he dropped on one knee and applied his eye to the keyhole.

'Key is in the lock all right, sir,' he said, rising. 'On the inside. Mr Ackroyd must have locked himself in and possibly just dropped off to sleep.'

I bent down and verified Parker's statement.

'It seems all right,' I said, 'but, all the same, Parker, I'm going to wake your master up. I shouldn't be satisfied to go home without hearing from his own lips that he's quite all right.'

So saying, I rattled the handle and called out, 'Ackroyd, Ackroyd, just a minute.'

But still there was no answer. I glanced over my shoulder.

'I don't want to alarm the household,' I said hesitatingly.

Parker went across and shut the door from the big hall through which we had come.

'I think that will be all right now, sir. The billiard room is at the other side of the house, and so are the kitchen quarters and the ladies' bedrooms.'

I nodded comprehendingly. Then I banged once more frantically on the door, and stooping down, fairly bawled through the keyhole:

'Ackroyd, Ackroyd! It's Sheppard. Let me in.'

And still – silence. Not a sign of life from within the locked room. Parker and I glanced at each other.

'Look here, Parker,' I said, 'I'm going to break this door in – or rather, we are. I'll take the responsibility.'

'If you say so, sir,' said Parker, rather doubtfully.

'I do say so. I'm seriously alarmed about Mr Ackroyd.'

I looked round the small lobby and picked up a heavy oak chair. Parker and I held it between us and advanced to the assault. Once, twice, and three times we hurled it against the lock. At the third blow it gave, and we staggered into the room.

Ackroyd was sitting as I had left him in the armchair before the fire. His head had fallen sideways, and clearly visible, just below the collar of his coat, was a shining piece of twisted metalwork.

Parker and I advanced till we stood over the recumbent figure. I heard the butler draw in his breath with a sharp hiss.

'Stabbed from be'ind,' he murmured. ' 'Orrible!'

He wiped his moist brow with his handkerchief, then stretched out a gingerly hand towards the hilt of the dagger.

'You mustn't touch that,' I said sharply. 'Go at once to the telephone and ring up the police station. Inform them of what has happened. Then tell Mr Raymond and Major Blunt.'

'Very good, sir.'

Parker hurried away, still wiping his perspiring brow.

I did what little had to be done. I was careful not to disturb the position of the body, and not to handle the dagger at all. No object was to be attained by moving it. Ackroyd had clearly been dead some little time.

Then I heard young Raymond's voice, horror-stricken and incredulous, outside.

'What do you say? Oh! impossible! Where's the doctor?'

He appeared impetuously in the doorway, then stopped dead, his face very white. A hand put him aside, and Hector Blunt came past him into the room.

'My God!' said Raymond from behind him; 'it's true, then.'

Blunt came straight on till he reached the chair. He bent over the body, and I thought that, like Parker, he was going to lay hold of the dagger hilt. I drew him back with one hand.

'Nothing must be moved,' I explained. 'The police must see him exactly as he is now.'

Blunt nodded in instant comprehension. His face was expressionless as ever, but I thought I detected signs of emotion beneath the stolid mask. Geoffrey Raymond had joined us now, and stood peering over Blunt's shoulder at the body.

'This is terrible,' he said in a low voice.

He had regained his composure, but as he took off the pince-nez he habitually wore and polished them I observed that his hand was shaking.

'Robbery, I suppose,' he said. 'How did the fellow get in? Through the window? Has anything been taken?'

He went towards the desk.

'You think it's burglary?' I said slowly.

'What else could it be? There's no question of suicide, I suppose?'

'No man could stab himself in such a way,' I said confidently. 'It's murder right enough. But with what motive?'

'Roger hadn't an enemy in the world,' said Blunt quietly. 'Must have been burglars. But what was the thief after? Nothing seems to be disarranged?'

He looked round the room. Raymond was still sorting the papers on the desk.

'There seems nothing missing, and none of the drawers show signs of having been tampered with,' the secretary observed at last. 'It's very mysterious.'

Blunt made a slight motion with his head.

'There are some letters on the floor here,' he said.

I looked down. Three or four letters still lay where Ackroyd had dropped them earlier in the evening.

But the blue envelope containing Mrs Ferrars's letter had disappeared. I half opened my mouth to speak, but at that moment the sound of a bell pealed through the house. There was a confused murmur of voices in the hall, and then Parker appeared with our local inspector and a police constable.

'Good-evening, gentlemen,' said the inspector. 'I'm terribly sorry for this! A good kind gentleman like Mr Ackroyd. The butler says it is murder. No possibility of accident or suicide, doctor?'

'None whatever,' I said.

'Ah! A bad business.'

He came and stood over the body.

'Been moved at all?' he asked sharply.

'Beyond making certain that life was extinct – an easy matter – I have not disturbed the body in any way.'

'Ah! And everything points to the murderer having got clear away – for the moment, that is. Now then, let me hear all about it. Who found the body?'

I explained the circumstances carefully.

'A telephone message, you say? From the butler?'

'A message that I never sent,' declared Parker earnestly. 'I've not been near the telephone the whole evening. The others can bear me out that I haven't.'

'Very odd, that. Did it sound like Parker's voice, doctor?'

'Well – I can't say I noticed. I took it for granted, you see.'

'Naturally. Well, you got up here, broke in the door, and found poor Mr Ackroyd like this. How long should you say he had been dead, doctor?'

'Half an hour at least – perhaps longer,' I said.

'The door was locked on the inside, you say? What about the window?'

'I myself closed and bolted it earlier in the evening at Mr Ackroyd's request.'

The inspector strode across to it and threw back the curtains.

'Well, it's open now, anyway,' he remarked.

True enough, the window was open, the lower sash being raised to its fullest extent.

The inspector produced a pocket torch and flashed it along the sill outside.

'This is the way he went all right,' he remarked, '*and* got in. See here.'

In the light of the powerful torch, several clearly defined footmarks could be seen. They seemed to be those of shoes with rubber studs in the soles. One particularly clear one pointed inwards, another, slightly overlapping it, ponted outwards.

'Plain as a pikestaff,' said the inspector. 'Any valuables missing?'

Geoffrey Raymond shook his head.

'Not so far that we can discover. Mr Ackroyd never kept anything of particular value in this room.'

'H'm,' said the inspector. 'Man found an open window. Climbed in, saw Mr Ackroyd sitting there — maybe he'd fallen asleep. Man stabbed him from behind, then lost his nerve and made off. But he's left his tracks pretty clearly. We ought to get hold of *him* without much difficulty. No suspicious strangers been hanging about anywhere?'

'Oh!' I said suddenly.

'What is it, doctor?'

'I met a man this evening — just as I was turning out of the gate. He asked me the way to Fernly Park.'

'What time would that be?'

'Just nine o'clock. I heard it chime the hour as I was turning out of the gate.'

'Can you describe him?'

I did so to the best of my ability.

The inspector turned to the butler.

'Anyone answering that description come to the front door?'

'No, sir. No one has been to the house at all this evening.'

'What about the back?'

'I don't think so, sir, but I'll make inquiries.'

He moved towards the door, but the inspector held up a large hand.

45

'No, thanks. I'll do my own inquiring. But first of all I want to fix the times a little more clearly. When was Mr Ackroyd last seen alive?'

'Probably by me,' I said, 'when I left at – let me see – about ten minutes to nine. He told me that he didn't wish to be disturbed, and I repeated the order to Parker.'

'Just so, sir,' said Parker respectfully.

'Mr Ackroyd was certainly alive at half-past nine,' put in Raymond, 'for I heard his voice in here talking.'

'Who was he talking to?'

'That I don't know. Of course, at the time I took it for granted that it was Dr Sheppard who was with him. I wanted to ask him a question about some papers I was engaged upon, but when I heard the voices I remembered that he had said he wanted to talk to Dr Sheppard without being disturbed, and I went away again. But now it seems that the doctor had already left?'

I nodded.

'I was at home by a quarter past nine,' I said. 'I didn't go out again until I received the telephone call.'

'Who could have been with him at half-past nine?' queried the inspector. 'It wasn't you, Mr – er—'

'Major Blunt,' I said.

'Major Hector Blunt?' asked the inspector, a respectful tone creeping into his voice.

Blunt merely jerked his head affirmatively.

'I think we've seen you down here before, sir,' said the inspector. 'I didn't recognise you for the moment, but you were staying with Mr Ackroyd a year ago last May.'

'June,' corrected Blunt.

'Just so, June it was. Now, as I was saying, it wasn't you with Mr Ackroyd at nine-thirty this evening?'

Blunt shook his head.

'Never saw him after dinner,' he volunteered.

The inspector turned once more to Raymond.

'You didn't overhear any of the conversation going on, did you, sir?'

'I did catch just a fragment of it,' said the secretary, 'and, supposing as I did that it was Dr Sheppard who was with Mr Ackroyd, that fragment struck me as distinctly odd. As far as I can remember, the exact words were these. Mr Ackroyd was speaking. "The calls on my purse have been so frequent of late" – that is what he was saying – "of late, that I fear it is impossible for me to accede to your request. . . ." I went away again at once, of course, so I did not hear any more. But I rather wondered because Dr Sheppard—'

'—Does not ask for loans for himself or subscriptions for others,' I finished.

'A demand for money,' said the inspector musingly. 'It may be that here we have a very important clue.' He turned to the butler. 'You say, Parker, that nobody was admitted by the front door this evening?'

'That's what I say, sir.'

'Then it seems almost certain that Mr Ackroyd himself must have admitted this stranger. But I don't quite see—'

The inspector went into a kind of day-dream for some minutes.

'One thing's clear,' he said at length, rousing himself from his absorption, 'Mr Ackroyd was alive and well at nine-thirty. That is the last moment at which he is known to have been alive.'

Parker gave vent to an apologetic cough which brought the inspector's eyes on him at once.

'Well?' he said sharply.

'If you'll excuse me, sir, Miss Flora saw him after that.'

'Miss Flora?'

'Yes, sir. About a quarter to ten that would be. It was after that that she told me Mr Ackroyd wasn't to be disturbed again tonight.'

'Did he send her to you with that message?'

'Not exactly, sir. I was bringing a tray with soda and whisky when Miss Flora, who was just coming out of this room, stopped me and said her uncle didn't want to be disturbed.'

The inspector looked at the butler with rather closer attention than he had bestowed on him up to now.

'You'd already been told that Mr Ackroyd didn't want to be disturbed, hadn't you?'

Parker began to stammer. His hands shook.

'Yes, sir. Yes, sir. Quite so, sir.'

'And yet you were proposing to do so?'

'I'd forgotten, sir. At least I mean, I always bring the whisky and soda about that time, sir, and ask if there's anything more, and I thought – well, I was doing as usual without thinking.'

It was at this moment that it began to dawn upon me that Parker was most suspiciously flustered. The man was shaking and twitching all over.

'H'm,' said the inspector. 'I must see Miss Ackroyd at once. For the moment we'll leave this room exactly as it is. I can return here after I've heard what Miss Ackroyd has to tell me. I shall just take the precaution of shutting and bolting the window.'

This precaution accomplished, he led the way into the hall and we followed him. He paused a moment, as he glanced up at the little staircase, then spoke over his shoulder to the constable.

'Jones, you'd better stay here. Don't let anyone go into that room.'

Parker interposed deferentially.

'If you'll excuse me, sir. If you were to lock the door into the main hall, nobody could gain access to this part. That staircase leads only to Mr Ackroyd's bedroom and bathroom. There is no communication with the other part of the house. There once was a door through, but Mr Ackroyd had it blocked up. He liked to feel that his suite was entirely private.'

To make things clear and explain the position, I have appended a rough sketch of the right-hand wing of the house. The small staircase leads, as Parker explained, to a big bedroom made by two being knocked into one, and an adjoining bathroom and lavatory.

The inspector took in the position at a glance. We went through into the large hall and he locked the door behind him, slipping the key into his pocket. Then he gave the constable some low-voiced instructions, and the latter prepared to depart.

'We must get busy on those shoe tracks,' explained the inspector. 'But first of all, I must have a word with Miss Ackroyd. She was the last person to see her uncle alive. Does she know yet?'

Raymond shook his head.

'Well, no need to tell her for another five minutes. She can answer my questions better without being upset by knowing the truth about her uncle. Tell her there's been a burglary, and ask her if she would mind dressing and coming down to answer a few questions.'

It was Raymond who went upstairs on this errand.

'Miss Ackroyd will be down in a minute,' he said, when he returned. 'I told her just what you suggested.'

In less than five minutes Flora descended the staircase. She was wrapped in a pale pink silk kimono. She looked anxious and excited.

The inspector stepped forward.

'Good-evening, Miss Ackroyd,' he said civilly. 'We're afraid there's been an attempt at robbery, and we want you to help us. What's this room – the billiard room? Come in here and sit down.'

Flora sat down composedly on the wide divan which ran the length of the wall, and looked up at the inspector.

'I don't quite understand. What has been stolen? What do you want me to tell you?'

'It's just this, Miss Ackroyd. Parker here says you came out of your uncle's study at about a quarter to ten. Is that right?'

'Quite right. I had been to say good-night to him.'

'And the time is correct?'

'Well, it must have been about then. I can't say exactly. It might have been later.'

'Was your uncle alone, or was there anyone with him?'

'He was alone. Dr Sheppard had gone.'

'Did you happen to notice whether the window was open or shut?'

Flora shook her head.

'I can't say. The curtains were drawn.'

'Exactly. And your uncle seemed quite as usual?'

'I think so.'

'Do you mind telling us exactly what passed between you?'

Flora paused a minute, as though to collect her recollections.

'I went in and said, "Good-night, Uncle, I'm going to bed now. I'm tired to-night." He gave a sort of grunt, and – I went over and kissed him, and he said something about my looking nice in the frock I had on, and then he told me to run away as he was busy. So I went.'

'Did he ask specially not to be disturbed?'

'Oh! yes, I forgot. He said: "Tell Parker I don't want anything more to-night, and that he's not to disturb me." I met Parker just outside the door and gave him Uncle's message.'

'Just so,' said the inspector.

'Won't you tell me what it is that has been stolen?'

'We're not quite – certain,' said the inspector hesitatingly.

A wide look of alarm came into the girl's eyes. She started up.

'What is it? You're hiding something from me?'

Moving in his usual unobtrusive manner, Hector Blunt came between her and the inspector. She half stretched out her hand, and he took it in both of his, patting it as though she were a very small child, and she turned to him as though something in his stolid, rocklike demeanour promised comfort and safety.

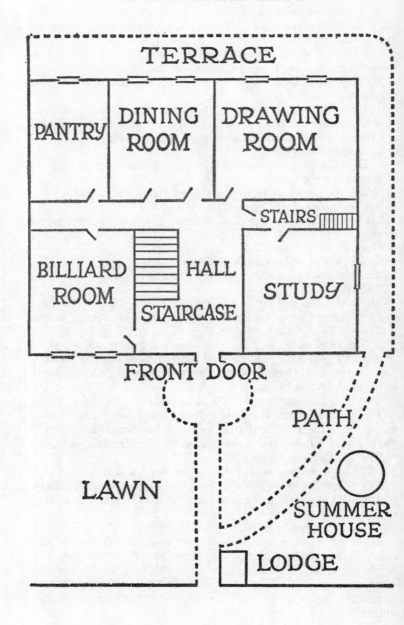

'It's bad news, Flora,' he said quietly. 'Bad news for all of us. Your Uncle Roger—'

'Yes?'

'It will be a shock to you. Bound to be. Poor Roger's dead.'

Flora drew away from him, her eyes dilating with horror. 'When?' she whispered. 'When?'

'Very soon after you left him, I'm afraid,' said Blunt gravely.

Flora raised her hand to her throat, gave a little cry, and I hurried to catch her as she fell. She had fainted, and Blunt and I carried her upstairs and laid her on her bed. Then I got him to wake Mrs Ackroyd and tell her the news. Flora soon revived, and I brought her mother to her, telling her what to do for the girl. Then I hurried downstairs again.

6

THE TUNISIAN DAGGER

I met the inspector just coming from the door which led into the kitchen quarters.

'How's the young lady, doctor?'

'Coming round nicely. Her mother's with her.'

'That's good. I've been questioning the servants. They all declare that no one has been to the back door to-night. Your description of that stranger was rather vague. Can't you give us something more definite to go upon?'

'I'm afraid not,' I said regretfully. 'It was a dark night, you see, and the fellow had his coat collar well pulled up and his hat squashed down over his eyes.'

'H'm,' said the inspector. 'Looked as though he wanted to conceal his face. Sure it was no one you know?'

I replied in the negative, but not as decidedly as I might have done. I remembered my impression that the stranger's voice was not unfamiliar to me. I explained this rather haltingly to the inspector.

'It was a rough, uneducated voice, you say?'

I agreed, but it occurred to me that the roughness had been of an almost exaggerated quality. If, as the inspector thought, the man had wished to hide his face, he might equally well have tried to disguise his voice.

'Do you mind coming into the study with me again, doctor? There are one or two things I want to ask you.'

I acquiesced. Inspector Davis unlocked the door of the lobby, we passed through, and he locked the door again behind him.

'We don't want to be disturbed,' he said grimly. 'And we don't want any eavesdropping either. What's all this about blackmail?'

'Blackmail!' I exclaimed, very much startled.

'Is it an effort of Parker's imagination? Or is there something in it?'

'If Parker heard anything about blackmail,' I said slowly, 'he must have been listening outside this door with his ear glued against the keyhole.'

Davis nodded.

'Nothing more likely. You see, I've been instituting a few inquiries as to what Parker has been doing with himself this evening. To tell the truth, I didn't like his manner. The man knows something. When I began to question him, he got the wind up, and plumped out some garbled story of blackmail.'

I took an instant decision.

'I'm rather glad you've brought the matter up,' I said. 'I've been trying to decide whether to make a clean breast of things or not. I'd already practically decided to tell you everything, but I was going to wait for a favourable opportunity. You might as well have it now.'

And then and there I narrated the whole events of the evening as I have set them down here. The inspector listened keenly, occasionally interjecting a question.

'Most extraordinary story I ever heard,' he said, when I had finished. 'And you say that letter has completely disappeared? It looks bad – it looks very bad indeed. It gives us what we've been looking for – a motive for the murder.'

I nodded.

'I realise that.'

'You say that Mr Ackroyd hinted at a suspicion he had that some member of his household was involved? Household's rather an elastic term.'

'You don't think that Parker himself might be the man we're after?' I suggested.

'It looks very like it. He was obviously listening at the door when you came out. Then Miss Ackroyd came across him later bent on entering the study. Say he tried again when she was safely out of the way. He stabbed Ackroyd, locked the door on the inside, opened the window, and got out that way, and went round to a side door which he had previously left open. How's that?'

'There's only one thing against it,' I said slowly. 'If Ackroyd went on reading that letter as soon as I left, as he intended to do, I don't see him continuing to sit on here and turn things over in his mind for another hour. He'd have had Parker in at once, accused him then and there, and there would have been a fine old uproar. Remember, Ackroyd was a man of choleric temper.'

'Mightn't have had time to go on with the letter just then,' suggested the inspector. 'We know someone was with him at half-past nine. If that visitor turned up as soon as you left, and after he went, Miss Ackroyd came in to say good-night – well, he wouldn't be able to go on with the letter until close upon ten o'clock.'

'And the telephone call?'

'Parker sent that all right – perhaps before he thought of the locked door and open window. Then he changed his mind – or got in a panic – and decided to deny all knowledge of it. That was it, depend upon it.'

'Ye – es,' I said rather doubtfully.

'Anyway, we can find out the truth about the telephone call from the exchange. If it was put through from here, I don't see how anyone else but Parker could have sent it. Depend upon it, he's our man. But keep it dark – we don't want to alarm him just yet, till we've got all the evidence. I'll see to it he doesn't give us the slip. To all appearances we'll be concentrating on your mysterious stranger.'

He rose from where he had been sitting astride the chair belonging to the desk, and crossed over to the still form in the armchair.

'The weapon ought to give us a clue,' he remarked, looking up. 'It's something quite unique – a curio, I should think, by the look of it.'

He bent down, surveying the handle attentively, and I heard him give a grunt of satisfaction. Then, very gingerly, he pressed his hands down below the hilt and drew the blade out from the wound. Still carrying it so as not to touch the handle, he placed it in a wide china mug which adorned the mantelpiece.

'Yes,' he said, nodding at it. 'Quite a work of art. There can't be many of them about.'

It was indeed a beautiful object. A narrow, tapering blade, and a hilt of elaborately intertwined metals of curious and careful workmanship. He touched the blade gingerly with his finger, testing its sharpness, and made an appreciative grimace.

'Lord, what an edge,' he exclaimed. 'A child could drive that into a man – as easy as cutting butter. A dangerous sort of toy to have about.'

'May I examine the body properly now?' I asked.

He nodded.

'Go ahead.'

I made a thorough examination.

'Well?' said the inspector, when I had finished.

'I'll spare you the technical language,' I said. 'We'll keep that for the inquest. The blow was delivered by a right-handed man standing behind him, and death must have been instantaneous. By the expression on the dead man's face, I should say the blow was quite unexpected. He may have died without knowing who his assailant was.'

'Butlers can creep about as soft-footed as cats,' said Inspector Davis. 'There's not going to be much mystery about this crime. Take a look at the hilt of that dagger.'

I took the look.

'I dare say they're not apparent to you, but *I* can see them clearly enough.' He lowered his voice. '*Fingerprints!*'

He stood off a few steps to judge of his effect.

'Yes,' I said mildly. 'I guessed that.'

I do not see why I should be supposed to be totally devoid of intelligence. After all, I read detective stories, and the newspapers, and am a man of quite average ability. If there had been toe marks on the dagger handle, now, that would have been quite a different thing. I would then have registered any amount of surprise and awe.

I think the inspector was annoyed with me for declining to get thrilled. He picked up the china mug and invited me to accompany him to the billiard room.

'I want to see if Mr Raymond can tell us anything about this dagger,' he explained.

Locking the outer door behind us again, we made our way to the billiard room, where we found Geoffrey Raymond. The inspector held up his exhibit.

'Ever seen this before, Mr Raymond?'

'Why – I believe – I'm almost sure that is a curio given to Mr Ackroyd by Major Blunt. It comes from Morocco – no, Tunis. So the crime was committed with that? What an extraordinary thing. It seems almost impossible, and yet there could hardly be two daggers the same. May I fetch Major Blunt?'

Without waiting for an answer, he hurried off.

'Nice young fellow that,' said the inspector. 'Something honest and ingenuous about him.'

I agreed. In the two years that Geoffrey Raymond has been secretary to Ackroyd, I have never seen him ruffled or out of temper. And he has been, I know, a most efficient secretary.

In a minute or two Raymond returned, accompanied by Blunt.

'I was right,' said Raymond excitedly. 'It *is* the Tunisian dagger.'

'Major Blunt hasn't looked at it yet,' objected the inspector.

'Saw it the moment I came into the study,' said the quiet man.

'You recognised it, then?'

Blunt nodded.

'You said nothing about it,' said the inspector suspiciously.

'Wrong moment,' said Blunt. 'Lot of harm done by blurting out things at the wrong time.'

He returned the inspector's stare placidly enough.

The latter grunted at last and turned away. He brought the dagger over to Blunt.

'You're quite sure about it, sir. You identify it positively?'

'Absolutely. No doubt whatever.'

'Where was this – er – curio usually kept? Can you tell me that, sir?'

It was the secretary who answered.

'In the silver table in the drawing-room.'

'What?' I exclaimed.

The others looked at me.

'Yes, doctor?' said the inspector encouragingly.

'It's nothing,' said the inspector again, still encouragingly.

'It's so trivial,' I explained apologetically. 'Only that when I arrived last night for dinner I heard the lid of the silver table being shut down in the drawing-room.'

I saw profound scepticism and a trace of suspicion on the inspector's countenance.

'How did you know it was the silver table lid?'

I was forced to explain in detail – a long, tedious explanation which I would infinitely rather not have had to make.

The inspector heard me to the end.

'Was the dagger in its place when you were looking over the contents?' he asked.

'I don't know,' I said. 'I can't say I remember noticing it – but, of course, it may have been there all the time.'

'We'd better get hold of the housekeeper,' remarked the inspector, and pulled the bell.

A few minutes later Miss Russell, summoned by Parker, entered the room.

'I don't think I went near the silver table,' she said, when the inspector had posed his question. 'I was looking to see that all the flowers were fresh. Oh! yes, I remember now. The silver table was open – which it had no business to be, and I shut the lid down as I passed.'

She looked at him aggressively.

'I see,' said the inspector. 'Can you tell me if this dagger was in its place then?'

Miss Russell looked at the weapon composedly.

'I can't say I'm sure,' she replied. 'I didn't stop to look. I knew the family would be down any minute, and I wanted to get away.'

'Thank you,' said the inspector.

There was just a trace of hesitation in his manner, as though he would have liked to question her further, but Miss Russell clearly accepted the words as a dismissal, and glided from the room.

'Rather a Tartar, I should fancy, eh?' said the inspector, looking after her. 'Let me see. This silver table is in front of one of the windows, I think you said, doctor?'

Raymond answered for me.

'Yes, the left-hand window.'

'And the window was open?'

'They were both ajar.'

'Well, I don't think we need go into the question much further. Somebody – I'll just say somebody – could get that dagger any time he liked, and exactly when he got it doesn't matter in the least. I'll be coming up in the morning with the chief constable, Mr Raymond. Until then, I'll keep the key of that door. I want Colonel Melrose to see everything exactly as it is. I happen to know that he's dining out the other side of the country, and, I believe, staying the night. . . .'

We watched the inspector take up the jar.

'I shall have to pack this carefully,' he observed. 'It's going to be an important piece of evidence in more ways than one.'

A few minutes later as I came out of the billiard room with Raymond, the latter gave a low chuckle of amusement.

I felt the pressure of his hand on my arm, and followed the direction of his eyes. Inspector Davis seemed to be inviting Parker's opinion of a small pocket diary.

'A little obvious,' murmured my companion. 'So Parker is the suspect, is he? Shall we oblige Inspector Davis with a set of our fingerprints also?'

He took two cards from the card tray, wiped them with his silk handkerchief, then handed one to me and took the other himself. Then, with a grin, he handed them to the police inspector.

'Souvenirs,' he said. 'No. 1, Dr Sheppard; No 2, my humble self. One from Major Blunt will be forthcoming in the morning.'

Youth is very buoyant. Even the brutal murder of his friend and employer could not dim Geoffrey Raymond's spirits for long. Perhaps that is as it should be. I do not know. I have lost the quality of resilience long since myself.

It was very late when I got back, and I hoped that Caroline would have gone to bed. I might have known better.

She had hot cocoa waiting for me, and whilst I drank it, she extracted the whole history of the evening from me. I said nothing of the blackmailing business, but contented myself with giving her the facts of the murder.

'The police suspect Parker,' I said, as I rose to my feet and prepared to ascend to bed. 'There seems a fairly clear case against him.'

'Parker!' said my sister. 'Fiddlesticks! That inspector must be a perfect fool. Parker indeed! Don't tell me.'

With which obscure pronouncement we went up to bed.

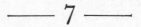

7

I LEARN MY NEIGHBOUR'S PROFESSION

On the following morning I hurried unforgivably over my round. My excuse can be that I had no very serious cases to attend. On my return Caroline came into the hall to greet me.

'Flora Ackroyd is here,' she announced in an excited whisper.

'What?'

I concealed my surprise as best as I could.

'She's very anxious to see you. She's been here half an hour.'

Caroline led the way into our small sitting-room, and I followed.

Flora was sitting on the sofa by the window. She was in

black and she sat nervously twisting her hands together. I was shocked by the sight of her face. All the colour had faded away from it. But when she spoke her manner was as composed and resolute as possible.

'Dr Sheppard, I have come to ask you to help me?'

'Of course he'll help you, my dear,' said Caroline.

I don't think Flora really wished Caroline to be present at the interview. She would, I am sure, have infinitely preferred to speak to me privately. But she also wanted to waste no time, so she made the best of it.

'I want you to come to The Larches with me.'

'The Larches?' I queried, surprised.

'To see that funny little man?' exclaimed Caroline.

'Yes. You know who he is, don't you?'

'We fancied,' I said, 'that he might be a retired hairdresser.'

Flora's blue eyes opened very wide.

'Why, he's Hercule Poirot! You know who I mean – the private detective. They say he's done the most wonderful things – just like detectives do in books. A year ago he retired and came to live down here. Uncle knew who he was, but he promised not to tell anyone, because M. Poirot wanted to live quietly without being bothered by people.'

'So that's who he is,' I said slowly.

'You've heard of him, of course?'

'I'm rather an old fogey, as Caroline tells me,' I said, 'but I *have* just heard of him.'

'Extraordinary!' commented Caroline.

I don't know what she was referring to – possibly her own failure to discover the truth.

'You want to go and see him?' I asked slowly. 'Now why?'

'To get him to investigate this murder, of course,' said Caroline sharply. 'Don't be so stupid, James.'

I was not really being stupid. Caroline does not always understand what I am driving at.

'You haven't got confidence in Inspector Davis?' I went on.

'Of course she hasn't,' said Caroline. 'I haven't either.'

Anyone would have thought it was Caroline's uncle who had been murdered.

'And how do you know he would take up the case?' I asked. 'Remember he has retired from active work.'

'That's just it,' said Flora simply. 'I've got to persuade him.'

'You are sure you are doing wisely?' I asked gravely.

'Of course she is,' said Caroline. 'I'll go with her myself if she likes.'

'I'd rather the doctor came with me if you don't mind, Miss Sheppard,' said Flora.

She knows the value of being direct on certain occasions. Any hints would certainly have been wasted on Caroline.

'You see,' she explained, following directness with tact, 'Dr Sheppard being the doctor, and having found the body, he would be able to give all the details to M. Poirot.'

'Yes,' said Caroline grudgingly, 'I see that.'

I took a turn or two up and down the room.

'Flora,' I said gravely, 'be guided by me. I advise you not to drag this detective into the case.'

Flora sprang to her feet. The colour rushed into her cheeks.

'I know why you say that,' she cried. 'But it's exactly for that reason I'm so anxious to go. You're afraid! But I'm not. I know Ralph better than you do.'

'Ralph!' said Caroline. 'What has Ralph got to do with it?' Neither of us heeded her.

'Ralph may be weak,' continued Flora. 'He may have done foolish things in the past – wicked things even – but he wouldn't murder anyone.'

'No, no,' I exclaimed. 'I never thought it of him.'

'Then why did you go to the Three Boars last night?' demanded Flora, 'on your way home – after Uncle's body was found?'

I was momentarily silenced. I had hoped that that visit of mine would remain unnoticed.

'How did you know about that?' I countered.

'I went there this morning,' said Flora. 'I heard from the servants that Ralph was staying there—'

I interrupted her.

'You had no idea that he was in King's Abbot?'

'No. I was astounded. I couldn't understand it. I went there and asked for him. They told me, what I suppose they told you last night, that he went out at about nine o'clock yesterday evening – and – and never came back.'

Her eyes met mine defiantly, and as though answering something in my look, she burst out:

'Well, why shouldn't he? He might have gone – anywhere. He may even have gone back to London.'

'Leaving his luggage behind?' I asked gently.

Flora stamped her foot.

'I don't care. There must be a simple explanation.'

'And that's why you want to go to Hercule Poirot? Isn't it better to leave things as they are? The police don't suspect

Ralph in the least, remember. They're working on quite another tack.'

'But that's just *it*,' cried the girl. 'They *do* suspect him. A man from Cranchester turned up this morning – Inspector Raglan, a horrid, weaselly little man. I found he had been to the Three Boars this morning before me. They told me all about his having been there, and the questions he had asked. He must think Ralph did it.'

'That's a change of mind from last night, if so,' I said slowly. 'He doesn't believe in Davis's theory that it was Parker then?'

'Parker indeed,' said my sister, and snorted.

Flora came forward and laid her hand on my arm.

'Oh! Dr Sheppard, let us go at once to this M. Poirot. He will find out the truth.'

'My dear Flora,' I said gently, laying my hand on hers. 'Are you quite sure it is the truth we want?'

She looked at me, nodding her head gravely.

'You're not sure,' she said. 'I am. I know Ralph better than you do.'

'Of course he didn't do it,' said Caroline, who had been keeping silent with great difficulty. 'Ralph may be extravagant, but he's a dear boy, and has the nicest manners.'

I wanted to tell Caroline that large numbers of murderers have had nice manners, but the presence of Flora restrained me. Since the girl was determined, I was forced to give in to her and we started at once, getting away before my sister was able to fire off any more pronouncements beginning with her favourite words, 'Of course.'

An old woman with an immense Breton cap opened the door of The Larches to us. M. Poirot was at home, it seemed.

We were ushered into a little sitting-room arranged with formal precision, and there, after the lapse of a minute or so, my friend of yesterday came to us.

'Monsieur le docteur,' he said, smiling. 'Mademoiselle.'

He bowed to Flora.

'Perhaps,' I began, 'you have heard of the tragedy which occurred last night.'

His face grew grave.

'But certainly I have heard. It is horrible. I offer mademoiselle all my sympathy. In what way can I serve you?'

'Miss Ackroyd,' I said, 'wants you to – to—'

'To find the murderer,' said Flora in a clear voice.

'I see,' said the little man. 'But the police will do that, will they not?'

'They might make a mistake,' said Flora. 'They are on their way to make a mistake now, I think. Please, M. Poirot, won't you help us? If – if it is a question of money—'

Poirot held up his hand.

'Not that, I beg of you, mademoiselle. Not that I do not care for money.' His eyes showed a momentary twinkle. 'Money, it means much to me and always has done. No, if I go into this, you must understand one thing clearly. *I shall go through with it to the end.* The good dog, he does not leave the scent, remember! You may wish that, after all, you had left it to the local police.'

'I want the truth,' said Flora, looking him straight in the eyes.

'All the truth?'

'All the truth.'

'Then I accept,' said the little man quietly. 'And I hope you will not regret those words. Now, tell me all the circumstances.'

'Dr Sheppard had better tell you,' said Flora. 'He knows more than I do.'

Thus enjoined, I plunged into a careful narrative, embodying all the facts I have previously set down. Poirot listened carefully, inserting a question here and there, but for the most part sitting in silence, his eyes on the ceiling.

I brought my story to a close with the departure of the inspector and myself from Fernly Park the previous night.

'And now,' said Flora, as I finished, 'tell him all about Ralph.'

I hesitated, but her imperious glance drove me on.

'You went to this inn – this Three Boars – last night on your way home?' asked Poirot, as I brought my tale to a close. 'Now exactly why was that?'

I paused a moment to choose my words carefully.

'I thought someone ought to inform the young man of his uncle's death. It occurred to me after I had left Fernly that possibly no one but myself and Mr Ackroyd were aware that he was staying in the village.'

Poirot nodded.

'Quite so. That was your only motive in going there, eh?'

'That was my only motive,' I said stiffly.

'It was not to – shall we say – reassure yourself about *ce jeune homme?*'

'Reassure myself?'

'I think, M. le docteur, that you know very well what I mean, though you pretend not to do so. I suggest that it would have been a relief to you if you had found that Captain Paton had been at home all the evening.'

'Not at all,' I said sharply.

The little detective shook his head at me gravely.

'You have not the trust in me of Miss Flora,' he said. 'But no matter. What we have to look at is this – Captain Paton is missing, under circumstances which call for an explanation. I will not hide from you that the matter looks grave. Still, it may admit of a perfectly simple explanation.'

'That's just what I keep saying,' cried Flora eagerly.

Poirot touched no more upon that theme. Instead he suggested an immediate visit to the local police. He thought it better for Flora to return home, and for me to be the one to accompany him there and introduce him to the officer in charge of the case.

We carried out this plan forthwith. We found Inspector Davis outside the police station looking very glum indeed. With him was Colonel Melrose, the Chief Constable, and another man whom, from Flora's description of 'weaselly,' I had no difficulty in recognising as Inspector Raglan from Cranchester.

I know Melrose fairly well, and I introduced Poirot to him and explained the situation. The chief constable was clearly vexed, and Inspector Raglan looked as black as thunder. Davis, however, seemed slightly exhilarated by the sight of his superior officer's annoyance.

'The case is going to be plain as a pikestaff,' said Raglan. 'Not the least need for amateurs to come butting in. You'd think any fool would have seen the way things were last night, and then we shouldn't have lost twelve hours.'

He directed a vengeful glance at poor Davis, who received it with perfect stolidity.

'Mr Ackroyd's family must, of course, do what they see fit,' said Colonel Melrose. 'But we cannot have the official investigation hampered in any way. I know M. Poirot's great reputation, of course,' he added courteously.

'The police can't advertise themselves, worse luck,' said Raglan.

It was Poirot who saved the situation.

'It is true that I have retired from the world,' he said. 'I never intended to take up a case again. Above all things, I have a horror of publicity. I must beg, that in the case of my being able to contribute something to the solution of the mystery, my name may not be mentioned.'

Inspector Raglan's face lightened a little.

'I've heard of some very remarkable successes of yours,' observed the colonel, thawing.

'I have had much experience,' said Poirot quietly. 'But most of my successess have been obtained by the aid of the police. I admire enormously your English police. If Inspector Raglan permits me to assist him, I shall be both honoured and flattered.'

The inspector's countenance became still more gracious.

Colonel Melrose drew me aside.

'From all I hear, this little fellow's done some really remarkable things,' he murmured. 'We're naturally anxious not to have to call in Scotland Yard. Raglan seems very sure of himself, but I'm not quite certain that I agree with him. You see, I – er – know the parties concerned better than he does. This fellow doesn't seem out after kudos, does he? Would work in with us unobtrusively, eh?'

'To the greater glory of Inspector Raglan,' I said solemnly.

'Well, well,' said Colonel Melrose breezily in a louder voice, 'we must put you wise to the latest developments, M. Poirot.'

'I thank you,' said Poirot. 'My friend, Doctor Sheppard, said something of the butler being suspected?'

'That's all bunkum,' said Raglan instantly. 'These high-class servants get in such a funk that they act suspiciously for nothing at all.'

'The fingerprints?' I hinted.

'Nothing like Parker's.' He gave a faint smile, and added: 'And yours and Mr Raymond's didn't fit either, doctor.'

'What about those of Captain Ralph Paton?' asked Poirot quietly.

I felt a secret admiration for the way he took the bull by the horns. I saw a look of respect creep into the inspector's eye.

'I see you don't let the grass grow under your feet, Mr Poirot. It will be a pleasure to work with you, I'm sure. We're going to take that young gentleman's fingerprints as soon as we can lay hands upon him.'

'I can't help thinking you're mistaken, Inspector,' said Colonel Melrose warmly. 'I've known Ralph Paton from a boy upward. He'd never stoop to murder.'

'Maybe not,' said the inspector tonelessly.

'What have you got against him?' I asked.

'Went out just on nine o'clock last night. Was seen in the neighbourhood of Fernly Park somewhere about nine-thirty.

Not been seen since. Believed to be in serious money difficulties. I've got a pair of his shoes here – shoes with rubber
studs in them. He had two pairs, almost exactly alike. I'm
going up now to compare them with those footmarks. The
constable is up there seeing that no one tampers with them.'

'We'll go at once,' said Colonel Melrose. 'You and M. Poirot
will accompany us, will you not?'

We assented, and all drove up in the colonel's car. The inspector was anxious to get at once to the footmarks, and asked
to be put down at the lodge. About half-way up the drive, on
the right, a path branched off which led round to the terrace
and the window of Ackroyd's study.

'Would you like to go with the inspector, M. Poirot?' asked
the chief constable, 'or would you prefer to examine the study?'

Poirot chose the latter alternative. Parker opened the door
to us. His manner was smug and deferential, and he seemed
to have recovered from his panic of the night before.

Colonel Melrose took a key from his pocket, and unlocking
the door which led into the lobby, he ushered us through into
the study.

'Except for the removal of the body, M. Poirot, this room
is exactly as it was last night.'

'And the body was found – where?'

As precisely as possible, I described Ackroyd's position. The
armchair still stood in front of the fire.

Poirot went and sat down in it.

'The blue letter you speak of, where was it when you left
the room?'

'Mr Ackroyd had laid it down on this little table at his
right hand.'

Poirot nodded.

'Except for that, everything was in its place?'

'Yes, I think so.'

Colonel Melrose, would you be so extremely obliging as
to sit down in this chair a minute. I thank you. Now M. le
docteur, will you kindly indicate to me the exact position of
the dagger?'

I did so, whilst the little man stood in the doorway.

'The hilt of the dagger was plainly visible from the door
then. Both you and Parker could see it at once?'

'Yes.'

Poirot went next to the window.

'The electric light was on, of course, when you discovered
the body?' he asked over his shoulder.

I assented, and joined him where he was studying the marks on the window-sill.

'The rubber studs are the same pattern as those in Captain Paton's shoes,' he said quietly.

Then he came back once more to the middle of the room. His eye travelled round, searching everything in the room with a quick, trained glance.

'Are you a man of good observation, Doctor Sheppard?' he asked at last.

'I think so,' I said, surprised.

'There was a fire in the grate, I see. When you broke the door down and found Mr Ackroyd dead, how was the fire? Was it low?'

I gave a vexed laugh.

'I – I really can't say. I didn't notice. Perhaps Mr Raymond or Major Blunt—'

The little man opposite me shook his head with a faint smile.

'One must always proceed with method. I made an error of judgment in asking you that question. To each man his own knowledge. You could tell me the details of the patient's appearance – nothing there would escape you. If I wanted information about the papers on that desk, Mr Raymond would have noticed anything there was to see. To find out about the fire, I must ask the man whose business it is to observe such things. You permit—'

He moved swiftly to the fireplace and rang the bell.

After a lapse of a minute or two Parker appeared.

'The bell rang, sir,' he said hesitatingly.

'Come in, Parker,' said Colonel Melrose. 'This gentleman wants to ask you something.'

Parker transferred a respectful attention to Poirot.

'Parker,' said the little man, 'when you broke down the door with Dr Sheppard last night, and found your master dead, what was the state of the fire?'

Parker replied without a pause.

'It had burned very low, sir. It was almost out.'

'Ah!' said Poirot. The exclamation sounded almost triumphant. He went on:

'Look round you, my good Parker. Is this room exactly as it was then?'

The butler's eye swept round. It came to rest on the windows.

'The curtains were drawn, sir, and the electric light was on.'

Poirot nodded approval.

'Anything else?'

'Yes, sir, this chair was drawn out a little more.'

He indicated a big grandfather chair to the left of the door between it and the window. I append a plan of the room with the chair in question marked with an X.

'Just show me,' said Poirot.

The butler drew the chair in question out a good two feet from the wall, turning it so that the seat faced the door.

'*Voilà ce qui est curieux,*' murmured Poirot. 'No one would want to sit in a chair in such a position, I fancy. Now who pushed it back into place again, I wonder? Did you, my friend?'

'No, sir,' said Parker. 'I was too upset with seeing the master and all.'

Poirot looked across at me.

'Did you, doctor?'

'It was back in position when I arrived with the police, sir,' put in Parker. 'I'm sure of that.'

'Curious,' said Poirot again.

'Raymond or Blunt must have pushed it back,' I suggested. 'Surely it isn't important?'

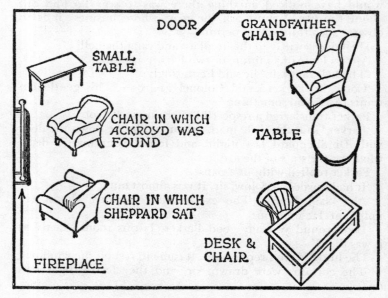

'It is completely unimportant,' said Poirot. 'That is why it is so interesting,' he added softly.

'Excuse me a minute,' said Colonel Melrose. He left the room with Parker.

'Do you think Parker is speaking the truth?' I asked.

'About the chair, yes. Otherwise I do not know. You will find, M. le docteur, if you have much to do with cases of this kind, that they all resemble each other in one thing.'

'What is that?' I asked curiously.

'Everyone concerned in them has something to hide.'

'Have I?' I asked, smiling.

Poirot looked at me attentively.

'I think you have,' he said quietly.

'But—'

'Have you told me everything known to you about this young man Paton?' He smiled as I grew red. 'Oh! do not fear. I will not press you. I shall learn it in good time.'

'I wish you'd tell me something of your methods,' I said hastily, to cover my confusion. 'The point about the fire, for instance?'

'Oh! that was very simple. You leave Mr Ackroyd at – ten minutes to nine, was it not?'

'Yes, exactly, I should say.'

'The window is then closed and bolted and the door unlocked. At a quarter past ten when the body is discovered, the door is locked and the window is open. Who opened it? Clearly only Mr Ackroyd himself could have done so, and for one of two reasons. Either because the room became unbearably hot but since the fire was nearly out and there was a sharp drop in temperature last night, that cannot be the reason, or because he admitted someone that way. And if he admitted someone that way, it must have been someone well known to him, since he had previously shown himself uneasy on the subject of that same window.'

'It sounds very simple,' I said.

'Everything is simple, if you arrange the facts methodically. We are concerned now with the personality of the person who was with him at nine-thirty last night. Everything goes to show that that was the individual admitted by the window, and though Mr Ackroyd was seen alive later by Miss Flora, we cannot approach a solution of the mystery until we know who that visitor was. The window may have been left open after his departure and so afforded entrance to the murderer, or the same person may have returned a second time. Ah! here is the colonel who returns.'

Colonel Melrose entered with an animated manner.

'The telephone call has been traced at last,' he said. 'It did not come from here. It was put through to Dr Sheppard at 10.15 last night from a public call office at King's Abbot station. And at 10.23 the night mail leaves for Liverpool.'

———— 8 ————

INSPECTOR RAGLAN IS CONFIDENT

We looked at each other.

'You'll have inquiries made at the station, of course?' I said.

'Naturally, but I'm not over sanguine as to the result. You know what that station is like.'

I did. King's Abbott is a mere village, but its station happens to be an important junction. Most of the big expresses stop there, and trains are shunted, re-sorted, and made up. It has two or three public telephone boxes. At that time of night, three local trains come in close upon each other, to catch the connection with the express for the north which comes in at 10.19 and leaves at 10.23. The whole place is in a bustle, and the chances of one particular person being noticed telephoning or getting into the express are very small indeed.

'But why telephone at all?' demanded Melrose. 'That is what I find so extraordinary. There seems no rhyme or reason in the thing.'

Poirot carefully straightened a china ornament on one of the bookcases.

'Be sure there was a reason,' he said over his shoulder.

'But what reason could it be?'

'When we know that, we shall know everything. This case is very curious and very interesting.'

There was something almost indescribable in the way he said those last words. I felt that he was looking at the case from some peculiar angle of his own, and what he saw I could not tell.

He went to the window and stood there, looking out.

'You say it was nine o'clock, Dr Sheppard, when you met this stranger outside the gate?'

He asked the question without turning round.

'Yes,' I replied. 'I heard the church clock chime the hour.'

'How long would it take him to reach the house – to reach this window, for instance?'

'Five minutes at the outside. Two or three minutes only if he took the path at the right of the drive and came straight here.'

'But to do that he would have to know the way. How can I explain myself? – it would mean that he had been here before – that he knew his surroundings.'

'That is true,' replied Colonel Melrose.

'We could find out, doubtless, if Mr Ackroyd had received any strangers during the past week?'

'Young Raymond could tell us that,' I said.

'Or Parker,' suggested Colonel Melrose.

'*Ou tous les deux*,' suggested Poirot, smiling.

Colonel Melrose went in search of Raymond, and I rang the bell once more for Parker.

Colonel Melrose returned almost immediately, accompanied by the young secretary, whom he introduced to Poirot. Geoffrey Raymond was fresh and debonair as ever. He seemed surprised and delighted to make Poirot's acquaintance.

'No idea you'd been living among us incognito, M. Poirot,' he said. 'It will be a great privilege to watch you at work – Hallo, what's this?'

Poirot had been standing just to the left of the door. Now he moved aside suddenly, and I saw that while my back was turned he must have swiftly drawn out the arm-chair till it stood in the position Parker had indicated.

'Want me to sit in the chair whilst you take a blood test?' asked Raymond good-humouredly. 'What's the idea?'

'M. Raymond, this chair was pulled out – so – last night when Mr Ackroyd was found killed. Someone moved it back again into place. Did you do so?'

The secretary's reply came without a second's hesitation.

'No, indeed I didn't. I don't even remember that it was in that position, but it must have been if you say so. Anyway, somebody else must have moved it back to its proper place. Have they destroyed a clue in doing so? Too bad!'

'It is of no consequence,' said the detective. 'Of no consequence whatever. What I really want to ask you is this, M. Raymond: Did any stranger come to see Mr Ackroyd during this past week?'

The secretary reflected for a minute or two, knitting his

brows, and during the pause Parker appeared in answer to the bell.

'No,' said Raymond at last. 'I can't remember anyone. Can you, Parker?'

'I beg your pardon, sir?'

'Any strangers coming to see Mr Ackroyd this week?'

The butler reflected for a minute or two.

'There was the young man who came on Wednesday, sir,' he said at last. 'From Curtis and Troute, I understood he was.'

Raymond moved this aside with an impatient hand.

'Oh! yes, I remember, but that is not the kind of stranger this gentleman means.' He turned to Poirot. 'Mr Ackroyd had some idea of purchasing a dictaphone,' he explained. 'It would have enabled us to get through a lot more work in a limited time. The firm in question sent down their representative, but nothing came of it. Mr Ackroyd did not make up his mind to purchase.'

Poirot turned to the butler.

'Can you describe this young man to me, my good Parker?'

'He was fair-haired, sir, and short. Very neatly dressed in a blue serge suit. A very presentable young man, sir, for his station in life.'

Poirot turned to me.

'The man you met outside the gate, doctor, was tall, was he not?'

'Yes,' I said. 'Somewhere about six feet, I should say.'

'There is nothing in that, then,' declared the Belgian. 'I thank you, Parker.'

The butler spoke to Raymond.

'Mr Hammond has just arrived, sir,' he said. 'He is anxious to know if he can be of any service, and he would be glad to have a word with you.'

'I'll come at once,' said the young man. He hurried out. Poirot looked inquiringly at the chief constable.

'The family solicitor, M. Poirot,' said the latter.

'It is a busy time for this young M. Raymond,' murmured M. Poirot. 'He has the air efficient, that one.'

'I believe Mr Ackroyd considered him a most able secretary.'

'He has been here – how long?'

'Just on two years, I fancy.'

'His duties he fulfils punctiliously. Of that I am sure. In what manner does he amuse himself? Does he go in for *le sport*?'

'Private secretaries haven't much time for that sort of thing,' said Colonel Melrose, smiling. 'Raymond plays golf, I believe. And tennis in the summer time.'

'He does not attend the courses – I should say the running of the horses?'

'Race meetings? No, I don't think he's interested in racing.'

Poirot nodded and seemed to lose interest. He glanced slowly round the study.

'I have seen, I think, all that there is to be seen here.'

I, too, looked round.

'If those walls could speak,' I murmured.

Poirot shook his head.

'A tongue is not enough,' he said. 'They would have to have also eyes and ears. But do not be too sure that these dead things' – he touched the top of the bookcase as he spoke – 'are always dumb. To me they speak sometimes – chairs, tables – they have their message!'

He turned away towards the door.

'What message?' I cried. 'What have they said to you to-day?'

He looked over his shoulder and raised one eyebrow quizzically.

'An opened window,' he said. 'A locked door. A chair that apparently moved itself. To all three I say, "Why?" and I find no answer.'

He shook his head, puffed out his chest, and stood blinking at us. He looked ridiculously full of his own importance. It crossed my mind to wonder whether he was really any good as a detective. Had his big reputation been built up on a series of lucky chances?

I think the same thought must have occurred to Colonel Melrose, for he frowned.

'Anything more you want to see, M. Poirot?' he inquired brusquely.

'You would perhaps be so kind as to show me the silver table from which the weapon was taken? After that, I will trespass on your kindness no longer.'

We went to the drawing-room, but on the way the constable waylaid the colonel, and after a muttered conversation the latter excused himself and left us together. I showed Poirot the silver table, and after raising the lid once or twice and letting it fall, he pushed open the window and stepped out on the terrace. I followed him.

Inspector Raglan had just turned the corner of the house, and was coming towards us. His face looked grim and satisfied.

'So there you are, M. Poirot,' he said. 'Well, this isn't going to be much of a case. I'm sorry, too. A nice enough young fellow gone wrong.'

Poirot's face fell, and he spoke very mildly.

'I'm afraid I shall not be able to be of much aid to you, then?'

'Next time, perhaps,' said the inspector soothingly. 'Though we don't have murders every day in this quiet little corner of the world.'

Poirot's gaze took on an admiring quality.

'You have been of a marvellous promptness,' he observed. 'How exactly did you go to work, if I may ask?'

'Certainly,' said the inspector. 'To begin with – method. That's what I always say – method!'

'Ah!' cried the other. 'That, too, is my watchword. Method, order, and the little grey cells.'

'The cells?' said the inspector, staring.

'The little grey cells of the brain,' explained the Belgian.

'Oh, of course; well, we all use them, I suppose.'

'In a greater or lesser degree,' murmured Poirot. 'And there are, too, differences in quality. Then there is the psychology of a crime. One must study that.'

'Ah!' said the inspector, 'you've been bitten with all this psycho-analysis stuff? Now, I'm a plain man—'

'Mrs Raglan would not agree, I am sure, to that,' said Poirot, making him a little bow.

Inspector Raglan, a little taken aback, bowed.

'You don't understand,' he said, grinning broadly. 'Lord, what a lot of difference language makes. I'm telling you how I set to work. First of all, method. Mr Ackroyd was last seen alive at a quarter to ten by his niece, Miss Flora Ackroyd. That's fact number one, isn't it?'

'If you say so.'

'Well, it is. At half-past ten, the doctor here says that Mr Ackroyd had been dead at least half an hour. You stick to that, doctor?'

'Certainly,' I said. 'Half an hour or longer.'

'Very good. That gives us exactly a quarter of an hour in which the crime must have been committed. I make a list of everyone in the house, and work through it, setting down opposite their names where they were and what they were doing between the hour of 9.45 and 10 p.m.'

He handed a sheet of paper to Poirot. I read it over his shoulder. It ran as follows, written in a neat script:

72

Major Blunt. – In billiard room with Mr Raymond. (Latter confirms.)

Mr Raymond. – Billiard room. (See above.)

Mrs Ackroyd. – 9.45 watching billiard match. Went up to bed 9.55. (Raymond and Blunt watched her up staircase.)

Miss Ackroyd. – Went straight from her uncle's room upstairs. (Confirmed by Parker, also housemaid, Elsie Dale.)

Servants:

> *Parker. – Went straight to butler's pantry. (Confirmed by housekeeper, Miss Russell, who came down to speak to him about something at 9.45, and remained at least ten minutes.)*
>
> *Miss Russell. – As above. Spoke to housemaid, Elsie Dale, upstairs at 9.45.*
>
> *Ursula Bourne (parlourmaid). – In her own room until 9.55. Then in Servants' Hall.*
>
> *Mrs Cooper (cook). – In Servants' Hall.*
>
> *Gladys Jones (second housemaid). – In Servants' Hall.*
>
> *Elsie Dale. – Upstairs in bedroom. Seen there by Miss Russell and Miss Flora Ackroyd.*
>
> *Mary Thripp (kitchenmaid). – Servants' Hall.*

'The cook has been here seven years, the parlourmaid eighteen months, and Parker just over a year. The others are new. Except for something fishy about Parker, they all seem quite all right.'

'A very complete list,' said Poirot, handing it back to him. 'I am quite sure that Parker did not do the murder,' he added gravely.

'So is my sister,' I struck in. 'And she's usually right.' Nobody paid any attention to my interpolation.

'That disposes pretty effectually of the household,' continued the inspector. 'Now we come to a very grave point. The woman at the lodge – Mary Black – was pulling the curtains last night when she saw Ralph Paton turn in at the gate and go up towards the house.'

'She is sure of that?' I asked sharply.

'Quite sure. She knows him well by sight. He went past very quickly and turned off by the path to the right, which is a short cut to the terrace.'

'And what time was that?' asked Poirot, who had sat with an immovable face.

'Exactly twenty-five minutes past nine,' said the inspector gravely.

73

There was a silence. Then the inspector spoke again.

'It's all clear enough. It fits in without a flaw. At twenty-five minutes past nine, Captain Paton is seen passing the lodge; at nine-thirty or thereabouts, Mr Geoffrey Raymond hears someone in here asking for money and Mr. Ackroyd refusing. What happens next? Captain Paton leaves the same way – through the window. He walks along the terrace, angry and baffled. He comes to the open drawing-room window. Say it's now a quarter to ten. Miss Flora Ackroyd is saying good-night to her uncle. Major Blunt, Mr Raymond, and Mrs Ackroyd are in the billiard room. The drawing-room is empty. He steals in, takes the dagger from the silver table, and returns to the study window. He slips off his shoes, climbs in, and – well, I don't need to go into details. Then he slips out again and goes off. Hadn't the nerve to go back to the inn. He makes for the station, rings up from there—'

'Why?' said Poirot softly.

I jumped at the interruption. The little man was leaning forward. His eyes shone with a queer green light.

For a moment Inspector Raglan was taken aback by the question.

'It's difficult to say exactly why he did that,' he said at last. 'But murderers do funny things. You'd know that if you were in the police force. The cleverest of them make stupid mistakes sometimes. But come along and I'll show you those footprints.'

We followed him round the corner of the terrace to the study window. At a word from Raglan a police constable produced the shoes which had been obtained from the local inn.

The inspector laid them over the marks.

'They're the same,' he said confidently. 'That is to say, they're not the same pair that actually made these prints. He went away in those. This is a pair just like them, but older – see how the studs are worn down.'

'Surely a great many people wear shoes with rubber studs in them?' asked Poirot.

'That's so, of course,' said the inspector. 'I shouldn't put so much stress on the footmarks if it wasn't for everything else.'

'A very foolish young man, Captain Ralph Paton,' said Poirot thoughtfully. 'To leave so much evidence of his presence.'

'Ah! well,' said the inspector, 'it was a dry, fine night, you know. He left no prints on the terrace or on the gravelled path. But, unluckily for him, a spring must have welled up just lately at the end of the path from the drive. See here.'

A small gravelled path joined the terrace a few feet away. In one spot, a few yards from its termination, the ground was wet and boggy. Crossing this wet place there were again the marks of footsteps, and amongst them the shoes with rubber studs.

Poirot followed the path on a little way, the inspector by his side.

'You noticed the women's footprints?' he said suddenly.

The inspector laughed.

'Naturally. But several different women have walked this way – and men as well. It's a regular short cut to the house, you see. It would be impossible to sort out all the footsteps. After all, it's the ones on the window-sill that are really important.'

Poirot nodded.

'It's no good going farther,' said the inspector, as we came in view of the drive. 'It's all gravelled again here, and hard as it can be.'

Again Poirot nodded, but his eyes were fixed on a small garden house – a kind of superior summer-house. It was a little to the left of the path ahead of us, and a gravelled walk ran up to it.

Poirot lingered about until the inspector had gone back towards the house. Then he looked at me.

'You must have indeed been sent from the good God to replace my friend Hastings,' he said, with a twinkle. 'I observe that you do not quit my side. How say you, Doctor Sheppard, shall we investigate that summer-house? It interests me.'

He went up to the door and opened it. Inside, the place was almost dark. There were one or two rustic seats, a croquet set, and some folded deck-chairs.

I was startled to observe my new friend. He had dropped to his hands and knees and was crawling about the floor. Every now and then he shook his head as though not satisfied. Finally, he sat back on his heels.

'Nothing,' he murmured. 'Well, perhaps it was not to be expected. But it would have meant so much—'

He broke off, stiffening all over. Then he stretched out his hand to one of the rustic chairs. He detached something from one side of it.

'What is it?' I cried. 'What have you found?'

He smiled, unclosing his hand so that I should see what lay in the palm of it. A scrap of stiff white cambric.

I took it from him, looked at it curiously, and then handed it back.

'What do you make of it, eh, my friend?' he asked, eyeing me keenly.

'A scrap torn from a handkerchief,' I suggested, shrugging my shoulders.

He made another dart and picked up a small quill – a goose quill by the look of it.

'And that?' he cried triumphantly. 'What do you make of that?'

I only stared.

He slipped the quill into his pocket, and looked again at the scrap of white stuff.

'A fragment of a handkerchief?' he mused. 'Perhaps you are right. But remember this – *a good laundry does not starch a handkerchief.*'

He nodded at me triumphantly, then he put away the scrap carefully in his pocket-book.

— 9 —

THE GOLDFISH POND

We walked back to the house together. There was no sign of the inspector. Poirot paused on the terrace and stood with his back to the house, slowly turning his head from side to side.

'*Une belle propriété,*' he said at last appreciatively. 'Who inherits it?'

His words gave me almost a shock. It is an odd thing, but until that moment the question of inheritance had never come into my head. Poirot watched me keenly.

'It is a new idea to you, that,' he said at last. 'You had not thought of it before – eh?'

'No,' I said truthfully. 'I wish I had.'

He looked at me again curiously.

'I wonder just what you mean by that,' he said thoughtfully. 'Oh! no,' as I was about to speak. '*Inutile!* You would not tell me your real thought.'

'Everyone has something to hide,' I quoted, smiling.

'Exactly.'

'You still believe that?'

'More than ever, my friend. But it is not easy to hide things from Hercule Poirot. He has a knack of finding out.'

He descended the steps of the Dutch garden as he spoke.

'Let us walk a little,' he said over his shoulder. 'The air is pleasant to-day.'

I followed him. He led me down a path to the left enclosed in yew hedges. A walk led down the middle, bordered each side with formal flower beds, and at the end was a round paved recess with a seat and a pond of goldfish. Instead of pursuing the path to the end, Poirot took another which wound up the side of a wooded slope. In one spot the trees had been cleared away, and a seat had been put. Sitting there one had a splendid view over the countryside, and one looked right down on the paved recess and the goldfish pond.

'England is very beautiful,' said Poirot, his eyes straying over the prospect. Then he smiled. 'And so are English girls,' he said in a lower voice. 'Hush, my friend, and look at the pretty picture below us.'

It was then that I saw Flora. She was moving along the path we had just left and she was humming a little snatch of song. Her step was more dancing than walking, and, in spite of her black dress, there was nothing but joy in her whole attitude. She gave a sudden pirouette on her toes, and her black draperies swung out. At the same time she flung her head back and laughed outright.

As she did so a man stepped out from the trees. It was Hector Blunt.

The girl started. Her expression changed a little.

'How you startled me – I didn't see you.'

Blunt said nothing, but stood looking at her for a minute or two in silence.

'What I like about you,' said Flora, with a touch of malice, 'is your cheery conversation.'

I fancy that at that Blunt reddened under his tan. His voice, when he spoke, sounded different – it had a curious sort of humility in it.

'Never was much of a fellow for talking. Not even when I was young.'

'That was a very long time ago, I suppose,' said Flora gravely.

I caught the undercurrent of laughter in her voice, but I don't think Blunt did.

'Yes,' he said simply, 'it was.'

'How does it feel to be Methuselah?' asked Flora.

This time the laughter was more apparent, but Blunt was following out an idea of his own.

'Remember the johnny who sold his soul to the devil? In return for being made young again? There's an opera about it.'

'Faust, you mean?'

'That's the beggar. Rum story. Some of us would do it if we could.'

'Anyone would think you were creaking at the joints to hear you talk,' cried Flora, half vexed, half amused.

Blunt said nothing for a minute or two. Then he looked away from Flora into the middle distance and observed to an adjacent tree trunk that it was about time he got back to Africa.

'Are you going on another expedition – shooting things?'

'Expect so. Usually do, you know – shoot things, I mean.'

'You shot that head in the hall, didn't you?'

Blunt nodded. Then he jerked out, going rather red as he did so:

'Care for some decent skins any time? If so, I could get 'em for you.'

'Oh! please do,' cried Flora. 'Will you really? You won't forget?'

'I shan't forget,' said Hector Blunt.

He added, in a sudden burst of communicativeness:

'Time I went. I'm no good in this sort of life. Haven't got the manners for it. I'm a rough fellow, no use in society. Never remember the things one's expected to say. Yes, time I went.'

'But you're not going at once,' cried Flora. 'No – not while we're in all this trouble. Oh! please. If you go—'

She turned away a little.

'You want me to stay?' asked Blunt.

He spoke deliberately but quite simply.

'We all—'

'I meant you personally,' said Blunt, with directness.

Flora turned slowly back again and met his eyes.

'I want you to stay,' she said, 'if – if that makes any difference.'

'It makes all the difference,' said Blunt.

There was a moment's silence. They sat down on the stone seat by the goldfish pond. It seemed as though neither of them knew quite what to say next.

'It – it's such a lovely morning,' said Flora at last. 'You

know, I can't help feeling happy, in spite – in spite of everything. That's awful, I suppose?'

'Quite natural,' said Blunt. 'Never saw your uncle until two years ago, did you? Can't be expected to grieve very much. Much better to have no humbug about it.'

'There's something awfully consoling about you,' said Flora. 'You make things seem so simple.'

'Things are simple as a rule,' said the big-game hunter.

'Not always,' said Flora.

Her voice had lowered itself, and I saw Blunt turn and look at her, bringing his eyes back from (apparently) the coast of Africa to do so. He evidently put his own construction on her change of tone, for he said, after a minute or two, in rather an abrupt manner:

'I say, you know, you mustn't worry. About that young chap, I mean. Inspector's an ass. Everybody knows – utterly absurd to think he could have done it. Man from outside. Burglar chap. That's the only possible solution.'

Flora turned to look at him.

'You really think so?'

'Don't you?' said Blunt quickly.

'I – oh, yes, of course.'

Another silence, and then Flora burst out:

'I'm – I'll tell you why I felt so happy this morning. However heartless you think me, I'd rather tell you. It's because the lawyer has been – Mr Hammond. He told us about the will. Uncle Roger has left me twenty thousand pounds. Think of it – twenty thousand beautiful pounds.'

Blunt looked surprised.

'Does it mean so much to you?'

'Mean much to me? Why, it's everything. Freedom – life – no more scheming and scraping and lying—'

'Lying?' said Blunt, sharply interrupting.

Flora seemed taken aback for a minute.

'You know what I mean,' she said uncertainly. 'Pretending to be thankful for all the nasty cast-off things rich relations give you. Last year's coats and skirts and hats.'

'Don't know much about ladies' clothes; should have said you were always very well turned out.'

'It's cost me something, though,' said Flora in a low voice. 'Don't let's talk of horrid things. I'm so happy. I'm free. Free to do what I like. Free not to—'

She stopped suddenly.

'Not to what?' asked Blunt quickly.

'I forget now. Nothing important.'

Blunt had a stick in his hand, and he thrust it into the pond, poking at something.

'What are you doing, Major Blunt?'

'There's something bright down there. Wondered what it was – looks like a gold brooch. Now I've stirred up the mud and it's gone.'

'Perhaps it's a crow,' suggested Flora. 'Like the one Melisande saw in the water.'

'Melisande,' said Blunt reflectively – 'she's in an opera, isn't she?'

'Yes, you seem to know a lot about operas.'

'People take me sometimes,' said Blunt sadly. 'Funny idea of pleasure – worse racket than the natives make with their tom-toms.'

Flora laughed.

'I remember Melisande,' continued Blunt, 'married an old chap old enough to be her father.'

He threw a small piece of flint into the goldfish pond. Then, with a change of manner, he turned to Flora.

'Miss Ackroyd, can I do anything? About Paton, I mean. I know how dreadfully anxious you must be.'

'Thank you,' said Flora in a cold voice. 'There is really nothing to be done. Ralph will be all right. I've got hold of the most wonderful detective in the world, and he's going to find out all about it.'

For some time I had felt uneasy as to our position. We were not exactly eavesdropping, since the two in the garden below had only to lift their heads to see us. Nevertheless, I should have drawn attention to our presence before now, had not my companion put a warning pressure on my arm. Clearly he wished me to remain silent. Now, however, he acted briskly.

He rose quickly to his feet, clearing his throat.

'I demand pardon,' he cried. 'I cannot allow mademoiselle thus extravagantly to compliment me, and not draw attention to my presence. They say the listener hears no good of himself, but that is not the case this time. To spare my blushes, I must join you and apologise.'

He hurried down the path with me close behind him, and joined the others by the pond.

'This is M. Hercule Poirot,' said Flora. 'I expect you've heard of him.'

Poirot bowed.

'I know Major Blunt by reputation,' he said politely. 'I am

glad to have encountered you, monsieur. I am in need of some information that you can give me.'

Blunt looked at him inquiringly.

'When did you last see M. Ackroyd alive?'

'At dinner.'

'And you neither saw nor heard anything of him after that?'

'Didn't see him. Heard his voice.'

'How was that?'

'I strolled out on the terrace—'

'Pardon me, what time was that?'

'About half-past nine. I was walking up and down smoking in front of the drawing-room window. I heard Ackroyd talking in his study—'

Poirot stooped and removed a microscopic weed.

'Surely you couldn't hear voices in the study from that part of the terrace,' he murmured.

He was not looking at Blunt, but I was, and to my intense surprise, I saw the latter flush.

'Went as far as the corner,' he explained unwillingly.

'Ah! indeed?' said Poirot.

In the mildest manner he conveyed an impression that more was wanted.

'Thought I saw – a woman disappearing into the bushes. Just a gleam of white, you know. Must have been mistaken. It was while I was standing at the corner of the terrace that I heard Ackroyd's voice speaking to that secretary of his.'

'Speaking to Mr Geoffrey Raymond?'

'Yes – that's what I supposed at the time. Seems I was wrong.'

'Mr Ackroyd didn't address him by name?'

'Oh, no.'

'Then, if I may ask, why did you think—?'

Blunt explained laboriously.

'Took it for granted that it *would* be Raymond, because he had said just before I came out that he was taking some papers to Ackroyd. Never thought of it being anybody else.'

'Can you remember what the words you heard were?'

'Afraid I can't. Something quite ordinary and unimportant. Only caught a scrap of it. I was thinking of something else at the time.'

'It is of no importance,' murmured Poirot. 'Did you move a chair back against the wall when you went into the study after the body was discovered?'

'Chair? No, why should I?'

Poirot shrugged his shoulders but did not answer. He turned to Flora.

'There is one thing I should like to know from you, mademoiselle. When you were examining the things in the silver table with Dr Sheppard, was the dagger in its place, or was it not?'

Flora's chin shot up.

'Inspector Raglan has been asking me that,' she said resentfully. 'I've told him, and I'll tell you. I'm perfectly certain the dagger was *not* there. He thinks it was and that Ralph sneaked it later in the evening. And – and he doesn't believe me. He thinks I'm saying it so – to shield Ralph.'

'And aren't you?' I asked gravely.

Flora stamped her foot.

'You, too, Dr Sheppard! Oh! it's too bad.'

Poirot tactfully made a diversion.

'It is true what I heard you say, Major Blunt. There is something that glitters in this pond. Let us see if I can reach it.'

He knelt down by the pond, baring his arm to the elbow, and lowered it in very slowly, so as not to disturb the bottom of the pond. But in spite of all his precautions the mud eddied and swirled, and he was forced to draw his arm out again empty-handed.

He gazed ruefully at the mud upon his arm. I offered him my handkerchief, which he accepted with fervent protestations of thanks. Blunt looked at his watch.

'Nearly lunch time,' he said. 'We'd better be getting back to the house.'

'You will lunch with us, M. Poirot?' asked Flora. 'I should like you to meet my mother. She is – very fond of Ralph.'

The little man bowed.

'I shall be delighted, mademoiselle.'

'And you will stay, too, won't you, Dr Sheppard?'

I hesitated.

'Oh, do!'

I wanted to, so I accepted the invitation without further ceremony.

We set out towards the house, Flora and Blunt walking ahead.

'What hair,' said Poirot to me in a low tone, nodding towards Flora. 'The real gold! They will make a pretty couple. She and the dark, handsome Captain Paton. Will they not?'

I looked at him inquiringly, but he began to fuss about a

few microscopic drops of water on his coat sleeve. The man reminded me in some ways of a cat. His green eyes and his finicking habits.

'And all for nothing, too,' I said sympathetically. 'I wonder what it was in the pond?'

'Would you like to see?' asked Poirot.

I stared at him. He nodded.

'My good friend,' he said gently and reproachfully, 'Hercule Poirot does not run the risk of disarranging his costume without being sure of attaining his object. To do so would be ridiculous and absurd. I am never ridiculous.'

'But you brought your hand out empty,' I objected.

'There are times when it is necessary to have discretion. Do you tell your patients everything – but everything, doctor? I think not. Nor do you tell your excellent sister everything either, is it not so? Before showing my empty hand, I dropped what it contained into my other hand. You shall see what that was.'

He held out his left hand, palm open. On it lay a little circlet of gold. A woman's wedding ring.

I took it from him.

'Look inside,' commanded Poirot.

I did so. Inside was an inscription in fine writing:

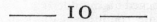

From R., March 13th.

I looked at Poirot, but he was busy inspecting his appearance in a tiny pocket glass. He paid particular attention to his moustaches, and none at all to me. I saw that he did not intend to be communicative.

------ I O ------

THE PARLOURMAID

We found Mrs Ackroyd in the hall. With her was a small dried-up little man, with an aggressive chin and sharp grey eyes, and 'lawyer' written all over him.

'Mr Hammond is staying to lunch with us,' said Mrs Ackroyd. 'You know Major Blunt, Mr Hammond? And dear Doctor Sheppard – also a close friend of poor Roger's. And, let me see—'

She paused, surveying Hercule Poirot in some perplexity.

'This is M. Poirot, Mother,' said Flora. 'I told you about him this morning.'

'Oh! yes,' said Mrs Ackroyd vaguely. 'Of course, my dear, of course. He is to find Ralph, is he not?'

'He is to find out who killed Uncle,' said Flora.

'Oh! my dear,' cried her mother. 'Please! My poor nerves. I am a wreck this morning, a positive wreck. Such a dreadful thing to happen. I can't help feeling that it must have been an accident of some kind. Roger was so fond of handling queer curios. His hand must have slipped, or something.'

This theory was received in polite silence. I saw Poirot edge up to the lawyer, and speak to him in a confidential undertone. They moved aside into the embrasure of the window. I joined them – then hesitated.

'Perhaps I'm intruding,' I said.

'Not at all,' cried Poirot heartily. 'You and I, M. le docteur, we investigate this affair side by side. Without you I should be lost. I desire a little information from the good Mr Hammond.'

'You are acting on behalf of Captain Ralph Paton, I understand,' said the lawyer cautiously.

Poirot shook his head.

'Not so. I am acting in the interests of justice. Miss Ackroyd has asked me to investigate the death of her uncle.'

Mr Hammond seemed slightly taken aback.

'I cannot seriously believe that Captain Paton can be concerned in this crime,' he said, 'however strong the circumstantial evidence against him may be. The mere fact that he was hard pressed for money—'

'Was he hard pressed for money?' interpolated Poirot quickly.

The lawyer shrugged his shoulders.

'It was a chronic condition with Ralph Paton,' he said dryly. 'Money went through his hands like water. He was always applying to his stepfather.'

'Had he done so of late? During the last year, for instance?'

'I cannot say. Mr Ackroyd did not mention the fact to me.'

'I comprehend. Mr Hammond, I take it that you are acquainted with the provisions of Mr Ackroyd's will?'

'Certainly. That is my principal business here to-day.'

'Then, seeing that I am acting for Miss Ackroyd, you will not object to telling me the terms of that will?'

'They are quite simple. Shorn of legal phraseology, and after paying certain legacies and bequests—'

'Such as—?' interrupted Poirot.

Mr Hammond seemed a little surprised.

'A thousand pounds to his housekeeper, Miss Russell; fifty pounds to the cook, Emma Cooper; five hundred pounds to his secretary, Mr Geoffrey Raymond. Then to various hospitals—'

Poirot held up his hand.

'Ah! the charitable bequests, they interest me not.'

'Quite so. The income on ten thousand pounds' worth of shares to be paid to Mrs Cecil Ackroyd during her lifetime. Miss Flora Ackroyd inherits twenty thousand pounds outright. The residue – including this property, and the shares in Ackroyd and Son – to his adopted son, Ralph Paton.'

'Mr Ackroyd possessed a large fortune?'

'A very large fortune. Captain Paton will be an exceedingly wealthy young man.'

There was a silence. Poirot and the lawyer looked at each other.

'Mr Hammond,' came Mrs Ackroyd's voice plaintively from the fireplace.

The lawyer answered the summons. Poirot took my arm and drew me right into the window.

'Regard the irises,' he remarked in rather a loud voice. 'Magnificent, are they not? A straight and pleasing effect.'

At the same time I felt the pressure of his hand on my arm, and he added in a low tone:

'Do you really wish to aid me? To take part in this investigation?'

'Yes, indeed,' I said eagerly. 'There's nothing I should like better. You don't know what a dull old fogey's life I lead. Never anything out of the ordinary.'

'Good, we will be colleagues then. In a minute or two I fancy Major Blunt will join us. He is not happy with the good mamma. Now there are some things I want to know – but I do not wish to seem to want to know them. You comprehend? So it will be your part to ask the questions.'

'What questions do you want me to ask?' I asked apprehensively.

'I want you to introduce the name of Mrs Ferrars.'

'Yes?'

'Speak of her in a natural fashion. Ask him if he was down here when her husband died. You understand the kind of thing I mean. And while he replies, watch his face without seeming to watch it. *C'est compris?*'

There was no time for more, for at that minute, as Poirot

had prophesied, Blunt left the others in his abrupt fashion and came over to us.

I suggested strolling on the terrace, and he acquiesced. Poirot stayed behind.

I stopped to examine a late rose.

'How things change in the course of a day or so,' I observed. 'I was up here last Wednesday, I remember, walking up and down this same terrace. Ackroyd was with me – full of spirits. And now – three days later – Ackroyd's dead, poor fellow. Mrs Ferrars dead – you knew her, didn't you? But of course you did.'

Blunt nodded his head.

'Had you seen her since you'd been down this time?'

'Went with Ackroyd to call. Last Tuesday, think it was. Fascinating woman – but something queer about her. Deep – one would never know what she was up to.'

I looked into his steady grey eyes. Nothing there surely. I went on:

'I suppose you'd met her before.'

'Last time I was here – she and her husband had just come here to live.' He paused a minute and then added: 'Rum thing, she had changed a lot between then and now.'

'How – changed?' I asked.

'Looked ten years older.'

'Were you down here when her husband died?' I asked, trying to make the question sound as casual as possible.

'No. From all I heard it would be a good riddance. Uncharitable, perhaps, but the truth.'

I agreed.

'Ashley Ferrars was by no means a pattern husband,' I said cautiously.

'Blackguard, I thought,' said Blunt.

'No,' I said, 'only a man with more money that was good for him.'

'Oh! money! All the troubles in the world can be put down to money – or the lack of it.'

'Which has been your particular trouble?' I asked.

'I've enough for what I want. I'm one of the lucky ones.'

'Indeed.'

'I'm not too flush just now, as a matter of fact. Came into a legacy a year ago, and like a fool let myself be persuaded into putting it into some wild-cat scheme.'

I sympathised, and narrated my own similar trouble.

Then the gong pealed out, and we all went in to lunch. Poirot drew me back a little.

'*Eh! bien*?'

'He's all right,' I said. 'I'm sure of it.'

'Nothing – disturbing?'

'He had a legacy just a year ago,' I said. 'But why not? Why shouldn't he? I'll swear the man is perfectly square and above board.'

'Without doubt, without doubt,' said Poirot soothingly. 'Do not upset yourself.'

He spoke as though to a fractious child.

We all trooped into the dining-room. It seemed incredible that less than twenty-four hours had passed since I last sat at that table.

Afterwards, Mrs Ackroyd took me aside and sat down with me on a sofa.

'I can't help feeling a little hurt,' she murmured, producing a handkerchief of the kind obviously not meant to be cried into. 'Hurt, I mean, by Roger's lack of confidence in me. That twenty thousand pounds ought to have been left to *me* – not to Flora. A mother could be trusted to safeguard the interests of her child. A lack of trust, I call it.'

'You forget, Mrs Ackroyd,' I said, 'Flora was Ackroyd's own niece, a blood relation. It would have been different had you been his sister instead of his sister-in-law.'

'As poor Cecil's widow, I think my feelings ought to have been considered,' said the lady, touching her eyelashes gingerly with the handkerchief. 'But Roger was always most peculiar – not to say *mean* – about money matters. It has been a most difficult position for both Flora and myself. He did not even give the poor child an allowance. He would pay her bills, you know, and even that with a good deal of reluctance and asking what she wanted all those fal-lals for – so like a man – but – now I've forgotten what it was I was going to say! Oh, yes, not a penny we could call our own, you know. Flora resented it – yes, I must say she resented it – very strongly. Though devoted to her uncle, of course. But any girl would have resented it. Yes, I must say Roger had very strange ideas about money. He wouldn't even buy new face towels, though I told him the old ones were in holes. And then,' proceeded Mrs Ackroyd, with a sudden leap highly characteristic of her conversation, 'to leave all that money – a thousand pounds, fancy, a thousand pounds! – to that woman.'

'What woman?'

'That Russell woman. Something very queer about her, and so I've always said. But Roger wouldn't hear a word against her. Said she was a woman of great force of character, and that he admired and respected her. He was always going on about her rectitude and independence and moral worth. *I* think there's something fishy about her. She was certainly doing her best to marry Roger. But I soon put a stop to that. She's always hated me. Naturally. *I* saw through her.'

I began to wonder if there was any chance of stemming Mrs Ackroyd's eloquence, and getting away.

Mr Hammond provided the necessary diversion by coming up to say good-bye. I seized my chance and rose also.

'About the inquest,' I said. 'Where would you prefer it to be held? Here, or at the Three Boars?'

Mrs Ackroyd stared at me with a dropped jaw.

'The inquest?' she asked, the picture of consternation. 'But surely there won't have to be an inquest?'

Mr Hammond gave a dry little cough and murmured, 'Inevitable. Under the circumstances,' in two short little barks.

'But surely Dr Sheppard can arrange—'

'There are limits to my powers of arrangement,' I said dryly.

'If his death was an accident—'

'He was murdered, Mrs Ackroyd,' I said brutally.

She gave a little cry.

'No theory of accident will hold water for a minute.'

Mrs Ackroyd looked at me in distress. I had no patience with what I though was her silly fear of unpleasantness.

'If there's an inquest, I – shan't have to answer questions and all that, shall I?' she asked.

'I don't know what will be necessary,' I answered. 'I imagine Mr Raymond will take the brunt of it off you. He knows all the circumstances, and can give formal evidence of identification.'

The lawyer assented with a little bow.

'I really don't think there is anything to dread, Mrs Ackroyd,' he said. 'You will be spared all unpleasantness. Now, as to the question of money, have you all you need for the present? I mean,' he added, as she looked at him inquiringly, 'ready money. Cash, you know. If not, I can arrange to let you have whatever you require.'

'That ought to be all right,' said Raymond, who was standing by. 'Mr Ackroyd cashed a cheque for a hundred pounds yesterday.'

'A hundred pounds?'

'Yes. For wages and other expenses due to-day. At the moment it is still intact.'

'Where is this money? In his desk?'

'No, he always kept his cash in his bedroom. In an old collar box, to be accurate. Funny idea, wasn't it?'

'I think,' said the lawyer, 'we ought to make sure the money is there before I leave.'

'Certainly,' agreed the secretary. 'I'll take you up now . . . Oh! I forgot. The door's locked.'

Inquiry from Parker elicited the information that Inspector Raglan was in the housekeeper's room asking a few supplementary questions. A few minutes later the inspector joined the party in the hall, bringing the key with him. He unlocked the door and we passed into the lobby and up the small staircase. At the top of the stairs the door into Ackroyd's bedroom stood open. Inside the room it was dark, the curtains were drawn, and the bed was turned down just as it had been last night. The inspector drew the curtains, letting in the sunlight, and Geoffrey Raymond went to the top drawer of a rosewood bureau.

'He kept his money like that, in an unlocked drawer. Just fancy,' commented the inspector.

The secretary flushed a little.

'Mr Ackroyd had perfect faith in the honesty of all the servants,' he said hotly.

'Oh! quite so,' said the inspector hastily.

Raymond opened the drawer, took out a round leather collar-box from the back of it, and opening it, drew out a thick wallet.

'Here is the money,' he said, taking out a fat roll of notes. 'You will find the hundred intact, I know, for Mr Ackroyd put it in the collar-box in my presence last night when he was dressing for dinner, and of course it has not been touched since.'

Mr Hammond took the roll from him and counted it. He looked up sharply.

'A hundred pounds, you said. But there is only sixty here.'

Raymond stared at him.

'Impossible,' he cried, springing forward. Taking the notes from the other's hand, he counted them aloud.

Mr Hammond had been right. The total amounted to sixty pounds.

'But – I can't understand it,' cried the secretary, bewildered.

Poirot asked a question.

'You saw Mr Ackroyd put this money away last night when he was dressing for dinner? You are sure he had not paid away any of it already?'

'I'm sure he hadn't. He even said, "I don't want to take a hundred pounds down to dinner with me. Too bulgy." '

'Then the affair is very simple,' remarked Poirot. 'Either he paid out that forty pounds sometime last evening, or else it has been stolen.'

'That's the matter in a nutshell,' agreed the inspector. He turned to Mrs Ackroyd. 'Which of the servants would come in here yesterday evening?'

'I suppose the housemaid would turn down the bed.'

'Who is she? What do you know about her?'

'She's not been here very long,' said Mrs Ackroyd. 'But she's a nice ordinary country girl.'

'I think we ought to clear this matter up,' said the inspector. 'If Mr Ackroyd paid that money away himself, it may have a bearing on the mystery of the crime. The other servants all right, as far as you know?'

'Oh, I think so.'

'Not missed anything before?'

'No.'

'None of them leaving, or anything like that?'

'The parlourmaid is leaving.'

'When?'

'She gave notice yesterday, I believe.'

'To you?'

'Oh, no. *I* have nothing to do with the servants. Miss Russell attends to the household matters.'

The inspector remained lost in thought for a minute or two. Then he nodded his head and remarked, 'I think I'd better have a word with Miss Russell, and I'll see the girl Dale as well.'

Poirot and I accompanied him to the housekeeper's room. Miss Russell received us with her usual sang-froid.

Elsie Dale had been at Fernly five months. A nice girl, quick at her duties, and most respectable. Good references. The last girl in the world to take anything not belonging to her.

'What about the parlourmaid?'

'She, too, was a most superior girl. Very quiet and lady-like. An excellent worker.'

'Then why is she leaving?' asked the inspector.

Miss Russell pursed up her lips.

'It was none of my doing. I understand Mr Ackroyd found fault with her yesterday afternoon. It was her duty to do the study, and she disarranged some of the papers on his desk, I believe. He was very annoyed about it, and she gave notice. At least, that is what I understood from her, but perhaps you'd like to see her yourselves?'

The inspector assented. I had already noticed the girl when she was waiting on us at lunch. A tall girl, with a lot of brown hair rolled tightly away at the back of her neck, and very steady grey eyes. She came in answer to the housekeeper's summons, and stood very straight with those same grey eyes fixed on us.

'You are Ursula Bourne?' asked the inspector.

'Yes, sir.'

'I understand you are leaving?'

'Yes, sir.'

'Why is that?'

'I disarranged some papers on Mr Ackroyd's desk. He was very angry about it, and I said I had better leave. He told me to go as soon as possible.'

'Were you in Mr Ackroyd's bedroom at all last night? Tidying up or anything?'

'No, sir. That is Elsie's work. I never went near that part of the house.'

'I must tell you, my girl, that a large sum of money is missing from Mr Ackroyd's room.'

At last I saw her roused. A wave of colour swept over her face.

'I know nothing about any money. If you think I took it, and that that is why Mr Ackroyd dismissed me, you are wrong.'

'I'm not accusing you of taking it, my girl,' said the inspector. 'Don't flare up so.'

The girl looked at him coldly.

'You can search my things if you like,' she said disdainfully. 'But you won't find anything.'

Poirot suddenly interposed.

'It was yesterday afternoon that Mr Ackroyd dismissed you – or you dismissed yourself, was it not?' he asked.

The girl nodded.

'How long did the interview last?'

'The interview?'

'Yes, the interview between you and Mr Ackroyd in the study?'

'I – I don't know.'

'Twenty minutes? Half an hour?'

'Something like that.'

'Not longer?'

'Not longer than half an hour, certainly.'

'Thank you, mademoiselle.'

I looked curiously at him. He was rearranging a few objects on the table, setting them straight with precise fingers. His eyes were shining.

'That'll do,' said the inspector.

Ursula Bourne disappeared. The inspector turned to Miss Russell.

'How long has she been here? Have you got a copy of the reference you had with her?'

Without answering the first question, Miss Russell moved to an adjacent bureau, opened one of the drawers, and took out a handful of letters clipped together with a patent fastener. She selected one and handed it to the inspector.

'H'm,' said he. 'Reads all right. Mrs Richard Folliott, Marby Grange, Marby. Who's this woman?'

'Quite good county people,' said Miss Russell.

'Well,' said the inspector, handing it back, 'let's have a look at the other one, Elsie Dale.'

Elsie Dale was a big fair girl, with a pleasant but slightly stupid face. She answered our questions readily enough, and showed much distress and concern at the loss of the money.

'I don't think there's anything wrong with her,' observed the inspector, after he had dismissed her. 'What about Parker?'

Miss Russell pursed her lips together and made no reply.

'I've a feeling there's something wrong about that man,' the inspector continued thoughtfully. 'The trouble is that I don't quite see when he got his opportunity. He'd be busy with his duties immediately after dinner, and he'd got a pretty good alibi all through the evening. I know, for I've been devoting particular attention to it. Well, thank you very much, Miss Russell. We'll leave things as they are for the present. It's highly probable Mr Ackroyd paid that money away himself.'

The housekeeper bade us a dry good-afternoon, and we took our leave.

I left the house with Poirot.

'I wonder,' I said, breaking the silence, 'what the papers the girl disarranged could have been for Ackroyd to have got into such a state about them? I wonder if there is any clue there to the mystery.'

'The secretary said there were no papers of particular importance on the desk,' said Poirot quietly.

'Yes, but—' I paused.

'It strikes you as odd that Ackroyd should have flown into a rage about so trivial a matter?'

'Yes, it does rather.'

'But was it a trivial matter?'

'Of course,' I admitted, 'we don't know what those papers may have been. But Raymond certainly said—'

'Leave M. Raymond out of it for a minute. What did you think of that girl?'

'Which girl? The parlourmaid?'

'Yes, the parlourmaid. Ursula Bourne.'

'She seemed a nice girl,' I said hesitatingly.

Poirot repeated my words, but whereas I had laid a slight stress on the fourth word, he put it on the second.

'She *seemed* a nice girl – yes.'

Then after a minute's silence, he took something from his pocket and handed it to me.

'See, my friend, I will show you something. Look there.'

The paper he had handed me was that compiled by the inspector and given by him to Poirot that morning. Following the pointing finger, I saw a small cross marked in pencil opposite the name Ursula Bourne.

'You may not have noticed it at the time, my good friend, but there was one person on this list whose alibi had no kind of confirmation. Ursula Bourne.'

'You don't think—'

'Dr Sheppard, I dare to think anything. Ursula Bourne may have killed Mr Ackroyd, but I confess I can see no motive for her doing so. Can you?'

He looked at me very hard – so hard that I felt uncomfortable.

'Can you?' he repeated.

'No motive whatsoever,' I said firmly.

His gaze relaxed. He frowned and murmured to himself:

'Since the blackmailer was a man, it follows that she cannot be the blackmailer, then—'

I coughed.

'As far as that goes—' I began doubtfully.

He spun round on me.

'What? What are you going to say?'

'Nothing. Nothing. Only that, strictly speaking, Mrs Ferrars in her letter mentioned a *person* – she didn't actually specify a man. But we took it for granted, Ackroyd and I, that it *was* a man.'

Poirot did not seem to be listening to me. He was muttering to himself again.

'But then it is possible after all – yes, certainly it is possible – but then – ah! I must rearrange my ideas. Method, order, never have I needed them more. Everything must fit in – in its appointed place – otherwise I am on the wrong track.'

He broke off, and whirled round upon me again.

'Where is Marby?'

'It's on the other side of Cranchester.'

'How far away?'

'Oh! – fourteen miles, perhaps.'

'Would it be possible for you to go there? To-morrow, say?'

'To-morrow? Let me see, that's Sunday. Yes, I could arrange it. What do you want me to do there?'

'See this Mrs Folliott. Find out all you can about Ursula Bourne.'

'Very well. But – I don't much care for the job.'

'It is not the time to make difficulties. A man's life may hang on this.'

'Poor Ralph,' I said with a sigh. 'You believe him to be innocent, though?'

Poirot looked at me very gravely.

'Do you want to know the truth?'

'Of course.'

'Then you shall have it. My friend, everything points to the assumption that he is guilty.'

'What!' I exclaimed.

Poirot nodded.

'Yes, that stupid inspector – for he is stupid – has everything pointing his way. I seek for the truth – and the truth leads me every time to Ralph Paton. Motive, opportunity, means. But I will leave no stone unturned. I promised Mademoiselle Flora. And she was very sure, that little one. But very sure indeed.'

POIROT PAYS A CALL

I was slightly nervous when I rang the bell at Marby Grange
the following afternoon. I wondered very much what Poirot
expected to find out. He had entrusted the job to me. Why?
Was it because, as in the case of questioning Major Blunt, he
wished to remain in the background? The wish, intelligible in
the first case, seemed to me quite meaningless here.

My meditations were interrupted by the advent of a smart
parlourmaid.

Yes, Mrs Folliott was at home. I was ushered into a big
drawing-room, and looked round me curiously as I waited for
the mistress of the house. A large bare room, some good bits
of old china, and some beautiful etchings, shabby covers and
curtains. A lady's room in every sense of the term.

I turned from the inspection of a Bartolozzi on the wall as
Mrs Folliott came into the room. She was a tall woman, with
untidy brown hair, and a very winning smile.

'Dr Sheppard,' she said hesitatingly.

'That is my name,' I replied. 'I must apologise for calling
upon you like this, but I wanted some information about a
parlourmaid previously employed by you, Ursula Bourne.'

With the utterance of the name the smile vanished from her
face, and all the cordiality froze out of her manner. She looked
uncomfortable and ill at ease.

'Ursula Bourne?' she said hesitatingly.

'Yes,' I said. 'Perhaps you don't remember the name?'

'Oh, yes, of course. I – I remember perfectly.'

'She left you just over a year ago, I understand?'

'Yes. Yes, she did. That is quite right.'

'And you were satisfied with her whilst she was with you?
How long was she with you, by the way?'

'Oh! a year or two – I can't remember exactly how long.
She – she is very capable. I'm sure you will find her quite
satisfactory. I didn't know she was leaving Fernly. I hadn't
the least idea of it.'

'Can you tell me anything about her?' I asked.

'Anything about her?'

'Yes, where she comes from, who her people are – that sort
of thing?'

Mrs Folliott's face wore more than ever its frozen look.

'I don't know at all.'

'Who was she with before she came to you?'

'I'm afraid I don't remember.'

There was a spark of anger now underlying her nervousness. She flung up her head in a gesture that was vaguely familiar.

'Is it really necessary to ask all these questions?'

'Not at all,' I said, with an air of surprise and a tinge of apology in my manner. 'I had no idea you would mind answering them. I am very sorry.'

Her anger left her and she became confused again.

'Oh! I don't mind answering them. I assure you I don't. Why should I? It – it just seemed a little odd, you know. That's all. A little odd.'

One advantage of being a medical practitioner is that you can usually tell when people are lying to you. I should have known from Mrs Folliott's manner, if from nothing else, that she did mind answering my questions – minded intensely. She was thoroughly uncomfortable and upset, and there was plainly some mystery in the background. I judged her to be a woman quite unused to deception of any kind, and consequently rendered acutely uneasy when forced to practise it. A child could have seen through her.

But it was also clear that she had no intention of telling me anything further. Whatever the mystery centring round Urusla Bourne might be, I was not going to learn it through Mrs Folliott.

Defeated, I apologised once more for disturbing her, took my hat and departed.

I went to see a couple of patients and arrived home about six o'clock. Caroline was sitting beside the wreck of tea things. She had that look of suppressed exultation on her face which I know only too well. It is a sure sign with her, of either the getting or the giving of information. I wondered which it had been.

'I've had a very interesting afternoon,' began Caroline, as I dropped into my own particular easy-chair and stretched out my feet to the inviting blaze in the fireplace.

'Have you?' I said. 'Miss Gannett drop in to tea?'

Miss Gannett is one of the chief of our newsmongers.

'Guess again,' said Caroline, with intense complacency.

I guessed several times, working slowly through all the members of Caroline's Intelligence Corps. My sister received each guess with a triumphant shake of the head. In the end she volunteered the information herself.

'M. Poirot!' she said. 'Now, what do you think of that?'

I thought a good many things of it, but I was careful not to say them to Caroline.

'Why did he come?' I asked.

'To see me, of course. He said that, knowing my brother so well, he hoped he might be permitted to make the acquaintance of his charming sister – your charming sister, I've got mixed up – but you know what I mean.'

'What did he talk about?' I asked.

'He told me a lot about himself and his cases. You know that Prince Paul of Mauretania – the one who's just married a dancer?'

'Yes?'

'I saw a most intriguing paragraph about her in *Society Snippets* the other day, hinting that she was really a Russian Grand Duchess – one of the Czar's daughters who managed to escape from the Bolsheviks. Well, it seems that M. Poirot solved a baffling murder mystery that threatened to involve them both. Prince Paul was beside himself with gratitude.'

'Did he give him an emerald tie pin the size of a plover's egg?' I inquired sarcastically.

'He didn't mention it. Why?'

'Nothing,' I said. 'I thought it was always done. It is in detective fiction anyway. The super-detective always has his rooms littered with rubies and pearls and emeralds from grateful Royal clients.'

'It's very interesting to hear about these things from the inside,' said my sister complacently.

It would be – to Caroline. I could not but admire the ingenuity of M. Hercule Poirot, who had selected unerringly the case of all others that would most appeal to an elderly lady living in a small village.

'Did he tell you if the dancer was really a Grand Duchess?' I inquired.

'He was not at liberty to speak,' said Caroline importantly.

I wondered how far Poirot had strained the truth in talking to Caroline – probably not at all. He had conveyed his innuendoes by means of his eyebrows and his shoulders.

'And after all this,' I remarked, 'I suppose you were ready to eat out of his hand?'

'Don't be coarse, James. I don't know where you get these vulgar expressions from.'

'Probably from my only link with the outside world – my patients. Unfortunately, my practice does not lie amongst Royal princes and interesting Russian *émigrés*.'

Caroline pushed her spectacles up and looked at me.

'You seem very grumpy, James. It must be your liver. A blue pill, I think, to-night.'

To see me in my own home, you would never imagine that I was a doctor of medicine. Caroline does the home prescribing both for herself and me.

'Damn my liver,' I said irritably. 'Did you talk about the murder at all?'

'Well, naturally, James. What else is there to talk about locally? I was able to set M. Poirot right upon several points. He was very grateful to me. He said I had the makings of a born detective in me – and a wonderful psychological insight into human nature.'

Caroline was exactly like a cat that is full to overflowing with rich cream. She was positively purring.

'He talked a lot about the little grey cells of the brain, and of their functions. His own, he says, are of the first quality.'

'He would say so,' I remarked bitterly. 'Modesty is certainly not his middle name.'

'I wish you wouldn't be so horribly American, James. He thought it every important that Ralph should be found as soon as possible, and induced to come forward and give an account of himself. He says that his disappearance will produce a very unfortunate impression at the inquest.'

'And what did you say to that?'

'I agreed with him,' said Caroline importantly. 'And I was able to tell him the way people were talking already about it.'

'Caroline,' I said sharply, 'did you tell M. Poirot what you overheard in the wood that day?'

'I did,' said Caroline complacently.

I got up and began to walk about.

'You realise what you're doing, I hope,' I jerked out. 'You're putting a halter round Ralph Paton's neck as surely as you're sitting in that chair.'

'Not at all,' said Caroline, quite unruffled. 'I was surprised *you* hadn't told him.'

'I took very good care not to,' I said. 'I'm fond of that boy.'

'So am I. That's why I say you're talking nonsense. I don't believe Ralph did it, and so the truth can't hurt him, and we ought to give M. Poirot all the help we can. Why, think, very

98

likely Ralph was out with that identical girl on the night of the murder, and if so, he's got a perfect alibi.'

'If he's got a perfect alibi,' I retorted, 'why doesn't he come forward and say so?'

'Might get the girl into trouble,' said Caroline sapiently. 'But if M. Poirot gets hold of her, and puts it to her as her duty, she'll come forward of her own accord and clear Ralph.'

'You seem to have invented a romantic fairy story of your own,' I said. 'You read too many trashy novels, Caroline. I've always told you so.'

I dropped into my chair again.

'Did Poirot ask you any more questions?' I inquired.

'Only about the patients you had that morning.'

'The patients?' I demanded, unbelievingly.

'Yes, your surgery patients. How many and who they were?'

'Do you mean to say you were able to tell him that?' I demanded.

Caroline is really amazing.

'Why not?' asked my sister triumphantly. 'I can see the path up to the surgery door perfectly from this window. And I've got an excellent memory, James. Much better than yours, let me tell you.'

'I'm sure you have,' I murmured mechanically.

My sister went on, checking the names on her fingers.

'There was old Mrs Bennett, and that boy from the farm with the bad finger, Dolly Grice to have a needle out of her finger; that American steward off the liner. Let me see – that's four. Yes, and old George Evans with his ulcer. And lastly—'

She paused significantly.

'Well?'

Caroline brought out her climax triumphantly. She hissed it in the most approved style – aided by the fortunate number of s's at her disposal.

'*Miss Russell!*'

She sat back in her chair and looked at me meaningly, and when Caroline looks at you meaningly, it is impossible to miss it.

'I don't know what you mean,' I said, quite untruthfully. 'Why shouldn't Miss Russell consult me about her bad knee?'

'Bad knee,' said Caroline. 'Fiddlesticks! No more bad knee than you and I. She was after something else.'

'What?' I asked.

Caroline had to admit that she didn't know.

'But depend upon it, that was what he was trying to get at

– M. Poirot, I mean. There's something fishy about that woman, and he knows it.'

'Precisely the remark Mrs Ackroyd made to me yesterday,' I said. 'That there was something fishy about Miss Russell.'

'Ah!' said Caroline darkly, 'Mrs Ackroyd! There's another!'

'Another what?'

Caroline refused to explain her remarks. She merely nodded her head several times, rolling up her knitting, and went upstairs to don the high mauve silk blouse and the gold locket which she calls dressing for dinner.

I stayed there staring into the fire and thinking over Caroline's words. Had Poirot really come to gain information about Miss Russell, or was it only Caroline's tortuous mind that interpreted everything according to her own ideas?

There had certainly been nothing in Miss Russell's manner that morning to arouse suspicion. At least—

I remembered her persistent conversation on the subject of drug-taking – and from that she had led the conversation to poisons and poisoning. But there was nothing in that. Ackroyd had not been poisoned. Still, it was odd. . . .

I heard Caroline's voice, rather acid in tone, calling from the top of the stairs.

'James, you will be late for dinner.'

I put some coal on the fire and went upstairs obediently. It is well at any price to have peace in the home.

—— 12 ——

ROUND THE TABLE

A joint inquest was held on Monday.

I do not propose to give the proceedings in detail. To do so would only be to go over the same ground again and again. By arrangement with the police, very little was allowed to come out. I gave evidence as to the cause of Ackroyd's death and the probable time. The absence of Ralph Paton was commented on by the coroner, but not unduly stressed.

Afterwards, Poirot and I had a few words with Inspector Raglan. The inspector was very grave.

'It looks bad, Mr Poirot,' he said. 'I'm trying to judge the thing fair and square. I'm a local man, and I've seen Captain

Paton many times in Cranchester. I'm not wanting him to be the guilty one – but it's bad whichever way you look at it. If he's innocent, why doesn't he come forward? We've got evidence against him, but it's just possible that the evidence could be explained away. Then why doesn't he give an explanation?'

A lot more lay behind the inspector's words than I knew at the time. Ralph's description had been wired to every port and railway station in England. The police everywhere were on the alert. His rooms in town were watched, and any houses he had been known to be in the habit of frequenting. With such a *cordon* it seemed impossible that Ralph should be able to evade detection. He had no luggage, and, as far as anyone knew, no money.

'I can't find anyone who saw him at the station that night,' continued the inspector. 'And yet he's well known down here, and you'd think somebody would have noticed him. There's no news from Liverpool either.'

'You think he went to Liverpool?' queried Poirot.

'Well, it's on the cards. That telephone message from the station, just three minutes before the Liverpool express left – there ought to be something in that.'

'Unless it was deliberately intended to throw you off the scent. That might just possibly be the point of the telephone message.'

'That's an idea,' said the inspector eagerly. 'Do you really think that's the explanation of the telephone call?'

'My friend,' said Poirot gravely, 'I do not know. But I will tell you this: I believe that when we find the explanation of that telephone call we shall find the explanation of the murder.'

'You said something like that before, I remember,' I observed, looking at him curiously.

Poirot nodded.

'I always come back to it,' he said seriously.

'It seems to me utterly irrelevant,' I declared.

'I wouldn't say that,' demurred the inspector. 'But I must confess I think Mr Poirot here harps on it a little too much. We've better clues than that. The fingerprints on the dagger, for instance.'

Poirot became suddenly very foreign in manner, as he often did when excited over anything.

'M. l'inspecteur,' he said, 'beware of the blind – the blind – *comment dire?* – the little street that has no end to it.'

Inspector Raglan stared, but I was quicker.

'You mean a blind alley?' I said.

'That is it – the blind street that leads nowhere. So it may be with those fingerprints – they may lead you nowhere.'

'I don't see how that can well be,' said the police officer. 'I suppose you're hinting that they're faked? I've read of such things being done, though I can't say I've ever come across it in my experience. But fake or true – they're bound to lead *somewhere.*'

Poirot merely shrugged his shoulders, flinging out his arms wide.

The inspector then showed us various enlarged photographs of the fingerprints, and proceeded to become technical on the subject of loops and whorls.

'Come now,' he said at last, annoyed by Poirot's detached manner, 'you've got to admit that those prints were made by someone who was in the house that night?'

'*Bien entendu,*' said Poirot, nodding his head.

'Well, I've taken the prints of every member of the household, everyone, mind you, from the old lady down to the kitchenmaid.'

'I don't think Mrs Ackroyd would enjoy being referred to as the old lady. She must spend a considerable amount on cosmetics.'

'Everyone's,' repeated the inspector fussily.

'Including mine,' I said dryly.

'Very well. None of them correspond. That leave us two alternatives. Ralph Paton, or the mysterious stranger the doctor here tells us about. When we get hold of those two—'

'Much valuable time may have been lost,' broke in Poirot.

'I don't quite get you, Mr Poirot.'

'You have taken the prints of everyone in the house, you say,' murmured Poirot. 'Is that the exact truth you are telling me there, M. l'Inspecteur?'

'Certainly.'

'Without overlooking anyone?'

'Without overlooking anyone.'

'The quick or the dead?'

For a moment the inspector looked bewildered at what he took to be a religious observation. The he reacted slowly.

'You mean—?'

'The dead, M. l'Inspecteur.'

The inspector still took a minute or two to understand.

'I am suggesting,' said Poirot placidly, 'that the fingerprints on the dagger handle are those of Mr Ackroyd himself. It is an easy matter to verify. His body is still available.'

'But why? What would be the point of it. You're surely not suggesting suicide, Mr Poirot?'

'Ah! no. My theory is that the murderer wore gloves or wrapped something round his hand. After the blow was struck, he picked up the victim's hand and closed it round the dagger handle.'

'But why?'

Poirot shrugged his shoulders again.

'To make a confusing case even more confusing.'

'Well,' said the inspector, 'I'll look into it. What gave you the idea in the first place?'

'When you were so kind as to show me the dagger and draw attention to the fingerprints. I know very little of loops and whorls — see, I confess my ignorance frankly. But it did occur to me that the position of the prints was somewhat awkward. Not so would I have held a dagger in order to strike. Naturally, with the right hand brought up over the shoulder backwards, it would have been difficult to put it in exactly the right position.'

Inspector Raglan stared at the litle man. Poirot, with an air of great concern, flecked a speck of dust from his coat sleeve.

'Well,' said the inspector, 'it's an idea. I'll look into it all right, but don't you be disappointed if nothing comes of it.'

He endeavoured to make his tone kindly and patronising. Poirot watched him go off. Then he turned to me with twinkling eyes.

'Another time,' he observed, 'I must be more careful of his *amour propre*. And now that we are left to our own devices, what do you think, my good friend, of a little reunion of the family?'

The 'little reunion,' as Poirot called it, took place about half an hour later. We sat round the table in the dining-room at Fernly. Poirot at the head of the table, like the chairman of some ghastly board meeting. The servants were not present, so we were six in all. Mrs Ackroyd, Flora, Major Blunt, young Raymond, Poirot, and myself.

When everyone was assembled, Poirot rose and bowed.

'Messieurs, mesdames, I have called you together for a certain purpose.' He paused. 'To begin with, I want to make a very special plea to mademoiselle.'

'To me?' said Flora.

'Mademoiselle, you are engaged to Captain Ralph Paton. If anyone is in his confidence, you are. I beg you, most earnestly, if you know of his whereabouts, to persuade him to come forward. One little minute' – as Flora raised her head to speak – 'say nothing till you have well reflected. Mademoiselle, his position grows daily more dangerous. If he had come forward at once, no matter how damning the facts, he might have had a chance of explaining them away. But this silence – this flight – what can it mean? Surely only one thing, knowledge of guilt. Mademoiselle, if you really believe in his innocence, persuade him to come forward before it is too late.'

Flora's face had gone very white.

'Too late!' she repeated, very low.

Poirot leant forward, looking at her.

'See now, mademoiselle,' he said very gently, 'it is Papa Poirot who asks you this. The old Papa Poirot who has much knowledge and much experience. I would not seek to entrap you, mademoiselle. Will you not trust me – and tell me where Ralph Paton is hiding?'

The girl rose, and stood facing him.

'M. Poirot,' she said in a clear voice, 'I swear to you – swear solemnly – that I have no idea where Ralph is, and that I have neither seen him nor heard from him either on the day of – of the murder, or since.'

She sat down again. Poirot gazed at her in silence for a minute or two, then he brought his hand down on the table with a sharp rap.

'*Bien*! That is that,' he said. His face hardened. 'Now I appeal to these others who sit round this table, Mrs Ackroyd, Major Blunt, Dr Sheppard, Mr Raymond. You are all friends and intimates of the missing man. If you know where Ralph Paton is hiding, speak out.'

There was a long silence. Poirot looked to each in turn.

'I beg of you,' he said in a low voice, 'speak out.'

But still there was silence, broken at last by Mrs Ackroyd.

'I must say,' she observed in a plaintive voice, 'that Ralph's absence is most peculiar – most peculiar indeed. Not to come forward at such a time. It looks, you know, as though there were something *behind* it. I can't help thinking, Flora dear, that it was a very fortunate thing your engagement was never formally announced.'

'Mother!' cried Flora angrily.

'Providence,' declared Mrs Ackroyd. 'I have a devout belief

in Providence – a divinity that shapes our ends, as Shake-speare's beautiful line runs.'

'Surely you don't make the Almighty directly responsible for thick ankles. Mrs Ackroyd, do you?' asked Geoffrey Raymond, his irresponsible laugh ringing out.

His idea was, I think, to loosen the tension, but Mrs Ackroyd threw him a glance of reproach and took out her handkerchief.

'Flora has been saved a terrible amount of notoriety and unpleasantness. Not for a moment that I think dear Ralph had anything to do with poor Roger's death. I *don't* think so. But then I have a trusting heart – I always have had, ever since a child. I am loath to believe the worst of anyone. But, of course, one must remember that Ralph was in several air raids as a young boy. The results are apparent long after, some-times, they say. People are not responsible for their actions in the least. They lose control, you know, without being able to help it.'

'Mother,' cried Flora, 'you don't think Ralph did it?'

'Come, Mrs Ackroyd,' said Blunt.

'I don't know what to think,' said Mrs Ackroyd tearfully. 'It''s all very upsetting. What would happen to the estate, I wonder, if Ralph were found guilty?'

Raymond pushed his chair away from the table violently. Major Blunt remained very quiet, looking thoughtfully at her.

'Like shell-shock, you know,' said Mrs Ackroyd obstinately, 'and I dare say Roger kept him very short of money – with the best intentions, of course. I can see you are all against me, but I do think it is very odd that Ralph has not come forward, and I must say I am thankful Flora's engagement was never announced formally.'

'It will be to-morrow,' said Flora in a clear voice.

'Flora!' cried her mother, aghast.

Flora had turned to the secretary.

'Will you send the announcement to the *Morning Post*. And *The Times*, please, Mr Raymond.'

'If you are sure that it is wise, Miss Ackroyd,' he replied gravely.

She turned impulsively to Blunt.

'You understand,' she said. 'What else can I do? As things are, I must stand by Ralph. Don't you see that I must?'

She looked very searchingly at him, and after a long pause he nodded abruptly.

Mrs Ackroyd burst out into shrill protests. Flora remained unmoved. Then Raymond spoke.

'I appreciate your motives, Miss Ackroyd. But don't you think you're being rather precipitate? Wait a day or two.'

'To-morrow,' said Flora in a clear voice. 'It's no good, Mother, going on like this. Whatever else I am, I'm not disloyal to my friends.'

'M. Poirot,' Mrs Ackroyd appealed tearfully. 'Can't you say anything at all?'

'Nothing to be said,' interpolated Blunt. 'She's doing the right thing. I'll stand by her through thick and thin.'

Flora held out her hand to him.

'Thank you, Major Blunt,' she said.

'Mademoiselle,' said Poirot, 'will you let an old man congratulate you on your courage and your loyalty? And will you not misunderstand me if I ask you – ask you most solemnly – to postpone the announcement you speak of for at least two days more?'

Flora hesitated.

'I ask it in Ralph Paton's interests as much as in yours, mademoiselle. You frown. You do not see how that can be. But I assure you that it is so. *Pas de blagues.* You put the case into my hands – you must not hamper me now.'

Flora paused a few minutes before replying.

'I do not like it,' she said at last, 'but I will do what you say.' She sat down again at the table.

'And now, messieurs et mesdames,' said Poirot rapidly, 'I will continue with what I was about so say. Understand this, I mean to arrive at the truth. The truth, however ugly in itself, is always curious and beautiful to the seeker after it. I am much aged, my powers may not be what they were.' Here he clearly expected a contradiction. 'In all probability this is the last case I shall ever investigate. But Hercule Poirot does not end with a failure. Messieurs et mesdames, I tell you, I mean to *know.* And I shall know – in spite of you all.'

He brought out the last words provocatively, hurling them in our faces as it were. I think we all flinched back a little, excepting Geoffrey Raymond, who remained good-humoured and imperturbable as usual.

'How do you mean – in spite of us all?' he asked, with slightly raised eyebrows.

'But – just that, monsieur. Every one of you in this room is concealing something from me.' He raised his hand as a faint murmur of protest arose. 'Yes, yes, I know what I am saying. It may be something unimportant – trivial – which is supposed to have no bearing on the case, but there it is. *Each one of you has something to hide.* Come now, am I right?'

His glance, challenging and accusing, swept round the table. And every pair of eyes dropped before his. Yes, mine as well.

'I am answered,' said Poirot, with a curious laugh. He got up from his seat. 'I appeal to you all. Tell me the truth – the whole truth.' There was a silence. 'Will no one speak?'

He gave the same short laugh again.

'*C'est dommage,*' he said, and went out.

—— 13 ——

THE GOOSE QUILL

That evening, at Poirot's request, I went over to his house after dinner. Caroline saw me depart with visible reluctance. I think she would have liked to have accompanied me.

Poirot greeted me hospitably. He had placed a bottle of Irish whisky (which I detest) on a small table, with a soda water siphon and a glass. He himself was engaged in brewing hot chocolate. It was a favourite beverage of his, I discovered later.

He inquired politely after my sister, whom he declared to be a most interesting woman.

'I'm afraid you've been giving her a swelled head,' I said dryly. 'What about Sunday afternoon?'

He laughed and twinkled.

'I always like to employ the expert,' he remarked obscurely, but he refused to explain the remark.

'You got all the local gossip anyway,' I remarked. 'True, and untrue.'

'And a great deal of valuable information,' he added quietly.

'Such as—?'

He shook his head.

'Why not have told me the truth?' he countered. 'In a place like this, all Ralph Paton's doings were bound to be known. If your sister had not happened to pass through the wood that day somebody else would have done so.'

'I suppose they would,' I said grumpily. 'What about this interest of yours in my patients?'

Again he twinkled.

'Only one of them, doctor. Only one of them.'

'The last?' I hazarded.

'I find Miss Russell a study of the most interesting,' he said evasively.

'Do you agree with my sister and Mrs Ackroyd that there is something fishy about her?' I asked.

'Eh? What do you say – fishy?'

I explained to the best of my ability.

'And they say that, do they?'

'Didn't my sister convey as much to you yesterday afternoon?'

'*C'est possible.*'

'For no reason whatever,' I declared.

'*Les femmes,*' generalised Poirot. 'They are marvellous! They invent haphazard – and by miracle they are right. Not that it is that, really. Women observe subconsciously a thousand little details, without knowing that they are doing so. Their subconscious mind adds these little things together – and they call the result intuition. Me, I am very skilled in psychology. I know these things.'

He swelled his chest out importantly, looking so ridiculous, that I found it difficult not to burst out laughing. Then he took a small sip of his chocolate, and carefully wiped his moustache.

'I wish you'd tell me,' I burst out, 'what you really think of it all?'

He put down his cup.

'You wish that?'

'I do.'

'You have seen what I have seen. Should not our ideas be the same?'

'I'm afraid you're laughing at me,' I said stiffly. 'Of course, I've no experience of matters of this kind.'

Poirot smiled at me indulgently.

'You are like the little child who wants to know the way the engine works. You wish to see the affair, not as the family doctor sees it, but with the eye of a detective who knows and cares for no one – to whom they are all strangers and all equally liable to suspicion.'

'You put it very well,' I said.

'So I give you, then, a little lecture. The first thing is to get a clear history of what happened that evening – always bearing in mind that the person who speaks may be lying.'

I raised my eyebrows.

'Rather a suspicious attitude.'

But necessary – I assure you, necessary. Now first – Dr Sheppard leaves the house at ten minutes to nine. How do I know that?'

'Because I told you so.'

'But you might not be speaking the truth – or the watch you went by might be wrong. But Parker also says that you left the house at ten minutes to nine. So we accept that statement and pass on. At nine o'clock you run into a man – and here we come to what we will call the Romance of the Mysterious Stranger – just outside the Park gates. How do I know that that is so?'

'I told you so,' I began again, but Poirot interrupted me with a gesture of impatience.

'Ah! but it is that you are a little stupid to-night, my friend. *You* know that it is so – but how am *I* to know? *Eh bien,* I am able to tell you that the Mysterious Stranger was not a hallucination on your part, because the maid of a Miss Gannett met him a few minutes before you did, and of her too he inquired the way to Fernly Park. We accept his presence, therefore, and we can be fairly sure of two things about him – that he was a stranger to the neighbourhood, and that whatever his object in going to Fernly, there was no great secrecy about it, since he twice asked the way there.'

'Yes,' I said, 'I see that.'

'Now I have made it my business to find out more about this man. He had a drink at the Three Boars, I learn, and the barmaid there says that he spoke with an American accent and mentioned having just come over from the States. Did it strike you that he had an American accent?'

'Yes, I think he had,' I said, after a minute or two, during which I cast my mind back; 'but a very slight one.'

'*Précisement.* There is also this, which, you will remember, I picked up in the summer-house.'

He held out to me the little quill. I looked at it curiously. Then a memory of something I had read stirred in me.

Poirot, who had been watching my face, nodded.

'Yes, heroin, "snow." Drug-takers carry it like this, and sniff it up the nose.'

Diamorphine hydrochloride,' I murmured mechanically.

'This method of taking the drug is very common on the other side. Another proof, if we wanted one, that the man came from Canada or the States.'

'What first attracted your attention to that summer-house?' I asked curiously.

'My friend the inspector took it for granted that anyone using that path did so as a short cut to the house, but as soon as I saw the summer-house, I realised that the same path would be taken by anyone using the summer-house as a rendezvous. Now it seems fairly certain that the stranger came neither to the front nor to the back door. Then did someone from the house go out and meet him? If so, what could be a more convenient place than that little summer-house? I searched it with the hope that I might find some clue inside. I found two, the scrap of cambric and the quill.'

'And the scrap of cambric?' I asked curiously. 'What about that?'

Poirot raised his eyebrows.

'You do not use your little grey cells,' he remarked dryly. 'The scrap of starched cambric should be obvious.'

'Not very obvious to me.' I changed the subject. 'Anyway,' I said, 'this man went to the summer-house to meet somebody. Who was that somebody?'

'Exactly the question,' said Poirot. 'You will remember that Mrs Ackroyd and her daughter came over from Canada to live here?'

'Is that what you meant to-day when you accused them of hiding the truth?'

'Perhaps. Now another point. What did you think of the parlourmaid's story?'

'What story?'

'The story of her dismissal. Does it take half an hour to dismiss a servant? Was the story of those important papers a likely one? And remember, though she says she was in her bedroom from nine-thirty until ten o'clock, there is no one to confirm her statement.'

'You bewilder me,' I said.

'To me it grows clearer. But tell me now your own ideas and theories.'

I drew a piece of paper from my pocket.

'I just scribbled down a few suggestions,' I said apologetically.

'But excellent – you have method. Let us hear them.'

I read out in a somewhat embarrassed voice.

'To begin with, one must look at the thing logically—'

'Just what my poor Hastings used to say,' interrupted Poirot, 'but alas! he never did so.'

'*Point No.* 1. – Mr Ackroyd was heard talking to someone at half-past nine.

'*Point No.* 2. – At some time during the evening Ralph Paton must have come in through the window, as evidenced by the prints of his shoes.

'*Point No.* 3. – Mr. Ackroyd was nervous that evening, and would only have admitted someone he knew.

'*Point No.* 4. – The person with Mr Ackroyd at nine-thirty was asking for money. We know Ralph Paton was in a scrape.

'*These four points go to show that the person with Mr Ackroyd at nine-thirty was Ralph Paton. But we know that Mr Ackroyd was alive at a quarter to ten, therefore it was not Ralph who killed him. Ralph left the window open. Afterwards the murderer came in that way.*'

'And who was the murderer?' inquired Poirot.

'The American stranger. He may have been in league with Parker, and possibly in Parker we have the man who blackmailed Mrs Ferrars. If so, Parker may have heard enough to realise the game was up, have told his accomplice so, and the latter did the crime with the dagger which Parker gave him.'

'It is a theory that,' admitted Poirot. 'Decidedly you have cells of a kind. But it leaves a good deal unaccounted for.'

'Such as—?'

'The telephone call, the pushed-out chair—'

'Do you really think the latter important?' I interrupted.

'Perhaps not,' admitted my friend. 'It may have been pulled out by accident, and Raymond or Blunt may have shoved it into place unconsciously under the stress of emotion. Then there is the missing forty pounds.'

'Given by Ackroyd to Ralph,' I suggested. 'He may have reconsidered his first refusal.'

'That still leaves one thing unexplained.'

'What?'

'Why was Blunt so certain in his own mind that it was Raymond with Mr Ackroyd at nine-thirty?'

'He explained that,' I said.

'You think so? I will not press the point. Tell me, instead, what were Ralph Paton's reasons for disappearing?'

'That's rather more difficult,' I said slowly. 'I shall have to speak as a medical man. Ralph's nerves must have gone phut! If he suddenly found out that his uncle had been murdered within a few minutes of his leaving him – after, perhaps, a rather stormy interview – well, he might get the wind up and clear right out. Men have been known to do that – act guiltily when they're perfectly innocent.'

'Yes, that is true,' said Poirot. 'But we must not lose sight of one thing.'

'I know what you're going to say,' I remarked: 'motive. Ralph Paton inherits a great fortune by his uncle's death.'

'That is one motive,' agreed Poirot.

'One?'

'*Mais oui*. Do you realise that there are three separate motives staring us in the face. Somebody certainly stole the blue envelope and its contents. That is one motive. Blackmail! Ralph Paton may have been the man who blackmailed Mrs Ferrars. Remember, as far as Hammond knew, Ralph Paton had not applied to his uncle for help of late. That looks as though he were being supplied with money elsewhere. Then there is the fact that he was in some – how do you say – scrape? – which he feared might get to his uncle's ears. And finally there is the one you have just mentioned.'

'Dear me,' I said, rather taken aback. 'The case does seem black against him.'

'Does it?' said Poirot. 'That is where we disagree, you and I. Three motives it is almost too much. I am inclined to believe that, after all, Ralph Paton is innocent.'

—— 14 ——

MRS ACKROYD

After the evening talk I have just chronicled, the affair seemed to me to enter on a different phase. The whole thing can be divided into two parts, each clear and distinct from the other. Part I ranges from Ackroyd's death on the Friday evening to the following Monday night. It is the straightforward narrative of what occurred, as presented to Hercule Poirot. I was at Poirot's elbow the whole time. I saw what he saw. I tried my best to read his mind. As I know now, I failed in this latter task. Though Poirot showed me all his discoveries – as, for instance, the gold wedding-ring – he held back the vital and yet logical impressions that he formed. As I came to know later, this secrecy was characteristic of him. He would throw out hints and suggestions, but beyond that he would not go.

As I say, up till the Monday evening, my narrative might have been that of Poirot himself. I played Watson to his Sherlock. But after Monday our ways diverged. Poirot was busy on his own account. I got to hear of what he was doing, because in King's Abbot, you get to hear of everything, but he did not take me into his confidence beforehand. And I, too, had my own preoccupations.

On looking back, the thing that strikes me most is the piece-meal character of this period. Everyone had a hand in the elucidation of the mystery. It was rather like a jig-saw puzzle to which everyone contributed their own little piece of knowledge or discovery. But their task ended there. To Poirot alone belongs the renown of fitting those pieces into their correct place.

Some of the incidents seemed at the time irrelevant and unmeaning. There was, for instance, the question of the black boots. But that cames later. . . . To take things strictly in chronological order, I must begin with the summons from Mrs Ackroyd.

She sent for me early on Tuesday morning, and since the summons sounded an urgent one, I hastened there, expecting to find her *in extremis*.

The lady was in bed. So much did she concede to the etiquette of the situation. She gave me her bony hand, and indicated a chair drawn up to the bedside.

'Well, Mrs Ackroyd,' I said, 'and what's the matter with you?'

I spoke with that kind of spurious geniality which seems to be expected of general practitioners.

'I'm prostrated,' said Mrs Ackroyd in a faint voice. 'Absolutely prostrated. It's the shock of poor Roger's death. They say these things often aren't felt at the *time*, you know. It's the reaction afterwards.'

It is a pity that a doctor is precluded by his profession from being able sometimes to say what he really thinks.

I would have given anything to be able to answer 'Bunkum!'

Instead, I suggested a tonic. Mrs Ackroyd accepted the tonic. One move in the game seemed to be concluded. Not for a moment did I imagine that I had been sent for because of the shock occasioned by Ackroyd's death. But Mrs Ackroyd is totally incapable of pursuing a straightforward course on any subject. She always approaches her object by tortuous means. I wondered very much why it was she had sent for me.

'And then that scene – yesterday,' continued my patient.

She paused as though expecting me to take up a cue.

'What scene?'

'Doctor, how can you? Have you forgotten? That dreadful little Frenchman – or Belgian – or whatever he is. Bullying us all like he did. It has quite upset me. Coming on the top of Roger's death.'

'I'm very sorry, Mrs Ackroyd,' I said.

'I don't know what he meant – shouting at us like he did. I should hope I know my duty too well to *dream* of concealing anything. I have given the police *every* assistance in my power.'

Mrs Ackroyd paused, and I said, 'Quite so.' I was beginning to have a glimmering of what all the trouble was about.

'No one can say that I have failed in my duty,' continued Mrs Ackroyd. 'I am sure Inspector Raglan is perfectly satisfied. Why should this little upstart of a foreigner make a fuss? A most ridiculous-looking creature he is too – just like a comic Frenchman in a revue. I can't think why Flora insisted on bringing him into the case. She never said a word to me about it. Just went off and did it on her own. Flora is too independent. I am a woman of the world and her mother. She should have come to me for advice first.'

I listened to all this in silence.

'What does he think? That's what I want to know. Does he actually imagine I'm hiding something? He – he – positively *accused* me yesterday.'

I shrugged my shoulders.

'It is surely of no consequence, Mrs Ackroyd,' I said. 'Since you are not concealing anything, any remarks he may have made do not apply to you.'

Mrs Ackroyd went off at a tangent, after her usual fashion.

'Servants are so tiresome,' she said. 'They gossip, and talk amongst themselves. And then it gets round – and all the time there's probably nothing in it at all.'

'Have the servants been talking?' I asked. 'What about?'

Mrs Ackroyd cast a very shrewd glance at me. It quite threw me off my balance.

'I was sure *you'd* know, doctor, if anyone did. You were with M. Poirot all the time, weren't you?'

'I was.'

'Then of course you know. It was that girl, Ursula Bourne, wasn't it? Naturally – she's leaving. She *would* want to make all the trouble she could. Spiteful, that's what they are. They're all alike. Now, you being there, doctor, you must know exactly what she did say? I'm most anxious that no wrong impression should get about. After all, you don't repeat every little detail to the police, do you? There are family matters sometimes – nothing to do with the question of the murder. But if the girl was spiteful, she may have made out all sorts of things.'

I was shrewd enough to see that a very real anxiety lay behind these outpourings. Poirot had been justified in his premises. Of the six people round the table yesterday, Mrs Ackroyd at least had had something to hide. It was for me to discover what that something might be.

'If I were you, Mrs Ackroyd,' I said brusquely, 'I should make a clean breast of things.'

She gave a little scream.

'Oh! doctor, how can you be so abrupt. It sounds as though – as though— And I can explain everything so simply.'

'Then why not do so?' I suggested.

Mrs Ackroyd took out a frilled handkerchief, and became tearful.

'I thought, doctor, that you might put it to M. Poirot – explain it, you know – because it's so difficult for a foreigner to see our point of view. And you don't know – nobody could know – what I've had to contend with. A martyrdom – a long martyrdom. That's what my life has been. I don't like to speak ill of the dead – but there it is. Not the smallest bill but it had all to be gone over – just as though Roger had had a few miserly hundreds a year instead of being (as Mr Hammond told me yesterday) one of the wealthiest men in these parts.'

Mrs Ackroyd paused to dab her eyes with the frilled handkerchief.

'Yes,' I said encouragingly. 'You were talking about bills?'

'Those dreadful bills. And some I didn't like to show Roger at all. They were things a man wouldn't understand. He would have said the things weren't necessary. And of course they mounted up, you know, and they kept coming in—'

She looked at me appealingly, as though asking me to condole with her on this striking peculiarity.

'It's a habit they have,' I agreed.

And the tone altered – became quite abusive. 'I assure you, doctor, I was becoming a nervous wreck. I couldn't sleep at nights. And a dreadful fluttering round the heart. And then I got a letter from a Scotch gentleman – as a matter of fact there were two letters – both Scotch gentlemen. Mr Bruce MacPherson was one, and the other was Colin MacDonald. Quite a coincidence.'

'Hardly that,' I said dryly. 'They are usually Scotch gentlemen, but I suspect a Semitic train in their ancestry.'

'Ten pounds to ten thousand on note of hand alone,' murmured Mrs Ackroyd reminiscently. 'I wrote to one of them, but it seemed there were difficulties.'

She paused.

I gathered that we were just coming to delicate ground. I have never known anyone more difficult to bring to the point.

'You see,' murmured Mrs Ackroyd, 'it's all a question of expectations, isn't it? Testamentary expectations. And though, of course, I expected that Roger would provide for me, I didn't *know*. I thought that if only I could glance over a copy of his will – not in any sense of vulgar prying – but just so that I could make my own arrangements.'

She glanced sideways at me. The position was now very delicate indeed. Fortunately words, ingeniously used, will serve to mask the ugliness of naked facts.

'I could only tell this to you, dear Doctor Sheppard,' said Mrs Ackroyd rapidly. 'I can trust you not to misjudge me, and to represent the matter in the right light to M. Poirot. It was on Friday afternoon—'

She came to a stop and swallowed uncertainly.

'Yes,' I repeated encouragingly. 'On Friday afternoon. Well?'

'Everyone was out, or so I thought. And I went into Roger's study – I had some real reason for going there – I mean, there was nothing underhand about it. And as I saw all the papers heaped on the desk, it just came to me, like a flash: "I wonder if Roger keeps his will in one of the drawers of the desk." I'm so impulsive, always was, from a child. I do things on the spur of the moment. He'd left his keys – very careless of him – in the lock of the top drawer.'

'I see,' I said helpfully. 'So you searched the desk. Did you find the will?'

Mrs Ackroyd gave a little scream, and I realised that I had not been sufficiently diplomatic.

'How dreadful it sounds. But it wasn't at all like that really.'

'Of course it wasn't,' I said hastily. 'You must forgive my unfortunate way of putting things.'

'Of course, men are so peculiar. In dear Roger's place, I should have not objected to revealing the provisions of my will. But men are so secretive. One is forced to adopt little subterfuges in self-defence.'

'And the result of the little subterfuge?' I asked.

'That's just what I'm telling you. As I got to the bottom drawer, Bourne came in. Most awkward. Of course I shut the drawer and stood up, and I called her attention to a few specks of dust on the surface. But I didn't like the way she looked – quite respectful in manner, but a very nasty light in her eyes. Almost contemptuous, if you know what I mean. I never have liked that girl very much. She's a good servant, and she says Ma'am, and doesn't object to wearing caps and aprons (which I declare to you a lot of them do nowadays), and she can say "Not at home" without scruples if she has to answer the door instead of Parker, and she doesn't have those peculiar gurgling noises inside which so many parlourmaids seem to have when they wait on table – Let me see, where was I?'

'You were saying, that in spite of several valuable qualities, you never liked Bourne.'

'No more I do. She's – odd. There's something different about her from the others. Too well educated, that's my opinion. You can't tell who are ladies and who aren't nowadays.'

'And what happened next?' I asked.

'Nothing. At least, Roger came in. And I thought he was out for a walk. And he said: "What's all this?" and I said, "Nothing. I just came in to fetch *Punch*." And I took *Punch* and went out with it. Bourne stayed behind. I heard her asking Roger if she could speak to him for a minute. I went straight up to my room, to lie down. I was very upset.'

There was a pause.

'You will explain to M. Poirot, won't you? You can see for yourself what a trivial matter the whole thing was. But, of course, when he was so stern about concealing things, I thought of this at once. Bourne may have made some extraordinary story out of it, but you can explain, can't you?'

'That is all?' I said. 'You have told me everything?'

'Ye-es,' said Mrs Ackroyd. 'Oh! yes,' she added firmly.

But I had noted the momentary hesitation, and I knew that there was still something she was keeping back. It was nothing less than a flash of sheer genius that prompted me to ask the question I did.

'Mrs Ackroyd,' I said, 'was it you who left the silver table open?'

I had my answer in the blush of guilt that even rouge and powder could not conceal.

'How did you know?' she whispered.

'It was you, then?'

'Yes – I – you see – there were one or two pieces of old silver – very interesting. I had been reading up the subject and there was an illustration of quite a small piece which had fetched an immense sum at Christy's. It looked to be just the same as the one in the silver table. I thought I would take it up to London with me when I went – and – and have it valued. Then if it really was a valuable piece, just think what a charming surprise it would have been for Roger.'

I refrained from comments, accepting Mrs Ackroyd's story on its merits. I even forbore to ask her why it was necessary to abstract what she wanted in such a surreptitious manner.

'Why did you leave the lid open?' I asked. 'Did you forget?'

'I was startled,' said Mrs Ackroyd. 'I heard footsteps coming along the terrace outside. I hastened out of the room and just got up the stairs before Parker opened the front door to you.'

'That must have been Miss Russell,' I said thoughtfully. Mrs Ackroyd had revealed to me one fact that was extremely interesting. Whether her designs upon Ackroyd's silver had been strictly honourable I neither knew nor cared. What did interest me was the fact that Miss Russell must have entered the drawing-room by the window, and that I had not been wrong when I judged her to be out of breath with running. Where had she been? I thought of the summer-house and the scrap of cambric.

'I wonder if Miss Russell has her handkerchiefs starched!' I exclaimed on the spur of the moment.

Mrs Ackroyd's start recalled me to myself, and I rose.

'You think you can explain to M. Poirot?' she asked anxiously.

'Oh, certainly. Absolutely.'

I got away at last, after being forced to listen to more justifications of her conduct.

The parlourmaid was in the hall, and it was she who helped me on with my overcoat. I observed her more closely than I had done heretofore. It was clear that she had been crying.

'How is it,' I asked, 'that you told us that Mr Ackroyd sent for you on Friday to his study? I hear now that it was *you* who asked to speak to *him*.'

For a minute the girl's eyes dropped before mine.

Then she spoke.

'I meant to leave in any case,' she said uncertainly.

I said no more. She opened the front door for me. Just as I was passing out, she said suddenly in a low voice:

'Excuse me, sir, is there any news of Captain Paton?'

I shook my head, looking at her inquiringly.

'He ought to come back,' she said. 'Indeed – indeed he ought to come back.'

She was looking at me with appealing eyes.

'Does no one know where he is?' she asked.

'Do you?' I said sharply.

She shook her head.

'No, indeed I know nothing. But anyone who was a friend to him would tell him this: he ought to come back.'

I lingered, thinking that perhaps the girl would say more. Her next question surprised me.

'When do they think the murder was done? Just before ten o'clock?'

'That is the idea,' I said. 'Between a quarter to ten and the hour.'

'Not earlier? Not before a quarter to ten?'

I looked at her attentively. She was so clearly eager for a reply in the affirmative.

'That's out of the question,' I said. 'Miss Ackroyd saw her uncle alive at a quarter to ten.'

She turned away, and her whole figure seemed to drop.

'A handsome girl,' I said to myself as I drove off. 'An exceedingly handsome girl.'

Caroline was at home. She had had a visit from Poirot and was very pleased and important about it.

'I am helping him with the case,' she explained.

I felt rather uneasy. Caroline is bad enough as it is. What will she be like with her detective instincts encouraged?

'Are you going round the neighbourhood looking for Ralph Paton's mysterious girl?' I inquired.

'I might do that on my own account,' said Caroline. 'No, this is a special thing M. Poirot wants me to find out for him.'

'What is it?' I asked.

'He wants to know whether Ralph Paton's boots were black or brown,' said Caroline with tremendous solemnity.

I stared at her. I see now that I was unbelievably stupid about these boots. I failed altogether to grasp the point.

'They were brown shoes,' I said. 'I saw them.'

'Not shoes, James, boots. M. Poirot wants to know whether a pair of boots Ralph had with him at the hotel were brown or black. A lot hangs on it.'

Call me dense if you like. I didn't see.

'And how are you going to find out?' I asked.

Caroline said there would be no difficulty about that. Our

Annie's dearest friend was Miss Gannett's maid, Clara. And Clara was walking out with the Boots at the Three Boars. The whole thing was simplicity itself, and by the aid of Miss Gannett, who co-operated loyally, at once giving Clara leave of absence, the matter was rushed through at express speed.

It was when we were sitting down to lunch that Caroline remarked, with would-be unconcern:

'About those boots of Ralph Paton's.'

'Well,' I said, 'what about them?'

'M. Poirot thought they were probably brown. He was wrong. They're black.'

And Caroline nodded her head several times. She evidently felt that she had scored a point over Poirot.

I did not answer. I was puzzling over what colour of a pair of Ralph Paton's boots had to do with the case.

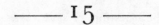

GEOFFREY RAYMOND

I was to have a further proof that day of the success of Poirot's tactics. That challenge of his had been a subtle touch born of his knowledge of human nature. A mixture of fear and guilt had wrung the truth from Mrs Ackroyd. She was the first to react.

That afternoon when I returned from seeing my patients, Caroline told me that Geoffrey Raymond had just left.

'Did he want to see me?' I asked, as I hung up my coat in the hall.

Caroline was hovering by my elbow.

'It was M. Poirot he wanted to see,' she said. 'He'd just come from The Larches. Mr Poirot was out. Mr Raymond thought that he might be here, or that you might know where he was.'

'I haven't the least idea.'

'I tried to make him wait,' said Caroline, 'but he said he would call back at The Larches in half an hour, and went away down the village. A great pity, because M. Poirot came in practically the minute after he left.'

'Came in here?'

'No, to his own house.'

'How do you know?'

'The side window,' said Caroline briefly.

It seemed to me that we had now exhausted the topic. Caroline thought otherwise.

'Aren't you going across?'

'Across where?'

'To The Larches, of course.'

'My dear Caroline,' I said, 'what for?'

'Mr Raymond wanted to see him very particularly,' said Caroline. 'You might hear what it's all about.'

I raised my eyebrows.

'Curiosity is not my besetting sin,' I remarked coldly. 'I can exist comfortably without knowing exactly what my neighbours are doing and thinking.'

'Stuff and nonsense, James,' said my sister. 'You want to know just as much as I do. You're not so honest, that's all. You always have to pretend.'

'Really, Caroline,' I said, and retired into my surgery.

Ten minutes later Caroline tapped at the door and entered. In her hand she held what seemed to be a pot of jam.

'I wonder, James,' she said, 'if you would mind taking this pot of medlar jelly across to M. Poirot? I promised it to him. He has never tasted any home-made medlar jelly.'

'Why can't Annie go?' I asked coldly.

'She's doing some mending. I can't spare her.'

Caroline and I looked at each other.

'Very well,' I said, rising. 'But if I take the beastly thing, I shall just leave it at the door. You understand that?'

My sister raised her eyebrows.

'Naturally,' she said. 'Who suggested you should do anything else?'

The honours were with Caroline.

'If you *do* happen to see M. Poirot,' she said, as I opened the front door, 'you might tell him about the boots.'

It was a most subtle parting shot. I wanted dreadfully to understand the enigma of the boots. When the old lady with the Breton cap opened the door to me, I found myself asking if M. Poirot was in, quite automatically.

Poirot sprang up to meet me, with every appearance of pleasure.

'Sit down, my good friend,' he said. 'The big chair? This small one? The room is not too hot, no?'

I thought it was stifling, but refrained from saying so. The windows were closed, and a large fire burned in the grate.

'The English people, they have a mania for the fresh air,' declared Poirot. 'The big air, it is all very well outside, where it belongs. Why admit it to the house? But let us not discuss such banalities. You have something for me, yes?'

'Two things,' I said. 'First – this – from my sister.'

I handed over the pot of medlar jelly.

'How kind of Mademoiselle Caroline. She has remembered her promise. And the second thing?'

'Information – of a kind.'

And I told him of my interview with Mrs Ackroyd. He listened with interest, but not much excitement.

'It clears the ground,' he said thoughtfully. 'And it has a certain value as confirming the evidence of the housekeeper. She said, you remember, that she found the silver table lid open and closed it down in passing.'

'What about her statement that she went into the drawing-room to see if the flowers were fresh?'

'Ah! we never took that very seriously, did we, my friend? It was patently an excuse, trumped up in a hurry, by a woman who felt it urgent to explain her presence – which, by the way, you would probably never have thought of questioning. I considered it possible that her agitation might arise from the fact that she had been tampering with the silver table, but I think now that we must look for another cause.'

'Yes,' I said. 'Whom did she go out to meet? And why?'

'You think she went to meet someone?'

'I do.'

Poirot nodded.

'So do I,' he said thoughtfully.

There was a pause.

'By the way,' I said, 'I've got a message for you from my sister. Ralph Paton's boots were black, not brown.'

I was watching him closely as I gave the message, and I fancied that I saw a momentary flicker of discomposure. If so, it passed almost immediately.

'She is absolutely positive they are not brown?'

'Absolutely.'

'Ah!' said Poirot regretfully. 'That is a pity.'

And he seemed quite crestfallen.

He entered into no explanations, but at once started a new subject of conversation.

'The housekeeper, Miss Russell, who came to consult you on that Friday morning – is it indiscreet to ask what passed at the interview – apart from the medical details, I mean?'

'Not at all,' I said. 'When the professional part of the conversation was over, we talked for a few minutes about poisons, and the ease or difficulty of detecting them, and about drug-taking and drug-takers.'

'With special reference to cocaine?' asked Poirot.

'How did you know?' I asked, somewhat surprised.

For answer, the little man rose and crossed the room to where newspapers were filed. He brought me a copy of the *Daily Budget,* dated Friday, 16th September, and showed me an article dealing with the smuggling of cocaine. It was a somewhat lurid article, written with an eye to picturesque effect.

'That is what put cocaine into her head, my friend,' he said.

I would have catechised him further, for I did not quite understand his meaning, but at that moment the door opened and Geoffrey Raymond was announced.

He came in fresh and debonair as ever, and greeted us both.

'How are you, doctor? M. Poirot, this is the second time I've been here this morning. I was anxious to catch you.'

'Perhaps I'd better be off,' I suggested rather awkwardly.

'Not on my account, doctor. No, it's just this,' he went on, seating himself at a wave of invitation from Poirot, 'I've got a confession to make.'

'*En verite?*' said Poirot, with an air of polite interest.

'Oh, it's of no consequence, really. But, as a matter of fact, my conscience has been pricking me ever since yesterday afternoon. You accused us all of keeping back something, M. Poirot. I plead guilty. I've had something up my sleeve.'

'And what is that, M. Raymond?'

'As I say, it's nothing of consequence – just this. I was in debt – badly, and that legacy came in the nick of time. Five hundred pounds puts me on my feet again with a little to spare.'

He smiled at us both with that engaging frankness that made him such a likeable youngster.

'You know how it is. Suspicious-looking policemen – don't like to admit you were hard up for money – think it will look bad to them. But I was a fool, really, because Blunt and I were in the billiard room from a quarter to ten onwards, so I've got a watertight alibi and nothing to fear. Still, when you thundered out that stuff about concealing things, I felt a nasty prick of conscience, and I thought I'd like to get it off my mind.'

He got up again and stood smiling at us.

'You are a very wise young man,' said Poirot, nodding at him with approval. 'See you, when I know that anyone is hiding things from me, I suspect that the thing hidden may be something very bad indeed. You have done well.'

'I'm glad I'm cleared from suspicion,' laughed Raymond. 'I'll be off now.'

'So that is that,' I remarked, as the door closed behind the young secretary.

'Yes,' agreed Poirot. 'A mere bagatelle – but if he had not been in the billiard room – who knows? After all, many crimes have been committed for the sake of less than five hundred pounds. It all depends on what sum is sufficient to break a man. A question of relativity, is it not so? Have you reflected, my friend, that many people in that house stood to benefit by Mr Ackroyd's death? Mrs Ackroyd, Miss Flora, young Mr Raymond, the housekeeper, Miss Russell. Only one, in fact, does not, Major Blunt.'

His tone in uttering that name was so peculiar that I looked up, puzzled.

'I don't quite understand you,' I said.

'Two of the people I accused have given me the truth.'

'You think Major Blunt has something to conceal also?'

'As for that,' remarked Poirot nonchalantly, 'there is a saying, is there not, that Englishmen conceal only one thing – their love? And Major Blunt, I should say, is not good at concealments.'

'Sometimes,' I said, 'I wonder if we haven't rather jumped to conclusions on one point.'

'What is that?'

'We've assumed that the blackmailer of Mrs Ferrars is necessarily the murderer of Mr Ackroyd. Mightn't we be mistaken?'

Poirot nodded energetically.

'Very good. Very good indeed. I wondered if that idea would come to you. Of course it is possible. But we must remember one point. The letter disappeared. Still, that, as you say, may not necessarily mean that the murderer took it. When you first found the body, Parker may have abstracted the letter unnoticed by you.'

'Parker?'

'Yes, Parker. I always come back to Parker – not as the murderer – no, he did not commit the murder; but who is more suitable than he as the mysterious scoundrel who

terrorised Mrs Ferrars? He may have got his information
about Mr Ferrars's death from one of the King's Paddock
servants. At any rate, he is more likely to have come upon it
than a casual guest such as Blunt, for instance.'

'Parker might have taken the letter,' I admitted. 'It wasn't
till later that I noticed it was gone.'

'How much later? After Blunt and Raymond were in the
room, or before?'

'I can't remember,' I said slowly. 'I think it was before – no,
afterwards. Yes, I'm almost sure it was afterwards.'

'That widens the field to three,' said Poirot thoughtfully.
'But Parker is the most likely. It is in my mind to try a little
experiment with Parker. How say you, my friend, will you
accompany me to Fernly?'

I acquiesced, and we set out at once. Poirot asked to see
Miss Ackroyd, and presently Flora came to us.

'Mademoiselle Flora,' said Poirot, 'I have to confide in you
a little secret. I am not yet satisfied of the innocence of Parker.
I propose to make a little experiment with your assistance. I
want to reconstruct some of his actions on that night. But we
must think of something to tell him – ah! I have it. I wish to
satisfy myself as to whether voices in the little lobby could have
been heard outside on the terrace. Now, ring for Parker, if
you will be so good.'

I did so, and presently the butler appeared, suave as ever.

'You rang, sir?'

'Yes, my good Parker. I have in mind a little experiment.
I have placed Major Blunt on the terrace outside the study
window. I want to see if anyone there could have heard the
voices of Miss Ackroyd and yourself in the lobby that night. I
want to enact that little scene over again. Perhaps you would
fetch the tray or whatever it was you were carrying?'

Parker vanished, and we repaired to the lobby outside the
study door. Presently we heard a chink in the outer hall, and
Parker appeared in the doorway carrying a tray with a siphon,
a decanter of whisky, and two glasses on it.

'One moment,' cried Poirot, raising his hand and seemingly
very excited. 'We must have everything in order. Just as it
occurred. It is a little method of mine.'

'A foreign custom, sir,' said Parker. 'Reconstruction of the
crime they call it, do they not?'

He was quite imperturbable as he stood there politely waiting on Poirot's orders.

'Ah! he knows something, the good Parker,' cried Poirot.

'He has read of these things. Now, I beg you, let us have everything of the most exact. You came from the outer hall – so. Mademoiselle was – where?'

'Here,' said Flora, taking up her stand just outside the study door.

'Quite right. sir,' said Parker.

'I had just closed the door,' continued Flora.

'Yes, miss.' agreed Parker. 'Your hand was still on the handle as it is now.'

'Then *allez*,' said Poirot. 'Play me the little comedy.'

Flora stood with her hand on the door handle, and Parker came stepping through the door from the hall, bearing the tray.

He stopped just inside the door. Flora spoke.

'Oh! Parker. Mr Ackroyd doesn't want to be disturbed again to-night.'

'Is that right?' she added in an undertone.

'To the best of my recollection, Miss Flora,' said Parker, 'but I fancy you used the word evening instead of night.' Then, raising his voice in a somewhat theatrical fashion: 'Very good, miss. Shall I lock up as usual?'

'Yes, please.'

Parker retired through the door, Flora followed him, and started to ascend the main staircase.

'Is that enough?' she asked over her shoulder.

'Admirable,' declared the little man, rubbing his hands. 'By the way, Parker, are you sure there were two glasses on the tray that evening? Who was the second one for?'

'I always bring two glasses, sir,' said Parker. 'Is there anything further?'

'Nothing. I thank you.'

Parker withdrew, dignified to the last.

Poirot stood in the middle of the hall frowning. Flora came down and joined us.

'Has your experiment been successful?' she asked. 'I don't quite understand, you know—'

Poirot smiled admirably at her.

'It is not necessary that you should,' he said. 'But tell me, were there indeed two glasses on Parker's tray that night?'

Flora wrinkled her brows a minute.

'I really can't remember,' she said. 'I think there were. Is – is that the object of your experiment?'

Poirot took her hand and patted it.

'Put it this way,' he said. 'I am always interested to see if people will speak the truth.'

'And did Parker speak the truth?'

'I rather think he did,' said Poirot thoughtfully.

A few minutes later saw us retracing our steps to the village.

'What was the point of that question about the glasses?' I asked curiously.

Poirot shrugged his shoulders.

'One must say something,' he remarked. 'That particular question did as well as any other.'

I stared at him.

'At any rate, my friend,' he said more seriously, 'I know now something I wanted to know. Let us leave it at that.'

—— 16 ——

AN EVENING AT MAH JONG

That night we had a little Mah Jong party. This kind of simple entertainment is very popular in King's Abbot. The guests arrive in goloshes and waterproofs after dinner. They partake of coffee and later of cake, sandwiches, and tea.

On this particular night our guests were Miss Gannett and Colonel Carter, who lives near the church. A good deal of gossip is handed round at these evenings, sometimes seriously interfering with the game in progress. We used to play bridge – chatty bridge of the worst description. We find Mah Jong much more peaceful. The irritated demand as to why on earth your partner did not lead a certain card is entirely done away with, and though we still express criticisms frankly, there is not the same acrimonious spirit.

'Very cold evening, eh, Sheppard?' said Colonel Carter, standing with his back to the fire. Caroline had taken Miss Gannett to her own room, and was there assisting her to disentangle herself from her many wraps. 'Reminds me of the Afghan passes.'

'Indeed?' I said politely.

'Very mysterious business this about poor Ackroyd,' continued the colonel, accepting a cup of coffee. 'A deuce of a lot behind it – that's what I say. Between you and me, Sheppard, I've heard the word blackmail mentioned!'

The colonel gave me the look which might be tabulated 'one man of the world to another.'

'A woman in it, no doubt,' he said. 'Depend upon it, a woman in it.'

Caroline and Miss Gannett joined us at this minute. Miss Gannett drank coffee whilst Caroline got out the Mah Jong box and poured out the tiles upon the table.

'Washing the tiles,' said the colonel facetiously. 'That's right – washing the tiles, as we used to say in the Shanghai Club.'

It is the private opinion of both Caroline and myself that Colonel Carter has never been in the Shanghai Club in his life. More, that he has never been farther east than India, where he juggled with tins of bully beef and plum and apple jam during the Great War. But the colonel is determinedly military, and in King's Abbot we permit people to indulge their little idiosyncrasies freely.

'Shall we begin?' said Caroline.

We sat round the table. For some five minutes there was complete silence, owing to the fact that there is tremendous secret competition amongst us as to who can build their wall quickest.

'Go on, James,' said Caroline at last. 'You're East Wind.'

I discarded a tile. A round or two proceeded, broken by the monotonous remarks of 'Three Bamboos,' 'Two Circles,' 'Pung,' and frequently from Miss Gannett 'Unpung,' owing to that lady's habit of too hastily claiming tiles to which she had no right.'

'I saw Flora Ackroyd this morning,' said Miss Gannett. 'Pung – no – Unpung. I made a mistake.'

'Four Circles,' said Caroline. 'Where did you see her?'

'She didn't see *me*,' said Miss Gannett, with that tremendous significance only to be met with in small villages.

'Ah!' said Caroline interestedly. 'Chow.'

'I believe,' said Miss Gannett, temporarily diverted, 'that it's the right thing nowadays to say "Chee" not "Chow." '

'Nonsense,' said Caroline. 'I have always said *"Chow."* '

'In the Shanghai Club,' said Colonel Carter, 'they say *"Chow."* '

Miss Gannett retired, crushed.

'What were you saying about Flora Ackroyd?' asked Caroline, after a moment or two devoted to the game. 'Was she with anyone?'

'Very much so,' said Miss Gannett.

The eyes of the two ladies met, and seemed to exchange information.

'Really,' said Caroline interestedly. 'Is that it? Well, it doesn't surprise me in the least.'

'We're waiting for you to discard, Miss Caroline,' said the colonel. He sometimes affects the pose of the bluff male, intent on the game and indifferent to gossip. But nobody is deceived.

'If you ask me,' said Miss Gannett. ('Was that a Bamboo you discarded, dear? Oh! no, I see now – it was a Circle.) As I was saying, if you ask me, Flora's been exceedingly lucky. Exceedingly lucky she's been.'

'How's that, Miss Gannett?' asked the colonel. 'I'll Pung that Green Dragon. How do you make out that Miss Flora's been lucky? Very charming girl and all that, I know.'

'I mayn't know very much about crime,' said Miss Gannett, with the air of one who knows everything there is to know, 'but I can tell you one thing. The first question that's always asked is "who last saw the deceased alive?" and the person who did is regarded with suspicion. Now, Flora Ackroyd last saw her uncle alive. It might have looked very nasty for her – very nasty indeed. It's my opinion – and I give it for what it's worth, that Ralph Paton is staying away on her account, to draw suspicion away from her.'

'Come, now,' I protested mildly, 'you surely can't suggest that a young girl like Flora Ackroyd is capable of stabbing her uncle in cold blood?'

'Well, I don't know,' said Miss Gannett. 'I've just been reading a book from the library about the underworld of Paris, and it says that some of the worst women criminals are young girls with the faces of angels.'

'That's in France,' said Caroline instantly.

'Just so,' said the colonel. 'Now, I'll tell you a very curious thing – a story that was going round the Bazaars in India. . . .'

The colonel's story was one of interminable length, and of curiously little interest. A thing that happened in India many years ago cannot compare for a moment with an event that took place in King's Abbot the day before yesterday.

It was Caroline who brought the colonel's story to a close by fortunately going Mah Jong. After the slight unpleasantness always occasioned by my corrections of Caroline's somewhat faulty arithmetic, we started a new hand.

'East Wind passes,' said Caroline. 'I've got an idea of my own about Ralph Paton. Three Characters. But I'm keeping it to myself for the present.'

'Are you, dear?' said Miss Gannett. 'Chow – I mean Pung.'

'Yes,' said Caroline firmly.

'Was it all right about the boots?' asked Miss Gannett. 'Their being black, I mean?'

'Quite all right,' said Caroline.

'What was the point, do you think?' asked Miss Gannett. Caroline pursed up her lips, and shook her head with an air of knowing all about it.

'Pung,' said Miss Gannett. 'No – Unpung. I suppose that now the doctor's in with M. Poirot he knows all the secrets?'

'Far from it,' I said.

'James is so modest,' said Caroline. 'Ah! a concealed Kong.'

The colonel gave vent to a whistle. For the moment gossip was forgotten.

'Your own wind, too,' he said. '*And* you've got two Pungs of Dragons. We must be careful. Miss Caroline's out for a big hand.'

We played for some minutes with no irrelevant conversation.

'This M. Poirot now,' said Colonel Carter, 'is he really such a great detective?'

'The greatest the world has ever known,' said Caroline solemnly. 'He has to come here incognito to avoid publicity.'

'Chow,' said Miss Gannett. 'Quite wonderful for our little village, I'm sure. By the way, Clara – my maid, you know – is great friends with Elsie, the housemaid at Fernly, and what do you think Elsie told her? That there's been a lot of money stolen, and it's her opinion – Elsie's – I mean, that the parlourmaid had something to do with it. She's leaving at the month, and she's crying a good deal at night. If you ask me, the girl is very likely in league with a *gang*. She's always been a queer girl – she's not friends with any of the girls round here. She goes off by herself on her days out – very unnatural, I call it, and most suspicious. I asked her once to come to our Friendly Girls' Evenings, but she refused, and then I asked her a few questions about her home and her family – all that sort of thing, and I'm bound to say I considered her manner most impertinent. Outwardly very respectful – but she shut me up in the most barefaced way.'

Miss Gannett stopped for breath, and the colonel, who was totally uninterested in the servant question, remarked that in the Shanghai Club brisk play was the invariable rule.

We had a round of brisk play.

'That Miss Russell,' said Caroline. 'She came here pretending to consult James on Friday morning. It's my opinion she wanted to see where the poisons were kept. Five Characters.'

'Chow,' said Miss Gannett. 'What an extraordinary idea! I wonder if you can be right.'

'Talking of poisons,' said the colonel. 'Eh —what? Haven't I discarded? Oh! Eight Bamboos.'

'Mah Jong!' said Miss Gannett.

Caroline was very much annoyed.

'One Red Dragon,' she said regretfully, 'and I should have had a hand of three doubles.'

'I've had two Red Dragons all the time,' I mentioned.

'So exactly like you, James,' said Caroline reproachfully. 'You've no conception of the spirit of the game.'

I myself thought I had played rather cleverly. I should have had to pay Caroline an enormous amount if she had gone Mah Jong. Miss Gannett's Mah Jong was of the poorest variety possible, as Caroline did not fail to point out to her.

East Wind passed, and we started a new hand in silence.

'What I was going to tell you just now was this,' said Caroline.

'Yes?' said Miss Gannett encouragingly.

'My idea about Ralph Paton, I mean.'

'Yes, dear,' said Miss Gannett, still more encouragingly. 'Chow!'

'It's a sign of weakness to Chow so early,' said Caroline severely. 'You should go for a big hand.'

'I know,' said Miss Gannett. 'You were saying – about Ralph Paton, you know?'

'Yes. Well, I've a pretty shrewd idea where he is.'

We all stopped to stare at her.

'This is very interesting, Miss Caroline,' said Colonel Carter. 'All your own idea, eh?'

'Well, not exactly. I'll tell you about it. You know that big map of the county we have in the hall?'

We all said Yes.

'As M. Poirot was going out the other day, he stopped and looked at it, and he made some remark – I can't remember exactly what it was. Something about Cranchester being the only big town anywhere near us – which is true, of course. But after he had gone – it came to me suddenly.'

'What came to you?'

'His meaning. Of course Ralph is in Cranchester.'

It was at that moment that I knocked down the rack that

held my pieces. My sister immediately reproved me for clumsiness, but half-heartedly. She was intent on her theory.

'Cranchester, Miss Caroline?' said Colonel Carter. 'Surely not Cranchester! It's so near.'

'That's exactly it,' cried Caroline triumphantly. 'It seems quite clear by now that he didn't get away from here by train. He must simply have walked into Cranchester. And I believe he's there still. No one would dream of his being so near at hand.'

I pointed out several objections to the theory, but when once Caroline has got something firmly into her head, nothing dislodges it.

'And you think M. Poirot has the same idea,' said Miss Gannett thoughtfully. 'It's a curious coincidence, but I was out for a walk this afternoon on the Cranchester road, and he passed me in a car coming from that direction.'

We all looked at each other.

'Why, dear me,' said Miss Gannett suddenly, 'I'm Mah Jong all the time, and I never noticed it.'

Caroline's attention was distracted from her own inventive exercises. She pointed out to Miss Gannett that a hand consisting of mixed suits and too many Chows was hardly worth going Mah Jong on. Miss Gannett listened imperturbably and collected her counters.

'Yes, dear, I know what you mean,' she said. 'But it rather depends on what kind of a hand you have to start with, doesn't it?'

'You'll never get the big hands if you don't go for them,' urged Caroline.

'Well, we must all play our own way, mustn't we?' said Miss Gannett. She loked down at her counters. 'After all, I'm up, so far.'

Caroline, who was considerably down, said nothing.

East Wind passed, and we set to once more. Annie brought in the tea things. Caroline and Miss Gannett were both slightly ruffled as is often the case during one of these festive evenings.

'If you would only play a leetle quicker, dear,' said Caroline, as Miss Gannett hesitated over her discard. 'The Chinese put down the tiles so quickly it sounds like little birds pattering.'

For some minutes we played like the Chinese.

'You haven't contributed much to the sum of information, Sheppard,' said Colonel Carter genially. 'You're a sly dog.

Hand in glove with the great detective, and not a hint as to the way things are going.'

'James is an extraordinary creature,' said Caroline. 'He can *not* bring himself to part with information.'

She looked at me with some disfavour.

'I assure you,' I said, 'that I don't know anything. Poirot keeps his own counsel.'

'Wise man,' said the colonel with a chuckle. 'He doesn't give himself away. But they're wonderful fellows, these foreign detectives. Up to all sorts of dodges, I believe.'

'Pung,' said Miss Gannett, in a tone of quiet triumph. 'And Mah Jong.'

The situation became more strained. It was annoyance at Miss Gannett's going Mah Jong for the third time running which prompted Caroline to say to me as we built a fresh wall:

'You are too tiresome, James. You sit there like a dead-head, and say nothing at all!'

'But, my dear,' I protested, 'I have really nothing to say – that is, of the kind you mean.'

'Nonsense,' said Caroline, as she sorted her hand. 'You *must* know something interesting.'

I did not answer for a moment. I was overwhelmed and intoxicated. I had read of there being such a thing as The Perfect Winning – going Mah Jong on one's original hand. I had never hoped to hold the hand myself.

With suppressed triumph I laid my hand face upwards on the table.

'As they say in the Shanghai Club,' I remarked – 'Tin-ho – the Perfect Winning!'

The colonel's eyes nearly bulged out of his head.

'Upon my soul,' he said. 'What an extraordinary thing. I never saw that happen before!'

It was then that I went on, goaded by Caroline's gibes, and rendered reckless by my triumph.

'And as to anything interesting,' I said. 'What about a gold wedding ring with a date and "From R." inside.'

I pass over the scene that followed. I was made to say exactly where this treasure was found. I was made to reveal the date.

'March 13th,' said Caroline. 'Just six months ago. Ah!'

Out of a babel of excited suggestions and suppositions three theories were evolved:

1. That of Colonel Carter: that Ralph was secretly married to Flora. The first or most simple solution.

2. That of Miss Gannett: that Roger Ackroyd had been secretly married to Mrs Ferrars.

3. That of my sister: that Roger Ackroyd had married his housekeeper, Miss Russell.

A fourth or super-theory was propounded by Caroline later as we went up to bed.

'Mark my words,' she said suddenly, 'I shouldn't be at all surprised if Geoffrey Raymond and Flora weren't married.'

'Surely it would be "From G," not "From R" then,' I suggested.

'You never know. Some girls call men by their surnames. And you heard what Miss Gannett said this evening – about Flora's carryings on.'

Strictly speaking, I had not heard Miss Gannett say anything of the kind, but I respected Caroline's knowledge of innuendoes.

'How about Hector Blunt?' I hinted. 'If it's anybody—'

'Nonsense,' said Caroline. 'I dare say he admires her – may even be in love with her. But depend upon it a girl isn't going to fall in love with a man old enough to be her father when there's a good-looking young secretary about. She may encourage Major Blunt just as a blind. Girls are very artful. But there's one thing I *do* tell you, James Sheppard. Flora Ackroyd does not care a penny piece for Ralph Paton, and never has. You can take it from me.'

I took it from her meekly.

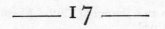

PARKER

It occurred to me the next morning that under the exhilaration produced by Tin-ho or the Perfect Winning, I might have been slightly indiscreet. True, Poirot had not asked me to keep the discovery of the ring to myself. On the other hand, he had said nothing about it whilst at Fernly, and as far as I knew, I was the only person aware that it had been found. I felt distinctly guilty. The fact was by now spreading through King's Abbot like wildfire. I was expecting wholesale reproaches from Poirot any minute.

The joint funeral of Mrs Ferrars and Roger Ackroyd was

fixed for eleven o'clock. It was a melancholy and impressive ceremony. All the party from Fernly were there.

After it was over, Poirot, who had also been present, took me by the arm, and invited me to accompany him back to The Larches. He was looking very grave, and I feared that my indiscretion of the night before had got round to his ears. But it soon transpired that his thoughts were occupied by something of a totally different nature.

'See you,' he said. 'We must act. With your help I propose to examine a witness. We will question, we will put such fear into him that the truth is bound to come out.'

'What witness are you talking of?' I asked, very much surprised.

'Parker!' said Poirot. 'I asked him to be at my house this morning at twelve o'clock. He should await us there at this very minute.'

'What do you think?' I ventured, glancing sideways at his face.

'I know this – that I am not satisfied.'

'You think that it was he who blackmailed Mrs Ferrars?'

'Either that, or—'

'Well?' I said, after waiting a minute or two.

'My friend, I will say this to you – I hope it was he.'

The gravity of his manner, and something indefinable that tinged it, reduced me to silence.

On arrival at The Larches, we were informed that Parker was already there awaiting our return. As we entered the room, the butler rose respectfully.

'Good-morning, Parker,' said Poirot pleasantly. 'One instant, I pray of you.'

He removed his overcoat and gloves.

'Allow me, sir,' said Parker, and sprang forward to assist him. He deposited the articles neatly on a chair by the door. Poirot watched him with approval.

'Thank you, my good Parker,' he said. 'Take a seat, will you not? What I have to say may take some time.'

Parker seated himself with an apologetic bend of the head.

'Now what do you think I asked you to come here for this morning – eh?'

Parker coughed.

'I understood, sir, that you wished to ask me a few questions about my late master – private like.'

'*Précisément*,' said Poirot, beaming. 'Have you made many experiments in blackmail?'

'Sir!'

The butler sprang to his feet.

'Do not excite yourself,' said Poirot placidly. 'Do not play the farce of the honest, injured man. You know all there is to know about the blackmail, is it not so?'

'Sir, I – I've never – never been—'

'Insulted,' suggested Poirot, 'in such a way before. Then why, my excellent Parker, were you so anxious to overhear the conversation in Mr Ackroyd's study the other evening, after you had caught the word blackmail?'

'I wasn't – I—'

'Who was your last master?' rapped out Poirot suddenly.

'My last master?'

'Yes, the master you were with before you came to Mr Ackroyd.'

'A Major Ellerby, sir—'

Poirot took the words out of his mouth.

'Just so, Major Ellerby. Major Ellerby was addicted to drugs, was he not? You travelled about with him. When he was in Bermuda there was some trouble – a man was killed. Major Ellerby was partly responsible. It was hushed up. But you knew about it. How much did Major Ellerby pay you to keep your mouth shut?'

Parker was staring at him open-mouthed. The man had gone to pieces, his cheeks shook flabbily.

'You see, me, I have made inquiries,' said Poirot pleasantly. 'It is as I say. You got a good sum then as blackmail, and Major Ellerby went on paying you until he died. Now I want to hear about your latest experiment.'

Parker still stared.

'It is useless to deny. Hercules Poirot *knows*. It is so, what I have said about Major Ellerby, is it not?'

As though against his will, Parker nodded reluctantly once. His face was ashen pale.

'But I never hurt a hair of Mr Ackroyd's head,' he moaned. 'Honest to God, sir, I didn't. I've been afraid of this coming all the time. And I tell you I didn't – I didn't kill him.'

His voice rose almost to a scream.

'I am inclined to believe you, my friend,' said Poirot. 'You have not the nerve – the courage. But I must have the truth.'

'I'll tell you anything, sir, anything you want to know. It's true that I tried to listen that night. A word or two I heard made me curious. And Mr Ackroyd's wanting not to be disturbed, and shutting himself up with the doctor the way he did. It's God's own truth what I told the police. I heard the word blackmail, sir, and well—'

He paused.

'You thought there might be something in it for you?' suggested Poirot smoothly.

'Well – well, yes, I did, sir. I thought that if Mr Ackroyd was being blackmailed, why shouldn't I have a share of the pickings?'

A very curious expression passed over Poirot's face. He leaned forward.

'Had you any reason to suppose before that night that Mr Ackroyd was being blackmailed?'

'No, indeed, sir. It was a great surprise to me. Such a regular gentleman in all his habits.'

'How much did you overhear?'

'Not very much, sir. There seemed what I might call a spite against me. Of course I had to attend to my duties in the pantry. And when I did creep along once or twice to the study it was no use. The first time Dr Sheppard came out and almost caught me in the act, and another time Mr Raymond passed me in the big hall and went that way, so I knew it was no use; and when I went with the tray, Miss Flora headed me off.'

Poirot stared for a long time at the man, as if to test his sincerity. Parker returned his gaze earnestly.

'I hope you believe me, sir. I've been afraid all along the police would rake up that old business with Major Ellerby and be suspicious of me in consequence.'

'*Eh bien*,' said Poirot at last. 'I am disposed to believe you. But there is one thing I must request of you – to show me your bank-book. You have a bank-book, I presume?'

'Yes, sir, as a matter of fact, I have it with me now.'

With no sign of confusion, he produced it from his pocket. Poirot took the slim, green-covered book and perused the entries.

'Ah! I perceive you have purchased £500 worth of National Savings Certificates this year?'

'Yes, sir. I have already over a thousand pounds saved – the result of my connection with – er – my late master, Major Ellerby. And I have had quite a little flutter on some horses this year – very successful. If you remember, sir, a rank outsider won the Jubilee. I was fortunate enough to back it – £20.'

Poirot handed him back the book.

'I will wish you good-morning. I believe that you have told

me the truth. If you have not – so much the worse for you, my friend.'

When Parker had departed, Poirot picked up his overcoat once more.

'Going out again?' I asked.

'Yes, we will pay a little visit to the good M. Hammond.'

'You believe Parker's story?'

'It is credible enough on the face of it. It seems clear that – unless he is a very good actor indeed – he genuinely believes it was Ackroyd himself who was the victim of blackmail. If so, he knows nothing at all about the Mrs Ferrars business.'

'Then in that case – who—?'

'*Précisément*! Who? But our visit to M. Hammond will accomplish one purpose. It will either clear Parker completely or else—'

'Well?'

'I fall into the bad habit of leaving my sentences unfinished this morning,' said Poirot apologetically. 'You must bear with me.'

'By the way,' I said, rather sheepishly. 'I've got a confession to make. I'm afraid I have inadvertently let out something about that ring.'

'What ring?'

'The ring you found in the goldfish pond.'

'Ah! yes,' said Poirot, smiling broadly.

'I hope you're not annoyed? It was very careless of me.'

'But not at all, my good friend, not at all. I laid no commands upon you. You were at liberty to speak of it if you so wished. She was interested, your sister?'

'She was indeed. It created a sensation. All sorts of theories are flying about.'

'Ah! And yet it is so simple. The true explanation leapt to the eye, did it not?'

'Did it?' I said dryly.

Poirot laughed.

'The wise man does not commit himself,' he observed. 'Is not that so? But here we are at Mr Hammond's.'

The lawyer was in his office, and we were ushered in without any delay. He rose and greeted us in his dry, precise manner.

Poirot came at once to the point.

'Monsieur, I desire from you certain information, that is, if you will be so good as to give it to me. You acted, I understand, for the late Mrs Ferrars of King's Paddock?'

I noticed the swift gleam of surprise which showed in the lawyer's eyes, before his professional reserve came down once more like a mask over his face.

'Certainly. All her affairs passed through our hands.'

'Very good. Now, before I ask you to tell me anything, I should like you to listen to the story Dr Sheppard will relate to you. You have no objection, have you, my friend, to repeating the conversation you had with Mr Ackroyd last Friday night?'

'Not in the least,' I said, and straightway began the recital of that strange evening.

Hammond listened with close attention.

'That is all,' I said, when I had finished.

'Blackmail,' said the lawyer thoughtfully.

'You are surprised?' asked Poirot.

The lawyer took off his pince-nez and polished them with his handkerchief.

'No,' he replied, 'I can hardly say that I am surprised. I have suspected something of the kind for some time.'

'That brings us,' said Poirot, 'to the information for which I am asking. If anyone can give us an idea of the actual sums paid, you are the man, monsieur.'

'I see no object in withholding the information,' said Hammond, after a moment or two. 'During the past year, Mrs Ferrars has sold out certain securities, and the money for them was paid into her account and not re-invested. As her income was a large one, and she lived very quietly after her husband's death, it seems certain that these sums of money were paid away for some special purpose. I once sounded her on the subject, and she said that she was obliged to support several of her husband's poor relations. I let the matter drop, of course. Until now, I have always imagined that the money was paid to some woman who had had a claim on Ashley Ferrars. I never dreamed that Mrs Ferrars herself was involved.'

'And the amount?' asked Poirot.

'In all, I should say the various sums totalled at least twenty thousand pounds.'

'Twenty thousand pounds!' I exclaimed. 'In one year!'

'Mrs Ferrars was a very wealthy woman,' said Poirot dryly. 'And the penalty for murder is not a pleasant one.'

'Is there anything else that I can tell you?' inquired Mr Hammond.

'I thank you, no,' said Poirot rising. 'All my excuses for having deranged you.'

'Not at all, not at all.'

'The word derange,' I remarked, when we were outside again, 'is applicable to mental disorder only.'

'Ah!' cried Poirot, 'never will my English be quite perfect. A curious language. I should then have said disarranged, *n'est-ce pas?*'

'Disturbed is the word you had in mind.'

'I thank you, my friend. The word exact, you are zealous for it. *Eh bien*, what about our friend, Parker now? With twenty thousand pounds in hand, would he have continued being a butler? *Je ne pense pas.* It is, of course, possible that he banked the money under another name, but I am disposed to believe he spoke the truth to us. If he is a scoundrel, he is a scoundrel on a mean scale. He has not the big ideas. That leaves us as a possibility, Raymond, or – well – Major Blunt.'

'Surely not Raymond,' I objected. 'Since we know that he was desperately hard up for a matter of five hundred pounds.'

'That is what he says, yes.'

'And as to Hector Blunt—'

'I will tell you something as to the good Major Blunt,' interrupted Poirot. 'It is my business to make inquiries. I make them. *Eh bien* – that legacy of which he speaks, I have discovered that the amount of it was close upon twenty thousand pounds. What do you think of that?'

I was so taken aback that I could hardly speak.

'It's impossible,' I said at last. 'A well-known man like Hector Blunt.'

Poirot shrugged his shoulders.

'Who knows? At least he is a man with big ideas. I confess that I hardly see him as a blackmailer, but there is another possibility that you have not even considered.'

'What is that?'

'The fire, my friend. Ackroyd himself may have destroyed that letter, blue envelope and all, after you left him.'

'I hardly think that likely,' I said slowly. 'And yet – of course, it may be so. He might have changed his mind.'

We had just arrived at my house, and on the spur of the moment I invited Poirot to come in and take pot luck.

I thought Caroline would be pleased with me, but it is hard to satisfy one's womenfolk. It appears that we were eating chops for lunch – the kitchen staff being regaled on tripe and onions. And two chops set before three people are productive of embarrassment.

But Caroline is seldom daunted for long. With magnificent

mendacity, she explained to Poirot that although James laughed at her for doing so, she adhered strictly to a vegetarian diet. She descanted ecstatically on the delights of nut cutlets (which I am quite sure she has never tasted) and ate a Welsh rarebit with gusto and frequent cutting remarks as to the dangers of 'fresh' foods.

Afterwards, when we were sitting in front of the fire and smoking, Caroline attacked Poirot directly.

'Not found Ralph Paton yet?' she asked.

'Where should I find him, mademoiselle?'

'I thought, perhaps, you'd found him in Cranchester,' said Caroline, with intense meaning in her tone.

Poirot looked merely bewildered.

'In Cranchester? But why in Cranchester?'

I enlightened him with a touch of malice.

'One of our ample staff of private detectives happened to see you in a car on the Cranchester road yesterday,' I explained.

Poirot's bewilderment vanished. He laughed heartily.

'Ah, that! A simple visit to the dentist, *c'est tout*. My tooth, it aches. I go there. My tooth, it is at once better. I think to return quickly. The dentist, he says No. Better to have it out. I argue. He insists. He has his way! That particular tooth, it will never ache again.'

Caroline collapsed rather like a pricked balloon.

We fell to discussing Ralph Paton.

'A weak nature,' I insisted. 'But not a vicious one.'

'Ah!' said Poirot. 'But weakness, where does it end?'

'Exactly,' said Caroline. 'Take James here – weak as water, if I weren't about to look after him.'

'My dear Caroline,' I said irritably, 'can't you talk without dragging in personalities?'

'You *are* weak, James,' said Caroline, quite unmoved. 'I'm eight years older than you are – oh! I don't mind M. Poirot knowing that—'

'I should never have guessed it, mademoiselle,' said Poirot, with a gallant little bow.

'Eight years older. And I've always considered it my duty to look after you. With a bad bringing up, Heaven knows what mischief you might have got into by now.'

'I might have married a beautiful adventuress,' I murmured, gazing at the ceiling, and blowing smoke rings.

'Adventuress!' said Caroline, with a snort. 'If we're talking of adventuresses—'

She left the sentence unfinished.

'Well?' I said, with some curiosity.

'Nothing. But I can think of someone not a hundred miles away.'

Then she turned to Poirot suddenly.

'James sticks to it that you believe someone in the house committed the murder. All I can say is, you're wrong.'

'I should not like to be wrong,' said Poirot. 'It is not – how do you say – my *métier?*'

'I've got the facts pretty clearly,' continued Caroline, taking no notice of Poirot's remarks, 'from James and others. As far as I can see, of the people in the house, only two *could* have had the chance of doing it. Ralph Paton and Flora Ackroyd.'

'My dear Caroline—'

'Now, James, don't interrupt me. I know what I'm talking about. Parker met her *outside* the door, didn't he? He didn't hear her uncle saying good-night to her. She could have killed him then and there.'

'Caroline!'

'I'm not saying she *did*, James. I'm saying she *could* have done. As a matter of fact, though, Flora is like all these young girls nowadays, with no veneration for their betters and thinking they know best on every subject under the sun, I don't for a minute believe she'd kill even a chicken. But there it is. Mr Raymond and Major Blunt have alibis. Mrs Ackroyd's got an alibi. Even that Russell woman seems to have one – and a good job for her it is she has. Who is left? Only Ralph and Flora! And say what you will, I don't believe Ralph Paton is a murderer. A boy we've known all our lives.'

'Let us take a man – a very ordinary man. A man with no idea of murder in his heart. There is in him somewhere a strain of weakness – deep down. It has so far never been called into play. Perhaps it never will be – and if so he will go to his grave honoured and respected by everyone. But let us suppose that something occurs. He is in difficulties – or perhaps not that even. He may stumble by accident on a secret – a secret involving life or death to someone. And his first impulse will be to speak out – to do his duty as an honest citizen. And then the strain of weakness tells. Here is a chance of money – a great amount of money. He wants money – he desires it – and it is so easy. He has to do nothing for it – just keep silence. That is the beginning. The desire for money grows. He must have more – and more! He is intoxicated by the gold mine which has opened at his feet. He becomes greedy.

And in his greed he overreaches himself. One can press a man as far as one likes – but with a woman one must not press too far. For a woman has at heart a great desire to speak the truth. How many husbands who have deceived their wives go comfortably to their graves, carrying their secret with them! How many wives who have deceived their husbands wreck their lives by throwing the fact in those same husbands' teeth! They have been pressed too far. In a reckless moment (which they will afterwards regret, *bien entendu*) they fling safety to the winds and turn at bay, proclaiming the truth with great momentary satisfaction to themselves. So it was, I think, in this case. The strain was too great. And so there came your proverb, the death of the goose that laid the golden eggs. But that is not the end. Exposure faced the man of whom we are speaking. And he is not the same man he was – say, a year ago. His moral fibre is blunted. He is desperate. He is fighting a losing battle, and he is prepared to take any means that come to his hand, for exposure means ruin to him. And so – the dagger strikes!'

He was silent for a moment. It was as though he had laid a spell upon the room. I cannot try to describe the impression his words produced. There was something in the merciless analysis, and the ruthless power of vision which struck fear into both of us.

'Afterwards,' he went on softly, 'the dagger removed, he will be himself again, normal, kindly. But if the need again arises, then once more he will strike.'

Caroline roused herself at last.

'You are speaking of Ralph Paton,' she said. 'You may be right, you may not, but you have no business to condemn a man unheard!'

The telephone bell rang sharply. I went out into the hall, and took off the receiver.

'What?' I said. 'Yes. Dr Sheppard speaking.'

I listened for a minute or two, then replied briefly. Replacing the receiver, I went back into the drawing-room.

'Poirot,' I said, 'they have detained a man at Liverpool. His name is Charles Kent, and he is believed to be the stranger who visited Fernly that night. They want me to go to Liverpool at once and identfy him.'

18

CHARLES KENT

Half an hour later saw Poirot, myself, and Inspector Raglan in the train on the way to Liverpool. The inspector was clearly very excited.

'We may get a line on the blackmailing part of the business, if on nothing else,' he declared jubilantly. 'He's a rough customer, this fellow, by what I heard over the phone. Takes dope, too. We ought to find it easy to get what we want out of him. If there was the shadow of a motive, nothing's more likely than that he killed Mr Ackroyd. But in that case, why is young Paton keeping out of the way. The whole thing's a muddle – that's what it is. By the way, M. Poirot, you were quite right about those fingerprints. They were Mr Ackroyd's own. I had rather the same idea myself, but I dismissed it as hardly feasible.'

I smiled to myself. Inspector Raglan was so very plainly saving his face.

'As regard this man,' said Poirot, 'he is not yet arrested, eh?'

'No, detained under suspicion.'

'And what account does he give of himself?'

'Precious little,' said the inspector, with a grin. 'He's a wary bird, I gather. A lot of abuse, but very little more.'

On arrival at Liverpool I was surprised to find that Poirot was welcomed with acclamation. Superintendent Hayes, who met us, had worked with Poirot over some case long ago, and had evidently an exaggerated opinion of his powers.

'Now we've got M. Poirot here we shan't be long,' he said cheerfully. 'I thought you'd retired, moosior?'

'So I had, my good Hayes, so I had. But how tedious is retirement! You cannot imagine to yourself the monotony with which day comes after day?'

'Very likely. So you've come to have a look at our own particular find? Is this Dr Sheppard? Think you'll be able to identify him, sir?'

'I'm not very sure,' I said doubtfully.

'How did you get hold of him?' inquired Poirot.

'Description was circulated, as you know. In the press and privately. Not much to go on, I admit. This fellow has an American accent all right, and he doesn't deny that he was near King's Abbot that night. Just asks what the hell it is to do with us, and that he'll see us in— before he answeres any questions.'

'Is it permitted that I, too, see him?' asked Poirot.

The superintendent closed one eye knowingly.

'Very glad to have you, sir. You've got permission to do anything you please. Inspector Japp of Scotland Yard was asking after you the other day. Said he'd heard you were connected unofficially with this case. Where's Captain Paton hiding, sir, can you tell me that?'

'I doubt if it would be wise at the present juncture,' said Poirot primly, and I bit my lips to prevent a smile.

The little man really did it very well.

After some further parley, we were taken to interview the prisoner.

He was a young fellow, I should say not more than twenty-two or three. Tall, thin, with slightly shaking hands, and the evidence of considerable physical strength somewhat run to seed. His hair was dark, but his eyes were blue and shifty, seldom meeting a glance squarely. I had all along cherished the illusion that there was something familiar about the figure I had met that night, but if this were indeed he, I was completely mistaken. He did not remind me in the least of anyone I knew.

'Now then, Kent,' said the superintendent. 'Stand up. Here are some visitors come to see you. Recognise any of them?'

Kent glared at us sullenly, but did not reply. I saw his glance waver over the three of us, and come back to rest on me.

'Well, sir,' said the superintendent to me, what do you say?'

'The height's the same,' I said, 'and as far as general appearance goes it might well be the man in question. Beyond that, I couldn't go.'

'What the hell's the meaning of all this?' asked Kent. 'What have you got against me? Come on, out with it! What am I supposed to have done?'

I nodded my head.

'It's the man,' I said. 'I recognise the voice.'

'Recognise my voice, do you? Where do you think you heard it before?'

'On Friday evening last, outside the gates of Fernly Park. You asked me the way there.'

'I did, did I?'

'Do you admit it?' asked the inspector.

'I don't admit anything. Not till I know what you've got on me.'

'Have you not read the papers in the last few days?' asked Poirot, speaking for the first time.

The man's eyes narrowed.

'So that's it, is it? I saw an old gent had been croaked at Fernly. Trying to make out I did the job, are you?'

'You were there that night,' said Poirot quietly.

'How do you know, mister?'

'By this.' Poirot took something from his pocket and held it out.

It was the goose quill we had found in the summer-house.

At the sight of it the man's face changed. He half held out his hand.

'Snow,' said Poirot thoughtfully. 'No, my friend, it is empty. It lay where you dropped it in the summer-house that night.'

Charles Kent looked at him uncertainly.

'You seem to know a hell of a lot about everything, you little foreign cock duck. Perhaps you remember this: the papers say that the old gent was croaked between a quarter to ten and ten o'clock?'

'That is so,' agreed Poirot.

'Yes, but is it really so? That's what I'm getting at.'

'This gentleman will tell you,' said Poirot.

He indicated Inspector Raglan. The latter hesitated, glanced at Superintendent Hayes, then at Poirot, and finally, as though receiving sanction, he said:

'That's right. Between a quarter to ten and ten o'clock.'

'Then you've nothing to keep me here for,' said Kent. 'I was away from Fernly Park by twenty-five minutes past nine. You can ask at the Dog and Whistle. That's a saloon about a mile out of Fernly on the road to Cranchester. I kicked up a bit of a row there, I remember. As near as nothing to quarter to ten, it was. How about that?'

Inspector Raglan wrote down something in his note-book.

'Well?' demanded Kent.

'Inquiries will be made,' said the inspector. 'If you've spoken the truth, you won't have anything to complain about. What were you doing at Fernly Park anyway?'

'Went there to meet someone.'

'Who?'

'That's none of your business.'

'You'd better keep a civil tongue in your head, my man,' the superintendent warned him.

146

'To hell with a civil tongue. I went there on my own business, and that's all there is to it. If I was clear away before the murder was done, that's all that concerns the cops.'

'Your name, it is Charles Kent,' said Poirot. 'Where were you born?'

The man stared at him, then he grinned.

'I'm a full-blown Britisher all right,' he said.

'Yes,' said Poirot meditatively, 'I think you are. I fancy you were born in Kent.'

The man stared.

'Why's that? Because of my name? What's that to do with it? Is a man whose name is Kent bound to be born in that particular county?'

'Under certain circumstances, I can imagine he might be,' said Poirot very deliberately. 'Under certain circumstances, you comprehend.'

There was so much meaning in his voice as to surprise the two police officers. As for Charles Kent, he flushed a brick red, and for a moment I thought he was going to spring at Poirot. He thought better of it, however, and turned away with a kind of laugh.

Poirot nodded as though satisfied, and made his way out through the door. He was joined presently by the two officers.

'We'll verify that statement,' remarked Raglan. 'I don't think he's lying, though. But he's got to come clean with a statement as to what he was doing at Fernly. It looks to me as though we'd got our blackmailer all right. On the other hand, granted his story's correct, he couldn't have had anything to do with the actual murder. He'd got ten pounds on him when he was arrested – rather a large sum. I fancy that forty pounds went to him – the numbers of the notes didn't correspond, but of course he'd have changed them first thing. Mr Ackroyd must have given him the money, and he made off with it as fast as possible. What was that about Kent being his birthplace? What's that got to do with it?'

'Nothing whatever,' said Poirot mildly. 'A little idea of mine, that was all. Me, I am famous for my little ideas.'

'Are you really?' said Raglan, studying him with a puzzled expression.

The superintendent went into a roar of laughter.

'Many's the time I've heard Inspector Japp say that. M. Poirot and his little ideas! Too fanciful for me, he'd say, but always something in them.'

'You mock yourself at me,' said Poirot, smiling; 'but never

'mind. The old ones they laugh last sometimes, when the young, clever ones do not laugh at all.'

And nodding his head at them in a sage manner he walked out into the street.

He and I lunched together at an hotel. I know now that the whole thing lay clearly unravelled before him. He had got the last thread he needed to lead him to the truth.

But at the time I had no suspicion of the fact. I over-estimated his general self-confidence, and I took it for granted that the things which puzzled me must be equally puzzling to him.

My chief puzzle was what the man Charles Kent could have been doing at Fernly. Again and again I put the question to myself and could get no satisfactory reply. At last I ventured a tentative query to Poirot. His reply was immediate.

'*Mon ami*, I do not think, I know.'

'Really?' I said incredulously.

'Yes, indeed. I suppose now that to you it would not make sense if I said that he went to Fernly that night because he was born in Kent?'

I stared at him.

'It certainly doesn't seem to make sense to me,' I said dryly.

'Ah!' said Poirot pityingly. 'Well, no matter. I have still my little idea.'

─── 19 ───

FLORA ACKROYD

As I was returning from my round the following morning, I was hailed by Inspector Raglan. I pulled up, and the inspector mounted on the step.

'Good-morning, Doctor Sheppard,' he said. 'Well, that alibi is all right enough.'

'Charles Kent's?'

'Charles Kent's. The barmaid at the Dog and Whistle, Sally Jones, she remembers him perfectly. Picked out his photograph from among five others. It was just a quarter to ten when he came into the bar, and the Dog and Whistle is well over a mile from Fernly Park. The girl mentions that he had a lot of money on him – she saw him take a handful of notes out of his pocket. Rather surprised her, it did, seeing the class of fellow he was, with a pair of boots clean dropping off him. That's where that forty pounds went right enough.'

'The man still refuses to give an account of his visit to Fernly?'

'Obstinate as a mule he is. I had a chat with Hayes at Liverpool over the wire this morning.'

'Hercule Poirot says he knows the reason the man went there that night,' I observed.

'Does he?' cried the inspector eagerly.

'Yes,' I said maliciously. 'He says he went there because he was born in Kent.'

I felt a distinct pleasure in passing on my own discomfiture.

Raglan stared at me for a moment or two uncomprehendingly. Then a grin overspread his weaselly countenance and he tapped his forehead significantly.

'But gone here,' he said. 'I've thought so for some time. Poor old chap, so that's why he had to give up and come down here. In the family, very likely. He's got a nephew who's quite off his crumpet.'

'Poirot has?' I said, very surprised.

'Yes. Hasn't he ever mentioned him to you? Quite docile, I believe, and all that, but mad as a hatter, poor lad.'

'Who told you that?'

Again a grin showed itself on Inspector Raglan's face.

'Your sister, Miss Sheppard, she told me all about it.'

Really, Caroline is amazing. She never rests until she knows the last details of everybody's family secrets. Unfortunately, I have never been able to instil into her the decency of keeping them to herself.

'Jump in, Inspector,' I said, opening the door of the car. 'We'll go up to The Larches together, and acquaint our Belgian friend with the latest news.'

'Might as well, I suppose. After all, even if he is a bit balmy, it was a useful tip he gave me about those fingerprints. He's got a bee in his bonnet about the man Kent, but who knows – there may be something useful behind it.'

Poirot received us with his usual smiling courtesy.

He listened to the information we had brought him, nodding his head now and then.

'Seems quite O.K., doesn't it?' said the inspector rather gloomily. 'A chap can't be murdering someone in one place when he's drinking in the bar in another place a mile away.'

'Are you going to release him?'

'Don't see what else we can do. We can't very well hold him

for obtaining money on false pretences. Can't prove a ruddy thing.'

The inspector tossed a match into the grate in a disgruntled fashion. Poirot retrieved it and put it neatly in a little receptacle designed for the purpose. His action was purely mechanical. I could see that his thoughts were on something very different.

'If I were you,' he said at last, 'I should not release the man Charles Kent yet.'

'What do you mean?'

Raglan stared at him.

'What I say. I should not release him yet.'

'You don't think he can have had anything to do with the murder, do you?'

'I think probably not – but one cannot be certain yet.'

'But haven't I just told you—?'

Poirot raised a hand protestingly.

'*Mais oui, mais oui.* I heard. I am not deaf – nor stupid, thank the good God! But see you, you approach the matter from the wrong – the wrong – premises, is not that the word?'

The inspector stared at him heavily.

'I don't see how you make that out. Look here, we know Mr Ackroyd was alive at a quarter to ten. You admit that, don't you?'

Poirot looked at him for a moment, then shook his head with a quick smile.

'I admit nothing that is not – *proved*!'

'Well, we've got proof enough of that. We've got Miss Flora Ackroyd's evidence.'

'That she said good-night to her uncle? But me – I do not always believe what a young lady tells me – no, not even when she is charming and beautiful.'

'But hang it all, man, Parker saw her coming out of the door.'

'No.' Poirot's voice rang out with sudden sharpness. 'That is just what he did not see. I satisfied myself of that by a little experiment the other day – you remember, doctor? Parker saw her *outside* the door, with her hand on the handle. He did not see her come out of the room.'

'But – where else could she have been?'

'Perhaps on the stairs.'

'The stairs?'

'That is my little idea – yes.'

'But those stairs only lead to Mr Ackroyd's bedroom.'

'Precisely.'

And still the inspector stared.

'You think she'd been up to her uncle's bedroom? Well, why not? Why should she lie about it?'

'Ah! that is just the question. It depends on what she was doing there, does it not?'

'You mean – the money? Hang it all, you don't suggest that it was Miss Ackroyd who took that forty pounds?'

'I suggest nothing,' said Poirot. 'But I will remind you of this. Life was not very easy for that mother and daughter. There were bills – there was constant trouble over small sums of money. Roger Ackroyd was a peculiar man over money matters. The girl might be at her wits' end for a comparatively small sum. Figure to yourself then what happens. She has taken the money, she descends the little staircase. When she is half-way down she hears the chink of glasses from the hall. She has not a doubt of what it is – Parker coming to the study. At all costs she must not be found on the stairs – Parker will not forget it, he will think it odd. If the money is missed, Parker is sure to remember having seen her come down those stairs. She has just time to rush down to the study door – with her hand on the handle to show that she has just come out, when Parker appears in the doorway. She says the first thing that comes into her head, a repetition of Roger Ackroyd's orders earlier in the evening, and then goes upstairs to her own room.'

'Yes, but later,' protested the inspector, 'she must have realised the vital importance of speaking the truth? Why, the whole case hinges on it!'

'Afterwards,' said Poirot dryly, 'it was a little difficult for Mademoiselle Flora. She is told simply that the police are here and that there has been a robbery. Naturally she jumps to the conclusion that the theft of the money has been discovered. Her one idea is to stick to her story. When she learns that her uncle is dead she is panic-stricken. Young women do not faint nowadays, monsieur, without considerable provocation. *Eh bien*! there it is. She is bound to stick to her story, or else confess everything. And a young and pretty girl does not like to admit that she is a thief – especially before those whose esteem she is anxious to retain.'

Raglan brought his fist down with a thump on the table.

'I'll not believe it,' he said. 'It's – it's not credible. And you – you've known this all along?'

'The possibility has been in my mind from the first,' admitted Poirot. 'I was always convinced that Mademoiselle Flora was hiding something from us. To satisfy myself, I made the little experiment I told you of. Dr Sheppard accompanied me.'

'A test for Parker, you said it was,' I remarked bitterly.

'*Mon ami,*' said Poirot apologetically, 'as I told you at the time, one must say something.'

The inspector rose.

'There's only one thing for it,' he declared. 'We must tackle the young lady right away. You'll come up to Fernly with me, M. Poirot?'

'Certainly. Dr Sheppard will drive us up in his car.'

I acquiesced willingly.

On inquiry for Miss Ackroyd, we were shown into the billiard room. Flora and Major Hector Blunt were sitting on the long window seat.

'Good-morning, Miss Ackroyd,' said the inspector. 'Can we have a word or two alone with you?'

Blunt got up at once and moved to the door.

'What is it?' asked Flora nervously. 'Don't go, Major Blunt. He can stay, can't he?' she asked, turning to the inspector.

'That's as you like,' said the inspector dryly. 'There's a question or two it's my duty to put to you, miss, but I'd prefer to do so privately, and I dare say you'd prefer it also.'

Flora looked keenly at him. I saw her face grow whiter. Then she turned and spoke to Blunt.

'I want you to stay – please – yes, I mean it. Whatever the inspector has to say to me, I'd rather you heard it.'

Raglan shrugged his shoulders.

'Well, if you will have it so, that's all there is to it. Now, Miss Ackroyd, M. Poirot here has made a certain suggestion to me. He suggests that you weren't in the study at all last Friday night, that you never saw Mr Ackroyd to say good-night to him, that instead of being in the study you were on the stairs leading down from your uncle's bedroom when you heard Parker coming across the hall.'

Flora's gaze shifted to Poirot. He nodded back at her.

'Mademoiselle, the other day, when we sat round the table, I implored you to be frank with me. What one does not tell to Papa Poirot he finds out. It was that, was it not? See, I will make it easy for you. You took the money, did you not?'

'The money?' said Blunt sharply.

There was a silence which lasted for at least a minute.

Then Flora drew herself up and spoke.

'M. Poirot is right. I took that money. I stole. I am a thief

– yes, a common, vulgar little thief. Now you know! I am glad it has come out. It's been a nightmare, these last few days!' She sat down suddenly and buried her face in her hands. She spoke huskily through her fingers. 'You don't know what my life has been since I came here. Wanting things, scheming for them, lying, cheating, running up bills, promising to pay – oh! I hate myself when I think of it all! That's what brought us together, Ralph and I. We were both weak! I understood him, and I was sorry – because I'm the same underneath. We're not strong enough to stand alone, either of us. We're weak, miserable, despicable things.'

She looked at Blunt and suddenly stamped her foot.

'Why do you look at me like that – as though you couldn't believe? I may be a thief – but at any rate I'm real now. I'm not lying any more. I'm not pretending to be the kind of girl you like, young and innocent and simple. I don't care if you never want to see me again. I hate myself, despise myself – but you've got to believe one thing, if speaking the truth would have made things better for Ralph, I would have spoken out. But I've seen all along that it wouldn't be better for Ralph – it makes the case against him blacker than ever. I was not doing him any harm by sticking to my lie.'

'Ralph,' said Blunt. 'I see – always Ralph.'

'You don't understand,' said Flora hopelessly. 'You never will.'

She turned to the inspector.

'I admit everything; I was at my wits' end for money. I never saw my uncle that evening after he left the dinner-table. As to the money, you can take what steps you please. Nothing could be worse than it is now!'

Suddenly she broke down again, hid her face in her hands, and rushed from the room.

'Well,' said the inspector in a flat tone, 'so that's that.'

He seemed rather at a loss what to do next.

Blunt came forward.

'Inspector Raglan,' he said quietly, 'that money was given to me by Mr Ackroyd for a special purpose. Miss Ackroyd never touched it. When she says she did, she is lying with the idea of shielding Captain Paton. The truth is as I said, and I am prepared to go into the witness-box and swear to it.'

He made a kind of jerky bow, then turning abruptly he left the room.

Poirot was after him in a flash. He caught the other up in the hall.

'Monsieur – a moment, I beg of you, if you will be so good.'

'Well, sir?'

Blunt was obviously impatient. He stood frowning down on Poirot.

'It is this,' said Poirot rapidly: 'I am not deceived by your little fantasy. No, indeed. It was truly Miss Flora who took the money. All the same it is well imagined what you say – it pleases me. It is very good what you have done there. You are a man quick to think and to act.'

'I'm not in the least anxious for your opinion, thank you,' said Blunt coldly.

He made once more as though to pass on, but Poirot, not at all offended, laid a detaining hand on his arm.

'Ah! but you are to listen to me. I have more to say. The other day I spoke of concealments. Very well, all along I have seen what you are concealing. Mademoiselle Flora, you love her with all your heart. From the first moment you saw her, is it not so? Oh! let us not mind saying these things – why must one in England think it necessary to mention love as though it were some disgraceful secret? You love Mademoiselle Flora. You seek to conceal that fact from all the world. That is very good – that is as it should be. But take the advice of Hercule Poirot – do not conceal it from mademoiselle herself.'

Blunt had shown several signs of restlessness whilst Poirot was speaking, but the closing words seemed to rivet his attention.

'What d'you mean by that?' he said sharply.

'You think that she loves the Capitaine Ralph Paton – but I, Hercule Poirot, tell you that that is not so. Mademoiselle Flora accepted Captain Paton to please her uncle, and because she saw in the marriage a way of escape from her life here which was becoming frankly insupportable to her. She liked him, and there was much sympathy and understanding between them. But love – no! It is not Captain Paton Mademoiselle Flora loves.'

'What the devil do you mean?' asked Blunt.

I saw the dark flush under his tan.

'You have been blind, monsieur. Blind! She is loyal, the little one. Ralph Paton is under a cloud, she is bound in honour to stick by him.'

I felt it was time I put in a word to help on the good work.

'My sister told me the other night,' I said encouragingly, that Flora had never cared a penny piece for Ralph Paton, and never would. My sister is always right about these things.'

Blunt ignored my well-meant offers. He spoke to Poirot.

'D'you really think—?' he began, and stopped.

He is one of those inarticulate men who find it hard to put things into words.

Poirot knows no such disability.

'If you doubt me, ask her yourself, monsieur. But perhaps you no longer care to – the affair of the money——'

Blunt gave a sound like an angry laugh.

'Think I'd hold that against her? Roger was always a queer chap about money. She got in a mess and didn't dare tell him. Poor kid. Poor lonely kid.'

Poirot looked thoughtfully at the side door.

'Mademoiselle Flora went into the garden, I think,' he murmured.

'I've been every kind of a fool,' said Blunt abruptly. 'Rum conversation we've been having. Like one of those Danish plays. But you're a sound fellow, M. Poirot. Thank you.'

He took Poirot's hand and gave it a grip which caused the other to wince in anguish. Then he strode to the side-door and passed out into the garden.

'Not every kind of a fool,' murmured Poirot, tenderly nursing the injured member. 'Only one kind – the fool in love.'

20

MISS RUSSELL

Inspector Raglan had received a bad jolt. He was not deceived by Blunt's valiant lie any more than we had been. Our way back to the village was punctuated by his complaints.

'This alters everything, this does. I don't know whether you've realised it, Monsieur Poirot?'

'I think so, yes, I think so,' said Poirot. 'You see, me, I have been familiar with the idea for some time.'

Inspector Raglan, who had only had the idea presented to him a short half-hour ago, looked at Poirot unhappily, and went on with his discoveries.

'Those alibis now. Worthless! Absolutely worthless. Got to start again. Find out what everyone was doing from nine-thirty onwards. Nine-thirty – that's the time we've got to hang on to. You were quite right about the man Kent – we don't release *him* yet awhile. Let me see now – nine-forty-five at the Dog and Whistle. He might have got there in a quarter of an hour if he ran. It's just possible that it was *his* voice Mr Raymond heard talking to Mr Ackroyd – asking for money which Mr Ackroyd refused. But one thing's clear – it wasn't he who sent the telephone message. The station is half a mile in the other direction – over a mile and a half from the Dog and Whistle, and he was at the Dog and Whistle until about ten minutes past ten. Dang that telephone call! We always come up against it.'

'We do indeed,' agreed Poirot. 'It is curious.'

'It's just possible that if Captain Paton climbed into his uncle's room and found him there murdered, *he* may have sent it. Got the wind up, thought he'd be accused, and cleared out. That's possible, isn't it?'

'Why should he have telephoned?'

'May have had doubts if the old man was really dead. Thought he'd get the doctor up there as soon as possible, but didn't want to give himself away. Yes, I say now, how's that for a theory? Something in that, I should say.'

The inspector swelled his chest out importantly. He was so plainly delighted with himself that any words of ours would have been quite superfluous.

We arrived back at my house at this minute, and I hurried in to my surgery patients, who had all been waiting a considerable time, leaving Poirot to walk to the police station with the inspector.

Having dismissed the last patient, I strolled into the little room at the back of the house which I call my workshop – I am rather proud of the home-made wireless set I turned out. Caroline hates my workroom. I keep my tools there, and Annie is not allowed to wreck havoc with a dustpan and brush. I was just adjusting the interior of an alarm clock which had been denounced as wholly unreliable by the household, when the door opened and Caroline put her head in.

'Oh! there you are, James,' she said, with deep disapproval. 'M. Poirot wants to see you.'

'Well,' I said, rather irritably, for her sudden entrance had startled me and I had let go of a piece of delicate mechanism. 'If he wants to see me, he can come in here.'

'In here?' said Caroline.

'That's what I said – in here.'

Caroline gave a sniff of disapproval and retired. She re-

turned in a moment or two, ushering in Poirot, and then retired again, shutting the door with a bang.

'Aha! my friend,' said Poirot, coming forward and rubbing
his hands. 'You have not got rid of me so easily, you see!'

'Finished with the inspector?' I asked.

'For the moment, yes. And you, you have seen all the
patients?'

'Yes.'

Poirot sat down and looked at me, tilting his egg-shaped
head on one side, with the air of one who savours a very
delicious joke.

'You are in error,' he said at last. 'You have still one patient
to see.'

'Not you?' I exclaimed in surprise.

'Ah, not me, *bien entendu*. Me, I have the health magnificent. No, to tell you the truth, it is a little *complot* of mine.
There is someone I wish to see, you understand – and at the
same time it is not necessary that the whole village should
intrigue itself about the matter – which is what would happen
if the lady were seen to come to my house – for it is a lady. But
to you she has already come as a patient before.'

'Miss Russell!' I exclaimed.

'*Précisement*. I wish much to speak with her, so I send her
the little note and make the appointment in your surgery. You
are not annoyed with me?'

'On the contrary,' I said. 'That is, presuming I am allowed
to be present at the interview?'

'But naturally! In your own surgery!'

'You know,' I said, throwing down the pincers I was holding, 'it's extraordinary intriguing, the whole thing. Every new
development that arises is like the shake you give to a kaleidoscope – the thing changes entirely in aspect. Now, why are you
so anxious to see Miss Russell?'

Poirot raised his eyebrows.

'Surely it is obvious?' he murmured.

'There you go again,' I grumbled. 'According to you everything is obvious. But you leave me walking about in a fog.'

Poirot shook his head genially at me.

'You mock yourself at me. Take the matter of Mademoiselle
Flora. The inspector was surprised – but you – you were not.'

'I never dreamed of her being the thief,' I expostulated.

'That – perhaps no. But I was watching your face and you
were not – like Inspector Raglan – startled and incredulous.'

I thought for a minute or two.

'Perhaps you are right,' I said at last. 'All along I've felt that Flora was keeping back something – so the truth, when it came, was subconsciously expected. It upset Inspector Raglan very much indeed, poor man.'

'Ah! *pour ça, oui!* The poor man must rearrange all his ideas. I profited by his state of mental chaos to induce him to grant me a little favour.'

'What was that?'

Poirot took a sheet of notepaper from his pocket. Some words were written on it, and he read them aloud.

'The police have, for some days, been seeking for Captain Ralph Paton, the nephew of Mr Ackroyd of Fernly Park, whose death occurred under such tragic circumstances last Friday. Captain Paton has been found at Liverpool, where he was on the point of embarking for America.'

He folded up the piece of paper again.

'That, my friend, will be in the newspapers to-morrow morning.'

I stared at him, dumbfounded.

'But – but it isn't true! He's not at Liverpool!'

Poirot beamed on me.

'You have the intelligence so quick! No, he has not been found at Liverpool. Inspector Raglan was very loath to let me send this paragraph to the press, especially as I could not take him into my confidence. But I assured him most solemnly that very interesting results would follow its appearance in print, so he gave in, after stipulating that he was, on no account, to bear the responsibility.'

I stared at Poirot. He smiled back at me.

'It beats me,' I said at last, what you expect to get out of that.'

'You should employ your little grey cells,' said Poirot gravely.

He rose and came across the bench.

'It is that you have really the love of the machinery,' he said, after inspecting the débris of my labours.

Every man has his hobby. I immediately drew Poirot's attenion to my home-made wireless. Finding him sympathetic, I showed him one or two little inventions of my own – trifling things, but useful in the house.

'Decidedly,' said Poirot, 'you should be an inventor by trade, not a doctor. But I hear the bell – that is your patient. Let us go into the surgery.'

Once before I had been struck by the remnants of beauty in the housekeeper's face. This morning I was struck anew. Very simply dressed in black, tall, upright and independent as ever, with her big dark eyes and an unwonted flush of colour in her usually pale cheeks, I realised that as a girl she must have been startlingly handsome.

'Good-morning, mademoiselle,' said Poirot. 'Will you be seated? Dr Sheppard is so kind as to permit me the use of his surgery for a little conversation I am anxious to have with you.'

Miss Russell sat down with her usual composure. If she felt any inward agitation, it did not display itself in any outward manifestation.

'It seems a queer way of doing things, if you'll allow me to say so,' she remarked.

'Miss Russell – I have news to give you.'

'Indeed!'

'Charles Kent has been arrested at Liverpool.'

Not a muscle of her face moved. She merely opened her eyes a trifle wider, and asked, with a tinge of defiance:

'Well, what of it?'

But at that moment it came to me – the resemblance that had haunted me all along, something familiar in the defiance of Charles Kent's manner. The two voices, one rough and coarse, the other painfully ladylike – were strangely the same in timbre. It was of Miss Russell that I had been reminded that night outside the gates of Fernly Park.

I looked at Poirot, full of my discovery, and he gave me an imperceptible nod.

In answer to Miss Russell's question, he threw out his hands in a thoroughly French gesture.

'I thought you might be interested, that is all,' he said mildly.

'Well, I'm not particularly,' said Miss Russell. 'Who is this Charles Kent anyway?'

'He is a man, mademoiselle, who was at Fernly on the night of the murder.'

'Really?'

'Fortunately for him, he has an alibi. At a quarter to ten he was at a public-house a mile from here.'

'Lucky for him,' commented Miss Russell.

'But we still do not know what he was doing at Fernly – who it was he went to meet, for instance.'

'I'm afraid I can't help you at all,' said the housekeeper politely. 'Nothing came to *my* ears. If that is all—'

She made a tentative movement as though to rise. Poirot stopped her.

'It is not quite all,' he said smoothly. 'This morning fresh developments have arisen. It seems now that Mr Ackroyd was murdered, not at a quarter to ten, but *before*. Between ten minutes to nine, when Dr Sheppard left, and a quarter to ten.'

I saw the colour drain from the housekeeper's face, leaving it dead white. She leaned forward, her figure swaying.

'But Miss Ackroyd said – Miss Ackroyd said—'

'Miss Ackroyd has admitted that she was lying. She was never in the study at all that evening.'

'Then—?'

'Then it would seem that in this Charles Kent we have the man we are looking for. He came to Fernly, can give no account of what he was doing there—'

'I can tell you what he was doing there. He never touched a hair of old Ackroyd's head – he never went near the study. He didn't do it, I tell you.'

She was leaning forward. That iron self-control was broken through at last. Terror and desperation was in her face.

'M. Poirot! M. Poirot! Oh, do believe me.'

Poirot got up and came to her. He patted her reassuringly on the shoulder.

'But yes – but yes, I will believe. I had to make you speak, you know.'

For an instant suspicion flared up in her.

'Is what you said true?'

'That Charles Kent is suspected of the crime? Yes, that is true. You alone can save him, by telling the reason for his being at Fernly.'

'He came to see me.' She spoke in a low, hurried voice. 'I went out to meet him—'

'In the summer-house, yes, I know.'

'How do you know?'

'Mademoiselle, it is the business of Hercule Poirot to know things. I know that you went out earlier in the evening, that you left a message in the summer-house to say what time you would be there.'

'Yes, I did. I had heard from him – saying he was coming. I dared not let him come to the house. I wrote to the address he gave me and said I would meet him in the summer-house, and described it to him so that he would be able to find it. Then I was afraid he might not wait there patiently, and I ran out and left a piece of paper to say I would be there about ten minutes past nine. I didn't want the servants to see me, so I slipped out through the drawing-room window. As I came back, I met Dr Sheppard, and I fancied that he would think it queer. I was out of breath, for I had been running. I had no idea that he was expected to dinner that night.'

She paused.

'Go on.' said Poirot. 'You went out to meet him at ten minutes past nine. What did you say to each other?'

'It's difficult. You see—'

'Mademoiselle,' said Poirot, interrupting her, 'in this matter I must have the whole truth. What you tell us need never go beyond these four walls. Dr Sheppard will be discreet, and so shall I. See, I will help you. This Charles Kent, he is your son, is he not?'

She nodded. The colour had flamed into her cheeks.

'No one has ever known. It was long ago – long ago – down in Kent. I was not married. . . .'

'So you took the name of the county as a surname for him. I understand.'

'I got work. I managed to pay for his board and lodging. I never told him that I was his mother. But he turned out badly, he drank, then took to drugs. I managed to pay his passage out to Canada. I didn't hear of him for a year or two. Then, somehow or other, he found out that I was his mother. He wrote asking me for money. Finally, I heard from him back in this country again. He was coming to see me at Fernly, he said. I dared not let him come to the house. I have always been considered so – so very respectable. If anyone got an inkling – it would have been all up with my post as house-keeper. So I wrote to him in the way I have just told you.'

'And in the morning you came to see Dr Sheppard?'

'Yes. I wondered if something could be done. He was not a bad boy – before he took to drugs.'

'I see,' said Poirot. 'Now let us go on with the story. He came that night to the summer-house?'

'Yes, he was waiting for me when I got there. He was very rough and abusive. I had brought with me all the money I had, and I gave it to him. We talked a little, and then he went away.'

'What time was that?'

'It must have been between twenty and twenty-five minutes past nine. It was not yet half-past when I got back to the house.'

'Which way did he go?'

'Straight out the same way he came, by the path that joined the drive just inside the lodge gates.'

Poirot nodded.

'And you, what did you do?'

'I went back to the house. Major Blunt was walking up and down the terrace smoking, so I made a detour to get round to the side door. It was just then on half-past nine, as I tell you.'

Poirot nodded again. He made a note or two in a microscopic pocket-book.

'I think that is all,' he said thoughtfully.

'Ought I—?' she hesitated. 'Ought I to tell all this to Inspector Raglan?'

'It may come to that. But let us not be in a hurry. Let us proceed slowly, with due order and method. Charles Kent is not yet formally charged with murder. Circumstances may arise which will render your story unnecessary.'

Miss Russell rose.

'Thank you very much, M. Poirot,' she said. 'You have been very kind – very kind indeed. You – you do believe me, don't you? That Charles had nothing to do with this wicked murder!'

'There seems no doubt that the man who was talking to Mr Ackroyd in the library at nine-thirty could not possibly have been your son. Be of good courage, mademoiselle. All will yet be well.'

Miss Russell departed. Poirot and I were left together.

'So that's that,' I said. 'Every time we come back to Ralph Paton. How did you manage to spot Miss Russell as the person Charles Kent came to meet? Did you notice the resemblance?'

'I had connected her with the unknown man long before we actually came face to face with him. As soon as we found that quill. The quill suggested dope, and I remembered your account of Miss Russell's visit to you. Then I found the article on cocaine in that morning's paper. It all seemed very clear. She had heard from someone that morning – someone addicted to drugs, she read the article in the paper, and she came to you to ask a few tentative questions. She mentioned cocaine, since the article in question was on cocaine. Then, when you seemed too interested, she switched hurriedly to the subject of detective stories and untraceable poisons. I suspected a son or a brother, or some other undesirable male relation. Ah! but I must go. It is the time of the lunch.'

'Stay and lunch with us,' I suggested.

Poirot shook his head. A faint twinkle came into his eye.

'Not again today. I should not like to force Mademoiselle Caroline to adopt a vegetarian diet two days in succession.'

It ocurred to me that there was not much which escaped Hercule Poirot.

———— 21 ————

THE PARAGRAPH IN THE PAPER

Caroline, of course, had not failed to see Miss Russell come to the surgery door. I had anticipated this, and had ready an eloborate account of the lady's bad knee. But Caroline was not in a cross-questioning mood. Her point of view was that she knew what Miss Russell had really come for and that *I* didn't.

'Pumping you, James,' said Caroline. 'Pumping you in the most shameless manner, I've no doubt. It's no good interrupting. I dare say you hadn't the least idea she was doing it even. Men *are* so simple. She knows that you are in M. Poirot's confidence, and she wants to find out things. Do you know what I think, James?'

'I couldn't begin to imagine. You think so many extraordinary things.'

'It's no good being sarcastic. I think Miss Russell knows more about Mr Ackroyd's death than she is prepared to admit.'

Caroline leaned back triumphantly in her chair.

'Do you really think so?' I said absently.

'You are very dull today, James. No animation about you. It's that liver of yours.'

Our conversation then dealt with purely personal matters.

The paragraph inspired by Poirot duly appeared in our daily paper the next morning. I was in the dark as to its purpose, but its effect on Caroline was immense.

She began by stating, most untruly, that she had said as much all along. I raised my eyebrows, but did not argue. Caroline, however, must have felt a prick of conscience, for she went on:

'I mayn't have actually mentioned Liverpool, but I knew he'd try to get away to America. That's what Crippen did.'

'Without much success,' I reminded her.

'Poor boy, and so they've caught him. I consider, James, that it's your duty to see that he isn't hung.'

'What do you expect me to do?'

'Why, you're a medical man, aren't you? You've known him from a boy upwards. Not mentally responsible. That's the line to take, clearly. I read only the other day that they're very happy in Broadmoor – it's quite like a high-class club.'

But Caroline's words had reminded me of something.

'I never knew that Poirot had an imbecile nephew?' I said curiously.

'Didn't you? Oh, he told me all about it. Poor lad. It's a great grief to all the family. They've kept him at home so far, but it's getting to such a pitch that they're afraid he'll have to go into some kind of institution.'

'I suppose you know pretty well everything there is to know about Poirot's family by this time,' I said, exasperated.

'Pretty well,' said Caroline complacently. 'It's a great relief to people to be able to tell all their troubles to someone.'

'It might be,' I said, 'if they were ever allowed to do so spontaneously. Whether they enjoy having confidences screwed out of them by force is another matter.'

Caroline merely looked at me with the air of a Christian martyr enjoying martyrdom.

'You are so self-contained, James,' she said. 'You hate speaking out, or parting with any information yourself, and you think everybody else must be just like you. I should hope that I never screw confidences out of anybody. For instance, if M. Poirot comes in this afternoon, as he said he might do, I shall not dream of asking him who it was arrived at his house early this morning.'

'Early this morning?' I queried.

'Very early,' said Caroline. 'Before the milk came. I just happened to be looking out of the window – the blind was flapping. It was a man. He came in a closed car, and he was all muffled up. I couldn't get a glimpse of his face. But I will tell you *my* idea, and you'll see that I'm right.'

'What's your idea?'

Caroline dropped her voice mysteriously.

'A Home Office expert,' she breathed.

'A Home Office expert,' I said, amazed. 'My dear Caroline!'

'Mark my words, James, you'll see that I'm right. That Russell woman was here that morning after your poisons. Roger Ackroyd might easily have been poisoned in his food that night.'

I laughed out loud.

'Nonsense,' I cried. 'He was stabbed in the neck. You know that as well as I do.'

'After death, James,' said Caroline; 'to make a false clue.'

'My good woman,' I said, 'I examined the body, and I know what I'm talking about. That wound wasn't inflicted after death – it was the cause of death, and you need make no mistake about it.'

Caroline merely continued to look omniscient, which so annoyed me that I went on:

'Perhaps you will tell me, Caroline, if I have a medical degree or if I have not?'

'You have the medical degree, I dare say, James – at least, I mean I know you have. But you've no imagination whatever.'

'Having endowed you with a treble portion, there was none left over for me,' I said dryly.

I was amused to notice Caroline's manœuvres that afternoon when Poirot duly arrived. My sister, without asking a direct question, skirted the subject of the mysterious guest in every way imaginable. By the twinkle in Poirot's eyes, I saw that he realised her object. He remained blandly impervious, and blocked her bowling so successfully that she herself was at a loss how to proceed.

Having, I suspect, quietly enjoyed the little game, he rose to his feet and suggested a walk.

'It is that I need to reduce the figure a little,' he explained. 'You will come with me, doctor? And perhaps later, Miss Caroline will give us some tea.'

'Delighted,' said Caroline. 'Won't your – er – guest come in also?'

'You are too kind,' said Poirot. 'But no, my friend reposes himself. Soon you must make his acquaintance.'

'Quite an old friend of yours, so somebody told me,' said Caroline, making one last valiant effort.

'Did they?' murmured Poirot. 'Well, we must start.'

Our tramp took us in the direction of Fernly. I had guessed beforehand that it might do so. I was beginning to understand Poirot's methods. Every little irrelevancy had a bearing upon the whole.

'I have a commission for you, my friend,' he said at last. 'Tonight, at my house. I desire to have a little conference. You will attend, will you not?'

'Certainly,' I said.

'Good. I need also all those in the house – that is to say: Mrs Ackroyd, Mademoiselle Flora, Major Blunt, Mr Raymond.

I want you to be my ambassador. This little reunion is fixed for nine o'clock. You will ask them – yes?'

'With pleasure; but why not ask them yourself?'

'Because they will then put the questions: Why? What for? They will demand what my idea is. And, as you know, my friend, I much dislike to have to explain my little ideas until the time comes.'

I smiled a little.

'My friend Hastings, he of whom I told you, used to say of me that I was the human oyster. But he was unjust. Of facts, I keep nothing to myself. But to everyone his own interpretation of them.'

'When do you want me to do this?'

'Now, if you will. We are close to the house.'

'Aren't you coming in?'

'No, me, I will promenade myself in the grounds. I will rejoin you by the lodge gates in a quarter of an hour's time.'

I nodded, and set off on my task. The only member of the family at home proved to be Mrs Ackroyd, who was sipping an early cup of tea. She received me very graciously.

'So grateful to you, doctor,' she murmured, 'for clearing up that little matter with M. Poirot. But life is one trouble after another. You have heard about Flora, of course?'

'What exactly?' I asked cautiously.

'This new engagement. Flora and Hector Blunt. Of course not such a good match as Ralph would have been. But after all, happiness comes first. What dear Flora needs is an older man – someone steady and reliable, and then Hector is really a very distinguished man in his way. You saw the news of Ralph's arrest in the paper this morning?'

'Yes,' I said, 'I did.'

'Horrible.' Mrs Ackroyd closed her eyes and shuddered. 'Geoffrey Raymond was in a terrible way. Rang up Liverpool. But they wouldn't tell him anything at the police station there. In fact, they said they hadn't arrested Ralph at all. Mr Raymond insists that it's all a mistake – a – what do they call it? – canard of the newspaper's. I've forbidden it to be mentioned before the servants. Such a terrible disgrace. Fancy if Flora had actually been married to him.'

Mrs Ackroyd shut her eyes in anguish. I began to wonder how soon I should be able to deliver Poirot's invitation.

Before I had time to speak, Mrs Ackroyd was off again.

'You were here yesterday, weren't you, with that dreadful Inspector Raglan? Brute of a man – he terrified Flora into saying she took that money from poor Roger's room. And the matter was so simple, really. The dear child wanted to borrow a few pounds, didn't like to disturb her uncle since he'd given strict orders against it. But knowing where he kept his notes she went there and took what she needed.'

'Is that Flora's account of the matter?' I asked.

'My dear doctor, you know what girls are nowadays. So easily acted on by suggestion. You, of course, know all about hypnosis and that sort of thing. The inspector shouts at her, says the word "steal" over and over again, until the poor child gets an inhibition – or is it a complex? – I always mix up those two words – and actually thinks herself that she has stolen the money. I saw at once how it was. But I can't be too thankful for the whole misunderstanding in one way – it seems to have brought those two together – Hector and Flora, I mean. And I assure you that I have been very much worried about Flora in the past: why, at one time I actually thought there was going to be some kind of understanding between her and young Raymond. Just think of it!' Mrs Ackroyd's voice rose in shrill horror. 'A private secretary – with practically no means of his own.'

'It would have been a severe blow to you,' I said. 'Now, Mrs Ackroyd, I've got a message for you from M. Hercule Poirot.'

'For me?'

Mrs Ackroyd looked quite alarmed.

I hastened to reassure her, and I explained what Poirot wanted.

'Certainly,' said Mrs Ackroyd rather doubtfully. 'I suppose we must come if M. Poirot says so. But what is it all about? I like to know beforehand.'

I assured the lady truthfully that I myself did not know any more than she did.

'Very well,' said Mrs Ackroyd at last, rather grudgingly, 'I will tell the others, and we will be there at nine o'clock.'

Thereupon I took my leave, and joined Poirot at the agreed meeting-place.

'I've been longer than a quarter of an hour, I'm afraid,' I remarked. 'But once that good lady starts talking it's a matter of the utmost difficulty to get a word in edgeways.'

'It is of no matter,' said Poirot. 'Me, I have been well amused. This park is magnificent.'

We set off homewards. When we arrived, to our great surprise Caroline, who had evidently been watching for us, herself opened the door.

She put her finger to her lips. Her face was full of importance and excitement.

'Ursula Bourne,' she said, 'the parlourmaid from Fernly. She's here! I've put her in the dining-room. She's in a terrible way, poor thing. Says she must see M. Poirot at once. I've done all I could. Taken her a cup of hot tea. It really goes to one's heart to see anyone in such a state.'

'In the dining-room?' asked Poirot.

'This way,' I said, and flung open the door.

Ursula Bourne was sitting by the table. Her arms were spread out in front of her, and she had evidently just lifted her head from where it had been buried. Her eyes were red with weeping.

'Ursula Bourne,' I murmured.

But Poirot went past me with outstretched hands.

'No,' he said, 'that is not quite right, I think. It is not Ursula Bourne, is it, my child – but Ursula Paton? Mrs Ralph Paton.'

—— 22 ——

URSULA'S STORY

For a moment or two the girl looked mutely at Poirot. Then, her reserve breaking down completely, she nodded her head once, and burst into an outburst of sobs.

Caroline pushed past me, and putting her arm round the girl, patted her on the shoulder.

'There, there, my dear,' she said soothingly, 'it will be all right. You'll see – everything will be all right.'

Buried under curiosity and scandal-mongering there is a lot of kindness in Caroline. For the moment, even the interest of Poirot's revelation was lost in the sight of the girl's distress.

Presently Ursula sat up and wiped her eyes.

'This is very weak and silly of me,' she said.

'No, no, my child,' said Poirot kindly. 'We can all realise the strain of this last week.'

'It must have been a terrible ordeal,' I said.

'And then to find that you knew,' continued Ursula. 'How did you know? Was it Ralph who told you?'

Poirot shook his head.

'You know what brought me to you tonight,' went on the girl. '*This*—'

She held out a crumpled piece of newspaper, and I recognised the paragraph that Poirot had had inserted.

'It says that Ralph has been arrested. So everything is useless. I need not pretend any longer.'

'Newspaper paragraphs are not always true, mademoiselle,' murmured Poirot, having the grace to look ashamed of himself. 'All the same, I think you will do well to make a clean breast of things. The truth is what we need now.'

The girl hesitated, looking at him doubtfully.

'You do not trust me,' said Poirot gently. 'Yet all the same you came here to find me, did you not? Why was that?'

'Because I don't believe that Ralph did it,' said the girl in a very low voice. 'And I think that you are clever, and will find out the truth. And also—'

'Yes?'

'I think you are kind.'

Poirot nodded his head several times.

'It is very good that – yes, it is very good. Listen, I do in verity believe that this husband of yours is innocent – but the affair marches badly. If I am to save him, I must know all there is to know – even if it should seem to make the case against him blacker than before.'

'How well you understand,' said Ursula.

'So you will tell me the whole story, will you not? From the beginning.'

'You're not going to send *me* away, I hope,' said Caroline, settling herself comfortably in an arm-chair. 'What I want to know,' she continued, 'is why this child was masquerading as a parlourmaid?'

'Masquerading?' I queried.

'That's what I said. Why did you do it, child? For a wager?'

'For a living,' said Ursula dryly.

And encouraged, she began the story which I reproduce here in my own words.

Ursula Bourne, it seemed, was one of a family of seven – impoverished Irish gentlefolk. On the death of her father, most of the girls were cast out into the world to earn their own living. Ursula's eldest sister was married to Captain Folliott. It was she whom I had seen that Sunday, and the cause of her embarrassment was clear enough now. Determined to earn her living and not attracted to the idea of being a nursery governess

– the one profession open to an untrained girl, Ursula preferred the job of parlourmaid. She scorned to label herself a 'lady parlourmaid.' She would be the real thing, her reference being supplied by her sister. At Fernly, despite an aloofness which, as has been seen, caused some comment, she was a success at her job – quick, competent, and thorough.

'I enjoyed the work,' she explained. 'And I had plenty of time to myself.'

And them came her meeting with Ralph Paton, and the love affair which culminated in a secret marriage. Ralph had persuaded her into that, somewhat against her will. He had declared that his stepfather would not hear of his marrying a penniless girl. Better to be married secretly, and break the news to him at some later and more favourable minute.

And so the deed was done, and Ursula Bourne became Ursula Paton. Ralph had declared that he meant to pay off his debts, find a job, and then, when he was in a position to support her, and independent of his adopted father, they would break the news to him.

But to people like Ralph Paton, turning over a new leaf is easier in theory than in practice. He hoped that his step-father, whilst still in ignorance of the marriage, might be persuaded to pay his debts and put him on his feet again. But the revelation of the amount of Ralph's liabilities merely enraged Roger Ackroyd, and he refused to do anything at all. Some months passed, and then Ralph was bidden once more to Fernly. Roger Ackroyd did not beat about the bush. It was the desire of his heart that Ralph should marry Flora, and he put the matter plainly before the young man.

And here it was that the innate weakness of Ralph Paton showed itself. As always, he grasped at the easy, the immediate solution. As far as I could make out, neither Flora nor Ralph made any pretence of love. It was, on both sides, a business arrangement. Roger Ackroyd dictated his wishes – they agreed to them. Flora accepted a chance of liberty, money, and an enlarged horizon, Ralph of course, was playing a different game. But he was in a very awkward hole financially. He seized at the chance. His debts would be paid. He could start again with a clean sheet. His was not a nature to envisage the future, but I gather that he saw vaguely the engagement with Flora being broken off after a decent interval had elapsed. Both Flora and he stipulated that it should be kept a secret for the present. He was anxious to conceal it from Ursula. He felt instinctively that her nature, strong and resolute, with an in-

herent distaste for duplicity, was not one to welcome such a
course.

Then came the crucial moment when Roger Ackroyd, always
high-handed, decided to announce the engagement. He said
no word of his intention to Ralph – only to Flora, and Flora,
apathetic, raised no objection. On Ursula, the news fell like a
bombshell. Summoned by her, Ralph came hurriedly down
from town. They met in the wood, where part of their conversation was overheard by my sister. Ralph implored her to
keep silent for a little while longer, Ursula was equally determined to have done with concealments. She would tell Mr
Ackroyd the truth without any further delay. Husband and
wife parted acrimoniously.

Ursula, steadfast in her purpose, sought an interview with
Roger Ackroyd that very afternoon, and revealed the truth to
him. Their interview was a stormy one – it might have been
even more stormy had not Roger Ackroyd been already obsessed with his own troubles. It was bad enough, however.
Ackroyd was not the kind of man to forgive the deceit that
had been practised upon him. His rancour was mainly directed
to Ralph, but Ursula came in for her share, since he regarded
her as a girl who had deliberately tried to 'entrap' the adopted
son of a very wealthy man. Unforgivable things were said on
both sides.

That same evening Ursula met Ralph by appointment in
the small summer-house, stealing out from the house by the
sidedoor in order to do so. Their interview was made up of
reproaches on both sides. Ralph charged Ursula with having
irretrievably ruined his prospects by her ill-timed revelation.
Ursula reproached Ralph with his duplicity.

They parted at last. A little over half an hour later came
the discovery of Roger Ackroyd's body. Since that night Ursula
had neither seen nor heard from Ralph.

As the story unfolded itself, I realised more and more what
a damning series of facts it was. Alive, Ackroyd could hardly
have failed to alter his will – I knew him well enough to
realise that to do so would be his first thought. His death
came in the nick of time for Ralph and Ursula Paton. Small
wonder the girl had held her tongue, and played her part so
consistently.

My meditations were interrupted. It was Poirot's voice speaking, and I knew from the gravity of his tone that he, too, was
fully alive to the implications of the position.

'Mademoiselle, I must ask you one question, and you must

answer it truthfully, for on it everything may hang: What time was it when you parted from Captain Ralph Paton in the summer-house? Now, take a little minute so that your answer may be very exact.'

The girl gave a half laugh, bitter enough in all conscience.

'Do you think I haven't gone over that again and again in my own mind? It was half-past nine when I went out to meet him. Major Blunt was walking up and down the terrace, so I had to go round through the bushes to avoid him. It must have been about twenty-seven minutes to ten when I reached the summer-house. Ralph was waiting for me. I was with him ten minutes – not longer, for it was just a quarter to ten when I got back to the house.'

I saw now the insistence of her question the other day. If only Ackroyd could have been proved to have been killed before a quarter to ten, and not after.

I saw the reflection of that thought in Poirot's next question.

'Who left the summer-house first?'

'I did.'

'Leaving Ralph Paton in the summer-house?'

'Yes – but you don't think—'

'Mademoiselle, it is of no importance what I think. What did you do when you got back to the house?'

'I went up to my room.'

'And stayed there until when?'

'Until about ten o'clock.'

'Is there anyone who can prove that?'

'Prove? That I was in my room, you mean? Oh! no. But surely – oh! I see, they might think – they might think—'

I saw the dawning horror in her eyes.

Poirot finished the sentence for her.

'That it was *you* who entered by the window and stabbed Mr Ackroyd as he sat in his chair? Yes, they might think just that.'

'Nobody but a fool would think any such thing,' said Caroline indignantly.

She patted Ursula on the shoulder.

The girl had her face hidden in her hands.

'Horrible,' she was murmuring. 'Horrible.'

Caroline gave her a friendly shake.

'Don't worry, my dear,' she said. 'M. Poirot doesn't think that really. As for that husband of yours, I don't think much of him, and I tell you so candidly. Running away and leaving you to face the music.'

But Ursula shook her head energetically.

'Oh, no,' she cried. 'It wasn't like that at all. Ralph would not run away on his own account. I see now. If he heard of his stepfather's murder, he might think himself that I had done it.'

'He wouldn't think any such thing,' said Caroline.

'I was so cruel to him that night – so hard and bitter. I wouldn't listen to what he was trying to say – wouldn't believe that he really cared. I just stood there telling him what I thought of him, and saying the coldest, cruellest things that came into my mind – trying my best to hurt him.'

'Do him no harm,' said Caroline. 'Never worry about what you say to a man. They're so conceited that they never believe you mean it if it's unflattering.'

Ursula went on nervously twisting and untwisting her hands.

'When the murder was discovered and he didn't come forward, I was terribly upset. Just for a moment I wondered – but then I knew he couldn't – he couldn't. . . . But I wished he would come forward and say openly that he'd had nothing to do with it. I knew that he was fond of Dr Sheppard, and I fancied that perhaps Dr Sheppard might know where he was hiding.'

She turned to me.

'That's why I said what I did to you that day. I thought, if you knew where he was, you might pass on the message to him.'

'I?' I exclaimed.

'Why should James know where he was?' demanded Caroline sharply.

'It was very unlikely, I know,' admitted Ursula, 'but Ralph had often spoken of Dr Sheppard, and I knew that he would be likely to consider him as his best friend in King's Abbot.'

'My dear child,' I said, 'I have not the least idea where Ralph Paton is at the present moment.'

'That is true enough,' said Poirot.

'But—' Ursula held out the newspaper cutting in a puzzled fashion.

'Ah! that,' said Poirot, slightly embarrassed; 'a *bagatelle*, mademoiselle. A *rien du tout*. Not for a moment do I believe that Ralph Paton has been arrested.'

'But then—' began the girl slowly.

Poirot went on quickly:

'There is one thing I should like to know – did Captain Paton wear shoes or boots that night?'

Ursula shook her head.

'I can't remember.'

'A pity! But how should you? Now, madame,' he smiled at her, his head on one side, his forefinger wagging eloquently, 'no questions. And do not torment yourself. Be of good courage, and place your faith in Hercule Poirot.'

—— 23 ——

POIROT'S LITTLE REUNION

'And now,' said Caroline, rising, 'that child is coming upstairs to lie down. Don't you worry, my dear. M. Poirot will do everything he can for you – be sure of that.'

'I ought to go back to Fernly,' said Ursual uncertainly.

But Caroline silenced her protests with a firm hand.

'Nonsense. You're in my hands for the time being. You'll stay here for the present, anyway – eh, M. Poirot?'

'It will be the best plan,' agreed the little Belgian. 'This evening I shall want mademoiselle – I beg her pardon, madame – to attend my little reunion. Nine o'clock at my house. It is most necessary that she should be there.'

Caroline nodded, and went with Ursula out of the room. The door shut behind them. Poirot dropped down into a chair again.

'So far, so good,' he said. 'Things are straightening themselves out.'

'They're getting to look blacker and blacker against Ralph Paton,' I observed gloomily.

Poirot nodded.

'Yes, that is so. But it was to be expected, was it not?'

I looked at him, slightly puzzled by the remark. He was leaning back in the chair, his eyes half closed, the tips of his fingers just touching each other. Suddenly he sighed and shook his head.

'What is it?' I asked.

'It is that there are moments when a great longing for my friend Hastings comes over me. That is the friend of whom I spoke to you – the one who resides now in the Argentine. Always, when I have had a big case, he has been by my side. And he has helped me –yes, often he has helped me. For he

had a knack, that one, of stumbling over the truth unawares
– without noticing it himself, *bien entendu*. At times, he has
said something particularly foolish, and behold that foolish
remark has revealed the truth to me! And then, too, it was
his practice to keep a written record of the cases that proved
interesting.'

I gave a slightly embarrassed cough.

'As far as that goes,' I began, and then stopped.

Poirot sat upright in his chair. His eyes sparkled.

'But yes? What is it that you would say?'

'Well, as a matter of fact, I've read some of Captain Hast-
ing's narratives, and I thought, why not try my hand at something of the same kind? Seemed a pity not to – unique opportunity – probably the only time I'll be mixed up with anything of this kind.'

I felt myself getting hotter and hotter, and more and more
incoherent, as I floundered through the above speech.

Poirot sprang from his chair. I had a moment's terror that
he was going to embrace me French fashion, but mercifully
he refrained.

'But this is magnificent – you have then written down your
impressions of the case as you went along?'

I nodded.

'*Epatant!*' cried Poirot. 'Let me see them – this instant.'

I was not quite prepared for such a sudden demand. I
racked my brains to remember certain details.

'I hope you won't mind,' I stammered. 'I may have been
a little – er – *personal* now and then.'

'Oh! I comprehend perfectly; you have referred to me as
comic – as, perhaps, ridiculous now and then? It matters not
at all. Hastings, he also was not always polite. Me, I have the
mind above such trivialities.'

Still somewhat doubtful, I rummaged in the drawers of my
desk and produced an untidy pile of manuscripts which I
handed over to him. With an eye on possible publication in
the future, I had divided the work into chapters, and the night
before I had brought it up to date with an account of Miss
Russell's visit. Poirot had therefore twenty chapters.

I left him with them.

I was obliged to go out to a case at some distance away, and
it was past eight o'clock when I got back, to be greeted with
a plate of hot dinner on a tray, and the announcement that
Poirot and my sister had supped together at half-past seven,

and that the former had then gone to my workshop to finish his reading of the manuscript.

'I hope, James,' said my sister, 'that you've been careful in what you say about me in it?'

My jaw dropped. I had not been careful at all.

'Not that it matters very much,' said Caroline, reading my expression correctly. 'M. Poirot will know what to think. He understands me much better than you do.'

I went into the workshop. Poirot was sitting by the window. The manuscript lay neatly piled on a chair beside him. He laid his hand on it and spoke.

'*Eh bien,*' he said, 'I congratulate you – on your modesty!'

'Oh!' I said, rather taken aback.

'And on your reticence,' he added.

I said 'Oh!' again.

'Not so did Hastings write,' continued my friend. 'On every page, many, many times was the word "I." What *he* thought – what *he* did. But you – you have kept your personality in the background; only once or twice does it obtrude – in scenes of home life, shall we say?'

I blushed a little before the twinkle in his eye.

'What do you really think of the stuff?' I asked nervously.

'You want my candid opinion?'

'Yes.'

Poirot laid his jesting manner aside.

'A very meticulous and accurate account,' he said kindly. 'You have recorded all the facts faithfully and exactly – though you have shown yourself becomingly reticent as to your own share in them.'

'And it has helped you?'

'Yes. I may say that it has helped me considerably. Come, we must go over to my house and set the stage for my little performance.'

Caroline was in the hall. I think she hoped that she might be invited to accompany us. Poirot dealt with the situation tactfully.

'I should much like to have had you present, mademoiselle,' he said regretfully, 'but at this juncture it would not be wise. See you, all these people tonight are suspects. Amongst them, I shall find the person who killed Mr Ackroyd.'

'You really believe that?' I said incredulously.

'I see that you do not,' said Poirot dryly. 'Not yet do you appreciate Hercule Poirot at his true worth.'

At that moment Ursula came down the staircase.

'You are ready, my child?' said Poirot. 'That is good. We will go to my house together. Mademoiselle Caroline, believe me. I do everything possible to render you service. Good evening.'

We went off, leaving Caroline rather like a dog who has been refused a walk, standing on the front door step gazing after us.

The sitting-room at The Larches had been got ready. On the table were various *siropes* and glasses. Also a plate of biscuits. Several chairs had been brought in from the other room.

Poirot ran to and fro rearranging things. Pulling out a chair here, altering the position of a lamp there, occasionally stooping to straighten one of the mats that covered the floor. He was specially fussing over the lighting. The lamps were arranged in such a way as to throw a clear light on the side of the room where the chairs were grouped, at the same time leaving the other end of the room, where I presumed Poirot himself would sit, in a dim twilight.

Ursula and I watched him. Presently a bell was heard.

'They arrive,' said Poirot. 'Good, all is in readiness.'

The door opened and the party from Fernly filed in. Poirot went forward and greeted Mrs Ackroyd and Flora.

'It is most good of you to come,' he said. 'And Major Blunt and Mr Raymond.'

The secretary was debonair as ever.

'What's the great idea?' he said, laughing. 'Some scientific machine? Do we have bands round our wrists which register guilty heart-beats? There is such an invention, isn't there?'

'I have read of it, yes,' admitted Poirot. 'But me, I am old-fashioned. I use the old methods. I work only with the little grey cells. Now let us begin – but first I have an announcement to make to you all.'

He took Ursula's hand and drew her forward.

'This lady is Mrs Ralph Paton. She was married to Captain Paton last March.'

A little shriek burst from Mrs Ackroyd.

'Ralph! Married! Last March! Oh! but it's absurd. How could he be?'

She stared at Ursula as though she had never seen her before.

'Married to Bourne?' she said. 'Really, M. Poirot, I don't believe you.'

Ursula flushed and began to speak, but Flora forestalled her.

Going quickly to the other girl's side, she passed her hand through her arm.

'You must not mind our being surprised,' she said. 'You see, we had no idea of such a thing. You and Ralph have kept your secret very well. I am – very glad about it.'

'You are very kind, Miss Ackroyd,' said Ursula in a low voice, 'and you have every right to be exceedingly angry. Ralph behaved very badly – especially to you.'

'You needn't worry about that,' said Flora, giving her arm a consoling little pat. 'Ralph was in a corner and took the only way out. I should probably have done the same in his place. I do think he might have trusted me with the secret, though. I wouldn't have let him down.'

Poirot rapped gently on a table and cleared his throat significantly.

'The board meeting's going to begin,' said Flora. 'M. Poirot hints that we mustn't talk. But just tell me one thing. Where is Ralph? You must know if anyone does.'

'But I don't,' cried Ursula, almost in a wail. 'That's just it, I don't.'

'Isn't he detained at Liverpool?' asked Raymond. 'It said so in the paper.'

'He is not at Liverpool,' said Poirot shortly.

'In fact,' I remarked, 'no one knows where he is.'

'Excepting Hercule Poirot, eh?' said Raymond.

Poirot replied seriously to the other's banter.

'Me, I know everything. Remember that.'

Geoffrey Raymond lifted his eyebrows.

'Everything?' He whistled. 'Whew! that's a tall order.'

'Do you mean to say you can really guess where Ralph Paton is hiding?' I asked incredulously.

'You call it guessing. I call it knowing, my friend.'

'In Cranchester?' I hazarded.

'No,' replied Poirot gravely, 'not in Cranchester.'

He said no more, but at a gesture from him the assembled party took their seats. As they did so, the door opened once more and two other people came in and sat down near the door. They were Parker and the housekeeper.

'The number is complete,' said Poirot. 'Everyone is here.'

There was a ring of satisfaction in his tone. And with the sound of it I saw a ripple of something like uneasiness pass over all thoses faces grouped at the other end of the room. There was a suggestion in all this as of a trap – a trap that had closed.

Poirot read from a list in an important manner.

'Mrs Ackroyd, Miss Flora Ackroyd, Major Blunt, Mr Geoffrey Raymond, Mrs Ralph Paton, John Parker, Elizabeth Russell.'

He laid the paper down on the table.

'What's the meaning of all this?' began Raymond.

'The list I have just read,' said Poirot, 'is a list of suspected persons. Every one of you present had the opportunity to kill Mr Ackroyd—'

With a cry Mrs Ackroyd sprang up, her throat working.

'I don't like it,' she wailed. 'I don't like it. I would much prefer to go home.'

'You cannot go home, madame,' said Poirot sternly, 'until you have heard what I have to say.'

He paused a moment, then cleared his throat.

'I will start at the beginning. When Miss Ackroyd asked me to investigate the case, I went up to Fernly Park with the good Doctor Sheppard. I walked with him along the terrace, where I was shown the footprints on the window-sill. From there Inspector Raglan took me along the path which leads to the drive. My eye was caught by a little summer-house, and I searched it thoroughly. I found two things – a scrap of starched cambric and an empty goose quill. The scrap of cambric immediately suggested to me a maid's apron. When Inspector Raglan showed me his list of the people in the house, I noticed at once that one of the maids – Ursula Bourne, the parlourmaid – had no real alibi. According to her own story, she was in her bedroom from nine-thirty until ten. But supposing that instead she was in the summer-house? If so, she must have gone there to meet someone. Now we know from Dr Sheppard that someone from outside *did* come to the house that night – the stranger whom he met just by the gate. At first glance it would seem that our problem was solved, and that the stranger went to the summer-house to meet Ursula Bourne. It was fairly certain that he *did* go to the summer-house because of the goose quill. That suggested at once to my mind a taker of drugs – and one who had acquired the habit on the other side of the Atlantic where sniffing "snow" is more common than in this country. The man whom Dr Sheppard met had an American accent, which fitted in with that supposition.

'But I was held up by one point. *The times did not fit.* Ursula Bourne could certainly not have gone to the summer-house before nine-thirty, whereas the man must have got there by a few minutes past nine. I could, of course, assume that he waited there for half an hour. The only alternative supposition was that there had been two separate meetings in the summer-house that night. *Eh bien*, as soon as I went into that alternative I found several significant facts. I discovered that Miss Russell, the houskeeper, had visited Dr Sheppard that morning, and had displayed a good deal of interest in cures for victims of the drug habit. Taking that in conjunction with the goose quill, I assumed that the man in question came to Fernly to meet the housekeeper, and not Ursula Bourne. Who, then, did Ursula Bourne come to the rendezvous to meet? I was not long in doubt. First I found a ring – a wedding ring – with "From R." and a date inside it. Then I learnt that Ralph Paton had been seen coming up the path which led to the summer-house at twenty-five minutes past nine, and I also heard of a certain conversation which had taken place in the wood near the village that very afternoon – a conversation between Ralph Paton and some unknown girl. So I had my facts succeeding each other in a neat and orderly manner. A secret marriage, an engagement announced on the day of the tragedy, the stormy interview in the wood, and the meeting arranged for the summer-house that night.

'Incidentally this proved to me one thing, that both Ralph Paton and Ursula Bourne (or Paton) had the strongest motives for wishing Mr Ackroyd out of the way. And it also made one other point unexpectedly clear. It could not have been Ralph Paton who was with Mr Ackroyd in the study at nine-thirty.

'So we come to another and most interesting aspect of the crime. Who was it in the room with Mr Ackroyd at nine-thirty? Not Ralph Paton, who was in the summer-house with his wife. Not Charles Kent, who had already left. Who, then? I posed my cleverest – my most audacious question: *Was anyone with him?*'

Poirot leaned forward and shot the last words triumphantly at us, drawing back afterwards with the air of one who has made a decided hit.

Raymond, however, did not seem impressed, and lodged a mild protest.

'I don't know if you're trying to make me out a liar, M. Poirot, but the matter does not rest on my evidence alone – except perhaps as to the exact words used. Remember, Major Blunt also heard Mr Ackroyd talking to someone. He was on the terrace outside, and couldn't catch the words clearly, but he distinctly heard the voices.'

Poirot nodded.

'I have not forgotten,' he said quietly. 'But Major Blunt

was under the impression that it was *you* to whom Mr Ackroyd was speaking.'

For a moment Raymond seemed taken aback. Then he recovered himself.

'Blunt knows now that he was mistaken,' he said.

'Exactly,' agreed the other man.

'Yet there must have been some reason for his thinking so,' mused Poirot. 'Oh! no,' he held up his hand in protest, 'I know the reason you will give – but it is not enough. We must seek elsewhere. I will put it this way. From the beginning of the case I have been struck by one thing – the nature of those words which Mr Raymond overheard. It has been amazing to me that no one has commented on them – has seen anything odd about them.'

He paused a minute, and then quoted softly:

'. . . *the calls on my purse have been so frequent of late that I fear it is impossible for me to accede to your request.* Does nothing strike you as odd about that?'

'I don't think so,' said Raymond. 'He has frequently dictated letters to me, using almost exactly those same words.'

'Exactly,' cried Poirot. 'That is what I seek to arrive at. Would any man use such a phrase in *talking* to another? Impossible that that should be part of a real conversation. Now, if he had been dictating a letter—'

'You mean he was reading a letter aloud,' said Raymond slowly. 'Even so, he must have been reading to someone.'

'But why? We have no evidence that there was anyone else in the room. No other voice but Mr Ackroyd's was heard, remember.'

'Surely a man wouldn't read letters of that type aloud to himself – not unless he was – well – going balmy.'

'You have all forgotten one thing,' said Poirot softly: 'the stranger who called at the house the preceding Wednesday.'

They all stared at him.

'But yes,' said Poirot, nodding encouragingly, 'on Wednesday. The young man was not of himself important. But the firm he represented interested me very much.'

'The Dictaphone Company,' gasped Raymond. 'I see it now. A dictaphone. That's what you think?'

Poirot nodded.

'Mr Ackroyd had promised to invest in a dictaphone, you remember. Me, I had the curiosity to inquire of the company in question. Their reply is that Mr Ackroyd *did* purchase a dictaphone from their representative. Why he concealed the matter from you, I do not know.'

'He must have meant to surprise me with it,' murmured Raymond. 'He had quite a childish love of surprising people. Meant to keep it up his sleeve for a day or so. Probably was playing with it like a new toy. Yes, it fits in. You're quite right no one would use quite those words in casual conversation.'

'It explains, too,' said Poirot, 'why Major Blunt thought it was you who were in the study. Such scraps as came to him were fragments of dictation, and so his subconscious mind deducted that you were with him. His conscious mind was occupied with something quite different – the white figure he had caught a glimpse of. He fancied it was Miss Ackroyd. Really, of course, it was Ursula Bourne's white apron he saw as she was stealing down to the summer-house.'

Raymond had recovered from his first surprise.

'All the same,' he remarked, 'this discovery of yours, brilliant though it is (I'm quite sure I should never have thought of it), leaves the essential position unchanged. Mr Ackroyd was alive at nine-thirty, since he was speaking into the dictaphone. It seems clear that the man Charles Kent was really off the premises by then. As to Ralph Paton—?'

He hesitated, glancing at Ursula.

Her colour flared up, but she answered steadily enough.

'Ralph and I parted just before a quarter to ten. He never went near the house, I am sure of that. He had no intention of doing so. The last thing on earth he wanted was to face his stepfather. He would have funked it badly.'

'It isn't that I doubt your story for a moment,' explained Raymond. 'I've always been quite sure Captain Paton was innocent. But one has to think of a court of law – and the questions that would be asked. He is in a most unfortunate position, but if he were to come forward—'

Poirot interrupted.

'That is your advice, yes? That he should come forward?'

'Certainly. If you know where he is—'

'I perceive that you do not believe that I do know. And yet I have told you just now that I know everything. The truth of the telephone call, of the footprints on the window-sill, of the hiding-place of Ralph Paton—'

'Where is he?' said Blunt sharply.

'Not very far away,' said Poirot, smiling.

'In Cranchester?' I asked.

Poirot turned towards me.

'Always you ask me that. The idea of Cranchester it is with you an *idée fixé*. No, he is not in Cranchester. He is – *there*!'

He pointed a dramatic forefinger. Everyone's head turned.

Ralph Paton was standing in the doorway.

——— 24 ———

RALPH PATON'S STORY

It was a very uncomfortable minute for *me*. I hardly took in what happened next, but there were exclamations and cries of surprise! When I was sufficiently master of myself to be able to realise what was going on, Ralph Paton was standing by his wife, her hand in his, and he was smiling across the room at me.

Poirot, too, was smiling, and at the same time shaking an eloquent finger at me.

'Have I not told you at least thirty-six times that it is useless to conceal things from Hercule Poirot?' he demanded. 'That in such a case he find out?'

He turned to the others.

'One day, you remember, we held a little séance about a table – just the six of us. I accused the other five persons present of concealing something from me. Four of them gave up their secret. Dr Sheppard did not give up his. But all along I have had my suspicions. Dr Sheppard went to the Three Boars that night hoping to find Ralph. He did not find him there; but supposing, I said to myself, that he met him in the street on his way home? Dr Sheppard was a friend of Captain Paton's, and he had come straight from the scene of the crime. He must know that things looked very black against him. Perhaps he knew more than the general public did—'

'I did,' I said ruefully. 'I suppose I might as well make a clean breast of things now. I went to see Ralph that afternoon. At first he refused to take me into his confidence, but later he told me about his marriage, and the hole he was in. As soon as the murder was discovered, I realised that once the facts were known, suspicion could not fail to attach to Ralph – or, if not to him, to the girl he loved. That night I put the facts plainly before him. The thought of having possibly to give evidence which might incriminate his wife made him resolve at all costs to – to—'

I hesitated, and Ralph filled up the gap.

'To do a bunk,' he said graphically. 'You see, Ursula left me to go back to the house. I thought it possible that she might have attempted to have another interview with my stepfather. He had already been very rude to her that afternoon. It occurred to me that he might have so insulted her – in such an unforgivable manner – that without knowing what she was doing—'

He stopped. Ursula released her hand from his, and stepped back.

'You thought that, Ralph! You actually thought that I might have done it?'

'Let us get back to the culpable conduct of Dr Sheppard,' said Poirot dryly. 'Dr Sheppard consented to do what he could to help him. He was successful in hiding Captain Paton from the police.'

'Where?' asked Raymond. 'In his own house?'

'Ah, no, indeed,' said Poirot. 'You should ask yourself the question that I did. If the good doctor is concealing the young man, what place would he choose? It must necessarily be somewhere near at hand. I think of Cranchester. A hotel? No. Lodgings? Even more emphatically, no. Where, then? Ah! I have it. A nursing home. A home for the mentally unfit. I test my memory. I invent a nephew with mental trouble. I consult Mademoiselle Sheppard as to suitable homes. She gives me the names of two near Cranchester to which her brother has sent patients. I make inquiries. Yes, at one of them a patient was brought there by the doctor himself early on Saturday morning. The patient, though known by another name, I had no difficulty in identifying as Captain Paton. After certain necessary formalities, I was allowed to bring him away. He arrived at my house in the early hours of yesterday morning.'

I looked at him ruefully.

'Caroline's Home Office expert,' I murmured. 'And to think I never guessed!'

'You see now why I drew attention to the reticence of your manuscript,' murmured Poirot. 'It was strictly truthful as far as it went – but it did not go very far, eh, my friend?'

I was too abashed to argue.

'Dr Sheppard has been very loyal,' said Ralph. 'He has stood by me through thick and thin. He did what he thought was best. I see now, from what M. Poirot has told me, that it was not really the best. I should have come forward and faced the music. You see, in the home, we never saw a newspaper. I knew nothing of what was going on.'

'Dr Sheppard has been a model of discretion,' said Poirot dryly. 'But me, I discover all the little secrets. It is my business.'

'Now we can have your story of what happened that night,' said Raymond impatiently.

'You know it already,' said Ralph. 'There's very little for me to add. I left the summer-house about nine forty-five, and tramped about the lanes, trying to make up my mind as to what to do next – what line to take. I'm bound to admit that I've not the shadow of an alibi, but I give you my solemn word that I never went to the study, that I never saw my stepfather alive – or dead. Whatever the world thinks, I'd like all of you to believe me.'

'No alibi,' murmured Raymond. 'That's bad. I believe you, of course, but – it's a bad business.'

'It makes things very simple, though,' said Poirot, in a cheerfull voice. 'Very simple indeed.'

We all stared at him.

'You see what I mean? No? Just this – to save Captain Paton the real criminal must confess.'

He beamed round at us all.

'But yes – I mean what I say. See now, I did not invite Inspector Raglan to be present. That was for a reason. I did not want to tell him all that I knew – at least I did not want to tell him to-night.'

He leaned forward, and suddenly his voice and his whole personality changed. He suddenly became dangerous.

'I who speak to you – I know the murderer of Mr Ackroyd is in this room now. It is to the murderer I speak. *To-morrow the truth goes to Inspector Raglan.* You understand?'

There was a tense silence. Into the midst of it came the old Breton woman with a telegram on a salver. Poirot tore it open.

Blunt's voice rose abrupt and resonant.

'The murderer is amongst us, you say? You know – which?'

Poirot had read the message. He crumpled it up in his hand.

'I know – now.'

He tapped the crumpled ball of paper.

'What is that?' said Raymond sharply.

'A wireless message – from a steamer now on her way to the United States.'

There was a dead silence. Poirot rose to his feet bowing.

'Messieurs et Mesdames, this reunion of mine is at an end. Remember – *the truth goes to Inspector Raglan in the morning.*'

—— 25 ——

THE WHOLE TRUTH

A slight gesture from Poirot enjoined me to stay behind the rest. I obeyed, going over to the fire and thoughtfully stirring the big logs on it with the toe of my boot.

I was puzzled. For the first time I was absolutely at sea as to Poirot's meaning. For a moment I was inclined to think that the scene I had just witnessed was a gigantic piece of bombast – that he had been what he called 'playing the comedy' with a view to making himself interesting and important. But, in spite of myself, I was forced to believe in an underlying reality. There had been real menace in his words – a certain indisputable sincerity. But I still believed him to be on entirely the wrong tack.

When the door shut behind the last of the party he came over to the fire.

'Well, my friend,' he said quietly, 'and what do you think of it all?'

'I don't know what to think,' I said frankly. 'What was the point? Why not go straight to Inspector Raglan with the truth instead of giving the guilty person this elaborate warning?'

Poirot sat down and drew out his case of tiny Russian cigarettes. He smoked for a minute or two in silence. Then:

'Use your little grey cells,' he said. 'There is always a reason behind my actions.'

I hesitated for a moment, and then I said slowly:

'The first one that occurs to me is that you yourself do not know who the guilty person is, but that you are sure that he is to be found amongst the people here to-night. Therefore your words were intended to force a confession from the unknown murderer?'

Poirot nodded approvingly.

'A clever idea, but not the truth.'

'I thought, perhaps, that by making him believe you knew, you might force him out into the open – not necessarily by confession. He might try to silence you as he formerly silenced Mr Ackroyd – before you could act to-morrow morning.'

'A trap with myself as the bait! *Merci, mon ami*, but I am not sufficiently heroic for that.'

'Then I fail to understand you. Surely you are running the risk of letting the murderer escape by thus putting him on his guard?'

Poirot shook his head.

'He cannot escape,' he said gravely. 'There is only one way out – and that way does not lead to freedom.'

'You really believe that one of those people here to-night committed the murder?' I asked incredulously.

'Yes, my friend.'

'Which one?'

There was a silence for some minutes. Then Poirot tossed the stump of his cigarette into the grate and began to speak in a quiet, reflective tone.

'I will take you the way that I have travelled myself. Step by step you shall accompany me, and see for yourself that all the facts point indisputably to one person. Now, to begin with, there were two facts and a little discrepancy in time which especially attracted my attention. The first fact was the telephone call. If Ralph Paton were indeed the murderer the telephone call became meaningless and absurd. Therefore, I said to myself, Ralph Paton is not the murderer.

'I satisfied myself that the call could not have been sent by anyone in the house, yet I was convinced that it was amongst those present on the fatal evening that I had to look for my criminal. Therefore I concluded that the telephone call must have been sent by an accomplice. I was not quite pleased with that deduction, but I let it stand for the minute.

'I next examined the *motive* for the call. That was difficult. I could only get at it by judging its *results*. Which was – that the murder was discovered that night instead of – in all probability – the following morning. You agree with that?'

'Ye-es,' I admitted. 'Yes. As you say, Mr Ackroyd, having given orders that he was not to be disturbed, nobody would have been likely to go to the study that night.'

'*Très bien*. The affair marches, does it not? But matters were still obscure. What was the advantage of having the crime discovered that night in preference to the following morning? The only idea I could get hold of was that the murderer, knowing the crime was to be discovered at a certain time, could make sure of being present when the door was broken in – or at any rate immediately afterwards. And now we come to the second fact – the chair pulled out from the wall. Inspector Raglan dismissed that as of no importance. I, on the contrary, have always regarded it as of supreme importance.

'In your manuscript you have drawn a neat little plan of the study. If you had it with you this minute you would see that – the chair being drawn out in the position indicated by Parker – it would stand in a direct line between the door and the window.'

'The window!' I said quickly.

'You, too, have my first idea. I imagined that the chair was drawn out so that something connected with the window should not be seen by anyone entering through the door. But I soon abandoned that supposition, for though the chair was a grandfather with a high back, it obscured very little of the window – only the part between the sash and the ground. No, *mon ami* – but remember that just in front of the window there stood a table with books and magazines upon it. Now that table *was* completely hidden by the drawn-out chair – and immediately I had my first shadowy suspicion of the truth.

'Supposing that there had been something on that table not intended to be seen? Something placed there by the murderer? As yet I had no inkling of what that something might be. But I knew certain very interesting facts about it. For instance, it was something that the murderer had not been able to take away with him at the time that he committed the crime. At the same time it was vital that it should be removed as soon as possible after the crime had been discovered. And so – the telephone message, and the opportunity for the murderer to be on the spot when the body was discovered.

'Now four people were on the scene before the police arrived. Yourself, Parker, Major Blunt, and Mr Raymond. Parker I eliminated at once, since at whatever time the crime was discovered, he was the one person certain to be on the spot. Also it was he who told me of the pulled-out chair. Parker, then, was cleared (of the murder, that is. I still thought it possible that he had been blackmailing Mrs Ferrars). Raymond and Blunt, however, remained under suspicion since, if the crime had been discovered in the early hours of the morning, it was quite possible that they might have arrived on the scene too late to prevent the object on the round table being discovered.

'Now what was that object? You heard my arguments tonight in reference to the scrap of conversation overheard? As soon as I learned that a representative of a dictaphone company had called, the idea of a dictaphone took root in my mind. You heard what I said in this room not half an hour ago? They all agreed with my theory – but one vital fact seems to have escaped them. Granted that a dictaphone was being used by Mr Ackroyd that night – why was no dictaphone found?'

'I never thought of that,' I said.

'We know that a dictaphone was supplied to Mr Ackroyd. But no dictaphone has been found amongst his effects. So, if something was taken from that table – why should not that something be the dictaphone? But there were certain difficulties in the way. The attention of everyone was, of course, focused on the murdered man. I think anyone could have gone to the table unnoticed by the other people in the room. But a dictaphone has a certain bulk – it cannot be slipped casually into a pocket. There must have been a receptacle of some kind capable of holding it.

'You see where I am arriving? The figure of the murderer is taking shape. A person who was on the scene straightaway, but who might not have been if the crime had been discovered the following morning. A person carrying a receptacle into which the dictaphone might be fitted—'

I interrutped.

'But why remove the dictaphone? What was the point?'

'You are like Mr Raymond. You take it for granted that what was heard at nine-thirty was Mr Ackroyd's voice speaking into a dictaphone. But consider this useful invention for a little minute. You dictate into it, do you not? And at some later time a secretary or a typist turns it on, and the voice speaks again.'

'You mean—?' I gasped.

Poirot nodded.

'Yes, I mean that. *At nine-thirty Mr Ackroyd was already dead*. It was the dictaphone speaking – not the man.'

'And the murderer switched it on. Then he must have been in the room at that minute?'

'Possibly. But we must not exclude the likelihood of some mechanical device having been applied – something after the nature of a time lock, or even of a simple alarm clock. But in that case we must add two qualifications to our imaginary portrait of the murderer. It must be someone who knew of Mr Ackroyd's purchase of the dictaphone and also someone with the necessary mechanical knowledge.

'I had got thus far in my own mind when we came to the

footprints on the window ledge. Here there were three conclusions open to me. (1) They might really have been made by
Ralph Paton. He had been at Fernly that night, and might
have climbed into the study and found his uncle dead there.
That was one hypothesis. (2) There was the possibility that the
footmarks might have been made by somebody else who happened to have the same kind of studs in his shoes. But the
inmates of the house had shoes soled with crêpe rubber, and I
decided to believe in the coincidence of someone from outside
having the same kind of shoes as Ralph Paton wore. Charles
Kent, as we know from the barmaid of the Dog and Whistle,
had on a pair of boots "clean dropping off him." (3) Those
prints were made by someone deliberately trying to throw suspicion on Ralph Paton. To test this last conclusion, it was
necessary to ascertain certain facts. One pair of Ralph's shoes
had been obtained from the Three Boars by the police. Neither
Ralph nor anyone else could have worn them that evening,
since they were downstairs being cleaned. According to the
police theory, Ralph was wearing another pair of the same
kind, and I found out that it was true that he had two pairs.
Now for my theory to be proved correct it was necessary for
the murderer to have worn Ralph's shoes that evening – in
which case Ralph must have been wearing yet a *third* pair of
footwear of some kind. I could hardly suppose that he would
bring three pairs of shoes all alike – the third pair of footwear
were more likely to be boots. I got your sister to make inquiries
on this point – laying some stress on the colour, in order – I
admit it frankly – to obscure the real reason for my asking.

'You know the result of her investigations. Ralph Paton *had*
had a pair of boots with him. The first question I asked him
when he came to my house yesterday morning was what he was
wearing on his feet on the fatal night. He replied at once that
he had worn *boots* – he was still wearing them, in fact – having
nothing else to put on.

'So we get a step further in our description of the murderer
– a person who had the opportunity to take these shoes of
Ralph Paton's from the Three Boars that day.'

He paused, and then said, with a slightly raised voice:

'There is one further point. The murderer must have been
a person who had the opportunity to purloin that dagger from
the silver table. You might argue that anyone in the house
might have done so, but I will recall to you that Flora Ackroyd
was very positive that the dagger was not there when she examined the silver table.'

He paused again.

'Let us recapitulate – now that all is clear. A person who was at the Three Boars earlier that day, a person who knew Ackroyd well enough to know that he had purchased a dictaphone, a person who was of a mechanical turn of mind, who had the opportunity to take the dagger from the silver table before Miss Flora arrived, who had with him a receptacle suitable for hiding the dictaphone – such as a black bag, and who had the study to himself for a few minutes after the crime was discovered while Parker was telephoning for the police. In fact – *Dr Sheppard*!'

—— 26 ——

AND NOTHING BUT THE TRUTH

There was a dead silence for a minute and a half.

Then I laughed.

'You're mad,' I said.

'No,' said Poirot placidly. 'I am not mad. It was the little discrepancy in time that first drew my attention to you – right at the beginning.'

'Discrepancy in time?' I queried, puzzled.

'But yes. You will remember that everyone agreed – you yourself included – that it took five minutes to walk from the lodge to the house – less if you took the short cut to the terrace. But you left the house at ten minutes to nine – both by your own statement and that of Parker, and yet it was nine o'clock when you passed through the lodge gates. It was a chilly night – not an evening a man would be inclined to dawdle; why had you taken ten minutes to do a five minutes' walk? All along I realised that we had only your statement for it that the study window was ever fastened. Ackroyd asked you if you had done so – he never looked to see. Supposing, then, that the study window was unfastened? Would there be time in that ten minutes for you to run round the outside of the house, change your shoes, climb in through the window, kill Ackroyd, and get to the gate by nine o'clock? I decided against that theory since in all probability a man as nervous as Ackroyd was that night would hear you climbing in, and then there would have been a struggle. But supposing that you killed Ackroyd *before* you left – as you were standing beside his chair? Then you got out of the front door, run round to the summer-house, take Ralph Paton's shoes out of the bag you brought up with you that night, slip them on, walk through the mud in them, and leave prints on the window ledge, you climb in, lock the study door on the inside, run back to the summer-house, change back into your own shoes, and race down to the gate. (I went through similar actions the other day, when you were with Mrs Ackroyd – it took ten minutes exactly.) Then home – and an alibi – since you had timed the dictaphone for half-past nine.'

'My dear Poirot,' I said in a voice that sounded strange and forced to my own ears, 'you've been brooding over this case too long. What on earth had I to gain by murdering Ackroyd?'

'Safety. It was you who blackmailed Mrs Ferrars. Who could have had a better knowledge of what killed Mr Ferrars than the doctor who was attending him? When you spoke to me that first day in the garden, you mentioned a legacy received about a year ago. I have been unable to discover any trace of a legacy. You had to invent some way of accounting for Mrs Ferrars's twenty thousand pounds. It has not done you much good. You lost most of it in speculation – then you put the screw on too hard, and Mrs Ferrars took a way out that you had not expected. If Ackroyd had learnt the truth he would have had no mercy on you – you were ruined for ever.'

'And the telephone call?' I asked, trying to rally. 'You have a plausible explanation of that also, I suppose?'

'I will confess to you that it was my greatest stumbling block when I found that a call had actually been put through to you from King's Abbot station. I at first believed that you had simply invented the story. It was a very clever touch, that. You must have some excuse for arriving at Fernly, finding the body, and so getting the chance to remove the dictaphone on which your alibi depended. I had a very vague notion of how it was worked when I came to see your sister that first day and inquired as to what patients you had seen on Friday morning. I had no thought of Miss Russell in my mind at that time. Her visit was a lucky coincidence, since it distracted your mind from the real object of my questions. I found what I was looking for. Among your patients that morning was the steward of an American liner. Who more suitable than he to be leaving for Liverpool by the train that evening? And afterwards he would be on the high seas, well out of the way. I noted that the *Orion* sailed on Saturday, and having obtained the name of the steward I sent him a wireless message asking a certain question. This is his reply you saw me receive just now.'

He held out the message to me. It ran as follow:

'Quite correct. Dr Sheppard asked me to leave a note at a patient's house. I was to ring him up from the station with the reply. Reply was "No answer." '

'It was a clever idea,' said Poirot. 'The call was genuine. Your sister saw you take it. But there was only one man's word as to what was actually said – your own!'

I yawned.

'All this,' I said, is very interesting – but hardly in the sphere of practical politics.'

'You think not? Remember what I said – the truth goes to Inspector Raglan in the morning. But, for the sake of your good sister, I am willing to give you the chance of another way out. There might be, for instance, an overdose of a sleeping draught. You comprehend me? But Captain Ralph Paton must be cleared – *ça va sans dire*. I should suggest that you finish that very interesting manuscript of yours – but abandoning your former reticence.'

'You seem to be very prolific of suggestions,' I remarked. 'Are you sure you've quite finished?'

'Now that you remind me of the fact, it is true that there is one thing more. It would be most unwise on your part to attempt to silence me as you silenced M. Ackroyd. That kind of business does not succeed against Hercule Poirot, you understand.'

'My dear Poirot,' I said, smiling a little, 'whatever else I may be, I am not a fool.'

I rose to my feet.

'Well, well,' I said, with a slight yawn, 'I must be off home. Thank you for a most interesting and instructive evening.'

Poirot also rose and bowed with his accustomed politeness as I passed out of the room.

27

APOLOGIA

Five a.m. I am very tired – but I have finished my task. My arm aches from writing.

A strange end to my manuscript. I meant it to be published some day as the history of one of Poirot's failures! Odd, how things pan out.

All along I've had a premonition of disaster, from the moment I saw Ralph Paton and Mrs Ferrars with their heads together. I thought then that she was confiding in him; as it happened I was quite wrong there, but the idea persisted even after I went into the study with Ackroyd that night, until he told me the truth.

Poor old Ackroyd. I'm always glad that I gave him a chance. I urged him to read that letter before it was too late. Or let me be honest – didn't I subconsciously realise that with a pig-headed chap like him, it was my best chance of getting him *not* to read it? His nervousness that night was interesting psychologically. He knew danger was close at hand. And yet he never suspected *me*.

The dagger was an afterthought. I'd brought up a very handy little weapon of my own, but when I saw the dagger lying in the silver table, it occurred to me at once how much better it would be to use a weapon that couldn't be traced to me.

I suppose I must have meant to murder him all along. As soon as I heard of Mrs Ferrars's death, I felt convinced that she would have told him everything before she died. When I met him and he seemed so agitated, I thought that perhaps he knew the truth, but that he couldn't bring himself to believe it, and was going to give me the chance of refuting it.

So I went home and took my precautions. If the trouble were after all only something to do with Ralph – well, no harm would have been done. The dictaphone he had given me two days before to adjust. Something had gone a little wrong with it, and I persuaded him to let me have a go at it, instead of sending it back. I did what I wanted to it, and took it up with me in my bag that evening.

I am rather pleased with myself as a writer. What could be neater, for instance, than the following:

'The letters were brought in at twenty minutes to nine. It was just on ten minutes to nine when I left him, the letter still unread. I hesitated with my hand on the door handle, looking back and wondering if there was anything I had left undone.'

All true, you see. But suppose I had put a row of stars after the first sentence! Would somebody then have wondered what exactly happened in the blank ten minutes?

When I looked round the room from the door, I was quite satisfied. Nothing had been left undone. The dictaphone was on the table by the window, timed to go off at nine-thirty (the mechanism of that little device was rather clever – based on the principle of an alarm clock), and the arm-chair was pulled out so as to hide it from the door.

I must admit that it gave me rather a shock to run into Parker just outside the door. I have faithfully recorded that fact.

Then later, when the body was discovered, and I had sent Parker to telephone for the police, what a judicious use of words: *'I did what little had to be done!'* It was quite little – just to shove the dictaphone into my bag and push back the chair against the wall in its proper place. I never dreamed that Parker would have noticed that chair. Logically, he ought to have been so agog over the body as to be blind to everything else. But I hadn't reckoned with the trained servant complex.

I wish I could have known beforehand that Flora was going to say she'd seen her uncle alive at a quarter to ten. That puzzled me more than I can say. In fact, all through the case there have been things that puzzled me hopelessly. Everyone seems to have taken a hand.

My greatest fear all through has been Caroline. I have fancied she might guess. Curious the way she spoke that day of my 'strain of weakness.'

Well, she will never know the truth. There is, as Poirot said, one way out. . . .

I can trust him. He and Inspector Raglan will manage it between them. I should not like Caroline to know. She is fond of me, and then, too, she is proud. . . . My death will be a grief to her, but grief passes. . . .

When I have finished writing, I shall enclose this whole manuscript in an envelope and address it to Poirot.

And then – what shall it be? Veronal? There would be a kind of poetic justice. Not that I take any responsibility for

Mrs Ferrar's death. It was the direct consequence of her own actions. I feel no pity for her.

I have no pity for myself either.

So let it be veronal.

But I wish Hercule Poirot had never retired from work and come here to grow vegetable marrows.

THE
MYSTERY
OF THE
BLUE TRAIN

I

THE MAN WITH THE WHITE HAIR

It was close on midnight when a man crossed the Place de la Concorde. In spite of the handsome fur coat which garbed his meagre form, there was something essentially weak and paltry about him.

A little man with a face like a rat. A man, one would say, who could never play a conspicuous part, or rise to prominence in any sphere. And yet, in leaping to such a conclusion, an onlooker would have been wrong. For this man, negligible and inconspicuous as he seemed, played a prominent part in the destiny of the world. In an Empire where rats ruled, he was the king of the rats.

Even now, an Embassy awaited his return. But he had business to do first – business of which the Embassy was not officially cognizant. His face gleamed white and sharp in the moonlight. There was the least hint of a curve in the thin nose. His father had been a Polish Jew, a journeyman tailor. It was business such as his father would have loved that took him abroad tonight.

He came to the Seine, crossed it, and entered one of the less reputable quarters of Paris. Here he stopped before a tall, dilapidated house and made his way up to an apartment on the fourth floor. He had barely time to knock before the door was opened by a woman who had evidently been awaiting his arrival. She gave him no greeting, but helped him off with his overcoat and then led the way into the tawdrily furnished sitting-room. The electric light was shaded with dirty pink festoons, and it softened, but could not disguise, the girl's face with its mask of crude paint. Could not disguise, either, the broad Mongolian cast of her countenance. There was no doubt of Olga Demiroff's profession, nor of her nationality.

'All is well, little one?'

'All is well, Boris Ivanovitch.'

He nodded, murmuring: 'I do not think I have been followed.'

But there was anxiety in his tone. He went to the window,

drawing the curtains aside slightly, and peering carefully out. He started away violently.

'There are two men – on the opposite pavement. It looks to me—' he broke off and began gnawing at his nails – a habit he had when anxious.

The Russian girl was shaking her head with a slow, reassuring action.

'They were here before you came.'

'All the same, it looks to me as though they were watching this house.'

'Possibly,' she admitted indifferently.

'But then—'

'What of it? Even if they *know* – it will not be *you* they will follow from here.'

A thin, cruel smile came to his lips.

'No,' he admitted, 'that is true.'

He mused for a minute or two, and then observed.

'This damned American – he can look after himself as well as anybody.'

'I suppose so.'

He went again to the window.

'Tough customers,' he muttered, with a chuckle. 'Known to the police, I fear. Well, well, I wish Brother Apache good hunting.'

Olga Demiroff shook her head.

'If the American is the kind of man they say he is, it will take more than a couple of cowardly apaches to get the better of him.' She paused. 'I wonder—'

'Well?'

'Nothing. Only twice this evening a man has passed along this street – a man with white hair.'

'What of it?'

'This. As he passed those two men, he dropped his glove. One of them picked it up and returned it to him. A threadbare device.'

'You mean – that the white-haired man is – their employer?'

'Something of the kind.'

The Russian looked alarmed and uneasy.

'You are sure – the parcel is safe? It has not been tampered with? There has been too much talk . . . much too much talk.'

He gnawed his nails again.

'Judge for yourself.'

She bent to the fireplace, deftly removing the coals. Underneath, from amongst the crumpled balls of newspaper, she selected from the very middle an oblong package wrapped round with grimy newspaper, and handed it to the man.

'Ingenious,' he said, with a nod of approval.

'The apartment has been searched twice. The mattress on my bed was ripped open.'

'It is as I said,' he muttered. 'There has been too much talk. This haggling over the price – it was a mistake.'

He had unwrapped the newspaper. Inside was a small brown paper parcel. This in turn he unwrapped, verified the contents, and quickly wrapped it up once more. As he did so, an electric bell rang sharply.

'The American is punctual,' said Olga, with a glance at the clock.

She left the room. In a minute she returned ushering in a stranger, a big, broad-shouldered man whose transatlantic origin was evident. His keen glance went from one to the other.

'M. Krassnine?' he inquired politely.

'I am he,' said Boris. 'I must apologise for – for the unconventionality of this meeting-place. But secrecy is urgent. I – I cannot afford to be connected with this business in any way.'

'Is that so?' said the American politely.

'I have your word, have I not, that no details of this transaction will be made public? That is one of the conditions of – sale.'

The American nodded.

'That has already been agreed upon,' he said indifferently. 'Now, perhaps, you will produce the goods.'

'You have the money – in notes?'

'Yes,' replied the other.

He did not, however, make any attempt to produce it. After a moment's hesitation, Krassnine gestured towards the small parcel on the table.

The American took it up and unrolled the wrapping paper. The contents he took over to a small electric lamp and submitted them to a very thorough examination. Satisfied, he drew from his pocket a thick leather wallet and extracted from it a wad of notes. These he handed to the Russian, who counted them carefully.

'All right?'

'I thank you, Monsieur. Everything is correct.'

'Ah!' said the other. He slipped the brown paper parcel negligently into his pocket. He bowed to Olga. 'Good evening, Mademoiselle. Good evening, M. Krassnine.'

He went out, shutting the door behind him. The eyes of

the two in the room met. The man passed his tongue over his dry lips.

'I wonder – will he ever get back to his hotel?' he muttered.

By common accord, they both turned to the window. They were just in time to see the American emerge into the street below. He turned to the left and marched along at a good pace without once turning his head. Two shadows stole from a doorway and followed noiselessly. Pursuers and pursued vanished into the night. Olga Demiroff spoke.

'He will get back safely,' she said. 'You need not fear – or hope – whichever it is.'

'Why do you think he will be safe?' asked Krassnine curiously.

'A man who has made as much money as he has could not possibly be a fool,' said Olga. 'And talking of money—'

She looked significantly at Krassnine.

'Eh?'

'My share, Boris Ivanovitch.'

With some reluctance, Krassnine handed over two of the notes. She nodded her thanks, with a complete lack of emotion, and tucked them away in her stocking.

'That is good,' she remarked, with satisfaction.

He looked at her curiously.

'You have no regrets, Olga Vassilovna?'

'Regrets? For what?'

'For what has been in your keeping. There are women – most women, I believe, who go mad over such things.'

She nodded reflectively.

'Yes, you speak true there. Most women have that madness. I – have not. I wonder now—' She broke off.

'Well?' asked the other curiously.

'The American will be safe with them – yes, I am sure of that. But afterwards—'

'Eh? What are you thinking of?'

'He will give them, of course, to some woman,' said Olga thoughtfully. 'I wonder what will happen then. . . .'

She shook herself impatiently and went over to the window. Suddenly she uttered an exclamation and called to her companion.

'See, he is going down the street now – the man I mean.'

They both gazed down together. A slim, elegant figure was progressing along at a leisurely pace. He wore an opera hat and a cloak. As he passed a street lamp, the light illuminated a thatch of thick white hair.

M. LE MARQUIS

The man with the white hair continued on his course, unhurried, and seemingly indifferent to his surroundings. He took a side turning to the right and another one to the left. Now and then he hummed a little air to himself.

Suddenly he stopped dead and listened intently. He had heard a certain sound. It might have been the bursting of a tyre or it might have been – a shot. A curious smile played round his lips for a minute. Then he resumed his leisurely walk.

On turning a corner he came upon a scene of some activity. A representative of the law was making notes in a pocket-book, and one or two late passers-by had collected on the spot. To one of these the man with the white hair made a polite request for information.

'Something has been happening, yes?'

'*Mais oui*, Monsieur. Two apaches set upon an elderly American gentleman.'

'They did him no injury?'

'No, indeed.' The man laughed. 'The American, he had a revolver in his pocket, and before they could attack him, he fired shots so closely round them that they took alarm and fled. The police, as usual, arrived too late.'

'Ah!' said the inquirer.

He displayed no emotion of any kind.

Placidly and unconcernedly he resumed his nocturnal strolling. Presently he crossed the Seine and came into the richer areas of the city. It was some twenty minutes later that he came to a stop before a certain house in a quiet but aristocratic thoroughfare.

The shop, for shop it was, was a restrained and unpretentious one. D. Papopolous, dealer in antiques, was so known to fame that he needed no advertisement, and indeed most of his business was not done over a counter. M. Papopolous had a very handsome apartment of his own overlooking the Champs Elysées, and it might reasonably be supposed that he would have been found there and not at his place of business at such an hour, but the man with the white hair seemed confident of success as he pressed the obscurely placed bell, having first given a quick glance up and down the deserted street.

His confidence was not misplaced. The door opened and a man stood in the aperture. He wore gold rings in his ears and was of a swarthy cast of countenance.

'Good evening,' said the stranger. 'Your master is within?'

'The master is here, but he does not see chance visitors at this time of night,' growled the other.

'I think he will see me. Tell him that his friend M. le Marquis is here.'

The man opened the door a little wider and allowed the visitor to enter.

The man who gave his name as M. le Marquis had shielded his face with his hand as he spoke. When the man-servant returned with the information that M. Papopolous would be pleased to receive the visitor a further change had taken place in the stranger's appearance. The man-servant must have been very unobservant or very well trained, for he betrayed no surprise at the small black satin mask which hid the other's features. Leading the way to a door at the end of the hall, he opened it and announced in a respectful murmur: 'M. le Marquis.'

The figure which rose to receive this strange guest was an imposing one. There was something venerable and patriarchal about M. Papopolous. He had a high domed forehead and a beautiful white beard. His manner had in it something ecclesiastical and benign.

'My dear friend,' said M. Papopolous.

He spoke in French and his tones were rich and unctuous.

'I must apologise,' said the visitor, 'for the lateness of the hour.'

'Not at all. Not at all,' said M. Papopolous – 'an interesting time of night. You have had, perhaps, an interesting evening?'

'Not personally,' said M. le Marquis.

'Not personally,' repeated M. Papopolous, 'no, no, of course not. And there is news, eh?'

He cast a sharp glance sideways at the other, a glance that was not ecclesiastical or benign in the least.

'There is no news. The attempt failed. I hardly expected anything else.'

'Quite so,' said M. Papopolous; 'anything crude—'

He waved his hand to express his intense distaste for crudity in any form. There was indeed nothing crude about M. Papopolous nor about the goods he handled. He was well

known in most European courts, and kings called him Deme-
trius in a friendly manner. He had the reputation for the most
exquisite discretion. That, together with the nobility of his
aspect, had carried him through several very questionable
transactions.

'The direct attack –' said M. Papopolous. He shook his head.
'It answers something – but very seldom.'

The other shrugged his shoulders.

'It saves time,' he remarked, 'and to fail costs nothing – or
next to nothing. The other plan – will not fail.'

'Ah,' said M. Papopolous, looking at him keenly.

The other nodded slowly.

'I have great confidence in your – er – reputation,' said the
antique dealer.

M. le Marquis smiled gently.

'I think I may say,' he murmured, 'that your confidence will
not be misplaced.'

'You have unique opportunities,' said the other, with a note
of envy in his voice.

'I make them,' said M. le Marquis.

He rose and took up the cloak which he had thrown carelessly on the back of a chair.

'I will keep you informed, M. Papopolous, through the usual
channels, but there must be no hitch in your arrangements.'

M. Papopolous was pained.

'There is *never* a hitch in my arrangements,' he complained.

The other smiled, and without any further words of adieu
he left the room, closing the door behind him.

M. Papopolous remained in thought for a moment stroking
his venerable white beard, and then moved across to a second
door which opened inwards. As he turned the handle, a young
woman, who only too clearly had been leaning against it with
her ear to the keyhole, stumbled headlong into the room. M.
Papopolous displayed neither surprise nor concern. It was
evidently all quite natural to him.

'Well, Zia?' he asked.

'I did not hear him go,' explained Zia.

She was a handsome young woman, built on Junoesque lines,
with dark flashing eyes and such a general air of resemblance
to M. Papopolous that it was easy to see they were father and
daughter.

'It is annoying.' she continued vexedly, 'that one cannot see
through a keyhole and hear through it at the same time.'

'It has often annoyed me,' said M. Papopolous, with great simplicity.

'So that is M. le Marquis,' said Zia slowly. 'Does he always wear a mask, Father?'

'Always.'

There was a pause.

'It is the rubies, I suppose?' asked Zia.

Her father nodded.

'What do you think, my little one?' he inquired, with a hint of amusement in his beady black eyes.

'Of M. le Marquis?'

'Yes.'

'I think,' said Zia slowly, 'that it is a very rare thing to find a well-bred Englishman who speaks French as well as that.'

'Ah!' said M. Papopolous, 'so that is what you think.'

As usual, he did not commit himself, but he regarded Zia with benign approval.

'I thought, too,' said Zia, 'that his head was an odd shape.'

'Massive,' said her father – 'a trifle massive. But then that effect is always created by a wig.'

They both looked at each other and smiled.

— 3 —

HEART OF FIRE

Rufus Van Aldin passed through the revolving doors of the Savoy, and walked to the reception desk. The desk clerk smiled a respectful greeting.

'Pleased to see you back again, Mr Van Aldin,' he said.

The American millionaire nodded his head in a casual greeting.

'Everything all right?' he asked.

'Yes, sir. Major Knighton is upstairs in the suite now.'

Van Aldin nodded again.

'Any mail?' he vouchsafed.

'They have all been sent up, Mr Van Aldin. Oh! wait a minute.'

He dived into a pigeon hole, and produced a letter.

'Just come this minute,' he explained.

Rufus Van Aldin took the letter from him, and as he saw

the handwriting, a woman's flowing hand, his face was suddenly transformed. The harsh contours of it softened, and the hard line of his mouth relaxed. He looked a different man. He walked across to the lift with the letter in his hand and the smile still on his lips.

In the drawing-room of his suite, a young man was sitting at a desk nimbly sorting correspondence with the ease born of long practice. He sprang up as Van Aldin entered.

'Hallo, Knighton!'

'Glad to see you back, sir. Had a good time?'

'So so!' said the millionaire unemotionally. 'Paris is rather a one-horse city nowadays. Still — I got what I went over for.'

He smiled to himself rather grimly.

'You usually do, I believe,' said the secretary, laughing.

'That's so,' agreed the other.

He spoke in a matter-of-fact manner, as one stating a well-known fact. Throwing off his heavy overcoat, he advanced to the desk.

'Anything urgent?'

'I don't think so, sir. Mostly the usual stuff. I have not quite finished sorting it out.'

Van Aldin nodded briefly. He was a man who seldom expressed either blame or praise. His methods with those he employed were simple; he gave them a fair trial and dismissed promptly those who were inefficient. His selections of people were unconventional. Knighton, for instance, he had met casually at a Swiss resort two months previously. He had approved of the fellow, looked up his war record, and found in it the explanation of the limp with which he walked. Knighton had made no secret of the fact that he was looking for a job, and indeed diffidently asked the millionaire if he knew of any available post. Van Aldin remembered, with a grim smile of amusement, the young man's complete astonishment when he had been offered the post of secretary to the great man himself.

'But — but I have no experience of business,' he had stammered.

'That doesn't matter a cuss,' Van Aldin had replied. 'I have got three secretaries already to attend to that kind of thing. But I am likely to be in England for the next six months, and I want an Englishman who — well, knows the ropes — and can attend to the social side of things for me.'

So far, Van Aldin had found his judgment confirmed.

Knighton had proved quick, intelligent, and resourceful, and he had a distinct charm of manner.

The secretary indicated three or four letters placed by themselves on the top of the desk.

'It might perhaps be as well, sir, if you glanced at these,' he suggested. 'The top one is about the Colton agreement—'

But Rufus Van Aldin held up a protesting hand.

'I am not going to look at a durned thing tonight,' he declared. 'They can all wait till the morning. Except this one,' he added, looking down at the letter he held in his hand. And again that strange transforming smile stole over his face.

Richard Knighton smiled sympathetically.

'Mrs Kettering?' he murmured. 'She rang up yesterday and today. She seems very anxious to see you at once, sir.'

'Does she, now!'

The smile faded from the millionaire's face. He ripped open the envelope which he held in his hand and took out the enclosed sheet. As he read it his face darkened, his mouth set grimly in the line which Wall Street knew so well, and his brows knit themselves ominously. Knighton turned tactfully away, and went on opening letters and sorting them. A muttered oath escaped the millionaire, and his clenched fist hit the table sharply.

'I'll not stand for this,' he muttered to himself. 'Poor little girl, it's a good thing she has her old father behind her.'

He walked up and down the room for some minutes, his brows drawn together in a scowl. Knighton still bent assiduously over the desk. Suddenly Van Aldin came to an abrupt halt. He took up his overcoat from the chair where he had thrown it.

'Are you going out again, sir?'

'Yes, I'm going round to see my daughter.'

'If Colton's people ring up—?'

'Tell them to go to the devil,' said Van Aldin.

'Very well,' said the secretary unemotionally.

Van Aldin had his overcoat on by now. Cramming his hat upon his head, he went towards the door. He paused with his hand upon the handle.

'You are a good fellow, Knighton,' he said. 'You don't worry me when I am rattled.'

Knighton smiled a little, but made no reply.

'Ruth is my only child,' said Van Aldin, 'and there is no one on this earth who knows quite what she means to me.'

A faint smile irradiated his face. He slipped his hand into his pocket.

'Care to see something, Knighton?'

He came back towards the secretary.

From his pocket he drew out a parcel carelessly wrapped in brown paper. He tossed off the wrapping and disclosed a big, shabby, red velvet case. In the centre of it were some twisted initials surmounted by a crown. He snapped the case open, and the secretary drew in his breath sharply. Against the slightly dingy white of the interior, the stones glowed like blood.

'My God! sir,' said Knighton. 'Are they – are they real?'

Van Aldin laughed a quiet little cackle of amusement.

'I don't wonder at your asking that. Amongst these rubies are the three largest in the world. Catherine of Russia wore them, Knighton. That centre one there is known as Heart of Fire. It's perfect – not a flaw in it.'

'But,' the secretary murmured, 'they must be worth a fortune.'

'Four or five hundred thousand dollars,' said Van Aldin nonchalantly, 'and that is apart from the historical interest.'

'And you carry them about – like that, loose in your pocket?'

Van Aldin laughed amusedly.

'I guess so. You see, they are my little present for Ruthie.'

The secretary smiled discreetly.

'I can understand now Mrs Kettering's anxiety over the telephone,' he murmured.

But Van Aldin shook his head. The hard look returned to his face.

'You are wrong there,' he said. 'She doesn't know about these; they are my little surprise for her.'

He shut the case, and began slowly to wrap it up again.

'It's a hard thing, Knighton,' he said, 'how little one can do for those one loves. I can buy a good portion of the earth for Ruth, if it would be any use to her, but it isn't. I can hang these things round her neck and give her a moment or two's pleasure, maybe, but—'

He shook his head.

'When a woman is not happy in her home—'

He left the sentence unfinished. The secretary nodded discreetly. He knew, none better, the reputation of the Hon. Derek Kettering. Van Aldin sighed. Slipping the parcel back in his coat pocket, he nodded to Knighton and left the room.

4

IN CURZON STREET

The Hon. Mrs Derek Kettering lived in Curzon Street. The butler who opened the door recognised Rufus Van Aldin at once and permitted himslf a discreet smile of greeting. He led the way upstairs to the big double drawing-room on the first floor.

A woman who was sitting by the window started up with a cry.

'Why, Dad, if that isn't too good for anything! I've been telephoning Major Knighton all day to try and get hold of you, but he couldn't say for sure when you were expected back.'

Ruth Kettering was twenty-eight years of age. Without being beautiful, or in the real sense of the word even pretty, she was striking good looking because of her colouring. Van Aldin had been called Carrots and Ginger in his time, and Ruth's hair was almost pure auburn. With it went dark eyes and very black lashes – the effect somewhat enhanced by art. She was tall and slender, and moved well. At a careless glance it was the face of a Raphael Madonna. Only if one looked closely did one perceive the same line of jaw and chin as in Van Aldin's face, bespeaking the same hardness and determination. It suited the man, but suited the woman less well. From her childhood upward Ruth Van Aldin had been accustomed to having her own way, and anyone who ever stood up against her soon realised that Rufus Van Aldin's daughter never gave in.

'Knighton told me you'd 'phoned him,' said Van Aldin. 'I only got back from Paris half an hour ago. What's all this about Derek?'

Ruth Kettering flushed angrily.

'It's unspeakable. It's beyond all limits,' she cried. 'He – he doesn't seem to listen to anything I say.'

There was bewilderment as well as anger in her voice.

'He'll listen to me,' said the millionaire grimly.

Ruth went on.

'I've hardly seen him for the last month. He goes about everywhere with that woman.'

'With what woman?'

'Mirelle. She dances at the Parthenon, you know.'

Van Aldin nodded.

'I was down at Leconbury last week. I – I spoke to Lord Leconbury. He was awfully sweet to me, sympathised entirely. He said he'd give Derek a good talking to.'

'Ah!' said Van Aldin.

'What do you mean by "Ah!" Dad?'

'Just what you think I mean, Ruthie. Poor old Leconbury is a wash out. Of course he sympathised with you, of course he tried to soothe you down. Having got his son and heir married to the daughter of one of the richest men in the States, he naturally doesn't want to mess the thing up. But he's got one foot in the grave already, everyone knows that, and anything he may say will cut darned little ice with Derek.'

'Can't *you* do anything, Dad?' urged Ruth, after a minute or two.

'I might,' said the millionaire. He waited a second reflectively, and then went on. 'There are several things I might do, but there's only one that will be any real good. How much pluck have you got, Ruthie?'

She stared at him. He nodded back at her.

'I mean just what I say. Have you got the grit to admit to all the world that you've made a mistake. There's only one way out of this mess, Ruthie. Cut your losses and start afresh.'

'You mean—?'

'Divorce.'

'Divorce!'

Van Aldin smiled drily.

'You say that word, Ruth, as though you'd never heard it before. And yet your friends are doing it all round you every day.'

'Oh! I know that. But—'

She stopped, biting her lip. Her father nodded comprehendingly.

'I know, Ruth. You're like me, you can't bear to let go. But I've learnt, and you've got to learn, that there are times when it's the only way. I might find ways of whistling Derek back to you, but it would all come to the same in the end. *He's no good*, Ruth; he's rotten through and through. And mind you, I blame myself for ever letting you marry him. But you were kind of set on having him, and he seemed in earnest about turning over a new leaf – and well, I'd crossed you once, honey...'

He did not look at her as he said the last words. Had he

done so, he might have seen the swift colour that came up in her face.

'You did,' she said in a hard voice.

'I was too durned soft-hearted to do it a second time. I can't tell you how I wish I had, though. You've led a poor kind of life for the last few years, Ruth.'

'It has not been very – agreeable,' agreed Mrs Kettering.

'That's why I say to you that this thing has got to *stop*!' He brought his hand down with a bang on the table. 'You may have a hankering after the fellow still. *Cut it out*. Face facts. Derek Kettering married you for your money. That's all there is to it. Get rid of him, Ruth.'

Ruth Kettering looked down at the ground for some moments, then she said, without raising her head:

'Supposing he doesn't consent?'

Van Aldin looked at her in astonishment.

'He won't have a say in the matter.'

She flushed and bit her lip.

'No – no – of course not. I only meant—'

She stopped. Her father eyed her keenly.

'What did you mean?'

'I meant—' She paused, choosing her words carefully. 'He mayn't take it lying down.'

The millionaire's chin shot out grimly.

'You mean he'll fight the case? Let him! But, as a matter of fact, you're wrong. He won't fight. Any solicitor he consults will tell him he hasn't got a leg to stand upon.'

'You don't think' – she hesitated – I mean – out of sheer spite against me – he might, well, try to make it awkward?'

Her father looked at her in some astonishment.

'Fight the case, you mean?'

He shook his head.

'Very unlikely. You see, he would have to have something to go upon.'

Mrs Kettering did not answer. Van Aldin looked at her sharply.

'Come, Ruth, out with it. There's something troubling you – what is it?'

'Nothing, nothing at all.'

But her voice was unconvincing.

'You are dreading the publicity, eh? Is that it? You leave it to me, I'll put the whole thing through so smoothly that there will be no fuss at all.'

'Very well, Dad, if you really think it's the best thing to be done.'

'Got a fancy for the fellow still, Ruth? Is that it?'

'No.'

The word came with no uncertain emphasis. Van Aldin seemed satisfied. He patted his daughter on the shoulder.

'It will be all right, little girl. Don't you worry any. Now let's forget about all this. I have brought you a present from Paris.'

'For me? Something very nice?'

'I hope you'll think so,' said Van Aldin, smiling.

He took the parcel from his coat pocket and handed it to her. She unwrapped it eagerly, and snapped open the case. A long-drawn 'Oh!' came from her lips. Ruth Kettering loved jewels – always had done so.'

'Dad, how – how wonderful!'

'Rather in a class by themselves, aren't they?' said the millionaire with satisfaction. 'You like them, eh.'

'Like them? Dad, they're unique. How did you get hold of them?'

Van Aldin smiled.

'Ah! that's my secret. They had to be bought privately, of course. They are rather well known. See that big stone in the middle? You have heard of it, maybe; that's the historic "Heart of Fire."'

'Heart of Fire!' repeated Mrs Kettering.

She had taken the stones from the case and was holding them against her breast. The millionaire watched her. He was thinking of the series of women who had worn the jewels. The heartaches, the despairs, the jealousies. 'Heart of Fire,' like all famous stones, had left behind it a trail of tragedy and violence. Held in Ruth Kettering's assured hand, it seemed to lose its potency of evil. With her cool, equable poise, this woman of the western world seemed a negation to tragedy or heart-burnings. Ruth returned the stones to their case; then, jumping up, she flung her arms round her father's neck.

'Thank you, thank you, thank you, Dad. They are wonderful! You do give me the most marvellous presents always.'

'That's all right,' said Van Aldin, patting her shoulder. 'You are all I have, you know, Ruthie.'

'You will stay to dinner, won't you, Father?'

'I don't think so. You were going out, weren't you?'

'Yes, but I can easily put that off. Nothing very exciting.'

'No,' said Van Aldin. 'Keep your engagement. I have got a

good deal to attend to. See you tomorrow, my dear. Perhaps if I 'phone you, we can meet at Galbraiths'?'

Messrs Galbraith, Galbraith, Cuthbertson & Galbraith were Van Aldin's London solicitors.

'Very well, Dad.' She hesitated. 'I suppose it – this – won't keep me from going to the Riviera?'

'When are you off?'

'On the fourteenth.'

'Oh, that will be all right. These things take a long time to mature. By the way, Ruth, I shouldn't take those rubies abroad if I were you. Leave them at the bank.'

Mrs Kettering nodded.

'We don't want to have you robbed and murdered for the sake of "Heart of Fire," ' said the millionaire jocosely.

'And yet you carried it about in your pocket loose,' retorted his daughter, smiling.

'Yes—'

Something, some hesitation, caught her attention.

'What is it, Dad?'

'Nothing.' He smiled. 'Thinking of a little adventure of mine in Paris.'

'An adventure?'

'Yes, the night I bought these things.'

He made a gesture towards the jewel case.

'Oh, do tell me.'

'Nothing to tell, Ruthie. Some apache fellows got a bit fresh and I shot at them and they got off. That's all.'

She looked at him with some pride.

'You're a tough proposition, Dad.'

'You bet I am, Ruthie.'

He kissed her affectionately and departed. On arriving back at the Savoy, he gave a curt order to Knighton.

'Get hold of a man called Goby; you'll find his address in my private book. He's to be here tomorrow morning at half-past nine.'

'Yes, sir.'

'I also want to see Mr Kettering. Run him to earth for me if you can. Try his Club – at any rate, get hold of him some-how, and arrange for me to see him here tomorrow morning. Better make it latish, about twelve. His sort aren't early risers.'

The secretary nodded in comprehension of these instructions. Van Aldin gave himself into the hands of his valet. His bath was prepared, and as he lay luxuriating in the hot water, his mind went back over the conversation with his daughter. On the whole he was well satisfied. His keen mind had long since accepted the fact that divorce was the only possible way out. Ruth had agreed to the proposed solution with more readiness than he had hoped for. Yet, in spite of her acquiescence, he was left with a vague sense of uneasiness. Something about her manner, he felt, had not been quite natural. He frowned to himself.

'Maybe I'm fanciful,' he muttered, 'and yet – I bet there's something she has not told me.'

— 5 —

A USEFUL GENTLEMAN

Rufus Van Aldin had just finished the sparse breakfast of coffee and dry toast, which was all he ever allowed himself, when Knighton entered the room.

'Mr Goby is below, sir, waiting to see you.'

The millionaire glanced at the clock. It was just half-past nine.

'All right,' he said curtly. 'He can come up.'

A minute or two later, Mr Goby entered the room. He was a small, elderly man, shabbily dressed, with eyes that looked carefully all round the room, and never at the person he was addressing.

'Good morning, Goby,' said the millionaire. 'Take a chair.'

'Thank you, Mr Van Aldin.'

Mr Goby sat down with his hands on his knees, and gazed earnestly at the radiator.

'I have got a job for you.'

'Yes, Mr Van Aldin?'

'My daughter is married to the Hon. Derek Kettering, as you may perhaps know.'

Mr Goby transferred his gaze from the radiator to the left-hand drawer of the desk, and permitted a deprecating smile to pass over his face. Mr Goby knew a great many things, but he always hated to admit the fact.

'By my advice, she is about to file a petition for divorce. That, of course, is a solicitor's business. But, for private reasons, I want the fullest and most complete information.'

Mr Goby looked at the cornice and murmured:

'About Mr Kettering?'

'About Mr Kettering.'

'Very good, sir.'

Mr Goby rose to his feet.

'When will you have it ready for me?'

'Are you in a hurry, sir?'

'I'm always in a hurry,' said the millionaire.

Mr Goby smiled understandingly at the fender.

'Shall we say two o'clock this afternoon, sir?' he asked.

'Excellent,' approved the other. 'Good morning, Goby.'

'Good morning, Mr Van Aldin.'

'That's a very useful man,' said the millionaire as Goby went out and his secretary came in. 'In his own line he's a specialist.'

'What is his line?'

'Information. Give him twenty-four hours and he would lay the private life of the Archbishop of Canterbury bare for you.'

'A useful sort of chap,' said Knighton, with a smile.

'He has been useful to me once or twice,' said Van Aldin. 'Now then, Knighton, I'm ready for work.'

The next few hours saw a vast quantity of business rapidly transacted. It was half-past twelve when the telephone bell rang, and Mr Van Aldin was informed that Mr Kettering had called. Knighton looked at Van Aldin, and interpreted his brief nod.

'Ask Mr Kettering to come up, please.'

The secretary gathered up his papers and departed. He and the visitor passed each other in the doorway, and Derek Kettering stood aside to let the other go out. Then he came in, shutting the door behind him.

'Good morning, sir. You are very anxious to see me, I hear.'

The lazy voice with its slightly ironic inflection roused memories in Van Aldin. There was charm in it – there had always been charm in it. He looked piercingly at his son-in-law. Derek Kettering was thirty-four, lean of build, with a dark, narrow face, which had even now something indescribably boyish in it.

'Come in,' said Van Aldin curtly. 'Sit down.'

Kettering flung himself lightly into an arm-chair. He looked at his father-in-law with a kind of tolerant amusement.

'Not seen you for a long time, sir,' he remarked pleasantly. 'About two years, I should say. Seen Ruth yet?'

'I saw her last night,' said Van Aldin.

'Looking very fit, isn't she?' said the other lightly.

'I didn't know you had had much opportunity of judging,' said Van Aldin drily.

Derek Kettering raised his eyebrows.

'Oh, we sometimes meet at the same night club, you know,' he said airily.

'I am not going to beat about the bush,' Van Aldin said curtly. 'I have advised Ruth to file a petition for divorce.'

Derek Kettering seemed unmoved.

'How drastic!' he murmured. 'Do you mind if I smoke, sir?'

He lit a cigarette, and puffed out a cloud of smoke as he added nonchalantly:

'And what did Ruth say?'

'Ruth proposes to take my advice,' said her father.

'Does she really?'

'Is that all you have got to say?' demanded Van Aldin sharply.

Kettering flicked his ash into the grate.

'I think, you know,' he said, with a detached air, 'that she's making a great mistake.'

'From your point of view she doubtless is,' said Van Aldin grimly.

'Oh, come now,' said the other; 'don't let's be personal. I really wasn't thinking of myself at the moment. I was thinking of Ruth. You know my poor old Governor really can't last much longer; all the doctors say so. Ruth had better give it a couple more years, then I shall be Lord Leconbury, and she can be châtelaine of Leconbury, which is what she married me for.'

'I won't have any of your darned impudence,' roared Van Aldin.

Derek Kettering smiled at him unmoved.

'I agree with you. It's an obsolete idea,' he said. 'There's nothing in a title nowadays. Still, Leconbury is a very fine old place, and, after all, we are one of the oldest families in England. It will be very annoying for Ruth if she divorces me to find me marrying again, and some other woman queening it at Leconbury instead of her.'

'I am serious, young man,' said Van Aldin.

'Oh, so am I,' said Kettering. 'I am in very low water financially; it will put me in a nasty hole if Ruth divorces me, and, after all, if she has stood it for ten years, why not stand it a little longer? I give you my word of honour that the old man can't possibly last out another eighteen months, and, as I said before, it's a pity Ruth shouldn't get what she married me for.'

'You suggest that my daughter married you for your title and position?'

Derek Kettering laughed a laugh that was not all amusement.

'You don't think it was a question of a love match?' he asked.

'I know,' said Van Aldin slowly, 'that you spoke very differently in Paris ten years ago.'

'Did I? Perhaps I did. Ruth was very beautiful, you know – rather like an angel or a saint, or something that had stepped down from a niche in a church. I had fine ideas, I remember, of turning over a new leaf, of settling down and living up to the highest traditions of English home-life with a beautiful wife who loved me.'

He laughed again, rather more discordantly.

'But you don't believe that, I suppose?' he said.

'I have no doubt at all that you married Ruth for her money,' said Van Aldin unemotionally.

'And that she married me for love?' asked the other ironically.

'Certainly,' said Van Aldin.

Derek Kettering stared at him for a minute or two, then he nodded reflectively.

'I see you believe that,' he said. 'So did I at the time. I can assure you, my dear father-in-law, I was very soon undeceived.'

'I don't know what you are getting at,' said Van Aldin, 'and I don't care. You have treated Ruth darned badly.'

'Oh, I have,' agreed Kettering lightly, 'but she's tough, you know. She's your daughter. Underneath the pink-and-white softness of her she's as hard as granite. You have always been known as a hard man, so I have been told, but Ruth is harder than you are. You, at any rate, love one person better than yourself. Ruth never has and never will.'

'That is enough,' said Van Aldin. 'I asked you here so that I could tell you fair and square what I meant to do. My girl has got to have some happiness, and remember this, I am behind her.'

Derek Kettering got up and stood by the mantelpiece. He tossed away his cigarette. When he spoke, his voice was very quiet.

'What exactly do you mean by that, I wonder?' he said.

'I mean,' said Van Aldin, 'that you had better not try to defend the case.'

'Oh,' said Kettering, 'is that a threat?'

'You can take it any way you please,' said Van Aldin.

Kettering drew a chair up to the table. He sat down fronting the millionaire.

'And supposing,' he said softly, 'that, just for argument's sake, I did defend the case?'

Van Aldin shrugged his shoulders.

'You have not got a leg to stand upon, you young fool. Ask your solicitors, they will soon tell you. Your conduct has been notorious, the talk of London.'

'Ruth has been kicking up a row about Mirelle, I suppose. Very foolish of her. I don't interfere with her friends.'

'What do you mean?' said Van Aldin sharply.

Derek Kettering laughed.

'I see you don't know everything, sir,' he said. 'You are, perhaps naturally, prejudiced.'

He took up his hat and stick and moved towards the door.

'Giving advice is not much in my line.' He delivered his final thrust. 'But, in this case, I should advise most strongly perfect frankness between father and daughter.'

He passed quickly out of the room and shut the door behind him just as the millionaire sprang up.

'Now, what the hell did he mean by that?' said Van Aldin as he sank back into his chair again.

All his uneasiness returned in full force. There was something here that he had not yet got to the bottom of. The telephone was by his elbow; he seized it, and asked for the number of his daughter's house.

'Hallo! Hallo! Is that Mayfair 81907? Mrs Kettering in? Oh, she's out, is she? Yes, out to lunch. What time will she be in? You don't know? Oh, very good; no, there's no message.'

He slammed the receiver down again angrily. At two o'clock he was pacing the floor of his room waiting expectantly for Goby. The latter was ushered in at ten minutes past two.

'Well?' barked the millionaire sharply.

But little Mr Goby was not to be hurried. He sat down at the table, produced a very shabby pocket-book, and proceeded to read from it in a monotonous voice. The millionaire listened attentively, with an increasing satisfaction. Goby came to a full stop, and looked attentively at the wastepaper-basket.

'Um!' said Van Aldin. 'That seems pretty definite. The case will go through like winking. The hotel evidence is all right, I suppose?'

'Cast iron,' said Goby, and looked malevolently at a gilt arm-chair.

'And financially he's in very low water. He's trying to raise a loan now, you say? Has already raised practically all he can upon his expectations from his father. Once the news of the divorce gets about, he won't be able to raise another cent, and not only that, his obligations can be bought up and pressure can be put upon him from that quarter. We have got him, Goby; we have got him in a cleft stick.'

He hit the table a bang with his fist. His face was grim and triumphant.

'The information,' said Mr Goby in a thin voice, 'seems satisfactory.'

'I have to go round to Curzon Street now,' said the millionaire. 'I am much obliged to you, Goby. You are the goods all right.'

A pale smile of gratification showed itself on the little man's face.

'Thank you, Mr Van Aldin,' he said; 'I try to do my best.'

Van Aldin did not go direct to Curzon Street. He went first to the City, where he had two interviews which added to his satisfaction. From there he took the tube to Down Street. As he was walking along Curzon Street, a figure came out of No. 160, and turned up the street towards him, so that they passed each other on the pavement. For a moment, the millionaire had fancied it might be Derek Kettering himself; the height and build were not unlike. But as they came face to face, he saw that the man was a stranger to him. At least – no, not a stranger; his face awoke some call of recognition in the millionaire's mind, and it was associated definitely with something unpleasant. He cudgelled his brains in vain, but the thing eluded him. He went on, shaking his head irritably. He hated to be baffled.

Ruth Kettering was clearly expecting him. She ran to him and kissed him when he entered.

'Well, Dad, how are things going?'

'Very well,' said Van Aldin; 'but I have got a word or two to say to you, Ruth.'

Almost insensibly he felt the change in her; something shrewd and watchful replaced the impulsiveness of her greeting. She sat down in a big arm-chair.

'Well, Dad?' she asked. 'What is it?'

'I saw your husband this morning,' said Van Aldin.

'You saw Derek?'

'I did. He said a lot of things, most of which were darned cheek. Just as he was leaving, he said something that I didn't understand. He advised me to be sure that there was perfect frankness between father and daughter. What did he mean by that, Ruthie?'

Mrs Kettering moved a little in her chair.

'I – I don't know, Dad. How should I?'

'Of course you know,' said Van Aldin. 'He said something else, about his having his friends and not interfering with yours. What did he mean by that?'

'I don't know,' said Ruth Kettering again.

Van Aldin sat down. His mouth set itself in a grim line.

'See here, Ruth. I am not going into this with my eyes closed. I am not at all sure that that husband of yours doesn't mean to make trouble. Now, he can't do it, I am sure of that. I have got the means to silence him, to shut his mouth for good and all, but I have got to know if there's any need to use those means. What did he mean by your having your own friends?'

Mrs Kettering shrugged her shoulders.

'I have got lots of friends,' she said uncertainly. 'I don't know what he meant, I am sure.'

'You do,' said Van Aldin.

He was speaking now as he might have spoken to a business adversary.

'I will put it plainer. Who is the man?'

'What man?'

'*The man.* That's what Derek was driving at. Some special man who is a friend of yours. You needn't worry, honey, I know there is nothing in it, but we have got to look at everything as it might appear to the Court. They can twist these things about a good deal, you know. I want to know who the man is, and just how friendly you have been with him.'

Ruth didn't answer. Her hands were kneading themselves together in intense nervous absorption.

'Come, honey,' said Van Aldin in a softer voice. 'Don't be afraid of your old Dad. I was not too harsh, was I, even that time in Paris? – My gosh!'

He stopped, thunderstruck.

'That's who it was,' he murmured to himself. 'I thought I knew his face.'

'What are you talking about, Dad? I don't understand.'

The millionaire strode across to her and took her firmly by the wrist.

'See here, Ruth, have you been seeing that fellow again?'

'What fellow?'

'The one we had all that fuss about years ago. You know who I mean well enough.'

'You mean' – she hesitated – 'you mean the Comte de la Roche?'

'Comte de la Roche!' snorted Van Aldin. 'I told you at the time that the man was no better than a swindler. You had entangled yourself with him then very deeply, but I got you out of his clutches.'

'Yes, you did,' said Ruth bitterly. 'And I married Derek Kettering.'

'You wanted to,' said the millionaire sharply.

She shrugged her shoulders.

'And now,' said Van Aldin slowly, 'you have been seeing him again – after all I told you. He has been in the house to-day. I met him outside, and couldn't place him for the moment.'

Ruth Kettering had recovered her composure.

'I want to tell you one thing, Dad; you are wrong about Armand – the Comte de la Roche, I mean. Oh, I know there were several regrettable incidents in his youth – he has told me about them; but – well, he has cared for me always. It broke his heart when you parted us in Paris, and now—'

She was interrupted by the snort of indignation her father gave.

'So you fell for that stuff, did you? You, a daughter of mine! My God!'

He threw up his hands.

'That women can be such darned fools!'

6

MIRELLE

Derek Kettering emerged from Van Aldin's suite so precipitantly that he collided with a lady passing across the corridor. He apologised, and she accepted his apologies with a smiling reassurance and passed on, leaving with him a pleasant impression of a soothing personality and rather fine grey eyes.

For all his nonchalance, his interview with his father-in-law had shaken him more than he cared to show. He had a solitary lunch, and after it, frowning to himself a little, he went round to the sumptuous flat that housed the lady known as Mirelle. A trim Frenchwoman received him with smiles.

'But enter then, Monsieur. Madame reposes herself.'

He was ushered into the long room with its Eastern setting which he knew so well. Mirelle was lying on the divan, supported by an incredible number of cushions, all in varying shades of amber, to harmonise with the yellow ochre of her complexion. The dancer was a beautifully made woman, and if her face, beneath its mask of yellow, was in truth somewhat haggard, it had a bizarre charm of its own, and her orange lips smiled invitingly at Derek Kettering.

He kissed her, and flung himself into a chair.

'What have you been doing with yourself? Just got up, I suppose?'

The orange mouth widened into a long smile.

'No,' said the dancer. 'I have been at work.'

She flung out a long, pale hand towards the piano, which was littered with untidy music scores.

'Ambrose has been here. He has been playing me the new Opera.'

Kettering nodded without paying much attention. He was profoundly uninterested in Claud Ambrose and the latter's operatic setting of Ibsen's *Peer Gynt*. So was Mirelle, for that matter, regarding it merely as a unique opportunity for her own presentation as Anitra.

'It is a marvellous dance,' she murmured. 'I shall put all the passion of the desert into it. I shall dance hung over with jewels – ah! and, by the way, *mon ami*, there is a pearl that I saw yesterday in Bond Street – a black pearl.'

She paused, looking at him invitingly.

'My dear girl,' said Kettering, 'it's no use talking of black pearls to me. At the present minute, as far as I am concerned, the fat is in the fire.'

She was quick to respond to his tone. She sat up, her big black eyes widening.

'What is that you say, Derek? What has happened?'

'My esteemed father-in-law,' said Kettering, 'is preparing to go off the deep end.'

'Eh?'

'In other words, he wants Ruth to divorce me.'

'How stupid!' said Mirelle. 'Why should she want to divorce you?'

Derek Kettering grinned.

'Mainly because of you, *chérie*!' he said.

Mirelle shrugged her shoulders.

'That is foolish,' she observed in a matter-of-fact voice.

'Very foolish,' agreed Derek.

'What are you going to do about it?' demanded Mirelle.

'My dear girl, what can I do? On the one side, the man with unlimited money; on the other side, the man with unlimited debts. There is no question as to who will come out on top.'

'They are extraordinary, these Americans,' commented Mirelle. 'It is not as though your wife were fond of you.'

'Well,' said Derek, 'what are we going to do about it?'

She looked at him inquiringly. He came over and took both her hands in his.

'Are you going to stick to me?'

'What do you mean? After—?'

'Yes,' said Kettering. 'After, when the creditors come down like wolves on the fold. I am damned fond of you, Mirelle; are you going to let me down?'

She pulled her hands away from him.

'You know I adore you, Dereek.'

He caught the note of evasion in her voice.

'So that's that, is it? The rats will leave the sinking ship.'

'Ah, Dereek!'

'Out with it,' he said violently. 'You will fling me over; is that it?'

She shrugged her shoulders.

'I am very fond of you, *mon ami* – indeed I am fond of you. You are very charming – *un beau garçon*, but *ce n'est pas pratique*.'

'You are a rich man's luxury, eh? Is that it?'

'If you like to put it that way.'

She leaned back on the cushions, her head flung back.

'All the same, I am fond of you, Dereek.'

He went over to the window and stood there some time looking out, with his back to her. Presently the dancer raised herself on her elbow and stared at him curiously.

'What are you thinking of, *mon ami*?'

He grinned at her over his shoulder, a curious grin, that made her vaguely uneasy.

'As it happened, I was thinking of a woman, my dear.'

'A woman, eh?'

Mirelle pounced on something that she could understand.

'You are thinking of some other woman, is that it?'

'Oh, you needn't worry; it is purely a fancy portrait. "Portrait of a lady with grey eyes." '

Mirelle said sharply, 'When did you meet her?'

Derek Kettering laughed, and his laughter had a mocking, ironical sound.

'I ran into the lady in the corridor of the Savoy Hotel.'

'Well! What did she say?'

'As far as I can remember, I said "I beg your pardon," and she said, "It doesn't matter," or words to that effect.'

'And then?' persisted the dancer.

Kettering shrugged his shoulders.

'And then – nothing. That was the end of the incident.'

'I don't understand a word of what you are talking about,' declared the dancer.

'Portrait of a lady with grey eyes,' murmured Derek reflectively. 'Just as well I am never likely to meet her again.'

'Why?'

'She might bring me bad luck. Women do.'

Mirelle slipped quietly from her couch, and came across to him, laying one long, snake-like arm round his neck.

'You are foolish, Dereek,' she murmured. 'You are very foolish. You are *beau garçon*, and I adore you, but I am not made to be poor – no, decidedly I am not made to be poor. Now listen to me; everything is very simple. You must make it up with your wife.'

'I am afraid that's not going to be actually in the sphere of practical politics,' said Derek drily.

'How do you say? I do not understand.'

'Van Aldin, my dear, is not taking any. He is the kind of man who makes up his mind and sticks to it.'

'I have heard of him,' nodded the dancer. 'He is very rich, is he not? Almost the richest man in America. A few days ago, in Paris, he bought the most wonderful ruby in the world— "Heart of Fire" it is called.'

Kettering did not answer. The dancer went on musingly:

'It is a wonderful stone – a stone that should belong to a woman like me. I love jewels, Dereek; they say something to me. Ah! to wear a ruby like "Heart of Fire." '

She gave a little sigh, and then became practical once more.

'You don't understand these things, Dereek; you are only a man. Van Aldin will give these rubies to his daughter, I suppose. Is she his only child?'

'Yes.'

'Then when he dies, she will inherit all his money. She will be a rich woman.'

'She is a rich woman already,' said Kettering drily. 'He settled a couple of millions on her at her marriage.'

'A couple of million! But that is immense. And if she died suddenly, eh? That would all come to you?'

'As things stand at present,' said Kettering slowly, 'it would. As far as I know she has not made a will.'

'*Mon Dieu!*' said the dancer. 'If she were to die, what a solution that would be.'

There was a moment's pause, and then Derek Kettering laughed outright.

'I like your simple, practical mind, Mirelle, but I am afraid what you desire won't come to pass. My wife is an extremely healthy person.'

'*Eh bien!*' said Mirelle; 'there are accidents.'

He looked at her sharply but did not answer.

She went on.

'But you are right, *mon ami*, we must not dwell on possibilities. See now, my little Dereek, there must be no more talk of this divorce. Your wife must give up the idea.'

'And if she won't?'

The dancer's eyes narrowed to slits.

'I think she will, my friend. She is one of those who would not like the publicity. There are one or two pretty stories that she would not like her friends to read in the newspapers.'

'What do you mean?' asked Kettering sharply.

Mirelle laughed, her head thrown back.

'*Parbleu!* I mean the gentleman who calls himself the Comte de la Roche. I know all about him. I am Parisienne, you remember. He was her lover before she married you, was he not?'

Kettering took her sharply by the shoulders.

'That is a damned lie,' he said, 'and please remember that, after all, you are speaking of my wife.'

Mirelle was a little sobered.

'You are extraordinary, you English,' 'she complained. 'All the same, I dare say that you may be right. The Americans are so cold, are they not? But you will permit me to say, *mon ami*, that she was *in love with him* before she married you, and her father stepped in and sent the Comte about his business. And the little Mademoiselle, she wept many tears! But she obeyed. Still, you must know as well as I do, Dereek, that it is a very different story now. She sees him nearly every day, and on the fourteenth she goes to Paris to meet him.'

'How do you know all this?' demanded Kettering.

'Me? I have friends in Paris, my dear Dereek, who know the Comte intimately. It is all arranged. She is going to the Riviera, so she says, but in reality the Comte meets her in Paris and – who knows! Yes, yes, you can take my word for it, it is all arranged.'

Derek Kettering stood motionless.

'You see,' purred the dancer, 'if you are clever, you have her in the hollow of your hand. You can make things very awkward for her.'

'Oh, for God's sake be quiet,' cried Kettering. 'Shut your cursed mouth!'

Mirelle flung herself down again on the divan with a laugh. Kettering caught up his hat and coat and left the flat, banging the door violently. And still the dancer sat on the divan and laughed softly to herself. She was not displeased with her work.

—— 7 ——

LETTERS

Mrs Samuel Harfield presents her compliments to Miss Katherine Grey and wishes to point out that under the circumstances Miss Grey may not be aware—'

Mrs Harfield, having written so far fluently, came to a dead stop, held up by what has proved an insuperable difficulty to many other people – namely, the difficulty of expressing oneself fluently in the third person.

After a minute or two of hesitation, Mrs Harfield tore up the sheet of notepaper and started afresh.

'DEAR MISS GREY, – Whilst fully appreciating the adequate way you discharged your duties to my Cousin Emma (whose recent death has indeed been a severe blow to us all), I cannot but feel—'

Again Mrs Harfield came to a stop. Once more the letter was consigned to the wastepaper-basket. It was not until four false starts had been made that Mrs Harfield at last produced an epistle that satisfied her. It was duly sealed and stamped and addressed to Miss Katherine Grey, Little Crampton, St Mary Mead, Kent, and it lay beside the lady's plate on the following morning at breakfast-time in company with a more important-looking communication in a long blue envelope.

Katherine Grey opened Mrs Harfield's letter first. The finished production ran as follows:

'DEAR MISS GREY, – My husband and I wish to express our thanks to you for your services to my poor cousin, Emma. Her death has been a great blow to us, though we were, of course, aware that her mind has been failing for some time past. I understand that her latter testamentary dispositions have been of a most peculiar character, and they would not hold good, of course, in any court of law. I have no doubt that, with your usual good sense, you have already realised this fact. If these matters can be arranged privately it is always so much better, my husband says. We shall be pleased to recommend you most highly for a similar post, and hope that you will also accept a small present. Believe me, dear Miss Grey, yours cordially,

MARY ANNE HARFIELD.'

Katherine Grey read the letter through, smiled a little, and read it a second time. Her face as she laid the letter down after the second reading was distinctly amused. Then she took up the second letter. After one brief perusal she laid it down and stared very straight in front of her. This time she did not smile. Indeed, it would have been hard for anyone watching her to guess what emotions lay behind that quiet, reflective gaze.

Katherine Grey was thirty-three. She came of good family, but her father had lost all his money, and Katherine had had to work for her living from an early age. She had been just twenty-three when she had come to old Mrs Harfield as companion.

It was generally recognised that old Mrs Harfield was 'difficult.' Companions came and went with startling rapidity. They arrived full of hope and they usually left in tears. But from the moment Katherine Grey set foot in Little Crampton, ten years ago, perfect peace had reigned. No one knows how these things come about. Snake-charmers, they say, are born, not made. Katherine Grey was born with the power of managing old ladies, dogs, and small boys, and she did it without any apparent sense of strain.

At twenty-three she had been a quiet girl with beautiful eyes. At thirty-three she was a quiet woman, with those same grey eyes, shining steadily out on the world with a kind of happy serenity that nothing could shake. Moreover, she had been born with, and still possessed, a sense of humour.

As she sat at the breakfast-table, staring in front of her, there was a ring at the bell, accompanied by a very energetic rat-a-tat-tat at the knocker. In another minute the little maid-servant opened the door and announced rather breathlessly:

'Dr Harrison.'

The big, middle-aged doctor came bustling in with the energy and breeziness that had been fore-shadowed by his on-slaught on the knocker.

'Good morning, Miss Grey.'

'Good morning, Dr Harrison.'

'I dropped in early,' began the doctor, 'in case you should have heard from one of those Harfield cousins. Mrs Samuel, she calls herself – a perfectly poisonous person.'

Without a word, Katherine picked up Mrs Harfield's letter from the table and gave it to him. With a good deal of amuse-ment she watched his perusal of it, the drawing together of the bushy eyebrows, the snorts and grunts of violent disapproval. He dashed it down again on the table.

'Perfectly monstrous,' he fumed. 'Don't you let it worry you, my dear. They're talking through their hats. Mrs Harfield's intellect was as good as yours or mine, and you won't get any-one to say the contrary. They wouldn't have a leg to stand upon, and they know it. All that talk of taking it into court is pure bluff. Hence this attempt to get round you in a hole-and-corner way. And look here, my dear, don't let them get round you with soft soap either. Don't get fancying it's your duty to hand over the cash, or any tomfoolery of conscientious scruples.'

'I'm afraid it hasn't occurred to me to have scruples,' said Katherine. 'All these people are distant relatives of Mrs Har-field's husband, and they never came near her or took any notice of her in her lifetime.'

'You're a sensible woman,' said the doctor. 'I know, none better, that you've had a hard life of it for the last ten years. You're fully entitled to enjoy the old lady's savings, such as they were.'

Katherine smiled thoughtfully.

'Such as they were,' she repeated. 'You've no idea of the amount, doctor?'

'Well – enough to bring in five hundred a year or so, I suppose.'

Katherine nodded.

'That's what I thought,' she said. 'Now read this.'

She handed him the letter she had taken from the long blue envelope. The doctor read and uttered an exclamation of utter astonishment.

'Impossible,' he muttered. 'Impossible.'

'She was one of the original shareholders in Mortaulds. Forty years ago she must have had an income of eight or ten thousand a year. She has never, I am sure, spent more than four hundred a year. She was always terribly careful about money. I always believed that she was obliged to be careful about every penny.'

'And all the time the income has accumulated at compound interest. My dear, you're going to be a very rich woman.'

Katherine Grey nodded.

'Yes,' she said, 'I am.'

She spoke in a detached, impersonal tone, as though she were looking at the situation from outside.

'Well,' said the doctor, preparing to depart, 'you have all my congratulations.' He flicked Mrs Samuel Harfield's letter with his thumb. 'Don't worry about that woman and her odious letter.'

'It really isn't an odious letter,' said Miss Grey tolerantly. 'Under the circumstancess, I think it's really quite a natural thing to do.'

'I have the gravest suspicions of you sometimes,' said the doctor.

'Why?'

'The things that you find perfectly natural.'

Katherine Grey laughed.

Doctor Harrison retailed the great news to his wife at lunch-time. She was very excited about it.

'Fancy old Mrs Harfield – with all that money. I'm glad she left it to Katherine Grey. That girl's a saint.'

The doctor made a wry face.

'Saints I always imagined must have been difficult people. Katherine Grey is too human for a saint.'

'She's a saint with a sense of humour,' said the doctor's wife, twinkling. 'And, though I don't suppose you've ever noticed the fact, she's extremely good looking.'

'Katherine Grey?' The doctor was honestly surprised. 'She's got very nice eyes, I know.'

'Oh, you men!' cried his wife. 'Blind as bats. Katherine's got all the makings of a beauty in her. All she wants is clothes!'

'Clothes? What's wrong with her clothes? She always looks very nice.'

Mrs Harrison gave an exasperated sign, and the doctor rose preparatory to starting on his rounds.

'You might look in on her, Polly,' he suggested.

'I'm going to,' said Mrs Harrison promptly.

Shes made her call about three o'clock.

'My dear, I'm so glad,' she said warmly, as she squeezed Katherine's hand. 'And everyone in the village will be glad too.'

'It's very nice of you to come and tell me,' said Katherine. 'I hoped you would come in because I wanted to ask about Johnnie.'

'Oh! Johnnie. Well—'

Johnnie was Mrs Harrison's youngest son. In another minute she was off, retailing a long history in which Johnnie's adenoids and tonsils bulked largely. Katherine listened sympathetically. Habits die hard. Listening had been her portion for ten years now. 'My dear, I wonder if I ever told you about the naval ball at Portsmouth? When Lord Charles admired my gown?' And composedly, kindly, Katherine would reply: 'I rather think you have, Mrs Harfield, but I've forgotten about it. Won't you tell it me again?' And then the old lady would start off full swing, with numerous corrections, and stops, and remembered details. And half of Katherine's mind would be listening, saying the right things mechanically when the old lady paused . . .

Now, with the same curious feeling of duality to which she was accustomed, she listened to Mrs Harrison.

At the end of half an hour, the latter recalled herself suddenly.

'I've been talking about myself all this time,' she exclaimed. 'And I came her to talk about you and your plans.'

'I don't know that I've got any yet.'

'My dear – you're not going to stay on *here*.'

Katherine smiled at the horror in the other's tone.

'No; I think I want to travel. I've never seen much of the world, you know.'

'I should think not. It must have been an awful life for you cooped up here all these years.'

'I don't know,' said Katherine. 'It gave me a lot of freedom.'

She caught the other's gasp, and reddened a little.

'It must sound foolish – saying that. Of course, I hadn't much freedom in the downright physical sense—'

'I should think not,' breathed Mrs Harrison, remembering

that Katherine had seldom had that useful thing, a 'day off.'

'But in a way, being tied physically gives you lots of scope mentally. You're always free to think. I've had a lovely feeling always of mental freedom.'

Mrs Harrison shook her head.

'I can't understand that.'

'Oh! you would if you'd been in my place. But, all the same, I feel I want a change. I want – well, I want things to happen. Oh! not to me – I don't mean that. But to be in the midst of things – exciting things – even if I'm only the looker-on. You know, things don't happen in St Mary Mead.'

'They don't indeed,' said Mrs Harrison, with fervour.

'I shall go to London first,' said Katherine. 'I have to see the solicitors, anyway. After that, I shall go abroad, I think.'

'Very nice.'

'But, of course, first of all—'

'Yes?'

'I must get some clothes.'

'Exactly what I said to Arthur this morning,' cried the doctor's wife. 'You know, Katherine, you could look possibly positively beautiful if you tried.'

Miss Grey laughed unaffectedly.

'Oh! I don't think you could ever make a beauty out of me,' she said sincerely. 'But I shall enjoy having some really good clothes. I'm afraid I'm talking about myself an awful lot.'

Mrs Harrison looked at her shrewdly.

'It must be quite a novel experience for you,' she said drily.

Katherine went to say good-bye to old Miss Viner before leaving the village. Miss Viner was two years older than Mrs Harfield, and her mind was mainly taken up with her own success in out-living her dead friend.

'You wouldn't have thought I'd have outlasted Jane Harfield, would you?' she demanded triumphantly of Katherine. 'We were at school together, she and I. And here we are, she taken, and I left. Who would have thought it?'

'You've always eaten brown bread for supper, haven't you?' murmured Katherine mechanically.

'Fancy your remembering that, my dear. Yes; if Jane Harfield had had a slice of brown bread every evening and taken a little stimulant with her meals she might be here today.'

The old lady paused, nodding her head triumphantly; then added in sudden remembrance:

'And so you've come into a lot of money, I hear? Well, well. Take care of it. And you're going up to London to have a good time? Don't think you'll get married, though, my dear, because you won't. You're not the kind to attract the men. And, besides, you're getting on. How old are you now?'

'Thirty-three,' Katherine told her.

'Well,' remarked Miss Viner doubtfully, 'that's not so very bad. You've lost your first freshness, of course.'

'I'm afraid so,' said Katherine, much entertained.

'But you're a very nice girl,' said Miss Viner kindly. 'And I'm sure there's many a man might do worse than take you for a wife instead of one of these flibbertigibbets running about nowadays showing more of their legs than the Creator ever intended them to. Good-bye, my dear, and I hope you'll enjoy yourself, but things are seldom what they seem in this life.'

Heartened by these prophecies, Katherine took her departure. Half the village came to see her off at the station, including the little maid of all work, Alice, who brought a stiff wired nosegay and cried openly.

'There ain't a many like her,' sobbed Alice when the train had finally departed. 'I'm sure when Charlie went back on me with that girl from the Dairy, nobody could have been kinder than Miss Grey was, and though particular about the brasses and the dust, she was always one to notice when you'd give a thing an extra rub. Cut myself in little pieces for her, I would, any day. A real lady, that's what I call her.'

Such was Katherine's departure from St Mary Mead.

8

LADY TAMPLIN WRITES A LETTER

'Well,' said Lady Tamplin, 'well.'

She laid down the continental *Daily Mail* and stared out across the blue waters of the Mediterranean. A branch of golden mimosa, hanging just above her head, made an effective frame for a very charming picture. A golden-haired, blue-eyed lady in a very becoming *négligée*. That the golden hair owed something to art, as did the pink-and-white complexion, was undeniable, but the blue of the eyes was Nature's gift, and at forty-four Lady Tamplin could still rank as a beauty.

Charming as she looked, Lady Tamplin was, for once, not

thinking of herself. That is to say, she was not thinking of her appearance. She was intent on graver matters.

Lady Tamplin was a well-known figure on the Riviera, and her parties at the Villa Marguerite were justly celebrated. She was a woman of considerable experience, and had had four husbands. The first had been merely an indiscretion, and so was seldom referred to by the lady. He had had the good sense to die with commendable promptitude, and his widow thereupon espoused a rich manufacturer of buttons. He too had departed for another sphere after three years of married life – it was said after a congenial evening with some boon companions. After him came Viscount Tamplin, who had placed Rosalie securely on those heights where she wished to tread. She retained her title when she married for a fourth time. This fourth venture had been undertaken for pure pleasure. Mr Charles Evans, an extremely good-looking young man of twenty-seven, with delightful manners, a keen love of sport, and an appreciation of this world's goods, had no money of his own whatsoever.

Lady Tamplin was very pleased and satisfied with life generally, but she had occasional faint preoccupations about money. The button manufacturer had left his widow a considerable fortune, but, as Lady Tamplin was wont to say, 'what with one thing and another—' (one thing being the depreciation of stocks owing to the War, and the other the extravagances of the late Lord Tamplin). She was still comfortably off. But to be merely comfortably off was hardly satisfactory to one of Rosalie Tamplin's temperament.

So, on this particular January morning, she opened her blue eyes extremely wide as she read a certain item of news and uttered that noncommital monosyllable 'Well.' The only other occupant of the balcony was her daughter, the Hon. Lenox Tamplin. A daughter such as Lenox was a sad thorn in Lady Tamplin's side, a girl with no kind of tact, who actually looked older than her age, and whose peculiar sardonic form of humour was, to say the least of it, uncomfortable.

'Darling,' said Lady Tamplin, 'just fancy.'

'What is it?'

Lady Tamplin picked up the *Daily Mail*, handed it to her daughter, and indicated with an agitated forefinger the paragraph of interest.

Lenox read it without any of the signs of agitation shown by her mother. She handed back the paper.

'What about it?' she asked. 'It is the sort of thing that is always happening. Cheese-paring old women are always dying in villages and leaving fortunes to their humble companions.'

'Yes, dear, I know,' said her mother, 'and I dare say the fortune is not anything like as large as they say it is; news-papers are so inaccurate. But even if you cut it down by half—'

'Well,' said Lenox, 'it has not been left to us.'

'Not exactly, dear,' said Lady Tamplin; 'but this girl, this Katherine Grey, is actually a cousin of mine. One of the Worcestershire Greys, the Edgeworth lot. My very own cousin! Fancy!'

'Ah-ha,' said Lenox.

'And I was wondering—' said her mother.

'What there is in it for us,' finished Lenox, with that side-ways smile that her mother always found difficult to under-stand.

'Oh, darling,' said Lady Tamplin, on a faint note of re-proach.

It was very faint, because Rosalie Tamplin was used to her daughter's outspokenness and to what she called Lenox's un-comfortable way of putting things.

'I was wondering,' said Lady Tamplin, again drawing her artistically pencilled brows together, 'whether – oh, good morning, Chubby darling: are you going to play tennis? How nice!'

Chubby, thus addressed, smiled kindly at her, remarked perfunctorily, 'How topping you look in that peach-coloured thing,' and drifted past them and down the steps.

'The dear thing,' said Lady Tamplin, looking affectionately after her husband. 'Let me see, what was I saying? Ah!' She switched her mind back to business once more. 'I was wonder-ing—'

'Oh, for God's sake get on with it. That is the third time you have said that.'

'Well, dear,' said Lady Tamplin, 'I was thinking that it would be very nice if I wrote to dear Katherine and suggested that she should pay us a little visit out here. Naturally, she is quite out of touch with Society. It would be nicer for her to be launched by one of her own people. An advantage for her and an advantage for us.'

'How much do you think you would get her to cough up?' asked Lenox.

Her mother looked at her reproachfully and murmured:

'We should have to come to some financial arrangement, of

course. What with one thing and another – the War – your poor father—'

'And Chubby now,' said Lenox. 'He is an expensive luxury if you like.'

'She was a nice girl as I remember her,' murmured Lady Tamplin, pursuing her own line of thought – 'quiet, never wanted to shove herself forward, not a beauty, and never a man-hunter.'

'She will leave Chubby alone, then?' said Lenox.

Lady Tamplin looked at her in protest. 'Chubby would never—' she began.

'No,' said Lenox, 'I don't believe he would; he knows a jolly sight too well which way his bread is buttered.'

'Darling,' said Lady Tamplin, 'you have such a coarse way of putting things.'

'Sorry,' said Lenox.

Lady Tamplin gathered up the *Daily Mail* and her *négligée,* a vanity bag, and various odd letters.

'I shall write to dear Katherine at once,' she said, 'and remind her of the dear old days at Edgeworth.'

She went into the house, a light of purpose shining in her eyes.

Unlike Mrs Samuel Harfield, correspondence flowed easily from her pen. She covered four sheets without pause or effort, and on re-reading it found no occasion to alter a word.

Katherine received it on the morning of her arrival in London. Whether she read between the lines of it or not is another matter. She put it in her handbag and started out to keep the appointment she had made with Mrs Harfield's lawyers.

The firm was an old-established one in Lincoln's Inn Fields, and after a few minutes' delay Katherine was shown into the presence of the senior partner, a kindly, elderly man with shrewd blue eyes and a fatherly manner.

They discussed Mrs Harfield's will and various legal matters for some twenty minutes, then Katherine handed the lawyer Mrs Samuel's letter.

'I had better show you this, I suppose,' she said, 'though it is really rather ridiculous.'

He read it with a slight smile.

'Rather a crude attempt, Miss Grey. I need hardly tell you, I suppose, that these people have no claim of any kind upon the estate, and if they endeavour to contest the will no court will uphold them.'

'I thought as much.'

'Human nature is not always very wise. In Mrs Samuel Harfield's place, I should have been more inclined to make an appeal to your generosity.'

'That is one of the things I want to speak to you about. I should like a certain sum to go to these people.'

'There is no obligation.'

'I know that.'

'And they will not take it in the spirit it is meant. They will probably regard it as an attempt to pay them off, though they will not refuse it on that account.'

'I can see that, and it can't be helped.'

'I should advise you, Miss Grey, to put that idea out of your mind.'

Katherine shook her head. 'You are quite right, I know, but I should like it done all the same.'

'They will grab at the money and abuse you all the more afterwards.'

'Well,' said Katherine, 'let them if they like. We all have our own ways of enjoying ourselves. They were, after all, Mrs Harfield's only relatives, and though they despised her as a poor relation and paid no attention to her when she was alive, it seems to me unfair that they should be cut off with nothing.'

She carried her point, though the lawyer was still unwilling, and she presently went out into the streets of London with a comfortable assurance that she could spend money freely and make what plans she liked for the future. Her first action was to visit the establishment of a famous dressmaker.

A slim, elderly Frenchwoman, rather like a dreaming duchess, received her, and Katherine spoke with a certain naïveté.

'I want, if I may, to put myself in your hands. I have been very poor all my life and know nothing about clothes, but now I have come into some money and want to look really well dressed.'

The Frenchwoman was charmed. She had an artist's temperament, which had been soured earlier in the morning by a visit from an Argentine meat queen, who had insisted on having those models least suited to her flamboyant type of beauty. She scrutinised Katherine with keen, clever eyes. 'Yes – yes, it will be a pleasure. Mademoiselle has a very good figure; for her the simple lines will be best. She is also très anglaise. Some people it would offend them if I said that, but

Mademoiselle no. *Une belle Anglaise,* there is no style more delightful.'

The demeanour of a dreaming duchess was suddenly put off. She screamed out directions to various mannequins. 'Clothilde, Virginie, quickly, my little ones, the little *tailleur gris clair* and the *robe de soirée "soupir d'automme."* Marcelle, my child, the little mimosa suit of crêpe de chine.'

It was a charming morning. Marcelle, Clothilde, Virginie, bored and scornful, passed slowly round, squirming and wriggling in the time-honoured fashion of mannequins. The Duchess stood by Katherine and made entries in a small notebook.

'An excellent choice, Mademoiselle. Mademoiselle has great *goût.* Yes, indeed. Mademoiselle cannot do better than those little suits if she is going to the Riviera, as I suppose, this winter.'

'Let me see that evening dress once more,' said Katherine – 'the pinky mauve one.'

Virginie appeared, circling slowly.

'That is the prettiest of all,' said Katherine, as she surveyed the exquisite draperies of mauve and grey and blue. 'What do you call it?'

'*Soupir d'automne;* yes, yes, that is truly the dress of Mademoiselle.'

What was there in these words that came back to Katherine with a faint feeling of sadness after she had left the dressmaking establishment.

'*"Soupir d'automne; that is truly the dress of Mademoiselle."*' Autumn, yes, it was autumn for her. She who had never known spring or summer, and would never know them now. Something she had lost never could be given to her again. These years of servitude in St Mary Mead – and all the while life passing by.

'I am an idiot,' said Katherine. 'I am an idiot. What do I want? Why, I was more contented a month ago than I am now.'

She drew out from her handbag the letter she had received that morning from Lady Tamplin. Katherine was no fool. She understood the *nuances* of that letter as well as anybody and the reason of Lady Tamplin's sudden show of affection towards a long-forgotten cousin was not lost upon her. It was for profit and not for pleasure that Lady Tamplin was so anxious for the company of her dear cousin. Well, why not? There would be profit on both sides.

'I will go,' said Katherine.

She was walking down Piccadilly at the moment, and turned into Cook's to clinch the matter then and there. She had to wait for a few minutes. The man with whom the clerk was engaged was also going to the Riviera. Everyone, she felt, was going. Well, for the first time in her life, she, too, would be doing what 'everybody' did.

The man in front of her turned abruptly, and she stepped into his place. She made her demand to the clerk, but at the same time half of her mind was busy with something else. That man's face – in some vague way it was familiar to her. Where had she seen him before? Suddenly she remembered. It was in the Savoy outside her room that morning. She had collided with him in the passage. Rather an odd coincidence that she should run into him twice in a day. She glanced over her shoulder, rendered uneasy by something, she knew not what. The man was standing in the doorway looking back at her. A cold shiver passed over Katherine; she had a haunting sense of tragedy, of doom impending. . . .

Then she shook the impression from her with her usual good sense and turned her whole attention to what the clerk was saying.

––––– 9 –––––

AN OFFER REFUSED

It was rarely that Derek Kettering allowed his temper to get the better of him. An easy-going insouciance was his chief characteristic, and it stood him in good stead in more than one tight corner. Even now, by the time he had left Mirelle's flat, he had cooled down. He had need of coolness. The corner he was in now was a tighter one than he had ever been in before, and unforseen factors had arisen with which, for the moment, he did not know how to deal.

He strolled along deep in thought. His brow was furrowed, and there was none of the easy, jaunty manner which sat so well upon him. Various possibilities floated through his mind. It might have been said of Derek Kettering that he was less of a fool than he looked. He saw several roads that he might take – one in particular. If he shrank from it, it was for the moment only. Desperate ills need desperate remedies. He had gauged his father-in-law correctly. A war between Derek Kettering and Rufus Van Aldin could end only one way. Derek damned money and the power of money vehemently to himself. He walked up to St James's Street, across Piccadilly, and strolled along it in the direction of Piccadilly Circus. As he passed the offices of Messrs Thomas Cook and Sons his footsteps slackened. He walked on, however, still turning the matter over in his mind. Finally, he gave a brief nod of his head, turned sharply – so sharply as to collide with a couple of pedestrians who were following in his footsteps, and went back the way he had come. This time he did not pass Cook's, but went in. The office was comparatively empty, and he got attended to at once.

'I want to go to Nice next week. Will you give me particulars?'

'What date, sir?'

'The fourteenth. What is the best train?'

'Well, of course, *the* best train is what they call "The Blue Train." You avoid the tiresome Customs business at Calais.'

Derek nodded. He knew all this, none better.

'The fourteenth,' murmured the clerk; 'that is rather soon. The Blue Train is nearly always all booked up.'

'See if there is a berth left,' said Derek. 'If there is not—' He left the sentence unfinished, with a curious smile on his face.

The clerk disappeared for a few minutes, and presently returned. That is all right, sir; still three berths left. I will book you one of them. What name?'

'Pavett,' said Derek. He gave the address of his rooms in Jermyn Street.

The clerk nodded, finished writing it down, wished Derek good morning politely, and turned his attention to the next client.

'I want to go to Nice – on the fourteenth. Isn't there a train called the Blue Train?'

Derek looked round sharply.

Coincidence – a strange coincidence. He remembered his own half-whimsical words to Mirelle. *'Portrait of a lady with grey eyes. I don't suppose I shall ever see her again.'* But he *had* seen her again, and, what was more, she proposed to travel to the Riviera on the same day as he did.

Just for a moment a shiver passed over him; in some ways he was superstitious. He had said, half-laughingly, that this woman might bring him bad luck. Suppose – suppose that should prove to be true. From the doorway he looked back at her as she stood talking to the clerk. For once his memory had not played him false. A lady – a lady in every sense of the word. Not very young, not singularly beautiful. But with something – grey eyes that might perhaps see too much. He knew as he went out of the door that in some way he was afraid of this woman. He had a sense of fatality.

He went back to his rooms in Jermyn Street and summoned his man.

'Take this cheque, Pavett, and go round to Cook in Piccadilly. They will have some tickets there booked in your name, pay for them, and bring them back.'

'Very good, sir.'

Pavett withdrew.

Derek strolled over to a side-table and picked up a handful of letters. They were of a type only too familiar. Bills, small bills and large bills, one and all pressing for payment. The tone of the demands was still polite. Derek knew how soon that polite tone would change if – if certain news became public property.

He flung himself moodily into a large, leather-covered chair. A damned hole – that was what he was in. Yes, a damned hole! And ways of getting out of that damned hole were not too promising.

Pavett appeared with a discreet cough.

'A gentleman to see you – sir – Major Knighton.'

'Knighton, eh?'

Derek sat up, frowned, became suddenly alert. He said in a softer tone, almost to himself: 'Knighton – I wonder what is in the wind now?'

'Shall I – er – show him in, sir?'

His master nodded. When Knighton entered the room he found a charming and genial host awaiting him.

'Very good of you to look me up,' said Derek.

Knighton was nervous.

The other's keen eyes noticed that at once. The errand on which the secretary had come was clerly distasteful to him. He replied almost mechanically to Derek's easy flow of conversation. He declined a drink, and, if anything, his manner became stiffer than before. Derek appeared at last to notice it.

'Well,' he said cheerfully, 'what does my esteemed father-in-law want with me? You have come on his business, I take it?'

Knighton did not smile in reply.

'I have, yes,' he said carefully. 'I –I wish Mr Van Aldin had chosen someone else.'

Derek raised his eyebrows in mock dismay.

'Is it as bad as all that? I am not very thin skinned, I can assure you, Knighton.'

'No,' said Knighton; 'but this—'

He paused.

Derek eyed him keenly.

'Go on, out with it,' he said kindly. 'I can imagine my dear father-in-law's errands might not always be pleasant ones.'

Knighton cleared his throat. He spoke formally in tones that he strove to render free of embarrassment.

'I am directed by Mr Van Aldin to make you a definite offer.'

'An offer?' For a moment Derek showed his surprise. Knighton's opening words were clearly not what he had expected. He offered a cigarette to Knighton, lit one himself, and sank back in his chair, murmuring in a slightly sardonic voice:

'An offer? That sounds rather interesting.'

'Shall I go on?'

'Please. You must forgive my surprise, but it seems to me that my dear father-in-law has rather climbed down since our chat this morning. And climbing down is not what one associates with strong men, Napoleons of finance, etc. It shows – I think it shows that he finds his position weaker than he thought it.'

Knighton listened politely to the easy, mocking voice, but no sign of any kind showed itself on his rather stolid countenance. He waited until Derek had finished, and then he said quietly:

'I will state the proposition in the fewest possible words.'

'Go on.'

Knighton did not look at the other. His voice was curt and matter-of-fact.

'The matter is simply this. Mrs Kettering, as you know, is about to file a petition for divorce. If the case goes undefended you will receive one hundred thousand on the day that the decree is made absolute.'

Derek, in the act of lighting his cigarette, suddenly stopped dead. 'A hundred thousand!' he said sharply. 'Dollars?'

'Pounds.'

There was dead silence for at least two minutes. Kettering had his brows together thinking. A hundred thousand pounds.

It meant Mirelle and a continuance of his pleasant, careless life. It meant that Van Aldin knew something. Van Aldin did not pay for nothing. He got up and stood by the chimney-piece.

'And in the event of my refusing his handsome offer?' he asked, with a cold, ironical politeness.

Knighton made a deprecating gesture.

'I can assure you, Mr Kettering,' he said earnestly, 'that it is with the utmost unwillingness that I came here with this message.'

'That's all right,' said Kettering. 'Don't distress yourself; it's not your fault. Now then – I asked you a question, will you answer it?'

Knighton also rose. He spoke more reluctantly than before.

'In the event of your refusing this proposition,' he said, 'Mr Van Aldin wished me to tell you in plain words that he proposes to break you. Just that.'

Kettering raised his eyebrows, but he retained his light, amused manner.

'Well, well!' he said, 'I suppose he can do it. I certainly should not be able to put up much of a fight against America's man of many millions. A hundred thousand! If you are going to bribe a man there is nothing like doing it thoroughly. Supposing I were to tell you that for two hundred thousand I'd do what he wanted, what then?'

'I would take your message back to Mr Van Aldin,' said Knighton unemotionally. 'Is that your answer?'

'No,' said Derek; 'funnily enough it is not. You can go back to my father-in-law and tell him to take himself and his bribes to hell. Is that clear?'

'Perfectly,' said Knighton. He got up, hesitated, and then flushed. 'I – you will allow me to say, Mr Kettering, that I am glad you have answered as you have.'

Derek did not reply. When the other had left the room he remained for a minute or two lost in thought. A curious smile came to his lips.

'And that is that,' he said softly.

ON THE BLUE TRAIN

'Dad!'

Mrs Kettering started violently. Her nerves were not completely under control this morning. Very perfectly dressed in a long mink coat and a little hat of Chinese lacquer red, she had been walking along the crowded platform of Victoria deep in thought, and her father's sudden appearance and hearty greeting had an unlooked-for effect upon her.

'Why, Ruth, how you jumped!'

'I didn't expect to see you, I suppose, Dad. You said good-bye to me last night and said you had a conference this morning.'

'So I have,' said Van Aldin, 'but you are more to me than any number of darned conferences. I came to take a last look at you, since I am not going to see you for some time.'

'That is very sweet of you, Dad. I wish you were coming too.'

'What would you say if I did?'

The remark was merely a joking one. He was surprised to see the quick colour of flame in Ruth's cheeks. For a moment he almost thought he saw dismay flash out of her eyes. She laughed uncertainly and nervously.

'Just for a moment I really thought you meant it,' she said.

'Would you have been pleased?'

'Of course.' She spoke with exaggerated emphasis.

'Well,' said Van Aldin, 'that's good.'

'It isn't really for very long, Dad,' continued Ruth; 'you know, you are coming out next month.'

'Ah!' said Van Aldin unemotionally, 'sometimes I guess I will go to one of these big guys in Harley Street and have him tell me that I need sunshine and change of air right away.'

'Don't be so lazy,' cried Ruth; 'next month is ever so much nicer than this month out there. You have got all sorts of things you can't possibly leave just now.'

'Well, that's so, I suppose,' said Van Aldin, with a sigh. 'You had better be getting on board this train of yours, Ruth. Where is your seat?'

Ruth Kettering looked vaguely up at the train. At the door of one of the Pullman cars a thin, tall woman dressed in black was standing – Ruth Kettering's maid. She drew aside as her mistress came up to her.

'I have put your dressing-case under your seat, Madam, in case you should need it. Shall I take the rugs, or will you require one?'

'No, no, I shan't want one. Better go and find your own seat now, Mason.'

'Yes, Madam.'

The maid departed.

Van Aldin entered the Pullman car with Ruth. She found her seat, and Van Aldin deposited various papers and magazines on the table in front of her. The seat opposite to her was already taken, and the American gave a cursory glance at its occupant. He had a fleeting impression of attractive grey eyes and a neat travelling costume. He indulged in a little more desultory conversation with Ruth, the kind of talk peculiar to those seeing other people off by train.

Presently, as whistles blew, he glanced at his watch.

'I had best be clearing out of here. Good-bye, my dear. Don't worry. I will attend to things.'

'Oh, Father!'

He turned back sharply. There had been something in Ruth's voice, something so entirely foreign to her usual manner, that he was startled. It was almost a cry of despair. She had made an impulsive movement towards him, but in another minute she was mistress of herself once more.

'Till next month,' she said cheerfully.

Two minutes later the train started.

Ruth sat very still, biting her under lip and trying hard to keep the unaccustomed tears from her eyes. She felt a sudden sense of horrible desolation. There was a wild longing upon her to jump out of the train and to go back before it was too late. She, so calm, so self-assured, for the first time in her life felt like a leaf swept by the wind. If her father knew – what would he say?

Madness! Yes, just that, madness! For the first time in her life she was swept away by emotion, swept away to the point of doing a thing which even she knew to be incredibly foolish and reckless. She was enough Van Aldin's daughter to realise her own folly, and level-headed enough to condemn her own action. But she was his daughter in another sense also. She had that same iron determination that would have what it wanted, and once it had made up its mind would not be balked. From her cradle she had been self-willed; the very circumstances of her life had developed that self-will in her. It drove her now remorselessly. Well, the die was cast. She must go through with it now.

She looked up, and her eyes met those of the woman sitting opposite. She had a sudden fancy that in some way this other woman had read her mind. She saw in those grey eyes understanding and – yes – compassion.

It was only a fleeting impression. The faces of both women hardened to well-bred impassiveness. Mrs Kettering took up a magazine, and Katherine Grey looked out of the window and watched a seemingly endless vista of depressing streets and suburban homes.

Ruth found an increasing difficulty in fixing her mind on the printed page in front of her. In spite of herself, a thousand apprehensions preyed on her mind. What a fool she had been! What a fool she was! Like all cool and self-sufficient people, when she did lose her self-control she lost it thoroughly. It was too late. . . . Was it too late? Oh, for someone to speak to, for someone to advise her. She had never before had such a wish; she would have scorned the idea of relying on any judgment other than her own, but now – what was the matter with her? Panic. Yes, that would describe it best – panic. She, Ruth Kettering, was completely and utterly panic stricken.

She stole a covert glance at the figure opposite. If only she knew someone like that, some nice, cool, calm, sympathetic creature. That was the sort of person one could talk to. But you can't, of course, confide in a stranger. And Ruth smiled to herself a little at the idea. She picked up the magazine again. Really she must control herself. After all she had thought all this out. She had decided of her own free will. What happiness had she ever had in her life up to now? She said to herself restlessly: 'Why shouldn't I be happy? No one will ever know.'

It seemed no time before Dover was reached. Ruth was a good sailor. She disliked the cold, and was glad to reach the shelter of the private cabin she had telegraphed for. Although she would not have admitted the fact, Ruth was in some ways superstitious. She was of the order of people to whom coincidence appeals. After embarking at Calais and settling herself down with her maid in her double compartment in the Blue Train, she went along to the luncheon car. It was with a little shock of surprise that she found herself set down to a small table with, opposite her, the same woman who had been her *vis-à-vis* in the Pullman. A faint smile came to the lips of both women.

'This is quite a coincidence,' said Mrs Kettering.

'I know,' said Katherine; 'it is odd the way things happen.'

A flying attendant shot up to them with the wonderful velocity always displayed by the Compagnie Internationale des Wagons-Lits and deposited two cups of soup. By the time the omelette succeeded the soup they were chatting together in friendly fashion.

'It will be heavenly to get into the sunshine,' sighed Ruth.

'I am sure it will be a wonderful feeling.'

'You know the Riviera well?'

'No; this is my first visit.'

'Fancy that.'

'You go every year, I expect?'

'Practically. January and February in London are horrible.'

'I have always lived in the country. They are not very inspiring months there either. Mostly mud.'

'What made you suddenly decide to travel?'

'Money,' said Katherine. 'For ten years I have been a paid companion with just enough money of my own to buy myself strong country shoes; now I have been left what seems to me a fortune, though I dare say it would not seem so much to you.'

'Now I wonder why you said that – that it would not seem so to me.'

Katherine laughed. 'I don't really know. I suppose one forms impressions without thinking of it. I put you down in my own mind as one of the very rich of the earth. It was just an impression. I dare say I am wrong.'

'No,' said Ruth, 'you are not wrong.' She had suddenly become very grave. 'I wish you would tell me what other impressions you formed about me.'

'I—'

Ruth swept on disregarding the other's embarrassment. 'Oh, please, don't be conventional. I want to know. As we left Victoria I looked across at you, and I had the sort of feeling that you – well, understood what was going on in my mind.'

'I can assure you I am not a mind reader,' said Katherine smiling.

'No, but will you tell me, please, just what you thought.' Ruth's eagerness was so intense and so sincere that she carried her point.

'I will tell you if you like, but you must not think me impertinent. I thought that for some reason you were in great distress of mind, and I was sorry for you.'

'You are right. You are quite right. I am in terrible trouble. I – I should like to tell you something about it, if I may.'

'Oh, dear,' Katherine thought to herself, 'how extraordinarily alike the world seems to be everywhere! People were always telling me things in St Mary Mead, and it is just the same thing here, and I don't really want to hear anybody's troubles!'

She replied politely:

'Do tell me.'

They were just finishing their lunch. Ruth gulped down her coffee, rose from her seat, and quite oblivious of the fact that Katherine had not begun to sip her coffee, said: 'Come to my compartment with me.'

They were two single compartments with a communicating door between them. In the second of them a thin maid, whom Katherine had noticed at Victoria, was sitting very upright on the seat, clutching a big scarlet morocco case with the initials R. V. K. on it. Mrs Kettering pulled the communicating door to and sank down on the seat. Katherine sat down beside her.

'I am in trouble and I don't know what to do. There is a man whom I am fond of – very fond of indeed. We cared for each other when we were thrust apart most brutally and unjustly. Now we have come together again.'

'Yes?'

'I – I am going to meet him now. Oh! I dare say you think it is all wrong, but you don't know the circumstances. My husband is impossible. He has treated me disgracefully.'

'Yes,' said Katherine again.

'What I feel so badly about is this. I have deceived my father – it was he who came to see me off at Victoria today. He wishes me to divorce my husband, and, of course, he has no idea – that I am going to meet this other man. He would think it extraordinarily foolish.'

'Well, don't you think it is?'

'I – I suppose it is.'

Ruth Kettering looked down at her hands; they were shaking violently.

'But I can't draw back now.'

'Why not?'

'I – it is all arranged, and it would break his heart.'

'Don't you believe it,' said Katherine robustly; 'hearts are pretty tough.'

'He will think I have no courage, no strength of purpose.'

'It seems to me an awfully silly thing that you are going to do,' said Katherine. 'I think you realise that yourself.'

Ruth Kettering buried her face in her hands. 'I don't know – I don't know. Ever since I left Victoria I have had a horrible feeling of something – something that is coming to me very soon – that I can't escape.'

She clutched convulsively at Katherine's hand.

'You must think I am mad talking to you like this, but I tell you I know something horrible is going to happen.'

'Don't think it,' said Katherine; 'try to pull yourself together. You could send your father a wire from Paris, if you like, and he would come to you at once.'

The other brightened.

'Yes, I could do that. Dear old Dad. It is queer – but I never knew until today how terribly fond of him I am.' She sat up and dried her eyes with a handkerchief. 'I have been very foolish. Thank you so much for letting me talk to you. I don't know why I got into such a queer, hysterical state.'

She got up. 'I am quite all right now. I suppose, really, I just needed someone to talk to. I can't think now why I have been making such an absolute fool of myself.'

Katherine got up too.

'I am glad you feel better,' she said, trying to make her voice sound as conventional as possible. She was only too well aware that the aftermath of confidences is embarrassment. She added tactfully:

She emerged into the corridor at the same time as the maid

'I must be going back to my own compartment.'

was also coming out from the next door. The latter looked towards Katherine, over her shoulder, and an expression of intense surprise showed itself on her face. Katherine turned also, but by that time whoever it was who had aroused the maid's interest had retreated into his or her compartment, and the corridor was empty. Katherine walked down it to regain her own place, which was in the next coach. As she passed the end compartment the door opened and a woman's face looked out for a moment and then pulled the door to sharply. It was a face not easily forgotten, as Katherine was to know when she saw it again. A beautiful face, oval and dark, very heavily made up in bizarre fashion. Katherine had a feeling that she had seen it before somewhere.

She regained her own compartment without other adventure and sat for some time thinking of the confidence which had just been made to her. She wondered idly who the woman in the mink coat might be, wondered also how the end of her story would turn out.

'If I had stopped anyone from making an idiot of themselves, I suppose I have done good work,' she thought to herself. 'But who knows? That is the kind of woman who is hardheaded and egotistical all her life, and it might be good for her to do the other sort of thing for a change. Oh, well – I don't suppose I shall ever see her again. She certainly won't want to see *me again*. That is the worst of letting people tell you things. They never do.'

She hoped that she would not be given the same place at dinner. She reflected, not without humour, that it might be awkward for both of them. Leaning back with her head against a cushion she felt tired and vaguely depressed. They had reached Paris, and the slow journey round the *ceinture*, with its interminable stops and waits, was very wearisome. When they arrived at the Gare de Lyon she was glad to get out and walk up and down the platform. The keen cold air was refreshing after the steam-heated train. She observed with a smile that her friend of the mink coat was solving the possible awkwardness of the dinner problem in her own way. A dinner basket was being handed up and received through the window by the maid.

When the train started once more, and dinner was announced by a violent ringing of bells, Katherine went along to it much relieved in mind. Her *vis-à-vis* tonight was of an entirely different kind – a small man, distinctly foreign in appearance, with a rigidly waxed moustache and an egg-shaped head which he carried rather on one side. Katherine had taken in a book to dinner with her. She found the little man's eyes fixed upon it with a kind of twinkling amusement.

'I see, Madame, that you have a *roman policier*. You are fond of such things?'

'They amuse me,' Katherine admitted.

The little man nodded with the air of complete understanding.

'They have a good sale always, so I am told. Now why is that, eh, Mademoiselle? I ask you as a student of human nature – why should that be?'

Katherine felt more and more amused.

'Perhaps they give one the illusion of living an exciting life,' she suggested.

He nodded gravely.

'Yes; there is something in that.'

'Of course, one knows that such things don't really happen,' Katherine was continuing, but he interrupted her sharply.

'Sometimes, Mademoiselle! Sometimes! I who speak to you – they have happened to *me*.'

She threw him a quick, interested glance.

'Some day, who knows, *you* might be in the thick of things,' he went on. 'It is all chance.'

'I don't think it is likely,' said Katherine. 'Nothing of that kind ever happens to me.'

He leaned forward.

'Would you like it to?'

The question startled her, and she drew in her breath sharply.

'It is my fancy, perhaps,' said the little man, as he dexterously polished one of the forks, 'but I think that you have a yearning in you for interesting happenings. *Eh bien*, Mademoiselle, all through my life I have observed one thing – "All one wants one gets!" Who knows?' His face screwed itself up comically. 'You may get more than you bargain for.'

'Is that a prophecy?' asked Katherine, smiling as she rose from the table.

The little man shook his head.

'I never prophesy,' he declared pompously. 'It is true that I have the habit of being always right – but I do not boast of it. Good-night, Mademoiselle, and may you sleep well.'

Katherine went back along the train amused and entertained by her little neighbour. She passed the open door of her friend's compartment and saw the conductor making up the bed. The lady in the mink coat was standing looking out of the window. The second compartment, as Katherine saw through the communicating door, was empty, with rugs and bags heaped up on the seat. The maid was not there.

Katherine found her own bed prepared, and since she was tired, she went to bed and switched off her light about half-past nine.

She woke with a sudden start; how much time had passed she did not know. Glancing at her watch, she found that it had stopped. A feeling of intense uneasiness pervaded her and grew stronger moment by moment. At last she got up, threw her dressing-gown round her shoulders, and stepped out into the corridor. The whole train seemed wrapped in slumber. Katherine let the window down and sat by it for some minutes, drinking in the cool night air and trying vainly to calm her

uneasy fears. She presently decided that she would go along
to the end and ask the conductor for the right time so that she
could set her watch. She found, however, that his little chair
was vacant. She hesitated for a moment and then walked
through into the next coach. She looked down the long, dim
line of the corridor and saw, to her surprise, that a man was
standing with his hand on the door of the compartment
occupied by the lady in the mink coat. That is to say, she
thought it was the compartment. Probably, however, she was
mistaken. He stood there for a moment or two with his back
to her, seeming uncertain and hesitating in his attitude.
Then he slowly turned, and with an odd feeling of fatality,
Katherine recognised him as the same man whom she had
noticed twice before – once in the corridor of the Savoy Hotel
and once in Cook's offices. Then he opened the door of the
compartment and passed in, drawing it to behind him.

An idea flashed across Katherine's mind. Could this be the
man of whom the other woman had spoken – the man she was
journeying to meet.

Then Katherine told herself that she was romancing. In all
probability she had mistaken the compartment.

She went back to her own carriage. Five minutes later the
train slackened speed. There was the long plaintive hiss of the
Westinghouse brake, and a few minutes later the train came
to a stop at Lyons.

I I

MURDER

Katherine wakened the next morning to brilliant sunshine.
She went along to breakfast early, but met none of her acquaintances of the day before. When she returned to her compartment it had just been restored to its daytime appearance
by the conductor, a dark man with a drooping moustache and
melancholy face.

'Madame is fortunate,' he said; 'the sun shines. It is always
a great disappointment to passengers when they arrive on a
grey morning.'

'I should have been disappointed, certainly,' said Katherine.

The man prepared to depart.

'We are rather late, Madame,' he said. 'I will let you know
just before we get to Nice.'

Katherine nodded. She sat by the window, entranced by the sunlit panorama. The palm trees, the deep blue of the sea, the bright yellow mimosa came with all the charm of novelty to the woman who for fourteen years had known only the drab winters of England.

When they arrived at Cannes, Katherine got out and walked up and down the platform. She was curious about the lady in the mink coat, and looked up at the windows of her compartment. The blinds were still drawn down – the only ones to be so on the whole train. Katherine wondered a little, and when she re-entered the train she passed along the corridor and noticed that these two compartments were still shuttered and closed. The lady of the mink coat was clearly no early riser.

Presently the conductor came to her and told her that in a few minutes the train would arrive at Nice. Katherine handed him a tip; the man thanked her, but still lingered. There was something odd about him. Katherine, who had at first wondered whether the tip had not been big enough, was now convinced that something far more serious was amiss. His face was of a sickly pallor, he was shaking all over, and looked as if he had been frightened out of his life. He was eyeing her in a curious manner. Presently he said abruptly: 'Madame will excuse me, but is she expecting friends to meet her at Nice?'

'Probably,' said Katherine. 'Why?'

But the man merely shook his head and murmured something that Katherine could not catch and moved away, not reappearing until the train came to rest at the station, when he started handing her belongings down from the window.

Katherine stood for a moment or two on the platform rather at a loss, but a fair young man with an ingenuous face came up to her and said rather hesitatingly:

'Miss Grey, is it not?'

Katherine said that it was, and the young man beamed upon her seraphically and murmured: 'I am Chubby, you know – Lady Tamplin's husband. I expect she mentioned me, but perhaps she forgot. Have you got your *billet de bagages*? I lost mine when I came out this year, and you would not believe the fuss they made about it. Regular French red tape!'

Katherine produced it, and was just about to move off beside him when a very gentle and insidious voice murmured in her ear:

'A little moment, Madame, if you please.'

Katherine turned to behold an individual who made up for

insignificance of stature by a large quantity of gold lace and uniform. The individual explained. 'There were certain formalities. Madame would perhaps be so kind as to accompany him. The regulations of the police—' He threw up his arms. 'Absurd, doubtless, but there it was.'

Mr Chubby Evans listened with a very imperfect comprehension, his French being of a limited order.

'So like the French,' murmured Mr Evans. He was one of those staunch patriotic Britons who, having made a portion of a foreign country their own, strongly resent the original inhabitants of it. 'Always up to some silly dodge or other. They've never tackled people on the station before, though. This is something quite new. I suppose you'll have to go.'

Katherine departed with her guide. Somewhat to her surprise, he led her towards a siding where a coach of the departed train had been shunted. He invited her to mount into this, and, preceding her down the corridor, held aside the door of one of the compartments. In it was a pompous-looking official personage, and with him a nondescript being who appeared to be a clerk. The pompous-looking personage rose politely, bowed to Katherine, and said:

'You will excuse me, Madame, but there are certain formalities to be complied with. Madame speaks French, I trust?'

'Sufficiently, I think, Monsieur,' replied Katherine in that language.

'That is good. Pray be seated, Madame. I am M. Caux, the Commissary of Police.' He blew out his chest importantly, and Katherine tried to look sufficiently impressed.

'You wish to see my passport?' she inquired. 'Here it is.'

The Commissary eyed her keenly and gave a little grunt.

'Thank you, Madame,' he said, taking the passport from her. He cleared his throat. 'But what I really desire is a little information.'

'Information?'

The Commissary nodded his head slowly.

'About a lady who has been a fellow-passenger of yours. You lunched with her yesterday.'

'I am afraid I can't tell you anything about her. We fell into conversation over our meal, but she is a complete stranger to me. I have never seen her before.'

'And yet,' said the Commissary sharply, 'you returned to her compartment with her after lunch and sat talking for some time?'

'Yes,' said Katherine; 'that is true.'

The Commissary seemed to expect her to say something more. He looked at her encouragingly.

'Yes, Madame?'

'Well, Monsieur?' said Katherine.

'You can, perhaps, give me some kind of idea of that conversation?'

'I could,' said Katherine, 'but at the moment I see no reason to do so.'

In a somewhat British fashion she felt annoyed. This foreign official seemed to her impertinent.

'No reason?' cried the Commissary. 'Oh yes, Madame, I can assure you there *is* a reason.'

'Then perhaps you will give it to me.'

The Commissary rubbed his chin thoughtfully for a minute or two without speaking.

'Madame,' he said at last, 'the reason is very simple. The lady in question was found dead in her compartment this morning.'

'Dead!' gasped Katherine. 'What was it – heart falure?'

'No,' said the Commissary in a reflective, dreamy voice. 'No – she was murdered.'

'Murdered!' cried Katherine.

'So you see, Madame, why we are anxious for any information we can possibly get.'

'But surely her maid—'

'The maid has disappeared.'

'Oh!' Katherine paused to assemble her thoughts.

'Since the conductor had seen you talking with her in her compartment, he quite naturally reported the fact to the police, and that is why, Madame, we have detained you, in the hope of gaining some information.'

'I am very sorry,' said Katherine; 'I don't even know her name.'

'Her name is Kettering. That we know from her passport and from the labels on her luggage. If we—'

There was a knock on the compartment door. M. Caux frowned. He opened it about six inches.

'What is the matter?' he said peremptorily. 'I cannot be disturbed.'

The egg-shaped head of Katherine's dinner acquaintance showed itself in the aperture. On his face was a beaming smile.

'My name,' he said, 'is Hercule Poirot.'

'Not,' the Commissary stammered, 'not *the* Hercule Poirot?'

'The same,' said M. Poirot. 'I remember meeting you once,

M. Caux, at the *Sûreté* in Paris, though doubtless you have forgotten me?'

'Not at all, Monsieur, not at all,' declared the Commissary heartily. 'But enter, I pray you. You know of this—?'

'Yes, I know,' said Hercule Poirot. 'I came to see if I might be of any assistance?'

'We should be flattered,' replied the Commissary promptly. 'Let me present you, M. Poirot, to' – he consulted the passport he still held in his hand – 'to Madame – er – Mademoiselle Grey.'

Poirot smiled across at Katherine.

'It is strange, is it not,' he murmured, 'that my words should have come true so quickly?'

'Mademoiselle, alas! can tell us very little,' said the Commissary.

'I have been explaining,' said Katherine, 'that this poor lady was a complete stranger to me.'

Poirot nodded.

'But she talked to you, did she not?' he said gently. 'You formed an impression – is it not so?'

'Yes,' said Katherine thoughtfully. 'I suppose I did.'

'And that impression was—?'

'Yes, Mademoiselle' – the Commissary jerked himself forward – 'let us by all means have your impressions.'

Katherine sat turning the whole thing over in her mind. She felt in a way as if she were betraying a confidence, but with that ugly word 'Murder' ringing in her ears she dared not keep anything back. Too much might hang upon it. So, as nearly as she could, she repeated word for word the conversation she had had with the dead woman.

'That is interesting,' said the Commissary, glancing at the other. 'Eh, M. Poirot, that is interesting? Whether it has anything to do with the crime—' He left the sentence unfinished.

'I suppose it could not be suicide,' said Katherine, rather doubtfully.

'No,' said the Commissary, 'it could not be suicide. She was strangled with a length of black cord.'

'Oh!' Katherine shivered. M. Caux spread out his hands apologetically. 'It is not nice – no. I think that our train robbers are more brutal than they are in your country.'

'It is horrible.'

'Yes, yes' – he was soothing and apologetic – 'but you have great courage, Mademoiselle. At once, as soon as I saw you, I said to myself, "Mademoiselle has great courage." That is why I am going to ask you to do something more – something distressing, but I assure you very necessary.'

Katherine looked at him apprehensively.

He spread out his hands apologetically.

'I am going to ask you, Mademoiselle, to be so good as to accompany me to the next compartment.'

'Must I?' asked Katherine in a low voice.

'Someone must identify her,' said the Commissary,' and since the maid has disappeared' – he coughed significantly – 'you appear to be the person who has seen most of her since she joined the train.'

'Very well,' said Katherine quietly; 'if it is necessary—'

She rose. Poirot gave a little nod of approval.

'Mademoiselle is sensible,' he said. 'May I accompany you, M. Caux?'

'Enchanted, my dear M. Poirot.'

They went out into the corridor, and M. Caux unlocked the door of the dead woman's compartment. The blinds on the far side had been drawn half-way up to admit light. The dead woman lay on the berth to their left, in so natural a posture that one could have thought her asleep. The bedclothes were drawn up over her, and her head was turned to the wall, so that only the red auburn curls showed. Very gently M. Caux laid a hand on her shoulder and turned the body back so that the face came into view. Katherine flinched a little and dug her nails into her palms. A heavy blow had disfigured the features almost beyond recognition. Poirot gave a sharp exclamation.

'When was that done, I wonder?' he demanded. 'Before death or after?'

'The doctor says after,' said M. Caux.

'Strange,' said Poirot, drawing his brows together. He turned to Katherine. 'Be brave, Mademoiselle; look at her well. Are you sure that this is the woman you talked to in the train yesterday?'

Katherine had good nerves. She steeled herself to look long and earnestly at the recumbent figure. Then she leaned forward and took up the dead woman's hand.

'I am quite sure,' she replied at length. 'The face is too disfigured to recognise, but the build and carriage and hair are exact, and besides I noticed *this*' – she pointed to a tiny mole on the dead woman's wrist – 'while I was talking to her.'

'*Bon,*' approved Poirot. 'You are an excellent witness, Mademoiselle. There is, then, no question as to the identity, but it is strange, all the same.' He frowned down on the dead woman in perplexity.

M. Caux shrugged his shoulders.

'The murderer was carried away by rage, doubtless,' he suggested.

'If she had been struck down, it would have been comprehensible,' mused Poirot, 'but the man who strangled her slipped up behind and caught her unawares. A little choke – a little gurgle – that is all that would be heard, and then afterwards – that smashing blow on her face. Now why? Did he hope that if the face were unrecognisable she might not be identified? Or did he hate her so much that he could not resist striking that blow even after she was dead?'

Katherine shuddered, and he turned at once to her kindly.

'You must not let me distress you, Mademoiselle,' he said. 'To you this is all very new and terrible. To me, alas! it is an old story. One moment, I pray of you both.'

They stood against the door watching him as he went quickly round the compartment. He noted the dead woman's clothes neatly folded on the end of the berth, the big fur coat that hung from a hook, and the little red lacquer hat tossed on the rack. Then he passed through into the adjoining compartment, that in which Katherine had seen the maid sitting. Here the berth had not been made up. Three or four rugs were piled loosely on the seat; there was a hat-box and a couple of suit-cases. He turned suddenly to Katherine.

'You were in here yesterday,' he said. 'Do you see anything changed, anything missing?'

Katherine looked carefully round both compartments.

'Yes,' she said, 'there is something missing – a scarlet morocco case. It had the initials "R. V. K." on it. It might have been a small dressing-case or a big jewel-case. When I saw it, the maid was holding it.'

'Ah!' said Poirot.

'But, surely,' said Katherine, 'I – of course, I don't know anything about such things, but surely it is plain enough, if the maid and the jewel-case are missing?'

'You mean that it was the maid who was the thief? No, Mademoiselle, there is a very good reason against that.'

'What?'

'The maid was left behind in Paris.'

He turned to Poirot. 'I should like you to hear the conductor's story yourself,' he murmured confidentially. 'It is very suggestive.'

'Mademoiselle would doubtless like to hear it also,' said Poirot. 'You do not object, Monsieur le Commissaire?'

'No,' said the Commissary, who clearly did object very much. 'No, certainly, M. Poirot, if you say so. You have finished here?'

'I think so. One little minute.'

He had been turning over the rugs, and now he took one to the window and looked at it, picking something off it with his fingers.

'What is it?' demanded M. Caux sharply.

'Four auburn hairs.' He bent over the dead woman. 'Yes, they are from the head of Madame.'

'And what of it? Do you attach importance to them?'

Poirot let the rug drop back on the seat.

'What is important? What is not? One cannot say at this stage. But we must note each little fact carefully.'

They went back again into the first compartment, and in a minute or two the conductor of the carriage arrived to be questioned.

'Your name is Pierre Michel?' said the Commissary.

'Yes, Monsieur le Commissaire.'

'I should like you to repeat to this gentleman' – he indicated Poirot – 'the story that you told me as to what happened in Paris.'

'Very good, Monsieur le Commissaire. It was after we had left the Gare de Lyon I came along to make the beds, thinking that Madame would be at dinner, but she had a dinner-basket in her compartment. She said to me that she had been obliged to leave her maid behind in Paris, so that I only need make up one berth. She took her dinner basket into the adjoining compartment, and sat there while I made up the bed; then she told me that she did not wish to be wakened early in the morning, that she liked to sleep on. I told her I quite understood, and she wished me "good-night." '

'You yourself did not go into the adjoining compartment?'

'No, Monsieur.'

'Then you did not happen to notice if a scarlet morocco case was amongst the luggage there?'

'No, Monsieur, I did not.'

'Would it have been possible for a man to have been concealed in the adjoining compartment?'

The conductor reflected.

'The door was half open,' he said. 'If a man had stood behind that door I should not have been able to see him, but he would, of course, have been perfectly visible to Madame when she went in there.'

'Quite so,' said Poirot. 'Is there anything more you have to tell us?'

'I think that is all, Monsieur. I can remember nothing else.'

'And now this morning?' prompted Poirot.

'As Madame had ordered, I did not disturb her. It was not until just before Cannes that I ventured to knock at the door. Getting no reply, I opened it. The lady appeared to be in her bed asleep. I took her by the shoulder to rouse her, and then—'

'And then you saw what had happened,' volunteered Poirot. '*Très bien*. I think I know all I want to know.'

'I hope, Monsieur le Commissaire, it is not that I have been guilty of any negligence,' said the man piteously. 'Such an affair to happen on the Blue Train! Is is horrible.'

'Console yourself,' said the Commissary. 'Everything will be done to keep the affair as quiet as possible, if only in the interests of justice. I cannot think you have been guilty of any negligence.'

'And Monsieur le Commissaire will report as much to the Company?'

'But certainly, but certainly,' said M. Caux, impatiently. 'That will do now.'

The conductor withdrew.

'According to the medical evidence,' said the Commissary, 'the lady was probably dead before the train reached Lyons. Who then was the murderer? From Mademoiselle's story, it seems clear that somewhere on her journey she was to meet this man of whom she spoke. Her action in getting rid of the maid seems significant. Did the man join the train at Paris, and did she conceal him in the adjoining compartment? If so, they may have quarrelled, and he may have killed her in a fit of rage. That is one possibility. The other, and the more likely to my mind, is that her assailant was a train robber travelling on the train; that he stole along the corridor unseen by the conductor, killed her, and went off with the red morocco case, which doubtless contained jewels of some value. In all probability he left the train at Lyons, and we have already telegraphed to the station there for full particulars of anyone seen leaving the train.'

'Or he may have come on to Nice,' suggested Poirot.

'He might,' agreed the Commissary, 'but that would be a very bold course.'

Poirot let a minute or two go by before speaking, and then he said:

'In the latter case you think the man was an ordinary train robber?'

The Commissary shrugged his shoulders.

'It depends. We must get hold of the maid. It is possible that she has the red morocco case with her. If so, then the man of whom she spoke to Mademoiselle may be concerned in the case, and the affair is a crime of passion. I myself think the solution of a train robber is the more probable. These bandits have become very bold of late.'

Poirot looked suddenly across at Katherine.

'And you, Mademoiselle,' he said, 'you heard and saw nothing during the night?'

'Nothing,' said Katherine.

Poirot turned to the Commissary.

'We need detain Mademoiselle no longer, I think,' he suggested.

The latter nodded.

'She will leave us her address?' he said.

Katherine gave him the name of Lady Tamplin's villa. Poirot made her a little bow.

'You permit that I see you again, Mademoiselle?' he said. 'Or have you so many friends that your time will be all taken up?'

'On the contrary,' said Katherine, 'I shall have plenty of leisure, and I shall be very pleased to see you again.'

'Excellent,' said Poirot, and gave her a little friendly nod. 'This shall be a *"roman policier"* à nous. We will investigate this affair together.'

----- 12 -----

AT THE VILLA MARGUERITE

'Then you were really in the thick of it all!' said Lady Tamplin enviously. 'My dear, how thrilling!' She opened her china blue eyes very wide and gave a little sigh.

'A real murder,' said Mr Evans gloatingly.

'Of course Chubby had no idea of anything of the kind,' went on Lady Tamplin; 'he simply could *not* imagine why the police wanted you. My dear, what an opportunity! I think, you know – yes, I certainly think something might be made out of this.'

A calculating look rather marred the ingenuousness of the blue eyes.

Katherine felt slightly uncomfortable. They were just finishing lunch, and she looked in turn at the three people sitting round the table. Lady Tamplin, full of practical schemes; Mr Evans, beaming with naïve appreciation, and Lenox with a queer crooked smile on her dark face.

'Marvellous luck,' murmured Chubby; 'I wish I could have gone along with you – and seen – all the exhibits.' His tone was wistful and childlike.

Katherine said nothing. The police had laid no injunctions of secrecy upon her, and it was clearly impossible to suppress the bare facts or try to keep them from her hostess. But she did rather wish it had been possible to do so.

'Yes,' said Lady Tamplin, coming suddenly out of her reverie, 'I do think something might be done. A little account, you know, cleverly written up. An eye-witness, a feminine touch: *"How I chatted with the dead woman, little thinking—"* that sort of thing, you know.'

'Rot!' said Lenox.

'You have no idea,' said Lady Tamplin in a soft, wistful voice, 'what newspapers will pay for a little titbit! Written, of course, by someone of really unimpeachable social position. You would not like to do it yourself, I dare say, Katherine dear, but just give me the bare bones of it, and *I* will manage the whole thing for you. Mr de Haviland is a special friend of mine. We have a little understanding together. A most delightful man – not at all reporterish. How does the idea strike you, Katherine?'

'I would much prefer to do nothing of the kind,' said Katherine bluntly.

Lady Tamplin was rather disconcerted at this uncompromising refusal. She sighed and turned to the elucidation of further details.

'A very striking-looking woman, you said? I wonder now who she could have been. You didn't hear her name?'

'It was mentioned,' Katherine admitted, 'but I can't remember it. You see, I was rather upset.'

'I should think so,' said Mr Evans; 'it must have been a beastly shock.'

It is to be doubted whether, even if Katherine had remembered the name, she would have admitted the fact. Lady

Tamplin's remorseless cross-examination was making her restive. Lenox, who was observant in her own way, noticed this, and offered to take Katherine upstairs to see her room. She left her there, remarking kindly before she went: 'You mustn't mind Mother; she would make a few pennies' profit out of her dying grandmother if she could.'

Lenox went down again to find her mother and her step-father discussing the newcomer.

'Presentable,' said Lady Tamplin, 'quite presentable. Her clothes are all right. That grey thing is the same model that Gladys Cooper wore in *Palm Trees in Egypt*.'

'Have you noticed her eyes – what?' interposed Mr Evans.

'Never mind her eyes, Chubby,' said Lady Tamplin tartly; 'we are discussing things that really matter.'

'Oh, quite,' said Mr Evans, and retired into his shell.

'She doesn't seem to me very – malleable,' said Lady Tamplin, rather hesitating to choose the right word.

'She has all the instincts of a lady, as they say in books,' said Lenox, with a grin.

'Narrow-minded,' murmured Lady Tamplin. 'Inevitable under the circumstances, I suppose.'

'I expect you will do your best to broaden her,' said Lenox, with a grin, 'but you will have your work cut out. Just now, you noticed, she stuck down her fore feet and laid back her ears and refused to budge.'

'Anyway,' said Lady Tamplin hopefully, 'she doesn't look to me at all mean. Some people, when they come into money, seem to attach undue importance to it.'

'Oh, you'll easily touch her for what you want,' said Lenox; 'and, after all, that is all that matters, isn't it? That is what she is here for.'

'She is my own cousin,' said Lady Tamplin, with dignity.

'Cousin, eh?' said Mr Evans, waking up again. 'I suppose I call her Katherine, don't I?'

'It is of no importance at all what you call her, Chubby,' said Lady Tamplin.

'Good,' said Mr Evans; 'then I will. Do you suppose she plays tennis?' he added hopefully.

'Of course not,' said Lady Tamplin. 'She has been a companion, I tell you. Companions don't play tennis – or golf. They might possibly play golf-croquet, but I have always understood that they wind wool and wash dogs most of the day.'

'O God!' said Mr Evans; 'do they really?'

Lenox drifted upstairs again to Katherine's room. 'Can I help you?' she asked rather perfunctorily.

On Katherine's disclaimer, Lenox sat on the edge of the bed and stared thoughtfully at her guest.

'Why did you come?' she said at last. 'To us, I mean. We're not your sort.'

'Oh, I am anxious to get into Society.'

'Don't be an ass,' said Lenox promptly, detecting the flicker of a smile. 'You know what I mean well enough. You are not a bit what I thought you would be. I say, you *have* got some decent clothes.' She sighed. 'Clothes are no good to me. I was born awkward. It's a pity, because I love them.'

'I love them too,' said Katherine, 'but it has not been much use my loving them up to now. Do you think this is nice?'

She and Lenox discussed several models with artistic fervour.

'I like you,' said Lenox suddenly. 'I came up to warn you not to be taken in by Mother, but I think now that there is no need to do that. You are frightfully sincere and upright and all those queer things, but you are not a fool. Oh hell! what is it now?'

Lady Tamplin's voice was calling plaintively from the hall:

'Lenox, Derek has just rung up. He wants to come to dinner to-night. Will it be all right? I mean, we haven't got anything awkward, like quails, have we?'

Lenox reassured her and came back into Katherine's room. Her face looked brighter and less sullen.

'I'm glad old Derek is coming,' she said; 'you'll like him.'

'Who is Derek?'

'He is Lord Leconbury's son, married a rich American woman. Women are simply potty about him.'

'Why?'

'Oh, the usual reason – very good-looking and a regular bad lot. Everyone goes off their head about him.'

'Do you?'

'Sometimes I do,' said Lenox, 'and sometimes I think I would like to marry a nice curate and live in the country and grow things in frames.' She paused a minute, and then added, 'An Irish curate would be best, and then I should hunt.'

After a minute or two she reverted to her former theme. 'There is something queer about Derek. All that family are a bit potty – mad gamblers, you know. In the old days they used to gamble away their wives and their estates, and did most reckless things just for the love of it. Derek would have made a perfect highwayman – debonair and gay, just the right manner.' She moved to the door. 'Well, come down when you feel like it.'

Left alone, Katherine gave herself up to thought. Just at present she felt thoroughly ill at ease and jarred by her surroundings. The shock of the discovery in the train and the reception of the news by her new friends jarred upon her susceptibilities. She thought long and earnestly about the murdered woman. She had been sorry for Ruth, but she could not honestly say that she had liked her. She had divined only too well the ruthless egoism that was the keynote of her personality, and it repelled her.

She had been amused and a trifle hurt by the other's cool dismissal of her when she had served her turn. That she had come to some decision, Katherine was quite certain, but she wondered now what that decision had been. Whatever it was, death had stepped in and made all decisions meaningless. Strange that it should have been so, and that a brutal crime should have been the ending of that fateful journey. But suddenly Katherine remembered a small fact that she ought, perhaps, to have told the police – a fact that had for the moment escaped her memory. Was it of any real importance? She had certainly thought that she had seen a man going into that particular compartment, but she realised that she might easily have been mistaken. It might have been the compartment next door, and certainly the man in question could be no train robber. She recalled him very clearly as she had seen him on those two previous occasions – once at the Savoy and once at Cook's office. No, doubtless she had been mistaken. He had not gone into the dead woman's compartment, and it was perhaps as well that she had said nothing to the police. She might have done incalculable harm by doing so.

She went down to join the others on the terrace outside. Through the branches of mimosa, she looked out over the blue of the Mediterranean, and, whilst listening with half an ear to Lady Tamplin's chatter, she was glad that she had come. This was better than St Mary Mead.

That evening she put on the mauvy pink dress that went by the name of *soupir d'automne*, and after smiling at her reflection in the mirror, went downstairs with, for the first time in her life, a faint feeling of shyness.

Most of Lady Tamplin's guests had arrived, and since noise was the essential of Lady Tamplin's parties, the din was already terrific. Chubby rushed up to Katherine, pressed a cocktail upon her, and took her under his wing.

'Oh, here you are, Derek,' cried Lady Tamplin, as the door opened to admit the last comer. 'Now at last we can have something to eat. I am starving.'

Katherine looked across the room. She was startled. So this – was Derek, and she realised that she was not surprised. She had always known that she would some day meet the man whom she had seen three times by such a curious chain of co-incidences. She thought, too, that he recognised her. He paused abruptly in what he was saying to Lady Tamplin, and went on again as though with an effort. They all went in to dinner, and Katherine found that he was placed beside her. He turned to her at once with a vivid smile.

'I knew I was going to meet you soon,' he remarked, 'but I never dreamt that it would be here. It had to be, you know. Once at the Savoy and once at Cook's – never twice without three times. Don't say you can't remember me or never noticed me. I insist upon your pretending that you noticed me, anyway.'

'Oh, I did,' said Katherine; 'but this is not the third time. It is the fourth. I saw you on the Blue Train.'

'On the Blue Train!' Something undefinable came over his manner; she could not have said just what it was. It was as though he had received a check, a set-back. Then he said carelessly:

'What was the rumpus this morning? Somebody had died, hadn't they?'

'Yes,' said Katherine slowly; 'somebody had died.'

'You shouldn't die on a train,' remarked Derek flippantly. 'I believe it causes all sorts of legal and international complications, and it gives the train an excuse for being even later than usual.'

'Mr Kettering?' A stout American lady, who was sitting opposite, leaned forward and spoke to him with the deliberate intonation of her race. 'Mr Kettering, I do believe you have forgotten me, and I thought you such a perfectly lovely man.'

Derek leaned forward, answering her, and Katherine sat almost dazed.

Kettering! That was the name, of course! She remembered it now – but what a strange, ironical situation! Here was this man whom she had seen go into his wife's compartment last night, who had left her alive and well, and now he was sitting at dinner, quite unconscious of the fate that had befallen her. Of that there was no doubt. He did not know.

A servant was leaning over Derek, handing him a note and

murmuring in his ear. With a word of excuse to Lady Tamplin, he broke it open, and an expression of utter astonishment came over his face as he read; then he looked at his hostess.

'This is most extraordinary. I say, Rosalie, I am afraid I will have to leave you. The Prefect of Police wants to see me at once. I can't think what about.'

'Your sins have found you out,' remarked Lenox.

'They must have,' said Derek; 'probably some idiotic nonsense, but I suppose I shall have to push off to the Prefecture. How dare the old boy rout me out from dinner? It ought to be something deadly serious to justify that,' and he laughed as he pushed back his chair and rose to leave the room.

—— 13 ——

VAN ALDIN GETS A TELEGRAM

On the afternoon of the 15th February a thick yellow fog had settled down on London. Rufus Van Aldin was in his suite at the Savoy and was making the most of the atmospheric conditions by working double time. Knighton was overjoyed. He had found it difficult of late to get his employer to concentrate on the matters in hand. When he had ventured to urge certain courses, Van Aldin had put him off with a curt word. But now Van Aldin seemed to be throwing himself into work with redoubled energy, and the secretary made the most of his opportunities. Always tactful, he plied the spur so unobtrusively that Van Aldin never suspected it.

Yet in the middle of this absorption in business matters, one little fact lay at the back of Van Aldin's mind. A chance remark of Knighton's, uttered by the secretary in all unconsciousness, had given rise to it. It now festered unseen, gradually reaching further and further forward into Van Aldin's consciousness, until at last, in spite of himself, he had to yield to its insistence.

He listened to what Knighton was saying with his usual air of keen attention, but in reality not one word of it penetrated his mind. He nodded automatically, however, and the secretary turned to some other paper. As he was sorting them out, his employer spoke:

'Do you mind telling me that over again, Knighton?'

For a moment Knighton was at a loss.

'You mean about this, sir?' He held up a closely written Company report.

'No, no,' said Van Aldin; 'what you told me about seeing Ruth's maid in Paris last night. I can't make it out. You must have been mistaken.'

'I can't have been mistaken, sir; I actually spoke to her.'

'Well, tell me the whole thing again.'

Knighton complied.

'I had fixed up the deal with Bartheimers,' he explained, 'and had gone back to the Ritz to pick up my traps preparatory to having dinner and catching the nine o'clock train from the Gare du Nord. At the reception desk I saw a woman whom I was quite sure was Mrs Kettering's maid. I went up to her and asked if Mrs Kettering was staying there.'

'Yes, yes,' said Van Aldin. 'Of course. Naturally. And she told you that Ruth had gone on to the Riviera and had sent her to the Ritz to await further orders there?'

'Exactly that, sir.'

'It is very odd,' said Van Aldin. 'Very odd, indeed, unless the woman had been impertinent or something of that kind.'

'In that case,' objected Knighton, 'surely Mrs Kettering would have paid her down a sum of money, and told her to go back to England. She would hardly have sent her to the Ritz.'

'No,' muttered the millionaire; 'that's true.'

He was about to say something further, but checked himself. He was fond of Knighton and liked and trusted him, but he could hardly discuss his daughter's private affairs with his secretary. He had already felt hurt by Ruth's lack of frankness, and this chance information which had come to him did nothing to allay his misgivings.

Why had Ruth got rid of her maid in Paris? What possible object or motive could she have had in so doing?

He reflected for a moment or two on the curious combination of chance. How should it have occurred to Ruth, except as the wildest coincidence, that the first person that the maid should run across in Paris should be her father's secretary? Ah, but that was the way things happened. That was the way things got found out.

He winced at the last phrase; it had arisen with complete naturalness to his mind. Was there then 'something to be found out'? He hated to put this question to himself; he had no doubt of the answer. The answer was – he was sure of it – Armand de la Roche.

It was bitter to Van Aldin that a daughter of his should be gulled by such a man, yet he was forced to admit that she was in good company – that other well-bred and intelligent women had succumbed just as easily to the Count's fascination. Men saw through him, women did not.

He sought now for a phrase that would allay any suspicion that his secretary might have felt.

'Ruth is always changing her mind about things at a moment's notice,' he remarked, and then he added in a would-be careless tone: 'The maid didn't give any – er – reason for this change of plan?'

Knighton was careful to make his voice as natural as possible as he replied:

'She said, sir, that Mrs Kettering had met a friend unexpectedly.'

'Is that so?'

The secretary's practised ears caught the note of strain underlying the seemingly casual tone.

'Oh, I see. Man or woman?'

'I think she said a man, sir.'

Van Aldin nodded. His worst fears were being realised. He rose from his chair, and began pacing up and down the room, a habit of his when agitated. Unable to contain his feelings any longer, he burst forth:

'There is one thing no man can do, and that is to get a woman to listen to reason. Somehow or other, they don't seem to have any kind of *sense*. Talk of woman's instinct – why, it is well known all the world over that a woman is the surest mark for any rascally swindler. Not one in ten of them knows a scoundrel when she meets one; they can be preyed on by any good-looking fellow with a soft side to his tongue. If I had my way—'

He was interrupted. A page-boy entered with a telegram. Van Aldin tore it open, and his face went a sudden chalky white. He caught hold of the back of a chair to steady himself, and waved the page-boy from the room.

'What's the matter, sir?'

Knighton had risen in concern.

'Ruth!' said Van Aldin hoarsely.

'Mrs Kettering?'

'Killed!'

'An accident to the train?'

Van Aldin shook his head.

'No. From this it seems she has been robbed as well. They

don't use the word, Knighton, but my poor girl has been murdered.'

'Oh, my God, sir!'

Van Aldin tapped the telegram with his forefinger.

'This is from the police at Nice. I must go out there by the first train.'

Knighton was efficient as ever. He glanced at the clock.

'Five o'clock from Victoria, sir.'

'That's right. You will come with me, Knighton. Tell my man, Archer, and pack your own things. See to everything here. I want to go round to Curzon Street.'

The telephone rang sharply, and the secretary lifted the receiver.

'Yes; who is it?'

Then to Van Aldin:

'Mr Goby, sir.'

'Goby? I can't see him now. No – wait, we have plenty of time. Tell them to send him up.'

Van Aldin was a strong man. Already he had recovered that iron calm of his. Few people would have noticed anything amiss in his greeting to Mr Goby.

'I am pressed for time, Goby. Got anything important to tell me?'

Mr Goby coughed.

'The movements of Mr Kettering, sir. You wished them reported to you.'

'Yes – well?'

'Mr Kettering, sir, left London for the Riviera yesterday morning.'

'What?'

Something in his voice must have startled Mr Goby. That worthy gentleman departed from his usual practice of never looking at the person to whom he was talking, and stole a fleeting glance at the millionaire.

'What train did he go on?' demanded Van Aldin.

'The Blue Train, sir.'

Mr Goby coughed again and spoke to the clock on the mantelpiece.

'Mademoiselle Mirelle, the dancer from the Parthenon, went by the same train.'

14

ADA MASON'S STORY

'I cannot repeat to you often enough, Monsieur, our horror, our consternation, and the deep sympathy we feel for you.'

Thus M. Carrège, the Juge d'Instruction, addressed Van Aldin. M. Caux the Commissary, made sympathetic noises in his throat. Van Aldin brushed away horror, consternation, and sympathy with an abrupt gesture. The scene was the Examining Magistrate's room at Nice. Besides M. Carrège, the Commissary, and Van Aldin, there was a further person in the room. It was that person who now spoke.

'M. Van Aldin,' he said, 'desires action – swift action.'

'Ah!' cried the Commissary, 'I have not yet presented you. M. Van Aldin, this is M. Hercule Poirot; you have doubtless heard of him. Although he has retired from his profession for some years now, his name is still a household word as one of the greatest living detectives.'

'Pleased to meet you, M. Poirot,' said Van Aldin, falling back mechanically on a formula that he had discarded some years ago. 'You have retired from your profession?'

'That is so, Monsieur. Now I enjoy the world.'

The little man made a grandiloquent gesture.

'M. Poirot happened to be travelling on the Blue Train,' explained the Commissary, 'and he has been so kind as to assist us out of his vast experience.'

The millionaire looked at Poirot keenly. Then he said unexpectedly:

'I am a very rich man, M. Poirot. It is usually said that a rich man labours under the belief that he can buy everything and everyone. That is not true. I am a big man in my way, and one big man can ask a favour from another big man.'

Poirot nodded a quick appreciation.

'That is very well said, M. Van Aldin. I place myself entirely at your service.'

'Thank you,' said Van Aldin. 'I can only say call upon me at any time, and you will not find me ungrateful. And now, gentlemen, to business.'

'I propose,' said M. Carrège, 'to interrogate the maid, Ada Mason. You have her here, I understand?'

'Yes,' said Van Aldin. 'We picked her up in Paris in passing through. She was very upset to hear of her mistress's death, but she tells her story coherently enough.'

'We will have her in, then,' said M. Carrège.

He rang the bell on his desk, and in a few minutes Ada Mason entered the room.

She was very neatly dressed in black, and the tip of her nose was red. She had exchanged her grey travelling gloves for a pair of black suède ones. She cast a look round the Examining Magistrate's office in some trepidation, and seemed relieved at the presence of her mistress's father. The Examining Magistrate prided himself on his geniality of manner, and did his best to put her at her ease. He was helped in this by Poirot, who acted as interpreter, and whose friendly manner was reassuring to the Englishwoman.

'Your name is Ada Mason; is that right?'

'Ada Beatrice I was christened, sir,' said Mason primly.

'Just so. And we can understand, Mason, that this has all been very distressing.'

'Oh, indeed it has, sir. I have been with many ladies and always given satisfaction, I hope, and I never dreamt of anything of this kind happening in any situation where I was.'

'No, no,' said M. Carrège.

'Naturally, I have read of such things, of course, in the Sunday papers. And then I always have understood that those foreign trains—' She suddenly checked her flow, remembering that the gentlemen who were speaking to her were of the same nationality as the trains.

'Now let us talk this affair over,' said M. Carrège. 'There was, I understand, no question of your staying in Paris when you started from London?'

'Oh no, sir. We were to go straight through to Nice.'

'Have you ever been abroad with your mistress before?'

'No, sir. I had only been with her two months, you see.'

'Did she seem quite as usual when starting on this journey?'

'She was worried like and a bit upset, and she was rather irritable and difficult to please.'

M. Carrège nodded.

'Now then, Mason, what was the first you heard of your stopping in Paris?'

'It was at the place they call the Gare de Lyon, sir. My mistress was thinking of getting out and walking up and down the platform. She was just going out into the corridor when she gave a sudden exclamation, and came back into her compartment with a gentleman. She shut the door between her carriage and mine, so that I didn't see or hear anything, till she suddenly opened it again and told me that she had changed her plans. She gave me some money and told me to get out and go to the Ritz. They knew her well there, she said, and would give me a room. I was to wait there until I heard from her; she would wire me what she wanted me to do. I had just time to get my things together and jump out of the train before it started off. It was a rush.'

'While Mrs Kettering was telling you this, where was the gentleman?'

'He was standing in the other compartment, sir, looking out of the window.'

'Can you describe him to us?'

'Well, you see, sir, I hardly saw him. He had his back to me most of the time. He was a tall gentleman and dark; that's all I can say. He was dressed very like another gentleman in a dark blue overcoat and a grey hat.'

'Was he one of the passengers on the train?'

'I don't thing so, sir; I took it that he had come to the station to see Mrs Kettering in passing through. Of course he might have been one of the passengers; I never thought of that.'

Mason seemed a little flurried by the suggestion.

'Ah!' M. Carrège passed lightly to another subject. 'Your mistress later requested the conductor not to rouse her early in the morning. Was that a likely thing for her to do, do you think?'

'Oh yes, sir. The mistress never ate any breakfast and she didn't sleep well at nights, so that she liked sleeping on in the morning.'

Again M. Carrège passed to another subject.

'Amongst the luggage there was a scarlet morocco case, was there not?' he asked. 'Your mistress's jewel-case?'

'Yes, sir.'

'Did you take that case to the Ritz?'

'*Me* take the mistress's jewel-case to the Ritz! Oh no, indeed, sir.' Mason's tones were horrified.

'You left it behind you in the carriage?'

'Yes, sir.'

'Had your mistress many jewels with her, do you know?'

'A fair amount, sir; made me a bit uneasy sometimes, I can tell you, with those nasty tales you hear of being robbed in foreign countries. They were insured, I know, but all the same it seemed a frightful risk. Why, the rubies alone, the mistress told me, were worth several hundred thousand pounds.'

'The rubies! What rubies?' barked Van Aldin suddenly.

Mason turned to him. 'I think it was you who gave them to her, sir, not very long ago.'

'My God!' cried Van Aldin. 'You don't say she had those rubies with her? I told her to leave them at the bank.'

Mason gave once more the discreet cough which was apparently part of her stock-in-trade as a lady's maid. This time it expressed a good deal. It expressed far more clearly than words could have done, that Mason's mistress had been a lady who took her own way.

'Ruth must have been mad,' muttered Van Aldin. 'What on earth could have possessed her?'

M. Carrège in turn gave vent to a cough, again a cough of significance. It riveted Van Aldin's attention on him.

'For the moment,' said M. Carrège, addressing Mason, 'I think that is all. If you will go into the next room, Mademoiselle, they will read over to you the questions and answers and you will sign accordingly.'

Mason went out escorted by the clerk, and Van Aldin said immediately to the Magistrate:

'Well?'

M. Carrège opened a drawer in his desk, took out a letter, and handed it across to Van Aldin.

'This was found in Madame's handbag.'

'CHERE AMIE' (the letter ran), – 'I will obey you; I will be prudent, discreet – all those things that a lover most hates. Paris would perhaps have been unwise, but the Isles d'Or are far away from the world, and you may be assured that nothing will leak out. It is like you and your divine sympathy to be so interested in the work on famous jewels that I am writing. It will, indeed, be an extraordinary privilege to actually see and handle these historic rubies. I am devoting a special passage to "Heart of Fire." My wonderful one! Soon I will make up to you for all those sad years of separation and emptiness. – Your ever-adoring,

'ARMAND.'

15

THE COMTE DE LA ROCHE

Van Aldin read the letter through in silence. His face turned a dull angry crimson. The men watching him saw the veins start out on his forehead, and his big hands clench themselves unconsciously. He handed back the letter without a word. M. Carrège was looking with close attention at his desk, M. Caux's eyes were fixed upon the ceiling, and M. Hercule Poirot was tenderly brushing a speck of dust from his coat sleeve. With the greatest tact they none of them looked at Van Aldin.

It was M. Carrège, mindful of his status and his duties, who tackled the unpleasant subject.

'Perhaps, Monsieur,' he murmured, 'you are aware by whom – er – this letter was written?'

'Yes, I know,' said Van Aldin heavily.

'Ah?' said the magistrate inquiringly.

'A scoundrel who calls himself the Comte de la Roche.'

There was a pause; then M. Poirot leaned forward, straightened a ruler on the judge's desk, and addressed the millionaire directly.

'M. Van Aldin, we are all sensible, deeply sensible, of the pain it must give you to speak of these matters, but believe me, Monsieur, it is not the time for concealments. If justice is to be done, we must know everything. If you will reflect a little minute you will realise the truth of that clearly for yourself.'

Van Aldin was silent for a moment or two, then almost reluctantly he nodded his head in agreement.

'You are quite right, M. Poirot,' he said. 'Painful as it is, I have no right to keep anything back.'

The Commissary gave a sigh of relief, and the Examining Magistrate leaned back in his chair and adjusted a pince-nez on his long thin nose.

'Perhaps you will tell us in your own words. M. Van Aldin,' he said, 'all that you know of this gentleman.'

'It began eleven or twelve years ago – in Paris. My daughter was a young girl then, full of foolish, romantic notions, like all young girls are. Unknown to me, she made the acquaintance of this Comte de la Roche. You have heard of him, perhaps?'

The Commissary and Poirot nodded in assent.

'He calls himself the Comte de la Roche,' continued Van Aldin, 'but I doubt if he has any right to the title.'

'You would not have found his name in the *Almanac de Gotha*,' agreed the Commissary.

'I discovered as much,' said Van Aldin. 'The man was a good-looking, plausible scoundrel, with a fatal fascination for women. Ruth was infatuated with him, but I soon put a stop to the whole affair. The man was no better than a common swindler.'

'You are quite right,' said the Commissary. 'The Comte de la Roche is well known to us. If it were possible, we should have laid him by the heels before now, but *ma foi*! it is not easy; the fellow is cunning, his affairs are always conducted with ladies of high social position. If he obtains money from them under false pretences or as the fruit of blackmail, *eh bien*! naturally they will not prosecute. To look foolish in the eyes of the world, oh no, that would never do, and he has an extraordinary power over women.'

'That is so,' said the millionaire heavily. 'Well, as I told you, I broke the affair up pretty sharply. I told Ruth exactly what he was, and she had, perforce, to believe me. About a year afterwards, she met her present husband and married him. As far as I knew, that was the end of the matter; but only a week ago, I discovered, to my amazement, that my daughter had resumed her acquaintance with the Comte de la Roche. She had been meeting him frequently in London and Paris. I remonstrated with her on her imprudence, for I may tell you gentlemen that, on my insistence, she was preparing to bring a suit for divorce against her husband.'

'That is interesting,' murmured Poirot softly, his eyes on the ceiling.

Van Aldin looked at him sharply, and then went on.

'I pointed out to her the folly of continuing to see the Comte under the circumstances. I thought she agreed with me.'

The Examining Magistrate coughed delicately.

'But according to this letter—' he began, and then stopped.

Van Aldin's jaw set itself squarely.

'I know. It's no good mincing matters. However unpleasant, we have got to face facts. It seems clear that Ruth had arranged to go to Paris and meet de la Roche there. After my warnings to her, however, she must have written to the Count suggesting a change of rendezvous.'

'The Isles d'Or,' said the Commissary thoughtfully, 'are situated just opposite Hyères, a remote and idyllic spot.'

Van Aldin nodded.

'My God! How could Ruth be such a fool?' he exclaimed bitterly. 'All this talk about writing a book on jewels! Why, he must have been after the rubies from the first.'

'There are some very famous rubies,' said Poirot, 'originally part of the Crown jewels of Russia; they are unique in character, and their value is almost fabulous. There has been a rumour that they have lately passed into the possession of an American. Are we right in concluding, Monsieur, that you were the purchaser?'

'Yes,' said Van Aldin. 'They came into my possession in Paris about ten days ago.'

'Pardon me, Monsieur, but you have been negotiating for their purchase for some time?'

'A little over two months. Why?'

'These things became known,' said Poirot. 'There is always a pretty formidable crowd on the track of jewels such as these.'

A spasm distorted the other's face.

'I remember,' he said brokenly, 'a joke I made to Ruth when I gave them to her. I told her not to take them to the Riviera with her, as I could not afford to have her robbed and murdered for the sake of the jewels. My God! the things one says — never dreaming or knowing they will come true.'

There was a sympathetic silence, and then Poirot spoke in a detached manner.

'Let us arrange our facts with order and precision. According to our present theory, this is how they run. The Comte de la Roche knows of your purchase of these jewels. By an easy stratagem he induces Madame Kettering to bring the stones with her. He, then, is the man Mason saw in the train at Paris.'

The other three nodded in agreement.

'Madame is surprised to see him, but he deals with the situation promptly. Mason is got out of the way; a dinner basket is ordered. We know from the conductor that he made up the berth for the first compartment, but he did not go into the second compartment, and that a man could quite well have been concealed from him. So far the Comte could have been hidden to a marvel. No one knows of his presence on the train except Madame; he has been careful that the maid did not see his face. All that she could say is that he was tall and dark. It is all most conveniently vague. They are alone — and the train rushes through the night. There would be no outcry, no struggle, for the man is, so she thinks, her lover.'

He turned gently to Van Aldin.

'Death, Monsieur, must have been almost instantaneous. We will pass over that quickly. The Comte takes the jewel-case which lies ready to his hand. Shortly afterwards the train draws into Lyons.'

M. Carrège nodded his approval.

'Precisely. The conductor without descends. It would be easy for our man to leave the train unseen; it would be easy to catch a train back to Paris or anywhere he pleases. And the crime would be put down as an ordinary train robbery. But for the letter found in Madame's bag, the Comte would not have been mentioned.'

'It was an oversight on his part not to search that bag,' declared the Commissary.

'Without doubt he thought she had destroyed that letter. It was – pardon me, Monsieur – it was in indiscretion of the first water to keep it.'

'And yet,' murmured Poirot, 'it was an indiscretion the Comte must have foreseen.'

'You mean?'

'I mean we are all agreed on one point, that is that the Comte de la Roche knows one subject *à fond*: Women. How was it that, knowing women as he does, he did not foresee that Madame would have kept that letter?'

'Yes – yes,' said the Examining Magistrate doubtfully, 'there is something in what you say. But at such times, you understand, a man is not master of himself. He does not reason calmly. *Mon Dieu!*' he added, with feeling, 'if our criminals kept their heads and acted with intelligence, how should we capture them?'

Poirot smiled to himself.

'It seems to me a clear case,' said the other, 'but a difficult one to prove. The Comte is a slippery customer, and unless the maid can identify him—'

'Which is most unlikely,' said Poirot.

'True, true.' The Examining Magistrate rubbed his chin. 'It is going to be difficult.'

'If he did indeed commit the crime—' began Poirot. M. Caux interrupted.

'If – you say *if*?'

'Yes, Monsieur le Commissaire, I say *if*.'

The other looked at him sharply. 'You are right,' he said at last, 'we go too fast. It is possible that the Comte may have an alibi. Then we should look foolish.'

'*Ah, ça par exemple,*' replied Poirot, 'that is of no importance whatever. Naturally, if he committed the crime he will have an alibi. A man with the Comte's experience does not neglect to take precautions. No, I said *if* for a very definite reason.'

'And what was that?'

Poirot wagged an emphatic forefinger. 'The psychology.'

'Eh?' said the Commissary.

'The psychology is at fault. The Comte is a scoundrel – yes. The Comte is a swindler – yes. The Comte preys upon women – yes. He proposes to steal Madame's jewels – again yes. Is he the kind of man to commit murder? I say *no*! A man of the type of the Comte is always a coward; he takes no risks. He plays the safe, the mean, what the English call the lowdown game; but murder, a hundred times no!' He shook his head in a dissatisfied manner.

The Examining Magistrate, however, did not seem disposed to agree with him.

'The day always comes when such gentry lose their heads and go too far,' he observed sagely. 'Doubtless that is the case here. Without wishing to disagree with you, M. Poirot—'

'It was only an opinion,' Poirot hastened to explain. 'The case is, of course, in your hands, and you will do what seems fit to you.'

'I am satisfied in my own mind the Comte de la Roche is the man we need to get hold of,' said M. Carrège. 'You agree with me, Monsieur le Commissaire?'

'Perfectly.'

'And you, M. Van Aldin?'

'Yes,' said the millionaire. 'Yes; the man is a thorough paced villain, no doubt about it.'

'It will be difficult to lay hands on him, I am afraid,' said the Magistrate, 'but we will do our best. Telegraphed instructions shall go out at once.'

'Permit me to assist you,' said Poirot. 'There need be no difficulty.'

'Eh?'

The others stared at him. The little man smiled beamingly back at them.

'It is my business to know things,' he explained. 'The Comte is a man of intelligence. He is at present at a villa he has leased, the Villa Marina at Antibes.'

16

POIROT DISCUSSES THE CASE

Everybody looked respectfully at Poirot. Undoubtedly the little man had scored heavily. The Commissary laughed – on a rather hollow note.

'You teach us all our business,' he cried. 'M. Poirot knows more than the police.'

Poirot gazed complacently at the ceiling, adopting a mock-modest air.

'What will you; it is my little hobby,' he murmured, 'to know things. Naturally I have the time to indulge it. I am not overburdened with affairs.'

'Ah!' said the Commissary shaking his head portentously. 'As for me—'

He made an exaggerated gesture to represent the cares that lay on his shoulders.

Poirot turned suddenly to Van Aldin.

'You agree, Monsieur, with this view? You feel certain that the Comte de la Roche is the murderer?'

'Why, it would seem so – yes, certainly.'

Something guarded in the answer made the Examining Magistrate look at the American curiously. Van Aldin seemed aware of his scrutiny and made an effort as though to shake off some preoccupation.

'What about my son-in-law?' he asked. 'You have acquainted him with the news? He is in Nice, I understand.'

'Certainly, Monsieur.' The Commissary hesitated, and then murmured very discreetly: 'You are doubtless aware, M. Van Aldin, that M. Kettering was also one of the passengers on the Blue Train that night?'

The millionaire nodded.

'Heard it just before I left London,' he vouchsafed laconically.

'He tells us,' continued the Commissary, 'that he had no idea his wife was travelling on the train.'

'I bet he hadn't,' said Van Aldin grimly. 'It would have been rather a nasty shock to him if he'd come across her on it.'

The three men looked at him questioningly.

'I'm not going to mince matters,' said Van Aldin savagely.

'No one knows what my poor girl has had to put up with. Derek Kettering wasn't alone. He had a lady with him.'

'Ah?'

'Mirelle – the dancer.'

M. Carrège and the Commissary looked at each other and nodded as though confirming some previous conversation. M. Carrège leaned back in his chair, joined his hands, and fixed his eyes on the ceiling.

'Ah!' he murmured again. 'One wondered.' He coughed. 'One has heard rumours.'

'The lady,' said M. Caux, 'is very notorious.'

'And also,' murmured Poirot softly, 'very expensive.'

Van Aldin had gone very red in the face. He leant forward and hit the table a bang with his fist.

'See here,' he cried, 'my son-in-law is a damned scoundrel!'

He glared at them, looking from one face to another.

'Oh, I don't know,' he went on. 'Good looks and a charming, easy manner. It took me in once upon a time. I suppose he pretended to be broken-hearted when you broke the news to him – that is, if he didn't know it already.'

'Oh, it came as a surprise to him. He was overwhelmed.'

'Darned young hypocrite,' said Van Aldin. 'Simulated great grief, I suppose?'

'N – no,' said the Commissary cautiously. 'I would not quite say that – eh, M. Carrège?'

The Magistrate brought the tips of his fingers together, and half closed his eyes.

'Shock, bewilderment, horror – these things, yes,' he declared judicially. 'Great sorrow – no – I should not say that.'

Hercule Poirot spoke once more.

Permit me to ask, M. Van Aldin, does M. Kettering benefit by the death of his wife?'

'He benefits to the tune of a couple of millions,' said Van Aldin.

'Dollars?'

'Pounds. I settled that sum on Ruth absolutely on her marriage. She made no will and leaves no children, so the money will go to her husband.'

'Whom she was on the point of divorcing,' murmured Poirot. 'Ah, yes – *précisément*.'

The Commissary turned and looked sharply at him.

'Do you mean—?' he began.

'I mean nothing,' said Poirot. 'I arrange the facts, that is all.'

Van Aldin stared at him with awakening interest.

The little man rose to his feet.

'I do not think I can be of any further service to you, M. le Juge,' he said politely, bowing to M. Carrège. 'You will keep me informed of the course of events? It will be a kindness.'

'But certainly – most certainly.'

Van Aldin rose also.

'You don't want me any more at present?'

'No, Monsieur; we have all the information we need for the moment.'

'Then I will walk a little way with M. Poirot. That is, if he does not object?'

'Enchanted, Monsieur,' said the little man, with a bow.

Van Aldin lighted a large cigar, having first offered one to Poirot, who declined it and lit one of his own tiny cigarettes. A man of great strength of character, Van Aldin already appeared to be his everyday, normal self once more. After strolling along for a minute or two in silence, the millionaire spoke:

'I take it, M. Poirot, that you no longer exercise your profession?'

'That is so, Monsieur. I enjoy the world.'

'Yet you are assisting the police in this affair?'

'Monsieur, if a doctor walks along the street and an accident happens, does he say, "I have retired from my profession, I will continue my walk," when there is someone bleeding to death at his feet? If I had been already in Nice and the police had sent to me and asked me to assist them, I should have refused. But this affair, the good God thrust it upon me.'

'You were on the spot,' said Van Aldin thoughtfully. 'You examined the compartment, did you not?'

Poirot nodded.

'Doubtless you found things that were, shall we say, suggestive to you?'

'Perhaps,' said Poirot.

'I hope you see what I am leading up to?' said Van Aldin. 'It seems to me that the case against this Comte de la Roche is perfectly clear, but I am not a fool. I have been watching you for this last hour or so, and I realise that for some reason of your own you don't agree with that theory?'

Poirot shrugged his shoulders.

'I may be wrong.'

'So we come to the favour I want to ask you. Will you act in this matter for me?'

'For you, personally?'

'That was my meaning.'

Poirot was silent for a moment or two. Then he said:

'You realise what you are asking?'

'I guess so,' said Van Aldin.

'Very well,' said Poirot. 'I accept. But in that case, I must have frank answers to my questions.'

'Why, certainly. That is understood.'

Poirot's manner changed. He became suddenly brusque and business-like.

'This question of a divorce,' he said. 'It was you who advised your daughter to bring the suit?'

'Yes.'

'When?'

'About ten days ago. I had had a letter from her complaining of her husband's behaviour, and I put it to her very strongly that divorce was the only remedy.'

'In what way did she complain of his behaviour?'

'He was being seen about with a *very* notorious lady – the one we have been speaking of – Mirelle.'

'The dancer. Ah-ha! And Madame Kettering objected? Was she very devoted to her husband?'

'I would not say that,' said Van Aldin, hesitating a little.

'It was not her heart that suffered, it was her pride – is that what you would say?'

'Yes, I suppose you might put it like that.'

'I gather that the marriage has not been a happy one from the beginning?'

'Derek Kettering is rotten to the core,' said Van Aldin. 'He is incapable of making any woman happy.'

'He is, as you say in England, a bad lot. That is right, is it not?'

Van Aldin nodded.

'*Très bien*! You advise Madame to seek a divorce, she agrees; you consult your solicitors. When does M. Kettering get news of what is in the wind?'

'I sent for him myself, and explained the course of action I proposed to take.'

'And what did he say?' murmured Poirot softly.

Van Aldin's face darkened at the remembrance.

'He was infernally impudent.'

'Excuse the question, Monsieur, but did he refer to the Comte de la Roche.'

'Not by name,' growled the other unwillingly, 'but he showed himself cognizant of the affair.'

'What, if I may ask, was Mr Kettering's financial position at the time?'

'How do you suppose I should know that?' asked Van Aldin, after a very brief hesitation.

'It seemed likely to me that you would inform yourself on that point.'

'Well – you are quite right, I did. I discovered that Kettering was on the rocks.'

'And now he has inherited two million pounds! *La vie* – it is a strange thing, is it not?'

Van Aldin looked at him sharply.

'What do you mean?'

'I moralise,' said Poirot, 'I reflect, I speak the philosophy. But to return to where we were. Surely M. Kettering did not propose to allow himself to be divorced without making a fight for it?'

Van Aldin did not answer for a minute or two, then he said:

'I don't exactly know what his intentions were.'

'Did you hold any further communications with him?'

Again a slight pause, then Van Aldin said:

'No.'

Poirot stopped dead, took off his hat, and held out his hand.

'I must wish you good-day, Monsieur. I can do nothing for you.'

'What are you getting at?' demanded Van Aldin angrily.

'If you do not tell me the truth, I can do nothing.'

'I don't know what you mean.'

'I think you do. You may rest assured, M. Van Aldin, that I know how to be discreet.'

'Very well, then,' said the millionaire. 'I'll admit that I was not speaking the truth just now. I *did* have further communications with my son-in-law.'

'Yes?'

'To be exact, I sent my secretary, Major Knighton, to see him, with instructions to offer him the sum of one hundred thousand pounds in cash if the divorce went through undefended.'

'A pretty sum of money,' said Poirot appreciatively: 'and the answer of Monsieur your son-in-law?'

'He sent back word that I could go to hell,' replied the millionaire succinctly.

'Ah!' said Poirot.

He betrayed no emotion of any kind. At the moment he was engaged in methodically recording facts.

'Monsieur Kettering has told the police that he neither saw nor spoke to his wife on the journey from England. Are you inclined to believe that statement, Monsieur?'

'Yes, I am,' said Van Aldin. 'He would take particular pains to keep out of her way, I should say.'

'Why?'

'Because he had got that woman with him.'

'Mirelle?'

'Yes.'

'How did you come to know that fact?'

'A man of mine, whom I had put on to watch him, reported to me that they both left by train.'

'I see,' said Poirot. 'In that case, as you said before, he would not be likely to attempt to hold any communication with Madame Kettering.'

The little man fell silent for some time. Van Aldin did not interrupt his meditation.

17

AN ARISTOCRATIC GENTLEMAN

'You have been to the Riviera before, Georges?' said Poirot to his valet the following morning.

George was an intensely English, rather wooden-faced individual.

'Yes, sir. I was here two years ago when I was in the service of Lord Edward Frampton.'

'And to-day,' murmured his master, 'you are here with Hercule Poirot. How one mounts in the world!'

The valet made no reply to this observation. After a suitable pause he asked:

'The brown lounge suit, sir? The wind is somewhat chilly to-day.'

'There is a grease spot on the waistcoat,' objected Poirot. 'A *morceau* of *Filet de sole à la Jeanette* alighted there when I was lunching at the Ritz last Tuesday.'

'There is no spot there now, sir,' said George reproachfully. 'I have removed it.'

'*Très bien!*' said Poirot, 'I am pleased with you, Georges.'

'Thank you, sir.'

There was a pause, and then Poirot murmured dreamily:

'Supposing, my good Georges, that you had been born in the same social sphere as your late master, Lord Edward Frampton – that, penniless yourself, you had married an extremely wealthy wife, but that wife proposed to divorce you, with excellent reasons, what would you do about it?'

'I should endeavour, sir,' replied George, 'to make her change her mind.'

'By peaceful or by forcible methods?'

George looked shocked.

'You will excuse me, sir,' he said, 'but a gentleman of the aristocracy would not behave like a Whitechapel coster. He would not do anything low.'

'Would he not, Georges? I wonder now. Well, perhaps you are right.'

There was a knock on the door. George went to it and opened it a discreet inch or two. A low murmured colloquy went on, and then the valet returned to Poirot.

'A note, sir.'

Poirot took it. It was from M. Caux, the Commissary of Police.

'We are about to interrogate the Comte de la Roche. The Juge d'Instruction begs that you will be present.'

'Quickly, my suit, Georges! I must hasten myself.'

A quarter of an hour later, spick and span in his brown suit, Poirot entered th Examining Magistrate's room. M. Caux was already there, and both he and M. Carrège greeted Poirot with polite *empressement*.

'The affair is somewhat discouraging,' murmured M. Caux. 'It appears that the Comte arrived in Nice the day before the murder.'

'If that is true, it will settle your affair nicely for you,' responded Poirot.

M. Carrège cleared his throat.

'We must not accept this alibi without very cautious inquiry,' he declared. He struck the bell upon the table with his hand.

In another minute a tall dark man, exquisitely dressed, with a somewhat haughty cast of countenance, entered the room. So very aristocratic-looking was the Count, that it would have seemed sheer heresy even to whisper that his father had been an obscure corn-chandler in Nantes – which, as a matter of fact, was the case. Looking at him, one would have been prepared to swear that innumerable ancestors of his must have perished by the guillotine in the French Revolution.

'I am here, gentlemen,' said the Count haughtily. 'May I ask why you wish to see me?'

'Pray be seated, Monsieur le Comte,' said the Examining Magistrate politely. 'It is the affair of the death of Madame Kettering that we are investigating.'

'The death of Madame Kettering? I do not understand.'

'You were – ahem! – acquainted with the lady, I believe, Monsieur le Comte?'

'Certainly I was acquainted with her. What has that to do with the matter?'

Sticking an eyeglass in his eye, he looked coldly round the room, his glance resting longest on Poirot, who was gazing at him with a kind of simple, innocent admiration which was most pleasing to the Count's vanity. M. Carrège leaned back in his chair and cleared his throat.

'You do not perhaps know, Monsieur le Comte' – he paused – 'that Madame Kettering was murdered?'

'Murdered? *Mon Dieu*, how terrible!'

The surprise and the sorrow were excellently done – so well done, indeed, as to seem wholly natural.

'Madame Kettering was strangled between Paris and Lyons,' continued M. Carrège, 'and her jewels were stolen.'

'It is iniquitous!' cried the Count warmly; 'the police should do something about these train bandits. Nowadays no one is safe.'

'In Madame's handbag,' continued the Judge, 'we found a letter to her from you. She had, it seemed, arranged to meet you?'

The Count shrugged his shoulders and spread out his hands.

'Of what use are concealments,' he said frankly. 'We are all men of the world. Privately and between ourselves, I admit the affair.'

'You met her in Paris and travelled down with her, I believe?' said M. Carrège.

'That was the original arrangement, but by Madame's wish it was changed. I was to meet her at Hyères.'

'You did not meet her on the train at Gare de Lyon on the evening of the 14th?'

'On the contrary, I arrived in Nice on the morning of that day, so what you suggest is impossible.'

'Quite so, quite so,' said M. Carrège. 'As a matter of form, you would perhaps give me an account of your movements during the evening and night of the 14th.'

The Count reflected for a minute.

'I dined in Monte Carle at the Café de Paris. Afterwards I went to the Le Sporting. I won a few thousand francs,' he shrugged his shoulders. 'I returned home at perhaps one o'clock.'

'Pardon me, Monsieur, but how did you return home?'

'In my own two-seater car.'

'No one was with you?'

'No one.'

'You could produce witnesses in support of this statement?'

'Doubtless many of my friends saw me there that evening. I dined alone.'

'Your servant admitted you on your return to your villa?'

'I let myself in with my own latch-key.'

'Ah!' murmured the Magistrate.

Again he struck the bell on the table with his hand. The door opened, and a messenger appeared.

'Bring in the maid, Mason,' said M. Carrège.

'Very good, Monsieur le Juge.'

Ada Mason was brought in.

'Will you be so good, Mademoiselle, as to look at this gentleman. To the best of your ability was it he who entered your mistress's compartment in Paris?'

The woman looked long and searchingly at the Count, who was, Poirot fancied, rather uneasy under this scrutiny.

'I could not say, sir, I am sure,' said Mason at last. 'It might be and again it might not. Seeing as how I only saw his back, it's hard to say. I rather think it *was* the gentleman.'

'But you are not sure?'

'No – o,' said Mason unwillingly; 'n – no, I am not sure.'

'You have seen this gentleman before in Curzon Street?'

Mason shook her head.

'I should not be likely to see any visitors that come to Curzon Street,' she explained, 'unless they were staying in the house.'

'Very well, that will do,' said the Examining Magistrate sharply.

Evidently he was disappointed.

'One moment,' said Poirot. 'There is a question I would like to put to Mademoiselle, if I may?'

'Certainly, M. Poirot – certainly, by all means.'

Poirot addressed himself to the maid.

'What happened to the tickets?'

'The tickets, sir?'

'Yes; the tickets from London to Nice. Did you or your mistress have them?'

'The mistress had her own Pullman ticket, sir; the others were in my charge.'

'What happened to them?'

'I gave them to the conductor on the French train, sir; he said it was usual. I hope I did right, sir?'

'Oh, quite right, quite right. A mere matter of detail.'

Both M. Caux and the Examining Magistrate looked at him curiously. Mason stood uncertainly for a minute or two, and then the magistrate gave her a brief nod of dismissal, and she went out. Poirot scribbled something on a scrap of paper and handed it across to M. Carrège. The latter read it and his brow cleared.

'Well, gentlemen,' demanded the Count haughtily, 'am I to be detained further?'

'Assuredly not, assuredly not,' M. Carrège hastened to say, with a great deal of amiability. 'Everything is now cleared up as regards your own position in this affair. Naturally, in view of Madame's letter, we were bound to question you.'

The Count rose, picked up his handsome stick from the corner, and, with rather a curt bow, left the room.

'And that is that,' said M. Carrège. 'You were quite right, M. Poirot – much better to let him feel he is not suspected. Two of my men will shadow him night and day, and at the same time we will go into the question of the alibi. It seems to me rather – er – a fluid one.'

'Possibly,' agreed Poirot thoughtfully.

'I asked M. Kettering to come here this morning,' continued the Magistrate, 'though really I doubt if we have much to ask him, but there are one or two suspicious circumstances—' He paused, rubbing his nose.

'Such as?' asked Poirot.

'Well' – the Magistrate coughed – 'this lady with whom he is said to be travelling – Mademoiselle Mirelle. She is staying at one hotel and he at another. That strikes me – er – as rather odd.'

'It looks,' said M. Caux, 'as though they were being careful.'

'Exactly,' said M. Carrège triumphantly; 'and what should they have to be careful about?'

'An excess of caution is suspicious, eh?' said Poirot.

'*Précisément.*'

'We might, I think,' murmured Poirot, 'ask M. Kettering one or two questions.'

The Magistrate gave instructions. A moment or two later, Derek Kettering, debonair as ever, entered the room.

'Good morning, Monsieur,' said the Judge politely.

'Good morning,' said Derek Kettering curtly. 'You sent for me. Has anything fresh turned up?'

'Pray sit down, Monsieur.'

Derek took a seat and flung his hat and stick on the table.

'Well?' he asked impatiently.

'We have, so far, no fresh data,' said M. Carrège cautiously.

'That's very interesting,' said Derek drily. 'Did you send for me here in order to tell me that?'

'We naturally thought, Monsieur, that you would like to be informed of the progress of the case,' said the Magistrate severely.

'Even if the progress is non-existent.'

'We also wished to ask you a few questions.'

'Ask away.'

'You are quite sure that you neither saw nor spoke with your wife on the train.'

'I've answered that already. I did not.'

'You had, no doubt, your reasons.'

Derek stared at him suspiciously.

'I – did – not – know – she – was – on – the – train,' he explained, spacing his words elaborately, as though to someone dull of intellect.

'That is what you say, yes,' murmured M. Carrège.

A quick frown suffused Derek's face.

'I should like to know what you are driving at. Do you know what I think, M. Carrège?'

'What do you think, Monsieur?'

'I think the French police are vastly overrated. Surely you must have some data as to these gangs of train robbers. It's outrageous that such a thing could happen on a *train de luxe* like that, and that the French police should be helpless to deal with the matter.'

'We are dealing with it, Monsieur, never fear.'

'Madame Kettering, I understand, did not leave a will,' interposed Poirot suddenly. His finger-tips were joined together, and he was looking intently at the ceiling.

'I don't think she ever made one,' said Kettering. 'Why?'

'It is a very pretty little fortune that you inherit there,' said Poirot – 'a very pretty little fortune.'

Although his eyes were still on the ceiling, he managed to see the dark flush that rose to Derek Kettering's face.

'What do you mean, and who are you?'

Poirot gently uncrossed his knees, withdrew his gaze from the ceiling, and looked the young man full in the face.

'My name is Hercule Poirot,' he said quietly, 'and I am probably the greatest detective in the world. You are quite sure that you did not see or speak to your wife on that train?'

'What are you getting at? Do you – do you mean to insinuate that I – I killed her?'

He laughed suddenly.

'I mustn't lose my temper; it's too palpably absurd. Why, if I killed her I should have had no need to steal her jewels, would I?'

'That is true,' murmured Poirot, with a rather crestfallen air. 'I did not think of that.'

'If ever there were a clear case of murder and robbery this is it,' said Derek Kettering. 'Poor Ruth, it was those damned rubies did for her. It must have got about she had them with her. There has been murder done for those same stones before now, I believe.'

Poirot sat up suddenly in his chair. A very faint green light glowed in his eyes. He looked extraordinarily like a sleek, well-fed cat.

'One more question, M. Kettering,' he said. 'Will you give me the date when you last saw your wife?'

'Let me see,' Kettering reflected. 'It must have been – yes, over three weeks ago. I am afraid I can't give you the date exactly.'

'No matter,' said Poirot drily; 'that is all I wanted to know.'

'Well,' said Derek Kettering impatiently, 'anything further?'

He looked towards M. Carrège. The latter sought inspiration from Poirot, and received it in a very faint shake of the head.

'No, M. Kettering,' he said politely; 'no, I do not think we need trouble you any further. I wish you good morning.'

'Good morning,' said Kettering. He went out, banging the door behind him.

Poirot leaned forward and spoke sharply, as soon as the young man was out of the room.

'Tell me,' he said peremptorily, 'when did you speak of these rubies to M. Kettering?'

'I have not spoken of them,' said M. Carrège. 'It was only yesterday afternoon that we learnt about them from M. Van Aldin.'

'Yes; but there was a mention of them in the Comte's letter.'

M. Carrège looked pained.

'Naturally I did not speak of that letter to M. Kettering,' he said in a shocked voice. 'It would have been most indiscreet at the present juncture of affairs.'

Poirot leaned forward and tapped the table.

'*Then how did he know about them*?' he demanded softly. 'Madame could not have told him, for he has not seen her for three weeks. It seems unlikely that either M. Van Aldin or his secretary would have mentioned them; their interviews with him have been on entirely different lines, and there has not been any hint or reference to them in the newspapers.'

He got up and took his hat and stick.

'And yet,' he murmured to himself, 'our gentleman knows all about them. I wonder now, yes, I wonder!'

——— 18 ———

DEREK LUNCHES

Derek Kettering went straight to the Negresco, where he ordered a couple of cocktails and disposed of them rapidly; then he stared moodily out over the dazzling blue sea. He noted the passers-by mechanically – a damned dull crowd, badly dressed, and painfully uninteresting; one hardly ever saw anything worthwhile nowadays. Then he corrected this last impression rapidly, as a woman placed herself at a table a little distance away from him. She was wearing a marvellous confection of orange and black, with a little hat that shaded her face. He ordered a third cocktail; again he stared out to sea, and then suddenly he started. A well-known perfume assailed his nostrils, and then he looked up to see the orange-and-black lady standing beside him. He saw her face now, and recognised her. It was Mirelle. She was smiling that insolent, seductive smile he knew so well.

'Dereek!' she murmured. 'You are pleased to see me, no?' She dropped into a seat the other side of the table.

'But welcome me, then, stupid one,' she mocked.

'This is an unexpected pleasure,' said Derek, 'When did you leave London?'

She shrugged her shoulders.

'A day or two ago?'

'And the Parthenon?'

'I have, how do you say it? – given them the chuck!'

'Really?'

'You are not very amiable, Dereek.'

'Do you expect me to be?'

Mirelle lit a cigarette and puffed at it for a few minutes before saying:

'You think, perhaps, that it is not prudent so soon?'

Derek stared at her, then shrugged his shoulders, and remarked formally:

'You are lunching here?'

'*Mais oui*. I am lunching with you.'

'I am exceedingly sorry,' said Derek. 'I have a very important engagement.'

'*Mon Dieu*! But you men are like children,' exclaimed the dancer. 'But yes, it is the spoilt child that you act to me, ever since that day in London when you flung yourself out of my flat, you sulk. Ah! *mais c'est inouï*!'

'My dear girl,' said Derek, 'I really don't know what you are talking about. We agreed in London that rats desert a sinking ship, that is all that there is to be said.'

In spite of his careless words, his face looked haggard and strained. Mirelle leaned forward suddenly.

'You cannot deceive me,' she murmured. 'I know – I know what you have done for me.'

He looked up at her sharply. Some undercurrent in her voice arrested his attention. She nodded her head at him.

'Ah! have no fear; I am discreet. You are magnificent! You have a superb courage, but, all the same, it was I who gave you the idea that day, when I said to you in London that accidents sometimes happened. And you are not in danger? The police do not suspect you?'

'What the devil—?'

'Hush!'

She held up a slim olive hand with one big emerald on the little finger.

'You are right, I should not haves spoken so in a public place. We will not speak of the matter again, but our troubles are ended; our life together will be wonderful – wonderful!'

Derek laughed suddenly – a harsh, disagreeable laugh.

'So the rats come back, do they? Two million makes a difference – of course it does. I ought to have known that.' He laughed again. 'You will help me to spend that two million, won't you, Mirelle? You know how, no woman better.' He laughed again.

'Hush!' cried the dancer. 'What is the matter with you, Dereek? See – people are turning to stare at you.'

'Me? I will tell you what is the matter. I have finished with you, Mirelle. Do you hear? Finished!'

Mirelle did not take it as he expected her to do. She looked at him for a minute or two, and then she smiled softly.

'But what a child! You are angry – you are sore, and all because I am practical. Did I not always tell you that I adored you?'

She leaned forward.

'But I know you, Dereek. Look at me – see, it is Mirelle who speaks to you. You cannot live without her, you know it. I loved you before, I will love you a hundred times more now. I will make life wonderful for you – but wonderful. There is no one like Mirelle.'

Her eyes burned into his. She saw him grow pale and draw in his breath, and she smiled to herself contentedly. She knew her own magic and power over men.

'That is settled,' she said softly, and gave a little laugh. 'And now, Dereek, will you give me lunch?'

'No.'

He drew in his breath sharply and rose to his feet.

'I am sorry, but I told you – I have got an engagement.'

'You are lunching with someone else? Bah! I don't believe it.'

'I am lunching with that lady over there.'

He crossed abruptly to where a lady in white had just come up the steps. He addressed her a little breathlessly.

'Miss Grey, will you – will you have lunch with me? You met me at Lady Tamplin's, if you remember.'

Katherine looked at him for a mimute or two with those thoughtful grey eyes that said so much.

'Thank you,' she said, after a moment's pause; 'I should like to very much.'

19

AN UNEXPECTED VISITOR

The Comte de la Roche had just finished *déjeuner,* consisting of an *omelette fines herbes,* an *entrecôte Bearnaise,* and a *Savarin au Rhum.* Wiping his fine black moustache delicately with his table napkin, the Comte rose from the table. He passed through the salon of the villa, noting with appreciation the few *objets d'art* which were carelessly scattered about. The Louis XV snuff-box, the satin shoe worn by Marie Antoinette, and the other historic trifles that were part of the Comte's *mise en scène.* They were, he would explain to his fair visitors, heirlooms in his family. Passing through on to the terrace the Comte looked out on to the Mediterranean with an unseeing eye. He was in no mood for appreciating the beauties of scenery. A fully matured scheme had been rudely brought to naught, and his plans had to be cast afresh. Stretching himself out in a basket chair, a cigarette held between his white fingers, the Comte pondered deeply.

Presently Hipolyte, his man-servant, brought out coffee and a choice of liqueurs. The Comte selected some very fine old brandy.

As the man-servant was preparing to depart, the Comte arrested him with a slight gesture. Hipolyte stood respectfully to attention. His countenance was hardly a prepossessing one, but the correctitude of his demeanour went far to obliterate the fact. He was now the picture of respectful attention.

'It is possible,' said the Comte, 'that in the course of the next few days various strangers may come to the house. They will endeavour to scrape acquaintance with you and with Marie. They will probably ask you various questions concerning me.'

'Yes, Monsieur le Comte.'

'Perhaps this has already happened?'

'No, Monsieur le Comte.'

'There have been no strangers about the place? You are certain?'

'There has been no one, Monsieur le Comte.'

'That is well,' said the Comte drily; 'nevertheless they will come – I am sure of it. They will ask questions.'

Hipolyte looked at his master in intelligent anticipation.

The Comte spoke slowly, without looking at Hipolyte.

'As you know, I arrived here last Tuesday morning. If the police or any other inquirer should question you, do not forget that fact. I arrived on Tuesday, the 14th – not Wednesday, the 15th. You understand?'

'Perfectly, Monsieur le Comte.'

'In an affair where a lady is concerned, it is always necessary to be discreet. I feel certain, Hipolyte, that you can be discreet.'

'I can be discreet, Monsieur.'

'And Marie?'

'Marie also. I will answer for her.'

'That is well then,' murmured the Comte.

When Hipolyte had withdrawn, the Comte sipped his black coffee with a reflective air. Occasionally he frowned, once he shook his head slightly, twice he nodded it. Into the midst of these cogitations came Hipolyte once more.

'A lady, Monsieur.'

'A lady?'

The Comte was surprised. Not that a visit from a lady was an unusual thing at the Villa Marina, but at this particular moment the Comte could not think who the lady was likely to be.

'She is, I think, a lady not know to Monsieur,' murmured the valet helpfully.

The Comte was surprised. Not that a visit from a lady was an 'Show her out here, Hipolyte,' he commanded.

A moment later a marvellous vision in orange and black stepped out in the terrace, accompanied by a strong perfume of exotic blossoms.

'Monsieur le Comte de la Roche?'

'At your service, Mademoiselle,' said the Comte, bowing.

'My name is Mirelle. You may have heard of me.'

'Ah, indeed, Mademoiselle, but who has not been enchanted by the dancing of Mademoiselle Mirelle? Exquisite!'

The dancer acknowledged this compliment with a brief mechanical smile.

'My descent upon you is unceremonious,' she began.

'But seat yourself, I beg of you, Mademoiselle,' cried the Comte, bringing forward a chair.

Behind the gallantry of his manners he was observing her narrowly. There were very few things that the Comte did not know about women. True, his experience had not lain much in ladies of Mirelle's class, who were themselves predatory. He and the dancer were, in a sense, birds of a feather. His arts, the Comte knew, would be thrown away on Mirelle. She was a

Parisienne, and a shrewd one. Nevertheless, there was one thing that the Comte could recognise infallibly when he saw it. He knew at once that he was in the presence of a very angry woman, and an angry woman, as the Comte was well aware, always says more than is prudent, and is occasionally a source of profit to a level-headed gentleman who keeps cool.

'It is most amiable of you, Mademoiselle, to honour my poor abode thus.'

'We have mutual friends in Paris,' said Mirelle. 'I have heard of you from them, but I come to see you today for another reason. I have heard of you since I came to Nice – in a different way, you understand.'

'Ah?' said the Comte softly.

'I will be brutal,' continued the dancer; 'nevertheless, believe that I have your welfare at heart. They are saying in Nice, Monsieur le Comte, that you are the murderer of the English lady, Madame Kettering.'

'I! – the murderer of Madame Kettering? Bah! But how absurd!'

He spoke more languidly than indignantly, knowing that he would thus provoke her further.

'But yes,' she insisted, 'it is as I tell you.'

'It amuses people to talk,' murmured the Comte indifferently. 'It would be beneath me to take such wild accusations seriously.'

'You do not understand.' Mirelle bent forward, her dark eyes flashing. 'It is not the idle talk of those in the streets. It is the police.'

'The police – ah?'

The Comte sat up, alert once more.

Mirelle nodded her head vigorously several times.

'Yes, yes. You comprehend me – I have friends everywhere. The Prefect himself—' She left the sentence unfinished, with an eloquent shrug of the shoulders.

'Who is not indiscreet where a beautiful woman is concerned?' murmured the Count politely.

'The police believe that you killed Madame Kettering. But they are wrong.'

'Certainly they are wrong,' agreed the Comte easily.

'You say that, but you do not know the truth. I do.'

The Comte looked at her curiously.

'You know who killed Madame Kettering? Is that what you would say, Mademoiselle?'

Mirelle nodded vehemently.

'Yes.'

'Who was it?' asked the Comte sharply.

'Her husband.' She leant across to the Comte, speaking in a low voice that vibrated with anger and excitement. 'It was her husband who killed her.'

The Comte leaned back in his chair. His face was a mask.

'Let me ask you, Mademoiselle – how do you know this?'

'How do I know it?' Mirelle sprang to her feet, with a laugh. 'He boasted of it beforehand. He was ruined, bankrupt, dishonoured. Only the death of his wife could save him. He told me so. He travelled on the same train – but she was not to know it. Why was that, I ask you? So that he might creep upon her in the night— Ah!' – she shut her eyes – 'I can see it happening . . .'

The Count coughed.

'Perhaps – perhaps,' he murmured. 'But surely, Mademoiselle, in that case he would not steal the jewels?'

'The jewels!' breathed Mirelle. 'The jewels. Ah! Those rubies . . .'

Her eyes grew misty, a far-away light in them. The Comte looked at her curiously, wondering for the hundredth time at the magical influence of precious stones on the female sex. He recalled her to practical matters.

'What do you want me to do, Mademoiselle?'

Mirelle became alert and business-like once more.

'Surely it is simple. You will go to the police. You will say to them that M. Kettering committed this crime.'

'And if they do not believe me? If they ask for proof?' He was eying her closely.

Mirelle laughed softly, and drew her orange-and-black wrap closer around her.

'Send them to me, Monsieur le Comte,' she said softly; 'I will give them the proof they want.'

Upon that she was gone, an impetuous whirlwind, her errand accomplished.

The Comte looked after her, his eyebrows delicately raised.

'She is in a fury,' he murmured. 'What has happened now to upset her? But she shows her hand plainly. Does she really believe that Mr Kettering killed his wife? She would like me to believe it. She would even like the police to believe it.'

He smiled to himself. He had no intention whatsoever of going to the police. He saw various other possibilities; to judge by his smile, an agreeable vista of them.

Presently, however, his brow clouded. According to Mirelle,

he was suspected by the police. That might be true or it might not. An angry woman of the type of the dancer was not likely to bother about the strict veracity of her statements. On the other hand, she might easily have obtained – inside information. In that case – his mouth set grimly – in that case he must take certain precautions.

He went into the house and questioned Hipolyte closely once more as to whether any strangers had been to the house. The valet was positive in his assurances that this was not the case. The Comte went up to his bedroom and crossed over to an old bureau that stood against the wall. He let down the lid of this, and his delicate fingers sought for a spring at the back of one of the pigeon-holes. A secret drawer flew out; in it was a small brown paper package. The Comte took this out and weighed it in his hand carefully for a minute or two. Raising his hand to his head, with a single grimace he pulled out a single hair. This he placed on the lip of the drawer and shut it carefully. Still carrying the small parcel in his hand, he went downstairs and out of the house to the garage, where stood a scarlet two-seater car. Ten minutes later he had taken the road for Monte Carlo.

He spent a few hours at the Casino, then sauntered out into the town. Presently he re-entered the car and drove off in the direction of Mentone. Earlier in the afternoon he had noticed an inconspicuous grey car some little distance behind him. He noticed it again now. He smiled to himself. The road was climbing steadily upwards. The Comte's foot pressed hard on the accelerator. The little red car had been specially built to the Comte's design, and had a far more powerful engine than would have been suspected from its appearance. It shot ahead.

Presently he looked back and smiled; the grey car was following behind. Smothered in dust, the little red car leaped along the road. It was travelling now at a dangerous pace, but the Comte was a first-class driver. Now they were going down hill, twisting and curving unceasingly. Presently the car slackened speed, and finally came to a standstill before a Bureau de Poste. The Comte jumped out, lifted the lid of the tool chest, extracted the small brown paper parcel and hurried into the post office. Two minutes later he was driving once more in the direction of Mentone. When the grey car arrived there, the Comte was drinking English five o'clock tea on the terrace of one of the hotels.

Later, he drove back to Monte Carlo, dined there, and

reached home once more at eleven o'clock. Hipolyte came out to meet him with a disturbed face.

'Ah! Monsieur le Comte has arrived. Monsieur le Comte did not telephone me, by any chance?'

The Comte shook his head.

'And yet at three o'clock I received a summons from Monsieur le Comte, to present myself to him at Nice, at the Negresco.'

'Really,' said the Comte; 'and you went?'

'Certainly, Monsieur, but at the Negresco they knew nothing of Monsieur le Comte. He had not been there.'

'Ah,' said the Comte, 'doubtless at that hour Marie was out doing her afternoon marketing?'

'That is so, Monsieur le Comte.'

'Ah, well,' said the Comte, 'it is of no importance. A mistake.' He went upstairs, smiling to himself.

Once within his own room, he bolted his door and looked sharply round. Everything seemed as usual. He opened various drawers and cupboards. Then he nodded to himself. Things had been replaced almost exactly as he had left them, but not quite. It was evident that a very thorough search had been made.

He went over to the bureau and pressed the hidden spring. The drawer flew open, but the hair was no longer where he had placed it. He nodded his head several times.

'They are excellent, our French police,' he murmured to himself – 'excellent. Nothing escapes them.'

20

KATHERINE MAKES A FRIEND

On the following morning Katherine and Lenox were sitting on the terrace of the Villa Marguerite. Something in the nature of a friendship was springing up between them, despite the difference in age. But for Lenox, Katherine would have found life at the Villa Marguerite quite intolerable. The Kettering case was the topic of the moment. Lady Tamplin frankly exploited her guest's connection with the affair for all it was worth. The most persistent rebuffs that Katherine could administer quite failed to pierce Lady Tamplin's self-esteem.

Lenox adopted a detached attitude, seemingly amused at her mother's manœuvres, and yet with a sympathetic understanding of Katherine's feelings. The situation was not helped by Chubby, whose naïve delight was unquenchable, and who introduced Katherine to all and sundry as:

'This is Miss Grey. You know that Blue Train business? She was in it up to the ears! Had a long talk with Ruth Kettering a few hours before the murder! Bit of luck for her, eh?'

A few remarks of this kind had provoked Katherine that morning to an unusually tart rejoinder, and when they were alone together Lenox observed in her slow drawl:

'Not used to exploitation, are you? You have a lot to learn, Katherine.'

'I am sorry I lost my temper. I don't, as a rule.'

'It is about time you learnt to blow off steam. Chubby is only an ass; there is no harm in him. Mother, of course, is trying, but you can lose your temper with her until Kingdom come, and it won't make any impression. She will open large, sad blue eyes at you and not care a bit.'

Katherine made no reply to this filial observation, and Lenox presently went on:

'I am rather like Chubby. I delight in a good murder, and besides – well, knowing Derek makes a difference.'

Katherine nodded.

'So you lunched with him yesterday,' pursued Lenox reflectively. 'Do you like him, Katherine?'

Katherine considered for a minute or two.

'I don't know,' she said very slowly.

'He is very attractive.'

'Yes, he is attractive.'

'What don't you like about him?'

Katherine did not reply to the question, or at any rate not directly. 'He spoke of his wife's death,' she said. 'He said he would not pretend that it had been anything but a bit of most marvellous luck for him.'

'And that shocked you, I suppose,' said Lenox. She paused, and then added in rather a queer tone of voice: 'He likes you, Katherine.'

'He gave me a very good lunch,' said Katherine, smiling.

Lenox refused to be side-tracked.

'I saw it the night he came here,' she said thoughtfully. 'The way he looked at you; and you are not his usual type – just the opposite. Well, I suppose it is like religion – you get it at a certain age.'

'Mademoiselle is wanted at the telephone,' said Marie, appearing at the window of the salon. 'M. Hercule Poirot desires to speak with her.'

'More blood and thunder. Go on, Katherine; go and dally with your detective.'

M. Hercule Poirot's voice came neat and precise in its intonation to Katherine's ear.

'That is Mademoiselle Grey who speaks? *Bon*. Mademoiselle, I have a word for you from M. Van Aldin, the father of Madame Kettering. He wishes very much to speak with you, either at the Villa Marguerite or at his hotel, whichever you prefer.'

Katherine reflected for a moment, but she decided that for Van Aldin to come to the Villa Marguerite would be both painful and unnecessary. Lady Tamplin would have hailed his advent with far too much delight. She never lost a chance to cultivate millionaires. She told Poirot that she would much rather come to Nice.

'Excellent, Mademoiselle. I will call for you myself in an auto. Shall we say in about three-quarters of an hour?'

Punctually to the moment Poirot appeared. Katherine was waiting for him, and they drove off at once.

'Well, Mademoiselle, how goes it?'

She looked at his twinkling eyes, and was confirmed in her first impression that there was something very attractive about M. Hercule Poirot.

'This is our own *roman policier*, is it not?' said Poirot. 'I made you the promise that we should study it together. And me, I always keep my promises.'

'You are too kind,' murmured Katherine.

'Ah, you mock yourself at me; but you do want to hear the developments of the case, or do you not?'

Katherine admitted that she did, and Poirot proceeded to sketch for her a thumbnail portrait of the Comte de la Roche.

'You think he killed her,' said Katherine thoughtfully.

'That is the theory,' said Poirot guardedly.

'Do you yourself believe that?'

'I did not say so. And you, Mademoiselle, what do you think?'

Katherine shook her head.

'How should I know? I don't know anything about those things, but I should say that—'

'Yes,' said Poirot encouragingly.

'Well – from what you say the Count does not sound the kind of man who would actually kill anybody.'

'Ah! Very good,' cried Poirot. 'You agree with me; that is just what I have said.' He looked at her sharply. 'But tell me, you have met Mr Derek Kettering?'

'I met him at Lady Tamplin's, and I lunched with him yesterday.'

'A *mauvais sujet*,' said Poirot, shaking his head; but *les femmes* – they like that, eh?'

He twinkled at Katherine and she laughed.

'He is the kind of man one would notice anywhere,' continued Poirot. 'Doubtless you observed him on the Blue Train?'

'Yes, I noticed him.'

'In the restaurant car?'

'No. I didn't notice him at meals at all. I only saw him once – going into his wife's compartment.'

Poirot nodded. 'A strange business,' he murmured. 'I believe you said you were awake, Mademoiselle, and looked out of your window at Lyons? You saw no tall dark man such as the Comte de la Roche leave the train?'

Katherine shook her head. 'I don't think I saw anyone at all,' she said. 'There was a youngish lad in a cap and overcoat who got out, but I don't think he was leaving the train, only walking up and down the platform. There was a fat Frenchman with a beard, in pyjamas and an overcoat, who wanted a cup of coffee. Otherwise, I think there were only the train attendants.'

Poirot nodded his head several times. 'It is like this, you see,' he confided, 'the Comte de la Roche has an alibi. An alibi, it is a very pestilential thing, and always open to the gravest suspicion. But here we are!'

They went straight up to Van Aldin's suite, where they found Knighton. Poirot introduced him to Katherine. After a few commonplaces had been exchanged, Knighton said: 'I will tell Mr Van Aldin that Miss Grey is here.'

He went through a second door into an adjoining room. There was a low murmur of voices, and then Van Aldin came into the room and advanced towards Katherine with outstretched hand, giving her at the same time a shrewd and penetrating glance.

'I am pleased to meet you, Miss Grey,' he said simply. 'I have been wanting very badly to hear what you can tell me about Ruth.'

The quiet simplicity of the millionaire's manner appealed to Katherine strongly. She felt herself in the presence of a very genuine grief, the more real for its absence of outward sign.

He drew forward a chair.

'Sit here, will you, and just tell me all about it.'

Poirot and Knighton retired discreetly into the other room, and Katherine and Van Aldin were left alone together. She found no difficulty in her task. Quite simply and naturally she related her conversation with Ruth Kettering, word for word as nearly as she could. He listened in silence, leaning back in his chair, with one hand shading his eyes. When she had finished he said quietly:

'Thank you, my dear.'

They both sat silent for a minute or two. Katherine felt that words of sympathy would be out of place. When the millionaire spoke, it was in a different tone:

'I am very grateful to you, Miss Grey. I think you did something to ease my poor Ruth's mind in the last hours of her life. Now I want to ask you something. You know – M. Poirot will have told you – about the scoundrel that my poor girl had got herself mixed up with. He was the man of whom she spoke to you – the man she was going to meet. In your judgment, do you think she might have changed her mind after her conversation with you? Do you think she meant to go back on her word?'

'I can't honestly tell you. She had certainly come to some decision, and seemed more cheerful in consequence of it.'

'She gave you no idea where she intended to meet the skunk – whether in Paris or at Hyères?'

Katherine shook her head.

'She said nothing as to that.'

'Ah!' said Van Aldin thoughtfully, 'and that is the important point. Well, time will show.'

He got up and opened the door of the adjoining room. Poirot and Knighton came back.

Katherine declined the millionaire's invitation to lunch, and Knighton went down with her and saw her into the waiting car. He returned to find Poirot and Van Aldin deep in conversation.

'If we only knew,' said the millionaire thoughtfully, 'what decision Ruth came to. It might have been any of half a dozen. She might have meant to leave the train at Paris and cable to me. She may have meant to have gone on to the south of France and have an explanation with the Count there. We are in the dark – absolutely in the dark. But we have the maid's word for it that she was both startled and dismayed at the Count's appearance at the station in Paris. That was clearly not part of the preconceived plan. You agree with me, Knighton?'

The secretary started. 'I beg your pardon, Mr Van Aldin. I was not listening.'

'Day-dreaming, eh?' said Van Aldin. 'That's not like you. I believe that girl has bowled you over.'

Knighton blushed.

'She is a remarkably nice girl,' said Van Aldin thoughtfully, 'very nice. Did you happen to notice her eyes?'

'Any man,' said Knighton, 'would be bound to notice her eyes.'

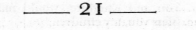

21

AT THE TENNIS

Several days had elapsed. Katherine had been for a walk by herself one morning, and came back to find Lenox grinning at her expectantly.

'Your young man has been ringing you up, Katherine!'

'Who do you call my young man?'

'A new one – Rufus Van Aldin's secretary. You seem to have made rather an impression there. You are becoming a serious breaker of hearts, Katherine. First Derek Kettering, and now this young Knighton. The funny thing is that I remember him quite well. He was in Mother's War Hospital that she ran out here. I was only a kid of about eight at the time.'

'Was he badly wounded?'

'Shot in the leg, if I remember rightly – rather a nasty business. I think the doctors messed it up a bit. They said he wouldn't limp or anything, but when he left here he was still completely dot and go one.'

Lady Tamplin came out and joined them.

'Have you been telling Katherine about Major Knighton?' she asked. 'Such a dear fellow! Just at first I didn't remember him – one has so many – but now it all comes back.'

'He was a bit too unimportant to be remembered before,' said Lenox. 'Now that he is a secretary to an American millionaire, it is a very different matter.'

'Darling!' said Lady Tamplin in her vague reproachful voice.

'What did Major Knighton ring up about?' inquired Katherine.

'He asked if you would like to go to the tennis this afternoon. If so, he would call for you in a car. Mother and I accepted for you with *empressement*. Whilst you dally with a millionaire's secretary, you might give me a chance with the millionaire, Katherine. He is about sixty, I suppose, so that he will be looking about for a nice sweet young thing like me.'

'I should like to meet Mr Van Aldin,' said Lady Tamplin earnestly; 'one has heard so much of him. Those fine rugged figures of the Western world' – she broke off – 'so fascinating,' she murmured.

'Major Knighton was very particular to say it was Mr Van Aldin's invitation,' said Lenox. 'He said it so often that I began to smell a rat. You and Knighton would make a very nice pair, Katherine. Bless you, my children.'

Katherine laughed, and went upstairs to change her clothes.

Knighton arrived soon after lunch and endured manfully Lady Tamplin's transports of recognition.

When they were driving together towards Cannes he remarked to Katherine: 'Lady Tamplin has changed wonderfully little.'

'In manner or appearance?'

'Both. She must be, I suppose, well over forty, but she is a remarkably beautiful woman still.'

'She is,' agreed Katherine.

'I am very glad you could come today,' went on Knighton. 'M. Poirot is going to be there also. What an extraordinary little man he is. Do you know him well, Miss Grey?'

Katherine shook her head. 'I met him on the train on the way here. I was reading a detective novel, and I happened to say something about such things not happening in real life. Of course, I had no idea of who he was.'

'He is a very remarkable person,' said Knighton slowly, 'and has done some very remarkable things. He has a kind of genius for going to the root of the matter, and right up to the end no one has any idea of what he is really thinking. I remember I was staying at a house in Yorkshire, and Lady Clanravon's jewels were stolen. It seemed at first to be a simple robbery, but it completely baffled the local police. I wanted them to call in Hercule Poirot, and said he was the only man who could help them, but they pinned their faith to Scotland Yard.'

'And what happened?' said Katherine curiously.

'The jewels were never recovered,' said Knighton drily.

'You really do believe in him?'

'I do indeed. The Comte de la Roche is a pretty wily customer. He has wriggled out of most things. But I think he has met his match in Hercule Poirot.'

'The Comte de la Roche,' said Katherine thoughtfully; 'so you really think he did it?'

'Of course.' Knighton looked at her in astonishment. 'Don't you?'

'Oh yes,' said Katherine hastily; 'that is, I mean, if it was not just an ordinary train robbery.'

'It might be, of course,' agreed the other, 'but it seems to me that the Comte de la Roche fits into this business particularly well.'

'And yet he has an alibi.'

'Oh, alibis!' Knighton laughed, his face broke into his attractive boyish smile.

'You confess that you have read detective stories, Miss Grey. You must know that anyone who has a perfect alibi is always open to grave suspicion.'

'Do you think that real life is like that?' asked Katherine, smiling.

'Why not? Fiction is founded on fact.'

'But is rather superior to it,' suggested Katherine.

'Perhaps. Anyway, if I was a criminal I should not like to have Hercule Poirot on my track.'

'No more should I,' said Katherine, and laughed.

They were met on arrival by Poirot. As the day was warm he was attired in a white duck suit, with a white camellia in his buttonhole.

'*Bonjour*, Mademoiselle,' said Poirot. 'I look very English do I not?'

'You look wonderful,' said Katherine tactfully.

'You mock yourself at me,' said Poirot genially. 'But no matter. Papa Poirot, he always laughs the last.'

'Where is Mr Van Aldin?' asked Knighton.

'He will meet us at our seats. To tell you the truth, my friend, he is not too well pleased with me. Oh, those Americans – the repose, the calm, they know it not! Mr Van Aldin, he would that I fly myself in the pursuit of criminals through all the byways of Nice.'

'I should have thought myself that it would not have been a bad plan,' observed Knighton.

'You are wrong,' said Poirot; 'in these matters one needs not energy but finesse. At the tennis one meets everyone. That is so important. Ah, there is Mr Kettering.'

Derek came abruptly up to them. He looked reckless and angry, as though something had arisen to upset him. He and Knighton greeted each other with some frigidity. Poirot alone seemed unconscious of any sense of strain, and chatted pleasantly in a laudable attempt to put everyone at their ease. He paid little compliments.

'It is amazing, M. Kettering, how well you speak the French,' he observed – 'so well that you could be taken for a French-man if you chose. That is a very rare accomplishment among Englishmen.'

'I wish I did,' said Katherine. 'I am only too well aware that my French is of a painfully British order.'

They reached their seats and sat down, and almost immedi-ately Knighton perceived his employer signalling to him from the other end of the court, and went off to speak to him.

'Me, I approve of that young man,' said Poirot, sending a beaming smile after the departing secretary; 'and you, Made-moiselle?'

'I like him very much.'

'And you, M. Kettering?'

Some quick rejoinder was springing to Derek's lips, but he checked it as though something in the little Belgian's twinkling eyes had made him suddenly alert. He spoke carefully, choosing his words.

'Knighton is a very good fellow,' he said.

Just for a moment Katherine fancied that Poirot looked dis-appointed.

'He is a great admirer of yours, M. Poirot,' she said, and she related some of the things that Knighton had said. It amused her to see the little man plume himself like a bird, thrusting out his chest, and assuming an air of mock modesty that would have deceived no one.

'That reminds me, Mademoiselle,' he said suddenly, 'I have a little matter of business I have to speak to you about. When you were sitting talking to that poor lady in the train, I think you must have dropped a cigarette case.'

Katherine looked rather astonished. 'I don't think so,' she said. Poirot drew from his pocket a cigarette case of soft blue leather, with the initial 'K' on it in gold.

'No, that is not mine,' Katherine said.

'Ah, a thousand apologies. It was doubtless Madame's own.

"K", of course, stands for Kettering. We were doubtful, because she had another cigarette case in her bag, and it seemed odd that she should have two.' He turned to Derek suddenly. 'You do not know, I suppose, whether this was your wife's case or not?'

Derek seemed momentarily taken aback. He stammered a little in his reply: 'I – I don't know. I suppose so.'

'It is not yours by any chance?'

'Certainly not. If it were mine it would hardly have been in my wife's possession.'

Poirot looked more ingenuous and childlike than ever.

'I thought perhaps you might have dropped it when you were in your wife's compartment,' he explained guilelessly.

'I never was there. I have already told the police that a dozen times.'

'A thousand pardons,' said Poirot, with his most apologetic air. 'It was Mademoiselle here who mentioned having seen you going in.'

He stopped with an air of embarrassment.

Katherine looked at Derek. His face had gone rather white, but perhaps that was her fancy. His laugh, when it came, was natural enough.

'You made a mistake, Miss Grey,' he said easily. 'From what the police have told me, I gather that my own compartment was only a door or two away from that of my wife's – though I never suspected the fact at the time. You must have seen me going into my own compartment.' He got up quickly as he saw Van Aldin and Knighton approaching.

'I'm going to leave you now,' he announced. 'I can't stand my father-in-law at any price.'

Van Aldin greeted Katherine very courteously, but was clearly in a bad humour.

'You seem fond of watching tennis, M. Poirot,' he growled.

'It is a pleasure to me, yes,' replied Poirot placidly.

'It is as well you are in France,' said Van Aldin. 'We are made of sterner stuff in the States. Business comes before pleasure there.'

Poirot did not take offence; indeed, he smiled gently and confidingly at the irate millionaire.

'Do not enrage yourself, I beg of you. Everyone his own methods. Me, I have always found it a delightful and pleasing idea to combine business and pleasure together.'

He glanced at the other two. They were deep in conversation, absorbed in each other. Poirot nodded his head in satisfaction, and then leant towards the millionaire, lowering his voice as he did so.

'It is not only for pleasure that I am here, M. Van Aldin. Observe just opposite us that old man – the one with the yellow face and the venerable beard.'

'Well, what of him?'

'That,' Poirot said, 'is M. Papopolus.'

'A Greek, eh?'

'As you say – a Greek. He is a dealer in antiques of world-wide reputation. He has a small shop in Paris, and he is suspected by the police of being something more.'

'What?'

'A receiver of stolen goods, especially jewels. There is nothing as to the re-cutting and re-setting of gems that he does not know. He deals with the highest in Europe and with the lowest of the riff-raff of the underworld.'

Van Aldin was looking at Poirot with suddenly awakened attention.

'Well?' he demanded, a new note in his voice.

'I ask myself,' said Poirot, 'I, Hercule Poirot' – he thumped himself dramatically on the chest – 'ask myself *why is M. Papopolous suddenly come to Nice?*'

Van Aldin was impressed. For a moment he had doubted Poirot and suspected the little man of being past his job, a *poseur* only. Now, in a moment, he switched back to his original opinion. He looked straight at the little detective.

'I must apologise to you, M. Poirot.'

Poirot waved the apology aside with an extravagant gesture.

'Bah!' he cried, 'all that is of no importance. Now listen, M. Van Aldin; I have news for you.'

The millionaire looked sharply at him, all his interest aroused.

Poirot nodded.

'It is as I say. You will be interested. As you know, M. Van Aldin, the Comte de la Roche has been under surveillance ever since his interview with the Juge d'Instruction. The day after that, during his absence, the Villa Marina was searched by the police.'

'Well,' said Van Aldin, 'did they find anything? I bet they didn't.'

Poirot made him a little bow.

'Your acumen is not at fault, M. Van Aldin. They found nothing of an incriminating nature. It was not to be expected that they would. The Comte de la Roche, as your expressive idiom has it, was not born on the preceding day. He is an astute gentleman with great experience.'

'Well, go on,' growled Van Aldin.

'It may be, of course, that the Comte had nothing of a compromising nature to conceal. But we must not neglect the possibility. If, then, he has something to conceal, where is it? Not in his house – the police searched thoroughly. Not on his person, for he knows that he is liable to arrest at any minute. There remains – his car. As I say, he was under surveillance. He was followed on that day to Monte Carlo. From there he went by road to Mentone, driving himself. His car is a very powerful one, it outdistanced his pursuers, and for about a quarter of an hour they completely lost sight of him.'

'And during that time you think he concealed something by the roadside?' asked Van Aldin, keenly interested.

'By the roadside, no. *Ca n'est pas pratique.* But listen now – me, I have made a little suggestion to M. Carrège. He is graciously pleased to approve of it. In each Bureau de Poste in the neighbourhood it has been seen to that there is someone who knows the Comte de la Roche by sight. Because, you see, Messieurs, the best way of hiding a thing is by sending it away by the post.'

'Well?' demanded Van Aldin; his face was keenly alight with interest and expectation.

'Well – *voilà!* ' With a dramatic flourish Poirot drew out from his pocket a loosely wrapped brown paper package from which the string had been removed.

'During that quarter of an hour's interval, our good gentleman mailed this.'

'The address?' asked the other sharply.

Poirot nodded his head.

'Might have told us something, but unfortunately it does not. The package was addressed to one of these little newspaper shops in Paris where letters and parcels are kept until called for on payment of a small commission.'

'Yes, but what is inside?' demanded Van Aldin impatiently.

Poirot unwrapped the brown paper and disclosed a square cardboard box. He looked round him.

'It is a good moment,' he said quietly. 'All eyes are on the tennis. Look, Monsieur!'

He lifted the lid of the box for a fraction of a second. An exclamation of utter astonishment came from the millionaire. His face turned as white as chalk.

'My God!' he breathed, 'the rubies.'

He sat for a moment as though dazed. Poirot restored the box to his pocket and beamed placidly. Then suddenly the millionaire seemed to come out of his trance; he leaned across to Poirot and wrung his hand so heartily that the little man winced with pain.

'This is great,' said Van Aldin. 'Great! You are the goods, M. Poirot. Once and for all, you are the goods.'

'It is nothing,' said Poirot modestly. 'Order, method, being prepared for eventualities beforehand – that is all there is to it.'

'And now, I suppose, the Comte de la Roche has been arrested?' continued Van Aldin eagerly.

'No,' said Poirot.

A look of utter astonishment came over Van Aldin's face.

'But why? What more do you want?'

'The Comte's alibi is still unshaken.'

'But that is nonsense.'

'Yes,' said Poirot; 'I rather think it is nonsense, but unfortunately we have to prove it so.'

'In the meantime he will slip through your fingers.'

Poirot shook his head very energetically.

'No,' he said, 'he will not do that. The one thing the Comte cannot afford to sacrifice is his social position. At all costs he must stop and brazen it out.'

Van Aldin was still dissatisfied.

'But I don't see—'

Poirot raised a hand. 'Grant me a little moment, Monsieur. Me, I have a little idea. Many people have mocked themselves at the little ideas of Hercule Poirot – and they have been wrong.'

'Well,' said Van Aldin, 'go ahead. What is this little idea?'

Poirot paused for a moment and then he said:

'I will call upon you at your hotel at eleven o'clock tomorrow morning. Until then, say nothing to anyone.'

22

M. PAPOPOLOUS BREAKFASTS

M. Papopolous was at breakfast. Opposite him sat his daughter, Zia.

There was a knock at the sitting-room door, and a chasseur entered with a card which he brought to M. Papopolous. The latter scrutinised it, raised his eyebrows, and passed it over to his daughter.

'Ah!' said M. Papopolous, scratching his left ear thoughtfully, 'Hercule Poirot. I wonder now.'

Father and daughter looked at each other.

'I saw him yesterday at the tennis,' said M. Papopolous. 'Zia, I hardly like this.'

'He was very useful to you once,' his daughter reminded him.

'That is true,' acknowledged M. Papopolous; 'also he has retired from active work, so I hear.'

These interchanges between father and daughter had passed in their own language. Now M. Papopolous turned to the chasseur and said in French:

'Faîtes monter ce monsieur.'

A few minutes later Hercule Poirot, exquisitely attired, and swinging a cane with a jaunty air, entered the room.

'My dear M. Papopolous.'

'My dear M. Poirot.'

'And Mademoiselle Zia.' Poirot swept her a low bow.

'You will excuse us going on with our breakfast,' said M. Papopolous, pouring himself out another cup of coffee. 'Your call is – ahem! – a little early.'

'It is scandalous,' said Poirot, 'but you see, I am pressed.'

'Ah!' murmured M. Papopolous, 'you are on an affair then?'

'A very serious affair,' said Poirot: 'the death of Madame Kettering.'

'Let me see,' M. Papopolous looked innocently up at the ceiling, 'that was the lady who died on the Blue Train, was it not? I saw a mention of it in the papers, but there was no suggestion of foul play.'

'In the interests of justice,' said Poirot, 'it was thought best to suppress that fact.'

There was a pause.

'And in what way can I assist you, M. Poirot?' asked the dealer politely.

'*Voilà*,' said Poirot. 'I shall come to the point.' He took from his pocket the same box that he had displayed at Cannes, and, opening it, he took out the rubies and pushed them across the table to Papopolous.

Although Poirot was watching him narrowly, not a muscle of the old man's face moved. He took up the jewels and examined them with a kind of detached interest, then he looked across at the detective inquiringly:

'Superb, are they not?' asked Poirot.

'Quite excellent,' said M. Papopolous.

'How much should you say they are worth?'

The Greek's face quivered a little.

'Is it really necessary to tell you, M. Poirot?' he asked.

'You are shrewd, M. Papopolous. No, it is not. They are not, for instance, worth five hundred thousand dollars.'

Papopolous laughed, and Poirot joined with him.

'As an imitation,' said Papopolous, handing them back to Poirot, 'they are, as I said, quite excellent. Would it be indiscreet to ask, M. Poirot, where you came across them?'

'Not at all,' said Poirot; 'I have no objection to telling an old friend like yourself. They were in the possession of the Comte de la Roche.'

M. Papopolous' eyebrows lifted themselves eloquently.

'In-deed,' he murmured.

Poirot leaned forward and assumed his most innocent and beguiling air.

'M. Papopolous,' he said, 'I am going to lay my cards upon the table. The original of these jewels was stolen from Madame Kettering on the Blue Train. Now I will say to you first this: *I am not concerned with the recovery of these jewels. This is the affair of the police.* I am working not for the police but for M. Van Aldin. I want to lay hands on the man who killed Madame Kettering. I am interested in the jewels only in so far as they may lead me to the man. You understand?'

The last two words were uttered with great significance. M. Papopolous, his face quite unmoved, said quietly:

'Go on.'

'It seems to me probable, Monsieur, that the jewels will change hands in Nice – may already have done so.'

'Ah!' said M. Papopolous.

He sipped his coffee reflectively, and looked a shade more noble and patriarchal than usual.

314

'I say to myself,' continued Poirot, with animation, 'what good fortune! My old friend, M. Papopolous, is in Nice. He will aid me.'

'And how do you think I can aid you?' inquired M. Papopolous coldly.

'I said to myself, without doubt M. Papopolous is in Nice on business.'

'Not at all,' said M. Papopolous, 'I am here for my health – by the doctor's orders.'

He coughed hollowly.

'I am desolated to hear it,' replied Poirot, with somewhat insincere sympathy. 'But to continue. When a Russian Grand Duke, an Austrian Archduchess, or an Italian Prince wish to dispose of their family jewels – to whom do they go? To M. Papopolous, is it not? He who is famous all over the world for the discretion with which he arranges these things.'

The other bowed.

'You flatter me.'

'It is a great thing, discretion,' mused Poirot, and was rewarded by the fleeting smile which passed across the Greek's face. 'I, too, can be discreet.'

The eyes of the two men met.

Then Poirot went on speaking very slowly, and obviously picking his words with care.

'I say to myself, this: if these jewels have changed hands in Nice, M. Papopolous would have heard of it. He has knowledge of all that passes in the jewel world.'

'Ah!' said M. Papopolous, and helped himself to a *croissant*.

'The police, you understand,' said M. Poirot, 'do not enter into the matter. It is a personal affair.'

'One hears rumours,' admitted M. Papopolous cautiously.

'Such as?' prompted Poirot.

'Is there any reason why I should pass them on?'

'Yes,' said Poirot, 'I think there is. You may remember, M. Papopolous, that seventeen years ago there was a certain article in your hands, left there as security by a very – er – Prominent Person. It was in your keeping and it unaccountably disappeared. You were, if I may use the English expression, in the soup.'

His eyes came gently round to the girl. She had pushed her cup and plate aside, and with both elbows on the table and her chin resting on her hands, was listening eagerly. Still keeping an eye on her he went on:

'I am in Paris at the time. You send for me. You place yourself in my hands. If I restore to you that – article, you say I shall earn your undying gratitude. *Eh bien*! I did restore it to you.'

A long sigh came from M. Papopolous.

'It was the most unpleasant moment of my career,' he murmured.

'Seventeen years is a long time,' said Poirot thoughtfully, 'but I believe that I am right in saying, Monsieur, that your race does not forget.'

'A Greek?' murmured Papopolous, with an ironical smile.

'It was not as a Greek I meant,' said Poirot.

There was a silence, and then the old man drew himself up proudly.

'You are right, M. Poirot,' he said quietly. 'I am a Jew. And, as you say, our race does not forget.'

'You will aid me then?'

'As regards the jewels, Monsieur, I can do nothing.'

The old man, as Poirot had done just now, picked his words carefully.

'I know nothing. I have heard nothing. But I can perhaps do you a good turn – that is, if you are interested in racing.'

'Under certain circumstances I might be,' said Poirot, eyeing him steadily.

'There is a horse running at Longchamps that would, I think, repay attention. I cannot say for certain, you understand; this news passed through so many hands.'

He stopped, fixing Poirot with his eye, as though to make sure that the latter was comprehending him.

'Perfectly, perfectly,' said Poirot, nodding.

'The name of the horse,' said Papopolous, leaning back and joining the tips of his fingers together, 'is the Marquis. I think, but I am not sure, that it is an English horse, eh, Zia?'

'I think so too,' said the girl.

Poirot got up briskly.

'I thank you, Monsieur,' he said. 'It is a great thing to have what the English call a tip from the stable. Au revoir, Monsieur, and many thanks.'

He turned to the girl.

'Au revoir, Mademoiselle Zia. It seems to me but yesterday that I saw you in Paris. One would say that two years had passed at most.'

'There is a difference between sixteen and thirty-three,' said Zia ruefully.

'Not in your case,' declared Poirot gallantly. 'You and your father will perhaps dine with me one night.'

'We shall be delighted,' replied Zia.

'Then we will arrange it,' declared Poirot, 'and now – *je me sauve.*'

Poirot walked along the street humming a little tune to himself. He twirled his stick with a jaunty air, once or twice he smiled to himself quietly. He turned into the first Bureau de Poste he came to and sent off a telegram. He took some time in wording it, but it was in code and he had to call upon his memory. It purported to deal with a missing scarf-pin, and was addressed to Inspector Japp, Scotland Yard.

Decoded, it was short and to the point. *'Wire me everything known about man whose soubriquet is the Marquis.'*

—— 23 ——

A NEW THEORY

It was exactly eleven o'clock when Poirot presented himself at Van Aldin's hotel. He found the millionaire alone.

'You are punctual, M. Poirot,' he said, with a smile, as he rose to greet the detective.

'I am always punctual,' said Poirot. 'The exactitude – always do I observe it. Without order and method—'

He broke off. 'Ah, but it is possible that I have said these things to you before. Let us come at once to the object of my visit.'

'Your little idea?'

'Yes, my little idea.' Poirot smiled.

'First of all, Monsieur, I should like to interview once more the maid, Ada Mason. She is here?'

'Yes, she's here.'

'Ah!'

Van Aldin looked at him curiously. He rang the bell, and a messenger was despatched to find Mason.

Poirot greeted her with his usual politeness, which was never without effect on that particular class.

'Good afternoon, Mademoiselle,' he said cheerfully. 'Be seated, will you not, if Monsieur permits.'

'Yes, yes, sit down, my girl,' said Van Aldin.

'Thank you, sir,' said Mason primly, and she sat down on the extreme edge of a chair. She looked bonier and more acid than ever.

'I have come to ask you yet more questions,' said Poirot. 'We must get to the bottom of this affair. Always I return to the question of the man in the train. You have been shown the Comte de la Roche. You say that it is possible he was the man, but you are not sure.'

'As I told you, sir, I never saw the gentleman's face. That is what makes it so difficult.'

Poirot beamed and nodded.

'Precisely, exactly. I comprehend well the difficulty. Now, Mademoiselle, you have been in the service of Madame Kettering two months, you say. During that time, how often did you see your master?'

Mason reflected a minute or two, and then said:

'Only twice, sir.'

'And was that near to, or far away?'

'Well once, sir, he came to Curzon Street. I was upstairs, and I looked over the banisters and saw him in the hall below. I was a bit curious like, you understand, knowing the way things – er – were.' Mason finished up with her discreet cough.

'And the other time?'

'I was in the Park, sir, with Annie – one of the housemaids, sir, and she pointed out the master to me walking with a foreign lady.'

Again Poirot nodded.

'Now listen, Mason, this man whom you saw in the carriage talking to your mistress at the Gare de Lyon, how do you know it was not your master?'

'The master, sir? Oh, I don't think it could have been.'

'But you are not sure,' Poirot persisted.

'Well – I never thought of it, sir.'

Mason was clearly upset at the idea.

'You have heard that your master was also on the train. What more natural than that it should be he who came along the corridor?'

'But the gentleman who was talking to the mistress must have come from outside, sir. He was dressed for the street. In an overcoat and soft hat.'

'Just so, Mademoiselle, but reflect a minute. The train has just arrived at the Gare de Lyon. Many of the passengers promenade themselves upon the quay. Your mistress was about to do so, and for that purpose had doubtless put on her fur coat, eh?'

'Yes, sir,' agreed Mason.

'Your master, then, does the same. The train is heated, but outside in the station it is cold. He puts on his overcoat and his hat and he walks along beside the train, and looking up at the lighted windows he suddenly sees Madame Kettering. Until then he has had no idea that she was on the train. Naturally, he mounts the carriage and goes to her compartment. She gives an exclamation of surprise at seeing him and quickly shuts the door between the two compartments since it is possible that their conversation may be of a private nature.'

He leaned back in his chair and watched the suggestion slowly take effect. No one knew better than Hercule Poirot that the class to which Mason belongs cannot be hurried. He must give her time to get rid of her own preconceived ideas. At the end of three minutes she spoke:

'Well, of course, sir, it might be so. I never thought of it that way. The master is tall and dark, and just about that build. It was seeing the hat and coat that made me say it was a gentle-man from outside. Yes, it might have been the master. I would not like to say either way I'm sure.'

'Thank you very much, Mademoiselle. I shall not require you any further. Ah, just one thing more.' He took from his pocket the cigarette case he had already shown to Katherine. 'Is that your mistress's case?' he said to Mason.

'No, sir, it is not the mistress – at least—'

She looked suddenly startled. An idea was clearly working its way to the forefront of her mind.

'Yes?' said Poirot encouragingly.

'I think, sir – I can't be sure, but I think – it is a case that the mistress bought to give to the master.'

'Ah,' said Poirot in a noncommittal manner.

'But whether she ever did give it to him or not, I can't say, of course.'

'Precisely,' said Poirot, 'precisely. That is all, I think, Mademoiselle. I wish you good afternoon.'

Ada Mason retired discreetly, closing the door noiselessly behind her.

Poirot looked across at Van Aldin, a faint smile upon his face. The millionaire looked thunderstruck.

'You think – you think it was Derek?' he queried, 'but – everything points the other way. Why, the Count has actually been caught red-handed with the jewels on him.'

'No.'

'But you told me—'

319

'What did I tell you?'

'That story about the jewels. You showed them to me.'

'No.'

Van Aldin stared at him.

'You mean to say you didn't show them to me?'

'No.'

'Yesterday – at the tennis?'

'No.'

'Are you crazy, M. Poirot, or am I?'

'Neither of us is crazy,' said the detective. 'You ask me a question; I answer it. You say have I not shown you the jewels yesterday? I reply – no. What I showed you, M. Van Aldin, was a first-class imitation, hardly to be distinguished except by an expert from the real ones.'

—— 24 ——

POIROT GIVES ADVICE

It took the millionaire some few minutes to take the thing in. He stared at Poirot as though dumbfounded. The little Belgian nodded at him gently.

'Yes,' he said, 'it alters the position, does it not?'

'Imitation!'

He leaned forward.

'All along, M. Poirot, you have had this idea? All along this is what you have been driving at? You never believed that the Comte de la Roche was the murderer?'

'I have had doubts,' said Poirot quietly. 'I said as much to you. Robbery with violence and murder' – he shook his head energetically – 'no, it is difficult to picture. It does not harmon-ise with the personality of the Comte de la Roche.'

'But you believe that he meant to steal the rubies?'

'Certainly. There is no doubt as to that. See, I will recount to you the affair as I see it. The Comte knew of the rubies and he laid his plans accordingly. He made up a romantic story of a book he was writing, so as to induce your daughter to bring them with her. He provided himself with an exact duplicate. It is clear, is it not, that substitution is what he was after. Madame, your daughter, was not an expert on jewels. It would probably be a long time before she discovered what had oc-curred. When she did so – well – I do not think she would prosecute the Comte. Too much would come out. He would have in his possession various letters of hers. Oh yes, a very safe scheme from the Comte's point of view – one that he has probably carried out before.'

'It seems clear enough, yes,' said Van Aldin musingly.

'It accords with the personality of the Comte de la Roche,' said Poirot.

'Yes, but now –' Van Aldin looked searchingly at the other. 'What actually happened? Tell me that, M. Poirot.'

Poirot shrugged his shoulders.

'It is quite simple,' he said; 'someone stepped in ahead of the Comte.'

There was a long pause.

Van Aldin seemed to be turning things over in his mind. When he spoke it was without beating about the bush.

'How long have you suspected my son-in-law, M. Poirot?'

'From the very first. He had the motive and the opportunity. Everyone took for granted that the man in Madame's compartment in Paris was the Comte de la Roche. I thought so, too. Then you happened to mention that you had once mistaken the Comte for your son-in-law. That told me that they were of the same height and build, and alike in colouring. It put some curious ideas in my head. The maid had only been with your daughter a short time. It was unlikely that she would know Mr Kettering well by sight, since he had not been living in Curzon Street; also the man was careful to keep his face turned away.'

'You believe he – murdered her?' said Van Aldin hoarsely.

Poirot raised a hand quickly.

'No, no, I did not say that – but it is a possibility – a very strong possibility. He was in a tight corner, a very tight corner, threatened with ruin. This was the one way out.'

'But why take the jewels?'

'To make the crime appear an ordinary one committed by train robbers. Otherwise suspicion might have fallen on him straight away.'

'If that is so, what has he done with the rubies?'

'That remains to be seen. There are several possibilities. There is a man in Nice who may be able to help, the man I pointed out at the tennis.'

He rose to his feet and Van Aldin rose also and laid his hand on the little man's shoulder. His voice when he spoke was harsh with emotion.

'Find Ruth's murderer for me,' he said, 'that is all I ask.'

Poirot drew himself up.

'Leave it in the hands of Hercule Poirot,' he said superbly; 'have no fears. I will discover the truth.'

He brushed a speck of fluff from his hat, smiled reassuringly at the millionaire, and left the room. Nevertheless, as he went down the stairs some of the confidence faded from his face.

'It is all very well,' he murmured to himself, 'but there are difficulties. Yes, there are great difficulties.' As he was passing out of the hotel he came to a sudden halt. A car had drawn up in front of the door. In it was Katherine Grey, and Derek Kettering was standing beside it talking to her earnestly. A minute or two later the car drove off and Derek remained standing on the pavement looking after it. The expression on his face was an odd one. He gave a sudden impatient gesture of the shoulders, sighed deeply, and turned to find Hercule Poirot standing at his elbow. In spite of himself he started. The two men looked at each other. Poirot steadily and un-waveringly and Derek with a kind of light-hearted defiance. There was a sneer behind the easy mockery of his tone when he spoke, raising his eyebrows slightly as he did so.

'Rather a dear, isn't she?' he asked easily.

His manner was perfectly natural.

'Yes,' said Poirot thoughtfully, 'that describes Mademoiselle Katherine very well. It is very English, that phrase there, and Mademoiselle Katherine, she also is very English.'

Derek remained perfectly still without answering.

'And yet she is *sympathique*, is it not so?'

'Yes,' said Derek; 'there are not many like her.'

He spoke softly as though to himself. Poirot nodded significantly. Then he leant towards the other and spoke in a different tone, a quiet, grave tone that was new to Derek Kettering.

'You will pardon an old man, Monsieur, if he says to you something that you may consider impertinent. There is one of your English proverbs that I would quote to you. It says that "it is well to be off with the old love, before being on with the new".'

Kettering turned on him angrily.

'What the devil do you mean?'

'You enrage yourself at me,' said Poirot placidly. 'I expected as much. As to what I mean – I mean, Monsieur, that there is a second car with a lady in it. If you turn your head you will see her.'

Derek spun round. His face darkened with anger.

'Mirelle, damn her!' he muttered. 'I will soon—'

Poirot arrested the movement he was about to make.

'Is it wise what you are about to do there?' he asked warningly. His eyes shone softly with a green light in them. But Derek was past noticing the warning signs. In his anger he was completely off his guard.

'I have broken with her utterly, and she knows it,' cried Derek angrily.

You have broken with her, yes, but has *she* broken with you?'

Derek gave a sudden harsh laugh.

'She won't break with two million pounds if she can help it,' he murmured brutally; 'trust Mirelle for that.'

Poirot raised his eyebrows.

'You have the outlook cynical,' he murmured.

'Have I?' There was no mirth in his sudden wide smile. 'I have lived in the world long enough, M. Poirot, to know that all women are pretty much alike.' His face softened suddenly.

He met Poirot's gaze defiantly. A look of alertness crept into his eyes, then faded again. 'That one,' he said, and jerked his head in the direction of Cap Martin.

'Ah!' said Poirot.

This quiescence was well calculated to provoke the impetuous temperament of the other.

'I know what you are going to say,' said Derek rapidly, 'the kind of life I have led, the fact that I am not worthy of her. You will say that I have no right to think even of such a thing. You will say that it is not a case of giving a dog a bad name – I know that it is not decent to be speaking like this with my wife dead only a few days, and murdered at that.'

He paused for breath, and Poirot took advantage of the pause to remark in his plaintive tone:

'But, indeed I have not said anything at all.'

'But you will.'

'Eh?' said Poirot.

'You will say that I have no earthly chance of marrying Katherine.'

'No,' said Poirot, 'I would not say that. Your reputation is bad, yes, but with women – never does that deter them. If you were a man of excellent character, of strict morality who had done nothing that he should not do, and – possibly everything that he should do – *eh bien*! then I should have grave doubts of your success. Moral worth, you understand, it is not romantic. It is appreciated, however, by widows.'

Derek Kettering stared at him, then he swung round on his heel and went up to the waiting car.

Poirot looked after him with some interest. He saw the lovely vision lean out of the car and speak.

Derek Kettering did not stop. He lifted his hat and passed straight on.

'*Ca y est,*' said M. Hercule Poirot, 'it is time, I think, that I return *chez moi.*'

He found an imperturbable George pressing trousers.

'A pleasant day, Georges, somewhat fatiguing, but not without interest,' he said.

George received these remarks in his usual wooden fashion.

'Indeed, sir.'

'The personality of a criminal, Georges, is an interesting matter. Many murderers are men of great personal charm.'

'I always heard, sir, that Dr Crippen was a pleasant-spoken gentleman. And yet he cut up his wife like so much mincemeat.'

'Your instances are always apt, Georges.'

The valet did not reply, and at that moment the telephone rang. Poirot took up the receiver.

' 'Allo – 'allo – yes, yes, it is Hercule Poirot who speaks.'

'This is Knighton. Will you hold the line a minute, M. Poirot. Mr Van Aldin would like to speak to you.'

There was a moment's pause, then the millionaire's voice came through.

'Is that you, M. Poirot? I just wanted to tell you that Mason came to me now of her own accord. She has been thinking it over, and she says that she is almost certain that the man at Paris was Derek Kettering. There was something familiar about him at the time, she says, but at the minute she could not place it. She seems pretty certain now.'

'Ah,' said Poirot, 'thank you, M. Van Aldin. That advances us.'

He replaced the receiver, and stood for a minute or two with a very curious smile on his face. George had to speak to him twice before obtaining an answer.

'Eh?' said Poirot. 'What is that that you say to me?'

'Are you lunching here, sir, or are you going out?'

'Neither,' said Poirot. 'I shall go to bed and take a *tisane.* The expected has happened, and when the expected happens, it always causes me emotion.'

DEFIANCE

As Derek Kettering passed the car, Mirelle leant out.

'Dereek – I must speak to you for a moment—'

But, lifting his hat, Derek passed straight on without stopping.

When he got back to his hotel, the concierge detached himself from his wooden pen and accosted him.

'A gentleman is waiting to see you, Monsieur.'

'Who is it?' asked Derek.

'He did not give his name, Monsieur, but he said his business with you was important, and that he would wait.'

'Where is he?'

'In the little salon, Monsieur. He preferred it to the lounge, he said, as being more private.'

Derek nodded, and turned his steps in that direction.

The small salon was empty except for the visitor, who rose and bowed with easy foreign grace as Derek entered. As it chanced, Derek had only seen the Comte de la Roche once, but found no difficulty in recognising that aristocratic nobleman, and he frowned angrily. Of all the consummate impertinence!

'The Comte de la Roche, is it not?' he said. 'I am afraid you have wasted your time in coming here.'

'I hope not,' said the Comte agreeably. His white teeth glittered.

The Comte's charm of manner was usually wasted on his own sex. All men, without exception, disliked him heartily. Derek Kettering was already conscious of a distinct longing to kick the Count bodily out of the room. It was only the realisation that scandal would be unfortunate just at present that restrained him. He marvelled anew that Ruth could have cared, as she certainly had, for this fellow. A bounder, and worse than a bounder. He looked with distaste at the Count's exquisitely manicured hands.

'I called,' said the Comte, 'on a little matter of business. It would be advisable, I think, for you to listen to me.'

Again Derek felt strongly tempted to kick him out, but again he refrained. The hint of a threat was not lost upon him, but he interpreted it in his own way. There were various reasons why it would be better to hear what the Comte had to say.

He sat down and drummed impatiently with his fingers on the table.

'Well,' he said sharply, 'what is it?'

It was not the Comte's way to come out into the open at once.

'Allow me, Monsieur, to offer you my condolences on your recent bereavement.'

'If I have any impertinence from you,' said Derek quietly, 'you go out by that window.'

He nodded his head towards the window beside the Comte, and the latter moved uneasily.

'I will send my friends to you, Monsieur, if that is what you desire,' he said haughtily.

Derek laughed.

'A duel, eh? My dear Count, I don't take you seriously enough for that. But I should take a good deal of pleasure in kicking you down the Promenade des Anglais.'

The Comte was not at all anxious to take offence. He merely raised his eyebrows and murmured:

'The English are barbarians.'

'Well,' said Derek, 'what is it you have to say to me?'

'I will be frank,' said the Comte, 'I will come immediately to the point. That will suit us both, will it not?'

Again he smiled in his agreeable fashion.

'Go on,' said Derek curtly.

The Comte looked at the ceiling, jointed the tips of his fingers together, and murmured softly:

'You have come into a lot of money, Monsieur.'

'What the devil has that got to do with you?'

The Comte drew himself up.

'Monsieur, my name is tarnished! I am suspected – accused – of foul crime.'

'The accusation does not come from me,' said Derek coldly; 'as an interested party I have not expressed any opinion.'

'I am innocent,' said the Comte. 'I swear before heaven' – he raised his hand to heaven – 'that I am innocent.'

'M. Carrège is, I believe, the Juge d'Instruction in charge of the case,' hinted Derek politely.

The Comte took no notice.

'Not only am I unjustly suspected of a crime that I did not commit, but I am also in serious need of money.'

He coughed softly and suggestively.

Derek rose to his feet.

'I was waiting for that,' he said softly; 'you blackmailing brute! I will not give you a penny. My wife is dead, and no scandal that you can make can touch her now. She wrote you foolish letters, I dare say. If I were to buy them from you for a round sum at this minute, I am pretty certain that you would manage to keep one or two back; and I will tell you this, M. de la Roche, blackmailing is an ugly word both in England and France. That is my answer to you. Good afternoon.'

'One moment' – the Comte stretched out a hand as Derek was turning to leave the room. 'You are mistaken, Monsieur. You are completely mistaken. I am, I hope, a "gentleman." ' Derek laughed. 'Any letters that a lady might write to me I should hold sacred.' He flung back his head with a beautiful air of nobility. 'The proposition that I was putting before you was of quite a different nature. I am, as I said, extremely short of money, and my conscience might impel me to go to the police with certain information.'

Derek came slowly back into the room.

'What do you mean?'

The Comte's agreeable smile flashed forth once more.

'Surely it is not necessary to go into details,' he purred. 'Seek whom the crime benefits, they say, don't they? As I said just now, you have come into a lot of money lately.'

Derek laughed.

'If that is all—' he said contemptuously.

But the Comte was shaking his head.

'But it is not all, my dear sir. I should not come to you unless I had much more precise and detailed information than that. It is not agreeable, Monsieur, to be arrested and tried for murder.

Derek came close up to him. His face expressed such furious anger that involuntarily the Comte drew back a pace or two.

'Are you threatening *me*?' the young man demanded angrily.

'You shall hear nothing more of the matter,' the Comte assured him.

'Of all the colossal bluffs that I have ever struck—'

The Comte raised a white hand.

'You are wrong. It is not a bluff. To convince you I will tell you this. My information was obtained from a certain lady. It is she who holds the irrefutable proof that you committed the murder.'

'She? Who?'

'Mademoiselle Mirelle.'

Derek drew back as though struck.

'Mirelle,' he muttered.

The Comte was quick to press what he took to be his advantage.

'A bagatelle of one hundred thousand francs,' he said. 'I ask no more.'

'Eh?' said Derek absently.

'I was saying, Monsieur, that a bagatelle of one hundred thousand francs would satisfy my – conscience.'

Derek seemed to recollect himself. He looked earnestly at the Comte.

'You would like my answer now?'

'If you please, Monsieur.'

'Then here it is. You can go to the devil. See?'

Leaving the Comte too astonished to speak, Derek turned on his heel and swung out of the room.

Once out of the hotel he hailed a taxi and drove to Mirelle's hotel. On inquiring, he learned that the dancer had just come in. Derek gave the concierge his card.

'Take this up to Mademoiselle and ask if she will see me.'

A very brief interval elapsed, and then Derek was bidden to follow a *chasseur*.

A wave of exotic perfume assailed Derek's nostrils as he stepped over the threshold of the dancer's apartments. The room was filled with carnations, orchids, and mimosa. Mirelle was standing by the window in a *peignoir* of foamy lace.

She came towards him, her hands outstretched.

'Dereek – you have come to me. I knew you would.'

He put aside the clinging arms and looked down on her sternly.

'Why did you send the Comte de la Roche to me?'

She looked at him in astonishment, which he took to be genuine.

'I? Send the Comte de la Roche to you? But for what?'

'Apparently – for blackmail,' said Derek grimly.

Again she stared. Then suddenly she smiled and nodded her head.

'Of course. It was to be expected. It is what he would do, *ce type là*. I might have known it. No, indeed, Dereek, I did not send him.'

He looked at her piercingly, as though seeking to read her mind.

'I will tell you,' said Mirelle. 'I am ashamed, but I will tell you. The other day, you comprehend, I was mad with rage, quite mad' – she made an eloquent gesture. 'My temperament, it is not a patient one. I want to be revenged on you, and so I go to the Comte de la Roche, and I tell him to go to the police and say so and so, and so and so. But have no fear, Dereek. Not completely did I lose my head; the proof rests with me alone. The police can do nothing without my word, you understand? And now – now?'

She nestled up close to him, looking at him with melting eyes.

He thrust her roughly away from him. She stood there, her breast heaving, her eyes narrowing to a cat-like slit.

'Be careful, Dereek, be very careful. You have come back to me, have you not?'

'I shall never come back to you,' said Derek steadily.

'Ah!'

More than ever the dancer looked like a cat. Her eyelids flickered.

'So there is another woman? The one with whom you lunched that day. Eh! am I right?'

'I intend to ask that lady to marry me. You might as well know.'

'That prim Englishwoman! Do you think that I will support that for one moment? Ah, no.' Here beautiful lithe body quivered. 'Listen, Dereek, do you remember that conversation we had in London? You said the only thing that could save you was the death of your wife. You regretted that she was so healthy. Then the idea of an accident came to your brain. And more than an accident.'

'I suppose,' said Derek contemptuously, 'that it was this conversation that you repeated to the Comte de la Roche.'

Mirelle laughed.

'Am I a fool? Could the police do anything with a vague story like that? See – I will give you a last chance. You shall give up this Englishwoman. You shall return to me. And then, *chéri*, never, never will I breathe—'

'Breathe what?'

She laughed softly. 'You thought no one saw you—'

'What do you mean?'

'As I say, you thought no one saw you – but *I* saw you, Dereek, *mon ami; I saw you coming out of the compartment of Madame your wife just before the train got into Lyons that night.* And I know more than that. I know that when you came out of her compartment she was dead.'

He stared at her. Then, like a man in a dream, he turned very slowly and went out of the room, swaying slightly as he walked.

—— 26 ——

A WARNING

'And so it is,' said Poirot, 'that we are the good friends and have no secrets from each other.'

Katherine turned her head to look at him. There was something in his voice, some undercurrent of seriousness, which she had not heard before.

They were sitting in the gardens of Monte Carlo. Katherine had come over with her friends, and they had run into Knighton and Poirot almost immediately on arrival. Lady Tamplin had seized upon Knighton and had overwhelmed him with reminiscences, most of which Katherine had a faint suspicion were invented. They had moved away together, Lady Tamplin with her hand on the young man's arm. Knighton had thrown a couple of glances back over his shoulder, and Poirot's eyes twinkled a little as he saw them.

'Of course we are friends,' said Katherine.

'From the beginning we have been sympathetic to each other,' mused Poirot.

'When you told me that a *"roman policier"* occurs in real life.'

'And I was right, was I not?' he challenged her, with an emphatic forefinger. 'Here we are, plunged in the middle of one. That is natural for me – it is my *métier* – but for you it is different. Yes,' he added in a reflective tone. 'for you it is different.'

She looked sharply at him. It was as though he were warning her, pointing out to her some menace that she had not seen.

'Why do you say that I am in the middle of it? It is true that I had that conversation with Mrs Kettering just before she died, but now – now all that is over. I am not connected with the case any more.'

'Ah, Mademoiselle, Mademoiselle, can we ever say, "I have finished with this or that"?'

Katherine turned defiantly round to face him.

'What is it?' she asked. 'You are trying to tell me something
– to convey it to me rather. But I am not clever at taking
hints. I would much rather that you said anything you have
to say straight out.'

Poirot look at her sadly. '*Ah, mais c'est anglais ça,*' he
murmured, 'everything in black and white, everything clear
cut and well refined. But life, it is not like that, Mademoiselle.
There are the things that are not yet, but which cast their
shadow before.'

He dabbed his brow with a very large silk pocket-handker-
chief and murmured:

'Ah, but it is that I become poetical. Let us, as you say,
speak only of facts. And, speaking of facts, tell me what you
think of Major Knighton.'

'I like him very much indeed,' said Katherine warmly; 'he
is quite delightful.'

Poirot sighed.

'What is the matter?' asked Katherine.

'You reply so heartily,' said Poirot. 'If you had said in an
indifferent voice, "Oh, quite nice," *eh bien*, do you know I
should have been better pleased.'

Katherine did not answer. She felt slightly uncomfortable.
Poirot went on dreamily:

'And yet, who knows? With *les femmes*, they have so many
ways of concealing what they feel – and heartiness is perhaps
as good a way as any other.'

He sighed.

'I don't see—' began Katherine.

He interrupted her.

'You do not see why I am being so impertinent, Mademoiselle? I am an old man, and now and then – not very often
– I come across someone whose welfare is dear to me. We are
friends, Mademoiselle. You have said so yourself. And it is just
this – I should like to see you happy.'

Katherine stared very straight in front of her. She had a
cretonne sunshade with her, and with its point she traced little
designs in the gravel at her feet.

'I have asked you a question about Major Knighton, now I
will ask you another. Do you like Mr Derek Kettering?'

'I hardly know him,' said Katherine.

'That is not an answer, that.'

'I think it is.'

He looked at her, struck by something in her tone. Then
he nodded his head gravely and slowly.

'Perhaps you are right, Mademoiselle. See you, I who speak to you have seen much of the world, and I know that there are two things which are true. A good man may be ruined by his love for a bad woman – but the other way holds good also. A bad man may equally be ruined by his love for a good woman.'

Katherine looked up sharply.

'When you say ruined—'

'I mean from his point of view. One must be wholehearted in crime as in everything else.'

'You are trying to warn me,' said Katherine in a low voice. 'Against whom?'

'I cannot look into your heart, Mademoiselle; I do not think you would let me if I could. I will just say this. There are men who have a strange fascination for women.'

'The Comte de la Roche,' said Katherine, with a smile.

'There are others – more dangerous than the Comte de la Roche. They have qualities that appeal – recklessness, daring, audacity. You are fascinated, Mademoiselle; I see that, but I think that it is no more than that. I hope so. This man of whom I speak, the emotion he feels is genuine enough, but all the same—'

'Yes?'

He got up and stood looking down at her. Then he spoke in a low, distinct voice:

'You could, perhaps, love a thief, Mademoiselle, *but not a murderer.*'

We wheeled sharply away on that and left her sitting there.

He heard the little gasp she gave and paid no attention. He had said what he meant to say. He left her there to digest that last unmistakable phrase.

Derek Kettering, coming out of the Casino into the sunshine, saw her sitting alone on the bench and joined her.

'I have been gambling,' he said, with a light laugh, gambling unsuccessfully. I have lost everything – everything, that is, that I have with me.'

Katherine looked at him with a troubled face. She was aware at once of something new in his manner, some hidden excitement that betrayed itself in a hundred different infinitesimal signs.

'I should think you were always a gambler. The spirit of gambling appeals to you.'

'Every day and in every way a gambler? You are about right.

Don't *you* find something stimulating in it? To risk all on one throw – there is nothing like it.'

Calm and stolid as she believed herself to be, Katherine felt a faint answering thrill.

'I want to talk to you,' went on Derek, 'and who knows when I may have another opportunity? There is an idea going about that I murdered my wife – no, please don't interrupt. It is absurd, of course.' He paused for a minute or two, then went on, speaking more deliberately. 'In dealing with the police and Local Authorities here I have had to pretend to – well – a certain decency. I prefer not to pretend with you. I meant to marry money. I was on the look out for money when I first met Ruth Van Aldin. She had the look of a slim Madonna about her, and – I – well – I made all sorts of good resolutions – and was bitterly disillusioned. My wife was in love with another man when she married me. She never cared for me in the least. Oh, I am not complaining; the thing was a perfectly respectable bargain. She wanted Leconbury and I wanted money. The trouble arose simply through Ruth's American blood. Without caring a pin for me, she would have liked me to be continually dancing attendance. Time and again she as good as told me that she had bought me and that I belonged to her. The result was that I behaved abominably to her. My father-in-law will tell you that, and he is quite right. At the time of Ruth's death, I was faced with absolute disaster.' He laughed suddenly. 'One *is* faced with absolute disaster when one is up against a man like Rufus Van Aldin.'

'And then?' asked Katherine in a low voice.

'And then,' Derek shrugged his shoulders, 'Ruth was murdered – very providentially.'

He laughed, and the sound of his laugh hurt Katherine. She winced.

'Yes,' said Derek, 'that wasn't in very good taste. But it is quite true. Now I am going to tell you something more. From the very first moment I saw you I knew you were the only woman in the world for me. I was – afraid of you. I thought you might bring me bad luck.'

'Bad luck?' said Katherine sharply.

He stared at her. 'Why do you repeat it like that? What have you got in your mind?'

'I was thinking of things that people have said to me.'

Derek grinned suddenly. 'They will say a lot to you about me, my dear, and most of it will be true. Yes, and worse things too – things that I shall never tell you. I have been a gambler always – and I have taken some long odds. I shan't confess to you now or at any other time. The past is done with. There is one thing I do wish you to believe. I swear to you solemnly that I did not kill my wife.'

He said the words earnestly enough, yet there was somehow a theatrical touch about them. He met her troubled gaze and went on:

'I know. I lied the other day. It *was* my wife's compartment I went into.'

'Ah,' said Katherine.

'It's difficult to explain just why I went in, but I'll try. I did it on an impulse. You see, I was more or less spying on my wife. I kept out of sight on the train. Mirelle had told me that my wife was meeting the Comte de la Roche in Paris. Well, as far as I had seen, that was not so. I felt ashamed, and I thought suddenly that it would be a good thing to have it out with her once and for all, so I pushed open the door and went in.'

He paused.

'Yes,' said Katherine gently.

'Ruth was lying on the bunk asleep – her face was turned away from me – I could only see the back of her head. I could have woken her up, of course. But suddenly I felt a reaction. What, after all, was there to say that we hadn't both of us said a hundred times before? She looked so peaceful lying there. I left the compartment as quietly as I could.'

'Why lie about it to the police?' asked Katherine.

'Because I'm not a complete fool. I've realised from the beginning that, from the point of view of motive, I'm the ideal murderer. If I once admitted that I had been in her compartment just before she was murdered, I'd do for myself once and for all.'

'I see.'

Did she see? She could not have told herself. She was feeling the magnetic attraction of Derek's personality, but there was something in her that resisted, that held back . . .

'Katherine—'

'I—'

'You know that I care for you. Do – do you care for me?'

'I –I don't know.'

Weakness there. Either she knew or she did not know. If – if only—

She cast a look round desperately as though seeking something that would help her. A soft colour rose in her cheeks as a tall fair man with a limp came hurrying along the path towards them – Major Knighton.

There was relief and an unexpected warmth in her voice as she greeted him.

Derek stood up, scowling, his face black as a thundercloud.

'Lady Tamplin having a flutter?' he said easily. 'I must join her and give her the benefit of my system.'

He swung round on his heel and left them together. Katherine sat down again. Her heart was beating rapidly and unevenly, but as she sat there, talking commonplaces to the quiet, rather shy man beside her, her self-command came back.

Then she realised with a shock that Knighton also was laying bare his heart, much as Derek had done, but in a very different manner.

He was shy and stammering. The words came haltingly with no eloquence to back them.

'From the first moment I saw you – I – I ought not to have spoken so soon – but Mr Van Aldin may leave here any day, and I might not have another chance. I know you can't care for me so soon – that is impossible. I dare say it is presumption anyway on my part. I have private means, but not very much – no, please don't answer now. I know what your answer would be. But in case I went away suddenly I just wanted you to know – that I care.'

She was shaken – touched. His manner was so gentle and appealing.

'There's one thing more. I just wanted to say that if – if you are ever in trouble, anything that I can do—'

He took her hand in his, held it tightly for a minute, then dropped it and walked rapidly away towards the Casino without looking back.

Katherine sat perfectly still, looking after him. Derek Kettering – Richard Knighton – two men so different – so very different. There was something kind about Knighton, kind and trustworthy. As to Derek—

Then suddenly Katherine had a very curious sensation. She felt that she was no longer sitting alone on the seat in the Casino gardens, but that someone was standing beside her, and that that someone was the dead woman, Ruth Kettering. She had a further impression that Ruth wanted – badly – to tell her something. The impression was so curious, so vivid, that it could not be driven away. She felt absolutely certain that the spirit of Ruth Kettering was trying to convey something of vital importance to her. The impression faded. Katherine got up, trembling a little. What was it that Ruth Kettering had wanted so badly to say?

—— 27 ——

INTERVIEW WITH MIRELLE

When Knighton left Katherine he went in search of Hercule Poirot, whom he found in the Rooms, jauntily placing the minimum stake on the even numbers. As Knighton joined him, the number thirty-three turned up, and Poirot's stake was swept away.

'Bad luck!' said Knighton; 'are you going to stake again?'

Poirot shook his head.

'Not at present.'

'Do you feel the fascination of gambling?' asked Knighton curiously.

'Not at roulette.'

Knighton shot a swift glance at him. His own face became troubled. He spoke haltingly, with a touch of deference.

'I wonder, are you busy, M. Poirot? There is something I would like to ask you about.'

'I am at your disposal. Shall we go outside? It is pleasant in the sunshine.'

They strolled out together, and Knighton drew a deep breath.

'I love the Riviera,' he said. 'I came here first twelve years ago, during the War, when I was sent to Lady Tamplin's Hospital. It was like Paradise, coming from Flanders to this.'

'It must have been,' said Poirot.

'How long ago the War seems now!' mused Knighton.

They walked on in silence for some little way.

'You have something on your mind?' said Poirot.

Knighton looked at him in some surprise.

'You are quite right,' he confessed. 'I don't know how you knew it, though.'

'It showed itself only too plainly,' said Poirot drily.

'I did not know that I was so transparent.'

'It is my business to observe the physiognomy,' the little man explained, with dignity.

'I will tell you, M. Poirot. You have heard of this dancer woman – Mirelle?'

'She who is the *chère amie* of M. Derek Kettering?'

'Yes, that is the one; and, knowing this, you will understand that Mr Van Aldin is naturally prejudiced against her. She wrote to him, asking for an interview. He told me to dictate a curt refusal, which of course I did. This morning she came to the hotel and sent up her card, saying that it was urgent and vital that she should see Mr Van Aldin at once.'

'You interest me,' said Poirot.

'Mr Van Aldin was furious. He told me what message to send down to her. I ventured to disagree with him. It seemed to me both likely and probable that this woman Mirelle might give us valuable information. We know that she was on the Blue Train, and she may have seen or heard something that it might be vital for us to know. Don't you agree with me, M. Poirot?'

'I do,' said Poirot drily. 'M. Van Aldin, if I may say so, behaved exceedingly foolishly.'

'I am glad you take that view of the matter,' said the secretary. 'Now I am going to tell you something, M. Poirot. So strongly did I feel the unwisdom of Mr Van Aldin's attitude that I went down privately and had an interview with the lady.'

'*Eh bien?*'

'The difficulty was that she insisted on seeing Mr Van Aldin himself. I softened his message as much as I possibly could. In fact – to be candid – I gave it in a very different form. I said that Mr Van Aldin was too busy to see her at present, but that she might make any communication she wished to me. That, however, she could not bring herself to do, and she left without saying anything further. But I have a strong impression, M. Poirot, that that woman knows something.'

'This is serious,' said Poirot quietly. 'You know where she is staying?'

'Yes.' Knighton mentioned the name of the hotel.

'Good,' said Poirot; 'we will go there immediately.'

The secretary looked doubtful.

'And Mr Van Aldin?' he queried doubtfully.

'M. Van Aldin is an obstinate man,' said' Poirot drily. 'I do not argue with obstinate men. I act in spite of them. We will go and see the lady immediately. I will tell her that you are empowered by M. Van Aldin to act for him, and you will guard yourself well from contradicting me.'

Knighton still looked slightly doubtful, but Poirot took no notice of his hesitation.

At the hotel, they were told that Mademoiselle was in, and

Poirot sent up both his and Knighton's cards, with 'From Mr Van Aldin' pencilled upon them.

Word came down that Mademoiselle Mirelle would receive them.

When they were ushered into the dancer's apartments, Poirot immediately took the lead.

'Mademoiselle,' he murmured, bowing very low, 'we are here on behalf of M. Van Aldin.'

'Ah! And why did he not come himself?'

'He is indisposed,' said Poirot mendaciously; 'the Riviera throat, it has him in its grip, but me I am empowered to act for him, as is Major Knighton, his secretary. Unless, of course, Mademoiselle would prefer to wait a fortnight or so.'

If there was one thing of which Poirot was tolerably certain, it was that to a temperament such as Mirelle's the mere word 'wait' was anathema.

'*Eh bien*, I will speak, Messieurs,' she cried. 'I have been patient. I have held my hand. And for what? That I should be insulted! Yes, insulted! Ah! Does he think to treat Mirelle like that? To throw her off like an old glove. I tell you never has a man tired of me. Always it is I who tire of them.'

She paced up and down the room, her slender body trembling with rage. A small table impeded her free passage, and she flung it from her into a corner, where it splintered against the wall.

'That is what I will do to him,' she cried, 'and that!'

Picking up a glass bowl filled with lilies she flung it into the grate, where it smashed into a hundred pieces.

Knighton was looking at her with cold British disapproval. He felt embarrassed and ill at ease. Poirot, on the other hand, with twinkling eyes was thoroughly enjoying the scene.

'Ah, it is magnificent!' he cried. 'It can be seen – Madame has a temperament.'

'I am an artist,' said Mirelle; 'every artist has a temperament. I told Dereek to beware, and he would not listen.' She whirled round on Poirot suddenly. 'It is true, is it not, that he wants to marry that English miss?'

Poirot coughed.

'*On m'a dit*,' he murmured, 'that he adores her passionately.'

Mirelle came towards them.

'He murdered his wife,' she screamed. 'There – now you have it! He told me beforehand that he meant to do it. He had got to an *impasse* – zut! he took the easiest way out.'

'You say that M. Kettering murdered his wife.'

'Yes, yes, yes. Have I not told you so?'

'The police,' murmured Poirot, 'will need proof of that – er – statement.'

'I tell you I saw him come out of her compartment that night on the train.'

'When?' asked Poirot sharply.

'Just before the train reached Lyons.'

'You will swear to that, Mademoiselle?'

It was a different Poirot who spoke now, sharp and decisive.

'Yes.'

There was a moment's silence. Mirelle was panting, and her eyes, half defiant, half frightened, went from the face of one man to the other.

'This is a serious matter, Mademoiselle,' said the detective. 'You realise how serious?'

'Certainly I do.'

'That is well,' said Poirot. 'Then you understand, Mademoiselle, that no time must be lost. You will, perhaps, accompany us immediately to the office of the Examining Magistrate.'

Mirelle was taken aback. She hesitated, but, as Poirot had foreseen, she had no loophole for escape.

'Very well,' she muttered, 'I will fetch a coat.'

Left alone together, Poirot and Knighton exchanged glances.

'It is necessary to act while – how do you say it? – the iron is hot,' murmured Poirot. 'She is temperamental; in an hour's time, maybe, she will repent, and she will wish to draw back. We must prevent that at all costs.'

Mirelle reappeared, wrapped in a sand-coloured velvet wrap trimmed with leopard skin. She looked not altogether unlike a leopardess, tawny and dangerous. Her eyes still flashed with anger and determination.

They found M. Caux and the Examining Magistrate together. A few brief introductory words from Poirot, and Mademoiselle Mirelle was courteously entreated to tell her tale. This she did in much the same words as she had done to Knighton and Poirot, though with far more soberness of manner.

'This is an extraordinary story, Mademoiselle,' said M. Carrège slowly. He leant back in his chair, adjusted his pince-nez, and looked keenly and searchingly at the dancer through them.

'You wish us to believe M. Kettering actually boasted of the crime to you beforehand?'

'Yes, yes. She was too healthy, he said. If she were to die it must be an accident – he would arrange it all.'

'You are aware, Mademoiselle,' said M. Carrège sternly, 'that you are making yourself out to be an accessory before the fact?'

'Me? But not the least in the world, Monsieur. Not for a moment did I take that statement seriously. Ah no indeed! I know men, Monsieur; they say many wild things. It would be an odd state of affairs if one were to take all they said *au pied de la lettre.*'

The Examining Magistrate raised his eyebrows.

'We are to take it, then, that you regarded M. Kettering's threats as mere idle words? May I ask, Mademoiselle, what made you throw up your engagements in London and come out to the Riviera?'

Mirelle looked at him with melting black eyes.

'I wished to be with the man I loved,' she said simply. 'Was it so unnatural?'

Poirot interpolated a question gently.

'Was it, then, at M. Kettering's wish that you accompanied him to Nice?'

Mirelle seemed to find a little difficulty in answering this. She hesitated perceptibly before she spoke. When she did, it was with a haughty indifference of manner.

'In such matters I please myself, Monsieur,' she said.

That the answer was not an answer at all was noted by all three men. They said nothing.

'When were you first convinced that M. Kettering had murdered his wife?'

'As I tell you, Monsieur, I saw M. Kettering come out of his wife's compartment just before the train drew in to Lyons. There was a look on his face – ah! at the moment I could not understand it – a look haunted and terrible. I shall never forget it.'

Her voice rose shrilly, and she flung out her arms in an extravagant gesture.

'Quite so,' said M. Carrège.

'Afterwards, when I found that Madame Kettering was dead when the train left Lyons, then – then I knew!'

'And still – you did not go to the police, Mademoiselle,' said the Commissary mildly.

Mirelle glanced at him superbly; she was clearly enjoying herself in the rôle she was playing.

'Shall I betray my lover?' she asked. 'Ah no; do not ask a woman to do that.'

'Yet now—' hinted M. Caux.

'Now it is different. He has betrayed me! Shall I suffer that in silence? . . .'

The Examining Magistrate checked her.

'Quite so, quite so,' he murmured soothingly. 'And now, Mademoiselle, perhaps you will read over the statement of what you have told us, see that it is correct, and sign it.'

Mirelle wasted no time on the document.

'Yes, yes,' she said, 'it is correct.' She rose to her feet. 'You require me no longer, Messieurs?'

'At present, no, Mademoiselle.'

'And Dereek will be arrested?'

'At once, Mademoiselle.'

Mirelle laughed cruelly and drew her fur draperies closer about her.

'He should have thought of this before he insulted me,' she cried.

'There is one little matter' – Poirot coughed apologetically – 'just a matter of detail.'

'Yes?'

'What makes you think that Madame Kettering was dead when the train left Lyons?'

Mirelle stared.

'But she *was* dead.'

'Was she?'

'Yes, of course. I—'

She came to an abrupt stop. Poirot was regarding her intently, and he saw the wary look that came into her eyes.

'I have been told so. Everybody says so.'

'Oh,' said Poirot, 'I was not aware that the fact had been mentioned outside the Examining Magistrate's office.'

Mirelle appeared somewhat discomposed.

'One hears those things,' she said vaguely; 'they get about. Somebody told me. I can't remember who it was.'

She moved to the door. M. Caux sprang forward to open it for her, and as he did so, Poirot's voice rose gently once more.

'And the jewels? Pardon, Mademoiselle. Can you tell me anything about those?'

'The jewels? What jewels?'

'The rubies of Catherine the Great. Since you hear so much, you must have heard of them.'

'I know nothing about any jewels,' said Mirelle sharply.

She went out, closing the door behind her. M. Caux came back to his chair; the Examining Magistrate sighed.

'What a fury!' he said, 'but *diablement chic*. I wonder if she is telling the truth? I think so.'

'There is *some* truth in her story, certainly,' said Poirot. 'We have confirmation of it from Miss Grey. She was looking down the corridor a short time before the train reached Lyons, and she saw M. Kettering go into his wife's compartment.'

'The case against him seems quite clear,' said the Commissary, sighing: 'it is a thousand pities,' he murmured.

'How do you mean?' asked Poirot.

'It has been the ambition of my life to lay the Comte de la Roche by the heels. This time, *ma foi*, I thought we had got him. This other – it is not nearly so satisfactory.'

M. Carrège rubbed his nose.

'If anything goes wrong,' he observed cautiously, 'it will be most awkward. M. Kettering is of the aristocracy. It will get into the newspapers. If we have made a mistake—' He shrugged his shoulders forebodingly.

'The jewels now,' said the Commissary, 'what do you think he has done with them?'

'He took them for a plant, of course,' said M. Carrège; 'they must have been a great inconvenience to him and very awkward to dispose of.'

Poirot smiled.

'I have an idea of my own about the jewels. Tell me, Messieurs, what do you know of a man called the Marquis?'

The Commissary leant forward excitedly.

'The Marquis,' he said, 'the Marquis? Do you think he is mixed up in this affair, M. Poirot?'

'I ask you what you know of him.'

The Commissary made an expressive grimace.

'Not as much as we should like to,' he observed ruefully. 'He works behind the scenes, you understand. He has underlings who do his dirty work for him. But he is someone high up. That we are sure of. He does not come from the criminal classes.'

'A Frenchman?'

'Y—es. At least we believe so. But we are not sure. He has worked in France, in England, in America. There was a series of robberies in Switzerland last autumn which were laid at his door. By all accounts he is a *grand seigneur*, speaking French and English with equal perfection, and his origin is a mystery.'

Poirot nodded and rose to take his departure.

'Can you tell us nothing more, M. Poirot?' urged the Commissary.

'At present, no,' said Poirot, 'but I may have news awaiting me at my hotel.'

M. Carrège looked uncomfortable. 'If the Marquis is concerned in this—' he began, and then stopped.

'It upsets our ideas,' complained M. Caux.

'It does not upset mine,' said Poirot. 'On the contrary, I think it agrees with them very well. Au revoir, Messieurs; if news of any importance comes to me I will communicate it to you immediately.'

He walked back to his hotel with a grave face. In his absence, a telegram had come for him. Taking a paper-cutter from his pocket, he slit it open. It was a long telegram, and he read it over twice before slowly putting it in his pocket. Upstairs, George was awaiting his master.

'I am fatigued, Georges, much fatigued. Will you order for me a small pot of chocolate?'

The chocolate was duly ordered and brought, and George set it at the little table at his master's elbow. As he was preparing to retire, Poirot spoke:

'I believe, Georges, that you have a good knowledge of the English aristocracy?' murmured Poirot.

George smiles apologetically.

'I think that I might say that I have' sir, he replied.

'I suppose that it is your opinion, Georges, that criminals are invariably drawn from the lower orders?'

'Not always, sir. There was great trouble with one of the Duke of Devize's younger sons. He left Eton under a cloud, and after that he caused great anxiety on several occasions. The police would not accept the view that it was kleptomania. A very clever young gentleman, sir, but vicious through and through, if you take my meaning. His Grace shipped him to Australia, and I hear he was convicted out there under another name. Very odd, sir, but there it is. The young gentleman, I need hardly say, was not in want financially.'

Poirot nodded his head slowly.

'Love of excitement,' he murmured, 'and a little kink in the brain somewhere. I wonder now—'

'Then there was Lady Mary Fox's daughter,' continued the valet in a mood of reminiscence. 'Swindled tradespeople something shocking, she did. Very worrying to the best families, if I may say so, and there are many other queer cases I could mention.'

'You have a wide experience, Georges,' murmured Poirot. I often wonder having lived so exclusively with titled families that you demean yourself by coming as a valet to me. I put it down to love of excitement on your part.'

'Not exactly, sir,' said George. 'I happened to see in *Society Snippets* that you had been received at Buckingham Palace. That was just when I was looking for a new situation. His Majesty, so it said, had been most gracious and friendly and thought very highly of your abilities.'

'Ah,' said Poirot, 'one always likes to know the reason for things.'

He remained in thought for a few moments and then said:

'You rang up Mademoiselle Papopolous?'

'Yes, sir; she and her father will be pleased to dine with you to-night.'

'Ah,' said Poirot thoughtfully. He drank off his chocolate, set the cup and saucer neatly in the middle of the tray, and spoke gently, more to himself than to the valet.

'The squirrel, my good Georges, collects nuts. He stores them up in the autumn so that they may be of advantage to him later. To make a success of humanity, Georges, we must profit by the lessons of those below us in the animal kingdom. I have always done so. I have been the cat, watching the mouse hole. I have been the good dog following up the scent, and not taking my nose from the trail. And also, my good Georges, I have been the squirrel. I have stored away the little fact here, the little fact there. I go now to my store and I take out one particular nut, a nut that I stored away – let me see, seventeen years ago. You follow me, Georges?'

'I should hardly have thought, sir,' said George, 'that nuts would have kept so long as that, though I know one can do wonders with preserving bottles.'

Poirot looked at him and smiled.

28

POIROT PLAYS THE SQUIRREL

Poirot started to keep his dinner appointment with a margin of three-quarters of an hour to spare. He had an object in this. The car took him, not straight to Monte Carlo, but to Lady Tamplin's house at Cap Martin, where he asked for Miss Grey. The ladies were dressing and Poirot was shown into a small salon to wait, and here, after a lapse of three or four minutes, Lenox Tamplin came to him.

'Katherine is not quite ready yet,' she said. 'Can I give her a message, or would you rather wait until she comes down?'

Poirot looked at her thoughtfully. He was a minute or two in replying, as though something of great weight hung upon his decision. Apparently the answer to such a simple question mattered.

'No,' he said at last, 'No, I do not think it is necessary that I should wait to see Mademoiselle Katherine. I think, perhaps, that it is better that I should not. These things are sometimes difficult.'

Lenox waited politely, her eyebrows slightly raised.

'I have a piece of news,' M. Kettering was arrested to-night for the murder of his wife.'

'You want me to tell Katherine that?' asked Lenox. She breathed rather hard, as though she had been running; her face, Poirot thought, looked white and strained – rather noticeably so.

'If you please, Mademoiselle.'

'Why?' said Lenox. 'Do you think Katherine will be upset? Do you think she cares?'

'I don't know, Mademoiselle,' said Poirot. 'See, I admit it frankly. As a rule I know everything, but in this case, I – well, I do not. You, perhaps, know better than I do.'

'Yes,' said Lenox, 'I know – but I am not going to tell you all the same.'

She paused for a minute or two, her dark brows drawn together in a frown.

'You believe he did it?' she said abruptly.

'The police say so.'

'Ah,' said Lenox, 'hedging, are you? So there is something to hedge about.'

Again she was silent, frowning. Poirot said gently:

'You have known Derek Kettering a long time, have you not?'

'Off and on ever since I was a kid,' said Lenox gruffly. Poirot nodded his head several times without speaking.

With one of her brusque movements Lenox drew forward a chair and sat down on it, her elbows on the table and her face supported by her hands. Sitting thus, she looked directly across the table at Poirot.

'What have they got to go on?' she demanded. 'Motive, I suppose. Probably came into money at her death.'

'He came into two million.'

'And if she had not died he would have been ruined?'

'Yes.'

'But there must have been more than that,' persisted Lenox. He travelled by the same train, I know, but – that would not be enough to go on by itself.'

'A cigarette case with the letter "K" on it which did not belong to Mrs Kettering was found in her carriage, and he was seen by two people entering and leaving the compartment just before the train got into Lyons.'

'What two people?'

'Your friend Miss Grey was one of them. The other was Mademoiselle Mirelle, the dancer.'

'And he, Derek, what has he got to say about it?' demanded Lenox sharply.

'He denies having entered his wife's compartment at all,' said Poirot.

'Fool!' said Lenox crisply, frowning. 'Just before Lyons, you say? Does nobody know when – when she died?'

'The doctors' evidence necessarily cannot be very definite,' said Poirot; 'they are inclined to think that death was unlikely to have occurred after leaving Lyons. And we know this much, that a few moments after leaving Lyons Mrs Kettering was dead.'

'How do you know that?'

Poirot was smiling rather oddly to himself.

'Someone else went into her compartment and found her dead.'

'And they did not rouse the train?'

'No.'

'Why was that?'

'Doubtless they had their reasons.'

Lenox looked at him sharply.

'Do you know the reason?'

'I think so – yes.'

Lenox sat still turning things over in her mind. Poirot watched her in silence. At last she looked up. A soft colour had come into her cheeks and her eyes were shining.

'You think someone on the train must have killed her, but that need not be so at all. What is to stop anyone swinging themselves on to the train when it stopped at Lyons? They could go straight to her compartment, strangle her, and take the rubies and drop off the train again without anyone being the wiser. She may have been actually killed while the train was in Lyons station. Then she would have been alive when Derek went in, and dead when the other person found her.'

Poirot leant back in his chair. He drew a deep breath. He looked across at the girl and nodded his head three times, then he heaved a sigh.

'Mademoiselle,' he said, 'what you have said there is very just – very true. I was struggling in the darkness, and you have shown me a light. There was a point that puzzled me and you have made it plain.'

He got up.

'And Derek?' said Lenox.

'Who knows?' said Poirot, with a shrug of his shoulders. 'But I tell you this, Mademoiselle. I am not satisfied; no, I, Hercule Poirot, am not yet satisfied. It may be that this very night I shall learn something more. At least, I go to try.'

'You are meeting someone?'

'Yes.'

'Someone who knows something?'

'Someone who might know something. In these matters one must leave no stone unturned. Au revoir, Mademoiselle.'

Lenox accompanied him to the door.

'Have I – helped?' she asked.

Poirot's face softened as he looked up at her standing on the doorstep above him.

'Yes, Mademoiselle, you have helped. If things are very dark, always remember that.'

When the car had driven off he relapsed into a frowning absorption, but in his eyes was that faint green light which was always the precursor of the triumph to be.

He was a few minutes late at the rendezvous, and found that M. Papopolous and his daughter had arrived before him. His apologies were abject, and he outdid himself in politeness and small attentions. The Greek was looking particularly benign and noble this evening, a sorrowful patriarch of blameless life. Zia was looking handsome and good humoured. The dinner was a pleasant one. Poirot was his best and most sparkling self. He told anecdotes, he made jokes, he paid graceful compliments to Zia Papopolous, and he told many interesting incidents of his career. The menu was a carefully selected one, and the wine was excellent.

At the close of dinner M. Papopolous inquired politely:

'And the tip I gave you? You have had your little flutter on the horse?'

'I am in communication with – er – my bookmaker,' replied Poirot.

The eyes of the two men met.

'A well-known horse, eh?'

'No,' said Poirot; it is what our friends, the English, call a dark horse.'

'Ah!' said M. Papopolous thoughtfully.

'Now we must step across to the Casino and have our little flutter at the roulette table,' cried Poirot gaily.

At the Casino the party separated, Poirot devoting himself solely to Zia, whilst Papopolous himself drifted away.

Poirot was not fortunate, but Zia had a run of good luck, and had soon won a few thousand francs.

'It would be as well,' she observed drily to Poirot, 'if I stopped now.'

Poirot's eyes twinkled.

'Superb!' he exclaimed. 'You are the daughter of your father, Mademoiselle Zia. To know when to stop. Ah! that is the art.'

He looked round the rooms.

'I cannot see your father anywhere about,' he remarked carelessly. 'I will fetch your cloak for you, Mademoiselle, and we will go out in the gardens.'

He did not, however, go straight to the cloakroom. His sharp eyes had seen but a little while before the departure of M. Papopolous. He was anxious to know what had become of the wily Greek. He ran him to earth unexpectedly in the big entrance hall. He was standing by one of the pillars, talking to a lady who had just arrived. The lady was Mirelle.

Poirot sidled unostentatiously round the room. He arrived at the other side of the pillar, and unnoticed by the two who were talking together in an animated fashion – or rather, that is to say, the dancer was talking, Papopolous contributing an occasional monosyllable and a good many expressive gestures.

'I tell you I must have time,' the dancer was saying. 'If you give me time I will get the money.'

'To wait' – the Greek shrugged his shoulders – 'it is awkward.'

'Only a very little while,' pleaded the other. 'Ah! but you must! A week – ten days – that is all I ask. You can be sure of your affair. The money will be forthcoming.'

Papopolous shifted a little and looked round him uneasily – to find Poirot almost at his elbow with a beaming innocent face.

'Ah! vous voilà, M. Papopolous. I have been looking for you.

It is permitted that I take Mademoiselle Zia for a little turn in the gardens? Good evening, Mademoiselle.' He bowed very low to Mirelle. 'A thousand pardons that I did not see you immediately.'

The dancer accepted his greetings rather impatiently. She was clearly annoyed at the interruption of her *tête-à-tête*. Poirot was quick to take the hint. Papopolous had already murmured: 'Certainly – but certainly,' and Poirot withdrew forthwith.

He fetched Zia's cloak, and together they strolled out into the gardens.

'This is where the suicides take place,' said Zia.

Poirot shrugged his shoulders. 'So it is said. Men are foolish, are they not, Mademoiselle? To eat, to drink, to breathe the good air, it is a very pleasant thing, Mademoiselle. One is foolish to leave all that simply because one has no money – or because the heart aches. *L'amour*, it causes many fatalities, does it not?'

Zia laughed.

'You should not laugh at love, Mademoiselle,' said Poirot, shaking an energetic forefinger at her. 'You who are young and beautiful.'

'Hardly that,' said Zia; 'you forget that I am thirty-three, M. Poirot. I am frank with you, because it is no good being otherwise. As you told my father it is exactly seventeen years since you aided us in Paris that time.'

'When I look at you, it seems much less,' said Poirot gallantly. 'You were then very much as you are now, Mademoiselle, a little thinner, a little paler, a little more serious. Sixteen years old and fresh from your *pension*. Not quite the *petite pensionnaire*, not quite a woman. You were very delicious, very charming, Mademoiselle Zia; others thought so too, without doubt.'

'At sixteen,' said Zia, 'one is simple and a little fool.'

'That may be,' said Poirot; 'yes, that well may be. At sixteen one is credulous, is one not? One believes what one is told.'

If he saw the quick sideways glance that the girl shot at him, he pretended not to have done so. He continued dreamily: 'It was a curious affair that, altogether. Your father, Mademoiselle, has never understood the true inwardness of it.'

'No?'

'When he asked me for details, for explanations, I said to him thus: "Without scandal, I have got back for you that which was lost. You must ask no questions." Do you know, Mademoiselle, why I said these things?'

'I have no idea,' said the girl coldly.

'It was because I had a soft spot in my heart for a little *pensionnaire,* so pale, so thin, so serious.'

'I don't understand what you are talking about,' cried Zia angrily.

'Do you not, Mademoiselle? Have you forgotten Antonio Pirezzio?' He heard the quick intake of her breath – almost a gasp.

'He came to work as an assistant in the shop, but not thus could he have got hold of what he wanted. An assistant can lift his eyes to his master's daughter, can he not? If he is young and handsome with a glib tongue. And since they cannot make love all the time, they must occasionally talk of things that interest them both – such as that very interesting thing which was temporarily in M. Papopolous' possession. And since, as you say, Mademoiselle, the young are foolish and credulous, it was easy to believe him and to give him a sight of that particular thing, to show him where it was kept. And afterwards when it is gone – when the unbelievable catastrophe has happened. Alas! the poor little *pensionnaire.* What a terrible position she is in. She is frightened, the poor little one. To speak or not to speak? And then there comes along that excellent fellow, Hercule Poirot. Almost a miracle it must have been, the way things arranged themselves. The priceless heirlooms are restored and there are no awkward questions.'

Zia turned on him fiercely.

'You have known all the time? Who told you? Was it – was it Antonio?'

Poirot shook his head.

'No one told me,' he said quietly. 'I guessed. It was a good guess, was it not, Mademoiselle? You see, unless you are good at guessing, it is not much use being a detective.'

The girl walked along beside him for some minutes in silence. Then she said in a hard voice:

'Well, what are you going to do about it; are you going to tell my father?'

'No,' said Poirot sharply. 'Certainly not.'

She looked at him curiously.

'You want something from me?'

'I want your help, Mademoiselle.'

'What makes you think that I can help you?'

'I do not think so. I only hope so.'

'And if I do not help you, then – you will tell my father?'

'But no, but no! Debarrass yourself of that idea, Mademoiselle. I am not a blackmailer. I do not hold your secret over your head and threaten you with it.'

'If I refuse to help you—?' began the girl slowly.

'Then you refuse, and that is that.'

'Then why—?' she stopped.

'Listen, and I will tell you why. Women, Mademoiselle, are generous. If they can render a service to one who has rendered a service to them, they will do it. I was generous once to you, Mademoiselle. When I might have spoken, I held my tongue.'

There was another silence; then the girl said, 'My father gave you a hint the other day.'

'It was very kind of him.'

'I do not think,' said Zia slowly, 'that there is anything that I can add to that.'

If Poirot was disappointed he did not show it. Not a muscle of his face changed.

'*Eh bien!*' he said cheerfully, 'then we must talk of other things.'

And he proceeded to chat gaily. The girl was *distraite*, however, and her answers were mechanical and not always to the point. It was when they were approaching the Casino once more that she seemed to come to a decision.

'M. Poirot?'

'Yes, Mademoiselle?'

'I – I should like to help you if I could.'

'You are very amiable, Mademoiselle – very amiable.'

Again there was a pause. Poirot did not press her. He was quite content to wait and let her take her own time.

'Ah bah,' said Zia, 'after all, why should I not tell you? My father is cautious – always cautious in everything he says. But I know that with you it is not necessary. You have told us it is only the murderer you seek, and that you are not concerned over the jewels. I believe you. You were quite right when you guessed that we were in Nice because of the rubies. They have been handed over here according to plan. My father has them now. He gave you a hint the other day as to who our mysterious client was.'

'The Marquis?' murmured Poirot softly.

'Yes, the Marquis.'

'Have you ever seen the Marquis, Mademoiselle Zia?'

'Once,' said the girl. 'But not very well,' she added. 'It was through a keyhole.'

351

'That always presents difficulties,' said Poirot sympatheti-cally, 'but all the same you saw him. You would know him again?'

Zia shook her head.

'He wore a mask,' she explained.

'Young or old?'

'He had white hair. It may have been a wig, it may not. It fitted very well. But I do not think he was old. His walk was young, and so was his voice.'

'His voice?' said Poirot thoughtfully. 'Ah, his voice! Would you know it again, Mademoiselle Zia?'

'I might,' said the girl.

'You were interested in him, eh? It was that that took you to the keyhole?'

Zia nodded.

'Yes, yes. I was curious. One had heard so much – he is not the ordinary thief – he is more like a figure of history or romance.'

'Yes,' said Poirot thoughtfully; 'yes, perhaps so.'

'But it is not this that I meant to tell you,' said Zia. 'It was just one other little fact that I thought might be – well – use-ful to you.'

'Yes?' said Poirot encouragingly.

'The rubies, as I say, were handed over to my father here at Nice. I did not see the person who handed them over, but—'

'Yes?'

'I know one thing. *It was a woman.*'

—— 29 ——

A LETTER FROM HOME

'DEAR KATHERINE, – Living among grand friends as you are doing now, I don't suppose you will care to hear any of our news; but as I always thought you were a sensible girl, perhaps you are a trifle less swollen-headed than I suppose Everything goes on much the same here. There was great trouble about the new curate, who is scandalously high. In my view, he is neither more nor less than a Roman. Everybody has spoken to the Vicar about it, but you know what the Vicar is – all Christian charity and no proper spirit. I have had a lot of trouble with maids lately. That girl Annie was no good – skirts up to her knees and wouldn't wear sensible woollen stockings. Not one of them can bear being spoken to. I have had a lot of pain with my rheumatism one way and another, and Dr Harris persuaded me to go and see a London specialist – a waste of three guineas and a railway fare, as I told him; but by waiting until Wednesday I managed to get a cheap return. The London doctor pulled a long face and talked all round about and never straight out, until I said to him, "I'm a plain woman, Doctor, and I like things to be plainly stated. Is it cancer, or is it not?" And then, of course, he had to say it was. They say a year with care, and not too much pain, though I'm sure I can bear pain as well as any other Christian woman. Life seems rather lonely at times, with most of my friends dead or gone before. I wish you were in St Mary Mead, my dear, and that is a fact. If you hadn't come into this money and gone off into grand society, I would have offered you double the salary poor Jane gave you to come and look after me; but there – there's no good wanting what we can't get. However, if things should go ill with you – and that is always possible. I have heard no end of tales of bogus noblemen marrying girls and getting hold of their money and then leaving them at the church door. I dare say you are too sensible for anything of the kind to happen to you, but one never knows; and never having had much attention of any kind it might easily go to your head now. So just in case, my dear, remember there is always a home for you here; and though a plain-spoken woman I am a warm-hearted one too. – Your affectionate old friend,

'AMELIA VINER.

'PS. – I saw a mention of you in the paper with your cousin, Viscountess Tamplin, and I cut it out and put it with my cuttings. I prayed for you on Sunday that you might be kept from pride and vainglory.'

Katherine read this characteristic epistle through twice, then she laid it down and stared out of her bedroom window across the blue waters of the Mediterranean. She felt a curious lump in her throat. A sudden wave of longing for St Mary Mead swept over her. So full of familiar, everyday, stupid little things – and yet – home. She felt very inclined to lay her head down on her arms and indulge in a real good cry.

Lenox, coming in at the moment, saved her.

'Hello, Katherine,' said Lenox. 'I say – what is the matter?'

'Nothing,' said Katherine, grabbing up Miss Viner's letter and thrusting it into her handbag.

'You looked rather queer,' said Lenox. 'I say – I hope you don't mind – I rang up your detective friend, M. Poirot, and asked him to lunch with us in Nice. I said you wanted to see him, as I thought he might not come for me.'

'Did you want to see him then?' asked Katherine.

'Yes,' said Lenox 'I have rather lost my heart to him. I never met a man before whose eyes were really green like a cat's.'

'All right,' said Katherine. She spoke listlessly. The last few days had been trying. Derek Kettering's arrest had been the topic of the hour, and the Blue Train Mystery had been thrashed out from every conceivable standpoint.

'I have ordered the car,' said Lenox, 'and I have told Mother some lie or other – unfortunately I can't remember exactly what; but it won't matter, as she never remembers. If she knew where we were going, she would want to come too, to pump M. Poirot.'

The two girls arrived at the Negresco to find Poirot waiting.

He was full of Gallic politeness, and showered so many compliments upon the two girls that they were soon helpless with laughter; yet for all that the meal was not a gay one. Katherine was dreamy and distracted, and Lenox made bursts of conversation, interspersed by silences. As they were sitting on the terrace sipping their coffee she suddenly attacked Poirot bluntly.

'How are things going? You know what I mean?'

Poirot shrugged his shoulders. 'They take their course,' he said.

'And you are just letting them take their course?'

He looked at Lenox a little sadly.

'You are young, Mademoiselle, but there are three things that cannot be hurried – *le bon Dieu,* Nature, and old people.'

'Nonsense!' said Lenox. 'You are not old.'

'Ah, it is pretty, what you say there.'

'Here is Major Knighton,' said Lenox.

Katherine looked round quickly and then turned back again.

'He is with Mr Van Aldin,' continued Lenox. 'There is something I want to ask Major Knighton about. I won't be a minute.'

Left alone together, Poirot bent forward and murmured to Katherine:

'You are *distraite*, Mademoiselle; your thoughts, they are far away, are they not?'

'Just as far as England, no farther.'

Guided by a sudden impulse, she took the letter she had received that morning and handed it across to him to read.

'That is the first word that has come to me from my old life; somehow or other – it hurts.'

He read it through and then handed it back to her.

'So you are going back to St Mary Mead?' he said.

'No, I am not,' said Katherine; 'why should I?'

'Ah,' said Poirot, 'it is my mistake. You will excuse me one little minute.'

He strolled across to where Lenox Tamplin was talking to Van Aldin and Knighton. The American looked old and haggard. He greeted Poirot with a curt nod but without any other sign of animation.

As he turned to reply to some observation made by Lenox, Poirot drew Knighton aside.

'M. Van Aldin looks ill,' he said.

'Do you wonder?' asked Knighton 'The scandal of Derek Kettering's arrest has about put the lid on things, as far as he is concerned He is even regretting that he asked you to find out the truth.'

'He should go back to England,' said Poirot.

'We are going the day after tomorrow.'

'That is good news,' said Poirot.

He hesitated, and looked across the terrace to where Katherine was sitting.

'I wish,' he murmured, 'that you could tell Miss Grey that.'

'Tell her what?'

'That you – I mean that M. Van Aldin is returning to England.'

Knighton looked a little puzzled, but he readily crossed the terrace and joined Katherine.

Poirot saw him go with a satisfied nod of the head, and then joined Lenox and the American. After a minute or two they joined the others. Conversation was general for a few minutes, then the millionaire and his secretary departed. Poirot also prepared to take his departure.

'A thousand thanks for your hospitality, Mesdemoiselles,' he cried; 'it has been a most charming luncheon. *Ma foi*, I needed it!' He swelled out his chest and thumped it. 'I am now a lion – a giant. Ah, Mademoiselle Katherine, you have not seen me as I can be. You have seen the gentle, the calm Hercule Poirot; but there is another Hercule Poirot. I go now to bully, to threaten, to strike terror into the hearts of those who listen to me.'

He looked at them in a self-satisfied way, and they both appeared to be duly impressed, though Lenox was biting her underlip, and the corners of Katherine's mouth had a suspicious twitch.

'And I shall do it,' he said gravely. 'Oh yes, I shall succeed.'

He had gone but a few steps when Katherine's voice made him turn.

'M. Poirot, I – I want to tell you. I think you were quite right in what you said. I am going back to England almost immediately.'

Poirot stared at her very hard, and under the directness of his scrutiny she blushed.

'I see,' he said gravely.

'I don't believe you do,' said Katherine.

'I know more than you think, Mademoiselle,' he said quietly.

He left her, with an odd little smile upon his lips. Entering a waiting car, he drove to Antibes.

Hipolyte, the Comte de la Roche's wooden-faced man-servant, was busy at the Villa Marina polishing his master's beautiful cut table glass. The Comte de la Roche himself had gone to Monte Carlo for the day. Chancing to look out of the window, Hipolyte espied a visitor walking briskly up to the hall door, a visitor of so uncommon a type that Hipolyte, experienced as he was, had some difficulty in placing him. Calling to his wife, Marie, who was busy in the kitchen, he drew her attention to what he called *ce type là*.

'It is not the police again?' said Marie anxiously.

'Look for yourself,' said Hipolyte.

Marie looked.

'Certainly not the police,' she declared. 'I am glad.'

'They have not really worried us much,' said Hipolyte. 'In fact, but for Monsieur le Comte's warning, I should never have guessed that stranger at the wine-shop to be what he was.'

The hall bell pealed and Hipolyte, in a grave and decorous manner, went to open the door.

'M. le Comte, I regret to say, is not at home.'

The little man with the large moustaches beamed placidly.

'I know that,' he replied. 'You are Hipolyte Flavelle, are you not?'

'Yes, Monsieur, that is my name.'

'And you have a wife, Marie Flavelle?'

'Yes, Monsieur, but—'

'I desire to see you both,' said the stranger, and he stepped nimbly past Hipolyte into the hall.

'Your wife is doubtless in the kitchen,' he said. 'I will go there.'

Before Hipolyte could recover his breath, the other had selected the right door at the back of the hall and passed along the passage and into the kitchen, where Marie paused open-mouthed to stare at him.

'*Voilà*,' said the stranger, and sank into a wooden armchair; 'I am Hercule Poirot.'

'Yes, Monsieur?'

'You do not know the name?'

'I have never heard it,' said Hipolyte.

'Permit me to say that you have been badly educated. It is the name of one of the great ones of this world.'

He sighed and folded his hands across his chest.

Hipolyte and Marie were staring at him uneasily. They were at a loss what to make of this unexpected and extremely strange visitor. 'Monsieur desires—?' murmured Hipolyte mechanically.

'I desire to know why you have lied to the police.'

'Monsieur' cried Hipolyte: 'I – lied to the police? Never have I done such a thing.'

M. Poirot shook his head.

'You are wrong,' he said; 'you have done it on several occasions. Let me see.' He took a small notebook from his pocket and consulted it. 'Ah, yes; on seven occasions at least. I will recite them to you.'

In a gentle unemotional voice he preceeded to outline the seven occasions.

Hipolyte was taken aback.

'But it is not of these past lapses that I wish to speak,' continued Poirot, 'only, my dear friend, do not get into the habit of thinking yourself too clever. I come now to the particular lie in which I am concerned – your statement that the Comte de la Roche arrived at this villa on the morning of 14th January.'

'But that was no lie, Monsieur; that was the truth. Monsieur le Comte arrived here on the morning of Tuesday, the 14th. That is so, Marie, is it not?'

Marie assented eagerly.

'Ah, yes, that is quite right. I remember it perfectly.'

'Oh,' said Poirot, 'and what did you give your good master for *déjeuner* that day?'

'I—' Marie paused, trying to collect herself.

'Odd,' said Poirot, 'how one remembers some things – and forgets others.'

He leant forward and struck the table a blow with his fist; his eyes flashed with anger.

'Yes, yes, it is as I say. You tell your lies and you think nobody knows. But there are two people who know. Yes – two people. One is *le bon Dieu*—'

He raised a hand to heaven, and then settling himself back in his chair and shutting his eyelids, he murmured comfortably:

'And the other is Hercule Poirot.'

'I assure you, Monsieur, you are completely mistaken. Monsieur le Comte left Paris on Monday night—'

'True,' said Poirot – 'by the Rapide. I do not know where he broke his journey. Perhaps you do not know that. What I do know is that he arrived here on Wednesday morning, and not on Tuesday morning.'

'Monsieur is mistaken,' said Marie stolidly.

Poirot rose to his feet.

'Then the law must take its course,' he murmured. 'A pity.'

'What do you mean, Monsieur?' asked Marie, with a shade of uneasiness.

'You will be arrested and held as accomplices concerned in the murder of Mrs Kettering, the English lady who was killed.'

'Murder!'

The man's face had gone chalk white, his knees knocked together. Marie dropped the rolling-pin and began to weep.

'But it is impossibue – impossible. I thought—'

'Since you stick to your story, there is nothing to be said. I think you are both foolish.'

He was turning towards the door when an agitated voice arrested him.

'Monsieur, Monsieur, just a little moment. I – I had no idea that it was anything of this kind. I – I thought it was just a matter concerning a lady. There have been little awkwardnesses with the police over ladies before. But murder – that is very different.'

'I have no patience with you,' cried Poirot. He turned round on them and angrily shook his fist in Hipolyte's face. 'Am I to stop here all day, arguing with a couple of imbeciles thus? It is the truth I want. If you will not give it to me, that is your lookout. *For the last time, when did Monsieur le Comte arrive at the Villa Marina – Tuesday morning or Wednesday morning?'*

'Wednesday,' gasped the man, and behind him Marie nodded confirmation.

Poirot regarded them for a minute or two, then inclined his head gravely.

'You are wise, my children,' he said quietly. 'Very nearly you were in serious trouble.'

He left the Villa Marina, smiling to himself.

'One guess confirmed,' he murmured to himself. 'Shall I take a chance on the other?'

It was six o'clock when the card of Monsieur Hercule Poirot was brought up to Merille. She stared at it for a moment or two, and then nodded. When Poirot entered, he found her walking up and down the room feverishly. She turned on him furiously.

'Well?' she cried. 'Well? What is it now? Have you not tortured me enough, all of you? Have you not made me betray my poor Dereek? What more do you want?'

'Just one little question, Mademoiselle. After the train left Lyons, when you entered Mrs Kettering's compartment—'

'What is that?'

Poirot looked at her with an air of mild reproach and began again.

'I say when you entered Mrs Kettering's compartment—'

'I never did.'

'And found her—'

'I never did.'

'*Ah, sacré!*'

He turned on her in a rage and shouted at her, so that she cowered back before him.

'Will you lie to me? I tell you I know what happened as well as though I had been there. You went into her compartment and you found her dead. I tell you I know it. To lie to me is dangerous. Be careful, Mademoiselle Mirelle.'

Her eyes wavered beneath his gaze and fell.

'I – I didn't—' she began uncertainly, and stopped.

'There is only one thing about which I wonder,' said Poirot – 'I wonder, Mademoiselle, if you found what you were looking for or whether—'

'Whether what?'

'Or whether someone else had been before you.'

'I will answer no more questions,' screamed the dancer. She tore herself away from Poirot's restraining hand, and flinging herself down on the floor in a frenzy, she screamed and sobbed. A frightened maid came rushing in.

Hercule Poirot shrugged his shoulders, raised his eyebrows, and quietly left the room.

But he seemed satisfied.

—— 30 ——

MISS VINER GIVES JUDGMENT

Katherine looked out of Miss Viner's bedroom window. It was raining, not violently, but with a quiet, well-bred persistence. The window looked out on a strip of front garden with a path down to the gate and neat little flower-beds on either side, where later roses and pinks and blue hyacinths would bloom.

Miss Viner was lying in a large Victorian bedstead. A tray with the remains of breakfast had been pushed to one side and she was busy opening her correspondence and making various caustic comments upon it.

Katherine had an open letter in her hand and was reading it through for the second time. It was dated from the Ritz Hotel, Paris.

'CHERE MADEMOISELLE KATHERINE' (It began) – 'I trust that you are in good health and that the return to the English winter has not proved too depressing. Me, I prosecute my inquiries with the utmost diligence. Do not think that it is the holiday that I take here. Very shortly I shall be in England, and I hope then to have the pleasure of meeting you once more. It shall be so, shall it not? On arrival in London I shall write to you. You remember that we are the colleagues in this affair? But indeed I think you know that very well. Be assured, Mademoiselle, of my most respectful and devoted sentiments.

HERCULE POIROT.'

Katherine frowned slightly. It was as though something in the letter puzzled and intrigued her.

'A choirboys' picnic indeed,' came from Miss Viner, 'Tommy Saunders and Albert Dykes ought to be left behind, and I shan't subscribe to it unless they are. What those two boys think they are doing in church on Sundays I don't know.

Tommy sang, "O God, make speed to save us," and never opened his lips again, and if Albert Dykes wasn't sucking a mint humbug, my nose is not what it is and always has been.'

'I know, they are awful,' agreed Katherine.

She opened her second letter, and a sudden flush came to her cheeks. Miss Viner's voice in the room seemed to recede into the far distance.

When she came back to a sense of her surroundings Miss Viner was bringing a long speech to a triumphant termination.

'And I said to her, "Not at all. As it happens, Miss Grey is Lady Tamplin's own cousin." What do you think of that?'

'Were you fighting my battles for me? That was very sweet of you.'

'You can put it that way if you like. There is nothing to me in a title. Vicar's wife or no vicar's wife, that woman is a cat. Hinting you had bought your way into Society.'

'Perhaps she was not so very far wrong.'

'And look at you,' continued Miss Viner. 'Have you come back a stuck-up fine lady, as well you might have done? No, there you are, as sensible as ever you were, with a pair of good Balbriggan stockings on and your sensible shoes. I spoke to Ellen about it only yesterday. "Ellen," I said, "you look at Miss Grey. She has been hobnobbing with some of the greatest in the land, and does she go about as you do with skirts up to her knees and silk stockings that ladder when you look at them, and the most ridiculous shoes that ever I set eyes on?"'

Katherine smiled a little to herself, it had apparently been worth while to conform to Miss Viner's prejudices. The old lady went on with increasing gusto.

'It has been a great relief to me that you have not had your head turned. Only the other day I was looking for my cuttings. I have several about Lady Tamplin and her War Hospital and what not, but I cannot lay my hand upon them. I wish you would look, my dear; your eyesight is better than mine. They are all in a box in the bureau drawer.'

Katherine glanced down at the letter in her hand and was about to speak, but checked herself, and going over to the bureau found the box of cuttings and began to look over them. Since her return to St Mary Mead, her heart had gone out to Miss Viner in admiration of the old woman's stoicism and pluck. She felt that there was little she could do for her old friend, but she knew from experience how much those seemingly small trifles meant to old people.

'Here is one,' she said presently. ' "Viscountess Tamplin,

who is running her villa at Nice as an Officers' Hospital, has just been the victim of a sensational robbery, her jewels having been stolen. Amongst them were some very famous emeralds, heirlooms of the Tamplin family." '

'Probably paste,' said Miss Viner; 'a lot of these Society women's jewels are.'

'Here is another,' said Katherine. 'A picture of her. "A charming camera study of Viscountess Tamplin with her little daughter Lenox." '

'Let me look,' said Miss Viner. 'You can't see much of the child's face, can you? But I dare say that is just as well. Things go by contraries in this world and beautiful mothers have hideous children. I dare say the photographer realised that to take the back of the child's head was the best thing he could do for her.'

Katherine laughed.

' "One of the smartest hostesses on the Riviera this season is Viscountess Tamplin, who has a villa at Cap Martin. Her cousin, Miss Grey, who recently inherited a vast fortune in a most romantic manner, is staying with her there." '

'That is the one I wanted,' said Miss Viner. 'I expect there has been a picture of you in one of the papers that I have missed; you know the kind of thing. Mrs Somebody or other Jones-Williams, at the something or other Point-to-Point, usually carrying a shooting-stick and having one foot lifted up in the air. It must be a trial to some of them to see what they look like.'

Katherine did not answer. She was smoothing out the cutting with her finger, and her face had a puzzled, worried look. Then she drew the second letter out of its envelope and mastered its contents once more. She turned to her friend.

'Miss Viner? I wonder – there is a friend of mine, someone I met on the Riviera, who wants very much to come down and see me here.'

'A man?' said Miss Viner.

'Yes.'

'Who is he?'

'He is secretary to Mr Van Aldin, the American millionaire.'

'What is his name?'

'Knighton. Major Knighton.'

'H'm – secretary to a millionaire. And wants to come down here. Now, Katherine, I am going to say something to you for your own good. You are a nice girl and a sensible girl, and though you have your head screwed on the right way about most things, every woman makes a fool of herself once in her life. Ten to one what this man is after is your money.'

With a gesture she arrested Katherine's reply. 'I have been waiting for something of this kind. What is a secretary to a millionaire? Nine times out of ten it is a young man who likes living soft. A young man with nice manners and a taste for luxury and no brains and no enterprise, and if there is anything that is a softer job than being secretary to a millionaire it is marrying a rich woman for her money I am not saying that you might not be some man's fancy. But you are not young, and though you have a very good complexion you are not a beauty, and what I say to you is, don't make a fool of yourself; but if you are determined to do so, do see that your money is properly tied up on yourself. There, now I have finished. What have you got to say?'

'Nothing,' said Katherine; 'but would you mind if he did come down to see me?'

'I wash my hands of it,' said Miss Viner. 'I have done my duty, and whatever happens now is on your own head. Would you like him to lunch or to dinner? I dare say Ellen could manage dinner – that is, if she didn't lose her head.'

'Lunch would be very nice,' said Katherine. 'It is awfully kind of you, Miss Viner. He asked me to ring him up, so I will do so and say that we shall be pleased if he will lunch with us. He will motor down from town.'

'Ellen does a steak with grilled tomatoes pretty fairly,' said Miss Viner. 'She doesn't do it well, but she does it better than anything else. It is no good having a tart because she is heavy-handed with pastry; but her little castle puddings are not bad, and I dare say you could find a nice piece of Stilton at Abbot's. I have always heard that gentlemen like a nice piece of Stilton, and there is a good deal of Father's wine left, a bottle of sparkling Moselle, perhaps.'

'Oh no, Miss Viner; that is really not necessary.'

'Nonsense, my child. No gentleman is happy unless he drinks something with his meal. There is some good pre-war whisky if you think he would prefer that. Now do as I say and don't argue. The key of the wine-cellar is in the third drawer down in the dressing-table, in the second pair of stockings on the left-hand side.'

Katherine went obediently to the spot indicated.

'The second pair, now mind,' said Miss Viner. 'The first pair has my diamond earrings and my filigree brooch in it.'

'Oh,' said Katherine, rather taken aback, 'wouldn't you like them put in your jewel-case?'

Miss Viner gave vent to a terrific and prolonged snort.

'No, indeed! I have much too much sense for that sort of thing, thank you. Dear, dear, I well remember how my poor father had a safe built in downstairs. Pleased as Punch he was with it, and he said to my mother, "Now, Mary, you bring me your jewels in their case every night and I will lock them away for you.' My mother was a very tactful woman, and she knew that gentlemen like having their own way, and she brought him the jewel-case locked up just as he said.

And one night burglars broke in, and of course – naturally – the first thing they went for was the safe– It would be, with my father talking up and down the village and bragging about it until you might have thought he kept all King Solomon's diamonds there. They made a clean sweep, got the tankards, the silver cups, and the presentation gold plate that my father had had presented to him, *and* the jewel-case.'

She sighed reminiscently. 'My father was in a great state over my mother's jewels. There was the Venetian set and some very fine cameos, and some pale pink corals, and two diamond rings with quite large stones in them. And then, of course, she had to tell him that, being a sensible woman, she had kept her jewellery rolled up in a pair of corsets, and there it was still as safe as anything.'

'And the jewel-case had been quite empty?'

'Oh, no, dear,' said Miss Viner, 'it would have been too light a weight then. My mother was a very intelligent woman; she saw to that. She kept her buttons in the jewel-case, and a very handy place it was. Boot buttons in the top tray, trouser buttons in the second tray, and assorted buttons below. Curiously enough, my father was quite annoyed with her. He said he didn't like deceit. But I mustn't go chattering on; you want to go and ring up your friend, and mind you choose a nice piece of steak, and tell Ellen she is not to have holes in her stockings when she waits at lunch.'

'Is her name Ellen or Helen, Miss Viner? I thought—'

Miss Viner closed her eyes.

'I can sound my h's, dear, as well as anyone, but Helen is *not* a suitable name for a servant. I don't know what the mothers in the lower classes are coming to nowadays.'

The rain had cleared away when Knighton arrived at the cottage. The pale fitful sunshine shone down on it and burnished Katherine's head as she stood in the doorway to welcome him. He came up to her quickly, almost boyishly.

'I say, I hope you don't mind. I simply had to see you again soon. I hope the friend you are staying with does not mind.'

'Come in and make friends with her,' said Katherine. 'She can be most alarming, but you will find that she has the softest heart in the world.'

Miss Viner was enthroned majestically in the drawing-room, wearing a complete set of the cameos which had been so providentially preserved in the family. She greeted Knighton with dignity and an austere politeness which would have damped many men. Knighton, however, had a charm of manner which was not easily set aside, and after about ten minutes Miss Viner thawed perceptibly. Luncheon was a merry meal, and Ellen, or Helen, in a new pair of silk stockings devoid of ladders, performed prodigies of waiting. Afterwards, Katherine and Knighton went for a walk, and they came back to have tea *tête-à-tête*, since Miss Viner had gone to lie down.

When the car had finally driven off Katherine went slowly upstairs. A voice called her and she went in to Miss Viner's bedroom.

'Friend gone?'

'Yes. Thank you so much for letting me ask him down.'

'No need to thank me. Do you think I am the sort of old curmudgeon who never will do anything for anybody?'

'I think you are a dear,' said Katherine affectionately.

'Humph,' said Miss Viner, mollified.

As Katherine was leaving the room she called her back.

'Katherine?'

'Yes.'

'I was wrong about that young man of yours. A man when he is making up to anybody can be cordial and gallant and full of little attentions and altogether charming. But when a man is really in love he can't help looking like a sheep. Now, whenever that young man looked at you he looked like a sheep. I take back all I said this morning. It is genuine.'

MR AARONS LUNCHES

'Ah!' said Mr Joseph Aarons appreciatively.

He took a long draught from his tankard, set it down with a sigh, wiped the froth from his lips, and beamed across the table at his host, Monsieur Hercule Poirot.

'Give me,' said Mr Aarons, 'a good Porterhouse steak and a tankard of something worth drinking, and anyone can have your French fallals and whatnots, your ordoovres and your omelettes and your little bits of quail. Give me,' he reiterated, 'a Porterhouse steak.'

Poirot, who had just complied with this request, smiled sympathetically.

'Not that there is much wrong with a steak and kidney pudding,' continued Mr Aarons. 'Apple tart? Yes, I will take apple tart, thank you, Miss, and a jug of cream.'

The meal proceeded. Finally, with a long sigh, Mr Aarons laid down his spoon and fork preparatory to toying with some cheese before turning his mind to other matters.

'There was a little matter of business I think you said, Monsieur Poirot,' he remarked. 'Anything I can do to help you I am sure I shall be most happy.'

'That is very kind of you,' said Poirot. 'I said to myself, "If you want to know anything about the dramatic profession there is one person who knows all that is to be known and that is my old friend, Mr Joseph Aarons." '

'And you don't say far wrong,' said Mr Aarons complacently; 'whether it is past, present, or future, Joe Aarons is the man to come to.'

'*Précisément*. Now I want to ask you, Monsieur Aarons, what you know about a young woman called Kidd.'

'Kidd? Kitty Kidd?'

'Kitty Kidd.'

'Pretty smart, she was. Male impersonator, song and dance – That one?'

'That is the one.'

'*Very* smart, she was. Made a good income. Never out of an engagement. Male impersonation mostly, but as a matter of fact, you could not touch her as a character actress.'

'So I have heard,' said Poirot; 'but she has not been appearing lately, has she?'

'No. Dropped right out of things. Went over to France and took up with some swell nobleman there. She quitted the stage then for good and all, I guess.'

'How long ago was that?'

'Let me see. Three years ago. And she has been a loss – let me tell you that.'

'She was clever?'

'Clever as a cartload of monkeys.'

'You don't know the name of the man she became friends with in Paris?'

'He was a swell, I know that. A Count – or was it a Marquis? Now I come to think of it, I believe it was a Marquis.'

'And you know nothing about her since?'

'Nothing. Never even run across her accidentally like. I bet she is tooling it round some of these foreign resorts. Being a Marquise to the life. You couldn't put one over on Kitty. She would give as good as she got any day.'

'I see,' said Poirot thoughtfully.

'I am sorry I can't tell you more, Monsieur Poirot,' said the other. 'I would like to be of use to you if I could. You did me a good turn once.'

'Ah, but we are quits on that; you, too, did me a good turn.'

'One good turn deserves another. Ha, ha!' said Mr Aarons.

'Your profession must be a very interesting one,' said Poirot.

'So-so,' said Mr Aarons non-committally. 'Taking the rough with the smooth, it is all right. I don't do so badly at it, all things considered, but you have to keep your eyes skinned. Never know what the public will jump for next.'

'Dancing has come very much to the fore in the last few years,' murmured Poirot reflectively.

'*I* never saw anything in this Russian ballet, but people like it. Too highbrow for me.'

'I met one dancer out on the Riviera – Mademoiselle Mirelle.'

'Mirelle? She is hot stuff, by all accounts. There is always money going to back her – though, so far as that goes, the girl can dance; I have seen her, and I know what I am talking about. I never had much to do with her myself, but I hear she is a terror to deal with. Tempers and tantrums all the time.'

'Yes,' said Poirot thoughtfully; 'yes, so I should imagine.'

'Temperament!' said Mr Aarons, 'temperament! That is what they call it themselves. My missus was a dancer before she married me, but I am thankful to say she never had any temperament. You don't want temperament in the home, Monsieur Poirot.'

'I agree with you, my friend; it is out of place there.'

'A woman should be calm and sympathetic, and a good cook,' said Mr Aarons.

'Mirelle has not been long before the public, has she?' asked Poirot.

'About two and a half years, that is all,' said Mr Aarons. 'Some French duke started her. I hear now that she has taken up with the ex-Prime Minister of Greece. These are the chaps who manage to put money away quietly.'

'That is news to me,' said Poirot.

'Oh, she's not one to let the grass grow under her feet. They say that young Kettering murdered his wife on her account. I don't know, I am sure. Anyway, he is in prison, and she had to look round for herself, and pretty smart she has been about it. They say she is wearing a ruby the size of a pigeon's egg – not that I have ever seen a pigeon's egg myself, but that is what they always call it in works of fiction.

'A ruby the size of a pigeon's egg!' said Poirot. His eyes were green and catlike. 'How interesting!'

'I had it from a friend of mine,' said Mr Aarons. 'But for all I know, it may be coloured glass. They are all the same, these women – they never stop telling tall stories about their jewels. Mirelle goes about bragging that it has got a curse on it. "Heart of Fire," I think she calls it.'

'But if I remember rightly,' said Poirot, 'the ruby that is named "Heart of Fire" is the centre stone in a necklace.'

'There you are! Didn't I tell you there is no end to the lies women will tell about their jewellery? This is a single stone, hung on a platinum chain round her neck; but, as I said before, ten to one it is a bit of coloured glass.'

'No,' said Poirot gently; 'no – somehow I do not think it is coloured glass.'

32

KATHERINE AND POIROT COMPARE NOTES

'You have changed, Mademoiselle,' said Poirot suddenly. He and Katherine were seated opposite each other at a small table at the Savoy.

'Yes, you have changed,' he continued.

'In what way?'

'Mademoiselle, these *nuances* are difficult to express.'

'I am older.'

'Yes, you are older. And by that I do not mean that the wrinkles and the crows' feet are coming. When I first saw you, Mademoiselle, you were a looker-on at life. You had the quiet, amused look of one who sits back in the stalls and watches the play.'

'And now?'

'Now you no longer watch. It is an absurd thing, perhaps, that I say here, but you have the wary look of a fighter who is playing a difficult game.'

'My old lady is difficult sometimes,' said Katherine, with a smile; 'but I can assure you that I don't engage in deadly contests with her. You must go down and see her some day, Monsieur Poirot. I think you are one of the people who would appreciate her pluck and her spirit.'

There was a silence while the waiter deftly served them with chicken *en casserole*. When he had departed, Poirot said: 'You have heard me speak of my friend Hastings? – he who said that I was a human oyster. *Eh bien*, Mademoiselle, I have met my match in you. You, far more than I, play a lone hand.'

'Nonsense,' said Katherine lightly.

'Never does Hercule Poirot talk nonsense. It is as I say.'

Again there was a silence. Poirot broke it by inquiring:

'Have you seen any of our Riviera friends since you have been back, Mademoiselle?'

'I have seen something of Major Knighton.'

'A-ha. Is that so?'

Something in Poirot's twinkling eyes made Katherine lower hers.

'So Mr Van Aldin remains in London?'

'Yes.'

'I must try to see him tomorrow or the next day.'

'You have news for him?'

'What makes you think that?'

'I – wondered, that is all.'

Poirot looked across at her with twinkling eyes.

'And now, Mademoiselle, there is much that you wish to ask me, I can see that. And why not? Is not the affair of the Blue Train our own *"roman policier"*?'

'Yes, there are things I should like to ask you.'

'Eh bien?'

Katherine looked up with a sudden air of resolution.

'What were you doing in Paris, Monsieur Poirot?'

Poirot smiled slightly.

'I made a call at the Russian Embassy.'

'Oh.'

'I see that that tells you nothing. But I will not be a human oyster. No, I will lay my cards on the table, which is assuredly a thing that oysters never do. You suspect, do you not, that I am not satisfied with the case against Derek Kettering?'

'That is what I have been wondering. I thought, in Nice, that you had finished with the case.'

'You do not say all that you mean, Mademoiselle. But I admit everything. It was I – my researches – which placed Derek Kettering where he now is. But for me the Examining Magistrate would still be vainly trying to fasten the crime on the Comte de la Roche. *Eh bien*, Mademoiselle, what I have done I do not regret. I have only one duty – to discover the truth, and that way led straight to Mr Kettering. But did it end there? The police say yes, but I, Hercule Poirot, am not satisfied.'

He broke off suddenly. 'Tell me, Mademoiselle, have you heard from Mademoiselle Lenox lately?'

'One very short, scrappy letter. She is, I think, annoyed with me for coming back to England.'

Poirot nodded.

'I had an interview with her the night that Monsieur Kettering was arrested. It was an interesting interview in more ways than one.'

Again he fell silent, and Kettering did not interrupt his train of thought 'Mademoiselle,' he said at last, 'I am now on delicate ground, yet I will say this to you. There is, I think someone who loves Monsieur Kettering – correct me if I am wrong – and for her sake – well – for her sake I hope that I am right and the police are wrong. You know who that someone is?'

There was a pause, then Katherine said:

'Yes – I think I know.'

Poirot leant across the table towards her.

'I am not satisfied, Mademoiselle; no, I am not satisfied. The facts, the main facts, led straight to Monsieur Kettering. But there is one thing that has been left out of account.'

'And what is that?'

'Ths disfigured face of the victim. I have asked myself, Mademoiselle, a hundred times, "Was Derek Kettering the kind of man who would deal that smashing blow after having committed the murder?" What end would it serve? What purpose would it accomplish? Was it a likely action for one of Monsieur Kettering's temperament? And, Mademoiselle, the answer to these questions is profoundly unsatisfactory. Again and again I go back to that one point – "why?" And the only things I have to help me to a solution of the problem are these.'

He whipped out his pocket-book and extracted something from it which he held between his finger and thumb.

'Do you remember, Mademoiselle? You saw me take these hairs from the rug in the railway carriage.'

Katherine leant forward, scrutinising the hairs keenly.

Poirot nodded his head slowly several times.

'They suggest nothing to you, I see that, Mademoiselle. And yet – I think somehow that you see a good deal.'

'I have had ideas,' said Katherine slowly, 'curious ideas. That is why I ask you what you were doing in Paris, Monsieur Poirot.'

'When I wrote to you—'

'From the Ritz?'

A curious smile came over Poirot's face.

'Yes, as you say, from the Ritz. I am a luxurious person sometimes – when a millionaire pays.'

'The Russian Embassy,' said Katherine, frowning. 'No, I don't see where that comes in.'

'It does not come in directly, Mademoiselle. I went there to get certain information. I saw a particular personage and I threatened him – yes, Mademoiselle, I, Hercule Poirot, threatened him.'

'With the police?'

'No,' said Poirot drily, 'with the Press – a much more deadly weapon.'

He looked at Katherine and she smiled at him, just shaking her head.

'Are you not just turning back into an oyster again, Monsieur Poirot?'

'No, no; I do not wish to make mysteries. See, I will tell you everything. I suspect this man of being the active party in the sale of the jewels of Monsieur Van Aldin. I tax him with it, and in the end I get the whole story out of him. I learn where the jewels were handed over, and I learn, too, of the man who paced up and down outside in the street – a man with a venerable head of white hair, but who walked with the light, springy step of a young man – and I give that man a name in my own mind – the name of "Monsieur le Marquis." '

'And now you have come to London to see Mr Van Aldin?'

'Not entirely for that reason. I had other work to do. Since I have been in London I have seen two more people – a theatrical agent and a Harley Street doctor. From each of them I have got certain information. Put these things together, Mademoiselle, and see if you can make of them the same as I do.'

'I?'

'Yes, you. I will tell you one thing, Mademoiselle. There has been a doubt all along in my mind as to whether the robbery and the murder were done by the same person. For a long time I was not sure—'

'And now?'

'And now I *know*.'

There was a silence. Then Katherine lifted her head. Her eyes were shining.

'I am not clever like you, Monsieur Poirot. Half the things that you have been telling me don't seem to me to point anywhere at all. The ideas that came to me came from such an entirely different angle—'

'Ah, but that is always so,' said Poirot quietly. 'A mirror shows the truth, but everyone stands in a different place for looking into the mirror.'

'My ideas may be absurd – they may be entirely different from yours, but—'

'Yes?'

'Tell me, does this help you at all?'

He took a newspaper cutting from her outstretched hand. He read it and, looking up, he nodded gravely.

'As I told you, Mademoiselle, one stands at a different angle for looking into the mirror, but it is the same mirror and the same things are reflected there.'

Katherine got up. 'I must rush,' she said. 'I have only just time to catch my train. Monsieur Poirot—'

'Yes, Mademoiselle.'

'It – it mustn't be much longer, you understand. I – I can't
go on much longer.'

There was a break in her voice.

He patted her hand reassuringly.

'Courage, Mademoiselle, you must not fail now; the end is
very near.'

33

A NEW THEORY

'Monsieur Poirot wants to see you, sir.'

'Damn the fellow!' said Van Aldin.

Knighton remained sympathetically silent.

Van Aldin got up from his chair and paced up and down.

'I suppose you have seen the cursed newspapers this morning?'

'I have glanced at them, sir.'

'Still at it hammer and tongs?'

'I am afraid so, sir.'

The millionaire sat down again and pressed his hands to his
forehead.

'If I had had an idea of this,' he groaned. 'I wish to God I
had never got that little Belgian to ferret out the truth. Find
Ruth's murderer – that was all I thought about.'

'You wouldn't have liked your son-in-law to go scot free?'

Van Aldin sighed.

'I would have preferred to take the law into my own hands.'

'I don't think that would have been a very wise proceeding,
sir.'

'All the same – are you sure the fellow wants to see me?'

'Yes, Mr Van Aldin. He is very urgent about it.'

'Then I suppose he will have to. He can come along this
morning if he likes.'

It was a very fresh and debonair Poirot who was ushered in.
He did not seem to see any lack of cordiality in the millionaire's manner, and chatted pleasantly about various trifles. He
was in London, he explained, to see his doctor. He mentioned
the name of an eminent surgeon.

'No, no, *pas la guerre* – a memory of my days in the police
force, a bullet of a rascally apache.'

He touched his left shoulder and winced realistically.

'I always consider you a lucky man, Monsieur Van Aldin;

you are not like our popular idea of American millionaires, martyrs to dyspepsia.'

'I am pretty tough,' said Van Aldin. 'I lead a very simple life, you know; plain fare and not too much of it.'

'You have seen something of Miss Grey, have you not?' inquired Poirot, innocently turning to the secretary.

'I – yes; once or twice,' said Knighton.

He blushed sligtly and Van Aldin exclaimed in surprise:

'Funny you never mentioned to me that you had seen her, Knighton.'

'I didn't think you would be interested, sir.'

'I like that girl very much,' said Van Aldin.

'It is a thousand pities that she should have buried herself once more in St Mary Mead,' said Poirot.

'It is very fine of her,' said Knighton hotly. 'There are very few people who would bury themselves down there to look after a cantankerous old woman who has no earthly claim on her.'

'I am silent,' said Poirot, his eyes twinkling a little; 'but all the same I say it is a pity. And now, Messieurs, let us come to business.'

Both the other men looked at him in some surprise.

'You must not be shocked or alarmed at what I am about to say. Supposing, Monsieur Van Aldin, that, after all, Monsieur Derek Kettering did not murder his wife?'

'What?'

Both men stared at him in blank surprise.

'Supposing, I say, that Monsieur Kettering did not murder his wife?'

'Are you mad, Monsieur Poirot?'

It was Van Aldin who spoke.

'No,' said Poirot, 'I am not mad. I am eccentric, perhaps – at least certain people say so; but as regards my profession, I am very much, as one says, "all there." I ask you, Monsieur Van Aldin, whether you would be glad or sorry if what I tell you should be the case?'

Van Aldin stared at him.

'Naturally I should be glad,' he said at last. 'Is this an exercise in suppositions, Monsieur Poirot, or are there any facts behind it?'

Poirot looked at the ceiling.

'There is an off-chance,' he said quietly, 'that it might be the Comte de la Roche after all. At least I have succeeded in upsetting his alibi'

374

'How did you manage that?'

Poirot shrugged his shoulders modestly.

'I have my own methods. The exercise of a little tact, a little cleverness – and the thing is done.'

'But the rubies,' said Van Aldin, 'these rubies that the Count had in his possession were false.'

'And clearly he would not have committed the crime except for the rubies. But you are overlooking one point, Monsieur Van Aldin. Where the rubies were concerned, someone might have been before him.'

'But this is an entirely new theory,' cried Knighton.

'Do you really believe all this rigmarole, Monsieur Poirot?' demanded the millionaire.

'The thing is not proved,' said Poirot quietly. 'It is as yet only a theory, but I tell you this, Monsieur Van Aldin, the facts are worth investigating. You must come out with me to the south of France and go into the case on the spot.'

'You really think this is necessary – that I should go, I mean?'

'I thought it would be what you yourself would wish,' said Poirot.

There was a hint of reproach in his tone which was not lost upon the other.

'Yes, yes, of course,' he said. 'When do you wish to start, Monsieur Poirot?'

'You are very busy at present, sir,' murmured Knighton.

But the millionaire had now made up his mind, and he waved the other's objections aside.

'I guess this business comes first,' he said. 'All right, Monsieur Poirot, tomorrow. What train?'

'We will go, I think, by the Blue Train,' said Poirot, and he smiled.

—— 34 ——

THE BLUE TRAIN AGAIN

'The Millionaires' Train,' as it is sometimes called, swung round a curve of line at what seemed a dangerous speed. Van Aldin, Knighton, and Poirot sat together in silence. Knighton and Van Aldin had two compartments connecting with each other, as Ruth Kettering and her maid had had on the fateful journey. Poirot's own compartment was farther along the coach.

The journey was a painful one for Van Aldin, recalling as it did the most agonising memories. Poirot and Knighton conversed occasionally in low tones without disturbing him.

When, however, the train had completed its slow journey round the *ceinture* and reached the Gare de Lyon, Poirot became suddenly galvanised into activity. Van Aldin realised that part of his object in travelling by the train had been to attempt to reconstruct the crime. Poirot himself acted every part. He was in turn the maid, hurriedly shut into her own compartment, Mrs Kettering, recognising her husband with surprise and a trace of anxiety, and Derek Kettering discovering that his wife was travelling on the train. He tested various possibilities, such as the best way for a person to conceal himself in the second compartment.

Then suddenly an idea seemed to strike him. He clutched at Van Aldin's arm.

'*Mon Dieu*, but that is something I have not thought of! We must break our journey in Paris. Quick, quick, let us alight at once.'

Seizing suit-cases he hurried from the train. Van Aldin and Knighton, bewildered but obedient, followed him. Van Aldin having once more formed his opinion of Poirot's ability was slow to depart from it. At the barrier they were held up. Their tickets were in charge of the conductor of the train, a fact which all three of them had forgotten.

Poirot's explanations were rapid, fluent, and impassioned, but they produced no effect upon the stolid-faced official.

'Let us get quit of this,' said Van Aldin abruptly. 'I gather you are in a hurry, Monsieur Poirot. For God's sake pay the fares from Calais and let us get right on with whatever you have got on your mind.'

But Poirot's flood of language had suddenly stopped dead, and he had the appearance of a man turned to stone. His arm still outflung in an impassioned gesture, remained there as though stricken with paralysis.

'I have been an imbecile,' he said simply. '*Ma foi*, I lose my head nowadays. Let us return and continue our journey quietly. With reasonable luck the train will not have gone.'

They were only just in time, the train moving off as Knighton, the last of the three, swung himself and his suitcase on board.

The conductor remonstrated with them, feelingly, and assisted them to carry their luggage back to their compartments. Van Aldin said nothing, but he was clearly disgusted at Poirot's extraordinary conduct. Alone with Knighton for a moment or two, he remarked:

'This is a wildgoose chase. The man has lost his grip on things. He has got brains up to a point, but any man who loses his head and scuttles round like a frightened rabbit is no earthly darned good.'

Poirot came to them in a moment or two, full of abject apologies and clearly so crestfallen that harsh words would have been superfluous. Van Aldin received his apologies gravely, but managed to restrain himself from making acid comments.

They had dinner on the train, and afterwards, somewhat to the surprise of the other two, Poirot suggested that they should all three sit up in Van Aldin's compartment.

The millionaire looked at him curiously.

'Is there anything that you are keeping back from us, Monsieur Poirot?'

'I?' Poirot opened his eyes in innocent surprise. 'But what an idea.'

Van Aldin did not answer, but he was not satisfied. The conductor was told that he need not make up the beds. Any surprise he might have felt was obliterated by the largeness of the tip which Van Aldin handed to him. The three men sat in silence. Poirot fidgeted and seemed restless. Presently he turned to the secretary.

'Major Knighton, is the door of your compartment bolted? The door into the corridor, I mean.'

'Yes; I bolted it myself just now.'

'Are you sure?' said Poirot.

'I will go and make sure, if you like,' said Knighton, smiling.

'No, no, do not derange yourself. I will see for myself.'

He passed through the connecting door and returned in a second or two, nodding his head.

'Yes, yes, it is as you said. You must pardon an old man's fussy ways.' He closed the connecting door and resumed his place in the right-hand corner.

The hours passed. The three men dosed fitfully, waking with uncomfortable starts. Probably never before had three people booked berths on the most luxurious train available, then declined to avail themselves of the accommodation they had paid for. Every now and then Poirot glanced at his watch, and then nodded his head and composed himself to slumber once more. On one occasion he rose from his seat and opened the connecting door, peered sharply into the adjoining compartment, and then returned to his seat, shaking his head.

'What is the matter?' whispered Knighton. 'You are expecting something to happen, aren't you?'

'I have the nerves,' confessed Poirot. 'I am like the cat upon the hot tiles. Every little noise it makes me jump.'

Knighton yawned.

'Of all the darned uncomfortable journeys,' he murmured. 'I suppose you know what you are playing at, Monsieur Poirot.'

He composed himself to sleep as best he could. Both he and Van Aldin had succumbed to slumber, when Poirot, glancing for the fourteenth time at his watch, leant across and tapped the millionaire on the shoulder.

'Eh? What is it?'

'In five or ten minutes, Monsieur, we shall arrive at Lyons.'

'My God!' Van Aldin's face looked white and haggard in the dim light. 'Then it must have been about this time that poor Ruth was killed.'

He sat staring straight in front of him. His lips twitched a little, his mind reverting back to the terrible tragedy that had saddened his life.

There was the usual long screaming sigh of the brake, and the train slackened speed and drew into Lyons. Van Aldin let down the window and leant out.

'If it wasn't Derek – if your new theory is correct, it is here that the man left the train?' he asked over his shoulder.

Rather to his surprise Poirot shook his head.

'No,' he said thoughtfully, 'no *man* left the train, but I think – yes, I think, a *woman* may have done so.'

Knighton gave a gasp.

'A woman?' demanded Van Aldin sharply.

'Yes, a woman,' said Poirot, nodding his head. 'You may not remember, Monsieur Van Aldin, but Miss Grey in her evidence mentioned that a youth in a cap and overcoat descended on to the platform ostensibly to stretch his legs. Me, I think that that youth was most probably a woman.'

'But who was she?'

Van Aldin's face expressed incredulity, but Poirot replied seriously and categorically:

'Her name – or the name under which she was known, for many years – is Kitty Kidd, but you, Monsieur Van Aldin, knew her by another name – *that of Ada Mason.*'

Knighton sprang to his feet.

'What?' he cried.

Poirot swung round to him.

'Ah! – before I forget it.' He whipped something from a pocket and held it out.

'Permit me to offer you a cigarette – out of your own cigarette-case. It was careless of you to drop it when you boarded the train on the *ceinture* at Paris.'

Knighton stood staring at him as though stupefied. Then he made a movement, but Poirot flung up his hand in a warning gesture.

'No, don't move,' he said in a silky voice; 'the door into the next compartment is open, and you are being covered from there this minute. I unbolted the door into the corridor when we left Paris, and our friends the police were told to take their places there. As I expect you know, the French police want you rather urgently, Major Knighton – or shall we say – Monsieur le Marquis?'

—— 35 ——

EXPLANATIONS

'Explanations?'

Poirot smiled. He was sitting opposite the millionaire at a luncheon table in the latter's private suite at the Negresco. Facing him was a relieved but very puzzled man. Poirot leant back in his chair, lit one of his tiny cigarettes, and stared reflectively at the ceiling.

'Yes, I will give you explanations. It began with the one point that puzzled me. You know what that point was? *The disfigured face.* It is not an uncommon thing to find when investigating a crime and it rouses an immediate question, the question of identity. That naturally was the first thing that occurred to me. Was the dead woman really Mrs Kettering? But that line led me nowhere, for Miss Grey's evidence was positive and very reliable, so I put that idea aside. The dead woman *was* Ruth Kettering.'

'When did you first begin to suspect the maid?'

'Not for some time, but one peculiar little point drew my attention to her. The cigarette-case found in the railway carriage and which she told us was one which Mrs Kettering had given to her husband. Now that was, on the face of it, most improbable, seeing the terms they were on. It awakened a doubt in my mind as to the general veracity of Ada Mason's statements. There was the rather suspicious fact to be taken into consideration, that she had only been with her mistress for two months. Certainly it did not seem as if she could have had anything to do with the crime since she had been left behind in Paris and Mrs Kettering had been seen alive by several people afterwards, but—'

Poirot leant forward. He raised an emphatic forefinger and wagged it with intense emphasis at Van Aldin.

'But I am a good detective. I suspect. There is nobody and nothing that I do not suspect. I believe nothing that I am told. I say to myself: how do we know that Ada Mason was left behind in Paris? And at first the answer to that question seemed completely satisfactory. There was the evidence of your secretary, Major Knighton, a complete outsider, whose testimony might be supposed to be entirely impartial, and there were the dead woman's own words to the conductor of the train. But I put the latter point aside for the moment, because a very curious idea – an idea perhaps fantastic and impossible – was growing up in my mind. If by an outside chance it happened to be true, that particular piece of testimony was worthless.

'I concentrated on the chief stumbling-block to my theory, Major Knighton's statement that he saw Ada Mason at the Ritz after the Blue Train had left Paris. That seemed conclusive enough, but yet, on examining the facts carefully, I noted two things. First, that by a curious coincidence he, too, had been exactly two months in your service. Secondly, his initial letter was the same – K.' Supposing – just supposing – that it was *his* cigarette-case which had been found in the carriage. Then, if Ada Mason and he were working together, and she recognised it when we showed it to her, would she not act precisely as she had done? At first, taken aback, she quickly evolved a plausible theory that would agree with Mr Kettering's guilt. *Bien entendu*, that was not the original idea. The Comte de la Roche was to be the scapegoat, though Ada Mason would not make her recognition of him too certain, in case he should be able to prove an alibi. Now, if you will cast your mind back to that time, you will remember a significant thing that happened. I suggested to Ada Mason that the man she had seen was not the Comte de la Roche, but Derek Kettering. She seemed uncertain at the time, but after I had got back to my hotel you rang me up and told me that she had come to you and said that, on thinking it over, she was now quite convinced that the man in question *was* Mr Kettering. I had been expecting something of the kind. There could be but one explanation of this sudden certainty on her part. After leaving your hotel, she had had time to consult with somebody, and had received instructions which she acted upon. Who had given her these instructions? Major Knighton. And there was another very small point, which might mean nothing or might mean a great deal. In casual conversation Knighton had talked of a jewel robbery in Yorkshire in a house where he was staying. Perhaps a mere coincidence – perhaps another small link in the chain.'

'But there is one thing I do not understand, Monsieur Poirot. I guess I must be dense or I would have seen it before now. Who was the man in the train at Paris? Derek Kettering or the Comte de la Roche?'

'That is the simplicity of the whole thing. *There was no man.* Ah – *mille tonnerres*! – do you not see the cleverness of it all? Whose word have we for it that there ever was a man there? Only Ada Mason's. And we believe in Ada Mason because of Knighton's evidence that she was left behind in Paris.'

'But Ruth herself told the conductor that she had left her maid behind there,' demurred Van Aldin.

'Ah! I am coming to that. We have Mrs Kettering's own evidence there, but, on the other hand, we have not really got her evidence, because, Monsieur Van Aldin, a dead woman cannot give evidence. It is not *her* evidence, but the evidence of the conductor of the train – a very different affair altogether.'

'So you think the man was lying?'

'No, no, not at all. He spoke what he thought to be the truth. But the woman who told him that she had left her maid in Paris was not Mrs Kettering.'

Van Aldin stared at him.

'Monsieur Van Aldin, Ruth Kettering was dead before the train arrived at the Gare de Lyon. It was Ada Mason, dressed in her mistress's very distinctive clothing, who purchased a dinner basket and who made that very necessary statement to the conductor.'

'Impossible!'

'No, no, Monsieur Van Aldin; not impossible. *Les femmes*, they look so much alike nowadays that one identifies them more by their clothing than by their faces. Ada Mason was the same height as your daughter. Dressed in that very sumptuous fur coat and the little red lacquer hat jammed down over her eyes, with just a bunch of auburn curls showing over each ear, it was no wonder that the conductor was deceived. He had not previously spoken to Mrs Kettering, you remember. True, he had seen the maid just for a moment when she handed him the tickets, but his impression had been merely that of a gaunt, black-clad female. If he had been an unusually intelligent man, he might have gone so far as to say that mistress and maid were not unlike, but it is extremely unlikely that he would even think that. And remember, Ada Mason, or Kitty Kidd, was an actress, able to change her appearance and tone of voice at a moment's notice. No, no; there was no danger of his recognising the maid in the mistress's clothing, but there *was* the danger that when he came to discover the body he might realise it was not the woman he had talked to the night before. And now we see the reason for the disfigured face. The chief danger that Ada Mason ran was that Katherine Grey might visit her compartment after the train left Paris, and she provided against that difficulty by ordering a dinner basket and by locking herself in her compartment.'

'But who killed Ruth — and when?'

'First, bear it in mind that the crime was planned and undertaken by the two of them — Knighton and Ada Mason, working together. Knighton was in Paris that day on your business. He boarded the train somewhere on its way round the *ceinture*. Mrs Kettering would be surprised, but she would be quite unsuspicious. Perhaps he draws her attention to something out of the window, and as she turns to look he slips the cord round her neck — and the whole thing is over in a second or two. The door of the compartment is locked, and he and Ada Mason set to work. They strip off the dead woman's outer clothes. Mason and Knighton roll the body up in a rug and put it on the seat in the adjoining compartment amongst the bags and suit-cases. Knighton drops off the train, taking the jewel case containing the rubies with him. Since the crime is not supposed to have been committed until nearly twelve hours later he is perfectly safe, and his evidence and the supposed Mrs Kettering's words to the conductor will provide a perfect alibi for his accomplice.

'At the Gare de Lyon Ada Mason gets a dinner basket and, shutting herself into the toilet compartment she quickly changes into her mistress's clothes, adjusts two false bunches of aburn curls, and generally makes up to resemble her as closely as possible. When the conductor comes to make up the bed, she tells him the prepared story about having left her maid behind in Paris; and whilst he is making up the berth, she stands looking out of the window, so that her back is towards the corridor and people passing along there. That was a wise precaution, because, as we know, Miss Grey was one of those passing, and she, among others, was willing to swear that Mrs Kettering was still alive at that hour.'

'Go on,' said Van Aldin.

'Before getting to Lyons, Ada Mason arranged her mistress's body in the bunk, folded up the dead woman's clothes neatly on the end of it, and herself changed into a man's clothes and prepared to leave the train. When Derek Kettering entered his wife's compartment, and, as he thought, saw her asleep in her berth, the scene had been set, and Ada Mason was hidden in the next compartment waiting for the moment to leave the train unobserved. As soon as the conductor had swung himself down on to the platform at Lyons, she follows, slouching along as though just taking a breath of air. At a moment when she is unobserved, she hurriedly crosses to the other platform, and takes the first train back to Paris and the Ritz Hotel. Her name has been registered there as taking a room the night before by one of Knighton's female accomplices. She has nothing to do but wait there placidly for your arrival. The jewels are not, and never have been, in her possession. No suspicion attaches to him, and, as your secretary, he brings them to Nice without the least fear of discovery. Their delivery there to Monsieur Papopolous is already arranged for, and they are entrusted to Mason at the last moment to hand over to the Greek. Altogether a very neatly planned coup, as one would expect from a master of the game such as the Marquis.'

'And you honestly mean that Richard Knighton is a well-known criminal, who has been at this business for years?'

Poirot nodded.

'One of the chief assets of the gentleman called the Marquis was his plausible, ingratiating manner. You fell a victim to his charm, Monsieur Van Aldin, when you engaged him as a secretary on such a slight acquaintanceship.'

'I could have sworn that he never angled for the post,' cried the millionaire.'

'It was very astutely done – so astutely done that it deceived a man whose knowledge of other men as as great as yours is.'

'I looked up his antecedents too. The fellow's record was excellent.'

'Yes, yes; that was part of the game. As Richard Knighton his life was quite free from reproach. He was well born, well connected, did honourable service in the War, and seemed altogether above suspicion; but when I came to glean information about the mysterious Marquis, I found many points of similarity. Knighton spoke French like a Frenchman, he had been in America, France, and England at much the same time as the Marquis was operating. The Marquis was last heard of as engineering various jewel robberies in Switzerland, and it was in Switzerland that you had come across Major Knighton; and it was at precisely that time that the first rumours were going round of your being in treaty for the famous rubies.'

'But why murder?' murmured Van Aldin brokenly. 'Surely a clever thief could have stolen the jewels without running his head into a noose.'

Poirot shook his head. 'This is not the first murder that lies to the Marquis's charge. He is a killer by instinct; he believes, too, in leaving no evidence behind him. Dead men and women tell no tales.

'The Marquis had an intense passion for famous and historical jewels. He laid his plans far beforehand by installing himself as your secretary and getting his accomplice to obtain the situation of maid with your daughter, for whom he guessed the jewels were destined. And, though this was his matured and carefully thought-out plan, he did not scruple to attempt a short-cut by hiring a couple of apaches to waylay you in Paris on the night you bought the jewels. The plan failed, which hardly surprised him, I think. This plan was, so he thought, completely safe. No possible suspicion could attach to Richard Knighton. But like all great men – and the Marquis was a great man – he had his weaknesses. He fell genuinely in love with Miss Grey, and suspecting her liking for Derek Kettering, he could not resist the temptation to saddle him with the crime when the opportunity presented itself. And now, Monsieur Van Aldin, I am going to tell you something very curious. Miss Grey is not a fanciful woman by any means, yet she firmly believes that she felt your daughter's presence beside her one day in the Casino Gardens at Monte Carlo, just after she had been having a long talk with Knighton. She was convinced, she says, that the dead woman was urgently trying to tell her something, and it suddenly came to her that what the dead woman was trying to say was that Knighton was her murderer! The idea seemed so fantastic at the time that Miss Grey spoke of it to no one. But she was so convinced of its truth that she acted on it – wild as it seemed. She did not encourage Knighton's advances, and she pretended to him that she was convinced of Derek Kettering's guilt.'

'Extraordinary,' said Van Aldin.

'Yes, it is very strange. One cannot explain these things.

Oh, by the way, there is one little point that baffled me considerably. Your secretary has a decided limp – the result of a wound that he received in the War. Now the Marquis most decidedly did not limp. That was a stumbling block. But Miss Lenox Tamplin happened to mention one day that Knighton's limp had been a surprise to the surgeon who had been in charge of the case in her mother's hospital. That suggested camouflage. When I was in London I went to the surgeon in question, and I got several technical details from him which confirmed me in that belief. I mentioned the name of that surgeon in Knighton's hearing the day before yesteraday. The natural thing would have been for Knighton to mention that he had been attended by him during the War, but he said nothing – and that little point, if nothing else, gave me the last final assurance that my theory of the crime was correct. Miss Grey, too, provided me with a cutting, showing that there had been a robbery at Lady Tamplin's hospital during the time that Knighton had been there. She realised that I was on the same track as herself when I wrote to her from the Ritz in Paris.

'I had some trouble in my inquiries there, but I got what I wanted – evidence that Ada Mason arrived on the morning after the crime and not on the evening of the day before.'

There was a long silence, then the millionaire stretched out a hand to Poirot across the table.

'I guess you know what this means to me, Monsieur Poirot,' he said huskily. 'I am sending you round a cheque in the morning, but no cheque in the world will express what I feel about what you have done for me. You are the goods, Monsieur Poirot. Every time, you are the goods.'

'Poirot rose to his feet; his chest swelled.

'I am only Hercule Poirot,' he said modestly, 'yet, as you say, in my own way I am a big man, even as you also are a big man. I am glad and happy to have been of service to you. Now I go to repair the damages caused by travel. Alas! My excellent Georges is not with me.'

In the lounge of the hotel he encountered a friend – the venerable Monsieur Papopolous, his daughter Zia beside him.

'I thought you had left Nice, Monsieur Poirot,' murmured the Greek as he took the detective's affectionately proffered hand.

'Business compelled me to return, my dear Monsieur Papopolous.'

'Business?'

'Yes, business. And talking of business, I hope your health is better, my dear friend?'

'Much better. In fact, we are returning to Paris tomorrow.'

'I am enchanted to hear such good news. You have not completely ruined the Greek ex-Minister, I hope.'

'I?'

'I understand you sold him a very wonderful ruby which – strictly *entre nous* – is being worn by Mademoiselle Mirelle, the dancer?'

'Yes,' murmured Monsieur Papopolous; 'yes, that is so.'

'A ruby not unlike the famous "Heart of Fire." '

'It has points of resemblance, certainly,' said the Greek casually

'You have a wonderful hand with jewels, Monsieur Papopolous. I congratulate you. Mademoiselle Zia, I am desolate that you are returning to Paris so speedily. I had hoped to see some more of you now that my business is accomplished.'

'Would one be indiscreet if one asked what that business was?' asked Monsieur Papopolous.

'Not at all, not at all. I have just succeeded in laying the Marquis by the heels.'

A far-away look came over Monsieur Papopolous' noble countenance.

'The Marquis?' he murmured; 'now why does that seem familiar to me? No – I cannot recall it.'

'You would not, I am sure,' said Poirot. 'I refer to a very notable criminal and jewel robber. He has just been arrested for the murder of the English lady, Madame Kettering.'

'Indeed? How interesting these things are!'

A polite exchange of farewells followed, and when Poirot was out of earshot, Monsieur Papopolous turned to his daughter.

'Zia,' he said, with feeling, 'that man is the devil!'

'I like him.'

'I like him myself,' admitted Monsieur Papopolous. 'But he is the devil, all the same.'

36

BY THE SEA

The mimosa was nearly over. The scent of it in the air was faintly unpleasant. There were pink geraniums twining along the balustrade of Lady Tamplin's villa, and masses of carnations below sent up a sweet, heavy perfume. The Mediterranean was at its bluest. Poirot sat on the terrace with Lenox Tamplin. He had just finished telling her the same story that he had told to Van Aldin two days before. Lenox had listened to him with absorbed attention, her brows knitted and her eyes sombre.

When he had finished she said simply:

'And Derek?'

'He was released yesterday.'

'And he has gone – where?'

'He left Nice last night.'

'For St Mary Mead?'

'Yes, for St Mary Mead.'

There was a pause.

'I was wrong about Katherine,' said Lenox. 'I thought she did not care.'

'She is very reserved. She trusts no one.'

'She might have trusted me,' said Lenox, with a shade of bitterness.

'Yes,' said Poirot gravely, 'she might have trusted you. But Mademoiselle Katherine has spent a great deal of her life listening, and those who have listened do not find it easy to talk, they keep their sorrows and joys to themselves and tell no one.'

'I was a fool,' said Lenox; 'I thought she really cared for Knighton. I ought to have known better. I suppose I thought so because – well, I hoped so.'

Poirot took her hand and gave it a little friendly squeeze. 'Courage, Mademoiselle,' he said gently.

Lenox looked very straight out across the sea, and her face, in its ugly rigidity, had for the moment a tragic beauty.

'Oh, well,' she said at last, 'it would not have done. I am too young for Derek; he is like a kid that has never grown up. He wants the Madonna touch.'

There was a long silence then Lenox turned to him quickly

and impulsively. 'But I *did* help, Monsieur Poirot – at any rate I did help.'

'Yes, Mademoiselle. It was you who gave me the first inkling of the truth when you said that the person who committed the crime need not have been on the train at all. Before that, I could not see how the thing had been done.'

Lenox drew a deep breath.

'I am glad,' she said; 'at any rate – that is something.'

From far behind them there came a long-drawn-out scream of an engine's whistle.

'That is that damned Blue Train,' said Lenox. 'Trains are relentless things, aren't they, Monsieur Poirot? People are murdered and die, but they go on just the same. I am talking nonsense, but you know what I mean.'

'Yes, yes, I know. Life is like a train, Mademoiselle. It goes on. And it is a good thing that that is so.'

'Why?'

'Because the train gets to its journey's end at last, and there is a proverb about that in your language, Mademoiselle.'

' "Journeys end in lovers meeting." ' Lenox laughed. 'That is not going to be true for me.'

'Yes – yes, it is true. You are young, younger than you yourself know. Trust the train, Mademoiselle, for it is *le bon Dieu* who drives it.'

The whistle of the engine came again.

'Trust the train Mademoiselle,' murmured Poirot again. 'And trust Hercule Poirot – *He knows.*'

DUMB WITNESS

I

THE MISTRESS OF LITTLEGREEN HOUSE

Miss Arundell died on May 1st. Though her illness was short, her death did not occasion much surprise in the little country town of Market Basing, where she had lived since she was a girl of sixteen. For Emily Arundell was well over seventy, the last of a family of five, and she had been known to be in delicate health for many years, and had, indeed, nearly died some eighteen months before of a similar attack to the one that killed her.

But though Miss Arundell's death surprised no one, something else did. The provisions of her will gave rise to varying emotions: astonishment, pleasurable excitement, deep condemnation, fury, despair, anger and general gossip. For weeks and even months Market Basing was to talk of nothing else! Everyone had their own contribution to make to the subject, from Mr Jones the grocer, who held that 'blood was thicker than water', to Mrs Lamphrey at the post office, who repeated *ad nauseam* that 'there's something behind it, depend upon it! You mark my words'.

What added zest to the speculations on the subject was the fact that the will had been made as late as April 21st. Add to this the further fact that Emily Arundell's near relations had been staying with her just before that date over Easter Bank Holiday, and it will be realized that the most scandalous theories could be propounded, pleasurably relieving the monotony of everyday life in Market Basing.

There was one person who was shrewdly suspected of knowing more about the matter than she was willing to admit. That was Miss Wilhelmina Lawson, Miss Arundell's companion. Miss Lawson, however, professed herself just as much in the dark as everyone else. She, too, she declared, had been dumbfounded when the will was read out.

A lot of people, of course, did not believe this. Nevertheless, whether Miss Lawson was or was not as ignorant as she declared herself to be, only one person really knew the true facts. That person was the dead woman herself. Emily Arundell had kept her own counsel, as she was in the habit of doing. Even to her lawyer she had said nothing of the motives underlying her action. She was content with making her wishes clear.

In that reticence could be found the keynote of Emily Arundell's character. She was, in every respect, a typical product of her generation. She had both its virtues and its vices. She was autocratic and often overbearing, but she was also intensely warm-hearted. Her tongue was sharp, but her actions were kind. She was outwardly sentimental, but inwardly shrewd. She had a succession of companions whom she bullied unmercifully, but treated with great generosity. She had a great sense of family obligation.

On the Friday before Easter, Emily Arundell was standing in the hall of Littlegreen House giving various directions to Miss Lawson.

Emily Arundell had been a handsome girl, and she was now a well-preserved, handsome old lady with a straight back and a brisk manner. A faint yellowness in her skin was a warning that she could not eat rich food with impunity.

Miss Arundell was saying: 'Now then, Minnie, where have you put them all?'

'Well, I thought – I hope I've done right – Dr and Mrs Tanios in the Oak room and Theresa in the Blue room and Mr Charles in the Old Nursery—'

Miss Arundell interrupted:

'Theresa can have the Old Nursery and Charles will have the Blue room.'

'Oh, yes – I'm sorry – I thought the Old Nursery being rather more inconvenient—'

'It will do very nicely for Theresa.'

In Miss Arundell's day, women took second place. Men were the important members of society.

'I'm so sorry the dear little children aren't coming,' murmured Miss Lawson sentimentally.

She loved children and was quite incapable of managing them.

'Four visitors will be quite enough,' said Miss Arundell. 'In any case, Bella spoils her children abominably. They never dream of doing what they are told.'

Minnie Lawson murmured:

'Mrs Tanios is a very devoted mother.'

Miss Arundell said with grave approval:

'Bella is a good woman.'

Miss Lawson sighed and said:

'It must be very hard for her sometimes – living in an outlandish place like Smyrna.'

Emily Arundell replied:

'She has made her bed and she must lie on it.' And having uttered this final Victorian pronouncement she went on: 'I am going to the village now to speak about the orders for the weekend.'

'Oh, Miss Arundell, do let me. I mean—'

'Nonsense! I prefer to go myself. Rogers needs a sharp word. The trouble with you Minnie, is, that you're not *emphatic* enough. Bob! Where *is* the dog?'

A wire-haired terrier came tearing down the stairs. He circled round and round his mistress, uttering short, staccato barks of delight and expectation.

Together mistress and dog passed out of the front door and down the short path to the gate.

Miss Lawson stood in the doorway smiling rather foolishly after them, her mouth a little open. Behind her a voice said tartly:

'Them pillowcases you gave me, miss, isn't a pair.'

'What? How stupid of me . . .'

Minnie Lawson plunged once more into household routine.

Emily Arundell, attended by Bob, made a royal progress down the main street of Market Basing.

It was very much of a royal progress. In each shop she entered the proprietor always hurried forward to attend to her.

She was Miss Arundell of Littlegreen House. She was 'one of our oldest customers'. She was 'one of the old school. Not many about like her nowadays.'

'Good morning, Miss. What can I have the pleasure of doing for you? Not tender? Well, I'm sorry to hear that. I thought myself it was as nice a little saddle – Yes, of course, Miss Arundell. If you say so, it is so – No, indeed, I wouldn't think of sending Canterbury to *you*, Miss Arundell – Yes, I'll see to it myself, Miss Arundell.'

Bob and Spot, the butcher's dog, circled slowly round each other, hackles raised, growling gently. Spot was a stout dog of nondescript breed. He knew that he must not fight with customers' dogs, but he permitted himself to tell them, by subtle indication, just exactly what mincemeat he would make of them were he free to do so.

Bob, a dog of spirit, replied in kind.

Emily Arundell said 'Bob!' sharply and passed on.

In the greengrocer's there was a meeting of heavenly bodies.

Another old lady, spherical in outline, but equally distinguished by that air of royalty, said:

'Mornin', Emily.'

'Good morning, Caroline.'

Caroline Peabody said:

'Expecting any of your young people down?'

'Yes, all of them. Theresa, Charles and Bella.'

'So Bella's home, is she? Husband too?'

'Yes.'

It was a simple monosyllable, but underlying it was knowledge common to both ladies.

For Bella Winter, Emily Arundell's niece, had married a Greek. And Emily Arundell's people, who were what is known as 'all service people', simply did not marry Greeks.

By way of being obscurely comforting (for, of course, such a matter could not be referred to openly), Miss Peabody said:

'Bella's husband's got brains. *And* charming manners!'

'His manners are delightful,' agreed Miss Arundell.

Moving out into the street Miss Peabody asked:

'What's this about Theresa being engaged to young Donaldson?'

Miss Arundell shrugged her shoulders.

'Young people are so casual nowadays. I'm afraid it will have to be a rather long engagement – that is, if anything comes of it. He has no money.'

'Of course Theresa has her own money,' said Miss Peabody.

Miss Arundell said stiffly:

'A man could not possibly wish to live on his wife's money.'

Miss Peabody gave a rich, throaty chuckle.

'They don't seem to mind doing it nowadays. You and I are out of date, Emily. What I can't understand is what the child sees in him. Of all the namby-pamby young men!'

'He's a clever doctor, I believe.'

'Those pince-nez – and that stiff way of talking! In my young days we'd have called him a poor stick!'

There was a pause while Miss Peabody's memory, diving into the past, conjured up visions of dashing, bewhiskered young men . . .

She said with a sigh:

'Send that young dog Charles along to see me – if he'll come.'

'Of course; I'll tell him.'

The two ladies parted.

They had known each other for considerably over fifty years. Miss Peabody knew of certain regrettable lapses in the life of

General Arundell, Emily's father. She knew just precisely what a shock Thomas Arundell's marriage had been to his sisters. She had a very shrewd idea of certain troubles connected with the younger generation.

But no word had ever passed between the two ladies on any of these subjects. They were both upholders of family dignity, family solidarity, and complete reticence on family matters.

Miss Arundell walked home, Bob trotting sedately at her heels. To herself, Emily Arundell admitted what she would never have admitted to another human being, her dissatisfaction with the younger generation of her family.

Theresa, for instance. She had no control over Theresa since the latter had come into her own money at the age of twenty-one. Since then the girl had achieved a certain notoriety. Her picture was often in the papers. She belonged to a young, bright, go-ahead set in London – a set that had freak parties and occasionally ended up in the police-courts. It was not the kind of notoriety that Emily Arundell approved of for an Arundell. In fact, she disapproved very much of Theresa's way of living. As regards the girl's engagement, her feelings were slightly confused. On the one hand, she did not consider an upstart Dr Donaldson good enough for an Arundell. On the other, she was uneasily conscious that Theresa was a most unsuitable wife for a quiet country doctor.

With a sigh her thoughts passed on to Bella. There was no fault to find with Bella. She was a good woman – a devoted wife and mother, quite exemplary in behaviour – and extremely dull! But even Bella could not be regarded with complete approval. For Bella had married a foreigner – and not only a foreigner, but a Greek. In Miss Arundell's prejudiced mind a Greek was almost as bad as an Argentine or a Turk. The fact that Dr Tanios had a charming manner and was said to be extremely able in his profession only prejudiced the old lady slightly more against him. She distrusted charm and easy compliments. For this reason, too, she found it difficult to be fond of the two children. They had both taken after their father in looks – there was really nothing English about them.

And then Charles . . .

Yes, Charles . . .

It was no use blinding one's eyes to facts. Charles, charming though he was, was not to be trusted . . .

Emily Arundell sighed. She felt suddenly tired, old, depressed . . .

She supposed that she couldn't last much longer . . .

Her mind reverted to the will she had made some years ago.

Legacies to the servants – to charities – and the main bulk of her considerable fortune to be divided equally between these, her three surviving relations . . .

It still seemed to her that she had done the right and equitable thing. It just crossed her mind to wonder whether there might not be some way of securing Bella's share of the money so that her husband could not touch it . . . She must ask Mr Purvis.

She turned in at the gate of Littlegreen House.

Charles and Theresa Arundell arrived by car – the Tanioses by train.

The brother and sister arrived first. Charles, tall and good-looking, with his slightly mocking manner, said:

'Hallo, Aunt Emily; how's the girl? You look fine.'

And he kissed her.

Theresa put an indifferent young cheek against her withered one.

'How are you, Aunt Emily?'

Theresa, her aunt thought, was looking far from well. Her face, beneath its plentiful make-up, was slightly haggard and there were lines around her eyes.

They had tea in the drawing room. Bella Tanios, her hair inclined to straggle in wisps from below the fashionable hat that she wore at the wrong angle, stared at her cousin Theresa with a pathetic eagerness to assimilate and memorize her clothes. It was poor Bella's fate in life to be passionately fond of clothes without having any clothes sense. Theresa's clothes were expensive, slightly bizarre, and she herself had an exquisite figure.

Bella, when she arrived in England from Smyrna, had tried earnestly to copy Theresa's elegance at an inferior price and cut.

Dr Tanios, who was a big, bearded, jolly-looking man, was talking to Miss Arundell. His voice was warm and full – an atractive voice that charmed a listener almost against his or her will. Almost in spite of herself, it charmed Miss Arundell.

Miss Lawson was fidgeting a good deal. She jumped up and down, handing plates, fussing over the tea-table. Charles, whose manners were excellent, rose more than once to help her, but she expressed no gratitude.

When, after tea, the party went out to make a tour of the garden, Charles murmured to his sister:

'Lawson doesn't like me. Odd, isn't it?'

Theresa said mockingly:

'Very odd. So there *is* one person who can withstand your fatal fascination?'

Charles grinned – an engaging grin – and said:

'Lucky it's only Lawson . . .'

In the garden Miss Lawson walked with Mrs Tanios and asked her questions about the children. Bella Tanios' rather drab face lighted up. She forgot to watch Theresa. She talked eagerly and animatedly. Mary had said such a *quaint* thing on the boat . . .

She found Minnie Lawson a most sympathetic listener.

Presently a fair-haired young man with a solemn face and pince-nez was shown into the garden from the house. He looked rather embarrassed. Miss Arundell greeted him politely.

Theresa said:

'Hallo, Rex!'

She slipped an arm through his. They wandered away.

Charles made a face. He slipped away to have a word with the gardener, an ally of his from the old days.

When Miss Arundell re-entered the house, Charles was playing with Bob. The dog stood at the top of the stairs, his ball in his mouth, his tail gently wagging.

'Come on, old man,' said Charles.

Bob sank down on his haunches, nosed his ball slowly and slowly nearer the edge. As he finally bunted it over he sprang to his feet in great excitement. The ball bumped slowly down the stairs. Charles caught it and tossed it up to him. Bob caught it neatly in his mouth. The performance was repeated.

'Regular game of his, this,' said Charles.

Emily Arundell smiled.

'He'll go on for hours,' said she.

She turned into the drawing room, and Charles followed her. Bob gave a disappointed bark.

Glancing through the window, Charles said:

'Look at Theresa and her young man. They *are* an odd couple!'

'You think Theresa is really serious over this?'

'Oh, she's crazy about him!' said Charles with confidence. 'Odd taste, but there it is. I think it must be the way he looks at her, as though she were a scientific specimen and not a live woman. That's rather a novelty for Theresa. Pity the fellow's so poor. Theresa's got expensive tastes.'

Miss Arundell said dryly:

'I've no doubt she can change her way of living – if she wants to! And after all she has her own income.'

'Eh? Oh, yes, yes, of course.'

Charles shot an almost guilty look at her.

That evening, as the others were assembled in the drawing room waiting to go in to dinner, there was a scurry and a burst of profanity on the stairs. Charles entered with his face rather red.

'Sorry, Aunt Emily. Am I late? That dog of yours nearly made me take the most frightful toss. He'd left that ball of his on the top of the stairs.'

'Careless little doggie,' cried Miss Lawson, bending down to Bob.

Bob looked at her contemptuously and turned his head away.

'I know,' said Miss Arundell. 'It's most dangerous. Minnie, fetch the ball and put it away.'

Miss Lawson hurried out.

Dr Tanios monopolized the conversation at the dinner-table most of the time. He told amusing stories of his life in Smyrna.

The party went to bed early. Miss Lawson, carrying wool, spectacles, a large velvet bag and a book, accompanied her employer to her bedroom chattering happily.

'Really *most* amusing, Dr Tanios. He is such *good* company! Not that I should quite care for that kind of life myself . . . One would have to boil the water, I expect . . . And goat's milk, perhaps – such a disagreeable taste—'

Miss Arudell snapped:

'Don't be a fool, Minnie. You told Ellen to call me at half past six?'

'Oh, yes, Miss Arundell. I said no tea, but don't you think it might be wiser – You know, the vicar at Southbridge – a most conscientious man – told me distinctly that there was no obligation to come fasting—'

Once more Miss Arundell cut her short.

'I've never yet taken anything before Early Service, and I'm not going to begin now. *You* can do as you like.'

'Oh, no – I didn't mean – I'm sure—'

Miss Lawson was flustered and upset.

'Take Bob's collar off,' said Miss Arundell.

The slave hastened to obey.

Still trying to please, she said:

'Such a *pleasant* evening. They all seem so *pleased* to be here.'

'Hmph,' said Emily Arundell. 'All here for what they can get.'

'Oh, dear Miss Arundell—'

'My good Minnie, I'm not a fool, whatever else I am! I just wonder which of them will open the subject first.'

She was not long left in doubt on that point. She and Miss Lawson returned from attending Early Service just after nine. Dr and Mrs Tanios were in the dining-room, but there were no signs of the two Arundells. After breakfast, when the others had left, Miss Arundell sat on, entering up some accounts in a little book.

Charles entered the room about ten.

'Sorry I'm late, Aunt Emily. But Theresa's worse. She's not unclosed an eyelid yet.'

'At half past ten breakfast will be cleared away,' said Miss Arundell. 'I know it is the fashion not to consider servants nowadays, but that is not the case in *my* house.'

'Good. That's the true diehard spirit!'

Charles helped himself to kidneys and sat down beside her.

His grin, as always, was very attractive. Emily Arundell soon found herself smiling indulgently at him. Emboldened by this sign of favour, Charles plunged.

'Look here, Aunt Emily, sorry to bother you, but I'm in the devil of a hole. Can you possibly help me out? A hundred would do it.'

His aunt's face was not encouraging. A certain grimness showed itself in her expression.

Emily Arundell was not afraid of speaking her mind. She spoke it.

Miss Lawson, bustling across the hall, almost collided with Charles as he left the dining-room. She glanced at him curiously. She entered the dining-room to find Miss Arundell sitting very upright with a flushed face.

2

THE RELATIONS

Charles ran lightly up the stairs and tapped on his sister's door. Her answering 'Come in' came promptly, and he entered.

Theresa was sitting up in bed yawning.

Charles took a seat on the bed.

'What a decorative female you are, Theresa,' he remarked appreciatively.

Theresa said sharply:

'What's the matter?'

Charles grinned.

'Sharp, aren't you? Well, I stole a march on you, my girl! Thought I'd make my touch before *you* got to work.'

'Well?'

Charles spread his hands downwards in negation.

'Nothing doing! Aunt Emily ticked me off good and proper. She intimated that she was under no illusions as to why her affectionate family had gathered round her! And she also intimated that the said affectionate family would be disappointed. Nothing being handed out but affection – and not so much of that.'

'You might have waited a bit,' said Theresa dryly.

Charles grinned again.

'I was afraid you or Tanios might get in ahead of me. I'm sadly afraid, Theresa my sweet, that there'll be nothing doing this time. Old Emily is by no means a fool.'

'I never thought she was.'

'I even tried to put the wind up her.'

'What d'you mean?' asked her sister sharply.

'Told her she was going about it the right way to get bumped off. After all, she can't take the dibs to heaven with her. Why not loosen up a bit?'

'Charles, you are a fool!'

'No, I'm not. I'm a bit of a psychologist in my way. It's never a bit of good sucking up to the old girl. She much prefers you to stand up to her. And after all, I was only talking sense. We get the money when she dies – she might just as well part with a little beforehand! Otherwise the temptation to help her out of the way might become overwhelming.'

'Did she see your point?' asked Theresa, her delicate mouth curling up scornfully.

'I'm not sure. She didn't admit it. Just thanked me rather nastily for my advice and said she was perfectly capable of taking care of herself. "Well," I said, "I've warned you." "I'll remember it," she said.'

Theresa said angrily:

'Really, Charles, you are an utter fool.'

'Damn it all, Theresa, I was a bit ratty myself! The old girl's rolling – simply rolling. I bet she doesn't spend a tenth part of her income – what has she got to spend it on, anyway? And here we are – young, able to enjoy life – and to spite us she's capable of living to a hundred. I want my fun now . . . So do you . . .'

Theresa nodded.

She said in a low, breathless voice:

'They don't understand – old people don't . . . they can't . . . They don't know what it is to *live*!'

Brother and sister were silent for some minutes.

Charles got up.

'Well, my love, I wish you better success than I've had. But I rather doubt it.'

Theresa said:

'I'm rather counting on Rex to do the trick. If I can make old Emily realize how brilliant he is, and how it matters terrifically that he should have his chance and not have to sink into a rut as a general practitioner . . . Oh, Charles, a few thousands of capital just at this minute would make all the difference in the world to our lives!'

'Hope you get it, but I don't think you will. You've got through a bit too much capital in riotous living in your time. I say, Theresa, you don't think the dreary Bella or the dubious Tanios will get anything, do you?'

'I don't see that money would be any good to Bella. She goes about looking like a rag-bag, and her tastes are purely domestic.'

'Oh, well,' said Charles vaguely. 'I expect she wants things for those unprepossessing children of hers, schools, and plates for their front teeth, and music lessons. And, anyway, it isn't Bella – it's Tanios. I bet *he's* got a nose for money all right! Trust a Greek for that. You know he's got through most of Bella's? Speculated with it and lost it all.'

'Do you think he'll get something out of old Emily?'

'He won't if I can prevent him,' said Charles grimly.

He left the room and wandered downstairs. Bob was in the hall. He fussed up to Charles agreeably. Dogs liked Charles.

He ran towards the drawing-room door and looked back at Charles.

'What's the matter?' said Charles, strolling after him.

Bob hurried into the drawing-room and sat down expectantly by a small bureau.

Charles strolled over to him.

'What's it all about?'

Bob wagged his tail, looked hard at the drawers of the bureau and uttered an appealing squeak.

'Want something that's in here?'

Charles pulled open the top drawer. His eyebrows rose. 'Dear, dear,' he said.

At one side of the drawer was a little pile of treasury notes.

Charles picked up the bundle and counted them. With a grin he removed three one-pound notes, two ten-shilling ones and put them in his pocket. He replaced the rest of the notes carefully in the drawer where he had found them.

'That was a good idea, Bob,' he said. 'Your uncle Charles will be able at any rate to cover expenses. A little ready cash always comes in handy.'

Bob uttered a faint reproachful bark as Charles shut the drawer.

'Sorry, old man,' Charles apologized. He opened the next drawer. Bob's ball was in the corner of it. He took it out. 'Here you are. Enjoy yourself with it.'

Bob caught the ball, trotted out of the room and presently bump, bump, bump, was heard down the stairs.

Charles strolled out into the garden. It was a fine sunny morning with a scent of lilac.

Miss Arundell had Dr Tanios by her side. He was speaking of the advantage of an English education – a good education – for children and how deeply he regretted that he could not afford such luxury for his own children.

Charles smiled with satisfied malice. He joined in the conversation in a light-hearted manner, turning it adroitly into entirely different channels.

Emily Arundell smiled at him quite amiably. He even fancied that she was amused by his tactics and was subtly encouraging them.

Charles's spirits rose. Perhaps, after all, before he left—

Charles was an incurable optimist.

Dr Donaldson called for Theresa in his car that afternoon

and drove her to Worthem Abbey, one of the local beauty spots. They wandered away from the Abbey itself into the woods.

There Rex Donaldson told Theresa at length about his theories and some of his recent experiments. She understood very little, but listened in a spellbound manner, thinking to herself:

'How clever Rex is – and how absolutely adorable!'

Her fiancé paused once and said rather doubtfully:

'I'm afraid this is dull stuff for you, Theresa.'

'Darling, it's too thrilling,' said Theresa firmly. 'Go on. You take some of the blood of the infected rabbit—'

Dr Donaldson went on.

Presently Theresa said with a sigh:

'Your work means a terrible lot to you, my sweet.'

'Naturally,' said Dr Donaldson.

It did not seem at all natural to Theresa. Very few of her friends did any work at all, and if they did they made extremely heavy weather about it.

She thought, as she had thought once or twice before, how singularly unsuitable it was that she should have fallen in love with Rex Donaldson. Why did these things, these ludicrous and amazing madnesses, happen to one? A profitless question. This had happened to her.

She frowned, wondering at herself. Her crowd had been so gay, so cynical. Love affairs were necessary to live, of course; but why take them seriously? One loved and passed on.

But this feeling of hers for Rex Donaldson was different; it went deeper. She felt instinctively that here there would be no passing on . . . Her need of him was simple and profound. Everything about him fascinated her. His calmness and detachment, so different from her own hectic, grasping life; the clear, logical coldness of his scientific mind, and something else, imperfectly understood – a secret force in the man masked by his unassuming, slightly pedantic manner, but which she nevertheless felt and sensed instinctively.

In Rex Donaldson there was genius, and the fact that his profession was the main preoccupation of his life and that she was only a part – though a necessary part – of existence to him only heightened his attraction for her. She found herself, for the first time in her selfish pleasure-loving life, content to take second place. The prospect fascinated her. For Rex she would do anything – anything!

'What a damned nuisance money is!' she said petulantly.

'If only Aunt Emily were to die, we could get married at once, and you could come to London and have a laboratory full of test-tubes and guinea-pigs, and never bother any more about children with mumps and old ladies with livers.'

Donaldson said:

'There's no reason why your aunt shouldn't live for many years to come – if she's careful.'

Theresa said despondently:

'I know that . . .'

In the big double-bedded room with the old-fashioned oak furniture, Dr Tanios said to his wife:

'I think that I have prepared the ground sufficiently. It is now your turn, my dear.'

He was pouring water from the old-fashioned copper can into the rose-patterned china basin.

Bella Tanios sat in front of the dressing-table, wondering why, when she combed her hair as Theresa did, it should not look like Theresa's!

There was a moment before she replied. Then she said:

'I don't think I want – to ask Aunt Emily for money.'

'It's not for yourself, Bella; it's for the sake of the children. Our investments have been so unlucky.'

His back was turned; he did not see the swift glance she gave him – a furtive, shrinking glance.

She said with mild obstinacy:

'All the same, I think I'd rather not . . . Aunt Emily is rather difficult. She can be generous, but she doesn't like being asked.'

Drying his hands, Tanios came across from the washstand

'Really, Bella, it isn't like you to be so obstinate. After all, what have we come down here for?'

She murmured:

'I didn't – I never meant – it wasn't to ask for money . . .'

'Yet you agreed that the only hope, if we are to educate the children properly, is for your aunt to come to the rescue.'

Bella Tanios did not answer. She moved uneasily.

But her face bore the mild, mulish look that many clever husbands of stupid wives know to their cost.

She said:

'Perhaps Aunt Emily herself may suggest—'

'It is possible, but I've seen no signs of it so far.'

Bella said:

'If we could have brought the children with us. Aunt Emily couldn't have helped loving Mary. And Edward is *so* intelligent.'

Tanios said dryly:

'I don't think your aunt is a great child-lover. It is probably just as well the children aren't here.'

'Oh, Jacob, but—'

'Yes, yes, my dear. I know your feelings. But these desiccated English spinsters – bah! they are not human. We want to do the best we can, do we not, for our Mary and our Edward? To help us a little would involve no hardship to Miss Arundell.'

Mrs Tanios turned; there was a flush in her cheeks.

'Oh, please, please, Jacob, not this time. I'm sure it would be unwise. I would so very, very much rather not.'

Tanios stood close behind her, his arm encircling her shoulders. She trembled a little and then was still – almost rigid.

He said – and his voice was still pleasant:

'All the same, Bella, I think – I think you will do what I ask . . . You usually do, you know – in the end . . . Yes, I think you will do what I say . . .'

—— 3 ——

THE ACCIDENT

It was Tuesday afternoon. The side door to the garden was open. Miss Arundell stood on the threshold and threw Bob's ball the length of the garden path. The terrier rushed after it.

'Just one more, Bob,' said Emily Arundell. 'A good one.'

Once again the ball sped along the ground, with Bob racing at full speed in pursuit.

Miss Arundell stooped down, picked up the ball from where Bob laid it at her feet and went into the house, Bob following her closely. She shut the side door, went into the drawing-room, Bob still at her heels, and put the ball away in the drawer.

She glanced at the clock on the mantelpiece. It was half-past six.

'A little rest before dinner, I think, Bob.'

She ascended the stairs to her bedroom. Bob accompanied her. Lying on the big chintz-covered couch with Bob at her feet, Miss Arundell sighed. She was glad that it was Tuesday and that her guests would be going tomorrow. It was not that this weekend had disclosed anything to her that she had not known before. It was more the fact that it had not permitted her to forget her own knowledge.

She said to herself:

'I'm getting old, I suppose . . .' And then, with a little shock of surprise: 'I *am* old . . .'

She lay with her eyes closed for half an hour, then the elderly house-parlourmaid, Ellen, brought hot water, and she rose and prepared for dinner.

Dr Donaldson was to dine with them that night. Emily Arundell wished to have an opportunity of studying him at close quarters. It still seemed to her a little incredible that the exotic Theresa should want to marry this rather stiff and pedantic young man. It also seemed a little odd that this stiff and pedantic young man should want to marry Theresa.

She did not feel, as the evening progressed, that she was getting to know Dr Donaldson any better. He was very polite, very formal and, to her mind, intensely boring. In her own mind she agreed with Miss Peabody's judgement. The thought flashed across her brain, 'Better stuff in our young days.'

Dr Donaldson did not stay late. He rose to go at ten o'clock. After he had taken his departure Emily Arundell herself announced that she was going to bed. She went upstairs, and her young relations went up also. They all seemed somewhat subdued tonight. Miss Lawson remained downstairs performing her final duties: letting Bob out for his run, poking down the fire, putting the guard up and rolling back the hearth-rug in case of fire.

She arrived rather breathless in her employer's room about five minutes later.

'I think I've got everything,' she said, putting down wool, working bag, and a library book. 'I do hope the book will be all right. She hadn't got any of the ones on your list, but she said she was sure you'd like this one.'

'That girl's a fool,' said Emily Arundell. 'Her taste in books is the worst I've ever come across.'

'Oh dear. I'm so sorry. Perhaps I ought—'

'Nonsense, it's not your fault,' Emily Arundell added kindly. 'I hope you enjoyed yourself this afternoon.'

Miss Lawson's face lighted up. She looked eager and almost youthful.

'Oh, yes, thank you very much. So *kind* of you to spare me. I had the most interesting time. We had the planchette; and really, it wrote the most *interesting* things. There were several messages . . . Of course, it's not *quite* the same thing as the sittings . . . Julia Tripp has been having a lot of success with the automatic writing. Several messages from Those who have Passed Over. It – it really makes me feel so grateful – that such things should be permitted . . .'

Miss Arundell said with a slight smile:

'Better not let the vicar hear you.'

'Oh, but indeed, dear Miss Arundell, I am convinced – quite convinced – there can be *nothing* wrong about it. I only wish dear Mr Lonsdale would *examine* the subject. It seems to me so narrow-minded to condemn a thing that you have not even *investigated*. Both Julia and Isabel Tripp are such truly *spiritual* women.'

'Almost too spiritual to be alive,' said Miss Arundell.

She did not care much for Julia and Isabel Tripp. She thought their clothes ridiculous, their vegetarian and un-cooked fruit meals absurd, and their manner affected. They were women of no traditions, no roots – in fact, no breeding! But she got a certain amount of amusement out of their earnestness, and she was at bottom kind-hearted enough not to grudge the pleasure that their friendship obviously gave to poor Minnie.

Poor Minnie! Emily Arundell looked at her companion with mingled affection and contempt. She had had so many of these foolish middle-aged women to minister to her – all much the same, kind, fussy, subservient and almost entirely mindless.

Really, poor Minnie was looking quite excited tonight. Her eyes were shining. She fussed about the room, vaguely touch-ing things here and there without the least idea of what she was doing, her eyes all bright and shining.

She stammered out rather nervously:

'I – I do wish you'd been there . . . I feel, you know, that you're not quite a believer yet. But tonight there was a mes-sage – for E.A., the initials came *quite* definitely. It was from a man who had passed over many years ago – a very good-looking military man – Isabel saw him quite distinctly. It must have been dear General Arundell. Such a beautiful mes-sage, so full of love and comfort, and how through patience all could be attained.'

'Those sentiments sound very unlike Papa,' said Miss Arun-dell.

'Oh, but our Dear Ones change so – on the other side. Everything is love and understanding. And then the planchette spelt out something about a *key* – I think it was the key of the Boule cabinet – could that be it?'

'The key of the Boule cabinet?' Emily Arundell's voice sounded sharp and interested.

'I think that was it. I thought perhaps it might be important papers – something of the kind. There was a well-authenticated case where a message came to look in a certain piece of furniture, and actually a *will* was discovered there.'

'There wasn't a will in the Boule cabinet,' said Miss Arundell. She added abruptly: 'Go to bed, Minnie. You're tired. So am I. We'll ask the Tripps in for an evening soon.'

'Oh, that *will* be nice! Goodnight, dear. Sure you've got everything? I hope you haven't been tired, with so many people here. I must tell Ellen to air the drawing-room *very well* tomorrow, and shake out the curtains – all this smoking leaves such a smell. I must say I think it's very good of you to let them all smoke in the drawing-room!'

'I must make some concessions to modernity,' said Emily Arundell. 'Goodnight, Minnie.'

As the other woman left the room, Emily Arundell wondered if this spiritualistic business was really good for Minnie. Her eyes had been popping out of her head, and she had looked so restless and excited.

Odd about the Boule cabinet, thought Emily Arundell as she got into bed. She smiled grimly as she remembered the scene of long ago. The key that had come to light after Papa's death, and the cascade of empty brandy bottles that had tumbled out when the cabinet had been unlocked! It was little things like that, things that surely neither Minnie Lawson nor Isabel and Julia Tripp could possibly know, which made one wonder whether, after all, there wasn't something in this spiritualistic business . . .

She felt wakeful lying on her big four-poster bed. Nowadays she found it increasingly difficult to sleep. But she scorned Dr Grainger's tentative suggestion of a sleeping draught. Sleeping draughts were for weaklings, for people who couldn't bear a finger-ache, or a little toothache, or the tedium of a sleepless night.

Often she would get up and wander noiselessly round the house, picking up a book, fingering an ornament, rearranging a vase of flowers, writing a letter or two. In those midnight hours she had a feeling of the equal liveliness of the house through which she wandered. They were not disagreeable, those nocturnal wanderings. It was as though ghosts walked

beside her: the ghosts of her sisters, Arabella, Matilda, and
Agnes; the ghost of her brother Thomas, the dear fellow, as
he was before That Woman got hold of him! Even the ghost
of General John Laverton Arundell, that domestic tyrant with
the charming manners who shouted and bullied his daughters,
but who nevertheless was an object of pride to them, with his
experiences in the Indian Mutiny and his knowledge of the
world. What if there were days when he was 'not quite so well,'
as his daughters put it evasively?

Her mind reverting to her niece's fiancé, Miss Arundell
thought. 'I don't suppose *he'll* ever take to drink! Calls himself a *man*, and drank *barley*-water this evening! Barley-water!
And I opened Papa's special port.'

Charles had done justic to the port all right. Oh, if only
Charles were to be trusted. If only one didn't know that with
him—

Her thoughts broke off . . . Her mind ranged over the events
of the weekend . . .

Everything seemed vaguely disquieting . . .

She tried to put worrying thoughts out of her mind. It was
no good.

She raised herself on her elbow, and by the light of the
night-light that always burned in a little saucer she looked at
the time.

One o'clock, and she had never felt less like sleep.

She got out of bed and put on her slippers and her warm
dressing-gown. She would go downstairs and just check over
the weekly books ready for the paying of them the following
morning.

Like a shadow she slipped from her room and along the
corridor, where one small electric bulb was allowed to burn
all night.

She came to the head of the stairs, stretched out one hand
to the baluster rail and then, unaccountably, she stumbled,
tried to recover her balance, failed and went headlong down
the stairs.

The sound of her fall, the cry she gave, stirred the sleeping
house to wakefulness. Doors opened, lights flashed on.

Miss Lawson popped out of her room at the head of the
staircase.

Uttering little cries of distress, she pattered down the stairs.
One by one the others arrived – Charles, yawning, in a resplen-
dent dressing-gown. Theresa, wrapped in dark silk. Bella in a

navy-blue kimono, her hair bristling with combs, to 'set the wave'.

Dazed and confused, Emily Arundell lay in a crushed heap. Her shoulder hurt her, and her ankle – her whole body was a confused mass of pain. She was conscious of people standing over her, of that fool Minnie Lawson crying and making ineffectual gestures with her hands, of Theresa with a startled look in her dark eyes, of Bella standing with her mouth open looking expectant, of the voice of Charles saying from somewhere – very far away, so it seemed:

'It's that damned dog's ball! He must have left it here, and she tripped over it. See? Here it is!'

And then she was conscious of authority, putting the others aside, kneeling beside her, touching her with hands that did not fumble, but *knew*.

A feeling of relief swept over her. It would be all right now.

Dr Tanios was saying in firm, reassuring tones:

'No, it's all right. No bones broken . . . Just badly shaken and bruised – and of course she's had a bad shock. But she's been very lucky that it's no worse.'

Then he had cleared the others off a little and picked her up quite easily and carried her to her bedroom, where he had held her wrist for a minute, counting, then nodded his head, sent Minnie (who was still crying, and generally a nuisance) out of the room to fetch brandy and to heat water for a hot bottle.

Confused, shaken, and racked with pain, she felt acutely grateful to Jacob Tanios in that moment: the relief of feeling oneself in capable hands. He gave you just that feeling of assurance – of confidence – that a doctor ought to give.

There was something – something she couldn't quite get hold of – something vaguely disquieting – but she wouldn't think of it now. She would drink this and go to sleep, as they told her.

But surely there was something missing – some one.

Oh, well, she wouldn't think . . . Her shoulder hurt her. She drank down what she was given.

She heard Dr Tanios say – and in what a comfortable, assured voice: 'She'll be all right, now.'

She closed her eyes.

She awoke to a sound that she knew – a soft, muffled bark.

She was wide awake in a minute.

Bob – naughty Bob! He was barking outside the front door – his own particular 'out all night very ashamed of myself' bark, pitched in a subdued key, but repeated hopefully.

Miss Arundell strained her ears. Ah, yes, that was all right. She could hear Minnie going down to let him in. She heard the creak of the opening front door, a confused, low murmur – Minnie's futile reproaches: 'Oh, you naughty little doggie – a very naughty little Bobsie—' She heard the pantry door open. Bob's bed was under the pantry table.

And at that moment Emily realized what it was she had subconsciously missed at the moment of her accident. It was Bob! All that commotion – her fall, people running – normally Bob would have responded by a crescendo of barking from inside the pantry.

So *that* was what had been worrying her at the back of her mind. But it was explained now – Bob, when he had been let out last night, had shamelessly and deliberately gone off on pleasure bent. From time to time he had these lapses from virtue – though his apologies afterwards were always all that could be desired.

So that was all right. But was it? What else was there worrying her, nagging at the back of her head? Her accident – something to do with her accident.

Ah, yes, somebody had said – Charles – that she had slipped on Bob's ball, which he had left on the top of the stairs . . .

The ball had been there – he had held it up in his hand . . .

Emily Arundell's head ached. Her shoulder throbbed. Her bruised body suffered . . .

But in the midst of her suffering her mind was clear and lucid. She was no longer confused by shock. Her memory was perfectly clear.

She went over in her mind all the events from six o'clock yesterday evening . . . She retraced every step . . . till she came to the moment when she arrived at the stairhead and started to descend the stairs . . .

A thrill of incredulous horror shot through her . . .

Surely – surely, she must be mistaken . . . One often had queer fancies after an event had happened. She tried – earnestly she tried – to recall the slippery roundness of Bob's ball under her foot . . .

But she could recall nothing of the kind.

Instead—

'Sheer nerves,' said Emily Arundell. 'Ridiculous fancies.'

But her sensible, shrewd, Victorian mind would not admit

411

that for a moment. There was no foolish optimism about the Victorians. They could believe the worst with the utmost ease. Emily Arundell believed the worst.

------ 4 ------

MISS ARUNDELL WRITES A LETTER

It was Friday.

The relations had left.

They left on the Wednesday, as originally planned. One and all they had offered to stay on. One and all they had been steadfastly refused. Miss Arundell explained that she preferred to be 'quite quiet'.

During the two days that had elapsed since their departure Emily Arundell had been alarmingly meditative. Often she did not hear what Minnie Lawson said to her. She would stare at her and curtly order her to begin all over again.

'It's the *shock*, poor dear,' said Miss Lawson.

And she added, with the kind of gloomy relish in disaster which brightens so many otherwise drab lives:

'I dare say she'll never be quite herself again.'

Dr Grainger, on the other hand, rallied her heartily.

He told her that she'd be downstairs again by the end of the week, that it was a positive disgrace she had no bones broken, and what kind of a patient was she for a struggling medical man. If all his patients were like her, he might as well take down his shingle straight away.

Emily Arundell replied with spirit – she and old Dr Grainger were allies of long standing. He bullied and she defied – they always got a good deal of pleasure out of each other's company!

But now, after the doctor had stumped away, the old lady lay with a frown on her face, thinking – thinking – responding absent-mindedly to Minnie Lawson's well-meant fussing, and then suddenly coming back to consciousness and rending her with a vitriolic tongue.

'Poor little Bobsie!' twittered Miss Lawson, bending over Bob, who had a rug spread on the corner of his mistress's bed. 'Wouldn't little Bobsie be unhappy if he knew what he'd done to his poor, poor Missus?'

Miss Arundell snapped:

'Don't be idiotic, Minnie! And where's your English sense of justice? Don't you know that everyone in this country is accounted innocent until he or she is proved guilty?'

'Oh, but we do know—'

Emily snapped:

'We don't know anything at all. Do stop fidgeting, Minnie. Pulling this and pulling that. Haven't you any idea how to behave in a sick-room? Go away, and send Ellen to me.'

Meekly Miss Lawson crept away.

Emily Arundell looked after her with a slight feeling of self-reproach. Maddening as Minnie was, she did her best.

Then the frown settled down again on her face.

She was desperately unhappy. She had all a vigorous, strong-minded old lady's dislike of inaction in any given situation. But in this particular situation she could not decide upon her line of action.

There were moments when she distrusted her own faculties, her own memory of events. And there was no one, absolutely no one, in whom she could confide.

Half an hour later, when Miss Lawson tiptoed creakingly into the room, carrying a cup of beef-tea, and then paused irresolute at the view of her employer lying with closed eyes, Emily Arundell suddenly spoke two words with such force and decision that Miss Lawson nearly dropped the cup.

'Mary Fox,' said Miss Arundell.

'A box, dear?' said Miss Lawson. 'Did you say you wanted a box?'

'You're getting deaf, Minnie. I didn't say anything about a box. I said Mary Fox. The woman I met at Cheltenham last year. She was the sister of one of the Canons of Exeter Cathedral. Give me that cup. You've split it into the saucer. And don't tiptoe when you come into a room. You don't know how irritating it is. Now go downstairs and get me the London telephone book.'

'Can I find the number for you, dear? Or the address?'

'If I'd wanted you to do that I'd have told you so. Do what I tell you. Bring it here, and put my writing things by the bed.'

Miss Lawson obeyed orders.

As she was going out of the room after having done everything required of her, Emily Arundell said unexpectedly:

'You're a good, faithful creature, Minnie. Don't mind my bark. It's a good deal worse than my bite. You're very patient and good to me.'

Miss Lawson went out of the room with her face pink, and incoherent words burbling from her lips.

Sitting up in bed, Miss Arundell wrote a letter. She wrote it slowly and carefully, with numerous pauses for thought and copious underlining. She crossed and recrossed the page – for she had been brought up in a school that was taught never to waste notepaper. Finally, with a sigh of satisfaction, she signed her name and put it into an envelope. She wrote a name upon the envelope. Then she took a fresh sheet of paper. This time she made a rough draft, and after having re-read it and made certain alterations and erasures, she wrote out a fair copy. She read the whole thing through very carefully, then, satisfied that she had expressed her meaning, she enclosed it in an envelope and addressed it to William Purvis, Esq, Messrs Purvis, Purvis, Charlesworth and Purvis, Solicitors, Harchester.

She took up the first envelope again, which was addressed to M. Hercule Poirot, and opened the telephone directory. Having found the address, she added it.

A tap sounded at the door.

Miss Arundell hastily thrust the letter she had just finished addressing – the letter to Hercule Poirot – inside the flap of her writing-case.

She had no intention of rousing Minnie's curiosity. Minnie was a great deal too inquisitive.

She called 'Come in' and lay back on her pillows with a sigh of relief.

She had taken steps to deal with the situation.

—— 5 ——

HERCULE POIROT RECEIVES A LETTER

The events which I have just narrated were not, of course, known to me until a long time afterwards. But by questioning various members of the family in detail, I have, I think, set them down accurately enough.

Poirot and I were only drawn into the affair when we received Miss Arundell's letter.

I remember the day well. It was a hot, airless morning towards the end of June.

Poirot had a particular routine when opening his morning

correspondence. He picked up each letter, scrutinized it carefully, and neatly slit the envelope open with his paper-cutter. Its contents were perused and it was then placed in one of four piles beyond the chocolate-pot. (Poirot always drank chocolate for breakfast – a revolting habit.) All this with a machine-like regularity!

So much was this the case that the least interruption of the rhythm attracted one's attention.

I was sitting by the window, looking out at the passing traffic. I had recently returned from the Argentine, and there was something particularly exciting to me in being once more in the roar of London.

Turning my head, I said with a smile:

'Poirot, I – the humble Watson – am going to hazard a deduction.'

'Enchanted, my friend. What is it?'

I struck an attitude and said pompously:

'You have received this morning *one* letter of particular interest!'

'You are indeed the Sherlock Holmes! Yes, you are perfectly right.' I laughed.

'You see, *I know your methods*, Poirot. If you read a letter through twice it must mean that it is of special interest.'

'You shall judge for yourself, Hastings.'

With a smile my friend tendered me the letter in question.

I took it with no little interest, but immediately made a slight grimace. It was written in one of those old-fashioned spidery handwritings, and it was, moreover, crossed on two pages.

'Must I read this, Poirot?' I complained.

'Ah, no, there is no compulsion. Assuredly not.'

'Can't you tell me what it says?'

'I would prefer you to form your own judgement. But do not trouble if it bores you.'

'No, no, I want to know what it's all about,' I protested.

My friend remarked dryly:

'You can hardly do *that*. In effect, the letter says nothing at all.'

Taking this as an exaggeration, I plunged without more ado into the letter.

M. Hercule Poirot.
Dear Sir,
    After much doubt and indecision, I am writing [the last

415

word was crossed out and the letter went on] *I am emboldened to write to you in the hope that you may be able
to assist me in a matter of a strictly private nature.* [The
words *strictly private* were underlined three times.] *I may say
that your name is not unknown to me. It was mentioned to
me by a Miss Fox of Exeter, and although Miss Fox was not
herself acquainted with you, she mentioned that her brother-
in-law's sister (whose name I cannot, I am sorry to say, recall) had spoken of your kindness and discretion in the
highest terms* [*highest terms* underlined once.] *I did not inquire, of course, as to the nature* [*nature* underlined] *of the
inquiry you had conducted on her behalf, but I understood
from Miss Fox that it was of a painful and confidential
nature* [last four words underlined heavily].

I broke off my difficult task of spelling out the spidery words.
'Poirot,' I said, 'must I go on? Does she ever get to the point?'
'Continue, my friend. Patience.'
'Patience!' I grumbled. 'It's exactly as though a spider had
got into an inkpot and were walking over a sheet of notepaper!
I remember my great-aunt Mary's writing used to be much the
same!'
Once more I plunged into the epistle.

*In my present dilemma, it occurs to me that you might
undertake the necessary investigations on my behalf. The
matter is such, as you will readily understand, as calls for the
utmost discretion and I may, in fact — and I need hardly say
how sincerely I hope and pray* [*pray* underlined twice] *that
this may be the case — I may, in fact, be completely mistaken.
One is apt sometimes to attribute too much significance to
facts capable of a natural explanation.*

'I haven't left out a sheet?' I murmured in some perplexity.
Poirot chuckled.
'No, no.'
'Because this doesn't seem to make sense. What is it she is
talking about?'

'*Continuez toujours.*'

The matter is such, as you will readily understand — No,
I'd got past that. Oh! Here we are. *In the circumstances, as
I am sure you will be the first to appreciate, it is quite im-
possible for me to consult anyone in Market Basing* [I

glanced back at the heading of the letter. Littlegreen House, Market Basing, Berks], *but at the same time you will naturally understand that I feel uneasy [uneasy* underlined]. *During the last few days I have reproached myself with being unduly fanciful [fanciful* underlined three times] *but have only felt increasingly perturbed. I may be attaching undue importance to what is, after all, a trifle [trifle* underlined twice], *but my uneasiness remains. I feel definitely that my mind must be set at rest on the matter. It is actually preying on my mind and affecting my health, and naturally I am in a difficult position, as I can say nothing to anyone [nothing to anyone* underlined with heavy lines]. *In your wisdom you may say, of course, that the whole thing is nothing but a mare's nest. The facts may be capable of a perfectly innocent explanation [innocent* underlined]. *Nevertheless, however trivial it may seem, ever since the incident of the dog's ball, I have felt increasingly doubtful and alarmed. I should therefore welcome your views and counsel on the matter. It would, I feel sure, take a great weight off my mind. Perhaps you would kindly let me know what your fees are and what you advise me to do in the matter?*

I must impress on you again that nobody here knows anything at all. The facts are, I know, very trivial and unimportant, but my health is not too good and my nerves [nerves underlined three times] *are not what they used to be. Worry of this kind, I am convinced, is very bad for me, and the more I think over the matter, the more I am convinced that I was quite right and no mistake was possible. Of course, I shall not dream of saying anything* [underlined] *to anyone* [underlined].

Hoping to have your advice in the matter at an early date,
I remain,
Yours faithfully,
EMILY ARUNDELL

I turned the letter over and scanned each page closely.
'But, Poirot,' I expostulated, 'what is it all *about?*'
My friend shrugged his shoulders.
'What, indeed?'
I tapped the sheets with some impatience.
'What a woman! Why can't Mrs – or Miss Arundell—'
'Miss, I think. It is typically the letter of a spinster.'
'Yes,' I said. 'A real fussy old maid. Why can't she say what she's talking about?'

Poirot sighed.

'As you say, a regrettable failure to employ order and method in the mental processes; and without order and method, Hastings—'

'Quite so,' I interrupted hastily. 'Little grey cells practically non-existent.'

'I would not say that, my friend.'

'I would! What's the *sense* of writing a letter like that?'

'Very little – that is true,' Poirot admitted.

'A long rigmarole all about nothing,' I went on. 'Probably some upset to her fat lapdog – an asthmatic pug or a yapping Pekingese!' I looked at my friend curiously. 'And yet you read that letter through twice. I do not understand you, Poirot.'

Poirot smiled.

'You, Hastings, you would have put it straight in the waste-paper basket?'

'I'm afraid I should.' I frowned down on the letter. 'I suppose I'm being dense, as usual, but *I* can't see anything of interest in this letter!'

'Yet there is one point in it of great interest – a point that struck me at once.'

'Wait,' I cried. 'Don't tell me. Let me see if I can't discover it for myself.' It was childish of me, perhaps. I examined the letter very thoroughly. Then I shook my head.

'No, I don't see it. The old lady's got the wind up, I realize that – but then, old ladies often do! It may be about nothing – it may conceivably be about something; but I don't see that you can tell that that is so. Unless your instinct—'

Poirot raised an offended hand.

'Instinct! You know how I dislike that word. "Something seems to tell me" – that is what you infer. *Jamais de la vie*! Me, I *reason*. I employ the little grey cells. There is one interesting point about that letter which you have overlooked utterly, Hastings.'

'Oh, well,' I said wearily, 'I'll buy it.'

'Buy it? Buy what?'

'An expression. Meaning that I will permit you to enjoy yourself by telling me just where I have been a fool.'

'Not a fool, Hastings; merely unobservant.'

'Well, out with it. What's the interesting point? I suppose, like the "incident of the dog in the night-time," the point *is* that there is no interesting point!'

Poirot disregarded this sally on my part. He said quietly and calmly:

'The interesting point is the *date*.'

'The date?'

I picked up the letter. On the top left-hand corner was written 'April 17th.'

'Yes,' I said slowly. 'That is odd. April 17th.'

'And we are today June 28th. *C'est curieux, n'est-ce pas?* Over two months ago.'

I shook my head doubtfully.

'It probably doesn't mean anything. A slip. She meant to put June and wrote April instead.'

'Even then it would be ten or eleven days old – an odd fact. But actually you are in error. Look at the colour of the ink. That letter was written more than ten or eleven days ago. No, April 17th is the date assuredly. But why was the letter not sent?'

I shrugged my shoulders.

'That's easy. The old pussy changed her mind.'

'Then why did she not destroy the letter? Why keep it over two months and post it now?'

I had to admit that that was harder to answer. In fact, I couldn't think of a really satisfactory answer. I merely shook my head and said nothing.

Poirot nodded.

'You see – it is a point? Yes, decidedly a curious point.'

He went over to his writing-table and took up a pen.

'You are answering the letter?' I asked.

'*Oui, mon ami.*'

The room was silent except for the scratching of Poirot's pen. It was a hot, airless morning. A smell of dust and tar came in through the window.

Poirot rose from his desk, the completed letter in his hand. He opened a drawer and drew out a little square box. From this he took out a stamp. Moistening this with a little sponge, he prepared to affix it to the letter.

Then suddenly he paused, stamp in hand, shaking his head with vigour.

'*Non!*' he exclaimed. 'That is the wrong thing I do.' He tore the letter across and threw it into the waste-paper basket. 'Not so must we tackle this matter! We will *go*, my friend.'

'You mean to go down to Market Basing?'

'Precisely. Why not? Does not one stifle in London today? Would not the country air be agreeable?'

'Well, if you put it like that,' I said. 'Shall we go in the car?'

I had acquired a secondhand Austin.

'Excellent. A very pleasant day for motoring. One will hardly need the muffler. A light overcoat, a silk scarf—'

'My dear fellow, you're not going to the North Pole!' I protested.

'One must be careful of catching the chill,' said Poirot sententiously.

'On a day like this?'

Disregarding my protests, Poirot proceeded to don a fawn-coloured overcoat and wrap his neck up with a white silk handkerchief. Having carefully placed the wetted stamp face downwards on the blotting-paper to dry, we left the room together.

—— 6 ——

WE GO TO LITTLEGREEN HOUSE

I don't know what Poirot felt like in his coat and muffler, but I myself felt roasted before we got out of London. An open car in traffic is far from being a refreshing place on a hot summer's day.

Once we were outside London, however, and getting a bit of pace on the Great West Road, my spirits rose.

Our drive took us about an hour and a half, and it was close upon twelve o'clock when we came into the little town of Market Basing. Originally on the main road, a modern by-pass now left it some three miles to the north of the main stream of traffic, and in consequence it had kept an air of old-fashioned dignity and quietude about it. Its one wide street and ample market square seemed to say, 'I was a place of importance once, and to any person of sense and breeding I am still the same. Let this modern speeding world dash along their new-fangled road; I was built to endure in a day when solidarity and beauty went hand in hand.'

There was a parking area in the middle of the big square, though there were only a few cars occupying it. I duly parked the Austin, Poirot divested himself of his superfluous garments, assured himself that his moustaches were in their proper condition of symmetrical flamboyance, and we were then ready to proceed.

For once in a way our first tentative inquiry did not meet with the usual response, 'Sorry, but I'm a stranger in these

parts'. It would indeed seem probable that there were no
strangers in Market Basing! It had that effect. Already, I felt,
Poirot and myself (and especially Poirot) were somewhat
noticeable. We tended to stick out from the mellow background of an English market town secure in its traditions.

'Littlegreen House?' The man, a burly, ox-eyed fellow,
looked us over thoughtfully. 'You go straight up the High
Street, and you can't miss it. On your left. There's no name on
the gate, but it's the first big house after the Bank.' He repeated. 'You can't miss it.'

His eyes followed us as we started on our course.

'Dear me,' I complained. 'There is something about this
place that makes me feel extremely conspicuous. As for you,
Poirot, you look positively exotic.'

'You think it is noticed that I am a foreigner – yes?'

'The fact cries aloud to heaven,' I assured him.

'And yet my clothes are made by an English tailor,' mused
Poirot.

'Clothes are not everything,' I said. 'It cannot be denied,
Poirot, that you have a noticeable personality. I have often
wondered that it has not hindered you in your career.'

Poirot sighed.

'That is because you have the mistaken idea implanted in
your head that a detective is necessarily a man who puts on a
false beard and hides behind a pillar! The false beard, is *vieux
jeu*, and shadowing is only done by the lowest branch of my
profession. The Hercule Poirots, my friend, need only to sit
back in a chair and think.'

'Which explains why we are walking along this exceedingly
hot street on an exceedingly hot morning.'

'That is very neatly replied, Hastings. For once, I admit, you
have made the score off me.'

We found Littlegreen House easily enough, but a shock
awaited us – a house-agent's board.

As we were staring at it, a dog's bark attracted my attention.
The bushes were thin at that point, and the dog could be easily
seen. He was a wire-haired terrier, somewhat shaggy as to coat.
His feet were planted wide apart, slightly to one side, and he
barked with an obvious enjoyment of his own performance
that showed him to be actuated by the most amiable motives.

'Good watchdog, aren't I?' he seemed to be saying. 'Don't
mind me! This is just my fun! My duty, too, of course. Just
have to let 'em know there's a dog about the place! Deadly
dull morning. Quite a blessing to have something to do. Com-

ing into our place? Hope so. It's darned dull. I could do with a little conversation.'

'Hallo, old man,' I said, and shoved forward a fist.

Craning his neck through the railings, he sniffed suspiciously, then gently wagged his tail, uttering a few sharp, staccato barks.

'Not been properly introduced, of course; have to keep this up! But I see you know the proper advances to make.'

'Good old boy,' I said.

'Wuff,' said the terrier amiably.

'Well, Poirot?' I said, desisting from this conversation and turning to my friend.

There was an odd expression on his face – one that I could not quite fathom. A kind of deliberately suppressed excitement seems to describe it best.

'The Incident of the Dog's Ball,' he murmured. 'Well, at least, we have here a dog.'

'Wuff,' observed our new friend. Then he sat down, yawned widely and looked at us hopefully.

'What next?' I asked.

The dog seemed to be asking the same question.

'*Parbleu*, to Messrs – what is it – Messrs Gabler and Stretcher.'

'That does seem indicated,' I agreed.

We turned and retraced our steps, our canine acquaintance sending a few disgusted barks after us.

The premises of Messrs Gabler and Stretcher were situated in the Market Square. We entered a dim outer office where we were received by a young woman with adenoids and a lacklustre eye.

'Good morning,' said Poirot politely.

The young woman was at the moment speaking into a telephone, but she indicated a chair, and Poirot sat down. I found another and brought it forward.

'I couldn't say, I'm sure,' said the young woman into the telephone vacantly. 'No, I don't know what the rates would be . . . Pardon? Oh, main water, I think; but, of course, I couldn't be certain . . . I'm very sorry, I'm sure . . . No, he's out . . . No, I couldn't say . . . Yes, of course I'll ask him . . . Yes . . . 8135? I'm afraid I haven't quite got it. Oh . . . 8935 . . . 39 . . . Oh, 5135 . . . Yes, I'll ask him to ring you . . . after six . . . Oh, pardon, before six . . . Thank you so much.'

She replaced the receiver, scribbled 5319 on the blotting-pad and turned a mildly inquiring but uninterested gaze on Poirot.

Poirot began briskly:

'I observe that there is a house to be sold just on the out-skirts of this town. Littlegreen House, I think is the name.'

'Pardon?'

'A house to be let or sold,' said Poirot slowly and distinctly. 'Littlegreen House.'

'Oh, Littlegreen House,' said the young woman vaguely. '*Littlegreen* House, did you say?'

'That is what I said.'

'Littlegreen House,' said the young woman, making a tre-mendous mental effort. 'Oh, well, I expect Mr Gabler would know about that.'

'Can I see Mr Gabler?'

'He's out,' said the young woman with a kind of faint, anaemic satisfaction, as of one who says, 'A point to me.'

'Do you know when he will be in?'

'I couldn't say, I'm sure,' said the young woman.

'You comprehend, I am looking for a house in this neigh-bourhood,' said Poirot.

'Oh, yes,' said the young woman, uninterested.

'And Littlegreen House seems to me just what I am looking for. Can you give me particulars?'

'Particulars?' The young woman seemed startled.

'Particulars of Littlegreen House.'

Unwillingly, she opened a drawer and took out an untidy file of papers. Then she called 'John'.

A lanky youth sitting in a corner looked up.

'Yes, miss.'

'Have we got any particulars of – what did you say?'

'Littlegreen House,' said Poirot distinctly.

'You've got a large bill of it here,' I remarked, pointing to the wall.

She looked at me coldly. Two to one, she seemed to think, was an unfair way of playing the game. She called up her own reinforcements.

'You don't know anything about Littlegreen House, do you, John?'

'No, miss. Should be in the file.'

'I'm sorry,' said the young woman, without looking so in the least. 'I rather fancy we must have sent all the particulars out.'

'*C'est dommage.*'

'Pardon?'

'A pity.'

'We've a nice bungalow at Hemel End, two bed, one sit.'

She spoke without enthusiasm, but with the air of one willing to do her duty by her employer.

'I thank you, no.'

'And a semi-detached with small conservatory. I could give you particulars of that.'

'No, thank you. I desired to know what rent you were asking for Littlegreen House.'

'It's not to be rented,' said the young woman, abandoning her position of complete ignorance of anything to do with Littlegreen House in the pleasure of scoring a point. 'Only to be sold outright.'

'The board says, "To be Let or Sold." '

'I couldn't say as to that, but it's for sale only.'

At this stage in the battle the door opened and a grey-haired, middle-aged man entered with a rush. His eye, a militant one, swept over us with a gleam. His eyebrows asked a question of his employee.

'This is Mr Gabler,' said the young woman.

Mr Gabler opened the door of an inner sanctum with a flourish.

'Step in here, gentlemen.' He ushered us in, an ample gesture swept us into chairs and he himself was facing us across a flat-topped desk.

'And now what can I do for you?'

Poirot began again perseveringly:

'I desired a few particulars of Littlegreen House—'

He got no further. Mr Gabler took command.

'Ah! Littlegreen House – *there's* a property! An absolute bargain. Only just come on to the market. I can tell you, gentlemen, we don't often get a house of that class going at the price. Taste's swinging round. People are fed up with jerry-building. They want sound stuff. Good, honest building. A beautiful property – character – feeling – Georgian through-out. That's what people want nowadays – there's a feeling for period houses, if you understand what I mean. Ah, yes, Little-green House won't be long in the market. It'll be snapped up. Snapped up! A Member of Parliament came to look at it only last Saturday. Liked it so much he's coming down again this weekend. And there's a Stock Exchange gentleman after it, too. People want quiet nowadays when they come to the country, want to be well away from main roads. That's all very well for some people, but we attract class here. And that's what that house has got. Class! You've got to admit, they knew how to

424

build for gentlemen in those days. Yes, we shan't have Little-green long on our books.'

Mr Gabler, who, it occurred to me, lived up to his name very happily, paused for breath.

'Has it changed hands often in the last few years?' inquired Poirot.

'On the contrary. Been in one family over fifty years. Name of Arundell. Very much respected in the town. Ladies of the old school.' He shot up, opened the door and called: 'Particulars of Littlegreen House, Miss Jenkins. Quickly now.' He returned to the desk.

'I require a house about this distance from London,' said Poirot. 'In the country, but not in the dead country, if you understand me—'

'Perfectly – perfectly. Too much in the country doesn't do. Servants don't like it, for one thing. Here you have the advantages of the country, but not the disadvantages.'

Miss Jenkins flitted in with a typewritten sheet of paper, which she placed in front of her employer, who dismissed her with a nod.

'Here we are,' said Mr Gabler, reading with practised rapidity. 'Period house of character: four recep., eight bed and dressing, usual offices, commodious kitchen premises, ample outbuildings, stables, etc. Main water, old-world gardens, inexpensive upkeep, amounting in all to three acres, two summer-houses, etc., etc. Price £2,850 or near offer.'

'You can give me an order to view?'

'Certainly, my dear sir.' Mr Gabler began writing in a flourishing fashion. 'Your name and address?'

Slightly to my surprise, Poirot gave his name as Mr Parotti.

'We have one or two other properties on our books which might interest you,' Mr Gabler went on.

Poirot allowed him to make further additions.

'Littlegreen House can be viewed any time?' he inquired.

'Certainly, my dear sir. There are servants in residence. I might perhaps ring up to make certain. You will be going there immediately? Or after lunch?'

'Perhaps after lunch would be better.'

'Certainly – certainly. I'll ring up and tell them to expect you about two o'clock – eh? Is that right?'

'Thank you. Did you say the owner of the house – a Miss Arundell, I think you said?'

'Lawson. Miss Lawson. That is the name of the present owner. Miss Arundell, I am sorry to say, died a short time ago.

That is how the place has come on to the market. And I can assure you it will be snapped up. Not a doubt of it. Between you and me, just in confidence, if you do think of making an offer I should make it quickly. As I've told you, there are two gentlemen after it already, and I shouldn't be surprised to get an offer for it any day from one or other of them. Each of them knows the other's after it, you see. And there's no doubt that competition spurs a man on. Ha, ha! I shouldn't like you to be disappointed.'

'Miss Lawson is anxious to sell, I gather.'

Mr Gabler lowered his voice confidentially.

'That's just it. The place is larger than she wants – one middle-aged lady living by herself. She wants to get rid of this and take a house in London. Quite understandable. That's why the place is going so ridiculously cheap.'

'She would be open, perhaps to an offer?'

'That's the idea, sir. Make an offer and set the ball rolling. But you can take it from me that there will be no difficulty in getting a price very near the figure named. Why, it's ridiculous! To build a house like that nowadays would cost every penny of six thousand, let alone the land value and valuable front-ages.'

'Miss Arundell died very suddenly, didn't she?'

'Oh, I wouldn't say that. Anno domini – anno domini. She had passed her three-score years and ten some time ago. And she'd been ailing for a long time. The last of her family – you know something about the family, perhaps?'

'I know some people of the same name who have relations in this part of the world. I fancy it must be the same family.'

'Very likely. Four sisters there were. One married fairly late in life, and the other three lived on here. Ladies of the old school. Miss Emily was the last of them. Very highly thought of in the town.'

He leapt forward and handed Poirot the orders.

'You'll drop in again and let me know what you think of it, eh? Of course, it may need a little modernizing here and there. That's only to be expected. But I always said, "What's a bath-room or two? That's easily done." '

We took our leave, and the last thing we heard was the vacant voice of Miss Jenkins saying:

'Mrs Samuels rang up, sir. She'd like you to ring her – Holland 5391.'

As far as I could remember that was neither the number

Miss Jenkins had scribbled on her pad nor the number finally arrived at through the telephone.

I felt convinced that Miss Jenkins was having her revenge for have been forced to find the particulars of Littlegreen House.

—— 7 ——

LUNCH AT THE GEORGE

As we emerged into the Market Square, I remarked that Mr Gabler lived up to his name. Poirot assented with a smile.

'He'll be rather disappointed when you don't return,' I said. 'I think he feels he has as good as sold you that house already.'

'Indeed, yes; I fear there is a deception in store for him.'

'I suppose we might as well have lunch here before returning to London, or shall we lunch at some more likely spot on our way back?'

'My dear Hastings, I am not proposing to leave Market Basing so quickly. We have not yet accomplished that which we came to do.'

I stared.

'Do you mean – but my dear fellow, that's all a washout. The old lady is dead.'

'Exactly.'

The tone of that one word made me stare at him harder than ever. It was evident that he had some bee in his bonnet over this incoherent letter.

'But if she's dead, Poirot,' I said gently, 'what's the use? She can't tell you anything now. Whatever the trouble was, it's over and finished with.'

'How lightly and easily you put the matter aside! Let me tell you that *no* matter is finished with until Hercule Poirot ceases to concern himself with it!'

I should have known from experience that to argue with Poirot is quite useless. Unwarily I proceeded:

'But since she is dead—'

'Exactly, Hastings. Exactly – exactly – exactly . . . You keep repeating the significant point with a magnificently obtuse disregard of its significance. Do you not see the importance of the point? Miss Arundell is *dead*.'

'But, my dear Poirot, her death was perfectly natural and

ordinary! There wasn't anything odd or unexplained about it. We have old Gabler's word for that.'

'We have his word that Littlegreen House is a bargain at £2,850. Do you accept that as gospel also?'

'No, indeed. It struck me that Gabler was all out to get the place sold – it probably needs modernizing from top to toe. I'd swear he – or rather his client – will be willing to accept a very much lower figure than that. These large Georgian houses fronting right on the street must be the devil to get rid of.'

'*Eh bien*, then,' said Poirot. 'Do not say, "But Gabler says so!" as though he were an inspired prophet who could not lie.'

I was about to protest further, but at this minute we passed the threshold of The George, and with an emphatic 'Chut!' Poirot put a damper on further conversation.

We were directed to the coffee-room, a room of fine proportions, tightly shut windows and an odour of stale food. An elderly waiter attended to us, a slow, heavy-breathing man. We appeared to be the only lunchers. We had some excellent mutton, large slabs of watery cabbage and some dispirited potatoes. Some rather tasteless stewed fruit and custard followed. After gorgonzola and biscuits the waiter brought us two cups of a doubtful fluid called coffee.

At this point Poirot produced his orders to view and invited the waiter's aid.

'Yes, sir, I know where most of these are. Hemel Down is three miles away – on the Much Benham road – quite a little place. Naylor's Farm is about a mile away. There's a kind of lane goes off to it not long after the King's Head. Bissett Grange? No, I've never heard of that. Littlegreen House is just close by, not more than a few minutes' walk.'

'Ah, I think I have already seen it from the outside. That is the most possible one, I think. It is in good repair – yes?'

'Oh, yes, sir. It's in good condition – roof and drains and all that. Old-fashioned, of course. It's never been modernized in any way. The gardens are a picture. Very fond of her garden Miss Arundell was.'

'It belongs, I see, to a Miss Lawson.'

'That's right, sir. Miss Lawson, she was Miss Arundell's companion, and when the old lady died everything was left to her – house and all.'

'Indeed? I suppose she had no relations to whom to leave it.'

'Well, it was not quite like that, sir. She *had* nieces and nephews living. But, of course, Miss Lawson was with her all the time. And, of course, she was an old lady – and well – that's how it was.'

'In any case, I suppose there was just the house, and not much money?'

I have often had occasion to notice how, where a direct question would fail to elicit a response, a false assumption brings instant information in the form of a contradiction.

'Very far from that, sir. Very far indeed. Every one was surprised at the amount the old lady left. The will was in the paper and the amount and everything. It seems she hadn't lived up to her income for many a long year. Something like three or four hundred thousand pounds she left.'

'You astonish me,' cried Poirot. 'It is like a fairy tale – eh? The poor companion suddenly becomes unbelievably wealthy. Is she still young, this Miss Lawson? Can she enjoy her new-found wealth?'

'Oh, no, sir; she's a middle-aged person, sir.'

His enunciation of the word 'person' was quite an artistic performance. It was clear that Miss Lawson, ex-companion, had cut no kind of a figure in Market Basing.

'It must have been disappointing for the nephews and nieces,' mused Poirot.

'Yes, sir. I believe it came as somewhat of a shock to them. Very unexpected. There's been feeling over it here in Market Basing. There are those who hold it isn't right to leave things away from your own flesh and blood. But, of course, there's others as hold that everyone's got a right to do as they like with their own. There's something to be said for both points of view, of course.'

'Miss Arundell had lived for many years here, had she not?'

'Yes, sir. She and her sisters and old General Arundell, their father, before them. Not that I remember him, naturally, but I believe he was quite a character. Was in the Indian Mutiny.'

'There were several daughters?'

'Three of them that I remember, and I believe there was one that married. Yes, Miss Matilda, Miss Agnes, and Miss Emily. Miss Matilda, she died first, and then Miss Agnes, and finally Miss Emily.'

'That was quite recently?'

'Beginning of May – or it may have been the end of April.'

'Had she been ill some time?'

'On and off – on and off. She was on the sickly side. Nearly went off a year ago with that there jaundice. Yellow as an orange she was for some time after. Yes, she'd had poor health for the last five years of her life.'

'I suppose you have some good doctors down here?'

'Well, there's Dr Grainger. Been here close on twenty years, he has, and folks mostly go to him. He's a bit crotchety and he has his fancies; but he's a good doctor, none better. He's got a young partner, Dr Donaldson. He's more the new-fangled kind. Some folk prefer him. Then, of course, there's Dr Harding; but he doesn't do much.'

'Dr Grainger was Miss Arundell's doctor, I suppose?'

'Oh, yes. He'd pulled her through many a bad turn. He's the kind that fair bullies you into living whether you want to or not.'

Poirot nodded. 'One should learn a little about a place before one comes to settle in it,' he remarked. 'A good doctor is one of the most important people.'

'That's very true, sir.'

Poirot then asked for his bill, to which he added a substantial tip.

'Thank you, sir. Thank you very much, sir. I'm sure I hope you'll settle here, sir.'

'I hope so, too,' said Poirot mendaciously.

We set forth from The George.

'Satisfied yet, Poirot?' I asked as we emerged into the street.

'Not in the least, my friend.'

He turned in an unexpected direction.

'Where are you off to now, Poirot?'

'The church, my friend. It may be interesting. Some brasses – an old monument.'

I shook my head doubtfully.

Poirot's scrutiny of the interior of the church was brief. Though an attractive specimen of what the guide-book calls Early Perp., it had been so conscientiously restored in Victorian vandal days that little of interest remained.

Poirot next wandered seemingly aimlessly about the church-yard reading some of the epitaphs, commenting on the number of deaths in certain families, occasionally exclaiming over the quaintness of a name.

I was not surprised, however, when he finally halted before what I was pretty sure had been his objective from the beginning.

An imposing marble slab bore a partly effaced inscription:

SACRED
TO THE MEMORY OF
JOHN LAVERTON ARUNDELL
GENERAL 24th SIKHS
WHO FELL ASLEEP IN CHRIST MAY 19, 1888
AGED 69
'FIGHT THE GOOD FIGHT WITH ALL THY MIGHT'

ALSO OF
MATILDA ANN ARUNDELL
DIED MARCH 10, 1912
'I WILL ARISE AND GO UNTO MY FATHER'

ALSO OF
AGNES GEORGINA MARY ARUNDELL
DIED NOVEMBER 20, 1921
'ASK AND YE SHALL RECEIVE'

The came a brand-new piece of lettering, evidently just done:

ALSO OF
EMILY HARRIET LAVERTON ARUNDELL
DIED MAY 1, 1936
'THY WILL BE DONE'

Poirot stood looking for some time.

He murmured softly:

'May 1st . . . May 1st . . . And today, June 28th, I receive her letter. You see, do you not, Hastings, that that fact has got to be explained?'

I saw that it had.

That is to say, I saw that Poirot was determined that it should be explained.

8

INTERIOR OF LITTLEGREEN HOUSE

On leaving the churchyard, Poirot led the way briskly in the direction of Littlegreen House. I gathered that his role was still that of the prospective purchaser. Carefully holding the various orders to view in his hand, with the Littlegreen House one uppermost, he pushed open the gate and walked up the path to the front door.

On this occasion our friend the terrier was not to be seen, but the sound of barking could be heard inside the house, though at some distance – I guessed in the kitchen quarters.

Presently we heard footsteps crossing the hall and the door was opened by a pleasant-faced woman of between fifty and sixty, clearly the old-fashioned type of servant seldom seen nowadays.

Poirot presented his credentials.

'Yes, sir, the house-agent telephoned. Will you step this way, sir?'

The shutters, which I had noticed were closed on our first visit to spy out the land, were now all thrown open in preparation for our visit. Everything, I observed, was spotlessly clean and well kept. Clearly our guide was a thoroughly conscientious woman.

'This is the morning room, sir.'

I glanced round approvingly. A pleasant room with its long windows giving on the street. It was furnished with good, solid, old-fashioned furniture, mostly Victorian, but there was a Chippendale bookcase and a set of attractive Hepplewhite chairs.

Poirot and I behaved in the customary fashion of people being shown over houses. We stood stock still, looking a little ill at ease, murmuring remarks such as: 'Very nice.' 'A very pleasant room.' 'The morning room, you say?'

The maid conducted us across the hall and into the corresponding room on the other side. This was much larger.

'The dining room, sir.'

This room was definitely Victorian. A heavy mahogany dining-table, a massive sideboard of almost purplish mahogany with great clusters of carved fruit, solid leather-covered dining room chairs. On the wall hung what were obviously family portraits.

The terrier had continued to bark in some sequestered spot. Now the sound suddenly increased in volume. With a crescendo of barking he could be heard galloping across the hall.

'*Who's* come into the house? *I'll* tear him limb from limb,' was clearly the 'burden of his song'.

He arrived in the doorway, sniffing violently.

'Oh, Bob, you naughty dog,' exclaimed our conductress. 'Don't mind him, sir. He won't do you no harm.'

Bob, indeed, having discovered the intruders, completely changed his manner. He fussed in and introduced himself to us in an agreeable manner.

'Pleased to meet you, I'm sure,' he observed as he sniffed round our ankles. 'Excuse the noise, won't you? but I have my job to do. Got to be careful who we let in, you know. But it's a dull life, and I'm really quite pleased to see a visitor. Dogs of your own, I fancy?'

This last was addressed to me, and I stooped and patted him.

'Nice little fellow,' I said to the woman. 'Needs plucking a bit, though.'

'Yes, sir, he's usually plucked three times a year.'

'Is he an old dog?'

'Oh no, sir. Bob's not more than six. And sometimes he behaves just like a puppy. Gets hold of cook's slippers and prances about with them. And he's very gentle, though you wouldn't believe it, to hear the noise he makes sometimes. The only person he goes for is the postman. Downright scared of him, the postman is.'

Bob was now investigating the legs of Poirot's trousers. Having learned all he could, he gave vent to a prolonged sniff ('H'm, not too bad, but not really a doggy person') and returned to me, cocking his head on one side and looking at me expectantly.

'I don't know why dogs always go for postmen, I'm sure,' continued our guide.

'It's a matter of reasoning,' said Poirot. 'The dog, he argues from reason. He is intelligent; he makes his deductions according to his point of view. There are people who may enter a house and there are people who may not – that a dog soon learns. *Eh bien*, who is the person who most persistently tries to gain admission, rattling on the door twice or three times a day – and who is never by any chance admitted? The postman. Clearly, then, an undesirable guest from the point of view of the master of the house. He is always sent about his business, but he persistently returns and tries again. Then a dog's duty is clear: to aid in driving this undesirable man away, and to bite him if possible. A most reasonable proceeding.'

He beamed on Bob.

'And a most intelligent person, I fancy.'

'Oh, he is, sir. He's almost human, Bob is.'

She flung open another door.

'The drawing room, sir.'

The drawing room conjured up memories of the past, A faint fragrance of pot-pourri hung about it. The chintzes were worn, their pattern faded garlands of roses. On the walls were prints and water-colour drawings. There was a good deal of china – fragile shepherds and shepherdesses. There were cushions worked in a crewel stitch. There were faded photographs in handsome silver frames. There were many inlaid workboxes and tea-caddies. Most fascinating of all to me were two ex-quisitely cut tissue-paper ladies under glass stands. One with a spinning-wheel, one with a cat on her knee.

The atmosphere of a bygone day, a day of leisure, of refine-ment, of 'ladies and gentlemen', closed round me. This was in-deed a 'withdrawing room'. Here ladies sat and did their fancy-work, and if a cigarette was ever smoked by a favoured mem-ber of the male sex, what a shaking out of curtains and general airing of the room there would be afterwards!

My attention was drawn by Bob. He was sitting in an attiude of rapt attention close beside an elegant little table with two drawers in it.

As he saw that I was noticing him, he gave a short, plaintive yelp, looking from me to the table.

'What does he want?' I asked.

Our interest in Bob was clearly pleasing to the maid, who obviously was very fond of him.

'It's his ball, sir. It was always kept in that drawer. That's why he sits there and asks.' Her voice changed. She addressed Bob in a high falsetto. 'It isn't there any longer, beautiful. Bob's ball is in the kitchen. In the kitchen, Bobsie.'

Bob shifted his gaze impatiently to Poirot.

'This woman's a fool,' he seemed to be saying. 'You look a brainy sort of chap. Balls are kept in certain places – this drawer is one of those places. There always has been a ball there. Therefore there should be a ball there now. That's ob-vious dog-logic, isn't it?'

'It's not there now, boy,' I said.

He looked at me doubtfully. Then as we went out of the room he followed slowly in an unconvinced manner.

We were shown various cupboards, a downstairs cloakroom, and a small pantry place, 'Where the mistress used to do the flowers, sir.'

'You were with your mistress a long time?' asked Poirot.

'Twenty-two years sir.'

'You are alone here caretaking?'

'Me and cook, sir.'

'She was also a long time with Miss Arundell?'

'Four years, sir. The old cook died.'

'Supposing I were to buy the house, would you be prepared to stay on?'

She blushed a little.

'It's very kind of you, sir, I'm sure, but I'm going to retire from service. The mistress left me a nice little sum, you see, and I'm going to my brother. I'm only remaining here as a convenience to Miss Lawson until the place is sold – to look after everything.'

Poirot nodded.

In the momentary silence a new sound was heard: Bump, bump, BUMP. A monotonous sound increasing in volume and seeming to descend from above.

'It's Bob, sir.' She was smiling. 'He's got hold of his ball and he's bumping it down the stairs. It's a little game of his.'

As we reached the bottom of the stairs a black rubber ball arrived with a thud on the last step. I caught it and looked up. Bob was lying on the top step, his paws splayed out, his tail gently wagging. I threw it up to him. He caught it neatly, chewed it for a minute or two with evident relish, then laid it between his paws and gently edged it forward with his nose till he finally bunted it over and it bumped once more down the stairs, Bob wagging his tail furiously as he watched its progress.

'He'll stay like that for hours, sir. Regular game of his. He'd go on all day at it. That'll do now, Bob. The gentlemen have got something else to do than play with you.'

A dog is a great promoter of friendly intercourse. Our interest and liking for Bob had quite broken down the natural stiffness of the good servant. As we went up to the bedroom floors, our guide was talking quite garrulously as she gave us accounts of Bob's wonderful sagacity. The ball had been left at the foot of the stairs. As we passed him, Bob gave us a look of deep disgust and stalked down in a dignified fashion to retrieve it. As we turned to the right I saw him slowly coming up again

435

with it in his mouth, his gait that of an exremely old man
forced by unthinking persons to exert himself unduly.

As we went round the bedrooms, Poirot began gradually to
draw our conductress out.

'There were four Miss Arundells lived here, did they not?'
he asked.

'Originally, yes, sir; but that was before my time. There was
only Miss Agnes and Miss Emily when I came and Miss Agnes
died a few years afterwards. She was the youngest of the family.
It seemed odd she should go before her sister.'

'I suppose she was not so strong as her sister?'

'No, sir, it's odd that. My Miss Arundell, Miss Emily, she was
always the delicate one. She's had a lot to do with doctors all
her life. Miss Agnes was always strong and robust, and yet she
went first, and Miss Emily, who'd been delicate from a child,
outlived all the family. Very odd the way things happen.'

'Astonishing how often that is the case.'

Poirot plunged into (I felt sure) a wholly mendacious story
of an invalid uncle which I will not trouble to repeat here. It
suffices to say that it had its effect. Discussions of death and
such matters do more to unlock the human tongue than any
other subject. Poirot was in a position to ask questions that
would have been regarded with suspicious hostility twenty
minutes earlier.

'Was Miss Arundell's illness a long and painful one?'

'No, I wouldn't say that, sir. She'd been ailing, if you know
what I mean for a long time – ever since two winters before.
Very bad she was then – this here jaundice. Yellow in the face
they go and the whites of their eyes—'

'Ah yes, indeed—' (Anecdote of Poirot's cousin, who appeared to have been the Yellow Peril in person.)

'That's right – just as you say, sir. Terribly ill she was, poor
dear. Couldn't keep anything down. If you ask me, Dr Grainger
hardly thought she'd pull through. But he'd a wonderful way
with her – bullying, you know. "Made up your mind to lie back
and order your tombstone?" he'd say. 'And she'd say, "I've a
bit of fight in me still, Doctor," and he'd say, "That's right –
that's what I like to hear." A hospital nurse we had, and she
made up her mind that it was all over – even said to the doctor
once that she supposed she'd better not worry the old lady too
much by forcing her to take food – but the doctor rounded on
her. "Nonsense," he said. "Worry her? You've got to bully her
into taking nourishment." Valentine's beef-juice at such and
such a time, Brand's essence – teaspoonfuls of brandy. And at

the end he said something that I've never forgotten. "You're young, my girl," he said to her. "You don't realize what fine fighting material there is in age. It's young people who turn up their toes and die because they're not interested enough to live. You show me anyone who's lived to over seventy and you show me a fighter – someone who's got the will to live." And it's true, sir – we're always saying how wonderful old people are – their vitality and the way they've kept their faculties – but, as the doctor put it, that's just *why* they've lived so long and got to be so old.'

'But it is profound what you say there – very profound! And Miss Arundell was like that? Very alive? Very interested in life?'

'Oh, yes, indeed, sir. Her health was poor, but her brain was as keen as anything. And as I was saying, she got over that illness of hers – surprised the nurse, it did. A stuck-up young thing she was, all starched collars and cuffs, and the waiting on she had to have, and tea at all hours.'

'A fine recovery.'

'Yes indeed, sir. Of course, the mistress had to be careful as to diet at first: everything boiled and steamed, no grease in the cooking; and she wasn't allowed to eat eggs either. Very monotonous it was for her.'

'Still, the main thing is she got well.'

'Yes, sir. Of course, she had her little turns. What I'd call bilious attacks. She wasn't always very careful about her food after a time – but still, they weren't very serious until the last attack.'

'Was it like her illness of two years before?'

'Yes, just the same sort of thing, sir. That nasty jaundice – an awful yellow colour again and terrible sickness and all the rest of it. Brought it on herself, I'm afraid she did, poor dear. Ate a lot of things she shouldn't have done. That very evening she was took bad she'd had curry for supper and, as you know, sir, curry's rich and a bit oily.'

'Her illness came on suddenly, did it?'

'Well, it seemed so, sir; but Dr Grainger, he said it had been working up for some time. A chill – the weather had been very changeable – and too rich feeding.'

'Surely her companion – Miss Lawson was her companion, was she not? – could have dissuaded her from rich dishes?'

'Oh, I don't think Miss Lawson would have much say. Miss Arundell wasn't one to take orders from anyone.'

'Had Miss Lawson been with her during her previous illness?'

'No, she came after that. She'd been with her about a year.'

'I suppose she'd had companions before that?'

'Oh, quite a number, sir.'

'Her companions didn't stay as long as her servants,' said Poirot, smiling.

The woman flushed.

'Well, you see, sir, it was different. Miss Arundell didn't get out much, and what with one thing and another—' She paused.

Poirot eyed her for a minute, then he said:

'I understand a little the mentality of elderly ladies. They crave, do they not, for novelty? They get, perhaps, to the end of a person.'

'Well, now, that's very clever of you sir. You've hit it exactly. When a new lady came Miss Arundell was always interested to start with – about her life and her childhood and where she'd been and what she thought about things, and then, when she knew all about her, well, she'd get – well, I suppose bored is the real word.'

'Exactly. And between you and me, these ladies who go as companions, they are not usually very interesting – very amusing, eh?'

'No, indeed, sir. They're poor-spirited creatures, most of them. Downright foolish, now and then. Miss Arundell soon got through with them, so to speak. And then she'd make a change and have someone else.'

'She must have been unusually attached to Miss Lawson, though.'

'Oh, I don't think so, sir.'

'Miss Lawson was not in any way remarkable?'

'I shouldn't have said so, sir. Quite an ordinary person.'

'You liked her, yes?'

The woman shrugged her shoulders slightly.

'There wasn't anything to like or dislike. Fussy she was – a regular old maid, and full of this nonsense about spirits.'

'*Spirits?*' Poirot looked alert.

'Yes, sir, spirits. Sitting in the dark round a table and dead people came back and spoke to you. Downright irreligious I call it – as if we didn't know departed souls had their rightful place and aren't likely to leave it.'

'So Miss Lawson was a spiritualist! Was Miss Arundell a believer, too?'

'Miss Lawson would have liked her to be!' snapped the other. There was a spice of satisfied malice in her tone.

'But she wasn't?' Poirot persisted.

'The mistress had too much sense.' She snorted. 'Mind you, I don't say it didn't *amuse* her. "I'm willing to be convinced," she'd say. But she'd often look at Miss Lawson as much as to say, "My poor dear, what a fool you are to be so taken in!"'

'I comprehend. She did not believe in it, but it was a source of amusement to her.'

'That's right, sir. I sometimes wondered if she didn't – well, have a bit of fun, so to speak, pushing the table and that sort of thing. And the others all as serious as death.'

'The others?'

'Miss Lawson and the two Miss Tripps.'

'Miss Lawson was a convinced spiritualist?'

'Took it all for gospel sir.'

'And Miss Arundell was very attached to Miss Lawson, of course?'

It was the second time Poirot had made this remark, and he got the same response.

'Well, hardly that, sir.'

'But surely,' said Poirot, 'if she left her everything— She did, did she not?'

The change was immediate. The human being vanished. The correct maid-servant returned. The woman drew herself up and said in a colourless voice that held reproof for familiarity in it:

'The way the mistress left her money is hardly my business, sir.'

I felt that Poirot had bungled the job. Having got the woman in a friendly mood, he was now proceeding to throw away his advantage. He was wise enough to make no immediate attempt to recover lost ground. After a commonplace remark about the size and number of the bedrooms. he went towards the head of the stairs.

Bob had disappeared, but as I came to the stair-head, I stumbled and nearly fell. Catching at the baluster to steady myself, I looked down, and saw that I had inadvertently placed my foot on Bob's ball, which he had left lying on the top of the stairs.

The woman apologized quickly.

'I'm sorry, sir. It's Bob's fault. He leaves his ball there. And you can't see it against the dark carpet. Death of someone some day it'll be. The poor mistress had a nasty fall through it. Might easily have been the death of her.'

Poirot stopped suddenly on the stairs.

'She had an accident, you say?'

'Yes, sir. Bob left his ball there, as he often did, and the mistress came out of her room and fell over it and went right down the stairs. Might have been killed.'

'Was she much hurt?'

'Not as much as you'd think. Very lucky she was, Dr Grainger said. Cut her head a little, and strained her back, and of course there were bruises and it was a nasty shock. She was in bed for about a week, but it wasn't serious.'

'Was this long ago?'

'Just a week or two before she died.'

Poirot stooped to recover something he had dropped.

'Pardon – my fountain pen – ah, yes, there it is.'

He stood up again.

'He is careless, this Master Bob,' he observed.

'Ah, well, he don't know no better, sir,' said the woman in an indulgent voice. 'Nearly human he may be, but you can't have everything. The mistress, you see, usedn't to sleep well at nights, and often she'd get up and wander downstairs and round and about the house.'

'She did that often?'

'Most nights. But she wouldn't have Miss Lawson or any one fussing after her.'

Poirot had turned into the drawing room again.

'A beautiful room this,' he observed. 'I wonder, would there be space in this recess for my bookcase? What do you think, Hastings?'

Quite fogged, I remarked cautiously that it would be difficult to say.

'Yes, sizes are so deceptive. Take, I pray you, my little rule and measure the width of it, and I will write it down.'

Obediently I took the folding rule that Poirot handed me and took various measurements under his direction whilst he wrote on the back of an envelope.

I was just wondering why he adopted such an untidy and uncharacteristic method instead of making a neat entry in his little pocket-book when he handed the envelope to me, saying:

'That is right, is it not? Perhaps you had better verify it.'

There were no figures on the envelope. Instead was written: 'When we go upstairs again, pretend to remember an appointment and ask if you can telephone. Let the woman come with you, and delay her as long as you can.'

'That's all right,' I said pocketing the envelope. 'I should say both bookcases would go in perfectly.'

'It is as well to be sure, though. I think, if it is not too much trouble, I would like to look at the principal bedroom again. I am not quite sure of the wall space there.'

'Certainly, sir. It's no trouble.'

We went up again. Poirot measured a portion of wall, and was just commenting aloud on the respective possible positions of bed, wardrobe and writing-table, when I looked at my watch, gave a somewhat exaggerated start and exclaimed:

'By Jove! do you know it's three o'clock already? What will Anderson think? I ought to telephone to him.' I turned to the woman. 'I wonder if I might use your telephone if you have one.'

'Why, certainly, sir. It's in the little room off the hall. I'll show you.'

She bustled down with me, indicating the instrument, and then I got her to help me in finding a number in the telephone directory. In the end I made a call – to a Mr Anderson in the neighbouring town of Harchester. Fortunately he was out, and I was able to leave a message saying it was unimportant and that I would ring up later!

When I emerged Poirot had descended the staircase and was standing in the hall. His eyes had a slightly green tinge. I had no clue to his excitement, but I realized that he *was* excited.

Poirot said:

'That fall from the top of the stairs must have given your mistress a great shock. Did she seem perturbed about Bob and his ball after it?'

'It's funny your saying that, sir. It worried her a lot. Why, just as she was dying, she was delirious, and she rambled on a lot about Bob and his ball and something about a picture that was ajar.'

'A picture that was ajar,' said Poirot thoughtfully.

'Of course, it didn't make sense, sir; but she was rambling, you see.'

'One moment – I must go into the drawing room once more.'

He wandered round the room, examining the ornaments. In especial, one big jar with a lid on it seemed to attract him. It was not, I fancy, a particularly good bit of china. A piece of Victorian humour – it had on it a rather crude picture of a bulldog sitting outside a front door with a mournful expression on its face. Below was written: *Out all night and no key.*

Poirot, whose taste I have always been convinced is hopelessly bourgeois, seemed lost in admiration.

'*Out all night and no key,*' he murmured. 'It is amusing

441

that! Is that true of our Master Bob? Does he sometimes stay out all night?'

'Very occasional, sir. Oh, very occasional. He's a very good dog, Bob is.'

'I am sure he is. But even the best of dogs—'

'Oh, it's quite true, sir. Once or twice he's gone off and come home perhaps at four in the morning. Then he sits down on the step and barks till he's let in.'

'Who lets him in – Miss Lawson?'

'Well, anyone who hears him, sir. It was Miss Lawson, sir, last time. It was the night of the mistress's accident. And Bob came home about five. Miss Lawson hurried down to let him in before he could make a noise. She was afraid of waking up the mistress, and hadn't told her Bob was missing for fear of worrying her.'

'I see. She thought it was better Miss Arundell shouldn't be told?'

'That's what she said, sir. She said, "He's sure to come back. He always does; but she might worry, and that would never do.' So we didn't say anything.'

'Was Bob fond of Miss Lawson?'

'Well, he was rather contemptuous of her, if you know what I mean, sir. Dogs can be. She was kind to him. Called him a good doggie and a nice doggie, but he used to look at her kind of scornful like, and he didn't pay any attention at all to what she told him to do.'

Poirot nodded. 'I see,' he said.

Suddenly he did something which startled me.

He pulled a letter from his pocket – the letter he had received this morning.

'Ellen,' he said, 'do you know anything about this?'

The change that came over Ellen's face was remarkable.

Her jaw dropped and she stared at Poirot with an almost comical expression of bewilderment.

'Well,' she ejaculated, 'I never did!'

The observation lacked coherency, perhaps, but it left no doubt of Ellen's meaning.

Gathering her wits about her, she said slowly:

'Are you the gentleman that letter was written to, then?'

'I am. I am Hercule Poirot.'

Like most people, Ellen had not glanced at the name on the order Poirot had held out to her on his arrival. She nodded her head slowly.

'That was it,' she said. 'Hercule Poirot.' She added an S to

the Christian name and sounded the T of the surname. 'My
word!' she exclaimed. 'Cook *will* be surprised.'

Poirot said quickly:

'Would it not be advisable, perhaps, for us to go to the
kitchen and there, in company with your friend, we could talk
the matter over?'

'Well – if you don't mind, sir.'

Ellen sounded just a little doubtful. This particular social
dilemma was clearly new to her. But Poirot's matter-of-fact
manner reassured her, and we departed forthwith to the
kitchen, Ellen elucidating the situation to a large, pleasant-
faced woman who was just lifting a kettle from a gas ring.

'You'll never believe it, Annie. This is actually the gentleman
that letter was to. You know, the one I found in the blotter.'

'You must remember I am in the dark,' said Poirot. 'Perhaps
you will tell me how the letter came to be posted so late in the
day?'

'Well, sir, to tell the truth, I didn't know what to do. Neither
of us did, did we?'

'Indeed, we didn't,' the cook confirmed.

'You see, sir, when Miss Lawson was turning out things after
the mistress's death a good lot of things were given away or
thrown away. Among them was a little papermatchie, I think
they call it, blotter. Very pretty it was, with a lily of the valley
on it. The mistress always used it when she wrote in bed. Well,
Miss Lawson didn't want it, so she gave it to me along with a
lot of other little odds and ends that had belonged to the mistress. I put it away in a drawer, and it wasn't till yesterday that
I took it out. I was going to put some new blotting-paper in it
so that it was ready for me to use. There was a sort of pocket
inside, and I just slipped my hand in it, when what should I
find but a letter in the mistress's handwriting, tucked away.

'Well, as I say, I didn't know rightly what to do about it. It
was the mistress's hand all right, and I saw as she'd written it
and slipped it in there waiting to post it the next day, and then
she'd forgot, which is the kind of thing she did many a time,
poor dear. Once it was a dividend warrant to her bank, and no
one could think where it had got to, and at last it was found
pushed right back in the pigeon-holes of the desk.'

'Was she untidy?'

'Oh, no, sir, just the opposite. She was always putting things
away and clearing them up. That was half the trouble. If she'd
left things about it would really have been better. It was their

being tidied away and then forgotten that was always happening.'

'Things like Bob's ball, for instance?' asked Poirot, with a smile.

The sagacious terrier had just trotted in from outdoors and greeted us anew in a very friendly manner.

'Yes, indeed, sir. As soon as Bob finished playing with his ball she'd put it away. But that was all right, because it had its own place – in the drawer I showed you.'

'I see. But I interrupted you. Pray go on. You discovered the letter in the blotter?'

'Yes, sir, that was the way of it, and I asked Annie what she thought I'd better do. I didn't like to put it in the fire – and, of course, I couldn't take upon myself to open it, and neither Annie nor I could see that it was any business of Miss Lawson's, so after we'd talked it over a bit, I just put a stamp on it and ran out to the post-box and posted it.'

Poirot turned slightly to me. '*Voilà*,' he murmured.

I could not help saying maliciously:

'Amazing how simple an explanation can be!'

I thought he looked a little crestfallen and rather wished I hadn't been so quick to try to rub it in.

He turned again to Ellen.

'As my friend says: How simple an explanation can be! You understand, when I received a letter dated over two months ago, I was somewhat surprised.'

'Yes, I suppose you must have been, sir. We didn't think of that.'

'Also' – Poirot coughed – 'I am in a little dilemma. That letter, you see – it was a commission with which Miss Arundell wished to entrust me. A matter of a somewhat private character.' He cleared his throat importantly. 'Now that Miss Arundell is dead, I am in some doubt how to act. Would Miss Arundell have wished me to undertake the commission in these circumstances or not? It is difficult – very difficult.'

Both women were looking at him respectfully.

'I shall have, I think, to consult Miss Arundell's lawyer. She had a lawyer, did she not?'

Ellen answered quickly:

'Oh, yes, sir. Mr Purvis from Harchester.'

'He knew all her affairs?'

'I think so, sir. He's done everything for her ever since I can remember. It was him she sent for after the fall she had.'

'The fall down the stairs?'

'Yes, sir.'

'Now let me see, when was that exactly?'

'The cook broke in:

'Day after Bank Holiday it was, I remember that well. I stayed in to oblige on Bank Holiday, seeing she had all those people staying, and I had the day on Wednesday instead.'

Poirot had whipped out his pocket almanac.

'Precisely – precisely. Easter Bank Holiday, I see, fell on the thirteenth this year. Then Miss Arundell had her accident on the fourteenth. This letter to me was written three days later. A pity that it was never sent. However, it may still not be too late—' He paused. 'I rather fancy that the – er – commission she wished me to perform was connected with one of the – er – guests you mentioned just now.'

This remark, which could only have been a pure shot in the dark, met with immediate response. A quick look of intelligence passed across Ellen's face. She turned to the cook, who gave her back an answering glance.

'That'll be Mr Charles,' she said.

'If you would tell me just who was there—' Poirot suggested.

'Dr Tanios and his wife – Miss Bella that was – and Miss Theresa and Mr Charles.'

'They were all nephews and nieces?'

'That's right, sir. Dr Tanios, of course, is no relation. In fact, he's a foreigner – a Greek or something of the sort, I believe. He married Miss Bella, Miss Arundell's niece, her sister's child. Mr Charles and Miss Theresa are brother and sister.'

'Ah, yes, I see. A family party. And when did they leave?'

'On the Wednesday morning, sir. And Dr Tanios and Miss Bella came down again the next weekend because they were worried about Miss Arundell.'

'And Mr Charles and Miss Theresa?'

'They came the weekend after. The weekend before she died.'

Poirot's curiosity, I felt, was quite insatiable. I could see no point in these continued questions. He had got the explanation of his mystery, and in my opinion the sooner he retired with dignity the better.

The thought seemed to go from my brain to his.

'*Eh bien*,' he said. 'This information you have given me is very helpful. I must consult this Mr Purvis, I think you said? Thank you very much for all your help.'

He stooped and patted Bob.

'*Brave chien, va!* You loved your mistress.'

Bob responded amiably to these overtures and, hopeful of a

445

little play, went and fetched a large piece of coal. For this he was reproved and the coal removed from him. He sent me a glance in search of sympathy.

'These women,' it seemed to say. 'Generous with the food, but not really sportsmen!'

——— 9 ———

RECONSTRUCTION OF THE DOG'S BALL INCIDENT

'Well, Poirot,' I said, as the gate of Littlegreen House closed behind us. 'You are satisfied now, I hope!'

'Yes, my friend. I am satisfied.'

'Thank Heaven for that! All the mysteries explained! The Wicked Companion and the Rich Old Lady myth exploded. The delayed letter and even the famous incident of the dog's ball shown in their true colours. Everything settled satisfactorily and according to Cocker!'

Poirot gave a dry little cough and said:

'I would not use the word *satisfactorily*, Hastings.'

'You did a minute ago.'

'No, no. I did not say the matter was *satisfactory*. I said that, personally, my curiosity was *satisfied*. I know the truth of the Dog's Ball incident.'

'And very simple it was too!'

'Not quite so simple as you think.' He nodded his head several times. Then he went on: 'You see, I know one little thing which you do not.'

'And what is that?' I asked somewhat sceptically.

'*I know that there is a nail driven into the skirting-board at the top of the stairs.*'

I stared at him. His face was quite grave.

'Well,' I said, after a minute or two. 'Why shouldn't there be?'

'The question is, Hastings, why should there be?'

'How do I know? Some household reason, perhaps. Does it matter?'

'Certainly it matters. And I can think of no household reason for a nail to be driven in at the top of the skirting-board in that particular place. It was carefully varnished, too, so as not to show.'

'What are you driving at, Poirot? Do *you* know the reason?'

'I can imagine it quite easily. If you wanted to stretch a piece of strong thread or wire across the top of the stairs about a foot from the ground, you could tie it one side to the balusters, but on the inner wall side you would need something like a nail to attach the thread to.'

'Poirot!' I cried. 'What on earth are you driving at?'

'*Mon cher ami*, I am reconstructing *the incident of the Dog's Ball!* Would you like to hear my reconstruction?'

'Go ahead.'

'*Eh bien*, here it is. Someone had noticed the habit Bob had of leaving his ball at the top of the stairs. A dangerous thing to do – it might lead to an accident.' Poirot paused a minute, then said in a slightly different tone, 'If you wished to kill someone, Hastings, how would you set about it?'

'I – well, really – I don't know. Fake up some *alibi* or something, I suppose.'

'A proceeding, I assure you, both difficult and dangerous, but, then, you are not the type of a cold-blooded, cautious murderer. Does it not strike you that the *easiest* way of removing someone you want to remove from your path is to take advantage of *accident*? Accidents are happening all the time. And sometimes – Hastings – *they can he helped to happen!*'

He paused a minute, then went on:

'I think the dog's ball left fortuitously at the top of the stairs gave our murderer an idea. Miss Arundell was in the habit of coming out of her room in the night and wandering about. Her eyesight was not good; it was quite within the bounds of probability that she might stumble over it and fall headlong down those stairs. But a careful murderer does not leave things to chance. A *thread* stretched across the top of the stairs would be a much better way. It would send her pitching head foremost. Then, when the household came rushing out – there, plain to see, is the *cause* of the accident – *Bob's ball!*'

'How horrible!' I cried.

Poirot said gravely:

'Yes, it was horrible . . . It was also unsuccessful . . . Miss Arundell was very little hurt, though she might easily have broken her neck. Very disappointing for our unknown friend! But Miss Arundell was a sharp-witted old lady. Everyone told her she had slipped on the ball, and there the ball was as evidence; but she herself, recalling the happening, felt that the accident had arisen differently. She had *not* slipped on the ball. And in addition she remembered something else. *She remem-*

bered hearing Bob barking for admission at five o'clock the next morning.

'This, I admit, is something in the way of guess-work, but I believe I am right. *Miss Arundell had put away Bob's ball herself* the evening before in its drawer. After that he went out *and did not return.* In that case, *it was not Bob* who put that ball on the top of the stairs.'

'That is pure guess-work, Poirot,' I objected.

He demurred.

'Not quite, my friend. There are the significant words uttered by Miss Arundell when she was delirious – something about Bob's ball and a "picture ajar". You see the point, do you not?'

'Not in the least.'

'Curious. I know your language well enough to realize that one does not talk of a picture being *ajar*. A *door* is *ajar*. A picture is *awry*.

'Or simply crooked.'

'Or simply crooked, as you say. So I realize at once that Ellen has mistaken the meaning of the words she heard. It is not ajar – but a or the jar that was meant. Now, in the drawing room there is a rather noticeable china jar. There is, I have already observed, a picture of a dog on it. With the remembrance of these delirious ravings in my mind, I go up and examine it more closely. I find that it deals with the subject of *a dog who has been out all night.* You see the trend of the feverish woman's thoughts? Bob was like the dog in the picture on the jar – out all night – *so it was not he who left the ball on the stairs.*'

I cried out, feeling some admiration in spite of myself.

'You're an ingenious devil, Poirot! How you think of these things beats me!'

'I do not "think of them". They are *there* – plain for anyone to see. *Eh bien*, you realize the position? Miss Arundell, lying in bed after her fall, becomes suspicious. That suspicion she feels is perhaps fanciful and absurd, but there it is. *"Since the incident of the Dog's Ball I have been increasingly uneasy."* And so – and so she writes to me, and by a piece of bad luck her letter does not reach me until two months have gone by. Tell me, does her letter not fit in *perfectly* with these facts?'

'Yes,' I admitted. 'It does.'

Poirot went on:

'There is another point worthy of consideration. Miss Lawson was exceedingly anxious that the fact of Bob's being out all night should not get to Miss Arundell's ears.'

'You think that she—'

'I think that the fact should be noted very carefully.'

I turned the thing over in my mind for a minute or two.

'Well,' I said at last with a sigh, 'it's all very interesting – as a mental exercise, that is. And I take off my hat to you. It's been a masterful piece of reconstruction. It's almost a pity really that the old lady has died.'

'A pity – yes. She wrote to me that someone had attempted to murder her (that is what it amounts to, after all), and a very short time after, she was dead.'

'Yes, I said, 'and it's a grand disappointment to you that she died a natural death, isn't it? Come, admit it.'

Poirot shrugged his shoulders.

'Or perhaps you think she was poisoned,' I said maliciously.

Poirot shook his head, somewhat despondently.

'It certainly seems,' he admitted, 'as though Miss Arundell died from natural causes.'

'And therefore,' I said, 'we return to London with our tail between our legs.'

'*Pardon*, my friend, but we do *not* return to London.'

'What do you mean, Poirot?' I cried.

'If you show the dog the rabbit, my friend, does he return to London? No, he goes into the rabbit hole.'

'What do you mean?'

'The dog hunts rabbits. Hercule Poirot hunts murderers. We have here a murderer – a murderer whose crime failed. Yes, perhaps; but nevertheless a murderer. And I, my friend, am going into the burrow after him – or her, as the case may be.'

He turned sharply in at the gate.

'Where are you off to, Poirot?'

'Into the burrow, my friend. This is the house of Dr Grainger, who attended Miss Arundell in her last illness.'

Dr Grainger was a man of sixty odd. His face was thin and bony with an aggressive chin, bushy eyebrows, and a pair of very shrewd grey eyes. He looked keenly from me to Poirot.

'Well, what can I do for you?' he asked abruptly.

Poirot swept into speech in the most flamboyant manner.

'I must apologize, Dr Grainger, for this intrusion. I must confess straightaway that I do not come to consult you professionally.'

Dr Grainger said dryly:

'Glad to hear it. You look healthy enough.'

'I must explain the purpose of my visit,' went on Poirot. 'The truth of the matter is that I am writing a book – the life of the late General Arundell, who I understand lived in Market Basing for some years before his death.'

The doctor looked rather surprised.

'Yes, General Arundell lived here till his death. At Little-green House – just up the road past the Bank – you've been there, perhaps?' Poirot nodded assent. 'But you understand that was a good bit before my time. I came here in 1919.'

'You knew his daughter, however, the late Miss Arundell?'

'I knew Emily Arundell well.'

'You comprehend, it has been a severe blow to me to find that Miss Arundell has recently died.'

'On May 1st.'

'So I discovered. I counted, you see, on her giving me various personal details and reminiscences of her father.'

'Quite – quite. But I don't see what I can do about it.'

Poirot asked:

'General Arundell has no other sons or daughters living?'

'No. All dead, the lot of them.'

'How many were there?'

'Five. Four daughters, one son.'

'And in the next generation?'

'Charles Arundell and his sister Theresa. You could get on to them. I doubt, though, if it would be much use to you. The young generation doesn't take much interest in its grandfathers. And there's a Mrs Tanios, but I doubt if you'd get much there either.'

'They might have family papers – documents?'

'They might have. Doubt it, though. A lot of stuff was cleared out and burnt after Miss Emily's death, I know.'

Poirot uttered a groan of anguish.

Grainger looked at him curiously.

'What's the interest in old Arundell? I never heard he was a big pot in any way?'

'My dear sir.' Poirot's eyes gleamed with the excitement of the fanatic. 'Is there not a saying that history knows nothing of its greatest men? Recently certain papers have come to light which throw an entirely different light on the whole subject of the Indian Mutiny. There is secret history there. And in that secret history John Arundell played a big part. The whole thing is fascinating – fascinating! And let me tell you, my dear sir, it is of especial interest at the present time. India – the English policy in regard to it – is the burning question of the hour.'

'H'm,' said the doctor. 'I have heard that old General Arundell used to hold forth a good deal on the subject of the Mutiny. As a matter of fact, he was considered a prize bore on the subject.'

'Who told you that?'

'A Miss Peabody. You might call on her, by the way. She's our oldest inhabitant – knew the Arundells intimately. And gossip is her chief recreation. She's worth seeing for her own sake – a character.'

'Thank you. That is an excellent idea. Perhaps, too, you would give me the address of young Mr Arundell, the grandson of the late General Arundell.'

'Charles? Yes, I can put you on to him. But he's an irreverent young devil. Family history means nothing to him.'

'He is quite young?'

'He's what an old fogy like me calls young,' said the doctor, with a twinkle. 'Early thirties. The kind of young man that's born to be a trouble and responsibility to their families. Charm of personality and nothing else. He's been shipped about all over the world, and done no good anywhere.'

'His aunt was doubtless fond of him?' ventured Poirot. 'It is often that way.'

'H'm – I don't know. Emily Arundell was no fool. As far as I knew, he never succeeded in getting any money out of her. Bit of a tartar, that old lady. I liked her. Respected her, too. An old soldier every inch of her.'

'Was her death sudden?'

'Yes, in a way. Mind you, she'd been in poor health for some years. But she'd pulled through some narrow squeaks.'

'There was some story – I apologize for repeating gossip' – Poirot spread out his hands deprecatingly – 'that she had quarrelled with her family.'

'She didn't exactly *quarrel* with them,' said Dr Grainger slowly. 'No, there was no open quarrel, as far as I know.'

'I beg your pardon. I am, perhaps, being indiscreet.'

'No, no. After all, the information's public property.'

'She left her money away from her family, I understand?'

'Yes, left it all to a frightened, fluttering hen of a companion. Odd thing to do. Can't understand it myself. Not like her.'

'Ah, well,' said Poirot thoughtfully. 'One can imagine such a thing happening. An old lady, frail and in ill-health. Very dependent on the person who attends and cares for her. A clever woman with a certain amount of personality could gain a great ascendency that way.'

The word 'ascendency' seemed to act like a red rag to a bull.
Dr Grainger snorted out:

'Ascendency? Ascendency? Nothing of the kind! Emily
Arundell treated Minnie Lawson worse than a dog. Characteristic of that generation. Anyway, women who earn their living
as companions are usually fools. If they've got brains they're
earning a better living some other way. Emily Arundell didn't
suffer fools gladly. She usually wore out one poor devil a year.
Ascendency? Nothing of the sort!'

Poirot hastened off the treacherous ground.

'It is possible, perhaps,' he suggested, 'that there are old
family letters and documents in this Miss – er – Lawson's possession?'

'Might be,' agreed Grainger. 'Usually are a lot of things
tucked away in an old maid's house. I don't suppose Miss Lawson's been through half of it yet.'

Poirot rose.

'Thank you very much, Dr Grainger. You have been most
kind.'

'Don't thank me,' said the doctor. 'Sorry I can't do anything
helpful. Miss Peabody's your best chance. Lives at Morton
Manor – about a mile out.'

Poirot was sniffing at a large bouquet of roses on the doctor's
table.

'Delicious,' he murmured.

'Yes, I suppose so. Can't smell 'em myself. Lost my sense of
smell when I had flu four years ago. Nice admission for a
doctor, eh? "Physician, heal thyself." Damned nuisance. Can't
enjoy a smoke as I used to.'

'Unfortunate, yes. By the way, you *will* give me young Arundell's address?'

'I can get it for you, yes.' He ushered us out into the hall and
called, 'Donaldson. My partner,' he explained. 'He should have
it all right. He's by way of being engaged to Charles's sister,
Theresa.'

He called again: 'Donaldson.'

A young man came out from a room at the back of the house.
He was of medium height and of rather colourless appearance.
His manner was precise. A greater contrast to Dr Grainger
could not be imagined.

The latter explained what he wanted.

Dr Donaldson's eyes – very pale blue eyes slightly prominent
– swept over us, appraisingly. When he spoke it was in a dry,
precise manner.

'I don't know exactly where Charles is to be found,' he said. 'I can give you Miss Theresa Arundell's address. Doubtless she will be able to put you in touch with her brother.'

Poirot assured him that that would do perfectly.

The doctor wrote down an address on a page in his notebook, tore it out, and handed it to Poirot.

Poirot thanked him and said goodbye to both doctors. As we went out of the door I was conscious of Dr Donaldson standing in the hall peering after us with a slightly startled look on his face.

——— 1 0 ———

VISIT TO MISS PEABODY

'Is it really necessary to tell such elaborate lies, Poirot?' I asked as we walked away.

Poirot shrugged his shoulders.

'If one is going to tell a lie at all – and I notice, by the way, that your nature is very much averse to lying; now, me, it does not trouble me at all—'

'So I've noticed,' I interjected.

'—As I was remarking, *if* one is going to tell a lie at all, it might as well be an artistic lie, a romantic lie, a convincing lie!'

'Do you consider this a convincing lie? Do you think **Dr** Donaldson was convinced?'

'That young man is of a sceptical nature,' admitted Poirot thoughtfully.

'He looked definitely suspicious to me.'

'I do not see why he should be so. Imbeciles are writing the lives of other imbeciles every day. It is, as you say, done.'

'First time I've heard you call yourself an imbecile,' I said, grinning.

'I can adopt a role, I hope, as well as anyone,' said Poirot coldly. 'I am sorry you do not think my little fiction well imagined. I was rather pleased with it myself.'

I changed the subject.

'What do we do next?'

'That is easy. We get into your car and pay a visit to Morton Manor.'

Morton Manor proved to be an ugly, substantial house of

the Victorian period. A decrepit butler received us somewhat doubtfully, and presently returned to ask if we had an appointment.

'Please tell Miss Peabody that we come from Dr Grainger,' said Poirot.

After a wait of a few minutes, the door opened and a short, fat woman waddled into the room. Her sparse, white hair was neatly parted in the middle. She wore a black velvet dress, the nap of which was completely rubbed off in various places, and some really beautiful fine point lace was fastened at her neck with a large cameo brooch.

She came across the room peering at us short-sightedly. Her first words were somewhat of a surprise.

'Got anything to sell?'

'Nothing, madame,' said Poirot.

'Sure?'

'But absolutely.'

'No vacuum cleaners?'

'No.'

'No stockings?'

'No.'

'No rugs?'

'No.'

'Oh, well,' said Miss Peabody, settling herself in a chair, 'I suppose it's all right You'd better sit down, then.'

We sat obediently.

'You'll excuse my asking,' said Miss Peabody with a trace of apology in her manner. 'Got to be careful. You wouldn't believe the people who come along. Servants are no good. They can't tell. Can't blame 'em either. Right voices, right clothes, right names. How are they to tell? Commander Ridgeway. Mr Scot Edgerton, Captain D'Arcy Fitzherbert. Nice-looking fellows, some of 'em. But before you know where you are they've shoved a cream-making machine under your nose.'

Poirot said earnestly:

'I assure you, madame, that we have nothing whatever of that kind.'

'Well, you should know,' said Miss Peabody.

Poirot plunged into his story. Miss Peabody heard him out without comment, blinking once or twice out of her small eyes. At the end she said:

'Goin' to write a book, eh?'

'Yes.'

'In English?'

'Certainly – in English.'

'But you're a foreigner. Eh? Come now, you're a foreigner, aren't you?'

'That is true.'

She transferred her gaze to me.

'You are his secretary, I suppose?'

'Er – yes,' I said doubtfully.

'Can you write decent English?'

'I hope so.'

'H'm – where did you go to school?'

'Eton.'

'Then you can't.'

I was forced to let this sweeping charge against an old and venerable centre of education pass unchallenged as Miss Peabody turned her attention once more to Poirot.

'Goin' to write a life of General Arundell, eh?'

'Yes. You knew him, I think.'

'Yes, I knew John Arundell. He drank.'

There was a momentary pause. Then Miss Peabody went on musingly:

'Indian Mutiny, eh? Seems a bit like flogging a dead horse to me. But that's your business.'

'You know, madame, there is a fashion in these things. At the moment India is the mode.'

'Something in that. Things do come round. Look at sleeves.'

We maintained a respectful silence.

'Leg o' muttons were always ugly,' said Miss Peabody. 'But I always looked well in Bishops.' She fixed a bright eye on Poirot. 'Now then, what do you want to know?'

Poirot spread out his hands.

'Anything! Family history. Gossip. Home life.'

'Can't tell you anything about India,' said Miss Peabody. 'Truth is, I didn't listen. Rather boring these old men and their anecdotes. He was a very stupid man – but I dare say none the worse General for that. I've always heard that intelligence didn't get you far in the army. Pay attention to your Colonel's wife and listen respectfully to your superior officers and you'll get on – that's what my father used to say.'

Treating this dictum respectfully, Poirot allowed a moment or two to elapse before he said:

'You knew the Arundell family intimately, did you not?'

'Knew 'em all,' said Miss Peabody. 'Matilda, she was the eldest. A spotty girl. Used to teach in Sunday School. Was sweet on one of the curates. Then there was Emily. Good seat on a horse, she had. She was the only one who could do anything with her father when he had one of his bouts on. Cartloads of bottles used to be taken out of that house. Buried them at night, they did. Then, let me see, who came next, Arabella or Thomas? Thomas, I think. Always felt sorry for Thomas. One man and four women. Makes a man look a fool. He was a bit of an old woman himself, Thomas was. Nobody thought he'd ever marry. Bit of a shock when he did.'

She chuckled – a rich, Victorian, fruity chuckle.

It was clear that Miss Peabody was enjoying herself. As an audience we were almost forgotten. Miss Peabody was well away in the past.

'Then came Arabella. Plain girl. Face like a scone. She married all right though, even if she were the plainest of the family. Professor at Cambridge. Quite an old man. Must have been sixty if he was a day. He gave a series of lectures here – on the wonders of Modern Chemistry, I think it was. I went to 'em. He mumbled, I remember. Had a beard. Couldn't hear much of what he said. Arabella used to stay behind and ask questions. She wasn't a chicken herself. Must have been getting on for forty. Ah, well, they're both dead now. Quite a happy marriage it was. There's something to be said for marrying a plain woman – you know the worst at once and she's not so likely to be flighty. Then there was Agnes. She was the youngest – the pretty one. Rather gay we used to think her. Almost fast! Odd, you'd think if any of them had married it would have been Agnes, but she didn't. She died not long after the war.'

Poirot murmured: 'You said that Mr Thomas's marriage was rather unexpected.'

Again Miss Peabody produced that rich, throaty chuckle.

'Unexpected? I should say it was! Made a nine days' scandal. You'd never have thought it of him – such a quiet, timid, retiring man and devoted to his sisters.'

She paused a minute.

'Remember a case that made rather a stir in the late nineties? Mrs Varley? Supposed to have poisoned her husband with arsenic. Good-looking woman. Made a big to-do, that case. She was acquitted. Well, Thomas Arundell quite lost his head. Used to get all the papers and read about the case and cut out the photographs of Mrs Varley. And would you believe it, when the trial was over, off he went to London and asked her to marry him? Thomas! Quiet, stay-at-home Thomas! Never can tell with men, can you? They're always liable to break out.'

'And what happened?'

'Oh, she married him all right.'

'It was a great shock to his sisters?'

'I should think so! They wouldn't receive her. I don't know that I blame them, all things considered. Thomas was mortally offended. He went off to live in the Channel Islands and nobody heard any more of him. Don't know whether his wife poisoned her first husband. She didn't poison Thomas. He survived her by three years. There were two children, boy and girl. Good-looking pair – took after their mother.'

'I suppose they came here to their aunt a good deal?'

'Not till after their parents died. They were at school and almost grown-up by then. They used to come for holidays. Emily was alone in the world then, and they and Bella Biggs were the only kith and kin she had.'

'Biggs?'

'Arabella's daughter. Dull girl – some years older than Theresa. Made a fool of herself, though. Married some foreigner who was over at the University. A Greek doctor. Dreadful-looking man – got rather a charming manner, though, I must admit. Well, I don't suppose poor Bella had many chances. Spent her time helping her father or holding wool for her mother. This fellow was exotic. It appealed to her.'

'Has it been a happy marriage?'

Miss Peabody snapped out:

'I wouldn't like to say for certain about *any* marriage! They *seem* quite happy. Two rather yellow-looking children. They live in Smyrna.'

'But they are now in England, are they not?'

'Yes, they came over in March. I rather fancy they'll be going back soon.'

'Was Miss Emily Arundell fond of her niece?'

'Fond of Bella? Oh, quite. She's a dull woman – wrapped up in her children and that sort of thing.'

'Did she approve of the husband?'

Miss Peabody chuckled.

'She didn't *approve* of him, but I think she rather liked the rascal. He's got brains, you know. If you ask me, he was jockeying her along very nicely. Got a nose for money, that man.'

Poirot coughed.

'I understand Miss Arundell died a rich woman?' he murmured.

Miss Peabody settled herself more comfortably in her chair.

'Yes, that's what made all the pother! Nobody dreamed she was quite as well off as she was. How it came about was this way. Old General Arundell left quite a nice little income – divided equally among his son and daughters. Some of it was reinvested, and I think every investment has done well. There were some original shares of Mortauld. Now, of course, Thomas and Arabella took their shares with them when they married. The other three sisters lived here, and they didn't spend a tenth part of their joint income; it all went back and was re-invested. When Matilda died she left her money to be divided between Emily and Agnes, and when Agnes died she left hers to Emily. And Emily still went on spending very little. Result, she died a rich woman – and the Lawson woman gets it all!'

Miss Peabody brought out the last sentence as a kind of triumphal climax.

'Did that come as a surprise to you, Miss Peabody?'

'To tell you the truth, it did! Emily had always given out quite openly that at her death her money was to be divided between her nieces and her nephew. And as a matter of fact, that was the way it was in the original will. Legacies to the servants and so on and then to be divided between Theresa, Charles and Bella. My goodness, there *was* a to-do when, after her death, it was found she'd made a new will leaving it all to poor Miss Lawson!'

'Was the will made just before her death?'

Miss Peabody directed a sharp glance at him.

'Thinking of undue influence? No, I'm afraid that's no use. And I shouldn't think poor Lawson had the brains or the nerve to attempt anything of the sort. To tell you the truth, she seemed as much surprised as anybody – or said she was!'

Poirot smiled at the addition.

'The will was made about ten days before her death,' went on Miss Peabody. 'Lawyer says it's all right. Well – it may be.'

'You mean—' Poirot leaned forward.

'Hanky-panky, that's what I say,' said Miss Peabody. 'Something fishy somewhere.'

'Just what exactly is your idea?'

'Haven't got one. How should I know where the hanky-panky comes in? I'm not a lawyer. But there's something queer about it, mark my words.'

Poirot said slowly:

'Has there been any question of contesting the will?'

'Theresa's taken counsel's opinion, I believe. A lot of good that'll do her! What's a lawyer's opinion nine times out of ten? "Don't!" Five lawyers advised me once against bringing an action. What did I do? Paid no attention. Won my case too. They had me in the witness-box, and a clever young whipper-snapper from London tried to make me contradict myself. But he didn't manage it. "You can hardly identify these furs positively, Miss Peabody," he said. "There's no furrier's mark on them."

' "That may be," I said. "But there's a darn on the lining, and if anyone can do a darn like that nowadays I'll eat my umbrella." Collapsed utterly, he did.'

Miss Peabody chuckled heartily.

'I suppose,' said Poirot cautiously, 'that – er – feeling – runs rather high between Miss Lawson and members of Miss Arundell's family?'

'What do you expect? You know what human nature is. Always trouble after a death, anyway. A man or woman is hardly cold in their coffin before most of the mourners are scratching each other's eyes out.'

Poirot sighed.

'Too true.'

'That's human nature,' said Miss Peabody tolerantly.

Poirot changed to another subject.

'Is it true that Miss Arundell dabbled in spiritualism?'

Miss Peabody's penetrating eye observed him very acutely.

'If you think,' she said, 'that the spirit of John Arundell came back and ordered Emily to leave her money to Minnie Lawson and that Emily obeyed, I can tell you that you're very much mistaken. Emily wouldn't be that kind of fool. If you ask me, she found spiritualism one degree better than playing patience or cribbage. Seen the Tripps?'

'No.'

'If you had, you'd realize just the sort of silliness it was. Irritating woman. Always giving you messages from one or other of your relations – and always totally incongruous ones. They believe it all. So did Minnie Lawson. Oh, well, one way of passing your evenings is as good as another, I suppose.'

Poirot tried yet another tack.

'You know young Charles Arundell, I presume? What kind of a person is he?'

'He's no good. Charmin' fellow. Always hard up – always in debt – always returning like a bad penny from all over the world. Knows how to get round women all right.' She chuckled. 'I've seen too many like him to be taken in! Funny son for

Thomas to have had, I must say. He was a staid old fogy if you like. Model of rectitude. Ah, well, bad blood somewhere. Mind you, I *like* the rascal – but he's the kind who would murder his grandmother for a shilling or two quite cheerfully. No moral sense. Odd the way some people seem to be born without it.'

'And his sister?'

'Theresa?' Miss Peabody shook her head and said slowly, 'I don't know. She's an exotic creature. Not usual. She's engaged to that namby-pamby doctor down here. You've seen him, perhaps?'

'Dr Donaldson.'

'Yes. Clever in his profession, they say. But he's a poor stick in other ways. Not the sort of young man I'd fancy if I were a young girl. Well, Theresa should know her mind. She's had her experiences, I'll be bound.'

'Dr Donaldson did not attend Miss Arundell?'

'He used to when Grainger was away on holiday.'

'But not in her last illness?'

'Don't think so.'

Poirot said, smiling:

'I gather, Miss Peabody, that you don't think much of him as a doctor?'

'Never said so. As a matter of fact, you're wrong. He's sharp enough, and clever enough in his way – but it's not *my* way. Take an instance. In the old days when a child ate too many green apples it had a bilious attack and the doctor called it a bilious attack and went home and sent you along a few pills from the surgery. Nowadays, you're told the child suffers from pronounced acidosis, that its diet must be supervised, and you get the same medicine, only it's nice little white tablets put up by manufacturing chemists and costs you about three times as much! Donaldson belongs to that school, and, mind you, most young mothers prefer it. It *sounds* better. Not that that young man will be in this place long ministering to measles and bilious attacks. He's got his eye on London. He's ambitious. He means to specialize.'

'In any particular line?'

'Serum therapeutics. I think I've got it right. The idea being that you get one of these nasty hypodermic needles stuck into you no matter how well you feel, just in case you should catch something. I don't hold with all these messy injections myself.'

'Is Dr Donaldson experimenting with any particular disease?'

'Don't ask me. All I know is a general practitioner's practice isn't good enough for him. He wants to set up in London. But to do that he's got to have money, and he's as poor as a church mouse, whatever a church mouse may be.'

Poirot murmured: 'Sad that real ability is so often baulked by lack of money. And yet there are people who do not spend a quarter of their incomes.'

'Emily Arundell didn't,' said Miss Peabody. 'It was quite a surprise to some people when that will was read. The amount, I mean, not the way it was left.'

'Was it a surprise, do you think, to the members of her own family?'

'That's telling,' said Miss Peabody, screwing up her eyes with a good deal of enjoyment. 'I wouldn't say yes, and I wouldn't say no. One of 'em had a pretty shrewd idea.'

'Which one?'

'Master Charles. He'd done a bit of calculation on his own account. He's no fool, Charles.'

'But a little bit of a rogue, eh?'

'At any rate, he isn't a namby-pamby stick,' said Miss Peabody viciously.

She paused a minute and then asked:

'Going to get in touch with him?'

'That was my intention,' Poirot went on solemnly. 'It seems to me possible that he might have certain family papers relating to his grandfather?'

'More likely to have made a bonfire of them. No respect for his elders, that young man.'

'One must try all avenues,' said Poirot sententiously.

'So it seems,' said Miss Peabody dryly.

There was a momentary glint in her blue eyes that seemed to affect Poirot disagreeably. He rose.

'I must not trespass any longer on your time, madame. I am most grateful for what you have been able to tell me.'

'I've done my best,' said Miss Peabody. 'Seem to have got rather a long way from the Indian Mutiny, don't we?'

She shook hands with us both.

'Let me know when the book comes out,' was her parting remark. 'I shall be *so* interested.'

And the last thing we heard as we left the room was a rich, throaty chuckle.

VISIT TO THE MISSES TRIPP

'And now,' said Poirot as we re-entered the car, 'what do we do next?'

Warned by experience, I did not this time suggest a return to town. After all, if Poirot was enjoying himself in his own fashion, why should I object?'

I suggested some tea.

'Tea, Hastings? What an idea! Regard the time.'

'I have regarded it – looked at it, I mean. It's half past five. Tea is clearly indicated.'

Poirot sighed.

'Always the afternoon tea with you English! No, *mon ami*, no tea for us. In a book of etiquette I read the other day that one must not make the afternoon call after six o'clock. To do so is to commit the solecism. We have, therefore, but half an hour in which to accomplish our purpose.'

'How social you are today, Poirot! On whom are we calling now?'

'*Les demoiselles* Tripp.'

'Are you writing a book on spiritualism now? Or is it still the life of General Arundell?'

'It will be simpler than that, my friend. But we must inquire where these ladies live.'

Directions were forthcoming readily enough, but of a somewhat confused nature, involving as they did a series of lanes. The abode of the Misses Tripp turned out to be a picturesque cottage – so extremely old-world and picturesque that it looked as though it might collapse any minute.

A child of fourteen or thereabouts opened the door and with difficulty squeezed herself against the wall sufficiently to allow us to pass inside.

The interior was very rich in old oak beams – there was a big open fireplace and such very small windows that it was difficult to see clearly. All the furniture was of pseudo-simplicity – ye olde oake for ye cottage dweller – there was a good deal of fruit in wooden bowls and large numbers of photographs – most of them, I noticed, of the same two people represented in different poses – usually with bunches of flowers clasped to their breasts or clutching large leghorn picture-hats.

The child who admitted us had murmured something and disappeared, but her voice was clearly audible in an upper storey:

'Two gentlemen to see you, miss.'

A sort of twitter of female voices arose, and presently, with a good deal of creaking and rustling, a lady descended the staircase and came graciously towards us.

She was nearer fifty than forty, her hair was parted in the middle in Madonna fashion, her eyes were brown and slightly prominent. She wore a sprigged muslin dress that conveyed an odd suggestion of fancy dress.

Poirot stepped forward and started the conversation in his most flourishing manner.

'I must apologize for intruding upon you, mademoiselle, but I am in somewhat of a predicament. I came here to find a certain lady, but she has left Market Basing and I was told that you would certainly have her address.'

'Really? Who was that?'

'Miss Lawson.'

'Oh, Minnie Lawson. Of *course*! We are the *greatest* friends. Do sit down, Mr – er—'

'Parotti – my friend, Captain Hastings.'

Miss Tripp acknowledged the introductions and began to fuss a little.

'Sit here, won't you? No, please – really, I always prefer an *upright* chair myself. Now, are you sure you are comfortable there? Dear Minnie Lawson – Oh, here is my sister.'

More creaking and rustling, and we were joined by a second lady, dressed in green gingham that would have been suitable for a girl or sixteen.

'My sister Isabel – Mr – er – Parrot – and – Captain Hawkins. Isabel dear, these gentlemen are friends of Minnie Lawson's.'

Miss Isabel Tripp was less buxom than her sister. She might, indeed, have been described as scraggy. She had very fair hair done up into a large quantity of rather messy curls. She cultivated a girlish manner and was easily recognizable as the subject of most of the flower poses in photography. She clasped her hands now in girlish excitement.

'How delightful! Dear Minnie! You have seen her lately?'

'Not for some years,' explained Poirot. 'We have quite lost touch with each other. I have been travelling. That is why I was so astonished and delighted to hear of the good fortune that had befallen my old friend.'

'Yes, indeed. And so *well* deserved! Minnie is such a rare soul. So simple so earnest.'

'Julia,' cried Isabel.

'Yes, Isabel?'

'How remarkable. P. You remember the planchette distinctly insisted on P. last night. A visitor from over the water and the initial P.'

'So it did,' agreed Julia.

Both ladies looked at Poirot in rapt and delighted surprise.

'It never lies,' said Miss Julia softly. 'Are you interested at all in the occult, Mr Parrot?'

'I have little experience, mademoiselle, but – like anyone who has travelled much in the East – I am bound to admit that there is much one does not understand and that cannot be explained by natural means.'

'So true,' said Julia. 'Profoundly true.'

'The East,' murmured Isabel. 'The home of mysticism and the occult.'

Poirot's travelling in the East, as far as I knew, consisted of one journey to Syria extended to Iraq, and which occupied perhaps a few weeks. To judge by his present conversation one would swear that he had spent most of his life in jungles and bazaars and in intimate converse with fakirs, dervishes, and mahatmas.

As far as I could make out, the Misses Tripp were vegetarians, theosophists, British, Israelites, Christian Scientists and enthusiastic amateur photographers.

'One sometimes feels,' said Julia, with a sigh, 'that Market Basing is an impossible place to live. There is no beauty here – no *soul*. One must have soul, don't you think so, Captain Hawkins?'

'Quite,' I said, slightly embarrassed, 'Oh, quite.'

'*Where there is no vision the people perish,*' quoted Isabel, with a sigh. 'I have often tried to discuss things with the vicar, but I find him most painfully *narrow*. Don't you think, Mr Parrot, that any definite creed is bound to be *narrowing*?'

'And everything is so simple, really,' put in her sister. 'As we know so well, everything is joy and love!'

'As you say, as you say,' said Poirot. 'What a pity it seems that misunderstandings and quarrels should arise – especially over money.'

'Money is so sordid,' sighed Julia.

'I gather that the late Miss Arundell was one of your converts?' said Poirot.

The two sisters looked at each other.

'I wonder,' said Isabel.

'We were never quite sure,' breathed Julia. 'One minute she seemed to be convinced, and then she would say something – so – so ribald.'

'Ah, but you remember that last manifestation,' said Julia. 'That was really most remarkable.' She turned to Poirot. 'It was the night dear Miss Arundell was taken ill. My sister and I went round after dinner, and we had a sitting – just for the four of us. And you know we saw – we all three saw – *most* distinctly, a kind of halo around Miss Arundell's head.'

'*Comment?*'

'Yes. It was a kind of luminous haze.' She turned to her sister. 'Isn't that how you would describe it, Isabel?'

'Yes. Yes, just that. A luminous haze gradually surrounding Miss Arundell's head – an aureole of faint light. It was a *sign* – we know that now – a sign that she was about to pass over to the other side.'

'Remarkable,' said Poirot in a suitably impressed voice. 'It was dark in the room, yes?'

'Oh, yes, we always get better results in the dark, and it was quite a warm evening, so we didn't even have the fire on.'

'A most interesting spirit spoke to us,' said Isabel.

'Fatima, her name was. She told us she had passed over in the time of the Crusades. She gave us a most beautiful message.'

'She actually spoke to you?'

'No, not direct voice. She rapped it out. Love. Hope. Life. Beautiful words.'

'And Miss Arundell was actually taken ill at the *séance?*'

'It was just after. Some sandwiches and port wine were brought in, and dear Miss Arundell said she wouldn't have any, as she wasn't feeling very well. That was the beginning of her illness. Mercifully she did not have to endure much suffering.'

'She passed over four days later' said, Isabel.

'And we have already had messages from her, said Julia eagerly 'Saying that she is very happy and that everything is beautiful and that she hopes that there is love and peace among all her dear ones.'

'Poirot coughed.

'That – er – is hardly the case I fear.'

'The relations have behaved *disgracefully* to poor Minnie,' said Isabel. Her face flushed with indignation.

'Minnie is the most *unworldly* soul,' chimed in Julia.

'People have gone about saying the *unkindest* things – that she *schemed* for this money to be left her!'

'When really it was the *greatest* surprise to her—'

'She could hardly believe her *ears* when the lawyer read the will—'

'She told us so herself. "Julia," she said to me, "my dear, you could have knocked me over with a feather. Just a few bequests to the servants and then Littlegreen House and the residue of my estate to Wilhelmina Lawson." She was so flabbergasted she could hardly speak. And when she could she asked how much it would be – thinking perhaps it would be a few thousand pounds – and Mr Purvis, after humming and hawing and talking about confusing things like gross and net personalities, said it would be in the neighbourhood of three hundred and seventy-five thousand pounds. Poor Minnie nearly fainted, she told us.'

'She had no *idea*,' the other sister reiterated. 'She never thought of such a thing happening!'

'That is what she told you, yes?'

'Oh, yes, she repeated it several times. And that's what makes it so wicked of the Arundell family to go on as they have done – cold-shouldering her and treating her with suspicion. After all, this is a free country—'

'English people seem to labour under that misapprehension,' murmured Poirot.

'And I should hope *anyone* can leave their money exactly as they choose! *I* think Miss Arundell acted very *wisely*. Obviously she *mistrusted* her own relatives, and I dare say she had her reasons.'

'Ah?' Poirot leant forward with interest. 'Indeed?'

This flattering attention encouraged Isabel to proceed.

'Yes, indeed. Mr Charles Arundell, her nephew, is a thoroughly bad lot. That's well known! I believe he's even wanted by the police in some foreign country. Not at all a desirable character. As for his sister – well, I've not actually *spoken* to her, but she's a very queer-looking girl. Ultramodern, of course, but terribly made-up. Really, the sight of her mouth made me quite *ill*. It looked like *blood*. And I rather suspect she takes drugs – her manner was so *odd* sometimes. She's by way of being engaged to that nice young Dr Donaldson, but I fancy even *he* looked a little disgusted sometimes. Of course, she is attractive in her way, but I hope that he will come to his senses in time and marry some nice English girl who is fond of country life and outdoor pursuits.'

'And the other relations?'

'Well, there you are again. Very undesirable. Not that I've anything to say against Mrs Tanios – she's quite a nice woman, but absolutely stupid, and completely under her husband's thumb. Of course, he's really a Turk, I believe – rather dreadful for an English girl to marry a *Turk*, I think, don't you? It shows a certain lack of *fastidiousness*. Of course, Mrs Tanios is a very good mother, though the children are singularly unattractive, poor little things.'

'So altogether you think Miss Lawson was a more worthy recipient of Miss Arundell's fortune?'

Julia said serenely:

'Minnie Lawson is a thoroughly *good* woman. And so *unwordly*. It isn't as though she had ever *thought* about money. She was *never* grasping.'

'Still, she has never thought of refusing to accept the legacy?'

Isabel drew back a little.

'Oh, well – one would hardly do *that*.'

Poirot smiled.

'No, perhaps not . . .'

'You see, Mr Parrot,' put in Julia, 'she regards it as a *trust* – a sacred *trust*.'

'And she is quite willing to do something for Mrs Tanios or for the Tanios children,' went on Isabel. 'Only she doesn't want *him* to get hold of it.'

'She even said she would consider making Theresa an allowance.'

'And that, I think, was very generous of her – considering the off hand way that girl has always treated her.'

'Indeed, Mr Parrot, Minnie is the most *generous* of creatures. But there now, you know her, of course!'

'Yes,' said Poirot. 'I know her. But I still do not know – her address.'

'Of course! How stupid of me! Shall I write it down for you?'

'I can write it down.'

Poirot produced the invariable notebook.

'17 Clanroyden Mansions, W.2. Not very far from Whiteleys. You'll give her our love, won't you? We haven't heard from her just lately.'

Poirot rose, and I followed suit.

'I have to thank you both very much,' he declared, 'for a most charming talk, as well as for your kindness in supplying me with my friend's address.'

'I wonder they didn't give it to you at the house,' exclaimed Isabel. 'It must be that Ellen! Servants are so *jealous* and *so small-minded*. They used to be quite rude to Minnie sometimes.'

Julia shook hands in a *grande dame* manner.

'We have enjoyed your visit,' she declared graciously. 'I wonder—'

She flashed a glance of inquiry at her sister.

'You would, perhaps—' Isabel flushed a little. 'Would you, that is to say, stay and share our evening meal? A very simple one – some shredded, raw vegetables, brown bread and butter, fruit.'

'It sounds delicious,' Poirot said hastily. 'But alas! my friend and I have to return to London.'

With renewed handshaking and messages to be delivered to Miss Lawson, we at last made our exit.

—— 12 ——

POIROT DISCUSSES THE CASE

'Thank goodness, Poirot,' I said with fervour, 'you got us out of those raw carrots! What awful women!'

'*Pour nous un bon bifteck* – with the fried potatoes – and a good bottle of wine. What should we have had to drink there, I wonder?'

'Well-water, I should think,' I replied with a shudder. 'Or non-alcoholic cider. It was that kind of place! I bet there's no bath and no sanitation except an earth closet in the garden!'

'Strange how women enjoy living an uncomfortable life,' said Poirot thoughtfully. 'It is not always poverty, though they are good at making the best of straitened circumstances.'

'What orders for the chauffeur now?' I asked as I negotiated the last bend on the winding lanes, and we emerged on the road to Market Basing. 'On what local light do we call next? Or do we return to The George and interrogate the asthmatic waiter once more?'

'You will be glad to hear, Hastings, that we have finished with Market Basing—'

'Splendid!'

'For the moment only. I shall return!'

'Still on the track of your unsuccessful murderer?'

'Exactly.'

'Did you learn anything from the fandango of nonsense we've just been listening to?'

Poirot said precisely:

'There were certain points deserving of attention. The various characters in our drama begin to emerge more clearly. In some ways it resembles, does it not, a novelette of olden days? The humble companion, once despised, is raised to affluence and now plays the part of lady bountiful.'

'I should imagine that such a patronage must be very galling to people who regard themselves as the rightful heirs!'

'As you say, Hastings. Yes, that is very true.'

We drove on in silence for some minutes. We had passed through Market Basing and were now once more on the main road. I hummed to myself softly the tune of 'Little Man, You've Had a Busy Day.'

'Enjoyed yourself, Poirot?' I asked at last.

Poirot said coldly:

'I do not know quite what you mean by "enjoyed yourself", Hastings.'

'Well,' I said, 'it seemed to me you've been treating yourself to a busman's holiday!'

'You do not think that I am serious?'

'Oh, you're *serious* enough. But this business seems to be of the academic kind. You're tacking it for your own mental satisfaction. What I mean is – it's not *real*.'

'*Au contraire*, it is intensely real.'

'I express myself badly. What I mean is, if there were a question of *helping* our old lady, of protecting her against further attack – well, there would be some excitement then. But as it is, I can't help feeling that as she is dead, why worry?'

'In that case, *mon ami*, one would not investigate a murder case at all!'

'No, no, no. That's quite different. I mean, then you have a *body* ... Oh, dash it all!'

'Do not enrage yourself. I comprehend perfectly. You make a distinction between a *body* and a mere *decease*. Supposing, for instance, that Miss Arundell had died with sudden and alarming violence instead of respectably of a long-standing illness – then you would not remain indifferent to my efforts to discover the truth?'

'Of course I wouldn't.'

'But all the same, some one did attempt to murder her.'

'Yes, but they didn't *succeed*. That makes all the difference.'

'It does not intrigue you at all to know *who* attempted to kill her?'

'Well, yes, it does in a way.'

'We have a very restricted circle,' said Poirot musingly. 'That thread—'

'The thread which you merely deduce from a nail in the skirting-board!' I interrupted. 'Why, that nail may have been there for years!'

'No. The varnish was quite fresh.'

'Well, I still think there might be all sorts of explanations of it.'

'Give me one.'

At the moment I could not think of anything sufficiently plausible. Poirot took advantage of my silence to sweep on with his discourse.

'Yes, a restricted circle. That thread could only have been stretched across the top of the stairs after every one had gone to bed. Therfore we have *only the occupants of the house to consider*. That is to say, the guilt lies between seven people. Dr Tanios. Mrs Tanios. Theresa Arundell. Charles Arundell. Miss Lawson. Ellen. Cook.'

'Surely you can leave the servants out of it?'

'They received legacies, *mon cher*. And there *might* have been other reasons: spite – a quarrel – dishonesty – one cannot be *certain*.'

'It seems to me very unlikely.'

'Unlikely, I agree. But one must take all possibilities into consideration.'

'In that case, you must allow for eight people, not seven.'

'How so?'

I felt I was about to score a point.

'You must include *Miss Arundell* herself. How do you know she may not have stretched that thread across the stairs in order to trip up some other member of the house-party?'

Poirot shrugged his shoulders.

'It is a *bêtise* you say there, my friend. If Miss Arundell laid a trap, she would be careful not to fall into it herself. It was *she* who fell down the stairs, remember.'

I retired crestfallen.

Poirot went on in a thoughtful voice:

'The sequence of events is quite clear – the fall – the letter to me – the visit of the lawyer – but there is one doubtful point. Did Miss Arundell deliberately hold back the letter to me, hesitating to post it? Or did she, once having written it, assume it *was posted?*'

'That we can't possibly tell,' I said.

'No. We can only *guess.* Personally, I fancy that she assumed it had been posted. She must have been surprised at getting no reply . . .'

My thoughts had been busy in another direction.

'Do you think this spiritualistic nonsense counted at all?' I asked. 'I mean, do you think, in spite of Miss Peabody's ridiculing of the suggestion, that a command was given at one of these *séances* that she should alter her will and leave her money to the Lawson woman?'

Poirot shook his head doubtfully.

'That does not seem to fit in with the general impression I have formed of Miss Arundell's character.'

'The Tripp women say that Miss Lawson was completely taken aback when the will was read,' I said thoughtfully.

'That is what she told them, yes,' agreed Poirot.

'But you don't believe it?'

'*Mon ami* you know my suspicious nature! I believe nothing that any one says unless it can be confirmed or corroborated.'

'That's right, old boy,' I said affectionately. 'A thoroughly nice, trustful nature.'

' "He says," "she says," "they say." Bah! what does that mean? Nothing at all. It may be absolute truth. It may be useful falsehood. Me, I deal only with *facts.*'

'And the facts are?'

'Miss Arundell had a fall. That nobody disputes. The fall was not a natural one – it was contrived.'

'The evidence for that being that Hercule Poirot says so!'

'Not at all. There is the evidence of the nail. The evidence of Miss Arundell's letter to me. The evidence of the dog having been out that night. The evidence of Miss Arundell's words about the jar and the picture and Bob's ball. All these things are *facts.*'

'And the next fact, please?'

'The next fact is the answer to our usual question. Who benefits by Miss Arundell's death? Answer – Miss Lawson.'

'The wicked companion! On the other hand, the others thought they were going to benefit. And at the time of the accident they *would* have benefited.'

'Exactly, Hastings. That is why they all lie equally under suspicion. There is also the little fact that Miss Lawson took pains to prevent Miss Arundell learning that Bob had been out all night.'

'You call that suspicious?'

'Not at all. I merely note it. It may have been natural concern for the old lady's peace of mind. That is by far the most likely explanation.'

I looked at Poirot sideways. He is so confoundedly slippery.

'Miss Peabody expressed the opinion that there was "hanky-panky" about the will,' I said. 'What do you suppose she meant by that?'

'It was, I think, her way of expressing various nebulous and unformulated suspicions.'

'Undue influence, it seems, can be washed out,' I said thoughtfully. 'And it certainly looks as though Emily Arundell was much too sensible to believe in any tomfoolery like spiritualism.'

'What makes you say that spiritualism is tomfoolery, Hastings?'

I stared at him in astonishment.

'My dear Poirot – those appalling women——'

He smiled.

'I quite agree with your estimate of the Misses Tripp. But the mere fact that the Misses Tripp have adopted with enthusiasm Christian Science, vegetarianism, theosophy, and spiritualism does not really constitute a damning indictment of those subjects! Because a foolish woman will tell you a lot of nonsense about a fake scarab which she had bought from a rascally dealer, that does not necessarily bring discredit on the general subject of Egyptology!'

'Do you mean you *believe* in spiritualism, Poirot?'

'I have an open mind on the subject. I have never studied any of its manifestations myself, but it must be accepted that many men of science and learning have pronounced themselves satisfied that there are phenomena which cannot be accounted for by – shall we say the credulity of a Miss Tripp?'

'Then you believe in this rigmarole of an aureole of light surrounding Miss Arundell's head?'

Poirot waved a hand.

'I was speaking generally – rebuking your attitude of quite unreasoning scepticism. I may say that, having formed a certain opinion of Miss Tripp and her sister, I should examine very carefully any fact they presented for my notice. Foolish women, *mon ami*, are foolish women, whether they are talking about spiritualism or politics or the relation of the sexes or the tenets of the Buddhist faith.'

'Yet you listened to what they had to say very carefully.'

'That has been my task today – to listen. To hear what everyone has got to tell me about these seven people – and mainly, of course, the five people primarily concerned. Already we know certain aspects of these people. Take Miss Lawson. From the Misses Tripp we learn she was devoted, unselfish, unworldly and altogether a beautiful character. From Miss Peabody we learn that she was credulous, stupid, without the nerve or the brains to attempt anything criminal. From Dr Grainger we learn that she was down-trodden, that her position was precarious, and that she was a poor "frightened, fluttering hen" were, I think, the words he used. From our waiter we learned that Miss Lawson was a "a person", and from Ellen that Bob, the dog, despised her! Everyone, you see, saw her from a slightly different angle. That is the same with the others. Nobody's opinion of Charles Arundell's morals seems to have been high, but nevertheless they vary in their manner of speaking of him. Dr Grainger calls him indulgently "an irreverent young devil." Miss Peabody says he would murder his grandmother for twopence but clearly prefers a rascal to a "stick." Miss Tripp hints not only that he would do a criminal action but that he has done one – or more. These sidelights are all very useful and interesting. They lead to the next thing.'

'Which is?'

'To see for ourselves, my friend.'

—— 13 ——

THERESA ARUNDELL

On the following morning we made our way to the address given us by Dr Donaldson.

I suggested to Poirot that a visit to the lawyer, Mr Purvis, might be a good thing, but Poirot negatived the idea strongly.

'No, indeed, my friend. What could we say – what reason could we advance for seeking information?'

'You're usually pretty ready with reasons, Poirot! Any old lie would do, wouldn't it?'

'On the contrary, my friend, "any old lie," as you put it,

would *not* do. Not with a lawyer. We should be – how do you say it? – thrown out with the flea upon the ear.'

'Oh, well,' I said. 'Don't let us risk *that!*'

So, as I have said, we set out for the flat, occupied by Theresa Arundell. It was situated in a block at Chelsea overlooking the river. It was furnished expensively in the modern style, with gleaming chromium and thick rugs with geometric designs upon them.

We were kept waiting a few minutes and then a girl entered the room and looked at us inquiringly.

Theresa Arundell looked about twenty-eight or -nine. She was tall and very slender, and she looked rather like an exaggerated drawing in black and white. Her hair was jet black – her face heavily made-up, dead pale. Her eyebrows, freakishly plucked, gave her an air of mocking irony. Her lips were the only spot of colour, a brilliant gash of scarlet in a white face. She also conveyed the impression – how I do not quite know, for her manner was almost wearily indifferent – of being at least twice as much alive as most people. There hung about her the restrained energy of a whiplash.

With an air of cool inquiry she looked from me to Poirot.

Wearied (I hoped) of deceit, Poirot had on this occasion sent in his own card. She was holding it now in her fingers, twirling it to and fro.

'I suppose,' she said, 'you're M. Poirot?'

Poirot bowed in his best manner.

'At your service, mademoiselle. You permit me to trespass for a few moments of your valuable time?'

With a faint imitation of Poirot's manner, she replied:

'Enchanted, M. Poirot. Pray sit down.'

Poirot sat, rather gingerly, on a low square easy-chair. I took an upright one of webbing and chromium. Theresa sat negligently on a low stool in front of the fireplace. She offered us both cigarettes. We refused and she lighted one herself.

'You know my name perhaps, mademoiselle?'

She nodded.

'Little friend of Scotland Yard. That's right, isn't it?'

Poirot, I think, did not much relish this description. He said with some importance:

'I concern myself with problems of crime, mademoiselle.'

'How frightfully thrilling!' said Theresa Arundell in a bored voice. 'And to think I've lost my autograph book!'

'The matter with which I concern myself is this,' continued Poirot. 'Yesterday I received a letter from your aunt.'

Her eyes – very long, almond-shaped eyes – opened a little. She puffed smoke in a cloud.

'From my *aunt*, M. Poirot?'

'That is what I said, mademoiselle.'

She murmured:

'I'm sorry if I'm spoiling sport in any way; but really, you know, there isn't any such person! All my aunts are mercifully dead. The last died two months ago.'

'Miss Emily Arundell?'

'Yes, Miss Emily Arundell. You don't receive letters from corpses, do you, M. Poirot?'

'Sometimes I do, mademoiselle.'

'How *macabre*!'

But there was a new note in her voice – a note suddenly alert and watchful.

'And what did my aunt say, M. Poirot?'

'That, mademoiselle, I can hardly tell you just at present. It was, you see, a somewhat' – he coughed – 'delicate matter.'

There was silence for a minute or two. Theresa Arundell smoked. Then she said:

'It all sounds delightfully hush-hush. But where exactly do I come in?'

'I hoped, mademoiselle, that you might consent to answer a few questions.'

'Questions? What about?'

'Questions of a family nature.'

Again I saw her eyes widen.

'That sounds rather pompous! Supposing you give me a specimen.'

'Certainly. Can you tell me the present address of your brother Charles?'

The eyes narrowed again. Her latent energy was less apparent. It was as though she withdrew into a shell.

'I'm afraid I can't. We don't correspond much. I rather think he has left England.'

'I see.'

Poirot was silent for a minute or two.

'Was that all you wanted to know?'

'Oh, I have other questions. For one – are you satisfied with the ways in which your aunt disposed of her fortune? For another – how long have you been engaged to Dr Donaldson?'

'You do jump about, don't you?'

'*Eh bien?*'

'*Eh bien* – since we are so foreign! – my answer to both

475

those questions is that they are none of your business! *Ça ne vous regarde pas*, M. Hercule Poirot.'

Poirot studied her for a moment or two attentively. Then, with no trace of disappointment, he got up.

'So it is like that! Ah, well, perhaps it is not surprising. Allow me, mademoiselle, to congratulate you upon your French accent. And to wish you a very good morning. Come, Hastings.'

We had reached the door when the girl spoke. The simile of a whiplash came again into my mind. She did not move from her position, but the two words were like the flick of a whip.

'Come back!' she said.

Poirot obeyed slowly. He sat down again and looked at her inquiringly.

'Let's stop playing the fool,' she said. 'It's just possible that you might be useful to me, M. Hercule Poirot.'

'Delighted, mademoiselle – and how?'

Between two puffs of cigarette smoke she said very quietly and evenly:

'Tell me how to break that will.'

'Surely a lawyer—'

'Yes, a lawyer, perhaps – if I knew the right lawyer. But the only lawyers I know are respectable men! Their advice is that the will holds good in law and that any attempt to contest it will be useless expense.'

'But you do not believe them?'

'I believe there is always a way to do things – if you don't mind being unscrupulous and are prepared to pay. Well, *I am prepared to pay*.'

'And you take it for granted that I am prepared to be un-scrupulous if I am paid?'

'I've found that to be true of most people! I don't see why you should be an exception. People always protest about their honesty and their rectitude to begin with, of course.'

'Just so. That is part of the game, eh? But what, given that I was prepared to be – unscrupulous – do you think I could do?'

'I don't know. But you're a clever man. Everyone knows that. You could think out some scheme.'

'Such as?'

Theresa Arundell shrugged her shoulders.

'That's your business. Steal the will and substitute a forgery . . . Kidnap the Lawson woman and frighten her into saying she bullied Aunt Emily into making it. Produce a later will made on old Emily's deathbed.'

'Your fertile imagination takes my breath away, mademoiselle!'

'Well, what is your answer? I've been frank enough. If it's righteous refusal, there's the door.'

'It is not righteous refusal – yet—' said Poirot.

Theresa Arundell laughed. She looked at me.

'Your friend,' she observed, 'looks shocked. Shall we send him out to chase himself round the block?'

Poirot addressed himself to me with some slight irritation.

'Control, I pray you, your beautiful and upright nature, Hastings. I demand pardon for my friend, mademoiselle. He is, as you have perceived, honest. But he is also faithful. His loyalty to myself is absolute. In any case, let me emphasize this point' – he looked at her very hard – 'whatever we are about to do will be strictly within the law.'

She raised her eyebrows slightly.

'The law,' said Poirot thoughtfully, 'has a lot of latitude.'

'I see.' She smiled faintly. 'All right, we'll let that be understood. Do you want to discuss your share of the booty – if there turns out to be any booty?'

'That, also, can be understood. Some nice little pickings – that is all I ask.'

'Done,' said Theresa.

Poirot leant forward.

'Now listen, mademoiselle. Usually – in ninety-nine cases out of a hundred, shall we say – I am on the side of the law. The hundredth – well, the hundredth is different. For one thing, it is usually more lucrative . . . But it has to be done very quietly, you understand – very, very quietly. My reputation, it must not suffer. I have to be careful.'

Theresa Arundell nodded.

'And I must have *all* the facts of the case! I must have the truth! You comprehend that once one knows the truth it is an easier matter to know just what lies to tell!'

'That seems eminently reasonable.'

'Very well, then. Now, on what date was this will made?'

'On April 21st.'

'And the previous will?'

'Aunt Emily made a will five years ago.'

'Its provisions being—?'

'After a legacy to Ellen and one to a former cook, all her property was to be divided between the children of her brother Thomas and the children of her sister Arabella.'

'Was this money left in trust?'

477

'No, it was left to us absolutely.'

'Now be careful. Did you all know the provisions of this will?'

'Oh, yes. Charles and I knew – and Bella knew too. Aunt Emily made no secret of it. In fact, if any of us asked for a loan she would usually say, "You'll have all my money when I'm dead and gone. Be content with that fact." '

'Would she have refused a loan if there had been a case of illness or any dire necessity?'

'No, I don't think she would,' said Theresa slowly.

'But she considered you all had enough to live on?'

'She considered so – yes.'

There was bitterness in that voice.

'But you – did not?'

Theresa waited a minute or two before speaking. Then she said:

'My father left us thirty thousand pounds each. The interest on that, safely invested, amounts to about twelve hundred a year. Income-tax takes another wedge off it. A nice little income on which one can manage very prettily. But I—' her voice changed, her slim body straightened, her head went back – all the wonderful aliveness I had sensed in her came to the fore – 'but I want something better than that out of life! I want the best! The best food, the best clothes – something with line to it – beauty – not just suitable covering in the prevailing fashion. I want to live and enjoy – to go to the Mediterranean and lie in the warm summer sea – to sit round a table and play with exciting wads of money – to give parties – wild, absurd, extravagant parties – I want everything that's going in this rotten world – and I don't want it somes day – I want it now!'

Her voice was wonderfully exciting, warm, exhilarating, intoxicating.

Poirot was studying her intently.

'And you have, I fancy, had it now?'

'Yes, Hercule – I've had it!'

'And how much of the thirty thousand is left?'

She laughed suddenly.

'Two hundred and twenty-one pounds, fourteen and sevenpence. That's the exact balance. So you see, little man, you've got to be paid by results. No results – no fees.'

'In that case,' said Poirot in a matter-of-fact manner, 'There will certainly be results.'

'You're a great little man, Hercule. I'm glad we got together.'

Poirot went on in a business-like way:

'There are a few things that are actually necessary that I should know. Do you drug?'

'No, never.'

'Drink?'

'Quite heavily – but not for the love of it. My crowd drinks and I drink with them, but I could give it up tomorrow.'

'That is very satisfactory.'

'I shan't give the show away in my cups, Hercule.'

Poirot proceeded:

'Love affairs?'

'Plenty in the past.'

'And the present?'

'Only Rex.'

'That is Dr Donaldson?'

'Yes.'

'He seems, somehow, very alien from the life you mention.'

'Oh, he is.'

'And yet you care for him. Why, I wonder?'

'Oh, what are reasons? Why did Juliet fall for Romeo?'

'Well, for one thing, with all due deference to Shakespeare, he happened to be the first man she had seen.'

Theresa said slowly: 'Rex wasn't the first man I saw – not by a long way.' She added in a lower voice, 'But I think – I feel – he'll be the last man I'll ever see.'

'And he is a poor man, mademoiselle.'

She nodded.

'And he, too, needs money?'

'Desperately. Oh, not for the reasons I do. He doesn't want luxury – or beauty – or excitement – or any of these things. He'd wear the same suit until it went into holes, and eat a congealed chop every day for lunch quite happily, and wash in a cracked tin bath. If he had money it would go on test-tubes and a laboratory and all the rest of it. He's ambitious. His profession means everything to him. It means more to him than – I do.'

'He knew that you would come into money when Miss Arundell died?'

'I told him so. Oh! after we were engaged. He isn't really marrying me for my money, if that is what you are getting at.'

'You are still engaged?'

'Of course we are.'

Poirot did not reply. His silence seemed to disquiet her.

'Of course we are,' she repeated sharply. And then she added, 'You – have seen him?'

'I saw him yesterday – at Market Basing.'

'Why? What did you say to him?'

'I said nothing. I only asked him for your brother's address.'

'Charles?' Her voice was sharp again. 'What did you want with Charles?'

'Charles? Who wants Charles?'

It was a new voice – a delightful, man's voice.

A bronze-faced young man with an agreeable grin strolled into the room.

'Who is talking about me?' he asked. 'I heard my name in the hall, but I didn't eavesdrop. They were very particular about eavesdropping at Borstal. Now then, Theresa, my girl, what's all this? Spill the beans.'

—— 14 ——

CHARLES ARUNDELL

I must confess that from the moment I set eyes on him I entertained a sneaking liking for Charles Arundell. There was something so debonair and carefree about him. His eyes had an agreeable and humorous twinkle, and his grin was one of the most disarming I have ever encountered.

He came across the room and sat down on the arm of one of the massive, upholstered chairs.

'What's it all about, old girl?' he asked.

'This is M. Hercule Poirot, Charles. He is prepared to – er – do some dirty work for us in return for a small consideration.'

'I protest,' cried Poirot. '*Not* dirty work – shall we say a little harmless deception of some kind – so that the original intention of the testator is carried out? Let us put it that way.'

'Put it any way you like,' said Charles agreeably. 'What made Theresa think of you, I wonder?'

'She did not,' said Poirot quickly. 'I came here of my own accord.'

'Offering your services?'

'Not quite that. I was asking for you. Your sister told me you had gone abroad.'

'Theresa,' said Charles, 'is a very careful sister. She hardly ever makes a mistake. In fact, she's suspicious as the devil.'

He smiled at her affectionately, but she did not smile back. She looked worried and thoughtful.

'Surely,' said Charles, 'we've got things the wrong way round? Isn't M. Poirot famous for tracking down criminals? Surely not for aiding and abetting them?'

'We're not criminals,' said Theresa sharply.

'But we're quite willing to be,' said Charles affably. 'I'd thought of a spot of forgery myself – that's rather my line. I got sent down from Oxford because of a little misunderstanding about a cheque. That was childishly simple, though – merely a question of adding a nought. Then there was another little *fracas* with Aunt Emily and the local bank. Foolish on my part, of course. I ought to have realized the old lady was sharp as needles. However, all these incidents have been very small fry: fivers or tenners – that class. A deathbed will would be admittedly risky. One would have to get hold of the stiff and starched Ellen and – is suborn the word? – anyway, induce her to say she had witnessed it. It would take some doing, I fear. I might even marry her, and then she wouldn't be able to give evidence against me afterwards.'

He grinned amiably at Poirot.

'I feel sure you've installed a secret dictaphone, and Scotland Yard is listening in,' he said.

'Your problem interests me,' said Poirot with a touch of reproof in his manner. 'Naturally I could not connive at anything against the law. But there are more ways than one—' He stopped significantly.

Charles Arundell shrugged his graceful shoulders.

'I've no doubt there's an equal choice of devious ways inside the law,' he said agreeably. 'You should know.'

'By whom was the will witnessed? I mean the one made on April 21st?'

'Purvis brought down his clerk, and the second witness was the gardener.'

'It was signed, then, in Mr Purvis's presence?'

'It was.'

'And Mr Purvis, I fancy, is a man of the highest respectability?'

'Purvis, Purvis, Charlesworth and once more Purvis are just about as respectable and impeccable as the Bank of England,' said Charles.

'He didn't like making the will,' said Theresa. 'In an ultra-correct fashion I believe he even tried to dissuade Aunt Emily from making it.'

Charles said sharply:

'Did he tell you that, Theresa?'

'Yes. I went to see him again yesterday.'

'It's no good, my sweet – you ought to realize that. Only piles up the six and eightpences.'

Theresa shrugged her shoulders.

Poirot said:

'I will ask of you to give me as much information as you can about the last weeks of Miss Arundell's life. Now, to begin with, I understand that you and your brother and also Dr Tanios and his wife stayed there for Easter?'

'Yes, we did.'

'Did anything happen of significance during that weekend?'

'I don't think so.'

'Nothing? But I thought—'

Charles broke in:

'What a self-centred creature you are, Theresa. Nothing of significance happened to *you*! Wrapped in love's young dream! Let me tell you, M. Poirot, that Theresa has a blue-eyed boy in Market Basing. One of the local sawbones. She's got rather a faulty sense of proportion in consequence. As a matter of fact, my revered aunt took a header down the stairs and nearly passed out. Wish she had. It would have saved all this fuss.'

'She fell down the stairs?'

'Yes, tripped over the dog's ball. Intelligent little brute left it at the top of the stairs, and she took a header over it in the night.'

'This was – when?'

'Let me see – Tuesday – the evening before we left.'

'Your aunt was seriously injured?'

'Unfortunately, she didn't fall on her head. If she had we might have pleaded softening of the brain – or whatever it's called scientifically. No, she was hardly hurt at all.'

Poirot said dryly.

'Very disappointing for you!'

'Eh? Oh, I see what you mean. Yes, as you say, very disappointing. Tough nuts, these old ladies.'

'And you all left on the Wednesday morning?'

'That's right.'

'That was Wednesday, the fifteenth. When did you next see your aunt?'

'Well, it wasn't the next weekend. It was the weekend after that.'

'That would be – let me see – the twenty-fifth, would it not?'

'Yes, I think that was the date.'

'And your aunt died – when?'

'The following Friday.'

'Having been taken ill on the Monday night?'

'Yes.'

'That was the Monday that you left?'

'Yes.'

'You did not return during her illness?'

'Not until the Friday. We didn't realize she was really bad.'

'You got there in time to see her alive?'

'No, she died before we arrived.'

Poirot shifted his glance to Theresa Arundell.

'You accompanied your brother on both these occasions?'

'Yes.'

'And nothing was said during that second weekend about a new will having been made?'

'Nothing,' said Theresa.

Charles, however, had answered at the same moment.

'Oh, yes,' he said. 'It was.'

He spoke airily as ever, but there was something a little constrained, as though the airiness were more artificial than usual.

'It *was*?' said Poirot.

'Charles!' cried Theresa.

Charles seemed anxious not to meet his sister's eye.

He spoke to her without looking at her.

'Surely you remember, old girl? I told you. Aunt Emily made a kind of ultimatum of it. She sat there like a judge in court. Made a kind of speech. Said she thoroughly disapproved of all her relations – that is to say, of me and Theresa. Bella, she allowed, she had nothing against; but, on the other hand, she disliked and distrusted her husband. Buy British was ever Aunt Emily's motto. If Bella were to inherit any considerable sum of money, she said she was convinced that Tanios would somehow or other get possession of it. Trust a Greek to do that! "She's safer as she is," she went on to say. Then she said that neither I nor Theresa were fit people to be trusted with money. We would only gamble and squander it away. Therefore, she finished up, she had made a new will and had left the entire estate to Miss Lawson. "She is a fool," said Aunt Emily, "but she is a faithful soul. And I really believe she is devoted to me. She cannot help her lack of brains. I have thought it fairer to tell you this, Charles, as you may as well realize that it will not be possible for you to raise money on your expectations from me." Rather a nasty one, that. Just what I'd been trying to do.'

'Why didn't you tell me, Charles?' demanded Theresa fiercely.

'Thought I did.' Charles avoided her eye.

Poirot asked:

'And what did you say, Mr Arundell?'

'I?' said Charles airily. 'Oh, I just laughed. No good cutting up rough. That's not the way. "Just as you please, Aunt Emily," I said. "Bit of a blow, perhaps; but, after all, it's your own money, and you can do what you like with it." '

'And your aunt's reaction to that?'

'Oh, it went down well – very well indeed. She said, "Well, I will say you're a sportsman, Charles." And I said, "Got to take the rough with the smooth. As a matter of fact, if I've no expectations, what about giving me a tenner now?" And she said I was an impudent boy, and actually parted with a fiver.'

'You concealed your feelings very cleverly.'

'Well, as a matter of fact, I didn't take it very seriously.'

'You didn't?'

'No. I thought it was what you might call a gesture on the old bean's part. She wanted to frighten us all. I'd a pretty shrewd suspicion that after a few weeks or perhaps months she'd tear that will up. She was pretty hot on family, Aunt Emily. And, as a matter of fact, I believe that's what she *would* have done if she hadn't died so confoundedly suddenly.'

'Ah!' said Poirot. 'It is an interesting idea that.'

He remained silent for a minute or two, then went on:

'Could anyone – Miss Lawson, for instance – have overheard your conversation?'

'Rather. We weren't speaking any too low. As a matter of fact, the Lawson bird was hovering about outside the door when I went out. Been doing a bit of snooping, in my opinion.'

Poirot turned a thoughtful glance on Theresa.

'And you knew nothing of this?'

Before she could answer, Charles broke in:

'Theresa, old girl, I'm sure I told you – or hinted to you.'

There was a queer sort of pause. Charles was looking fixedly at Theresa and there was an anxiety, a fixity, about his gaze that seemed out of all proportion to the subject-matter.

Theresa said slowly:

'If you had told me, I don't think I could have forgotten – do you, M. Poirot?'

Her long, dark eyes turned to him.

Poirot said slowly:

'No, I don't think you could have forgotten, Miss Arundell.'
Then he turned sharply to Charles.

'Let me be quite clear on one point. Did Miss Arundell tell
you she was about to alter her will, or did she tell you specifically that she *had* altered it?'

Charles said quickly:

'Oh, she was quite definite. As a matter of fact, she showed
me the will.'

Poirot leaned forward. His eyes opened wide.

'This is very important. You say that Miss Arundell actually
showed you the will?'

Charles gave a sudden schoolboy wriggle – a rather disarming action. Poirot's gravity made him quite uncomfortable.

'Yes,' he said, 'she showed it to me.'

'You can swear definitely to that?'

'Of course I can.' Charles looked nervously at Poirot. 'I don't
see what is so significant about that.'

There was a sudden brusque movement from Theresa. She
had risen and was standing by the mantelpiece. She quickly
lit another cigarette.

'And you, mademoiselle?' Poirot whirled suddenly round on
her. 'Did your aunt say nothing of importance to you during
that weekend?'

'I don't think so. She was – quite amiable. That is, as amiable
as she usually was. Lectured me a bit about my way of life and
all that. But, then, she always did. She seemed perhaps a bit
more jumpy than usual.'

Poirot said, smiling:

'I suppose, mademoiselle, that you were more taken up with
your fiancé?'

Theresa said sharply:

'He wasn't there. He was away: he'd gone to some medical
congress.'

'You had not seen him, then, since the Easter weekend? Was
that the last time you had seen him?'

'Yes – on the evening before we left he came to dinner.'

'You had not – excuse me – had any quarrel with him then?'

'Certainly not.'

'I only thought, seeing that he was away on your second
visit—'

Charles broke in:

'Ah, but, you see, that second weekend was rather unpremeditated. We went down on the spur of the moment.'

'Really?'

'Oh, let's have the truth,' said Theresa wearily. 'You see, Bella and her husband were down the weekend before – fussing over Aunt Emily because of her accident. We thought they might steal a march on us—'

'We thought,' said Charles with a grin, 'that we'd better show a little concern for Aunt Emily's health, too. Really, though, the old lady was much too sharp to be taken in by the dutiful attention stunt. She knew very well how much it was worth. No fool, Aunt Emily.'

Theresa laughed suddenly.

'It's a pretty story, isn't it? All of us with our tongues hanging out for money.'

'Was that the case with your cousin and her husband?'

'Oh, yes. Bella's always hard up. Rather pathetic the way she tries to copy all my clothes at about an eighth of the price. Tanios speculated with her money, I believe. They're hard put to it to make both ends meet. They've got two children, and want to educate them in England.'

'Can you perhaps give me their address?' said Poirot.

'They're staying at the Durham Hotel in Bloomsbury.'

'What is she like, your cousin?'

'Bella? Well, she's a dreary woman. Eh, Charles?'

'Oh, definitely a dreary woman. Rather like an earwig. She's a devoted mother. So are earwigs, I believe.'

'And her husband?'

'Tanios? Well, he looks a bit odd, but he's really a thoroughly nice fellow. Clever, amusing and a thoroughly good sport.'

'You agree, mademoiselle?'

'Well, I must admit I prefer him to Bella. He's a damned clever doctor, I believe. All the same, I wouldn't trust him very far.'

'Theresa,' said Charles, 'doesn't trust anybody.' He put an arm round her. 'She doesn't trust me.'

'Anyone who trusted you, my sweet, would be mentally deficient,' said Theresa kindly.

The brother and sister moved apart and looked at Poirot. Poirot bowed and moved to the door.

'I am – as you say – on the job! It is difficult, but mademoiselle is right. There is always a way. Ah, by the way, this Miss Lawson, is she the kind that might conceivably lose her head under cross-examination in court?'

Charles and Theresa exchanged glances.

'I should say,' said Charles, 'that a really bullying KC could make her say black was white!'

'That,' said Poirot, 'may be very useful.'

He skipped out of the room, and I followed him. In the hall he picked up his hat, moved to the front door, opened it and shut it again quickly with a bang. Then he tiptoed to the door of the sitting room and unblushingly applied his ear to the crack. At whatever school Poirot was educated, there were clearly no unwritten rules about eavesdropping. I was horrified, but powerless. I made urgent signs to Poirot, but he took no notice.

And then, clearly, in Theresa Arundell's deep, vibrant voice, there came two words:

'You fool!'

There was the noise of footsteps along the passage, and Poirot quickly seized me by the arm, opened the front door and passed through it, closing it noiselessly behind him.

—— 15 ——

MISS LAWSON

'Poirot,' I said, 'have we *got* to listen at doors?'

'Calm yourself, my friend. It was only I who listened! It was not you who put your ear to the crack. On the contrary, you stood bolt upright, like a soldier.'

'But I heard, just the same.'

'True. Mademoiselle was hardly whispering.'

'Because she thought that we had left the flat.'

'Yes, we practised a little deception there.'

'I don't like that sort of thing.'

'Your moral attitude is irreproachable! But let us not repeat ourselves. This conversation has occurred on previous occasions. You are about to say that it is not playing the game. And my reply is that murder is not a game.'

'But there is no question of murder here.'

'Do not be sure of that.'

'The *intention* – yes, perhaps. But, after all, murder and *attempted* murder are not the same thing.'

'Morally they are exactly the same thing. But what I meant

was, are you so sure that it is only *attempted* murder that occupies our attention?'

I stared at him.

'But old Miss Arundell died a perfectly natural death.'

'I repeat again – *are you so sure?*'

'Everyone says so!'

'Everyone? Oh, *là là!*'

'The doctor says so,' I pointed out. 'Dr Grainger. He ought to know.'

'Yes, he ought to know.' Poirot's voice was dissatisfied. 'But remember, Hastings, again and again a body is exhumed – and in each case a certificate has been signed in all good faith by the doctor attending the case.'

'Yes, but in this case Miss Arundell died of a long-standing complaint.'

'It seems so – yes.'

Poirot's voice was still dissatisfied. I looked at him keenly. 'Poirot,' I said, 'I'll begin a sentence with "Are you sure?" Are you sure you are not being carried away by professional zeal? You *want* it to be murder, and so you think it *must* be murder.'

The shadow on his brow deepened. He nodded his head slowly.

'It is clever what you say there, Hastings. It is a weak spot on which you put your finger. Murder is my business. I am like a great surgeon who specializes in – say – appendicitis or some rarer operation. A patient comes to him, and he regards that patient solely from the standpoint of his own specialized subject. Is there any possible reason for thinking this man suffers from so and so . . .? Me, I am like that, too. I say to myself always, "Can this possibly be murder?" And you see, my friend, there is nearly always a possibility.'

'I shouldn't say there was much possibility here,' I remarked.

'But she died, Hastings! You cannot get away from that fact. She *died!*'

'She was in poor health. She was past seventy. It all seems perfectly natural to me.'

'And does it also seem natural to you that Theresa Arundell should call her brother a fool with that degree of intensity?'

'What has that got to do with it?'

'Everything! Tell me, what did you think of that statement of Mr Charles Arundell's – that his aunt had shown him her will?'

I looked at Poirot warily.

'What do *you* make of it?' I asked.

Why should Poirot always be the one to ask the questions?

'I call it very interesting – very interesting indeed. So was Miss Theresa Arundell's reaction to it. Their passage of arms was suggestive – very suggestive.'

'H'm,' I said in oracular fashion.

'It opens up two distinct lines of inquiry.'

'They seem a nice pair of crooks,' I remarked. 'Ready for anything. The girl's amazingly good-looking. As for young Charles, he's certainly an attractive scoundrel.'

Poirot was just hailing a taxi. It drew into the kerb and Poirot gave an address to the driver.

'17 Clanroyden Mansions, Bayswater.'

'So it's Lawson next,' I commented. 'And after that – the Tanioses?'

'Quite right, Hastings.'

'What role are you adopting here?' I inquired as the taxi drew up at Clanroyden Mansions. 'The biographer of General Arundell, a prospective tenant of Littlegreen House, or something more subtle still?'

'I shall present myself simply as Hercule Poirot.'

'How very disappointing!' I gibed.

Poirot merely threw me a glance and paid off the taxi.

Number 17 was on the second floor. A pert-looking maid opened the door and showed us into a room that really struck a ludicrous note after the one we had just left.

Theresa Arundell's flat had been bare to the point of emptiness. Miss Lawson's, on the other hand, was so crammed with furniture and odds and ends that one could hardly move about without the fear of knocking something over.

The door opened and a rather stout, middle-aged lady came in. Miss Lawson was very much as I had pictured her. She had an eager, rather foolish face, untidy greyish hair and pince-nez perched a little askew on her nose. Her style of conversation was spasmodic and consisted of gasps.

'Good morning – er – I don't think—'

'Miss Wilhelmina Lawson?'

'Yes – yes – that *is* my name . . .'

'My name is Poirot – Hercule Poirot. Yesterday I was looking over Littlegreen House.'

'Oh, yes?'

Miss Lawson's mouth fell a little wider open and she made some inefficient dabs at her untidy hair.

'Won't you sit down?' She went on: 'Sit here, won't you? Oh, dear, I'm afraid that table is in your way. I'm just a leetle bit crowded here. So difficult! These flats! Just a teeny bit on the small side. But *so* central! And I do like being central. Don't you?'

With a gasp she sat down on an uncomfortable-looking Victorian chair and, her pince-nez still awry, leaned forward breathlessly and looked at Poirot hopefully.

'I went to Littlegreen House in the guise of a purchaser,' went on Poirot. 'But I should like to say at once – this is in the strictest confidence—'

'Oh, yes,' breathed Miss Lawson, apparently pleasurably excited.

'The very strictest confidence,' continued Poirot, 'that I went there with another object . . . You may or may not be aware that shortly before she died Miss Arundell wrote to me—'

He paused and then went on:

'I am a well-known private detective.'

A variety of expressions chased themselves over Miss Lawson's slightly flushed countenance. I wondered which one Poirot would single out as relevant to his inquiry. Alarm, excitement, surprise, puzzlement . . .

'Oh,' she said. Then after a pause. 'Oh,' again.

And then, quite unexpectedly, she asked:

'Was it about the money?'

Poirot, even, was slightly taken aback. He said tentatively:

'You mean the money that was—'

'Yes, yes. The money that was taken from the drawer?'

Poirot said quietly:

'Miss Arundell didn't tell you she had written to me on the subject of that money?'

'No, indeed. I had no idea – well, really, I must say I'm very surprised—'

'You thought she should not have mentioned it to anyone?'

'I certainly didn't think so. You see, she had a very good idea—'

She stopped again. Poirot said quickly:

'She had a very good idea who took it. That is what you would say, is it not?'

Miss Lawson nodded and continued breathlessly:

'And I shouldn't have thought she would have wanted – well, I mean she said – that is, she seemed to feel—'

Again Poirot cut in neatly into the midst of these incoherencies.

'It was a family matter?'

'Exactly.'

'But me,' said Poirot, 'I specialize in family matters. I am, you see, very, very discreet.'

Miss Lawson nodded vigorously.

'Oh, of course – that makes a difference. It's not like the *police.*'

'No, no. I am not at all like the police. That would not have done at all.'

'Oh, no. Dear Miss Arundell was such a *proud* woman. Of course, there had been trouble with Charles, but it was always hushed up. Once, I believe, he had to go to Australia!'

'Just so,' said Poirot. 'Now, the facts of the case were as follows, were they not? Miss Arundell had a sum of money in a drawer—'

He paused. Miss Lawson hastened to confirm his statement.

'Yes – from the Bank. For the wages, you know, and the books.'

'And how much was missing exactly?'

'Four pound notes. No, no, I am wrong, three pound notes and two ten-shilling notes. One must be exact, I know, very exact, in such matters.' Miss Lawson looked at him earnestly, and absent-mindedly knocked her pince-nez a little farther awry. Her rather prominent eyes seemed to goggle at him.

'Thank you, Miss Lawson. I see you have an excellent business sense.'

Miss Lawson bridled a little and uttered a deprecatory laugh.

'Miss Arundell suspected, no doubt with reason, that her nephew Charles was responsible for this theft,' went on Poirot.

'Yes.'

'Although there was no particular evidence to show who actually took the money?'

'Oh, but it must have been Charles! Mrs Tanios wouldn't do such a thing, and her husband was quite a stranger and wouldn't have known where the money was kept – neither of them would. And I don't think Theresa Arundell would dream of such a thing. She's got plenty of money and always so beautifully dressed.'

'It might have been one of the servants,' Poirot suggested.

Miss Lawson seemed horrified by the idea.

'Oh, no, indeed; neither Ellen nor Annie would have *dreamed* of such a thing. They are both *most* superior women and *absolutely honest*, I am sure.'

Poirot waited a minute or two. Then he said:

'I wonder if you can give me any idea – I am sure you can, for if anyone possessed Miss Arundell's confidence you did—'

Miss Lawson murmured confusedly:

'Oh, I don't know about that, I'm sure—' But she was clearly flattered.

'I feel that you will be able to help me.'

'Oh, I'm sure, if I can – anything I can do—'

Poirot went on:

'This is in confidence—'

A sort of owlish expression appeared on Miss Lawson's face. The magical words 'in confidence' seemed to be a kind of Open Sesame.

'Have you any idea of the reason which caused Miss Arundell to alter her will?'

'Her will? Oh – her will?'

Miss Lawson seemed slightly taken aback.

Poirot said, watching her closely:

'It is true, is it not, that she made a new will shortly before her death, leaving all her fortune to you?'

'Yes, but I knew nothing about it. Nothing at all.' Miss Lawson was shrill in protest. 'It was the *greatest* surprise to me! A *wonderful* surprise, of course! So *good* of dear Miss Arundell. And she never even gave me a *hint*. Not the smallest hint! I was so taken aback, when Mr Purvis read it out, I didn't know where to look, or whether to laugh or cry! I assure you, Mr Poirot, the *shock* of it – the *shock*, you know. The *kindness* – the wonderful kindness of dear Miss Arundell. Of course, I'd hoped, perhaps, for just a little something – perhaps just a teeny, teeny legacy – though of course there was no *reason* she should have left me even that. I'd not been with her so very long. But this – it was like – it was like a fairy story! Even now I can't quite believe in it, if you know what I mean. And sometimes – well, sometimes I don't feel altogether comfortable about it. I mean – well, I mean—'

She knocked off her pince-nez, picked them up, fumbled with them and went on even more incoherently:

'Sometimes I feel that – well, flesh and blood is flesh and blood, after all, and I don't feel quite comfortable at Miss Arundell's leaving all her money away from her family. I mean, it doesn't seem *right*, does it? Not *all* of it. Such a *large* fortune, too! Nobody had any *idea*! But – well – it does make one feel uncomfortable – and everyone saying things, you know – and I'm sure I've never been an *ill-natured* woman! I mean I wouldn't have dreamed of influencing Miss Arundell in any way! And it's not as though I could, either. Truth to tell, I was always just a teeny weeny bit afraid of her! She was so *sharp,* you know, so inclined to *jump* on you. And quite rude sometimes! "Don't be a downright fool," she'd snap. And really, after all, I had my feelings, and sometimes I'd feel quite upset . . . And then to find out that all the time she'd really been fond of me – well, it was very wonderful, wasn't it? Only of course, as I say, there's been a lot of *unkindness,* and really in some ways one feels – I mean, well, it does seem a little *hard,* doesn't it, on some people?'

'You mean that you would prefer to relinquish the money?' asked Poirot.

Just for a moment I fancied a flicker of some quite different expression showed itself in Miss Lawson's dull, pale blue eyes. I imagined that, just for a moment, a shrewd, intelligent woman sat there instead of an amiable, foolish one.

She said with a little laugh:

'Well – of course, there is the other side of it too . . . I mean there are two sides to every question. What I say is, Miss Arundell meant me to have the money. I mean if I didn't take it I should be going against her *wishes.* And that wouldn't be right either, would it?'

'It is a difficult question,' said Poirot, shaking his head.

'Yes, indeed. I have worried over it a great deal. Mrs Tanios – Bella – she is such a nice woman – and those dear little children! I mean, I feel sure Miss Arundell wouldn't have wanted her to – I feel, you see, that dear Miss Arundell intended me to use my *discretion.* She didn't want to leave any money *outright* to Bella because she was afraid that man would get hold of it.'

'What man?'

'Her husband. You know, Mr Poirot, the poor girl is *quite* under his thumb. She does *anything* he tells her. I dare say she'd *murder* someone if he told her to! And she's afraid of him. I'm quite sure she's afraid of him. I've seen her look simply *terrified* once or twice. Now, that isn't right, Mr Poirot – you can't say that' right.'

Poirot did not say so. Instead he inquired:

'What sort of man is Dr Tanios?'

'Well,' said Miss Lawson hesitatingly, 'he's a very pleasant man.'

She stopped doubtfully.

'But you don't trust him?'

'Well – no, I don't. I don't know,' went on Miss Lawson doubtfully, 'that I'd trust *any* man very much! Such *dreadful* things one hears! And all their *poor* wives go through! It's really terrible! Of course, Dr Tanios pretends to be very fond of his wife and he's quite charming to her. His manners are really de*lightful*. But I don't trust foreigners. They're so *art-ful*! And I'm quite sure dear Miss Arundell didn't want her money to get into *his* hands!'

'It is hard on Miss Theresa Arundell and Mr Charles Arundell also to be deprived of their inheritance,' Poirot suggested.

A spot of colour came into Miss Lawson's face.

'I think Theresa has quite as much money as is good for her,' she said sharply. 'She spends hundreds of pounds on her clothes alone. And her underclothing – it's wicked! When one thinks of so many nice, well-bred girls who have to earn their own living—'

Poirot gently completed the sentence.

'You think it would do no harm for her to earn hers for a bit?'

Miss Lawson looked at him solemnly.

'It might do her a lot of *good*,' she said. 'It might bring her to her senses. Adversity teaches us many things.'

Poirot nodded slowly. He was watching her intently.

'And Charles?'

'Charles doesn't deserve a penny,' said Miss Lawson sharply. 'If Miss Arundell cut him out of her will, it was for a very good cause – after his wicked threats.'

'Threats?' Poirots eyebrows rose.

'Yes, threats.'

'What threats? When did he threaten her?'

'Let me see, it was – yes, of course, it was at Easter. Actually on *Easter Sunday* – which made it even worse!'

'What did he say?'

'He asked her for money, and she'd refused to give it him! And then he told her that it wasn't wise of her. He said if she kept up that attitude he would – now what was the phrase? – a very vulgar American one – oh, yes, he said he would bump her off!'

'He threatened to bump her off?'

'Yes.'

'And what did Miss Arundell say?'

'She said: "I think you'll find, Charles, that I can look after myself." '

'You were in the room at the time?'

'Not exactly in the room,' said Miss Lawson after a momentary pause.

'Quite, quite,' said Poirot hastily. 'And Charles, what did he say to that?'

'He said: "Don't be too sure." '

Poirot said slowly:

'Did Miss Arundell take this threat seriously?'

'Well, I don't know . . . She didn't say anything to me about it . . . But, then, she wouldn't do that, anyway.'

Poirot said quietly:

'You knew, of course, that Miss Arundell was making a new will?'

No, no. I've told you, it was a complete surprise. I never dreamt—'

Poirot interrupted.

'You did not know the *contents*. But you knew the *fact* – that there *was* a will being made?'

'Well – I suspected – I mean her sending for the lawyer when she was laid up—'

'Exactly. That was after she had a fall, was it not?'

'Yes, Bob – Bob was the dog – he had left his ball at the top of the stairs and she tripped over it and fell.'

'A nasty accident.'

'Oh, yes; why, she might easily have broken her leg or her arm. The doctor said so.'

'She might quite easily have been killed.'

'Yes, indeed.'

Her answer seemed quite natural and frank.

Poirot said, smiling:

'I think I saw Master Bob at Littlegreen House.'

'Oh, yes, I expect you did. He's a dear little doggie.'

Nothing annoys me more than to hear a sporting terrier called a dear little doggie. No wonder, I thought, that Bob despised Miss Lawson and refused to do anything she told him.

'And he is very intelligent?' went on Poirot.

'Oh, yes, very.'

'How upset he'd be if he knew he had nearly killed his mistress.'

Miss Lawson did not answer. She merely shook her head and sighed.

Poirot asked:

'Do you think it possible that that fall influenced Miss Arundell to remake her will?'

We were getting perilously near the bone here, I thought, but Miss Lawson seemed to find the question quite natural.

'You know,' she said, 'I shouldn't wonder if you weren't

495

right. It gave her a *shock* – I'm sure of that. Old people never like to think there's any chance of their dying. But an accident like that makes one *think*. Or perhaps she might have had a *premonition* that her death wasn't far off.'

Poirot said casually:

'She was in fairly good health, was she not?'

'Oh, yes. Very well, indeed.'

'Her illness must have come on very suddenly?'

'Oh, it did. It was quite a shock. We had some friends that evening—' Miss Lawson paused.

'Your friends, the Missess Tripp. I have met those ladies. They are quite charming.'

Miss Lawson's face flushed with pleasure.

'Yes, aren't they? Such *cultured* women! Such wide interests. And so very *spiritual*! They told you, perhaps, about our sittings? I expect you are a sceptic – but, indeed, I wish I could tell you the inexpressible joy of getting into touch with those who passed over!'

'I am sure of it. I am sure of it.'

'Do you know, Mr Poirot, my mother has spoken to me – more than once. It is such a joy to know that one's dear ones are still thinking of one and watching over one.'

'Yes, yes, I can well understand that,' said Poirot gently. 'And was Miss Arundell also a believer?'

Miss Lawson's face clouded over a little.

'She was willing to be convinced,' she said doubtfully. 'But I do not think she always approached the matter in the right frame of mind. She was sceptical and unbelieving – and once or twice her attitude attracted a most *undesirable* type of spirit! There were some very ribald messages – all due, I am *convinced*, to Miss Arundell's attitude.'

'I should think very likely due to Miss Arundell,' agreed Poirot.

'But on that last evening—' continued Miss Lawson, 'perhaps Isabel and Julia told you? – then were distinct phenomena. Actually the beginning of materialization. Ectoplasm – you know what ectoplasm is, perhaps?'

'Yes, yes, I am acquainted with its nature.'

'It proceeds, you know, from the medium's mouth in the form of a *ribbon* and builds itself up into a *form*. Now I am *convinced*, Mr Poirot, that *unknown to herself* Miss Arundell was a *medium*. On that evening I distinctly saw a *luminous ribbon* issuing from dear Miss Arundell's mouth! Then her head became enveloped in a luminous mist.'

'Most interesting!'

'And then, unfortunately, Miss Arundell was suddenly taken ill and we had to break up the *séance*.'

'You sent for the doctor – when?'

'First thing the following morning.'

'Did he think the matter grave?'

'Well, he sent in a hospital nurse the following evening, but I think he hoped she would pull through.'

'The – excuse me – the relatives were not sent for?'

Miss Lawson flushed.

'They were notified as soon as possible – that is to say, when Dr Grainger pronounced her to be in danger.'

'What was the cause of the attack? Something she had eaten?'

'No, I don't think there was anything in particular. Dr Grainger said she hadn't been quite as careful in diet as she should have been. I think he thought the attack was probably brought on by a chill. The weather had been very treacherous.'

'Theresa and Charles Arundell had been down that weekend, had they not?'

Miss Lawson pursed her lips together.

'They had.'

'The visit was not a success,' Poirot suggested, watching her.

'It was not.' She added quite spitefully: 'Miss Arundell knew what they'd come for!'

'Which was?' asked Poirot, watching her.

'Money!' snapped Miss Lawson. 'And they didn't get it.'

'No?' said Poirot.

'And I believe that's what Dr Tanios was after too,' she went on.

'Dr Tanios. He was not down that same weekend, was he?'

'Yes, he came down on the Sunday. He only stayed about an hour.'

'Everyone seems to have been after poor Miss Arundell's money,' hazarded Poirot.

'I know, it is not very nice to think of, is it?'

'No, indeed,' said Poirot. 'It must have been a shock to Charles and Theresa Arundell that weekend when they learned that Miss Arundell had definitely disinherited them!'

Miss Lawson stared at him.

Poirot said:

'Is that not so? Did she not specifically inform them of the fact?'

'As to that, I couldn't say. *I* didn't hear anything about it!

There wasn't any *fuss*, or anything, as far as I know. Both Charles and his sister seemed to go away *quite* cheerful.'

'Ah! Possibly I have been misinformed. Miss Arundell actually kept her will in the house, did she not?'

Miss Lawson dropped her pince-nez and stooped to pick them up.

'I really couldn't say. No, I think it was with Mr Purvis.'

'Who was the executor?'

'Mr Purvis was.'

'After the death, did he come over and look through her papers?'

'Yes, he did.'

Poirot looked at her keenly and asked her an unexpected question.

'Do you like Mr Purvis?'

Miss Lawson was flustered.

'Like Mr Purvis? Well, really, that's difficult to say, isn't it? I mean, I'm sure he's a very *clever* man – that is, a clever lawyer, I mean. But rather a brusque *manner*! I mean, it's not very pleasant always to have someone speaking to you as though – well, really, I can't explain what I mean – he was quite civil, and yet at the same time almost *rude,* if you know what I mean.'

'A difficult situation for you,' said Poirot sympathetically.

'Yes, indeed, it was.'

Miss Lawson sighed and shook her head.

Poirot rose to his feet.

'Thank you very much, mademoiselle, for all your kindness and help.'

Miss Lawson rose too. She sounded slightly flustered.

'I'm sure there's nothing to thank *me* for – nothing at all! So glad if I've been able to do anything – if there's anything more I *can* do—'

Poirot came back from the door. He lowered his voice.

'I think, Miss Lawson, that there is something you ought to be told. Charles and Theresa Arundell are hoping to upset this will.'

A sharp flush of colour came into Miss Lawson's cheek.

'They can't do that,' she said sharply. 'My lawyer says so.'

'Ah,' said Poirot. 'You have consulted a lawyer, then?'

'Certainly. Why shouldn't I?'

'No reason at all. A very wise proceeding. Good-day to you, mademoiselle.'

When we emerged from Clanroyden Mansions into the street Poirot drew a deep breath.

'Hastings, *mon ami,* that woman is either exactly what she seems or else she is a very good actress.'

'She doesn't believe Miss Arundell's death was anything but natural. You can see that,' I said.

Poirot did not answer. There are moments when he is conveniently deaf. He hailed a taxi.

'Durham Hotel, Bloomsbury,' he told the driver.

—— 16 ——

MRS TANIOS

'Gentleman to see you, madam.'

The woman who was sitting writing at one of the tables in the writing room of the Durham Hotel turned her head and then rose, coming towards us uncertainly.

Mrs Tanios might have been any age over thirty. She was a tall, thin woman with dark hair, rather prominent light 'boiled gooseberry' eyes and a worried face. A fashionable hat was perched on her head at an unfashionable angle and she wore a rather depressed-looking cotton frock.

'I don't think—' she began vaguely.

Poirot bowed.

'I have just come from your cousin, Miss Theresa Arundell.'

'Oh, from Theresa? Yes?'

'Perhaps I could have a few minutes' private conversation?'

Mrs Tanios looked about her rather vacantly. Poirot suggested a leather sofa at the far end of the room.

As we made our way there a high voice squeaked out:

'Mother, where are you going?'

'I shall be just over here. Go on with your letter, darling.'

The child, a thin, peaky-looking girl of about seven, settled down again to what was evidently a laborious task. Her tongue showed through her parted lips in the effort of composition.

The far end of the room was quite deserted. Mrs Tanios sat down; we did the same. She looked inquiringly at Poirot.

He began:

'It is in reference to the death of your aunt, the late Miss Emily Arundell.'

Was I beginning to fancy things, or did a look of alarm spring up suddenly in those pale, prominent eyes?

'Yes?'

'Miss Arundell,' said Poirot, 'altered her will a very short time before she died. By the new will everything was left to Miss Wilhelmina Lawson. What I want to know, Mrs Tanios, is whether you will join your cousins, Miss Theresa and Mr Charles Arundell, in trying to contest that will?'

'Oh!' Mrs Tanios drew a deep breath. 'But I don't think that's possible, is it? I mean, my husband consulted a lawyer, and he seemed to think that it was better not to attempt it.'

'Lawyers, madame, are cautious people. Their advice is usually to avoid litigation at all costs – and no doubt they are usually right. But there are times when it pays to take a risk. I am not a lawyer myself, and therefore I look at the matter rather differently. Miss Arundell – Miss Theresa Arundell, I mean – is prepared to fight. What about you?'

'I – Oh, I really don't know.' She twisted her fingers nervously together. 'I should have to consult my husband.'

'Certainly, you must consult your husband before anything definite is undertaken. But what are your *own* feelings in the matter?'

'Well, really, I don't know.' Mrs Tanios looked more worried than ever. 'It depends so much on my husband.'

'But you *yourself*, what do you think, madame?'

Mrs Tanios frowned, then she said slowly:

'I don't think I like the idea very much. It seems – it seems rather indecent, doesn't it?'

'Does it, madame?'

'Yes – after all, if Aunt Emily chose to leave her money away from her family, I suppose we must put up with it.'

'You do not feel aggrieved in the matter, then?'

'Oh, yes, I do.' A quick flush showed in her cheeks. 'I think it was most unfair! *Most* unfair! And so unexpected. It was so unlike Aunt Emily. And so very unfair to the children.'

'You think it is very unlike Miss Arundell?'

'I think it was extraordinary of her!'

'Then isn't it possible that she was not acting of her own free will? Don't you think that perhaps she was being unduly influenced?'

Mrs Tanios frowned again. Then she said almost unwillingly:

'The difficult thing is that I can't see Aunt Emily being influenced by *anybody*! She was such a decided old lady.'

Poirot nodded approvingly.

'Yes, what you say is true. And Miss Lawson is hardly what one would describe as a strong character.'

'No, she's a nice creature, really – rather foolish, perhaps – but very, very kind. That's partly why I feel—'

'Yes, madame?' said Poirot as she paused.

Mrs Tanios twisted her fingers nervously again as she answered:

'Well, that it would be mean to try to upset the will. I feel certain that it wasn't in any way Miss Lawson's doing – I'm sure she'd be quite incapable of scheming and intriguing—'

'Again I agree with you, madame.'

'And that's why I feel that to go to law would be – well, would be undignified and spiteful; and besides, it would be very expensive, wouldn't it?'

'It would be expensive, yes.'

'And probably useless, too. But you must speak to my husband about it. He's got a much better head for business than I have.'

Poirot waited a minute or two, then he said:

'What reason do you think lay behind the making of that will?'

A quick colour rose in Mrs Tanios's cheeks as she murmured: 'I haven't the least idea.'

'Madame, I have told you I am not a lawyer. But you have not asked me what my profession is.'

She looked at him inquiringly.

'I am a detective. And, a short time before she died, Miss Emily Arundell wrote me a letter.'

Mrs Tanios leaned forward; her hands pressed themselves together.

'A letter?' she asked abruptly. 'About my husband?'

Poirot watched her for a minute or two, then he said slowly:

'I am afraid I am not at liberty to answer that question.'

'Then it *was* about my husband.' Her voice rose slightly. 'What did she say? I can assure you, Mr – er – I don't know your name.'

'Poirot is my name, Hercule Poirot.'

'I can assure you, Mr Poirot, that if anything was said in that letter against my husband, it was entirely untrue! I know, too, who will have inspired that letter! And that is another reason why I would rather have nothing to do with *any* action undertaken by Teresa and Charles! Theresa has never liked my husband. She has said things! I know she has said things! Aunt

501

Emily was prejudiced against my husband because he was not an Englishman, and she may therefore have believed things that Theresa said about him. But they are *not true*, Mr Poirot, you can take my word for that!'

'Mother – I've finished my letter.'

Mrs Tanios turned quickly. With an affectionate smile she took the letter the little girl held out to her.

'That's very nice, darling, very nice indeed. And that's a beautiful drawing of Mickey Mouse.'

'What shall I do now, mother?'

'Would you like to get a nice postcard with a picture on it? Here's the money. You go to the gentleman in the hall and choose one and then you can send it to Selim.'

The child moved away. I remembered what Charles Arundell had said. Mrs Tanios was evidently a devoted wife and mother. She was also, as he had said, a little like an earwig.

'That is your only child, madame?'

'No, I have a little boy also. He is out with his father at the moment.'

'They did not accompany you to Littlegreen House on your visits?'

'Oh, yes, sometimes; but you see, my aunt was rather old and children were inclined to worry her. But she was very kind, and always sent them out nice presents at Christmas.'

'Let me see, when did you last see Miss Emily Arundell?'

'I think it was just about ten days before she died.'

'You and your husband and your two cousins were all down there together, were you not?'

'Oh, no, that was the weekend before – at Easter.'

'And you and your husband were down there the weekend after Easter as well?'

'Yes.'

'And Miss Arundell was in good health and spirits then?'

'Yes, she seemed much as usual.'

'She was not ill in bed?'

'She was laid up with a fall she had had, but she came downstairs again while we were there.'

'Did she say anything to you about having made a new will?'

'No, nothing at all.'

'And her manner to you was quite unchanged?'

A slightly longer pause this time before Mrs Tanios said: 'Yes.'

I feel sure that at that moment Poirot and I had the same conviction. Mrs Tanios was lying!

Poirot paused a minute and then said:

'Perhaps I should explain that when I asked if Miss Arundell's manner to you was unchanged, I was not using the "you" plural. I referred to *you* personally.'

Mrs Tanios replied quickly:

'Oh, I see. Aunt Emily was very nice to me. She gave me a little pearl-and-diamond brooch and she sent ten shillings to each of the children.'

There was no constraint in her manner now. The words came freely with a rush.

'And as regards your husband – was there no change in her manner to him?'

The constraint had returned. Mrs Tanios did not meet Poirot's eyes as she replied:

'No, of course not – why should there be?'

'But since you suggest that your cousin Theresa Arundell might have tried to poison your aunt's mind—'

'She did! I'm sure she did!' Mrs Tanios leaned forward eagerly. 'You are quite right. There *was* a change! Aunt Emily was suddenly far more distant to him. And she behaved very oddly. There was a special digestive mixture he recommended – even went to the trouble of getting her some – going to the druggist and having it made up. She thanked him and all that – but rather stiffly, and later I actually saw her pouring the stuff from the bottle down the sink!'

Her indignation was quite fierce.

Poirot's eyes flickered.

'A very odd procedure,' he said. His voice was carefully unexcited.

'I thought it *most* ungrateful,' said Dr Tanios's wife hotly.

'As you say, elderly ladies distrust foreigners sometimes,' said Poirot. 'I am sure they think that English doctors are the only doctors in the world. Insularity accounts for a lot.'

'Yes, I suppose it does.' Mrs Tanios looked slightly mollified.

'When do you return to Smyrna, madame?'

'In a few weeks' time. My husband – ah! here is my husband and Edward with him.'

17

DR TANIOS

I must say that my first sight of Dr Tanios was rather a shock. I had been imbuing him in my mind with all sorts of sinister attributes. I had been picturing to myself a dark beaded foreigner with a swarthy aspect and a sinister cast of countenance.

Instead, I saw a rotund, jolly, brown-haired, brown-eyed man. And though it is true he had a beard, it was a modest brown affair that made him look more like an artist.

He spoke English perfectly. His voice had a pleasant timbre and matched the cheerful good-humour of his face.

'Here we are,' he said, smiling to his wife. 'Edward has been passionately thrilled by his first ride in the tube. He has always been in buses until today.'

Edward was not unlike his father in appearance, but both he and his little sister had a definitely foreign-looking appearance, and I understood what Miss Peabody had meant when she described them as rather yellow-looking children.

The presence of her husband seemed to make Mrs Tanios nervous. Stammering a little, she introduced Poirot to him. Me she ignored.

Dr Tanios took up the name sharply.

'Poirot? Monsieur Hercule Poirot? But I know that name well. And what brings you to us, M. Poirot?'

'It is the affair of a lady lately deceased. Miss Emily Arundell,' replied Poirot.

'My wife's aunt? Yes – what of her?'

Poirot said slowly:

'Certain matters have arisen in connexion with her death—'

Mrs Tanios broke in suddenly:

'It's about the will, Jacob. M. Poirot has been conferring with Theresa and Charles.'

Some of the tensity went out of Dr Tanios's attitude. He dropped into a chair.

'Ah, the will! An iniquitous will – but there, it is not my business, I suppose.'

Poirot sketched an account of his interview with the two Arundells (hardly a truthful one, I may say) and cautiously hinted at a fighting chance of upsetting the will.

'You interest me, M. Poirot, very much. I may say I am of your opinion. Something could be done. I actually went as far as to consult a lawyer on the subject, but his advice was not encouraging. Therefore—' He shrugged his shoulders.

'Lawyers, as I have told your wife, are cautious people. They do not like taking chances. But me, I am different! And you?'

Dr Tanios laughed – a rich, rollicking laugh.

'Oh, I'd take a chance all right! Often have, haven't I, Bella, old girl?' He smiled across at her, and she smiled back at him – but in a rather mechanical manner, I thought.

He turned his attention to Poirot.

'I am not a lawyer,' he said. 'But in my opinion it is perfectly clear that that will was made when the old lady was not responsible for what she was doing. The Lawson woman is both clever and cunning.'

Mrs Tanios moved uneasily. Poirot looked at her quickly. 'You do not agree, madame?'

She said rather weakly:

'She has always been very kind. I shouldn't call her clever.'

'She's been kind to you,' said Tanios, 'because she had nothing to fear from you, my dear Bella. You're easily taken in!'

He spoke quite good-humouredly, but his wife flushed.

'With me it was different,' he went on. 'She didn't like me. And she made no bones about showing it! I'll give you an instance. The old lady had a fall down the stairs when we were staying there. I insisted on coming back the following weekend to see how she was. Miss Lawson did her utmost to prevent us. She didn't succeed, but she was annoyed about it, I could see. The reason was clear. *She wanted the old lady to herself.*'

Again Poirot turned to the wife.

'You agree, madame?'

Her husband did not give her time to answer.

'Bella's too kind-hearted,' he said. 'You won't get her to impute bad motives to anybody. But I'm quite sure I was right. I'll tell you another thing, M. Poirot. The secret of her ascendency over old Miss Arundell was spiritualism. That's how it was done, depend upon it!'

'You think so?'

'Sure of it, my dear fellow. I've seen a lot of that sort of thing. It gets hold of people. You'd be amazed. Especially anyone of Miss Arundell's age. I'd be prepared to bet that that's how the suggestion came. Some spirit – possibly her dead father – ordered her to alter her will and leave her money to the Lawson woman. She was in bad health – credulous—'

There was a very faint movement from Mrs Tanios. Poirot turned to her.

'You think it possible – yes?'

'Speak up, Bella,' said Dr Tanios. 'Tell us your views.'

He looked at her encouragingly. Her quick look back at him was an odd one. She hesitated, then said:

'I know so little about these things. I dare say you're right, Jacob.'

'Depend upon it I'm all right, eh, M. Poirot?'

Poirot nodded his head.

'It may be – yes.' Then he said, 'You were down at Market Basing, I think, the weekend before Miss Arundell's death?'

'We were down at Easter and again the weekend after – that is right.'

'No, no, I meant the weekend after that – on the 26th. You were there on the Sunday, I think?'

'Oh, Jacob, were you?' Mrs Tanios looked at him wide-eyed. He turned quickly.

'Yes, you remember? I just ran down in the afternoon. I told you about it.'

Both Poirot and I were looking at her. Nervously she pushed her hat a little farther back on her head.

'Surely you remember, Bella,' her husband continued. 'What a terrible memory you've got.'

'Of course!' she apologized, a thin smile on her face. 'It's quite true; I have a shocking memory. And it's more than two months ago now.'

'Miss Theresa Arundell and Mr Charles Arundell were there then, I believe?' said Poirot.

'They may have been,' said Tanios easily. 'I didn't see them.'

'You were not there very long, then?'

'Oh, no – just half an hour or so.'

Poirot's inquiring gaze seemed to make him a little uneasy.

'Might as well confess,' he said with a twinkle. 'I hoped to get a loan – but I didn't get it. I'm afraid my wife's aunt didn't take to me as much as she might. Pity, because I liked her. She was a sporting old lady.'

'May I ask you a frank question, Dr Tanios?'

Was there or was there not a momentary apprehension in Tanios's eye? 'Certainly, M. Poirot.'

'What is your opinion of Charles and Theresa Arundell?'

The doctor loked slightly relieved.

'Charles and Theresa?' He looked at his wife with an affec-

tionate smile. 'Bella, my dear, I don't suppose you mind my
being frank about your family?'

She shook her head, smiling faintly.

'Then it's my opinion they're rotten to the core, both of
them! Funnily enough, I like Charles the best, He's a rogue,
but he's a likeable rogue. He's no moral sense, but he can't
help that. People are born that way.'

'And Theresa?'

He hesitated.

'I don't know. She's an amazingly attractive young woman.
But she's quite ruthless. I should say. She'd murder anyone in
cold blood if it suited her book. At least, that's my fancy. You
may have heard, perhaps, that her mother was tried for murder.'

'And acquitted,' said Poirot.

'As you say, "and acquitted," ' said Tanios quickly, 'But all
the same, it makes one – wonder sometimes.'

'You met the young man to whom she is engaged?'

'Donaldson? Yes, he came to supper one night.'

'What do you think of him?'

'A very clever fellow. I fancy he'll go far – if he gets the
chance. It takes money to specialize.'

'You mean that he is clever in his profession?'

'That is what I mean, yes. A first-class brain.' He smiled. 'Not
quite a shining light in society yet. A little precise and prim in
manner. He and Theresa make a comic pair. The attraction of
opposites. She's a social butterfly and he's a recluse.'

The two children were bombarding their mother.

'Mother, can't we go in to lunch? I'm so hungry. We'll be
late.'

Poirot looked at his watch and gave an exclamation.

'A thousand pardons! I delay your lunch hour.'

Glancing at her husband, Mrs Tanios said uncertainly:

'Perhaps we can offer you—'

Poirot said quickly:

'You are most amiable, madame; but I have a luncheon engagement for which I am already late.'

He shook hands with both the Tanioses and with the children I did the same.

We delayed for a minute or two in the hall. Poirot wanted to
put through a telephone call. I waited for him by the hall
porter's desk. I was standing there when I saw Mrs Tanios
come out into the hall and look searchingly around. She had a
hunted, harried look. She saw me and came swiftly across to me.

'Your friend – M. Poirot – I suppose he has gone?'

'No, he is in the telephone box.'

'Oh.'

'You wanted to speak to him?'

She nodded. Her air of nervousness increased.

Poirot came out of the box at that moment and saw us standing together. He came quickly across to us.

'M. Poirot,' she began quickly in a low, hurried voice. 'There is something that I would like to say – that I *must* tell you—'

'Yes, madame.'

'It is important – very important. You see—'

She stopped. Dr Tanios and the two children had just emerged from the writing room. He came across and joined us.

'Having a few last words with M. Poirot, Bella?'

His tone was good-humoured, the smile on his face pleasantness itself.

'Yes—' She hesitated, then said, 'Well, that is really all, M. Poirot. I just wanted you to tell Theresa that we will back her up in anything she decides to do. I quite see that the family *must* stand together.'

She nodded brightly to us, then, taking her husband's arm, she moved off in the direction of the dining room.

I caught Poirot by the shoulder.

'That wasn't what she started to say Poirot!'

He shook his head slowly, watching the retreating couple.

'She changed her mind,' I went on.

'Yes, *mon ami,* she changed her mind.'

'Why?'

'I wish I knew,' he murmured.

'She will tell us some other time,' I said hopefully.

'I wonder. I rather fear – she may not . . .'

—— 18 ——

'A NIGGER IN THE WOODPILE'

We had lunch at a small restaurant not far away. I was eager to learn what he made of the various members of the Arundell family.

'Well, Poirot?' I asked impatiently.

With a look of reproof Poirot turned his whole attention to

the menu. When he had ordered he leaned back in his chair, broke his roll of bread in half and said with a slightly mocking intonation:

'Well, Hastings?'

'What do you think of them now you've seen them all?'

Poirot said slowly:

'*Ma foi*, I think they are an interesting lot! Really this case is an enchanting study! It is, how do you say, the box of surprises? Look how each time I say, "I got a letter from Miss Arundell before she died," something crops up. From Miss Lawson I learn about the missing money. Mrs Tanios says at once, "About my husband?" Why about her husband? Why should Miss Arundell write to me, Hercule Poirot, about Dr Tanios?'

'That woman has something on her mind,' I said.

'Yes, she knows something. But *what*? Miss Peabody tells us that Charles Arundell would murder his grandmother for twopence. Miss Lawson says that Mrs Tanios would murder anyone if her husband told her to do so. Dr Tanios says that Charles and Theresa are rotten to the core, and he hints that their mother was a murderess and says apparently carelessly that Theresa is capable of murdering anyone in cold blood.

'They have a pretty opinion of each other, all these people! Dr Tanios thinks, or *says* he thinks, that there was undue influence. His wife, before he came in, evidently did *not* think so. She does not want to contest the will at first. Later she veers round. See you, Hastings – it is a pot that boils and seethes, and every now and then a significant fact comes to the surface and can be seen. There is *something* in the depths there – yes, there is *something*! I swear it, by my faith as Hercule Poirot, I swear it!'

I was impressed in spite of myself by his earnestness.

After a minute or two I said:

'Perhaps you are right, but it seems so vague – so nebulous.'

'But you agree with me that there is *something*?'

'Yes,' I said hesitatingly. 'I believe I do.'

Poirot leaned across the table. His eyes bored into mine.

'Yes – you have changed. You are no longer amused, superior – indulging me in my academic pleasures. But what is it that has convinced you? It is not my excellent reasoning – *non, ce n'est pas ça*! But *something* – something quite independent – has produced an effect on you. Tell me, my friend, what is it that has suddenly induced you to take this matter seriously?'

'I think,' I said slowly, 'it was Mrs Tanios. She looked – she looked – *afraid* . . . '

'Afraid of me?'

'No – no, not of you. It was something else. She spoke so quietly and sensibly to begin with – a natural resentment at the terms of the will, perhaps, but otherwise she seemed so resigned and willing to leave things as they are. It seemed the natural attitude of a well-bred but rather apathetic woman. And then that sudden change – the eagerness with which she came over to Dr Tanios's point of view. The way she came out into the hall after us – the – almost *furtive* way—'

Poirot nodded encouragingly.

'And another little thing which you may not have noticed—'

'I notice everything!'

'I mean the point about her husband's visit to Littlegreen House on that last Sunday. I could swear she knew nothing of it – that it was the most complete surprise to her – and yet she took her cue so quickly –agreed that he had told her about it and that she had forgotten. I – I don't like it, Poirot.'

'You are quite right, Hastings – it was significant – that.'

'It left an ugly impression of – of fear on me.'

Poirot nodded his head slowly.

'You felt the same?' I asked.

'Yes – that impression was very definitely in the air.' He paused and then went on: 'And yet you liked Tanios, did you not? You found him an agreeable man, open-hearted, good-natured, genial. attractive in spite of your insular prejudice against the Argentines, the Portuguese and the Greeks – a thoroughly congenial personality?'

'Yes,' I admitted. 'I did.'

'In the silence that ensued, I watched Poirot. Presently I said: 'What are you thinking of, Poirot?'

'I am reflecting on various people: handsome young Norman Gale, bluff, hearty Evelyn Howard, the pleasant Dr Shepherd, the quiet, reliable Knighton.'

For a moment I did not understand these references to people who had figured in past cases.

'What of them?' I asked.

'They were all delightful personalities . . .'

'My goodness, Poirot, do you really think Tanios—'

'No, no. Do not jump to conclusions, Hastings. I am only pointing out that one's own personal reactions to people are singularly unsafe guides. One must go not by one's feelings, but by facts.'

'H'm,' I said. Facts are not our strong suit. No, no, Poirot, don't go over it all again!'

'I will be brief, my friend, do not fear. To begin with, we have quite certainly a case of attempted murder. You admit, do you not?'

'Yes,' I said slowly. 'I do.'

I had up to now, been a little sceptical over Poirot (as I thought) somewhat fanciful reconstruction of the events on the night of Easter Tuesday. I was forced to admit, however, that his deductions were perfectly logical.

'*Très bien.* Now one cannot have attempted murder without a murderer. One of the people present on that evening was a murderer – in intention, if not in fact.'

'Granted.'

'Then that is our starting point – a murderer. We make a few inquiries – we, as you would say, stir the mud – and what do we get – several very interesting accusations uttered apparently casually in the course of conversations.'

'You think they were not casual?'

'Impossible to tell at the moment! Miss Lawson's innocent-seeming way of bringing out the fact that Charles threatened his aunt may have been quite innocent or it may not. Dr Tanios's remarks about Theresa Arundell may have absolutely no malice behind them, but be merely a physician's opinion. Miss Peabody, on the other hand, is probably quite genuine in her opinion of Charles Arundell's proclivities – but it is, after all, merely an opinion. So it goes on. There is a saying, is there not, a nigger in the woodpile? *Eh bien,* that is just what I find here. There is – not a nigger – but a murderer in our woodpile.'

'What I'd like to know is what you yourself really think, Poirot.'

'Hastings – Hastings – I do not permit myself to "think" – not, that is, in the sense that you are using the word. At the moment I only make certain reflections.'

'Such as?'

'I consider the questions of motive. What are the likely *motives* for Miss Arundell's death? Clearly the most obvious one is *gain*. Who would have gained by Miss Arundell's death – if she had died on Easter Tuesday?'

'Everyone – with the exception of Miss Lawson.'

'Precisely.'

'Well, at any rate, one person is automatically cleared.'

'Yes,' said Poirot thoughtfully. 'It would seem so. But the interesting thing is that the person who would have gained nothing if death had occurred on Easter Tuesday gains everything when death occurs two weeks later.'

'What are you getting at, Poirot?' I said, slightly puzzled.

'Cause and effect, my friend, cause and effect.'

I looked at him doubtfully.

He went on:

'Proceed logically! What exactly happened – after the accident?'

I hate Poirot in this mood. Whatever one says is bound to be wrong! I proceeded with intense caution.

'Miss Arundell was laid up in bed.'

'Exactly. With plenty of time to think. What next?'

'She wrote to you.'

Poirot nodded.

'Yes, she wrote to me. And the letter was not posted. A thousand pities, that.'

'Do you suspect that there was something fishy about that letter not being posted?'

Poirot frowned.

'There, Hastings, I have to confess that I do not know. I think – in view of everything I am almost sure – that the letter was genuinely mislaid. I believe – but I cannot be sure – that the fact that such a letter was written was unsuspected by anybody. Continue – what happened next?'

I reflected. 'The lawyer's visit,' I suggested.

'Yes – she sent for her lawyer, and in due course he arrived.'

'And she made a new will,' I continued.

'Precisely. She made a new and very unexpected will. Now, in view of that will we have to consider very carefully a statement made to us by Ellen. Ellen said, if you remember, that Miss Lawson was particularly anxious that the news that Bob had been out all night should not get to Miss Arundell's ears.'

'But – oh, I see – no, I don't. Or do I begin to see what you are hinting at? . . .'

'I doubt it!' said Poirot. 'But if you do, you realize, I hope, the *supreme importance* of that statement.'

He fixed me with a fierce eye.

'Of course. Of course,' I said hurriedly.

'And then,' continued Poirot, 'various other things happen. Charles and Theresa come for the weekend, and Miss Arundell shows the new will to Charles – er – so he *says*.'

'Don't you believe him?'

'I only believe statements that are *checked*. Miss Arundell does not show it to Theresa.'

'Because she thought Charles would tell her.'

'But he doesn't. *Why* doesn't he?'

'According to Charles himself he *did* tell her.'

'Theresa said quite positively that he *didn't* – a very interesting and suggestive little clash. And when we depart she calls him a fool.'

'I'm getting fogged, Poirot,' I said plaintively.

'Let us return to the sequence of events. Dr Tanios comes down on Sunday – possibly without the knowledge of his wife.'

'I should say certainly without her knowledge.'

'Let us say *probably*. To proceed! Charles and Theresa leave on the Monday. Miss Arundell is in good health and spirits. She eats a good dinner and sits in the dark with the Tripps and Miss Lawson. Towards the end of the *séance* she is taken ill. She retires to bed and dies four days later and Miss Lawson inherits all her money, and Captain Hastings says she died a natural death!'

'Whereas Hercule Poirot says she was given poison in her dinner on no evidence at all!'

'I have *some* evidence, Hastings. Think over our conversation with the Misses Tripp. And also one statement that stood out from Miss Lawson's somewhat rambling conversation.'

'Do you mean the fact that she had curry for dinner? Curry would mask the taste of a drug. Is that what you meant?'

Poirot said slowly:

'Yes, the curry has a certain significance, perhaps.'

'But,' I said, 'if what you advance (in defiance of all the medical evidence) is true, only Miss Lawson or one of the maids could have killed her.'

'I wonder.'

'Or the Tripp women? Nonsense. I can't believe that! All these people are palpably innocent.'

Poirot shrugged his shoulders.

'Remember this, Hastings. Stupidity – or even silliness, for that matter – can go hand in hand with intense cunning. And do not forget the original attempt at murder. That was not the handiwork of a particularly clever or complex brain. It was a very *simple* little murder, suggested by Bob and his habit of leaving the ball at the top of the stairs. The thought of putting a thread across the stairs was quite simple and easy – a child could have thought of it!'

I frowned.

'You mean—'

'I mean that what we are seeking to find here is just one thing – the wish to kill. Nothing more than that.'

'But the poison must have been a very skilful one, to leave no trace,' I argued. 'Something that the ordinary person would have difficulty in getting hold of. Oh, damn it all, Poirot, I simply can't believe it now. You can't *know*! It's all pure hypothesis.'

'You are wrong, my friend. As the result of our various conversations this morning I have now something definite to go upon. Certain faint but unmistakable indications. The only thing is – I am afraid.'

'Afraid? Of what?'

He said gravely:

'Of disturbing the dogs that sleep. That is one of your proverbs, is it not? To let the sleeping dogs lie! That is what our murderer does at present – sleeps happily in the sun . . . Do we not know, you and I, Hastings, how often a murderer, his confidence disturbed, turns and kills a second – or even a *third* time!'

'You are afraid of that happening?'

He nodded.

'Yes. *If* there is a murderer in the woodpile – and I think there is, Hastings. Yes, I think there is . . .'

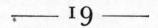

19

VISIT TO MR PURVIS

Poirot called for his bill and paid it.

'What do we do next?' I asked.

'We are going to do what you suggested this morning. We are going to Harchester to interview Mr Purvis. That is why I telephoned from the Durham Hotel.'

'You telephoned to Purvis?'

'No, to Theresa Arundell. I asked her to write me a letter of introduction to him. To approach him with any chance of success we must be accredited by the family. She promised to send it round to my flat by hand. It should be awaiting us there now.'

We found not only the letter but Charles Arundell, who had brought it round in person.

'Nice place you have here, M. Poirot,' he remarked, glancing round the sitting room of the flat.

At that moment my eye was caught by an imperfectly shut drawer in the desk. A small slip of paper was preventing it from shutting.

Now, if there was one thing absolutely incredible it was that Poirot should shut a drawer in such a fashion! I looked thoughtfully at Charles. He had been alone in this room awaiting our arrival. I had no doubt that he had been passing the time by snooping among Poirot's papers. What a young crook the fellow was! I felt myself burning with indignation.

Charles himself was in a most cheerful mood.

'Here we are,' he remarked, presenting a letter. 'All present and correct – and I hope you'll have more luck with old Purvis than we did.'

'He held out very little hope, I suppose?'

'Definitely discouraging . . . In his opinion the Lawson bird had clearly got away with the doings.'

'You and your sister have never considered an appeal to the lady's feelings?'

Charles grinned.

'I considered it – yes. But there seemed to be nothing doing. My eloquence was in vain. The pathetic picture of the disinherited black sheep – and a sheep not so black as he was painted (or so I endeavoured to suggest) – failed to move the woman! You know, she definitely seems to dislike me! I don't know why.' He laughed. 'Most old women fall for me quite easily. They think I've never been properly understood and that I've never had a fair chance!'

'A useful point of view.'

'Oh, it's been extremely useful before now. But, as I say, with the Lawson bird, nothing doing. I thing she's rather anti-man. Probably used to chain herself to railings and wave a suffragette flag in good old pre-war days.'

'Ah, well,' said Poirot, shaking his head. 'If simpler methods fail—'

'We must take to crime,' said Charles cheerfully.

'Aha,' said Poirot. 'Now, speaking of crime, young man, is it true that you threatened your aunt – that you said that you would "bump her off," or words to that affect?'

Charles sat down in a chair, stretched his legs out in front of him and stared hard at Poirot.

'Now, who told you that?' he said.

'No matter. Is it true?'

'Well, there are elements of truth about it.'

'Come, come, let me hear the true story – the *true* story, mind.'

'Oh, you can have it, sir. There was nothing melodramatic about it. I'd been attempting a touch – if you gather what I mean.'

'I comprehend.'

'Well, that didn't go according to plan. Aunt Emily intimated that any efforts to separate her and her money would be quite unavailing! Well, I didn't lose my temper, but I put it to her plainly, 'Now look here, Aunty Emily," I said. "You know, you're going about things in such a way that you'll end by getting bumped off!" She said, rather sniffly, what did I mean? "Just that," I said. "Here are your friends and relations all hanging around with their mouths open, all as poor as church mice – whatever church mice may be – all hoping. And what do you do? Sit down on the dibs and refuse to part. That's the way people get themselves murdered. Take it from me, if you're bumped off, you'll only have yourself to blame."

'She looked at me then, over the top of her spectacles in a way she had. Looked at me rather nastily. "Oh," she said dryly enough, "so that's your opinion, is it?" "It is," I said. "You loosen up a bit, that's my advice to you." "Thank you, Charles," she said, "for your well-meant advice. But I think you'll find I'm well able to take care of myself." "Please yourself, Aunt Emily," I said. I was grinning all over my face – and I fancy she wasn't as grim as she tried to look. "Don't say I didn't warn you." "I'll remember it," she said.'

He paused.

'That's all there was to it.'

'And so,' said Poirot, 'you contented yourself with a few pound notes you found in a drawer.'

Charles stared at him, then burst out laughing.

'I take off my hat to you,' he said. 'You're some sleuth! How did you get hold of *that*?'

'It is true, then?'

'Oh, it's true enough! I was damned hard up. Had to get money somehow. Found a nice little wad of notes in a drawer and helped myself to a few. I was very modest – didn't think my little subtraction would be noticed. Even then, they'd probably think it was the servants.'

Poirot said dryly:

'It would be very serious for the servants if such an idea had been entertained.'

Charles shrugged his shoulders.

'Every one for himself,' he murmured.

'And *le diable* takes the hindermost,' said Poirot. 'That is your creed, is it?'

Charles was looking at him curiously.

'I didn't know the old lady had ever spotted it. How did you come to know about it – and about the bumping-off conversation?'

'Miss Lawson told me.'

'The sly old pussy cat!' He looked, I thought, just a shade disturbed. 'She doesn't like me and she doesn't like Theresa,' he said presently. 'You don't think – she's got anything more up her sleeve?'

'What could she have?'

'Oh, I don't know. It's just that she strikes me as a malicious old devil.' He paused. 'She hates Theresa . . .' he added.

'Did you know, Mr Arundell, that Dr Tanios came down to see your aunt on the Sunday before she died?'

'What – on the Sunday that we were there?'

'Yes. You did not see him?'

'No. We were out for a walk in the afternoon. I suppose he must have come then. Funny that Aunt Emily didn't mention his visit. Who told you?'

'Miss Lawson.'

'Lawson again? She seems to be a mine of information.'

He paused and then said: 'You know, Tanios is a nice fellow. I like him. Such a jolly, smiling chap.'

'He has an attractive personality, yes,' said Poirot.

Charles rose to his feet.

'If I'd been him I'd have murdered the dreary Bella years ago! Doesn't she strike you as the type of woman who is marked out by fate to be a victim? You know, I should never be surprised if bits of her turned up in a trunk at Margate or somewhere!'

'It is not a pretty action that you attribute there to her husband the good doctor,' said Poirot severely.

'No,' said Charles meditatively. 'And I don't think really that Tanios would hurt a fly. He's much too kind-hearted.'

'And what about you? Would you do murder if it were made worth your while?'

Charles laughed – a ringing, genuine laugh.

'Thinking about a spot of blackmail, M. Poirot? Nothing

doing. I can assure you that I didn't put' – he stopped, suddenly and then went on – 'strychnine in Aunt Emily's soup.'

With a careless wave of his hand he departed.

'Were you trying to frighten him, Poirot?' I asked. 'If so, I don't think you succeeded. He showed no guilty reactions whatsoever.'

'No?'

'No. He seemed quite unruffled.'

'Curious that pause he made,' said Poirot.

'A pause?'

'Yes. A pause before the word "strychnine". Almost as though he had been about to say something else and thought better of it.'

I shrugged my shoulders.

'He was probably thinking of a good, venomous-sounding poison.'

'It is possible. It is possible. But let us set off. We will, I think, stay the night at The George in Market Basing.'

Ten minutes later saw us speeding through London, bound more for the country.

We arrived in Harchester about four o'clock, and made our way straight to the offices of Purvis, Purvis, Charlesworth, and Purvis.

Mr Purvis was a big, solidly built man with white hair and a rosy complexion. He had a little the look of a country squire. His manner was courteous but reserved.

He read the letter we had brought and then looked at us across the top of his desk. It was a shrewd look and a somewhat searching one.

'I know you by name, of course, M. Poirot,' he said politely. 'Miss Arundell and her brother have, I gather engaged your services in this manner but exactly in what capacity you propose to be of use to them I am at a loss to imagine.'

'Shall we say, Mr Purvis, a fuller investigation of all the circumstances?'

The lawyer said dryly: 'Miss Arundell and her brother have already had my opinion as to the legal position. The circumstances were perfectly clear and admit of no misrepresentation.'

'Perfectly, perfectly,' said Poirot quickly. 'But you will not, I am sure, object to just repeating them so that I can envisage the situation clearly.'

The lawyer bowed his head.

'I am at your service.'

Poirot began:

'Miss Arundell wrote to you giving you instructions on the seventeenth of April, I believe?'

Mr Purvis consulted some papers on the table before him.

'Yes, that is correct.'

'Can you tell me what she said?'

'She asked me to draw up a will. There were to be legacies to two servants and to three or four charities. The rest of her estate was to pass to Wilhelmina Lawson absolutely.

'You will pardon me, Mr Purvis, but you were surprised?'

'I will admit that – yes, I was surprised.'

'Miss Arundell had made a will previously?'

'Yes, she made a will five years ago.'

'That will, after certain small legacies, left her property to her nephew and nieces?'

'The bulk of her estate was to be divided equally between the children of her brother Thomas and the daughter of Arabella Biggs, her sister.'

'What has happened to that will?'

'At Miss Arundell's request I brought it with me when I visited her at Littlegreen House on April 21st.'

'I should be much obliged to you, Mr Purvis, if you would give me a full description of everything that occurred on that occasion.'

The lawyer paused for a minute or two. Then he said, very precisely:

'I arrived at Littlegreen House at three o'clock in the afternoon. One of my clerks accompanied me. Miss Arundell received me in the drawing room.'

'How did she look to you?'

'She seemed to me in good health in spite of the fact that she was walking with a stick. That, I understand, was on account of a fall she had recently. Her general health, as I say, seemed good. She struck me as slightly nervous and over-excited in manner.'

'Was Miss Lawson with her?'

'She was with her when I arrived. But she left us immediately.'

'And then?'

'Miss Arundell asked me if I had done what she had asked me to do, and if I had brought the new will with me for her to sign.

'I said I had done so. I – er—' He hesitated for a minute or two, then went on stiffly: 'I may as well say that, as far as it was proper for me to do so, I remonstrated with Miss Arundell. I pointed out to her that this new will might be regarded as grossly unfair to her family, who were, after all, her own flesh and blood.'

'And her answer?'

'She asked me if the money was or was not her own to do with as she liked. I replied that certainly that was the case. "Very well, then," she said. I reminded her that she had known this Miss Lawson a very short time, and I asked her if she was quite sure that the injustice she was doing to her own family was legitimate. Her reply was, "My dear friend, I know perfectly what I am doing." '

'Her manner was excited, you say.'

'I think I can definitely say that it was, but understand me M. Poirot, she was in full possession of her faculties. She was in every sense of the word fully competent to manager her own affairs. Though my sympathies are entirely with Miss Arundell's family, I should be obliged to maintain that in any court of law.'

'That is quite understood. Proceed. I pray of you.'

'Miss Arundell read through her existing will. Then she stretched out her hand for the one I had drawn up. I may say that I would have preferred to submit a draft first, but she had impressed upon me that the will must be brought her ready to sign. That presented no difficulties, as its provisions were so simple. She read it through, nodded her head, and said she would sign it straightaway. I felt it my duty to enter one last protest. She heard me out quite patiently, but said that her mind was quite made up. I called in my clerk, and he and the gardener acted as witness to her signature. The servants, of course, were ineligible owing to the fact that they were beneficaries under the will.'

'And afterwards, did she entrust the will to you for safe keeping?'

'No, she placed it in a drawer of her desk, which drawer she locked.'

'What was done with the original will? Did she destroy it?'

'No, she locked it away with the other.'

'After her death, where was the will found?'

'In the same drawer. As executor I had her keys, and went through her papers and business documents.'

'Were both wills in the drawer?'

'Yes, exactly as she had placed them there.'

'Did you question her at all as to the motive for this rather surprising action?'

'I did. But I got no satisfactory answer. She merely assured me that "she knew what she was doing".'

'Nevertheless you were surprised at the proceeding?'

'Very surprised. Miss Arundell, I should say, had always shown herself to have a strong sense of family feeling.'

Poirot was silent a minute, then he asked:

'You did not, I suppose, have any conversation with Miss Lawson on the subject?'

'Certainly not. Such a proceeding would have been highly improper.'

Mr Purvis looked scandalized at the mere suggestion.

'Did Miss Arundell say anything to indicate that Miss Lawson knew that a will was being drawn in her favour?'

'On the contrary. I asked her if Miss Lawson was aware of what was being done, and Miss Arundell snapped out that she knew nothing about it.

'It was advisable, I thought, that Miss Lawson should not be aware of what had happened. I endeavoured to hint as much, and Miss Arundell seemed quite of my opinion.'

'Just why did you stress that point, Mr Purvis?'

The old gentleman returned his glance with dignity.

'Such things, in my opinion, are best undiscussed. Also it might have led to future disappointment.'

'Ah!' Poirot drew a long breath. 'I take it that *you thought it probable that Miss Arundell might change her mind in the near future?*'

The lawyer bowed his head.

'That is so. I fancied that Miss Arundell had had some violent altercation with her family. I thought it probable that when she cooled down she would repent of her rash decision.'

'In which case she would have done – what?'

'She would have given me instructions to prepare a new will.'

'She might have taken the simpler course of merely destroying the will lately made, in which case the older will would have been good?'

'That is a somewhat debatable point. All earlier wills, you understand, had been definitely revoked by the testator.'

'But Miss Arundell would not have had the legal knowledge to appreciate that point. She may have thought that by destroying the later will, the earlier one would stand.'

'It is quite possible.'

'Actually, if she died intestate, her money would pass to her family?'

'Yes. One half to Mrs Tanios, one half divisible between Charles and Theresa Arundell. But the fact remains, however, that she did *not* change her mind! She died with her decision unchanged.'

'But that,' said Poirot, 'is where I come in.'

The lawyer looked at him inquiringly.

Poirot leaned forward.

'Supposing,' he said, that Miss Arundell, on her deathbed, *wished to destroy that will.* Supposing that she believed that she *had* destroyed it – but that, in reality, she only destroyed the *first* will.'

Mr Purvis shook his head.

'No, *both* wills were intact.'

'Then supposing she destroyed a *dummy* will – *under the impression that she was destroying the genuine document.* She was very ill, remember; it would be easy to deceive her.'

'You would have to bring evidence to that effect,' said the lawyer sharply.

'Oh, undoubtedly – undoubtedly . . .'

'Is there – may I ask – is there any reason to believe something of the kind happened?'

Poirot drew back a little.

'I should not like to commit myself at this stage—'

'Naturally, naturally,' said Mr Purvis, agreeing with a phrase that was familiar to him.

'But I may say, strictly in confidence, that there are some curious features about this business!'

'Really? You don't say so?'

Mr Purvis rubbed his hands together with a kind of pleasurable anticipation.

'What I wanted from you and what I have got,' continued Poirot, 'is your opinion that Miss Arundell would, sooner or later, have changed her mind and relented towards her family.'

'That is only my personal opinion, of course,' the lawyer pointed out.

'My dear sir, I quite understand. You do not, I believe, act for Miss Lawson?'

'I advised Miss Lawson to consult an independent solicitor,' said Mr Purvis.

His tone was wooden.

Poirot shook hands with him, thanking him for his kindness and the information he had given us.

— 20 —

SECOND VISIT TO LITTLEGREEN HOUSE

On our way from Harchester to Market Basing, a matter of some ten miles we discussed the situation.

'Have you any grounds at all, Poirot, for that suggestion you threw out?'

'You mean that Miss Arundell may have believed that that particular will was destroyed? No, *mon ami* – frankly, no. But it was incumbent upon me – you must perceive that – to make *some* sort of suggestion! Mr Purvis is a shrewd man. Unless I threw out some hint of the kind I did, he would ask himself what I could be doing in this affair.'

'Do you know what you remind me of, Poirot?'

'No, *mon ami.*'

'Of a juggler juggling with a lot of different-coloured balls! They are all in the air at once.'

'The different-coloured balls are the different lies I tell – eh?'

'That's about th size of it.'

'And some day, you think, there will come the grand crash?'

'You can't keep it up for ever,' I pointed out.

'That is true. There will come the grand moment when I catch the balls one by one, make my bow, and walk off the stage.'

'To the sound of thunderous applause from the audience.'

Poirot looked at me suspiciously.

'That well may be, yes.'

'We didn't learn very much from Mr Purvis,' I remarked, edging away from the danger-point.

'No, except that it confirmed our general ideas.'

'And it confirmed Miss Lawson's statement that she knew nothing about the will until after the old lady's death.'

'Me, I do not see that it confirmed anything of the sort.'

'Purvis advised Miss Arundell not to tell her, and Miss Arundell replied that she had no intention of doing so.'

'Yes, that is all very nice and clear. But there are keyholes, my friend, and keys that unlock locked drawers.'

'Do you really think that Miss Lawson would eavesdrop and poke and pry around?' I asked, rather shocked.

Poirot smiled.

'Miss Lawson – she is not an old school tie, *mon cher.* We

know that she overheard *one* conversation which she was not supposed to have heard – I refer to the one in which Charles and his aunt discussed the question of bumping off miserly relatives.'

I admitted the truth of that.

'So you see, Hastings, she may easily have overheard some of the conversation between Mr Purvis and Miss Arundell. He has a good, resonant voice. As for poking and prying,' went on Poirot, 'more people do it than you would suppose. Timid and easily frightened people such as Miss Lawson often acquire a number of mildly dishonourable habits which are a great solace and recreation to them.'

'Really, Poirot!' I protested.

He nodded his head a good many times.

'But yes, it is so, it is so.'

We arrived at The George and took a couple of rooms. Then we strolled off in the direction of Littlegreen House.

When we rang the bell, Bob immediately answered the challenge. Dashing across the hall, barking furiously, he flung himself against the front door.

'I'll have your liver and your lights!' he snarled. 'I'll tear you limb from limb! I'll teach you to try to get into *this* house! Just wait until I get my teeth into you.'

A soothing murmur added itself to the clamour.

'Now then, boy. Now then, there's a good doggie. Come in here.'

Bob, dragged by the collar, was immured in the morning room, much against his will.

'Always spoiling a fellow's sport,' he grumbled. 'First chance I've had of giving anyone a really good fight for ever so long. Just aching to get my teeth into a trouser leg. You be careful for yourself without me to protect you.'

The door of the morning room was shut on him, and Ellen drew back bolts and bars and opened the front door.

'Oh, it's you, sir,' she exclaimed.

She drew the door right back. A look of highly pleasurable excitement spread over her face.

'Come in, sir, if you please, sir.'

We entered the hall. From beneath the door on the left, loud snuffling sounds proceeded, interspersed with growls. Bob was endeavouring to 'place' us correctly.

'You can let him out,' I suggested.

'I will, sir. He's quite all right, really, but he makes such a noise and rushes at people so it frightens them. He's a splendid watchdog, though.'

She opened the morning room door, and Bob shot through like a suddenly projected cannon-ball.

'Who is it? Where are they? Oh, there you are. Dear me, don't I seem to remember—' Sniff – sniff – sniff – prolonged snort. 'Of course! We *have* met!'

'Hullo, old man,' I said. 'How goes it?'

Bob wagged its tail perfunctorily.

'Nicely, thank you. Let me just see—' He resumed his researches. 'Been talking to a spaniel lately, I smell. Foolish dogs, I think. What's this? A cat? That is interesting. Wish we had her here. We'd have a rare sport. H'm – not a bad bull-terrier.'

Having correctly diagnosed a visit I had lately paid to some doggy friends, he transferred his attentions to Poirot, inhaled a noseful of benzine and walked away reproachfully.

'Bob,' I called.

He threw me a look over his shoulder.

'It's all right. I know what I'm doing. I'll be back in a jiffy.'

'The house is all shut up. I hope you'll excuse—' Ellen hurried into the morning room and began to unfasten the shutters.

'Excellent, this is excellent,' said Poirot, following her in and sitting down.

As I was about to rejoin him, Bob reappeared from some mysterious region, ball in mouth. He dashed up the stairs and sprawled himself on the top step, his ball between his paws. His tail wagged slowly.

'Come on,' he said. 'Come on. Let's have a game.'

My interest in detection momentarily eclipsed, we played for some minutes, then with a feeling of guilt I hurried into the morning room.

Poirot and Ellen seemed to be well away on the subject of illness and medicines.

'Some little white pills, sir, that's all she used to take. Two or three after every meal. That was Dr Grainger's orders. Oh, yes, she was very good about it. Tiny little things they were. And then there was some stuff Miss Lawson swore by. Capsules, they were, Dr Loughbarrow's Liver Capsules. You can see advertisements of them on all the hoardings.'

'She took those too?'

'Yes. Miss Lawson got her them to begin with, and she thought they did her good.'

'Did Dr Grainger know?'

'Oh, sir, he didn't mind. 'You take 'em if you think they do you good,' he'd say to her. And she said, 'Well, you may laugh, but they *do* do me good. A lot better than any of *your* physic.' And Dr Grainger, he laughed, and said faith was worth all the drugs ever invented.'

'She didn't take anything else?'

'No. Miss Bella's husband, the foreign doctor, he went out and got her a bottle of something, but although she thanked him very politely she poured it away, and that I know for a fact! And I think she was right. You don't know where you are with these foreign things.'

'Mrs Tanios saw her pouring it away, didn't she?'

'Yes, and I'm afraid she was rather hurt about it, poor lady. I'm sorry, too, for no doubt it was kindly meant on the doctor's part.'

'No doubt. No doubt. I suppose any medicines that were left in the house were thrown away when Miss Arundell died?'

Ellen looked a little surprised at the question.

'Oh, yes, sir. The nurse threw away some, and Miss Lawson got rid of all the old lot in the medicine-cupboard in the bathroom.'

'Is that where the – er – Dr Loughbarrow's Liver Capsules were kept?'

'No, they were kept in the corner cupboard in the dining room, so as to be handy for taking after meals as directed.'

'What nurse attended Miss Arundell? Can you give me her name and address?'

Ellen could supply that at once and did.

Poirot continued to ask questions about Miss Arundell's last illness.

Ellen gave details with relish, describing the sickness, the pain, the onset of jaundice, and the final delirium. I don't know whether Poirot got any satisfaction out of the catalogue. He listened patiently enough and occasionally interpolated some pertinent little questions, usually about Miss Lawson and the amount of time she spent in the sick-room. He was also exceedingly interested in the diet administered to the ill woman, comparing it with that administered to some dead relative (non-existent) of his own.

Seeing that they were enjoying themselves so much, I stole out in the hall again. Bob had gone to sleep on the landing, his ball lying under his chin.

I whistled to him and he sprang up, alert at once. This time, however, doubtless out of offended dignity, he made a pro-

tracted business of dispatching the ball down to me, several
times catching it back at the last minute.

'Disappointed, aren't you? Well, perhaps I *will* let you have
it this time.'

When I next went back to the morning room, Poirot was talking about Dr Tanios's surprise visit on the Sunday before the
old lady's death.

'Yes, sir, Mr Charles and Miss Theresa were out for a walk.
Dr Tanios wasn't expected, I know. The mistress was lying
down, and she was very surprised when I told her who it was.
"Dr Tanios?" she said. 'Is Mrs Tanios with him?" I told her
no, the gentleman had come alone. So she said to tell him she'd
be down in a minute.'

'Did he stay long?'

'Not above an hour, sir. He didn't look too pleased when he
went away.'

'Have you any idea of the – er – purpose of his visit?'

'I couldn't say, I'm sure, sir.'

'You did not happen to hear anything?'

Ellen's face flushed suddenly.

'No, I did *not*, sir! I've never been one to listen at doors, no
matter what *some* people will do – and people who ought to
know better!'

'Oh, but you misunderstand me.' Poirot was eager, apologetic.
'It just occurred to me that perhaps you might have brought in
tea while the gentleman was there, and if so, you could hardly
have helped hearing what he and your mistress were talking
about.'

Ellen was mollified.

'I'm sorry, sir; I misunderstood you. No, Dr Tanios didn't
stay for tea.'

Poirot looked up at her and twinkled a little.

'And if I want to know what he came down for – well, it is
possible that Miss Lawson might be in a position to know? Is
that it?'

'Well, if she doesn't know, sir, nobody does,' said Ellen with
a sniff.

'Let me see.' Poirot frowned as though trying to remember.
'Miss Lawson's bedroom – was it next to Miss Arundell's?'

'No, sir. Miss Lawson's room is right at the top of the staircase. I can show you, sir.'

Poirot accepted the offer. As he went up the stairs he kept
close to the wall side, and just as he reached the top uttered an
exclamation and stooped to his trouser-leg.

'Ah – I have just caught a thread – ah, yes, there is a nail here in the skirting-board.'

'Yes, there is, sir. I think it must have worked loose or something. I've caught my dress on it once or twice.'

'Has it been like that long?'

'Well, some time, I'm afraid, sir. I noticed it first when the mistress was laid up – after her accident, that was, sir – I tried to pull it out but I couldn't.'

'It has had a thread round it some time, I think.'

'That's right, sir, there was a little loop of thread, I remember. I can't thing what for, I'm sure.'

But there was no suspicion in Ellen's voice. To her it was just one of the things that occur in houses and which one does not bother to explain!

Poirot had stepped into the room at the top of the stairs. It was of moderate size. There were two windows directly facing us. There was a dressing-table across one corner and between the windows was a wardrobe with a long mirror. The bed was to the right behind the door facing the windows. On the left-hand wall of the room was a big mahogany chest of drawers and a marble-topped washstand.

Poirot looked round the room thoughtfully and then came out again on the landing. He went along the passage, passing two other bedrooms, and then came to the large bed-chamber which had belonged to Emily Arundell.

'The nurse had the little room next door,' Ellen explained.

Poirot nodded thoughtfully.

As we descended the stairs, he asked if he might walk round the garden.

'Oh, yes, sir, certainly. It looks lovely just now.'

'The gardener is still employed?'

'Angus? Oh, yes, Angus is still here. Miss Lawson wants everything kept nice because she thinks it will sell better that way.'

'I think she is wise. To let a place run to seed is not the good policy.'

The garden was very peaceful and beautiful. The wide borders were full of lupins and delphiniums and great scarlet poppies. The peonies were in bud. Wandering along, we came presently to a potting-shed where a big, rugged old man was busy. He saluted us respectfully and Poirot engaged him in conversation.

A mention that we had seen Mr Charles that day thawed the old man and he became quite garrulous.

'Always a one, he was! I've known him come out here with half a gooseberry pie and the cook hunting high and low for it! And he'd go back with such an innocent face that durned if they wouldn't say it must have been the cat, though I've never known a cat eat a gooseberry pie! Oh, he's a one, Mr Charles is!'

'He was down here in April, wasn't he?'

'Yes, down here two weekends. Just before the missus died, it was.'

'Did you see much of him?'

'A good bit, I did. There wasn't much for a young gentleman to do down here, and that's a fact. Used to stroll up to The George and have one. And then he'd potter round here, asking me questions about one thing and another.'

'About flowers?'

'Yes – flowers – and weeds too.' The old man chuckled.

'Weeds?'

Poirot's voice held a sudden, tentative note. He turned his head and looked searchingly along the shelves. His eye stopped at a tin.

'Perhaps he wanted to know how you got rid of them?'

'He did that!'

'I suppose this is the stuff you use.'

Poirot turned the tin gently round and read the label.

'That's it,' said Angus. 'Very handy stuff it is.'

'Dangerous stuff?'

'Not if you use it right. It's arsenic, of course. Had a bit of a joke about that, Mr Charles and I did. Said as how when he had a wife and didn't like her, he'd come to me and get a little of that stuff to put her away with! Maybe, I sez, *she'll* be the one that wants to do away with *you*! Ah, that made him laugh proper, that did! It was a good one, that!'

We laughed as in duty bound. Poirot prised up the lid of the tin.

'Nearly empty,' he murmured.

The old man had a look.

'Ay, there's more gone than I thought. No idea I'd used that much. I'll be having to order some more.'

'Yes,' said Poirot, smiling. 'I'm afraid there's hardly enough for you to spare me some for *my* wife!'

We all had another good laugh over this witticism.

'You're not married, I take it, mister?'

'No.'

'Ah! It's always them as isn't that can afford to joke about it. Those that isn't married don't know what trouble is!'

'I gather that your wife –?' Poirot paused delicately.

'She's alive all right – very much so.'

Angus seemed a little depressed about it.

Complimenting him on his garden, we bade him farewell.

—— 21 ——

THE CHEMIST. THE NURSE. THE DOCTOR

The tin of weed-killer had started a new train of thought in my mind. It was the first definite suspicious circumstance that I had encountered. Charles's interest in it, the old gardener's obvious surprise at finding the tin almost empty – it all seemed to point in the right direction.

Poirot was, as usual when I am excited, very non-committal.

'Even if some of the weed-killer *has* been taken, there is as yet no evidence that Charles was the person to take it, Hastings.'

'But he talked so much to the gardener about it!'

'Not a very wise procedure if he was going to help himself to some.'

Then he went on:

'What is the first and simplest poison to come into your mind if you were asked to name one quickly?'

'Arsenic, I suppose.'

'Yes. You understand, then, that very marked pause before the word "strychnine" when Charles was talking to us today.'

'You mean—?'

'That he was about to say "arsenic in the soup", and stopped himself.'

'Ah!' I said, 'and why did he stop himself?'

'Exactly. *Why*? I may say, Hastings, that it was to find the answer to that particular "why?" which made me go out into the garden in search of any likely source of weed-killer.'

'And you found it!'

'And I found it.'

I shook my head.

'It begins to look rather bad for young Charles. You had a

good talk with Ellen over the old lady's illness. Did her symptoms resemble those of arsenic poisoning?'

Poirot rubbed his nose.

'It is difficult to say. There was abdominal pain – sickness.'

'Of course – that's it!'

'H'm, I am not so sure.'

'What poison did it resemble?'

'*Eh bien*, my friend, it resembled not so much poison as disease of the liver and death from that cause!'

'Oh, Poirot,' I cried. 'It *can't* be natural death! It's got to be murder!'

'Oh, *là là*, we seem to have changed places, you and I.'

He turned abruptly into a chemist's shop. After a long discussion of Poirot's particular internal troubles, he purchased a small box of indigestion lozenges. Then, when his purchase was wrapped up and he was about to leave the shop, his attention was taken by an attractively wrapped package of Dr Loughbarrow's Liver Capsules.

'Yes, sir, a very good preparation.' The chemist was a middle-aged man of a chatty disposition. 'You'll find them very efficacious.'

'Miss Arundell used to take them, I remember. Miss Emily Arundell.'

'Indeed she did, sir. Miss Arundell of Littlegreen House. A fine old lady, one of the old school. I used to serve her.'

'Did she take many patent medicines?'

'Not really, sir. Not so many as some elderly ladies I could name. Miss Lawson, now, her companion, the one that's come into all the money—'

Poirot nodded.

'She was a one for this, that, and the other. Pills, lozenges, dyspepsia tablets, digestive mixtures, blood mixtures. Really enjoyed herself among the bottles.' He smiled ruefully. 'I wish there were more like her. People nowadays don't take to medicines as they used to. Still, we sell a lot of toilet preparations to make up for it.'

'Did Miss Arundell take these Liver Capsules regularly?'

'Yes, she'd been taking them for three months, I think, before she died.'

'A relative of hers, a Dr Tanios, came in to have a mixture made up one day, didn't he?'

'Yes, of course, the Greek gentleman that married Miss Arundell's niece. Yes, a very interesting mixture it was. One I've not previously become acquainted with.'

The man spoke as of a rare botanical trophy.

'It makes a change, sir, when you get something new. Very interesting combination of drugs, I remember. Of course, the gentleman is a doctor. Very nice he was – a pleasant way with him.'

'Did his wife do any shopping here?'

'Did she now? I don't recall. Oh, yes, came in for a sleeping draught – chloral it was, I remember. A double quantity the prescription was for. It's always a little difficult for us with hypnotic drugs. You see, most doctors don't prescribe much at a time.'

'Whose prescription was it?'

'Her husband's, I think. Oh, of course, it was quite all *right* – but, you know, we have to be careful nowadays. Perhaps you don't know the fact, but if a doctor makes a mistake in a prescription and we make it up in all good faith and anything goes wrong it's we who have to take the blame – not the doctor.'

'That seems very unfair!'

'It's worrying, I'll admit. Ah, well, I can't complain. No trouble has come *my* way – touching wood.'

He rapped the counter sharply with his knuckles.

Poirot decided to buy a package of Dr Loughbarrow's Liver Capsules.

'Thank you, sir. Which size – 25, 50, 100?'

'I suppose the larger ones are better value – but still—'

'Have the 50, sir. That's the size Miss Arundell had. Eight and six.'

Poirot agreed, paid over eight and six and received the parcel.

Then we left the shop.

'So, Mrs Tanios bought a sleeping-draught,' I exclaimed as we got out into the street. 'An overdose of that would kill anyone, wouldn't it?'

'With the greatest of ease.'

'Do you think old Miss Arundell—'

I was remembering Miss Lawson's words, '*I dare say she'd murder someone if he told her to!*'

Poirot shook his head.

'Chloral is a narcotic and a hypnotic. Used to alleviate pain and as a sleeping-draught. It can also become a habit.'

'Do you think Mrs Tanios had acquired the habit?'

Poirot shook his head perplexedly.

'No, I hardly think so. But it is curious. I can think of one explanation. But that would mean—'

He broke off and looked at his watch.

'Come, let us see if we can find this Nurse Carruthers who was with Miss Arundell in her last illness.'

Nurse Carruthers proved to be a sensible-looking, middle-aged woman.

Poirot now appeared in yet another role and with one more fictitious relative. This time he had an aged mother for whom he was anxious to find a sympathetic hospital nurse.

'You comprehend – I am going to speak to you quite frankly. My mother, she is difficult. We have had some excellent nurses, young women, fully competent, but the very fact that they are young has been against them. My mother dislikes young women, she insults them, she is rude and fractious, she fights against open windows and modern hygiene. It is very difficult.' He sighed mournfully.

'I know,' said Nurse Carruthers sympathetically. 'It's very trying sometimes. one has to use a lot of tact. It's no use upsetting a patient. Better to give in to them as far as you can. And once they feel you're not trying to force things on them, they very often relax and give in like lambs.'

'Ah, I see that you would be ideal in the part. You understand old ladies.'

'I've had to do with a few in my time,' said Nurse Carruthers with a laugh. 'You can do a lot with patience and good humour.'

'That is so wise. You nursed Miss Arundell, I believe. Now, she could not have been an easy old lady.'

'Oh, I don't know. She was strong-willed, but I didn't find her difficult at all. Of course, I wasn't there any length of time. She died on the fourth day.'

'I was talking to her niece, Miss Theresa Arundell, only yesterday.'

'Really. Fancy that now! What I always says is – the world's a small place!'

'You know her, I expect?'

'Well, of course, she came down after her aunt's death and she was here for the funeral. And, of course, I've seen her about before when she's been staying down here. A very handsome girl.'

'Yes, indeed – but too thin – definitely too thin.'

Nurse Carruthers, conscious of her own comfortable plumpness, preened herself slightly.

'Of course,' she said, one shouldn't be *too* thin.'

'Poor girl,' continued Poirot. 'I am sorry for her. *Entre nous,*' he leaned forward confidentially, 'her aunt's will was a great blow.'

'I suppose it must have been,' said Nurse Carruthers. 'I know it caused a good deal of *talk*.'

'I cannot imagine what induced Miss Arundell to disinherit all her family. It seems an extraordinary procedure.'

'Most extraordinary. I agree with you. And, of course, people say there must have been something behind it all.'

'Did you ever get any idea of the *reason*? Did old Miss Arundell say anything?'

No. Not to me – that is.'

'But to somebody else?'

'Well, I rather fancy she mentioned *something* to Miss Lawson because I heard Miss Lawson say, "Yes, dear, but you see it's at the lawyer's." And Miss Arundell said "I'm sure it's in the drawer downstairs. And Miss Lawson said, "No, you sent it to Mr Purvis. Don't you remember?" And then my patient had an attack of nausea again and Miss Lawson went away while I saw to her, but I've often wondered if it was the will they were talking about.'

'It certainly seems probable.'

Nurse Carruthers went on:

If so, I expect Miss Arundell was worried and perhaps wanted to alter it – but there, she was so ill, poor dear, after that – that she was past thinking of anything.'

'Did Miss Lawson take part in the nursing at all?' asked Poirot.

'Oh, dear no, she was no manner of good! Too fussy, you know. She only irritated my patient.'

'Did you, then, do all the nursing yourself? *C'est formidable ça.*'

'The maid – what was her name? – Ellen, helped me. Ellen was very good. She was used to illness and used to looking after the old lady. We managed pretty well between us. As a matter of fact, Dr Grainger was sending in a night nurse on the Friday, but Miss Arundell died before the night nurse arrived.'

'Perhaps Miss Lawson helped to prepare some of the invalid's food?'

'No, she didn't do anything at all. There wasn't really anything to prepare. I had the Valentine and the brandy – and the Brand's and glucose and all that. All Miss Lawson did was to go about the house crying and getting in everyone's way.'

The nurse's tone held distinct acrimony.

'I can see,' said Poirot, smiling, 'that you have not a very high opinion of Miss Lawson's usefulness.'

'Companions are usually a poor lot, in my opinion. They're not *trained*, you see, in any way. Just *amateurs*. And usually they're women who wouldn't be any good at anything else.'

Do you think Miss Lawson was very attached to Miss Arundell?'

'She seemed to be. Very upset and took on terribly when the old lady died. More than the relatives did, in *my* opinion,' Nurse Carruthers finished with a sniff.

'Perhaps, then,' said Poirot, nodding his head sagely, 'Miss Arundell knew what she was doing when she left her money as she did.'

'She was a very shrewd old lady,' said the nurse. 'There wasn't much *she* didn't take in and know about, I must say!'

'Did she mention the dog, Bob, at all?'

'It's funny you should say that! She talked about him a lot – when she was delirious. Something about his ball and a fall she'd had. A nice dog, Bob was – I'm very fond of dogs. Poor fellow, he was very miserable when she died. Wonderful, aren't they? Quite human.'

And on the note of the humanity of dogs, we parted.

'There is one who has clearly no suspicions,' remarked Poirot after we had left.

He sounded slightly discouraged.

We had a bad dinner at The George – Poirot groaning a good deal, especially over the soup.

'And it is so easy, Hastings, to make good soup. *Le pot au feu*—'

I avoided a disquisition on cookery with some difficulty.

After dinner we had a surprise.

We were sitting in the lounge', which we had to ourselves. There had been one other man at dinner – a commercial traveller, by his appearance – but he had gone out. I was just idly turning over the pages of an antiquated *Stock-Breeder's Gazette* or some such periodical when I suddenly heard Poirot's name being mentioned.

The voice in question was somewhere outside.

'Where is he? In here? Right – I can find him.'

The door was flung violently open, and Dr Grainger, his face rather red, his eyebrows working irritably, strode into the room. He paused to close the door and then advanced upon us in no uncertain fashion.

'Oh, here you are! Now then, M. Hercule Poirot, what the

devil do you mean by coming round to see me and telling me a
pack of lies?'

'One of the juggler's balls?' I murmured maliciously.

Poirot said in his oiliest voice:

'My dear doctor, you must allow me to explain—'

'Allow you? Allow you? Damn it, I'll *force* you to explain!
You're a detective, that's what you are! A nosing, prying detective! Coming round to me and feeding me up with a pack of
lies about writing old General Arundell's biography! More fool
me to be taken in by such a damn-fool story.'

'Who told you of my identity?' asked Poirot.

'Who told me? Miss Peabody told me. *She* saw through you
all right!'

'Miss Peabody – yes.' Poirot sounded reflective. 'I rather
thought—'

Dr Grainger cut in angrily.

Now then, sir, I'm waiting for your explanation!'

'Certainly. My explanation is very simple. *Attempted murder.*'

'What? What's that?'

Poirot said quietly:

'Miss Arundell had a fall, did she not? A fall down the stairs
shortly before her death?'

'Yes, what of it? She slipped on that damned dog's ball.'

Poirot shook his head.

'No Doctor, *she did not*. A *thread* was fastened across the top
of the stairs so as to trip her up.'

Dr Grainger stared.

'Then why didn't she tell me so?' he demanded. 'Never said
a word to me about it.'

'That is perhaps understandable – if it were *a member of her
own family* who placed that thread there!'

'H'm – I see.' Grainger cast a sharp glance at Poirot, then
threw himself into a chair. Well?' he said. 'How did you come
to be mixed up in this affair?'

'Miss Arundell wrote to me, stressing the utmost secrecy.
Unfortunately the letter was delayed.'

Poirot proceeded to give certain carefully edited details and
explained the finding of the nail driven into the skirting-board.

The doctor listened with a grave face. His anger had abated.

'You can comprehend my position was a difficult one,' Poirot
finished. 'I was employed, you see, by a dead woman. But I
counted the obligation none the less strong for that.'

Dr Grainger's brows were drawn together in thought.

'And you've no idea who it was stretched that thread across the head of the stairs?' he asked.

'I have no *evidence* as to who it was. I will not say I have no *idea*.'

'It's a nasty story,' said Grainger, his face grim.

'Yes. You can understand, can you not, that to begin with I was uncertain whether there had or had not been a sequel?'

'Eh? What's that?'

'To all intents and purposes Miss Arundell died a natural death, but could one be sure of that? There had been *one* attempt on her life. How could I be sure that there had not been a second? And this a successful one!'

Grainger nodded thoughtfully.

I suppose you are *sure*, Dr Grainger – please do not get angry – that Miss Arundell's death *was* a natural one? I have come across certain evidence today—'

He detailed the conversation he had had with old Angus, Charles Arundell's interest in the weed-killer, and finally the old man's surprise at the emptiness of the tin.

Grainger listened with keen attention. When Poirot had finished he said quietly:

'I see your point. Many a case of arsenical poisoning has been diagnosed as acute gastric enteritis and a certificate given – especially when there are no suspicious contributing circumstances. In any case, arsenical poisoning presents certain difficulties – it has so many different forms. It may be acute, subacute, nervous of chronic. There may be vomiting and abdominal pain – these symptoms may be entirely absent – the person may fall suddenly to the ground and expire shortly afterwards – there may be narcotism and paralysis. The symptoms vary widely.'

Poirot said:

'*Eh bien*, taking the facts into account, what is your opinion?'

Dr Grainger was silent for a minute or two. Then he said slowly:

'Taking everything into account, and without any bias whatever, I am of the opinion that no form of arsenical poisoning could account for the symptoms in Miss Arundell's case. She died, I am quite convinced, of yellow atrophy of the liver. I have, as you know, attended her for many years, and she had suffered previously from attacks similar to that which caused her death. That is my considered opinion, M. Poirot.'

And there, perforce, the matter had to rest.

It seemed rather an anticlimax when, somewhat apologetically, Poirot produced the package of Liver Capsules he had bought at the chemist's.

'Miss Arundell took these, I believe?' he said. 'I suppose they could not be injurious in any way?'

'That stuff? No harm in it. *Aloes – podophyllin* – all quite mild and harmless,' said Grainger. 'She liked trying the stuff. I didn't mind.'

He got up.

'You dispensed certain medicines for her yourself?' asked Poirot.

'Yes – a mild liver pill to be taken after food.' His eyes twinkled. She could have taken a boxfull without hurting herself. I'm not given to poisoning my patients, M. Poirot.'

Then, with a smile, he shook hands with us both and departed.

Poirot undid the package he had purchased at the chemist's. The medicament consisted of transparent capsules, three-quarters full of a dark brown powder.

'They look like a seasick remedy I once took,' I remarked.

Poirot opened a capsule, examined its contents and tasted it gingerly with his tongue. He made a grimace.

'Well,' I said, throwing myself back in my chair and yawning, 'everything seems harmless enough. Dr Loughbarrow's specialities, and Dr Grainger's pills! And Dr Grainger seems definitely to negative the arsenic theory. Are you convinced at last, my stubborn Poirot?'

'It is true that I am pig-headed – that is your expression, I think? Yes, definitely I have the head of the pig,' said my friend meditatively.

'Then, in spite of having the chemist, the nurse and the doctor against you, you still think that Miss Arundell was murdered?'

Poirot said quietly: 'That is what I believe. No – more than believe. I am *sure* of it, Hastings.'

'There's one way of proving it, I suppose,' I said slowly. Exhumation.'

Poirot nodded.

'Is that the next step?'

'My friend, I have to go carefully.'

'Why?'

'Because,' his voice dropped. 'I am afraid of a second tragedy.'

'You mean—?'

'I am afraid, Hastings, I am afraid. Let us leave it at that.'

THE WOMAN ON THE STAIRS

On the following morning a note arrived by hand. It was in a rather weak, uncertain handwriting, slanting very much uphill.

Dear M. Poirot,
 I hear from Ellen that you were at Littlegreen House yesterday. I shall be much obliged if you could call and see me sometime today.

Yours truly,
WILHELMINA LAWSON

'So *she's* down here,' I remarked.

'Yes.'

'Why has she come, I wonder?'

Poirot smiled. 'I do not suppose there is any sinister reason. After all, the house belongs to her.'

'Yes, that's true, of course. You know, Poirot, that's the worst of this game of ours. Every single little thing that anyone does is open to the most sinister constructions.'

'It is true that I myself have enjoined upon you the motto, "suspect every one".'

'Are you still in that state yourself?'

'No – for me it has boiled down to this. I suspect one particular person.'

'Which one?'

'Since, at the moment, it is only suspicion and there is no definite proof, I think I must leave you to draw your own deductions, Hastings. And do not neglect the psychology – that is important. The character of the murder – implying as it does a certain temperament in the murderer – that is an essential clue to the crime.'

'I can't consider the character of the murderer if I don't know who the murderer is!'

'No, no, you have not paid attention to what I have just said. If you reflect sufficiently on the character – the necessary character – of the *murder, then* you will realize *who* the murderer is!'

'Do you really know, Poirot?' I asked curiously.

'I cannot say I *know*, because I have no proofs. That is why I cannot say more at the present. But I am quite sure – yes, my friend, in my own mind I am very sure.'

'Well,' I said, laughing, 'mind he doesn't get *you*! That *would* be a tragedy!'

Poirot started a little. He did not take the matter as a joke. Instead he murmured: 'You are right. I must be careful – extremely careful.'

'You ought to wear a coat of chain mail,' I said chaffingly. 'And employ a taster, in case of poison! In fact, you ought to have a regular band of gunmen to protect you!'

'*Merci*, Hastings, I shall rely on my wits.'

He then wrote a note to Miss Lawson saying that he would call at Littlegreen House at eleven o'clock.

After that we breakfasted and then strolled out into the Square. It was about a quarter past ten and a hot, sleepy morning.

I was looking into the window of the antique shop at a very nice set of Hepplewhite chairs when I received a highly painful lunge in the ribs, and a sharp, penetrating voice said: 'Hi!'

I spun round indignantly, to find myself face to face with Miss Peabody. In her hand (the instrument of her assault upon me) was a large and powerful umbrella with a spiked point.

Apparently completely callous to the severe pain she had inflicted, she observed in a satisfied voice:

'Ha! Thought it was you. Don't often make a mistake.'

I said rather coldly:

'Er – good morning. Can I do anything for you?'

'You can tell me how that friend of yours is getting on with his book – *Life of General Arundell*?'

'He hasn't actually started to write it yet,' I said.

Miss Peabody indulged in a little silent but apparently satisfying laughter. She shook like a jelly. Recovering from that attack, she remarked:

'No, I don't supose he will be starting to write it.'

I said, smiling:

'So you saw through our little fiction?'

'What d'you take me for – a fool?' asked Miss Peabody. 'I saw soon enough what your downy friend was after! Wanted me to talk! Well, I didn't mind. I like talking. Hard to get anyone to listen nowadays. Quite enjoyed myself that afternoon.'

She cocked a shrewd eye at me.

'What's it all about, eh? What's it all about?'

I was hesitating what exactly to reply when Poirot joined us. He bowed with *empressement* to Miss Peabody.

'Good morning, Mademoiselle. Enchanted to encounter you.'

'Good morning,' said Miss Peabody. 'What are you this morning, Parotti or Poirot – eh?'

'It was very clever of you to pierce my disguise so rapidly,' said Poirot, smiling.

'Wasn't much disguise to pierce! Not many like you about, are there? Don't know if that's a good thing or a bad one. Difficult to say.'

'I prefer, mademoiselle, to be unique.'

'You've got your wish, I should say,' said Miss Peabody dryly. 'Now then, Mr Poirot, I gave you all the gossip you wanted the other day. Now it's my turn to ask questions. What's it all about? Eh? What's it all about?'

'Are you not asking a question to which you already know the answer?'

'I wonder.' She shot a sharp glance at him. 'Something fishy about that will? Or is it something else? Going to dig Emily up? Is that it?'

Poirot did not answer.

Miss Peabody nodded her head slowly and thoughtfully, as though she had received a reply.

'Often wondered,' she said inconsequently, 'what it would feel like . . . Readin' the papers, you know – wondered if anyone would ever be dug up in Market Basing . . . Didn't think it would be Emily Arundell . . .'

She gave him a sudden, piercing look.

'She wouldn't have liked it, you know. I suppose you've thought of that – hey?'

'Yes, I have thought of it.'

'I suppose you would do – you're not a fool! Don't think you're particularly officious either.'

Poirot bowed. 'Thank you, mademoiselle.'

'And that's more than most people would say – looking at your moustache. Why d'you have a moustache like that? D'you like it?'

I turned away convulsed with laughter.

'In England the cult of the moustache is lamentably neglected,' said Poirot. His hand surreptitiously caressed the hirsute adornment.

'Oh, I see! Funny,' said Miss Peabody. 'Knew a woman once who had a goitre and was proud of it! Wouldn't believe that, but it's true! Well, what I say is, it's lucky when you're pleased with what the Lord has given you. It's usually the other way about.'

She shook her head and sighed.

'Never thought there would be a murder in this out-of-the-world spot.' Again she shot a sudden, piercing look at Poirot. 'Which of 'em did it?'

'Am I to shout that to you here in the street?'

'Probably means you don't know. Or do you? Oh, well – bad blood. I'd like to know whether that Varley woman poisoned her husband or not. Makes a difference.'

'You believe in heredity?'

Miss Peabody said suddenly:

'I'd rather it was Tanios. An outsider! But wishes ain't horses, worst luck. Well, I'll be getting along. I can see you're not goin' to tell me anything . . . Who are you actin' for, by the way?'

Poirot said gravely:

'I am acting for the dead, mademoiselle.'

I am sorry to say that Miss Peabody received this remark with a sudden shiek of laughter. Quickly subduing her mirth she said:

'Excuse me. It sounded like Isabel Tripp – that's all! What an awful woman! Julia's worse, I think. So painfully girlish. Never did like mutton dressed lamb-fashion. Well, goodbye. Seen Dr Grainger at all?'

'Mademoiselle, I have the bone to pick with you. You betrayed my secret.'

Miss Peabody indulged in her peculiar throaty chuckle.

'Men are simple! He'd swallowed that preposterous tissue of lies you told him. Wasn't he mad when I told him! Went away snorting with rage! He's looking for you.'

'He found me last night.'

'Oh! I wish I'd been there.'

'I wish you had, mademoiselle,' said Poirot gallantly.

Miss Peabody laughed and prepared to waddle away. She addressed me over her shoulder.

'Goodbye, young man. Don't you go buying those chairs. They're a fake.'

She moved off, chuckling.

'That,' said Poirot, 'is a very clever old woman.'

'Even although she did not admire your moustaches?'

'Taste is one thing,' said Poirot coldly. 'Brains are another.'

We passed into the shop and spent a pleasant twenty minutes

looking round. We emerged unscathed in pocket and proceeded in the direction of Littlegreen House.

Ellen, rather redder in the face than usual, admitted us and showed us into the drawing room. Presently footsteps were heard descending the stairs and Miss Lawson came in. She seemed somewhat out of breath and flustered. Her hair was pinned up in a silk handkerchief.

'I hope you'll excuse my coming in like this, M. Poirot. I've been going through some locked-up cupboards – so many things – old people are inclined to *hoard* a little, I'm afraid – dear Miss Arundell was no exception – and one gets so much dust in one's *hair* –astonishing, you know, the things people collect – if you can believe me, two dozen needlebooks – actually two dozen.'

'You mean that Miss Arundell had bought two dozen needlebooks?'

'Yes, and put them away and forgot about them – and, of course, now the needles are all rusty – such a pity. She used to give them to the maids as Christmas presents.'

'She was very forgetful – yes?'

'Oh, *very*. Especially in the way of putting things away. Like a dog with a bone, you know. That's what we used to call it between us. 'Now don't go and dog and bone it,' I used to say to her.'

She laughed, and then, producing a small handkerchief from her pocket, suddenly began to sniff.

'Oh, dear,' she said tearfully. 'It seems so dreadful of me to be laughing here.'

'You have too much sensibility,' said Poirot. 'You feel things too much.'

'That's what my mother always used to say to me, M. Poirot. 'You take things to heart too much, Mina,' she used to say. It's a great drawback, M. Poirot, to be so sensitive. Especially when one has one's living to get.'

'Ah, yes, indeed; but that is all a thing of the past. You are now your own mistress. You can enjoy yourself – travel – you have absolutely no worries or anxieties.'

'I suppose that's true,' said Miss Lawson rather doubtfully.

'Assuredly it is true. Now, talking of Miss Arundell's forgetfulness, I see how it was that her letter to me never reached me for so long a time.'

He explained the circumstances of the finding of the letter. A red spot showed in Miss Lawson's cheek. She said:

'Ellen should have told *me*! To send that letter off to you

543

without a word was great impertinence! She should have consulted me first. *Great* impertinence, I call it! Not one word did I hear about the whole thing. Disgraceful!'

'Oh, my dear lady, I am sure it was done in all good faith.'

'Well, I think it was very *peculiar* myself! *Very* peculiar! Servants really do the oddest things. Ellen should have remembered that I am the mistress of the house now.'

She drew herself up importantly.

'Ellen was very devoted to her mistress, was she not?' said Poirot.

'Yes, I dare say; but that makes no difference. I should have been *told*!'

'The important thing is – that I received the letter,' said Poirot.

'Oh, I agree that it's no good making a fuss after things have happened, but all the same I think Ellen ought to be told that she mustn't take it upon herself to do things without asking first!'

She stopped, a red spot on each cheekbone.

Poirot was silent for a minute, then he said:

'You wanted to see me today? In what way can I be of service to you?'

Miss Lawson's annoyance subsided as promptly as it had arisen. She began to be flustered and incoherent again.

'Well, really – you see, I just *wondered* . . . Well, to tell the truth, M. Poirot, I arrived down here yesterday and, of course, Ellen told me you had been here, and I just wondered – well, as you hadn't *mentioned* to me that you were coming – well, it seemed rather *odd* – and I couldn't see—'

'You could not see what I was doing down here?' Poirot finished for her.

'I – well, – no, that's exactly it. I couldn't.'

She looked at him, flushed but inquiring.

'I must make a little confession to you,' said Poirot. 'I have permitted you to remain under a misapprehension, I am afraid. You assumed that the letter I received from Miss Arundell concerned itself with the question of a small sum of money abstracted by – in all possibility – Mr Charles Arundell.'

Miss Lawson nodded.

'But that, you see, was not the case . . . In fact, the first I heard of the stolen money was from you . . . Miss Arundell wrote to me on the subject of her accident.'

'Her accident?'

'Yes, she had a fall downstairs, I understand.'

'Oh, quite – quite—' Miss Lawson looked bewildered. She stared vacantly at Poirot. She went on: 'But – I'm sorry – I'm sure it's very stupid of me – but why should she write to *you*? I understand – in fact, I think you said so – that you are a detective. You're not a – doctor, too? Or a faith healer, perhaps?'

'No, I am not a doctor – nor a faith healer. But, like the doctor, I concern myself sometimes with so-called accidental deaths.'

'With accidental deaths?'

'With *so-called* accidental deaths, I said. It is true that Miss Arundell did not *die* – but she might have died!'

'Oh, dear me, yes; the doctor said so. But I don't understand—'

Miss Lawson sounded still bewildered.

'The cause of the accident was supposed to be the ball of the little Bob, was it not?'

'Yes, yes, that was it. It was Bob's ball.'

'Oh, no, it was not Bob's ball.'

'But excuse me, Mr Poirot, I saw it there myself – as we all ran down.'

'You saw it – yes, perhaps. But *it was not the cause of the accident. The cause of the accident, Miss Lawson, was a dark-coloured thread stretched about a foot above the top of the stairs!*'

'But – but a dog couldn't—'

'Exactly,' said Poirot quickly. 'A dog could not do that – he is not sufficiently intelligent – or, if you like, he is not sufficiently *evil* . . . *A human being* put that thread in position . . .'

Miss Lawson's face had gone deadly white. She raised a shaking hand to her face.

'Oh, Mr Poirot – I can't believe it – you don't mean – but that is awful – really awful. You mean it was done on *purpose*?'

'Yes, it was done on purpose.'

'But that's dreadful. It's almost like – like killing a person.'

'If it had succeeded it *would* have been killing a person! In other words, it would have been murder!'

Miss Lawson gave a little shrill cry.

Poirot went on in the same grave tone:

'A nail was driven into the skirting-board so that the thread could be attached. The nail was varnished so as not to show. Tell me, do you ever remember a smell of varnish that you could not account for?'

Miss Lawson gave a cry.

'Oh, how extraordinary! To think of that! Why, of course!

And to think I never thought – never dreamed – but then, how could I? And yet it did seem odd to me at the time.'

Poirot leant forward.

'So – you can help us, mademoiselle. Once again you can help us. *C'est épatant!*'

'To think that was it! Oh, well, it all fits in.'

'Tell me, I pray of you. You smelt varnish – yes?'

'Yes. Of course, I didn't know what it was. I thought – dear me – is it paint? – no, it's more like floor-stain, and then, of course, I thought I must have *imagined* it.'

'When was this?'

'Now let me see – when was it?'

'Was it during that Easter weekend, when the house was full of guests?'

'Yes, that was the time – but I'm trying to recall just which day it was . . . Now, let me see, it wasn't Sunday. No, and it wasn't on Tuesday – that was the night Dr Donaldson came to dinner. And on the Wednesday they had all left. No, of course, it was the *Monday* – Bank Holiday. I'd been lying awake – rather worried, you know. I always think Bank Holiday is such a worrying day! There had been only just enough cold beef to go round at supper, and I was afraid Miss Arundell might be annoyed about it. You see, *I'd* ordered the joint on the Saturday, and of course I ought to have said seven pounds, but I thought five pounds would do nicely, but Miss Arundell was always so vexed if there was any shortage – she was so hospitable—'

Miss Lawson paused to draw a deep breath and then rushed on:

'And so I was lying awake and wondering whether she'd say anything about it tomorrow, and what with one thing and another I was a long time dropping off – and then, just as I was going off, something seemed to wake me up – a sort of rap or tap – and I sat up in bed, and then I sniffed. Of course, I'm always terrified of fire – sometimes I think I smell fire two or three times a night (so awful, wouldn't it be, if one were *trapped*?). Anyway, there was a smell, and I sniffed hard; but it wasn't smoke or anything like that. And I said to myself, it's more like paint or floor-stain – but, of course, one wouldn't smell that in the middle of the night. But it was quite strong, and I sat up sniffing and sniffing, and then saw her in the glass—'

'Saw *her*? Saw whom?'

'In my looking glass, you know, it's really most convenient. I left my door open a little always, so as to hear Miss Arundell if she were to call, and if she went up and down stairs I could see her. The one light was always left switched on in the passage. That's how I came to see her kneeling on the stairs – Theresa, I mean. She was kneeling on about the third step, with her head bent down over something, and I was just thinking. "How odd! I wonder if she's *ill*?" when she got up and went away, so I supposed she'd just slipped or something. Or perhaps was stooping to pick something up. But, of course, I never thought about it again one way or another.

'The tap that aroused you would be the tap of the hammer on the nail,' mused Poirot.

'Yes, I suppose it would. But oh, M. Poirot, how *dreadful* – how truly dreadful! I've always felt Theresa was, perhaps, a little *wild*, but to do a thing like that—'

'You are sure it was Theresa?'

'Oh, dear me, yes.'

'It couldn't have been Mrs Tanios or one of the maids, for instance?'

'Oh, no, it was Theresa.'

Miss Lawson shook her head and murmured to herself. 'Oh, dear, oh, dear,' several times.

Poirot was staring at her in a way I found it hard to understand.

'Permit me,' he said suddenly, 'to make an experiment. Let us go upstairs and endeavour to reconstruct this little scene.'

'Reconstruct? Oh, really – I don't know – I mean I don't quite see—'

'I will show you,' said Poirot, cutting in upon these doubts in an authoritative manner.

Somewhat flustered, Miss Lawson led the way upstairs.

'I hope the room's tidy – so much to do – what with one thing and another—' She tailed off incoherently.

The room was indeed somewhat heavily littered with miscellaneous articles, obviously the result of Miss Lawson's turning out of cupboards. With her usual incoherence, Miss Lawson managed to indicate her own position, and Poirot was able to verify for himself the fact that a portion of the staircase was reflected in the wall-mirror.

'And now, mademoiselle,' he suggested, 'if you will be so good as to go out and reproduce the actions that you saw.'

Miss Lawson, still murmuring, 'Oh, dear—' bustled out to fulfil her part. Poirot acted the part of observer.

The performance concluded, he went out on the landing and asked which electric light had been left switched on.

'This one – this one along here. Just outside Miss Arundell's door.'

Poirot reached up, detached the bulb and examined it.

'A forty-watt lamp, I see. Not very powerful.'

'No, it was just so that the passage shouldn't be quite dark.'

Poirot retraced his steps to the top of the stairs.

'You will pardon me, mademoiselle, but with the light being fairly dim and the way that shadow falls it is hardly possible that you can have seen very clearly. Can you be positive it was Miss Theresa Arundell, and not just an indeterminate female figure in a dressing-gown?'

Miss Lawson was indignant.

'No, indeed, M. Poirot! I'm *perfectly* sure! I know Theresa well enough, I should hope! Oh, it was her all right. Her dark dressing-gown and that big shining brooch she wears with the initials – I saw that plainly.'

'So there is no possible doubt. You saw the initials?'

'Yes, T. A. I know the brooch. Theresa often wore it. Oh, yes, I could swear to its being Theresa – and I will swear to it, if necessary!'

There was a firmness and decision in those last two sentences that was quite at variance with her usual manner.

Poirot looked at her. Again there was something in his glance. It was aloof, appraising – and had also a queer appearance of finality about it.

'You would swear to that, yes?' he said.

'If – if – it's necessary. But I suppose it – will it be necessary?'

Again Poirot turned that appraising glance upon her.

'That will depend on the result of the exhumation,' he said.

'Ex – exhumation?'

Poirot put out a restraining hand. In her excitement Miss Lawson very nearly went headlong down the stairs.

'It may possibly be a question of exhumation,' he said.

'Oh, but surely – how *very* unpleasant! But I mean, I'm sure the family would oppose the idea very strongly – very strongly indeed.'

'Probably they will.'

'I'm quite sure they won't hear of such a thing!'

'Ah, but if it is an order from the Home Office.'

'But, M. Poirot – *why*? I mean it's not as though – not as though—'

'Not as though what?'

'Not as though there were anything – *wrong*.'

'You think not?'

'No, of course not. Why, there *couldn't* be! I mean the doctor and the nurse and everything—'

'Do not upset yourself,' said Poirot calmly and soothingly.

'Oh, but I can't help it! Poor dear Miss Arundell! It's not even as though Theresa had been here in the house when she died.'

'No, she left on the Monday before she was taken ill, did she not?'

'Quite early in the morning. So, you see, *she* can't have had anything to do with it!'

'Let us hope not,' said Poirot.

'Oh, dear. Miss Lawson clasped her hands together. 'I've never known *anything* so dreadful as all this. Really, I don't know whether I'm on my head or my heels.'

Poirot glanced at his watch.

'We must depart. We are returning to London. And you, mademoiselle, you are remaining down here some little time?'

'No – no . . . I have really no settled plans. Actually, I'm going back myself today . . . I only came down just for a night to – to settle things a little.'

'I see. Well, goodbye, mademoiselle, and forgive me if I have upset you at all.'

'Oh, M. Poirot. *Upset* me? I feel quite *ill*! Oh, dear – oh, dear! It's such a *wicked* world! Such a dreadfully wicked world!'

Poirt cut short her lamentations by taking her hand firmly in his.

'Quite so. And you are still ready to swear *that you saw Theresa Arundell kneeling on the stairs on the night of Easter Bank Holiday*?'

'Oh, yes, I can swear to that.'

'And you can also swear that you saw a halo of light round Miss Arundell's head during the *séance*?'

Miss Lawson's mouth fell open.

'Oh, M. Poirot, don't – don't joke about these things.'

'I am not joking. I am perfectly serious.'

Miss Lawson said with dignity:

'It wasn't exactly a halo. It was more like the beginning of a manifestation. A ribbon of some luminous material. I think it was beginning to form into a face.'

'Extremely interesting. *Au revoir*, mademoiselle, and please keep all this to yourself.'

'Oh, of course – of course. I shouldn't dream of doing anything else . . .'

The last we saw of Miss Lawson was her rather sheeplike face gazing after us from the front-door step.

———— 23 ————

DR TANIOS CALLS ON US

No sooner had we left the house than Poirot's manner changed. His face was grim and set.

'*Dépêchons nous,* Hastings,' he said. 'We must get back to London as soon as possible.'

'I'm willing.' I quickened my pace to suit his. I stole a look at his grave face.

'Who do you suspect, Poirot?' I asked. 'I wish you'd tell me. Do you believe it was Theresa Arundell on the stairs or not?'

Poirot did not reply to my question. Instead he asked a question of his own.

'Did it strike you – reflect before you answer – did it strike you that there was something *wrong* with that statement of Miss Lawson's?'

'How do you mean – wrong with it?'

'If I knew that I should not be asking you!'

'Yes, but wrong in what way?'

'That is just it. I cannot be precise. But as she was talking I had, somehow, a feeling of unreality . . . as though there was something – some small point that was wrong – that was, yes, that was the feeling – something that was *impossible* . . .'

'She seemed quite positive it was Theresa!'

'Yes, yes.'

'But, after all, the light couldn't have been very good. I don't see how she can be quite so sure.'

'No, no, Hastings, you are not helping me. It was some small point – something connected with – yes, I am sure of it – with the bedroom.'

'With the bedroom?' I repeated, trying to recall the details of the room. 'No,' I said at last. 'I can't help you.'

Poirot shook his head vexedly.

'Why did you bring up that spiritualistic business again?' I asked.

'Because it is important.'

'What is important? Miss Lawson's luminous "ribbon development"?'

'You remember the Misses Tripp's description of the *séance*?'

'I know they saw a halo round the old lady's head.' I laughed in spite of myself. '*I* shouldn't think she was a saint, by all accounts! Miss Lawson seems to have been terrified by her. I felt quite sorry for the poor woman when she described how she lay awake, worried to death because she might get into trouble over ordering too small a sirloin of beef.'

'Yes, it was an interesting touch that.'

'What are we going to do when we get to London?' I asked as we turned into The George and Poirot asked for the bill.

'We must go and see Theresa Arundell immediately.'

'And find out the truth? But won't she deny the whole thing, anyway?'

'*Mon cher*, it is not a criminal offence to kneel upon a flight of stairs! She may have been picking up a pin to bring her luck – something of that sort!'

'And the smell of varnish?'

We could say no more just then, as the waiter arrived with the bill.

On the way to London we talked very little. I am not fond of talking and driving, and Poirot was so busy protecting his moustaches with his muffler from the disastrous effects of wind and dust that speech was quite beyond him.

We arrived at the flat at about twenty to two.

George, Poirot's immaculate and extremely English manservant, opened the door.

'A Dr Tanios is waiting to see you, sir. He has been here for half an hour.'

'Dr Tanios? Where is he?'

'In the sitting room, sir. A lady also called to see you, sir. She seemed very distressed to find you were absent from home. It was before I received your telephone message, sir, so I could not tell her when you would be returning to London.'

'Dscribe this lady.'

'She was about five-foot-seven, sir, with dark hair and light blue eyes. She was wearing a grey coat and skirt and a hat worn very much to the back of the head instead of over the right eye.'

'Mrs Tanios,' I ejaculated in a low voice.

'She seemed in a condition of great nervous excitement, sir.

Said it was of the utmost importance she should find you quickly.'

'What time was this?'

'About half past ten, sir.'

Poirot shook his head as he passed on towards the sitting room.

'That is the second time I have missed hearing what Mrs Tanios has to say. What would you say, Hastings? Is there a fate in it?'

'Third time lucky,' I said consolingly.

Poirot shook his head doubtfully.

'Will there be a third time? I wonder. Come, let us hear what the husband has to say.'

Dr Tanios was sitting in an armchair reading one of Poirot's books on psychology. He sprang up and greeted us.

'You must forgive this intrusion. I hope you don't mind my forcing my way in and waiting for you like this.'

'*Du tout, du tout*. Pray sit down. Permit me to offer you a glass of sherry.'

'Thank you. As a matter of fact, I have an excuse. M. Poirot, I am worried, terribly worried about my wife.'

'About your wife? I'm very sorry. What's the matter?'

Tanios said: 'You have seen her perhaps, lately?'

It seemed quite a natural question, but the quick look that accompanied it was not so natural.

Poirot replied in the most matter-of-fact manner:

'No, not since I saw her at the hotel with you yesterday.'

'Ah – I thought perhaps she might have called upon you.'

Poirot was busy pouring out three glasses of sherry. He said in a slightly abstracted voice:

'No. Was there any – reason for her calling on me?'

'No, no.' Dr Tanios accepted his sherry. 'Thank you. Thank you very much. No, there was no exact *reason*, but, to be frank, I am very much concerned about my wife's state of health.'

'Ah, she is not strong?'

'Her bodily health,' said Tanios slowly, 'is good. I wish I could say the same for her mind.'

'Ah?'

'I fear, M. Poirot, that she is on the verge of a complete nervous breakdown.'

'My dear Dr Tanios, I am extremely sorry to hear this.'

'This condition has been growing for some time. During the last two months her manner towards me has completely changed. She is nervous, easily startled, and she has the oddest fancies – actually they are more than fancies – they are *delusions*!'

'Really?'

'Yes She is suffering from what is commonly known as persecution mainia – a fairly well-known condition.'

Poirot made a sympathetic noise with his tongue.

'You can understand my anxiety!'

'Naturally. Naturally. But what I do not quite understand is why you have come to me. How can I help you?'

Dr Tanios seemed a little embarrassed.

'It occurred to me that my wife might have – or may yet – come to you with some extraordinary tale. She may conceivably say that she is in danger from me – something of that kind.'

'But why should she come to *me*?'

Dr Tanios smiled – it was a charming smile, genial, yet wistful.

'You are a celebrated detective, M. Poirot. I saw – I could see at once – that my wife was very impressed at meeting you yesterday. The mere fact of meeting a detective would make a powerful impression on her in her present state. It seems to me highly probable that she might seek you out and – and – well confide in you. That is the way these nervous affections go! There is a tendency to turn against those nearest and dearest to you.'

'Very distressing.'

'Yes, indeed. I am very fond of my wife.' There was a rich tenderness in his voice. 'I always feel it was so brave of her to marry me – a man of another race – to come out to a far country – to leave all her own friends and surroundings. For the last few days I have been really distraught . . . I can see only one thing for it . . .'

'Yes?'

'Perfect rest and quiet and suitable psychological treatment. There is a splendid home I know of run by a first-class man. I want to take her down there – it is in Norfolk – straightaway. Perfect rest and isolation from outside influence – that is what is needed. I feel convinced that once she has been there a month or two under skilled treatment there will be a change for the better.'

'I see,' said Poirot.

He uttered the words in a matter-of-fact manner without any clue to the feelings that prompted him.

Tanios again shot a quick glance at him.

'That is why, if she should come to you, I should be obliged if you will let me know at once.'

'But certainly. I will telephone you. You are at the Durham Hotel still?'

'Yes. I am going back there now.'

'And your wife is not there?'

'She went out directly after breakfast.'

'Without telling you where she was going?'

'Without saying a word. That is most unlike her.'

'And the children?'

'She took them with her.'

'I see.'

Tanios got up.

'Thank you so much, M. Poirot. I need hardly say that if she does tell you any high-flown stories of intimidation and persecution, pay no attention to them. It is, unfortunately, a part of her malady.'

'Most distressing,' said Poirot with sympathy.

'It is indeed. Although one knows, medically speaking, that it is part of a recognized mental disease, yet one cannot help being hurt when a person very near and dear to you turns against you and all their affection changes to dislike.'

'You have my deepest sympathy,' said Poirot as he shook hands with his guest.

'By the way—' Poirot's voice recalled Tanios just as he was at the door.

'Yes?'

'Do you ever prescribe chloral for your wife?'

Tanios gave a startled movement.

'I – no – at least, I may have done. But not lately. She seems to have taken an aversion to any form of sleeping-draught.'

'Ah! I suppose because she does not trust you?'

'M. Poirot!'

Tanios came striding forward angrily.

'That would be part of the disease,' said Poirot smoothly. Tanios stopped.

'Yes, yes, of course.'

'She is probably highly suspicious of anything you give her to eat or drink. Probably suspects you of wanting to poison her?'

'Dear me, M. Poirot, you are quite right. You know something of such cases, then?'

'One comes across them now and then in my profession,

554

naturally. But do not let me detain you. You may find her waiting for you at the hotel.'

'True. I hope I shall. I feel terribly anxious.'

He hurried out of the room.

Poirot went swiftly to the telephone. He flicked over the pages of the telephone directory and asked for a number.

' 'Allo – 'allo – is that the Durham Hotel? Can you tell me if Mrs Tanios is in? What? T-A-N-I-O-S. Yes, that is right. Yes? Oh, I see.'

He replaced the receiver.

'Mrs Tanios left the hotel this morning early. She returned at eleven, waited in the taxi whilst her luggage was brought down and drove away with it.'

'Does Tanios know she took away her luggage?'

'I think not as yet.'

'Where has she gone?'

'Impossible to tell.'

'Do you think she will come back here?'

'Possibly I cannot tell.'

'Perhaps she will write.'

'Perhaps.'

'What can we do?'

Poirot shook his head. He looked worried and distressed.

'Nothing at the moment. A hasty lunch and then we will go and see Theresa Arundell.'

'Do you believe it *was* her on the stairs?'

'Impossible to tell. Ont thing I made sure of – Miss Lawson could not have seen her face. She saw a tall figure in a dark dressing-gown, that is all.'

'And the brooch?'

'My dear friend, a brooch is not a part of a person's anatomy! It can be detached from that person. It can be lost – or borrowed – or even stolen.'

'In other words, you don't want to believe Theresa Arundell guilty?'

'I want to hear what she has to say on the matter.'

'And if Mrs Tanios comes back?'

'I will arrange for that.'

George brought in an omelette.

'Listen, George,' said Poirot. 'If that lady comes back, you will ask her to wait. If Dr Tanios comes while she is here, on no account let him in. If he asks if his wife is here, you will tell him she is not. You understand?'

'Perfectly, sir.'

Poirot attacked the omelette.

'This business complicates itself,' he said. 'We must step very carefully. If not – the murderer will strike again.'

'If he did you might get him.'

'Quite possibly, but I prefer the life of the innocent to the conviction of the guilty. We must go very, very carefully.'

—— 24 ——

THERESA'S DENIAL

We found Theresa Arundell just preparing to go out.

She was looking extraordinarily attractive. A small hat of the most outrageous fashion descended rakishly over one eye. I recognized with momentary amusement that Bella Tanios had worn a cheap imitation of such a hat yesterday and had worn it – as George had put it – on the back of the head instead of over the right eye. I remembered well how she had pushed it farther and farther back on her untidy hair.

Poirot said politely:

'Can I have just a minute or two, mademoiselle, or will it delay you too much?'

Theresa laughed. 'Oh, it doesn't matter. I'm always three-quarters of an hour late for everything. I might as well make it an hour.'

She led him into the sitting room. To my surprise, Dr Donaldson rose from a chair by the window.

'You've met M. Poirot already, Rex, haven't you?'

'We met at Market Basing,' said Donaldson stiffly.

'You were pretending to write the life of my drunken grandfather, I understand,' said Theresa. 'Rex, my angel, will you leave us?'

'Thank you, Theresa, but I think that from every point of view it would be advisable for me to be present at this interview.'

There was a brief duel of eyes. Theresa's were commanding. Donaldson's were impervious. She showed a quick flash of anger.

'All right, stay then, damn you!'

Dr Donaldson seemed unperturbed.

He seated himself again in the chair by the window, laying down his book on the arm of it. It was a book on the pituitary gland, I noticed.

Theresa sat down on her favourite low stool and looked impatiently at Poirot.

'Well, you've seen Purvis? What about it?'

Poirot said in a non-committal voice:

'There are – possibilities, mademoiselle.'

She looked at him thoughtfully. Then she sent a very faint glance in the direction of the doctor. It was, I think, intended as a warning to Poirot.

'But it would be well, I think,' went on Poirot, 'for me to report later, when my plans are more advanced.'

A faint smile showed for a minute on Theresa's face.

Poirot continued:

'I have today come from Market Basing, and while there I have talked to Miss Lawson. Tell me, mademoiselle, did you on the night of April 13th (that was the night of the Easter Bank Holiday) kneel upon the stairs after everyone had gone to bed?'

'My dear Hercule Poirot, what an extraordinary question! Why should I?'

'The question, mademoiselle, is not why you *should*, but whether you *did*.'

'I'm sure I don't know. I should think it most unlikely.'

'You comprehend, mademoiselle, Miss Lawson *says you did*.'

Theresa shrugged her attractive shoulders.

'Does it matter?'

'It matters very much.'

She stared at him in a perfectly amiable fashion. Poirot stared back.

'Loopy!' said Theresa.

'*Pardon?*'

'Definitely loopy!' said Theresa. 'Don't you think so, Rex?'

Dr Donaldson coughed.

'Excuse me, M. Poirot, but what is the point of the question?'

My friend spread out his hands.

'It is most simple! Some one drove in a nail in a convenient position at the head of the stairs. The nail was just touched with brown varnish to match the skirting-board.'

'Is this a new kind of witchcraft?' asked Theresa.

'No, mademoiselle, it is much more homely and simple than that. On the following evening, the Tuesday, *someone* attached a string or thread from the nail to the balusters, with the result that when Miss Arundell came out of her room she caught her foot in it and went headlong down the stairs.'

Theresa drew in her breath sharply.

'That was Bob's ball!'

'*Pardon,* it was not.'

There was a pause. It was broken by Donaldson, who said in his quiet, precise voice:

'Excuse me, but what evidence have you in support of this statement?'

Poirot said quietly:

'The evidence of the nail, the evidence of Miss Arundell's own written words, and finally the evidence of Miss Lawson's eyes.'

Theresa found her voice.

'She says *I* did it, does she?'

Poirot did not answer except by bending his head a little.

'Well, it's a lie! I had nothing to do with it!'

'You were kneeling on the stairs for quite another reason?'

'I wasn't kneeling on the stairs at all!'

'Be careful, mademoiselle.'

'I wasn't there! I never came out of my room after I went to bed on any evening I was there.'

'Miss Lawson recognized you.'

'It was probably Bella Tanios or one of the maids she saw.'

'She says it was you.'

'She's a damned liar!'

'She recognized your dressing-gown and a brooch you wear.'

'A brooch – what brooch?'

'A brooch with your initials.'

'Oh, I know the one! What a circumstantial liar she is!'

'You will deny that it was you she saw?'

'If it's my word against hers—'

'You are a better liar than she is – eh?'

Theresa said calmly:

'That's probably quite true. But in this case I'm speaking the truth. I wasn't preparing a booby-trap, or saying my prayers, or picking up gold or silver, or doing anything at all on the stairs.'

'Have you this brooch that was mentioned?'

'Probably. Do you want to see it?'

'If you please, mademoiselle.'

Theresa got up and left the room. There was an awkward silence. Dr Donaldson looked at Poirot much as I imagined he might have looked at an anatomical specimen.

Theresa returned. 'Here it is.'

She almost flung the ornament at Poirot. It was a large, rather showy chromium or stainless steel brooch with T.A. enclosed in a circle. I had to admit that it was large enough and showy enough to be easily seen in Miss Lawson's mirror.

'I never wear it now. I'm tired of it,' said Theresa. 'London's been flooded with them. Every little skivvy wears one.'

'But it was expensive when you bought it?'

'Oh, yes. They were quite exclusive to begin with.'

'When was that?'

'Last Christmas, I think it was. Yes, about then.'

'Have you ever lent it to anyone?'

'No.'

'You had it with you at Littlegreen House?'

'I suppose I did. Yes, I did. I remember.'

'Did you leave it about at all? Was it out of your possession while you were there?'

'No, it wasn't. I wore it on a green jumper, I remember. And I wore the same jumper every day.'

'And at night?'

'It was still in the jumper.'

'And the jumper?'

'Oh, hell, the jumper was sitting on a chair.'

'You are sure no one removed the brooch and put it back again the next day?'

'We'll say so in court if you like – if you think that's the best lie to tell! Actually I'm *quite sure* that nothing like that happened! It's a pretty idea that somebody framed me – but I don't think it's true.'

Poirot frowned. Then he got up, attached the brooch carefully to his coat lapel and approached a mirror on a table at the other end of the room. He stood in front of it and then moved slowly backward, getting an effect of distance.

Then he uttered a grunt.

'Imbecile that I am! Of course!'

He came back and handed the brooch to Theresa with a bow.

'You are quite right, mademoiselle. The brooch did *not* leave your possession! I have been regrettably dense.'

'I do like modesty,' said Theresa, pinning the brooch on carelessly.

She looked up at him.

'Anything more? I ought to be going.'

'Nothing that cannot be discussed later.'

Theresa moved towards the door. Poirot went on in a quiet voice:

'There is a question of exhumation, it is true—'

Theresa stopped dead. The brooch fell from her hand to the ground.

'What's that?'

Poirot said clearly:

'It is possible that the body of Miss Emily Arundell may be exhumed.'

Theresa stood still, her hands clenched. She said in a low, angry voice:

'Is this *your* doing? It can't be done without an application from the family!'

'You are wrong, mademoiselle. It can be done on an order from the Home Office.'

'My God!' said Theresa.

She turned and walked swiftly up and down.

Donaldson said quietly:

'I really don't see that there is any need to be so upset, Tessa. I dare say that to an outsider the idea is not very pleasant, but—'

She interrupted him.

'Don't be a fool, Rex!'

Poirot asked:

'The idea disturbs you, mademoiselle?'

'Of course it does! It isn't decent. Poor old Aunt Emily! Why the devil *should* she be exhumed?'

'I presume,' said Donaldson, 'that there is some doubt as to the cause of death?' He looked inquiringly at Poirot. He went on: 'I confess that I am surprised. I think that there is no doubt that Miss Arundell died a natural death from a disease of long standing.'

'You told me something about a rabbit and liver trouble once,' said Theresa. 'I've forgotten it now, but you infect a rabbit with blood from a person with yellow atrophy of the liver, and then you inject that rabbit's blood into another rabbit, and then that second rabbit's blood into a person and the person gets a diseased liver. Something like that.'

'That was merely an illustration of serum therapeutics,' said Donaldson patiently.

'Pity there are so many rabbits in the story!' said Theresa with a reckless laugh. 'None of us keep rabbits.' She turned on Poirot and her voice altered. 'M. Poirot, is this *true*?' she asked.

'It is true enough, but – there are ways of avoiding such a contingency, mademoiselle.'

'Then avoid it!' Her voice sank almost to a whisper. It was urgent, compelling. 'Avoid it *at all costs!*'

Poirot rose to his feet.

'Those are your instructions?' His voice was formal.

'Those are my instructions.'

'But, Tessa—' Donaldson interruped.

She whirled round on her fiancé.

'Be quiet. She was *my* aunt, wasn't she? Why should *my* aunt be dug up? Don't you know there will be paragraphs in the papers and gossip and general unpleasantness?' She swung round again on Poirot. 'You must stop it! I give you *carte blanche*. Do anything you like, but *stop it!*'

Poirot bowed formally.

'I will do what I can. *Au revoir, mademoiselle, au revoir, Doctor.*'

'Oh, go away!' cried Theresa. 'And take St Leonards with you. I wish I'd never set eyes on either of you.'

We left the room. Poirot did not this time deliberately place his ear to the crack, but he dallied – yes, he dallied.

And not in vain. Theresa's voice rose clear and defiant:

'Don't look at me like that, Rex.' And then suddenly, with a break in her voice: 'Darling.'

Dr Donaldson's precise voice answered her.

He said very clearly:

'That man means mischief.'

Poirot grinned suddenly. He drew me through the front door.

'Come, St Leonards,' he said, *'c'est drôle, ça!'*

Personally I thought the joke a particularly stupid one.

25

I LIE BACK AND REFLECT

No, I thought, as I hurried after Poirot, there was no doubt about it now. Miss Arundell had been murdered, and Theresa knew it. But was she herself the criminal, or was there another explanation?

She was afraid – yes. But was she afraid for herself or for

someone else? Could that someone be the quiet, precise young doctor with the calm, aloof manner?

Had the old lady died of genuine disease *artificially induced*?

Up to a point it all fitted in – Donaldson's ambitions, his belief that Theresa would inherit money at her aunt's death. Even the fact that he had been at dinner there on the evening of the accident. How easy to leave a convenient window open and return in the dead of night to tie the murderous thread across the staircase. But then, what about the placing of the nail in position?

No, Theresa must have done that. Theresa, his fiancée and accomplice. With the two of them working it together, the whole thing seemed clear enough. In that case it was probably Theresa who had actually placed the thread in position. The *first* crime, the crime that failed, had been *her* work. The second crime, the crime that had succeeded, was Donaldson's more scientific masterpiece.

'Yes – it all fitted in.

Yet even now there were loose strands. Why had Theresa blurted out those facts about inducing liver disease in human beings? It was almost as though she did not realize the truth . . . But in that case – and I felt my mind growing bewildered, and I interrupted my speculations to ask:

'Where are we going, Poirot?'

'Back to my flat. It is possible that we may find Mrs Tanios there.'

My thoughts switched off on a different track.

Mrs Tanios! That was another mystery! If Donaldson and Theresa were guilty, where did Mrs Tanios and her smiling husband come in? What did the woman want to tell Poirot and what was Tanios's anxiety to prevent her doing so?

'Poirot,' I said humbly. 'I'm getting rather muddled. They're not *all* in it, are they?'

'Murder by a syndicate? A family syndicate? No, not this time. There is the mark of one brain and one brain only in this. The psychology is clear.'

'You mean that either Theresa or Donaldson did it – but not *both* of them? Did he get her to hammer that nail in on some entirely innocent pretext, then?'

'My dear friend, from the moment I heard Miss Lawson's story I realized that there were three possibilities: (1) That Miss Lawson was telling the exact truth. (2) That Miss Lawson had invented the story for reasons of her own. (3) That Miss Lawson actually believed her own story, but that her identification rested upon the brooch – and, as I have already pointed out to you, a brooch is easily detachable from its owner.'

'Yes, but Theresa insists that the brooch did not leave her possession.'

'And she is perfectly right. I had overlooked a small but intensely significant fact.'

'Very unlike you, Poirot,' I said solemnly.

'*N'est-ce pas*? But one has one's lapses.'

'Age will tell!'

'Age has nothing to do with it,' said Poirot coldly.

'Well, what is the significant fact?' I asked as we turned in at the entrance of the Mansions.

'I will show you.'

We had just reached the flat.

George opened the door to us. In reply to Poirot's anxious questions he shook his head.

'No, sir, Mrs Tanios has not called. Neither has she telephoned.'

Poirot went into the sitting room. He paced up and down for a few moments. Then he picked up the telephone. He got first on to the Durham Hotel.

'Yes – yes, please. Ah, Dr Tanios, this is Hercule Poirot speaking. Your wife has returned? Oh, not returned. Dear me . . . Taken her luggage, you say? . . . And the children . . . You have no idea where she has gone . . . Yes, quite . . . Oh, perfectly . . . if my professional services are of any use to you? I have a certain experience in these matters . . . Such things can be done quite discreetly . . . No, of course not . . . Yes, of course that is true . . . Certainly – certainly. I shall respect your wishes in the matter.'

He hung up the receiver thoughtfully.

'He does not know where she is,' he said thoughtfully. 'I think that is quite genuine. The anxiety in his voice is unmistakable. He does not want to go to the police; that is understandable. Yes, I understand that. He does not want my assistance either. That is, perhaps, not quite so understandable . . . He wants her found – but he does not want *me* to find her . . . No, definitely he does not want me to find her . . . He seems confident that he can manage the matter himself. He does not think she can remain long hidden, for she has very little money with her. Also she has the children. Yes, I fancy he will be able to hunt her down before long. But, I think, Hastings, that we shall be a little quicker than he is. It is important, I think, that we should be.'

'Do you think it's true that she is slightly batty?' I asked.

'I think that she is in a highly nervous, overwrought condition.'

'But not to such a point that she ought to be in a mental home?'

'That, very definitely, no.'

'You know, Poirot, I don't quite understand all this.'

'If you will pardon my saying so, Hastings, you do not understand at all!'

'There seems so many – well – side issues.'

'Naturally there are side issues. To separate the main issue from the side issues is the first task of the orderly mind.'

'Tell me, Poirot, have you realized all along that there were *eight* possible suspects and not seven!'

Poirot replied dryly:

'I have taken that fact into consideration from the moment that Theresa Arundell mentioned that the last time she saw Dr Donaldson was when he dined at Littlegreen House on April 14th.'

'I can't quite see—' I broke off.

'What is it you cannot quite see?'

'Well, if Donaldson had planned to do away with Miss Arundell by scientific means – by inoculation, that is to say – I can't see why he resorted to such a clumsy device as a string across the stairs.'

'*En vérité*, Hastings, there are moments when I lose patience with you! One method is a highly scientific one needing fully specialized knowledge. That is so, is it not?'

'Yes.'

'And the other is a homely simple method – "the kind that mother makes", as the advertisements say. Is that not right?'

'Yes, exactly.'

'Then think, Hastings – *think*. Lie back in your chair, close the eyes, employ the little grey cells.'

I obeyed. That is to say, I leant back in the chair and closed my eyes and endeavoured to carry out the third part of Poirot's instructions. The result, however, did not seem to clarify matters much.

I opened my eyes to find Poirot regarding me with the kindly attention a nurse might display towards a childish charge.

'*Eh bien?*'

I made a desperate attempt to emulate Poirot's manner.

'Well,' I said, 'it seems to me that the kind of person who laid the original booby-trap is not the kind of person to plan out a scientific murder.'

'Exactly.'

'And I doubt if a mind trained to scientific complexities would think of anything so childish as the accident plan – it would be altogether too haphazard.'

'Very clearly reasoned.'

Emboldened, I went on:

'Therefore, the only logical solution seems to be this – the two attempts were planned by two different people. We have here to deal with murder attempted by two entirely different people.'

'You do not think that is too much of a coincidence?'

'You said yourself once that one coincidence is nearly always found in a murder case.'

'Yes, that is true. I have to admit it.'

'Well, then.'

'And who do you suggest for your villains?'

'Donaldson and Theresa Arundell. A doctor is clearly indicated for the final and successful murder. On the other hand, we know that Theresa Arundell is concerned in the first attempt. I think it's possible that they acted quite independently of each other.'

'You are so fond of saying "we know", Hastings. I can assure you that no matter what *you* know, I do not know that Theresa was implicated.'

'But Miss Lawson's story.'

'Miss Lawson's story is Miss Lawson's story. Just that.'

'But she says—'

'She says – she says . . . Always you are so ready to take what people say for a proved and accepted fact. Now listen, *mon cher*. I told you at the time, did I not, that something struck me as wrong about Miss Lawson's story?'

'Yes, I remember you saying so. But you couldn't get hold of what it was.'

'Well, I have done so now. A little moment and I will show you what I, imbecile that I am, ought to have seen at once.'

He went over to the desk and, opening a drawer, took out a sheet of cardboard. He cut into this with a pair of scissors, motioning to me not to overlook what he was doing.

'Patience, Hastings. In a little moment we will proceed to our experiment.'

I averted my eyes obligingly.

In a minute of two Poirot uttered an exclamation of satisfaction. He put away the scissors, dropped the fragments of cardboard into the waste-paper basket and came across the room to me.

'Now, do not look. Continue to avert the eyes while I pin something to the lapel of your coat.'

I humoured him. Poirot completed the proceeding to his satisfaction, then, propelling me gently to my feet, he drew me across the room and into the adjoining bedroom.

'Now, Hastings, regard yourself in the glass. You are wearing, are you not a fashionable brooch with your initials on it – only, *bien entendu*, the brooch is made not of chromium nor stainless steel, nor gold, nor platinum – but of humble cardboard!'

I looked at myself and smiled. Poirot is uncommonly neat with his fingers. I was wearing a very fair representation of Theresa Arundell's brooch – a circle cut out of cardboard and enclosing my initials – A.H.

'*Eh bien,*' said Poirot. 'You are satisfied? You have there, have you not, a very smart brooch with your initials?'

'A most handsome affair,' I agreed.

'It is true it does not gleam and reflect the light, but all the same you are prepared to admit that that brooch could be seen plainly from some distance away?'

'I've never doubted it.'

'Quite so. Doubt is not your strong point. Simple faith is more characteristic of you. And now, Hastings, be so good as to remove your coat.'

Wondering a little, I did so. Poirot divested himself of his own coat and slipped on mine, turning away a little as he did so.

'And now,' said he, 'regard how the brooch – the brooch with *your* initials – becomes me?'

He whisked round. I stared at him – for the moment uncomprehendingly. Then I saw the point.

'What a blithering fool I am! Of course. It's H.A. in the brooch, not A.H. at all.'

Poirot beamed on me, as he reassumed his own clothes and handed me mine.

'Exactly – and now you see what struck me as wrong with Miss Lawson's story. She stated that she had seen Theresa's initials clearly on the brooch she was wearing. But she saw Theresa in the *glass*. So, *if she saw the initials at all*, she must have seen them *reversed*.'

'Well,' I argued. 'Perhaps she did, and realized that they were reversed.'

'*Mon cher*, did that occur to you just now? Did you exclaim, "Ha! Poirot, you've got it wrong – that's H.A. really – not A.H."? No, you did not. And yet you are a good deal more intelligent, I should say, than Miss Lawson. Do not tell me that a muddle-headed woman like that woke up suddenly, and still half-asleep, realized that A.T. was really T.A. No, that is not at all consistent with the mentality of Miss Lawson.'

'She was determined it should be Theresa,' I said slowly.

'You are getting nearer, my friend. You remember, I hint to her that she could not really see the face of anyone on the stairs, and immediately – what does she do?'

'Remembers Theresa's brooch and lugs that in – forgetting that the mere fact of having seen it in the glass gave her own story the lie.'

The telephone bell rang sharply. Poirot crossed to it.

He only spoke a few non-committal words.

'Yes? Yes . . . certainly. Yes, quite convenient. The afternoon, I think. Yes, two o'clock will do admirably.'

He replaced the receiver and turned to me with a smile.

'Dr Donaldson is anxious to have a talk with me. He is coming here tomorrow afternoon at two o'clock. We progress, *mon ami*, we progress.'

—— 26 ——

MRS TANIOS REFUSES TO SPEAK

When I came round after breakfast the following morning I found Poirot busy at the writing table.

He raised a hand in salutation, then proceeded with his task. Presently he gathered up the sheets, enclosed them in an envelope and sealed them up carefully.

'Well, old boy, what are you doing?' I asked facetiously. 'Writing an account of the case to be placed in safe-keeping in case someone bumps you off during the course of the day?'

'You know, Hastings, you are not so far wrong as you think.'

His manner was serious.

'Is our murderer really about to get dangerous?'

'A murderer is always dangerous,' said Poirot gravely. 'Astonishingly how often that fact is overlooked.'

'Any news?'

'Dr Tanios rang up.'

'Still no trace of his wife?'

'No.'

'Then that's all right.'

'I wonder.'

'Dash it all, Poirot, you don't think she's been bumped off do you?'

Poirot shook his head doubtfully.

'I confess,' he murmured, 'that I should like to know where she is.'

'Oh, well,' I said. 'She'll turn up.'

'Your cheerful optimism never fails to delight me, Hastings!'

'My goodness, Poirot, you don't think she'll turn up in parcels or dismembered in a trunk?'

Poirot said slowly: 'I find the anxiety of Dr Tanios somewhat excessive – but no more of that. The first thing to do is to interview Miss Lawson.'

'Are you going to point out that little error over the brooch?'

'Certainly not. That little fact remains up my sleeve until the right moment comes.'

'Then what are you going to say to her?'

'That *mon ami*, you will hear in due course.'

'More lies, I suppose?'

'You are really very offensive sometimes, Hastings. Anybody would think I enjoyed telling lies.'

'I rather think you do. In fact, I'm sure of it.'

'It is true that I sometimes compliment myself upon my ingenuity,' Poirot confessed naïvely.

I could not help giving a shout of laughter. Poirot looked at me reproachfully, and we set off for Clanroyden Mansions.

We were shown into the same crowded sitting room, and Miss Lawson came bustling in, her manner even more incoherent than usual.

'Oh, dear, M. Poirot, good morning. Such a to-do – rather untidy, I'm afraid. But then, everything is at sixes and sevens this morning. Ever since Bella arrived—'

'What is that you say? Bella?'

'Yes, Bella Tanios. She turned up half an hour ago – *and* the children – completely exhausted, poor soul! Really, I don't know what to do about it. You see, she's left her husband.'

'Left him?'

'So she says. Of course, I've no doubt she's fully *justified*, poor thing.'

'She had confided in you?'

'Well – not exactly *that*. In fact, she won't say anything at all. Just repeats that she's left him and that nothing will induce her to go back to him!'

'That is a very serious step to take.'

'Of course it is! In fact, if he'd been an Englishman. I would have advised her – but there, he isn't an Englishman . . . And she looks so peculiar, poor thing, so – well, so *scared*. What can he have been doing to her? I believe Turks are frightfully cruel sometimes.'

'Dr Tanios is a Greek.'

'Yes, of course, that's the other way about – I mean, they're usually the ones who get massacred by the Turks – or am I thinking of Armenians? But all the same, I don't like to think of it. I don't think she *ought* to go back to him, do you, M. Poirot? Anyway, I mean, she says she won't . . . She doesn't even want him to know where she is.'

'As bad as that?'

'Yes, you see, it's the *children*. She's so afraid he could take them back to Smyrna. Poor soul! she really is in a terrible way. You see, she's got no money – no money at all. She doesn't know where to go or what to do. She wants to try to earn her living; but, really, you know, M. Poirot, that's not so easy as it sounds. I know that. It's not as though she were *trained* for anything.'

'When did she leave her husband?'

'Yesterday. She spent last night in a little hotel near Paddington. She came to me because she couldn't think of anyone else to go to, poor thing.'

'And are you going to help her? That is very good of you.'

'Well, you see. M. Poirot, I really feel it's my *duty*. But, of course, it's all very difficult. This is a very small flat and there's no room – and what with one thing and another . . .'

'You could send her to Littlegreen House?'

'I suppose I could – but, you see, her husband might think of that. Just for the moment I've got her rooms at the Wellington Hotel in Queen's Road. She's staying there under the name of Mrs Peters.'

'I see,' said Poirot.

He paused for a minute, then said:

'I would like to see Mrs Tanios. You see, she called at my flat yesterday, but I was out.'

'Oh, did she? She didn't tell me that. I'll tell her, shall I?'

'If you would be so good.'

Miss Lawson hurried out of the room. We could hear her voice.

'Bella – Bella – my dear, will you come and see M. Poirot?'

We did not hear Mrs Tanios's reply, but a minute or two later she came into the room.

I was really shocked at her appearance. There were dark circles under her eyes and her cheeks were completely destitute of colour, but what struck me far more than this was her obvious air of terror. She started at the least provocation, and she seemed to be continually listening.

Poirot greeted her in his most soothing manner. He came forward, shook hands, arranged a chair for her and handed her a cushion. He treated the pale, frightened woman as though she had been a queen.

'And now, madame, let us have a little chat. You came to see me yesterday, I believe?'

She nodded.

'I regret very much that I was away from home.'

'Yes – yes, I wish you had been there.'

'You came because you wanted to tell me something?'

'Yes, I – I meant to—'

'*Eh bien*, I am here, at your service.'

Mrs Tanios did not respond. She sat quite still, twisting a ring round and round on her finger.

'Well, madame?'

'Slowly, almost reluctantly, she shook her head.

'No,' she said. 'I daren't.'

'You *daren't*, madame?'

'No. I – if he knew – he'd – oh, something would happen to me!'

'Come, come, madame – that is absurd.'

'Oh, but it isn't absurd – it isn't absurd at all. You don't know him . . .'

'By *him*, you mean your husband, madame?'

'Yes, of course.'

Poirot was silent a minute or two, then he said:

'Your husband came to see me yesterday, madame.'

A quick look of alarm sprang up in her face.

'Oh, no! You didn't tell him – but of course you didn't! You couldn't. You didn't know where I was. Did he – did he say I was *mad*?'

Poirot answered cautiously.

'He said that you were – highly nervous.'

But she shook her head, undeceived.

'No, he said that I was mad – or that I was going mad! He wants to shut me up so that I shan't be able to tell anyone ever.'

'Tell anyone – what?'

But she shook her head. Twisting her fingers nervously round and round, she muttered:

'I'm afraid . . .'

'But, madame, once you have *told* me – you are *safe*! The secret is out! The fact will protect you automatically.'

But she did not reply. She went on twisting – twisting at her ring.

'You must see that yourself,' said Poirot gently.

She gave a sort of gasp.

'How am I to know? . . . Oh, dear, it's terrible! He's so *plausible*! And he's a doctor. People will believe him, and not me. I know they will. I should myself. Nobody will believe me. How could they?'

'You will not even give me the chance?'

She shot a troubled glance at him.

'How do I know? You may be on his side.'

'I am on no one's side, madame. I am – always – on the side of the truth.'

'I don't know,' said Mrs Tanios hopelessly. 'Oh, I don't know.'

She went on, her words gathering volume, tumbling over each other:

'It's been so awful – for years now. I've seen things happening again and again. And I couldn't say anything or do anything. There have been the children. It's been like a long nightmare. And now this . . . But I won't go back to him. I won't let him have the children. I'll go somewhere where he can't find me. Minnie Lawson will help me. She's been so kind so wonderfully kind. Nobody could have been kinder.' She stopped, then shot a quick look at Poirot and asked: 'What did he say about me? Did he say I had delusions?'

'He said, madame, that you had – changed towards him.'

She nodded.

'And he said I had delusions. He *did* say that, didn't he?'

'Yes, madame, to be frank, he did.'

'That's it, you see. That's what it will sound like. And I've no proof – no real proof.'

Poirot leaned back in his chair. When he next spoke it was
with an entire change of manner.

He spoke in a matter-of-fact, business-like voice with as little
emotion as if he had been discussing some dry matter of
business.

'Do you suspect your husband of doing away with Miss Emily
Arundell?'

Her answer came quickly – a spontaneous flash.

'I don't suspect – I know.'

'Then, madame, it is your duty to speak.'

'Ah, but it isn't so easy – no, it isn't so easy.'

'How did he kill her?'

'I don't know exactly – but he did kill her.'

'But you don't know the method he employed?'

'No – it was something he did that last Sunday.'

'The Sunday he went down to see her?'

'Yes.'

'But you don't know what it was?'

'No.'

'Then how, forgive me, madame, can you be so sure?'

'Because he—' She stopped and said slowly. 'I *am* sure!'

'*Pardon,* madame, but there is something you are keeping
back. Something you have not yet told me?'

'Yes.'

'Come, then.'

Bella Tanios got up suddenly.

'No. No. I can't do that. The children. Their father. I can't.
I simply can't . . .'

'But, madame—'

'I can't, I tell you.'

Her voice rose almost to a scream. The door opened and
Miss Lawson came in, her head cocked on one side with a sort
of pleasurable excitement.

'May, I come in? Have you had your little talk? Bella, my
dear, don't you think you ought to have a cup of tea, or some
soup, or perhaps a little brandy, even?'

Mrs Tanios shook her head.

'I'm quite all right.' She gave a weak smile. 'I must be getting
back to the children. I have left them to unpack.'

'Dear little things,' said Miss Lawson. 'I'm so fond of children.'

Mrs Tanios turned to her suddenly.

'I don't know what I should do without you,' she said. 'You
– you've been wonderfully kind.'

'There, there, my dear, don't cry. Everything's going to be all right. You shall come round and see my lawyer – such a nice man, so sympathetic – and he'll advise you the best way to get a divorce. Divorce is so simple nowadays, isn't it? Everybody says so. Oh, dear, there's the bell. I wonder who that is.'

She left the room hurriedly. There was a murmur of voices in the hall. Miss Lawson reappeared. She tiptoed in and shut the door carefully behind her. She spoke in an excited whisper, mouthing the words exaggeratedly.

'Oh, dear, Bella, it's your husband. I'm sure I don't know—'

Mrs Tanios gave one bound towards a door at the other end of the room. Miss Lawson nodded her head violently.

'That's right, dear, go in there, and then you can slip out when I've brought him in here.'

Mrs Tanios whispered:

'Don't say I've been here. Don't say you've seen me.'

'No, no, of course I won't.'

Mrs Tanios slipped through the door. Poirot and I followed hastily. We found ourselves in a small dining room.

Poirost crossed to the door into the hall, opened it a crack and listened. Then he beckoned.

'All is clear. Miss Lawson has taken him into the other room.'

We crept through the hall and out by the front door. Poirot drew it to as noiselessly as possible after him.

Mrs Tanios began to run down the steps, stumbling and clutching at the banisters. Poirot steadied her with a hand under her arm.

'*Du calme – du calme*. All is well.'

We reached the entrance hall.

'Come with me,' said Mrs Tanios piteously. She looked as though she might be going to faint.

'Certainly I will come,' said Poirot reassuringly.

We crossed the road, turned a corner, and found ourselves in the Queen's Road. The Wellington was a small, inconspicuous hotel of the boarding-house variety.

When we were inside, Mrs Tanios sank down on a plush sofa. Her hand was on her beating heart.

Poirot patted her reassuringly on the shoulder.

'It was the narrow squeak – yes. Now, madame, you are to listen to me very carefully.'

'I can't tell you anything more, M. Poirot. It wouldn't be *right*. You – you know what I think – what I believe. You – you must be satisfied with that.'

'I asked you to listen, madame. Supposing – this is a supposition only – *that I already know the facts of the case.* Supposing that what you could tell me *I have already guessed* – that would make a difference, would it not?'

She looked at him doubtfully. Her eyes were painful in their intensity.

'Oh, believe me, madame, I am not trying to trap you into saying what you do not wish to. But it *would* make a difference – yes?'

'I – I suppose it would.'

'Good. Then let me say this. *I, Hercule Poirot, know the truth.* I am not going to ask you to accept my word for it. Take this.' He thrust upon her the bulky envelope I had seen him seal up that morning. 'The facts are there. After you have read them, if they satisfy you, ring me up. My number is on the notepaper.'

Almost reluctantly she accepted the envelope.

Poirot went on briskly:

'And now, one more point. You must leave this hotel at once.'

'But why?'

'You will go to the Coniston Hotel near Euston. Tell no one where you are going.'

'But surely – here – Minnie Lawson won't tell my husband where I am.'

'You think not?'

'Oh, no – she's entirely on my side.'

'Yes, but your husband, madame, is a very clever man. He will not find it difficult to turn a middle-aged lady inside out. It is essential – *essential,* you understand – that your husband should not know where you are.'

She nodded dumbly.

Poirot held out a sheet of paper.

'Here is the address. Pack up and drive there with the children as soon as possible. You understand?'

She nodded.

'I understand.'

'It is the children you must think of, madame, not yourself. You love your children.'

He had touched the right note.

A little colour crept into her cheeks, her head went back. She looked, not a frightened drudge, but an arrogant, almost handsome woman.

'It is arranged then,' said Poirot.

He shook hands, and he and I departed. But not far. From

the shelter of a convenient café, we sipped coffee and watched the entrance of the hotel. In about five minutes we saw Dr Tanios walking down the street. He did not even glance up at the Wellington. He passed it, his head bowed in thought, then he turned into the Underground station.

About ten minutes later we saw Mrs Tanios and the children get into the taxi with their luggage and drive away.

'*Bien*,' said Poirot, rising with the bill in his hand. 'We have done our part. Now it is on the knees of the gods.'

—— 27 ——

VISIT OF DR DONALDSON

Donaldson arrived punctually at two o'clock. He was as calm and precise as ever.

The personality of Donaldson had begun to intrigue me. I had started by regarding him as a rather nondescript young man. I had wondered what a vivid, compelling creature like Theresa could see in him. But now I began to realize that Donaldson was anything but negligible. Behind that pedantic manner there was force.

After our preliminary greetings were over, Donaldson said:

'The reason for my visit is this. I am at a loss to understand exactly what your position is in this matter, M. Poirot.'

Poirot replied guardedly: 'You know my profession, I think?'

'Certainly. I may say that I have taken the trouble to make inquiries about you.'

'You are a careful man, Doctor.'

Donaldson said dryly:

'I like to be sure of my facts.'

'You have the scientific mind!'

'I may say that all reports on you are the same. You are obviously a very clever man in your profession. You have also the reputation of being a scrupulous and honest one.'

'You are too flatterinug,' murmured Poirot.

'That is why I am at a loss to explain your connexion with this affair.'

'And yet it is so simple!'

'Hardly that,' said Donaldson. 'You first present yourself as a writer of biographies.'

'A pardonable deception, do you not think? One cannot go everywhere announcing the fact that one is a detective – though that, too, has its uses sometimes.'

'So I should imagine.' Again Donaldson's tone was dry. 'Your next proceeding,' he went on, 'was to call Miss Theresa Arundell and represent to her that her aunt's will might conceivably be set aside.'

Poirot merely bowed his head in assent.

'That, of course, was ridiculous.' Donaldson's voice was sharp. 'You knew perfectly well that that will was valid in law and that nothing could be done about it.'

'You think that is the case?'

'I am not a fool, M. Poirot—'

'No, Dr Donaldson, you are certainly not a fool.'

'I know something – not very much, but enough – of the law. That will can certainly not be upset. Why did you pretend it could? Clearly for reasons of your own – reasons which Miss Theresa Arundell did not for a moment grasp.'

'You seem very certain of her reactions.'

A very faint smile passed across the young man's face.

He said unexpectedly:

'I know a good deal more about Theresa than she suspects. I have no doubt that she and Charles think they have enlisted your aid in some questionable business. Charles is almost completely amoral. Theresa has a bad heredity and her upbringing has been unfortunate.'

'It is thus you speak of your fiancée – as though she was a guinea-pig?'

Donaldson peered at him through his pince-nez.

'I see no occasion to blink the truth. I love Theresa Arundell, and I love her for what she is and not for any imagined qualities.'

'Do you realize that Theresa Arundell is devoted to you and that her wish for money is mainly in order that your ambitions should be gratified?'

'Of course I realize it. I've already told you I'm not a fool. But I have no intention of allowing Theresa to embroil herself in any questionable situation on my account. In many ways Theresa is a child still. I am quite capable of furthering my career by my own efforts. I do not say that a substantial legacy would not have been acceptable. It would have been most acceptable. But it would merely have provided a short cut.'

'You have, in fact, full confidence in your own abilities?'

'It probably sounds conceited, but I have,' said Donaldson composedly.

'Let us proceed, then. I admit that I gained Miss Theresa's confidence by a trick. I let her think that I would be – shall we say, reasonably dishonest – for money. She believed that without the least difficulty.'

'Theresa believes that anyone would do anything for money,' said the young doctor in the matter-of-fact tone one uses when stating a self-evident truth.

'True. That seems to be her attitude – her brother's also.'

'Charles probably *would* do anything for money!'

'You have no illusions, I see, about your future brother-in-law.'

'No. I find him quite an interesting study. There is, I think, some deep-seated neurosis – but that is talking shop. To return to what we are discussing. I have asked myself *why* you should act in the way you have done, and I have found only one answer. It is clear that you suspect either Theresa or Charles of having a hand in Miss Arundell's death. No, please don't bother to contradict me! Your mention of exhumation was, I think, a mere device to see what reaction you would get. Have you, in actual fact, taken any steps towards getting a Home Office order for exhumation?'

'I will be quite frank with you. As yet, I have not.'

Donaldson nodded.

'So I thought. I suppose you have considered the possibility that Miss Arundell's death may turn out to be from natural causes?'

'I have considered the fact that it may appear to be so – yes.'

'But your own mind is made up?'

'Very definitely. If you have a case of – say – tuberculosis that looks like tuberculosis, behaves like tuberculosis, and in which the blood gives a positive reaction – *eh bien,* you consider it *is* tuberculosis, do you not?'

'You look at it that way? I see. Then what exactly are you waiting for?'

'I am waiting for a final piece of evidence.'

The telephone bell rang. At a gesture from Poirot I got up and answered it. I recognized the voice.

'Captain Hastings? This is Mrs Tanios speaking. Will you tell M. Poirot that he is perfectly right? If he will come here tomorrow morning at ten o'clock, I will give him what he wants.'

'At ten o'clock tomorrow?'

'Yes.'

'Right. I'll tell him.'

Poirot's eyes asked a question. I nodded.

He turned to Donaldson. His manner had changed. It was brisk – assured.

'Let me make myself clear,' he said. 'I have diagnosed this case of mine as a case of murder. It looked like murder, it gave all the characteristic reactions of murder – in fact, it *was* murder! Of that there is not the least doubt.'

'Where, then, does the doubt – for I perceive there *is* a doubt – lie?'

'The doubt lay in *the identity of the murderer* – but that is a doubt no longer!'

'Really? You know?'

'Let us say that I shall have definite proof in my hands tomorrow.'

Dr Donaldson's eyebrows rose in a slightly ironical fashion.

'Ah,' he said. 'Tomorrow! Sometimes, M. Poirot, tomorrow is a long way off.'

'On the contrary,' said Poirot, 'I always find that it succeeds today with monotonous regularity.'

Donaldson smiled. He rose.

'I fear I have wasted your time, M. Poirot.'

'Not at all. It is always as well to understand each other.'

With a slight bow, Dr Donaldson left the room.

—— 28 ——

ANOTHER VICTIM

'That is a clever man,' said Poirot thoughtfully.

'It's rather difficult to know what he's driving at.'

'Yes. He is a little inhuman. But extremely perceptive.'

'That telephone call was from Mrs Tanios.'

'So I gathered.'

I repeated the message. Poirot nodded approval.

'Good. All marches well. Twenty-four hours, Hastings, and I think we shall know exactly where we stand.'

'I'm still a little fogged. Who exactly do we suspect?'

'I really could not say who *you* suspect, Hastings! Everybody in turn, I should imagine!'

'Sometimes I think you *like* to get me into that state!'

'No, no. I would not amuse myself in such a way.'

'I wouldn't put it past you.'

Poirot shook his head, but somewhat absently. I studied him.

'Is anything the matter?' I asked.

'My friend, I am always nervous towards the end of a case. If anything should go wrong—'

'Is anything likely to go wrong?'

'I do not think so.' He paused, frowning. 'I have, I think, provided against every contingency.'

'Then, supposing that we forget crime and go to a show?'

'*Ma foi*, Hastings, that is a good idea!'

We passed a very pleasant evening, though I made the slight mistake of taking Poirot to a crook play. There is one piece of advice I offer to all my readers. Never take a soldier to a military play, a sailor to a naval play, a Scotsman to a Scottish play, a detective to a thriller – and an actor to any play whatsoever! The shower of destructive criticism in each case is somewhat devastating. Poirot never ceased to complain of faulty psychology, and the hero detective's lack of order and method nearly drove him demented. We parted that night with Poirot still explaining how the whole business might have been laid bare in the first half of the first act.

'But in that case, Poirot, there would have been no play,' I pointed out.

Poirot was forced to admit that perhaps that was so.

It was a few minutes past nine when I entered the sitting room the next morning. Poirot was at the breakfast table – as usual neatly slitting open his letters.

The telephone rang, and I answered it.

A heavy-breathing female voice spoke:

'Is that M. Poirot? Oh, it's you Captain Hastings.'

There was a sort of gasp and a sob.

'Is that Miss Lawson?' I asked.

'Yes, yes, such a terrible thing has happened!'

I grasped the receiver tightly.

'What is it?'

'She left the Wellington, you know – Bella, I mean. I went there late in the afternoon yesterday, and they said she'd left. Without a word to me, either! *Most* extraordinary! It makes me feel that perhaps, after all, Dr Tanios was *right*. He spoke

579

so *nicely* about her and seemed so *distressed,* and now it really looks as though he were right, after all.'

'But what's happened, Miss Lawson? Is it just that Mrs Tanios left the hotel without telling you?'

'Oh, no, it's not *that*! Oh, dear me, no. If that were all it would be *quite* all right. Though I do think it was *odd,* you know. Dr Tanios did say that he was afraid she wasn't quite – not *quite* – if you know what I mean. Persecution mania, he called it.'

'Yes.' (Damn the woman!) 'but what's *happened*?'

'Oh, dear – it is terrible. Died in her sleep. An overdose of some sleeping stuff! And those *poor* little children! It all seems so dreadfully *sad*! I've done nothing but cry since I heard.'

'How did you hear? Tell me all about it.'

Out of the tail of my eye I noticed that Poirot had stopped opening his letters. He was listening to my side of the conversation. I did not like to cede my place to him. If I did it seemed highly probable that Miss Lawson would start with lamentations all over again.

'They rang me up. From the hotel. The Coniston it's called. It seems they found my name and address in her bag. Oh, dear, M. Poirot – Captain Hastings, I mean – *isn't it terrible*? Those poor little children left motherless.'

'Look here,' I said. 'Are you sure it's an accident? They didn't think it could be suicide?'

'Oh, what a *dreadful* idea, Captain Hastings! Oh, dear, I don't know, I'm sure. Do you think it could be? That would be *dreadful*! Of course she *did* seem very depressed. But she needn't have been. I mean there wouldn't have been any difficulty about *money*. I was going to *share* with her – indeed I was! Dear Miss Arundell would have wished it. I'm sure of that! It seems so awful to think of her taking her own life – but perhaps she didn't . . . The hotel people seemed to think it was an accident.'

'What did she take?'

'One of those sleeping things. Veronal, I think. No, chloral. Yes, that was it. Chloral. Oh, dear, Captain Hastings, do you think—'

Unceremoniously I banged down the receiver. I turned to Poirot.

'Mrs Tanios—'

He raised a hand.

'Yes, yes, I know what you are going to say. She is dead, is she not?'

'Yes. Overdose of sleeping-draught. Chloral.'

Poirot got up.

'Come, Hastings, we must go there at once.'

'Is this what you feared – last night? When you said you were always nervous towards the end of a case?'

'I feared another death – yes.'

Poirot's face was set and stern. We said very little as we drove towards Euston. Once or twice Poirot shook his head.

I said timidly:

'You don't think—? Could it be an accident?'

'No, Hastings – no. It was not an accident.'

'How on earth did he find out where she had gone?'

Poirot only shook his head without replying.

The Coniston was an unsavoury-looking place quite near Euston station. Poirot, with his card, and a suddenly bullying manner, soon fought his way into the manager's office.

The facts were quite simple.

Mrs Peters, as she had called herself, and her two children had arrived about half past twelve. They had lunch at one o'clock.

At four o'clock a man had arrived with a note for Mrs Peters. The note had been sent up to her. A few minutes later she had come down with the two children and a suitcase. The children had then left with the visitor. Mrs Peters had gone to the office and explained that she should only want the one room, after all.

She had not appeared exceptionally distressed or upset; indeed, she had seemed quite calm and collected. She had had dinner about seven-thirty and had gone to her room soon afterwards.

On calling her in the morning the chambermaid had found her dead.

A doctor had been sent for and had pronounced her to have been dead for some hours. An empty glass was found on the table by the bed. It seemed fairly obvious that she had taken a sleeping-draught, and, by mistake, taken an overdose. Chloral hydrate, the doctor said, was a somewhat uncertain drug. There were no indications of suicide. No letter had been left. Searching for means of notifying her relations, Miss Lawson's name and address had been found and she had been communicated with by telephone.

Poirot asked if anything had been found in the way of letters or papers. The letter, for instance brought by the man who had called for the children.'

No papers of any kind had been found, the man said, but there was a pile of charred paper on the hearth.

Poirot nodded thoughtfully.

As far as anyone could say, Mrs Peters had had no visitors and no one had come to her room – with the solitary exception of the man who had called for the two children.

I questioned the porter myself as to his appearance, but the man was very vague. A man of medium height – he thought fair-haired – rather military build – of somewhat nondescript appearance. No, he was positive the man had no beard.

'It wasn't Tanios,' I murmured to Poirot.

'My dear Hastings! Do you really believe that Mrs Tanios, after all the trouble she was taking to get the children away from their father, would quite meekly hand them over to him without the least fuss or protest? Ah, that, no!'

'Then who was the man?'

'Clearly it was someone in whom Mrs Tanios had confidence, or rather it was someone sent by a third person in whom Mrs Tanios had confidence.'

'A man of medium height,' I mused.

'You need hardly trouble yourself about his appearance, Hastings. I am quite sure that the man who actually called for the children was some quite unimportant personage. The real agent kept himself in the background!'

'And the note was from this third person?'

'Yes.'

'Someone in whom Mrs Tanios had confidence?'

'Obviously.'

'And the note is now burnt?'

'Yes, she was instructed to burn it.'

'What about that *résumé* of the case that you gave her?'

Poirot's face looked unusually grim.

'That, too, is burned. But that does not matter!'

'No?'

'No. For you see – it is all in the head of Hercule Poirot.'

He took me by the arm.

'Come, Hastings, let us leave here. Our concern is not with the dead, but with the living. It is with them I have to deal.'

29

INQUEST AT LITTLEGREEN HOUSE

It was eleven o'clock the following morning.

Seven people were assembled at Littlegreen House. Hercule Poirot stood by the mantelpiece. Charles and Theresa Arundell were on the sofa, Charles on the arm of it with his hand on Theresa's shoulder. Dr Tanios sat in a grandfather chair. His eyes were red-rimmed, and he wore a black band round his arm.

On an upright chair by a round table sat the owner of the house, Miss Lawson. She, too, had red eyes. Her hair was even untidier than usual. Dr Donaldson sat directly facing Poirot. His face was quite expressionless.

My interest quickened as I looked at each face in turn.

In the course of my association with Poirot I had assisted at many such a scene. A little company of people, all outwardly composed, with well-bred masks for faces. And I had seen Poirot strip the mask from one face and show it for what it was – *the face of a killer!*

Yes, there was no doubt of it. *One of these people was a murderer!* But which? Even now I was not *sure.*

Poirot cleared his throat – a little pompously, as was his habit – and began to speak.

'We are assembled here, ladies and gentlemen, to inquire into the death of Emily Arundell on the first of May last. There are four possibilities: that she died naturally – that she died as the result of an accident – that she took her own life – or lastly that she met her death at the hands of some person known or unknown.

'No inquest was held at the time of her death, since it was assumed that she died from natural causes and a medical certificate to that effect was given by Dr Grainger.

'In a case where suspicion arises after burial has taken place it is usual to exhume the body of the person in question. There are reasons why I have not advocated that course. The chief of them is that my client would not have liked it.'

It was Dr Donaldson who interrupted. He said:

'Your client?'

Poirot turned to him. 'My client is Miss Emily Arundell. I

am acting for her. Her greatest desire was that there should be no scandal.'

I will pass over the next ten minutes, since it would involve much needless repetition. Poirot told of the letter he had received, and producing it he read it aloud. He went on to explain the steps he had taken on coming to Market Basing, and of his discovery of the means taken to bring about the accident.

Then he paused, cleared his throat once more, and went on:

'I am now going to take you over the ground I travelled to get at the truth. I am going to show you what I believe to be a true reconstruction of the facts of the case.

'To begin with, it is necessary to picture exactly what passed in Miss Arundell's mind. That, I think, is fairly easy. She has a fall, her fall is supposed to be occasioned by a dog's ball, but *she herself knows better*. Lying there on her bed her active and shrewd mind goes over the circumstances of her fall and she comes to a very definite conclusion about it. Someone has deliberately tried to injure – perhaps to kill – her.

'From that conclusion she passes to a consideration of who that person can be. There were *seven* people in the house – four guests, her companion and two servants. Of these seven people only one can be entirely exonerated – since to that one person no advantage could accrue. She does not seriously suspect the two servants, both of whom have been with her for years and whom she knows to be devoted to her. There remain, then, *four* persons, three of them members of her family, and one of them a connexion by marriage. *Each of those four persons benefits, three directly, one indirectly, by her death.*

'She is in a difficult position, since she is a woman with a strong sense of family feeling. Essentially she is not one who wishes to wash the dirty linen in public as the saying goes. On the other hand, she is not one to submit tamely to attempted murder!

'She takes her decision and writes to me. She also takes a further step. That further step was, I believe, actuated by two motives. One, I think, was a distinct feeling of *spite* against her entire family! She suspected them all impartially, and she determined at all costs to score off them! The second and more reasoned motive was a wish to protect herself and a realization of how this could be accomplished. As you know, she wrote to her lawyer, Mr Purvis, and directed him to draw up a will in favour of the one person in the house who, she felt convinced, could have had no hand in her accident.

'Now I may say that, from the terms of her letter to me and from her subsequent actions, I am quite sure that Miss Arundell passed from *indefinite* suspicion of four people to *definite* suspicion of *one* of those four. The whole tenor of her letter to me is an insistence that this business must be kept strictly private, since the honour of the family is involved.

'I think that, from a Victorian point of view, this means that a person of *her* own name was indicated – and preferably a *man*.

'If she had suspected Mrs Tanios she would have been quite as anxious to secure her own safety, but not quite as concerned for the family honour. She might have felt much the same about Theresa Arundell, but not nearly as intensely as she would feel about Charles.

'Charles was an *Arundell*. He bore the family *name*! Her reasons for suspecting him seem quite clear. To begin with, she had no illusions about Charles. He had come near to disgracing the family once before. That is, she knew him to be not only a *potential* but an *actual* criminal! He had already forged her name to a cheque. After forgery – a step further – murder!

'Also she had had a somewhat suggestive conversation with him only two days before her accident. He had asked her for money and she had refused and he had thereupon remarked – oh, lightly enough – that she was going the right way to get herself bumped off. To this she had responded that she could take care of herself! To this, we are told, her nephew responded: "Don't be too sure." *And two days later this sinister accident takes place.*

'It is hardly to be wondered at that lying there and brooding over the occurrence, Miss Arundell came definitely to the conclusion that it was *Charles Arundell* who had made an attempt upon her life.

'The sequence of events is perfectly clear. The conversation with Charles. The accident. The letter written to me in great distress of mind. The letter to the lawyer. On the following Tuesday, the 21st, Mr Purvis brings the will and she signs it.

'Charles and Theresa Arundell come down the following weekend, and Miss Arundell at once takes the necessary steps to safeguard herself. *She tells Charles about the will.* She not only *tells* him, but she actually *shows* it to him! That, to my mind, is *absolutely conclusive. She is making it quite clear to a would be murderer that murder would bring him nothing whatever!*

'She probably thought that Charles would pass on that information to his sister. But he did not do so. Why? I fancy that he had a very good reason – he felt guilty! He believed that it was *his* doing that the will had been made. But *why* did he feel guilty? Because he had really attempted murder? Or merely because he had helped himself to a small sum of ready cash? Either the serious crime or the petty one might account for his reluctance. He said nothing, hoping that his aunt would relent and change her mind.

'As far as Miss Arundell's state of mind was concerned I felt that I had reconstructed events with a fair amount of correctness. I had next to make up my mind if her suspicions were, in actual fact, justified.

'Just as she had done, I realized that my suspicions were limited to a narrow circle – seven people, to be exact. Charles and Theresa Arundell, Dr Tanios and Mrs Tanios, the two servants, and Miss Lawson. There was an eighth person who had to be taken into account – namely, Dr Donaldson, who dined there that night, but I did not learn of his presence until later.

'These seven persons that I was considering fell easily into two categories. Six of them stood to benefit in a greater or lesser degree by Miss Arundell's death. If anyone of those six had committed the crime the reason was probably a plain matter of *gain*. The second category contained one person only – Miss Lawson. Miss Lawson did *not* stand to gain by Miss Arundell's death, but, *as a result of the accident*, she did benefit considerably *later*!

'That meant that if Miss Lawson staged the so-called accident—'

'I never did anything of the kind!' Miss Lawson interrupted. 'It's disgraceful! Standing up there and saying such things!'

'A little patience, mademoiselle. And be kind enough not to interrupt,' said Poirot.

Miss Lawson tossed her head angrily.

'I insist on making my protest! Disgraceful, that's what it is! Disgraceful!'

Poirot went on, unheeding:

'I was saying that *if* Miss Lawson staged that accident, she did so for an entirely *different* reason – that is, she engineered it so that Miss Arundell *would naturally suspect her own family and become alienated from them*. That *was* a possibility! I searched to see if there were any confirmation or otherwise, and I unearthed one very definite fact. If Miss Lawson wanted Miss Arundell to suspect her own family, she would have stressed the fact of the dog, Bob, being *out* that night. But, on the contrary, Miss Lawson took the utmost pains to *prevent* Miss Arundell hearing of that. Therefore, I argued, Miss Lawson *must* be innocent.'

Miss Lawson said sharply:

'I should hope so!'

'I next considered the problem of Miss Arundell's death. If one attempt to murder a person is made, a second attempt usually follows. It seemed to me significant that within a fortnight of the first attempt Miss Arundell should have died. I began to make inquiries.

'Dr Grainger did not seem to think there was anything unusual about his patient's death. That was a little damping to my theory. But, inquiring into the happenings of the last evening before she was taken ill, I came across a rather significant fact. Miss Julia Tripp mentioned a halo of light that had appeared round Miss Arundell's head. Her sister confirmed her statement. They might, of course, be inventing – in a romantic spirit – but I did not think that the incident was quite a likely one to occur to them unprompted. When questioning Miss Lawson she also gave me an interesting piece of information. She referred to a luminous ribbon issuing from Miss Arundell's mouth and forming a luminous haze round her head.

'Obviously, though described somewhat differently by two different observers. the actual *fact* was the same. What it amounted to, shorn of spiritualistic significance, was this: *On the night in question Miss Arundell's breath was phosphorescent!*'

Dr Donaldson moved a little in his chair.

Poirot nodded to him.

'Yes, you begin to see. There are not very many phosphorescent substances. The first and most common one gave me exactly what I was looking for. I will read you a short extract from an article on phosphorus poisoning.

'*The person's breath may be phosphorescent before he feels in any way affected.* That is what Miss Lawson and the Misses Tripp saw in the dark – Miss Arundell's phophorescent breath – "a luminous haze". And here I will read you again. *The jaundice having thoroughly pronounced itself, the system may be considered as not only under the influence of the toxic action of phosphorus, but as suffering in addition from all the accidents incidental to the retention of the bilary secretion in the blood, nor is there from this point, any special difference between phosphorus poisoning and certain affections of the liver – such, for example, as yellow atrophy.*

'You see the cleverness of that? Miss Arundell has suffered for years from liver trouble. The symptoms of phosphorus poisoning would only look like *another attack of the same complaint.* There will be nothing new, nothing startling about it.

'Oh, it was well planned! Foreign matches – vermin paste? It is not difficult to get hold of phosphorus, and a very small dose will kill. The medicinal dose is from 1/100 to 1/30 grain.

'*Voilà.* How clear – how marvellously clear the whole business becomes! Naturally, the doctor is deceived – especially as I find his sense of smell is affected – the garlic odour of the breath is a distinct symptom of phosphorus poisoning. He had no suspicions – why should he have? There were no suspicious circumstances, and the one thing that might have given him a hint was the one thing he would never hear – or, if he did hear it, he would only class it as spiritualistic nonsense.

'I was now sure (from the evidence of Miss Lawson and the Misses Tripp) that murder had been committed. The question still was by *whom*? I eliminated the servants – their mentality was obviously not adapted to such a crime. I eliminated Miss Lawson, since she would hardly have prattled on about luminous ectoplasm if she had been connected with the crime. I eliminated Charles Arundell, *since he knew, having seen the will, that he would gain nothing by his aunt's death.*

'There remained his sister, Theresa, Dr Tanios, Mrs Tanios and Dr Donaldson, whom I discovered to have been dining in the house on the evening of the dog's ball incident.

'At this point I had very little to help me. I had to fall back upon the psychology of the crime and the *personality* of the murderer! Both crimes had roughly *the same outline.* They were both *simple.* They were cunning, and carried out with efficiency. They required a certain amount of knowledge, but not a great deal. The facts about phosphorus poisoning are easily learned, and the stuff itself, as I say, is quite easily obtained, especiallly abroad.

'I considered first the two men. Both of them were doctors, and both were clever men. Either of them might have thought of phosphorus and its suitability in this particular case, but the incident of the dog's ball did not seem to fit a masculine mind. The incident of the ball seemed to me essentially a *woman's* idea.

'I considered first of all Theresa Arundell. She had certain potentialities. She was bold, ruthless, and not over-scrupulous. She had led a selfish and greedy life. She had always had everything she wanted, and she had reached a point where she was desperate for money – both for herself and for the man she loved. Her manner, also, showed plainly that she knew her aunt had been murdered.

'There was an interesting little passage between her and her brother. I conceived the idea that *each suspected the other of the crime*. Charles endeavoured to make her say that *she knew of the existence of the new will*. Why? Clearly because if she knew of it she could not be suspected of the murder. She, on the other hand, clearly did not believe Charles's statement that Miss Arundell had shown it to him! She regarded it as a singularly clumsy attempt on his part to divert suspicion from himself.

'There was another significant point. Charles displayed a reluctance to use the word "arsenic". Later I found that he had questioned the old gardener at length upon the strength of some weed-killer. It was clear what had been in his mind.'

Charles Arundell shifted his position a little.

'I thought of it,' he said. 'But – well, I suppose I hadn't got the nerve.'

Poirot nodded at him.

'Precisely, *it is not in your psychology*. Your crimes will always be the crimes of weakness. To steal, to forge – yes, it is the easiest way – but to kill – *no*! To kill, one needs the type of mind that can be obsessed by an idea.'

He resumed his lecturing manner.

'Theresa Arundell, I decided, had quite sufficient strength of mind to carry such a design through, but there were other facts to take into consideration. She had never been thwarted, she had lived fully and selfishly. But that type of person is *not the type that kills* – except perhaps in sudden anger. And yet – I felt sure – *it was Theresa Arundell who had taken the weed-killer from the tin.*'

Theresa spoke suddenly:

'I'll tell you the truth. I thought of it. I actually took some weed-killer from a tin down at Littlegreen House. But I couldn't do it! I'm too fond of living – of being alive. I couldn't do that to anyone – take life from them . . . I may be bad and selfish, but there are things I can't do! I couldn't kill a living, breathing, human creature!'

Poirot nodded. 'No, that is true. And you are not as bad as

you paint yourself, mademoiselle. You are only young – and reckless.'

He went on:

'There remained Mrs Tanios. As soon as I saw her I realized that she was afraid. She saw that I realized that, and she very quickly made capital out of that momentary betrayal. She gave a very convincing portrait of a woman *who is afraid for her husband*. A little later she changed her tactics. It was very cleverly done – but the change did not deceive me. A woman can be afraid *for* her husband or she can be afraid *of* her husband – but she can hardly be *both*. Mrs Tanios decided on the latter role – and she played her part cleverly – even to coming out after me into the hall of the hotel and pretending that there was something she wanted to tell me. When her husband followed her, as she knew he would, she pretended that she could not speak before him.

'I realized at once, not that she feared her husband, but that she disliked him. And at once, summing the matter up, I felt convinced that here was the exact character I had been looking for. Here was – not a self-indulgent woman – but a thwarted one. A plain girl, leading a dull existence, unable to attract the men she would like to attract, finally accepting a man she did not care for rather than be left an old maid. I could trace her growing dissatisfaction with life, her life in Smyrna, exiled from all she cared for in life. Then the birth of her children and her passionate attachment to them.

'Her husband was devoted to her, but she came secretly to dislike him more and more. He had speculated with her money and lost it – another grudge against him.

'There was only one thing that illumined her drab life, the expectation of her Aunty Emily's death. Then she would have money, independence, the means to educate her children as she wished – and remember education means a lot to her: she was a professor's daughter.

'She may have already planned the crime, or had the idea of it in her mind, before she came to England. She had a certain knowledge of chemistry, having assisted her father in the laboratory. She knew the nature of Miss Arundell's complaint and she was well aware that phosphorus would be an ideal substance for her purpose.

'Then, when she came to Littlegreen House, a simpler method presented itself to her. The dog's ball – a thread of string across the top of the stairs. A simple, ingenious woman's idea.

'She made her attempt – and failed. I do not think that she

had any idea that Miss Arundell was aware of the true facts of the matter. Miss Arundell's suspicions were directed entirely against Charles. I doubt if her manner to Bella showed any alteration. And so, quietly and determinedly, this self-contained, unhappy, ambitious woman put her original plan into execution. She found an excellent vehicle for the poison, some patent capsules that Miss Arundell was in the habit of taking after meals. To open a capsule, place the phosphorus inside and close it again, was child's play. The capsule was replaced among the others. Sooner or later Miss Arundell would swallow it. Poison was not likely to be suspected. Even if by some unlikely chance it was, she herself would be nowhere near Market Basing at the time.

'Yet she took one precaution. She obtained a double supply of chloral hydrate at the chemist's, forging her husband's name to the prescription. I have no doubt of what that was for – to keep by her in case anything went wrong.

'As I say, I was convinced from the first moment I saw her that Mrs Tanios was the person I was looking for, but I had absolutely no *proof* of the fact. I had to proceed carefully. If Mrs Tanios had any idea I suspected her, I was afraid that she might proceed to a further crime. Furthermore, I believed that the idea of that crime had already occurred to her. Her one wish in life was to shake herself free of her husband.

'Her original murder had proved a bitter disappointment. The money, the wonderful all-intoxicating money, had all gone to Miss Lawson! It was a blow, but she set to work most intelligently. She began to work on Miss Lawson's conscience, which, I suspect, was already not too comfortable.'

There was a sudden outburst of sobs. Miss Lawson took out her handkerchief and cried into it.

'It's been dreadful,' she sobbed. 'I've been wicked! Very wicked. You see, I was very curious about the will – why Miss Arundell had made a new one, I mean. And one day, when Miss Arundell was resting, I managed to unlock the drawer in the desk. And then I found she'd left it all to *me*! Of course, I never dreamed it was so *much*. Just a few thousand – that's all I thought it was. And why not? After all, her own relations didn't *really care* for her! But then, when she was so ill, she asked for the will. I could see – I felt sure – she was going to destroy it . . . And that's when I was so wicked. I told her she'd sent it back to Mr Purvis. Poor dear, she was so forgetful. She never remembered what she'd done with things. She believed me. Said I must write for it, and I said I would.

'Oh, dear – oh, dear – and then she got worse and couldn't think of anything. And she died. And when the will was read and it was all that money, I felt *dreadful*. Three hundred and seventy-five thousand pounds. I'd never dreamed for a minute it was anything like that, or I wouldn't have done it.

'I felt just as though I'd *embezzled* the money – and I didn't know what to do. The other day, when Bella came to me, I told her that she should have half of it. I felt sure that then I would feel happy again.'

'You see?' said Poirot. 'Mrs Tanios was succeeding in her object. That is why she was so averse to any attempt to contest the will. She had her own plans, and the last thing she wanted to do was to antagonize Miss Lawson. She pretended, of course, to fall in at once with her husband's wishes, but she made it quite clear what her real feelings were.

'She had at that time two objects: to detach herself and her children from Dr Tanios and to obtain her share of the money. Then she would have what she wanted – a rich, contented life in England with her children.

'As time went on she could no longer conceal her dislike from her husband. In fact, she did not try to. He, poor man, was seriously upset and distressed. Her actions must have seemed quite incomprehensible to him. Really, they were logical enough. She was playing the part of the terrorized woman. If I had suspicions – and she was fairly sure that that must be the case – she wished me to believe that her husband had committed the murder. And at any moment that second murder, which I am convinced was already planned in her mind, might occur. I knew that she had a lethal dose of chloral in her possession. I feared that she would stage a pretended sucide and confession on his part.

'And still I had no evidence against her! And then, when I was quite in despair, I got something at last! Miss Lawson told me that she had seen Theresa Arundell kneeling on the stairs on the night of Easter Monday. I soon discovered that Miss Lawson could not have seen Theresa at all clearly – not nearly clearly enough to recognize her *features*. Yet she was quite positive in her identification. On being pressed she mentioned a brooch with Theresa's initials – T.A.

'On my request Miss Thersea Arundell showed me the brooch in question. At the same time she absolutely denied having been on the stairs at the time stated. At first I fancied someone else had borrowed her brooch, but when I looked at the brooch in the glass the truth leaped at me. Miss Lawson,

waking up, had seen a dim figure with the initials T.A. flashing
in the light. She had leapt to the conclusion that it was
Theresa.

'But if in the glass she had seen the initials T.A. – then the
real initials must have been A.T., since the glass naturally reversed the order.

'Of course Mrs Tanios's mother was Arabella Arundell. Bella
is only a contraction. A.T. stood for Arabella Tanios. There
was nothing odd in Mrs Tanios possessing a similar type of
brooch. It had been exclusive last Christmas, but by the spring
they were all the rage, and I had already observed that Mrs
Tanios copied her cousin Theresa's hats and clothes as far as
she was able with her limited means.

'In my own mind, at any rate, my case was proved.

'Now – what was I to do? Obtain a Home Office order for
the exhumation of the body? That could doubtless be managed.
I *might* prove that Miss Arundell had been poisoned with phosphorus, though there was a little doubt about that. The body
had been buried two months, and I understand that there have
been cases of phosphorus poisoning where no lesions have been
found and where the post-mortem appearances are very indecisive. Even then, could I connect Mrs Tanios with the purchase or possession of phosphorus? Very doubtful, since she
had probably obtained it abroad.

'At this juncture Mrs Tanios took a decisive action. She left
her husband, throwing herself on the pity of Miss Lawson. She
also definitely accused her husband of the murder.

'Unless I acted I felt convinced that he would be her next
victim. I took steps to isolate them one from the other on the
pretext that it was for her safety. She could not very well contradict that. Really, it was *his* safety I had in mind. And then
– and then—'

He paused – a long pause. His face had gone rather white.

'But that was only a temporary measure. I had to make sure
that the killer would kill no more. I had to assure the safety of
the innocent.

'So I wrote out my construction of the case and gave it to
Mrs Tanios.'

There was a long silence.

Dr Tanios cried out:

'Oh, my God, so that's why she killed herself.'

Poirot said gently:

'Was it not the best way? She thought so. There were you
see, the children to consider.'

Dr Tanios buried his face in his hands.

Poirot came forward and laid a hand on his shoulder.

'It had to be. Believe me, it was necessary. There would have been more deaths. First yours – then possibly, under certain circumstances, Miss Lawson's And so it goes on.'

He paused.

In a broken voice Tanios said:

'She wanted me – to take a sleeping-draught one night . . . There was something in her face – I threw it away. That was when I began to believe her mind was going . . .'

'Think of it that way. It is indeed partly true. But not in the legal meaning of the term. She knew the meaning of her action . . .'

Dr Tanios said wistfully:

'She was much too good for me – always.'

A strange epitaph on a self-confessed murderess!

30

THE LAST WORD

There is very little more to tell.

Theresa married her doctor shortly afterwards. I know them fairly well now, and I have learnt to appreciate Donaldson – his clarity of vision and the deep, underlying force and humanity of the man. His manner, I may say, is just as dry and precise as ever; Theresa often mimics him to his face. She is, I think, amazingly happy and absolutely wrapped up in her husband's career. He is already making a big name for himself and is an authority on the functions of ductless glands.

Miss Lawson, in an acute attack of conscience, had to be restrained forcibly from denuding herself of every penny. A settlement agreeable to all parties was run up by Mr Purvis whereby Miss Arundell's fortune was shared out between Miss Lawson, the two Arundells and the Tanios children.

Charles went through his share in a little over a year and, is now I believe, in British Columbia.

Just two incidents.

'You're a downy fellow, ain't you?' said Miss Peabody, stopping us as we emerged from the gate of Littlegreen House one

day. 'Managed to hush everything up! No exhumation. Everything done decently.'

'There seems to be no doubt that Miss Arundell died of
yellow atrophy of the liver,' said Poirot gently.

'That's very satisfactory,' said Miss Peabody. 'Bella Tanios
took an overdose of sleeping stuff, I hear.'

'Yes, it was very sad.'

'She was a miserable kind of woman – always wanting what
she hadn't got. People go a bit queer sometimes when they're
like that. Had a kitchen-maid once. Same thing. Plain girl. Felt
it. Started writing anonymous letters. Queer kinks people get.
Ah, well, I dare say it's all for the best.'

'One hopes so, madame. One hopes so.'

'Well,' said Miss Peabody, preparing to resume her walk. 'I'll
say this for you. You've hushed things up nicely. Very nicely
indeed.'

She walked on.

There was a plaintive 'Wuff' behind me.

I turned and opened the gate.

'Come on, old man.'

Bob bounced through. There was a ball in his mouth.

'You can't take that for a walk.'

Bob sighed, turned and slowly ejected the ball inside the
gate. He looked at it anxiously, then passed through.

He looked up at me.

'If you say so, master, I suppose it's all right.'

I drew a long breath.

'My word, Poirot, it's good to have a dog again.'

'The spoils of war,' said Poirot. 'But I would remind you,
my friend, that it was to *me* that Miss Lawson presented Bob,
not to *you*.'

'Possibly,' I said. 'But you're not really any good with a dog,
Poirot. You don't understand dog psychology! Now, Bob and
I understand each other perfectly, don't we?'

'Wuff,' said Bob in energetic assent.

AFTER THE FUNERAL

——— I ———

Old Lanscombe moved totteringly from room to room, pulling
up the blinds. Now and then he peered with screwed up
rheumy eyes through the windows.

Soon they would be coming back from the funeral. He
shuffled along a little faster. There were so many windows.

Enderby Hall was a vast Victorian house built in the Gothic
style. In every room the curtains were of rich faded brocade
or velvet. Some of the walls were still hung with faded silk.
In the green drawing-room, the old butler glanced up at the
portrait above the mantlepiece of old Cornelius Abernethie
for whom Enderby Hall had been built. Cornelius Abernethie's
brown beard stuck forward aggressively, his hand rested on
a terrestrial globe, whether by desire of the sitter, or as a sym-
bolic conceit on the part of the artist, no one could tell.

A very forceful looking gentleman, so old Lanscombe had
always thought, and was glad that he himself had never known
him personally. Mr Richard had been *his* gentleman. A good
master, Mr Richard. And taken very sudden, he'd been,
though of course the doctor had been attending him for some
little time. Ah, but the master had never recovered from the
shock of young Mr Mortimer's death. The old man shook
his head as he hurried through a connecting door into the
White Boudoir. Terrible, that had been, a real catastrophe.
Such a fine upstanding young gentleman, so strong and
healthy. You'd never have thought such a thing likely to
happen to him. Pitiful, it had been, quite pitiful. And Mr
Gordon killed in the war. One thing on top of another. That
was the way things went nowadays. Too much for the master,
it had been. And yet he'd seemed almost himself a week ago.

The third blind in the White Boudoir refused to go up as it
should. It went up a little way and stuck. The springs were
weak — that's what it was — very old, these blinds were, like
everything else in the house. And you couldn't get these old
things mended nowadays. Too old-fashioned, that's what they'd
say, shaking their heads in that silly superior way — as if the
old things weren't a great deal better than the new ones! *He*
could tell them that! Gimcrack, half the new stuff was — came

to pieces in your hands. The material wasn't good, or the craftsmanship either. Oh yes, *he* could tell them.

Couldn't do anything about this blind unless he got the steps. He didn't like climbing up the steps much, these days, made him come over giddy. Anyway, he'd leave the blind for now. It didn't matter, since the White Boudoir didn't face the front of the house where it would be seen as the cars came back from the funeral – and it wasn't as though the room was ever used nowadays. It was a lady's room, this, and there hadn't been a lady at Enderby for a long time now. A pity Mr Mortimer hadn't married. Always going off to Norway for fishing and to Scotland for shooting and to Switzerland for those winter sports, instead of marrying some nice young lady and settling down at home with children running about the house. It was a long time since there had been any children in the house.

And Lanscombe's mind went ranging back to a time that stood out clearly and distinctly – much more distinctly than the last twenty years or so, which were all blurred and confused and he couldn't really remember who had come and gone or indeed what they looked like. But he could remember the old days well enough.

More like a father to those young brothers and sisters of his, Mr Richard had been. Twenty-four when his father had died, and he'd pitched in right away to the business, going off every day as punctual as clockwork, and keeping the house running and everything as lavish as it could be. A very happy household with all those young ladies and gentlemen growing up. Fights and quarrels now and again, of course, and those governesses had had a bad time of it! Poor-spirited creatures, governesses, Lanscombe had always despised them. Very spirited the young ladies had been. Miss Geraldine in particular. Miss Cora, too, although she was so much younger. And now Mr Leo was dead, and Miss Laura gone too. And Mr Timothy such a sad invalid. And Miss Geraldine dying somewhere abroad. And Mr Gordon killed in the war. Although he was the eldest, Mr Richard himself turned out the strongest of the lot. Outlived them all, he had – at least not quite because Mr Timothy was still alive and little Miss Cora who'd married that unpleasant artist chap. Twenty-five years since he'd seen her and she'd been a pretty young girl when she went off with that chap, and now he'd hardly have known her, grown so stout – and so arty-crafty in her dress! A Frenchman her husband had been, or nearly a Frenchman – and no good ever came of marrying one of *them*! But Miss Cora had always been a bit − well *simple like* you'd call it if she'd lived in a village. Always one of them in a family.

She'd remembered *him* all right. 'Why, it's Lanscombe!' she'd said and seemed ever so pleased to see him. Ah, they'd all been fond of him in the old days and when there was a dinner party they'd crept down to the pantry and he'd given them jelly and Charlotte Russe when it came out of the dining-room. They'd all known old Lanscombe, and now there was hardly anyone who remembered. Just the younger lot whom he could never keep clear in his mind and who just thought of him as a butler who'd been there a long time. A lot of strangers, he had thought, when they all arrived for the funeral − and a seedy lot of strangers at that!

Not Mrs Leo − she was different. She and Mr Leo had come here off and on ever since Mr Leo married. She was a nice lady, Mrs Leo − a *real* lady. Wore proper clothes and did her hair well and looked what she was. And the master had always been fond of her. A pity that she and Mr Leo had never had any children. . . .

Lanscombe roused himself; what was he doing standing here and dreaming about old days with so much to be done? The blinds were all attended to on the ground floor now, and he'd told Janet to go upstairs and do the bedrooms. He and Janet and the cook had gone to the funeral service in the church but instead of going on to the Crematorium they'd driven back to the house to get the blinds up and the lunch ready. Cold lunch, of course, it had to be. Ham and chicken and tongue and salad. With cold lemon soufflé and apple tart to follow. Hot soup first − and he'd better go along and see that Marjorie had got it on ready to serve, for they'd be back in a minute or two now for certain.

Lanscombe broke into a shuffling trot across the room. His gaze, abstracted and uncurious, just swept up to the picture over this mantelpiece − the companion portrait to the one in the green drawing-room. It was a nice painting of white satin and pearls. The human being round whom they were draped and clasped was not nearly so impressive. Meek features, a rosebud mouth, hair parted in the middle. A woman both modest and unassuming. The only thing really worthy of note about Mrs Cornelius Abernethie had been her name − Coralie.

For over sixty years after their original appearance, Coral Cornplasters and the allied 'Coral' foot preparations still held their own. Whether there had ever been anything outstanding about Coral Cornplasters nobody could say – but they had appealed to the public fancy. On a foundation of Coral Corn-plasters there had arisen this neo-Gothic palace, its acres of gardens, and the money that had paid out an income to seven sons and daughters and had allowed Richard Abernethie to die three days ago a very rich man.

2

Looking into the kitchen with a word of admonition, Lans-combe was snapped at by Marjorie, the cook. Marjorie was young, only twenty-seven, and was a constant irritation to Lanscombe as being so far removed from what his conception of a proper cook should be. She had no dignity and no proper appreciation of his, Lanscombe's position. She frequently called the house 'a proper old mausoleum' and complained of the immense area of the kitchen, scullery and larder, saying that it was a 'day's walk to get round them all.' She had been at Enderby two years and only stayed because in the first place the money was good, and in the second because Mr Abernethie had really appreciated her cooking. She cooked very well. Janet, who stood by the kitchen table, refreshing herself with a cup of tea, was an elderly housemaid who, although enjoying frequent acid disputes with Lanscombe, was nevertheless usually in alliance with him against the younger generation as represented by Marjorie. The fourth person in the kitchen was Mrs Jacks, who 'came in' to lend assistance where it was wanted and who had much enjoyed the funeral.

'Beautiful it was,' she said with a decorous sniff as she re-plenished her cup. 'Nineteen cars and the church quite full and the Canon read the service beautiful, I thought. A nice fine day for it, too. Ah, poor dear Mr Abernethie, there's not many like him left in the world. Respected by all, he was.'

There was the note of a horn and the sound of a car coming up the drive, and Mrs Jacks put down her cup and exclaimed: 'Here they are.'

Marjorie turned up the gas under her large saucepan of creamy chicken soup. The large kitchen range of the days of Victorian grandeur stood cold and unused, like an altar to the past.

The cars drove up one after the other and the people issuing from them in their black clothes moved rather uncertainly across the hall and into the big green drawing-room. In the big steel grate a fire was burning, tribute to the first chill of the autumn days and calculated to counteract the further chill of standing about at a funeral.

Lanscombe entered the room, offering glasses of sherry on a silver tray.

Mr Entwhistle, senior partner of the old and respected firm of Bollard, Entwhistle, Entwhistle and Bollard, stood with his back to the fireplace warming himself. He accepted a glass of sherry, and surveyed the company with his shrewd lawyer's gaze. Not all of them were personally known to him, and he was under the necessity of sorting them out, so to speak. Introductions before the departure for the funeral had been hushed and perfunctory.

Appraising old Lanscombe first, Mr Entwhistle thought to himself, 'Getting very shaky, poor old chap – going on for ninety I shouldn't wonder. Well, he'll have that nice little annuity. Nothing for *him* to worry about. Faithful soul. No such thing as old-fashioned service nowadays. Household helps and baby sitters, God help us all! A sad world. Just as well, perhaps, poor Richard didn't last his full time. He hadn't much to live for.'

To Mr Entwhistle, who was seventy-two, Richard Abernethie's death at sixty-eight was definitely that of a man dead before his time. Mr Entwhistle had retired from active business two years ago, but as executor of Richard Abernethie's will and in respect for one of his oldest clients who was also a personal friend, he had made the journey to the North.

Reflecting in his own mind on the provisions of the will, he mentally appraised the family.

Mrs Leo, Helen, he knew well, of course. A very charming woman for whom he had both liking and respect. His eyes dwelt approvingly on her now as she stood near one of the windows. Black suited her. She had kept her figure well. He liked the clear cut features, the springing line of grey hair back from her temples and the eyes that had once been likened to cornflowers and which were still quite vividly blue.

How old was Helen now? About fifty-one or -two, he supposed. Strange that she had never married again after Leo's death. An attractive woman. Ah, but they had been very devoted, those two.

His eyes went on to Mrs Timothy. He had never known her very well. Black didn't suit her – country tweeds were her wear. A big sensible, capable-looking woman. She'd always been a good devoted wife to Timothy. Looking after his health, fussing over him – fussing over him a bit too much, probably. Was there really anything the matter with Timothy? Just a hypochondriac, Mr Entwhistle suspected. Richard Abernethie had suspected so, too. 'Weak chest, of course, when he was a boy,' he had said. 'But blest if I think there's much wrong with him now.' Oh well, everybody had to have some hobby. Timothy's hobby was the all absorbing one of his own health. Was Mrs Tim taken in? Probably not – but women never admitted that sort of thing. Timothy must be quite comfortably off. He'd never been a spendthrift. However, the extra would not come amiss – not in these days of taxation. He'd probably had to retrench his scale of living a good deal since the war.

Mr Entwhistle transferred his attention to George Crossfield, Laura's son. Dubious sort of fellow Laura had married. Nobody had ever known much about him. A stockbroker he had called himself. Young George was in a solicitor's office – not a very reputable firm. Good-looking young fellow – but something a little shifty about him. He couldn't have too much to live on. Laura had been a complete fool over her investments. She'd left next to nothing when she died five years ago. A handsome romantic girl she'd been, but no money sense.

Mr Entwhistle's eyes went on from George Crossfield. Which of the two girls was which? Ah yes, that was Rosamund, Geraldine's daughter, looking at the wax flowers on the malachite table. Pretty girl, beautiful, in fact – rather a silly face. On the stage. Repertory companies or some nonsense like that. Had married an actor, too. Good-looking fellow. '*And* knows he is,' thought Mr Entwhistle, who was prejudiced against the stage as a profession. 'Wonder what sort of a background *he* has and where he comes from.'

He looked disapprovingly at Michael Shane with his fair hair and his haggard charm.

Now Susan. Gordon's daughter, would do much better on the stage than Rosamund. More personality. A little too much personality for everyday life, perhaps. She was quite near him and Mr Entwhistle studied her covertly. Dark hair, hazel – almost golden-eyes, a sulky attractive mouth. Beside her was the husband she had just married – a chemist's assistant, he understood. Really, a chemist's assistant! In Mr Entwhistle's creed girls did not marry young men who served behind a counter. But now of course, they married *anybody*! The young man, who had a pale nondescript face and sandy hair, seemed very ill at ease. Mr Entwhistle wondered why, but decided charitably that it was the strain of meeting so many of his wife's relations.

Last in his survey Mr Entwhistle came to Cora Lansquenet. There was a certain justice in that, for Cora had decidedly been an afterthought in the family. Richard's youngest sister, she had been born when her mother was just on fifty, and that meek woman had not survived her tenth pregnancy (three children had died in infancy). Poor little Cora! All her life, Cora had been rather an embarrassment, growing up tall and gawky, and given to blurting out remarks that had always better have remained unsaid. All her elder brothers and sisters had been very kind to Cora, atoning for her deficiencies and covering her social mistakes. It had never really occurred to anyone that Cora would marry. She had not been a very attractive girl, and her rather obvious advances to visiting young men had usually caused the latter to retreat in some alarm. And then, Mr Entwhistle mused, there had come the Lansquenet business – Pierre Lansquenet, half French, whom she had come across in an Art school where she had been having very correct lessons in painting flowers in water colours. But somehow she had got into the Life class and there she had met Pierre Lansquenet and had come home and announced her intention of marrying him. Richard Abernethie had put his foot down – he hadn't liked what he saw of Pierre Lansquenet and suspected that the young man was really in search of a rich wife. But whilst he was making a few researches into Lansquenet's antecedents, Cora had bolted with the fellow and married him out of hand. They had spent most of their married life in Brittany and Cornwall and other painters' conventional haunts. Lansquenet had been a very bad painter and not, by all accounts, a very nice man, but Cora had remained devoted to him and had never forgiven her family for their attitude to him. Richard had generously made his young sister an allowance and on that they had, so Mr Entwhistle believed, lived. He doubted if Lansquenet had ever earned any money at all. He must have been dead now twelve years or more, thought Mr Entwhistle. And now here was his widow, rather cushion-like in shape and dressed in wispy artistic black with festoons of jet beads, back in the home of her girlhood, moving about and touching things and exclaiming with pleasure when she recalled some childish memory. She made very little pretence of grief at her brother's death. But then, Mr Entwhistle reflected, Cora had never pretended.

Re-entering the room Lanscombe murmured in muted tones suitable for the occasion:

'Luncheon is served.'

2

After the delicious chicken soup, and plenty of cold viands accompanied by an excellent *chablis*, the funeral atmosphere lightened. Nobody had really felt any deep grief for Richard Abernethie's death since none of them had any close ties with him. Their behaviour had been suitably decorous and subdued (with the exception of the uninhibited Cora who was clearly enjoying herself) but it was now felt that the decencies had been observed and that normal conversation could be resumed. Mr Entwhistle encouraged this attitude. He was experienced in funerals and knew exactly how to set correct funeral timing.

After the meal was over, Lanscombe indicated the library for coffee. This was his feeling for niceties. The time had come when business – in other words, The Will – would be discussed. The library had the proper atmosphere for that with its bookshelves and its very heavy red velvet curtains. He served coffee to them there and then withdrew, closing the door.

After a few desultory remarks, everyone began to look tentatively at Mr Entwhistle. He responded promptly after glancing at his watch.

'I have to catch the 3.30 train,' he began.

Others, it seemed, also had to catch that train.

'As you know,' said Mr Entwhistle, 'I am the executor of Richard Abernethie's will—'

He was interrupted.

'*I* didn't know,' said Cora Lansquenet brightly. 'Are you? Did he leave me anything?'

Not for the first time, Mr Entwhistle felt that Cora was too apt to speak out of turn.

Bending a repressive glance a her he continued:

'Up to a year ago, Richard Abernethie's will was very simple. Subject to certain legacies he left everything to his son Mortimer.'

'Poor Mortimer,' said Cora. 'I do think all this infantile paralysis is *dreadful*.

'Mortimer's death, coming so suddenly and tragically, was

a great blow to Richard. It took him some months to rally from it. I pointed out to him that it might be advisable for him to make new testamentary dispositions.'

Maude Abernethie asked in her deep voice:

'What would have happened if he *hadn't* made a new will? Would it – would it all have gone to Timothy – as the next of kin, I mean?'

Mr Entwhistle opened his mouth to give a disquisition on the subject of next of kin, thought better of it, and said crisply:

'On my advice, Richard decided to make a new will. First of all, however, he decided to get better acquainted with the younger generation.'

'He had us upon appro,' said Susan with a sudden rich laugh. 'First George and then Greg and me, and then Rosamund and Michael.'

Gregory Banks said sharply, his thin face flushing:

'I don't think you ought to put it like that, Susan. On appro, indeed!'

'But that was what it was, wasn't it, Mr Entwhistle?' 'Did he leave *me* anything?' repeated Cora.

Mr Entwhistle coughed and spoke rather coldly:

'I propose to send you all copies of the will. I can read it to you now if you like but its legal phraseology may seem to you rather obscure. Briefly it amounts to this: After certain small bequests and a substantial legacy to Lanscombe to purchase an annuity, the bulk of the estate – a very considerable one – is to be divided into six equal portions. Four of these, after all duties are paid, are to go to Richard's brother Timothy, his nephew George Crossfield, his niece Susan Banks, and his niece Rosamund Shane. The other two portions are to be held upon trust and the income from them paid to Mrs Helen Abernethie, the widow of his brother Leo; and to his sister Mrs Cora Lansquenet, during their lifetime. The capital after their death to be divided between the other four beneficiaries or their issue.'

'That's *very* nice!' said Cora Lansquenet with real appreciation. 'An income! How much?'

'I – er – can't say exactly at present. Death duties, of course, will be heavy and—'

'Can't you give me any idea?'

Mr Entwhistle realised that Cora must be appeased.

'Possibly somewhere in the neighbourhood of three to four thousand a year.'

'Goody!' said Cora. 'I shall go to Capri.'

Helen Abernethie said softly:

'How very kind and generous of Richard. I do appreciate his affection towards me.'

'He was very fond of you', said Mr Entwhistle. 'Leo was his favourite brother and your visits to him were always much appreciated after Leo died.'

'I wish I had realised how ill he was – I came up to see him not long before he died, but although I knew he had been ill, I did not think it was serious.'

'It was always serious,' said Mr Entwhistle. 'But he did not want it talked about and I do not believe that anybody expected the end to come as soon as it did. The doctor was quite surprised, I know.'

' "*Suddenly, at his residence*," that's what it said in the paper,' said Cora, nodding her head. 'I wondered then.'

'It was a shock to all of us,' said Maude Abernethie. 'It upset poor Timothy dreadfully. So sudden, he kept saying. So sudden.'

'Still, it's been hushed up very nicely, hasn't it?' said Cora.

Everybody stared at her and she seemed a little flustered.

'I think you're all quite right,' she said hurriedly. *Quite* right. I mean – it can't do any good – making it public. Very unpleasant for everybody. It should be kept strictly in the family.'

The faces turned towards her looked even more blank.

Mr Entwhistle leaned forward:

'Really, Cora, I'm afraid I don't quite understand what you mean.'

Cora Lansquenet looked round at the family in wide-eyed surprise. She tilted her head on one side with a bird-like movement.

'But he *was* murdered, wasn't he?' she said.

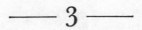

3

Travelling to London in the corner of a first-class carriage Mr Entwhistle gave himself up to somewhat uneasy thought over that extraordinary remark made by Cora Lansquenet. Of course Cora was a rather unbalanced and excessively stupid woman, and she had been noted, even as a girl, for the embarrassing manner in which she had blurted out unwelcome truths. At least, he didn't mean *truths* – that was *quite* the wrong word to use. Awkward statements – that was a much better term.

In his mind he went back over the immediate sequence to that unfortunate remark. The combined stare of many startled and disapproving eyes had roused Cora to a sense of the enormity of what she had said.

Maude had exclaimed, '*Really*, Cora!' George had said, 'My dear Aunt Cora.' Somebody else had said, 'What do you mean?'

And at once Cora Lansquenet, abashed, and convicted of enormity, had burst into fluttering phrases.

'Oh I'm sorry – I didn't mean – oh, of course, it was very stupid of me, but I did think from what he said— Oh, of course I know it's quite all right, but his death was so *sudden* – please forget that I said anything at all— I didn't mean to be so stupid – I know I'm always saying the wrong thing.'

And then the momentary upset had died down and there had been a practical discussion about the disposition of the late Richard Abernethie's personal effects. The house and its contents, Mr Entwhistle supplemented, would be put up for sale.

Cora's unfortunate *gaffe* had been forgotten. After all, Cora had always been, if not subnormal, at any rate embarrassingly *naïve*. She had never had any idea of what should or should not be said. At nineteen it had not mattered so much. The mannerisms of an *enfant terrible* can persist to then, but an *enfant terrible* of nearly fifty is decidedly disconcerting. To blurt out unwelcome truths—

Mr Entwhistle's train of thought came to an abrupt check. It was the second time that that disturbing word had occurred. *Truths*. And why was it so disturbing? Because, of course, that had always been at the bottom of the embarrassment that Cora's outspoken comments had caused. It was because her *naïve* statements had been either true or had contained some grain of truth that they had been so embarrassing!

Although in the plump woman of forty-nine, Mr Entwhistle had been able to see little resemblance to the gawky girl of earlier days, certain of Cora's mannerisms had persisted – the slight bird-like twist of the head as she brought out a particularly outrageous remark – a kind of air of pleased expectancy. In just such a way had Cora once commented on the figure of the kitchen-maid. 'Mollie can hardly get near the

kitchen table, her stomach sticks out so. It's only been like that
the last month or two. I wonder *why* she's getting so fat?'

Cora had been quickly hushed. The Abernethie household
was Victorian in tone. The kitchen-maid had disappeared from
the premises the next day, and after due inquiry the second
gardener had been ordered to make an honest woman of her
and had been presented with a cottage in which to do so.

Far-off memories – but they had their point . . .

Mr Entwhistle examined his uneasiness more closely. What
was there in Cora's ridiculous remarks that had remained to
tease his subconscious in this manner? Presently he isolated two
phrases. 'I did think from what he said—' and 'his death was
so sudden. . . .'

Mr Entwhistle examined that last remark first. Yes, Richard's death could, in a fashion, be considered sudden. Mr
Entwhistle had discussed Richard's health both with Richard
himself and his doctor. The latter had indicated plainly that
a long life could not be expected. If Mr Abernethie took
reasonable care of himself he might live two or even three
years. Perhaps longer – but that was unlikely. In any case the
doctor had anticipated no collapse in the near future.

Well, the doctor had been wrong — but doctors, as they were
the first to admit themselves, could never be sure about the
individual reaction of a patient to disease. Cases given up,
unexpectedly recovered. Patients on the way to recovery, relapsed and died. So much depended on the vitality of the
patient. On his own inner urge to live.

And Richard Abernethie, though a strong and vigorous
man, had had no great incentive to live.

For six months previously his only surviving son, Mortimer,
had contracted infantile paralysis and had died within a week.
His death had been a shock greatly augmented by the fact that
he had been such a particularly strong and vital young man.
A keen sportsman, he was also a good athlete and was one of
those people of whom it was said that he had never had a day's
illness in his life. He was on the point of becoming engaged to
a very charming girl and his father's hopes for the future were
centred in this dearly loved and thoroughly satisfactory son of
his.

Instead had come tragedy. And besides the sense of personal loss, the future had held little to stir Richard Abernethie's interest. One son had died in infancy, the second
without issue. He had no grandchildren. There was, in fact,

no one of the Abernethie name to come after him, and he was the holder of a vast fortune with wide business interests which he himself still controlled to a certain extent. Who was to succeed to that fortune and to the control of those interests?

That this had worried Richard deeply, Entwhistle knew. His only surviving brother was very much of an invalid. There remained the younger generation. It had been in Richard's mind, the lawyer thought, though his friend had not actually said so to choose one definite successor, though minor legacies would probably have been made. Anyway, as Entwhistle knew, within the last six months Richard Abernethie had invited to stay with him, in succession, his nephew George, his niece Susan and her husband, his niece Rosamund and her husband, and his sister-in-law, Mrs Leo Abernethie. It was amongst the first three, so the lawyer thought, that Abernethie had looked for his successor. Helen Abernethie, he thought, had been asked out of personal affection and even possibly as someone to consult, for Richard had always held a high opinion of her good sense and practical judgment. Mr Entwhistle also remembered that sometime during that six months period Richard had paid a short visit to his brother Timothy.

The net result had been the will which the lawyer now carried in his brief-case. An equable distribution of property. The only conclusion that could be drawn, therefore, was that he had been disappointed both in his nephew, and in his nieces or perhaps in his nieces' husbands.

As far as Mr Entwhistle knew, he had not invited his sister, Cora Lansquenet, to visit him – and that brought the lawyer back to that first disturbing phrase that Cora had let slip so incoherently – 'but I did think from what he said—'

What had Richard Abernethie said? And when had he said it? If Cora had not been to Enderby, then Richard Abernethie must have visited her at the artistic village in Berkshire where she had a cottage. Or was it something that Richard had said in a letter?

Mr Entwhistle frowned. Cora, of course, was a very stupid woman. She could easily have misinterpreted a phrase, and twisted its meaning. But he did wonder what the phrase could have been. . . .

There was enough uneasiness in him to make him consider the possibility of approaching Mrs Lansquenet on the subject. Not too soon. Better not make it seem of importance. But he *would* like to know just what it was that Richard Abernethie had said to her which had led her to pipe up so briskly with that outrageous question:

'But he was murdered, wasn't he?'

2

In a third-class carriage, farther along the train, Gregory Banks said to his wife:

'That aunt of yours must be completely bats!'

'Aunt Cora?' Susan was vague. 'Oh, yes, I believe she was always a bit simple or something.'

George Crossfield, sitting opposite, said sharply:

'She really ought to be stopped from going about saying things like that. It might put ideas into people's heads.'

Rosamund Shane, intent in outlining the cupid's bow of her mouth with lipstick, murmured vaguely:

'I don't suppose anyone would pay any attention to what a frump like that says. The most peculiar clothes and lashings and lashings of jet—'

'Well, I think it ought to be stopped,' said George.

'All right, darling' laughed Rosamund, putting away her lipstick and contemplating her image with satisfaction in the mirror. 'You stop it.'

Her husband said unexpectedly:

'I think George is right. It's so easy to set people talking.'

'Well, would it matter?' Rosamund contemplated the question. The cupid's bow lifted at the corners in a smile. 'It might really be rather fun.'

'Fun?' Four voices spoke.

'Having a murder in the family,' said Rosamund. 'Thrilling, you know!'

It occurred to that nervous and unhappy young man Gregory Banks that Susan's cousin, setting aside her attractive exterior might have some faint points of resemblance to her Aunt Cora. Her next words rather confirmed his impression.

'If he was murdered,' said Rosamund, 'who do you think did it?'

Her gaze travelled thoughtfully round the carriage.

'His death has been awfully convenient for all of us,' she said thoughtfully. 'Michael and I are absolutely on our beam ends. Mick's had a really good part offered to him in the Sandbourne show if he can afford to wait for it. Now we'll be in clover. We'll be able to back our own show if we want to. As a matter of fact there's a play with a simply wonderful part—'

Nobody listened to Rosamund's ecstatic disquisition. Their attention had shifted to their own immediate future.

'Touch and go,' thought George to himself. 'Now I can put that money back and nobody will ever know. . . . But it's been a near shave.'

Gregory closed his eyes as he lay back against the seat. Escape from bondage.

Susan said in her clear rather hard voice, 'I'm very sorry, of course, for poor old Uncle Richard. But then he *was* very old, and Mortimer had died, and he'd nothing to live for and it would have been awful for him to go on as an invalid year after year. *Much* better for him to pop off suddenly like this with no fuss.'

Her hard confident young eyes softened as they watched her husband's absorbed face. She adored Greg. She sensed vaguely that Greg cared for her less than she cared for him – but that only strengthened her passion. Greg was hers, she'd do anything for him. Anything at all. . . .

3

Maude Abernethie, changing her dress for dinner at Enderby, (for she was staying the night) wondered if she ought to have offered to stay longer to help Helen out with the sorting and clearing of the house. There would be all Richard's personal things . . . There might be letters . . . All important papers, she supposed, had already been taken possession of by Mr Entwhistle. And it really was necessary for her to get back to Timothy as soon as possible. He fretted so when she was not there to look after him. She hoped he would be pleased about the will and not annoyed. He had expected, she knew, that most of Richard's fortune would come to *him*. After all, he was the only surviving Abernethie. Richard could surely have trusted *him* to look after the younger generation. Yes, she was afraid Timothy *would* be annoyed. . . . And that was so bad for his digestion. And really, when he was annoyed, Timothy could become quite unreasonable. There were times when he seemed to lose his sense of proportion . . . She wondered if she ought to speak to Dr Barton about it . . . Those sleeping pills – Timothy had been taking far too many of them lately – he got so angry when she wanted to keep the bottle for him. But they could be dangerous – Dr Barton had said so – you could get drowsy and forget you'd taken them – and then take more. And then anything might happen! There certainly weren't as many left in the bottle as there ought to be . . . Timothy was really very naughty about medicines. He wouldn't listen to her . . . He was very difficult sometimes.

She sighed – then brightened. Things were going to be much easier now. The garden, for instance—

4

Helen Abernethie sat by the fire in the green drawing-room waiting for Maude to come down to dinner.

She looked round her, remembering old days here with Leo and the others. It had been a happy house. But a house like this needed *people*. It needed children and servants and big meals and plenty of roaring fires in winter. It had been a sad house when it had been lived in by one old man who had lost his son. . . .

Who would buy it, she wondered? Would it be turned into an hotel, or an institute, or perhaps one of those hostels for young people. That was what happened to these vast houses nowadays. No one would buy them to live in. It would be pulled down, perhaps, and the whole estate built over. It made her sad to think of that, but she pushed the sadness aside resolutely. It did one no good to dwell on the past. This house, and happy days here, and Richard, and Leo, all that was good, but it was over. She had her own activities and friends and interests. Yes, her interests. . . . And now, with the income Richard had left her, she would be able to keep on the villa in Cyprus and do all the things she had planned to do.

How worried she had been lately over money – taxation – all those investments going wrong. . . . Now, thanks to Richard's money, all that was over. . . .

Poor Richard. To die in his sleep like that had been really a great mercy. . . . *Suddenly on the 22nd* – she supposed that that was what had put the idea into Cora's head. Really Cora was outrageous! She always had been. Helen remembered meeting her once abroad, soon after her marriage to Pierre Lansquenet. She had been particularly foolish and fatuous that day, twisting her head sideways, and making dogmatic statements about painting, and particularly about her husband's painting, which must have been most uncomfortable for him.

No man could like his wife appearing such a fool. And Cora was a fool! Oh, well, poor thing, she couldn't help it, and that husband of hers hadn't treated her too well.

Helen's gaze rested absently on a bouquet of wax flowers that stood on a round malachite table. Cora had been sitting beside it when they had all been sitting round waiting to start for the church. She had been full of reminiscences and delighted recognitions of various things and was clearly so pleased at being back in her old home that she had completely lost sight of the reason for which they were assembled.

'But perhaps,' thought Helen, 'she was just less of a hypocrite than the rest of us. . . .'

Cora had never been one for observing the conventions. Look at the way she had plumped out that question: 'But he was murdered, wasn't he?'

The faces all round, startled, shocked, staring at her! Such a variety of expressions there must have been on those faces. . . .

And suddenly, seeing the picture clearly in her mind, Helen frowned. . . . There was something wrong with that picture. . . .

Something . . . ?

Somebody . . . ?

Was it an expression on someone's face? Was that it? Something that – how could she put it? – ought not to have been there . . . ?

She didn't know . . . she couldn't place it . . . but there had been something – somewhere – *wrong*.

5

Meanwhile, in the buffet at Swindon, a lady in wispy mourning and festoons of jet was eating bath buns and drinking tea and looking forward to the future. She had no premonitions of disaster. She was happy.

These cross-country journeys were certainly tiring. It would have been easier to get back to Lytchett St Mary via London – and not so very much more expensive. Ah, but expense didn't matter now. Still, she would have had to travel with the – family – probably having to talk all the way. Too much of an effort.

No, better to go home cross-country. These bath buns were really excellent. Extraordinary how hungry a funeral made you feel. The soup at Enderby had been delicious – and so was the cold soufflé.

How smug people were – and what hypocrites! All those faces – when she'd said that about murder! The way they'd all looked at her!

Well, it had been the right thing to say. She nodded her head in satisfied approval of herself. Yes, it had been the right thing to do.

She glanced up at the clock. Five minutes before her train went. She drank up her tea. Not very good tea. She made a grimace.

For a moment or two she sat dreaming. Dreaming of the future unfolding before her. . . . She smiled like a happy child.

She was really going to enjoy herself at last . . . She went out to the small branch line train busily making plans. . . .

—— 4 ——

Mr Entwhiste passed a very restless night. He felt so tired and so unwell in the morning that he did not get up.

His sister who kept house for him, brought up his breakfast on a tray and explained to him severely how wrong he had been to go gadding off to the North of England at his age and in his frail state of health.

Mr Entwhistle contented himself with saying that Richard Abernethie had been a very old friend.

'Funerals!' said his sister with deep disapproval. 'Funerals are absolutely fatal for a man of your age! You'll be taken off as suddenly as your precious Mr Abernethie was if you don't take more care of yourself.'

The word 'suddenly' made Mr Entwhistle wince. It also silenced him. He did not argue.

He was well aware of what had made him flinch at the word *suddenly*.

Cora Lansquenet! What she had suggested was definitely quite impossible, but all the same he would like to find out exactly why she had suggested it. Yes, he would go down to Lytchett St Mary and see her. He could pretend that it was business connected with probate, that he needed her signature. No need to let her guess that he had paid any attention to her silly remark. But he would go down and see her – and he would do it soon.

He finished his breakfast and lay back on his pillows and read *The Times*. He found *The Times* very soothing.

It was about a quarter to six that evening when his telephone rang.

He picked it up. The voice at the other end of the wire was that of Mr James Parrott, the present second partner of Bollard, Entwhistle, Entwhistle and Bollard.

'Look here Entwhistle,' said Mr Parrott. 'I've just been rung up by the police from a place called Lytchett St Mary.'

'Lytchett St Mary?'

'Yes. It seems—' Mr Parrott paused a moment. He seemed embarrassed. 'It's about a Mrs Cora Lansquenet. Wasn't she one of the heirs of the Abernethie estate?'

'Yes, of course. I saw her at the funeral yesterday.'

'Oh? She was at the funeral, was she?'

'Yes. What about her?'

'Well,' Mr Parrott sounded apologetic. 'She's – it's really most extraordinary – she's been well – *murdered.*'

Mr Parrott said the last word with the uttermost deprecation. It was not the sort of word, he suggested, that ought to mean anything to the firm of Bollard, Entwhistle, Entwhistle and Bollard.

'*Murdered?*'

'Yes – yes – I'm afraid so. Well, I mean, there's no doubt about it.'

'How did the police get on to us?'

'Her companion, or housekeeper, or whatever she is – a Miss Gilchrist. The police asked for the name of her nearest relative or her solicitors. And this Miss Gilchrist seemed rather doubtful about relatives and their addresses, but she knew about us. So they got through at once.'

'What makes them think she was murdered?' demanded Mr Entwhistle.

Mr Parrott sounded apologetic again.

'Oh well, it seems there can't be any doubt about *that* – I mean it was a hatchet or something of that kind – a very violent sort of crime.'

'Robbery?'

'That's the idea. A window was smashed and there are some trinkets missing and drawers pulled out and all that, but the police seem to think there might be something – well – phony about it."

'What time did it happen?'

'Sometime between two and four-thirty this afternoon.'

'Where was the housekeeper?'

'Changing library books in Reading. She got back about five o'clock and found Mrs Lansquenet dead. The police want to know if we've any idea of who could have been likely to attack her. I said,' Mr Parrott's voice sounded outraged, 'that I thought it was a most unlikely thing to happen.'

'Yes, of course.'

'It *must* be some half-witted local oaf – who thought there might be something to steal and then lost his head and attacked her. That must be it – eh, don't you think so, Entwhistle?'

'Yes, yes . . .' Mr Entwhistle spoke absentmindedly.

Parrott was right, he told himself. That was what must have happened. . . .

But uncomfortably he heard Cora's voice saying brightly:

'*He was murdered, wasn't he*?'

Such a fool, Cora. Always had been. Rushing in where angels fear to tread . . . Blurting out unpleasant truths . . .

Truths!

That blasted word again. . . .

2

Mr Entwhistle and Inspector Morton looked at each other appraisingly.

In his neat precise manner Mr Entwhistle had placed at the Inspector's disposal all the relevant facts about Cora Lansquenet. Her upbringing, her marriage, her widowhood, her financial position, her relatives.

'Mr Timothy Abernethie is her only surviving brother and her next of kin, but he is a recluse and an invalid, and is quite unable to leave home. He has empowered me to act for him and to make all such arrangments as may be necessary.'

The Inspector nodded. It was a relief for him to have this shrewd elderly solicitor to deal with. Moreover he hoped that the lawyer might be able to give him some assistance in solving what was beginning to look like a rather puzzling problem.

He said:

'I understand from Miss Gilchrist that Mrs Lansquenet had been North, to the funeral of an elder brother, on the day before her death?'

'That is so, Inspector. I myself was there.'

'There was nothing unusual in her manner – nothing strange – or apprehensive?'

Mr Entwhistle raised his eyebrows in well-simulated surprise.

'Is it customary for there to be something strange in the manner of a person who is shortly to be murdered?' he asked.

The Inspector smiled rather ruefully.

'I'm not thinking of her being "fey" or having a premonition. No, I'm just hunting around for something – well, something out of the ordinary.'

'I don't think I quite understand you, Inspector,' said Mr Entwhistle.

'It's not a very easy case to understand, Mr Entwhistle. Say someone watched the Gilchrist woman come out of the house at about two o'clock and go along to the village and the bus stop. This someone then deliberately takes the hatchet that was lying by the woodshed, smashes the kitchen window with it, gets into the house, goes upstairs, attacks Mrs Lansquenet with the hatchet – and attacks her savagely. Six or eight blows were struck.' Mr Entwhistle flinched – 'Oh, yes, quite a brutal crime. Then the intruder pulls out a few drawers, scoops up a few trinkets – worth perhaps a tenner in all, and clears off.'

'She was in bed?'

'Yes. It seems she returned late from the North the night before, exhausted and very excited. She'd come into some legacy as I understand?'

'Yes.'

'She slept very badly and woke with a terrible headache. She had several cups of tea and took some dope for her head and then told Miss Gilchrist not to disturb her till lunch-time. She felt no better and decided to take two sleeping pills. She then sent Miss Gilchrist into Reading by the bus to change some library books. She'd have been drowsy, if not already asleep, when this man broke in. He could have taken what he wanted by means of threats, or he could easily have gagged her. A hatchet, deliberately taken up with him from outside, seems excessive.'

'He may just have meant to threaten her with it,' Mr Entwhistle suggested. 'If she showed fight then—'

'According to the medical evidence there is no sign that she did. Everything seems to show that she was lying on her side sleeping peacefully when she was attacked.'

Mr Entwhistle shifted uneasily in his chair.

'One does hear of these brutal and rather senseless murders,' he pointed out.

'Oh yes, yes, that's probably what it will turn out to be. There's an alert out, of course, for any suspicious character. Nobody local is concerned, we're pretty sure of that. The locals are all accounted for satisfactorily. Most peope are at work at that time of day. Of course her cottage is up a lane outside the village proper. Anyone could get there easily without being seen. There's a maze of lanes all round the village. It was a fine morning and there has been no rain for some days, so there aren't any distinctive car tracks to go by – in case anyone came by car.'

'You think someone came by car?' Mr Entwhistle asked sharply.

The Inspector shrugged his shoulders. 'I don't know. All I'm saying is there are curious features about the case. These, for instance—' He shoved across his desk a handful of things – a trefoil-shaped brooch with small pearls, a brooch set with amethysts, a small string of seed pearls, and a garnet bracelet.

'Those are the things that were taken from her jewel box. They were found just outside the house shoved into a bush.'

'Yes – yes, that *is* rather curious. Perhaps if her assailant was frightened at what he had done—'

'Quite. But he would probably then have left them upstairs in her room. . . . Of course a panic may have come over him between the bedroom and the front gate.'

Mr Entwhistle said quietly:

'Or they may, as you are suggesting, have only been taken as a blind.'

'Yes, several possibilities . . . Of course this Gilchrist woman may have done it. Two women living alone together – you never know what quarrels or resentments or passions may have been aroused. Oh, yes, we're taking that possibility into consideration as well. But it doesn't seem very likely. From all accounts they were on quite amicable terms.' He paused before going on. 'According to you, nobody stands to gain by Mrs Lansquenet's death?'

The lawyer shifted uneasily.

'I didn't quite say that.'

Inspector Morton looked up sharply.

'I thought you said that Mrs Lansquenet's source of income was an allowance made to her by her brother and that as far as you knew she had no property or means of her own.'

'That is so. Her husband died a bankrupt, and from what I

620

knew of her as a girl and since, I should be surprised if she had ever saved or accumulated any money.'

'The cottage itself is rented, not her own, and the few sticks of furniture aren't anything to write home about, even in these days. Some spurious "cottage oak" and some arty painted stuff. Whoever she's left them to won't gain much — if she's made a will, that is to say.'

Mr Entwhistle shook his head.

'I know nothing about her will. I had not seen her for many years, you must understand.'

'Then what exactly did you mean just now? You had something in mind, I think?'

'Yes. Yes, I did. I wished to be strictly accurate.'

'Were you referring to the legacy you mentioned? The one that her brother left? Had she the power to dispose of that by will?'

'No, not in the sense you mean. She had no power to dispose of the capital. Now that she is dead, it will be divided amongst the five other beneficiaries of Richard Abernethie's will. That is what I meant. All five of them will benefit automatically by her death.'

The Inspector looked disappointed.

'Oh, I thought we were on to something. Well, there certainly seems no motive there for anyone to come and swipe her with a hatchet. Looks as though it's some chap with a screw loose — one of these adolescent criminals, perhaps — a lot of them about. And then he lost his nerve and bushed the trinkets and ran . . . Yes, it must be that. Unless it's the highly respectable Miss Gilchrist, and I must say that seems unlikely.'

'When did she find the body?'

'Not until just about five o'clock. She came back from Reading by the 4.50 bus. She arrived back at the cottage, let herself in by the front door, and went into the kitchen and put the kettle on for tea. There was no sound from Mrs Lansquenet's room, but Miss Gilchrist assumed that she was still sleeping. Then Miss Gilchrist noticed the kitchen window; the glass was all over the floor. Even then, she thought at first it might have been done by a boy with a ball or a catapult. She went upstairs and peeped very gently into Mrs Lansquenet's room to see if she were asleep or if she was ready for some tea. Then of course, she let loose, shrieked, and rushed down the lane to the nearest neighbour. Her story seems perfectly consistent and there was no trace of blood in her room or in the bathroom, or on her clothes. No, I don't think Miss Gilchrist had anything to do with it. The doctor got there at half-past five. He puts the time of death not later than four-thirty – and probably much nearer two o'clock, so it looks as though who-ever it was, was hanging round waiting for Miss Gilchrist to leave the cottage.'

The lawyer's face twitched slightly. Inspector Morton went on: 'You'll be going to see Miss Gilchrist, I suppose?'

'I thought of doing so.'

'I should be glad if you would. She's told us, I think, every-thing that she can, but you never know. Sometimes, in con-versation, some point or other may crop up. She's a trifle old maidish – but quite a sensible, practical woman – and she's really been most helpful and efficient.'

He paused and then said:

'The body's at the mortuary. If you would like to see it—'

Mr Entwhistle assented, though with no enthusiasm.

Some few minutes later he stood looking down at the mortal remains of Cora Lansquenet. She had been savagely attacked and the henna dyed fringe was clotted and stiffened with blood. Mr Entwhistle's lips tightened and he looked away queasily.

Poor little Cora. How eager she had been the day before yesterday to know whether her brother had left her anything. What rosy anticipations she must have had of the future. What a lot of silly things she could have done – and enjoyed doing – with the money.

Poor Cora. . . . How short a time those anticipations had lasted.

No one had gained by her death – not even the brutal assail-ant who had thrust away those trinkets as he fled. Five people had a few thousands more of capital – but the capital they had already received was probably more than sufficient for them. No, there could be no motive there.

Funny that murder should have been running in Cora's mind the very day before she herself was murdered.

'*He was murdered, wasn't he?*'

Such a ridiculous thing to say. Ridiculous! quite ridiculous! Much too ridiculous to mention to Inspector Morton.

Of course, after he had seen Miss Gilchrist . . .

Supposing that Miss Gilchrist, although it was unlikely, could throw any light on what Richard had said to Cora.

'*I thought from what he said—*' What *had* Richard said?

'I must see Miss Gilchrist at once,' said Mr Entwhistle to himself.

3

Miss Gilchrist was a spare faded-looking woman with short, iron-grey hair. She had one of those indeterminate faces that women around fifty so often acquire.

She greeted Mr Entwhistle warmly.

'Im *so* glad you have come, Mr Entwhistle. I really know so *little* about Mrs Lansquenet's family, and of course I've never never had anything to do with a *murder* before. It's too dreadful!'

Mr Entwhistle felt quite sure that Miss Gilchrist had never before had anything to do with murder. Indeed, her reaction to it was very much that of his partner.

'One *reads* about them, of course,' said Miss Gilchrist, relegating crimes to their proper sphere. And even *that* I'm not very fond of doing. So *sordid*, most of them.'

Following her into the sitting-room Mr Entwhistle was looking sharply about him. There was a strong smell of oil paint. The cottage was overcrowded, less by furniture, which was much as Inspector Morton had described it, than by pictures. The walls were covered with pictures, mostly very dark and dirty oil paintings. But there were water-colour sketches as well and one or two still lifes. Smaller pictures were stacked on the window-seat.

'Mrs Lansquenet used to buy them at sales,' Miss Gilchrist explained. 'It was a great interest to her, poor dear. She went to all the sales round about. Pictures go so cheap, nowadays, a mere song. She never paid more than a pound for any of them, sometimes only a few shillings, and there was a wonderful chance, she always said, of picking up something worth while. She used to say that this was an Italian Primitive that might be worth a lot of money.'

Mr Entwhistle looked at the Italian Primitive pointed out to him dubiously. Cora, he reflected, had never really known anything about pictures. He'd eat his hat if any of these daubs were worth a five pound note!

'Of course,' said Miss Gilchrist, noticing his expression, and quick to sense his reaction. 'I don't know much myself, though my father was a painter – not a very successful one, I'm afraid. But I used to do water-colours myself as a girl and I heard a lot of talk about painting and that made it nice for

Mrs Lansquenet to have someone she could talk to about painting and who'd understand. Poor dear soul, she cared so much about artistic things.'

'You were fond of her?'

A foolish question, he told himself. Could she possibly answer 'no'? Cora, he thought, must have been a tiresome woman to live with.

'Oh *yes*,' said Miss Gilchrist. 'We got on *very* well together. In some ways, you know, Mrs Lansquenet was just like a child. She said anything that came into her head. I don't know that her *judgement* was always very good—'

One does not say of the dead – 'She was a thoroughly silly woman' – Mr Entwhistle said, 'She was not in any sense an intellectual woman.

'No – no – perhaps not. But she was very shrewd, Mr Entwhistle. Really very shrewd. It quite surprised me sometimes – how she managed to hit the nail on the head.'

Mr Entwhistle looked at Miss Gilchrist with more interest. He thought that she was no fool herself.

'You were with Mrs Lansquenet for some years, I think?'

'Three and a half.'

'You – er – acted as companion and also did the – er – well – looked after the house?'

It was evident that he had touched on a delicate subject. Miss Gilchrist flushed a little.

'Oh yes, indeed. I did most of the cooking – I *quite* enjoy cooking – and did some dusting and light housework. None of the *rough*, of course.' Miss Gilchrist's tone expressed a firm principle. Mr Entwhistle who had no idea what 'the rough' was, made a soothing murmur.

'Mrs Panter from the village came in for that. Twice a week regularly. You see, Mr Entwhistle. I could not have contemplated being in any way a *servant*. When my little teashop failed – such a disaster – it was the war, you know. A delightful place. I called it the Willow Tree and all the china was blue willow pattern – sweetly pretty – and the cakes *really* good – I've always had a hand with cakes and scones. Yes, I was doing really well and then the war came and supplies were cut down and the whole thing went bankrupt – a war casualty, that is what I always say, and I try to think of it like that. I lost the little money my father left me that I had invested in it, and of course I had to look round for something to do. I'd never been trained for anything. So I went to one lady but it didn't answer at all – she was so rude and overbearing – and then I did some office work – but I didn't like that at all, and then I came to Mrs Lansquenet and we suited each other from the start – her husband being an artist and everything.' Miss Gilchrist came to a breathless stop and added mournfully: 'But how I loved my dear, dear little tea-shop. Such *nice* people used to come to it!'

Looking at Miss Gilchrist, Mr Entwhistle felt a sudden stab of recognition – a composite picture of hundreds of ladylike figures approaching him in numerous Bay Trees, Ginger Cats, Blue Parrots, Willow Trees and Cosy Corners, all chastely encased in blue or pink or orange overalls and taking orders for pots of china tea and cakes. Miss Gilchrist had a Spiritual Home – a lady-like tea-shop of Ye Olde Worlde variety with a suitable genteel clientèle. There must, he thought, be large numbers of Miss Gilchrists all over the country, all looking much alike with mild patient faces and obstinate upper lips and slightly wispy grey hair.

Miss Gilchrist went on:

'But really I must not talk about myself. The police have been very kind and considerate. Very kind indeed. An Inspector Morton came over from headquarters and he was most understanding. He even arranged for me to go and spend the night at Mrs Lake's down the lane but I said "No." I felt it my duty to stay here with all Mrs Lansquenet's nice things in the house. They took the – the—' Miss Gilchrist gulped a little – 'the body away, of course, and locked up the room, and the Inspector told me there would be a constable on duty in the kitchen all night – because of the broken window – it has been reglazed this morning, I am glad to say – where was I? Oh yes, so I said I should be *quite* all right in my own room, though I must confess I *did* pull the chest of drawers across the door and put a big jug of water on the window-sill. One never knows – and if by any chance it *was* a maniac – one does hear of such things . . .'

Here Miss Gilchrist ran down. Mr Entwhistle said quickly:

'I am in possession of all the main facts. Inspector Morton gave them to me. But if it would not distress you too much to give me your own account—?'

'Of course, Mr Entwhistle. I know *just* what you feel. The police are so impersonal, are they not? Rightly so, of course.'

'Mrs Lansquenet got back from the funeral the night before last,' Mr Entwhistle prompted.

'Yes, her train didn't get in until quite late. I had ordered a taxi to meet it as she told me to. She was very tired, poor dear

– as was only natural – but on the whole she was in quite good spirits.'

'Yes, yes. Did she talk about the funeral at all?'

'Just a little. I gave her a cup of hot milk – she didn't want anything else – and she told me that the church had been quite full and lots and lots of flowers – oh! and she said that she was sorry not to have seen her older brother – Timothy – was it?'

'Yes, Timothy.'

'She said it was over twenty years since she had seen him and that she hoped he would have been there, but she quite realised he would have thought it better not to come under the circumstances, but that his wife was there and that she'd never been able to stand Maude – oh dear, I *do* beg your pardon, Mr Entwhistle – it just slipped out – I never meant—'

'Not at all. Not at all,' said Mr Entwhistle encouragingly. 'I am no relation, you know. And I believe that Cora and her sister-in-law never hit it off very well.'

'Well, she almost said as much. 'I always knew Maude would grow into one of those bossy interfering women,' is what she said. And then she was very tired and said she'd go to bed at once – I'd got her hot-water bottle in all ready – and she went up.'

'She said nothing else that you can remember specially?'

'She had no *premonition*, Mr Entwhistle, if that is what you mean. I'm sure of that. She was really, you know, in remarkably good spirits – apart from tiredness and the – the sad occasion. She asked me how I'd like to go to Capri. To Capri! Of course I said it would be too wonderful – it's a thing I'd never dreamed I'd ever do – and she said, 'We'll go!' Just like that. I gathered – of course it wasn't actually *mentioned* – that her brother had left her an annuity or something of the kind.'

Mr Entwhistle nodded.

'Poor dear. Well, I'm glad she had the pleasure of planning – at all events.' Miss Gilchrist sighed and murmured wistfully. 'I don't suppose I shall ever go to Capri now . . .'

'And the next morning?' Mr Entwhistle prompted, oblivious of Miss Gilchrist's disappointments.

'The next morning Mrs Lansquenet wasn't at all well. Really, she looked dreadful. She'd hardly slept at all, she told me. Nightmares. "It's because you were overtired yesterday," I told her, and she said maybe it was. She had her breakfast in bed, and she didn't get up all the morning, but at

lunch-time she told me that she still hadn't been able to sleep.
"I feel so restless," she said, "I keep thinking of some things
and wondering." And then she said she'd take some sleeping
tablets and try and get a good sleep in the afternoon. And she
wanted me to go over by bus to Reading and change her two
library books, because she'd finished them both on the train
journey and she hadn't got anything to read. Usually two books
lasted her nearly a week. So I went off just after two and that
– that – was the last time—' Miss Gilchrist began to sniff. 'She
must have been asleep, you know. She wouldn't have heard anything and the Inspector assures me that she didn't suffer.
. . . He thinks the first blow killed her. Oh dear, it makes me
quite sick even to *think* of it!'

'Please, please. I've no wish to take you any further over
what happened. All I wanted was to hear what you could tell
me about Mrs Lansquenet before the tragedy.'

'Very natural, I'm sure. Do tell her relations that apart from
having such a bad night she was really very happy and looking forward to the future.'

Mr Entwhistle paused before asking his next question. He
wanted to be careful not to lead the witness.

'She did not mention any of her relations in particular?'

'No, no, I don't think so.' Miss Gilchrist considered. 'Except what she said about being sorry not to see her brother
Timothy.'

'She did not speak at all about her brother's decease? The
– er – cause of it? Anything like that?'

'No.'

There was no sign of alertness in Miss Gilchrist's face. Mr
Entwhistle felt certain there would have been if Cora had
plumped out her verdict of murder.

'He'd been ill for some time, I think,' said Miss Gilchrist
vaguely, 'though I must say I was surprised to hear it. He
looked so very vigorous.'

Mr Entwhistle said quickly:

'You saw him – when?'

'When he came down here to see Mrs Lansquenet. Let me
see – that was about three weeks ago.'

'Did he stay here?'

'Oh –no – just came for luncheon. It was quite a surprise.
Mrs Lansquenet hadn't expected him. I gather there had been
some family disagreement. She hadn't seen him for years she
told me.'

'Yes, that is so.'

'It quite upset her – seeing him again – and probably realising how ill he was—'

'She knew that he was ill?'

'Oh yes, I remember quite well. Because I wondered – only in my own mind, you understand – if perhaps Mr Abernethie might be suffering from softening of the brain. An aunt of mine—'

Mr Entwhistle deftly side-tracked the aunt.

'Something Mrs Lansquenet said caused you to think of softening of the brain?'

'Yes. Mrs Lansquenet said something like "Poor Richard. Mortimer's death must have aged him a lot. He sounds quite senile. All these fancies about persecution and that someone was poisoning him. Old people get like that." And of course, as I knew, that is only too *true*. This aunt that I was telling you about – was convinced the servants were trying to poison her in her food and at last would eat only boiled eggs – because she said, you couldn't get inside a boiled egg to poison it. We humoured her, but if it had been nowadays I don't know *what* we should have done. With eggs so scarce and mostly foreign at that, so that boiling is always risky.'

Mr Entwhistle listened to the saga of Miss Gilchrist's aunt with deaf ears. He was very much disturbed.

He said at last, when Miss Gilchrist had twittered into silence:

'I suppose Mrs Lansquenet didn't take all this too seriously?'

'Oh no, Mr Entwhistle, she *quite* understood.'

Mr Entwhistle found that remark disturbing too, though not quite in the sense in which Miss Gilchrist had used it.

Had Cora Lansquenet understood? Not then, perhaps, but later. Had she understood only too well?

Mr Entwhiste knew that there had been no senility about Richard Abernethie. Richard had been in full possession of his faculties. He was not the man to have persecution mania in any form. He was, as he always had been, a hard-headed business man – and his illness made no difference in that respect.

It seemed extraordinary that he should have spoken to his sister in the terms that he had. But perhaps Cora, with her odd childlike shrewdness had read between the lines, and had crossed the t's and dotted the i's of what Richard Abernethie had actually said.

In most ways, thought Mr Entwhistle, Cora had been a complete fool. She had no judgment, no balance, and a crude childish point of view, but she had also the child's uncanny knack of sometimes hitting the nail on the head in a way that seemed quite startling.

Mr Entwhistle left it at that. Miss Gilchrist, he thought, knew no more than she had told him. He asked whether she knew if Cora Lansquenet had left a will. Miss Gilchrist replied promptly that Mrs Lansquenet's will was at the Bank.

With that and after making certain further arrangements he took his leave. He insisted on Miss Gilchrist's accepting a small sum in cash to defray present expenses and told her he would communicate with her again, and in the meantime he would be grateful if she would stay on at the cottage while she was looking about for a new post. That would be, Miss Gilchrist said, a great convenience and really she was not at all nervous.

He was able to escape without being shown round the cottage by Miss Gilchrist, and introduced to various pictures by the late Pierre Lansquenet which were crowded into the small dining-room and which made Mr Entwhistle flinch – they were mostly nudes executed with a singular lack of draughtsmanship but with much fidelity to detail. He was also made to admire various small oil sketches of picturesque fishing ports done by Cora herself.

'Polperro,' said Miss Gilchrist proudly. 'We were there last year and Mrs Lansquenet was delighted with its picturesqueness.'

Mr Entwhistle, viewing Polperro from the south-west, from the north-west, and presumably from the several other points of the compass, agreed that Mrs Lansquenet had certainly been enthusiastic.

'Mrs Lansquenet promised to leave me her sketches,' said Miss Gilchrist wistfully. 'I admired them so much. One can really see the waves breaking in this one, can't one? Even if she forgot, I might perhaps have just *one* as a souvenir, do you think?'

'I'm sure that could be arranged,' said Mr Entwhistle graciously.

He made a few further arrangements and then left to interview the Bank Manager and to have a further consultation with Inspector Morton.

───── 5 ─────

'Worn out, that's what you are,' said Miss Entwhistle in the indignant and bullying tones adopted by devoted sisters towards brothers for whom they keep house. 'You shouldn't do it at your age. What's it all got to do with you, I'd like to know? You've retired, haven't you?'

Mr Entwhistle said mildly that Richard Abernethie had been one of his oldest friends.

'I dare say. But Richard Abernethie's dead, isn't he? So I see no reason for you to go mixing yourself up in things that are no concern of yours and catching your death of cold in these nasty draughty railway trains. And murder, too! *I* can't see why they sent for you at all.'

'They communicated with me because there was a letter in the cottage signed by me, telling Cora the arrangements for the funeral.'

'Funerals! One funeral after another, and that reminds me. Another of these precious Abernethies has been ringing you up – Timothy, I think he said. From somewhere in Yorkshire – and *that's* about a funeral, too! Said he'd ring again later.'

A personal call for Mr Entwhistle came through that evening. Taking it, he heard Maude Abernethie's voice at the other end.

'Thank goodness I've got hold of you at last! Timothy has been in the most terrible state. This news about Cora has upset him dreadfully

'Quite understandable,' said Mr Entwhistle.

'What did you say?'

'I said it was quite understandable.'

'I suppose so.' Maude sounded more than doubtful. 'Do you mean to say it was really murder?'

(*'It was murder, wasn't it?'* Cora had said. But this time there was no hesitation about the answer.)

'Yes, it was murder, said Mr Entwhistle.

'And with a hatchet, so the papers say?'

'Yes.'

'It seems *quite* incredible to me," said Maude, 'that Timothy's sister – his own sister – can have been murdered with a *hatchet*!

It seemed no less incredible to Mr Entwhistle. Timothy's life was so remote from violence that even his relations, one felt, ought to be equally exempt.

"I'm afraid one has to face the fact," said Mr Entwhistle mildly.

'I am really *very* worried about Timothy. It's so bad for him all this! I've got him to bed now but he insists on my persuading you to come up and see him. He wants to know a hundred things – whether there will be an inquest, and who ought to attend, and how soon after that the funeral can take place, and where, and what funds there are, and if Cora expressed any wishes about being cremated or what, and if she left a will—'

Mr Entwhistle interrupted before the catalogue got too long. 'There is a will, yes. She left Timothy her executor.'

'Oh dear, I'm afraid Timothy can't undertake anything—'

'The firm will attend to all the necessary business. The will's very simple. She left her own sketches and an amethyst brooch to her companion, Miss Gilchrist, and everything else to Susan.'

'To Susan? Now I wonder why Susan? I don't believe she ever saw Susan – not since she was a baby anyway.'

'I imagine that it was because Susan was reported to have made a marriage not wholly pleasing to the family.'

Maude snorted.

'Even Gregory is a great deal better than Pierre Lansquenet ever was! Of course marrying a man who serves in a shop would have been unheard of in my day – but a chemist's shop is much better than a haberdasher's – and at least Gregory seems quite respectable.' She paused and added: 'Does this mean that Susan gets the income Richard left to Cora?'

'Oh no. The capital of that will be divided according to the instructions of Richard's will. No, poor Cora had only a few hundred pounds and the furniture of her cottage to leave. When outstanding debts are paid and the furniture sold I doubt if the whole thing will amount to more than at most five hundred pounds.' He went on: 'There will have to be an inquest, of course. That is fixed for next Thursday. If Timothy is agreeable, we'll send down young Lloyd to watch the proceedings on behalf of the family.' He added apologetically: 'I'm afraid it may attract some notoriety owing to the – er – circumstances.'

'How very unpleasant! Have they caught the wretch who did it?'

'Not yet.'

'One of these dreadful halfbaked young men who go about the country roving and murdering, I suppose. The police are so incompetent.'

'No, no,' said Mr Entwhistle. 'The police are by no means incompetent. Don't imagine that, for a moment.'

'Well, it all seems to me quite extraordinary. And *so* bad for Timothy. I suppose you couldn't possibly come down here, Mr Entwhistle? I should be *most* grateful if you could. I think Timothy's mind might be set at rest if you were here to re-assure him.'

Mr Entwhistle was silent for a moment. The invitation was not unwelcome.

'There is something in what you say,' he admitted. 'And I shall need Timothy's signature as executor to certain documents. Yes, I think it might be quite a good thing.'

'That is splendid. I am so relieved. To-morrow? And you'll stay the night? The best train is the 11.20 from St Pancras.'

'It will have to be an afternoon train, I'm afraid. I have,' said Mr Entwhistle, 'other business in the morning. . . .'

2

George Crossfield greeted Mr Entwhistle heartily but with, perhaps, just a shade of surprise.

Mr Entwhistle said, in an explanatory way, although it really explained nothing:

'I've just come up from Lytchett St Mary.'

'Then it really was Aunt Cora? I read about it in the papers and I just couldn't believe it. I thought it must be someone of the same name.'

'Lansquenet is not a common name.'

'No, of course it isn't. I suppose there is a natural aversion to believing that anyone of one's own family can be murdered. Sounds to me rather like that case last month on Dartmoor.'

'Does it?'

'Yes. Same circumstances. Cottage in a lonely position. Two elderly women living together. Amount of cash taken really quite pitifully inadequate one would think.'

'The value of money is always relative,' said Mr Entwhistle. 'It is the need that counts.'

'Yes – yes, I suppose you're right.'

'If you need ten pounds desperately – then fifteen is more than adequate. And inversely also. If your need is for a hundred pounds, forty-five would be worse than useless. And if it's thousands you need, then hundreds are not enough.'

George said with a sudden flicker of the eyes: 'I'd say *any* money came in useful these days. Everyone's hard up.'

'But not desperate,' Mr Entwhistle pointed out. 'It's the desperation that counts.'

'Are you thinking of something in particular?'

'Oh no, not at all.' He paused then went on: 'It will be a little time before the estate is settled; would it be convenient for you to have an advance?'

'As a matter of fact, I was going to raise the subject. However, I saw the Bank this morning and referred them to you and they were quite obliging about an overdraft.'

Again there came that flicker in George's eyes, and Mr Entwhistle, from the depths of his experience, recognised it. George he felt certain, had been, if not desperate, then in very sore straits for money. He knew at that moment, what he had felt subconsciously all along, that in money matters he would not trust George. He wondered if old Richard Abernethie, who also had had great experience in judging men, had felt that. Mr Entwhistle was also sure that after Mortimer's death, Richard Abernethie had formed the intention of making George his heir. George was not an Abernethie, but he was the only male of the younger generation. He was the natural successor to Mortimer. Richard Abernethie had sent for George, had had him staying in the house for some days. It seemed probable that at the end of the visit the older man had not found George satisfactory. Had he felt instinctively, as Mr Entwhistle felt, that George was not straight? George's father, so the family had thought, had been a poor choice on Laura's part. A stockbroker who had had other rather mysterious activities. George took after his father rather than after the Abernethies.

Perhaps misinterpreting the old lawyer's silence, George said with an uneasy laugh:

'Truth is, I've not been very lucky with my investments lately. I took a bit of a risk and it didn't come off. More or less cleaned me out. But I'll be able to recoup myself now. All one needs is a bit of capital. Ardens Consolidated are pretty good, don't you think?'

Mr Entwhistle neither agreed not dissented. He was wondering if by any chance George had been speculating with money that belonged to clients and not with his own? If George had been in danger of criminal prosecution—

Mr Entwhistle said precisely:

'I tried to reach you the day after the funeral, but I suppose you weren't in the office.'

'Did you? They never told me. As a matter of fact, I thought I was entitled to a day off after the good news!'

'The good news?'

George reddened.

'Oh look here, I didn't mean Uncle Richard's death. But knowing you've come into money does give one a bit of a kick. One feels one must celebrate. As a matter of fact I went to Hurst Park. Backed two winners. It never rains but it pours! If your luck's in, it's in! Only a matter of fifty quid, but it all helps.'

'Oh yes,' said Mr Entwhistle. 'It all helps. And there will now be an additional sum coming to you as a result of your Aunt Cora's death.'

George looked concerned.

'Poor old girl,' he said. 'It does seem rotten luck, doesn't it? Probably just when she was all set to enjoy herself.'

'Let us hope the police will find the person responsible for her death,' said Mr Entwhistle.

'I expect they'll get him all right. They're good, our police. They round up all the undesirables in the neighbourhood and go through 'em with a tooth comb – make them account for their actions at the time it happened.'

'Not so easy if a little time has elapsed,' said Mr Entwhistle. He gave a wintry little smile that indicated he was about to make a joke. 'I myself was in Hatchard's bookshop at 3.30 on the day in question. Should I remember that if I were questioned by the police in ten days' time? I very much doubt it. And you, George, you were at Hurst Park. Would you remember which day you went to the races in – say – a month's time?'

'Oh I could fix it by the funeral – the day after.'

'True – true. And then you backed a couple of winners. Another aid to memory. One seldom forgets the name of a horse on which one has won money. Which were they, by the way?'

'Let me see. Gaymarck and Frogg II. Yes, I shan't forget them in a hurry.'

Mr Entwhistle gave his dry little cackle of laughter and took his leave.

It's lovely to see you, of course,' said Rosamund without any marked enthusiasm. 'But it's frightfully early in the morning.'

She yawned heavily.

'It's eleven o'clock,' said Mr Entwhistle.

Rosamund yawned again. She said apologetically:

'We had the hell of a party last night. Far too much to drink. Michael's got a terrible hangover still.'

Michael appeared at this moment, also yawning. He had a cup of black coffee in his hand and was wearing a very smart dressing-gown. He looked haggard and attractive – and his smile had the usual charm. Rosamund was wearing a black skirt, a rather dirty yellow pullover, and nothing else as far as Mr Entwhistle could judge.

The precise and fastidious lawyer did not approve at all of the young Shanes' way of living. The rather ramshackle flat on the first floor of a Chelsea house – the bottles and glasses and cigarette ends that lay about in profusion – the stale air, and the general air of dust and dishevelment.

In the midst of this discouraging setting Rosamund and Michael bloomed with their wonderful good looks. They were certainly a very handsome couple and they seemed, Mr Entwhistle thought, very fond of each other. Rosamund was certainly adoringly fond of Michael.

'Darling,' she said. 'Do you think just a teeny sip of champagne? Just to pull us together and toast the future. Oh, Mr Entwhistle, it really is the most marvellous luck Uncle Richard leaving us all that lovely money just now—'

Mr Entwhistle noted the quick, almost scowling frown that Michael gave, but Rosamund went on serenely:

'Because there's the most wonderful chance of a play. Michael's got an option on it. It's a most wonderful part for him and even a small part for me, too. It's about one of these young criminals, you know, they are really saints – it's absolutely full of the latest modern ideas.'

'So it would seem,' said Mr Entwhistle stiffly.

'He robs, you know, and he kills, and he's hounded by the police and by society – and then in the end, he does a miracle.'

Mr Entwhistle sat in outraged silence. Pernicious nonsense these young fools talked! *And* wrote.

Not that Michael Shane was talking much. There was still a faint scowl on his face.

'Mr Entwhistle doesn't want to hear all our rhapsodies,

Rosamund,' he said. 'Shut up for a bit and let him tell us why he's come to see us.'

'There are just one or two little matters to straighten out,' said Mr Entwhistle. 'I have just come back from Lytchett St Mary.'

'Then it *was* Aunt Cora who was murdered? We saw it in the paper. And I said it must be because it's a very uncommon name. Poor old Aunt Cora. I was looking at her at the funeral that day and thinking what a frump she was and that really one might as well be dead if one looked like that – and now she *is* dead. They absolutely wouldn't *believe* it last night when I told them that that murder with the hatchet in the paper was actually *my aunt*! They just laughed, didn't they, Michael?'

Michael Shane did not reply and Rosamund with every appearance of enjoyment said:

'Two murders one after another. It's almost too much, isn't it?'

'Don't be a fool, Rosamund, your Uncle Richard wasn't murdered.'

'Well, Cora thought he was.'

Mr Entwhistle intervened to ask:

'You came back to London after the funeral, didn't you?'

'Yes, we came back by the same train as you did.'

'Of course . . . of course. I ask because I tried to get hold of you,' he shot a quick glance at the telephone – 'on the following day – several times in fact, and couldn't get an answer.'

'Oh dear – I'm so sorry. What were we doing that day? The day before yesterday. We were here until about twelve, weren't we? And then you went round to try and get hold of Rosenheim and you went on to lunch with Oscar and I went out to see if I could get some nylons and round the shops. I was to meet Janet but we missed each other. Yes, I had a lovely afternoon shopping – and then we dined at the *Castile,* We got back here about ten o'clock, I suppose.'

'About that,' said Michael. He was looking thoughtfully at Mr Entwhistle. 'What did you want to get hold of us for, sir?'

'Oh! Just some points that had arisen about Richard Abernethie's estate – papers to sign – all that.'

Rosamund asked: 'Do we get the money now, or not for ages,'

'I'm afraid,' said Mr Entwhistle, 'that the law is prone to delays.'

'But we can get an advance, can't we?' Rosamund looked alarmed. 'Michael said we could. Actually it's terribly important. Because of the play.'

Michael said pleasantly:

'Oh, there's no real hurry. It's just a matter of deciding whether or not to take up the option.'

'It will be quite easy to advance you some money,' said Mr Entwhistle. 'As much as you need.'

'Then that's all right.' Rosamund gave a sigh of relief. She added as an afterthought: 'Did Aunt Cora leave any money?'

'A little. She left it to your cousin Susan.'

'Why Susan, I should like to know! Is it much?'

'A few hundred pounds and some furniture.'

'Nice furniture?'

'No,' said Mr Entwhistle.

Rosamund lost interest. 'It's all very odd, isn't it?' she said. 'There was Cora, after the funeral, suddenly coming out with "He *was* murdered!" and then, the very next day, *she* goes and gets *herself* murdered? I mean, it is *odd*, isn't it?

There was a moment's rather uncomfortable silence before Mr Entwhistle said quietly:

'Yes, it is indeed very odd. . . .'

4

Mr Entwhistle studied Susan Banks as she leant forward across the table talking in her animated manner.

None of the loveliness of Rosamund here. But it was an attractive face and its attraction lay, Mr Entwhistle decided, in its vitality. The curves of the mouth were rich and full. It was a woman's mouth and her body was very decidedly a woman's – emphatically so. Yet in many ways Susan reminded him of her uncle, Richard Abernethie. The shape of her head, the line of her jaw, the deep-set reflectve eyes. She had the same kind of dominant personality that Richard had had, the same driving energy, the same foresightedness and forthright judgment. Of the three members of the younger generation she alone seemed to be made of the metal that had raised up the vast Abernethie fortunes. Had Richard recognised in this niece a kindred spirit of his own? Mr Entwhistle thought he must have done. Richard had always had a keen appreciation of character. Here, surely, were exactly the qualities of which he was in search. And yet, in his will, Richard Abernethie had made no distinction in her favour. Distrustful, as Mr Entwhistle believed, of George, passing over that lovely dimwit, Rosamund – could he not have found in Susan what he was seeking – an heir of his own mettle?

If not, the cause must be – yes, it followed logically – the husband. . . .

Mr Entwhistle's eyes slid gently over Susan's shoulder to where Gregory Banks stood absently whittling at a pencil.

A thin, pale, nondescript young man with reddish sandy hair. So overshadowed by Susan's colourful personality that it was difficult to realise what he himself was really like. Nothing to take hold of in the fellow – quite pleasant, ready to be agreeable – a 'yes' man, as the modern term went. And yet that did not seem to describe him satisfactorily. There was something vaguely disquieting about the unobtrusiveness of Gregory Banks. He had been an unsuitable match – yet Susan had insisted on marrying him – had overborne all opposition – why? What had she seen in him?

And now, six months after the marriage – 'She's crazy about the fellow,' Mr Entwhistle said to himself. He knew the signs. A large number of wives with matrimonial troubles had passed through the office of Bollard, Entwhistle, Entwhistle and Bollard. Wives madly devoted to unsatisfactory and often what appeared quite unprepossessing husbands, wives contemptuous of, and bored by, apparently attractive and impeccable husbands. What any woman saw in some particular man was beyond the comprehension of the average intelligent male. It just was so. A woman who could be intelligent about everything else in the world could be a complete fool when it came to some particular man. Susan, thought Mr Entwhistle, was one of those women. For her the world revolved around Greg. And that had its dangers in more ways than one.

Susan was talking with emphasis and indignation.

'—because it is disgraceful. You remember that woman who was murdered in Yorkshire last year? Nobody was ever arrested. And the old woman in the sweet shop who was killed with a crowbar. They detained some man, and then they let him go!'

'There has to be evidence, my dear,' said Mr Entwhistle. Susan paid no attention.

'And that other case – a retired nurse – that was a hatchet or an axe – just like Aunt Cora.'

'Dear me, you appear to have made quite a study of these crimes, Susan,' said Mr Entwhistle mildly.

'Naturally one remembers these things – and when someone in one's own family is killed – and in very much the same way – well it shows that there must be a lot of these sorts of people going round the countryside, breaking into places and attacking lonely women – and that the police just don't *bother*!'

Mr Entwhistle shook his head.

'Don't belittle the police, Susan. They are a very shrewd and patient body of men – persistent, too. Just because it isn't still mentioned in the newspapers doesn't mean that a case is closed Far from it.'

'And yet there are hundreds of unsolved crimes every year.'

'Hundreds?' Mr Entwhistle looked dubious. 'A certain number, yes. But there are many occasions when the police know who has committed a crime but where the evidence is insufficient for a prosecution.'

'I don't believe it,' said Susan. 'I believe if you knew definitely *who* committed a crime you could always get the evidence.'

'I wonder now.' Mr Entwhistle sounded thoughtful. 'I very much wonder . . .'

'Have they any idea *at all* – in Aunt Cora's case – of who it might be?'

'That I couldn't say. Not as far as I know. But they would hardly confide in me – and it's early days yet – the murder took place only the day before yesterday, remember.'

'It's definitely got to be a certain kind of person,' Susan mused. 'A brutal, perhaps slightly half-witted type – a discharged soldier or a gaol bird. I mean, using a hatchet like that.'

Looking slightly quizzical, Mr Entwhistle raised his eyebrows and murmured:

> 'Lizzie Borden with an axe
> Gave her father fifty whacks
> When she saw what she had done
> She gave her mother fifty-one.'

'Oh,' Susan flushed angrily, 'Cora hadn't got any relations living with her – unless you mean the companion. And anyway Lizzie Borden was acquitted. Nobody knows for certain she killed her father and stepmother.'

'The rhyme is quite definitely libellous,' Mr Entwhistle agreed.

'You mean the companion did do it? Did Cora leave her anything?'

'An amethyst brooch of no great value and some sketches of fishing villages of sentimental value only.'

'One has to have a motive for murder – unless one is half-witted.'

Mr Entwhistle gave a little chuckle.

'As far as one can see, the only person who had a motive is *you*, my dear Susan.'

'What's that?' Greg moved forward suddenly. He was like a sleeper coming awake. An ugly light showed in his eyes. He was suddenly no longer a negligible feature in the background. 'What's Sue got to do with it? What do you mean – saying things like that?'

Susan said sharply:

'Shut up, Greg. Mr Entwhistle doesn't mean anything—'

'Just my little joke,' said Mr Entwhistle apologetically. 'Not in the best taste, I'm afraid. Cora left her estate, such as it was, to you, Susan. But to a young lady who has just inherited several thousand pounds, an estate, amounting at the most to a few hundreds, can hardly be said to represent a motive for murder.'

'She left her money to me?' Susan sounded surprised. 'How extraordinary. She didn't even know me? Why did she do it, do you think?'

'I think she had heard rumours that there had been a little difficulty – er – over your marriage.' Greg, back again at sharpening his pencil, scowled. 'There had been a certain amount of trouble over her own marriage – and I think she experienced a fellow feeling.'

Susan asked with a certain amount of interest:

'She married an artist, didn't she, whom none of the family liked? Was he a good artist?

Mr Entwhistle shook his head very decidedly.

'Are there any of his paintings in the cottage?'

'Yes.'

'Then I shall judge for myself,' said Susan.

Mr Entwhistle smiled at the resolute tilt of Susan's chin.

'So be it. Doubtless I am an old fogey and hopelessly old-fashioned in matters of art, but I really don't think you will dispute my verdict.'

'I suppose I ought to go down there, anyway? And look over what there is. Is there anybody there now?'

'I have arranged with Miss Gilchrist to remain there until further notice.'

Greg said: 'She must have a pretty good nerve – to stay in a cottage where a murder's been committed."

'Miss Gilchrist is quite a sensible woman, I should say. Besides,' added the lawyer dryly, 'I don't think she has anywhere else to go until she gets another situation.'

'So Aunt Cora's death left her high and dry? Did she – were she and Aunt Cora – on intimate terms—?'

Mr Entwhistle looked at her rather curiously, wondering just what exactly was in her mind.

'Moderately so, I imagine,' he said. 'She never treated Miss Gilchrist as a servant.'

'Treated her a damned sight worse, I dare say,' said Susan. 'These wretched so called "ladies" are the ones who get it taken out of them nowadays. I'll try and find her a decent post somewhere. It won't be difficult. Anyone who's willing to do a bit of housework and cook is worth their weight in gold – she does cook, doesn't she?'

'Oh yes. I gather it is something she called, er *"the rough"* that she objected to. I'm afraid I don't quite know what "the rough" is.'

Susan appeared to be a good deal amused.

Mr Entwhistle, glancing at his watch, said:

'Your aunt left Timothy her executor.'

'Timothy,' said Susan with scorn. 'Uncle Timothy is practically a myth. Nobody ever sees him.'

'Quite.' Mr Entwhistle glanced at his watch. 'I am travelling up to see him this afternoon. I will acquaint him with your decision to go down to the cottage.'

'It will only take me a day or two, I imagine. I don't want to be long away from London. I've got various schemes in hand. I'm going into business.'

Mr Entwhistle looked round him at the cramped sitting-room of the tiny flat. Greg and Susan were evidently hard up. Her father, he knew, had run through most of his money. He had left his daughter badly off.

'What are your plans for the future, if I may ask?'

'I've got my eye on some premises in Cardigan Street. I suppose, if necessary, you can advance me some money? I may have to pay a deposit.'

'That can be managed,' said Mr Entwhistle. 'I rang you up the day after the funeral several times – but could get no answer. I thought perhaps you might care for an advance. I wondered whether you might perhaps have gone out of Town.'

'Oh no,' said Susan quickly. 'We were in all day. Both of us. We didn't go out at all.'

Greg said gently: 'You know Susan, I think our telephone must have been out of order that day. You remember how I couldn't get through to Hard and Co. in the afternoon. I meant to report it, but it was all right the next morning.'

'Telephones,' said Mr Entwhistle, 'can be very unreliable sometimes.'

Susan said suddenly:

'How did Aunt Cora know about our marriage? It was at a Registry Office and we didn't tell anyone until afterwards!'

'I fancy Richard may have told her about it. She remade her will about three weeks ago (it was formerly in favour of the Theosophical Society) – just about the time he had been down to see her.'

Susan loked startled.

'Did Uncle Richard go down to see her? I'd no idea of that?'

'I hadn't any idea of it myself,' said Mr Entwhistle.

'So that was when—'

'When what?'

'Nothing,' said Susan.

———— 6 ————

'Very good of you to come along,' said Maude gruffly, as he greeted Mr Entwhistle on the platform of Bayham Compton station. 'I can assure you that both Timothy and I much appreciate it. Of course the truth is that Richard's death was the worst thing possible for Timothy.'

Mr Entwhistle had not yet considered his friend's death from this particular angle. But it was, he knew, the only angle from which Mrs Timothy Abernethie was likely to regard it.

As they proceeded towards the exit, Maude developed the theme.

'To begin with, it was a *shock* – Timothy was really very attached to Richard. And then unfortunately it put the idea of death into Timothy's head. Being such an invalid has made him rather nervous about himself. He realised that he was the only one of the brothers left alive – and he started saying that he'd be the next to go – and that it wouldn't be long now – all very morbid talk, as I told him.'

They emerged from the station and Maude led the way to a dilapidated car of almost fabulous antiquity.

'Sorry about our old rattletrap,' she said. 'We've wanted a new car for years, but really we couldn't afford it. This has had a new engine twice – and these old cars really stand up to a lot of hard work.

'I hope it will start,' she added. 'Sometimes one has to wind it.'

She pressed the starter several times but only a meaningless whirr resulted. Mr Entwhistle, who had never wound a car in his life, felt rather apprehensive, but Maude herself descended, inserted the starting handle and with a vigorous couple of turns woke the motor to life. It was fortunate, Mr Entwhistle reflected, that Maude was such a powerfully built woman.

'That's that,' she said. 'The old brute's been playing me up lately. Did it when I was coming back after the funeral. Had to walk a couple of miles to the nearest garage and they weren't good for much – just a village affair. I had to put up at the local inn while they tinkered at it. Of course that upset Timothy, too. I had to phone through to him and tell him I couldn't be back till the next day. Fussed him terribly. One tries to keep things from him as much as possible – but some things one can't do anything about – Cora's murder, for instance. I had to send for Dr Barton to give him a sedative. Things like murder are too much for a man in Timothy's state of health. I gather Cora was always a fool.'

Mr Entwhistle digested this remark in silence. The inference was not quite clear to him.

'I don't think I'd seen Cora since our marriage,' said Maude. 'I didn't like to say to Timothy at the time: "Your youngest sister's batty," not just like that. But it's what I *thought*. There she was saying the most extraordinary things! One didn't know whether to resent them or whether to laugh. I suppose the truth is she lived in a kind of imaginary world of her own – full of melodrama and fantastic ideas about other people. Well, poor soul, she's paid for it now. She didn't have any protégés, did she?'

'Protégés? What do you mean?'

'I just wondered. Some young cadging artist, or musician – or something of that kind. Someone she might have let in that day, and who killed her for her loose cash. Perhaps an adolescent – they're so queer at that age sometimes – especially if they're the neurotic arty type. I mean, it seems so odd to break in and murder her in the middle of the afternoon. If you break into a house surely you'd do it at night.'

'There would have been two women there then.'

'Oh yes, the companion. But really I can't believe that anyone would deliberately wait until she was out of the way and then break in and attack Cora. What for? He can't have expected she'd have any cash or stuff to speak of, and there must have been times when both the women were out and the house was empty. That would have been much safer. It seems so stupid to go and commit a murder unless it's absolutely necessary.'

'And Cora's murder, you feel, was unnecessary?'

'It all seems so stupid.'

Should murder make sense? Mr Entwhistle wondered. Academically the answer was yes. But many pointless crimes were on record. It depended, Mr Entwhistle reflected, on the mentality of the murder.

What did he really know about murderers and their mental processes? Very little. His firm had never had a criminal practice. He was no student of criminology himself. Murderers, as far as he could judge, seemed to be of all sorts and kinds. Some had had over-weening vanity, some had had a lust for power, some, like Seddon, had been mean and avaricious, others, like Smith and Rowse had had an incredible fascination for women; some, like Armstrong, had been pleasant fellows to meet. Edith Thompson had lived in a world of violent unreality, Nurse Waddington had put her elderly patients out of the way with business-like cheerfulness.

Maude's voice broke into his meditations.

'If I could only keep the newspapers from Timothy! But he will insist on reading them – and then, of course, it upsets him. You do understand, don't you, Mr Entwhistle, that there can be *no question* of Timothy's attending the inquest? If necessary, Dr Barton can write out a certificate or whatever it is.'

'You can set your mind at rest about that.'

'Thank goodness!'

They turned in through the gates of Stansfield Grange, and up a neglected drive. It had been an attractive small property once – but had now a doleful and neglected appearance. Maude sighed as she said:

"We had to let this go to seed during the war. Both gardeners called up. And now we've only got one old man – and he's not much good. Wages have gone up so terribly. I must say it's a blessing to realise that we'll be able to spend a little money on the place now. We're both so fond of it. . . . Not that I suggested anything of the kind to Timothy. It would have upset him – dreadfully.'

They drew up before the portico of a very lovely old Georgian house which badly needed a coat of paint.

'No servants,' said Maude bitterly, as she led the way in. 'Just a couple of women who come in. We had a resident maid until a month ago – slightly hunchbacked and terribly adenoidal and in many ways not too bright, but she was there which was such a comfort – and quite good at plain cooking. And would you believe it, she gave notice and went to a fool of a woman who keeps six Pekinese dogs (it's a larger house than this and more work) because she was "so fond of little doggies," she said. Dogs, indeed! Being sick and making messes all the time I've no doubt! Really, these girls are *mental*! So there we are and if I have to go out any afternoon, Timothy is left quite alone in the house and if anything should happen, how could he get help? Though I do leave the telephone close by his chair so that if he felt faint he could dial Dr Barton immediately.'

Maude led the way into the drawing-room where tea was laid ready by the fireplace, and establishing Mr Entwhistle there, disappeared, presumably to the back regions. She returned in a few minutes' times with a teapot and silver kettle, and proceeded to minister to Mr Entwhistle's needs. It was a good tea with home-made cake and fresh buns. Mr Entwhistle murmured:

'What about Timothy?' and Maude explained briskly that she had taken Timothy his tray before she set out for the station.

'And now,' said Maude, 'he will have had his little nap and it will be the best time for him to see you. Do try and not let him excite himself too much.'

Mr Entwhistle assured her that he would exercise every precaution.

Studying her in the flickering fire-light, he was seized by a feeling of compassion. This big, stalwart matter-of-fact woman so healthy, so vigorous, so full of common sense, and yet so strangely, almost pitifully, vulnerable in one spot. Her love for her husband was maternal love, Mr Entwhistle decided. Maude Abernethie had borne no child and she was a woman built for motherhood. Her invalid husband had become her child, to be shielded, guarded, watched over. And perhaps, being the stronger character of the two, she had unconsciously imposed on him a state of invalidism greater than might otherwise have been the case.

'Poor Mrs Tim,' thought Mr Entwhistle to himself.

2

'Good of you to come, Entwhistle.'

Timothy raised himself up in his chair as he held out a hand. He was a big man with a marked resemblance to his brother Richard. But what was strength in Richard, in Timothy was weakness. The mouth was irresolute, the chin very slightly receding, the eyes less deep-set. Lines of peevish irritability showed on his forehead.

His invalid status was emphasised by the rug across his knees and a positive pharmacopœia of little bottles and boxes, on a table at his right hand.

'I mustn't exert myself,' he said warningly. 'Doctor's forbidden it. Keeps telling me not to worry! Worry! If *he'd* had a murder in his family *he'd* do a bit of worrying, I bet! It's too much for a man – first Richard's death – then hearing all about his funeral and his will – what a will! – and on top of that poor little Cora killed with a hatchet. Hatchet! Ugh! This country's full of gangsters nowadays – thugs – left over from the war! Going about killing defenceless women. Nobody's got the guts to put these things down – to take a strong hand. What's the country coming to, I'd like to know? What's the damned country coming to?'

Mr Entwhistle was familiar with this gambit. It was a question almost invariably asked sooner or later by his clients for the last twenty years and he had his routine for answering it. The non-committal words he uttered could have been classified under the headings of soothing noises.

'It all began with that damned Labour Government,' said Timothy. Sending the whole country to blazes. And the Government we've got now is no better. Mealy-mouthed, milk-and-water socialists! Look at the state *we're* in! Can't get a decent gardener, can't get servants – poor Maude here has to work herself to a shadow messing about in the kitchen (by the way, I think a custard pudding would go well with the sole tonight, my dear – and perhaps a little clear soup first?) I've got to keep my strength up – Doctor Barton said so – let me see, where was I? Oh yes, *Cora*. It's a shock, I can tell you, to a man when he hears his sister – his own sister – has been *murdered*! Why, I had palpitations for twenty minutes! You'll have to attend to everything for me Entwhistle. *I* can't go to the inquest or be bothered by business of any kind connected with Cora's estate. I want to forget the whole thing. What happens by the way to Cora's share of Richard's money? Comes to me I suppose?'

Murmuring something about clearing away tea, Maude left the room.

Timothy lay back in his chair and said:

'Good thing to get rid of the women. Now we can talk business without any silly interruptions.'

'The sum left in trust for Cora,' said Mr Entwhistle, 'goes equally to you and the nieces and nephew.'

'But look here,' Timothy's cheeks assumed a purplish hue of indignation. 'Surely I'm her next of kin? Only surviving brother.'

Mr Entwhistle explained with some care the exact provisions of Richard Abernethie's will, reminding Timothy gently that he had had a copy sent him.

'Don't expect me to understand all that legal jargon, do you?' said Timothy ungratefully. 'You lawyers! Matter of fact, I couldn't believe it when Maude came home and told me the gist of it. Thought she'd got it wrong. Women are never clear headed. Best woman in the world, Maude – but women don't understand finance. I don't believe Maude even realises that if Richard hadn't died when he did, we might have had to clear out of here. Fact!'

'Surely if you had applied to Richard—'

Timothy gave a short bark of harsh laughter.

'That's not my style. Our father left us all a perfectly reasonable share of his money – that is, if we didn't want to go into the family concern. I didn't. I've a soul above cornplasters, Entwhistle! Richard took my attitude a bit hard. Well, what with taxes, depreciation of income, one thing and another – it hasn't been easy to keep things going. I've had to realise a good deal of capital. Best thing to do these days. I did hint once to Richard that this place was getting a bit hard to run. He took the attitude that we'd be much better off in a smaller place altogether. Easier for Maude, he said, more labour saving – labour saving, what a term! Oh no, I wouldn't have asked Richard for help. But I can tell you, Entwhistle, that the worry affected my health most unfavourably. A man in my state of health oughtn't to have to worry. Then Richard

died and though of course naturally I was cut up about it –
my brother and all that – I couldn't help feeling relieved about
future prospects. Yes, it's all plain sailing now – and a great
relief. Get the house painted – get a couple of really good men
on the garden – you can get them at a price. Restock the rose
garden completely. And – where was I—'

'Detailing your future plans.'

'Yes, yes – but I mustn't bother you with all that. What did
hurt me – and hurt me cruelly – were the terms of Richard's
will.'

'Indeed?' Mr Entwhistle looked inquiring. 'They were not
– as you expected?'

'I should say they weren't! Naturally, after Mortimer's
death, I assumed that Richard would leave everything to *me*.'

'Ah – did he – ever – indicate that to you?'

'He never said so – not in so many words. Reticent sort of
chap, Richard. But he asked himself here – not long after
Mortimer's death. Wanted to talk over family affairs generally.
We discussed young George – and the girls and their husbands.
Wanted to know my views – not that I could tell him much.
I'm an invalid and I don't get about, and Maudie and I live
out of the world. Rotten silly marriages both of those girls
made, if you ask me. Well, I ask you, Entwhistle, naturally I
thought he was consulting me as the head of the family after
he was gone and naturally I thought the control of the money
would be mine. Richard could surely trust me to do the right
thing by the younger generation. And to look after poor old
Cora. Dash it all, Entwhistle, I'm an Abernethie – the last
Abernethie. Full control should have been left in my hands.'

In his excitement Timothy had kicked aside his rug and had
sat up in his chair. There were no signs of weakness or fragility
about him. He looked, Mr Entwhistle thought, a perfectly
healthy man, even if a slightly excitable one. Moreover the
old lawyer realised very clearly that Timothy Abernethie had
probably always been secretly jealous of his brother Richard.
They had been sufficiently alike for Timothy to resent his
brother's strength of character and firm grasp of affairs. When
Richard had died, Timothy had exulted in the prospect of
succeeding at this late date to the power to control the des-
tinies of others.

Richard Abernethie had not given him that power. Had he
thought of doing so and then decided against it?

A sudden squalling of cats in the garden brought Timothy
up out of his chair. Rushing to the window he threw up the

sash, bawled out 'Stop it, you!' and picking up a large book
hurled it out at the marauders.

'Beastly cats,' he grumbled, returning to his visitor. 'Ruin
the flower beds and I can't stand that damned yowling.'

He sat down again and asked:

'Have a drink, Entwhistle?'

'Not quite so soon. Maude has just given me an excellent
tea.'

Timothy grunted.

'Capable woman, Maude. But she does too much. Even has
to muck about with the inside of that old car of ours – she's
quite a mechanic in her way, you know.'

'I hear she had a breakdown coming back from the funeral?'

'Yes. Car conked out. She had the sense to telephone
through about it, in case I should be anxious, but that ass of a
daily woman of ours wrote down the message in a way that
didn't make sense. I was out getting a bit of fresh air – I'm
advised by the doctor to take what exercise I can if I feel like
it – I got back from my walk to find scrawled on a bit of
paper: 'Madam's sorry car gone wrong got to stay night.'
Naturally I thought she was still at Enderby. Put a call
through and found Maude had left that morning. Might have
had the breakdown *anywhere*! Pretty kettle of fish! Fool of a
daily woman only left me a lumpy macaroni cheese for supper.
I had to go down to the kitchen and warm it up *myself – and*
make myself a cup of tea – to say nothing of stoking the
boiler. I might have had a heart attack – but does that class
of woman care? Not she? With any decent feelings she'd have
come back that evening and looked after me properly. No
loyalty any more in the lower classes—'

He brooded sadly.

'I don't know how much Maude told you about the funeral
and the relatives,' said Mr Entwhistle. 'Cora produced rather
an awkward moment. Said brightly that Richard had been
murdered, hadn't he? Perhaps Maude told you.'

Timothy chuckled easily.

'Oh yes, I heard about that. Everybody looked down their
noses and pretended to be shocked. Just the sort of thing Cora
would say! You know how she always managed to put her foot
in it when she was a girl, Entwhistle? Said something at our
wedding that upset Maude, I remember. Maude never cared
for her very much. Yes, Maude rang me up that evening after
the funeral to know if I was all right and if Mrs Jones had
come in to give me my evening meal and then she told me

it had all gone off very well, and I said "What about the will?" and she tried to hedge a bit, but of course I had the truth out of her. I couldn't believe it, and I said she must have made a mistake, but she stuck to it. It hurt me, Entwhistle – it really *wounded* me, if you know what I mean. If you ask me, it was just *spite* on Richard's part. I know one shouldn't speak ill of the dead, but upon my word—'

Timothy continued on this theme for some time.

Then Maude came back into the room and said firmly:

'I think dear, Mr Entwhistle has been with you quite long enough. You really *must* rest. If you have settled everything—'

'Oh, we've settled things. I leave it all to you, Entwhistle. Let me know when they catch the fellow – if they ever do. I've no faith in the police nowadays – the Chief Constables aren't the right type. You'll see to the – er – interment – won't you? We shan't be able to come, I'm afraid. But order an expensive wreath – and there must be a proper stone put up in due course – she'll be buried locally, I suppose? No point in bringing her North and I've no idea where Lansquenet is buried, somewhere in France I believe. I don't know what one puts on a stone when it's murder. . . . Can't very well say "entered into rest" or anything like that. One will have to choose a text – something appropriate. RIP? No, that's only for Catholics.'

'O Lord, thou hast seen my wrong. Judge thou my case,' murmured Mr Entwhistle.

The startled glance Timothy bent on him made Mr Entwhistle smile faintly.

'From Lamentations,,' he said. 'It seems appropriate if somewhat melodramatic. However, it will be some time before the question of the Memorial stone comes up. The – er – ground has to settle, you know. Now don't worry about anything. We will deal with things and keep you fully informed.'

Mr Entwhistle left for London by the breakfast train on the following morning.

When he got home, after a little hesitation, he rang up a friend of his.

7

'I can't tell you how much I appreciate your invitation.'

Mr Entwhistle pressed his host's hand warmly.

Hercule Poirot gestured hospitably to a chair by the fire.

Mr Entwhistle sighed as he sat down.

On one side of the room a table was laid for two.

'I returned from the country this morning,' he said.

'And you have a matter on which you wish to consult me?'

'Yes. It's a long rambling story, I'm afraid.'

'Then we will not have it until after we have dined. *Georges?*'

The efficient Georges materialised with some *Pâté de Foie Gras* accompanied by hot toast in a napkin.

'We will have our *Pâté* by the fire,' said Poirot. 'Afterwards we will move to the table.'

It was an hour and a half later that Mr Entwhistle stretched himself comfortably out in his chair and sighed a contented sigh.

'You certainly know how to do yourself well, Poirot. Trust a Frenchman.'

'I am a Belgian. But the rest of your remark applies. At my age the chief pleasure, almost the *only* pleasure that still remains, is the pleasure of the table. Mercifull I have an excellent stomach.'

'Ah,' murmured Mr Entwhistle.

They had dined off *Sole Veronique*, followed by *Escalope de Veau Milanaise*, proceeding to *Poire Flambée* with ice-cream.

They had drunk a *Pouilly Fuisse* followed by a *Corton*, and a very good port now reposed at Mr Entwhistle's elbow. Poirot, who did not care for port, was sipping *Crème de Cacao*.

'I don't know,' murmured Mr Entwhistle reminiscently, 'how you manage to get hold of an escalope like that! It melted in the mouth!'

'I have a friend who is a Continental butcher. For him I solve a small domestic problem. He is appreciative – and ever since then he is most sympathetic to me in the matters of the stomach.'

'A domestic problem.' Mr Entwhistle sighed. 'I wish you had not reminded me . . . This is such a perfect moment . . .'

'Prolong it, my friend. We will have presently the *demi tasse* and the fine brandy, and then, when digestion is peacefully under way, *then* you shall tell why you need my advice.'

The clock struck the half hour after nine before Mr Entwhistle stirred in his chair. The psychological moment had come. He no longer felt reluctant to bring forth his perplexities – he was eager to do so.

'I don't know,' he said, 'whether I'm making the most colossal fool of myself. In any case I don't see that there's anything that can possibly be done. But I'd like to put the facts before you, and I'd like to know what you think.'

He paused for a moment or two, then in his dry meticulous way, he told his story. His trained legal brain enabled him to put the facts clearly, to leave nothing out, and to add nothing extraneous. It was a clear succinct account, and as such appreciated by the little elderly man with the egg-shaped head who sat listening to him.

When he had finished there was a pause. Mr Entwhistle was prepared to answer questions, but for some few moments no question came. Hercule Poirot was reviewing the evidence.

He said at last:

'It seems very clear. You have in your mind the suspicion that your friend, Richard Abernethie, may have been murdered? That suspicion, or assumption, rests on the basis of one thing only – *the words spoken by Cora Lansquenet at Richard Abernethie's funeral*. Take those away – and there is nothing left. The fact that she herself was murdered the day afterwards may be the purest coincidence. It is true that Richard Abernethie died suddenly, but he was attended by a reputable doctor who knew him well, and that doctor had no suspicions and gave a death certificate. Was Richard buried or cremated?'

'Cremated – according to his own request.'

'Yes, that is the law. And it means that a second doctor signed the certificate – but there would be no difficulty about that. So we come back to the essential point, *what Cora Lansquenet said*. You were there and you heard her. She said: 'But he was murdered, wasn't he?'' '

'Yes.'

'And the real point is – that you believe she was speaking the truth.'

The lawyer hesitated for a moment, then he said:

'Yes, I do.'

'Why?'

'Why?' Entwhistle repeated the word, slightly puzzled.

'But yes, *why*? Is it because, already, deep down, you had an uneasiness about the manner of Richard's death?'

The lawyer shook his head. 'No, no, not in the least.'

'Then it is because of *her* – of Cora herself. You knew her well?'

'I had not seen her for – oh – over twenty years.'

'Would you have known her if you had met her in the street?'

Mr Entwhistle reflected.

'I might have passed her by in the street without recognising her. She was a thin slip of a girl when I saw her last and she had turned into a stout, shabby, middle-aged woman. But I think that the moment I spoke to her face to face I should have recognised her. She wore her hair in the same way, a bang cut straight across the forehead and she had a trick of peering up at you through her fringe like a rather shy animal, and she had a very characteristic, abrupt way of talking, and a way of putting her head on one side and then coming out with something quite outrageous. She had *character*, you see, and character is always highly individual.'

'She was, in fact, the same Cora you had known years ago. And she still said outrageous things! The things, the outrageous things, she had said in the past – were they usually – justified?'

'That was always the awkward thing about Cora. When truth would have been better left unspoken, she spoke it.'

'And that characteristic remained unchanged. Richard Abernethie was murdered – so Cora at once mentioned the fact."

Mr Entwhistle stirred.

'You think he *was* murdered?'

'Oh, no, no, my friend, we cannot go so fast. We agree on this – Cora *thought* he had been murdered. She was quite sure he had been murdered. It was, to her, more a certainty than a surmise. And so, we come to this, *she must have had some reason for the belief*. We agree, by your knowledge of her, that it was not just a bit of mischief making. Now tell me – when she said what she did, there was, at once, a kind of chorus of protest – that is right?'

'Quite right.'

'And she then became confused, abashed, and retreated from the position – saying – as far as you can remember, something like "But I thought – from what he told me—" '

The lawyer nodded.

'I wish I could remember more clearly. But I am fairly sure of that. She used the words "he told me" or "he said—" '

'And the matter was then smoothed over and everyone spoke of something else. You can remember, looking back, no special expression on anyone's face? Anything that remains in your memory as – shall we say – *unusual?*'

'No.'

'And the very next day, *Cora is killed* – and you ask yourself: "Can it be cause and effect?" '

The lawyer stirred.

'I suppose that seems to you quite fantastic?'

'Not at all,' said Poirot. 'Given that the original assumption is correct, it is logical. The perfect murder, the murder of Richard Abernethie, has been committed, all has gone off smoothly – and suddenly it appears that there is one person who has a knowledge of the truth! Clearly that person must be silenced *as quickly as possible.*'

'Then you do think that – it was murder?'

Poirot said gravely:

'I think, *mon cher*, exactly as you thought – that there is a case for investigation. Have you taken any steps? You have spoken of these matters to the police?'

'No.' Mr Entwhistle shook his head. 'It did not seem to me that any good purpose could be achieved. My position is that I represent the family. If Richard Abernethie was murdered, there seems only one method by which it could be done.'

'By poison?'

'Exactly. *And the body has been cremated.* There is now no evidence available. But I decided that I, myself, *must* be satisfied on the point. That is why, Poirot, I have come to *you.*'

'Who was in the house at the time of his death?'

'An old butler who has been with him for years, a cook and a housemaid. It would seem, perhaps, as though it must necessarily be one of them—'

'Ah! do not try to pull the wool upon my eyes. This Cora, she knows Richard Abernethie was killed, yet she acquiesces in the hushing up. She says "I think you are all quite right." Therefore it *must* be one of the family who is concerned, someone whom the victim himself might prefer not to have openly accused. Otherwise, since Cora was fond of her brother, she would not agree to let the sleeping murderer lie. You agree to that, yes?'

'It was the way I reasoned – yes,' confessed Mr Entwhistle. 'Though how any of the family could possibly—'

Poirot cut him short.

'Where poison is concerned there all all sorts of possibilities. It must, presumably, have been a narcotic of some sort if he died in his sleep and if there were no suspicious appearances. Possibly he was already having some narcotic administered to him.'

'In any case,' said Mr Entwhistle, 'the *how* hardly matters. We shall never be able to prove anything.'

'In the case of Richard Abernethie, no. But the murder of Cora Lansquenet is different. Once we know "who" then evidence ought to be possible to get.' He added with a sharp glance, 'You have, perhaps, already done something.'

'Very little. My purpose was mainly, I think, *elimination*. It is distasteful to me to think that one of the Abernethie family is a murderer. I still can't quite believe it. I hoped that by a few apparently idle questions I could exonerate certain members of the family beyond question. Perhaps, who knows, *all* of them? In which case, Cora would have been wrong in her assumption and her own death could be ascribed to some casual prowler who broke in. After all, the issue is very simple. What were the members of the Abernethie family doing on the afternoon that Cora Lansquenet was killed?'

'*Eh bien*,' said Poirot, 'what were they doing?'

'George Crossfield was at Hurst Park races. Rosamund Shane was out shopping in London. Her husband – for one must include husbands—'

'Assuredly.'

'Her husband was fixing up a deal about an option on a play, Susan and Gregory Banks were at home all day, Timothy Abernethie, who is an invalid, was at his home in Yorkshire, and his wife was driving herself home from Enderby.'

He stopped.

Hercule Poirot looked at him and nodded comprehendingly. 'Yes, that is what they *say*. And is it all true?'

'I simply don't know, Poirot. Some of the statements are capable of proof or disproof – but it would be difficult to do so without showing one's hand pretty plainly. In fact to do so would be tantamount to an accusation. I will simply tell you certain conclusions of my own. George may have been at Hurst Park races, but I do not think he was. He was rash enough to boast that he had backed a couple of winners. It is my experience that so many offenders against the law ruin their own case by saying too much. I asked him the name of the winners, and he gave the names of two horses without any apparent hesitation. Both of them, I found, had been heavily tipped on the day in question and one had duly won. The other, though an odds on favourite, had unaccountably failed even to get a place.'

'Interesting. Had this George any urgent need for money at the time of his uncle's death?'

'It is my impression that his need was very urgent. I have no evidence for saying so, but I strongly suspect that he has been speculating with his clients' funds and that he was in danger of prosecution. It is only my impression but I have some experience in these matters. Defaulting solicitors, I regret to say, are not entirely uncommon. I can only tell you that I suspect that Richard Abernethie, a very shrewd judge of men, was dissatisfied with his nephew and placed no reliance on him.'

'His mother,' the lawyer continued, 'was a good-looking rather foolish girl and she married a man of what I should call dubious character.' He sighed. 'The Abernethie girls were not good choosers.'

He paused and then went on:

'As for Rosamund, she is a lovely nitwit. I really cannot see her smashing Cora's head in with a hatchet! Her husband, Michael Shane, is something of a dark horse – he's a man with ambition and also a man of overweening vanity I should say. But really I know very little about him. I have no reason to suspect him of a brutal crime or of a carefully planned poisoning, but until I know that he really was doing what he says he was doing I cannot rule him out.'

'But you have no doubts about the wife?'

'No – no – there is a certain rather startling callousness . . . but no, I really cannot envisage the hatchet. She is a fragile looking creature.'

'And beautiful!' said Poirot with a faint cynical smile. 'And the other niece?'

'Susan? She is a very different type from Rosamund – a girl of remarkable ability, I should say. She and her husband were at home together that day. I said (falsely) that I had tried to get them on the telephone on the afternoon in question. Greg said very quickly that the telephone had been out of order all day. He had tried to get someone and failed.'

'So again it is not conclusive. . . . You cannot eliminate as you hoped to do. . ..What is the husband like?'

'I find him hard to make out. He has a somewhat unpleasing personality though one cannot say exactly why he makes this impression. As for Susan—'

'Yes?'

'Susan reminds me of her uncle. She has the vigour, the drive, the mental capacity of Richard Abernethie. It may be my fancy that she lacks some of the kindliness and the warmth of my old friend.'

'Women are never kind,' remarked Poirot. 'Though they can sometimes be tender. She loves her husband?'

'Devotedly, I should say. But really, Poirot, I can't believe – I *won't* believe for one moment that Susan—'

'You prefer George?' said Poirot. 'It is natural! As for me, I am not so sentimental about beautiful young ladies. Now tell me about your visit to the older generation?'

Mr Entwhistle described his visit to Timothy and Maude at some length. Poirot summarised the result.

'So Mrs Abernethie is a good mechanic. She knows all about the inside of a car. And Mr Abernethie is not the invalid he likes to think himself. He goes out for walks and is, according to you, capable of vigorous action. He is also a bit of an ego maniac and he resented his brother's success and superior character.'

'He spoke very affectionately of Cora.'

'And ridiculed her silly remark after the funeral. What of the sixth beneficiary?'

'Helen? Mrs Leo? I do not suspect her for a moment. In any case, her innocence will be easy to prove. She was at Ender-by. With three servants in the house.'

'*Eh bien*, my friend, said Poirot. 'Let us be practical. What do you want me to do?'

'I want to know the truth, Poirot.'

'Yes. Yes, I should feel the same in your place.'

'And you're the man to find it out for me. I know you don't take cases any more, but I ask you to take this one. This is a matter of business. I will be responsible for your fees. Come now, money is always useful.'

Poirot grinned.

'Not if it all goes in the taxes! But I will admit, your problem interests me! Because it is not easy. . . . It is all so nebulous . . . One thing, my friend, had better be done by you. After that, I will occupy myself of everything. But I think it will be best if you yourself seek out the doctor who attended Mr Richard Abernethie. You know him?'

'Slightly.'

'What is he like?'

'Middle-aged GP. Quite competent. On very friendly terms with Richard. A thoroughly good fellow.'

'Then seek him out. He will speak more freely to you than to me. Ask him about Mr Abernethie's illness. Find out what medicines Mr Abernethie was taking at the time of his death and before. Find out if Richard Abernethie ever said anything to his doctor about fancying himself being poisoned. By the way, this Miss Gilchrist is sure that he used the term *poisoned* in talking to his sister?'

Mr Entwhistle reflected.

'It was the word she used – but she is the type of witness who often changes the actual words used, because she is convinced she is keeping to the sense of them. If Richard had said he was afraid someone wanted to kill him, Miss Gilchrist might have assumed poison because she connected his fears with those of an aunt of hers who thought her food was being tampered with. I can take up the point with her again some time.'

'Yes. Or I will do so.' He paused and then said in a different voice: 'Has it occurred to you, my friend, that your Miss Gilchrist may be in some danger herself?'

Mr Entwhistle looked surprised.

'I can't say that it had.'

'But, yes. Cora voiced her suspicions on the day of the funeral. The question in the murderer's mind will be, did she voice them to anybody when she first heard of Richard's death? And the most likely person for her to have spoken to about them will be Miss Gilchrist. I think, *mon cher*, that she had better not remain alone in that cottage.'

'I believe Susan is going down.'

'Ah, so Mrs Banks is going down?'

'She wants to look through Cora's things.'

'I see . . . I see . . . Well, my friend, do what I have asked of you. You might also prepare Mrs Abernethie – Mrs Leo Abernethie, for the possibility that I may arrive in the house. We will see. From now on I occupy myself with everything.'

And Poirot twirled his moustaches with enormous energy.

8

Mr Entwhistle looked at Dr Larraby thoughtfully.

He had had a lifetime of experience in summing people up. There had been frequent occasions on which it had been necessary to tackle a difficult situation or a delicate subject. Mr Entwhistle was an adept by now in the art of how exactly to make the proper approach. How would it be best to tackle Dr Larraby on what was certainly a very difficult subject and one which the doctor might very well resent as reflecting upon his own professional skill?

Frankness, Mr Entwhistle thought — or at least a modified frankness. To say that suspicions had arisen because of a haphazard suggestion thrown out by a silly woman would be ill-advised. Dr Larraby had not known Cora.

Mr Entwhistle cleared his throat and plunged bravely.

'I want to consult you on a very delicate matter,' he said. 'You may be offended, but I sincerely hope not. You are a sensible man and you will realise, I'm sure, that a – er – preposterous suggestion is best dealt with by finding a reasonable answer and not by condemning it out of hand. It concerns my client, the late Mr Abernethie. I'll ask you my question flat out. Are you certain, *absolutely certain*, that he died what is termed a natural death?'

Dr Larraby's good-humoured, rubicund middle-aged face turned in astonishment on his questioner.

'What on earth— Of course he did. I gave a certificate, didn't I? If I hadn't been satisfied—'

Mr Entwhistle cut in adroitly:

'Naturally, naturally. I assure you that I am not assuming anything to the contrary. But I would be glad to have your positive assurance – in face of the – er – rumours that are flying around.'

'Rumours? What rumours?'

'One doesn't know quite how these things start,' said Mr Entwhistle mendaciously. 'But my feeling is that they should be stopped – authoritatively, if possible.'

'Abernethie was a sick man. He was suffering from a disease that would have proved fatal within, I should say, at the earliest, two years. It might have come much sooner. His son's death had weakened his will to live, and his powers of resistance. I admit that I did not expect his death to come so soon, or indeed so suddenly, but there are precedents – plenty of precedents. Any medical man who predicts exactly when a patient will die, or exactly how long he will live, is bound to make a fool of himself. The human factor is always incalculable. The weak have often unexpected powers of resistance, the strong sometimes succumb.'

'I understand all that. I am not doubting your diagnosis. Mr Abernethie was, shall we say (rather melodramatically, I'm afraid) under sentence of death. All I'm asking you is, is it quite possible that a man, knowing or suspecting that he is doomed, might of his own accord shorten that period of life? Or that someone else might do it for him?'

Dr Larraby frowned.

'Suicide, you mean? Abernethie wasn't a suicidal type."

'I see. You can assure me, medically speaking, that such a suggestion is impossible.'

The doctor stirred uneasily.

'I wouldn't use the word impossible. After his son's death life no longer held the interest for Abernethie that it had done. I certainly don't feel that suicide is likely – but I can't say that it's *impossible.*'

'You are speaking from the psychological angle. When I say medically, I really meant; do the circumstances of his death make such a suggestion impossible?'

'No, oh no. No, I can't say that. He died in his sleep, as people often do. There was no reason to suspect suicide, no evidence of his state of mind. If one were to demand an autopsy every time a man who is seriously ill died in his sleep—'

The doctor's face was getting redder and redder. Mr Entwhistle hastened to interpose.

'Of course. Of course. But if there *had* been evidence – evidence of which you yourself were not aware? If, for instance, he had said something to someone—'

'Indicating that he was contemplating suicide? Did he? I must say it surprises me.'

'But if it *were* so – my case is purely hypothetical – could you rule out the possibility?'

Dr Larraby said slowly:

'No – not – I could not do that. But I say again, I should be very much surprised.'

Mr Entwhistle hastened to follow up his advantage.

'If, then, we assume that his death was *not* natural – all this is *purely* hypothetical – what could have caused it? What kind of drug, I mean?'

'Several. Some kind of a narcotic would be indicated. There was no sign of cyanosis, the attitude was quite peaceful.'

'He had sleeping draughts or pills? Somthing of that kind?'

'Yes. I had prescribed Slumberyl – a very safe and dependable hypnotic. He did not take it every night. And he only had a small bottle of tablets at a time. Three or even four times the prescribed dose would not have caused death. In fact, I remember seeing the bottle on his wash-stand after his death still nearly full.'

'What else had you prescribed for him?'

'Various things – a medicine containing a small quantity of morphia to be taken when he had an attack of pain. Some vitamin capsules. An indigestion mixture.'

Mr Entwhistle interrupted.

'Vitamin capsules? I think I was once prescribed a course of those. Small round capsules of gelatine.'

'Yes. Containing adexoline.'

'Could anything else have been introduced into – say – one of those capsules?'

'Something lethal, you mean?' The doctor was looking more and more surprised. 'But surely no man would ever – look here, Entwhistle, what are you getting at? My God man, are you suggesting *murder*?'

'I don't quite know what I'm suggesting. . . . I just want to know what would be *possible*.'

'But what evidence have you for even suggesting such a thing?'

'I haven't any evidence,' said Mr Entwhistle in a tired voice. 'Mr Abernethie is dead – and the person to whom he spoke is also dead. The whole thing is rumour – vague, unsatisfactory rumour, and I want to scotch it if I can. If you tell me that no one could possibly have poisoned Abernethie in any way whatsoever, I'll be delighted! It would be a big weight off my mind, I can assure you.'

Dr Larraby got up and walked up and down.

'I can't tell you what you want me to tell you,' he said at last. 'I wish I could. Of course it could have been done. Anybody could have extracted the oil from a capsule and replaced it with – say – pure nicotine or half a dozen other things. Or something could have been put in his food or drink? Isn't that more likely?'

'Possibly. But you see, there were only the servants in the

house when he died – and I don't think it was any of them
– in fact I'm quite sure it wasn't. So I'm looking for some delayed action possibility. There's no drug, I suppose, that you
can administer and then the person dies weeks later?'

'A convenient idea – but untenable, I'm afraid,' said the
doctor dryly. 'I know you're a responsible person, Entwhistle,
but who *is* making this suggestion? It seems to be widely far
fetched.'

'Abernethie never said anything to you? Never hinted that
one of his relations might be wanting him out of the way?'

The doctor looked at him curiously.

'No, he never said anything to me. Are you sure, Entwhistle,
that somebody hasn't been – well, playing up the sensational?
Some hysterical subjects can give an appearence of being quite
reasonable and normal, you know.'

'I hope it was like that. It might well be.'

'Let me understand. Someone claims that Abernethie told
her – it was a woman, I suppose?'

'Oh yes, it was a woman.'

'—told her someone was trying to kill him?'

Cornered, Mr Entwhistle reluctantly told the tale of Cora's
remark at the funeral. Dr Larraby's face lightened.

'My dear fellow. I shouldn't pay any attention! The explanation is quite simple. The woman's at a certain time of
life – craving for sensation, unbalanced, unreliable – might
say anything. They do, you know!'

Mr Entwhistle resented the doctor's easy assumption. He
himself had had to deal with plenty of sensation-hunting and
hysterical women.

'You may be quite right,' he said rising. 'Unfortunately we
can't tackle her on the subject, as she's been murdered herself.'

'What's that – murdered?' Dr Larraby looked as though he
had grave suspicions of Mr Entwhistle's own stability of mind.

'You've probably read about it in the paper. Mrs Lansquenet at Lytchett St Mary in Berkshire.'

'Of course – I'd no idea she was a relation of Richard Abernethie's!' Dr Larraby was looking quite shaken.

Feeling that he had revenged himself for the doctor's professional superiority, and unhappily conscious that his own
suspicions had not been assuaged as a result of the visit, Mr
Entwhistle took his leave.

Back at Enderby, Mr Entwhistle decided to talk to Lanscombe. He started by asking the old butler what his plans were.

'Mrs Leo has asked me to stay on here until the house is sold, sir, and I'm sure I shall be very pleased to oblige her. We are all very fond of Mrs Leo.' He sighed. 'I feel it very much, sir, if you will excuse me mentioning it, that the house has to be sold. I've known it for so very many years and seen all the young ladies and gentlemen grow up in it. I always thought that Mr Mortimer would come after his father and perhaps bring up a family here, too. It was arranged, sir, that I should go to the North Lodge when I got past doing my work here. A very nice little place, the North Lodge – and I looked forward to having it very spick and span. But I suppose that's all over now.'

'I'm afraid so, Lanscombe. The estate will all have to be sold together. But with your legacy—'

'Oh I'm not complaining, sir, and I'm very sensible of Mr Abernethie's generosity. I'm well provided for, but it's not so easy to find a little place to buy nowadays and though my married niece has asked me to make my home with them, well, it won't be quite the same thing as living on the estate.'

'I know,' said Mr Entwhistle 'It's a hard new world for us old fellows. I wish I'd seen more of my old friend before he went. How did he seem those last few months?'

'Well, he wasn't himself, sir, not since Mr Mortimer's death.'

'No, it broke him up. And then he was a sick man – sick men have strange fancies sometimes. I imagine Mr Abernethie suffered from that sort of thing in his last days. He spoke of enemies sometimes, of somebody wishing to do him harm – perhaps? He may even have thought his food was being tampered with?'

Old Lanscombe looked surprised – surprised and offended.

'I cannot recall anything of that kind, sir.'

Entwhistle looked at him keenly.

'You're a very loyal servant, Lanscombe, I know that. But such fancies on Mr Abernethie's part would be quite – er – unimportant – a natural sympton in some – er diseases.'

'Indeed, sir? I can only say Mr Abernethie never said anything like that to me, or in my hearing.'

Mr Entwhistle slid gently to another subject.

'He had some of his family down to stay with him, didn't he, before he died. His nephew and two nieces and their husbands?'

'Yes, sir, that is so.'

'Was he satisfied with those visits? Or was he disappointed?'

Lanscombe's eyes became remote, his old back stiffened.

'I really could not say, sir.'

'I think you could, you know,' said Mr Entwhistle gently. 'It's not your place to say anything of that kind – that's what you really mean. But there are times when one has to do violence to one's sense of what is fitting. I was one of your master's oldest friends. I cared for him very much. So did you. That's why I'm asking you for your opinion as a *man*, not as a butler.'

Lanscombe was silent for a moment, then he said in a colourless voice:

'Is there anything – wrong, sir?'

Mr Entwhistle replied truthfully.

'I don't know,' he said. 'I hope not. I would like to make sure. Have you yourself felt that something was – wrong?'

'Only since the funeral, sir. And I couldn't say exactly what it is. But Mrs Leo and Mrs Timothy, too, they didn't seem quite themselves that evening after the others had gone.'

'You know the contents of the will?'

'Yes, sir. Mrs Leo thought I would like to know. It seemed to me, if I may permit myself to comment, a very fair will.'

'Yes, it was a fair will. Equal benefits. But it is not, I think the will that Mr Abernethie originally intended to make after his son died. Will you answer now the question that I asked you just now?'

'As a matter of personal opinion—'

'Yes, yes, that is understood.'

'The master, sir, was very much disappointed after Mr George had been here. . . . He had hoped, I think, that Mr George might resemble Mr Mortimer. Mr George, if I may say so, did not come up to standard. Miss Laura's husband was always considered unsatisfactory, and I'm afraid Mr George took after him.' Lanscombe paused and then went on, 'Then the young ladies came with their husbands. Miss Susan he took to at once – a very spirited and handsome young lady, but it's my opinion he couldn't abide her husband. Young ladies make funny choices nowadays, sir.'

'And the other couple?'

'I couldn't say much about that. A very pleasant and good-looking young pair. I think the master enjoyed having them here – but I don't think—' The old man hesitated.

'Yes, Lanscombe?'

'Well, the master had never had much truck with the stage. He said to me one day, "I can't understand why anyone gets stage-struck. It's a foolish kind of life. Seems to deprive people of what little sense they have. I don't know what it does to your moral sense. You certainly lose your sense of proportion." Of course he wasn't referring directly—'

'No, no, I quite understand. Now after these visits, Mr Abernethie himself went away – first to his brother, and afterwards to his sister Mrs Lansquenet.'

'That I did not know, sir. I mean he mentioned to me that he was going to Mr Timothy and afterwards to Something St Mary.'

'That is right. Can you remember anything he said on his return in regard to those visits?'

Lanscombe frowned.

'I really don't know – nothing direct. He was glad to be back. Travelling and staying in strange houses tired him very much – that I do remember his saying.'

'Nothing else? Nothing about either of them?'

Lanscombe frowned.

'The master used to – well, to *murmur*, if you get my meaning – speaking to me and yet more to himself – hardly noticing I was there – because he knew me so well.'

'Knew you and trusted you, yes.'

'But my recollection is very vague as to what he said – something about he couldn't think what he'd done with his money – that was Mr Timothy, I take it. And then he said something about "Women can be fools in ninty nine different ways but be pretty shrewd in the hundredth." Oh yes, and he said, "You can only say what you really think to someone of your own generation. They don't think you're fancying things as the younger ones do." And later he said – but I don't know in what connection – "It's not very nice to have to set traps for people, but I don't see what else I can do." But I think it possible, sir, that he may have been thinking of the second gardener – a question of the peaches being taken.'

But Mr Entwhistle did not think that it was the second gardener who had been in Richard Abernethie's mind. After a few more questions he let Lanscombe go and reflected on what he had learned. Nothing, really – nothing, that is, that he had not deduced before. Yet there were suggestive points.

It was not his sister-in-law, Maude, but his sister Cora of whom he had been thinking when he made the remark about women who were fools and yet shrewd. And it was to her he had confided his 'fancies.' And he had spoken of setting a trap. For whom?

3

Mr Entwhistle had meditated a good deal over how much he should tell Helen. In the end he decided to take her wholly into his confidence.

First he thanked her for sorting out Richard's things and for making various household arrangements. The house had been advertised for sale and there were one or two prospective buyers who would be coming to look over it.

'Private buyers?'

'I'm afraid not. The YWCA are considering it, and there is a young people's club, and the Trustees of the Jefferson Trust are looking for a suitable place to house their Collection.'

'It seems sad that the house will not be lived in, but of course it is not a practicable proposition nowadays.'

'I am going to ask you if it would be possible for you to remain here until the house is sold. Or would it be a great inconvenience?'

'No – actually it would suit me very well. I don't want to go to Cyprus until May, and I much prefer being here than to being in London as I had planned. I love this house, you know; Leo loved it, and we were always happy when we were here together.'

'There is another reason why I should be grateful if you would stay on. There is a friend of mine, a man called Hercule Poirot—'

Helen said sharply: 'Hercule Poirot? Then you think—'

'You know of him?'

'Yes. Some friends of mine – but I imagined that he was dead long ago.'

'He is very much alive. Not young, of course.'

'No, he could hardly be young.'

She spoke mechanically. Her face was white and strained. She said with an effort:

'You think – that Cora was right? That Richard was – *murdered*?'

Mr Entwhistle unburdened himself. It was a pleasure to unburden himself to Helen with her clear calm mind.

When he had finished she said:

'One ought to feel it's fantastic – but one doesn't. Maude and I, that night after the funeral – it was in both our minds, I'm sure. Saying to ourselves what a silly woman Cora was – and yet being uneasy. And then – Cora was killed – and I told myself it was just coincidence – and of course it may be – but oh! if one can only be sure. It's all so difficult.'

'Yes, it's difficult. But Poirot is a man of great originality and he has something really approaching genius. He understands perfectly what we need – assurance that the whole thing is a mare's nest.'

'And suppose it isn't?'

'What makes you say that?' asked Mr Entwhistle sharply.

'I don't know. I've been uneasy . . . Not just about what Cora said that day – something else. Something that I felt at the time to be wrong.'

'Wrong? In what way?'

'That's just it. I don't know.'

'You mean it was something about one of the people in the room?'

'Yes – yes – something of that kind. But I don't know who or what . . . Oh that sounds absurd—'

'Not at all. It is interesting – very interesting. You are not a fool, Helen. If you noticed something, that something has significance.'

'Yes, but I can't remember what it *was*. The more I think—'

'Don't think. That is the wrong way to bring anything back. Let it go. Sooner or later it will flash into your mind. And when it does – let me know – at once.'

'I will.'

9

Miss Gilchrist pulled her black hat down firmly on her head and tucked in a wisp of grey hair. The inquest was set for twelve o'clock and it was not quite twenty past eleven. Her grey coat and skirt looked quite nice, she thought, and she had bought herself a black blouse. She wished she could have been all in black, but that would have been far beyond her means. She looked round the small neat bedroom and at the walls hung with representations of Brixham harbour, Cockington Forge, Anstey's Cove, Kyance Cove, Polflexan harbour, Babbacombe Bay, etc, all signed in a dashing way, Cora Lansquenet. Her eyes rested with particular fondness on Polflexan harbour. On the chest of drawers a faded photograph carefully framed represented the Willow Teashop. Miss Gilchrist looked at it lovingly and sighed.

She was disturbed from her reverie by the sound of the door bell below.

'Dear me,' murmured Miss Gilchrist, 'I wonder who—'

She went out of her room and down the rather rickety stairs. The bell sounded again and there was a sharp knock.

For some reason Miss Gilchrist felt nervous. For a moment or two her steps slowed up, then she went rather unwillingly to the door, adjuring herself not to be so silly.

A young woman dressed smarly in black and carrying a small suitcase was standing on the step. She noticed the alarmed look on Miss Gilchrist's face and said quickly:

'Miss Gilchrist? I am Mrs Lansquenet's niece – Susan Banks.'

'Oh dear, yes, of course. I didn't know. Do come in, Mrs Banks. Mind the hall-stand – it sticks out a little. In here, yes. I didn't know you were coming down for the inquest. I'd have had something ready – some coffee or something.'

Susan Banks said briskly:

'I don't want anything. I'm so sorry if I startled you.'

'Well, you know you *did*, in a way. It's very silly of me. I'm not usually nervous. In fact I told the lawyer that I *wasn't* nervous and that I wouldn't be nervous staying on here alone, and really I'm *not* nervous. Only – perhaps it's just the inquest and – thinking of things, but I have been jumpy all this morning, just about half an hour ago the bell rang and I could hardly bring myself to open the door – which was really very stupid and so unlikely that a murderer would come *back* – and why should he? – and actually it was only a nun, collecting for an orphanage – and I was so relieved I gave her two shillings although I'm *not* a Roman Catholic and indeed have no sympathy with the Roman Catholic Church and all these monks and nuns though I believe the Little Sisters of the Poor really do good work. But do please sit down, Mrs – Mrs—'

'Banks.'

'Yes, of course, Banks. Did you come down by train?'

'No, I drove down. The lane seemed so narrow I ran the car

on a little way and found a sort of old quarry I backed it into.'

'This lane is very narrow, but there's hardly ever any traffic along here. It's rather a lonely road.'

Miss Gilchrist gave a little shiver as she said those last words. Susan Banks was looking round the room.

'Poor old Aunt Cora,' she said. 'She left what she had to me, you know.'

'Yes, I know. Mr Entwhistle told me. I expect you'll be glad of the furniture. You're newly married, I understand, and furnishing is such an expense nowadays. Mrs Lansquenet had some very nice things.'

Susan did not agree. Cora had had no taste for the antique. The contents varied between 'modernistic' pieces and the 'arty' type.

'I shan't want any of the furniture,' she said. 'I've got my own, you know. I shall put it up for auction. Unless — is there any of it you would like? I'd be very glad . . .'

She stopped a little embarrassed. But Miss Gilchrist was not at all embarrassed. She beamed.

'Now really, that's *very* kind of you, Mrs Banks — yes, very kind indeed. I really do appreciate it. But actually, you know, I have my own things. I put them in store in case — some day — I should need them. There are some pictures my father left too. I had a small tea-shop at one time, you know — but then the war came — it was all very unfortunate. But I didn't sell up everything, because I did hope to have my own little home again one day, so I put the best things in store with my father's pictures and some relics of our old home. But I *would* like very much, if you *really* wouldn't mind, to have that little painted tea table of dear Mrs Lansquenet's. Such a pretty thing and we always had tea on it.'

Susan, looking with a slight shudder at a small green table painted with large purple clematis, said quickly that she would be delighted for Miss Gilchrist to have it.

'Thank you *very* much, Mrs Banks. I feel a little greedy. I've got all her beautiful pictures, you know, and a lovely amethyst brooch, but I feel that perhaps I ought to give *that* back to you.'

'No, no, indeed.'

'You'll want to go through her things? After the inquest, perhaps?'

'I thought I'd stay here a couple of days, go through things, and clear everything up.'

'Sleep here, you mean?'

'Yes. Is there any difficulty?'

'Oh no, Mrs Banks, of course not. I'll put fresh sheets on my bed, and I can doss down here on the couch quite well.'

'But there's Aunt Cora's room, isn't there? I can sleep in that.'

'You – you wouldn't mind?'

'You mean because she was murdered there? Oh no, I wouldn't mind. I'm very tough, Miss Gilchrist. It's been – I mean – it's all right again?'

Miss Gilchrist understood the question.

'Oh *yes*, Mrs Banks. All the blankets sent away to the cleaners and Mrs Panter and I scrubbed the whole room out thoroughly. And there are plenty of spare blankets. But come up and see for yourself.'

She led the way upstairs and Susan followed her.

The room where Cora Lansquenet had died was clean and fresh and curiously devoid of any sinister atmosphere. Like the sitting-room it contained a mixture of modern utility and elaborately painted furniture. It represented Cora's cheerful tasteless personality. Over the mantelpiece an oil painting showed a buxom young woman about to enter her bath.

Susan gave a slight shudder as she looked at it and Miss Gilchrist said:

'That was painted by Mrs Lansquenet's husband. There are a lot more of his pictures in the dining-room downstairs.'

'How terrible.'

'Well, I don't care very much for that style of painting *myself* – but Mrs Lansquenet was very proud of her husband as an artist and thought that his work was sadly unappreciated.'

'Where are Aunt Cora's own pictures?'

'In my room. Would you like to see them?'

Miss Gilchrist displayed her treasures proudly.

Susan remarked that Aunt Cora seemed to have been fond of sea coast resorts.

'Oh yes. You see, she lived for many years with Mr Lansquenet at a small fishing village in Brittany. Fishing boats are always so picturesque, are they not?'

'Obviously,' Susan murmured. A whole series of picture postcards could, she thought, have been made from Cora Lansquenet's paintings which were faithful to detail and very highly coloured. They gave rise to the suspicion that they might actually have been painted from picture postcards.

But when she hazarded this opinion Miss Gilchrist was indignant. Mrs Lansquenet *always* painted from Nature! Indeed, once she had had a touch of the sun from reluctance to leave a subject when the light was just right.

'Mrs Lansquenet was a real artist,' said Miss Gilchrist reproachfully.

She glanced at her watch and Susan said quickly:

'Yes, we ought to start for the inquest. Is it far? Shall I get the car?'

It was only five minutes' walk. Miss Gilchrist assured her. So they set out together on foot. Mr Entwhistle, who had come down by train, met them and shepherded them into the Village Hall.

There seemed to be a large number of strangers present. The inquest was not sensational. There was evidence of identification of the deceased. Medical evidence as to the nature of the wounds that had killed her. There were no signs of a struggle. Deceased was probably under a narcotic at the time she was attacked and would have been taken quite unawares. Death was unlikely to have occurred later than four-thirty. Between two and four-thirty was the nearest approximation. Miss Gilchrist testified to finding the body. A police constable and Inspector Morton gave their evidence. The Coroner summed up briefly. The jury made no bones about the verdict. *'Murder by some person or persons unknown.'*

It was over. They came out again into the sunlight. Half a dozen cameras clicked. Mr Entwhistle shepherded Susan and Miss Gilchrist into the King's Arms, where he had taken the precaution to arrange for lunch to be served in a private room behind the bar.

'Not a very good lunch, I'm afraid,' he said apologetically. But the lunch was not at all bad. Miss Gilchrist sniffed a little and murmured that 'it was all so dreadful,' but cheered up and tackled the Irish stew with appetite after Mr Entwhistle had insisted on her drinking a glass of sherry. He said to Susan:

'I'd no idea you were coming down today Susan. We could have come together.'

'I know I said I wouldn't. But it seemed rather mean for none of the family to be there. I rang up George but he said he was very busy and couldn't possibly make it, and Rosamund had an audition and Uncle Timothy, of course, is a crock. So it had to be me.'

'Your husband didn't come with you?'

671

'Greg had to settle up with his tiresome shop.'

Seeing a startled look in Miss Gilchrist's eye, Susan said: 'My husband works in a chemist's shop.'

A husband in retail trade did not quite square with Miss Gilchrist's impression of Susan's smartness, but she said valiantly: 'Oh yes, just like Keats.'

'Greg's no poet,' said Susan.

She added:

'We've got great plans for the future – a double-barrelled establishment – Cosmetics and Beauty parlour and a laboratory for special preparations.'

'That will be much nicer,' said Miss Gilchrist approvingly. 'Something like Elizabeth Arden who is really a Countess, so I have been told – or is that Helena Rubinstein? In any case,' she added kindly, 'a pharmacist's is not in the least like an ordinary shop – a *draper*, for instance, or a *grocer*.'

'You kept a tea-shop, you said, didn't you?'

'Yes, indeed,' Miss Gilchrist's face lit up. That the Willow Tree had ever been 'trade' in the sense that a shop was trade, would never have occurred to her. To keep a tea-shop was in her mind the essence of gentility. She started telling Susan about the Willow Tree.

Mr Entwhistle, who had heard about it before, let his mind drift to other matters. When Susan had spoken to him twice without his answering he hurriedly apologised.

'Forgive me, my dear, I was thinking, as a matter of fact, about your Uncle Timothy. I am a little worried.'

'About Uncle Timothy? I shouldn't be. I don't believe really there's anything the matter with him. He's just a hypochondriac.'

'Yes – yes, you may be right. I confess it was not his health that was worrying me. It's Mrs Timothy. Apparently she's fallen downstairs and twisted her ankle. She's laid up and your uncle is in a terrible state.'

'Because he'll have to look after her instead of the other way about? Do him a lot of good,' said Susan.

'Yes – yes, I dare say. But will your poor aunt *get* any looking after? That is really the question. With no servants in the house?'

'Life is really hell for elderly people,' said Susan. 'They live in a kind of Georgian Manor house, don't they?'

Mr Entwhistle nodded.

They came rather warily out of the King's Arms, but the Press seemed to have dispersed.

A couple of reporters were lying in wait for Susan by the cottage door. Shepherded by Mr Entwhistle she said a few necessary and non-committal words. Then she and Miss Gilchrist went into the cottage and Mr Entwhistle returned to the King's Arms where he had booked a room. The funeral was to be on the following day.

'My car's still in the quarry,' said Susan. 'I'd forgotten about it. I'll drive it along to the village later.'

Miss Gilchrist said anxiously:

'Not too late. You won't go out after dark, will you?'

Susan looked at her and laughed.

'You don't think there's a murderer still hanging about, do you?'

'No – no, I suppose not.'' Miss Gilchrist looked embarrased.

'But it's exactly what she does think,' thought Susan.

'How amazing!'

Miss Gilchrist had vanished towards the kitchen.

'I'm sure you'd like tea early. In about half an hour, do you think, Mrs Banks?'

Susan thought that tea at half-past three was overdoing it, but she was charitable enough to realise that 'a nice cup of tea' was Miss Gilchrist's idea of restoration for the nerves and she had her own reasons for wishing to please Miss Gilchrist, so she said:

'Whenever you like, Miss Gilchrist.'

A happy clatter of kitchen implements began and Susan went into the sitting-room. She had only been there a few minutes when the bell sounded and was succeeded by a very precise little rat-tat-tat.

Susan came out into the hall and Miss Gilchrist appeared at the kitchen door wearing an apron and wiping floury hands on it.

'Oh dear, who do you think that can be?'

'More reporters, I expect,' said Susan.

'Oh dear, how annoying for you, Mrs Banks.'

'Oh well, never mind, I'll attend to it.'

'I was just going to make a few scones for tea.'

Susan went towards the front door and Miss Gilchrist hovered uncertainly. Susan wondered whether she thought a man with a hatchet was waiting outside.

The visitor, however, proved to be an elderly gentleman who raised his hat when Susan opened the door and said, beaming at her in avuncular style.

'Mrs Banks, I think?'

'Yes.'

'My name is Guthrie – Alexander Guthrie. I was a friend – a very old friend, of Mrs Lansquenet's. You, I think, are her niece, formerly Miss Susan Abernethie?'

'That's quite right.'

'Then since we know who we are, I may come in?'

'Of course.'

Mr Guthrie wiped his feet carefully on the mat, stepped inside, divested himself of his overcoat, laid it down with his hat on a small oak chest and followed Susan into the sitting-room.

'This is a melancholy occasion,' said Mr Guthrie, to whom melancholy did not seem to come naturally, his own inclination being to beam. 'Yes, a very melancholy occasion. I was in this part of the world and I felt the least I could do was to attend the inquest – and of course the funeral. Poor Cora – poor foolish Cora. I have known her, my dear Mrs Banks, since the early days of her marriage. A high-spirited girl – and she took art very seriously – took Pierre Lansquenet seriously, too – as an artist, I mean. All things considered he didn't make her too bad a husband. He strayed, if you know what I mean, yes, he strayed – but fortunately Cora took it as part of the artistic temperament. He was an artist and therefore immoral! In fact, I'm not sure she didn't go further: he was immoral and therefore he must be an artist! No kind of sense in artistic matters, poor Cora – though in other ways, mind you, Cora had a lot of sense – yes, a surprising lot of sense.'

'That's what everybody seems to say,' Said Susan. 'I didn't really know her.'

'No, no, cut herself off from her family because they didn't appreciate her precious Pierre. She was never a pretty girl – but she had *something*. She was good company! You never knew what she'd say next and you never knew if her *naiveté* was genuine or whether she was doing it deliberately. She made us all laugh a good deal. The eternal child – that's what we always felt about her. And really the last time I saw her (I have seen her from time to time since Pierre died) she struck me as still behaving very much like a child.'

Susan offered Mr Guthrie a cigarette, but the old gentleman shook his head.

'No, thank you, my dear. I don't smoke. You must wonder why I've come? To tell you the truth I was feeling rather conscience-stricken. I promised Cora to come and see her some weeks ago. I usually called upon her once a year, and just lately she'd taken up the hobby of buying pictures at local sales, and wanted me to look at some of them. My profession is that of art critic, you know. Of course most of Cora's purchases were horrible daubs, but take it all in all, it isn't such a bad speculation. Pictures go for next to nothing at these country sales and the frames alone are worth more than you pay for the picture. Naturally any important sale is attended by dealers and one isn't likely to get hold of masterpieces. But only the other day, a small Cuyp was knocked down for a few pounds at a farmhouse sale. The history of it was quite interesting. It had been given to an old nurse by the family she had served faithfully for many years – they had no idea of its value. Old nurse gave it to farmer nephew who liked the horse in it but thought it was a dirty old thing! Yes, yes, these things sometimes happen, and Cora was convinced that she had an eye for pictures. She hadn't, of course. Wanted me to come and look at a Rembrandt she had picked up last year. A Rembrandt! Not even a respectable copy of one! But she had got hold of a quite nice Bartolozzi engraving – damp spotted unfortunately. I sold it for her for thirty pounds and of course that spurred her on. She wrote to me with great gusto about an Italian Primitive she had bought at some sale and I promised I'd come along and see it.'

'That's it over there, I expect,' said Susan, gesturing to the wall behind him.

Mr Guthrie got up, put on a pair of spectacles, and went over to study the picture.

'Poor dear Cora,' he said at last.

'There are a lot more,' said Susan.

Mr Guthrie proceeded to a leisurely inspection of the art treasures acquired by the hopeful Mrs Lansquenet. Occasionally he said, 'Tchk, Tchk,' occasionally he sighed.

Finally he removed his spectacles.

'Dirt,' he said, 'is a wonderful thing, Mrs Banks! It gives a patina of romance to the most horrible examples of the painter's art. I'm afraid that Bartolozzi was beginner's luck. Poor Cora. Still it gave her an interest in life. I am really thankful that I did not have to disillusion her.'

'There are some pictures in the dining-room,' said Susan, 'but I think they are all her husband's work.'

Mr Guthrie shuddered slightly and held up a protesting hand.

'Do not force me to look at those again. Life classes have much to answer for! I always tried to spare Cora's feelings.

A devoted wife – a very devoted wife. Well, dear Mrs Banks, I must not take up more of your time.'

'Oh, do stay and have some tea. I think it's nearly ready.'

'That is very kind of you.' Mr Guthrie sat down again promptly.

'I'll just go and see.'

In the kitchen, Miss Gilchrist was just lifting a last batch of scones from the oven. The tea-tray stood ready and the kettle was just gently rattling its lid.

'There's a Mr Guthrie here, and I've asked him to stay for tea.'

'Mr Guthrie? Oh, yes, he was a friend of dear Mrs Lansquenet's. He's the celebrated art critic. How fortunate; I've made a nice lot of scones and that's some home-made strawberry jam, and I just whipped up some little drop cakes. I'll just make the tea – I've warmed the pot. Oh, please, Mrs Banks, don't carry that heavy tray. I can manage *everything*.'

However, Susan took in the tray and Miss Gilchrist followed with teapot and kettle, greeted Mr Guthrie, and they set to.

'Hot scones, that *is* a treat,' said Mr Guthrie, 'and what delicious jam! Really, the stuff one buys nowadays.'

Miss Gilchrist was flushed and delighted. The little cakes were excellent and so were the scones, and everyone did justice to them. The ghost of the Willow Tree hung over the party. Here, it was clear, Miss Gilchrist was in her element.

'Well, thank you, perhaps I will,' said Mr Guthrie as he accepted the last cake, pressed upon him by Miss Gilchrist. 'I do feel rather guilty, though – enjoying my tea here, where poor Cora was so brutally murdered.'

Miss Gilchrist displayed an unexpected Victorian reaction to this.

'Oh, but Mrs Lansquenet would have wished you to take a good tea. You've got to keep your strength up.'

'Yes, yes, perhaps you are right. The fact is, you know, that one cannot really bring oneself to believe that someone you knew – actually knew – *can* have been murdered!'

'I agree,' said Susan. 'It just seems – fantastic.'

'And certainly not by some casual tramp who broke in and attacked her. I *can* imagine, you know, reasons why Cora might have been murdered—'

Susan said quickly, 'Can you? What reasons?'

'Well, she wasn't discreet,' said Mr Guthrie. 'Cora was never discreet. And she enjoyed – how shall I put it – showing how sharp she could be? Like a child who's got hold of somebody's secret. If Cora got hold of a secret she'd want to talk about it. Even if she promised not to, she'd still do it. She wouldn't be able to help herself.'

Susan did not speak. Miss Gilchrist did not either. She looked worried. Mr Guthrie went on:

'Yes, a little dose of arsenic in a cup of tea – *that* would not have surprised me, or a box of chocolates by post. But sordid robbery and assault – that seems highly incongruous. I may be wrong but I should have thought she had very little to take that would be worth a burglar's while. She didn't keep much money in the house, did she?'

Miss Gilchrist said, 'Very little.'

Mr Guthrie sighed and rose to his feet.

'Ah! Well, there's a lot of lawlessness about since the war. Times have changed.'

Thanking them for the tea he took a polite farewell of the two women. Miss Gilchrist saw him out and helped him on with his overcoat. From the window of the sitting-room, Susan watched him trot briskly down the front path to the gate.

Miss Gilchrist came back into the room with a small parcel in her hand.

'The postman must have been while we were at the inquest. He pushed it through the letter-box and it had fallen in the corner behind the door. Now I wonder – why, of course, it must be wedding cake.'

Happily Miss Gilchrist ripped off the paper. Inside was a small white box tied with silver ribbon.

'It is!' She pulled off the ribbon, inside was a modest wedge of rich cake with almond paste and white icing. 'How nice! Now who—' She consulted the card attached. '*John and Mary*. Now who *can* that be? How silly to put no surname.'

Susan, rousing herself from contemplation, said vaguely:

'It's quite difficult sometimes with people just using Christian names. I got a postcard the other day signed Joan. I counted up I knew eight Joans – and with telephoning so much, one often doesn't know their handwriting.'

Miss Gilchrist was happily going over the possible Johns or Marys of her acquaintance.

'It might be Dorothy's daughter – *her* name was Mary, but I hadn't heard of an engagement, still less of a marriage. Then there's little John Banfield – I suppose he's grown up and old enough to be married – or the Enfield girl – no, her name was Margaret. No address or anything. Oh well, I dare say it will come to me . . .'

She picked up the trap and went out to the kitchen.

Susan roused herself and said:

'Well – I suppose I'd better go and put the car somewhere.'

10

Susan retrieved the car from the quarry where she had left it and drove into the village. There was a petrol pump but no garage and she was advised to take it to the King's Arms. They had room for it there and she left it by a big Diamler which was preparing to go out. It was chauffeur driven and inside it, very much muffled up, was an elderly foreign gentleman with a large moustache.

The boy to whom Susan was talking about the car was staring at her with such rapt attention that he did not seem to be taking in half of what she said.

Finally he said in an awe-stricken voice:

'You're her niece, aren't you?'

'What?'

'You're the victim's niece,' the boy repeated with relish.

'Oh – yes – yes, I am.'

'Ar! Wondered where I'd seen you before.'

'Ghoul,' thought Susan as she retraced her steps to the cottage.

Miss Gilchrist greeted her with:

'Oh, you're safely back,' in tones of relief which further annoyed her. Miss Gilchrist added anxiously:

'You *can* eat spaghetti, can't you? I thought for tonight—'

'Oh yes, anything. I don't want much.'

'I really flatter myself that I can make a very tasty spaghetti *au gratin*.'

The boast was not an idle one. Miss Gilchrist, Susan reflected, was really an excellent cook. Susan offered to help wash up but Miss Gilchrist, though clearly gratified by the offer, assured Susan that there was very little to do.

She came in a little while after with coffee. The coffee was less excellent, being decidedly weak. Miss Gilchrist offered Susan a piece of the wedding cake which Susan refused.

'It's really very good cake,' Miss Gilchrist insisted, tasting it. She had settled to her own satisfaction that it must have been sent by someone whom she alluded to as 'dear Ellen's daughter who I know was engaged to be married but I can't remember her name.'

Susan let Miss Gilchrist chirrup away into silence before starting her own subject of conversation. This moment, after supper, sitting before the fire, was a companionable one.

She said at last:

'My Uncle Richard came down here before he died, didn't he?'

'Yes, he did.'

'When was that exactly?'

'Let me see – it must have been, one, two – nearly three weeks before his death was announced.'

'Did he seem – ill?'

'Well, no, I wouldn't say he seemed exactly ill. He had a very hearty vigorous manner. Mrs Lansquenet was very surprised to see him. She said, "Well, really, Richard, after all these years!" and he said, "I came to see for myself exactly how things are with you." And Mrs Lansquenet said, "*I'm* all right." I think, you know, she was a teeny bit offended by his turning up so casually – after the long break. Anyway Mr Abernethie said, "No use keeping up old grievances. You and I and Timothy are the only ones left – and nobody can talk to Timothy except about his own health." And he said, "Pierre seems to have made you happy, so it seems I was in the wrong. There, will that content you?" Very nicely he said it. A handsome man, though elderly, of course.'

'How long was he here?'

'He stayed for lunch. Beef olives, I made. Fortunately it was the day the butcher called.'

Miss Gilchrist's memory seemed to be almost wholly culinary.

'They seemed to be getting on well together?'

'Oh, yes.'

Susan paused and then said:

'Was Aunt Cora surprised when – he died?'

'Oh yes, it was quite sudden, wasn't it?'

'Yes, it was sudden . . . I meant – she *was* surprised. He hadn't given her any indication how ill he was.

'Oh – I see what you mean.' Miss Gilchrist paused a moment. 'No, no, I think perhaps you are right. She did say that he had got very old – I think she said senile . . .'

'But *you* didn't think he was senile?'

'Well, not to *look* at. But I didn't talk to him much, naturally I left them alone together.'

Susan looked at Miss Gilchrist speculatively. Was Miss Gilchrist the kind of woman who listened at doors? She was honest, Susan felt sure, she wouldn't ever pilfer, or cheat over the housekeeping, or open letters. But inquisitiveness can drape itself in a mantle of rectitude. Miss Gilchrist might have found it necessary to garden near an open window, or to dust the hall . . . That would be within the permitted lengths. And then, of course, she could not have helped hearing something. . . .

'You didn't hear any of their conversation?' Susan asked.

Too abrupt. Miss Gilchrist flushed angrily.

'No, indeed, Mrs Banks. It has never been my custom to listen at doors!'

That means she does, thought Susan, otherwise she'd just say 'No.'

Aloud she said: 'I'm so sorry, Miss Gilchrist. I didn't mean it that way. But sometimes, in these small flimsily built cottages, one simply can't help overhearing nearly everything that goes on, and now that they are both dead, it's really rather important to the family to know just what was said at that meeting between them.'

The cottage was anything but flimsily built – it dated from a sturdier era of building, but Miss Gilchrist accepted the bait, and rose to the suggestion held out.

'Of course what you say is quite true, Mrs Banks – this *is* a very small place and I do appreciate that you would want to know what passed between them, but really I'm afraid I can't help very much. I think they were talking about Mr Abernethie's health – and certain – well, *fancies* he had. He didn't look it, but he must have been a sick man and as is so often the case, he put his ill-health down to *outside agencies*. A common sympton, I believe. My aunt—'

Miss Gilchrist described her aunt.

Susan, like Mr Entwhistle, side-tracked the aunt.

'Yes,' she said. 'That is just what we thought. My uncle's servants were all very attached to him and naturally they are upset by his thinking—' She paused.

'Oh, of course! Servants are *very* touchy about anything of that kind. I remember that my aunt—'

Again Susan interrupted.

'It *was* the servants he suspected, I suppose? Of poisoning him, I mean?'

'I don't know . . . I – really—'

Susan noted her confusion.

'It wasn't the servants. Was it one particular person?'

'I don't know, Mrs Banks. Really I don't know—'

But her eye avoided Susan's. Susan thought to herself that Miss Gilchrist knew more than she was willing to admit.

It was possible that Miss Gilchrist knew a good deal . . .

Deciding not to press the point for the moment, Susan said:

'What are your own plans for the future, Miss Gilchrist?'

'Well, really, I was going to speak to you about that, Mrs Banks. I told Mr Entwhistle I would be willing to stay on until everything here was cleared up.'

'I know. I'm very grateful.'

'And I wanted to ask you how long that was likely to be, because, of course, I must start looking about for another post.'

Susan considered.

'There's really not very much to be done here. In a couple of days I can get things sorted out and notify the auctioneer.'

'You have decided to sell up everything, then?'

'Yes. I don't suppose there will be any difficulty in letting the cottage?'

'Oh, no – people will queue up for it, I'm sure. There are so few cottages to rent. One nearly always has to buy.'

'So it's all very simple, you see.' Susan hesitated a moment before saying, 'I wanted to tell you – that I hope you'll accept three months' salary.'

'That's very generous of you, I'm sure, Mrs Banks. I do appreciate it. And you would be prepared to – I mean I could ask you – if necessary – to – recommend me? To say that I had been with a relation of yours and that I had – proved satisfactory?'

'Oh, of course.'

'I don't know whether I ought to ask it.' Miss Gilchrist's hands began to shake and she tried to steady her voice. 'But would it be possible not to – to mention the circumstances – or even the *name*?'

Susan stared.

'I don't understand.'

'That's because you haven't thought, Mrs Banks. It's *murder*. A murder that's been in the papers and that everybody has read about. Don't you see? People might think. "Two women living together, and one of them is killed – and *perhaps the companion did it*." Don't you see, Mrs Banks? I'm sure that if I was looking for someone, I'd – well, I'd think twice before engaging myself – if you understand what I mean

Because one never *knows*! It's been worrying me dreadfully, Mrs Banks; I've been lying awake at night thinking that perhaps I'll never get another job – not of this kind. And what else is there that I can do?'

The question came out with unconscious pathos. Susan felt suddenly stricken. She realised the desperation of this pleasant-spoken commonplace woman who was dependent for existence on the fears and whims of employers. And there was a lot of truth in what Miss Gilchrist had said. You wouldn't, if you could help it, engage a woman to share domestic intimacy who had figured, however innocently, in a murder case.

Susan said: 'But if they find the man who did it—'

'Oh *then* of course, it will be quite all right. But will they find him? I don't think, myself, the police have the *least idea*. And if he's *not* caught – well, that leaves me as – as not quite the most likely person, but as a person who *could* have done it.'

Susan nodded thoughtfully. It was true that Miss Gilchrist did not benefit from Cora Lansquenet's death – but who was to know that? And besides, there were so many tales – ugly tales – of animosity arising between women who lived together – strange pathological motives for sudden violence. Someone who had not known them might imagine that Cora Lansquenet and Miss Gilchrist had lived on those terms. . . .

Susan spoke with her usual decision.

'Don't worry, Miss Gilchrist,' she said, speaking briskly and cheerfully. 'I'm sure I can find you a post amongst my friends. There won't be the least difficulty.'

'I'm afraid,' said Miss Gilchrist, regaining some of her customary manner, 'that I couldn't undertake any really rough work. Just a little plain cooking and housework—'

The telephone rang and Miss Gilchrist jumped.

'Dear me, I wonder who *that* can be.'

'I expect it's my husband,' said Susan, jumping up. 'He said he'd ring me to-night.

She went to the telephone.

'Yes? – yes, this is Mrs Banks speaking personally . . .'

There was a pause and then her voice changed. It became soft and warm. 'Hallo, darling – yes, it's me . . . Oh, quite well . . . Murder by someone unknown . . . the usual thing . . . Only Mr Entwhistle . . . What? . . . it's difficult to say, but I think so . . . Yes, just as we thought . . . Absolutely according to plan . . . I shall sell the stuff. There's nothing *we'd* want . . Not for a day or two . . . Absolutely frightful . . . Don't fuss I know

what I'm doing . . . Greg, you didn't . . . You were careful to
. . . No, it's nothing. Nothing at all. Good night, darling.'

She rang off. The nearness of Miss Gilchrist had hampered
her a little. Miss Gilchrist could probably hear from the
kitchen, where she had tactfully retired, exactly what went on.
There were things she had wanted to ask Greg, but she hadn't
liked to.

She stood by the telephone, frowning abstractedly. Then
suddenly an idea came to her.

'Of course,' she murmured. 'Just the thing.'

Lifting the receiver she asked for Trunk Enquiry.

Some quarter of an hour later a weary voice from the exchange was saying:

'I'm afraid there's no reply.'

'Please go on ringing them.'

Susan spoke autocratically. She listened to the far off buzzing of a telephone bell. Then, suddenly it was interrupted and
a man's voice, pevish and slightly indignant, said:

'Yes, yes, what is it?'

'Uncle Timothy?'

'What's that? I can't hear you.'

'Uncle Timothy? I'm Susan Banks.'

'Susan who?'

'Banks. Formerly Abernethie. Your niece Susan.'

'Oh, you're Susan, are you? What's the matter? What are
you ringing up for at this time of night?'

'It's quite early still.'

'It isn't. I was in bed.'

'You must go to bed early. How's Aunt Maude?'

'Is that all you rang up to ask? Your's aunt's in a good deal
of pain and she can't do a thing. Not a thing. She's helpless.
We're in a nice mess, I can tell you. That fool of a doctor
says he can't even get a nurse. He wanted to cart Maude off
to hospital. I stood out against *that*. He's trying to get hold
of someone for us. I can't do anything – I daren't even try.
There's a fool from the village staying in the house to-night
– but she's murmuring about getting back to her husband.
Don't know *what* we're going to do.'

'That's what I rang up about. Would you like Miss Gilchrist?'

'Who's she? Never heard of her.'

'Aunt Cora's companion. She's very nice and capable.'

'Can she cook?'

'Yes, she cooks very well, and she could look after Aunt Maude.'

'That's all very well, but when could she come? Here I am, all on my own, with only these idiots of village women popping in and out at odd hours, and it's not good for me. My heart's playing me up.'

'I'll arrange for her to get off to you as soon as possible. The day after tomorrow, perhaps?'

'Well, thanks very much,' said the voice rather grudgingly. 'You're a good girl, Susan – er – thank you.'

Susan rang off and went into the kitchen.

'Would you be willing to go up to Yorkshire and look after my aunt? She fell and broke her ankle and my uncle is quite useless. He's a bit of a pest but Aunt Maude is a very good sort. They have help in from the village, but you could cook and look after Aunt Maude.'

Miss Gilchrist dropped the coffee pot in her agitation.

'Oh, thank you, thank you – that really is kind. I think I can say of myself that I am really good in the sickroom, and I'm sure I can manage your uncle and cook him nice little meals. It's really very kind of you, Mrs Banks, and I *do* appreciate it.'

--- I I ---

Susan lay in bed and waited for sleep to come. It had been a long day and she was tired. She had been quite sure that she would go to sleep at once. She never had any difficulty in going to sleep. And yet here she lay, hour after hour, wide awake, her mind racing.

She had said she did not mind sleeping in this room, in this bed. This bed were Cora Abernethie—

No, no, she must put all that out of her mind. She had always prided herself on having no nerves. Why think of that afternoon less than a week ago? Think ahead – the future. Her future and Greg's. Those premises in Cardigan Street – just what they wanted. The business on the ground floor and a charming flat upstairs. The room out at the back a laboratory for Greg. For purposes of income tax it would be an excellent set-up. Greg would get calm and well again. There would be no more of those alarming brain-storms. The times when he looked at her without seeming to know who she was. Once or twice she's been quite frightened . . . And old Mr Cole – he'd hinted – threatened: 'If this happens again . . .' And it might have happened again – it *would* have happened again. If Uncle Richard hadn't died just when he did . . .

Uncle Richard – but really why look at it like that? He'd nothing to live for. Old and tired and ill. His son dead. It was a mercy really. To die in his sleep quietly like that. Quietly . . . in his sleep. . . If only she could sleep: It was so stupid lying awake hour after hour . . . hearing the furniture creak, and the rustling of trees and bushes outside the window and the occasional queer melancholy hoot – an owl, she supposed. How sinister the country was, somehow. So different from the big noisy indifferent town. One felt so safe there – surrounded by people – never alone. Whereas here . . .

Houses where a murder had been committed were sometimes haunted. Perhaps this cottage would come to be known as the haunted cottage. Haunted by the spirit of Cora Lansquenet . . . Aunt Cora. Odd, really, how ever since she had arrived she had felt as though Aunt Cora were quite close to her . . . within reach. All nerves and fancy. Cora Lansquenet was dead, tomorrow she would be buried. There was no one in the cottage except Susan herself and Miss Gilchrist. Then why did she feel that there was someone in this room, someone close beside her . . .

She had lain on this bed when the hatchet fell. . . . Lying there trustingly asleep . . . Knowing nothing till the hatchet fell . . . And now she wouldn't let Susan sleep . . .

The furniture creaked again . . . was that a stealthy step? Susan switched on the light. Nothing Nerves, nothing but nerves. Relax . . . close your eyes . . .

Surely that was a groan – a groan or a faint moan . . . Someone in pain – someone dying . . .

'I mustn't imagine things, I mustn't, I mustn't,' Susan whispered to herself.

Death was the end – there was no existence after death. Under no circumstances could anyone come back. Or was she reliving a scene from the past – a dying woman groaning . . .

There it was again . . . stronger . . . someone groaning in acute pain . . .

But – this was real. Once again Susan switched on the light, sat up in bed and listened The groans were real groans and she was hearing them through the wall. They came from the room next door.

Susan jumped out of bed, flung on a dressing-gown and crossed to the door. She went out on to the landing, tapped for a moment on Miss Gilchrist's door and then went in. Miss Gilchrist's light was on. She was sitting up in bed. She looked ghastly. Her face was distorted with pain.

'Miss Gilchrist, what's the mater? Are you ill?'

'Yes I don't know what – I –' she tried to get out of bed, was seized with a fit of vomiting and then collapsed back on the pillows.

She murmured: 'Please – ring up doctor. Must have eaten something. . . .'

'I'll get you some bicarbonate. We can get the doctor in the morning if you're not better.'

Miss Gilchrist shook her head.

'No, get the doctor now. I – I feel dreadful.'

'Do you know his number? Or shall I look in the book?'

Miss Gilchrist gave her the number. She was interrupted by another fit of retching.

Susan's call was answered by a sleepy male voice.

'Who? Gilchrist? In Mead's Lane? Yes, I know. I'll be right along.'

He was as good as his word. Ten minutes later Susan heard his car draw up outside and she went to open the door to him.

She explained the case as she took him upstairs. 'I think,' she said, 'she must have eaten something that disagreed with her. But she seems pretty bad.'

The doctor had had the air of one keeping his temper in leash and who has had some experience of being called out unnecessarily on more than one occasion. But as soon as he examined the moaning woman his manner changed. He gave various curt orders to Susan and presently came down and telephoned. Then he joined Susan in the sitting-room.

'I've sent for an ambulance. Must get her into hospital.'

'She's really bad then?'

'Yes. I've given her a shot of morphia to ease the pain. But it looks—' He broke off. 'What's she eaten?'

'We had macaroni *au gratin* for supper and a custard pudding. Coffee afterwards.'

'You have the same things?'

'Yes.'

'And you're all right? No pain or discomfort?'

'No.'

'She's taken nothing else? No tinned fish? Or sausages?'

'No. We had lunch at the King's Arms – after the inquest.'

'Yes, of course. You're Mrs Lansquenet's niece?'

'Yes.'

'That was a nasty business. Hope they catch the man who did it.'

'Yes, indeed.'

The ambulance came. Miss Gilchrist was taken away and the doctor went with her. He told Susan he would ring her up in the morning. When he had left she went upstairs to bed.

This time she fell asleep as soon as her head touched the pillow.

2

The funeral was well attended. Most of the village had turned out. Susan and Mr Entwhistle were the only mourners, but various wreaths had been sent by the other members of the family. Mr Entwhistle asked where Miss Gilchrist was, and Susan explained the circumstances in a hurried whisper. Mr Entwhistle raised his eyebrows.

'Rather an odd occurrence?'

'Oh, she's better this morning. They rang me from the hospital. People do get these bilious turns. Some make more fuss than others.'

Mr Entwhistle said no more. He was returning to London immediately after the funeral.

Susan went back to the cottage. She found some eggs and made herself an omelette. Then she went up to Cora's room and started to sort through the dead woman's things.

She was interrupted by the arrival of the doctor.

The doctor was looking worried. He replied to Susan's inquiry by saying that Miss Gilchrist was much better.

'She'll be out and around in a couple of days,' he said. 'But it was lucky I got called in so promptly. Otherwise – it might have been a near thing.'

Susan stared. 'Was she really so bad?'

'Mrs Banks, will you tell me again exactly what Miss Gilchrist had to eat and drink yesterday. Everything.'

Susan reflected and gave a meticulous account. The doctor shook his head in a dissatisfied manner.

'There must have been something she had and you didn't?'

'I don't think so . . . Cakes, scones, jam, tea – and then supper. No, I can't remember anything.'

The doctor rubbed his nose. He walked up and down the room.

'Was it definitely something she ate? Definitely food poisoning?'

The doctor threw her a sharp glance. Then he seemed to come to a decision.

'It was arsenic,' he said.

'Arsenic?' Susan started. 'You mean somebody gave her arsenic?'

'That's what it looks like.'

'Could she have taken it herself? Deliberately, I mean?'

'Suicide? She says not and she should know. Besides, if she wanted to commit suicide she wouldn't be likely to choose arsenic. There are sleping pills in this house. She could have taken an overdose of them.'

'Could the arsenic have got into something by accident?'

'That's what I'm wondering. It seems very unlikely, but such things have been known. But if you and she ate the same things—'

Susan nodded. She said, 'It all seems impossible—' then she gave a sudden gasp. 'Why, of course, the wedding cake!'

'What's that? Wedding cake?'

Susan explained. The doctor listened with close atention.

'Odd. And you say she wasn't sure who sent it? Any of it left. Or is the box it came in lying around?'

'I don't know I'll look.'

They searched together and finally found the white cardboard box with a few crumbs of cake still in it lying on the kitchen dresser. The doctor packed it away with some care.

'I'll take charge of this. Any idea where the wrapping paper it came in might be?'

Here they were not successful and Susan said that it had probably gone into the Ideal boiler.

'You won't be leaving here just yet, Mrs Banks?'

His tone was genial, but it made Susan feel a little uncomfortable.

'No, I have to go through my aunt's things. I shall be here for a few days.'

'Good. You understand the police will probably want to ask some questions. You don't know of anyone who – well, might have had it in for Miss Gilchrist?'

Susan shook her head.

'I don't really know much about her. She was with my aunt for some years – that's all I know.'

'Quite, quite. Always seemed a pleasant unassuming woman – quite ordinary. Not the kind, you'd say, to have enemies or anything melodramatic of that kind. Wedding cake through the post. Sounds like some jealous woman – but who'd be jealous of Miss Gilchrist? Doesn't seem to fit.'

'No.'

'Well, I must be on my way. I don't know what's happening to us in quiet little Lytchett St Mary. First a brutal murder and now attempted poisoning through the post. Odd, the one following the other.'

He went down the path to his car. The cottage felt stuffy and Susan left the door standing open as she went slowly upstairs to resume her task.

Cora Lansquenet had not been a tidy or methodical woman. Her drawers held a miscellaneous assortment of things. There were toilet accessories and letters and old handkerchiefs and paint brushes mixed up together in one drawer. There were a few old letters and bills thrust in amongst a bulging drawer of underclothes. In another drawer under some woollen jumpers was a cardboard box holding two false fringes. There was another drawer full of old photographs and sketching books. Susan lingered over a group taken evidently at some French place many years ago and which showed a younger, thinner Cora clinging to the arm of a tall lanky man with a straggling beard dressed in what seemed to be a velveteen coat and whom Susan took to be the late Pierre Lansquenet.

The photographs interested Susan, but she laid them aside, sorted all the papers she had found into a heap and began to go through them methodically. About a quarter way through she came on a letter. She read it through twice and was still staring at it when a voice speaking behind her caused her to give a cry of alarm.

'And what may you have got hold of there, Susan? Hallo, what's the matter?'

Susan reddened with annoyance. Her cry of alarm had been quite involuntary and she felt ashamed and anxious to explain.

'George? How you startled me!'

Her cousin smiled lazily.

'So it seems.'

'How did you get here?'

'Well, the door downstairs was open, so I walked in. There seemed to be nobody about on the ground floor, so I came up here. If you mean how did I get to this part of the world, I started down this morning to come to the funeral.'

'I didn't see you there?'

'The old bus played me up. The petrol feed seemed choked. I tinkered with it for some time and finally it seemed to clear itself. I was too late for the funeral by then, but I thought I might as well come on down. I knew you were here.'

He paused, and then went on:

'I rang you up, as a matter of fact and Greg told me you'd come down to take possession, as it were. I thought I might give you a hand.'

Susan said, 'Aren't you needed in the office? Or can you take days off whenever you like?'

'A funeral has always been a recognised excuse for absenteeism. And this funeral is indubitably genuine. Besides, a murder always fascinates people. Anyway, I shan't be going much to the office in future – not now that I'm a man of means. I shall have better things to do.'

He paused and grinned, 'Same as Greg,' he said.

Susan looked at George thoughtfully. She had never seen much of this cousin of hers and when they did meet she had always found him rather difficult to make out.

She asked, 'Why did you really come down here, George?'

'I'm not sure it wasn't to do a little detective work. I've been thinking a good deal about the last funeral we attended. Aunt Cora certainly threw a spanner into the works that day. I've wondered whether it was sheer irresponsibility and auntly *joie de vivre* that prompted her words, or whether she really had something to go upon. What actually is in that letter that you were reading so attentively when I came in?'

Susan said slowly, 'It's a letter that Uncle Richard wrote to Cora after he'd been down here to see her.'

How very black George's eyes were. She'd thought of them as brown but they were black, and there was something curiously inpenetrable about black eyes. They concealed the thoughts that lay behind them.

George drawled slowly, 'Anything interesting in it?'

'No, not exactly . . .'

'Can I see?'

She hesitated for a moment, then put the letter into his outstretched hand.

He read it, skimming over the contents in a low monotone.

'*Glad to have seen you again after all these years . . . looking very well . . . had a good journey home and arrived back not too tired. . . .*'

His voice changed suddenly, sharpened:

'Please don't say anything to anyone about what I told you. It may be a mistake. Your loving brother, Richard.'

He looked up at Susan. 'What does that mean?'

'It might mean anything . . . It might be just about his health. Or it might be some gossip about a mutual friend.'

'Oh yes, it might be a lot of things. It isn't conclusive – but it's suggestive. . . . What did he tell Cora? Does anyone know what he told her?'

'Miss Gilchrist might know,' said Susan thoughtfully. 'I think she listened.'

'Oh, yes, the companion help. Where is she, by the way?'

'In hospital, suffering from arsenic poisoning.'

George stared.

'You don't mean it?'

'I do. Someone sent her some poisoned wedding cake.'

George sat down on one of the bedroom chairs and whistled. 'It looks,' he said, 'as though Uncle Richard was not mistaken.'

3

On the following morning Inspector Morton called at the cottage.

He was a quiet middle-aged man with a soft country burr in his voice. His manner was quiet and unhurried, but his eyes were shrewd.

'You realise what this is all about, Mrs Banks?' he said. 'Dr Proctor has already told you about Miss Gilchrist. The few crumbs of wedding cake that he took from here have been analysed and show traces of arsenic.'

'So someone deliberately wanted to poison her?'

'That's what it looks like. Miss Gilchrist herself doesn't seem able to help us. She keeps repeating that it's impossible – that nobody would do such a thing. But somebody did. *You* can't throw any light on the matter?'

Susan shook her head.

'I'm simply dumbfounded,' she said. 'Can't you find out anything from the postmark? Or the handwriting?'

'You've forgotten – the wrapping paper was presumably burnt. And there's a little doubt whether it came through the post at all. Young Andrews, the driver of the postal van, doesn't seem able to remember delivering it. He's got a big round, and he can't be sure – but there it is – there's a doubt about it.'

'But – what's the alternative?'

'The alternative, Mrs Banks, is that an old piece of brown paper was used that already had Miss Gilchrist's name and address on it and a cancelled stamp, and that the package was pushed through the letter box or deposited inside the door by hand to create the impression that it had come by post.'

He added dispassionately:

'It's quite a clever idea, you know, to choose wedding cake. Lonely middle-aged women are sentimental about wedding cake, pleased at having been remembered. A box of sweets, or something of that kind *might* have awakened suspicion.'

Susan said slowly:

'Miss Gilchrist speculated a good deal about who could have sent it, but she wasn't at all suspicious – as you say, she was pleased and yes – flattered.'

She added: 'Was there enough poison in it to – kill?'

'That's difficult to say until we get the quantitative analysis. It rather depends on whether Miss Gilchrist ate the whole of the wedge. She seems to think that she didn't. Can you remember?'

'No – no, I'm not sure. She offered me some and I refused and then she ate some and said it was a very good cake, but I don't remember if she finished it or not.'

'I'd like to go upstairs if you don't mind, Mrs Banks.'

'Of course.'

She followed him up to Miss Gilchrist's room. She said apologetically:

'I'm afraid it's in a rather disgusting state. But I didn't have time to do anything about it with my aunt's funeral and everything, and then after Dr Proctor came I thought perhaps I ought to leave it as it was.'

'That was very intelligent of you, Mrs Banks. It's not everyone who would have been so intelligent.'

He went to the bed and slipping his hand under the pillow raised it carefully. A slow smile spread over his face.

'There you are,' he said.

A piece of wedding cake lay on the sheet looking somewhat the worse for wear.

'How extraordinary,' said Susan.

'Oh no, it's not. Perhaps your generation doesn't do it. Young ladies nowadays mayn't set so much store on getting married. But it's an old custom. Put a piece of wedding cake under your pillow and you'll dream of your future husband.'

'But surely Miss Gilchrist—'

'She didn't want to tell us about it because she felt foolish doing such a thing at her age. But I had a notion that's what it might be.' His face sobered. 'And if it hadn't been for an old maid's foolishness, Miss Gilchrist mightn't be alive today.'

'But who could have possibly wanted to kill her?'

His eyes met hers, a curious speculative look in them that made Susan feel uncomfortable.

'You don't know?' he asked.

'No – of course I don't.'

'It seems then as though we shall have to find out,' said Inspector Morton.

——— 12 ———

Two elderly men sat together in a room whose furnishings were of the most modern kind. There were no curves in the room. Everything was square. Almost the only exception was Hercule Poirot himself who was full of curves. His stomach was pleasantly rounded, his head resembled an egg in shape, and his moustaches curved upwards in a flamboyant flourish.

He was sipping a glass of *sirop* and looking thoughtfully at Mr Goby.

Mr Goby was small and spare and shrunken. He had always been refreshingly nondescript in appearance and he was now so nondescript as practically not to be there at all. He was not looking at Poirot because Mr Goby never looked at anybody.

Such remarks as he was now making seemed to be addressed to the left-hand corner of the chromium-plated fireplace curb.

Mr Goby was famous for the acquiring of information. Very few people knew about him and very few employed his services – but those few were usually extremely rich. They had to be, for Mr Goby was very expensive. His speciality was the acquiring of information quickly. At the flick of Mr Goby's double-jointed thumb, hundreds of patient questioning plodding men and women, old and young, of all apparent stations in life, were despatched to question, and probe, and achieve results.

Mr Goby had now practically retired from business. But he occasionally 'obliged' a few old patrons. Hercule Poirot was one of these.

'I've got what I could for you,' Mr Goby told the fire curb

in a soft confidential whisper. 'I sent the boys out. They do what they can – good lads – good lads all of them, but not what they used to be in the old days. They don't come that way nowadays. Not willing to learn, that's what it is. Think they know everything after they've only been a couple of years on the job. And they work to time. Shocking the way they work to time.'

He shook his head sadly and shifted his gaze to an electric plug socket.

'It's the Government,' he told it. 'And all this education racket. It gives them ideas. They come back and tell us what they think. They *can't* think, most of them, anyway. All they know is things out of books. That's no good in our business. Bring in the answers – that's all that's needed – no thinking.'

Mr Goby flung himself back in his chair and winked at a lampshade.

'Mustn't crab the Government, though! Don't know really what we'd do without it. I can tell you that nowadays you can walk in most anywhere with a notebook and pencil, dressed right, and speaking BBC, and ask people all the most intimate details of their daily lives and all their back history, and what they had for dinner on November 23rd because that was a test day for middle-class incomes – or whatever it happens to be (making it a grade above to butter them up!) – ask 'em any mortal thing you can; and nine times out of ten they'll come across pat, and even the tenth time though they may cut up rough, they won't doubt for a minute that you're what you say you are – and that the Government really wants to know – for some completely unfathomable reason! I can tell you, M. Poirot,' said Mr Goby, still talking to the lampshade, 'that it's the best line we've ever had; much better than taking the electric meter or tracing a fault in the telephone – yes, or than calling as nuns, or the Girl Guides or the Boy Scouts asking for subscriptions – though we use all those too. Yes, Government snooping is God's gift to investigators and long may it continue!'

Poirot did not speak. Mr Goby had grown a little garrulous with advancing years, but he would come to the point in his own good time.

'Ar,' said Mr Goby, and took out a very scrubby little notebook. He licked his finger and flicked over the pages. 'Here we are. Mr George Crossfield. We'll take him first. Just the plain facts. You won't want to know how I got them. He's been in Queer Street for quite a while now. Horses, mostly, and gambling – he's not a great one for women. Goes over to France now and then, and Monte too. Spends a lot of time at the Casino. Too downy to cash cheques there, but gets hold of a lot more money than his travelling allowance would account for. I didn't go into that, because it wasn't what you want to know. But he's not scrupulous about evading the law – and being a lawyer he knows how to do it. Some reason to believe that he's been using trust funds entrusted to him to invest. Plunging pretty wildly of late – on the Stock Exchange *and* on the gee-gees! Bad judgment and bad luck. Been off his feed badly for three months. Worried, bad-tempered and irritable in the office. *But* since his uncle's death that's all changed. He's like the breakfast eggs (if we had 'em). Sunny side up!

'Now, as to particular information asked for. Statement that he was at Hurst Park races on day in question almost certainly untrue. Almost invariably places bets with one or other of two bookies on the course. They didn't see him that day. Possible that he left Paddington by train for destination unknown. Taxi-driver who took fare to Paddington made doubtful identification of his photograph. But I wouldn't bank on it. He's a very common type – nothing outstanding about him. No success with porters, etc, at Paddington. Certainly didn't arrive at Cholsey Station – which is nearest for Lytchett St Mary. Small station, strangers noticeable. Could have got out at Reading and taken bus. Buses there crowded, frequent and several routes go within a mile or so of Lytchett St Mary as well as the bus service that goes right into the village. He wouldn't take that – not if he meant business. All in all, he's a downy card. Wasn't seen in Lytchett St Mary but he needn't have been. Other ways of approach than through the village. Was in the OUDS at Oxford, by the way. If he went to the cottage that day he mayn't have looked quite like the usual George Crossfield. I'll keep him in my book, shall I? There's a black market angle I'd like to play up.'

'You may keep him in,' said Hercule Poirot.

Mr Goby licked his finger and turned another page of his notebook.

'Mr Michael Shane. He's thought quite a lot of in the profession. Has an even better idea of himself than other people have. Wants to star and wants to star quickly. Fond of money and doing himself well. Very attractive to women. They fall for him right and left. He's partial to them himself – but business comes first, as you might say. He's been run-

ning around with Sorrel Dainton who was playing the lead
in the last show he was in. He only had a minor part but made
quite a hit in it, and Miss Dainton's husband doesn't like him.
His wife doesn't know about him and Miss Dainton. Doesn't
know much about anything, it seems. Not much of an actress
I gather, but easy on the eye. Crazy about her husband. Some
rumour of a bust-up likely between them not long ago, but
that seems out now. Out since Mr Richard Abernethie's death.'

Mr Goby emphasised the last point by nodding his head
significantly at a cushion on the sofa.

'On the day in question, Mr Shane says he was meeting a
Mr Rosenheim and a Mr Oscar Lewis to fix up some stage
business. He didn't meet them. Sent them a wire to say he
was terribly sorry he couldn't make it. What he *did* do was
to go to the Emeraldo Car people, who hire out "drive yourself" cars. He hired a car about twelve o'clock and drove away
in it. He returned it about six in the evening. According to
the speedometer it had been driven just about the right
number of miles for what we're after. No confirmation from
Lytchett St Mary. No strange car seems to have been observed there that day. Lots of places it could be left unnoticed
a mile or so away. And there's even a disused quarry a few
hundred yards down the lane from the cottage. Three market
towns within walking distance where you can park in side
streets, without the police bothering about you. All right, we
keep Mr Shane in?'

'Most certainly.'

'Now Mrs Shane.' Mr Goby rubbed his nose and told his
left cuff about Mrs Shane. 'She says she was shopping. Just
shopping . . .' Mr Goby raised his eyes to the ceiling. 'Women
who are shopping – just scatty, that's what they are. And she'd
heard she'd come into money the day before. Naturally there'd
be no holding her. She has one or two charge accounts but
they're overdrawn and they've been pressing her for payment
and she didn't put any more on the sheet. It's quite on the
cards that she went in here and there and everywhere, trying
on clothes, looking at jewellery, pricing this, that, and the
other – and as likely as not, not buying anything! She's easy
to approach – I'll say that. I had one of my young ladies who's
knowledgeable on the theatrical line do a hook up. Stopped
by her table in a restaurant and exclaimed the way they do:
"Darling, I haven't seen you since *Way Down Under*. You were
wonderful in that! Have you seen Hubert lately?" That was
the producer and Mrs Shane was a bit of a flop in the play –

but that makes it go all the better. They're chatting theatrical stuff at once, and my girl throws the right names about, and then she says, "I believe I caught a glimpse of you at so and so, on so and so," giving the day – and most ladies fall for it and say, "Oh no, I was—" whatever it may be. But not Mrs Shane. Just looks vacant and says, "Oh, I dare say." What can you do with a lady like that?' Mr Goby shook his head severely at the radiator.

'Nothing,' said Hercule Poirot with feeling. 'Do I not have cause to know it? Never shall I forget the killing of Lord Edgware. I was nearly defeated – yes, I, Hercule Poirot – by the extremely simple cunning of a vacant brain. The very simple-minded have often the genius to commit an uncomplicated crime and then leave it alone. Let us hope that our murderer – if there is a murderer in this affair — is intelligent and superior and thoroughly pleased with himself and unable to resist painting the lily. *Enfin* – but continue.'

Once more Mr Goby applied himself to his little book.

'Mr and Mrs Banks – who said they were at home all day. *She* wasn't anyway! Went round to the garage, got out her car, and drove off in it about 1 o'clock. Destination unknown. Back about five. Can't tell about mileage because she's had it out every day since and it's been nobody's business to check.

'As to Mr Banks, we've dug up something curious. To begin with. I'll mention that on the day in question we don't know *what* he did. He didn't go to work. Seems he'd already asked for a couple of days off on account of the funeral. And since then he's chucked his job – with no consideration for the firm. Nice well-established small pharmacy it is. They're not too keen on Master Banks. Seems he used to get into rather queer excitable states.

'Well, as I say, we don't know what he was doing on the day of Mrs L's death. He didn't go with his wife. It *could* be that he stopped in their little flat all day. There's no porter there, and nobody knows whether tenants are in or out. But his back history is interesting. Up till about four months ago – just before he met his wife, he was in a Mental Home. Not certified – just what they call a mental breakdown. Seems he made some slip up in dispensing a medicine. (He was working with a Mayfair firm then.) The woman recovered, and the firm were all over themselves apologising, and there was no prosecution. After all, these accidental slips do occur, and most decent people are sorry for a poor chap who's done it – so long as there's no permanent harm done, that is. The firm didn't sack him, but he resigned – said it had shaken his nerve. But afterwards, it seems, he got into a very low state and told the doctor he was obsessed by guilt – that it had all been deliberate – the woman had been overbearing and rude to him when she came into the shop, had complained that her last prescription had been badly made up – and that he had resented this and had deliberately added a near lethal dose of some drug or other He said "She had to be punished for daring to speak to me like that!" And then wept and said he was too wicked to live and a lot of things like that. The medicos have a long word for that sort of thing – guilt complex or something – and don't believe it was deliberate at all, just carelessness, but that he wanted to make it important and serious.'

'*Ca se peut*,' said Hercule Poirot.

'Pardon? Anyway, he went into this Sanatorium and they treated him and discharged him as cured, and he met Miss Abernethie as she was then. And he got a job in this respectable but rather obscure little chemist's shop. Told them he'd been out of England for a year and a half, and gave them his former reference from some shop in Eastbourne. Nothing against him in that shop, but a fellow dispenser said he had a very queer temper and was odd in his manner sometimes. There's a story about a customer saying once as a joke, 'Wish you'd sell me something to poison my wife, ha ha!' And Banks says to him, very soft and quiet: "I could . . . It would cost you two hundred pounds." The man felt uneasy and laughed it off. *May* have been all a joke, but it doesn't seem to me that Banks is the joking kind.

'*Mon ami*,' said Hercule Poirot. 'It really amazes me how you get your information! Medical and highly confidential most of it.!'

Mr Goby's eyes swivelled right round the room and he murmured, looking expectantly at the door, that there were *ways. . . .*

'Now we come to the country department. Mr and Mrs Timothy Abernethie. Very nice place they've got, but sadly needing money spent on it. Very straitened they seem to be, very straitened. Taxation and unfortunate investments. Mr Abernethie enjoys ill health and the emphasis is on the enjoyment. Complains a lot and has everyone running and fetching and carrying. Eats hearty meals, and seems quite strong physically if he likes to make the effort. There's no one in the house after the daily woman goes and no one's allowed into

Mr Abernethie's room unless he rings his bell. He was in a very bad temper the morning of the day after the funeral. Swore at Mrs Jones. Ate only a little of his breakfast and said he wouldn't have any lunch – he'd had a bad night. He said the supper she had left out for him was unfit to eat and a good deal more. He was alone in the house and unseen by anybody from 9.30 that morning until the following morning.'

'And Mrs Abernethie?'

'She started off from Enderby by car at the time you mentioned. Arrived on foot at a small local garage in a place called Cathstone and explained her car had broken down a couple of miles away.

'A mechanic drove her out to it, made an investigation and said they'd have to tow it in and it would be a long job – couldn't promise to finish it that day. The lady was very put out, but went to a small inn, arranged to stay the night, and asked for some sandwiches as she said she'd like to see something of the countryside – it's on the edge of the moorland country. She didn't come back to the inn till quite late that evening. My informant said he didn't wonder. It's a sordid little place!'

'And the times?'

'She got the sandwiches at eleven. If she'd walked to the main road, a mile, she could have hitch-hiked into Wallcaster and caught a special South Coast express which stops at Reading West. I won't go into details of buses etcetera. It *could* have been done if you could make the – er – attack fairly late in the afternoon.'

'I understand the doctor stretched the time limit to possibly 4.30.'

'Mind you,' said Mr Goby, 'I shouldn't say it was likely. She seems to be a nice lady, liked by everybody. She's devoted to her husband, treats him like a child.'

'Yes, yes, the maternal complex.'

'She's strong and hefty, chops the wood and often hauls in great baskets of logs. Pretty good with the inside of a car, too.'

'I was coming to that. What exactly *was* wrong with the car?'

'Do you want the exact details, M. Poirot?'

'Heaven forbid. I have no mechanical knowledge.'

'It was a difficult thing to spot. And also to put right. And it *could* have been done maliciously by someone without very

much trouble. By someone who was familiar with the insides
of a car.'

'*C'est magnifique!*' said Poirot with bitter enthusiasm. 'All
so convenient, all so possible. *Bon dieu*, can we eliminate *nobody*? And Mrs Leo Abernethie?'

'She's a very nice lady, too. Mr Abernethie deceased was
very fond of her. She came there to stay about a fortnight
before he died.'

'After he had been to Lytchett St Mary to see his sister?'

'No, just before. Her income is a good deal reduced since
the war. She gave up her house in England and took a small
flat in London. She has a villa in Cyprus and spends part of
the year there. She has a young nephew whom she is helping
to educate, and there seems to be one or two young artists
whom she helps financially from time to time.'

'St Helen of the blameless life,' said Poirot, shutting his
eyes. 'And it was quite impossible for her to have left
Enderby that day without the servants knowing? Say that
that is so, I implore you!'

Mr Goby brought his glance across to rest apologetically on
Poirot's polished patent leather shoe, the nearest he had come
to a direct encounter, and murmured:

'I'm afraid I can't say that, M. Poirot. Mrs Abernethie went
to London to fetch some extra clothes and belongings as she
had agreed with Mr Entwhistle to stay on and see to things.'

'*Il ne manquait que ça!*' said Poirot with strong feeling.

—— 13 ——

When the card of Inspector Morton of the Berkshire County
Police was brought to Hercule Poirot, his eyebrows went up.

'Show him in, Georges, show him in. And bring – what is
it that the police prefer?'

'I would suggest beer, sir.'

'How horrible! But how British. Bring beer, then.'

Inspector Morton came straight to the point.

'I had to come to London,' he said. 'And I got hold of your
address, M. Poirot. I was interested to see you at the inquest on
Thursday.'

'So you saw me there?'

'Yes. I was surprised – and, as I say, interested. You won't remember me but I remember you very well. In that Pang-bourne Case.'

'Ah, you were connected with that?'

'Only in a very junior capacity. It's a long time ago but I've never forgotten you.'

'And you recognised me at once the other day?'

'That wasn't difficult, sir.' Inspector Morton repressed a slight smile. 'Your appearance is – rather unusual.'

His gaze took in Poirot's satorial perfection and rested finally on the curving moustaches.

'You stick out in a country place,' he said.

'It is possible, it is possible,' said Poirot with complacency.

'It interested me *why* you should be there. That sort of crime – robbery – assault – doesn't usually interest you.'

'Was it the usual ordinary brutal type of crime?'

'That's what I've been wondering.'

'You have wondered from the beginning, have you not?'

'Yes, M. Poirot. There were some unusual features. Since then we've worked along the routine lines. Pulled in one or two people for questioning, but everyone has been able to account quite satisfactorily for his time that afternoon. It wasn't what you'd call an "ordinary" crime, M. Poirot – we're quite sure of that. The Chief Constable agrees. It was done by someone who wished to make it appear that way. It could have been the Gilchrist woman, but there doesn't seem to be any motive – and there wasn't any emotional background. Mrs Lansquenet was perhaps a bit mental – or "simple," if you like to put it that way, but it was a household of mistress and dogs-body with no feverish feminine friendship about it. There are dozens of Miss Gilchrists about, and they're not usually the murdering type.'

He paused.

'So it looks as though we'd have to look farther afield. I came to ask if you could help us at all. *Something* must have brought you down there, M. Poirot.'

'Yes, yes, something did. An excellent Daimler car. But not only that.'

'You had – information?'

'Hardly in your sense of the word. Nothing that could be used as evidence.'

'But something that could be – a pointer?'

'Yes.'

'You see, M. Poirot, there have been developments.'

Meticulously, in detail, he told of the poisoned wedge of wedding cake

Poirot took a deep, hissing breath.

'Ingenious – yes, ingenious . . . I warned Mr Entwhistle to look after Miss Gilchrist. An attack on her was always a possibility. But I must confess that I did *not* expect poison. I anticipated a repetition of the hatchet *motif*. I merely thought that it would be inadvisable for her to walk alone in unfrequented lanes after dark.'

'But *why* did you anticipate an attack on her? I think, M. Poirot, you ought to tell me that.'

Poirot nodded his head slowly.

'Yes, I will tell you. Mr Entwhistle will not tell you, because he is a lawyer and lawyers do not like to speak of suppositions, or inferences made from the character of a dead woman, or from a few irresponsible words. But he will not be averse to *my* telling you – no, he will be relieved. He does not wish to appear foolish or fanciful, but he wants you to know what may – only *may* – be the facts.'

Poirot paused as Georges entered with a tall glass of beer.

'Some refreshment, Inspector. No, no, I insist.'

'Won't you join me?'

'I do not drink the beer. But I will myself have a glass of *sirop de cassis* – the English they do not care for it, I have noticed.'

Inspector Morton looked gratefully at his beer.

Poirot, sipping delicately from his glass of dark purple fluid, said:

'It begins, all this, at a funeral. Or rather, to be exact, *after* the funeral.'

Graphically, with many gestures, he set forth the story as Mr Entwhistle had told it to him, but with such embellishments as his exuberant nature suggested. One almost felt that Hercule Poirot had himself been an eye-witness of the scene.

Inspector Morton had an excellent clear-cut brain. He seized at once on what were, for his purposes, the salient points.

'This Mr Abernethie may have been poisoned?'

'It is a possibility.'

'And the body has been cremated and there is no evidence?'

'Exactly.'

Inspector Morton ruminated.

'Interesting. There's nothing in it for us. Nothing, that is, to make Richard Abernethie's death worth investigating. It would be a waste of time.'

'Yes.'

'But there are the *people* – the people who were there – the people who heard Cora Lansquenet say what she did, and one of whom may have thought that she might say it again and with more detail.'

'As she undoubtedly would have. There are, Inspector, as you say, *the people*. And now you see why I was at the inquest, why I interest myself in the case – because it is, always, *people* in whom I interest myself.'

'Then the attack on Miss Gilchrist—'

'Was always indicated. Richard Abernethie had been down to the cottage. He had talked to Cora. He had, perhaps, actually mentioned a *name*. The only person who might possibly have known or overheard something was Miss Gilchrist. After Cora is silenced, the murderer might continue to be anxious. Does the other woman know something – anything? Of course, if the murderer is wise he will let well alone, but murderers, Inspector, are seldom wise. Fortunately for us. They brood, they feel uncertain, they desire to make sure – quite sure. They are pleased with their own cleverness. And so, in the end, they protrude their necks, as you say.'

Inspector Morton smiled faintly.

Poirot went on:

'This attempt to silence Miss Gilchrist, already it is a mistake. For now there are *two* occasions about which you make inquiry. There is the handwriting on the wedding label also. It is a pity the wrapping paper was burnt.'

'Yes, I could have been certain then, whether it came by post or whether it didn't.'

'You have reason for thinking the latter, you say?'

'It's only what the postman thinks – he's not sure. If the parcel had gone through a village post office, it's ten to one the postmistress would have noticed it, but nowadays the mail is delivered by van from Market Keynes and of course the young chap does quite a round and delivers a lot of things. He thinks it was letters only and no parcel at the cottage – but he isn't sure. As a matter of fact he's having a bit of girl trouble and he can't think about anything else. I've tested his memory and he isn't reliable in any way. If he *did* deliver it, it seems to me odd that the parcel shouldn't have been noticed until after this Mr – whatshisname – Guthrie—'

'Ah, Mr Guthrie.'

Inspector Morton smiled.

'Yes, M. Poirot. We're checking up on him. After all, it

would be easy, wouldn't it, to come along with a plausible tale of having been a friend of Mrs Lansquenet's. Mrs Banks wasn't to know if he was or he wasn't. He could have dropped that little parcel, you know. It's easy to make a thing look as though it's been through the post. Lamp black a little smudged, makes quite a good postmark cancellation mark over a stamp.'

He paused and then added:

'And there are other possibilities.'

Poirot nodded.

'You think—?'

'Mr George Crossfield was down in that part of the world – but not until the next day. Meant to attend the funeral, but had a little engine trouble on the way. Know anything about him, M. Poirot?'

'A little. But not as much as I would like to know.'

'Like that, is it? Quite a little bunch interested in the late Mr Abernethie's will, I understand. I hope it doesn't mean going after all of them.'

'I have accumulated a little information. It is at your disposal. Naturally I have no authority to ask these people questions. In fact, it would not be wise for me to do so.'

'I shall go slowly myself. You don't want to fluster your bird too soon. But when you do fluster it, you want to fluster it well.'

'A very sound technique. For you then, my friend, the routine – with all the machinery you have at your disposal. It is slow – but sure. For myself—'

'Yes, M. Poirot?'

'For myself, I go North. As I have told you, it is *people* in whom I interest myself. Yes – a little preparatory *camouflage* – and I go North.

'I intend,' added Hercule Poirot, 'to purchase a country mansion for foreign refugees. I represent U.N.A.R.C.O.'

'And what's U.N.A.R.C.O?'

'United Nations Aid for Refugee Centre Organisation. It sounds well, do you not think?'

Inspector Morton grinned.

14

Hercule Poirot said to a grim-faced Janet:

'Thank you very much. You have been most kind.'

Janet, her lips still fixed in a sour line, left the room. These foreigners! The questions they asked. Their impertinence! All very well to say that he a specialist interested in unsuspected heart conditions such as Mr Abernethie must have suffered from. That was very likely true – gone very sudden the master had, and the doctor had been surprised. But what business was it of some foreign doctor coming along and nosing around?

All very well for Mrs Leo to say: 'Please answer Monsieur Pontarlier's questions. He has a good reason for asking.'

Questions. Always questions. Sheets of them sometimes to fill in as best you could – and what did the Government or anyone else want to know about your private affairs for? Asking your age at that census – downright impertinent and she hadn't told them, either! Cut off five years she had. Why not? If she only felt fifty-four, she'd *call* herself fifty-four!

At any rate Monsieur Pontarlier hadn't wanted to know her age. He'd had *some* decency. Just questions about the medicines the master had taken, and where they were kept, and if, perhaps, he might have taken too much of them if he was feeling not quite the thing – or if he'd been forgetful. As though she could remember all that rubbish – the master knew what he was doing! And asking if any of the medicines he took were still in the house. Naturally they'd all been thrown away. Heart condition – and some long word he'd used. Always thinking of something new they were, these doctors. Look at them telling old Rogers he had a disc or some such in his spine. Plain lumbago, that was all that was the matter with him. Her father had been a gardener and *he'd* suffered from lumbago. Doctors!

The self-appointed medical man sighed and went downstairs in search of Lanscombe. He had not got very much out of Janet but he had hardly expected to do so. All he had really wanted to do was check such information as could unwillingly be extracted from her with that given him by Helen Abernethie and which had been obtained from the same source – but with much less difficulty, since Janet was ready to admit that Mrs Leo had a perfect right to ask such questions and indeed Janet herself had enjoyed dwelling at length on the last few weeks of her master's life. Illness and death were congenial subjects to her.

Yes, Poirot thought, he could have relied on the information that Helen had got for him. He had done so really. But by nature and long habit he trusted nobody until he himself had tried and proved them.

In any case the evidence was slight and unsatisfactory. It boiled down to the fact that Richard Abernethie had been prescribed vitamin oil capsules. That these had been in a large bottle which had been nearly finished at the time of his death. Anybody who had wanted to, could have operated on one or more of those capsules with a hypodermic syringe and could have rearranged the bottle so that the fatal dose would only be taken some weeks after that somebody had left the house. Or someone might have slipped into the house on the day before Richard Abernethie died and have doctored a capsule then – or, which was more likely – have substituted something else for a sleeping tablet in the little bottle that stood beside the bed. Or again he might have quite simply tampered with the food or drink.

Hercule Poirot had made his own experiments. The front door was kept locked, but there was a side door giving on the garden which was not locked until evening. At about quarter-past one, when the gardeners had gone to lunch and when the household was in the dining-room, Poirot had entered the grounds, come to the side door, and mounted the stairs to Richard Abernethie's bedroom without meeting anybody. As a variant he had pushed through a baize door and slipped into the larder. He had heard voices from the kitchen at the end of the passage but no one had seen him.

Yes, it could have been done. But had it been done? There was nothing to indicate that that was so. Not that Poirot was really looking for evidence – he wanted only to satisfy himself as to possibilities. The murder of Richard Abernethie could only be a hypothesis. It was Cora Lansquenet's murder for which evidence was needed. What he wanted was to study the people who had been assembled for the funeral that day, and to form his own conclusions about them. He had already had his plan, but first he wanted a few more words with old Lanscombe.

Lanscombe was courteous but distant. Less resentful than Janet, he nevertheless regarded this upstart foreigner as the materialisation of the Writing on the Wall. This was What We are Coming to!

He put down the leather with which he was lovingly polishing the Georgian teapot and straightened his back.

'Yes, sir?' he said politely.

Poirot sat down gingerly on a pantry stool.

'Mrs Abernethie tells me that you hoped to reside in the lodge by the north gate when you retired from service here?'

'That is so, sir. Naturally all that is changed now. When the property is sold—'

Poirot interrupted deftly:

'It might still be possible. There are cottages for the gardeners. The lodge is not needed for the guests or their attendants. It might be possible to make an arrangement of some kind.'

'Well, thank you, sir, for the suggestion. But I hardly think— The majority of the – guests would be foreigners, I presume?'

'Yes, they will be foreigners. Amongst those who fled from Europe to this country are several who are old and infirm. There can be no future for them if they return to their own countries, for these persons, you understand, are those whose relatives there have perished. They cannot earn their living here as an able-bodied man or woman can do. Funds have been raised and are being administered by the organisation which I represent to endow various country homes for them. This place is, I think, eminently suitable. The matter is practically settled'

Lanscombe sighed.

'You'll understand, sir, that it's sad for me to think that this won't be a private dwelling-house any longer. But I know how things are nowadays. None of the family could afford to live here – and I don't think the young ladies and gentlemen would even want to do so. Domestic help is too difficult to obtain these days, and even if obtained is expensive and unsatisfactory. I quite realise that these fine mansions have served their turn.' Lanscombe sighed again. 'If it has to be an – an institution of some kind, I'll be glad to think that it's the kind you're mentioning. We were Spared in This Country, sir owing to our Navy and Air Force and our brave young men and being fortunate enough to be an island. If Hitler had landed here we'd all have turned out and given him short shrift. My sight isn't good enough for shooting, but I could have used a pitchfork, sir, and I intended to do so if necessary.

We've always welcomed the unfortunate in this country, sir, it's been our pride. We shall continue so to do.'

'Thank you, Lanscombe,' said Poirot gently. 'Your master's death must have been a great blow to you.'

'It was, sir. I'd been very fortunate in my life, sir. No one could have had a better master.'

'I have been conversing with my friend and – er colleague, Dr Larraby. We were wondering if your master could have had any extra worry – any unpleasant interview – on the day before he died? You do not remember if any visitors came to the house that day?'

'I think not, sir I do not recall any.'

'No one called at just about that time?'

'The vicar was here to tea the day before. Otherwise some nuns called for a subscription – and a young man came to the back door and wanted to sell Marjorie some brushes and saucepan cleaners. Very persistent he was. Nobody else.'

A worried expression had appeared on Lanscombe's face. Poirot did not press him further. Lanscombe had already unburdened himself to Mr Entwhistle. He would be far less forthcoming with Hercule Poirot.

With Marjorie, on the other hand, Poirot had had instant success. Marjorie had none of the conventions of 'good service.' Marjorie was a first-class cook and the way to her heart lay through her cooking. Poirot had visited her in the kitchen, praised certain dishes with discernment, and Marjorie, realising that here was someone who knew what he was talking about, hailed him immediately as a fellow spirit. He had no difficulty in finding out exactly what had been served the night before Richard Abernethie had died. Marjorie, indeed, was inclined to view the matter as 'It was the night I made that chocolate soufflé that Mr Abernethie died. Six eggs I'd saved up for it. The dairyman he's a friend of mine. Got hold of some cream too. Better not ask how. Enjoyed it, Mr Abernethie did.' The rest of the meal was likewise detailed. What had come out from the dining-room had been finished in the kitchen. Ready as Marjorie was to talk, Poirot had learned nothing of value from her.

He went now to fetch his overcoat and a couple of scarves, and thus padded against the North Country air he went out on the terrace and joined Helen Abernethie, who was clipping some late roses.

'Have you found out anything fresh?' she asked.

'Nothing. But I hardly expected to do so.'

'I know. Ever since Mr Entwhistle told me you were coming, I've been ferreting around, but there's really been nothing.'

She paused and said hopefully:

'Perhaps it *is* a mare's nest?'

'To be attacked with a hatchet?'

'I wasn't thinking of Cora.'

'But it is of Cora that I think. Why was it necessary for someone to kill her? Mr Entwhistle has told me that on that day, at the moment that she came out suddenly with her *gaffe*, you yourself felt that something was wrong. That is so?'

'Well – yes, but I don't know—'

Poirot swept on.

'How "wrong"? Unexpected? Surprising? Or – what shall we say – uneasy? Sinister?'

'Oh no, not sinister. Just something that wasn't – oh, I don't know. I can't remember and it wasn't important.'

'But why cannot you remember – because something else put it out of your head – something more important?'

'Yes – yes – I think you're right there. It was the mention of murder, I suppose. That swept away everything else.'

'It was, perhaps, the reaction of some particular person to the word "murder"?'

'Perhaps . . . But I don't remember looking at anyone in particular. We were all staring at Cora.'

'It may have been something you heard – something dropped perhaps . . . or broken . . .'

Helen frowned in an effort of remembrance.

'No . . . I don't think so. . . .'

'Ah well, someday it will come back. And it may be of no consequence. Now tell me, Madame, of those here, who knew Cora best?'

Helen considered.

'Lanscombe, I suppose. He remembers her from a child. The housemaid, Janet, only came after she had married and gone away.'

'And next to Lanscombe?'

Helen said thoughtfully: 'I suppose – *I* did. Maude hardly knew her at all.'

'Then, taking you as the person who knew her best, why do you think she asked that question as she did?'

Helen smiled.

'It was very characteristic of Cora!'

'What I mean is, was it a *bêtise* pure and simple? Did she

just blurt out what was in her mind without thinking? Or was she being malicious – amusing herself by upsetting everyone?'

Helen reflected.

'You can't ever be quite sure about a person, can you? I never have known whether Cora was just ingenious – or whether she counted, childishly, on making an effect. That's what you mean, isn't it?'

'Yes. I was thinking: Suppose this Mrs Cora says to herself "What fun it would be to ask if Richard was murdered and see how they all look!" That would be like her, yes?'

Helen looked doubtful.

'It might be. She certainly had an impish sense of humour as a child. But what difference does it make?'

'It would underline the point that it is unwise to make jokes about murder,' said Poirot dryly.

Helen shivered.

'Poor Cora.'

Poirot changed the subject.

'Mrs Timothy Abernethie stayed the night after the funeral?'
'Yes.'

'Did she talk to you at all about what Cora had said?'

'Yes, she said it was outrageous and just like Cora!'

'She didn't take it seriously?'

'Oh, no. No, I'm sure she didn't.'

'The second 'no,' Poirot thought, had sounded suddenly doubtful. But was not that almost always the case when you went back over something in your mind?

'And you, Madame, did you take it seriously?'

Helen Abernethie, her eyes looking very blue and strangely young under the sideways sweep of crisp grey hair, said thoughtfully:

'Yes, M. Poirot, I think I did.'

'Because of your feeling that something was wrong?'

'Perhaps.'

He waited – but as she said nothing more, he went on:

'There had been an estrangement, lasting many years, between Mrs Lansquenet and her family?'

'Yes. None of us liked her husband and she was offended about it, and so the estrangement grew.'

'And then, suddenly, your brother-in-law went to see her. Why?'

'I don't know – I suppose he knew, or guessed that he

hadn't very long to live and wanted to be reconciled – but I really don't know.'

'He didn't tell you?'

'Tell *me*?'

'Yes. You were here staying with him, just before he went there. He didn't even mention his intention to you?'

He thought a slight reserve came into her manner.

'He told me he was going to see his brother Timothy – which he did. He never mentioned Cora at all. Shall we go in? It must be nearly lunchtime.'

She walked beside him carrying the flowers she had picked. As they went in by the door, Poirot said:

'You are sure, quite sure that during your visit Mr Abernethie said nothing to you about any member of the family which might be relevant?'

A faint resentment in her manner Helen said:

'You are speaking like a policeman.'

'I *was* a policeman – once. I have no status – no right to question you. But you want the truth – or so I have been led to believe?'

They entered the green drawing-room. Helen said with a sigh:

'Richard was disappointed in the younger generation. Old men usually are. He disparaged them in various ways – but there was nothing – *nothing,* do you understand – that could possibly suggest a motive for murder.'

'Ah,' said Poirot. She reached for a Chinese bowl, and began to arrange the roses in it. When they were disposed to her satisfaction she looked round for a place to put it.

'You arrange flowers admirably, Madame,' said Hercule. 'I think that anything you undertook you would manage to do with perfection.'

'Thank you. I am fond of flowers. I think this would look well on that green malachite table.'

There was a bouquet of wax flowers under a glass shade on the malachite table. As she shifted it off, Poirot said casually:

'Did anyone tell Mr Abernethie that his niece Susan's husband had come near to poisoning a customer when making up a prescription? Ah, *pardon!*'

He sprang forward.

The Victorian ornament had slipped from Helen's fingers. Poirot's spring forward was not quick enough. It dropped on the floor and the glass shade broke. Helen gave an expression of annoyance.

'How careless of me. However, the flowers are not damaged. I can get a new glass shade made for it. I'll put it away in the big cupboard under the stairs.'

It was not until Poirot had helped her to lift it on to a shelf in the dark cupboard and had followed her back to the drawing-room that he said:

'It was my fault. I should not have startled you.'

'What was it that you asked me? I have forgotten.'

'Oh, there is no need to repeat my question. Indeed – I have forgotten what it was'

Helen came up to him. She laid her hand on his arm.

'M. Poirot, is there anyone whose life would really bear close investigation? *Must* people's lives be dragged into this when they have nothing to do with – with —'

'With the death of Cora Lansquenet? Yes, because one has to examine *everything*. Oh! it is true enough – it is an old maxim – *everyone has something to hide*. It is true of all of us – it is perhaps true of you, too, Madame. But I say to you, nothing can be ignored. That is why your friend, Mr Entwhistle, he has come to me. For I am not the police. I am discreet and what I learn does not concern me. But I have to *know*. And since in this matter it is not so much *evidence* as *people* – then it is *people* with whom I occupy myself. I need, Madame, to meet everyone who was here on the day of the funeral. And it would be a great convenience – yes, and it would be strategically satisfactory – if I could meet them *here*.'

'I'm afraid,' said Helen slowly, 'that would be too difficult—'

'Not so difficult as you think. Already I have devised a means. The house, it is sold. So Mr Entwhistle will declare. (*Entendu*, sometimes these things fall through!) He will invite the various members of the family to assemble here and to choose what they want from the furnishings before it is all put up to auction. A suitable week-end can be selected for that purpose.'

He paused and then said:

'You see, it is easy, is it not?'

Helen looked at him. The blue eyes were cold – almost frosty.

'Are you laying a trap for someone, M. Poirot?'

'Alas! I wish I knew enough. No, I have still the open mind.

'There may,' Hercule Poirot added thoughtfully, 'be certain tests . . .'

'Tests? What kind of tests?'

'I have not yet formulated them to myself. And in any case, Madame, it would be better that you should not know them.'

'So that I can be tested too?'

'You, Madame, have been taken behind the scenes. Now there is one thing that is doubtful. The young people will, I think, come readily. But it may be difficult, may it not, to secure the presence here of Mr Timothy Abernethie. I hear that he never leaves home.'

Helen smiled suddenly.

'I believe you may be lucky there, M. Poirot. I heard from Maude yesterday. The workmen are in painting the house and Timothy is suffering terribly from the smell of the paint. He says that it is seriously affecting his health. I think that he and Maude would both be pleased to come here – perhaps for a week or two. Maude is still not able to get about very well – you know she broke her ankle?'

'I had not heard. How unfortunate.'

'Luckily they have got Cora's companion, Miss Gilchrist. It seems that she has turned out a perfect treasure.'

'What is that?' Poirot turned sharply on Helen. 'Did they ask for Miss Gilchrist to go to them? Who suggested it?'

'I think Susan fixed it up. Susan Banks.'

'Aha,' said Poirot in a curious voice. 'So it was the little Susan who suggested it. She is fond of making the arrangements.'

'Susan struck me as being a very competent girl.'

'Yes. She is competent. Did you hear that Miss Gilchrist had a narrow escape from death with a piece of poisoned wedding cake?'

'No!' Helen looked startled. 'I do remember now that Maude said over the telephone that Miss Gilchrist had just come out of hospital. Poisoned? But, M. Poirot – *why*—'

'Do you really ask that?'

Helen said with sudden vehemence:

'Oh! get them all here! Find out the truth! There mustn't be any more murders'

'So you will co-operate?'

'Yes – I will co-operate.'

15

'That linoleum does look nice, Mrs Jones. What a hand you have with lino. The teapot's on the kitchen table, so go and help yourself I'll be there as soon as I've taken up Mr Abernethie's elevenses.'

Miss Gilchrist trotted up the staircase, carrying a daintily set out tray. She tapped on Timothy's door, interpreted a growl from within as an invitation to enter, and tripped briskly in.

'Morning coffee and biscuits, Mr Abernethie. I do hope you're feeling brighter today. Such a lovely day.'

Timothy grunted and said suspiciously:

'Is there skim on that milk?'

'Oh no, Mr Abernethie. I took it off very carefully, and anyway I've brought up the little strainer in case it should form again. Some people like it, you know, they say it's the *cream* – an so it is really.'

'Idiots!' said Timothy. 'What kind of biscuits are those?'

'They're those nice digestive biscuits.'

'Digestive tripe. Ginger-nuts are the only biscuits worth eating.'

'I'm afraid the grocer hadn't got any this week. But these are really very nice. You try them and see.'

'I know what they're like, thank you. Leave those curtains alone, can't you?'

'I thought you might like a little sunshine. It's such a nice sunny day.'

'I want the room kept dark. My head's terrible. It's this paint. I've always been sensitive to paint. It's poisoning me.'

Miss Gilchrist sniffed experimentally and said brightly:

'One really can't smell it much in here. The workmen are over on the other side.'

'You're not sensitive like I am. Must I have *all* the books I'm reading taken out of my reach?'

'I'm so sorry, Mr Abernethie, I didn't know you were reading all of them.'

'Where's my wife? I haven't seen her for over an hour.'

'Mrs Abernethie is resting on the sofa.'

'Tell her to come and rest up here.'

'I'll tell her, Mr Abernethie. But she may have dropped off to sleep. Shall we say in about a quarter of an hour?'

'No, tell her I want her now. Don't monkey about with that rug. It's arranged the way I like it.'

'I'm so sorry. I thought it was slipping off the far side.'

'I like it slipping off. Go and get Maude. I want her.'

Miss Gilchrist departed downstairs and tiptoed into the drawing-room where Maude Abernethie was sitting with her feet up reading a novel.

'I'm so sorry, Mrs Abernethie,' she said apologetically. 'Mr Abernethie is asking for you.'

Maude thrust aside her novel with a guilty expression.

'Oh dear,' she said, 'I'll go up at once.'

She reached for her stick.

Timothy burst out as soon as his wife entered the room:

'So there you are at last!'

'I'm so sorry dear, I didn't know you wanted me.'

'That woman you've got into the house will drive me mad. Twittering and fluttering round like a demented hen. Real typical old maid, that's what she is.'

'I'm sorry she annoys you. She tries to be kind, that's all.'

'I don't want anybody kind. I don't want a blasted old maid always chirruping over me. She's so damned arch, too—'

'Just a little, perhaps.'

'Treats me as though I was a confounded kid! It's maddening.'

'I'm sure it must be. But please, *please*, Timothy, do try not to be rude to her. I'm really very helpless still – and you yourself say she cooks well.'

'Her cooking's all right,' Mr Abernethie admitted grudgingly. 'Yes, she's a decent enough cook. But keep her in the kitchen, that's all I ask. Don't let her come fussing round me.

'No, dear, of course not. How are you feeling?'

'Not at all well. I think you'd better send for Barton to come and have a look at me. This paint affects my heart. Feel my pulse – the irregular way it's beating.'

Maude felt it without comment.

'Timothy, shall we go to an hotel until the house painting is finished?'

'It would be a great waste of money.'

'Does that matter much – now?'

'You're just like all women – hopelessly extravagant! Just because we've come into a ridiculously small part of my brother's estate, you think we can go and live indefinitely at the Ritz.'

'I didn't quite say that, dear.'

'I can tell you that the difference Richard's money will make will be hardly appreciable. This bloodsucking Government will see to that. You mark my words, the whole lot will go in taxation'

Mrs Abernethie shook her head sadly.

'This coffee's cold,' said the invalid, looking with distaste at the cup which he had not as yet tasted. 'Why can't I ever get a cup of really hot coffee?'

'I'll take it down and warm it up.'

In the kitchen Miss Gilchrist was drinking tea and conversing affably, though with slight condescension, with Mrs Jones.

'I'm so anxious to spare Mrs Abernethie all I can,' she said. 'All this running up and down stairs is so painful for her.'

'Waits on him hand and foot, she does,' said Mrs Jones, stirring the sugar in her cup.

'It's very sad his being such an invalid.'

'Not such an invalid either,' Mrs Jones said darkly. 'Suits him very well to lie up and ring bells and have trays brought up and down. But he's well able to get up and go about. Even seen him out in the village, I have, when *she's* been away. Walking as hearty as you please Anything. he *really* needs — like his tobacco or a stamp — he can come and get. And that's why when *she* was off at that funeral and got held up on the way back, and *he* told me I'd got to come in and stay, the night again, I refused. "I'm sorry, sir," I said, "but I've got my husband to think of. Going out to oblige in the mornings is all very well, but I've got to be there to see him when he comes back from work." Nor I wouldn't budge, I wouldn't. Do him good, I thought, to get about the house and look after himself for once. Might make him see what a lot he gets done for him. So I stood firm, I did. He didn't half create.'

Mrs Jones drew a deep breath and took a long satisfying drink of sweet inky tea. 'Ar,' she said.

Though deeply suspicious of Miss Gilchrist, and considering her as a finicky thing and a 'regular fussy old maid,' Mrs Jones approved of the lavish way in which Miss Gilchrist dispensed her employer's tea and sugar ration.

She set down the cup and said affably:

'I'll give the kitchen floor a nice scrub down and then I'll be getting along. The potatoes is all ready peeled, dear, you'll find them by the sink.'

Though slightly affronted by the 'dear,' Miss Gilchrist was

appreciative of the goodwill which had divested an enormous quantity of potatoes of their outer coverings.

Before she could say anything the telephone rang and she hurried out in the hall to answer it. The telephone, in the style of fifty-odd years ago, was situated inconveniently in a draughty passage behind the staircase.

Maude Abernethie appeared at the top of the stairs while Miss Gilchrist was still speaking. The latter looked up and said:

'It's Mrs – Leo – is it? – Abernethie speaking.'

'Tell her I'm just coming.'

Maude descended the stairs slowly and painfully.

Miss Gilchrist murmured, 'I'm so sorry you've had to come down again, Mrs Abernethie. Has Mr Abernethie finished his elevenses? I'll just nip up and get the tray.'

She trotted up the stairs as Mrs Abernethie said into the receiver:

'Helen? This is Maude here.'

The invalid received Miss Gilchrist with a baleful glare. As she picked up the tray he asked fretfully:

'Who's that on the telephone?'

'Mrs Leo Abernethie.'

'Oh? Suppose they'll go gossiping for about an hour. Women have no sense of time when they get on the phone. Never think of the money they're wasting'

Miss Gilchrist said brightly that it would be Mrs Leo who had to pay, and Timothy grunted.

'Just pull that curtain aside, will you? No, not that one, the *other* one. I don't want the light slap in my eyes. That's better. No reason because I'm an invalid that I should have to sit in the dark all day.'

He went on:

'And you might look in that bookcase over there for a green— What's the matter *now*? What are you rushing off for?'

'It's the front door, Mr Abernethie.'

'I didn't hear anything. You've got that woman downstairs, haven't you? Let her go and answer it.'

'Yes, Mr Abernethie. What was the book you wanted me to find?'

The invalid closed his eyes.

'I can't remember now. You've put it out of my head. You'd better go.'

Miss Gilchrist seized the tray and hurriedly departed.

Putting the tray on the pantry table she hurried into the front hall, passing Mrs Abernethie who was still at the telephone.

She returned in a moment to ask in a muted voice:

'I'm so sorry to interrupt. It's a nun. Collecting. The Heart of Mary Fund, I think she said. She has a book. Half a crown or five shillings most people seem to have given.'

Maude Abernethie said:

'Just a moment, Helen,' into the telephone, and to Miss Gilchrist, 'I don't subscribe to Roman Catholics. We have our own Church charities.'

Miss Gilchrist hurried away again.

Maude terminated her conversation after a few minutes with the phrase, 'I'll talk to Timothy about it.'

She replaced the receiver and came into the front hall. Miss Gilchrist was standing quite still by the drawing-room door. She was frowning in a puzzled way and jumped when Maude Abernethie spoke to her.

'There's nothing the matter, is there, Miss Gilchrist?'

'Oh no, Mrs Abernethie, I'm afraid I was just wool gathering. So stupid of me when there's so much to be done.'

Miss Gilchrist resumed her imitation of a busy ant and Maude Abernethie climbed the stairs slowly and painfully to her husband's room.

'That was Helen on the telephone. It seems that the place is definitely sold – some Institution for Foreign Refugees—'

She paused whilst Timothy expressed himself forcibly on the subject of Foreign Refugees, with side issues as to the house in which he had been born and brought up. 'No decent standards left in this country. My old home! I can hardly bear to think of it.'

Maude went on:

'Helen quite appreciates what you – we – will feel about it. She suggests that we might like to come there for a visit before it goes. She was very distressed about your health and the way the painting is affecting it. She thought you might prefer coming to Enderby to going to an hotel. The servants are there still, so you could be looked after comfortably.'

Timothy, whose mouth had been open in outraged protests half-way through this, had closed it again. His eyes had become suddenly shrewd. He now nodded his head approvingly.

'Thoughtful of Helen,' he said. 'Very thoughtful. I don't know, I'm sure, I'll have to think it over. . . . There's no doubt that this paint is poisoning me – there's arsenic in paint, I believe. I seem to have heard something of the kind. On the other hand the exertion of moving might be too much for me. It's difficult to know what would be the best.'

'Perhaps you'd prefer an hotel, dear,' said Maude. 'A good hotel is very expensive, but where your health is concerned—'

Timothy interrupted.

'I wish I could make you understand, Maude, that we *are not millionaires*. Why go to an hotel when Helen has very kindly suggested that we should go to Enderby? Not that it's really for her to suggest! The house isn't hers. I don't understand legal subtleties, but I presume it belongs to us equally until it's sold and the proceeds divided. Foreign Refugees! It would have made old Cornelius turn in his grave. Yes,' he sighed, 'I should like to see the old place again before I die.'

Maude played her last card adroitly.

'I understand that Mr Entwhistle has suggested that the members of the family might like to choose certain pieces of furniture or china or something – before the contents are put up for auction.'

Timothy heaved himself briskly upright.

'We must certainly go. There must be a very exact valuation of what is chosen by each person. Those men the girls have married – I wouldn't trust either of them from what I've heard. There might be some sharp practice. Helen is far too amiable. As the head of the family, it is my duty to be present!'

He got up and walked up and down the room with a brisk vigorous tread.

'Yes, it is an excellent plan. Write to Helen and accept. What I am really thinking about is you, my dear. It will be a nice rest and change for you. You have been doing far too much lately. The decorators can get on with the painting while we are away and that Gillespie woman can stay here and look after the house.'

'Gilchrist,' said Maude.

Timothy waved a hand and said that it was all the same.

2

'I can't do it,' said Miss Gilchrist.

Maude looked at her in surprise.

Miss Gilchrist was trembling. Her eyes looked pleadingly into Maude's.

719

'It's stupid of me, I know . . . But I simply can't. Not stay here all alone in the house. If there was any one who could come and – and sleep here too?'

She looked hopefully at the other woman, but Maude shook her head. Maude Abernethie knew only too well how difficult it was to get anyone in the neighbourhood to 'live in.'

Miss Gilchrist went on, a kind of desperation in her voice. 'I know you'll think it nervy and foolish – and I wouldn't have dreamed once that I'd ever feel like this. I've never been a nervous woman – or fanciful. But now it all seems different. I'd be terrified – yes, literally terrified – to be all alone here.'

'Of course,' said Maude. 'It's stupid of me. After what happened at Lytchett St Mary.'

'I suppose that's it . . . It's not logical, I know. And I didn't feel it at first. I didn't mind being alone in the cottage after – after it had happened. The feeling's grown up gradually. You'll have no opinion of me at all, Mrs Abernethie, but ever since I've been here I've been feeling it – *frightened*, you know. Not of anything in particular – but just *frightened*. . . . It's so silly and I really am ashamed It's just as though all the time I was expecting something awful to happen . . . Even that nun coming to the door startled me. Oh dear, I *am* in a bad way . . .'

'I suppose it's what they call delayed shock,' said Maude vaguely.

'Is it? I don't know. Oh, dear, I'm so sorry to appear so – so ungrateful, and after all your kindness. What you will think—'

Maude soothed her.

'We must think of some other arrangements,' she said.

—— 16 ——

George Crossfield paused irresolutely for a moment as he watched a particular feminine back disappear through a doorway. Then he nodded to himself and went in pursuit.

The doorway in question was that of a double-fronted shop – a shop that had gone out of business. The plate-glass window showed a disconcerting emptiness within. The door was closed, but George rapped on it. A vacuous faced young man with spectacles opened it and stared at George.

'Excuse me,' said George. 'But I think my cousin just came in here.'

The young man drew back and George walked in.

'Hallo Susan,' he said.

Susan, who was standing on a packing-case and using a foot-rule, turned her head in some surprise.

'Hallo, George. Where did you spring from?'

'I saw your back. I was sure it was yours.'

'How clever of you. I suppose backs are distinctive.'

'Much more so than faces. Add a beard and pads in your cheeks and do a few things to your hair and nobody will know you when you come face to face with them – but beware of the moment when you walk away.'

'I'll remember. Can you remember seven feet five inches until I've got time to write it down.'

'Certainly. What is this, book shelves?'

'No, cubicle space. Eight feet nine – and three seven . . .'

The young man with the spectacles who had been fidgeting from one foot to the other, coughed apologetically.

'Excuse me, Mrs Banks, but if you want to be here for some time—'

'I do, rather,' said Susan. 'If you leave the keys, I'll lock the door and return them to the office when I go past. Will that be all right?'

'Yes, thank you. If it weren't that we're short staffed this morning—'

Susan accepted the apologetic intent of the half-finished sentence and the young man removed himself to the outer world of the street.

'Im glad we've got rid of him,' said Susan. 'House agents are a bother. They will keep talking just when I want to do sums.'

'Ah,' said George. 'Murder in an empty shop. How exciting it would be for the passers-by to see the dead body of a beautiful young woman displayed behind plate glass. How they would goggle. Like goldfish.

'There wouldn't be any reason for you to murder me, George.'

'Well, I should get a fourth part of your share of our esteemed uncle's estate. If one were sufficiently fond of money that should be a reason.'

Susan stopped taking measurements and turned to look at him. Her eyes opened a little.

'You look a different person, George. It's really – extra-ordinary.'

'Different? How different?'

'Like an advertisement. *This is the same man that you saw overleaf, but now he has taken Uppington's Health Salts.*'

She sat down on another packing-case and lit a cigarette.

'You must have wanted your share of old Richard's money pretty badly, George?'

'Nobody could honestly say that money isn't welcome these days.'

George's tone was light.

Susan said: 'You were in a jam, weren't you?'

'Hardly your business, is it Susan?'

'I was just interested.'

'Are you renting this shop as a place of business?'

'I'm buying the whole house.'

'With possession?'

'Yes. The two upper floors were flats. One's empty and went with the shop. The other I'm buying the people out.'

'Nice to have money, isn't it, Susan?'

There was a malicious tone in George's voice. But Susan merely took a deep breath and said:

'As far as I'm concerned, it's wonderful. An answer to prayer.'

'Does prayer kill off elderly relatives?'

Susan paid no atention.

'This place is exactly *right*. To begin with, it's a very good piece of period architecture. I can make the living part upstairs something quite unique. There are two lovely moulded ceilings and the rooms are a beautiful shape. This part down here which has already been hacked about I shall have completely modern.'

'What is this? A dress business?'

'No. Beauty culture. Herbal preparations. Face creams!'

'The full racket?'

'The racket as before. It pays. It always pays. What you need to put it over is personality. I can do it.'

George looked at his cousin appreciatively. He admired the slanting planes of her face, the generous mouth, the radiant colouring. Altogether an unusual and vivid face. And he recognised in Susan that odd, indefinable quality, the quality of success.

'Yes,' he said, 'I think you've got what it takes, Susan. You'll get back your outlay on this scheme and you'll get places with it.'

'It's the right neighbourhood, just off a main shopping street *and* you can park a car right in front of the door.'

Again Susan nodded.

'Yes, Susan, you're going to succeed. Have you had this in mind for a long time?'

'Over a year.'

'Why didn't you put it up to old Richard? He might have staked you.'

'I did put it up to him.'

'And he didn't see his way? I wonder why. I should have thought he'd have recognised the same mettle that he himself was made of.'

Susan did not answer, and into George's mind there leapt a swift bird's eye view of another figure. A thin, nervous, suspicious-eyed young man.

'Where does – what's his name – Greg – come in on all this?' he asked. 'He'll give up dishing out pills and powders, I take it?'

'Of course. There will be a laboratory built out at the back. We shall have our own formulas for face creams and beauty preparations.'

George suppressed a grin. He wanted to say: 'So baby is to have his play pen,' but he did not say it. As a cousin he did not mind being spiteful, but he had an uneasy sense that Susan's feeling for her husband was a thing to be treated with care. It had all the qualities of a dangerous explosive. He wondered, as he had wondered on the day of the funeral, about that queer fish, Gregory. Something odd about the fellow. So nondescript in appearance – and yet, in some way, not nondescript . . .

He looked again at Susan, calmly and radiantly triumphant.

'You've got the true Abernethie touch,' he said. 'The only one of the family who has. Pity as far as old Richard was concerned that you're a woman. If you'd been a boy, I bet he'd have left you the whole caboodle.'

Susan said slowly: 'Yes, I think he would.'

She paused and then went on:

'He didn't like Greg, you know . . .'

'Ah.' George raised his eyebrows. 'His mistake.'

'Yes.'

'Oh, well. Anyway, things are going well now – all going according to plan.'

As he said the words he was struck by the fact that they seemed particularly applicable to Susan.

The idea made him, just for a moment, a shade uncomfortable.

He didn't really like a woman who was so cold-bloodedly efficient.

Changing the subject he said:

'By the way, did you get a letter from Helen? About Enderby?'

'Yes, I did. This morning. Did you?'

'Yes. What are you going to do about it?'

'Greg and I thought of going up the week-end after next – if that suits everyone else. Helen seemed to want us all together.'

George laughed shrewdly.

'Or somebody might choose a more valuable piece of furniture than somebody else?'

Susan laughed.

'Oh, I suppose there is a proper valuation. But a valuation for probate will be much lower than the things would be in the open market. And besides, I'd quite like to have a few relics of the founder of the family fortunes. Then I think it would be amusing to have one or two really absurd and charming specimens of the Victorian age in this place. Make a kind of *thing* of them! That period's coming in now. There was a green malachite table in the drawing-room. You could build quite a colour scheme around it. And perhaps a case of stuffed humming birds or one of those crowns made of waxed flowers. Something like that – just as a key-note – can be very effective.'

'I trust your judgment.'

'You'll be there, I suppose?'

'Oh, I shall be there – to see fair play if nothing else.'

Susan laughed.

'What do you bet there will be a grand family row?' she asked.

'Rosamund will probably want your green malachite table for a stage set!'

Susan did not laugh. Instead she frowned.

'Have you seen Rosamund lately?'

'I have not seen beautiful Cousin Rosamund since we all came back third-class from the funeral.'

'I've seen her once or twice . . . She – she seemed rather odd—'

'What was the matter with her? Trying to think?'

'No. She seemed – well – upset.'

'Upset about coming into a lot of money and being able to put on some perfectly frightful play in which Michael can make an ass of himself?'

'Oh, that's going ahead and it *does* sound frightful – but all the same, it may be a success. Michael's good, you know. He can put himself across the footlights – or whatever the term is. He's not like Rosamund, who's just beautiful and ham.'

'Poor beautiful ham Rosamund.'

'All the same Rosamund is not quite so dumb as one might think. She says things that are quite shrewd, sometimes. Things that you wouldn't have imagined she'd even noticed. It's – it's quite disconcerting.'

'Quite like our Aunt Cora—'

'Yes . . .'

A momentary uneasiness descended on them both – conjured up it seemed, by the mention of Cora Lansquenet.

Then George said with a rather elaborate air of unconcern:

'Talking of Cora – what about that companion woman of hers? I rather think something ought to be done about her.'

'Done about her? What do you mean?'

'Well, it's up to the family, so to speak. I mean I've been thinking Cora was our Aunt – and it occurred to me that his woman mayn't find it easy to get another post.'

'That occurred to you, did it?'

'Yes. People are so careful of their skins. I don't say they'd **actually** think that this Gilchrist female would take a hatchet to them – but at the back of their minds they'd feel that it might be unlucky. People are superstitious.'

'How odd that you should have thought of all that, George? How would you know about things like that?'

George said dryly:

'You forget that I'm a lawyer. I see a lot of the queer illogical side of people. What I'm getting at is, that I think we might do something about the woman, give her a small allowance or something, to tide her over, or find some office post for her if she's capable of that sort of thing. I feel rather as though we ought to keep in touch with her.'

'You needn't worry,' said Susan. Her voice was dry and ironic. 'I've seen to things. She's gone to Timothy and Maude.'

George looked startled.

'I say, Susan – is that wise?'

'It was the best thing I could think of – at the moment.'

George looked at her curiously.

'You're very sure of yourself, aren't you, Susan? You know what you're doing and you don't have – regrets.'

Susan said lightly:

'It's a waste of time – having regrets.'

—— 17 ——

Michael tossed the letter across the table to Rosamund.

'What about it?'

'Oh, we'll go. Don't you think so?'

Michael said slowly:

'It might be as well.'

'There might be some jewellery . . . Of course all the things in the house are quite hideous – stuffed birds and wax flowers – ugh!'

'Yes. Bit of a mausoleum. As a matter of fact I'd like to make a sketch or two – particularly in that drawing-room. The mantelpiece, for instance, and that very odd shaped couch.

They'd be just right for *The Baronet's Progress* – if we revive it."

He got up and looked at his watch.

'That reminds me. I must go round and see Rosenheim. Don't expect me until rather late this evening. I'm dining with Oscar and we're going into the question of taking up that option and how it fits in with the American offer.'

'Darling Oscar. He'll be pleased to see you after all this time. Give him my love.'

Michael looked at her sharply. He no longer smiled and his face had an alert predatory look.

'What do you mean – after all this time? Anyone would think I hadn't seen him for months.'

'Well, you haven't, have you?' murmured Rosamund.

'Yes, I have. We lunched together only a week ago.'

'How funny. He must have forgotten about it. He rang up yesterday and said he hadn't seen you since the first night of *Tilly Looks West.*'

'The old fool must be off his head.'

Michael laughed. Rosamund, her eyes wide and blue, looked at him without emotion.

'You think I'm a fool, don't you, Mick?'

Michael protested.

'Darling, of course I don't.'

'Yes, you do. But I'm not an absolute nitwit. You didn't go near Oscar that day. I know where you did go.'

'Rosamund darling – what do you mean?'

'I mean I know where you really were . . .'

Michael, his atractive face uncertain, stared at his wife. She stared back at him, placid unruffled.

How very disconcerting, he suddenly thought, a really empty stare could be.

He said rather unsuccessfully:

'I don't know what you're driving at . . .'

'I just meant it's reather silly telling me a lot of lies.'

'Look here, Rosamund—'

He had started to bluster – but he stopped, taken aback as his wife said softly:

'We do want to take up this option and put this play on, don't we?'

'Want to? It's the part I've always dreamed must exist somewhere.'

'Yes – that's what I mean.'

'Just what do you mean?'

'Well – it's worth a good deal, isn't it? But one mustn't take *too* many risks.'

He stared at her and said slowly:

'It's your money – I know that. If you don't want to risk it—'

'It's *our* money, darling.' Rosamund stressed it. 'I think that's rather important.'

'Listen, darling. The part of Eileen – it would bear writing up.'

Rosamund smiled.

'I don't think – really – I want to play it.'

'My dear girl.' Michael was aghast. 'What's come over you?'

'Nothing.'

'Yes, there is, you've been different lately – moody – nervous, what is it?'

'Nothing. I only want you to be – careful, Mick.'

'Careful about what? I'm always careful.'

'No, I don't think you are. You always think you can get away with things and that everyone will believe whatever you want them to. You were stupid about Oscar that day.'

Michael flushed angrily.

'And what about you? You said you were going shopping with Jane. You didn't. Jane's in America, has been for weeks.'

'Yes,' said Rosamund. 'That was stupid, too. I really just went for a walk – in Regent's Park.'

Michael looked at her curiously.

'Regent's Park? You never went for a walk in Regent's Park in your life. What's it all about? Have you got a boy friend? You may say what you like, Rosamund, you *have* been different lately. Why?'

'I've been – thinking about things. About what to do . . .'

Michael came round the table to her in a satisfying spontaneous rush. His voice held fervour as he cried:

'Darling – you know I love you madly!'

She responded satisfactorily to the embrace, but as they drew apart he was struck again disagreeably by the odd calculation in those beautiful eyes.

'Whatever I've done, you'd always forgive me, wouldn't you?' he demanded.

'I suppose so,' said Rosamund vaguely. 'That's not the point. You see, it's all different now. We've got to think and plan.'

'Think and plan – what?'

Rosamund, frowning, said:

'Things aren't over when you've done them. It's really a sort of beginning and then one's got to arrange what to do next, and what's important and what is not.'

'Rosamund . . .'

She sat, her face perplexed, her wide gaze on a middle distance in which Michael, apparently, did not feature.

At the third repetition of her name, she started slightly and came out of her reverie.

'What did you say?'

'I asked you what you were thinking about . . .'

'Oh? Oh yes, I was wondering if I'd go down to – what is it? – Lytchett St Mary, and see that Miss Somebody – the one who was with Aunt Cora.'

'But why?'

'Well, she'll be going away soon, won't she? To relatives or someone. I don't think we ought to let her go away until we've asked her.'

'Asked her what?'

'Asked her who killed Aunt Cora.'

Michael stared.

'You mean – you think she *knows*?'

Rosamund said rather absently:

'Oh yes, I *expect* so . . . She lived there, you see.'

But she'd have told the police.'

'Oh, I don't mean she knows *that* way – I just mean that she's probably quite sure. Because of what Uncle Richard said when he went down there. He did go down there, you know, Susan told me so.'

'But she wouldn't have heard what he said.'

'Oh yes, she would, darling.' Rosamund sounded like someone arguing with an unreasonable child.

'Nonsense, I can hardly see old Richard Abernethie discussing his suspicions of his family before an outsider.'

'Well, of course. She'd have heard it through the door.'

'Eavesdropping, you mean?'

'I expect so – in fact I'm sure. It must be deadly dull shut up, two women in a cottage and nothing ever happening except washing up and the sink and putting the cat out and things like that. Of course she listened and read letters – anyone would.'

Michael looked at her with something faintly approaching dismay.

'Would you?' he demanded bluntly.

'I wouldn't go and be a companion in the country.' Rosamund shuddered. 'I'd rather die.'

'I mean – would you read letters and – all that?'

Rosamund said calmly:

'If I wanted to know, yes. Everybody does, don't you think so?'

The limpid gaze met his.

'One just wants to know,' said Rosamund. 'One doesn't want to do anything about it. I expect that's how *she* feels – Miss Gilchrist, I mean. But I'm certain she *knows*.'

Michael said in a stifled voice:

'Rosamund, who do you think killed Cora? And old Richard?'

Once again that limpid blue gaze met his.

'Darling – don't be absurd . . . You know as well as I do. But it's much, much better *never* to mention it. So we won't.'

From his seat by the fireplace in the library, Hercule Poirot looked at the assembled company.

His eyes passed thoughtfully over Susan, sitting upright, looking vivid and animated, over her husband, sitting near her, his expression rather vacant and his fingers twisting a loop of string; they went on to George Crossfield, debonair and distinctly pleased with himself, talking about card sharpers on Atlantic cruises to Rosamund, who said mechanically, 'How extraordinary, darling. But why?' in a completely uninterested voice; went on to Michael with his very individual type of haggard good looks and his very apparent charm; to Helen, poised and slightly remote; to Timothy, comfortably settled in the best armchair with an extra cushion at his back; and Maude, sturdy and thick-set, in devoted attendance, and finally to the figure sitting with a tinge of apology just beyond the range of the family circle – the figure of Miss Gilchrist wearing a rather peculiar 'dressy' blouse. Presently, he judged, she would get up, murmur an excuse and leave the family gathering and go up to her room. Miss Gilchrist, he thought, knew her place. She had learned it the hard way.

Hercule Poirot sipped his after-dinner coffee and between half-closed lids made his appraisal.

He had wanted them there – all together, and he had got them. And what, he thought to himself, was he going to do with them now? He felt a sudden weary distaste for going on with the business. Why was that, he wondered? Was it the influence of Helen Abernethie? There was a quality of passive resistance about her that seemed unexpectedly strong. Had she, while apparently graceful and unconcerned, managed to impress her own reluctance upon him? She was averse to this raking up of the details of old Richard's death, he knew that. She wanted it left alone, left to die out into oblivion. Poirot was not surprised by that. What did surprise him was his own disposition to agree with her.

Mr Entwhistle's account of the family had, he realised, been admirable. He had described all these people shrewdly and well. With the old lawyer's knowledge and appraisal to guide him, Poirot had wanted to see for himself. He had fancied that, meeting these people intimately, he would have a very shrewd idea – not of *how* and *when* – (those were questions with which he did not propose to concern himself. Murder had been possible – that was all he needed to know!) – but of who. For Hercule Poirot had a lifetime of experience behind him, and as a man who deals with pictures can recognise the artist, so Poirot believed he could recognise a likely type of the amateur criminal who will – if his own particular need arises – be prepared to kill.

But it was not to be so easy.

Because he could visualise almost all of these people as a possible – though not a probable – murderer. George might kill – as the cornered rat kills. Susan calmly – efficiently – to further a plan. Gregory because he had that queer morbid streak which discounts and invites, almost craves, punishment. Michael because he was ambitious and had a murderer's cock-sure vanity. Rosamund because she was frighteningly simple in outlook. Timothy because he had hated and resented his brother and had craved the power his brother's money would give. Maude because Timothy was her child and where her child was concerned she would be ruthless. Even Miss Gilchrist, he thought, might have contemplated murder if it could have restored to her the Willow Tree in its lady-like glory!

And Helen? He could not see Helen as committing murder. She was too civilised – too removed from violence. And she and her husband had surely loved Richard Abernethie.

Poirot sighed to himself. There were to be no short cuts to the truth. Instead he would have to adopt a longer, but a reasonably sure method. There would have to be conversation. Much conversation. For in the long run, either through a lie, or through truth, people were bound to give themselves away. . . .

He had been introduced by Helen to the gathering, and had set to work to overcome the almost universal annoyance caused by his presence – a foreign stranger! – in this family gathering. He had used his eyes and his ears. He had watched and listened openly and behind doors! He had noticed affinities, antagonism, the unguarded words that arose as always when property was to be divided. He had engineered adroitly tête-à-têtes, walks upon the terrace, and had made his deductions and observations. He had talked with Miss Gilchrist about the vanished glories of her tea-shop and about the correct composition of *brioches* and chocolate *éclairs* and has visited the kitchen garden with her to discuss the proper use of herbs in cooking. He had spent some long half-hours listening to Timothy talking about his own health and about the effect upon it of paint.

Paint? Poirot frowned. Somebody else had said something about paint – Mr Entwhistle?

There had also been discussion of a different kind of painting. Pierre Lansquenet as a painter. Cora Lansquenet's paintings, rapturised over by Miss Gilchrist, dismissed scornfully by Susan. 'Just like picture postcards,' she had said. 'She did them from postcards, too.'

Miss Gilchrist had been quite upset by that and had said sharply that dear Mrs Lansquenet always painted from Nature.

'But I bet she cheated,' said Susan to Poirot when Miss Gilchrist had gone out of the room. 'In fact I know she did, though I won't upset the old pussy by saying so.'

'And how do you know?'

Poirot watched the strong confident line of Susan's chin.

'She will always be sure, this one,' he thought. 'And perhaps sometimes, she will be too sure . . .'

Susan was going on.

'I'll tell you, but don't pass it on to the Gilchrist. One picture is of Polflexan, the cove and the lighthouse and the pier – the usual aspect that all amateur artists sit down and sketch. But the pier was blown up in the war, and since Aunt Cora's sketch was done a couple of years ago, it can't very well be from Nature, can it? But the postcards they sell there still show the pier as it used to be. There was one in her bedroom drawer. So Aunt Cora started her "rough sketch" down there, I expect, and then finished it surreptitiously later at home from a postcard! It's funny, isn't it, the way people get caught out?'

'Yes, it is, as you say, funny.' He paused, and then thought that the opening was a good one.

'You do not remember me, Madame,' he said, 'but I remember you. This is not the first time that I have seen you.'

She stared at him. Poirot nodded with great gusto.

'Yes, yes, it is so. I was inside an automobile, well wrapped up and from the window I saw you. You were talking to one of the mechanics in the garage. You do not notice me – it is natural – I am inside the car – an elderly muffled-up foreigner! But *I* noticed you, for you are young and agreeable to look at and you stand there in the sun. So when I arrive here, I say to myself, "Tiens! What a coincidence!"'

'A garage? Where? When was this?'

'Oh, a little time ago – a week – no, more For the moment,' said Poirot disingenuously and with a full recollection of the King's Arm's garage in his mind, 'I cannot remember where. I travel so much all over this country.'

'Looking for a suitable house to buy for your refugees?'

'Yes. There is so much to take into consideration, you see. Price – neighbourhood – suitability for conversion.'

'I suppose you'll have to pull the house about a lot? Lots of horrible partitions.'

'In the bedrooms, yes, certainly. But most of the ground floor rooms we shall not touch.' He paused before going on. 'Does it sadden you, Madame, that this old family mansion of yours should go this way – to strangers?'

'Of course not.' Susan looked amused. 'I think it's an excellent idea. It's an impossible place for anybody to think of living in as it is. And I've nothing to be sentimental about. It's not *my* old home. My mother and father lived in London. We just came up here for Christmas sometimes. Actually I've always thought it quite hideous – an almost indecent temple to wealth.'

'The altars are different now. There is the building in, and the concealed lighting and the expensive simplicity. But wealth still has its temples, Madame. I understand – I am not, I hope, indiscreet – that you yourself are planning such an edifice? Everything *de luxe* – and no expense spared.'

Susan laughed.

'Hardly a temple – it's just a place of business.'

'Perhaps the name does not matter. . . . But it will cost much money – that is true, is it not?'

'Everything's wickedly expensive nowadays. But the initial outlay wil be worth while, I think.'

'Tell me something about these plans of yours. It amazes me to find a beautiful young woman so practical, so competent. In my young days – a long time ago, I admit – beautiful women thought only of their pleasures, of cosmetics – of *la toilette.*'

'Women still think a great deal about their faces – that's where I come in.'

'Tell me.'

And she told him. Told him with a wealth of detail and with a great deal of unconscious self-revelation. He appreciated her business acumen, her boldness of planning and her grasp of detail. A good bold planner, sweeping all side issues away. Perhaps a little ruthless as all those who plan boldly must be. . . .

Watching her, he had said:

'Yes, you will succeed. You will go ahead. How fortunate that you are not restricted, as so many are, by poverty. One cannot go far without the capital outlay. To have had these creative ideas and to have been frustrated by lack of means – that would have been unbearable.'

'I couldn't have borne it! But I'd have raised money somehow or other – got someone to back me.'

'Ah! of course. Your uncle, whose house this was, was rich. Even if he had not died, he would, as you express it, have "staked" you.'

'Oh no, he wouldn't. Uncle Richard was a bit of a stick-in-the-mud where women were concerned. If I'd been a man—' A quick flash of anger swept across her face. 'He made me very angry.'

'I see – yes, I see . . .'

'The old shouldn't stand in the way of the young. I – oh, I beg your pardon.'

Hercule Poirot laughed easily and twirled his moustache.

'I am old, yes. But I do not impede youth. There is no one who needs to wait for my death.'

'What a horrible idea.'

'But you are a realist, Madame. Let us admit without more ado that the world is full of the young – or even the middle-aged – who wait, patiently or impatiently, for the death of someone whose decease will give them if not affluence – then opportunity.'

'Opportunity!' Susan said, taking a deep breath. 'That's what one needs.'

Poirot who had been looking beyond her, said gaily:

'And here is your husband come to join our little discussion. . . . We talk, Mr Banks, of opportunity. Opportunity the golden – opportunity who must be grasped with both hands. How far in conscience can one go? Let us hear your views?'

But he was not destined to hear the views of Gregory Banks on opportunity or on anything else. In fact he had found it next to impossible to talk to Gregory Banks at all. Banks had a curious fluid quality. Whether by his own wish, or by that of his wife, he seemed to have no liking for tête-à-têtes or quiet discussions. No, 'conversation' with Gregory had failed.

Poirot had talked with Maude Abernethie – also about paint (the smell of) and how fortunate it had been that Timothy had been able to come to Enderby, and how kind it had been of Helen to extend an invitation to Miss Gilchrist also.

'For really she is *most* useful. Timothy so often feels like a snack – and one cannot ask too much of other people's servants but there is a gas ring in a little room off the pantry, so that Miss Gilchrist can warm up Ovaltine or Benger's there without disturbing anybody. And she's so willing about fetching things, she's quite willing to run up and down stairs a dozen times a day. Oh yes, I feel that it was really quite Providental that she should have lost her nerve about staying alone in the house as she did, though I admit it vexed me at the time.

'Lost her nerve?' Poirot was interested.

He listened whilst Maude gave him an account of Miss Gilchrist's sudden collapse.

'She was frightened, you say? And yet could not exactly say why? That is interesting. Very interesting.'

'I put it down myself to delayed shock.'

'Perhaps.'

'Once during the war, when a bomb dropped about a mile away from us, I remember Timothy—'

Poirot abstracted his mind from Timothy.

'Had anything particular happened that day?' he asked.

'On what day?' Maude looked blank.

'The day that Miss Gilchrist was upset.'

'Oh, that – no, I don't think so. It seems to have been coming on ever since she left Lytchett St Mary, or so she said. She didn't seem to mind when she was there.'

And the result, Poirot thought, had been a piece of poisoned wedding cake. Not so very surprising that Miss Gilchrist was frightened after that. . . . And even when she had removed herself to the peaceful country round Stansfield Grange, the fear had lingered. More than lingered. Grown. Why grown? Surely attending that nervous hypochondriac like Timothy must be so exhausting that nervous fears would be likely to be swallowed up in exasperation?

But something in that house had made Miss Gilchrist afraid. What? Did she know herself?

Finding himself alone with Miss Gilchrist for a brief space before dinner, Poirot had sailed into the subject with an exaggerated foreign curiosity.

'Impossible, you comprehend, for me to mention the matter of murder to members of the family. But I am intrigued. Who would not be? A brutal crime – a sensitive artist attacked in a lonely cottage. Terrible for her family. But terrible, also, I imagine, for *you*. Since Mrs Timothy Abernethie gives me to understand that you were there at the time?'

'Yes, I was. And if you'll excuse me, M. Pontarlier, I don't want to talk about it.'

'I understand – oh yes, I completely understand.'

Having said this, Poirot waited. And, as he had thought, Miss Gilchrist immediately *did* begin to talk about it.

He heard nothing from her that he had not heard before, but he played his part with perfect sympathy, uttering little cries of comprehension and listening with an absorbed interest which Miss Gilchrist could not but help enjoy.

Not until she had exhausted the subject of what she herself had felt, and what the doctor had said, and how kind Mr Entwhistle had been, did Poirot proceed cautiously to the next point.

'You were wise, I think, not to remain alone down in that cottage.'

'I couldn't have done it, M. Pontarlier. I really couldn't have done it.'

'No. I understand even that you were afraid to remain alone in the house of Mr Timothy Abernethie whilst they came here?'

Miss Gilchrist looked guilty.

'I'm terribly ashamed about that. So foolish really. It was just a kind of panic I had – really don't know *why*.'

'But of course one knows why. You had just recovered from a dastardly attempt to poison you—'

Miss Gilchrist here sighed and said she simply couldn't understand it. Why should anyone try to poison her?

'But obviously, my dear lady, because this criminal, this assassin, thought that you knew something that might lead to his apprehension by the police.'

'But what could *I* know? Some dreadful tramp, or semi-crazed creature.'

'If it *was* a tramp. It seems to me unlikely—'

'Oh, please, M. Pontarlier—' Miss Gilchrist became suddenly very upset. 'Don't suggest such things. I don't want to believe it.'

'You do not want to believe what?'

'I don't want to believe that it wasn't – I mean – that it was—'

She paused, confused.

'And yet,' said Poirot shrewdly, 'you *do* believe.'

'Oh, I don't. I *don't*!'

'But I think you do. That is why you are frightened . . . You are still frightened, are you not?'

'Oh, no, not since I came here. So many people. And such

a nice family atmosphere. Oh, no, everything seems quite all right here.'

'It seems to me – you must excuse my interest – I am an old man, somewhat infirm and a great part of my time is given to idle speculation on matters which interest me – it seems to me that there must have been some definite occurrence at Stansfield Grange which, so to speak, brought your fears to a *head*. Doctors recognise nowadays how much takes place in our subconscious.'

'Yes, yes – I know they say so.'

'And I think your subconscious fears might have been brought to a point by some small concrete happening, something, perhaps, quite extraneous, serving, shall we say, as a focal point.'

Miss Gilchrist seemed to lap this up eagerly.

'I'm sure you are right,' she said.

'Now what, should you think, was this – er – extraneous circumstance?'

Miss Gilchrist pondered a moment, and then said, unexpectedly:

'I think, you know, M. Pontarlier, it was the *nun*.'

Before Poirot could take this up, Susan and her husband came in, closely followed by Helen.

'A nun,' thought Poirot . . . 'Now where, in all this, have I heard something about a nun?'

He resolved to lead the conversation on to nuns sometime in the course of the evening.

—— 19 ——

The family had all been polite to M. Pontarlier, the representative of U.N.A.R.C.O. And how right he had been to have chosen to designate himself by initials. Everyone had accepted U.N.A.R.C.O. as a matter of course – had even pretended to know all about it! How averse human beings were ever to admit ignorance! An exception had been Rosamund, who had asked him wonderingly: 'But what *is* it? I never heard of it?' Fortunately no one else had been there at the time. Poirot had explained the organisation in such a way that anyone but Rosamund would have felt abashed at having displayed ignorance of such a well-known world-wide institution.

Rosamund, however, had only said vaguely, 'Oh! refugees all over *again*. I'm so *tired* of refugees.' Thus voicing the unspoken reaction of many, who were usually too conventional to express themselves so frankly.

M. Pontarlier was, therefore, now accepted – as a nuisance but also as a nonentity. He had become, as it were, a piece of foreign *décor*. The general opinion was that Helen should have avoided having him here this particular week-end, but as he was here they must make the best of it. Fortunately this queer little foreigner did not seem to know much English. Quite often he did not understand what you said to him, and when everyone was speaking more or less at once he seemed completely at sea. He appeared to be interested only in refugees and post-war conditions, and his vocabulary only included those subjects. Ordinary chit-chat appeared to bewilder him. More or less forgotten by all, Hercule Poirot leant back in his chair, sipped his coffee and observed, as a cat may observe, the twitterings and comings and goings of a flock of birds. The cat is not ready yet to make its spring.

After twenty-four hours of prowling round the house and examining its contents, the heirs of Richard Abernethie were ready to state their preferences, and, if need be, to fight for them.

The subject of conversation was, first, a certain Spode dinner dessert service off which they had just been eating dessert.

'I don't suppose I have long to live,' said Timothy in a faint melancholy voice. 'And Maude and I have no children. It is hardly worth while our burdening ourselves with useless possessions. But for sentiment's sake I *should* like to have the old dessert service. I remember it in the dear old days. It's out of fashion, of course, and I understand dessert services have little value nowadays – but there it is. I shall be *quite* content with that – and perhaps the Boule Cabinet in the White Boudoir.'

'You're too late, Uncle,' George spoke with debonair insouciance. 'I asked Helen to mark off the Spode service to me this morning.'

Timothy became purple in the face.

'Mark it off – mark it off? What do you mean? Nothing's been settled yet. And what do *you* want with a dessert service? You're not married.'

'As a matter of fact I collect Spode. And this is really a splendid specimen. But it's quite all right about the Boule Cabinet, Uncle. I wouldn't have that as a gift.'

Timothy waved aside the Boule Cabinet.

'Now look here, young George. You can't go butting in, in this way. I'm an older man than you are – and I'm Richard's only surviving brother. That dessert service is *mine*.'

'Why not take the Dresden service, Uncle? A very fine example and I'm sure just as full of sentimental memories. Anyway, the Spode's mine. First come, first served.'

'Nonsense – nothing of the kind!' Timothy spluttered.

Maude said sharply:

'Please don't upset your uncle, George. It's very bad for him. Naturally he will take the Spode if he wants to! The first choice is *his*, and you young people must come afterwards. He was Richard's brother, as he says, and you are only a nephew.'

'And I can tell you this, young man.' Timothy was seething with fury. 'If Richard had made a proper will, the disposal of the contents of this place would have been entirely in my hands. That's the way the property *should* have been left, and if it wasn't, I can only suspect *undue influence*. Yes – and I repeat it – *undue influence*.'

Timothy glared at his nephew.

'A preposterous will,' he said. 'Preposterous!'

He leant back, placed a hand to his heart, and groaned:

'This is very bad for me. If I could have – a little brandy.'

Miss Gilchrist hurried to get it and returned with the restorative in a small glass.

'Here you are, Mr Abernethie. Please – please don't excite yourself. Are you sure you oughtn't to go up to bed?'

'Don't be a fool.' Timothy swallowed the brandy. 'Go to bed? I intend to protect my interests.'

'Really, George, I'm surprised at you,' said Maude. 'What your uncle says is perfectly true. His wishes come first. If he wants the Spode dessert service he shall have it!'

'It's quite hideous anyway,' said Susan.

'Hold your tongue, Susan,' said Timothy.

The thin young man who sat beside Susan raised his head. In a voice that was a little shriller than his ordinary tones, he said:

'Don't speak like that to my wife!'

He half rose from his seat.

Susan said quickly: 'It's all right, Greg. I don't mind.'

'But *I* do.'

Helen said: 'I think it would be graceful on your part, George, to let your uncle have the dessert service.'

Timothy spluttered indignantly: 'There's no "letting" about it!'

But George, with a slight bow to Helen said, 'Your wish is law, Aunt Helen. I abandon my claim.'

'You didn't really want it, anyway, did you?' said Helen.

He cast a sharp glance at her, then grinned:

'The trouble with you, Aunt Helen, is that you're too sharp by half! You see more than you're meant to see. Don't worry, Uncle Timothy, the Spode is yours. Just my idea of fun.'

'Fun, indeed.' Maude Abernethie was indignant. 'Your uncle might have had a heart attack!'

'Don't you believe it,' said George cheerfully. 'Uncle Timothy will probably outlive us all. He's what is known as a creaking gate.'

Timothy leaned forward balefully.

'I don't wonder,' he said, 'that Richard was disappointed in *you*.'

'What's that?' The good humour went out of George's face.

'You came up here after Mortimer died, expecting to step into his shoes – expecting that Richard would make you his heir, didn't you? But my poor brother soon took *your* measure. He knew where the money would go if you had control of it. I'm surprised that he even left you a part of his fortune. He knew where it would go. Horses, Gambling, Monte Carlo, foreign Casinos. Perhaps worse. He suspected you of not being straight, didn't he?'

George, a white dint appearing each side of his nose, said quietly:

'Hadn't you better be careful of what you are saying?'

'I wasn't well enough to come here for the funeral,' said Timothy slowly, 'but Maude told me what *Cora said*. Cora always was a fool – but there *may* have been something in it! And if so, I know who *I'd* suspect—'

'Timothy!' Maude stood up, solid, calm, a tower of forcefulness. 'You have had a very trying evening. You must consider your health. I can't have you getting ill again. Come up with me. You must take a sedative and go straight to bed. Timothy and I, Helen, will take the Spode dessert service and the Boule Cabinet as mementoes of Richard. There is no objection to that, I hope?'

Her glance swept round the company. Nobody spoke, and she marched out of the room supporting Timothy with a hand under his elbow, waving aside Miss Gilchrist who was hovering half-heartedly by the door.

George broke the silence after they had departed.

'*Femme formidable!*' he said. 'That describes Aunt Maude exactly. I should hate ever to impede her triumphal progress.'

Miss Gilchrist sat down again rather uncomfortably and murmured:

'Mrs Abernethie is always so kind.'

The remark fell rather flat.

Michael Shane laughed suddenly and said: 'You know, I'm enjoying all this! "The Voysey Inheritance" to the life. By the way, Rosamund and I want that malachite table in the drawing-room.'

'Oh, no,' cried Susan. '*I* want that.'

'Here we go again,' said George, raising his eyes to the ceiling.

'Well, we needn't get angry about it,' said Susan. 'The reason I want it is for my new Beauty shop. Just a note of colour – and I shall put a great bouquet of wax flowers on it. It would look wonderful. I can find wax flowers easily enough, but a green malachite table isn't so common.'

'But, darling,' said Rosamund, 'that's just why *we* want it. For the new set. As you say, a note of colour – and so *absolutely* period. And either wax flowers or stuffed humming birds. It will be absolutely *right*.'

'I see what you mean, Rosamund,' said Susan. 'But I don't think you've got as good a case as I have. You could easily have a painted malachite table for the stage – it would look just the same. But for my *salon* I've *got* to have the genuine thing.'

'Now, ladies,' said George. 'What about a sporting decision? Why not toss for it? Or cut the cards? All quite in keeping with the period of the table.'

Susan smiled pleasantly.

'Rosamund and I will talk about it to-morrow,' she said.

She seemed, as usual, quite sure of herself. George looked with some interest from her face to that of Rosamund. Rosamund's face had a vague, rather far-away expression.

'Which one will you back, Aunt Helen?' he asked. 'An even money chance, I'd say. Susan has determination, but Rosamund is so wonderfully single-minded.'

'Or perhaps *not* humming birds,' said Rosamund. 'One of those big Chinese vases would make a lovely lamp, with a gold shade.'

Miss Gilchrist hurried into placating speech.

'This house is full of so many beautiful things,' she said.

'That green table would look wonderful in your new establishment, I'm sure, Mrs Banks. I've never seen one like it. It must be worth a lot of money.'

'It will be deducted from my share of the estate, of course,' said Susan.

'I'm so sorry – I didn't mean—' Miss Gilchrist was covered with confusion.

'It may be deducted from *our* share of the estate,' Michael pointed out. 'With the wax flowers thrown in.'

'They look so right on that table,' Miss Gilchrist murmured. 'Really artistic. Sweetly pretty.'

But nobody was paying any attention to Miss Gilchrist's well-meant trivialities.

Greg said, speaking again in that high nervous voice:

'Susan *wants* that table.'

There was a momentary stir of unease, as though, by his words, Greg had set a different musical key.

Helen said quickly:

'And what do you really want, George? Leaving out the Spode service.'

George grinned and the tension relaxed.

'Rather a shame to bait old Timothy,' he said. 'But he really is quite unbelievable. He's had his own way in everything so long that he's become quite pathological about it.'

'You have to humour an invalid, Mr Crossfield,' said Miss Gilchrist.

'Ruddy old hypochondriac, that's what he is,' said George.

'Of course he is,' Susan agreed. 'I don't believe there's anything whatever the matter with him, do you, Rosamund?'

'What?'

'Anything the matter with Uncle Timothy.'

'No – no, I shouldn't think so.' Rosamund was vague. She apologised. 'I'm sorry. I was thinking about what lighting would be right for the table.'

'You see?' said George. 'A woman of one idea. Your wife's a dangerous woman, Michael. I hope you realise it.'

'I realise it,' said Michael rather grimly.

George went on with every appearance of enjoyment.

'The Battle of the Table! To be fought tomorrow – politely – but with grim determination. We ought all to take sides. I back Rosamund who looks so sweet and yielding and isn't. Husbands, presumably back their own wives. Miss Gilchrist? On Susan's side, obviously.'

'Oh, really, Mr Crossfield, I wouldn't venture to—'

'Aunt Helen?' George paid no attention to Miss Gilchrist's flutterings. 'You have the casting vote. Oh, er – I forgot. M. Pontarlier?'

'*Pardon*?' Hercule Poirot looked blank.

George considered explanations, but decided against it. The poor old boy hadn't understood a word of what was going on. He said: 'Just a family joke.'

'Yes, yes, I comprehend.' Poirot smiled amiably.

'So yours is the casting vote, Aunt Helen. Whose side are you on?'

Helen smiled.

'Perhaps I want it myself, George.'

She changed the subject deliberately, turning to her foreign guest.

'I'm afraid this is all very dull for you, M. Pontarlier?'

'Not at all, Madame. I consider myself privileged to be admitted to your family life—' he bowed. 'I would like to say – I cannot quite express my meaning – my regret that this house had to pass out of your hands into the hands of strangers. It is without doubt – a great sorrow.'

'No, indeed, we don't regret at all,' Susan assured him.

'You are very amiable, Madame. It will be, let me tell you, perfection here for my elderly sufferers of persecution. What a haven! What peace! I beg you to remember that, when the harsh feelings come to you as assuredly they must. I hear that there was also the question of a school coming here – not a regular school, a convent – run by *religeuses* – by "nuns," I think you say? You would have preferred that, perhaps?'

'Not at all,' said George.

'The Sacred Heart of Mary,' continued Poirot. 'Fortunately, owing to the kindness of an unknown benefactory we were able to make a slightly higher offer.' He addressed Miss Gilchrist directly. 'You do not like nuns, I think?'

Miss Gilchrist flushed and looked embarrassed.

'Oh, really, Mr Pontarlier, you mustn't – I mean, it's nothing *personal*. But I never do see that it's right to shut yourself up from the world in that way – not necessary, I mean, and really almost selfish, though not teaching ones, of course, or the ones that go about amongst the poor – because I'm sure they're thoroughly unselfish women and do a lot of good.'

'I simply can't imagine wanting to be a nun,' said Susan.

'It's very becoming,' said Rosamund. 'You remember – when they revived *The Miracle* last year. Sonia Wells looked absolutely too glamorous for *words*.'

'What beats me,' said George, 'is why it should be pleasing to the Almighty to dress oneself up in medieval dress. For after all, that's all a nun's dress is. Thoroughly cumbersome, unhygienic and impractical.'

'And it makes them look so alike, doesn't it?' said Miss Gilchrist. 'It's silly, you know, but I got quite a turn when I was at Mrs Abernethie's and a nun came to the door, collecting. I got it into my head she was the same as a nun who came to the door on the day of the inquest on poor Mrs Lansquenet at Lytchett St Mary. I felt, you know, almost as though she had been following me round!'

'I thought nuns always collected in couples,' said George. 'Surely a detective story hinged on that point once?'

'There was only one this time,' said Miss Gilchrist. 'Perhaps they've got to economise,' she added vaguely. 'And anyway it couldn't have been the same nun, for the other one was collecting for an organ for St – Barnabas, I think – and this one was for something quite different – something to do with children.'

'But they both had the same type of features?' Hercule Poirot asked. He sounded intersted. Miss Gilchrist turned to him.

'I suppose that must be it. The upper lip – almost as though she had a moustache. I think you know, that *that* is really what alarmed me – being in a rather nervous state at the time, and remembering those stories during the war of nuns who were really men and in the Fifth Column and landed by parachute. Of course it was very foolish of me. I knew that afterwards.'

'A nun would be a good disguise,' said Susan thoughtfully. 'It hides your feet.'

'The truth is,' said George, 'that one very seldom looks properly at anyone. That's why one gets such wildly differing accounts of a person from different witnesses in court. You'd be surprised. A man is often described as tall – short; thin – stout; fair – dark; dressed in a dark – light – suit, and so on. There's usually *one* reliable observer, but one has to make up one's mind who that is.'

'Another queer thing,' said Susan, 'is that you sometimes catch sight of yourself in a mirror unexpectedly and don't know who it is. It just looks vaguely familiar. And you say to yourself, "There's somebody I know quite well . . ." and then suddenly realise it's yourself!'

George said: 'It would be more difficult still if you could really see yourself – and not a mirror image.

'Why?' asked Rosamund, looking puzzled.

'Because, don't you see, nobody ever sees themselves – *as they appear to other people*. They always see themselves in a *glass* – that is – as a reversed image.'

'But does that look any different?'

'Oh, yes,' said Susan quickly. 'It must. Because people's faces aren't the same both sides. Their eyebrows are different, and their mouths go up one side, and their noses aren't really straight. You can see with a pencil – who's got a pencil?'

Somebody produced a pencil, and they experimented, holding a pencil each side of the nose and laughing to see the ridiculous variation in angle.

The atmosphere had now lightened a good deal. Everybody was in a good humour. They were no longer the heirs of Richard Abernethie gathered together for a division of property. They were a cheerful and normal set of people gathered together for a week-end in the country.

Only Helen Abernethie remained silent and abstracted.

With a sigh, Hercule Poirot rose to his feet and bade his hostess a polite good night.

'And perhaps, Madame, I had better say good-bye. My train departs itself at nine o'clock to-morrow morning. That is very early. So I will thank you now for all your kindness and hospitality. The date of possession – that will be arranged with the good Mr Entwhistle. To suit your convenience, of course.'

'It can be any time you please, M. Pontarlier. I – I have finished all that I came here to do.'

'You will return now to your villa at Cyprus?'

'Yes.' A little smile curved Helen Abernethie's lips.

Poirot said:

'You are glad, yes. You have no regrets?'

'At leaving England? Or leaving here, do you mean?'

'I meant – leaving here?'

'Oh – no. It's no good, is it, to cling on to the past? One must leave that behind one.'

'If one can.' Blinking his eyes innocently Poirot smiled apologetically round on the group of polite faces that surrounded him.

'Sometimes, is it not, the Past will not be left, will not suffer itself to pass into oblivion? It stands at one's elbow – it says "*I am not done with yet.*" '

Susan gave a rather doubtful laugh. Poirot said:

'But I am serious – yes.'

'You mean,' said Michael, 'that your refugees when they come here wil not be able to put their past sufferings completely behind them?'

'I did not mean my Refugees.'

'He meant us, darling,' said Rosamund. 'He means Uncle Richard and Aunt Cora and the hatchet and all that.'

She turned to Poirot.

'Didn't you?'

Poirot looked at her with a blank face. Then he said:

'Why do you think that, Madame?'

'Because you're a detective, aren't you? That's why you're here. N.A.R.C.O., or whatever you call it, is just nonsense, isn't it?'

—— 20 ——

There was a moment of extraordinary tenseness. Poirot felt it, though he himself did not remove his eyes from Rosamund's lovely placid face.

He said with a little bow, 'You have great perspicacity, Madame.'

'Not really,' said Rosamund. 'You were pointed out to me once in a restaurant. I remembered.'

'But you have not mentioned it – until now?'

'I thought it would be more fun not to,' said Rosamund. Michael said in an imperfectly controlled voice:

'My – dear girl.'

Poirot shifted his gaze then to look at him.

Michael was angry. Angry and something else – apprenhensive?

Poirot's eyes went slowly round all the faces. Susan's, angry and watchful; Gregory's dead and shut in; Miss Gilchrist's, foolish, her mouth wide open; George, wary; Helen, dismayed and nervous. . . .

All those expressions were normal ones under the circumstances. He wished he could have seen their faces a split second earlier, when the words 'a detective' fell from Rosamund's lips. For now, inevitably, it could not be quite the same. . . .

He squared his shoulders and bowed to them. His language and his accent became less foreign.

'Yes,' he said. 'I am a detective.'

George Crossfield said, the white dints showing once more each side of his nose, 'Who sent you here?'

'I was commissioned to inquire into the circumstances of Richard Abernethie's death.'

'By whom?'

'For the moment, that does not concern you. But it would be an advantage, would it not, if you could be assured *beyond any possible doubt* that Richard Abernethie died a natural death?'

'Of course he died a natural death. Who says anything else?'

'Cora Lansquenet said so. And Cora Lansquenet is dead herself.'

A little wave of uneasiness seemed to sigh through the room like an evil breeze.

'She said it here – in this room,' said Susan. 'But I didn't really think—'

'Didn't you, Susan?' George Crossfield turned his sardonic glance upon her. 'Why pretend any more? You won't take M. Pontarlier in?'

'We all thought so really,' said Rosamund. 'And his name isn't Pontarlier – it's Hercules something.'

'Hercule Poirot – at your service.'

Poirot bowed.

There were no gasps of astonishment or of apprehension. His name seemed to mean nothing at all to them.

They were less alarmed by it than they had been by the single word '*detective.*'

'May I ask what conclusions you have come to?' asked George.

'He won't tell you darling,' said Rosamund. 'Or if he does tell you, what he says won't be true.'

Alone of all the company she appeared to be amused.

Hercule Poirot looked at her thoughtfully.

2

Hercule Poirot did not sleep well that night. He was perturbed, and he was not quite sure *why* he was perturbed. Elusive snatches of conversation, various glances, odd movements – all seemed fraught with a tantalising significance in the loneliness of the night. He was on the threshold of sleep, but sleep would not come. Just as he was about to drop off, something flashed into his mind and woke him up again. Paint – Timothy and paint. Oil paint – the smell of oil paint – connected somehow with Mr Entwhistle. Paint and Cora. Cora's paintings – picture postcards. . . . Cora was deceitful about her painting . . . No, back to Mr Entwhistle – something Mr Entwhistle had said – or was it Lanscombe? A nun who came to the house on the day that Richard Abernethie died. A nun with a moustache. A nun at Stansfield Grange – and at Lytchett St Mary. Altogether too many nuns! Rosamund looking glamorous as a nun on the stage. Rosamund – saying that he was a detective – and everyone staring at her when she had said it. That was the way that they must all have stared at Cora that day when she said 'But he was murdered, wasn't he?' What was it Helen Abernethie felt to be 'wrong' on that occasion? Helen Abernethie – leaving the past behind – going to Cyprus . . . Helen dropping the wax flowers with a crash when he had said – *what* was it he had said? He couldn't quite remember . . .

He slept then, and as he slept he dreamed . . .

He dreamed of the green malachite table. On it was the glass-covered stand of wax flowers – only the whole thing had been painted over with thick crimson oil paint. Paint the colour of blood. He could smell the paint, and Timothy was groaning, was saying 'I'm dying – dying . . . this is the end.' And Maude, standing by, tall and stern, with a large knife in her hand was echoing him, saying 'Yes, it's the end. . . .' The end – a deathbed, with candles and a nun praying. If he could just see the nun's face, he would know. . . .

Hercule Poirot woke up – and he did know!

Yes, it *was* the end. . . .

Though there was still a long way to go.

He sorted out the various bits of the mosaic.

Mr Entwhistle, the smell of paint, Timothy's house and something that must be in it – or might be in it . . . the wax flowers . . . Helen . . . Broken glass . . .

3

Helen Abernethie, in her room, took some time in going to bed. She was thinking.

Sitting in front of her dressing-table, she stared at herself unseeingly in the glass.

She had been forced into having Hercule Poirot in the house. She had not wanted it. But Mr Entwhistle had made it hard for her to refuse. And now the whole thing had come out into the open. No question any more of letting Richard Abernethie lie quiet in his grave. All started by those few words of Cora's. . . .

That day after the funeral . . . How had they all looked, she wondered? How had they looked to Cora? How had she herself looked?

What was it George had said? About seeing oneself?

There was some quotation, too. *To see ourselves as others see us.* . . . As others see us.

The eyes that were staring into the glass unseeingly suddenly focused. She was seeing herself – but not really herself – not herself as others saw her – not as Cora had seen her that day.

Her right – no, her left eyebrow was arched a little higher than the right. The mouth? No, the curve of the mouth was symmetrical. If she met herself she would surely not see much difference from this mirror image. Not like Cora.

Cora – the picture came quite clearly . . . Cora, on the day of the funeral, her head tilted sideways – asking her question – looking at Helen . . .

Suddenly Helen raised her hands to her face. She said to herself, '*It doesn't make sense . . . it can't make sense . . .*'

4

Miss Entwhistle was aroused from a delightful dream in which she was playing Piquet with Queen Mary, by the ringing of the telephone.

She tried to ignore it – but it persisted. Sleepily she raised her head from the pillow and looked at the watch beside her bed. Five minutes to seven – who on earth could be ringing up at that hour? It must be a wrong number.

The irritating ding-dong continued. Miss Entwhistle sighed, snatched up a dressing-gown and marched into the sitting-room.

'This is Kensington 675498,' she said with asperity as she picked up the receiver.

'This is Mrs Abernethie speaking. Mrs *Leo* Abernethie. Can I speak to Mr Entwhistle.?'

'Oh, good morning, Mrs Abernethie.' The 'good morning'

was not cordial. 'This is Miss Entwhistle. My brother is still asleep I'm afraid. I was asleep myself.'

'I'm so sorry,' Helen was forced to the apology. 'But it's very important that I should speak to your brother at once.'

'Wouldn't it do later?'

'I'm afraid not.'

'Oh, very well then.'

Miss Entwhistle was tart.

She tapped at her brother's door and went in.

'Those Abernethies again!' she said bitterly.

'Eh! The Abernethies?'

'Mrs Leo Abernethie. Ringing up before seven in the morning! Really!

'Mrs Leo, is it? Dear me. How remarkable. Where is my dressing-gown? Ah, thank you.'

Presently he was saying:

'Entwhistle speaking. Is that you, Helen?'

'Yes. I'm terribly sorry to get you out of bed like this. But you did tell me once to ring you up at once if I remembered what it was that struck me as having been wrong somehow on the day of the funeral when Cora electrified us all by suggesting that Richard had been murdered.'

'Ah! You *have* remembered?'

Helen said in a puzzled voice:

'Yes, but it doesn't make sense.'

'You must allow me to be the judge of that. Was it something you noticed about one of the people?'

'Yes.'

'Tell me.'

'It seems absurd.' Helen's voice sounded apologetic. 'But I'm quite sure of it. It came to me when I was looking at myself in the glass last night. Oh . . .

The little startled half cry was succeeded by a sound that came oddly through the wires – a dull heavy sound that Mr Entwhistle couldn't place at all.

He said urgently:

'Hallo – hallo – are you there? Helen, are you there? . . . Helen . . .'

21

It was not until nearly an hour later that Mr Entwhistle, after a great deal of conversation with supervisors and others, found himself at last speaking to Hercule Poirot.

'Thank heaven!' said Mr Entwhistle with pardonable exasperation. 'The Exchange seems to have had the greatest difficulty in getting the number.'

'That is not surprising. The receiver was off the hook.'

There was a grim quality in Poirot's voice which carried through to the listener.

Mr Entwhistle said sharply:

'Has something happened?'

'Yes. Mrs Leo Abernethie was found by the housemaid about twenty minutes ago lying by the telephone in the study. She was unconscious. A serious concussion.'

'Do you mean she was struck on the head?'

'I think so. It is *just* possible that she fell and struck her head on a marble doorstop, but me I do not think so, and the doctor, he does not think so either.'

'She was telephoning to me at the time. I wondered when we were cut off so suddenly.'

'So it was to you she was telephoning? What did she say?'

'She mentioned to me some time ago that on the occasion when Cora Lansquenet suggested her brother had been murdered, she herself had a feeling of something being wrong – odd – she did not quite know how to put it – unfortunately she could not remember *why* she had that impression.'

'And suddenly, she did remember?'

'Yes.'

'And rang up to tell you?'

'Yes.'

'*Eh bien?*'

'There's no *eh bien* about it,' said Mr Entwhistle testily. 'She started to tell me, but was interrupted.'

'How much had she said?'

'Nothing pertinent.'

'You will excuse me, *mon ami*, but *I* am the judge of that, not you. What exactly did she say?'

'She reminded me that I had asked her to let me know at once if she remembered what it was that had struck her as peculiar. She said she had remembered – but that it "didn't make sense."

'I asked her if it was something about one of the people who were there that day, and she said, yes, it was. She said it had come to her when she was looking in the glass—'

'Yes?'

'That was all?'

'She gave no hint as to – which of the people concerned it was?'

'I should hardly fail to let you know if she had told me *that*,' said Mr Entwhistle acidly.

'I apologise, *mon ami*. Of course you would have told me.' Mr Entwhistle said :

'We shall just have to wait until she recovers consciousness before we know.'

Poirot said gravely :

'That may not be for a very long time. Perhaps never.'

'Is it as bad as that?' Mr Entwhistle's voice shook a little.

'Yes, it is as bad as that.'

'But – that's terrible, Poirot.'

'Yes, it is terrible. And it is why we cannot afford to wait. For it shows that we have to deal with someone who is either completely ruthless or so frightened that it comes to the same thing.'

'But look here, Poirot, what about Helen? I feel worried. Are you sure she will be safe at Enderby?'

'No, she would not be safe. So she is not at Enderby. Already the ambulance has come and is taking her to a nursing home where she will have special nurses and where *no one*, family or otherwise, will be allowed in to see her.'

Mr Entwhistle sighed.

'You relieve my mind. She might have been in danger.'

'She assuredly would have been in danger !'

Mr Entwhistle's voice sounded deeply moved.

'I have a great regard for Helen Abernethie. I always have had. A woman of very exceptional character. She may have had certain – what shall I say? – reticences in her life.'

'Ah, there were reticences?'

'I have always had an idea that such was the case.'

'Hence the villa in Cyprus. Yes, that explains a good deal. . . .'

'I don't want you to begin thinking—'

'You cannot stop me thinking. But now, there is a little commission that I have for you. One moment.'

There was a pause, then Poirot's voice spoke again.

'I had to make sure that nobody was listening. All is well. Now here is what I want you to do for me. You must prepare to make a journey.'

'A journey?' Mr Entwhistle sounded faintly dismayed. 'Oh, I see – you want me to come down to Enderby?'

'Not at all. *I* am in charge here. No, you will not have to travel so far. Your journey will not take you very far from London. You will travel to Bury St Edmunds – (*Ma foi!* what names your English towns have!) and there you will hire a car and drive to Forsdyke House. It is a Mental Home. Ask for Dr Penrith and inquire of him particulars about a patient who was recently discharged.'

'What patient? Anyway, surely—'

Poirot broke in:

'The name of the patient is Gregory Banks. Find out for what form of insanity he was being treated.'

'Do you mean that Gregory Banks is insane?'

'Sh! Be careful what you say. And now – I have not yet breakfasted and you, too, I suspect have not breakfasted?'

'Not yet. I was too anxious—'

'Quite so. Then, I pray you, eat your breakfast, repose yourself. There is a good train to Bury St Edmunds at twelve o'clock. If I have any more news I will telephone you before you start.'

'Be careful of *yourself*, Poirot,' said Mr Entwhistle with some concern.

'Ah that, yes! Me, I do not want to be hit on the head with a marble doorstop. You may be assured that I will take every precaution. And now – for the moment – good-bye.'

Poirot heard the sound of the receiver being replaced at the other end, then he heard a very faint second click – and smiled to himself. Somebody had replaced the receiver on the telephone in the hall.

He went out there. There was no one about. He tiptoed to the cupboard at the back of the stairs and looked inside. At that moment Lanscombe came through the service door carrying a tray with toast and a silver coffee pot. He looked slightly surprised to see Poirot emerge from the cupboard.

'Breakfast is ready in the dining-room, sir,' he said.

Poirot surveyed him thoughtfully.

The old butler looked white and shaken.

'Courage,' said Poirot, clapping him on the shoulder. 'All

will yet be well. Would it be too much trouble to serve me a cup of coffee in my bedroom?'

'Certainly, sir. I will send Janet up with it, sir.'

Lanscombe looked disapprovingly at Hercule Poirot's back as the latter climbed the stairs. Poirot was attired in an exotic silk dressing-gown with a pattern of triangles and squares.

'Foreigners!' thought Lanscombe bitterly. 'Foreigners in the house! And Mrs Leo with concussion! I don't know what we're coming to. Nothing's the same since Mr Richard died.'

Hercule Poirot was dressed by the time he received his coffee from Janet. His murmurs of sympathy were well received, since he stressed the shock her discovery must have given her.

'Yes, indeed, sir, what I felt when I opened the door of the study and came in with the Hoover and saw Mrs Leo lying there I shall never forget. There she lay – and I made sure she was dead. She must have been taken faint as she stood at the phone – and fancy her being up at that time in the morning! I've never known her to do such a thing before.'

'Fancy, indeed!' He added casually: 'No one else was up, I suppose?'

'As it happens, sir, Mrs Timothy was up and about. She's a very early riser always – often goes for a walk before breakfast.'

'She is of the generation that rises early,' said Poirot nodding his head. 'The younger ones, now – *they* do not get up so early?'

'No, indeed, sir, all fast asleep when I brought them their tea – and very late I was, too, what with the shock and getting the doctor to come and having to have a cup first to steady myself.'

She went off and Poirot reflected on what she had said.

Maude Abernethie had been up and about, and the younger generation had been in bed – but that, Poirot reflected, meant nothing at all. Anyone could have heard Helen's door open and close, and have followed her down to listen – and would afterwards have made a point of being fast asleep in bed.

'But if I am right,' thought Poirot. 'And after all, it is natural to me to be right – it is a habit I have! – then there is no need to go into who was here and who was there. First, I must seek a proof where I have deduced the proof may be. And then – I make my little speech. And I sit back and see what happens . . .'

As soon as Janet had left the room, Poirot drained his coffee cup, put on his overcoat and his hat, left his room, ran nimbly down the back stairs and left the house by the side door. He walked briskly the quarter-mile to the post office where he demanded a trunk call. Presently he was once more speaking to Mr Entwhistle.

'Yes, it is I yet again! Pay no attention to the commission with which I entrusted you. *C'était une blague!* Someone was listening. Now, *mon vieux*, to the real commission. You must, as I said, take a train. But not to Bury St Edmunds. I want you to proceed to the house of Mr Timothy Abernethie.'

'But Timothy and Maude are at Enderby.'

'Exactly. There is no one in the house but a woman by the name of Jones who has been persuaded by the offer of considerable *largesse* to guard the house whilst they are absent. What I want you to do it to take something out of that house!'

'My dear Poirot! I really can't stoop to burglary!'

'It will not seem like burglary. You will say to the excellent Mrs Jones who knows you, that you have been asked by Mr or Mrs Abernethie to fetch this particular object and take it to London. She will not suspect anything amiss.'

'No, no, probably not. But I don't like it.' Mr Entwhistle sounded most reluctant. 'Why can't you go and get whatever it is yourself.'

'Because, my friend, I should be a stranger of foreign appearance and as such a suspicious character, and Mrs Jones would at once raise the difficulties! With you, she will not.'

'No, no – I see that. But what on earth are Timothy and Maude going to think when they hear about it? I have known them for forty odd years.'

'And you knew Richard Abernethie for that time also! And you knew Cora Lansquenet when she was a little girl!'

In a martyred voice Mr Entwhistle asked:

'You're sure this is really *necessary*, Poirot?'

'The old question they asked in wartime on the posters. *Is your journey really necessary?* I say to you, it *is* necessary. It is vital!'

'And what is this object I've got to get hold of?'

Poirot told him.

'But really, Poirot, I don't see—'

'It is not necessary for *you* to see. *I* am doing the seeing.'

'And what to you want me to do with the damned thing?'

'You will take it to London, to an address in Elm Park Gardens. If you have a pencil, note it down.'

Having done so, Mr Entwhistle said, still in his martyred voice:

'I hope you know what you are doing, Poirot?'

He sounded very doubtful – but Poirot's reply was not doubtful at all.

'Of course I know what I am doing. We are nearing the end.'

Mr Entwhistle sighed:

'If we could only guess what Helen was going to tell me.'

'No need to guess. I *know.*'

'You know? But my dear Poirot—'

'Explanations must wait. But let me assure you of this. *I know what Helen Abernethie saw when she looked in her mirror.*"

2

Breakfast had been an uneasy meal. Neither Rosamund nor Timothy had appeared, but the others were there and had talked in rather subdued tones, and eaten a little less than they normally would have done.

George was the first one to recover his spirits. His temperament was mercurial and optimistic.

'I expect Aunt Helen will be all right,' he said. 'Doctors always like to pull a long face. After all, what's concussion? Often clears up completely in a couple of days.'

'A woman I knew had concussion during the war,' said Miss Gilchrist conversationally. 'A brick or something hit her as she was walking down Tottenham Court Road – it was during fly bomb time – and she never felt *anything* at all. Just went on with what she was doing – and collapsed in a train to Liverpool twelve hours later. And would you believe it, she had no recollection at all of going to the station and catching the train or *anything*. She just couldn't understand it when she woke up in hospital. She was there for nearly three weeks.'

'What I can't make out,' said Susan, 'is what Helen was doing telephoning at that unearthly hour, and who she was telephoning to?'

'Felt ill,' said Maude with decision. 'Probably woke up feeling queer and came down to ring up the doctor. Then had a giddy fit and fell. That's the only thing that makes sense.'

'Bad luck hitting her head on that doorstop,' said Michael. 'If she'd just pitched over on to that thick pile carpet she'd have been all right.'

The door opened and Rosamund came in, frowning.

'I can't find those wax flowers,' she said. 'I mean the ones that were standing on the malachite table the day of Uncle

Richard's funeral.' She looked accusingly at Susan. '*You* haven't taken them?'

'Of course I haven't! Really, Rosamund, you're not *still* thinking about malachite tables with poor old Helen carted off to hospital with concussion?'

'I don't see why I shouldn't think about them. If you've got concussion you don't know what's happening and it doesn't matter to you. We can't do anything for Aunt Helen, and Michael and I have got to get back to London by to-morrow lunch-time because we're seeing Jackie Lygo about opening dates for *The Baronet's Progress*. So I'd like to fix up definitely about the table. But I'd like to have a look at those wax flowers again. There's a kind of Chinese vase on the table now – nice – but not nearly so period. I do wonder where they are – perhaps Lanscombe knows.'

Lanscombe had just looked in to see if they had finished breakfast.

'We're all through, Lanscombe,' said George getting up. 'What's happened to our foreign friend?'

'He is having his coffee and toast served upstairs, sir.'

'*Petit dejeuner* for N.A.R.C.O.'

'Lanscombe, do you know where those wax flowers are that used to be on that green table in the drawing-room?' asked Rosamund.

'I understand Mrs Leo had an accident with them, ma'am. She was going to have a new glass shade made, but I don't think she has seen about it yet.'

'Then where is the thing?'

'It would probably be in the cupboard behind the staircase, ma'am. That is where things are usually placed when awaiting repair. Shall I ascertain for you?'

'I'll go and look myself. Come with me, Michael sweetie. It's dark there, and I'm not going in any dark corners by myself after what happened to Aunt Helen.'

Everybody showed a sharp reaction. Maude demanded in her deep voice:

'What *do* you mean, Rosamund?'

'Well, she was coshed by someone, wasn't she?'

Gregory Banks said sharply:

'She was taken suddenly faint and fell.'

Rosamund laughed.

'Did she tell you so? Don't be silly, Greg, of course she was coshed.'

George said sharply:

'You shouldn't say things like that, Rosamund.'

'Nonsense,' said Rosamund. 'She *must* have been. I mean, it all adds up. A detective in the house looking for clues, and Uncle Richard poisoned, and Aunt Cora killed with a hatchet, and Miss Gilchrist given poisoned wedding cake, and now Aunt Helen struck down with a blunt instrument. You'll see, it will go on like that. One after another of us will be killed and the one that's left will be It – the murderer, I mean. But it's not going to be *me* – who's killed, I mean.'

'And why should anyone want to kill you, beautiful Rosamund?' asked George lightly.

Rosamund opened her eyes very wide.

'Oh,' she said. 'Because I know too much, of course.'

'What do you know?' Maude Abernethie and Gregory Banks spoke almost in unison.

Rosamund gave her vacant and angelic smile.

'Wouldn't you all like to know?' she said agreeably. 'Come on Michael.'

22

At eleven o'clock Hercule Poirot called an informal meeting in the library. Everyone was there and Poirot looked thoughtfully round the semi-circle of faces.

'Last night,' he said, 'Mrs Shane announced to you that I was a private detective. For myself, I hoped to retain my – *camouflage*, shall we say? – a little longer. But no matter! To-day – or at most the day after – I would have told you the truth. Please listen carefully now to what I have to say.

'I am in my own line a celebrated person – I may say a *most* celebrated person. My gifts, in fact, are unequalled!'

George Crossfield grinned and said:

'That's the stuff, M. Pont – no, it's M. Poirot, isn't it? Funny, isn't it, that I've never even heard of you?'

'It is not funny,' said Poirot severely. 'It is lamentable! Alas, there is no proper education nowadays. Apparently one learns nothing but economics – and how to set Intelligence Tests! But to continue. I have been a friend for many years of Mr Entwhistle's—'

'So *he's* the nigger in the wood pile!'

'If you like to put it that way, Mr Crossfield. Mr Entwhistle was greatly upset by the death of his old friend, Mr Richard Abernethie. He was particularly perturbed by some words spoken on the day of the funeral by Mr Abernethie's sister, Mrs Lansquenet. Words spoken in this very room.'

'Very silly – and just like Cora,' said Maude. 'Mr Entwhistle should have had more sense than to pay attention to them!'

Poirot went on:

'Mr Entwhistle was even more perturbed after the – the coincidence, shall I say? – of Mrs Lansquenet's death. He wanted one thing only – to be assured that that death *was* a coincidence. In other words he wanted to feel assured that Richard Abernethie had died a natural death. To that end he commissioned me to make the necessary investigations.'

There was a pause.

'I have made them . . .'

Again there was a pause. No one spoke.

Poirot threw back his head.

'*Eh bien*, you will all be delighted to hear that as a result of my investigations – *there is absolutely no reason to believe that Mr Abernethie died anything but a natural death*. There is no reason *at all* to believe that he was murdered!' He smiled. He threw out his hands in a triumphant gesture.

'That is good news, is it not?'

It hardly seemed to be, by the way they took it. They stared at him and in all but the eyes of one person there still seemed to be doubt and suspicion.

The exception was Timothy Abernethie, who was nodding his head in violent agreement.

'Of course Richard wasn't murdered,' he said angrily. 'Never could understand why anybody even thought of such a thing for a moment! Just Cora up to her tricks, that was all. Wanting to give you all a scare. Her idea of being funny. Truth is that although she was my own sister, she was always a bit mental, poor girl. Well, Mr whatever your name is, I'm glad you've had the sense to come to the right conclusion, though if you ask me, I call it damned cheek of Entwhistle to go commissioning you to come prying and poking about. And if he thinks he's going to charge the estate with your fee, I can tell you he won't get away with it! Damned cheek, and most uncalled for! Who's Entwhistle to set himself up? If the family's satisfied—'

'But the family wasn't, Uncle Timothy,' said Rosamund.

'Hey – what's that?'

Timothy peered at her under beetling brows of displeasure.

'We weren't satisfied. And what about Aunt Helen this morning?'

Maude said sharply:

'Helen's just the age when you're liable to get a stroke. That's all there is to that.'

'I see,' said Rosamund. 'Another coincidence, you think?'

She looked at Poirot.

'Aren't there rather too many coincidences?'

'Coincidences,' said Hercule Poirot, 'do happen.'

'Nonsense,' said Maude. 'Helen felt ill, came down and rang up the doctor, and then—'

'But she didn't ring up the doctor,' said Rosamund. 'I asked him—'

Susan said sharply:

'Who did she ring up?'

'I don't know,' said Rosamund, a shade of vexation passing over her face. 'But I dare say I can find out,' she added hopefully.

2

Hercule Poirot was sitting in the Victorian summer-house. He drew his large watch from his pocket and laid it on the table in front of him.

He had announced that he was leaving by the twelve o'clock train. There was still half an hour to go. Half an hour for someone to make up their minds and come to him. Perhaps more than one person. . . .

The summer-house was clearly visible from most of the windows of the house. Surely, soon, someone would come?

If not, his knowledge of human nature was deficient, and his main premises incorrect.

He waited – and above his head a spider in its web waited for a fly.

It was Miss Gilchrist who came first. She was flustered and upset and rather incoherent.

'Oh, Mr Pontarlier – I can't remember your other name,' she said. 'I had to come and speak to you although I *don't* like doing it – but really I feel I *ought* to. I mean, after what happened to poor Mrs Leo this morning – and I think myself Mrs Shane was *quite right* – and *not* coincidence, and certainly not a *stroke* – as Mrs Timothy suggested, because my own father had a stroke and it was quite a different appearance, and anyway the doctor *said* concussion quite clearly!'

She paused, took breath and looked at Poirot with appealing eyes.

'Yes,' said Poirot gently and encouragingly. 'You want to tell me something?'

'As I say, I don't like doing it – because she's been so kind. She found me the position with Mrs Timothy and everything. She's been really *very* kind. That's why I feel so ungrateful. And even gave me Mrs Lansquenet's musquash jacket which is really *most* handsome and fits beautifully because it never matters if fur is a little on the large side. And when I wanted to return her the amethyst brooch she wouldn't hear of it—'

'You are referring,' said Poirot gently, 'to Mrs Banks?'

'Yes, you see—' Miss Gilchrist looked down, twisting her fingers unhappily. She looked up and said with a sudden gulp: 'You see, I *listened*!'

'You mean you happened to overhear a conversation—'

'No.' Miss Gilchrist shook her head with an air of heroic determination. 'I'd rather speak the truth. And it's not so bad telling you because you're not English.'

Hercule Poirot understood her without taking offence.

'You mean that to a foreigner it is natural that people should listen at doors and open letters, or read letters that are left about?'

'Oh, I'd never open anybody else's letters,' said Miss Gilchrist in a shocked tone. 'Not *that*. But I *did* listen that day – the day that Mr Richard Abernethie came down to see his sister. I was curious, you know, about his turning up suddenly after all those years. And I did wonder why – and – and – you see when you haven't much life of your own or very many friends, you do tend to get interested – when you're living *with* anybody, I mean.'

'Most natural,' said Poirot.

'Yes, I do think it was natural . . . Though not, of course, at all *right*. But I did it! And I heard what he said!'

'You heard what Mr Abernethie said to Mrs Lansquenet?'

'Yes. He said something like – "It's no good talking to Timothy. He pooh-poohs everything. Simply won't listen. But I thought I'd like to get it off my chest to you, Cora. We three are the only ones left. And though you've always liked to play the simpleton you've got a lot of common sense. So what would *you* do about it, if you were me?"

'I couldn't quite hear what Mrs Lansquenet said, but I caught the word *police* – and then Mr Abernethie burst out quite loud, and said, "I can't do that. Not when it's a question of *my own niece.*" And then I had to run in the kitchen for something boiling over and when I got back Mr Abernethie was saying, "Even if I die an unnatural death I don't want the police called in, if it can possibly be avoided. You understand that, don't you my dear girl? But don't worry. Now that I *know*, I shall take all possible precautions." And he went on, saying he'd made a new will, and that she, Cora, would be quite all right. And then he said about her having been happy with her husband and how perhaps he'd made a mistake over that in the past.'

Miss Gilchrist stopped.

Poirot said : 'I see – I see . . .'

'But I never wanted to say – to tell. I didn't think Mrs Lansquenet would have wanted me to . . . But now – after Mrs Leo being attacked this morning – and then you saying so calmly it was coincidence. But, oh, M. Pontarlier, it *wasn't* co-incidence!'

Poirot smiled. He said :

'No, it wasn't coincidence. . . . Thank you, Miss Gilchrist, for coming to me. It was very necessary that you should.'

3

He had a little difficulty in getting rid of Miss Gilchrist, and it was urgent that he should, for he hoped for further confidences.

His instinct was right. Miss Gilchrist had hardly gone before Gregory Banks, striding across the lawn, came impetuously into the summer-house. His face was pale and there were beads of perspiration on his forehead. His eyes were curiously excited.

'At last!' he said. 'I thought that stupid woman would never go. You're all wrong in what you said this morning. You're wrong about everything. Richard Abernethie *was* killed. *I* killed him.'

Hercule Poirot let his eyes move up and down over the excited young man. He showed no surprise.

'So you killed him, did you? How?'

Gregory Banks smiled.

'It wasn't difficult for *me*. You can surely realise that. There were fifteen or twenty different drugs I could lay my hands on that would do it. The method of administration took rather more thinking out, but I hit on a very ingenious idea in the end. The beauty of it was that *I* didn't need to be anywhere near at the time.'

'Clever,' said Poirot.

'Yes.' Gregory Banks cast his eyes down modestly. He seemed pleased. 'Yes – I *do* think it was ingenious.'

Poirot asked with interest:

'Why did you kill him? For the money that would come to your wife?'

'No. No, of course not.' Greg was suddenly excitely indignant. 'I'm not a money grubber. I didn't marry Susan for her *money*!'

'Didn't you, Mr Banks?

'That's what *he* thought,' Greg said with sudden venom. 'Richard Abernethie! He liked Susan, he admired her, he was proud of her as an example of Abernethie blood! But he thought she'd married beneath her – he thought *I* was no good – he despised me! I dare say I hadn't the right accent – I didn't wear my clothes the right way. He was a snob – a filthy snob!'

'I don't think so,' said Poirot mildly. 'From all I have heard, Richard Abernethie was no snob.'

'He was. He was.' The young man spoke with something approaching hysteria. 'He thought nothing of me. He sneered at me – always very polite but underneath I could *see* that he didn't like me!'

'Possibly.'

'People can't treat me like that and get away with it! They've tried it before! A woman who used to come and have her medicines made up. She was rude to me. Do you know what I did?'

'Yes,' said Poirot.

Gregory looked startled.

'So you know that?'

'Yes.'

'She nearly died.' He spoke in a satisfied manner. 'That shows you I'm not the sort of person to be trifled with! Richard Abernethie despised me – and what happened to him? He died.'

'A most successful murder,' said Poirot with grave congratulation.

He added: 'But why come and give yourself away – to me?'

'Because you said you were through with it all! You said he *hadn't* been murdered. I had to show you that you're not as clever as you think you are – and besides – besides—'

'Yes,' said Poirot. 'And besides?'

Greg collapsed suddenly on to the bench. His face changed. It took on a sudden ecstatic quality.

'It was wrong – wicked . . . I must be punished . . . I must go back there – to the place of punishment . . . to atone . . . Yes, to *atone*! Repentance! Retribution!'

His face was alight now with a kind of glowing ecstasy. Poirot studied him for a moment or two curiously.

Then he asked:

'How badly do you want to get away from your wife?'

Gregory's face changed.

'Susan? Susan is wonderful – wonderful!'

'Yes. Susan is wonderful. That is a grave burden. Susan loves you devotedly. That is a burden, too?'

Gregory sat looking in front of him. Then he said, rather in the manner of a sulky child:

'Why couldn't she let me alone?'

He sprang up.

'She's coming now – across the lawn. I'll go now. But you'll tell her what I told you? Tell her I've gone to the police station. To confess.'

4

Susan came in breathlessly.

'Where's Greg? He was here! I saw him.'

'Yes.' Poirot paused a moment – before saying: 'He came to tell me that it was he who poisoned Richard Abernethie. . . .'

'What absolute *nonsense*! You didn't believe him, I hope?'

'Why should I not believe him?'

'He wasn't even near this place when Uncle Richard died!'

'Perhaps not. Where was he when Cora Lansquenet died?'

'In London. We both were.'

Hercule Poirot shook his head.

'No, no, that will not do. You, for instance, took out your car that day and were away all the afternoon. I think I know where you went. You went to Lytchett St Mary.'

'I did no such thing!'

Poirot smiled.

'When I first met you here, Madame, it was not, as I told you, the first time I had seen you. After the inquest on Mrs Lansquenet you were in the garage of the King's Arms. You talk there to a mechanic and close by you is a car containing an elderly foreign gentleman. You did not notice him, but he noticed you.'

'I don't see what you mean. That was the day of the inquest.'

'Ah, but remember what that mechanic said to you! He asked you if you were a relative of the victim, and you said you were her niece.'

'He was just being a ghoul. They're all ghouls.'

'And his next words were, "Ah, wondered where I'd seen you before." Where did he see you before, Madame? It must have been in Lytchett St Mary, since in his mind his seeing you before was accounted for by your being Mrs Lansquenet's niece. Had he seen you near her cottage? And when? It was a matter, was it not, that demands inquiry. And the result of the inquiry is, that you were there – in Lytchett St Mary – on the afternoon Cora Lansquenet died. You parked your car in the same quarry where you left it the morning of the inquest. The car was seen and the number was noted. By this time Inspector Morton knows whose car it was.'

Susan stared at him. Her breath came rather fast, but she showed no signs of discomposure.

'You're talking nonsense, M. Poirot. And you're making me forget what I came here to say – I wanted to try and find you alone—'

'To confess to me it was you and not your husband who committed the murder?'

'No, of course not. What kind of fool do you think I am? And I've already told you that Gregory never left London that day.'

'A fact which you cannot possibly know since you were away yourself. Why did you go down to Lytchett St Mary, Mrs Banks?'

Susan drew a deep breath.

'All right, if you must have it! What Cora said at the funeral worried me. I kept on thinking about it. Finally I decided to run down in the car and see her, and ask her what had put the idea into her head. Greg thought it a silly idea, so I didn't even tell him where I was going. I got there about three o'clock, knocked and rang, but there was no answer, so I thought she must be out or gone away. That's all there is to it. I didn't go round to the back of the cottage. If I had, I might have seen the broken window. I just went back to London without the faintest idea there was anything wrong.'

Poirot's face was non-committal. He said:

'Why does your husband accuse himself of the crime?'

'Because he's—' a word trembled on Susan's tongue and was rejected. Poirot seized on it.

'You were going to say "because he is batty" speaking in jest – but the jest was too near the truth, was it not?'

'Greg's all right. He is. He *is*.'

'I know something of his history,' said Poirot. 'He was for some months in Forsdyke House Mental Home before you met him.'

'He was never certified. He was a voluntary patient.'

'That is true. He is not, I agree, to be classed as insane. But he is, very definitely, unbalanced. He has a punishment complex – has had it, I suspect, since infancy.'

Susan spoke quickly and eagerly:

'You don't understand, M. Poirot. Greg has never had a *chance*. That's why I wanted Uncle Richard's money so badly. Uncle Richard was so matter-of-fact. He couldn't understand. I knew Greg had got to set up for himself. He had got to feel he was *someone* – not just a chemist's assistant, being pushed around. Everything will be different now. He will have his own laboratory. He can work out his own formulas.'

'Yes, yes – you will give him the earth – because you love him. Love him too much for safety or for happiness. But you cannot give to people what they are incapable of receiving. At the end of it all, he will still be something that he does not want to be. . . .'

'What's that?'

'*Susan's husband.*'

'How cruel you are! And what nonsense you talk!'

'Where Gregory Banks is concerned you are unscrupulous. You wanted your uncle's money – not for yourself – but for your husband. *How badly did you want it?*'

Angrily, Susan turned and dashed away.

5

'I thought,' said Michael Shane lightly, 'that I'd just come along and say goodbye.'

He smiled, and his smile had a singularly intoxicating quality.

Poirot was aware of the man's vital charm.

He studied Michael Shane for some moments in silence. He felt as though he knew this man least well of all the house party, for Michael Shane only showed the side of himself that he wanted to show.

'Your wife,' said Poirot conversationally, 'is a very unusual woman.'

Michael raised his eyebrows.

'Do you think so? She's a lovely, I agree. But not, or so I've found, conspicuous for brains.'

'She will never try to be too clever,' Poirot agreed. 'But she knows what she wants.' He sighed. 'So few people do.'

'Ah!' Michael's smile broke out again. 'Thinking of the malachite table?'

'Perhaps.' Poirot paused and added: *'And of what was on it.'*

'The wax flowers, you mean?'

'The wax flowers.'

Michael frowned.

'I don't always quite understand you, M. Poirot. However,' the smile was switched on again. 'I'm more thankful than I can say that we're all out of the wood. It's unpleasant, to say the least of it, to go around with the suspicion that somehow or other one of us murdered poor old Uncle Richard.'

'That is how he seemed to you when you met him?' Poirot inquired. 'Poor old Uncle Richard?'

'Of course he was very well preserved and all that—'

'And in full possession of his faculties—'

'Oh yes.'

'And, in fact, quite *shrewd*?'

'I dare say.'

'A shrewd judge of character.'

The smile remained unaltered.

'You can't expect me to agree with *that*, M. Poirot. He didn't approve of *me*.'

'He thought you, perhaps, the unfaithful type?' Poirot suggested.

Michael laughed.

'What an old-fashioned idea!'

'But it is true, isn't it?'

'Now I wonder what you meant by *that*?'

Poirot placed the tips of his fingers together.

'There have been inquiries made, you know,' he murmured.

'By you?'

'Not only by me.'

Michael Shane gave him a quick searching glance. His

reactions, Poirot noted, were quick. Michael Shane was no fool.

'You mean – the police are interested?'

'They have never been quite satisfied, you know, to regard the murder of Cora Lansquenet as a casual crime.'

'And they've been making inquiries about me?'

Poirot said primly:

'They are interested in the movements of Mrs Lansquenet's relations on the day that she was killed.'

'That's extremely awkward.' Michael spoke with a charming confidential rueful air.

'Is it, Mr Shane?'

'More so than you can imagine! I told Rosamund, you see, that I was lunching with a certain Oscar Lewis on that day.'

'When, in actual fact, you were not?'

'No. Actually I motored down to see a woman called Sorrel Dainton – quite a well-known actress. I was with her in her last show. Rather awkward, you see – for though it's quite satisfactory as far as the police are concerned, it won't go down very well with Rosamund.'

'Ah!' Poirot loked discreet. 'There has been a little trouble over this friendship of yours?'

'Yes . . . In fact – Rosamund made me promise I wouldn't see her any more.'

'Yes, I can see that may be awkward . . . *Entre nous*, you had an affair with the lady?'

'Oh, just one of those things! It's not as though I cared for the woman at all.'

'But she cares for you?'

'Well, she's been rather tiresome . . . Women do cling so. However, as you say, the police at any rate will be satisfied.'

'You think so?'

'Well, I could hardly be taking a hatchet to Cora if I was dallying with Sorrel miles and miles away. She's got a cottage in Kent.'

'I see – I see – and this Miss Dainton, she will testify for you?'

'She won't like it – but as it's murder, I suppose she'll have to do it.'

'She will do it, perhaps, even if you were *not* dallying with her.'

'What do you mean?' Michael looked suddenly black as thunder.

'The lady is fond of you. When they are fond, women will swear to what is true – and also to what is untrue.'

'Do you mean to say that you don't believe me?'

'It does not matter if *I* believe you or not. It is not *I* you have to satisfy.'

'Who then?'

'Inspector Morton – who has just come out on the terrace through the side door.'

Michael Shane wheeled round sharply.

23

'I heard you were here, M. Poirot,' said Inspector Morton.

The two men were pacing the terrace together.

'I came over with Superintendent Parwell from Matchfield. Dr Larraby rang him up about Mrs Leo Abernethie and he's come over here to make a few inquiries. The doctor wasn't satisfied.'

'And you, my friend,' inquired Poirot, 'where do you come in? You are a long way from your native Berkshire.'

'I wanted to ask a few questions – and the people I wanted to ask them of seemed very conveniently assembled here.' He paused before adding, 'Your doing?'

'Yes, my doing.'

'And as a result Mrs Leo Abernethie gets knocked out.'

'You must not blame me for that. If she had come to *me* . . . But she did not. Instead she rang up her lawyer in London.'

'And was in the process of spilling the beans to him when – Wonk!'

'When – as you say – Wonk!'

'And what had she managed to tell him?'

'Very little. She had only got as far as telling him that she was looking at herself in the glass.'

'Ah! well,' said Inspector Morton philosophically. 'Women will do it.' He looked sharply at Poirot. 'That suggests something to you?'

'Yes, I think I know what it was she was going to tell him.'

'Wonderful guesser, aren't you? You always were. Well, what was it?'

'Excuse me, are you inquiring into the death of Richard Abernethie?'

'Officially, no. Actually, of course, if it has a bearing on the murder of Mrs Lansquenet—'

'It has a bearing on that, yes. But I will ask you, my friend, to give me a few more hours. I shall know by then if what I have imagined – imagined only, you comprehend – is correct. If it *is*—'

'Well, if is is?'

'Then I may be able to place in your hands a piece of concrete evidence.'

'We could certainly do with it,' said Inspector Morton with feeling. He looked askance at Poirot. 'What have you been holding back?'

'Nothing. Absolutely nothing. Since the piece of evidence I have imagined may not in fact exist. I have only deduced its existence from various scraps of conversation. I may,' said Poirot in a completely unconvinced tone, 'be wrong.'

Morton smiled.

'But that doesn't often happen to you?'

'No. Though I will admit – yes, I am forced to admit – that it *has* happened to me.'

'I must say I'm glad to hear it! To be always right must be sometimes monotonous.'

'I do not find it so,' Poirot assured him.

Inspector Morton laughed.

'And you're asking me to hold off with my questioning?'

'No, no, not at all. Proceed as you had planned to do. I suppose you were not actually contemplating an arrest?'

Morton shook his head.

'Much too flimsy for that. We'd have to get a decision from the Public Prosecutor first – and we're a long way from that No, just statements from certain parties of their movements on the day in question – in one case with a caution, perhaps.'

'I see. Mrs Banks?'

'Smart, aren't you? Yes. She was there that day. Her car was parked in that quarry.'

'She was not seen actually *driving* the car?'

'No.'

The Inspector added, 'It's bad you know, that she's never said a word about being down there that day. She's got to explain that satisfactorily.'

'She is quite skilful at explanations,' said Poirot dryly.

'Yes. Clever young lady. Perhaps a thought too clever.'

'It is never wise to be too clever. That is how murderers get caught. Has anything more come up about George Crossfield?'

'Nothing definite. He's a very ordinary type. There are a lot of young men like him going about the country in trains and buses or on bicycles. People find it hard to remember when a week or so has gone by if it was Wednesday or Thursday when they were at a certain place or noticed a certain person.'

He paused and went on: 'We've had one piece of rather curious information – from the Mother Superior of some convent or other. Two of her nuns had been out collecting from door to door. It seems that they went to Mrs Lansquenet's cottage on the day *before* she was murdered, but couldn't make anyone hear when they knocked and rang. That's natural enough – she was up North at the Abernethie funeral and Gilchrist had been given the day off and had gone on an excursion to Bournemouth. The point is that they say *there was someone in the cottage*. They say they heard sighs and groans. I've queried whether it wasn't a day later but the Mother Superior is quite definite that that couldn't be so. It's all entered up in some book. Was there someone searching for something in the cottage that day, who seized the opportunity of both the women being away? And did that somebody not find what he or she was looking for and come back the next day? I don't set much store on the sighs and still less on the groans. Even nuns are suggestible and a cottage where murder has occurred positively *asks* for groans. The point is, was there someone in the cottage who shouldn't have been there? And if so, who was it? All the Abernethie crowd were at the funeral.'

Poirot asked a seemingly irrelevant question:

'These nuns who were collecting in that district, did they return at all at a later date to try again?'

'As a matter of fact they did come again – about a week later. Actually on the day of the inquest, I believe.'

'That fits,' said Hercule Poirot. 'That fits very well.'

Inspector Morton looked at him.

'Why this interest in nuns?'

'They have been forced on my attention whether I will or no. It will not have escaped your attention, Inspector, that the visit of the nuns was the same day that poisoned wedding cake found its way into that cottage.'

'You don't think— Surely that's a ridiculous idea?'

'My ideas are never ridiculous,' said Hercule Poirot severely. 'And now, *mon cher*, I must leave you to your questions and to the inquiries into the attack on Mrs Abernethie. I myself must go in search of the late Richard Abernethie's niece.'

'Now be careful what you go saying to Mrs Banks.'

'I do not mean Mrs Banks. I mean Richard Abernethie's other niece.'

2

Poirot found Rosamund sitting on a bench overlooking a little stream that cascaded down in a waterfall and then flowed through rhododendron thickets. She was staring into the water.

'I do not, I trust, disturb an Ophelia,' said Poirot as he took his seat beside her. 'You are, perhaps, studying the *rôle*?'

'I've never played in Shakespeare,' said Rosamund. 'Except once in Rep. I was Jessica in *The Merchant*. A lousy part.'

'Yet not without pathos. "*I am never merry when I hear sweet music.*" What a load she carried, poor Jessica, the daughter of the hated and despised Jew. What doubts of herself she must have had when she brought with her her father's ducats when she ran away to her lover. Jessica with gold was one thing – Jessica without gold might have been another.'

Rosamund turned her head to look at him.

'I thought you'd gone,' she said with a touch of reproach. She glanced down at her wrist-watch. 'It's past twelve o'clock.'

'I have missed my train,' said Poirot.

'Why?'

'You think I missed it for a reason?'

'I suppose so. You're rather precise, aren't you? If you wanted to catch a train, I should think you'd catch it.'

'Your judgment is admirable. Do you know, Madame, I have been sitting in the little summer-house hoping that you would, perhaps, pay me a visit there?'

Rosamund stared at him.

'Why should I? You more or less said good-bye to us all in the library.'

'Quite so. And there was nothing – *you* wanted to say to *me*?'

'No.' Rosamund shook her head. 'I had a lot I wanted to think about. Important things.'

'I see.'

'I don't often do much thinking,' said Rosamund. 'It seems a waste of time. But this *is* important. I think one ought to plan one's life just as one wants it to be.'

'And that is what you are doing?'

'Well, yes . . . I was trying to make a decision about something.'

'About your husband?'

'In a way.'

Poirot waited a moment, then he said:

'Inspector Morton has just arrived here.' He anticipated Rosamund's question by going on: 'He is the police officer in charge of the inquiries about Mrs Lansquenet's death. He has come here to get statements from you all about what you were doing on the day she was murdered.'

'I see. *Alibis*,' said Rosamund cheerfully.

Her beautiful face relaxed into an impish glee.

'That will be hell for Michael,' she said. 'He thinks I don't really know he went off to be with that woman that day.'

'How did you know?'

'It was obvious from the *way* he said he was going to lunch with Oscar. So frightfully casually, you know, and his nose twitching just a tiny bit like it always does when he tells lies.'

'How devoutly thankful I am I am not married to you, Madame!'

'And then, of course, I made sure by ringing up Oscar' continued Rosamund. 'Men always tell such silly lies.'

'He is not, I fear, a very faithful husband?' Poirot hazarded.

Rosamund, however, did not reject the statement.

'No.'

'But you do not mind?'

'Well, it's rather fun in a way,' said Rosamund. 'I mean, having a husband that all the other women want to snatch away from you. I should hate to be married to a man that nobody wanted – like poor Susan. Really Greg is so completely wet!'

Poirot was studying her.

'And suppose someone did succeed – in snatching your husband away from you?'

'They won't,' said Rosamund. 'Not now,' she added.

'You mean'—

'Not now that there's Uncle Richard's money. Michael falls for these creatures in a way – that Sorrel Dainton woman nearly got her hooks into him – wanted him for keeps – but with Michael the show will always come first. He can launch out now in a big way – put his own shows on. Do some production as well as acting. He's ambitious, you know, and he really is good. Not like me. I adore acting – but I'm ham, though I look nice. No, I'm not worried about Michael any more. Because it's my money, you see.'

Her eyes met Poirot's calmly. He thought how strange it was that both Richard Abernethie's nieces should have fallen deeply in love with men who were incapable of returning that love. And yet Rosamund was unusually beautiful and Susan was attractive and full of sex appeal. Susan needed and clung to the illusion that Gregory loved her. Rosamund, clear-sighted, had no illusions at all, but knew what she wanted.

'The point is,' said Rosamund, 'that I've got to make a big decision – about the future. Michael doesn't know yet.' Her face curved into a smile. 'He found out that I wasn't shopping that day and he's madly suspicious about Regent's Park.'

'What is this about Regent's Park?' Poirot looked puzzled.

'I went there, you see, after Harley Street. Just to walk about and think. Naturally Michael thinks that if I went there at all, I went to meet some man!'

Rosamund smiled beatifically and added:

'He didn't like that *at all*!'

'But why should you not go to Regent's Park?' asked Poirot.

'Just to walk there, you mean?'

'Yes. Have you never done it before?'

'Never. Why should I? What is there to go to Regent's Park *for*?'

Poirot looked at her and said:

'For you – nothing.'

He added:

'I think, Madame, that you must cede the green malachite table to your cousin Susan.'

Rosamund's eyes opened very wide.

'Why should I? I *want* it.'

'I know. I know. But you – you will keep your husband. And the poor Susan, she will lose hers.'

'Lose him? Do you mean Greg's going off with someone? I wouldn't have believed it of him. He looks so *wet*.'

'Infidelity is not the only way of losing a husband, Madame.'

'You don't mean—?' Rosamund stared at him. 'You're not thinking that Greg poisoned Uncle Richard and killed Aunt Cora and conked Aunt Helen on the head? That's ridiculous. Even *I* know better than that.'

'Who did, then?'

'George, of course. George is a wrong un, you know, he's mixed up in some sort of currency swindle – I heard about it from some friends of mine who were in Monte. I expect Uncle Richard got to know about it and was just going to cut him out of his will.'

Rosamund added complacently:

'I've always known it was George.'

—— 24 ——

The telegram came about six o'clock that evening.

As specially requested it was delivered by hand, not telephoned, and Hercule Poirot, who had been hovering for some time in the neighbourhood of the front door, was at hand to receive it from Lanscombe as the latter took it from the telegraph boy.

He tore it open with somewhat less than his usual precision. It consisted of three words and a signature.

Poirot gave vent to an enormous sigh of relief.

Then he took a pound note from his pocket and handed it to the dumbfounded boy.

'There are moments,' he said to Lanscombe, 'when economy should be abandoned.'

'Very possibly, sir,' said Lanscombe politely.

'Where is Inspector Morton?' asked Poirot.

'One of the police gentlemen,' Lanscombe spoke with distaste – and indicated subtly that such things as names for police officers were impossible to remember – 'has left. The other is, I believe, in the study.'

'Splendid,' said Poirot. 'I join him immediately.'

He once more clapped Lanscombe on the shoulder and said:

'Courage, we are on the point of arriving!'

Lanscombe looked slightly bewildered since departures, and not arrivals, had been in his mind.

He said:

'You do not, then, propose to leave by the nine-thirty train after all, sir?'

'Do not lose hope,' Poirot told him.

Poirot moved away, then wheeling round, he asked:

'I wonder, can you remember what were the first words Mrs Lansquenet said to you when she arrived here on the day of your master's funeral?'

'I remember very well, sir,' said Lanscombe, his face lighting up. 'Miss Cora – I beg pardon, Mrs Lansquenet – I always think of her as Miss Cora, somehow—'

'Very naturally.'

'She said to me: "Hallo, Lanscombe. It's a long time since you used to bring us our meringues to the huts." All the children used to have a hut of their own – down by the fence in the Park. In summer, when there was going to be a dinner party, I used to take the young ladies and gentlemen – the younger ones, you understand, sir – some meringues. Miss Cora, sir, was always very fond of her food.'

Poirot nodded.

'Yes,' he said, 'that was as I thought. Yes, it was very typical, that.'

He went into the study to find Inspector Morton and without a word handed him the telegram.

Morton read it blankly.

'I don't understand a word of this.'

'The time has come to tell you all.'

Inspector Morton grinned.

'You sound like a young lady in a Victorian melodrama. But it's about time you came across with something. I can't hold out on this set-up much longer. That Banks fellow is still insisting that he poisoned Richard Abernethie and boasting that we can't find out how. What beats me is why there's always somebody who comes forward when there's a murder and yells out that they did it! What do they think there is in it for them? I've never been able to fathom that.'

'In this case, probably shelter from the difficulties of being responsible for oneself – in other words – Forsdyke Sanatorium.'

'More likely to be Broadmoor.'

'That might be equally satisfactory.'

'*Did* he do it, Poirot? The Gilchrist woman came out with the story she'd already told you and it would fit with what Richard Abernethie said about his niece. If her husband did it, it would involve her. Somehow, you know, I can't visualise that girl committing a lot of crimes. But there's nothing she wouldn't do to try and cover *him*.'

'I will tell you all—'

'Yes, yes, tell me all! And for the Lord's sake hurry up and do it!'

This time it was in the big drawing-room that Hercule Poirot assembled his audience.

There was amusement rather than tension in the faces that were turned towards him. Menace had materialised in the shape of Inspector Morton and Superintendent Parwell. With the police in charge, questioning, asking for statements, Hercule Poirot, private detective, had receded into something closely resembling a joke.

Timothy was not far from voicing the general feeling when he remarked in an audible *sotto voce* to his wife:

'Damned little mountebank! Entwhistle must be *gaga*! — that's all I can say.'

It looked as though Hercule Poirot would have to work hard to make his proper effect.

He began in a slightly pompous manner.

'For the second time, I announce my departure! This morning I announced it for the twelve o'clock train. This evening I announce it for the nine-thirty — immediately, that is, after dinner. I go because there is nothing more here for me to do.'

'Could have told him that all along.' Timothy's commentary was still in evidence. 'Never was anything for him to do. The cheek of these fellows!'

'I came here originally to solve a riddle. The riddle is solved. Let me, first, go over the various points which were brought to my attention by the excellent Mr Entwhistle.

'First, Mr Richard Abernethie dies suddenly. Secondly, after his funeral, his sister Cora Lansquenet says, "He was murdered, wasn't he?" Thirdly Mrs Lansquenet is killed. The question is, are those three things part of a *sequence*? Let us observe what happens next? Miss Gilchrist, the dead woman's companion, is taken ill after eating a piece of wedding cake which contains arsenic. That, then, is the *next* step in the sequence.

'Now, as I told you this morning, in the course of my inquiries I have come across nothing — nothing at all, to substantiate the belief that Mr Abernethie was poisoned. Equally I may say, I have found nothing to prove conclusively that he was *not* poisoned. But as we proceed, things become easier. Cora Lansquenet undoubtedly asked that sensational question at the funeral. Everyone agrees upon *that*. And undoubtedly, on the following day, Mrs Lansquenet was murdered — a hatchet being the instrument employed. Now let us examine the fourth happening. The local post van driver is strongly of the belief – though he will not definitely swear to it – that he did not deliver that parcel of wedding cake in the usual way. And if that is so, then the parcel was left by hand and though we cannot exclude a "person unknown" – we must take particular notice of those people who were actually on the spot and in a position to put the parcel where it was subsequently found. Those were: Miss Gilchrist herself, of course; Susan Banks who came down that day for the inquest; Mr Entwhistle (but yes, we must consider Mr Entwhistle; he was present, remember, when Cora made her disquieting remark!) And there were two other people. An old gentleman who represented himself to be a Mr Guthrie, an art critic, and a nun or nuns who called early that morning to collect a subscription.

'Now I decided that I would start on the assumption that the postal van driver's recollection was correct. Therefore the little group of people under suspicion must be very carefully studied. Miss Gilchrist did not benefit in any way by Richard Abernethie's death and in only a very minute degree by Mrs Lansquenet's – in actual fact the death of the latter put her out of employment and left her with the possibility of finding it difficult to get new employment. Also Miss Gilchrist was taken to hospital definitely suffering from arsenical poisoning.

'Susan Banks *did* benefit from Richard Abernethie's death and in a small degree from Mrs Lansquenet's – though here her motive must almost certainly have been security. She might have had very good reason to believe that Miss Gilchrist had overheard a conversation between Cora Lansquenet and her brother which referred to her, and she might therefore decide that Miss Gilchrist must be eliminated. She herself, remember, refused to partake of the wedding cake and also suggested not calling in a doctor until the morning, when Miss Gilchrist was taken ill in the night.

'Mr Entwhistle did *not* benefit by either of the deaths – but he had had considerable control over Mr Abernethie's affairs, and the trust funds, and there will be some reason why Richard Abernethie should not live too long. But – you will say – if it is Mr Entwhistle who was concerned, why should he come to *me*?

'And to that I will answer – it is not the first time that a murderer has been too sure of himself.

'We now come to what I may call the two outsiders. Mr Guthrie and a nun. If Mr Guthrie is really Mr Guthrie, the art critic, then that clears him. The same applies to the nun,

if she is really a nun. The question is, are these people themselves, or are they somebody else?

'And I may say that there seems to be a curious – *motif* – one
might call it – of a nun running through this business. A nun
comes to the door of Mr Timothy Abernethie's house and
Miss Gilchrist believes it is the same nun she has seen at
Lytchett St Mary. Also a nun, or nuns, called here the day
before Mr Abernethie died . . .'

George Crossfield murmured, 'Three to one, the nun.'

Poirot went on:

'So here we have certain pieces of our pattern – the death
of Mr Abernethie, the murder of Cora Lansquenet, the
poisoned wedding cake, the "*motif*" of the "nun."

'I will add some other features of the case that engaged my
attention:

'The visit of an art critic, a smell of oil paint, a picture
postcard of Polflexan harbour, and finally a bouquet of wax
flowers standing on that malachite table where a Chinese vase
stands now.

'It was reflecting on these things that led me to the truth
– and I am now about to tell you the truth.

'The first part of it I told you this morning. Richard Abernethie died suddenly – but there would have been no reason
at all to suspect foul play had it not been for the words uttered
by his sister Cora at his funeral. *The whole case for the murder of Richard Abernethie rests upon those words.* As a result
of them you all believed that murder had taken place, and
you believed it, not really because of the words themselves but
because of the *character of Cora Lansquenet herself.* For Cora
Lansquenet had always been famous for speaking the truth at
awkward moments. So the case for Richard's murder rested
not only upon what Cora had *said* but upon Cora herself.

'And now I come to the question that I suddenly asked
myself:

'*How well did you all know Cora Lansquenet?*'

He was silent for a moment, and Susan asked sharply, 'What
do you mean?'

Poirot went on:

'*Not well at all* – that is the answer! The younger generation
had never seen her at all, or if so, only when they were very
young children. There were actually only three people present
that day who actually *knew* Cora. Lanscombe, the butler, who
is old and very blind; Mrs Timothy Abernethie who had
only seen her a few times round about the date of her own

wedding, and Mrs Leo Abernethie who had known her quite well, but who had not seen her for over twenty years.

'So I said to myself: "Supposing it was *not* Cora Lansquenet who came to the funeral that day?" '

'Do you mean that Aunt Cora – *wasn't* Aunt Cora?' Susan demanded incredulously. 'Do you mean that it wasn't Aunt Cora who was murdered, but someone else?'

'No, no, it was Cora Lansquenet who was murdered. *But it was not* Cora Lansquenet who came the day before to her brother's funeral. The woman who came that day came for one purpose only – to exploit, one may say, the fact that Richard died suddenly. And to create in the minds of his relations the belief that he had been murdered. Which she managed to do most successfully!'

'Nonsense! Why? What was the point of it?' Maude spoke bluffly.

'Why? *To draw attention away from the other murder* From the murder of Cora Lansquenet herself. For if Cora says that Richard has been murdered and the next day *she herself is killed*, the two deaths are bound to be at least considered as possible cause and effect. But if Cora is murdered and her cottage is broken into, and if the apparent robbery does not convince the police, then they will look – where? Close at home, will they not? Suspicion will tend to fall on the woman who shares the house with her.'

Miss Gilchrist protested in a tone that was almost bright:

'Oh come – really – Mr Pontarlier – you don't suggest I'd commit a murder for an amethyst brooch and a few worthless sketches?'

'No,' said Poirot. 'For a little more than that. There was one of those sketches, Miss Gilchrist, that represented Polflexan harbour and which, as Mrs Banks was clever enough to realise, had been copied from a picture postcard which showed the old pier still in position. But Mrs Lansquenet painted always from life. I remembered then that Mr Entwhistle had mentioned there being *a smell of oil paint* in the cottage when he first got there. You can paint, can't you, Miss Gilchrist? Your father was an artist and you know a good deal about pictures. Supposing that one of the pictures that Cora picked up cheaply at a sale was a valuable picture. Supposing that she herself did not recognise it for what it was, but that you did. You knew she was expecting, very shortly, a visit from an old friend of hers who was a well-known art critic. Then her brother died suddenly – and a plan leaps into your head.

Easy to administer a sedative to her in her early cup of tea that will keep her unconscious for the whole of the day of the funeral whilst you yourself are playing her part at Enderby. You know Enderby well from listening to her talk about it. She has talked, as people do when they get on in life, a great deal about her childhood days. Easy for you to start off by a remark to old Lanscombe about meringues and huts which will make him quite sure of your identity in case he was inclined to doubt. Yes, you used your knowledge of Enderby well that day, with allusions to this and that, and recalling memories. None of them suspected you were not Cora. You were wearing her clothes, slightly padded, and since she wore a false front of hair, it was easy for you to assume that. Nobody had seen Cora for twenty years – and in twenty years people change so much that one often hears the remark: 'I would never have known her!' But mannerisms, are remembered, and Cora had certain very definite mannerisms, all of which you had practised carefully before the glass.'

'And it was there, strangely enough, that you made your first mistake. *You forgot that a mirror image is reversed.* When you saw in the glass the perfect reproduction of Cora's birdlike sidewise tilt of the head, you didn't realise that it was actually the *wrong way round.* You saw, let us say, Cora inclining her head to the right – but you forgot that actually your own head was inclined to the *left* to produce that effect *in the glass.*

'That was what puzzled and worried Helen Abernethie at the moment when you made your famous insinuation. Something seemed to her "wrong." I realised myself the other night when Rosamund Shane made an unexpected remark what happens on such an occasion. Everybody inevitably looks at the *speaker.* Therefore, when Mrs Leo felt something was "wrong," it must be that something was wrong with *Cora Lansquenet.* The other evening, after talk about mirror images and "seeing oneself" I think Mrs Leo experimented before a looking-glass. Her own face is not particularly asymmetrical. She probably thought of Cora, remembered how Cora used to incline her head to the right, did so, and looked in the glass – when, of course, the image seemed to her "wrong" and she realised, in a flash, just what had been wrong on the day of the funeral. She puzzled it out – either Cora had taken to inclining her head in the opposite direction – most unlikely – or else *Cora had not been Cora.* Neither way seemed to her to make sense. But she was determined to tell

Mr Entwhistle of her discovery at once. Someone who was used to getting up early was already about, and followed her down, and fearful of what revelations she might be about to make struck her down with a heavy doorstop.'

Poirot paused and added :

'I may as well tell you now, Miss Gilchrist, that Mrs Abernethie's concussion is not serious. She will soon be able to tell us her own story.'

'I never did anything of the sort,' said Miss Gilchrist. 'The whole thing is a wicked lie.'

'It *was* you that day,' said Michael Shane suddenly. He had been studying Miss Gilchrist's face. 'I ought to have seen it sooner – I felt in a vague kind of way I had seen you before somewhere – but of course one never looks much at—' he stopped.

'No, one doesn't bother to look at a mere companion-help,' said Miss Gilchrist. Her voice shook a little. 'A drudge, a domestic drudge! Almost a servant! But go on, M. Poirot. Go on with this fantastic piece of nonsense!'

'The suggestion of murder thrown out at the funeral was only the first step, of course,' said Poirot. 'You had more in reserve. At any moment you were prepared to admit to having listened to a conversation between Richard and his sister. What he actually told her, no doubt, was the fact that he had not long to live, and that explains a cryptic phrase in the letter he wrote to her after getting home. The "nun" was another of your suggestions. The nun – or rather nuns – who called at the cottage on the day of the inquest suggested to you a mention of a nun who was "following you round," and you used that when you were anxious to hear what Mrs Timothy was saying to her sister-in-law at Enderby. And also because you wished to accompany her there and find out for yourself just how suspicions were going. Actually to poison *yourself*, badly but not fatally, with arsenic, is a very old device – and I may say that it served to awaken Inspector Morton's suspicions of you.'

'But the picture?' said Rosamund. 'What kind of a picture was it?'

Poirot slowly unfolded a telegram.

'This morning I rang up Mr Entwhistle, a respectable person, to go to Stansfield Grange and, acting on authority from Mr Abernethie himself' (here Poirot gave a hard stare at Timothy) 'to look amongst the pictures in Miss Gilchrist's room and select the one of Polflexan Harbour on pretext of having it reframed as a surprise for Miss Gilchrist. He was to take it back to London and call upon Mr Guthrie whom I had warned by telegram. The hastily painted sketch of Polflexan Harbour was removed and the original picture exposed.'

He held up the telegram and read:

'*Definitely a Vermeer, Guthrie.*'

Suddenly, with electrifying effect, Miss Gilchrist burst into speech.

'I knew it was a Vermeer. I *knew* it! *She* didn't know! Talking about Rembrandts and Italian Primitives and unable to recognise a Vermeer when it was under her nose! Always prating about Art – and really knowing nothing about it! She was a thoroughly stupid woman. Always maundering on about this place – about Enderby, and what they did there as children, and about Richard and Timothy and Laura and all the rest of them. Rolling in money always! Always the best of everything those children had. You don't know how boring it is listening to somebody going on about the same things, hour after hour and day after day. And saying, "Oh, yes, Mrs Lansquenet" and "Really, Mrs Lansquenet?" Pretending to be interested. And really bored – bored – *bored* . . . And nothing to look forward to . . . And then – a Vermeer! I saw in the papers that a Vermeer sold the other day for over five thousand pounds!'

'You killed her – in that brutal way – for five thousand pounds?' Susan's voice was incredulous.

'Five thousand pounds,' said Poirot, 'would have rented and equipped a *tea-shop* . . .'

Miss Gilchrist turned to him.

'At least,' she said. 'You *do* understand. It was the only chance I'd ever get. I *had* to have a capital sum.' Her voice vibrated with the force and obsession of her dream .'I was going to call it the Palm Tree. And have little camels as menu holders. One can occasionally get quite nice china – export rejects – not that awful white utility stuff. I meant to start it in some nice neighbourhood where nice people would come in. I had thought of Rye . . . Or perhaps Chichester . . . I'm sure I could have made a success of it.' She paused a minute, then added musingly, 'Oak tables – and little basket chairs with striped red and white cushions. . . .'

For a few moments, the tea-shop that would never be, seemed more real than the Victorian solidity of the drawing-room at Enderby . . .

It was Inspector Morton who broke the spell.

Miss Gilchrist turned to him quite politely.

'Oh, certainly,' she said. 'At once. I don't want to give any trouble, I'm sure. After all, if I can't have the Palm Tree, nothing really seems to matter very much. . . .

She went out of the room with him and Susan said, her voice still shaken:

'I've never imagined a *lady-like* murderer. It's horrible. . . .'

—— 25 ——

'But I don't understand about the wax flowers,' said Rosamund.

She fixed Poirot with large reproachful blue eyes.

They were at Helen's flat in London. Helen herself was resting on the sofa and Rosamund and Poirot were having tea with her.

'I don't see that *wax flowers* had anything to *do* with it,' said Rosamund. 'Or the malachite table.'

'The malachite table, no. But the wax flowers were Miss Gilchrist's second mistake. She said how nice they looked on the malachite table. And you see, Madame, *she* could not have seen them there. Because they had been broken and put away before she arrived with the Timothy Abernethies. So *she could only have seen them when she was there as Cora Lansquenet.*'

'That was stupid of her, wasn't it?' said Rosamund.

Poirot shook a forefinger at her.

'It shows you, Madame, the dangers of *conversation*. It is a profound belief of mine that if you can induce a person to talk to you for long enough, *on any subject whatever,* sooner or later they will give themselves away. Miss Gilchrist did.'

'I shall have to be careful,' said Rosamund thoughtfully.

Then she brightened up.

'Did you know? I'm going to have a baby.'

'Aha! So that is the meaning of Harley Street and Regent's Park?'

'Yes. I was so upset, you know, and so surprised – that I just had to go somewhere and *think*.'

'You said, I remember, that that does not very often happen.'

'Well, it's much easier not to. But this time I had to decide about the future. And I've decided to leave the stage and just be a mother.'

'A *role* that will suit you admirably. Already I foresee delightful pictures in the *Sketch* and the *Tatler*.'

Rosamund smiled happily.

'Yes, it's wonderful. Do you know, Michael is *delighted*. I didn't really think he would be.'

She paused and added:

'Susan's got the malachite table. I thought, as I was having a baby—'

She left the sentence unfinished.

'Susan's cosmetic business promises well,' said Helen. 'I think she is all set for a big success.'

'Yes, she was born to succeed,' said Poirot. 'She is like her uncle.'

'You mean Richard, I suppose,' said Rosamund. 'Not Timothy?'

'Assuredly not like Timothy,' said Poirot.

They laughed.

'Greg's away somewhere,' said Rosamund. 'Having a rest cure Susan *says*?'

She looked inquiringly at Poirot who said nothing.

'I can't think why he kept on saying he'd killed Uncle Richard,' said Rosamund. 'Do you think it was a form of Exhibitionism?'

Poirot reverted to the previous topic.

'I received a very amiable letter from Mr Timothy Abernethie,' he said. 'He expressed himself as highly satisfied with the services I had rendered the family.'

'I do think Uncle Timothy is quite awful,' said Rosamund.

'I am going to stay with them next week,' said Helen. 'They seem to be getting the gardens into order, but domestic help is still difficult.'

'They miss the awful Gilchrist, I suppose,' said Rosamund. 'But I dare say in the end, she'd have killed Uncle Timothy too. What fun if she had!'

'Murder has always seemed fun to you, Madame.'

'Oh! Not really,' said Rosamund vaguely. 'But I *did* think it was George.' She brightened up. 'Perhaps he will do one some day.'

'And that will be fun,' said Poirot sarcastically.

'Yes, won't it?' Rosamund agreed.

She ate another éclair from the plate in front of her.

Poirot turned to Helen.

'And you, Madame, are off to Cyprus?'

'Yes, in a fortnight's time.'

'Then let me wish you a happy journey.'

He bowed over her hand. She came with him to the door, leaving Rosamund dreamily stuffing herself with cream pastries.

Helen said abruptly:

'I should like you to know, M. Poirot, that the legacy Richard left me meant more to me than theirs did to any of the others.'

'As much as that, Madame?'

'Yes. You see – there is a child in Cyprus . . . My husband and I were very devoted – it was a great sorrow to us to have no children. After he died my loneliness was unbelievable. When I was nursing in London at the end of the war, I met someone . . . He was younger than I was and married, though not very happily. We came together for a little while. That was all. He went back to Canada – to his wife and his children. He never knew about – our child. He would not have wanted it. I did. It seemed like a miracle to me – a middle-aged woman with everything behind her. With Richard's money I can educate my so-called nephew, and give him a start in life.' She paused, then added, 'I never told Richard. He was fond of me and I of him – but he would not have understood. You know so much about us that I thought I would like you to know this about me.'

Once again Poirot bowed over her hand.

'Hallo, Poirot,' said Mr Entwhistle. 'I've just come back from the Assizes. They brought in a verdict of Guilty, of course. But I shouldn't be surprised if she ends up in Broadmoor. She's gone definitely over the edge since she's been in prison. Quite happy, you know, and most *gracious*. She spends most of her time making the most elaborate plans to run a chain of tea-shops. Her newest establishment is to be the Lilac Bush. She's opening it in Cromer.'

'One wonders if she was always a little mad? But me, I think not.'

'Good Lord, no! Sane as you and I when she planned that murder. Carried it out in cold blood. She's got a good head on her, you know, underneath the fluffy manner.'

Poirot gave a little shiver.

'I am thinking,' he said, 'of some words that Susan Banks said – that she had never imagined a *lady-like* murderer.'

'Why not?' said Mr Entwhistle. 'It takes all sorts.'

They were silent – and Poirot thought of murderers he had known . . .

DEATH ON THE NILE

—— **I** ——

'Linnet Ridgeway!'

'That's *her*!' said Mr Burnaby, the landlord of the Three Crowns.

He nudged his companion.

The two men stared with round bucolic eyes and slightly open mouths.

A big scarlet Rolls-Royce had just stopped in front of the local post office.

A girl jumped out, a girl without a hat and wearing a frock that looked (but only *looked*) simple. A girl with golden hair and straight autocratic features – a girl with a lovely shape – a girl such as was seldom seen in Malton-under-Wode.

With a quick imperative step she passed into the post office.

'That's her!' said Mr Burnaby again. And he went on in a low awed voice: 'Millions she's got . . . Going to spend thousands on the place. Swimming-pools there's going to be, and Italian gardens and a ballroom and half of the house pulled down and rebuilt. . . .'

'She'll bring money into the town,' said his friend. He was a lean, seedy-looking man. His tone was envious and grudging.

Mr Burnaby agreed.

'Yes, it's a great thing for Malton-under-Wode. A great thing it is.'

Mr Burnaby was complacent about it.

'Wake us all up proper,' he added.

'Bit of difference from Sir George,' said the other.

'Ah, it was the 'orses did for him,' said Mr Burnaby indulgently. 'Never 'ad no luck.'

'What did he get for the place?'

'A cool sixty thousand, so I've heard.'

The lean man whistled.

Mr Burnaby went on triumphantly: 'And they say she'll have spent another sixty thousand before she's finished!'

'Wicked!' said the lean man. 'Where'd she *get* all that money from?'

'America, so I've heard. Her mother was the only daughter of one of those millionaire blokes. Quite like the pictures, isn't it?'

The girl came out of the post office and climbed into the car.

As she drove off, the lean man followed her with his eyes. He muttered:

'It seems all wrong to me – her looking like that. Money *and* looks – it's too much! If a girl's as rich as that she's no right to be a good-looker as well. And she *is* a good-looker . . . Got everything, that girl has. Doesn't seem fair. . . .'

2

Extract from the Social column of the *Daily Blague*.

Among those supping at Chez Ma Tante I noticed beautiful Linnet Ridgeway. She was with the Hon. Joanna Southwood, Lord Windlesham and Mr Toby Bryce. Miss Ridgeway, as everyone knows, is the daughter of Melhuish Ridgeway who married Anna Hartz. She inherits from her grandfather, Leopold Hartz, an immense fortune. The lovely Linnet is the sensation of the moment and it is rumoured that an engagement may be announced shortly. Certainly Lord Windlesham seemed very épris! !

3

The Hon. Joanna Southwood said:

'Darling, I think it's going to be all perfectly *marvellous*!'

She was sitting in Linnet Ridgeway's bedroom at Wode Hall.

From the window the eye passed over the gardens to open country with blue shadows of woodlands.

'It's rather perfect, isn't it?' said Linnet.

She leaned her arms on the window sill. Her face was eager, alive, dynamic. Beside her, Joanna Southwood seemed, somehow, a little dim – a tall thin young woman of twenty-seven, with a long clever face and freakishly plucked eyebrows.

'And you've done so much in the time! Did you have lots of architects and things?'

'Three.'

'What are architects like? I don't think I've ever seen any.'

'They were all right. I found them rather unpractical sometimes.'

'Darling, you soon put *that* right! You are the *most* practical creature!'

Joanna picked up a string of pearls from the dressing-table.

'I suppose these are real, aren't they, Linnet?'

'Of course.'

'I know it's "of course" to you, my sweet, but it wouldn't be to most people. Heavily cultured or even Woolworth! Darling, they really are *incredible,* so exquisitely matched. They must be worth the *most* fabulous sums!'

'Rather vulgar, you think?'

'No, not at all – just pure beauty. What *are* they worth?'

'About fifty thousand.'

'What a lovely lot of money! Aren't you afraid of having them stolen?'

'No, I always wear them – and anyway they're insured.'

'Let me wear them till dinner-time, will you, darling? It would give me such a thrill.'

Linnet laughed.

'Of course, if you like.'

'You know, Linnet, I really do envy you. You've simply got *everything.* Here you are at twenty, your own mistress, with any amount of money, looks, superb health. You've even got *brains*! When are you twenty-one?'

'Next June. I shall have a grand coming-of-age party in London.'

'And then are you going to marry Charles Windlesham? All the dreadful little gossip writers are getting so excited about it. And he really is frightfully devoted.'

Linnet shrugged her shoulders.

'I don't know. I don't really want to marry anyone yet.'

'Darling, how right you are! It's never quite the same afterwards, is it?'

The telephone shrilled and Linnet went to it.

'Yes? Yes?'

The butler's voice answered her:

'Miss de Bellefort is on the line. Shall I put her through?'

'Bellefort? Oh, of course, yes, put her through.'

A click and a voice, an eager, soft, slightly breathless voice: 'Hullo, is that Miss Ridgeway? *Linnet*!'

'*Jackie darling*! I haven't heard anything of you for ages and *ages*!'

'I know. It's awful. Linnet, I want to see you terribly.'

'Darling, can't you come down here? My new toy. I'd love to show it to you.'

'That's just what I want to do.'

'Well, jump into a train or a car.'

'Right, I will. A frightfully dilapidated two-seater. I bought it for fifteen pounds, and some days it goes beautifully. But it has moods. If I haven't arrived by tea-time you'll know it's had a mood. So long, my sweet.'

Linnet replaced the receiver. She crossed back to Joanna.

'That's my oldest friend, Jacqueline de Bellefort. We were together at a convent in Paris. She's had the most terrible bad luck. Her father was a French Count, her mother was American – a Southerner. The father went off with some woman, and her mother lost all her money in the Wall Street crash. Jackie was left absolutely broke. I don't know how she's managed to get along the last two years.'

Joanna was polishing her deep-blood-coloured nails with her friend's nail pad. She leant back with her head on one side scrutinising the effect.

'Darling,' she drawled, 'won't that be rather *tiresome*? If any misfortunes happen to my friends I always drop them *at once*! It sounds heartless, but it saves such a lot of trouble later! They always want to borrow money off you, or else they start a dressmaking business and you have to get the most terrible clothes from them. Or they paint lampshades, or do batik scarves.'

'So, if I lost all my money, you'd drop me tomorrow?'

'Yes, darling, I would. You can't say I'm not honest about it! I only like successful people. And you'll find that's true of nearly everybody – only most people won't admit it. They just say that really they can't put up with Mary or Emily or Pamela any more! "Her troubles have made her so *bitter* and peculiar, poor dear!"'

'How beastly you are, Joanna!'

'I'm only on the make, like everyone else.'

'*I'm* not on the make!'

'For obvious reasons! You don't have to be sordid when good-looking, middle-aged American trustees pay you over a vast allowance every quarter.'

'And you're wrong about Jacqueline,' said Linnet. 'She's not a sponge. I've wanted to help her, but she won't let me. She's as proud as the devil.'

'What's she in such a hurry to see you for? I'll bet she wants something! You just wait and see.'

'She sounded excited about something,' admitted Linnet.

'Jackie always did get frightfully worked up over things. She once stuck a penknife into someone!'

'Darling, how thrilling!'

'A boy who was teasing a dog. Jackie tried to get him to stop. He wouldn't. She pulled him and shook him, but he was much stronger than she was, and at last she whipped out a penknife and plunged it right into him. There was the *most* awful row!'

'I should think so. It sounds most uncomfortable!'

Linnet's maid entered the room. With a murmured word of apology, she took down a dress from the wardrobe and went out of the room with it.

'What's the matter with Marie?' asked Joanna. 'She's been crying.'

'Poor thing! You know I told you she wanted to marry a man who has a job in Egypt. She didn't know much about him, so I thought I'd better make sure he was all right. It turned out that he had a wife already – and three children.'

'What a lot of enemies you must make, Linnet.'

'Enemies?' Linnet looked surprised.

Joanna nodded and helped herself to a cigarette.

'Enemies, my sweet. You're so devastatingly efficient. And you're so frightfully good at doing the right thing.'

Linnet laughed.

'Why, I haven't got an enemy in the world.'

4

Lord Windlesham sat under the cedar tree. His eyes rested on the graceful proportions of Wode Hall. There was nothing to mar its old-world beauty; the new buildings and additions were out of sight round the corner. It was a fair and peaceful sight bathed in the autumn sunshine. Nevertheless, as he gazed, it was no longer Wode Hall that Charles Windlesham saw. Instead, he seemed to see a more imposing Elizabethan mansion, a long sweep of park, a more bleak background. . . . It was his own family seat, Charltonbury, and in the foreground stood a figure – a girl's figure, with bright golden hair and an eager confident face . . . Linnet as mistress of Charltonbury!

He felt very hopeful. That refusal of hers had not been at all a definite refusal. It had been little more than a plea for time. Well, he could afford to wait a little. . . .

How amazingly suitable the whole thing was! It was certainly advisable that he should marry money, but not such a matter of necessity that he could regard himself as forced to put his own feelings on one side. And he loved Linnet. He would have wanted to marry her even if she had been practically penniless, instead of one of the richest girls in England. . . . Only, fortunately, she *was* one of the richest girls in England. . . .

His mind played with attractive plans for the future. The Mastership of the Roxdale perhaps, the restoration of the west wing, no need to let the Scotch shooting. . . .

Charles Windlesham dreamed in the sun.

5

It was four o'clock when the dilapidated little two-seater stopped with a sound of crunching gravel. A girl got out of it – a small slender creature with a mop of dark hair. She ran up the steps and tugged at the bell.

A few minutes later she was being ushered into the long stately drawing-room, and an ecclesiastical butler was saying with the proper mournful intonation: 'Miss de Bellefort.'

'Linnet!'

'Jackie!'

Windlesham stood a little aside, watching sympathetically as this fiery little creature flung herself open-armed upon Linnet.

'Lord Windlesham – Miss de Bellefort – my best friend.'

A pretty child, he thought – not really pretty but decidedly attractive, with her dark curly hair and her enormous eyes. He murmured a few tactful nothings and then managed unobtrusively to leave the two friends together.

Jacqueline pounced – in a fashion that Linnet remembered as being characteristic of her.

'Windlesham? Windlesham? *That's* the man the papers always say you're going to marry? Are you, Linnet? *Are* you?'

Linnet murmured: 'Perhaps.'

'Darling – I'm so glad! He looks nice.'

'Oh, don't make up your mind about it – I haven't made up my own mind yet.'

'Of course not! Queens always proceed with due deliberation to the choosing of a consort!'

'Don't be ridiculous, Jackie.'

'But you *are* a queen, Linnet! You always were. *Sa Majesté, la reine Linette. Linette la blonde*! And I – I'm the Queen's confidante! The trusted Maid of Honour.'

'What nonsense you talk, Jackie darling! Where have you been all this time? You just disappear. And you never write.'

'I hate writing letters. Where have I been? Oh, about three parts submerged, darling. In JOBS, you know. Grim jobs with grim women!'

'Darling, I wish you'd—'

'Take the Queen's bounty? Well, frankly, darling, that's what I'm here for. No, not to borrow money. It's not got to that yet! But I've come to ask a great big important favour!'

'Go on.'

'If you're going to marry the Windlesham man, you'll understand, perhaps.'

Linnet looked puzzled for a minute; then her face cleared.

'Jackie, do you mean—?'

'Yes, darling, *I'm engaged*!'

'So that's it! I thought you were looking particularly alive somehow. You always do, of course, but even more than usual.'

'That's just what I feel like.'

'Tell me all about him.'

'His name's Simon Doyle. He's big and square and incredibly simple and boyish and utterly adorable! He's poor – got no money. He's what you call "country" all right – but very impoverished country – a younger son and all that. His people come from Devonshire. He loves country and country things. And for the last five years he's been in the City in a stuffy office. And now they're cutting down and he's out of a job. Linnet, I shall *die* if I can't marry him! I shall die! I shall die! I shall *die*. . . .'

'Don't be ridiculous, Jackie.'

'I shall die, I tell you! I'm crazy about him. He's crazy about me. We can't live without each other.'

'Darling, you *have* got it badly!'

'I know. It's awful, isn't it? This love business gets hold of you and you can't do anything about it.'

She paused for a minute. Her dark eyes dilated, looked suddenly tragic. She gave a little shiver.

'It's – even frightening sometimes! Simon and I were made for each other. I shall never care for anyone else. And *you've* got to help us, Linnet. I heard you'd bought this place and it put an idea into my head. Listen, you'll have to have a land agent – perhaps two. I want you to give the job to Simon.'

'Oh!' Linnet was startled.

Jacqueline rushed on: 'He's got all that sort of thing at his fingertips. He knows all about estates – was brought up on one. And he's got his business training, too. Oh, Linnet, you will give him a job, won't you, for love of me? If he doesn't make good, sack him. But he will. And we can live in a little house, and I shall see lots of you, and everything in the garden will be too, too divine.'

She got up.

'Say you will, Linnet. Say you will. Beautiful Linnet! Tall golden Linnet! My own very special Linnet! Say you will!'

'Jackie—'

'You will?'

Linnet burst out laughing.

'Ridiculous Jackie! Bring along your young man and let me have a look at him and we'll talk it over.'

Jackie darted at her, kissing her exuberantly.

'*Darling Linnet* – you're a real friend! I knew you were. You wouldn't let me down – ever. You're just the loveliest thing in the world. Good-bye.'

'But, Jackie, you're *staying*.'

'Me? No, I'm not. I'm going back to London, and tomorrow I'll come back and bring Simon and we'll settle it all up. You'll adore him. He really is a *pet*.'

'But can't you wait and just have tea?'

'No, I can't wait, Linnet. I'm too excited. I must get back and tell Simon. I know I'm mad, darling, but can't help it. Marriage will cure me, expect. It always seems to have a very sobering effect on people.'

She turned at the door, stood a moment, then rushed back for a last quick birdlike embrace.

'Dear Linnet – there's no one like you.'

6

M. Gaston Blondin, the proprietor of that modish little restaurant Chez Ma Tante, was not a man who delighted to honour many of his clientèle. The rich, the beautiful, the notorious, and the well-born might wait in vain to be singled out and paid special attention. Only in the rarest cases did M. Blondin, with gracious condescension, greet a guest, accompany him to a privileged table, and exchange with him suitable and apposite remarks.

On this particular night, M. Blondin had exercised his royal prerogative three times – once for a Duchess, once for a famous racing peer, and once for a little man of comical appearance with immense black moustaches, who, a casual onlooker would have thought, could bestow no favour on Chez Ma Tante by his presence there.

M. Blondin, however, was positively fulsome in his attentions. Though clients had been told for the last half hour that a table was not to be had, one now mysteriously appeared, placed in a most favourable position. M. Blondin conducted the client to it with every appearance of *empressement*.

'But naturally, for *you* there is *always* a table, Monsieur Poirot! How I wish that you would honour us oftener!'

Hercule Poirot smiled, remembering that past incident wherein a dead body, a waiter, M. Blondin, and a very lovely lady had played a part.

'You are too amiable, Monsieur Blondin,' he said.

'And you are alone, Monsieur Poirot?'

'Yes, I am alone.'

'Oh, well, Jules here will compose for you a little meal that will be a poem – positively a poem! Women, however charming, have this disadvantage: they distract the mind from food! You will enjoy your dinner, Monsieur Poirot; I promise you that. Now as to wine—'

A technical conversation ensued, Jules, the *maître d'hôtel*, assisting.

Before departing, M. Blondin lingered a moment, lowering his voice confidentially.

'You have grave affairs on hand?'

Poirot shook his head.

'I am, alas, a man of leisure,' he said softly. 'I have made the economies in my time and I have now the means to enjoy a life of idleness.'

'I envy you.'

'No, no, you would be unwise to do so. I can assure you, it is not so gay as it sounds.' He sighed. 'How true is the saying that man was forced to invent work in order to escape the strain of having to think.'

M. Blondin threw up his hands.

'But there is so much! There is travel!'

'Yes, there is travel. Already I have not done so badly. This winter I shall visit Egypt, I think. The climate, they say, is superb! One will escape from the fogs, the greyness, the monotony of the constantly falling rain.'

'Ah! Egypt,' breathed M. Blondin.

'One can even voyage there now, I believe, by train, escaping all sea travel except the Channel.'

'Ah, the sea, it does not agree with you?'

Hercule Poirot shook his head and shuddered slightly.

'I, too,' said M. Blondin with sympathy. 'Curious the effect it has upon the stomach.'

'But only upon certain stomachs! There are people on whom the motion makes no impression whatever. They actually *enjoy* it!'

'An unfairness of the good God,' said M. Blondin.

He shook his head sadly, and, brooding on the impious thought, withdrew.

Smooth-footed, deft-handed waiters ministered to the table. Toast Melba, butter, an ice pail, all the adjuncts to a meal of quality.

The Negro orchestra broke into an ecstasy of strange discordant noises. London danced.

Hercule Poirot looked on, registered impressions in his neat orderly mind.

How bored and weary most of the faces were! Some of those stout men, however, were enjoying themselves . . . whereas a patient endurance seemed to be the sentiment exhibited on their partners' faces. The fat woman in purple was looking radiant. . . . Undoubtedly the fat had certain compensations in life . . . a zest – a gusto – denied to those of more fashionable contours.

A good sprinkling of young people – some vacant-looking – some bored – some definitely unhappy. How absurd to call youth the time of happiness – youth, the time of greatest vulnerability!

His glance softened as it rested on one particular couple. A well-matched pair – tall broad-shouldered man, slender delicate girl. Two bodies that moved in a perfect rhythm of happiness. Happiness in the place, the hour, and in each other.

The dance stopped abruptly. Hands clapped and it started again. After a second *encore* the couple returned to their table close by Poirot. The girl was flushed, laughing. As she sat, he could study her face, lifted laughing to her companion.

There was something else beside laughter in her eyes. Hercule Poirot shook his head doubtfully.

'She cares too much, that little one,' he said to himself. 'It is not safe. No, it is not safe.'

And then a word caught his ear, 'Egypt.'

Their voices came to him clearly – the girl's young, fresh,

arrogant, with just a trace of soft-sounding foreign R's, and the man's pleasant, low-toned, well-bred English.

'I'm *not* counting my chickens before they're hatched, Simon. I tell you Linnet won't let us down!'

'*I* might let *her* down.'

'Nonsense – it's just the right job for you.'

'As a matter of fact I think it is. . . . I haven't really any doubts as to my capability. And I mean to make good – for *your* sake!'

The girl laughed softly, a laugh of pure happiness.

'We'll wait three months – to make sure you don't get the sack – and then—'

'And then I'll endow thee with my worldly goods – that's the hang of it, isn't it?'

'And, as I say, we'll go to Egypt for our honeymoon. Damn the expense! I've always wanted to go to Egypt all my life. The Nile and the Pyramids and the sand . . .'

He said, his voice slightly indistinct: 'We'll see it together, Jackie . . . together. Won't it be marvellous?'

'I wonder. Will it be as marvellous to you as it is to me? Do you really care – as much as I do?'

Her voice was suddenly sharp – her eyes dilated – almost with fear.

The man's answer came quickly crisp: 'Don't be absurd, Jackie.'

But the girl repeated: 'I wonder . . .'

Then she shrugged her shoulders. 'Let's dance.'

Hercule Poirot murmured to himself:

'*Une qui aime et un qui se laisse aimer.* Yes, I wonder too.'

7

Joanna Southwood said: 'And suppose he's a terrible tough?'

Linnet shook her head. 'Oh, he won't be. I can Trust Jacqueline's taste.'

Joanna murmured: 'Ah, but people don't run true to form in love affairs.'

Linnet shook her head impatiently. Then she changed the subject.

'I must go and see Mr Pierce about those plans.'

'Plans?'

'Yes, some dreadful insanitary old cottages. I'm having them pulled down and the people moved.'

'How sanitary and public-spirited of you, darling!'

'They'd have had to go anyway. Those cottages would have overlooked my new swimming pool.'

'Do the people who live in them like going?'

'Most of them are delighted. One or two are being rather stupid about it – really tiresome in fact. They don't seem to realise how vastly improved their living conditions will be!'

'But you're being quite high-handed about it, I presume.'

'My dear Joanna, it's to their advantage really.'

'Yes, dear. I'm sure it is. Compulsory benefit.'

Linnet frowned. Joanna laughed.

'Come now, you *are* a tyrant, admit it. A beneficent tyrant if you like!'

'I'm not the least bit of a tyrant.'

'But you like your own way!'

'Not especially.'

'Linnet Ridgeway, can you look me in the face and tell me of *any one occasion* on which you've failed to do exactly as you wanted?'

'Heaps of times.'

'Oh, yes, "heaps of times" – just like that – but no concrete example. And you simply can't think up one, darling, however hard you try! The triumphal progress of Linnet Ridgeway in her golden car.'

Linnet said sharply: 'You think I'm selfish?'

'No – just irresistible. The combined effect of money and charm. Everything goes down before you. What you can't buy with cash you buy with a smile. Result: Linnet Ridgeway, the Girl Who Has Everything.'

'Don't be ridiculous, Joanna!'

'Well, haven't you got everything?'

'I suppose I have. . . . It sounds rather disgusting somehow!'

'Of course it's disgusting, darling! You'll probably get terribly bored and blasé by and by. In the meantime, enjoy the triumphal progress in the golden car. Only I wonder, I really do wonder, what will happen when you want to go down a street which has a board up saying "No Thoroughfare".'

'Don't be idiotic, Joanna.' As Lord Windlesham joined them, Linnet said, turning to him: 'Joanna is saying the nastiest things to me.'

'All spite, darling, all spite,' said Joanna vaguely as she got up from her seat.

She made no apology for leaving them. She had caught the glint in Windlesham's eye.

He was silent for a minute or two. Then he went straight to the point.

'Have you come to a decision, Linnet?'

Linnet said slowly: 'Am I being a brute? I suppose, if I'm not sure, I ought to say "No"—'

He interrupted her:

'Don't say it. You shall have time – as much time as you want. But I think, you know, we should be happy together.'

'You see,' Linnet's tone was apologetic, almost childish, 'I'm enjoying myself so much – especially with all this.' She waved a hand. 'I wanted to make Wode Hall into my real ideal of a country house, and I do think I've got it nice, don't you?'

'It's beautiful. Beautifully planned. Everything perfect. You're very clever, Linnet.'

He paused a minute and went on: 'And you like Charlton-bury, don't you? Of course it wants modernising and all that – but you're so clever at that sort of thing. You enjoy it.'

'Why, of course, Charltonbury's divine.'

She spoke with ready enthusiasm, but inwardly she was conscious of a sudden chill. An alien note had sounded, disturbing her complete satisfaction with life. She did not analyse the feeling at the moment, but later, when Windlesham had left her, she tried to probe the recesses of her mind.

Charltonbury – yes, that was it – she had resented the mention of Charltonbury. But why? Charltonbury was modestly famous. Windlesham's ancestors had held it since the time of Elizabeth. To be mistress of Charltonbury was a position unsurpassed in society. Windlesham was one of the most desirable peers in England.

Naturally he couldn't take Wode seriously. . . . It was not in any way to be compared with Charltonbury.

Ah, but Wode was *hers*! She had seen it, acquired it, rebuilt and re-dressed it, lavished money on it. It was her own possession – her kingdom.

But in a sense it wouldn't count if she married Windlesham. What would they want with two country places? And of the two, naturally Wode Hall would be the one to be given up.

She, Linnet Ridgeway, wouldn't exist any longer. She would be Countess of Windlesham, bringing a fine dowry to Charlton-bury and its master. She would be queen consort, not queen any longer.

'I'm being ridiculous,' said Linnet to herself.

But it was curious how she did hate the idea of abandoning Wode. . . .

And wasn't there something else nagging at her?

Jackie's voice with that queer blurred note in it saying: 'I shall *die* if I can't marry him! I shall die. I shall die . . .'

So positive, so earnest. Did she, Linnet, feel like that about Windlesham? Assuredly she didn't. Perhaps she could never feel like that about anyone. It must be – rather wonderful – to feel like that. . . .

The sound of a car came through the open window.

Linnet shook herself impatiently. That must be Jackie and her young man. She'd go out and meet them.

She was standing in the open doorway as Jacqueline and Simon Doyle got out of the car.

'Linnet!' Jackie ran to her. 'This is Simon. Simon, here's Linnet. She's just the most wonderful person in the world.'

Linnet saw a tall, broad-shouldered young man, with very dark blue eyes, crisply curling brown hair, a square chin, and a boyish, appealing, simple smile. . . .

She stretched out a hand. The hand that clasped hers was firm and warm. . . . She liked the way he looked at her, the naïve genuine admiration.

Jackie had told him she was wonderful, and he clearly thought that she was wonderful. . . .

A warm sweet feeling of intoxication ran through her veins.

'Isn't this all lovely?' she said. 'Come in, Simon, and let me welcome my new land agent properly.'

And as she turned to lead the way she thought: 'I'm frightfully – frightfully happy. I like Jackie's young man . . . I like him enormously. . . .'

And then with a sudden pang: 'Lucky Jackie. . . .'

8

Tim Allerton leant back in his wicker chair and yawned as he looked out over the sea. He shot a quick sidelong glance at his mother.

Mrs Allerton was a good-looking, white-haired woman of fifty. By imparting an expression of pinched severity to her mouth every time she looked at her son, she sought to disguise the fact of her intense affection for him. Even total strangers were seldom deceived by this device and Tim himself saw through it perfectly.

He said: 'Do you really like Majorca, Mother?'

'Well,' Mrs Allerton considered, 'it's cheap.'

'And cold,' said Tim with a slight shiver.

He was a tall, thin young man, with dark hair and a rather narrow chest. His mouth had a very sweet expression: his eyes were sad and his chin was indecisive. He had long delicate hands.

Threatened by consumption some years ago, he had never displayed a really robust physique. He was popularly supposed 'to write,' but it was understood among his friends that inquiries as to literary output were not encouraged.

'What are you thinking of, Tim?'

Mrs Allerton was alert. Her bright, dark-brown eyes looked suspicious.

Tim Allerton grinned at her:

'I was thinking of Egypt.'

'Egypt?' Mrs Allerton sounded doubtful.

'Real warmth, darling. Lazy golden sands. The Nile. I'd like to go up the Nile, wouldn't you?'

'Oh, I'd *like* it.' Her tone was dry. 'But Egypt's expensive, my dear. Not for those who have to count the pennies.'

Tim laughed. He rose, stretched himself. Suddenly he looked alive and eager. There was an excited note in his voice.

'The expense will be my affair. Yes, darling. A little flutter on the Stock Exchange. With thoroughly satisfactory results. I heard this morning.'

'This morning?' said Mrs Allerton sharply. 'You only had one letter and that—'

She stopped and bit her lip.

Tim looked momentarily undecided whether to be amused or annoyed. Amusement gained the day.

'And that was from Joanna,' he finished coolly. 'Quite right, Mother. What a queen of detectives you'd make! The famous Hercule Poirot would have to look to his laurels if you were about.'

Mrs Allerton looked rather cross.

'I just happened to see the handwriting—'

'And knew it wasn't that of a stockbroker? Quite right. As a matter of fact it was yesterday I heard from them. Poor Joanna's handwriting *is* rather noticeable – sprawls about all over the envelope like an inebriated spider.'

'What does Joanna say? Any news?'

Mrs Allerton strove to make her voice sound casual and ordinary. The friendship between her son and his second

cousin, Joanna Southwood always irritated her. Not, as she
put it to herself, that there was 'anything in it.' She was quite
sure there wasn't. Tim had never manifested a sentimental interest in Joanna, nor she in him. Their mutual attraction
seemed to be founded on gossip and the possession of a large
number of friends and acquaintances in common. They both
liked people and discussing people. Joanna had an amusing
if caustic tongue.

It was not because Mrs Allerton feared that Tim might fall
in love with Joanna that she found herself always becoming a
little stiff in manner if Joanna were present or when letters
from her arrived.

It was some other feeling hard to define – perhaps an un-
acknowledged jealousy in the unfeigned pleasure Tim always
seemed to take in Joanna's society. He and his mother were
such perfect companions that the sight of him absorbed and
interested in another woman always startled Mrs Allerton
slightly. She fancied, too, that her own presence on these
occasions set some barrier between the two members of the
younger generation. Often she had come upon them eagerly
absorbed in some conversation and, at sight of her, their
talk had wavered, had seemed to include her rather too pur-
posefully and as if duty bound. Quite definitely, Mrs Allerton
did not like Joanna Southwood. She thought her insincere,
affected, and essentially superficial. She found it very hard to
prevent herself saying so in unmeasured tones.

In answer to her question, Tim pulled the letter out of his
pocket and glanced through it. It was quite a long letter, his
mother noted.

'Nothing much,' he said. 'The Devenishes are getting a
divorce. Old Monty's been had up for being drunk in charge
of a car. Windlesham's gone to Canada. Seems he was pretty
badly hit when Linnet Ridgeway turned him down. She's definitely going to marry this land agent person.'

'How extraordinary! Is he very dreadful?'

'No, no, not at all. He's one of the Devonshire Doyles. No
money, of course – and he was actually engaged to one of Linnet's best friends. Pretty thick, that.'

'I don't think it's at all nice,' said Mrs Allerton, flushing.

Tim flashed her a quick affectionate glance.

'I know, darling. You don't approve of snaffling other
people's husbands and all that sort of thing.'

'In my day we had our standards,' said Mrs Allerton. 'And

a very good thing too! Nowadays young people seem to think they can just go about doing anything they choose.'

Tim smiled. 'They don't only think it. They do it. *Vide* Linnet Ridgeway!'

'Well, I think it's horrid!'

Tim twinkled at her.

'Cheer up, you old die-hard! Perhaps I agree with you. Anyway, *I* haven't helped myself to anyone's wife or fiancée yet.'

'I'm sure you'd never do such a thing,' said Mrs Allerton. She added with spirit, 'I've brought you up properly.'

'So the credit is yours, not mine.'

He smiled teasingly at her as he folded the letter and put it away again. Mrs Allerton let the thought just flash across her mind: 'Most letters he shows to me. He only reads me snippets from Joanna's.'

But she put the unworthy thought away from her, and decided, as ever, to behave like a gentlewoman.

'Is Joanna enjoying life?' she asked.

'So so. Says she thinks of opening a delicatessen shop in Mayfair.'

'She always talks about being hard up,' said Mrs Allerton with a tinge of spite, 'but she goes about everywhere and her clothes must cost her a lot. She's always beautifully dressed.'

'Ah, well,' said Tim, 'she probably doesn't pay for them. No, mother, I don't mean what your Edwardian mind suggests to you. I just mean quite literally that she leaves her bills unpaid.'

Mrs Allerton sighed.

'I never know how people manage to do that.'

'It's a kind of special gift,' said Tim. 'If only you have sufficient extravagant tastes, and absolutely no sense of money values, people will give you any amount of credit.'

'Yes, but you come to the Bankruptcy Court in the end like poor Sir George Wode.'

'You have a soft spot for that old horse coper – probably because he called you a rosebud in 1879 at a dance.'

'I wasn't born in 1879,' Mrs Allerton retorted with spirit. 'Sir George has charming manners, and I won't have you calling him a horse coper.'

'I've heard funny stories about him from people that know.'

'You and Joanna don't mind what you say about people; anything will do so long as it's sufficiently ill-natured.'

Tim raised his eyebrows.

'My dear, you're quite heated. I didn't know old Wode was such a favourite of yours.'

'You don't realise how hard it was for him, having to sell Wode Hall. He cared terribly about that place.'

Tim suppressed the easy retort. After all, who was he to judge? Instead he said thoughtfully:

'You know, I think you're not far wrong there. Linnet asked him to come down and see what she'd done to the place, and he refused quite rudely.'

'Of course. She ought to have known better than to ask him.'

'And I believe he's quite venomous about her – mutters things under his breath whenever he sees her. Can't forgive her for having given him an absolutely top price for the worm-eaten family estate.'

'And you can't understand that?' Mrs Allerton spoke sharply.

'Frankly,' said Tim calmly, 'I can't. Why live in the past? Why cling on to things that have been?'

'What are you going to put in their place?'

He shrugged his shoulders. 'Excitement, perhaps. Novelty. The joy of never knowing what may turn up from day to day. Instead of inheriting a useless tract of land, the pleasure of making money for yourself – by your own brains and skill.'

'A successful deal on the Stock Exchange, in fact!'

He laughed. 'Why not?'

'And what about an equal *loss* on the Stock Exchange?'

'That, dear, is rather tactless. And quite inappropriate to-day. . . . What about this Egypt plan?'

'Well—'

He cut in, smiling at her: 'That's settled. We've both always wanted to see Egypt.'

'When do you suggest?'

'Oh, next month. January's about the best time there. We'll enjoy the delightful society in this hotel a few weeks longer.'

'Tim,' said Mrs Allerton reproachfully. Then she added guiltily: 'I'm afraid I promised Mrs Leech that you'd go with her to the police station. She doesn't understand any Spanish.'

Tim made a grimace.

'About her ring? The blood-red ruby of the horse-leech's daughter? Does she still persist in thinking it's been stolen? I'll go if you like, but it's a waste of time. She'll only get some wretched chambermaid into trouble. I distinctly saw it on her finger when she went into the sea that day. It came off in the water and she never noticed.'

She says she is quite sure she took it off and left it on her dressing-table.'

'Well, she didn't. I saw it with my own eyes. The woman's a fool. Any woman's a fool who goes prancing into the sea in December, pretending the water's quite warm just because the sun happens to be shining rather brightly at the moment. Stout women oughtn't to be allowed to bathe anyway; they look so revolting in bathing dresses.'

Mrs Allerton murmured, 'I really feel I ought to give up bathing.'

Tim gave a shout of laughter.

'You? You can give most of the young things points and to spare.'

Mrs Allerton sighed and said, 'I wish there were a few more young people for you here.'

Tim Allerton shook his head decidedly.

'I don't. You and I get along rather comfortably without outside distractions.'

'You'd like it if Joanna were here.'

'I wouldn't.' His tone was unexpectedly resolute. 'You're all wrong there. Joanna amuses me, but I don't really like her, and to have her around much gets on my nerves. I'm thankful she isn't here. I should be quite resigned if I were never to see Joanna again.'

He added, almost below his breath, 'There's only one woman in the world I've got a real respect and admiration for, and I think, Mrs Allerton, you know very well who that woman is.'

His mother blushed and looked quite confused.

Tim said gravely: 'There aren't very many really nice women in the world. You happen to be one of them.'

9

In an apartment overlooking Central Park in New York, Mrs Robson exclaimed: 'If that isn't just too lovely! You really are the luckiest girl, Cornelia.'

Cornelia Robson flushed responsively. She was a big clumsy-looking girl with brown doglike eyes.

'Oh, it will be wonderful!' she gasped.

Old Miss Van Schuyler inclined her head in a satisfied fashion at this correct attitude on the part of poor relations. 'I've always dreamed of a trip to Europe,' sighed Cornelia, 'but I just didn't feel I'd ever get there.'

'Miss Bowers will come with me as usual, of course,' and Miss Van Schuyler, 'but as a social companion I find her limited – very limited. There are many little things that Cornelia can do for me.'

'I'd just love to, Cousin Marie,' said Cornelia eagerly.

'Well, well, then that's settled,' said Miss Van Schuyler. 'Just run and find Miss Bowers, my dear. It's time for my egg-nog.'

Cornelia departed. Her mother said: 'My dear Marie, I'm really *most* grateful to you! You know I think Cornelia suffers a lot from not being a social success. It makes her feel kind of mortified. If I could afford to take her to places – but you know how it's been since Ned died.'

'I'm very glad to take her,' said Miss Van Schuyler. 'Cornelia has always been a nice handy girl, willing to run errands, and not so selfish as some of these young people nowadays.'

Mrs Robson rose and kissed her rich relative's wrinkled and slightly yellow face.

'I'm just ever so grateful,' she declared.

On the stairs she met a tall capable-looking woman who was carrying a glass containing a yellow foamy liquid.

'Well, Miss Bowers, so you're off to Europe?'

'Why, yes, Mrs Robson.'

'What a lovely trip!'

'Why, yes, I should think it would be very enjoyable.'

'But you've been abroad before?'

'Oh, yes, Mrs Robson. I went over to Paris with Miss Van Schuyler last fall. But I've never been to Egypt before.'

Mrs Robson hesitated.

'I do hope – there won't be any – trouble.'

She had lowered her voice. Miss Bowers, however, replied in her usual tone:

'Oh, *no*, Mrs Robson; I shall take good care of *that*. I keep a very sharp look-out always.'

But there was still a faint shadow on Mrs Robson's face as she slowly continued down the stairs.

10

In his office down town Mr Andrew Pennington was opening her personal mail. Suddenly his fist clenched itself and came down on his desk with a bang; his face crimsoned and two big veins stood out on his forehead. He pressed a buzzer on his

desk and a smart-looking stenographer appeared with commendable promptitude.

'Tell Mr Rockford to step in here?'

'Yes, Mr Pennington.'

A few minutes later, Sterndale Rockford, Pennington's partner, entered the office. The two men were not unlike – both
tall, sparse, with greying hair and clean-shaven, clever faces.

'What's up, Pennington?'

Pennington looked up from the letter he was re-reading. He
said. 'Linnet's married . . .'

'*What?*'

'You heard what I said! Linnet Ridgeway's *married*!'

'How? When? Why didn't we hear about it?'

Pennington glanced at the calendar on his desk.

'She wasn't married when she wrote this letter, but she's
married now. Morning of the fourth. That's today.'

Rockford dropped into a chair.

'Whew! No warning! Nothing? Who's the man?'

Pennington referred again to the letter.

'Doyle. Simon Doyle.'

'What sort of a fellow is he? Ever heard of him?'

'No. She doesn't say much. . . .' He scanned the lines of clear,
upright handwriting. 'Got an idea there's something hole-and-
corner about the business . . . That doesn't matter. The whole
point is, she's married.'

The eyes of the two men met. Rockford nodded.

'This needs a bit of thinking out,' he said quietly.

'What are we going to do about it?'

'I'm asking you.'

The two men sat silent. Then Rockford asked. 'Got any
plan?'

Pennington said slowly: 'The *Normandie* sails today. One
of us could just make it.'

'You're crazy! What's the big idea?'

Pennington began: 'Those British lawyers—' and stopped.

'What about 'em. Surely you're not going over to tackle
'em? You're mad!'

'I'm not suggesting that you – or I – should go to England.'

'What's the big idea, then?'

Pennington smoothed out the letter on the table.

'Linnet's going to Egypt for her honeymoon. Expects to be
there a month or more. . . .'

'Egypt – eh?'

Rockford considered. Then he looked up and met the other's glance.

'Egypt,' he said; *'that's* your idea!'

'Yes – a chance meeting. Over on a trip. Linnet and her husband – honeymoon atmosphere. It might be done.'

Rockford said doubtfully: 'She's sharp, Linnet is . . . but—'

Pennington went on softly: 'I think there might be ways of – managing it.'

Again their eyes met. Rockford nodded.

'All right, big boy.'

Pennington looked at the clock.

'We'll have to hustle – whichever of us is going.'

'You go,' said Rockford promptly. 'You always made a hit with Linnet. "Uncle Andrew." That's the ticket!'

Pennington's face had hardened. He said: 'I hope I can pull it off.'

'You've got to pull it off,' his partner said. 'The situation's critical. . . .'

11

William Carmichael said to the thin, weedy youth who opened the door inquiringly: 'Send Mr Jim to me, please.'

Jim Fanthorp entered the room and looked inquiringly at his uncle. The older man looked up with a nod and a grunt.

'Humph, there you are.'

'You asked for me?'

'Just cast an eye over this.'

The young man sat down and drew the sheaf of papers towards him. The elder man watched him.

'Well?'

The answer came promptly. 'Looks fishy to me, sir.'

Again the senior partner of Carmichael, Grant & Carmichael uttered his characteristic grunt.

Jim Fanthorp re-read the letter which had just arrived by air mail from Egypt:

. . . It seems wicked to be writing business letters on such a day. We have spent a week at Mena House and made an expedition to the Fayum. The day after tomorrow we are going up the Nile to Luxor and Assuan by steamer, and perhaps on to Khartoum. When we went into Cook's this morning to see about our tickets who do you think was the first person I saw? – my American trustee, Andrew Pennington.

I think you met him two years ago when he was over. I had no idea he was in Egypt and he had no idea that I was! Nor that I was married! My letter, telling him of my marriage, must just have missed him. He is actually going up the Nile on the same trip that we are. Isn't it a coincidence? Thank you so much for all you have done in this busy time. I—

As the young man was about to turn the page, Mr Carmichael took the letter from him.

'That's all,' he said. 'The rest doesn't matter. Well, what do you think?'

His nephew considered for a moment– then he said:

'Well – I think – not a coincidence. . . .'

The other nodded approval.

'Like a trip to Egypt?' he barked out.

'You think that's advisable?'

'I think there's no time to lose.'

'But, why me?'

'Use your brains, boy; use your brains. Linnet Ridgeway has never met you; no more has Pennington. If you go by air you may get there in time.'

'I – I don't like it, sir. What am I to do?'

'Use your eyes. Use your ears. Use your brains – if you've got any. And, if necessary – act.'

'I – I don't like it.'

'Perhaps not – but you've got to do it.'

'It's – necessary?'

'In my opinion,' said Carmichael, 'it's absolutely vital.'

12

Mrs Otterbourne, readjusting the turban of native material that she wore draped round her head, said fretfully:

'I really don't see why we shouldn't go on to Egypt. I'm sick and tired of Jerusalem.'

As her daughter made no reply, she said, 'You might at least answer when you're spoken to.'

Rosalie Otterbourne was looking at a newspaper reproduction of a face. Below it was printed:

Mrs Simon Doyle, who before her marriage was the well-known society beauty, Miss Linnet Ridgeway. Mr and Mrs Doyle are spending their holiday in Egypt.

Rosalie said, 'You'd like to move on to Egypt, Mother?'

'Yes, I would', Mrs Otterbourne snapped. 'I consider they've treated us in a most cavalier fashion here. My being here is an advertisement – I ought to get a special reduction in terms. When I hinted as much, I consider they were most impertinent – *most* impertinent. I told them exactly what I thought of them.'

The girl sighed. She said: 'One place is very like another. I wish we could get right away.'

'And this morning,' went on Mrs Otterbourne, 'the manager actually had the impertinence to tell me that all the rooms had been booked in advance and that he would require ours in two days' time.'

'So we've got to go somewhere.'

'Not at all. I'm quite prepared to fight for my rights.'

Rosalie murmured: 'I suppose we might as well go on to Egypt. It doesn't make any difference.'

'It's certainly not a matter of life or death,' agreed Mrs Otterbourne.

But there she was quite wrong – for a matter of life and death was exactly what it was.

—— 2 ——

'That's Hercule Poirot, the detective,' said Mrs Allerton.

She and her son were sitting in brightly painted scarlet basket chairs outside the Cataract Hotel at Assuan. They were watching the retreating figures of two people – a short man dressed in a white silk suit and a tall slim girl.

Tim Allerton sat up in an unusually alert fashion.

'That funny little man?' he asked incredulously.

'That funny little man!'

'What on earth's he doing out here?' Tim asked.

His mother laughed. 'Darling, you sound quite excited. Why do men enjoy crime so much? I hate detective stories and never read them. But I don't think Monsieur Poirot is here with any ulterior motive. He's made a good deal of money and he's seeing life, I fancy.'

'Seems to have an eye for the best-looking girl in the place.'

Mrs Allerton tilted her head a little on one side as she considered the retreating backs of M. Poirot and his companion.

The girl by his side overtopped him by some three inches. She walked well, neither stiffly nor slouchingly.

'I suppose she *is* quite good-looking,' said Mrs Allerton. She shot a little glance sideways at Tim. Somewhat to her amusement the fish rose at once.

'She's more than quite. Pity she looks so bad-tempered and sulky.'

'Perhaps that's just expression, dear.'

'Unpleasant young devil, I think. But she's pretty enough.'

The subject of these remarks was walking slowly by Poirot's side. Rosalie Otterbourne was twirling an unopened parasol, and her expression certainly bore out what Tim had just said. She looked both sulky and bad-tempered. Her eyebrows were drawn together in a frown, and the scarlet line of her mouth was drawn downward.

They turned to the left out of the hotel gate and entered the cool shade of the public gardens.

Hercule Poirot was prattling gently, his expression that of beatific good humour. He wore a white silk suit, carefully pressed, and a panama hat, and carried a highly ornamental fly whisk with a sham amber handle.

'—it enchants me,' he was saying. 'The black rocks of Elephantine, and the sun, and the little boats on the river. Yes, it is good to be alive.'

He paused and then added: 'You do not find it so, Mademoiselle?'

Rosalie Otterbourne said shortly: 'It's all right, I suppose. I think Assuan's a gloomy sort of place. The hotel's half empty, and everyone's about a hundred—'

She stopped – biting her lip.

Hercule Poirot's eyes twinkled.

'It is true, yes, I have one leg in the grave.'

'I – I wasn't thinking of you,' said the girl. 'I'm sorry. That sounded rude.'

'Not at all. It is natural you should wish for companions of your own age. Ah, well, there is *one* young man, at least.'

'The one who sits with his mother all the time? I like *her* – but I think he looks dreadful – so conceited!'

Poirot smiled.

'And I – am I conceited?'

'Oh, I don't think so.'

She was obviously uninterested – but the fact did not seem to annoy Poirot. He merely remarked with placid satisfaction: 'My best friend says that I am very conceited.'

'Oh, well,' said Rosalie vaguely, 'I suppose you have something to be conceited about. Unfortunately crime doesn't interest me in the least.'

Poirot said solemnly, 'I am delighted to learn that you have no guilty secret to hide.'

Just for a moment the sulky mask of her face was transformed as she shot him a swift questioning glance. Poirot did not seem to notice it as he went on:

'Madame, your mother, was not at lunch today. She is not indisposed, I trust?'

'This place doesn't suit her,' said Rosalie briefly. 'I shall be glad when we leave.'

'We are fellow passengers, are we not? We both make the excursion up to Wâdi Halfa and the Second Cataract?'

'Yes.'

They came out from the shade of the gardens on to a dusty stretch of road bordered by the river. Five watchful bead-sellers, two vendors of postcards, three sellers of plaster scarabs, a couple of donkey boys and some detached but hopeful infantile riff-raff closed in upon them.

'You want beads, sir? Very good, sir. Very cheap. . . .'

'Lady, you want scarab? Look – great queen – very lucky. . . .'

'You look, sir – real lapis. Very good, very cheap. . . .'

'You want ride donkey, sir? This very good donkey. This donkey Whisky and Soda, sir . . .'

'You want to go granite quarries, sir? This very good donkey. Other donkey very bad, sir, that donkey fall down. . . .'

'You want postcard – very cheap – very nice. . . .'

'Look, lady. . . . Only ten piastres – very cheap – lapis – this ivory. . . .'

'This very good fly whisk – this all-amber. . . .'

'You go out in boat, sir? I got very good boat, sir. . . .'

'You go back to hotel, lady? This first-class donkey. . . .'

Hercule Poirot made vague gestures to rid himself of this human cluster of flies. Rosalie stalked through them like a sleep-walker.

'It's best to pretend to be deaf and blind,' she remarked.

The infantile riff-raff ran alongside murmuring plaintively: 'Bakshish? Bakshish? Hip hip hurrah – very good, very nice. . . .'

Their gaily coloured rags trailed picturesquely, and the flies lay in clusters on their eyelids. They were the most persistent. The others fell back and launched a fresh attack on the next comer.

Now Poirot and Rosalie only ran the gauntlet of the shops
– suave, persuasive accents here. . . .

'You visit my shop today, sir?' You want that ivory crocodile,
sir?' 'You not been in my shop yet, sir? I show you very beautiful things.'

They turned into the fifth shop and Rosalie handed over
several rolls of film – the object of the walk.

Then they came out again and walked towards the river's
edge.

One of the Nile steamers was just mooring. Poirot and
Rosalie looked interestedly at the passengers.

'Quite a lot, aren't there?' commented Rosalie.

She turned her head as Tim Allerton came up and joined
them. He was a little out of breath as though he had been
walking fast.

They stood there for a moment or two, and then Tim spoke.

'An awful crowd as usual, I suppose,' he remarked disparagingly, indicating the disembarking passengers.

'They're usually quite terrible,' agreed Rosalie.

All three wore the air of superiority assumed by people who
are already in a place when studying new arrivals.

'Hullo!' exclaimed Tim, his voice suddenly excited. 'I'm
damned if that isn't Linnet Ridgeway.'

If the information left Poirot unmoved, it stirred Rosalie's
interest. She leaned forward and her sulkiness quite dropped
from her as she asked: 'Where? That one in white?'

'Yes, there with the tall man. They're coming ashore now.
He's the new husband, I suppose. Can't remember his name
now.'

'Doyle,' said Rosalie. 'Simon Doyle. It was in all the newspapers. She's simply rolling, isn't she?'

'Only about the richest girl in England,' replied Tim cheerfully.

The three lookers-on were silent watching the passengers
come ashore. Poirot gazed with interest at the subject of the
remarks of his companions. He murmured: 'She is beautiful.'

'Some people have got everything,' said Rosalie bitterly.

There was a queer grudging expression on her face as she
watched the other girl come up the gangplank.

Linnet Doyle was looking as perfectly turned out as if she
were stepping on to the centre of the stage of a revue. She had
something too of the assurance of a famous actress. She was
used to being looked at, to being admired, to being the centre
of the stage wherever she went.

She was aware of the keen glances bent upon her – and at the same time almost unaware of them; such tributes were part of her life.

She came ashore playing a rôle, even though she played it unconsciously. The rich beautiful society bride on her honeymoon. She turned, with a little smile and a light remark, to the tall man by her side. He answered, and the sound of his voice seemed to interest Hercule Poirot. His eyes lit up and he drew his brows together.

The couple passed close to him. He heard Simon Doyle say:

'We'll try and make time for it, darling. We can easily stay a week or two if you like it here.'

His face was turned towards her, eager, adoring, a little humble.

Poirot's eyes ran over him thoughtfully – the square shoulders, the bronzed face, the dark blue eyes, the rather childlike simplicity of the smile.

'Lucky devil,' said Tim after they had passed. 'Fancy finding an heiress who hasn't got adenoids and flat feet!'

'They look frightfully happy,' said Rosalie with a note of envy in her voice. She added suddenly, but so low that Tim did not catch the words, 'It isn't fair.'

Poirot heard, however. He had been frowning somewhat perplexedly, but now he flashed a quick glance towards her.

Tim said: 'I must collect some stuff for my mother now.'

He raised his hat and moved off. Poirot and Rosalie retraced their steps slowly in the direction of the hotel, waving aside fresh proffers and donkeys.

'So it is not fair, Mademoiselle?' asked Poirot gently.

The girl flushed angrily.

'I don't know what you mean.'

'I am repeating what you said just now under your breath. Oh, yes, you did.'

Rosalie Otterbourne shrugged her shoulders.

'It really seems a little too much for one person. Money, good looks, marvellous figure and—'

She paused and Poirot said:

'And love? Eh? And love? But you do not know – she may have been married for her money!'

'Didn't you see the way he looked at her?'

'Oh, yes, Mademoiselle. I saw all there was to see – indeed I saw something that you did not.'

'What was that?'

Poirot said slowly: 'I saw, Mademoiselle, dark lines below

a woman's eyes. I saw a hand that clutched a sun-shade so tight that the knuckles were white. . . .'

Rosalie was staring at him.

'What do you mean?'

'I mean that all is not the gold that glitters. I mean that, though this lady is rich and beautiful and beloved, there is all the same *something* that is not right. And I know something else.'

'Yes?'

'I know,' said Poirot, frowning, 'that somewhere, at some time, I have heard that voice before – the voice of Monsieur Doyle – and I wish I could remember where.'

But Rosalie was not listening. She had stopped dead. With the point of her sunshade she was tracing patterns in the loose sand. Suddenly she broke out fiercely:

'I'm odious, I'm quite odious. I'm just a beast through and through. I'd like to tear the clothes off her back and stamp on her lovely, arrogant, self-confident face. I'm just a jealous cat – but that's what I feel like. She's so horribly successful and poised and assured.'

Hercule Poirot looked a little astonished by the outburst. He took her by the arm and gave her a friendly little shake.

'*Tenez* – you will feel better for having said that!'

'I just hate her! I've never hated anyone so much at first sight.'

'Magnificent!'

Rosalie looked at him doubtfully. Then her mouth twitched and she laughed.

'*Bien*,' said Poirot, and laughed too.

They proceeded amicably back to the hotel.

'I must find Mother,' said Rosalie, as they came into the cool dim hall.

Poirot passed out on the other side on to the terrace overlooking the Nile. Here were little tables set for tea, but it was early still. He stood for a few moments looking at the river, then strolled down through the garden.

Some people were playing tennis in the hot sun. He paused to watch them for a while, then went on down the steep path. It was here, sitting on a bench overlooking the Nile, that he came upon the girl of Chez Ma Tante. He recognised her at once. Her face, as he had seen it that night, was securely etched upon his memory. The expression on it now was very different. She was paler, thinner, and there were lines that told of a great weariness and misery of spirit.

He drew back a little. She had not seen him, and he watched her for a while without her suspecting his presence. Her small foot tapped impatiently on the ground. Her eyes, dark with a kind of smouldering fire, had a queer kind of suffering dark triumph in them. She was looking out across the Nile where the white-sailed boats glided up and down the river.

A face – and a voice. He remembered them both. This girl's face and the voice he had heard just now, the voice of a newly made bridegroom. . . .

And even as he stood there considering the unconscious girl, the next scene in the drama was played.

Voices sounded above. The girl on the seat started to her feet. Linnet Doyle and her husband came down the path. Linnet's voice was happy and confident. The look of strain and tenseness of muscle had quite disappeared, Linnet was happy.

The girl who was standing there took a step or two forward. The other two stopped dead.

'Hullo, Linnet,' said Jacqueline de Bellefort. 'So here you are! We never seem to stop running into each other. Hullo, Simon, how are you?'

Linnet Doyle had shrunk back against the rock with a little cry. Simon Doyle's good-looking face was suddenly convulsed with rage. He moved forward as though he would have liked to strike the slim girlish figure.

With a quick birdlike turn of her head she signalled her realisation of a stranger's presence. Simon turned his head and noticed Poirot. He said awkwardly: 'Hullo, Jacqueline; we didn't expect to see you here.'

The words were unconvincing in the extreme.

The girl flashed white teeth at them.

'Quite a surprise?' she asked. Then, with a little nod, she walked up the path.

Poirot moved delicately in the opposite direction. As he went, he heard Linnet Doyle say:

'Simon – for God's sake! Simon – what can we do?'

————— 3 —————

Dinner was over. The terrace outside the Cataract Hotel was
softly lit. Most of the guests staying at the hotel were there
sitting at little tables.

Simon and Linnet Doyle came out, a tall, distinguished-
looking grey-haired man, with a keen, clean-shaven American
face, beside them. As the little group hesitated for a moment in
the doorway, Tim Allerton rose from his chair near by and
came forward.

'You don't remember me, I'm sure,' he said pleasantly to
Linnet, 'but I'm Joanna Southwood's cousin.'

'Of course — how stupid of me! You're Tim Allerton. This
is my husband' — a faint tremor in the voice, pride, shyness?
— 'and this is my American trustee, Mr Pennington.'

Tim said: 'You must meet my mother.'

A few minutes later they were sitting together in a party —
Linnet in the corner, Tim and Pennington each side of her,
both talking to her, vying for her attention. Mrs Allerton talked
to Simon Doyle.

The swing doors revolved. A sudden tension came into the
beautiful upright figure sitting in the corner between the two
men. Then it relaxed as a small man came out and walked
across the terrace.

Mrs Allerton said: 'You're not the only celebrity here, my
dear. That funny little man is Hercule Poirot.'

She had spoken lightly, just out of instinctive social tact to
bridge an awkward pause, but Linnet seemed struck by the
information.

'Hercule Poirot? Of course — I've heard of him. . . .'

She seemed to sink into a fit of abstraction. The two men on
either side of her were momentarily at a loss.

Poirot had strolled across to the edge of the terrace, but his
attention was immediately solicited.

'Sit down, Monsieur Poirot. What a lively night!'

He obeyed.

'*Mais oui, Madame*, it is indeed beautiful.'

He smiled politely at Mrs Otterbourne. What draperies of
black ninon and that ridiculous turban effect! Mrs Otterbourne went on in her high complaining voice:

'Quite a lot of notabilities here now, aren't there? I expect

819

we shall see a paragraph about it in the papers soon. Society beauties, famous novelists—'

She paused with a slight mock-modest laugh.

Poirot felt, rather than saw, the sulky frowning girl opposite him flinch and set her mouth in a sulkier line than before.

'You have a novel on the way at present, Madame?' he inquired.

Mrs Otterbourne gave her little self-conscious laugh again.

'I'm being dreadfully lazy. I really must set to. My public is getting terribly impatient – and my publisher, poor man! Appeals by every post! Even cables!'

Again he felt the girl shift in the darkness.

'I don't mind telling you, Monsieur Poirot, I am partly here for local colour. *Snow on the desert's Face* – that is the title of my new book. Powerful – suggestive. Snow – on the desert – melted in the first flaming breath of passion.'

Rosalie got up, muttering something, and moved away down into the dark garden.

'One must be strong,' went on Mrs Otterbourne, wagging the turban emphatically. 'Strong meat – that is what my books are – all important. Libraries banned – no matter! I speak the truth. Sex – ah! Monsieur Poirot – why is everyone so afraid of sex? The pivot of the universe! You have read my books?'

'Alas, Madame! You comprehend, I do not read many novels. My work—'

Mrs Otterbourne said firmly: 'I must give you a copy of *Under the Fig Tree*. I think you will find it significant. It is outspoken – but it is *real*!'

'That is most kind of you, Madame. I will read it with pleasure.'

Mrs Otterbourne was silent a minute or two. She fidgeted with a long chain of beads that was wound twice round her neck. She looked swiftly from side to side.

'Perhaps – I'll just slip up and get it for you now.'

'Oh, Madame, pray do not trouble yourself. Later—'

'No, no. It's no trouble.' She rose. 'I'd like to show you—'

'What is it, Mother?'

Rosalie was suddenly at her side.

'Nothing, dear. I was just going up to get a book for Monsieur Poirot.'

'The *Fig Tree*? I'll get it.'

'You don't know where it is, dear. I'll go.'

'Yes, I do.'

The girl went swiftly across the terrace and into the hotel.

'Let me congratulate you, Madame, on a very lovely daughter,' said Poirot, with a bow.

'Rosalie? Yes, yes – she is good-looking. But she's very *hard*, Monsieur Poirot. And no sympathy with illness. She always thinks she knows best. She imagines she knows more about my health than I do myself—'

Poirot signalled to a passing waiter.

'A liquer, Madame? A chartreuse? A crème de menthe?'

Mrs Otterbourne shook her head vigorously.

'No, no. I am practically a teetotaller. You may have noticed I never drink anything but water – or perhaps lemonade. I cannot bear the taste of spirits.'

'Then may I order you a lemon squash, Madame?'

He gave the order – one lemon squash and one benedictine.

The swing door revolved. Rosalie passed through and came towards them, a book in her hand.

'Here you are,' she said. Her voice was quite expressionless – almost remarkably so.

'Monsieur Poirot has just ordered me a lemon squash,' said her mother.

'And you, Mademoiselle, what will you take?'

'Nothing.' She added, suddenly conscious of the curtness: 'Nothing, thank you.'

Poirot took the volume which Mrs Otterbourne held out to him. It still bore its original jacket, a gaily coloured affair representing a lady, with smartly shingled hair and scarlet fingernails, sitting on a tiger skin, in the traditional costume of Eve. Above her was a tree with the leaves of an oak, bearing large and improbably coloured apples.

It was entitled *Under the Fig Tree*, by Salome Otterbourne. On the inside was a publisher's blurb. It spoke enthusiastically of the superb courage and realism of this study of a modern woman's love life. 'Fearless, unconventional, realistic,' were the adjectives used.

Poirot bowed and murmured: 'I am honoured, Madame.'

As he raised his head, his eyes met those of the authoress's daughter. Almost involuntarily he made a little movement. He was astonished and grieved at the eloquent pain they revealed.

It was at that moment that the drinks arrived and created a welcome diversion.

Poirot lifted his glass gallantly.

'*A votre santé, Madame – Mademoiselle.*'

Mrs Otterbourne, sipping her lemonade, murmured, 'So refreshing – delicious!'

Silence fell on the three of them. They looked down to the shining black rocks in the Nile. There was something fantastic about them in the moonlight. They were like vast prehistoric monsters lying half out of the water. A little breeze came up suddenly and as suddenly died away. There was a feeling in the air of hush – of expectancy.

Hercule Poirot brought his gaze back to the terrace and its occupants. Was he wrong, or was there the same hush of expectancy there? It was like a moment on the stage when one is waiting for the entrance of the leading lady.

And just at that moment the swing doors began to revolve once more. This time it seemed as though they did so with a special air of importance. Everyone had stopped talking and was looking towards them.

A dark slender girl in a wine-coloured evening frock came through. She paused for a minute, then walked deliberately across the terrace and sat down at an empty table. There was nothing flaunting, nothing out of the way about her demeanour, and yet it had somehow the studied effect of a stage entrance.

'Well,' said Mrs Otterbourne. She tossed her turbaned head. 'She seems to think she is somebody, that girl!'

Poirot did not answer. He was watching. The girl had sat down in a place where she could look deliberately across at Linnet Doyle. Presently, Poirot noticed, Linnet Doyle leant forward and said something and a moment later got up and changed her seat. She was now sitting facing in the opposite direction.

Poirot nodded thoughtfully to himself.

It was about five minutes later that the other girl changed her seat to the opposite side of the terrace. She sat smoking and smiling quietly, the picture of contented ease. But always, as though unconsciously, her meditative gaze was on Simon Doyle's wife.

After a quarter of an hour Linnet Doyle got up abruptly and went into the hotel. Her husband followed her almost immediately.

Jacqueline de Bellefort smiled and twisted her chair round. She lit a cigarette and stared out over the Nile. She went on smiling to herself.

—— 4 ——

'Monsieur Poirot.'

Poirot got hastily to his feet. He had remained sitting out on the terrace alone after everyone else had left. Lost in meditation he had been staring at the smooth shiny black rocks when the sound of his name recalled him to himself.

It was a well-bred, assured voice, a charming voice, although perhaps a trifle arrogant.

Hercule Poirot, rising quickly, looked into the commanding eyes of Linnet Doyle. She wore a wrap of rich purple velvet over her white satin gown and she looked more lovely and more regal than Poirot had imagined possible.

'You are Monsieur Hercule Poirot?' said Linnet.

It was hardly a question.

'At your service, Madame.'

'You know who I am, perhaps?'

'Yes, Madame. I have heard your name. I know exactly who you are.'

Linnet nodded. that was only what she had expected. She went on, in her charming autocratic manner: 'Will you come with me into the card room, Monsieur Poirot? I am very anxious to speak to you.'

'Certainly, Madame.'

She led the way into the hotel. He followed. She led him into the deserted card room and motioned him to close the door. Then she sank down on a chair at one of the tables and he sat down opposite her.

She plunged straightaway into what she wanted to say. There were no hesitations. Her speech came flowingly.

'I have heard a great deal about you, Monsieur Poirot, and I know that you are a very clever man. It happens that I am urgently in need of someone to help me – and I think very possibly that you are the man who would do it.'

Poirot inclined his head.

'You are very amiable, Madame, but you see, I am on holiday, and when I am on holiday I do not take cases.'

'That could be arranged.'

It was not offensively said – only with the quiet confidence of a young woman who had always been able to arrange matters to her satisfaction.

Linnet Doyle went on: 'I am the subject, Monsieur Poirot,

of an intolerable persecution. That persecution has got to stop!
My own idea was to go to the police about it, but my – my
husband seems to think that the police would be powerless to
do anything.'

'Perhaps – if you would explain a little further?' murmured
Poirot politely.

'Oh, yes, I will do so. The matter is perfectly simple.'

There was still no hesitation – no faltering. Linnet Doyle
had a clear-cut businesslike mind. She only paused a minute
so as to present the facts as concisely as possible.

'Before I met my husband, he was engaged to a Miss de
Bellefort. She was also a friend of mine. My husband broke off
his engagement to her – they were not suited in any way. She,
I am sorry to say, took it rather hard. . . . I – am very sorry
about that – but these things cannot be helped. She made
certain – well, threats – to which I paid very little attention,
and which, I may say, she has not attempted to carry out. But
instead she has adopted the extraordinary course of – of following us about wherever we go.'

Poirot raised his eyebrows.

'Ah – rather an unusual – er –revenge.'

'Very unusual – and very ridiculous! But also – annoying.'
She bit her lip.

Poirot nodded.

'Yes, I can imagine that. You are, I understand, on your
honeymoon?'

'Yes. It happened – the first time – at Venice. She was there
– at Danielli's. I thought it was just coincidence. Rather embarrassing, but that was all. Then we found her on board the
boat at Brindisi. We – we understood that she was going on
to Palestine. We left her, as we thought, on the boat. But – but
when we got to Mena House she was there – waiting for us.'

Poirot nodded.

'And now?'

'We came up the Nile by boat. I – I was half expecting to
find her on board. When she wasn't there I thought she had
stopped being so – childish. But when we got here – she – she
was here – waiting.'

Poirot eyed her keenly for a moment. She was still perfectly
composed, but the knuckles of the hand that was gripping the
table were white with the force of her grip.

He said: 'And you are afraid this state of things may continue?'

'Yes.' She paused. 'Of course the whole thing is idiotic!

Jacqueline is making herself utterly ridiculous. I am surprised she hasn't got more pride – more dignity.'

Poirot made a slight gesture.

'There are times, Madame, when pride and dignity – they go by the board! There are other – stronger emotions.'

'Yes, possibly.' Linnet spoke impatiently. 'But what on earth can she hope to *gain* by all this?'

'It is not always a question of gain, Madame.'

Something in his tone struck Linnet disagreeably. She flushed and said quickly: 'You are right. A discussion of motives is beside the point. The crux of the matter is that this has got to be stopped.'

'And how do you propose that that should be accomplished, Madame?' Poirot asked.

'Well – naturally – my husband and I cannot continue being subjected to this annoyance. There must be some kind of legal redress against such a thing.'

She spoke impatiently. Poirot looked at her thoughtfully as he asked: 'Has she threatened you in actual words in public? Used insulting language? Attempted any bodily harm?'

'No.'

'Then, frankly, Madame, I do not see what you can do. If it is a young lady's pleasure to travel in certain places, and those places are the same where you and your husband find themselves – *eh bien* – what of it? The air is free to all! There is no question of her forcing herself upon your privacy? It is always in public that these encounters take place?'

'You mean there is nothing that I can do about it?'

Linnet sounded incredulous.

Poirot said placidly: 'Nothing at all, as far as I can see. Mademoiselle de Bellefort is within her rights.'

'But – but it is maddening! It is *intolerable* that I should have to put up with this!'

Poirot said dryly: 'I sympathise with you, Madame – especially as I imagine that you have not often had to put up with things.'

Linnet was frowning.

'The*re must* be some way of stopping it,' she murmured.

Poirot shrugged his shoulders.

'You can always leave – move on somewhere else,' he suggested.

'Then she will follow!'

'Very possibly – yes.'

'It's absurd!'

'Precisely.'

'Anyway, why should I – we – run away? As though – as though—'

She stopped.

'Exactly, Madame. As though—! It is all there, is it not?'

Linnet lifted her head and stared at him.

'What do you mean?'

Poirot altered his tone. He leant forward; his voice was confidential, appealing. He said very gently: 'Why do you mind so much, Madame?'

'Why? But it's maddening! Irritating to the last degree! I've told you why!'

Poirot shook his head.

'Not altogether.'

'What do you mean?' Linnet asked again.

Poirot leant back, folded his arms and spoke in a detached impersonal manner.

'*Ecoutez*, Madame. I will recount to you a little history. It is that one day, a month or two ago, I am dining in a restaurant in London. At the table next to me are two people, a man and a girl. They are very happy, so it seems, very much in love. They talk with confidence of the future. It is not that I listen to what is not meant for me; they are quite oblivious of who hears them and who does not. The man's back is to me, but I can watch the girl's face. It is very intense. She is in love – heart, soul, and body – and she is not of those who love lightly and often. With her it is clearly the life and the death. They are engaged to be married, these two; that is what I gather; and they talk of where they shall pass the days of their honeymoon. They plan to go to Egypt.'

He paused. Linnet said sharply: 'Well?'

Poirot went on: 'That is a month or two ago, but the girl's face – I do not forget it. I know that I shall remember if I see it again. And I remember too the man's voice. And I think you can guess, Madame, when it is I see the one and hear the other again. It is here in Egypt. The man is on his honeymoon, yes – but he is on his honeymoon with another woman.'

Linnet said sharply: 'What of it? I had already mentioned the facts.'

'The facts – yes.'

'Well then?'

Poirot said slowly: 'The girl in the restaurant mentioned a friend – a friend who, she was very positive, would not let her down. That friend, I think, was you, Madame.'

'Yes. I told you we had been friends.'

Linnet flushed.

'And she trusted you?'

'Yes.'

She hesitated for a moment, biting her lip impatiently; then, as Poirot did not seem disposed to speak, she broke out:

'Of course the whole thing was very unfortunate. But these things happen, Monsieur Poirot.'

'Ah! yes, they happen, Madame.' He paused. 'You are of the Church of England, I presume?'

'Yes.' Linnet looked slightly bewildered.

'Then you have heard portions of the Bible read aloud in church. You have heard of King David and of the rich man who had many flocks and herds and the poor man who had one ewe lamb – and of how the rich man took the poor man's one ewe lamb. That was something that happened, Madame.'

Linnet sat up. Her eyes flashed angrily.

'I see perfectly what you are driving at, Monsieur Poirot! You think, to put it vulgarly, that I stole my friend's young man. Looking at the matter sentimentally – which is, I suppose, the way people of your generation cannot help looking at things – that is possibly true. But the real hard truth is different. I don't deny that Jackie was passionately in love with Simon, but I don't think you take into account that he may not have been equally devoted to her. He was very fond of her, but I think that even before he met me he was beginning to feel that he had made a mistake. Look at it clearly, Monsieur Poirot. Simon discovers that it is I he loves, not Jackie. What is he to do? Be heroically noble and marry a woman he does not care for – and thereby probably ruin three lives – for it is doubtful where he could make Jackie happy under those circumstances? If he were actually married to her when he met me I agree that it *might* be his duty to stick to her – though I'm not really sure of that. If one person is unhappy the other suffers too. But an engagement is not really binding. If a mistake has been made, then surely it is better to face the fact before it is too late. I admit that it was very hard on Jackie, and I'm terribly sorry about it – but there it is. It was inevitable.'

'I wonder.'

She stared at him.

'What do you mean?'

'It is very sensible, very logical – all that you say! But it does not explain one thing.'

'What is that?'

'Your own attitude, Madame. See you, this pursuit of you, you might take it in two ways. It might cause you annoyance – yes, or it might stir your pity – that your friend should have been so deeply hurt as to throw all regard for the conventions aside. But that is not the way you react. No, to you this persecution is *intolerable* – and why? It can be for one reason only – that you feel a sense of guilt.'

Linnet sprang to her feet.

'How dare you? Really, Monsieur Poirot, this is going too far.'

'But I do dare, Madame! I am going to speak to you quite frankly. I suggest to you that, although you may have endeavoured to gloss over the fact to yourself, you did deliberately set about taking your husband from your friend. I suggest that you felt strongly attracted to him at once. But I suggest that there was a moment when you hesitated, when you realised that there was a *choice* – that you could refrain or go in. I suggest that the initiative rested with *you* – not with Monsieur Doyle. You are beautiful, Madame; you are rich; you are clever, intelligent – and you have charm. You could have exercised that charm or you could have restrained it. You had everything, Madame, that life can offer. Your friend's life was bound up in one person. You knew that, but, though you hesitated, you did not hold your hand. You stretched it out and, like the rich man in the Bible, you took the poor man's one ewe lamb.'

There was a silence. Linnet controlled herself with an effort and said in a cold voice: 'All this is quite beside the point!'

'No, it is not beside the point. I am explaining to you just why the unexpected appearances of Mademoiselle de Bellefort have upset you so much. It is because though she may be unwomanly and undignified in what she is doing, you have the inner conviction that she has right on her side.'

'That's not true.'

Poirot shrugged his shoulders.

'You refuse to be honest with yourself.'

'Not at all.'

Poirot said gently: 'I should say, Madame, that you have had a happy life, that you have been generous and kindly in your attitude towards others.'

'I have tried to be,' said Linnet. The impatient anger died out of her face. She spoke simply – almost forlornly.

'And that is why the feeling that you have deliberately caused injury to someone upsets you so much, and why you are so reluctant to admit the fact. Pardon me if I have been impertinent, but the psychology, it is the most important fact in a case.'

Linnet said slowly: 'Even supposing what you say were true – and I don't admit it, mind – what can be done about it now? One can't alter the past; one must deal with things as they are.'

Poirot nodded.

'You have the clear brain. Yes, one cannot go back over the past. One must accept things as they are. And sometimes, Madame, that is all one can do – accept the consequences of one's past deeds.'

'You mean,' asked Linnet incredulously, 'that I can do nothing – *nothing*?'

'You must have courage, Madame; that is what it seems like to me.'

Linnet said slowly:

'Couldn't you – talk to Jackie – to Miss de Bellefort? Reason with her?'

'Yes, I could do that. I will do that if you would like me to do so. But do not expect much result. I fancy that Mademoiselle de Bellefort is so much in the grip of a fixed idea that nothing will turn her from it.'

'You could, of course, return to England and establish yourself in your own house.'

'Even then, I suppose, Jacqueline is capable of planting herself in the village, so that I should see her every time I went out of the grounds.'

'True.'

'Besides,' said Linnet slowly, 'I don't think that Simon would agree to run away.'

'What is his attitude in this?'

'He's furious – simply furious.'

Poirot nodded thoughtfully.

Linnet said appealingly, 'You will – talk to her?'

'Yes, I will do that. But it is my opinion that I shall not be able to accomplish anything.'

Linnet said violently: 'Jackie is extraordinary! One can't tell what she will do!'

'You spoke just now of certain threats she had made. Would you tell me what those threats were?'

Linnet shrugged her shoulders.

'She threatened to – well – kill us both. Jackie can be rather – Latin sometimes.'

'I see.' Poirot's tone was grave.

Linnet turned to him appealingly.

'You will act for me?'

'No, Madame.' His tone was firm. 'I will not accept a commission from you. I will do what I can in the interests of humanity. That, yes. There is here a situation that is full of difficulty and danger. I will do what I can to clear it up – but I am not very sanguine as to my chance of success.'

Linnet Doyle said slowly: 'But you will not act for *me*?'

'No, Madame,' said Hercule Poirot.

5

Hercule Poirot found Jacqueline de Bellefort sitting on the rocks directly overlooking the Nile. He had felt fairly certain that she had not retired for the night and that he would find her somewhere about the grounds of the hotel.

She was sitting with her chin cupped in the palms of her hands, and she did not turn her head or look around at the sound of his approach.

'Mademoiselle de Bellefort?' asked Poirot. 'You permit that I speak to you for a little moment?'

Jacqueline turned her head slightly. A faint smile played round her lips.

'Certainly,' she said. 'You are Monsieur Hercule Poirot, I think? Shall I make a guess? You are acting for Mrs Doyle, who has promised you a large fee if you succeed in your mission.'

Poirot sat down on the bench near her.

'Your assumption is partially correct,' he said, smiling. 'I have just come from Madame Doyle, but I am not accepting any fee from her and, strictly speaking, I am not acting for her.'

'Oh!'

Jacqueline studied him attentively.

'Then why have you come?' she asked abruptly.

Hercule Poirot's reply was in the form of another question.

'Have you ever seen me before, Mademoiselle?'

She shook her head.

'No, I do not think so.'

'Yet I have seen you. I sat next to you once at Chez Ma Tante. You were there with Monsieur Simon Doyle.'

A strange masklike expression came over the girl's face. She said, 'I remember that evening. . . .'

'Since then,' said Poirot, 'many things have occurred.'

'As you say, many things have occurred.'

Her voice was hard with an undertone of desperate bitterness.

'Mademoiselle, I speak as a friend. Bury your dead!'

She looked startled.

'What do you mean?'

'Give up the past! Turn to the future! What is done is done. Bitterness will not undo it.'

'I'm sure that that would suit dear Linnet admirably.'

Poirot made a gesture.

'I am not thinking of her at this moment! I am thinking of *you*. You have suffered – yes – but what you are doing now will only prolong that suffering.'

She shook her head.

'You're wrong. There are times when I almost enjoy myself.'

'And that, Mademoiselle, is the worst of all.'

She looked up swiftly.

'You're not stupid,' she said. She added slowly, 'I believe you mean to be kind.'

'Go home, Mademoiselle. You are young; you have brains, the world is before you.'

Jacqueline shook her head slowly.

'You don't understand – or you won't. Simon is my world.'

'Love is not everything, Mademoiselle,' Poirot said gently. 'It is only when we are young that we think it is.'

But the girl still shook her head.

'You don't understand.' She shot him a quick look. 'You know all about it, of course? You've talked to Linnet? And you were in the restaurant that night . . . Simon and I loved each other.'

'I know that you loved him.'

She was quick to perceive the inflection of his words. She repeated with emphasis:

'*We loved each other*. And I loved Linnet. . . . I trusted her. She was my best friend. All her life Linnet has been able to buy everything she wanted. She's never denied herself anything. When she saw Simon she wanted him – and she just took him.'

'And he allowed himself to be – bought?'

Jacqueline shook her dark head slowly.

'No, it's not quite like that. If it were, I shouldn't be here now. . . . You're suggesting that Simon isn't worth caring for. . . . If he'd married Linnet for her money, that would be true. But he didn't marry her for her money. It's more complicated than that. There's such a thing as *glamour*, Monsieur Poirot. And money helps that. Linnet had an "atmosphere," you see. She was the queen of a kingdom – the young princess – luxurious to her fingertips. It was like a stage setting. She had the world at her feet, one of the richest and most sought-after peers in England wanting to marry her. And she stoops instead to the obscure Simon Doyle. . . . Do you wonder it went to his head?' She made a sudden gesture. 'Look at the moon up there. You see her very plainly, don't you? She's very real. But if the sun were to shine you wouldn't be able to see her at all. It was rather like that. I was the moon. . . . When the sun came out, Simon couldn't see me any more. . . . He was dazzled. He couldn't see anything but the sun – Linnet.'

She paused and then went on: 'So you see it was – glamour. She went to his head. And then there's her complete assurance – her habit of command. She's so sure of herself that she makes other people sure. Simon was weak, perhaps, but then he's a very simple person. He would have loved me and me only if Linnet hadn't come along and snatched him up in her golden chariot. And I know – I know perfectly – that he wouldn't ever have fallen in love with her if she hadn't made him.'

'That is what you think – yes.'

'I *know* it. He loved me – he will always love me.'

Poirot said: 'Even now?'

A quick answer seemed to rise to her lips, then she stifled. She looked at Poirot and a deep burning colour spread over her face. She looked away; her head dropped down. She said in a low stifled voice: 'Yes, I know. He hates me now. Yes, hates me. . . . He'd better be careful!'

With a quick gesture she fumbled in a little silk bag that lay on the seat. Then she held out her hand. On the palm of it was a small pearl-handled pistol – a dainty toy it looked.

'Nice little thing, isn't it?' she said. 'Looks too foolish to be real, but it is real! One of those bullets would kill a man or a woman. And I'm a good shot.' She smiled a faraway, reminiscent smile.

'When I went home as a child with my mother, to South Carolina, my grandfather taught me to shoot. He was the old-fashioned kind that believes in shooting – especially where honour is concerned. My father, too, he fought several duels as a young man. He was a good swordsman. He killed a man once. Thas was over a woman. So you see, Monsieur Poirot' – she met his eyes sharply – 'I've hot blood in me! I bought this when it first happened. I meant to kill one or other of them – the trouble was I couldn't decide which. Both of them would have been unsatisfactory. If I'd thought Linnet would have looked afraid – but she's got plenty of physical courage. She can stand up to physical action. And then I thought I'd – wait! That appeared to me more and more. After all, I could do it any time; it would be more fun to wait and – think about it! And then this idea came to my mind – to follow them! Whenever they arrived at some faraway spot and were together and happy, they should see *Me*! And it worked. It got Linnet badly – in a way nothing else could have done! It got right under her skin. . . . That was when I began to enjoy myself. . . . And there's nothing she can do about it! I'm always perfectly pleasant and polite! There's not a word they can take hold of! It's poisoning everything – everything – for them.' Her laugh rang out, clear and silvery.

Poirot grasped her arm.

'Be quiet. Quiet, I tell you.'

Jacqueline looked at him.

'Well?' she asked. Her smile was definitely challenging.

'Mademoiselle, I beseech you, do not do what you are doing.'

'Leave dear Linnet alone, you mean!'

'It is deeper than that. Do not open your heart to evil.'

Her lips fell apart; a look of bewilderment came into her eyes.

Poirot went on gravely: 'Because – if you do – evil will come. . . . Yes, very surely evil will come. . . . It will enter in and make its home within you, and after a little while it will no longer be possible to drive it out.'

Jacqueline stared at him. Her glance seemed to waver, to flicker uncertainly.

She said: 'I – don't know——' Then she cried definitely, 'You can't stop me.'

'No,' said Hercule Poirot. 'I cannot stop you.' His voice was sad.

'Even if I were to – kill her, you couldn't stop me.'

'No – not if you were willing to pay the price.'

Jacqueline de Bellefort laughed.

'Oh, I'm not afraid of death! What have I got to live for, after all? I suppose you believe it's very wrong to kill a person who has injured you – even if they've taken away everything you had in the world?'

Poirot said steadily: 'Yes, Mademoiselle. I believe it is the unforgivable offence – to kill.'

Jacqueline laughed again.

'Then you ought to approve of my present scheme of revenge; because, you see, as long as it works, I shan't use that pistol. . . . But I'm afraid – yes, afraid sometimes – it all goes red – I want to hurt her – to stick a knife into her, to put my dear little pistol close against her head and then – just press with my finger – *Oh*!'

The exclamation startled him.

'What is it, Mademoiselle?'

She had turned her head and was staring into the shadows.

'Someone – standing over there. He's gone now.'

Hercule Poirot looked round sharply.

The place seemed quite deserted.

'There seems no one here but ourselves, Mademoiselle.' He got up. 'In any case I have said all I came to say. I wish you good-night.'

Jacqueline got up too. She said almost pleadingly, 'You do understand – that I can't do what you ask me to do?'

Poirot shook his head.

'No – for you could do it! There is always a moment! Your friend Linnet – there was a moment, too, in which she could have held her hand. . . . She let it pass by. And if one does that, then one is committed to the enterprise and there comes no second chance.'

'No second chance . . .' said Jacqueline de Bellefort.

She stood brooding for a moment; then she lifted her head defiantly.

'Good-night, Monsieur Poirot.'

He shook his head sadly and followed her up the path to the hotel.

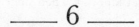

6

On the following morning Simon Doyle joined Hercule Poirot as the latter was leaving the hotel to walk down to the town.

'Good-morning, Monsieur Poirot.'

'Good-morning, Monsieur Doyle.'

'You are going to the town? Mind if I stroll along with you?'

'But certainly. I shall be delighted.'

The two men walked side by side, passed out through the

gateway and turned into the cool shade of the gardens. Then Simon removed his pipe from his mouth and said, 'I understand, Monsieur Poirot, that my wife had a talk with you last night?'

'That is so.'

Simon Doyle was frowning a little. He belonged to that type of men of action who find it difficult to put thoughts into words and who have trouble in expressing themselves clearly.

'I'm glad of one thing,' he said. 'You've made her realise that we're more or less powerless in the matter.'

'There is clearly no legal redress,' agreed Poirot.

'Exactly. Linnet didn't seem to understand that.' He gave a faint smile. 'Linnet's been brought up to believe that every annoyance can automatically be referred to the police.'

'It would be pleasant if such were the case,' said Poirot.

There was a pause. Then Simon said suddenly, his face going very red as he spoke:

'It's – it's infamous that she should be victimised like this! She's done nothing! If anyone likes to say I behaved like a cad, they're welcome to say so! I suppose I did. But I won't have the whole thing visited on Linnet. She had nothing whatever to do with it.'

Poirot bowed his head gravely but said nothing.

'Did you – er – have you – talked to Jackie – Miss de Bellefort?'

'Yes, I have spoken with her.'

'Did you get her to see sense?'

'I'm afraid not.'

Simon spoke out irritably: 'Can't she see what an ass she's making of herself? Doesn't she realise that no decent woman would behave as she is doing? Hasn't she got any pride or self-respect?'

Poirot shrugged his shoulders.

'She has only a sense of – injury, shall we say?' he replied.

'Yes, but damn it all, man, decent girls don't behave like this! I admit I was entirely to blame. I treated her damned badly and all that. I should quite understand her being thoroughly fed up with me and never wishing to see me again. But this following me round – it's – it's *indecent*! Making a show of herself! What the devil does she hope to get out of it?'

'Perhaps – revenge!'

'Idiotic! I'd really understand better if she'd tried to do something melodramatic – like taking a pot shot at me.'

'You think that would be more like her – yes?'

'Frankly I do. She's hot-blooded – and she's got an ungovernable temper. I shouldn't be surprised at her doing anything while she was in a white-hot rage. But this spying business –'
He shook his head.

'It is more subtle – yes! It is intelligent!'

Doyle stared at him.

'You don't understand. It's playing hell with Linnet's nerves.'

'And yours?'

Simon looked at him with momentary surprise.

'Me? I'd like to wring the little devil's neck.'

'There is nothing, then, of the old feeling left?'

'My dear Monsieur Poirot – how can I put it? It's like the moon when the sun comes out. You don't know it's there any more. When once I'd met Linnet – Jackie didn't exist.'

'*Tiens, c'est drôle, ça!*' muttered Poirot.

'I beg your pardon.'

'Your simile interested me, that is all.'

Again flushed, Simon said: 'I suppose Jackie told you that I'd only married Linnet for her money? Well, that's a damned lie! I wouldn't marry any woman for money! What Jackie doesn't understand is that it's difficult for a fellow when – when – a woman cares for him as she cared for me.'

'Ah?'

Poirot looked up sharply.

Simon blundered on: 'It – it – sounds a caddish thing to say, but Jackie was *too* fond of me!'

'*Une qui aime et un qui se laisse aimer,*' murmured Poirot.

'Eh? What's that you say? You see, a man doesn't want to feel that a woman cares more for him than he does for her.' His voice grew warm as he went on. 'He doesn't want to feel *owned*, body and soul. It's that damned *possessive* attitude! This man is *mine* – he *belongs* to me! That's the sort of thing I can't stick – no man could stick! He wants to get away – to get free. He wants to own his woman; he doesn't want *her* to own *him.*'

He broke off, and with fingers that trembled slightly he lit a cigarette.

Poirot said: 'And it is like that that you felt with Mademoiselle Jacqueline?'

'Eh?' Simon stared and then admitted: 'Er – yes – well, yes, as a matter of fact I did. She doesn't realise that, of course. And it's not the sort of thing I could ever tell her. But I *was* feeling restless – and then I met Linnet, and she just swept me off my feet! I'd never seen anything so lovely. It was all so amazing. Everyone kowtowing to her – and then her singling out a poor chump like me.'

His tone held boyish awe and astonishment.

'I see,' said Poirot. He nodded thoughtfully. 'Yes – I see.'

'Why can't Jackie take it like a man?' demanded Simon resentfully.

A very faint smile twitched Poirot's upper lip.

'Well, you see, Monsieur Doyle, to begin with she is *not* a man.'

'No, no – but I mean take it like a good sport! After all, you've got to take your medicine when it comes to you. The fault's mine, I admit. But there it is! If you no longer care for a girl, it's simply madness to marry her. And, now that I see what Jackie's really like and the lengths she is likely to go to, I feel I've had rather a lucky escape.'

'The lengths she is likely to go to,' Poirot repeated thoughtfully. 'Have you an idea, Monsieur Doyle, what those lengths are?'

Simon looked at him, rather startled.

'No – at least, what do you mean?'

'You know she carries a pistol about with her?'

Simon frowned, then shook his head.

'I don't believe she'll use that – now. She might have done so earlier. But I believe it's got past that. She's just spiteful now – trying to take it out of us both.'

Poirot shrugged his shoulders.

'It may be so,' he said doubtfully.

'It's Linnet I'm worrying about,' declared Simon, somewhat unnecessarily.

'I quite realise that,' said Poirot.

'I'm not really afraid of Jackie doing any melodramatic shooting stuff, but this spying and following business has absolutely got Linnet on the raw. I'll tell you the plan I've made, and perhaps you can suggest improvements on it. To begin with, I've announced fairly openly that we're going to stay here ten days. But tomorrow the steamer *Karnak* starts from Shellâl to Wâdi Halfa. I propose to book passages on that under an assumed name. Tomorrow we'll go on an excursion to Philae. Linnet's maid can take the luggage. We'll join the *Karnak* at Shellâl. When Jackie finds we don't come back, it will be too late – we shall be well on our way. She'll assume we have given her the slip and gone back to Cairo. In fact I might even bribe the porter to say so. Inquiry at the tourist offices won't help her, because our names won't appear. How does that strike you?'

'It is well imagined, yes. And suppose she waits here till you return?'

'We may not return. We would go on to Khartoum and then perhaps by air to Kenya. She can't follow us all over the globe.'

'No; there must come a time when financial reasons forbid. She has very little money, I understand.'

Simon looked at him with admiration.

'That's clever of you. Do you know, I hadn't thought of that. Jackie's as poor as they make them.'

'And yet she has manged to follow you so far?'

Simon said doubtfully:

'She's got a small income, of course. Something under two hundred a year, I imagine. I suppose – yes, I suppose she must have sold out the capital to do what she's doing.'

'So that the time will come when she has exhausted her resources and is quite penniless?'

'Yes. . . .'

Simon wriggled uneasily. The thought seemed to make him uncomfortable. Poirot watched him attentively.

'No,' he remarked. 'No, it is not a pretty thought. . . .'

Simon said rather angrily, 'Well, *I* can't help it!' Then he added, 'What do you think of my plan?'

'I think it may work, yes. But it is, of course, a *retreat.*'

Simon flushed.

'You mean, we're running away? Yes, that's true. . . . But Linnet—'

Poirot watched him, then gave a short nod.

'As you say, it may be the best way. But remember, Mademoiselle de Bellefort has brains.'

Simon said somberly: 'Some day, I feel, we've got to make a stand and fight it out. Her attitude isn't reasonable.'

'Reasonable, *mon Dieu!*' cried Poirot.

'There's no reason why women shouldn't behave like rational beings,' Simon asserted stolidly.

Poirot said dryly: 'Quite frequently they do. That is even more upsetting!' He added, 'I too, shall be on the *Karnak*. It is part of my itinerary.'

'Oh!' Simon hesitated, then said, choosing his words with some embarrassment: 'That isn't – isn't – er – on our account in any way? I mean I wouldn't like to think—'

Poirot disabused him quickly:

'Not at all. It was all arranged before I left London. I always make my plans well in advance.'

'You don't just move on from place to place as the fancy takes you? Isn't the latter really pleasanter?'

'Perhaps. But to succeed in life every detail should be arranged well beforehand.'

Simon laughed and said: 'That is how the more skilful murderer behaves, I suppose.'

'Yes – though I must admit that the most brilliant crime I remember and one of the most difficult to solve was committed on the spur of the moment.'

Simon said boyishly: 'You must tell us something about your cases on board the *Karnak*.'

'No, no; that would be to talk – what do you call it? – the shop.'

'Yes, but your kind of shop is rather thrilling. Mrs Allerton thinks so. She's longing to get a chance to cross-question you.'

'Mrs Allerton? That is the charming grey-haired woman who has such a devoted son?'

'Yes. She'll be on the *Karnak* too.'

'Does she know that you —?'

'Certainly not,' said Simon with emphasis. 'Nobody knows. I've gone on the principle that it's better not to trust anybody.'

'An admirable sentiment – and one which I always adopt. By the way, the third member of your party, the tall grey-haired man —'

'Pennington?'

'Yes. He is travelling with you?'

Simon said grimly: 'Not very usual on a honeymoon, you were thinking? Pennington is Linnet's American trustee. We ran across him by chance in Cairo.'

'*Ah, vraiment!* You permit a question? She is of age, Madame your wife?'

Simon looked amused.

'She isn't actually twenty-one yet – but she hadn't got to ask anyone's consent before marrying me. It was the greatest surprise to Pennington. He left New York on the *Carmanic* two days before Linnet's letter got there telling him of our marriage, so he knew nothing about it.'

'The *Carmanic* —' murmured Poirot.

'It was the greatest surprise to him when we ran into him at Shepherd's in Cairo.'

'That was indeed the coincident!'

'Yes, and we found that he was coming on this Nile trip – so naturally we foregathered; couldn't have done anything else decently. Besides that, it's been – well, a relief in some ways.'

He looked embarrassed again. 'You see, Linnet's been all strung up – expecting Jackie to turn up anywhere and everywhere. While we were alone together, the subject kept coming up. Andrew Pennington's a help that way, we have to talk of outside matters.'

'Your wife has not confided in Mr Pennington?'

'No.' Simon's jaw looked aggressive. 'It's nothing to do with anyone else. Besides, when we started on this Nile trip we thought we'd seen the end of the business.'

Poirot shook his head.

'You have not seen the end of it yet. No – the end is not yet at hand. I am very sure of that.'

'I say, Monsieur Poirot, you're not very encouraging.'

Poirot looked at him with a slight feeling of irritation. He thought to himself: 'The Anglo-Saxon, he takes nothing seriously but playing games! He does not grow up.'

Linnet Doyle – Jacqueline de Bellefort – both of them took the business seriously enough. But in Simon's attitude he could find nothing but male impatience and annoyance. He said: 'You will permit me an impertinent question? Was it your idea to come to Egypt for your honeymoon?'

Simon flushed.

'No, of course not. As a matter of fact I'd rather have gone anywhere else, but Linnet was absolutely set upon it. And so – and so –'

He stopped rather lamely.

'Naturally,' said Poirot gravely.

He appreciated the fact that, if Linnet Doyle was set upon anything, that thing had to happen.

He thought to himself: 'I have now heard three separate accounts of the affair – Linnet Doyle's, Jacqueline de Bellefort's, Simon Doyle's. Which of them is nearest to the truth?'

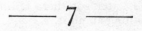

7

Simon and Linnet Doyle set off on their expedition to Philae about eleven o'clock the following morning. Jacqueline de Bellefort, sitting on the hotel balcony, watched them set off in the picturesque sailing-boat. What she did not see was the departure of a car – laden with luggage, and in which sat a demure-looking maid – from the front door of the hotel. It turned to the right in the direction of Shellâl.

Hercule Poirot decided to pass the remaining two hours before lunch on the island of Elephantine, immediately opposite the hotel.

He went down to the landing-stage. There were two men just stepping into one of the hotel boats, and Poirot joined them. The men were obviously strangers to each other. The younger of them had arrived by train the day before. He was a tall, dark-haired young man, with a thin face and a pugnacious chin. He was wearing an extremely dirty pair of grey flannel trousers and a high-necked polo jumper singularly unsuited to the climate. The other was a slightly podgy middle-aged man who lost no time in entering into conversation with Poirot in idiomatic but slightly broken English. Far from taking part in the conversation, the younger man merely scowled at them both and then deliberately turned his back on them and proceeded to admire the agility with which the Nubian boatman steered the boat with his toes as he manipulated the sail with his hands.

It was very peaceful on the water, the great smooth slippery black rocks gliding by and the soft breeze fanning their faces. Elephantine was reached very quickly and on going ashore Poirot and his loquacious acquaintance made straight for the Museum. By this time the latter had produced a card which he handed to Poirot with a little bow. It bore the inscription: 'Signor Guido Richetti, Archeologo.'

Not to be outdone, Poirot returned the bow and extracted his own card. These formalities completed, the two men stepped into the Museum together, the Italian pouring forth a stream of erudite information. They were by now conversing in French.

The young man in the flannel trousers strolled listlessly round the Museum, yawning from time to time, and then escaped to the outer air.

Poirot and Signor Richetti at last followed him. The Italian was energetic in examining the ruins, but presently Poirot, espying a green-lined sunshade which he recognised on the rocks down by the river, escaped in that direction.

Mrs Allerton was sitting on a large rock, a sketch-book by her side and a book on her lap.

Poirot removed his hat politely and Mrs. Allerton at once entered into conversation.

'Good-morning,' she said. 'I suppose it would be quite impossible to get rid of some of these awful children.'

A group of small black figures surrounded her, all grinning and posturing and holding out imploring hands as they lisped 'Bakshish' at intervals, hopefully.

'I thought they'd get tired of me,' said Mrs Allerton sadly. 'They've been watching me for over two hours now – and they close in on me little by little; and then I yell "Imshi" and brandish my sunshade at them and they scatter for a minute or two. And then they come back and stare and stare, and their eyes are simply disgusting, and so are their noses, and I don't believe I really like children – not unless they're more or less washed and have the rudiments of manners.'

She laughed ruefully.

Poirot gallantly attempted to disperse the mob for her, but without avail. They scattered and then reappeared, closing in once more.

'If there were only any peace in Egypt, I should like it better,' said Mrs Allerton. 'But you can never be alone anywhere. Someone is always pestering you for money, or offering you donkeys, or beads, or expeditions to native villages, or duck shooting.'

'It is the great disadvantage, that is true,' agreed Poirot.

He spread his handkerchief cautiously on the rock and sat somewhat gingerly upon it.

'Your son is not with you this morning?' he went on.

'No, Tim had some letters to get off before we leave. We're doing the trip to the Second Cataract, you know.'

'I, too.'

'I'm so glad. I want to tell you that I'm quite thrilled to meet you. When we were in Majorca, there was a Mrs Leech there, and she was telling us the most wonderful things about you. She'd lost a ruby ring bathing, and she was just lamenting that you weren't there to find it for her.'

'Ah, *parbleu*, but I am not the diving seal!'

They both laughed.

Mrs Allerton went on:

'I saw you from my window walking down the drive with Simon Doyle this morning. Do tell me what you make of him! We're all so excited about him.'

'Ah? Truly?'

'Yes. You know his marriage to Linnet Ridgeway was the greatest surprise. She was supposed to be going to marry Lord

Windlesham and then suddenly she gets engaged to this man no one had ever heard of!'

'You know her well, Madame?'

'No, but a cousin of mine, Joanna Southwood, is one of her best friends.'

'Ah, yes, I have read that name in the papers.' He was silent a moment and then went on, 'She is a young lady very much in the news, Mademoiselle Joanna Southwood.'

'Oh, she knows how to advertise herself all right,' snapped Mrs Allerton.

'You do not like her, Madame?'

'That was a nasty remark of mine.' Mrs Allerton looked penitent. 'You see I'm old-fashioned. I don't like her much. Tim and she are the greatest friends, though.'

'I see,' said Poirot.

His companion shot a quick look at him. She changed the subject.

'How very few young people there are out here! That pretty girl with the chestnut hair and the appalling mother in the turban is almost the only young creature in the place. You have talked to her a good deal, I notice. She interests me, that child.'

'Why is that, Madame?'

'I feel sorry for her. You can suffer so much when you are young and sensitive. I think she is suffering.'

'Yes, she is not happy, poor little one.'

'Tim and I call her the "sulky girl." I've tried to talk to her once or twice, but she's snubbed me on each occasion. However, I believe she's going on this Nile trip too, and I expect we'll have to be more or less all matey together, shan't we?'

'It is a possible contingency, Madame.'

'I'm very matey really – people interest me enormously. All the different types.' She paused, then said: 'Tim tells me that that dark girl – her name is de Bellefort – is the girl who was engaged to Simon Doyle. It's rather awkward for them – meeting like this.'

'It is awkward – yes,' agreed Poirot.

Mrs Allerton shot a quick glance at him.

'You know, it may sound foolish, but she almost frightened me. She looked so – intense.'

Poirot nodded his head slowly.

'You were not far wrong, Madame. A great force of emotion is always frightening.'

'Do people interest you too, Monsieur Poirot? Or do you reserve your interest for potential criminals?'

'Madame – that category would not leave many people outside it.'

Mrs Allerton looked a trifle startled.

'Do you really mean that?'

'Given the particular incentive, that is to say,' Poirot added.

'Which would differ?'

'Naturally.'

Mrs Allerton hesitated – a little smile on her lips.

'Even I perhaps?'

'Mothers, Madame, are particularly ruthless when their children are in danger.'

She said gravely, 'I think that's true – yes, you're quite right.'

She was silent a minute or two, then she said, smiling: 'I'm trying to imagine motives for crime suitable for everyone in the hotel. It's quite entertaining. Simon Doyle, for instance?'

Poirot said, smiling: 'A very simple crime – a direct short-cut to his objective. No subtlety about it.'

'And therefore very easily detected?'

'Yes; he would not be ingenious.'

'And Linnet?'

'That would be like the Queen in your *Alice in Wonderland*, "Off with her head." '

'Of course. The divine right of monarchy! Just a little bit of the Naboth's vineyard touch. And the dangerous girl – Jacqueline de Bellefort – could *she* do a murder?'

Poirot hesitated for a minute or two, then he said doubtfully, 'Yes, I think she could.'

'But you're not sure?'

'No. She puzzles me, that little one.'

'I don't think Mr Pennington could do one, do you? He looks so desiccated and dyspeptic – with no red blood in him.'

'But possibly a strong sense of self-preservation.'

'Yes, I suppose so. And poor Mrs Otterbourne in her turban?'

'There is always vanity.'

'As a motive for murder?' Mrs Allerton asked doubtfully.

'Motives for murder are sometimes very trivial, Madame.'

'What are the most usual motives, Monsieur Poirot?'

'Most frequent – money. That is to say, gain in its various ramifications. Then there is revenge – and love, and fear, and pure hate, and beneficence—'

'Monsieur Poirot!'

'Oh, yes, Madame. I have known of – shall we say A?— being removed by B solely in order to benefit C. Political murders often come under that heading. Someone is considered to be harmful to civilisation and is removed on that account. Such people forget that life and death are the affair of the good God.'

He spoke gravely.

Mrs Allerton said quietly: 'I am glad to hear you say that. All the same, God chooses his instruments.'

'There is danger in thinking like that, Madame.'

She adopted a lighter tone.

'After this conversation, Monsieur Poirot, I shall wonder that there is anyone left alive!'

She got up.

'We must be getting back. We have to start immediately after lunch.'

When they reached the landing-stage they found the young man in the polo jumper just taking his place in the boat. The Italian was already waiting. As the Nubian boatman cast the sail loose and they started, Poirot addressed a polite remark to the stranger.

'There are very wonderful things to be seen in Egypt, are there not?'

The young man was now smoking a somewhat noisome pipe. He removed it from his mouth and remarked briefly and very emphatically, in astonishingly well-bred accents: 'They make me sick.'

Mrs Allerton put on her pince-nez and surveyed him with pleasurable interest.

'Indeed? And why is that?' Poirot asked.

'Take the Pyramids. Great blocks of useless masonry, put up to minister to the egoism of a despotic bloated king. Think of the sweated masses who toiled to build them and died doing it. It makes me sick to think of the suffering and torture they represent.'

Mrs Allerton said cheerfully: 'You'd rather have no Pyramids, no Parthenon, no beautiful tombs or temples – just the solid satisfaction of knowing that people got three meals a day and died in their beds.'

The young man directed his scowl in her direction.

'I think human beings matter more than stones.'

'But they do not endure as well,' remarked Hercule Poirot.

'I'd rather see a well-fed worker than any so-called work of art. What matters is the future – not the past.'

This was too much for Signor Richetti, who burst into a torrent of impassioned speech not too easy to follow.

The young man retorted by telling everybody exactly what he thought of the capitalist system. He spoke with the utmost venom.

When the tirade was over they had arrived at the hotel landing-stage.

Mrs Allerton murmured cheerfully: 'Well, well,' and stepped ashore. The young man directed a baleful glance after her.

In the hall of the hotel Poirot encountered Jacqueline de Bellefort. She was dressed in riding clothes. She gave him an ironical little bow.

'I'm going donkey-riding. Do you recommend the native villages, Monsieur Poirot?'

'Is that your excursion to-day, Mademoiselle? *Eh bien,* they are picturesque – but do not spend large sums on native curios.'

'Which are shipped here from Europe? No, I am not so easy to deceive as that.'

With a little nod she passed out into the brilliant sunshine.

Poirot completed his packing – a very simple affair, since his possessions were always in the most meticulous order. Then he repaired to the dining-room and ate an early lunch.

After lunch the hotel bus took the passengers for the Second Cataract to the station where they were to catch the daily express from Cairo on to Shellâl – a ten-minute run.

The Allertons, Poirot, the young man in the dirty flannel trousers and the Italian were the passengers. Mrs Otterbourne and her daughter had made the expedition on the Dam and to Philae and would join the steamer at Shellâl.

The train from Cairo and Luxor was about twenty minutes late. However, it arrived at last, and the usual scenes of wild activity occurred. Native porters taking suitcases out of the train collided with other porters putting them in.

Finally, somewhat breathless, Poirot found himself, with an assortment of his own, the Allertons', and some totally unknown luggage, in one compartment, while Tim and his mother were elsewhere with the remains of the assorted baggage.

The compartment in which Poirot found himself was occupied by an elderly lady with a very wrinkled face, a stiff white stock, a good many diamonds and an expression of reptilian contempt for the majority of mankind.

She treated Poirot to an aristocratic glare and retired behind the pages of an American magazine. A big, rather clumsy young woman of under thirty was sitting opposite her. She had eager brown eyes, rather like a dog's, untidy hair, and a terrific air of willingness to please. At intervals the old lady looked over the top of her magazine and snapped an order at her.

'Cornelia, collect the rugs.' 'When we arrive look after my dressing-case. On no account let anyone else handle it.' 'Don't forget my paper-cutter.'

The train run was brief. In ten minutes' time they came to rest on the jetty where the S.S. *Karnak* was awaiting them. The Otterbournes were already on board.

The *Karnak* was a smaller steamer than the *Papyrus* and the *Lotus*, the First Cataract steamers, which are too large to pass through the locks of the Assuan dam. The passengers went on board and were shown their accommodation. Since the boat was not full, most of the passengers had accommodation on the promenade deck. The entire forward part of this deck was occupied by an observation saloon, all glass-enclosed, where the passengers could sit and watch the river unfold before them. On the deck below were a smoking-room and a small drawing-room and on the deck below that, the dining-saloon.

Having seen his possessions disposed in his cabin, Poirot came out on the deck again to watch the process of departure. He joined Rosalie Otterbourne, who was leaning over the side.

'So now we journey into Nubia. You are pleased, Mademoiselle?'

The girl drew a deep breath.

'Yes. I feel that one's really getting away from things at last.'

She made a gesture with her hand. There was a savage aspect about the sheet of water in front of them, the masses of rock without vegetation that came down to the water's edge – here and there a trace of houses, abandoned and ruined as a result of the damming up of the waters. The whole scene had a melancholy, almost sinister charm.

'Away from *people*,' said Rosalie Otterbourne.

'Except those of our own number, Mademoiselle?'

She shrugged her shoulders. Then she said: 'There's something about this country that makes me feel – wicked. It brings to the surface all the things that are boiling inside one. Everything's so unfair – so unjust.'

'I wonder. You cannot judge by material evidence.'

Rosalie muttered: 'Look at – at some people's mothers – and look at mine. There is no God but Sex, and Salome Otterbourne is its Prophet.' She stopped. 'I shouldn't have said that, I suppose.'

Poirot made a gesture with his hands.

'Why not say it – to me? I am one of those who hear many things. If, as you say, you boil inside – like the jam – *eh bien*, let the scum come to the surface, and then one can take it off with a spoon so.'

He made the gesture of dropping something into the Nile.

'Then, it has gone.'

'What an extraordinary man you are!' Rosalie said. Her sulky mouth twisted into a smile. Then she suddenly stiffened as she exclaimed: 'Well, here are Mrs Doyle and her husband! I'd no idea *they* were coming on this trip!'

Linnet had just emerged from a cabin half-way down the deck. Simon was behind her. Poirot was almost startled by the look of her – so radiant, so assured. She looked positively arrogant with happiness. Simon Doyle, too, was a transformed being. He was grinning from ear to ear and looking like a happy schoolboy.

'This is grand,' he said as he too leaned on the rail. 'I'm really looking forward to this trip, aren't you, Linnet? It feels, somehow so much less touristy – as though we were really going into the heart of Egypt.'

His wife responded quickly: 'I know. It's so much – wilder, somehow.'

Her hand slipped through his arm. He pressed it close to his side.

'We're off, Lin,' he murmured.

The steamer was drawing away from the jetty. They had started on their seven-day journey to the Second Cataract and back.

Behind them a light silvery laugh rang out. Linnet whipped round.

Jacqueline de Bellefort was standing there. She seemed amused.

'Hullo, Linnet! I didn't expect to find *you* here. I thought you said you were staying at Assuan another ten days. This is a surprise!'

'You – you didn't—' Linnet's tongue stammered. She forced a ghastly conventional smile. 'I – I didn't expect to see you either.'

'No?'

Jacqueline moved away to the other side of the boat. Linnet's grasp on her husband's arm tightened.

'Simon – Simon—'

All Doyle's good-natured pleasure had gone. He looked furious. His hands clenched themselves in spite of his effort at self-control.

The two of them moved a little away. Without turning his head Poirot caught scraps of disjointed words:

'. . . . turn back . . . impossible . . . we could . . .' and then, slightly louder, Doyle's voice, despairing but grim: 'We can't run away for ever Lin. We've got to go through with it now. . . .'

It was some hours later. Daylight was just fading. Poirot stood in the glass-enclosed saloon looking straight ahead. The *Karnak* was going through a narrow gorge. The rocks came down with a kind of sheer ferocity to the river flowing deep and swift between them. They were in Nubia now.

He heard a movement and Linnet Doyle stood by his side. Her fingers twisted and untwisted themselves; she looked as he had never yet seen her look. There was about her the air of a bewildered child. She said:

'Monsieur Poirot, I'm afraid – I'm afraid of everything. I've never felt like this before. All these wild rocks and the awful grimness and starkness. Where are we going? What's going to happen? I'm afraid, I tell you. Everyone hates me. I've never felt like that before. I've always been nice to people – I've done things for them – and they hate me – lots of people hate me. Except for Simon, I'm surrounded by enemies. . . . It's terrible to feel – that there are people who hate you. . . .'

'But what is all this, Madame?'

She shook her head.

'I suppose – it's nerves. . . . I just feel that – everything's unsafe all round me.'

She cast a quick nervous glance over her shoulder. Then she said abruptly: 'How will all this end? We're caught here. Trapped! There's no way out. We've got to go on. I – I don't know where I am.'

She slipped down on to a seat. Poirot looked down on her gravely; his glance was not untinged with compassion.

'How did she know we were coming on this boat?' she said. 'How could she have known?'

Poirot shook his head as he answered: 'She has brains, you know.'

'I feel as though I shall never escape from her.'

Poirot said: 'There is one plan you might have adopted. In fact I am surprised that it did not occur to you. After all, with you, Madame, money is no object. Why did you not engage your own private dahabiyeh?'

Linnet shook her head rather helplessly.

'If we'd known about all this – but you see we didn't – then. And it was difficult. . . .' She flashed out with sudden impatience: 'Oh! you don't understand half my difficulties. I've got to be careful with Simon. . . . He's – he's absurdly sensitive – about money. About my having so much! He wanted me to go to some little place in Spain with him – he – he wanted to pay all our honeymoon expenses himself. As if it *mattered*! Men are stupid! He's got to get used to – to – living comfortably. The mere idea of a dahabiyeh upset him – the – the needless expense. I've got to educate him – gradually.'

She looked up, bit her lip vexedly, as though feeling that she had been led into discussing her difficulties rather too unguardedly.

She got up.

'I must change. I'm sorry, Monsieur Poirot. I'm afraid I've been talking a lot of foolish nonsense.'

8

Mrs Allerton, looking quiet and distinguished in her simple black lace evening gown, descended two decks to the dining-room. At the door of it her son caught her up.

'Sorry, darling. I thought I was going to be late.'

'I wonder where we sit.' The saloon was dotted with little tables. Mrs Allerton paused till the steward, who was busy seating a party of people, could attend to them.

'By the way,' she added, 'I asked little Hercule Poirot to sit at our table.'

'Mother, you didn't!' Tim sounded really taken aback and annoyed.

His mother stared at him in surprise. Tim was usually so easy-going.

'My dear, do you mind?'

'Yes, I do. He's an unmitigated little bounder!'

'Oh, no, Tim! I don't agree with you.'

'Anyway, what do we want to get mixed up with an outsider

for? Cooped up like this on a small boat, that sort of thing is always a bore. He'll be with us morning, noon and night.'

'I'm sorry, dear.' Mrs Allerton looked distressed. 'I thought really it would amuse you. After all, he must have had a varied experience. And you love detective stories.'

Tim grunted.

'I wish you wouldn't have these bright ideas, Mother. We can't get out of it now, I suppose?'

'Really, Tim, I don't see how we can.'

'Oh, well, we shall have to put up with it, I suppose.'

The steward came to them at this minute and led them to a table. Mrs Allerton's face wore rather a puzzled expression as she followed him. Tim was usually so easy-going and good-tempered. This outburst was quite unlike him. It wasn't as though he had the ordinary Britisher's dislike – and mistrust – of foreigners. Tim was very cosmopolitan. Oh, well – she sighed. Men were incomprehensible! Even one's nearest and dearest had unsuspected reactions and feelings.

As they took their places, Hercule Poirot came quickly and silently into the dining-saloon. He paused with his hand on the back of the third chair.

'You really permit Madame, that I avail myself of your kind suggestion?'

'Of course. Sit down, Monsieur Poirot.'

'You are most amiable.'

She was uneasily conscious that, as he seated himself, he shot a swift glance at Tim, and that Tim had not quite succeeded in masking a somewhat sullen expression.

Mrs Allerton set herself to produce a pleasant atmosphere. As they drank their soup, she picked up the passenger list which had been placed beside her plate.

'Let's try and identify everybody,' she suggested cheerfully. 'I always think that's rather fun.'

She began reading: 'Mrs Allerton, Mr T. Allerton. That's easy enough! Miss de Bellefort. They've put her at the same table as the Otterbournes, I see. I wonder what she and Rosalie will make of each other. Who comes next? Dr Bessner. Dr Bessner? Who can identify Dr Bessner?'

She bent her glance on a table at which four men sat together.

'I think he must be the fat one with the closely shaved head and the moustache. A German, I should imagine. He seems to be enjoying his soup very much.' Certain succulent noises floated across to them.

Mrs Allerton continued: 'Miss Bowers? Can we make a guess at Miss Bowers? There are three or four women – no, we'll leave her for the present. Mr and Mrs Doyle. Yes, indeed, the lions of this trip. She really is very beautiful, and what a perfectly lovely frock she is wearing.'

Tim turned round in his chair. Linnet and her husband and Andrew Pennington had been given a table in the corner. Linnet was wearing a white dress and pearls.

'It looks frightfully simple to me,' said Tim. 'Just a length of stuff with a kind of cord round the middle.'

'Yes, darling,' said his mother. 'A very nice manly description of an eighty-guinea model.'

'I can't think why women pay so much for their clothes,' Tim said. 'It seems absurd to me.'

Mrs Allerton proceeded with her study of her fellow passengers.

'Mr Fanthorp must be one of the four at that table. The intensely young man who never speaks. Rathter a nice face, cautious but intelligent.'

Poirot agreed.

'He is intelligent – yes. He does not talk, but he listens very attentively, and he also watches. Yes, he makes good use of his eyes. Not quite the type you would expect to find travelling for pleasure in this part of the world. I wonder what he is doing here.'

'Mr Ferguson,' read Mrs Allerton. 'I feel that Ferguson must be our anti-capitalist friend. Mrs Otterbourne, Miss Otterbourne. We all know about them. Mr Pennington? Alias Uncle Andrew. He's a good-looking man, I think—'

'Now, Mother,' said Tim.

'I think he's very good-looking in a dry sort of way,' said Mrs Allerton. 'Rather a ruthless jaw. Probably the kind of man one reads about in the paper, who operates on Wall Street – or is it *in* Wall Street? I'm sure he must be extremely rich. Next – Monsieur Hercule Poirot – whose talents are really being wasted. Can't you get up a crime for Monsieur Poirot, Tim?'

But her well-meant banter only seemed to annoy her son anew. He scowled and Mrs Allerton hurried on: 'Mr Richetti. Our Italian archæological friend. Then Miss Robson and last of all Miss Van Schuyler. The last's easy. The very ugly old American lady who obviously feels herself the queen of the boat and who is clearly going to be very exclusive and speak to nobody who doesn't come up to the most exacting standards! She's rather marvellous, isn't she, really? A kind of period piece. The two women with her must be Miss Bowers and Miss Robson – perhaps a secretary, the thin one with pince-nez, and a poor relation, the rather pathetic young woman who is obviously enjoying herself in spite of being treated like a black slave. I think Robson's the secretary woman and Bowers is the poor relation.'

'Wrong, Mother,' said Tim, grinning. He had suddenly recovered his good humour.

'How do you know?'

'Because I was in the lounge before dinner and the old bean said to the companion woman: "Where's Miss Bowers? Fetch her at once, Cornelia." And away trotted Cornelia like an obedient dog.'

'I shall have to talk to Miss Van Schuyler,' mused Mrs Allerton.

Tim grinned again.

'She'll snub you, Mother.'

'Not at all. I shall pave the way by sitting near her and conversing, in low (but penetrating), well-bred tones, about any titled relations and friends I can remember. I think a casual mention of your second cousin, once removed, the Duke of Glasgow, would probably do the trick.'

'How unscrupulous you are, Mother!'

Events after dinner were not without their amusing side to a student of human nature.

The socialistic young man (who turned out to be Mr Ferguson as deduced) retired to the smoking-room, scorning the assemblage of passengers in the observation saloon on the top deck.

Miss Van Schuyler duly secured the best and most undraughty position there by advancing firmly on a table at which Mrs Otterbourne was sitting and saying, 'You'll excuse me, I am sure, but I *think* my knitting was left here!'

Fixed by a hypnotic eye, the turban rose and gave ground. Miss Van Schuyler established herself and her suite. Mrs Otterbourne sat down near by and hazarded various remarks, which were met with such chilling politeness that she soon gave up. Miss Van Schuyler then sat in glorious isolation. The Doyles sat with the Allertons. Dr Bessner retained the quiet Mr Fanthorp as a companion. Jacqueline de Bellefort sat by herself with a book. Rosalie Otterbourne was restless. Mrs Allerton spoke to her once or twice and tried to draw her into their group, but the girl responded ungraciously.

M. Hercule Poirot spent his evening listening to an account of Mrs Otterbourne's mission as a writer.

On his way to his cabin that night he encountered Jacqueline de Bellefort. She was leaning over the rail and, as she turned her head, he was struck by the look of acute misery on her face. There was now no insouciance, no malicious defiance, no dark flaming triumph.

'Good-night, Mademoiselle.'

'Good-night, Monsieur Poirot.' She hesitated, then said: 'You were surprised to find me here?'

'I was not so much surprised as sorry – very sorry. . . .'

He spoke gravely.

'You mean sorry – for *me*?'

'That is what I meant. You have chosen, Mademoiselle, the dangerous course. . . . As we here in this boat have embarked on a journey, so you too have embarked on your own private journey – a journey on a swift-moving river, between dangerous rocks, and heading for who knows what currents of disaster. . . .'

'Why do you say this?'

'Because it is true. . . . You have cut the bonds that moored you to safety. I doubt now if you could turn back if you would.'

She said very slowly: 'That is true. . . .'

Then she flung her head back.

'Ah, well – one must follow one's star, wherever it leads.'

'Beware, Mademoiselle, that it is not a false star. . . .'

She laughed and mimicked the parrot cry of the donkey boys:

'That very bad star, sir! That star fall down. . . .'

He was just dropping off to sleep when the murmur of voices awoke him. It was Simon Doyle's voice he heard, repeating the same words he had used when the steamer left Shellâl.

'We've got to go through with it now. . . .'

'Yes,' thought Hercule Poirot to himself, 'we have got to go through with it now. . . .'

He was not happy.

The steamer arrived early next morning at Ez-Sebûa.

Cornelia Robson, her face beaming, a large flapping hat on her head, was one of the first to hurry on shore. Cornelia was not good at snubbing people. She was of an amiable disposition and disposed to like all her fellow creatures.

The sight of Hercule Poirot, in a white suit, pink shirt, large black bow tie and a white topee, did not make her wince as the aristocratic Miss Van Schuyler would assuredly have winced. As they walked together up an avenue of sphinxes, she responded readily to his conventional opening, 'Your companions are not coming ashore to view the temple?'

'Well, you see, Cousin Marie — that's Miss Van Schuyler — never gets up very early. She has to be very, very careful of her health. And of course she wanted Miss Bowers, that's her hospital nurse, to do things for her. And she said, too, that this isn't one of the best temples — but she was frightfully kind and said it would be quite all right for me to come.'

'That was very gracious of her,' said Poirot dryly.

The ingenuous Cornelia agreed unsuspectingly.

'Oh, she's very kind. It's simply wonderful of her to bring me on this trip. I do feel I'm a lucky girl. I just could hardly believe it when she suggested to Mother that I should come too.'

'And you have enjoyed it — yes?'

'Oh, it's been wonderful! I've seen Italy — Venice and Padua and Pisa — and then Cairo — only Cousin Marie wasn't very well in Cairo, so I couldn't get round much, and now this wonderful trip up to Wâdi Halfa and back.'

Poirot said, smiling, 'You have the happy nature, Mademoiselle.'

He looked thoughtfully from her to silent, frowning Rosalie, who was walking ahead by herself.

'She's very nice-looking, isn't she?' said Cornelia, following his glance. 'Only kind of scornful-looking. She's very English, of course. She's not as lovely as Mrs Doyle. I think Mrs Doyle's the loveliest, the most elegant woman I've ever seen! And her husband just worships the ground she walks on, doesn't he? I think that grey-haired lady is kind of distinguished-looking, don't you? She's a cousin to a Duke, I believe. She was talking about him right near us last night. But she isn't actually titled herself, is she?'

She prattled on until the dragoman in charge called a halt and began to intone: 'This temple was dedicated to Egyptian God Amun and the Sun God Re-Harakhte – whose symbol was hawk's head. . . .'

It droned on. Dr Bessner, Baedeker in hand, mumbled to himself in German. He preferred the written word.

Tim Allerton had not joined the party. His mother was breaking the ice with the reserved Mr Fanthorp. Andrew Pennington, his arm through Linnet Doyle's, was listening attentively, seemingly most interested in the measurements as recited by the guide.

'Sixty-five feet high, is that so? Looks a little less to me. Great fellow, this Rameses. An Egyptian live wire.'

'A big business man, Uncle Andrew.'

Andrew Pennington looked at her appreciatively.

'You look fine this morning, Linnet. I've been a mite worried about you lately. You've looked kind of peaky.'

Chatting together, the party returned to the boat. Once more the *Karnak* glided up the river. The scenery was less stern now. There were palms, cultivation.

It was as though the change in the scenery had relieved some secret oppression that had brooded over the passengers. Tim Allerton had got over his fit of moodiness. Rosalie looked less sulky. Linnet seemed almost light-hearted.

Pennington said to her: 'It's tactless to talk business to a bride on her honeymoon, but there are just one or two things—'

'Why, of course, Uncle Andrew.' Linnet at once became businesslike. 'My marriage has made a difference, of course.'

'That's just it. Some time or other I want your signature to several documents.'

'Why not now?'

Andrew Pennington glanced round. Their corner of the observation saloon was quite untenanted. Most of the people were outside on the deck space between the observation saloon and the cabin. The only occupants of the saloon were Mr Ferguson – who was drinking beer at a small table in the middle, his legs, encased in their dirty flannel trousers, stuck out in front of him, whilst he whistled to himself in the intervals of drinking – M. Hercule Poirot, who was sitting close up to the front glass, intent on the panorama unfolding before him, and

Miss Van Schuyler, who was sitting in a corner reading a book on Egypt.

'That's fine,' said Andrew Pennington. He left the saloon.

Linnet and Simon smiled at each other – a slow smile that took a few minutes to come to full fruition.

'All right, sweet?' he asked.

'Yes, still all right. . . . Funny how I'm not rattled any more.'

Simon said with deep conviction in his tone: 'You're marvellous.'

Pennington came back. He brought with him a sheaf of closely written documents.

'Mercy!' cried Linnet. 'Have I got to sign all these?'

Andrew Pennington was apologetic.

'It's tough on you, I know, but I'd just like to get your affairs put in proper shape. First of all there's the lease of the Fifth Avenue property . . . then there are the Western Land Concessions . . . He talked on, rustling and sorting the papers. Simon yawned.

The door to the deck swung open and Mr Fanthorp came in. He gazed aimlessly round, then strolled forward and stood by Poirot looking out at the pale blue water and the yellow enveloping sands. . . .

'—you sign just there,' concluded Pennington, spreading a paper before Linnet and indicating a space.

Linnet picked up the document and glanced through it. She turned back once to the first page, then, taking up the fountain pen Pennington had laid beside her, she signed her name *Linnet Doyle*. . . .

Pennington took away the paper and spread out another.

Fanthorp wandered over in their direction. He peered out through the side window at something that seemed to interest him on the bank they were passing.

'That's just the transfer,' said Pennington. 'You needn't read it.'

But Linnet took a brief glance through it. Pennington laid down a third paper. Again Linnet perused it carefully.

'They're all quite straightforward,' said Andrew. 'Nothing of interest. Only legal phraseology.'

Simon yawned again.

'My dear girl, you're not going to read the whole lot through, are you? You'll be at it till lunch-time and longer.'

'I always read everything through,' said Linnet. 'Father taught me to do that. He said there might be some clerical error.'

Pennington laughed rather harshly.

'You're a grand woman of business, Linnet.'

'She's much more conscientious than I'd be,' said Simon, laughing. 'I've never read a legal document in my life. I sign where they tell me to sign on the dotted line – and that's that.'

'That's frightfully slipshod,' said Linnet disapprovingly.

'I've no business head,' declared Simon cheerfully. 'Never had. A fellow tells me to sign – I sign. It's much the simplest way.'

Andrew Pennington was looking at him thoughtfully. He said dryly, stroking his upper lip, 'A little risky sometimes, Doyle?'

'Nonsense,' replied Simon. 'I'm not one of those people who believe the whole world is out to do one down. I'm a trusting kind of fellow – and it pays, you know. I've hardly ever been let down.'

Suddenly, to everyone's surprise, the silent Mr Fanthorp swung round and addressed Linnet.

'I hope I'm not butting in, but you must let me say how much I admire your businesslike capacity. In my profession – er – I am a lawyer – I find ladies sadly unbusinesslike. Never to sign a document unless you read it through is admirable – altogether admirable.'

He gave a little bow. Then, rather red in the face, he turned once more to contemplate the banks of the Nile.

Linnet said rather uncertainly: 'Er – thank you. . . .' She bit her lip to repress a giggle. The young man had looked so preternaturally solemn.

Andrew Pennington looked seriously annoyed.

Simon Doyle looked uncertain whether to be annoyed or amused.

The backs of Mr Fanthorp's ears were bright crimson.

'Next, please,' said Linnet, smiling up at Pennington.

But Pennington was looking decidedly ruffled.

'I think perhaps some other time would be better,' he said stiffly. 'As – er – Doyle says, if you have to read through all these we shall be here till lunch-time. We mustn't miss enjoying the scenery. Anyway those first two papers were the only urgent ones. We'll settle down to business later.'

'It's frightfully hot in here,' Linnet said. 'Let's go outside.'

The three of them passed through the swing door. Hercule Poirot turned his head. His gaze rested thoughtfully on Mr Fanthorp's back; then it shifted to the lounging figure of Mr

Ferguson who had his head thrown back and was still whistling softly to himself.

Finally Poirot looked over at the upright figure of Miss Van Schuyler in her corner. Miss Van Schuyler was glaring at Mr Ferguson.

The swing door on the port side opened and Cornelia Robson hurried in.

'You've been a long time,' snapped the old lady. 'Where've you been?'

'I'm so sorry, Cousin Marie. The wool wasn't where you said it was. It was in another case altogether—'

'My dear child, you are perfectly hopeless at finding anything! You are willing, I know, my dear, but you must try to be a little cleverer and quicker. It only needs *concentration*.'

'I'm so sorry, Cousin Marie. I'm afraid I am very stupid.'

'Nobody need be stupid if they *try*, my dear. I have brought you on this trip, and I expect a little attention in return.'

Cornelia flushed.

'I'm very sorry, Cousin Marie.'

'And where is Miss Bowers? It was time for my drops ten minutes ago. Please go and find her at once. The doctor said it was most important—'

But at this stage Miss Bowers entered, carrying a small medicine glass.

'Your drops, Miss Van Schuyler.'

'I should have had them at eleven,' snapped the old lady. 'If there's one thing I detest it's unpunctuality.'

'Quite,' said Miss Bowers. She glanced at her wristwatch. 'It's exactly half a minute to eleven.'

'By my watch it's ten past.'

'I think you'll find my watch is right. It's a perfect time-keeper. It never loses or gains.' Miss Bowers was quite imperturbable.

Miss Van Schuyler swallowed the contents of the medicine glass.

'I feel definitely worse,' she snapped.

'I'm sorry to hear that, Miss Van Schuyler.'

Miss Bowers did not sound sorry. She sounded completely uninterested. She was obviously making the correct reply mechanically.

'It's too hot in here,' snapped Miss Van Schuyler. 'Find me a chair on the deck, Miss Bowers. Cornelia, bring my knitting. Don't be clumsy or drop it. And then I shall want you to wind some wool.'

The procession passed out.

Mr Ferguson sighed, stirred his legs and remarked to the world at large, 'Gosh, I'd like to scrag that dame.'

Poirot asked interestedly: 'She is a type you dislike, eh?'

'Dislike? I should say so. What good has that woman ever been to anyone or anything? She's never worked or lifted a finger. She's just battened on other people. She's a parasite – and a damned unpleasant parasite. There are a lot of people on this boat I'd say the world could do without.'

'Really?'

'Yes. That girl in here just now, signing share transfers and throwing her weight about. Hundreds and thousands of wretched workers slaving for a mere pittance to keep her in silk stockings and useless luxuries. One of the richest women in England, so someone told me – and never done a hand's turn in her life.'

'Who told you she was one of the richest women in England?'

Mr Ferguson cast a belligerent eye at him.

'A man you wouldn't be seen speaking to! A man who works with his hands and isn't ashamed of it! Not one of your dressed-up, foppish good-for-nothings.'

His eye rested unfavourably on the bow tie and pink shirt.

'Me, I work with my brains and am not ashamed of it,' said Poirot, answering the glance.

Mr Ferguson merely snorted.

'Ought to be shot – the lot of them!' he asserted.

'My dear young man,' said Poirot, 'what a passion you have for violence!'

'Can you tell me of any good that can be done without it? You've got to break down and destroy before you can build up.'

'It is certainly much easier and much noisier and much more spectacular.'

'What do *you* do for a living? Nothing at all, I bet. Probably call yourself a middle man.'

'I am not a middle man. I am a top man,' declared Hercule Poirot with a slight arrogance.

'What *are* you?'

'I am a detective,' said Hercule Poirot with the modest air of one who says 'I am a king.'

'Good God!' The young man seemed seriously taken aback. 'Do you mean that girl actually totes about a dumb dick? Is she as careful of her precious skin as *that*?'

'I have no connection whatever with Monsieur and Madame Doyle,' said Poirot stiffly. 'I am on a holiday.'

'Enjoying a vacation – eh?'

'And you? Is it not that you are on a holiday also?'

'Holiday!' Mr Ferguson snorted. Then he added cryptically: 'I'm studying conditions.'

'Very interesting,' murmured Poirot and moved gently out on to the deck.

Miss Van Schuyler was established in the best corner. Cornelia knelt in front of her, her arms outstretched with a skein of grey wool upon them. Miss Bowers was sitting very upright reading the *Saturday Evening Post*.

Poirot wandered gently onward down the starboard deck. As he passed round the stern of the boat he almost ran into a woman who turned a startled face towards him – a dark, piquant, Latin face. She was neatly dressed in black and had been standing talking to a big burly man in uniform – one of the engineers, by the look of him. There was a queer expression on both their faces – guilt and alarm. Poirot wondered what they had been talking about.

He rounded the stern and continued his walk along the port side. A cabin door opened and Mrs Otterbourne emerged and nearly fell into his arms. She was wearing a scarlet satin dressing-gown.

'So sorry,' she apologised. 'Dear Mr Poirot – so very sorry. The motion – just the motion, you know. Never did have any sea legs. If the boat would only keep still. . . .' She clutched at his arm. 'It's the pitching I can't stand. . . . Never really happy at sea. . . . And left all alone here hour after hour. That girl of mine – no sympathy – no understanding of her poor old mother who's done everything for her. . . .' Mrs Otterbourne began to weep. 'Slaved for her I have – worn myself to the bone – to the bone. *A grande amoureuse* – that's what I might have been – a *grande amoureuse* – sacrificed everything – everything. . . . And nobody cares! But I'll tell everyone – I'll tell them now – how she neglects me – how hard she is – making me come on this journey – bored to death. . . . I'll go and tell them now—'

She surged forward. Poirot gently repressed the action.

'I will send her to you, Madame. Re-enter your cabin. It is best that way—'

'No. I want to tell everyone – everyone on the boat—'

'It is too dangerous, Madame. The sea is too rough. You might be swept overboard.'

Mrs Otterbourne looked at him doubtfully.

'You think so. You really think so?'

'I do.'

He was successful. Mrs Otterbourne wavered, faltered and re-entered her cabin.

Poirot's nostrils twitched once or twice. Then he nodded and walked on to where Rosalie Otterbourne was sitting between Mrs Allerton and Tim.

'Your mother wants you, Mademoiselle.'

She had been laughing quite happily. Now her face clouded over. She shot a quick suspicious look at him and hurried along the deck.

'I can't make that child out,' said Mrs Allerton. 'She varies so. One day she's friendly; the next day, she's positively rude.'

'Thoroughly spoilt and bad-tempered,' said Tim.

Mrs Allerton shook her head.

'No. I don't think it's that. I think she's unhappy.'

Tim shrugged his shoulders.

'Oh, well, I suppose we've all got our private troubles.' His voice sounded hard and curt.

A booming voice was heard.

'Lunch,' cried Mrs Allerton delightedly. 'I'm starving.'

That evening, Poirot noticed that Mrs Allerton was sitting talking to Miss Van Schuyler. As he passed, Mrs Allerton closed one eye and opened it again. She was saying, 'Of course at Calfries Castle – the dear Duke—'

Cornelia, released from attendance, was out on the deck. She was listening to Dr Bessner, who was instructing her somewhat ponderously in Egyptology as culled from the pages of Baedeker. Cornelia listened with rapt attention.

Leaning over the rail Tim Allerton was saying: 'Anyhow, it's a rotten world. . . .'

Rosalie Otterbourne answered: 'It's unfair; some people have everything.'

Poirot sighed. He was glad that he was no longer young.

10

On the Monday morning various expressions of delight and appreciation were heard on the deck of the *Karnak*. The steamer was moored to the bank and a few hundred yards away, the morning sun just striking it, was a great temple carved out of the face of the rock. Four colossal figures, hewn out of the cliff, look out eternally over the Nile and face the rising sun.

Cornelia Robson said incoherently: 'Oh, Monsieur Poirot, isn't it wonderful? I mean they're so big and peaceful – and looking at them makes one feel that one's so small and – and rather like an insect – and that nothing matters very much really, does it?'

Mr Fanthorp, who was standing near by, murmured, 'Very – er – impressive.'

'Grand, isn't it?' said Simon Doyle, strolling up. He went on confidentially to Poirot: 'You know, I'm not much of a fellow for temples and sight-seeing and all that, but a place like this sort of gets you, if you know what I mean. Those old Pharaohs must have been wonderful fellows.'

The other had drifted away. Simon lowered his voice.

'I'm no end glad we came on this trip. It's – well, it's cleared things up. Amazing why it should – but there it is. Linnet's got her nerve back. She says it's because she's actually *faced* the business at last.'

'I think that is very probable,' said Poirot.

'She says that when she actually saw Jackie on the boat she felt terrible – and then, suddenly, it didn't matter any more. We're both agreed that we won't try to dodge her any more. We'll just meet her on her own ground and show her that this ridiculous stunt of hers doesn't worry us a bit. It's just damned bad form – that's all. She thought she'd got us badly rattled, but now, well, we just aren't rattled any more. That ought to show her.'

'Yes,' said Poirot thoughtfully.

'So that's splendid, isn't it?'

'Oh, yes, yes.'

Linnet came along the deck. She was dressed in a soft shade of apricot linen. She was smiling. She greeted Poirot with no particular enthusiasm, just gave him a cool nod and then drew her husband away.

Poirot realised with a momentary flicker of amusement that he had not made himself popular by his critical attitude. Linnet was used to unqualified admiration of all she was or did. Hercule Poirot had sinned noticeably against this creed.

Mrs Allerton, joining him, murmured:

'What a difference in that girl! She looked worried and not very happy at Assuan. Today she looks so happy that one might almost be afraid she was fey.'

Before Poirot could respond as he meant, the party was called to order. The official dragoman took charge and the party was led ashore to visit Abu Simbel.

Poirot himself fell into step with Andrew Pennington.

'It is your first visit to Egypt – yes?' he asked.

'Why, no, I was here in nineteen twenty-three. That is to say, I was in Cairo. I've never been this trip up the Nile before.'

'You came over on the *Carmanic,* I believe – at least so Madame Doyle was telling me.'

Pennington shot a shrewd glance in his direction.

'Why, yes, that is so,' he admitted.

'I wondered if you had happened to come across some friends of mine who were aboard – the Rushington Smiths.'

'I can't recall anyone of that name. The boat was full and we had bad weather. A lot of passengers hardly appeared, and in any case the voyage is so short one doesn't get to know who is on board and who isn't.'

'Yes, that is very true. What a pleasant surprise your running into Madame Doyle and her husband. You had no idea they were married?'

'No. Mrs Doyle had written me, but the letter was forwarded on and I only received it some days after our unexpected meeting in Cairo.'

'You have known here for very many years, I understand?'

'Why, I should say I have, Monsieur Poirot. I've known Linnet Ridgeway since she was just a cute little thing so high—' He made an illustrating gesture. 'Her father and I were lifelong friends. A very remarkable man, Melhuish Ridgeway – and a very successful one.'

'His daughter comes into a considerable fortune, I understand. . . . Ah, *pardon* – perhaps it is not delicate what I say there.'

Andrew Pennington seemed slightly amused.

'Oh, that's pretty common knowledge. Yes, Linnet's a wealthy woman.'

'I suppose, though, that the recent slump is bound to affect any stocks, however sound they may be?'

Pennington took a moment or two to answer. He said at last: 'That, of course, is true to a certain extent. The position is very difficult in these days.'

Poirot murmured: 'I should imagine, however, that Madame Doyle has a keen business head.'

'That is so. Yes, that is so. Linnet is a clever practical girl.'

They came to a halt. The guide proceeded to instruct them on the subject of the temple built by the great Rameses. The four colossi of Rameses himself, one pair on each side of the entrance, hewn out of the living rock, looked down on the little straggling party of tourists.

Signor Richetti, disdaining the remarks of the dragoman, was busy examining the reliefs of Negro and Syrian captives on the bases of the colossi on either side of the entrance.

When the party entered the temple, a sense of dimness and peace came over them. The still vividly coloured reliefs on some of the inner walls were pointed out, but the party tended to break up into groups.

Dr Bessner read sonorously in German from a Baedeker, pausing every now and then to translate for the benefit of Cornelia, who walked in a docile manner beside him. This was not to continue, however. Miss Van Schuyler, entering on the arms of the phlegmatic Miss Bowers, uttered a commanding: 'Cornelia, come here,' and the instruction had perforce to cease. Dr Bessner beamed after her vaguely through his thick lenses.

'A very nice maiden, that,' he announced to Poirot. 'She does not look so starved as some of these young women. No, she has the nice curves. She listens too very intelligently; it is a pleasure to instruct her.'

It fleeted across Poirot's mind that it seemed to be Cornelia's fate either to be bullied or instructed. In any case she was always the listener, never the talker.

Miss Bowers, momentarily released by the peremptory summons of Cornelia, was standing in the middle of the temple, looking about her with her cool, incurious gaze. Her reaction to the wonders of the past was succinct.

'The guide says the name of one of these gods or goddesses was Mut. Can you beat it?'

There was an inner sanctuary where sat four figures eternally presiding, strangely dignified in their dim aloofness.

Before them stood Linnet and her husband. Her arm was

in his, her face lifted – a typical face of the new civilisation, intelligent, curious, untouched by the past.

Simon said suddenly: 'Let's get out of here. I don't like these four fellows – especially the one in the high hat.'

'That's Amon, I suppose. And that one is Rameses. Why don't you like them? I think they're very impressive.'

'They're a damned sight too impressive; there's something uncanny about them. Come out into the sunlight.'

Linnet laughed but yielded.

They came out of the temple into the sunshine with the sand yellow and warm about their feet. Linnet began to laugh. At their feet in a row, presenting a momentarily gruesome appearance as though sawn from their bodies, were the heads of half a dozen Nubian boys. The eyes rolled, the heads moved rhythmically from side to side, the lips chanted a new invocation:

'Hip, hip *hurray*! Hip, hip *hurray*! Very good, very nice. Thank you very much.'

'How absurd! How do they do it? Are they really buried very deep?'

Simon produced some small change.

'Very good, very nice, very expensive,' he mimicked.

Two small boys in charge of the 'show' picked up the coins neatly.

Linnet and Simon passed on. They had no wish to return to the boat, and they were weary of sight-seeing. They settled themselves with their backs to the cliff and let the warm sun bake them through.

'How lovely the sun is,' thought Linnet. 'How warm – how safe. . . . How lovely it is to be happy. . . . How lovely to be me – me . . . me . . . Linnet . . .'

Her eyes closed. She was half asleep, half awake, drifting in the midst of thought that was like the sand drifting and blowing.

Simon's eyes were open. They too held contentment. What a fool he'd been to be rattled that first night. . . . There was nothing to be rattled about. . . . Everything was all right. . . . After all, one could trust Jackie—

There was a shout – people running towards him waving their arms – shouting. . . .

Simon stared stupidly for a moment. Then he sprang to his feet and dragged Linnet with him.

Not a minute too soon. A big boulder hurtling down the

cliff crashed past him. If Linnet had remained where she was she would have been crushed to atoms.

White-faced they clung together. Hercule Poirot and Tim Allerton ran up to them.

'*Ma foi*, Madame, that was a near thing.'

All four instinctively looked up at the cliff. There was nothing to be seen. But there was a path along the top. Poirot remembered seeing some natives walking along there when they had first come ashore.

He looked at the husband and wife. Linnet looked dazed still – bewildered. Simon, however, was inarticulate with rage.

'God damn her!' he ejaculated.

He checked himself with a quick glance at Tim Allerton.

The latter said: 'Phew, that was near! Did some fool bowl that thing over, or did it get detached on its own?'

Linnet was very pale. She said with difficulty: 'I think – some fool must have done it.'

'Might have crushed you like an eggshell. Sure you haven't got an enemy, Linnet?'

Linnet swallowed twice and found a difficulty in answering the light-hearted raillery.

'Come back to the boat, Madame,' Poirot said quickly. 'You must have a restorative.'

They walked there quickly, Simon still full of pent-up rage, Tim trying to talk cheerfully and distract Linnet's mind from the danger she had run, Poirot with a grave face.

And then, just as they reached the gangplank, Simon stopped dead. A look of amazement spread over his face.

Jacqueline de Bellefort was just coming ashore. Dressed in blue gingham, she looked childish this morning.

'Good God!' said Simon under his breath. 'So it *was* an accident, after all.'

The anger went out of his face. An overwhelming relief showed so plainly that Jacqueline noticed something amiss.

'Good-morning,' she said. 'I'm afraid I'm a little on the late side.'

She gave them all a nod and stepped ashore and proceeded in the direction of the temple.

Simon clutched Poirot's arm. The other two had gone on.

'My God, that's a relief. I thought – I thought—'

Poirot nodded. 'Yes, yes, I know what you thought.' But he himself still looked grave and preoccupied. He turned his head and noted carefully what had become of the rest of the party from the ship.

Miss Van Schuyler was slowly returning on the arm of Miss Bowers.

A little farther away Mrs Allerton was standing laughing at the little Nubian row of heads. Mrs Otterbourne was with her.

The others were nowhere in sight.

Poirot shook his head as he followed Simon slowly on to the boat.

—————— I I ——————

'Will you explain to me, Madame, the meaning of the word "fey"?'

Mrs Allerton looked slightly surprised. She and Poirot were toiling slowly up to the rock overlooking the Second Cataract. Most of the others had gone up on camels, but Poirot had felt that the motion of the camel was slightly reminiscent of that of a ship. Mrs Allerton had put it on the grounds of personal dignity.

They had arrived at Wâdi Halfa the night before. This morning two launches had conveyed all the party to the Second Cataract, with the exception of Signor Richetti, who had insisted on making an excursion of his own to a remote spot called Semna, which, he explained, was of paramount interest as being the gateway of Nubia in the time of Amenemhet III, and where there was a stele recording the fact that on entering Egypt Negroes must pay customs duties. Everything had been done to discourage this example of individuality, but with no avail. Signor Richetti was determined and had waved aside each objection: (1) that the expedition was not worth making, (2) that the expedition could not be made, owing to the impossibility of getting a car there, (3) that no car could be obtained to do the trip, (4) that a car would be a prohibitive price. Having scoffed at (1), expressed incredulity at (2), offered to find a car himself to (3), and bargained fluently in Arabic for (4), Signor Richetti had at last departed – his departure being arranged in a secret and furtive manner, in case some of the other tourists should take it into their heads to stray from the appointed paths of sight-seeing.

'Fey?' Mrs Allerton put her head on one side as she considered her reply. 'Well, it's a Scotch word, really. It means the kind of exalted happiness that comes before disaster. You know – it's too good to be true.'

She enlarged on the theme. Poirot listened attentively.

'I thank you, Madame. I understand now. It is odd that you should have said that yesterday – when Madame Doyle was to escape death so shortly afterwards.'

Mrs Allerton gave a little shiver.

'It must have been a very near escape. Do you think some of these little black wretches rolled it over for fun? It's the sort of thing boys might do all over the world – not perhaps really meaning any harm.'

Poirot shrugged his shoulders.

'It may be, Madame.'

He changed the subject, talking of Majorca and asking various practical questions from the point of view of a possible visit.

Mrs Allerton had grown to like the little man very much – partly perhaps out of a contradictory spirit. Tim, she felt, was always trying to make her less friendly to Hercule Poirot, whom he summarised firmly as ' the worst kind of bounder.' But she herself did not call him a bounder; she supposed it was his somewhat foreign exotic clothing which roused her son's prejudices. She herself found him an intelligent and stimulating companion. He was also extremely sympathetic. She found herself suddenly confiding in him her dislike of Joanna Southwood. It eased her to talk of the matter. And after all, why not? He did not know Joanna – would probably never meet her. Why should she not ease herself of that constantly borne burden of jealous thought?

At that same moment Tim and Rosalie Otterbourne were talking of her. Tim had just been half jestingly abusing his luck. His rotten health, never bad enough to be really interesting, yet not good enough for him to have led the life he would have chosen. Very little money, no congenial occupation.

'A thoroughly lukewarm, tame existence,' he finished discontentedly.

Rosalie said abruptly, 'You've got something heaps of people would envy you.'

'What's that?'

'Your mother.'

Tim was surprised and pleased.

'Mother? Yes, of course she is quite unique. It's nice of you to see it.'

'I think she's marvellous. She looks so lovely – so composed and calm – as though nothing could ever touch her, and yet –

and yet somehow she's always ready to be funny about things too. . . .'

Rosalie was stammering slightly in her earnestness.

Tim felt a rising warmth towards the girl. He wished he could return the compliment, but, lamentably, Mrs Otterbourne was his idea of the world's greatest menace. The inability to respond in kind made him embarrassed.

Miss Van Schuyler had stayed in the launch. She could not risk the ascent either on a camel or on her legs. She had said snappily:

'I'm sorry to have to ask you to stay with me, Miss Bowers. I intended you to go and Cornelia to stay, but girls are so selfish. She rushed off without a word to me. And I actually saw her talking to that very unpleasant and ill-bred young man, Ferguson. Cornelia has disappointed me sadly. She has absolutely no social sense.'

Miss Bowers replied in her usual matter-of-fact fashion:

'That's quite all right, Miss Van Schuyler. It would have been a hot walk up there, and I don't fancy the look of those saddles on the camels. Fleas, as likely as not.'

She adjusted her glasses, screwed up her eyes to look at the party descending the hill and remarked: 'Miss Robson isn't with that young man any more. She's with Dr Bessner.'

Miss Van Schuyler grunted.

Since she had discovered that Dr Bessner had a large clinic in Czechoslovakia and a European reputation as a fashionable physician, she was disposed to be gracious to him. Besides, she might need his professional services before the journey was over.

When the party returned to the *Karnak* Linnet gave a cry of surprise.

'A telegram for me.'

She snatched it off the board and tore it open.

'Why – I don't understand – potatoes, beetroots – what does it mean, Simon?'

Simon was just coming to look over her shoulder when a furious voice said: 'Excuse me, that telegram is for me.' and Signor Richetti snatched it rudely from her hand, fixing her with a furious glare as he did so.

Linnet stared in surprise for a moment, then turned over the envelope.

'Oh, Simon, what a fool I am! It's Richetti – not Ridgeway – and anyway of course my name isn't Ridgeway now. I must apologise.'

She followed the little archæologist up to the stern of the boat.

'I am so sorry, Signor Richetti. You see my name was Ridgeway before I married, and I haven't been married very long, and so—'

She paused, her face dimpled with smiles, inviting him to smile upon a young bride's *faux pas*.

But Richetti was obviously 'not amused.' Queen Victoria at her most disapproving could not have looked more grim. 'Names should be read carefully. It is inexcusable to be careless in these matters.'

Linnet bit her lip and her colour rose. She was not accustomed to have her apologies received in this fashion. She turned away and, rejoining Simon, said angrily, 'These Italians are really insupportable.'

'Never mind, darling; let's go and look at that big ivory crocodile you liked.'

They went ashore together.

Poirot, watching them walk up the landing-stage, heard a sharp indrawn breath. He turned to see Jacqueline de Bellefort at his side. Her hands were clenched on the rail. The expression on her face, as she turned it towards him, quite startled him. It was no longer gay or malicious. She looked devoured by some inner consuming fire.

'They don't care any more.' The words came low and fast. 'They've got beyond me. I can't reach them. . . . They don't mind if I'm here or not . . . I can't – I can't hurt them any more. . . .'

Her hands on the rail trembled.

'Mademoiselle—'

She broke in: 'Oh, it's too late now – too late for warning. . . . You were right. I ought not to have come. Not on this journey. What did you call it? A journey of the soul? I can't go back; I've got to go on. And I'm going on. They shan't be happy together; they shan't. I'd kill him sooner. . . .'

She turned abruptly away. Poirot, staring after her, felt a hand on his shoulder.

'Your girl friend seems a trifle upset, Monsieur Poirot.' Poirot turned. He stared in surprise, seeing an old acquaintance.

'Colonel Race.'

The tall bronzed man smiled.

'Bit of a surprise, eh?'

Hercule Poirot had come across Colonel Race a year previously in London. They had been fellow guests at a very strange dinner party – a dinner party that had ended in death for that strange man, their host.

Poirot knew that Race was a man of unadvertised goings and comings. He was usually to be found in one of the outposts of Empire where trouble was brewing.

'So you are here at Wâdi Halfa,' he remarked thoughtfully.

'I am here on this boat.'

'You mean?'

'That I am making the return journey with you to Shellâl.'

Hercule Poirot's eyebrows rose.

'That is very interesting. Shall we, perhaps, have a little drink?'

They went into the observation saloon, now quite empty. Poirot ordered a whisky for the Colonel and a double orange-ade full of sugar for himself.

'So you make the return journey with us,' said Poirot as he sipped. 'You would go faster, would you not, on the Government steamer, which travels by night as well as day?'

Colonel Race's face creased appreciatively.

'You're right on the spot as usual, Monsieur Poirot,' he said pleasantly.

'It is, then, the passengers?'

'One of the passengers.'

'Now which one, I wonder?' Hercule Poirot asked of the ornate ceiling.

'Unfortunately I don't know myself,' said Race Ruefully.

Poirot looked interested.

Race said: 'There's no need to be mysterious to you. We've had a good deal of trouble out here – one way and another. It isn't the people who ostensibly lead the rioters that we're after. It's the men who very cleverly put the match to the gun-powder. There were three of them. One's dead. One's in prison. I want the third man – a man with five or six cold-blooded murders to his credit. He's one of the cleverest paid agitators that ever existed. . . . He's on this boat. I know that from a passage in a letter that passed through our hands. Decoded it said: "X will be on the *Karnak* trip seventh to thirteenth." It didn't say under what name X would be passing.'

'Have you any description of him?'

'No. American, Irish, and French descent. Bit of a mongrel. That doesn't help us much. Have you got any ideas?'

'An idea – it is all very well,' said Poirot meditatively.

Such was the understanding between them that Race pressed

him no further. He knew that Hercule Poirot did not ever speak unless he was sure.

Poirot rubbed his nose and said unhappily: 'There passes itself something on this boat that causes me much inquietude.'

Race looked at him inquiringly.

'Figure to yourself,' said Poirot, 'a person A who has grievously wronged a person B. The person B desires the revenge. The person B makes the threats.'

'A and B being both on this boat?'

Poirot nodded. 'Precisely.'

'And B, I gather, being a woman?'

'Exactly.'

Race lit a cigarette.

'I shouldn't worry. People who go about talking of what they are going to do don't usually do it.'

'And particularly is that the case with *les femmes*, you would say! Yes, that is true.'

But he still did not look happy.

'Anything else?' asked Race.

'Yes, there is something. Yesterday the person A had a very near escape from death, the kind of death that might very conveniently be called an accident.'

'Engineered by B?'

'No, that is just the point. B could have had nothing to do with it.'

'Then it *was* an accident.'

'I suppose so – but I do not like such accidents.'

'You're quite sure B could have had no hand in it?'

'Absolutely.'

'Oh, well, coincidences do happen. Who is A, by the way? A particularly disagreeable person?'

'On the contrary. A is a charming, rich, and beautiful young lady.'

Race grinned.

'Sounds quite like a novelette.'

'*Peut-être*. But I tell you, I am not happy, my friend. If I am right, and after all I am constantly in the habit of being right' – Race smiled into his moustache at this typical utterance – 'then there is matter for grave inquietude. And now, *you* come to add yet another complication. You tell me that there is a man on the *Karnak* who kills.'

'He doesn't usually kill charming young ladies.'

Poirot shook his head in a dissatisfied manner.

'I am afraid, my friend,' he said. 'I am afraid. . . . Today, I

advised this lady, Madame Doyle, to go with her husband to
Khartoum, not to return on this boat. But they would not
agree. I pray to Heaven that we may arrive at Shellâl without
catastrophe.'

'Aren't you taking rather a gloomy view?'

Poirot shook his head.

'I am afraid,' he said simply. 'Yes, I, Hercule Poirot, I'm
afraid. . . .'

——— I 2 ———

Cornelia Robson stood inside the temple of Abu Simbel. It was
the evening of the following day – a hot still evening. The
Karnak was anchored once more at Abu Simbel to permit a
second visit to be made to the temple, this time by artificial
light. The difference this made was considerable, and Cornelia
commented wonderingly on the fact to Mr Ferguson, who was
standing by her side.

'Why, you see it ever so much better now!' she exclaimed.
'All those enemies having their heads cut off by the King –
they just stand right out. That's a cute kind of castle there that
I never noticed before. I wish Dr Bressner was here, he'd tell
me what it was.'

'How you can stand that old fool beats me,' said Ferguson
gloomily.

'Why, he's just one of the kindest men I've ever met.'

'Pompous old bore.'

'I don't think you ought to speak that way.'

The young man gripped her suddenly by the arm. They
were just emerging from the temple into the moonlight.

'Why do you stick being bored by fat old men – and bullied
and snubbed by a vicious old harridan?'

'Why, Mr Ferguson!'

'Haven't you got any spirit? Don't you know you're just as
good as she is?'

'But I'm not!' Cornelia spoke with honest conviction.

'You're not as rich; that's all you mean.'

'No, it isn't. Cousin Marie's very cultured, and—'

'Cultured!' The young man let go of her arm as suddenly
as he had taken it. 'That word makes me sick.'

Cornelia looked at him in alarm.

'She doesn't like you talking to me, does she?' asked the young man.

Cornelia blushed and looked embarrassed.

'Why? Because she thinks I'm not her social equal! Pah! Doesn't that make you see red?'

Cornelia faltered out: 'I wish you wouldn't get so mad about things.'

'Don't you realise – and you an American – that everyone is born free and equal?'

'They're not,' said Cornelia with calm certainty.

'My good girl, it's part of your constitution!'

'Cousin Marie says politicians aren't gentlemen,' said Cornelia. 'And of course people aren't equal. It doesn't make sense. I know I'm kind of homely-looking, and I used to feel mortified about it sometimes, but I've got over that. I'd like to have been born elegant and beautiful like Mrs Doyle, but I wasn't, so I guess it's no use worrying.'

'Mrs Doyle!' exclaimed Ferguson with deep contempt. 'She's the sort of woman who ought to be shot as an example.'

Cornelia looked at him anxiously.

'I believe it's your digestion,' she said kindly. 'I've got a special kind of pepsin that Cousin Marie tried once. Would you like to try it?'

Mr Ferguson said: 'You're impossible!'

He turned and strode away. Cornelia went on towards the boat. Just as she was crossing on to the gangway he caught her up once more.

'You're the nicest person on the boat,' he said. 'And mind you remember it.'

Blushing with pleasure Cornelia repaired to the observation saloon. Miss Van Schuyler was conversing with Dr Bessner – an agreeable conversation dealing with certain royal patients of his.

Cornelia said guiltily: 'I do hope I haven't been a long time, Cousin Marie.'

Glancing at her watch, the old lady snapped: 'You haven't exactly hurried, my dear. And what have you done with my velvet stole?'

Cornelia looked round.

'Shall I see if it's in the cabin, Cousin Marie?'

'Of course it isn't! I had it just after dinner in here, and I haven't moved out of the place. It was on that chair.'

Cornelia made a desultory search.

'I can't see it anywhere, Cousin Marie.'

'Nonsense!' said Miss Van Schuyler. 'Look about.' It was an order such as one might give to a dog, and in her doglike fashion Cornelia obeyed. The quiet Mr Fanthorp, who was sitting at a table near by, rose and assisted her. But the stole could not be found.

The day had been such an unusually hot and sultry one that most people had retired early after going ashore to view the temple. The Doyles were playing bridge with Pennington and Race at a table in a corner. The only other occupant of the saloon was Hercule Poirot, who was yawning his head off at a small table near the door.

Miss Van Schuyler, making a Royal Progress bedward, with Cornelia and Miss Bowers in attendance, paused by his chair. He sprang politely to his feet, stifling a yawn of gargantuan dimensions.

Miss Van Schuyler said: 'I have only just realised who you are, Monsieur Poirot. I may tell you that I have heard of you from my old friend Rufus Van Aldin. You must tell me about your cases sometime.'

Poirot, his eyes twinkling a little through their sleepiness, bowed in an exaggerated manner. With a kindly but condescending nod, Miss Van Schuyler passed on.

Poirot yawned once more. He felt heavy and stupid with sleep and could hardly keep his eyes open. He glanced over at the bridge players, absorbed in their game, then at young Fanthorp, who was deep in a book. Apart from them the saloon was empty.

He passed through the swinging door out on to the deck. Jacqueline de Bellefort, coming precipitately along the deck, almost collided with him.

'Pardon, Mademoiselle.'

She said: 'You look sleepy, Monsieur Poirot.'

He admitted it frankly:

'*Mais oui* – I am consumed with sleep. I can hardly keep my eyes open. It has been a day very close and oppressive.'

'Yes.' She seemed to brood over it. 'It's been the sort of day when things – snap! Break! When one can't go on. . . .'

Her voice was low and charged with passion. She looked not at him, but towards the sandy shore. Her hands were clenched, rigid. . . .

Suddenly the tension relaxed. She said: 'Good-night, Monsieur Poirot.'

'Good-night, Mademoiselle.'

Her eyes met his, just for a swift moment. Thinking it over

the next day, he came to the conclusion that there had been appeal in that glance. He was to remember it afterwards.

Then he passed on to his cabin and she went towards the saloon.

Cornelia, having dealt with Miss Van Schuyler's many needs and fantasies, took some needlework with her back to the saloon. She herself did not feel in the least sleepy. On the contrary she felt wide awake and slightly excited.

The bridge four were still at it. In another chair the quiet Fanthorp read a book. Cornelia sat down to her needlework.

Suddenly the door opened and Jacqueline de Bellefort came in. She stood in the doorway, her head thrown back. Then she pressed a bell and sauntered across to Cornelia and sat down.

'Been ashore?' she asked.

'Yes. I thought it was just fascinating in the moonlight.'

Jacqueline nodded.

'Yes, lovely night. . . . A real honeymoon night.'

Her eyes went to the bridge table – rested a moment on Linnet Doyle.

The boy came in answer to the bell. Jacqueline ordered a double gin. As she gave the order Simon Doyle shot a quick glance at her. A faint line of anxiety showed between his eyebrows.

His wife said: 'Simon, we're waiting for you to call.'

Jacqueline hummed a little tune to herself. When the drink came, she picked it up, said: 'Well, here's to crime,' drank it off and ordered another.

Again Simon looked across from the bridge table. His calls became slightly absent-minded. His partner, Pennington, took him to task.

Jacqueline began to hum again, at first under her breath, then louder:

'He was her man and he did her wrong. . . .'

'Sorry,' said Simon to Pennington. 'Stupid of me not to return your lead. That gives 'em rubber.'

Linnet rose to her feet.

'I'm sleepy. I think I'll go to bed.'

'About time to turn in,' said Colonel Race.

'I'm with you,' agreed Pennington.

'Coming, Simon?'

Doyle said slowly: 'Not just yet. I think I'll have a drink first.'

Linnet nodded and went out. Race followed her. Pennington finished his drink and then followed suit.

Cornelia began to gather up her embroidery.

'Don't go to bed, Miss Robson,' said Jacqueline. 'Please don't. I feel like making a night of it. Don't desert me.'

Cornelia sat down again.

'We girls must stick together,' said Jacqueline.

She threw back her head and laughed – a shrill laugh without merriment.

The second drink came.

'Have something,' said Jacqueline.

'No, thank you very much,' replied Cornelia.

Jacqueline tilted back her chair. She hummed now loudly: *'He was her man and he did her wrong . . .'*

Mr Fanthorp turned a page of *Europe from Within.*

Simon Doyle picked up a magazine.

'Really, I think I'll go to bed,' said Cornelia. 'It's getting very late.'

'You can't go to bed yet,' Jacqueline declared. 'I forbid you to. Tell me all about yourself.'

'Well – I don't know. There isn't much to tell,' Cornelia faltered. 'I've just lived at home, and I haven't been around much. This is my first trip to Europe. I'm just loving every minute of it.'

Jacqueline laughed.

'You're a happy sort of person, aren't you? God, I'd like to be you.'

'Oh, would you? But I mean – I'm sure—'

Cornelia felt flustered. Undoubtedly Miss de Bellefort was drinking too much. That wasn't exactly a novelty to Cornelia. She had seen plenty of drunkenness during Prohibition years. But there was something else. . . . Jacqueline de Bellefort was talking to her – was looking at her – and yet, Cornelia felt, it was as though, somehow, she was talking to someone else. . . .

But ther were only two other people in the room, Mr Fanthorp and Mr Doyle. Mr Fanthorp seemed quite absorbed in his book. Mr Doyle was looking rather odd – a queer sort of watchful look on his face. . . .

Jacqueline said again: 'Tell me all about yourself.'

Always obedient, Cornelia tried to comply. She talked, rather heavily, going into unnecessary small details about her daily life. She was so unused to being the talker. Her rôle was so constantly that of listener. And yet Miss de Bellefort seemed to want to know. When Cornelia faltered to a standstill, the other girl was quick to prompt her.

'Go on – tell me more.'

And so Cornelia went on ('Of course, Mother's very delicate – some days she touches nothing but cereals—') unhappily conscious that all she said was supremely uninteresting, yet flattered by the other girl's seeming interest. But was she interested? Wasn't she, somehow, listening to something else – or, perhaps, *for* something else? She was looking at Cornelia, yes, but wasn't there *someone else*, sitting in the room?

'And of course we get very good art classes, and last winter I had a course of—'

(How late was it? Surely very late. She had been talking and talking. If only something definite would happen—)

And immediately, as though in answer to the wish, something did happen. Only, at that moment, it seemed very natural.

Jacqueline turned her head and spoke to Simon Doyle.

'Ring the bell, Simon. I want another drink.'

Simon Doyle looked up from his magazine and said quietly: 'The stewards have gone to bed. It's after midnight.'

'I tell you I want another drink.'

Simon said: 'You've had quite enough drink, Jackie.'

She swung round at him.

'What damned business is it of yours?'

He shrugged his shoulders. 'None.'

She watched him for a minute or two. Then she said: 'What's the matter, Simon? Are you afraid?'

Simon did not answer. Rather elaborately he picked up his magazine again.

Cornelia murmured: 'Oh, dear – as late as that – I – must—'

She began to fumble, dropped a thimble. . . .

Jacqueline said: 'Don't go to bed. I'd like another woman here – to support me.' She began to laugh again. 'Do you know what Simon over there is afraid of? He's afraid *I'm* going to tell you the story of *my* life.'

'Oh, really?'

Cornelia was the prey of conflicting emotions. She was deeply embarrassed but at the same time pleasurably thrilled. How – how *black* Simon Doyle was looking.

'Yes, it's a very sad story,' said Jacqueline; her soft voice was low and mocking. 'He treated me rather badly, didn't you, Simon?'

Simon Doyle said brutally: 'Go to bed, Jackie. You're drunk.'

'If you're embarrassed, Simon dear, you'd better leave the room.'

Simon Doyle looked at her. The hand that held the magazine shook a little, but he spoke bluntly.

'I'm staying,' he said.

Cornelia murmured for the third time, 'I really must – it's so late—'

'You're not to go,' said Jacqueline. Her hand shot out and held the other girl in her chair. 'You're to stay and hear what I've got to say.'

'Jackie,' said Simon sharply, 'you're making a fool of yourself! For God's sake, go to bed.'

Jacqueline sat up suddenly in her chair. Words poured from her rapidly in a soft hissing stream.

'You're afraid of a scene, aren't you? That's because you're so English – so reticent! You want me to behave "decently," don't you? But I don't care whether I behave decently or not! You'd better get out of here quickly – because I'm going to talk – a lot.'

Jim Fanthorp carefully shut his book, yawned, glanced at his watch, got up and strolled out. It was a very British and utterly unconvincing performance.

Jacqueline swung round in her chair and glared at Simon.

'You damned fool,' she said thickly, 'do you think you can treat me as you have done and get away with it?'

Simon Doyle opened his lips, then shut them again. He sat quite still as though he were hoping that her outburst would exhaust itself if he said nothing to provoke her further.

Jacqueline's voice came thick and blurred. It fascinated Cornelia, totally unused to naked emotions of any kind.

'I told you,' said Jacqueline, 'that I'd kill you sooner than see you go to another woman. . . . You don't think I meant that? *You're wrong*. I've only been waiting! You're my man! Do you hear? You belong to me. . . .'

Still Simon did not speak. Jacqueline's hand fumbled a moment or two on her lap. She leant forward.

'I told you I'd kill you and I meant it. . . .' Her hand came up suddenly with something in it that flashed and gleamed. 'I'll shoot you like a dog – like the dirty dog you are. . . .'

Now at last Simon acted. He sprang to his feet, but at the same moment she pulled the trigger. . . .

Simon half twisted – fell across a chair. . . . Cornelia screamed and rushed to the door. Jim Fanthorp was on the deck leaning over the rail. She called to him.

'Mr Fanthorp . . . Mr Fanthorp . . .'

He ran to her; she clutched at him incoherently. . . .

'She's shot him – Oh! she's shot him. . . .'

Simon Doyle still lay as he had fallen half into and across a chair. . . . Jacqueline stood as though paralysed. She was trembling violently, and her eyes, dilated and frightened, were staring at the crimson stain slowly soaking through Simon's trouser leg just below the knee where he held a handkerchief close against the wound. . . .

She stammered out:

'I didn't mean . . . Oh, my God, I didn't really mean . . .'

The pistol dropped from her nervous fingers with a clatter on the floor. She kicked it away with her foot. It slid under one of the settees.

Simon, his voice faint, murmured: 'Fanthorp, for heaven's sake – there's someone coming . . . Say it's all right – an accident – something. There mustn't be a scandal over this.'

Fanthorp nodded in quick comprehension. He wheeled round to the door where a startled Nubian face showed. He said: 'All right – all right! Just fun!'

The black face looked doubtful, puzzled, then reassured. The teeth showed in a wide grin. The boy nodded and went off.

Fanthorp turned back.

'That's all right. Don't think anybody else heard. Only sounded like a cork, you know. Now the next thing—'

He was startled. Jacqueline suddenly began to weep hysterically.

'Oh, God, I wish I were dead. . . . I'll kill myself. I'll be better dead. . . . Oh, what have I done – what have I done?'

Cornelia hurried to her.

'Hush, dear, hush.'

Simon, his brow wet, his face twisted with pain, said urgently:

'Get her away. For God's sake, get her out of here! Get her to her cabin, Fanthorp. Look here, Miss Robson, get that hospital nurse of yours.' He looked appealingly from one to the other of them. 'Don't leave her. Make quite sure she's safe with the nurse looking after her. Then get hold of old Bessner and bring him here. For God's sake, don't let any news of this get to my wife.'

Jim Fanthorp nodded comprehendingly. The quiet young man was cool and competent in an emergency.

Between them he and Cornelia got the weeping, struggling girl out of the saloon and along the deck to her cabin. There they had more trouble with her. She fought to free herself; her sobs redoubled.

'I'll drown myself . . . I'll drown myself. . . . I'm not fit to live. . . . Oh, Simon – Simon!'

Fanthorp said to Cornelia: 'Better get hold of Miss Bowers. I'll stay while you get her.'

Cornelia nodded and hurried out.

As soon as she left, Jacqueline clutched Fanthorp.

'His leg – it's bleeding – broken. . . . He may bleed to death. I must go to him. . . . Oh, Simon – Simon – how could I?'

Her voice rose. Fanthorp said urgently: 'Quietly quietly. . . . He'll be all right.'

She began to struggle again.

'Let me go! Let me throw myself overboard. . . . Let me kill myself!'

Fanthorp, holding her by the shoulders, forced her back on to the bed.

'You must stay here. Don't make a fuss. Pull yourself together. It's all right, I tell you.'

To his relief, the distraught girl did manage to control herself a little, but he was thankful when the curtains were pushed aside and the efficient Miss Bowers, neatly dressed in a hideous kimono, entered, accompanied by Cornelia.

'Now then,' said Miss Bowers briskly, 'what's all this?'

She took charge without any sign of surprise and alarm.

Fanthorp thankfully left the overwrought girl in her capable hands and hurried along to the cabin occupied by Dr Bessner. He knocked and entered on top of the knock.

'Dr Bessner?'

A terrific snore resolved itself, and a startled voice asked: 'So? What is it?'

By this time Fanthorp had switched the light on. The doctor blinked up at him, looking rather like a large owl.

'It's Doyle. He's been shot. Miss de Bellefort shot him. He's in the saloon. Can you come?'

The stout doctor reacted promptly. He asked a few curt questions, pulled on his bedroom slippers and a dressing-gown, picked up a little case of necessaries and accompanied Fanthorp to the lounge.

Simon had managed to get the window beside him open. He was leaning his head against it, inhaling the air. His face was a ghastly colour.

Dr Bessner came over to him.

'Ha? So? What have we here?'

A handkerchief sodden with blood lay on the carpet, and on the carpet itself was a dark stain.

The doctor's examination was punctuated with Teutonic grunts and exclamations.

'Yes, it is bad this. . . . The bone is fractured. And a big loss
of blood. Herr Fanthorp, you and I must get him to my cabin.
So – like this. He cannot walk. We must carry him, thus.'

As they lifted him Cornelia appeared in the doorway. Catching sight of her, the doctor uttered a grunt of satisfaction.

'Ach, it is you? Goot. Come with us. I have need of assistance. You will be better than my friend here. He looks a little
pale already.'

Fanthorp emitted a rather sickly smile.

'Shall I get Miss Bowers?' he asked.

Dr Bessner threw a considering glance over Cornelia.

'You will do very vell, young lady,' he announced. 'You will
not faint or be foolish, hein?'

'I can do what you tell me,' said Cornelia eagerly.

Bessner nodded in a satisfied fashion.

The procession passed along the deck.

The next ten minutes were purely surgical and Mr Jim
Fanthorp did not enjoy it at all. He felt secretly ashamed of
the superior fortitude exhibited by Cornelia.

'So, that is the best I can do,' announced Dr Bessner at last.
'You have been a hero, my friend.' He patted Simon approvingly on the shoulder. Then he rolled up his sleeve and produced a hypodermic needle.

'And now I will give you something to make you sleep. Your
wife, what about her?'

Simon said weakly: 'She needn't know till the morning.
. . .' He went on: 'I – you mustn't blame Jackie. . . . It's been
all my fault. I treated her disgracefully . . . poor kid – she
didn't know what she was doing. . . .'

Dr Bessner nodded comprehendingly.

'Yes, yes – I understand. . . .'

'My fault—' Simon urged. His eyes went to Cornelia. 'Someone – ought to stay with her. She might – hurt herself—'

Dr Bessner injected the needle. Cornelia said, with quiet
competence: 'It's all right, Mr Doyle. Miss Bowers is going to
stay with her all night. . . .'

A grateful look flushed over Simon's face. His body relaxed.
His eyes closed. Suddenly he jerked them open. 'Fanthorp?'

'Yes, Doyle.'

'The pistol . . . ought not to leave it . . . lying about. The
boys will find it in the morning. . . .'

Fanthorp nodded. 'Quite right. I'll go and get hold of it
now.'

He went out of the cabin and along the deck. Miss Bowers appeared at the door of Jacqueline's cabin.

'She'll be all right now,' she announced. 'I've given her a morphine injection.'

'But you'll stay with her?'

'Oh, yes. Morphia excites some people. I shall stay all night.'

Fanthorp went on to the lounge.

Some three minutes later there was a tap on Bessner's cabin door.

'Dr Bessner?'

'Yes?' The stout man appeared.

Fanthorp beckoned him out on the deck.

'Look here – I can't find that pistol. . . .'

'What is that?'

'The pistol. It dropped out of the girl's hand. She kicked it away and it went under a settee. It isn't under that settee now.'

They stared at each other.

'But who can have taken it?'

Fanthorp shrugged his shoulders.

Bessner said: 'It is curious, that. But I do not see what we can do about it.'

Puzzled and vaguely alarmed, the two men separated.

—— I 3 ——

Hercule Poirot was just wiping the lather from his freshly shaved face when there was a quick tap on the door, and hard on top of it Colonel Race entered unceremoniously. He closed the door behind him.

He said: 'Your instinct was quite correct. It's happened.'

Poirot straightened up and asked sharply: 'What has happened?'

'Linnet Doyle's dead – shot through the head last night.'

Poirot was silent for a minute, two memories vividly before him – a girl in a garden at Assuan saying in a hard breathless voice: 'I'd like to put my dear little pistol against her head and just press the trigger,' and another more recent memory, the same voice saying: 'One feels one can't go on – the kind of day when something breaks' – and that strange momentary flash of appeal in her eyes. What had been the matter with him not to respond to that appeal? He had been blind, deaf, stupid with his need for sleep. . . .

Race went on: 'I've got some slight official standing; they sent for me, put it in my hands. The boat's due to start in half an hour, but it will be delayed till I give the word. There's a possibility, of course, that the murderer came from the shore.'

Poirot shook his head.

Race acquiesced in the gesture.

'I agree. One can pretty well rule that out. Well, man, it's up to you. This is your show.'

Poirot had been attiring himself with a neat-fingered celerity. He said now: 'I am at your disposal.'

The two men stepped out on the deck.

Race said: 'Bessner should be there by now. I sent the steward for him.'

There were four cabins de luxe, with bathrooms, on the boat. Of the two on the port side one was occupied by Dr Bessner, the other by Andrew Pennington. On the starboard side the first was occupied by Miss Van Schuyler, and the one next to it by Linnet Doyle. Her husband's dressing cabin was next door.

A white-faced steward was standing outside the door of Linnet Doyle's cabin. He opened the door for them and they passed inside. Dr Bessner was bending over the bed. He looked up and grunted as the other two entered.

'What can you tell us, Doctor, about this business?' asked Race.

Bessner rubbed his unshaven jaw meditatively.

'Ach! She was shot – shot at close quarters. See – here, just above the ear – that is where the bullet entered. A very little bullet – I should say a twenty-two. The pistol, it was held close against her head, see, there is blackening here, the skin is scorched.'

Again in a sick wave of memory Poirot thought of those words uttered at Assuan.

Bessner went on: 'She was asleep; there was no struggle; the murderer crept up in the dark and shot her as she lay there.'

'Ah! *non*!' Poirot cried out. His sense of psychology was outraged. Jacqueline de Bellefort creeping into a darkened cabin, pistol in hand – no, it did not 'fit,' that picture.

Bessner stared at him through his thick lenses.

'But that is what happened, I tell you.'

'Yes, yes. I did not mean what you thought. I was not contradicting you.'

Bessner gave a satisfied grunt.

Poirot came up and stood beside him. Linnet Doyle was lying on her side. Her attitude was natural and peaceful. But above the ear was a tiny hole with an incrustation of dried blood round it.

Poirot shook his head sadly.

Then his gaze fell on the white painted wall just in front of him and he drew in his breath sharply. It's white neatness was marred by a big wavering letter J scrawled in some brownish-red medium.

Poirot stared at it, then he leaned over the dead girl and very gently picked up her right hand. One finger of it was stained a brownish-red.

'*Nom d'un nom d'un nom!*' ejaculated Hercule Poirot.

'Eh? What is that?'

Dr Bessner looked up.

'Ach! *That.*'

Race said: 'Well, I'm damned. What do you make of that, Poirot?'

Poirot swayed a little on his toes.

'You ask me what I make of it. *Eh bien*, it is very simple, is it not? Madame Doyle is dying; she wishes to indicate her murderer, and so she writes with her finger, dipped in her own blood, the initial letter of her murderer's name. Oh, yes, it is astonishingly simple.'

'Ach, but—'

Dr Bessner was about to break out, but a peremptory gesture from Race silenced him.

'So it strikes you like that?' he asked slowly.

Poirot turned round on him nodding his head.

'Yes, yes. It is, as I say, of an astonishing simplicity! It is so familiar, is it not? It has been done so often, in the pages of the romance of crime! It is now, indeed, a little *vieux jeu*! It leads one to suspect that our murderer is – old-fashioned!'

Race drew a long breath.

'I see,' he said. 'I thought at first—' He stopped.

Poirot said with a very faint smile: 'That I believed in all the old clichés of melodrama? But pardon, Dr Bessner, you were about to say—?'

Bessner broke out gutturally: 'What do I say? Pah! I say it is absurd; it is the nonsense! The poor lady she died instantaneously. To dip her finger in the blood (and as you see, there is hardly any blood) and write the letter J upon the wall – Bah – it is the nonsense – the melodramatic nonsense!'

'*C'est de l'enfantillage,*' agreed Poirot.

886

'But it was done with a purpose,' suggested Race.

'That – naturally,' agreed Poirot, and his face was grave.

'What does J stand for?' asked Race.

Poirot replied promptly: 'J stands for Jacqueline de Belle-fort, a young lady who declared to me less than a week ago that she would like nothing better than to—' he paused and then deliberately quoted, ' "to put my dear little pistol close against her head and then just press with my finger—" '

'*Gott im Himmel*!' exclaimed Dr Bessner.

There was a momentary silence. Then Race drew a deep breath and said: 'Which is just what was done here?'

Bessner nodded.

'That is so, yes. It was a pistol of very small calibre – as I say, probably a twenty-two. The bullet has got to be extracted, of course, before we can say definitely.'

Race nodded in swift comprehension. Then he asked: 'What about time of death?'

Bessner stroked his jaw again. His fingers made a rasping sound.

'I would not care to be too precise. It is now eight o'clock. I will say, with due regard to the temperature last night, that she has been dead certainly six hours and probably not longer than eight.'

'That puts it between midnight and two a.m.'

'That is so.'

There was a pause. Race looked round.

'What about her husband? I suppose, he sleeps in the cabin next door.'

'At the moment,' said Dr Bessner, 'he is asleep in my cabin.'

Both men looked very surprised.

Bessner nodded his head several times.

'Ach, so. I see you have not been told about that. Mr Doyle was shot last night in the saloon.'

'Shot By whom?'

'By the young lady, Jacqueline de Bellefort.'

Race asked sharply, 'Is he badly hurt?'

'Yes, the bone was splintered. I have done all that is possible at the moment, but it is necessary, you understand, that the fracture should be X-rayed as soon as possible and proper treatment given such as is impossible on this boat.'

Poirot murmured: 'Jacqueline de Bellefort.'

His eyes went again to the J on the wall.

Race said abruptly: 'If there is nothing more we can do here for the moment, let's go below. The management has put the smoking-room at our disposal. We must get the details of what happened last night.'

They left the cabin. Race locked the door and took the key with him.

'We can come back later,' he said. 'The first thing to do is to get all the facts clear.'

They went down to the deck below, where they found the manager of the *Karnak* waiting uneasily in the doorway of the smoking-room. The poor man was terribly upset and worried over the whole business, and was eager to leave everything in Colonel Race's hands.

'I feel I can't do better than leave it to you, sir, seeing your official position. I'd had orders to put myself at your disposal in the – er – other matter. If you will take charge, I'll see that everything is done as you wish.'

'Good man! To begin with I'd like this room kept clear for me and for Monsieur Poirot during the inquiry.'

'Certainly, sir.'

'That's all at present. Go on with your own work. I know where to find you.'

Looking slightly relieved, the manager left the room.

Race said, 'Sit down, Bessner, and let's have the whole story of what happened last night.'

They listened in silence to the doctor's rumbling voice.

'Clear enough,' said Race, when he had finished. 'The girl worked herself up, helped by a drink or two, and finally took a pot shot at the man with a twenty-two pistol. Then she went along to Linnet Doyle's cabin and shot her as well.'

But Dr Bessner was shaking his head.

'No, no, I do not think so. I do not think that was *possible*. For one thing she would not write her own initial on the wall; it would be ridiculous, *nicht wahr?*'

'She might,' Race declared, 'if she were as blindly mad and jealous as she sounds; she might want to – well – sign her name to the crime, so to speak.'

Poirot shook his head. 'No, no, I do not think she would be as – as *crude* as that.'

'Then there's only one reason for that J. It was put there by someone else deliberately to throw suspicion on her.'

Bessner nodded. 'Yes, and the criminal was unlucky, because, you see, it is not only *unlikely* that the young Fräulein did the murder; it is also I think *impossible*.'

'How's that?'

Bessner explained Jacqueline's hysterics and the circumstances which had led Miss Bowers to take charge of her.

'And I think – I am sure – that Miss Bowers stayed with her all night.'

Race said: 'If that's so, it's going to simplify matters very much.'

'Who discovered the crime?' Poirot asked.

'Mrs Doyle's maid, Louise Bourget. She went to call her mistress as usual, found her dead, and came out and flopped into the steward's arms in a dead faint. He went to the manager, who came to me. I got hold of Bessner and then came for you.'

Poirot nodded.

Race said: 'Doyle's got to know. You say he's asleep still?'

Bessner nodded. 'Yes, he's still asleep in my cabin. I gave him a strong opiate last night.'

Race turned to Poirot.

'Well,' he said, 'I don't think we need detain the doctor any longer, eh? Thank you, Doctor.'

Bessner rose. 'I will have my breakfast yes. And then I will go back to my cabin and see if Mr Doyle is ready to wake.'

'Thanks.'

Bessner went out. The two men looked at each other.

'Well, what about it, Poirot?' Race asked. 'You're the man in charge. I'll take my orders from you. You say what's to be done.'

Poirot bowed.

'*Eh bien!*' he said, 'we must hold the court of inquiry. First of all, I think we must verify the story of the affair last night. That is to say, we must question Fanthorp and Miss Robson, who were the actual witnesses of what occurred. The disappearance of the pistol is very significant.'

Race rang a bell and sent a message by the steward.

Poirot sighed and shook his head. 'It is bad, this,' he murmured. 'It is bad.'

'Have you any ideas?' asked Race curiously.

'My ideas conflict. They are not well arranged; they are not orderly. There is, you see, the big fact that this girl hated Linnet Doyle and wanted to kill her.'

'You think she's capable of it?'

'I think so – yes.' Poirot sounded doubtful.

'But not in this way? That's what's worrying you, isn't it? Not to creep into her cabin in the dark and shoot her while she was sleeping. It's the cold-bloodedness that strikes you as not ringing true?'

'In a sense, yes.'

'You think that this girl, Jacqueline de Bellefort, is incapable of a premeditated cold-blooded murder?'

Poirot said slowly: 'I am not sure, you see. She would have the brains – yes. But I doubt if, physically, she could bring herself to do the *act*. . . .'

Race nodded. 'Yes, I see. . . . Well, according to Bessner's story, it would also have been physically impossible.'

'If that is true it clears the ground considerably. Let us hope it is true.' Poirot paused and then added simply: 'I shall be glad if it is so, for I have for that little one much sympathy.'

The door opened and Fanthorp and Cornelia came in. Bessner followed them.

Cornelia gasped out: 'Isn't this just awful? Poor, poor Mrs Doyle! And she was so lovely too. It must have been a real *fiend* who could hurt her! And poor Mr Doyle; he'll just go crazy when he knows? Why, even last night he was so frightfully worried lest she should hear about his accident.'

'That is just what we want you to tell us about, Miss Robson,' said Race. 'We want to know exactly what happened last night.'

Cornelia began a little confusedly, but a question or two from Poirot helped matters.

'Ah, yes, I understand. After the bridge, Madame Doyle went to her cabin. Did she really go to her cabin, I wonder?'

'She did,' said Race. 'I actually saw her. I said good-night to her at the door.'

'And the time?'

'Mercy, I couldn't say,' replied Cornelia.

'It was twenty past eleven,' said Race.

'*Bien*. Then at twenty past eleven, Madame Doyle was alive and well. At that moment there was, in the saloon, who?'

Fanthorp answered: 'Doyle was there. And Miss de Bellefort. Myself and Miss Robson.'

'That's so,' agreed Cornelia. 'Mr Pennington had a drink and then went off to bed.'

'That was how much later?'

'Oh, about three or four minutes.'

'Before half-past eleven, then?'

'Oh, yes.'

'So that there were left in the saloon you, Mademoiselle

Robson, Mademoiselle de Bellefort, Monsieur Doyle and Monsieur Fanthorp. What were you all doing?'

'Mr Fanthorp was reading a book. I'd got some embroidery. Miss de Bellefort was – she was—'

Fanthorp came to the rescue. 'She was drinking pretty heavily.'

'Yes,' agreed Cornelia. 'She was talking to me mostly and asking me about things at home. And she kept saying things – to me mostly. But I think they were kind of meant for Mr Doyle. He was getting kind of mad at her, but he didn't say anything. I think he thought if he kept quiet she might simmer down.'

'But she didn't?'

Cornelia shook her head.

'I tried to go once or twice, but she made me stay, and I was getting very, very uncomfortable. And then Mr Fanthorp got up and went out—'

'It was a little embarrassing,' said Fanthorp. 'I thought I'd make an unobtrusive exit. Miss de Bellefort was clearly working up for a scene.'

'And then she pulled out the pistol,' went on Cornelia, 'and Mr Doyle jumped up to try and get it away from her, and it went off and shot him through the leg; and then she began to sob and cry – and I was scared to death and ran out after Mr Fanthorp, and he came back with me, and Mr Doyle said not to make a fuss, and one of the Nubian boys heard the noise of the shot and came along, but Mr Fanthorp told him it was all right; and then we got Jacqueline away to her cabin, and Mr Fanthorp stayed with her while I got Miss Bowers.' Cornelia paused breathless.

'What time was this?' asked Race.

Cornelia said again, 'Mercy, I don't know,' but Fanthorp answered promptly:

'It must have been about twenty minutes past twelve. I know that it was actually half-past twelve when I finally got to my cabin.'

'Now let me be quite sure on one or two points,' said Poirot. 'After Madame Doyle left the saloon, did any of you four leave it?'

'No.'

'You are quite certain Mademoiselle de Bellefort did not leave the saloon at all?'

Fanthorp answered promptly: 'Positive. Neither Doyle, Miss de Bellefort, Miss Robson, nor myself left the saloon.'

'Good. That establishes the fact that Mademoiselle de Bellefort could not possibly have shot Madame Doyle before – let us
say – twenty past twelve. Now, Mademoiselle Robson, you went
to fetch Mademoiselle Bowers. Was Mademoiselle de Bellefort
alone in her cabin during that period?'

'No. Mr Fanthorp stayed with her.'

'Good! So far, Mademoiselle de Bellefort has a perfect alibi.
Mademoiselle Bowers is the next person to interview, but, before I send for her. I should like to have your opinion on one
or two points. Monsieur Doyle, you say, was very anxious that
Mademoiselle de Bellefort should not be left alone. Was he
afraid, do you think, that she was contemplating some further
rash act?'

'Thas is my opinion,' said Fanthorp.

'He was definitely afraid she might attach Madame Doyle?'

'No.' Fanthorp shook his head. 'I don't think that was his
idea at all. I think he was afraid she might – er – do something
rash to herself.'

'Suicide?'

'Yes. You see, she seemed completely sobered and heart-
broken at what she had done. She was full of self-reproach.
She kept saying she would be better dead.'

Cornelia said timidly: 'I think he was rather upset about
her. He spoke – quite nicely. He said it was all his fault – that
he'd treated her badly. He – he was really very nice.'

Hercule Poirot nodded thoughtfully. 'Now about the pistol,'
he went on. 'What happened to that?'

'She dropped it,' said Cornelia.

'And afterwards?'

Fanthorp explained how he had gone back to search for it,
but had not been able to find it.

'Aha!' said Poirot. 'Now we begin to arrive. Let us, I pray
you, be very precise. Describe to me exactly what happened.'

'Miss de Bellefort let it fall. Then she kicked it away from
her with her foot.'

'She sort of hated it,' explained Cornelia. 'I know just what
she felt.'

'And it went under a settee, you say. Now be very careful.
Mademoiselle de Bellefort did not recover that pistol before
she left the saloon?'

Both Fanthorp and Cornelia were positive on that point.

'Précisément. I seek only to be very exact, you comprehend.
Then we arrive at this point. When Mademoiselle de Bellefort
leaves the saloon the pistol is under the settee, and, since

Mademoiselle de Bellefort is not left alone – Monsieur Fanthorp, Mademoiselle Robson or Mademoiselle Bowers being with her – she has no opportunity to get back the pistol after she left the saloon. What time was it, Monsieur Fanthorp, when you went back to look for it?'

'It must have been just before half-past twelve.'

'And how long would have elapsed between the time you and Dr Bessner carried Monsieur Doyle out of the saloon until you returned to look for the pistol?'

'Perhaps five minutes – perhaps a little more.'

'Then in that five minutes someone removes that pistol from where it lay out of sight under the settee. That someone was *not* Mademoiselle de Bellefort. Who was it? It seems highly probable that the person who removed it was the murderer of Madame Doyle. We may assume, too, that that person had overheard or seen something of the events immediately preceding.'

'I don't see how you make that out,' objected Fanthorp.

'Because,' said Hercule Poirot, 'you have just told us that the pistol was out of sight under the settee. Therefore it is hardly credible that it was discovered by *accident*. It was taken by someone who knew it was there. Therefore that someone must have assisted at the scene.'

Fanthorp shook his head. 'I saw no one when I went out on the deck just before the shot was fired.'

'Ah, but you went out by the door on the starboard side.'

'Yes. The same side as my cabin.'

'Then if there had been anybody at the port door looking through the glass you would not have seen him?'

'No,' admitted Fanthorp.

'Did anyone hear the shot except the Nubian boy?'

'Not as far as I know.'

Fanthorp went on: 'You see, the windows in here were all closed. Miss Van Schuyler felt a draught earlier in the evening. The swing doors were shut. I doubt if the shot would be at all clearly heard. It would only sound like the pop of a cork.'

Race said: 'As far as I know, no one seems to have heard the other shot – the shot that killed Mrs Doyle.'

'That we will inquire into presently,' said Poirot. 'For the moment we will concern ourselves with Mademoiselle de Bellefort. We must speak to Mademoiselle Bowers. But first, before you go' – he arrested Fanthorp and Cornelia with a gesture – 'you will give me a little information about yourselves. Then it will not be necessary to call you again later. You first, Monsieur – your full name.'

'James Lechdale Fanthorp.'

'Address?'

'Glasmore House, Market Donnington, Northamptonshire.'

'Your profession?'

'I am a lawyer.'

'And your reasons for visiting this country?'

There was a pause. For the first time the impassive Mr Fanthorp seemed taken aback. He said at last, almost mumbling the words, 'Er – pleasure.'

'Aha!' said Poirot. 'You take the holiday; that is it, yes?'

'Er – yes.'

'Very well, Monsieur Fanthorp. Will you give me a brief account of your own movements last night after the events we have just been narrating?'

'I went straight to bed.'

'That was at—?'

'Just after half-past twelve.'

'Your cabin is number twenty-two on the starboard side – the one nearest the saloon?'

'Yes.'

'I will ask you one more question. Did you hear anything – anything at all – after you went to your cabin?'

Fanthorp considered.

'I turned in very quickly. I *think* I heard a kind of splash just as I was dropping off to sleep. Nothing else.'

'You heard a kind of splash? Near at hand?'

Fanthorp shook his head.

'Really, I couldn't say. I was half asleep.'

'And what time would that be?'

'It might have been about one o'clock. I can't really say.'

'Thank you, Monsieur Fanthorp. That is all.'

Poirot turned his attention to Cornelia.

'And now, Mademoiselle Robson. Your full name?'

'Cornelia Ruth. And my address is The Red House, Bellfield, Connecticut.'

'What brought you to Egypt?'

'Cousin Marie, Miss Van Schuyler, brought me along on a trip.'

'Had you ever met Madame Doyle previous to this journey?'

'No, never.'

'And what did you do last night?'

'I went right to bed after helping Dr Bessner with Mr Doyle's leg.'

'Your cabin is—?'

'Forty-three on the port side – right next door to Miss de Bellefort.'

'And did you hear anything?'

Cornelia shook her head. 'I didn't hear a thing.'

'No splash?'

'No, but then I wouldn't, because the boat's against the bank on my side.'

Poirot nodded. 'Thank you, Mademoiselle Robson. Now perhaps you will be so kind as to ask Mademoiselle Bowers to come here.'

Fanthorp and Cornelia went out.

'That seems clear enough,' said Race. 'Unless three independent witnesses are lying, Jacqueline de Bellefort couldn't have got hold of the pistol. But somebody did. And somebody overheard the scene. And somebody was B.F. enough to write a big J on the wall.'

There was a tap on the door and Miss Bowers entered. The hospital nurse sat down in her usual composed efficient manner. In answer to Poirot she gave her name, address, and qualifications, adding: 'I've been looking after Miss Van Schuyler for over two years now.'

'Is Mademoiselle Van Schuyler's health very bad?'

'Why, no, I wouldn't say that,' replied Miss Bowers. 'She's not very young, and she's nervous about herself and she likes to have a nurse around handy. There's nothing serious the matter with her. She just likes plently of attention and she's willing to pay for it.'

Poirot nodded comprehendingly. Then he said: 'I understand that Mademoiselle Robson fetched you last night?'

'Why, yes, that's so.'

'Will you tell me exactly what happened?'

'Well, Miss Robson just gave me a brief outline of what had occurred, and I came along with her. I found Miss de Bellefort in a very excited, hysterical condition.'

'Did she utter any threats against Madame Doyle?'

'No, nothing of that kind. She was in a condition of morbid self-reproach. She'd taken a good deal of alcohol, I should say, and she was suffering from reaction. I didn't think she ought to be left. I gave her a shot of morphia and sat up with her.'

'Now, Mademoiselle Bowers, I want you to answer this. Did Mademoiselle de Bellefort leave her cabin at all?'

'No, she did not.'

'And you yourself?'

'I stayed with her until early this morning.'

'You are quite sure of that?'

'Absolutely sure.'

'Thank you, Mademoiselle Bowers.'

The nurse went out. The two men looked at each other.

Jacqueline de Bellefort was definitely cleared of the crime. Who then had shot Linnet Doyle?

——— 14 ———

Race said: 'Someone pinched the pistol. It wasn't Jacqueline de Bellefort. Someone knew enough to feel that his crime would be attributed to her. But that someone did not know that a hospital nurse was going to give her morphia and sit up with her all night. And one thing more. Someone had already attempted to kill Linnet Doyle by rolling a boulder over the cliff; that someone was *not* Jacqueline de Bellefort. Who was it?'

Poirot said: 'It will be simpler to say who it could not have been. Neither Monsieur Doyle, Madame Allerton, Monsieur Allerton, Mademoiselle Van Schuyler, nor Mademoiselle Bowers could have had anything to do with it. They were all within my sight.'

'H'm' said Race; 'that leaves rather a large field. What about motive?'

'That is where I hope Monsieur Doyle may be able to help us. There have been several incidents—'

The door opened and Jacqueline de Bellefort entered. She was very pale and she stumbled a little as she walked.

'I didn't do it,' she said. Her voice was that of a frightened child. 'I didn't do it. Oh, please believe me. Everyone will think I did it – but I didn't – I didn't. It's – it's awful. I wish it hadn't happened. I might have killed Simon last night; I was mad, I think. But I didn't do the other. . . .'

She sat down and burst into tears.

Poirot patted her on the shoulder.

'There, there. We know that you did not kill Madame Doyle. It is proved – yes, proved, *mon enfant*. It was not you.'

Jackie sat up suddenly, her wet handkerchief clasped in her hand.

'But who did?'

'That,' said Poirot, 'is just the question we are asking ourselves. You cannot help us there, my child?'

Jacqueline shook her head.

'I don't know . . . I can't imagine. . . . No, I haven't the faintest idea.' She frowned deeply. 'No,' she said at last. 'I can't think of anyone who wanted her dead.' Her voice faltered a little. 'Except me.'

Race said: 'Excuse me a minute – just thought of something.' He hurried out of the room.

Jacqueline de Bellefort sat with her head downcast, nervously twisting her fingers. She broke out suddenly: 'Death's horrible – horrible! I – hate the thought of it.'

Poirot said: 'Yes. It is not pleasant to think, is it, that now, at this very moment, someone is rejoicing at the successful carrying out of his or her plan.'

'Don't – don't!' cried Jackie. 'It sounds horrible the way you put it.'

Poirot shrugged his shoulders. 'It is true.'

Jackie said in a low voice: 'I – I wanted her dead – and she *is* dead. . . . And, what is worse . . . she died – just like I said.'

'Yes, Mademoiselle. She was shot through the head.'

She cried out: 'Then I was right, that night at the Cataract Hotel. There *was* someone listening!'

'Ah!' Poirot nodded his head. 'I wondered if you would remember that. Yes, it is altogether too much of a coincidence – that Madame Doyle should be killed in just the way you described.'

Jackie shuddered.

'That man that night – who can he have been?'

Poirot was silent for a minute or two, then he said in quite a different tone of voice: 'You are sure it was a man, Mademoiselle?'

Jackie looked at him in surprise.

'Yes, of course. At least—'

'Well, Mademoiselle?'

She frowned, half closing her eyes in an effort to remember. She said slowly: 'I *thought* it was a man. . . .'

'But now you are not so sure?'

Jackie said slowly: 'No, I can't be certain. I just assumed it was a man – but it was really just a – a figure – a shadow. . . .'

She paused and then, as Poirot did not speak, she added:

'You think it must have been a woman? But surely none of the women on this boat can have wanted to kill Linnet?'

Poirot merely moved his head from side to side.

The door opened and Bessner appeared.

'Will you come and speak with Mr Doyle, please, Monsieur Poirot? He would like to see you.'

Jackie sprang up. She caught Bessner by the arm.

'How is he? Is he – all right?'

'Naturally he is not all right,' replied Dr Bessner reproachfully. 'The bone is fractured, you understand.'

'But he's not going to die?' cried Jackie.

'Ach, who said anything about dying? We will get him to civilisation and there we will have an X-ray and proper treatment.'

'Oh!' The girl's hands came together in convulsive pressure. She sank down again on a chair.

Poirot stepped out on to the deck with the doctor and at that moment Race joined them. They went up to the promenade deck and along to Bessner's cabin.

Simon Doyle was lying propped with cushions and pillows, an improvised cage over his leg. His face was ghastly in colour, the ravages of pain with shock on top of it. But the predominant expression on his face was bewilderment – the sick bewilderment of a child.

He muttered: 'Please come in. The doctor's told me – told me – about Linnet. . . . I can't believe it. I simply can't believe it's true.'

'I know. It's a bad knock,' said Race.

Simon stammered: 'You know – Jackie didn't do it. I'm certain Jackie didn't do it! It looks black against her, I dare say, but she *didn't* do it. She – she was a bit tight last night, and all worked up, and that's why she went for me. But she wouldn't – she wouldn't do *murder* . . . not cold-blooded murder. . . .'

Poirot said gently: 'Do not distress yourself, Monsieur Doyle. Whoever shot your wife, it was not Mademoiselle de Bellefort.'

Simon looked at him doubtfully.

'Is that on the square?'

'But since it was not Mademoiselle de Bellefort,' continued Poirot, 'can you give us any idea of who it might have been?'

Simon shook his head. The look of bewilderment increased.

'It's crazy – impossible. Apart from Jackie nobody could have wanted to do her in.'

'Reflect, Monsieur Doyle. Had she no enemies? Is there no one who had a grudge against her?'

Again Simon shook his head with the same hopeless gesture.

'It sounds absolutely fantastic. There's Windlesham, of course. She more or less chucked him to marry me – but I can't see a polite stick like Windlesham committing murder, and anyway he's miles away. Same thing with old Sir George Wode. He'd got a down in Linnet over the house – disliked the way she was pulling it about; but he's miles away in London, and anyway to think of murder in such a connection would be fantastic.'

'Listen, Monsieur Doyle.' Poirot spoke very earnestly. 'On the first day we came on board the *Karnak* I was impressed by a little conversation which I had with Madame your wife. She was very upset – very distraught. She said – mark this well – that *everybody* hated her. She said she felt afraid – unsafe – as though *everyone* round her were an enemy.'

'She was pretty upset at finding Jackie aboard. So was I,' said Simon.

'That is true, but it does not quite explain those words. When she said she was surrounded by enemies, she was almost certainly exaggerating, but all the same she did mean more than one person.'

'You may be right there,' admitted Simon. 'I thing I can explain that. It was a name in the passenger list that upset her.'

'A name in the passenger list? What name?'

'Well, you see, she didn't actually tell me. As a matter of fact I wasn't even listening very carefully. I was going over the Jacqueline business in my mind. As far as I remember, Linnet said something about doing people down in business, and that it made her uncomfortable to meet anyone who had a grudge against her family. You see, although I don't really know the family history very well, I gather that Linnet's mother was a millionaire's daughter. Her father was only just ordinary plain wealthy, but after his marriage he naturally began playing the markets or whatever you call it. And as a result of that, of course, several people got it in the neck. You know, affluence one day, the gutter the next. Well, I gather there was someone on board whose father had got up against Linnet's father and taken a pretty hard knock. I remember Linnet saying: "It's pretty awful when people hate you without even knowing you." '

'Yes,' said Poirot thoughtfully. 'That would explain what

she said to me. For the first time she was feeling the burden of her inheritance and not its advantages. You are quite sure, Monsieur Doyle, that she did not mention this man's name?'

Simon shook his head ruefully.

'I didn't really pay much attention. Just said: "Oh, nobody minds what happened to their fathers nowadays. Life goes too fast for that." Something of that kind.'

Bessner said dryly: 'Ach, but I can have a guess. There is certainly a young man with a grievance on board.'

'You mean Ferguson?' asked Poirot.

'Yes. He spoke against Mrs Doyle once or twice. I myself have heard him.'

'What can we do to find out?' asked Simon.

Poirot replied: 'Colonel Race and I must interview all the passengers. Until we have got their stories it would be unwise to form theories. Then there is the maid. We ought to interview her first of all. It would, perhaps, be as well if we did that here. Monsieur Doyle's presence might be helpful.'

'Yes, that's a good idea,' said Simon.

'Had she been with Mrs Doyle long?'

'Just a couple of months!' exclaimed Poirot.

'Why, you don't think—'

'Had Madame any valuable jewellery?'

'There were her pearls,' said Simon. 'She once told me they were worth forty or fifty thousand.' He shivered. 'My God, do you thing those damned pearls—?'

'Robbery is a possible motive,' said Poirot. 'All the same it seems hardly credible. . . . Well, we shall see. Let us have the maid here.'

Louise Bourget was that same vivacious Latin brunette whom Poirot had seen one day and noticed.

She was anything but vivacious now. She had been crying and looked frightened. Yet there was a kind of sharp cunning apparent in her face which did not prepossess the two men favourably towards her.

'You are Louise Bourget?'

'Yes, Monsieur.'

'When did you last see Madame Doyle alive?'

'Last night, Monsieur. I was in her cabin to undress her.'

'What time was that?'

'It was some time after eleven, Monsieur. I cannot say exactly when. I undress Madame and put her to bed, and then I leave.'

'How long did all that take?'

'Ten minutes, Monsieur. Madame was tired. She told me to put the lights out when I went.'

'And when you had left her, what did you do?'

'I went to my own cabin, Monsieur, on the deck below.'

'And you heard or saw nothing more that can help us?'

'How could I, Monsieur?'

'That, Mademoiselle, is for you to say, not for us,' Hercule Poirot retorted.

She stole a sideways glance at him.

'But Monsieur, I was nowhere near. . . . What could I have seen or heard? I was on the deck below. My cabin, it was on the other side of the boat, even. It is impossible that I should have heard anything. Naturally if I had been unable to sleep, if I had mounted the stairs, *then* perhaps I might have seen this assassin, this monster, enter or leave Madame's cabin, but as it is—'

She threw out her hands appealingly to Simon.

'Monsieur, I implore you – you see how it is? What can I say?'

'My good girl,' said Simon harshly, 'don't be a fool. Nobody thinks you saw or heard anything. You'll be quite all right. I'll look after you. Nobody's accusing you of anything.'

Louise murmured, 'Monsieur is very good,' and dropped her eyelids modestly.

'We take it, then, that you saw and heard nothing?' asked Race impatiently.

'That is what I said, Monsieur.'

'And you know of no one who had a grudge against your mistress?'

To the surprise of her listeners Louis nodded her head vigorously.

'Oh, yes. That I do know. To that question I can answer Yes most emphatically.'

Poirot said, 'You mean Mademoiselle de Bellefort?'

'She, certainly. But it is not of her I speak. There was someone else on this boat who disliked Madame, who was very angry because of the way Madame had injured him.'

'Good lord!' Simon exclaimed. 'What's all this?'

Louise went on, still emphatically nodding her head with the utmost vigour.

'Yes, yes, yes, it is as I say! It concerns the former maid of Madame – my predecessor. There was a man one of the engineers on this boat, who wanted her to marry him. And my predecessor, Marie her name was, she would have done so. But

Madame Doyle, she made inquiries and she discovered that this Fleetwood already had a wife – a wife of colour you understand, a wife of this country. She had gone back to her own people, but he was still married to her, you understand. And so Madame she told all this to Marie, and Marie she was very unhappy and she would not see Fleetwood any more. And this Fleetwood, he was infuriated, and when he found out that this Madame Doyle had formerly been Mademoiselle Linnet Ridgeway he tells me that he would like to kill her! Her interference ruined his life, he said.'

Louise paused triumphantly.

'This is interesting,' said Race.

Poirot turned to Simon.

'Had you any idea of this?'

'None whatever,' Simon replied with patient sincerity. 'I doubt if Linnet even knew the man was on the boat. She had probably forgotten all about the incident.'

He turned sharply to the maid.

'Did you say anything to Mrs Doyle about this?'

'No, Monsieur, of course not.'

Poirot asked: 'Do you know anything about your mistress's pearls?'

'Her pearls?' Louise's eyes opened very wide. 'She was wearing them last night.'

'You saw them when she came to bed?'

'Yes, Monsieur.'

'Where did she put them?'

'On the table by the side as always.'

'That is where you last saw them?'

'Yes, Monsieur.'

'Did you see them there this morning?'

A startled look came into the girl's face.

'*Mon Dieu*! I did not even look. I come up to the bed, I see – I see Madame; and then I cry out and rush out of the door, and I faint.'

Hercule Poirot nodded his head.

'You did not look. But I, I have the eyes which notice, and there were no pearls on the table beside the bed this morning.'

Hercule Poirot's observation had not been at fault. There were no pearls on the table by Linnet Doyle's bed.

Louise Bourget was bidden to make a search among Linnet's belongings. According to her, all was in order. Only the pearls had disappeared.

As they emerged from the cabin a steward was waiting to tell them that breakfast had been served in the smoking-room. As they passed along the deck, Race paused to look over the rail.

'Aha! I see you have had an idea, my friend.'

'Yes. It suddenly came to me, when Fanthorp mentioned thinking he heard a splash, that I too had been awakened some time last night by a splash. It's perfectly possible that, after the murder, the murderer threw the pistol overboard.'

Poirot said slowly: 'You really think that is possible, my friend?' Race shrugged his shoulders.

'It's a suggestion. After all, the pistol wasn't anywhere in the cabin. First thing I looked for.'

'All the same,' said Poirot, 'it is incredible that it should have been thrown overboard.'

Race asked: 'Where is it then?'

Poirot replied thoughtfully, 'If it is not in Madame Doyle's cabin, there is, logically, only one other place where it could be.'

'Where's that?'

'In Mademoiselle de Bellefort's cabin.'

Race said thoughtfully: 'Yes. I see—'

He stopped suddenly.

'She's out of her cabin. Shall we go and have a look now?'

Poirot shook his head. 'No my friend, that would be precipitate. It may not yet have been put there.'

'What about an immediate search of the whole boat?'

'That way we should show our hand. We must work with great care. It is very delicate, our position, at the moment. Let us discuss the situation as we eat.'

Race agreed. They went into the smoking-room.

'Well,' said Race as he poured himself out a cup of coffee, 'we've got two definite leads. There's the disappearance of the pearls. And there's the man Fleetwood. As regards the pearls, robbery seems indicated, but – I don't know whether you'll agree with me—'

Poirot said quickly: 'But it was an odd moment to choose?'

'Exactly. To steal the pearls at such a moment invites a close search of everybody on board. How then could the thief hope to get away with his booty?'

'He might have gone ashore and dumped it.'

'The company always has a watchman on the bank.'

'Then that is not feasible. Was the murder committed to divert attention from the robbery? No, that does not make sense; it is profoundly unsatisfactory. But supposing that Madame Doyle woke up and caught the thief in the act?'

'And therefore the thief shot her? But she was shot whilst she slept.'

'So that too does not make sense. . . . You know, I have a little idea about those pearls – and yet – no – it is impossible. Because if my idea was right the pearls would not have disappeared. Tell me, what did you think of the maid?'

'I wondered,' said Race slowly, 'if she knew more than she said.'

'Ah, you too had that impression?'

'Definitely not a nice girl,' said Race.

Hercule Poirot nodded. 'Yes, I would not trust her.'

'You think she had something to do with the murder?'

'No. I would not say that.'

'With the theft of the pearls, then?'

'That is more probable. She had only been with Madame Doyle a very short time. She may be a member of a gang that specialises in jewel robberies. In such a case there is often a maid with excellent references. Unfortunately we are not in a position to seek information on these points. And yet that explanation does not quite satisfy me. . . . Those pearls – ah, *sacré*, my little idea *ought* to be right. And yet nobody would be so imbecile—' He broke off.

'What about the man Fleetwood?'

'We must question him. It may be that we have there the solution. If Louise Bourget's story is true, he had a definite motive for revenge. He could have overheard the scene between Jacqueline and Monsieur Doyle, and when they had left the saloon he could have darted in and secured the gun. Yes, it is all quite possible. And that letter J scrawled in blood. That, too, would accord with a simple, rather crude nature.'

'In fact, he's just the person we are looking for?'

'Yes – only—' Poirot rubbed his nose. He said with a slight

grimace: 'See you, I recognise my own weaknesses. It has been said of me that I like to make a case difficult. This solution that you put to me – it is too simple, too easy. I cannot feel that it really happened. And yet, that may be sheer prejudice on my part.'

'Well, we'd better have the fellow here.'

Race rang the bell and gave the order. Then he asked, 'Any other – possibilities?'

'Plenty, my friend. There is, for example, the American trustee.'

'Pennington?'

'Yes, Pennington. There was a curious little scene in here the other day.' He narrated the happenings to Race. 'You see – it is significant. Madame, she wanted to read all the papers before signing. So he makes the excuse of another day. And then, the husband, he makes a very significant remark.'

'What was that?'

'He says – "I never read anything. I sign where I am told to sign." You perceive the significance of that. Pennington did. I saw it in his eye. He looked at Doyle as though an entirely new idea had come into his head. Just imagine, my friend, that you have been left trustee to the daughter of an intensely wealthy man. You use, perhaps, the money to speculate with. I know it is so in all detective novels – but you read of it too in the newspapers. It happens, my friend, it *happens.*'

'I don't dispute it,' said Race.

'There is, perhaps, still time to make good by speculating wildly. Your ward is not yet of age. And then – she marries! The control passes from your hands into hers at a moment's notice! A disaster! But there is still a chance. She is on a honeymoon. She will perhaps be careless about business. A casual paper, slipped in among others, signed without reading. . . . But Linnet Doyle was not like that. Honeymoon or no honeymoon, she was a business woman. And then her husband makes a remark, and a new idea comes to that desperate man who is seeking a way out from ruin. If Linnet Doyle were to die, her fortune would pass to her husband – and he would be easy to deal with; he would be a child in the hands of an astute man like Andrew Pennington. *Mon cher Colonel,* I tell you I *saw* the thought pass through Andrew Pennington's head. "If only it were *Doyle* I had got to deal with . . ." That is what he was thinking.'

'Quite possible, I daresay,' said Race dryly, 'but you've no evidence.'

'Alas, no.'

'Then there's young Ferguson,' said Race. 'He talks bitterly enough. Not that I go by talk. Still, he *might* be the fellow whose father was ruined by old Ridgeway. It's a little far-fetched but it's *possible*. People do brood over bygone wrongs sometimes.' He paused a minute and then said: 'And there's my fellow.'

'Yes, there is "your fellow" as you call him.'

'He's a killer,' said Race. 'We know that. On the other hand, I can't see any way in which he could have come up against Linnet Doyle. Their orbits don't touch.'

Poirot said slowly: 'Unless, accidentally, she had become possessed of evidence showing his identity.'

'That's possible, but it seems highly unlikely.' There was a knock at the door. 'Ah, here's our would-be bigamist.'

Fleetwood was a big, truculent-looking man. He looked suspiciously from one to the other of them as he entered the room. Poirot recognised him as the man he had seen talking to Louise Bourget.

Fleetwood asked suspiciously: 'You wanted to see me?'

'We did,' said Race. 'You probably know that a murder was committed on this boat last night?'

Fleetwood nodded.

'And I believe it is true that you had reason to feel anger against the woman who was killed.'

A look of alarm sprang up in Fleetwood's eyes.

'Who told you that?'

'You considered that Mrs Doyle had interfered between you and a young woman.'

'I know who told you that – that lying French hussy. She's a liar through and through, that girl.'

'But this particular story happens to be true.'

'It's a dirty lie!'

'You say that, although you don't know what it is yet.'

The shot told. The man flushed and gulped.

'It is true, is it not, that you were going to marry the girl Marie, and that she broke it off when she discovered that you were a married man already?'

'What business was it of hers?'

'You mean, what business was it of Mrs Doyle's? Well, you know, bigamy is bigamy.'

'It wasn't like that. I married one of the locals out here. It didn't answer. She went back to her people. I've not seen her for a half a dozen years.'

'Still you were married to her.'

The man was silent. Race went on: 'Mrs Doyle, or Miss Ridgeway as she then was, found out all this?'

'Yes, she did, curse her! Nosing about where no one ever asked her to. I'd have treated Marie right. I'd have done anything for her. And she'd never have known about the other, if it hadn't been for that meddlesome young lady of hers. Yes, I'll say it, I *did* have a grudge against the lady, and I felt bitter about it when I saw her on this boat, all dressed up in pearls and diamonds and lording it all over the place, with never a thought that she'd broken up a man's life for him! I felt bitter all right, but if you think I'm a dirty murderer – if you think I went and shot her with a gun, well, that's a damned lie! I never touched her. And that's God's truth.'

He stopped. The sweat was rolling down his face.

'Where were you last night between the hours of twelve and two?'

'In my bunk asleep – and my mate will tell you so.'

'We shall see,' said Race. He dismissed him with a curt nod. 'That'll do.'

'*Eh bien?*' inquired Poirot as the door closed behind Fleetwood.

Race shrugged his shoulders. 'He tells quite a straight story. He's nervous, of course, but not unduly so. We'll have to investigate his alibi – though I don't suppose it will be decisive. His mate was probably asleep, and this fellow could have slipped in and out if he wanted to. It depends whether anyone else saw him.'

'Yes, one must inquire as to that.'

'The next thing, I think,' said Race, 'is whether anyone heard anything which might give a clue as to the time of the crime. Bessner places it as having occurred between twelve and two. It seems reasonable to hope that someone among the passengers may have heard the shot – even if they did not recognise it for what it was. I didn't hear anything of the kind myself. What about you?'

Poirot shook his head.

'Me, I slept absolutely like the log. I heard nothing – but nothing at all. I might have been drugged, I slept so soundly.'

'A pity,' said Race. 'Well, let's hope we have a bit of luck with the people who have cabins on the starboard side. Fanthorp we've done. The Allertons come next. I'll send the steward to fetch them.'

Mrs Allerton came in briskly. She was wearing a soft grey striped silk dress. Her face looked distressed.

'It's too horrible,' she said as she accepted the chair that Poirot placed for her. 'I can hardly believe it. That lovely creature, with everything to live for – dead. I almost feel I can't believe it.'

'I know how you feel, Madame,' said Poirot sympathetically.

'I'm glad *you* are on board,' said Mrs Allerton simply. 'You'll be able to find out who did it. I'm so glad it isn't that poor tragic girl.'

'You mean Mademoiselle de Bellefort. Who told you she did not do it?'

'Cornelia Robson,' replied Mrs Allerton, with a faint smile. 'You know, she's simply thrilled by it all. It's probably the only exciting thing that has ever happened to her, and probably the only exciting thing that ever will happen to her. But she's so nice that she's terribly ashamed of enjoying it. She thinks it's awful of her.'

Mrs Allerton gave a look at Poirot and then added: 'But I mustn't chatter. You want to ask me questions.'

'If you please. You went to bed at what time, Madame?'

'Just after half-past ten.'

'And you went to sleep at once?'

'Yes. I was sleepy.'

'And did you hear anything – anything at all – during the night?'

Mrs Allerton wrinkled her brows.

'Yes, I think I heard a splash and someone running – or was it the other way about? I'm rather hazy. I just had a vague idea that someone had fallen overboard at sea – a dream, you know – and then I woke up and listened, but it was all quite quiet.'

'Do you know what time that was?'

'No, I'm afraid I don't. But I don't think it was very long after I went to sleep. I mean it was within the first hour or so.'

'Alas, Madame, that is not very definite.'

'No. I know it isn't. But it's no good my trying to guess, is it, when I haven't really the vaguest idea?'

'And that is all you can tell us, Madame?'

'I'm afraid so.'

'Had you ever actually met Madame Doyle before?'

'No, Tim had met her. And I'd heard a good deal about her – through a cousin of ours, Joanna Southwood, but I'd never spoken to her till we met at Assuan.'

'I have one other question, Madame, if you will pardon me for asking.'

Mrs Allerton murmured with a faint smile, 'I should love to be asked an indiscreet question.'

'It is this. Did you, or your family, ever suffer any financial loss through the operations of Madame Doyle's father, Melhuish Ridgeway?'

Mrs Allerton looked thoroughly astonished.

'Oh, no! The family finances have never suffered except by dwindling . . . you know, everything paying less interest than it used to. There's never been anything melodramatic about our poverty. My husband left very little money but what he left I still have, though it doesn't yield as much as it used to yield.'

'I thank you, Madame. Perhaps you will ask your son to come to us.'

Tim said lightly, when his mother came: 'Ordeal over? My turn now! What sort of things did they ask you?'

'Only whether I heard anything last night,' said Mrs Allerton. 'And unluckily I didn't hear anything at all. I can't think why not. After all, Linnet's cabin is only one away from mine. I should think I'd have been bound to hear the shot. Go along, Tim; they're waiting for you.'

To Tim Allerton Poirot repeated his previous questions.

Tim answerd: 'I went to bed early, half-past ten or so. I read for a bit. Put out my light just after eleven.'

'Did you hear anything after that?'

'Heard a man's voice saying good-night, I think, not far away.'

'That was me saying good-night to Mrs Doyle,' said Race.

'Yes. After that I went to sleep. Then, later, I heard a kind of hullabaloo going on, somebody calling Fanthorp, I remember.'

'Mademoiselle Robson when she ran out from the observation saloon.'

'Yes, I suppose that was it. And then a lot of different voices. And then somebody running along the deck. And then a splash. And then I heard old Bessner booming out something about "Careful now" and "Not too quick." '

'You heard a splash?'

'Well, something of that kind.'

'You are sure it was not a *shot* you heard?'

'Yes, I suppose it might have been . . . I did hear a cork pop. Perhaps that was the shot. I may have imagined the splash from connecting the idea of the cork with liquid pouring into a glass. . . . I know my foggy idea was that there was some kind of party on, and I wished they'd all go to bed and shut up.'

'Anything more after that?'

Tim thought. 'Only Fanthorp barging round in his cabin next door. I thought he'd never get to bed.'

'And after that?'

Tim shrugged his shoulders. 'After that – oblivion.'

'You heard nothing more?'

'Nothing whatever.'

'Thank you, Monsieur Allerton.'

Tim got up and left the cabin.

——— 16 ———

Race pored thoughtfully over a plan of the promenade deck of the *Karnak*.

'Fanthorp, young Allerton, Mrs Allerton. Then an empty cabin – Simon Doyle's. Now who's on the other side of Mrs Doyle's? The old American dame. If anyone heard anything she would have done. If she's up we'd better have her along.'

Miss Van Schuyler entered the room. She looked even older and yellower than usual this morning. Her small dark eyes had an air of venomous displeasure in them.

Race rose and bowed.

'We're very sorry to trouble you, Miss Van Schuyler. It's very good of you. Please sit down.'

Miss Van Schuyler said sharply: 'I dislike being mixed up in this. I resent it very much. I do not wish to be associated in any way with this – er – very unpleasant affair.'

'Quite – quite. I was just saying to Monsieur Poirot that the sooner we took your statement the better, as then you need have no further trouble.'

Miss Van Schuyler looked at Poirot with something approaching favour.

'I'm glad you both realise my feelings. I am not accustomed to anything of this kind.'

Poirot said soothingly: 'Precisely, Mademoiselle. That is why we wish to free you from unpleasantness as quickly as possible. Now you went to bed last night – at what time?'

'Ten o'clock is my usual time. Last night I was rather later, as Cornelia Robson, very inconsiderately, kept me waiting.'

'*Très bien,* Mademoiselle. Now what did you hear after you had retired?'

Miss Van Schuyler said: 'I sleep very lightly.'

'*A merveille!* That is very fortunate for us.'

'I was awakened by that rather flashy young woman, Mrs Doyle's maid, who said, *"Bonne nuit, Madame"* in what I cannot but think an unnecessarily loud voice.'

'And after that?'

'I went to sleep again. I woke up thinking someone was in my cabin, but I realised that it was someone in the cabin next door.'

'In Madame Doyle's cabin?'

'Yes. Then I heard someone outside on the deck and then a splash.'

'You have no idea what time this was?'

'I can tell you the time exactly. It was ten minutes past one.'

'You are sure of that?'

'Yes. I looked at my little clock that stands by my bed.'

'You did not hear a shot?'

'No, nothing of the kind.'

'But it might possibly have been a shot that awakened you?'

Miss Van Schuyler considered the question, her toadlike head on one side.

'It might,' she admitted rather grudgingly.

'And you have no idea what caused the splash you heard?'

'Not at all – I know perfectly.'

'Colonel Race sat up alertly. 'You know?'

'Certainly. I did not like this sound of prowling around. I got up and went to the door of my cabin. Miss Otterbourne was leaning over the side. She had just dropped something into the water.'

'Miss Otterbourne?' Race sounded really surprised.

'Yes.'

'You are quite sure it was Miss Otterbourne?'

'I saw her face distinctly.'

'She did not see you?'

'I do not think so.'

Poirot leant forward.

'And what did her face look like, Mademoiselle?'

'She was in a condition of considerable emotion.'

Race and Poirot exchanged a quick glance.

'And then?' Race prompted.

'Miss Otterbourne went away round the stern of the boat and I returned to bed.'

There was a knock at the door and the manager entered. He carried in his hand a dripping bundle.

'We've got it, Colonel.'

Race took the package. He unwrapped fold after fold of sodden velvet. Out of it fell a coarse handkerchief, faintly stained with pink, wrapped round a small pearl-handled pistol.

Race gave Poirot a glance of slightly malicious triumph.

'You see,' he said, 'my idea was right. It *was* thrown overboard.'

He held the pistol out on the palm of his hand.

'What do you say, Monsieur Poirot? Is this the pistol you saw at the Cataract Hotel that night?'

Poirot examined it carefully; then he said quietly: 'Yes – that is it. There is the ornamental work on it – and the initials J.B. It is an *article de luxe*, a very feminine production, but it is none the less a lethal weapon.'

'Twenty-two,' murmured Race. He took out the clip. 'Two bullets fired. Yes, there doesn't seem much doubt about it.'

Miss Van Schuyler coughed significantly.

'And what about my stole?' she demanded.

'Your stole, Mademoiselle?'

'Yes, that is my velvet stole you have here.'

Race picked up the dripping folds of material.

'This is yours, Miss Van Schuyler?'

'Certainly it's mine!' the old lady snapped. 'I missed it last night. I was asking everyone if they'd seen it.'

Poirot questioned Race with a glance, and the latter gave a slight nod of assent.

'Where did you see it last, Miss Van Schuyler?'

'I had it in the saloon yesterday evening. When I came to go to bed I could not find it anywhere.'

Race said quietly: 'You realise what its been used for?'

He spread it out, indicating with a finger the scorching and several small holes. 'The murderer wrapped it round the pistol to deaden the noise of the shot.'

'Impertinence!' snapped Miss Van Schuyler. The colour rose in her wizened cheeks.

Race said: 'I shall be glad, Miss Van Schuyler, if you will tell me the extent of your previous acquaintance with Mrs Doyle.'

'There was no previous acquaintance.'

'But you knew of her?'

'I knew who she was, of course.'

'But your families were not acquainted?'

'As a family we have always prided ourselves on being exclusive, Colonel Race. My dear mother would never have dreamed of calling upon any of the Hartz family, who, outside their wealth, were nobodies.'

'That is all you have to say, Miss Van Schuyler?'

'I have nothing to add to what I have told you. Linnet Ridgeway was brought up in England and I never saw her till I came aboard this boat.'

She rose. Poirot opened the door and she marched out.

The eyes of the two men met.

'That's her story,' said Race, 'and she's going to stick to it! It may be true. I don't know. But – Rosalie Otterbourne? I hadn't expected that.'

Poirot shook his head in a perplexed manner. Then he brought down his hand on the table with a sudden bang.

'But it does not make sense,' he cried. *'Nom d'un nom d'un nom*! It does not make sense.'

Race looked at him.

'What do you mean exactly?'

'I mean that up to a point it is all the clear sailing. Someone wished to kill Linnet Doyle. Someone overheard the scene in the saloon last night. Someone sneaked in there and retrieved the pistol – Jacqueline de Bellefort's pistol, remember. Somebody shot Linnet Doyle with that pistol and wrote the letter J on the wall. . . . All so clear, is it not? All pointing to Jacqueline de Bellefort as the murderess. And then what does the murderer do? Leave the pistol – the damning pistol – Jacqueline de Bellefort's pistol, for everyone to find? No, he – or she – throws the pistol, that particularly damning bit of evidence, overboard. Why, my friend, why?'

Race shook his head. 'It's odd.'

'It is more than odd – it is *impossible*!'

'Not impossible since it happened!'

'I do not mean that. I mean that the sequence of events is impossible. Something is wrong.'

17

Colonel Race glanced curiously at his colleague. He respected
– he had reason to respect – the brain of Hercule Poirot. Yet
for the moment he did not follow the other's process of
thought. He asked no questions, however. He seldom did ask
questions. He proceeded staightforwardly with the matter in
hand.

'What's the next thing to be done? Question the Otterbourne
girl?'

'Yes, that may advance us a little.'

Rosalie Otterbourne entered ungraciously. She did not look
nervous or frightened in any way – merely unwilling and sulky.

'Well,' she asked, 'what is it?'

Race was the spokesman.

'We're investigating Mrs Doyle's death,' he explained.

Rosalie nodded.

'Will you tell me what you did last night?'

Rosalie reflected a minute.

'Mother and I went to bed early – before eleven. We didn't
hear anything in particular, except a bit of fuss outside Dr
Bessner's cabin. I heard the old man's German voice booming away. Of course I didn't know what it was all about till
this morning.'

'You didn't hear a shot?'

'No.'

'Did you leave your cabin at all last night?'

'No.'

'You are quite sure of that?'

Rosalie stared at him.

'What do you mean? Of course I'm sure of it.'

'You did not, for instance, go round to the starboard side of
the boat and throw something overboard?'

The colour rose in her face.

'Is there any rule against throwing things overboard?'

'No, of course not. Then you did?'

'No, I didn't. I never left my cabin, I tell you.'

'Then if anyone says that they saw you—?'

She interrupted him. 'Who says they saw me?'

'Miss Van Schuyler.'

'Miss Van Schuyler?' She sounded genuinely astonished.

'Yes. Miss Van Schuyler says she looked out of her cabin and saw you throw something over the side.'

Rosalie said clearly. 'That's a damned lie.' Then, as though struck by a sudden thought, she asked: 'What time was this?'

It was Poirot who answered.

'It was ten minutes past one, Mademoiselle.'

She nodded her head thoughtfully. 'Did she see anything else?'

Poirot looked at her curiously. He stroked his chin.

'See – no,' he replied, 'but she heard something.'

'What did she hear?'

'Someone moving about in Madame Doyle's cabin.'

'I see,' muttered Rosalie.

She was pale now – deadly pale.

'And you persist in saying that you threw nothing overboard, Mademoiselle?'

'What on earth should I run about throwing things overboard for in the middle of the night?'

'There might be a reason – an innocent reason.'

'Innocent?' repeated the girl sharply.

'That's what I said. You see, Mademoiselle, something *was* thrown overboard last night – something that was not innocent.'

Race silently held out the bundle of stained velvet, opening it to display its contents.

Rosalie Otterbourne shrank back. 'Was that – what – she was killed with?'

'Yes, Mademoiselle.'

'And you think that I – I did it? What utter nonsense! Why on earth should I want to kill Linnet Doyle? I don't even know her!'

She laughed and stood up scornfully. 'The whole thing is too ridiculous.'

'Remember, Miss Otterbourne,' said Race, 'that Miss Van Schuyler is prepared to swear she saw your face quite clearly in the moonlight.'

Rosalie laughed again. 'That old cat? She's probably half blind anyway. It wasn't me she saw.' She paused. 'Can I go now?'

Race nodded and Rosalie Otterbourne left the room.

The eyes of the two men met. Race lighted a cigarette.

'Well, that's that. Flat contradiction. Which of 'em do we believe?'

Poirot shook his head. 'I have a little idea that neither of them was being quite frank.'

'That's the worst of our job,' said Race despondently. 'So many people keep back the truth for positively futile reasons. What's our next move? Get on with the questioning of the passengers?'

'I think so. It is always well to proceed with order and method.'

Race nodded.

Mrs Otterbourne, dressed in floating batik material, succeeded her daughter. She corroborated Rosalie's statement that they had both gone to bed before eleven o'clock. She herself had heard nothing of interest during the night. She could not say whether Rosalie had left their cabin or not. On the subject of the crime she was inclined to hold forth.

'The *crime passionel*!' she exclaimed. 'The primitive instinct – to kill! So closely allied to the sex instinct. That girl, Jacqueline, half Latin, hot-blooded, obeying the deepest instincts of her being, stealing forth, revolver in hand—'

'But Jacqueline de Bellefort did not shoot Madame Doyle. That we know for certain. It is proved' explained Poirot.

'Her husband, then,' said Mrs Otterbourne, rallying from the blow. 'The blood lust and the sex instinct – a sexual crime. There are many well-known instances.'

'Mr Doyle was shot through the leg and he was quite unable to move – the bone was fractured,' explained Colonel Race. 'He spent the night with Dr Bessner.'

Mrs Otterbourne was even more disappointed. She searched her mind hopefully.

'Of course!' she said. 'How foolish of me! Miss Bowers!'

'Miss Bowers?'

'Yes. Naturally. It's so *clear* psychologically. Repression! The repressed virgin! Maddened by the sight of these two – a young husband and wife passionately in love with each other. Of course it was her! She's just the type – sexually unattractive, innately respectable. In my book, *The Barren Vine*—'

Colonel Race interposed tactfully: 'Your suggestions have been most helpful, Mrs Otterbourne. We must get on with our job now. Thank you so much.'

He escorted her gallantly to the door and came back wiping his brow.

'What a poisonous woman! Whew! Why didn't somebody murder *her*!'

'It may yet happen,' Poirot consoled him.

'There might be some sense in that. Whom have we got left? Pennington – we'll keep him for the end, I think. Richetti – Ferguson.'

Signor Richetti was very voluble, very agitated.

'But what a horror, what an infamy – a woman so young and so beautiful – indeed an inhuman crime!'

Signor Richetti's hands flew expressively up in the air.

His answers were prompt. He had gone to bed early – very early. In fact immediately after dinner. He had read for a while – a very interesting pamphlet lately published – *Prähistorische Forschung in Kleinasien* – throwing an entirely new light on the painted pottery of the Anatolian foothills.

He had put out his light some time before eleven. No, he had not heard any shot. Not any sound like the pop of a cork. The only thing he had heard – but that was later, in the middle of the night – was a splash, a big splash, just near his porthole.

'Your cabin is on the lower deck, on the starboard side, is it not?'

'Yes, yes, that is so. And I heard the big splash.' His arms flew up once more to describe the bigness of the splash.

'Can you tell me at all what time that was?'

Signor Richetti reflected.

'It was one, two, three hours after I go to sleep. Perhaps two hours.'

'About ten minutes past one, for instance?'

'It might very well be, yes. Ah! But what a terrible crime – how inhuman . . . So charming a woman . . .'

Exit Signor Richetti, still gesticulating freely.

Race looked at Poirot. Poirot raised his eyebrows expressively, then shrugged his shoulders. They passed on to Mr Ferguson.

Ferguson was difficult. He sprawled insolently in a chair.

'Grand to-do about this business!' he sneered. 'What's it really matter? Lots of superfluous women in the world!'

Race said coldly: 'Can we have an account of your movements last night, Mr Ferguson?'

'Don't see why you should, but I don't mind. I mooched around a good bit. Went ashore with Miss Robson. When she went back to the boat I mooched around by myself for a while. Came back and turned in round about midnight.'

'Your cabin is on the lower deck, starboard side?'

'Yes. I'm not up among the nobs.'

'Did you hear a shot? It might only have sounded like the popping of a cork.'

Ferguson considered. 'Yes, I think I did hear something like a cork. . . . Can't remember when – before I went to sleep. But there was still a lot of people about then – commotion, running about on the deck above.'

'That was probably the shot fired by Miss de Bellefort. You didn't hear another?'

Ferguson shook his head.

'Nor a splash?'

'A splash? Yes, I believe I did hear a splash. But there was so much row going on I can't be sure about it.'

'Did you leave your cabin during the night?'

Ferguson grinned. 'No, I didn't. And I didn't participate in the good work, worse luck.'

'Come, come, Mr Ferguson, don't behave childishly.'

The young man reacted angrily.

'Why shouldn't I say what I think? I believe in violence.'

'But you don't practise what you preach?' murmured Poirot. 'I wonder.'

He leaned forward.

'It was the man, Fleetwood, was it not, who told you that Linnet Doyle was one of the richest women in England?'

'What's Fleetwood got to do with this?'

'Fleetwood, my friend, had an excellent motive for killing Linnet Doyle. He had a special grudge against her.'

Mr Ferguson came up out of his seat like a jack-in-the-box.

'So that's your dirty game, is it?' he demanded wrathfully. 'Put it on to a poor devil like Fleetwood, who can't defend himself, who's got no money to hire lawyers. But I tell you this – if you try and saddle Fleetwood with this business you'll have me to deal with.'

'And who exactly are you?' asked Poirot sweetly.

Mr Ferguson got rather red.

'I can stick by my friends anyway,' he said gruffly.

'Well, Mr Ferguson, I think that's all we need for the present,' said Race.

As the door closed behind Ferguson he remarked unexpectedly: 'Rather a likeable young cub, really.'

'You don't think he is the man *you* are after?' asked Poirot.

'I hardly think so. I suppose he *is* on board. The information was very precise. Oh, well, one job at a time. Let's have a go at Pennington.'

18

Andrew Pennington displayed all the conventional reactions of grief and shock. He was, as usual, carefully dressed. He had changed into a black tie. His long clean-shaven face bore a bewildered expression.

'Gentlemen,' he said sadly, 'this business has got me right down! Little Linnet – why, I remember her as the cutest little thing you can imagine. How proud of her Melhuish Ridgeway used to be, too! Well, there's no point in going into that. Just tell me what I can do; that's all I ask.'

Race said: 'To begin with, Mr Pennington, did you hear anything last night?'

'No, sir, I can't say I did. I have the cabin right next to Dr Bessner's number forty – forty-one, and I heard a certain commotion going on in there round about midnight or so. Of course I didn't know what it was at the time.'

'You heard nothing else? No shots?'

Andrew Pennington shook his head.

'Nothing whatever of that kind.'

'And you went to bed at what time?'

'Must have been some time after eleven.'

He leant forward.

'I don't suppose it's news to you to know that there's plenty of rumours going about the boat. That half-French girl – Jacqueline de Bellefort – there was something fishy there, you know. Linnet didn't tell me anything, but naturally I wasn't born blind and deaf. There'd been some affair between her and Simon, some time, hadn't there – *Cherchez la femme* – that's a pretty good sound rule, and I should say you wouldn't have to *cherchez* far.'

'You mean that in your belief Jacqueline de Bellefort shot Madame Doyle?' Poirot asked.

'That's what it looks like to me. Of course I don't *know* anything. . . .'

'Unfortunately we *do* know something!'

'Eh?' Mr Pennington looked startled.

'We know that it is quite impossible for Mademoiselle de Bellefort to have shot Madame Doyle.'

He explained carefully the circumstances. Pennington seemed reluctant to accept them.

'I agree it looks all right on the face of it – but this hospital nurse woman, I'll bet she didn't stay awake all night. She dozed off and the girl slipped out and in again.'

'Hardly likely, Monsieur Pennington. She had administered a strong opiate, remember. And anyway a nurse is in the habit of sleeping lightly and waking when her patient wakes.'

'It all sounds rather fishy to me,' declared Pennington.

Race said, in a gently authoritative manner: 'I think you must take it from me, Mr Pennington, that we have examined all the possibilities very carefully. The result is quite definite – Jacqueline de Bellefort did not shoot Mrs Doyle. So we are forced to look elsewhere. That is where we hope you may be able to help us.'

'I?' Pennington gave a nervous start.

'Yes. You were an intimate friend of the dead woman. You know the circumstances of her life, in all probability, much better than her husband does, since he only made her acquaintance a few months ago. You would know, for instance, of anyone who had a grudge against her. You would know, perhaps, whether there was anyone who had a motive for desiring her death.'

Andrew Pennington passed his tongue over rather dry-looking lips.

'I assure you, I have no idea. . . . You see Linnet was brought up in England. I know very little of her surroundings and associations.'

'And yet,' mused Poirot, 'there was someone on board who was interested in Madame Doyle's removal. She had a near escape before, you remember, at this very place, when that boulder crashed down – ah! but you were not there, perhaps?'

'No. I was inside the temple at the time. I heard about it afterwards, of course. A very near escape. But possibly an accident, don't you think?'

Poirot shrugged his shoulders.

'One thought so at the time. Now – one wonders.'

'Yes – yes, of course.' Pennington wiped his face with a fine silk handkerchief.

Colonel Race went on: 'Mr Doyle happened to mention someone being on board who bore a grudge – not against her personally, but against her family. Do you know who that could be?'

Pennington looked genuinely astonished.

'No, I've no idea.'

'She didn't mention the matter to you?'

'No.'

'You were an intimate friend of her father's – you cannot remember any business operations of his that might have resulted in ruin for some business opponent?'

Pennington shook his head helplessly. 'No outstanding case. Such operations were frequent, of course, but I can't recall anyone who uttered threats – nothing of that kind.'

'In short, Mr Pennington, you cannot help us?'

'It seems so. I deplore my inadequacy, gentlemen.'

Race interchanged a glance with Poirot, then he said: 'I'm sorry too. We'd had hopes.'

He got up as a sign the interview was at an end.

Andrew Pennington said: 'As Doyle's laid up, I expect he'd like me to see to things. Pardon me, Colonel, but what exactly are the arrangements?'

'When we leave here we shall make a non-stop run to Shellâl, arriving there tomorrow morning.'

'And the body?'

'Will be removed to one of the cold storage chambers.'

Andrew Pennington bowed his head. Then he left the room.

Poirot and Race again interchanged a glance.

'Mr Pennington,' said Race, lighting a cigarette, 'was not at all comfortable.'

Poirot nodded. 'And,' he said, 'Mr Pennington was sufficiently perturbed to tell a rather stupid lie. He was *not* in the temple of Abu Simbel when that boulder fell. I – *moi qui vous parle* – can swear to that. I had just come from there.'

'A very stupid lie,' said Race, 'and a very revealing one.'

Again Poirot nodded.

'But for the moment,' he said, and smiled, 'we handle him with the gloves of kid, is it not so?'

'That was the idea,' agreed Race.

'My friend, you and I understand each other to a marvel.'

There was a faint grinding noise, a stir beneath their feet. The *Karnak* has started on her homeward journey to Shellâl.

'The pearls,' said Race. 'That is the next thing to be cleared up.'

'You have a plan?'

'Yes.' He glanced at his watch. 'It will be lunch time in half an hour. At the end of the meal I propose to make an announcement – just state the fact that the pearls have been stolen, and that I must request everyone to stay in the dining-saloon while a search is conducted.'

Poirot nodded approvingly.

'It is well imagined. Whoever took the pearls still has them. By giving no warning beforehand, there will be no chance of their being thrown overboard in a panic.'

Race drew some sheets of paper towards him. He murmured apologetically: 'I'd like to make a brief précis of the facts as I go along. It keeps one's mind free of confusion.'

'You do well. Method and order, they are everything,' replied Poirot.

Race wrote for some minutes in his small neat script. Finally he pushed the result of his labours towards Poirot.

'Anything you don't agree with there?'

Poirot took up the sheets. They were headed:

MURDER OF MRS LINNET DOYLE

Mrs Doyle was last seen alive by her maid, Louise Bourget. Time: 11.30 (approx.).

From 11.30–12.20 following have alibis: Cornelia Robson, James Fanthorp, Simon Doyle, Jacqueline de Bellefort – *nobody else* – but crime almost certainly committed *after* that time, since it is practically certain that pistol used was Jacqueline de Bellefort's, which was then in her handbag. That her pistol was used is not *absolutely* certain until after post mortem and expert evidence re bullet – but it may be taken as overwhelmingly probable.

Probable course of events: X (murderer) was witness of scene between Jacqueline and Simon Doyle in observation saloon and noted where pistol went under settee. After the saloon was vacant, X procured pistol – his or her idea being that Jacqueline de Bellefort would be thought guilty of crime. On this theory certain people are automatically cleared of suspicion:

Cornelia Robson, since she had no opportunity to take pistol before James Fanthorp returned to search for it.

Miss Bowers – same.

Dr Bessner – same.

N.B. – Fanthorp is not definitely excluded from suspicion, since he could actually have pocketed pistol while declaring himself unable to find it.

Any other person could have taken the pistol during that ten minutes' interval.

Possible motives for the murder:

Andrew Pennington. This is on the assumption that he has been guilty of fradulent practices. There is a certain amount of evidence in favour of that assumption, but not enough to

justify making out a case against him. If it was he who rolled
down the boulder, he is a man who can seize a chance when
it presents itself. The crime, clearly, was not premeditated
except in a *general* way. Last night's shooting scene was an
ideal opportunity.

Objections to the theory of Pennington's guilt: *Why did he
throw the pistol overboard, since it constituted a valuable clue
against J.B.?*

Fleetwood. Motive, revenge. Fleetwood considered himself
injured by Linnet Doyle. Might have overheard scene and
noted position of pistol. He may have taken pistol because it
was a handy weapon, rather than with the idea of throwing
guilt on Jacqueline. This would fit in with throwing it overboard. *But if that were the case, why did he write J in blood
on the wall?*

N.B. – Cheap handkerchief found with pistol more likely to
have belonged to a man like Fleetwood than to one of the
well-to-do passengers.

Rosalie Otterbourne. Are we to accept Miss Van Schuyler's
evidence or Rosalie's denial? Something *was* thrown overboard
at that time and that something was presumably the pistol
wrapped up in the velvet stole.

Points to be noted. Had Rosalie any motive? She may have
disliked Linnet Doyle and even been envious of her – but as a
motive for murder that seems grossly inadequate. The evidence
against her can be convincing only if we discover an adequate
motive. As far as we know, there is no previous knowledge or
link between Rosalie Otterbourne and Linnet Doyle.

Miss Van Schuyler. The velvet stole in which pistol was
wrapped belongs to Miss Van Schuyler. According to her own
statement she last saw it in the observation saloon. She drew
attention to its loss during the evening, and a search was
made for it without success.

How did the stole come into the possession of X? Did X
purloin it some time early in the evening? But if so, why? Nobody could tell, in advance, that there was going to be a scene
between Jacqueline and Simon. Did X find the stole in the
saloon when he went to get the pistol from under the settee?
But if so, why was it not found when the search for it was
made? Did it never leave Miss Van Schuyler's possession? That
is to say: Did Miss Van Schuyler murder Linnet Doyle? Is her
accusation of Rosalie Otterbourne a deliberate lie? If she did
murder her, what was her motive?

Other possibilities:

Robbery as a motive. Possible, since the pearls have disappeared, and Linnet Doyle was certainly wearing them last night.

Someone with a grudge against the Ridgeway family. Possible – again no evidence.

We know that there is a dangerous man on board – a killer. Here we have a killer and a death. May not the two be connected? But we should have to show that Linnet Doyle possessed dangerous knowledge concerning this man.

Conclusions: We can group the persons on board into two classes – those who had a possible motive or against whom there is definite evidence, and those who, as far as we know, are free of suspicion.

Group I	*Group II*
Andrew Pennington	Mrs Allerton
Fleetwood	Tim Allerton
Rosalie Otterbourne	Cornelia Robson
Miss Van Schuyler	Miss Bowers
Louise Bourget (Robbery?)	Dr Bessner
Ferguson (Political?)	Signor Richetti
	Mrs Otterbourne
	James Fanthorp

Poirot pushed the paper back.

'It is very just, very exact, what you have written there.'

'You agree with it?'

'Yes.'

'And now what is your contribution?'

Poirot drew himself up in an important manner.

'Me, I pose to myself one question: "*Why* was the pistol thrown overboard?"'

'That's all?'

'At the moment, yes. Until I can arrive at a satisfactory answer to that question, there is no sense anywhere. That is – that *must* be the starting point. You will notice, my friend, that, in your summary of where we stand, you have not attempted to answer that point.'

Race shrugged his shoulders.

'Panic.'

Poirot shook his head perplexedly. He picked up the sodden velvet wrap and smoothed it out, wet and limp, on the table. His fingers traced the scorched marks and the burnt holes.

'Tell me, my friend,' he said suddenly. 'You are more conversant with firearms than I am. Would such a thing as this, wrapped round a pistol, make much difference in muffling the sound?'

'No, it wouldn't. Not like a silencer, for instance.'

Poirot nodded. He went on: 'A man – certainly a man who had had much handling of firearms – would know that. But a woman – a woman would *not* know.'

Race looked at him curiously. 'Probably not.'

'No. She would have read the detective stories where they are not always very exact as to details.'

Race flicked the little pearl-handled pistol with his finger. 'This little fellow wouldn't make much noise anyway,' he said. 'Just a pop, that's all. With any other noise around, ten to one you wouldn't notice it.'

'Yes, I have reflected as to that.'

Poirot picked up the handkerchief and examined it.

'A man's handkerchief – but not a gentleman's handkerchief. *Ce cher* Woolworth, I imagine. Threepence at most.'

'The sort of handkerchief a man like Fleetwood would own.'

'Yes. Andrew Pennington, I notice, carries a very fine silk handkerchief.'

'Ferguson?' suggested Race.

'Possibly. As a gesture. But then it ought to be a bandana.'

'Used it instead of a glove, I suppose, to hold the pistol and obviate fingerprints.' Race added, with slight facetiousness, ' "The Clue of the Blushing Handkerchief." '

'Ah, yes. Quite a *jeune fille* colour, is it not?' He laid it down and returned to the stole, once more examining the powder marks.

'All the same,' he murmured, 'it is odd . . .'

'What's that?'

Poirot said gently: '*Cette pauvre* Madame Doyle. Lying there so peacefully . . . with the little hole in her head. You remember how she looked?'

Race looked at him curiously. 'You know,' he said, 'I've got an idea you're trying to tell me something – but I haven't the faintest idea what it is.'

—— 19 ——

There was a tap on the door.

'Come in,' Race called.

A steward entered.

'Excuse me, sir,' he said to Poirot, 'but Mr Doyle is asking for you.'

'I will come.'

Poirot rose. He went out of the room and up the companion-way to the promenade deck and along it to Dr Bessner's cabin.

Simon, his face flushed and feverish, was propped up with pillows. He looked embarrassed.

'Awfully good of you to come along, Monsieur Poirot. Look here, there's something I want to ask you.'

'Yes?'

Simon got still redder in the face.

'It's — it's about Jackie. I want to see her. Do you think — would you mind — would she mind, d'you think, if you asked her to come along here? You know I've been lying here thinking. . . . That wretched kid — she is only a kid after all — and I treated her damn' badly — and—' He stammered to silence.

Poirot looked at him with interest.

'You desire to see Mademoiselle Jacqueline? I will fetch her.'

'Thanks. Awfully good of you.'

Poirot went on his quest. He found Jacqueline de Bellefort sitting huddled up in a corner of the observation saloon. There was an open book on her lap but she was not reading.

Poirot said gently: 'Will you come with me, Mademoiselle? Monsieur Doyle wants to see you.'

She started up. Her face flushed — then paled. She looked bewildered.

'Simon? He wants to see me — to see *me*?'

He found her incredulity moving.

'Will you come, Mademoiselle?'

She went with him in a docile fashion, like a child, but like a puzzled child.

'I — yes, of course I will.'

Poirot passed into the cabin.

'Here is Mademoiselle.'

She stepped in after him, wavered, stood still . . . standing there mute and dumb, her eyes fixed on Simon's face.

'Hullo, Jackie.' He, too, was embarrassed. He went on: 'Aw-

926

fully good of you to come. I wanted to say – I mean – what I
mean is—'

She interrupted him then. Her words came out in a rush –
breathless, desperate.

'Simon – I didn't kill Linnet. You know I didn't do that . . .
I – I was mad last night. Oh, can you ever forgive me?'

Words came more easily to him now.

'Of course. That's all right! Absolutely all right! That's
what I wanted to say. Thought you might be worrying a bit,
you know. . . .'

'*Worrying? A bit?* Oh! Simon!'

'That's what I wanted to see you about. It's quite all right,
see, old girl? You just got a bit rattled last night – a shade
tight. All perfectly natural.'

'Oh, Simon! I might have killed you!'

'Not you. Not with a rotten little peashooter like that. . . .'

'And your leg! Perhaps you'll never walk again. . . .'

'Now, look here, Jackie, don't be maudlin. As soon as we
get to Assuan they're going to put the X-ray to work, and dig
out that tin-pot bullet, and everything will be as right as rain.'

Jacqueline gulped twice, then she rushed forward and knelt
down by Simon's bed, burying her face and sobbing. Simon
patted her awkwardly on the head. His eyes met Poirot's and,
with a reluctant sigh, the latter left the cabin.

He heard broken murmurs as he went:

'How could I be such a devil? Oh, Simon! . . . I'm so dreadfully sorry.'

Outside Cornelia Robson was leaning over the rail. She
turned her head.

'Oh, it's you, Monsieur Poirot. It seems so awful somehow
that it should be such a lovely day.'

Poirot looked up at the sky.

'When the sun shines you cannot see the moon,' he said.
'But when the sun is gone – ah, when the sun is gone.'

Cornelia's mouth fell open.

'I beg your pardon?'

'I was saying, Mademoiselle, that when the sun has gone
down, we shall see the moon. That is so, is it not?'

'Why – why, yes – certainly.'

She looked at him doubtfully.

Poirot laughed gently.

'I utter the imbecilities,' he said. 'Take no notice.'

He strolled gently towards the stern of the boat. As he passed the next cabin he paused for a minute. He caught fragments of speech from within:

'Utterly ungrateful – after all I've done for you – no consideration for your wretched mother – no idea what I suffer. . . .'

Poirot's lips stiffened as he pressed them together. He raised a hand and knocked.

There was a startled silence and Mrs Otterbourne's voice called out: 'Who's that?'

'Is Mademoiselle Rosalie there?'

Rosalie appeared in the doorway. Poirot was shocked at her appearance. There were dark circles under her eyes and drawn lines round her mouth.

'What's the matter?' she said ungraciously. 'What do you want?'

'The pleasure of a few minutes' conversation with you, Mademoiselle. Will you come?'

Her mouth went sulky at once. She shot him a suspicious look.

'Why should I?'

'I entreat you, Mademoiselle.'

'Oh, I suppose—'

She stepped out on the deck, closing the door behind her. 'Well?'

Poirot took her gently by the arm and drew her along the deck, still in the direction of the stern. They passed the bathrooms and round the corner. They had the stern part of the deck to themselves. The Nile flowed away behind them.

Poirot rested his elbows on the rail. Rosalie stood up straight and stiff.

'Well?' she asked again, and her voice held the same ungracious tone.

Poirot spoke slowly, choosing his words. 'I could ask you certain questions, Mademoiselle, but I do not think for one moment that you would consent to answer them.'

'Seems rather a waste to bring me along here then.'

Poirot drew a finger slowly along the wooden rail.

'You are accustomed, Mademoiselle, to carrying your own burdens. . . . But you can do that too long. The strain becomes too great. For you, Mademoiselle, the strain is becoming too great.'

'I don't know what you are talking about,' said Rosalie.

'I am talking about facts, Mademoiselle – plain ugly facts. Let us call the spade the spade and say it in one little short sentence. Your mother drinks, Mademoiselle.'

Rosalie did not answer. Her mouth opened; then she closed it again. For once she seemed at a loss.

'There is no need for you to talk, Mademoiselle. I will do all the talking. I was interested at Assuan in the relations existing between you. I saw at once that, in spite of your carefully studied unfilial remarks, you were in reality passionately protecting her from something. I very soon knew what that something was. I knew it long before I encountered your mother one morning in an unmistakable state of intoxication. Moreover, her case, I could see, was one of secret bouts of drinking – by far the most difficult kind of case with which to deal. You were coping with it manfully. Nevertheless, she had all the secret drunkard's cunning. She managed to get hold of a secret supply of spirits and to keep it successfully hidden from you. I should not be surprised if you discovered its hiding place only yesterday. Accordingly, last night, as soon as your mother was really soundly asleep, you stole out with the contents of the *cache*, went round to the other side of the boat (since your own side was up against the bank) and cast it overboard into the Nile.'

He paused.

'I am right, am I not?'

'Yes – you're quite right.' Rosalie spoke with sudden passion. 'I was a fool not to say so, I suppose! But I didn't want everyone to know. It would go all over the boat. And it seemed so – so silly – I mean – that I—'

Poirot finished the sentence for her.

'So silly that you should be suspected of committing a murder?'

Rosalie nodded.

Then she burst out again: 'I've tried so hard to – keep everyone from knowing. . . . It isn't really her fault. She got discouraged. Her books didn't sell any more. People are tired of all that cheap sex stuff. . . . It hurt her – it hurt her dreadfully. And so she began to – to drink. For a long time I didn't know why she was so queer. Then, when I found out, I tried to – to stop it. She'd be all right for a bit, and then, suddenly, she'd start, and there would be dreadful quarrels and rows with people. It was awful.' She shuddered. 'I had always to be on the watch – to get her away. . . .

'And then – she began to dislike me for it. She – she's turned right against me. I think she almost hates me sometimes.'

'*Pauvre petite*,' said Poirot.

She turned on him vehemently.

929

'Don't be sorry for me. Don't be kind. It's easier if you're not.' She sighed – a long heartrending sigh. 'I'm so tired . . . I'm so deadly, deadly tired.'

'I know,' said Poirot.

'People think I'm awful. Stuck-up and cross and bad-tempered. I can't help it. I've forgotten how to be – to be nice.'

'That is what I said to you; you have carried your burden by yourself too long.'

Rosalie said slowly: 'It's a relief – to talk about it. You – you've always been kind to me, Monsieur Poirot. I'm afraid I've been rude to you often.'

'*La politesse*, it is not necessary between friends.'

The suspicion came back to her face suddenly.

'Are you – are you going to tell everyone? I suppose you must, because of those damned bottles I threw overboard.'

'No, no, it is not necessary. Just tell me what I want to know. At what time was this? Ten minutes past one?'

'About that, I should think. I don't remember exactly.'

'Now tell me, Mademoiselle. Mademoiselle Van Schuyler saw *you*, did you see *her*?'

Rosalie shook her head.

'No, I didn't.'

'She says that she looked out of the door of her cabin.'

'I don't think I should have seen her. I just looked along the deck and then out to the river.'

Poirot nodded.

'And did you see anyone – anyone at all, when you looked down the deck?'

There was a pause – quite a long pause. Rosalie was frowning. She seemed to be thinking earnestly.

At last she shook her head quite decisively.

'No,' she said. 'I saw nobody.'

Hercule Poirot slowly nodded his head. But his eyes were grave.

—— 20 ——

People crept into the dining-saloon by ones and twos in a very subdued manner. There seemed a general feeling that to sit down eagerly to food displayed an unfortunate heartlessness. It was with an almost apologetic air that one passenger after another came and sat down at their tables.

Tim Allerton arrived some few minutes after his mother had taken her seat. He was looking in a thoroughly bad temper.

'I wish we'd never come on this blasted trip,' he growled.

Mrs Allerton shook her head sadly.

'Oh, my dear, so do I. That beautiful girl! It all seems such a *waste*. To think that anyone could shoot her in cold blood. It seems awful to me that anyone could do such a thing. And that other poor child.'

'Jacqueline?'

'Yes; my heart aches for her. She looks so dreadfully unhappy.'

'Teach her not to go round loosing off toy firearms,' said Tim unfeelingly as he helped himself to butter.

'I expect she was badly brought up.'

'Oh, for God's sake, Mother, don't go all maternal about it.'

'You're in a shocking bad temper, Tim.'

'Yes, I am. Who wouldn't be?'

'I don't see what there is to be cross about. It's just frightfully sad.'

Tim said crossly: 'You're taking the romantic point of view! What you don't seem to realise is that it's no joke being mixed up in a murder case.'

Mrs Allerton looked a little startled.

'But surely—'

'That's just it. There's no "But surely" about it. Everyone on this damned boat is under suspicion – you and I as well as the rest of them.'

Mrs Allerton demurred. 'Technically we are, I suppose – but actually it's ridiculous!'

'There's nothing ridiculous where murder's concerned! You may sit there, darling, just exuding virtue and conscious rectitude, but a lot of unpleasant policemen at Shellâl or Assuan won't take you at your face value.'

'Perhaps the truth will be known before then.'

'Why should it be?'

'Monsieur Poirot may find out.'

'That old mountebank? He won't find out anything. He's all talk and moustaches.'

'Well, Tim,' said Mrs Allerton, 'I daresay everything you say is true, but, even if it is we've got to go through with it, so we might as well make up our minds to it and go through with it as cheerfully as we can.'

But her son showed no abatement of gloom.

'There's this blasted business of the pearls being missing, too.'

'Linnet's pearls?'

'Yes. It seems somebody must have pinched 'em.'

'I suppose that was the motive for the crime,' said Mrs Allerton.

'Why should it be? You're mixing up two perfectly different things.'

'Who told you that they were missing?'

'Ferguson. He got it from his tough friend in the engine room, who got it from the maid.'

'They were lovely pearls,' declared Mrs Allerton.

Poirot sat down at the table, bowing to Mrs Allerton.

'I am a little late,' he said.

'I expect you have been busy,' Mrs Allerton replied.

'Yes, I have been much occupied.'

He ordered a fresh bottle of wine from the waiter.

'We're very catholic in our tastes,' said Mrs Allerton. 'You drink wine always; Tim drinks whisky and soda, and I try all the different brands of mineral water in turn.'

'*Tiens!*' said Poirot. He stared at her for a moment. He murmured to himself: 'It is an idea, that . . .'

Then, with an impatient shrug of his shoulders, he dismissed the sudden preoccupation that had distracted him and began to chat lightly of other matters.

'Is Mr Doyle badly hurt?' asked Mrs Allerton.

'Yes, it is a fairly serious injury. Dr Bessner is anxious to reach Assuan so that his leg can be X-rayed and the bullet removed. But he hopes there will be no permanent lameness.'

'Poor Simon,' said Mrs Allerton. 'Once yesterday he looked such a happy boy, with everything in the world he wanted. And now his beautiful wife killed and he himself laid up and helpless. I do hope, though—'

'What do you hope, Madame?' asked Poirot as Mrs Allerton paused.

'I hope he's not too angry with that poor child.'

'With Mademoiselle Jacqueline? Quite the contrary. He was full of anxiety on her behalf.'

He turned to Tim.

'You know, it is a pretty little problem of psychology, that. All the time that Mademoiselle Jacqueline was following them from place to place, he was absolutely furious; but now, when she has actually shot him, and wounded him dangerously –

perhaps made him lame for like – all his anger seems to have evaporated. Can you understand that?'

'Yes,' said Tim thoughtfully, 'I think I can. The first thing made him feel a fool—'

Poirot nodded. 'You are right. It offended his male dignity.'

'But now – if you look at it a certain way, it's *she* who's made a fool of herself. Everyone's down on her, and so—'

'He can be generously forgiving,' finished Mrs Allerton. 'What children men are!'

'A profoundly untrue statement that women always make,' murmured Tim.

Poirot smiled. Then he said to Tim: 'Tell me, Madame Doyle's cousin, Miss Joanna Southwood, did she resemble Madame Doyle?'

'You've got it a little wrong, Monsieur Poirot. She was our cousin and Linnet's friend.'

'Ah, pardon – I was confused. She is a young lady much in the news, that. I have been interested in her for some time.'

'Why?' asked Tim sharply.

Poirot half rose to bow to Jacqueline de Bellefort, who had just come in and passed their table on the way to her own. Her cheeks were flushed and her eyes bright, and her breath came a little unevenly. As he resumed his seat Poirot seemed to have forgotten Tim's question. He murmured vaguely: 'I wonder if all young ladies with valuable jewels are as careless as Madame Doyle was?'

'It is true, then, that they were stolen?' asked Mrs Allerton.

'Who told you so, Madame?'

'Ferguson said so,' Tim volunteered.

Poirot nodded gravely.

'It is quite true.'

'I suppose,' said Mrs Allerton nervously, 'that this will mean a lot of unpleasantness for all of us. Tim says it will.'

Her son scowled, but Poirot had turned to him.

'Ah! you have had previous experience, perhaps? You have been in a house where there was a robbery?'

'Never,' said Tim.

'Oh, yes, darling, you were at the Portarlingtons' that time – when that awful woman's diamonds were stolen.'

'You always get things hopelessly wrong, Mother. I was there when it was discovered that the diamonds she was wearing round her fat neck were only paste! The actual substitution was probably done months earlier. As a matter of fact, a lot of people said she'd had it done herself!'

'Joanna said so, I expect.'

'Joanna wasn't there.'

'But she knew them quite well. And it's very like her to make that kind of suggestion.'

'You're always down on Joanna, Mother.'

Poirot hastily changed the subject. He had it in mind to make a really big purchase at one of the Assuan shops. Some very attractive purple and gold material at one of the Indian merchants. There would, of course, be the duty to pay, but—

'They tell me that they can – how do you say – expedite it for me. And that the charges will not be too high. How think you, will it arrive all right?'

Mrs Allerton said that many people, so she had heard, had had things sent straight to England from the shops in question and that everything had arrived safely.

'*Bien*. Then I will do that. But the trouble one has, when one is abroad, if a parcel comes out from England! Have you had experience of that? Have you had any parcels arrive since you have been on your travels?'

'I don't think we have, have we, Tim? You get books sometimes, but of course there is never any trouble about them.'

'Ah, no, books are different.'

Dessert had been served. Now, without any previous warning, Colonel Race stood up and made his speech.

He touched on the circumstances of the crime and announced the theft of the pearls. A search of the boat was about to be instituted, and he would be obliged if all the passengers would remain in the saloon until this was completed. Then, after that, if the passengers agreed, as he was sure they would, they themselves would be kind enough to submit to a search.

Poirot slipped nimbly along to his side. There was a little buzz and hum all round them. Voices doubtful, indignant, excited. . . .

Poirot reached Race's side and murmured something in his ear just as the latter was about to leave the dining-saloon.

Race listened, nodded assent, and beckoned a steward. He said a few brief words to him; then, together with Poirot he passed out on to the deck, closing the door behind him.

They stood for a minute or two by the rail. Race lit a cigarette.

'Not a bad idea of yours,' he said. 'We'll soon see if there's anything in it. I'll give 'em three minutes.'

The door of the dining-saloon opened and the same steward

to whom they had spoken came out. He saluted Race and said:
'Quite right, sir. There's a lady who says it's urgent she should
speak to you at once without delay.'

'Ah!' Race's face showed satisfaction. 'Who is it?'

'Miss Bowers, sir, the hospital nurse lady.'

A slight shade of surprise showed on Race's face. He said.
'Bring her to the smoking-room. Don't let anyone else leave.'

'No, sir – the other steward will attend to that.'

He went back into the dining-room. Poirot and Race went
to the smoking-room.

'Bowers, eh?' muttered Race.

They had hardly got inside the smoking-room before the
steward reappeared with Miss Bowers. He ushered her in and
left, shutting the door behind him.

'Well, Miss Bowers?' Colonel Race looked at her inquiringly.
'What's all this?'

Miss Bowers looked her usual composed, unhurried self. She
displayed no particular emotion.

'You'll excuse me, Colonel Race,' she said, 'but under the
circumstances I thought the best thing to do would be to speak
to you at once' – she opened her neat black handbag – 'and to
return you these.'

She took out a string of pearls and laid them on the table.

—— 2I ——

If Miss Bowers had been the kind of woman who enjoyed
creating a sensation, she would have been richly repaid by the
result of her action.

A look of utter astonishment passed over Colonel Race's
face as he picked up the pearls from the table.

'This is most extraordinary,' he said. 'Will you kindly explain, Miss Bowers?'

'Of course. That's what I've come to do.' Miss Bowers settled
herself comfortably in a chair. 'Naturally it was a little difficult
for me to decide what it was best for me to do. The family
would naturally be averse to scandal of any kind, and they
trusted my discretion, but the circumstances are so very unusual that it really leaves me no choice. Of course, when you
didn't find anything in the cabins, your next move would be
a search of the passengers, and, if the pearls were then found

in my possession, it would be rather an awkward situation and the truth would come out just the same.'

'And just what is the truth? Did you take these pearls from Mrs Doyle's cabin?'

'Oh, no, Colonel Race, of course not. Miss Van Schuyler did.'

'Miss Van Schuyler?'

'Yes. She can't help it, you know, but she does – er – take things. Especially jewellery. That's really why I'm always with her. It's not her health at all; it's this little idiosyncrasy. I keep on the alert, and fortunately there's never been any trouble since I've been with her. It just means being watchful, you know. And she always hides the things she takes in the same place – rolled up in a pair of stockings – so that it makes it very simple. I look each morning. Of course I'm a light sleeper, and I always sleep next door to her, and with the communicating door open if it's a hotel, so that I usually hear. Then I go after her and persuade her to go back to bed. Of course it's been rather more difficult on a boat. But she doesn't really do it at night. It's more just picking up things that she sees left about. Of course, pearls have a great attraction for her always.'

Miss Bowers ceased speaking.

Race asked: 'How did you discover they had been taken?'

'They were in her stockings this morning. I knew whose they were, of course. I've often noticed them. I went along to put them back, hoping that Mrs Doyle wasn't up yet and hadn't discovered her loss. But there was a steward standing there, and he told me about the murder and that no one could go in. So then, you see, I was in a regular quandary. But I still hoped to slip them back in the cabin later, before their absence had been noticed. I can assure you I've passed a very unpleasant morning wondering what was the best thing to do. You see, the Van Schuyler family is so *very* particular and exclusive. It would never do if this got into the newspapers. But that won't be necessary, will it?'

Miss Bowers really looked worried.

'That depends on circumstances,' said Colonel Race cautiously. 'But we shall do our best for you, of course. What does Miss Van Schuyler say to this?'

'Oh, she'll deny it, of course. She always does. Says some wicked person has put it there. She never admits taking anything. That's why if you catch her in time she goes back to bed like a lamb. Says she just went out to look at the moon. Something like that.'

'Does Miss Robson know about this – er – failing?'

'No, she doesn't. Her mother knows, but she's a very simple kind of girl and her mother thought it best she should know nothing about it. I was quite equal to dealing with Miss Van Schuyler,' added the competent Miss Bowers.

'We have to thank you, Mademoiselle, for coming to us so promptly,' said Poirot.

Miss Bowers stood up.

'I'm sure I hope I acted for the best.'

'Be assured that you have.'

'You see, what with there being a murder as well—'

Colonel Race interrupted her. His voice was grave.

'Miss Bowers, I am going to ask you a question, and I want to impress upon you that it has got to be answered truthfully. Miss Van Schuyler is unhinged mentally to the extent of being a kleptomaniac. Has she also a tendency to homicidal mania?'

Miss Bowers' answer came immediately: 'Oh, dear me, no! Nothing of that kind. You can take my word for it absolutely. The old lady wouldn't hurt a fly.'

The reply came with such positive assurance that there seemed nothing more to be said. Nevertheless Poirot did interpolate one mild inquiry.

'Does Miss Van Schuyler suffer at all from deafness?'

'As a matter of fact she does, Monsieur Poirot. Not so that you'd notice in any way, not if you were speaking to her, I mean. But quite often she doesn't hear you when you come into a room. Things like that.'

'Do you think she would have heard anyone moving about in Mrs Doyle's cabin, which is next door to her own?'

'Oh, I shouldn't think so – not for a minute. You see, the bunk is the other side of the cabin, not even against the partition wall. No, I don't think she would have heard anything.'

'Thank you, Miss Bowers.'

Race said: 'Perhaps you will now go back to the dining-saloon and wait with the others?'

He opened the door for her and watched her go down the staircase and enter the saloon. Then he shut the door and came back to the table. Poirot had picked up the pearls.

'Well,' said Race grimly, 'that reaction came pretty quickly. That's a very cool-headed and astute young woman – perfectly capable of holding out on us and still further if she thinks it suits her book. What about Miss Marie Van Schuyler now? I don't think we can eliminate her from the possible suspects. You know, she *might* have committed murder to get hold of those jewels. We can't take the nurse's word for it. She's all out to do the best for the family.'

Poirot nodded in agreement. He was very busy with the pearls, running them through his fingers, holding them up to his eyes.

He said: 'We may take it, I think, that part of the old lady's story to us was true. She *did* look out of her cabin and she *did* see Rosalie Otterbourne. But I don't think she *heard* anything or anyone in Linnet Doyle's cabin. I think she was just peering out from *her* cabin preparatory to slipping along and purloining the pearls.'

'The Otterbourne girl was there, then?'

'Yes. Throwing her mother's secret *cache* of drink overboard.'

Colonel Race shook his head sympathetically.

'So that's it! Tough on a young 'un.'

'Yes, her life has not been very gay, *cette pauvre petite Rosalie.*'

'Well, I'm glad that's been cleared up. *She* didn't see or hear anything?'

'I asked her that. She responded – after a lapse of quite twenty seconds – that she saw nobody.'

'Oh?' Race looked alert.

'Yes, it is suggestive, that.'

Race said slowly: 'If Linnet Doyle was shot round about ten minutes past one, or indeed any time after the boat had quieted down, it has seemed amazing to me that no one heard the shot. I grant you that a little pistol like that wouldn't make much noise, but all the same the boat would be deadly quiet, and any noise, even a gentle pop, should have been heard. But I begin to understand better now. The cabin on the forward side of hers was unoccupied – since her husband was in Dr Bessner's cabin. The one aft was occupied by the Van Schuyler woman, who was deaf. That leaves only—'

He paused and looked expectantly at Poirot, who nodded.

'The cabin next to her on the other side of the boat. In other words – Pennington. We always seem to come back to Pennington.'

'We will come back to him presently with the kid gloves removed! Ah, yes, I am promising myself that pleasure.'

'In the meantime we'd better get on with our search of the boat. The pearls still make a convenient excuse, even though they have been returned – but Miss Bowers is not likely to advertise that fact.'

'Ah, these pearls!' Poirot held them up against the light

once more. He stuck out his tongue and licked them; he even gingerly tried one of them between his teeth. Then, with a sigh, he threw them down on the table.

'Here are more complications, my friend,' he said. 'I am not an expert on precious stones, but I have had a good deal to do with them in my time and I am fairly certain of what I say. These pearls are only a clever imitation.'

——— 22 ———

Colonel Race swore hastily.

'This damned case gets more and more involved.' He picked up the pearls. 'I suppose you've not made a mistake? They look all right to me.'

'They are a very good imitation – yes.'

'Now where does that lead us? I suppose Linnet Doyle didn't deliberately have an imitation made and bring it aboard with her for safety. Many women do.'

'I think, if that were so, her husband would know about it.'

'She may not have told him.'

Poirot shook his head in a dissatisfied manner.

'No, I do not think that is so. I was admiring Madame Doyle's pearls the first evening on the boat – their wonderful sheen and lustre. I am sure that she was wearing the genuine ones then.'

'That brings us up against two possibilities. First, that Miss Van Schuyler only stole the imitation string after the real ones had been stolen by someone else. Second, that the whole kleptomaniac story is a fabrication. Either Miss Bowers is a thief, and quickly invented the story and allayed suspicion by handing over the false pearls, or else that whole party is in it together. That is to say, they are a gang of clever jewel thieves masquerading as an exclusive American family.'

'Yes,' Poirot murmured. 'It is difficult to say. But I will point out to you one thing – to make a perfect and exact copy of the pearls, clasp and all, good enough to stand a chance of deceiving Madame Doyle is a highly skilled technical performance. It could not be done in a hurry. Whoever copied those pearls must have had a good opportunity of studying the original.'

Race rose to his feet.

'Useless to speculate about it any further now. Let's get on with the job. We've got to find the real pearls. And at the same time we'll keep our eyes open.'

They disposed first of the cabins occupied on the lower deck. That of Signor Richetti contained various archæological works in different languages a varied assortment of clothing, hair lotions of a highly scented kind and two personal letters – one from an archæological expedition in Syria, and one from, apparently a sister in Rome. His handkerchiefs were all of coloured silk.

They passed on to Ferguson's cabin.

There was a sprinkling of communistic literature, a good many snapshots, Samuel Butler's *Erewhon* and a cheap edition of Pepys' *Diary*. His personal possessions were not many. Most of what outer clothing there was was torn and dirty; the under-clothing, on the other hand, was of really good quality. The handkerchiefs were expensive linen ones.

'Some interesting discrepancies,' murmured Poirot.

Race nodded. 'Rather odd that there are absolutely no personal papers, letters, etc.'

'Yes; that gives one to think. An odd young man, Monsieur Ferguson.' He looked thoughtfully at a signet ring he held in his hand, before replacing it in the drawer where he had found it.

They went along to the cabin, occupied by Louis Bourget. The maid had her meals after the other passengers but Race had sent word that she was to be taken to join the others. A cabin steward met them.

'I'm sorry, sir,' he apologised 'but I've not been able to find the young woman anywhere. I can't think where she can have got to.'

Race glanced inside the cabin. It was empty.

They went up to the promenade deck and started on the starboard side. The first cabin was that occupied by James Fanthorp. Here all was in meticulous order. Mr Fanthorp travelled light, but all that he had was of good quality.

'No letters,' said Poirot thoughtfully. 'He is careful, our Mr Fanthorp to destroy his correspondence.'

They passed on to Tim Allerton's cabin next door.

There were evidences here of an Anglo-Catholic turn of mind – an exquisite little triptych, and a big rosary of intricately carved wood. Besides personal clothing, there was a half-completed manuscript, a good deal annotated and scribbled over and a good collection of books, most of them recently published. There were also a quantity of letters thrown carelessly into a drawer. Poirot never in the least scrupulous about reading other people's correspondence, glanced through them. He noted that amongst them there were no letters from Joanna Southwood. He picked up a tube of Seccotine, fingered it absently for a minute or two, then said: 'Let us pass on.'

'No Woolworth handkerchiefs,' reported Race, rapidly replacing the contents of a drawer.

Mrs Allerton's cabin was the next. It was exquisitely neat, and a faint old-fashioned smell of lavender hung about it. The two men's search was soon over. Race remarked as they left it: 'Nice woman, that.'

The next cabin was that which had been used as a dressing-room by Simon Doyle. His immediate necessities – pyjamas, toilet things, etc. – had been moved to Bessner's cabin, but the remainder of his possessions were still there – two good-sized leather suitcases and a kitbag. There were also some clothes in the wardrobe.

'We will look carefully here, my friend,' said Poirot, 'for it is possible that the thief hid the pearls here.'

'You think it is likely?'

'But yes, indeed. Consider! The thief, whoever he or she may be, must know that sooner or later a search will be made, and therefore a hiding-place in his or her own cabin would be injudicious in the extreme. The public rooms present other difficulties. But here is a cabin belonging to a man who cannot possibly visit it himself so that, if the pearls are found here, it tells us nothing at all.' But the most meticulous search failed to reveal any trace of the missing necklace.

Poirot murmured 'Zut!' to himself and they emerged once more on the deck.

Linnet Doyle's cabin had been locked after the body was removed, but Race had the key with him. He unlocked the door and the two men stepped inside.

Except for the removal of the girl's body, the cabin was exactly as it had been that morning.

'Poirot,' said Race, 'if there's anything to be found here, for God's sake go ahead and find it. You can if anyone can – I know that.'

'This time you do not mean the pearls, *mon ami*?'

'No. The murder's the main thing. There may be something I overlooked this morning.'

Quietly, deftly, Poirot went about his search. He went down on his knees and scrutinised the floor inch by inch. He examined the bed. He went rapidly through the wardrobe and chest of drawers. He went through the wardrobe trunk and the two costly suitcases. He looked through the expensive gold-fitted dressing-case. Finally he turned his attention to the washstand. There were various creams, powders, face lotions. But the only thing that seemed to interest Poirot were two little bottles labelled Nailex. He picked them up at last and brought them to the dressing-table. One, which bore the inscription Nailex Rose, was empty but for a drop or two of dark red fluid at the bottom. The other, the same size, but labelled Nailex Cardinal, was nearly full. Poirot uncorked first the empty, then the full one, and sniffed them both delicately.

An odour of peardrops billowed into the room. With a slight grimace he recorked them.

'Get anything?' asked Race.

Poirot replied by a French proverb: *'On no prend pas les mouches avec le vinaigre.'* Then he said with a sigh: 'My friend, we have not been fortunate. The murderer has not been obliging. He has not dropped for us the cuff link, the cigarette end, the cigar ash – or, in the case of a woman, the handkerchief, the lipstick, or the hair slide.'

'Only the bottle of nail polish?'

Poirot shrugged his shoulders. 'I must ask the maid. There is something – yes – a little curious there.'

'I wonder where the devil the girl's got to?' said Race.

They left the cabin, locking the door behind them, and passed on to that of Miss Van Schuyler.

Here again were all the appurtenances of wealth, expensive toilet fittings, good luggage, a certain number of private letters and papers all perfectly in order.

The next cabin was the double one occupied by Poirot, and beyond it that of Race. 'Hardly like to hide 'em in either of these,' said the Colonel.

Poirot demurred. 'It might be. Once, on the Orient Express, I investigated a murder. There was a little matter of a scarlet kimono. It had disappeared, and yet it must be on the train. I found it – where do you think? In my own locked suitcase! Ah! it was an impertinence, that!'

'Well, let's see if anybody has been impertinent with you or me this time.'

But the thief of the pearls had not been impertinent with Hercule Poirot or with Colonel Race.

Rounding the stern they made a very careful search of Miss

Bowers' cabin but could find nothing of a suspicious nature. Her handkerchiefs were of plain linen with an initial.

The Otterbournes' cabin came next. Here, again, Poirot made a very meticulous search, but with no result.

The next cabin was Bessner's. Simon Doyle lay with an untasted tray of food beside him.

'Off my feed,' he said apologetically.

He was looking feverish and very much worse than earlier in the day. Poirot appreciated Bessner's anxiety to get him as swiftly as possible to hospital and skilled appliances. The little Belgian explained what the two of them were doing, and Simon nodded approval. On learning that the pearls had been restored by Miss Bowers, but proved to be merely imitation, he expressed the most complete astonishment.

'You are quite sure, Monsieur Doyle, that your wife did not have an imitation string which she brought aboard with her instead of the real ones?'

Simon shook his head decisively.

'Oh, no. I'm quite sure of that. Linnet loved those pearls and she wore 'em everywhere. They were insured against every possible risk, so I think that made her a bit careless.'

'Then we must continue our search.'

He started opening drawers. Race attacked a suitcase.

Simon stared. 'Look here, you surely don't suspect old Bessner pinched them?'

Poirot shrugged his shoulders.

'It might be so. After all, what do we know of Dr Bessner? Only what he himself gives out.'

'But he couldn't have hidden them in here without my seeing him.'

'He could not have hidden anything *today* without your having seen him. But we do not know when the substitution took place. He may have effected the exchange some days ago.'

'I never thought of that.'

But the search was unavailing.

The next cabin was Pennington's. The two men spent some time in their search. In particular, Poirot and Race examined carefully a case full of legal and business documents, most of them requiring Linnet's signature.

Poirot shook his head gloomily. 'These seem all square and aboveboard. You agree?'

'Absolutely. Still, the man isn't a born fool. If there *had* been a compromising document there – a power of attorney or something of that kind – he'd be pretty sure to have destroyed it first thing.'

'That is so, yes.'

Poirot lifted a heavy Colt revolver out of the top drawer of the chest of drawers, looked at it and put it back.

'So it seems there are still some people who travel with revolvers,' he murmured.

'Yes, a little suggestive, perhaps. Still, Linnet Doyle wasn't shot with a thing that size.' Race paused and then said: 'You know, I've thought of a possible answer to your point about the pistol being thrown overboard. Supposing that the actual murderer did leave it in Linnet Doyle's cabin, and that someone else – some second person – took it away and threw it into the river?'

'Yes, that is possible. I have thought of it. But it opens up a whole string of questions. Who was that second person? What interest had they in endeavouring to shield Jacqueline de Bellefort by taking away the pistol? What was the second person doing there? The only other person we know of who went into the cabin was Mademoiselle Van Schuyler. Was it conceivably Mademoiselle Van Schuyler who removed it? Why should *she* wish to shield Jacqueline de Bellefort? And yet – what other reason can there be for the removal of the pistol?'

Race suggested, 'She may have recognised the stole as hers, got the wind up, and thrown the whole bag of tricks over on that account.'

'The stole, perhaps, but would she have got rid of the pistol, too? Still, I agree that it is a possible solution. But it is always – *bon Dieu*! It is clumsy. And you still have not appreciated one point about the stole—'

As they emerged from Pennington's cabin Poirot suggested that Race should search the remaining cabins those occupied by Jacqueline, Cornelia and two empty ones at the end, while he himself had a few words with Simon Doyle. Accordingly he retraced his steps along the deck and re-entered Bessner's cabin.

Simon said: 'Look here, I've been thinking. I'm perfectly sure that those pearls were all right yesterday.'

'Why is that, Monsieur Doyle?'

'Because Linnet' – he winced as he uttered his wife's name – 'was passing them through her hands just before dinner and talking about them. She knew something about pearls. I feel certain she'd have known if they were a fake.'

'They were a very good imitation, though. Tell me, was

Madame Doyle in the habit of letting those pearls out of her hands? Did she ever lend them to a friend, for instance?'

Simon flushed with slight embarrassment.

'You see, Monsieur Poirot, it's difficult for me to say. . . . I – I – well, you see, I hadn't known Linnet very long.'

'Ah no, it was a quick romance – yours.'

Simon went on. 'And so – really – I shouldn't know a thing like that. But Linnet was awfully generous with her things. I should think she might have done.'

'She never, for instance' – Poirot's voice was very smooth – 'she never, for instance, lent them to Mademoiselle de Belle-fort?'

'What d'you mean?' Simon flushed brick-red, tried to sit up and, wincing, fell back. 'What are you getting at? That Jackie stole the pearls? She didn't. I'll swear she didn't. Jackie's as straight as a die. The mere idea of her being a thief is ridiculous – absolutely ridiculous.'

Poirot looked at him with gently twinkling eyes. 'Oh, la! la! la!' he said unexpectedly. 'That suggestion of mine, it has indeed stirred up the nest of hornets.'

Simon repeated doggedly, unmoved by Poirot's lighter note, 'Jackie's straight!'

Poirot remembered a girl's voice by the Nile in Assuan saying, 'I love Simon – and he loves me. . . .'

He had wondered which of the three statements he had heard that night was the true one. It seemed to him that it had turned out to be Jacqueline who had come closest to the truth.

The door opened and Race came in.

'Nothing,' he said brusquely. 'Well, we didn't expect it. I see the stewards coming along with their report as to the searching of the passengers.'

A steward and stewardess appeared in the doorway. The former spoke first. 'Nothing, sir.'

'Any of the gentlemen make any fuss?'

'Only the Italian gentleman, sir. He carried on a good deal. Said it was a dishonour – something of that kind. He'd got a gun on him, too.'

'What kind of a gun?'

'Mauser automatic twenty-five, sir.'

'Italians are pretty hot-tempered,' said Simon. 'Richetti got in no end of a stew at Wâdi Halfa just because of a mistake over a telegram. He was darned rude to Linnet over it.'

Race turned to the stewardess. She was a big handsome-looking woman.

'Nothing on any of the ladies, sir. They made a good deal of fuss – except for Mrs Allerton, who was as nice as nice could be. Not a sign of the pearls. By the way, the young lady, Miss Rosalie Otterbourne, had a little pistol in her handbag.'

'What kind?'

'It was a very small one, sir, with a pearl handle. A kind of toy.'

Race stared. 'Devil take this case,' he muttered. 'I thought we'd got *her* cleared of suspicion, and now— Does every girl on this blinking boat carry around pearl-handled toy pistols?'

He shot a question at the stewardess. 'Did you show any feeling over you finding it?'

The woman shook her head. 'I don't think she noticed. I had my back turned whilst I was going through the handbag.'

'Still, she must have known you'd come across it. Oh, well, it beats me. What about the maid?'

'We've looked all over the boat, sir. We can't find her anywhere.'

'What's this?' asked Simon.

'Mrs Doyle's maid – Louise Bourget. She's disappeared.'

'*Disappeared?*'

Race said thoughtfully: 'She might have stolen the pearls. She is the one person who had ample opportunity to get a replica made.'

'And then, when she found a search was being instituted, she threw herself overboard?' suggested Simon.

'Nonsense,' replied Race, irritably. 'A woman can't throw herself overboard in broad daylight, from a boat like this, without somebody realising the fact. She's bound to be somewhere on board.' He addressed the stewardess once more. 'When was she last seen?'

'About half an hour before the bell went for lunch, sir.'

'We'll have a look at her cabin anyway,' said Race. 'That may tell us something.'

He led the way to the deck below. Poirot followed him. They unlocked the door of the cabin and passed inside.

Louise Bourget, whose trade it was to keep other people's belongings in order, had taken a holiday where her own were concerned. Odds and ends littered the top of the chest of drawers; a suitcase gaped open, with clothes hanging out of the side of it and preventing it shutting; underclothing hung limply over the sides of the chairs.

As Poirot, with swift neat fingers, opened the drawers of the dressing-chest, Race examined the suitcase.

Louise's shoes were lined along by the bed. One of them, a black patent leather, seemed to be resting at an extraordinary angle, almost unsupported. The appearance of it was so odd that it attracted Race's attention.

He closed the suitcase and bent over the line of shoes. Then he uttered a sharp exclamation.

Poirot whirled round.

'*Qu'est-ce qu'il y a?*'

Race said grimly: 'She hasn't disappeared. She's here – under the bed. . . .'

—— 23 ——

The body of a dead woman, who in life had been Louise Bourget, lay on the floor of her cabin. The two men bent over it.

Race straightened himself first.

'Been dead close on an hour, I should say. We'll get Bessner on to it. Stabbed to the heart. Death pretty well instantaneous, I should imagine. She doesn't look pretty, does she?'

'No.'

Poirot shook his head with a slight shudder.

The dark feline face was convulsed, as though with surprise and fury, the lips drawn back from the teeth.

Poirot bent again gently and picked up the right hand. Something just showed within the fingers. He detached it and held it out to Race, a little sliver of flimsy paper coloured a pale mauvish pink.

'You see what it is?'

'Money,' said Race.

'The corner of a thousand-franc note, I fancy.'

'Well, it's clear what happened,' said Race. 'She knew something – and she was blackmailing the murderer with her knowledge. We thought she wasn't being quite straight this morning.'

Poirot cried out: 'We have been idiots – fools! We should have known – then. What did she say? "What could I have seen or heard? I was on the deck below. Naturally, if I had been unable to sleep, if I had mounted the stairs, *then* perhaps I might have seen this assassin, this monster, enter or leave

Madame's cabin, but as it is—' Of course, that is what did happen! She did come up. She did see someone gliding into Linnet Doyle's cabin – or coming out of it. And, because of her greed, her insensate greed, she lies here—'

'And we are no nearer to knowing who killed her,' finished Race disgustedly.

Poirot shook his head. 'No, no. We know much more now. We know – we know almost everything. Only what we know seems incredible. . . . Yet it must be so. Only I do not see. Pah! what a fool I was this morning! We felt – both of us felt – that she was keeping something back, and yet we never realised that logical reason, blackmail.'

'She must have demanded hush money straight away,' said Race. 'Demanded it with threats. The murderer was forced to accede to that request and paid her in French notes. Anything there?'

Poirot shook his head thoughtfully. 'I hardly think so. Many people take a reserve of money with them when travelling – sometimes five-pound notes, sometimes dollars, but very often French notes as well. Possibly the murderer paid her all he had in a mixture of currencies. Let us continue our reconstruction.'

'The murderer comes to her cabin, gives her the money, and then—'

'And then,' said Poirot, 'she counts it. Oh, yes, I know that class. She would count the money, and while she counted it she was completely off her guard. The murderer struck. Having done so successfully, he gathered up the money and fled – not noticing that the corner of one of the notes was torn.'

'We may get him that way,' suggested Race doubtfully.

'I doubt it,' said Poirot. 'He will examine those notes, and will probably notice the tear. Of course if he were of a parsimonious disposition he would not be able to bring himself to destroy a *mille* note – but I very much fear that his temperament is just the opposite.'

'How do you make that out?'

'Both this crime and the murder of Madame Doyle demanded certain qualities – courage, audacity, bold execution, lightning action; those qualities do not accord with a saving, prudent disposition.'

Race shook his head sadly. 'I'd better get Bessner down,' he said.

The stout doctor's examination did not take long. Accompanied by a good many *Ach's* and *So's,* he went to work.

'She has been dead not more than an hour,' he announced. 'Death it was very quick – at once.'

'And what weapon do you think was used?'

'Ach, it is interesting that. It was something very sharp, very thin, very delicate. I could show you the kind of thing.'

Back again in his cabin he opened a case and extracted a long, delicate, surgical knife.'

'It was something like that, my friend; it was not a common table knife.'

'I suppose,' suggested Race smoothly, 'that none of your own knives are – er – missing, Doctor?'

Bessner stared at him; then his face grew red with indignation.

'What is that you say? Do you think I – I, Carl Bessner – who is so well-known all over Austria – I with my clinics, my highly born patients – I have killed a miserable little *femme de chambre*? Ah, but it is ridiculous – absurd, what you say! None of my knives are missing – not one, I tell you. They are all here, correct, in their places. You can see for yourself. And this insult to my profession I will not forget.'

Dr Bessner closed his case with a snap, flung it down and stamped out on to the deck.

'Whew!' said Simon. 'You've put the old boy's back up.'

Poirot shrugged his shoulders. 'It is regrettable.'

'You're on the wrong tack. Old Bessner's one of the best, even though he is a kind of Boche.'

Dr Bessner reappeared suddenly.

'Will you be so kind as to leave me now my cabin? I have to do the dressing of my patient's leg.'

Miss Bowers had entered with him and stood, brisk and professional, waiting for the others to go.

Race and Poirot crept out meekly. Race muttered something and went off. Poirot turned to his left. He heard scraps of girlish conversation, a little laugh. Jacqueline and Rosalie were together in the latter's cabin.

The door was open and the two girls were standing near it. As his shadow fell on them they looked up. He saw Rosalie Otterbourne smile at him for the first time – a shy welcoming smile – a little uncertain in its lines, as of one who does a new and unfamiliar thing.

'You talk the scandal, Mesdemoiselles?' he accused them.

'No, indeed,' said Rosalie. 'As a matter of fact we were just comparing lipsticks.'

Poirot smiled. '*Les chiffons d'aujourd hui,*' he murmured.

But there was something a little mechanical about his smile, and Jacqueline de Bellefort, quicker and more observant than Rosalie, saw it. She dropped the lipstick she was holding and came out upon the deck.

'Has something – what has happened now?'

'It is as you guess, Mademoiselle; something has happened.'

'What?' Rosalie came out too.

'Another death,' said Poirot.

Rosalie caught her breath sharply. Poirot was watching her narrowly. He saw alarm and something more – consternation – show for a minute or two in her eyes.

'Madame Doyle's maid has been killed,' he told them bluntly.

'Killed?' cried Jacqueline. '*Killed*, do you say?'

'Yes, that is what I said.' Though his answer was nominally to her, it was Rosalie whom he watched. It was Rosalie to whom he spoke as he went on: 'You see, this maid she saw something she was not intended to see. And so – she was silenced, in case she should not hold her tongue.'

'What was it she saw?'

Again it was Jacqueline who asked, and again Poirot's answer was to Rosalie. It was an odd little three-cornered scene.

'There is, I think, very little doubt what it was she saw,' said Poirot. 'She saw someone enter and leave Linnet Doyle's cabin on that fatal night.'

His ears were quick. He heard the sharp intake of breath and saw the eyelids flicker. Rosalie Otterbourne had reacted just as he intended she should.

'Did she say who it was she saw?' Rosalie asked.

Gently – regretfully – Poirot shook his head.

Footsteps pattered up the deck. It was **Cornelia** Robson, her eyes wide and startled.

'Oh, Jacqueline,' she cried, 'something awful has happened! Another dreadful thing!'

Jacqueline turned to her. The two moved a few steps forward. Almost unconsciously Poirot and Rosalie Otterbourne moved in the other direction.

Rosalie said sharply: 'Why do you look at me? What have you got in your mind?'

'That is two questions you ask me. I will ask you only one in return. Why do you not tell me all the truth, Mademoiselle?'

'I don't know what you mean. I told you – everything – this morning.'

'No, there were things you did not tell me. You did not tell me that you carry about in your handbag a small-calibre pistol with a pearl handle. You did not tell me all that you saw last night.'

She flushed. Then she said sharply: 'It's quite untrue. I haven't got a revolver.'

'I did not say a revolver. I said a small pistol that you carry about in your handbag.'

She wheeled round, darted into her cabin and out again and thrust her grey leather handbag into his hands.

'You're talking nonsense. Look for yourself if you like.'

Poirot opened the bag. There was no pistol inside.

He handed the bag back to her, meeting her scornful triumphant glance.

'No,' he said pleasantly. 'It is not there.'

'You see. You're not always right, Monsieur Poirot. And you're wrong about that other ridiculous thing you said.'

'No, I do not think so.'

'You're infuriating!' She stamped an angry foot. 'You get an idea into your head, and you go on and on and on about it.'

Because I want you to tell me the truth.'

'What is the truth? You seem to know it better than I do.'

Poirot said: 'You want me to tell what it was you saw? If I am right, will you admit that I am right? I will tell you my little idea. I think that when you came round the stern of the boat you stopped involuntarily because you saw a man come out of a cabin about half-way down the deck – Linnet Doyle's cabin, as you realised next day. You saw him come out, close the door behind him, and walk away from you down the deck and – perhaps – enter one of the two end cabins. Now, then, am I right, Mademoiselle?'

She did not answer.

'Poirot said: 'Perhaps you think it wiser not to speak. Perhaps you are afraid that, if you do, you too will be killed.'

For a moment he thought she had risen to the easy bait, that the accusation against her courage would succeed where more subtle arguments would have failed.

Her lips opened – trembled – then, 'I saw no one,' said Rosalie Otterbourne.

Miss Bowers came out of Dr Bessner's cabin, smoothing her cuffs over her wrists.

Jacqueline left Cornelia abruptly and accosted the hospital nurse.

'How is he?' she demanded.

Poirot came up in time to hear the answer. Miss Bowers was looking rather worried.

'Things aren't going too badly,' she said.

Jacqueline cried: 'You mean, he's worse?'

'Well, I must say I shall be relieved when we get in and can get a proper X-ray done and the whole thing cleaned up under an anæsthetic. When do you think we shall get to Shellâl, Monsieur Poirot?'

'Tomorrow morning.'

Miss Bowers pursed her lips and shook her head.

'It's very unfortunate. We are doing all we can, but there's always such a danger of septicæmia.'

Jacqueline caught Miss Bowers' arm and shook it.

'Is he going to die? Is he going to die?'

'Dear me, no, Miss de Bellefort. That is, I hope not, I'm sure. The wound in itself isn't dangerous, but there's no doubt it ought to be X-rayed as soon as possible. And then, of course poor Mr Doyle ought to have been kept absolutely quiet today. He's had far too much worry and excitement. No wonder his temperature is rising. What with the shock of his wife's death, and one thing and another—'

Jacqueline relinquished her grasp of the nurse's arm and turned away. She stood leaning over the side, her back to the other two.

'What I say is, we've got to hope for the best always,' said Miss Bowers. 'Of course Mr Doyle has a very strong constitution – one can see that – probably never had a day's illness in his life. So that's in his favour. But there's no denying that this rise in temperature is a nasty sign and—'

She shook her head, adjusted her cuffs once more, and moved briskly away.

Jacqueline turned and walked gropingly, blinded by tears, towards her cabin. A hand below her elbow steadied and guided her. She looked up through the tears to find Poirot by her side. She leaned on him a little and he guided her through the cabin door.

She sank down on the bed and the tears came more freely, punctuated by great shuddering sobs.

'He'll die! He'll die! I know he'll die . . . And I shall have killed him. Yes, I shall have killed him. . . .'

Poirot shrugged his shoulders. He shook his head a little, sadly. 'Mademoiselle, what is done is done. One cannot take back the accomplished action. It is too late to regret.'

She cried out more vehemently: 'I shall have killed him! And I love him so . . . I love him so.'

Poirot sighed. 'Too much. . . .'

It had been his thought long ago in the restaurant of M. Blondin. It was his thought again now.

He said, hesitating a little: 'Do not, at all events, go by what Miss Bowers says. Hospital nurses, me, I find them always gloomy! The night nurse always, she is astonished to find her patient alive in the evening; the day nurse, always, she is surprised to find him alive in the morning! They know too much, you see, of the possibilities that may arise. When one is motoring one might easily say to oneself: "If a car came out from that cross-road – or if that lorry backed suddenly – or if the wheel came off the car that is approaching – or if a dog jumped off the hedge on to my driving arm – *eh bien*, I should probably be killed!" But one assumes, and usually rightly, that none of these things *will* happen, and that one will get to one's journey's end. But if, of course, one has been in an accident, or seen one or more accidents, then one is inclined to take the opposite point of view.'

Jacqueline asked, half smiling through her tears: 'Are you trying to console me, Monsieur Poirot?'

'The *bon Dieu* knows what I am trying to do! You should not have come on this journey.'

'No – I wish I hadn't. It's been – so awful. But – it will be soon over now.'

'*Mais oui – mais oui.*'

'And Simon will go to the hospital, and they'll give the propert treatment and everything will be all right.'

'You speak like the child! "And they lived happily ever afterward." That is it, is it not?'

She flushed suddenly scarlet.

'Monsieur Poirot, I never meant – never—'

'It is too soon to think of such a thing! That is the proper hypocritical thing to say, is it not? But you are partly a Latin,

Mademoiselle Jacqueline. You should be able to admit facts even if they do not sound very decorous. *Le roi est mort – vive le roi*! The sun has gone and the moon rises. That is so, is it not?'

'You don't understand. He's just sorry for me – awfully sorry for me, because he knows how terrible it is for me to know I've hurt him so badly.'

'Ah, well,' said Poirot. 'The pure pity, it is a very lofty sentiment.'

He looked at her half mockingly, half with some other emotion.

He murmured softly under his breath words in French:

> *'La vie est vaine.*
> *Un peu d'amour,*
> *Un peu de haine,*
> *Et puis bonjour.*
>
> *La vie est brève.*
> *Un peu d'espoir,*
> *Un peu de rêve,*
> *Et puis bonsoir.'*

He went out again on to the deck. Colonel Race was striding along the deck and hailed him at once.

'Poirot. Good man! I want you. I've got an idea.'

Thrusting his arm through Poirot's he walked him up the deck.

'Just a chance remark of Doyle's. I hardly noticed it at the time. Something about a telegram.'

'*Tiens – c'est vrai.*'

'Nothing in it, perhaps, but one can't leave an avenue un-explored. Damn it all, man, two murders, and we're still in the dark.'

Poirot shook his head. 'No not in the dark. In the light.'

Race looked at him curiously. 'You have an idea?'

'It is more than an idea now. *I am sure.*'

'Since – when?'

'Since the death of the maid, Louise Bourget.'

'Damned if I see it!'

'My friend, it is so clear – so clear. Only there are difficulties – embarrassments – impediments! See you, around a person like Linnet Doyle there is so much – so many conflicting hates and jealousies and envies and meannesses. It is like a cloud of flies, buzzing, buzzing. . . .'

'But you think you know?' The other looked at him curiously. 'You wouldn't say so unless you were sure. Can't say I've any real light, myself. I've suspicions, of course. . . .'

Poirot stopped. He laid an impressive hand on Race's arm.

'You are a great man, *mon Colonel*. . . . You do not say: "Tell me. What is it that you think?" You know that if I could speak now I would. But there is much to be cleared away first. But think, think for a moment along the lines that I shall indicate. There are certain points. . . . There is the statement of Mademoiselle de Bellefort that someone overheard our conversation that night in the garden at Assuan. There is the statement of Monsieur Tim Allerton as to what he heard and did on the night of the crime. There are Louise Bourget's significant answers to our questions this morning. There is the fact that Madame Allerton drinks water, that her son drinks whisky and soda and that I drink wine. Add to that the fact of two bottles of nail polish and the proverb I quoted. And finally we come to the crux of the whole business, the fact that the pistol was wrapped up in a cheap handkerchief and a velvet stole and thrown overboard. . . .'

Race was silent a minute or two, then he shook his head.

'No,' he said. 'I don't see it. Mind, I've got a faint idea what you're driving at, but as far as I can see, it doesn't work.'

'But yes – but yes. You are seeing only half the truth. And remember this – we must start again from the beginning, since our first conception was entirely wrong.'

Race made a slight grimace.

'I'm used to that. It often seems to me that's all detective work is, wiping out your false starts and beginning again.'

'Yes, it is very true, that. And it is just what some people will not do. They conceive a certain theory, and everything has to fit into that theory. If one little fact will not fit it, they throw it aside. But it is always the facts that will not fit in that are significant. All along I have realised the significance of that pistol being removed from the scene of the crime. I knew that it meant something, but what that something was I only realised one little half hour ago.'

'And I still don't see it!'

'But you will! Only reflect along the lines I indicated. And now let us clear up this matter of a telegram. That is, if the Herr Doktor will admit us.'

Dr Bessner was still in a very bad humour. In answer to their knock he disclosed a scowling face.

'What is it? Once more you wish to see my patient? But I tell you it is not wise. He has fever. He has had more than enough excitement today.'

'Just one question,' said Race. 'Nothing more, I assure you.'

With an unwilling grunt the doctor moved aside and the two men entered the cabin. Dr Bessner, growling to himself, pushed past them.

'I return in three minutes,' he said. 'And then – positively – you go!'

They heard him stumping down the deck.

Simon Doyle looked from one to the other of them inquiringly.

'Yes,' he said, 'what is it?'

'A very little thing,' Race replied. 'Just now, when the stewards were reporting to me, they mentioned that Signor Richetti had been particularly troublesome. You said that that didn't surprise you, as you knew he had a bad temper, and that he had been rude to your wife over some matter of a telegram. Now can you tell me about that incident?'

'Easily. It was a Wâdi Halfa. We'd just come back from the Second Cataract. Linnet thought she saw a telegram for her sticking up on the board. She'd forgotten, you see, that she wasn't called Ridgeway any longer, and Richetti and Ridgeway do look rather alike when written in an atrocious handwriting. So she tore it open, couldn't make head or tail of it, and was puzzling over it when this fellow Richetti came along, fairly tore it out of her hand and gibbered with rage. She went after him to apologise and he was frightfully rude to her about it.'

Race drew a deep breath. 'And do you know at all, Mr Doyle, what was in that telegram?'

'Yes. Linnet read part of it out aloud. It said—'

He paused. There was a commotion outside. A high-pitched voice was rapidly approaching.

'Where are Monsieur Poirot and Colonel Race? I must see them *immediately*! It is most important. I have vital information. I— Are they with Mr Doyle?'

Bessner had not closed the door. Only the curtain hung across the open doorway. Mrs Otterbourne swept it to one side and entered like a tornado. Her face was suffused with colour, her gait slightly unsteady, her command of words not quite under her control.

'Mr Doyle,' she said dramatically, 'I know who killed your wife!'

'What?'

Simon stared at her. So did the other two.

Mrs Otterbourne swept all three of them with a triumphant glance. She was happy – superbly happy.

'Yes,' she said. 'My theories are completely vindicated. The deep, primeval, primordial urges – it may appear impossible – fantastic – but it is the truth!'

Race said sharply: 'Do I understand that you have evidence in your possession to show who killed Mrs Doyle?'

Mrs Otterbourne sat down in a chair and leaned forward, nodding her head vigorously.

'Certainly I have. You will agree, will you not, that whoever killed Louise Bourget also killed Linnet Doyle – that the two crimes were committed by one and the same hand?'

'Yes, yes,' said Simon impatiently. 'Of course. That stands to reason. Go on.'

'Then my assertion holds. I know who killed Louise Bourget; therefore I know who killed Linnet Doyle.'

'You mean, you have a theory as to who killed Louise Bourget,' suggested Race sceptically.

Mrs Otterbourne turned on him like a tiger.

'No, I have exact knowledge. I *saw* the person with my own eyes.'

Simon, fevered, shouted out: 'For God's sake, start at the beginning. You know the person who killed Louise Bourget, you say.'

Mrs Otterbourne nodded.

'I will tell you exactly what occurred.'

Yes, she was very happy – no doubt of it! This was her moment, her triumph! What of it if her books were failing to sell, if the stupid public that once had bought them and devoured them voraciously now turned to newer favourites? Salome Otterbourne would once again be notorious. Her name would be in all the papers. She would be principal witness for the prosecution at the trial.

She took a deep breath and opened her mouth.

'It was when I went down to lunch. I hardly felt like eating – all the horror of the recent tragedy–– Well, I needn't go into that. Half-way down I remembered that I had – er – left something in my cabin. I told Rosalie to go on without me. She did.'

Mrs Otterbourne paused a minute.

The curtain across the door moved slightly as though lifted by the wind, but none of the three men noticed it.

'I – er—' Mrs Otterbourne paused. Thin ice to skate over here, but it must be done somehow. 'I – er – had an arrangement with one of the – er – *personnel* of the ship. He was to – er – get me something I needed, but I did not wish my daughter to know of it. She is inclined to be tiresome in certain ways—'

Not too good, this, but she could think of something that sounded better before it came to telling the story in court.

Race's eyebrows lifted as his eyes asked a question of Poirot.

Poirot gave an infinitesimal nod. His lips formed the word: 'Drink.'

The curtain across the door moved again. Between it and the door itself something showed with a faint steel-blue gleam. Mrs Otterbourne continued: 'The arrangement was that I should go round to the stern on the deck below this, and there I should find the man waiting for me. As I went along the deck a cabin door opened and somebody looked out. It was this girl Louise Bourget, or whatever her name is. She seemed to be expecting someone. When she saw it was me, she looked disappointed and went abruptly inside again. I didn't think anything of it, of course. I went along just as I had said I would and got the – the stuff from the man. I paid him and – er – just had a word with him. Then I started back. Just as I came around the corner I saw someone knock on the maid's door and go into the cabin.'

Race said, 'And that person was—?'

Bang!

The noise of the explosion filled the cabin. There was an acrid sour smell of smoke. Mrs Otterbourne turned slowly sideways, as though in supreme inquiry, then her body slumped forward and she fell to the ground with a crash. From just behind her ear the blood flowed from a round neat hole.

There was a moment's stupefied silence. Then both the able-bodied men jumped to their feet. The woman's body hindered their movements a little. Race bent over her while Poirot made a catlike jump for the door and the deck.

The deck was empty. On the ground just in front of the sill lay a big Colt revolver.

Poirot glanced in both directions. The deck was empty. He then sprinted towards the stern. As he rounded the corner he ran into Tim Allerton, who was coming full tilt from the opposite direction.

'What the devil was that?' cried Tim breathlessly.

Poirot said sharply: 'Did you meet anyone on your way here?'

'Meet anyone?' No.'

'Then come with me.' He took the young man by the arm and retraced his steps. A little crowd had assembled by now. Rosalie, Jacqueline, and Cornelia had rushed out of their cabins. More people were coming along the deck from the saloon – Ferguson, Jim Fanthorp, and Mrs Allerton.

Race stood by the revolver. Poirot turned his head and said sharply to Tim Allerton: 'Got any gloves in your pocket?'

Tim fumbled.

'Yes, I have.'

Poirot seized them from him, put them on, and bent to examine the revolver. Race did the same. The others watched breathlessly.

Race said: 'He didn't go the other way. Fanthorp and Ferguson were sitting on this deck lounge; they'd have seen him.'

Poirot responded, 'And Mrs Allerton would have met him if he'd gone aft.'

Race said, pointing to the revolver: 'Rather fancy we've seen this not so very long ago. Must make sure, though.'

He knocked on the door of Pennington's cabin. There was no answer. The cabin was empty. Race strode to the right-hand drawer of the chest and jerked it open. The revolver was gone.

'Settles that,' said Race. 'Now then, where's Pennington himself?'

They went out again on deck. Mrs Allerton had joined the group. Poirot moved swiftly over to her.

'Madame, take Miss Otterbourne with you and look after her. Her mother has been' – he consulted Race with an eye and Race nodded – 'killed.'

Dr Bessner came bustling along.

'*Gott im Himmel*! What is there now?'

They made way for him. Race indicated the cabin. Bessner went inside.

'Find Pennington,' said Race. 'Any fingerprints on that revolver?'

'None,' said Poirot.

They found Pennington on the deck below. He was sitting in the little drawing-room writing letters. He lifted a handsome, clean-shaven face.

'Anything new?' he asked.

'Didn't you hear a shot?'

'Why – now you mention it – I believe I did hear a kind of a bang. But I never dreamed—— Who's been shot?'

'Mrs Otterbourne.'

'*Mrs Otterbourne?*' Pennington sounded quite astounded. 'Well, you do surprise me. Mrs Otterbourne.' He shook his head. 'I can't see that at all.' He lowered his voice. 'Strikes me, gentlemen, we've got a homicidal maniac aboard. We ought to organise a defence system.'

'Mr Pennington,' said Race, 'how long have you been in this room?'

'Why, let me see.' Mr Pennington gently rubbed his chin. 'I should say a matter of twenty minutes or so.'

'And you haven't left it?'

'Why no – certainly not.'

He looked inquiringly at the two men.

'You see, Mr Pennington,' said Race, 'Mrs Otterbourne was shot with your revolver.'

—— 25 ——

Mr Pennington was shocked. Mr Pennington could hardly believe it.

'Why, gentlemen,' he said, 'this is a very serious matter. Very serious indeed.'

'Extremely serious for you, Mr Pennington.'

'For me?' Pennington's eyebrows rose in startled surprise. 'But, my dear sir, I was sitting quietly writing in here when that shot was fired.'

'You have, perhaps, a witness to prove that?'

Pennington shook his head.

'Why, no – I wouldn't say that. But it's clearly impossible that I should have gone to the deck above, shot this poor woman (and why should I shoot her anyway?) and come down again with no one seeing me. There are always plenty of people on the deck lounge this time of day.'

'How do you account for your pistol being used?'

'Well – I'm afraid I may be to blame there. Quite soon after getting aboard there was a conversation in the saloon one evening, I remember, about firearms, and I mentioned then that I always carried a revolver with me when I travel.'

'Who was there?'

'Well, I can't remember exactly. Most people, I think. Quite a crowd, anyway.'

He shook his head gently.

'Why, yes,' he said. 'I am certainly to blame there.'

He went on: 'First Linnet, then Linnet's maid, and now Mrs Otterbourne. There seems no reason in it all!'

'There *was* reason,' said Race.

'There was?'

'Yes. Mrs Otterbourne was on the point of telling us that she had seen a certain person go into Louise's cabin. Before she could name that person she was shot dead.'

Andrew Pennington passed a fine silk handkerchief over his brow.

'All this is terrible,' he murmured.

Poirot said: 'Monsieur Pennington, I would like to discuss certain aspects of the case with you. Will you come to my cabin in half an hour's time?'

'I should be delighted.'

Pennington did not sound delighted. He did not look delighted either. Race and Poirot exchanged glances and then abruptly left the room.

'Cunning old devil,' said Race, 'but he's afraid. Eh?'

Poirot nodded. 'Yes, he is not happy, our Monsieur Pennington.'

As they reached the promenade deck again Mrs Allerton came out of her cabin and, seeing Poirot, beckoned him imperiously.

'Madame?'

'That poor child! Tell me, Monsieur Poirot, is there a double cabin somewhere that I could share with her? She oughtn't to go back to the one she shared with her mother, and mine is only a single one.'

'That can be arranged, Madame. It is very good of you.'

'It's merely decency. Besides, I'm very fond of the girl. I've always liked her.'

'Is she very upset?'

'Terribly. She seems to have been absolutely devoted to that odious woman. That is what is so pathetic about it all. Tim says he believes she drank. Is that true?'

Poirot nodded.

'Oh, well, poor woman, one must not judge her, I suppose; but that girl must have had a terrible life.'

'She did Madame. She is very proud and she was very loyal.'

'Yes, I like that – loyalty, I mean. It's out of fashion

nowadays. She's an odd character, that girl – proud, reserved, stubborn and terribly warm-hearted underneath, I fancy.'

'I see that I have given her into good hands, Madame.'

'Yes, don't worry. I'll look after her. She's inclined to cling to me in the most pathetic fashion.'

Mrs Allerton went back into the cabin. Poirot returned to the scene of the tragedy.

Cornelia was still standing on the deck, her eyes wide. She said: 'I don't understand, Monsieur Poirot. How did the person who shot her get away without our seeing him?'

'Yes, how?' echoed Jacqueline.

'Ah,' said Poirot, 'it was not quite such a disappearing trick as you think, Mademoiselle. There were three distinct ways the murderer might have gone.'

Jacqueline looked puzzled. She said, 'Three?'

'He might have gone to the right, or he might have gone to the left, but I don't see any other way,' puzzled Cornelia.

Jacqueline too frowned. Then her brow cleared.

She said: 'Of course. He could move in two directions on one plane, but he could go at right angles to that plane too. That is, he couldn't go *up* very well, but he could go *down*.'

Poirot smiled. 'You have brains, Mademoiselle.'

Cornelia said: 'I know I'm just a plain mutt, but I still don't see.'

Jacqueline said: 'Monsieur Poirot means, darling, that he could swing himself over the rail and down on to the deck below.'

'My!' gasped Cornelia. 'I never thought of that. He'd have to be mighty quick about it, though. I suppose he could just do it?'

'He could do it easily enough,' said Tim Allerton. 'Remember, there's always a minute of shock after a thing like this. One hears a shot and one's too paralysed to move for a second or two.'

'That was your experience, Monsieur Allerton?'

'Yes, it was. I just stood like a dummy for quite five seconds. Then I fairly sprinted round the deck.'

Race came out of Bessner's cabin and said authoritatively: 'Would you mind all clearing off? We want to bring out the body.'

Everyone moved away obediently. Poirot went with them. Cornelia said to him with sad earnestness: 'I'll never forget this trip as long as I live. Three deaths. . . . It's just like living in a nightmare.'

Ferguson overheard her. He said aggressively: 'That's because you're over-civilised. You should look on death as the Oriental does. It's a mere incident – hardly noticeable.'

'That's all very well,' Cornelia said. 'They're not educated, poor creatures.'

'No, and a good thing too. Education has devitalised the white races. Look at America – goes in for an orgy of culture. Simply disgusting.'

'I think you're talking nonsense,' said Cornelia, flushing. 'I attend lectures very winter on Greek Art and the Renaissance, and I went to some on Famous Women of History.'

Mr Ferguson groaned in agony: 'Greek Art; Renaissance! Famous Women of History! It makes me quite sick to hear you. It's the *future* that matters, woman, not the past. Three women are dead on this boat. Well, what of it? They're no loss! Linnet Doyle and her money! The French maid – a domestic parasite. Mrs Otterbourne – a useless fool of a woman. Do you think anyone really cares whether they're dead or not? I don't. I think it's a damned good thing!'

'Then you're wrong!' Cornelia blazed out at him. 'And it makes me sick to hear you talk and talk, as though nobody mattered but *you*. I didn't like Mrs Otterbourne much, but her daughter was ever so fond of her, and she's all broken up over her mother's death. I don't know much about the French maid, but I expect somebody was fond of her somewhere; and as for Linnet Doyle – well, apart from everything else, she was just lovely! She was so beautiful when she came into a room that it made a lump come in your throat. I'm homely myself, and that makes me appreciate beauty a lot more. She was as beautiful –just as a woman – as anything in Greek Art. And when anything beautiful's dead, it's a loss to the world. So there!'

Mr Ferguson stepped back a space. He caught hold of his hair with both hands and tugged at it vehemently.

'I give it up,' he said. 'You're unbelievable. Just haven't got a bit of natural female spite in you anywhere.' He turned to Poirot. 'Do you know, sir, that Cornelia's father was practically ruined by Linnet Ridgeway's old man? But does the girl gnash her teeth when she sees the heiress sailing about in pearls and Paris models? No, she just bleats out: "Isn't she beautiful?" like a blessed Baa Lamb. I don't believe she even felt sore at her.'

Cornelia flushed. 'I did – just for a minute. Poppa kind of

died of discouragement, you know, because he hadn't made good.'

'Felt sore for a minute! I ask you.'

Cornelia flashed round on him.

'Well, didn't you say just now it was the future that mattered, not the past? All that was in the past, wasn't it? It's over.'

'Got me there,' said Ferguson. 'Cornelia Robson, you're the only nice woman I've ever come across. Will you marry me?'

'Don't be absurd.'

'It's a genuine proposal – even if it is made in the presence of Old Man Sleuth. Anyway, you're a witness, Monsieur Poirot. I've deliberately offered marriage to this female – against all my principles, because I don't believe in legal contracts between the sexes; but I don't think she'd stand for anything else, so marriage it shall be. Come on, Cornelia, say yes.'

'I think you're utterly ridiculous,' said Cornelia, flushing.

'Why won't you marry me?'

'You're not serious,' said Cornelia.

'Do you mean not serious in proposing or do you mean not serious in character?'

'Both, but I really meant character. You laugh at all sorts of serious things. Education and Culture – and – and Death. You wouldn't be *reliable*.'

She broke off, flushed again, and hurried along into her cabin.

Ferguson stared after her. 'Damn the girl! I believe she really means it. She wants a man to be reliable. *Reliable* – ye gods!' He paused and then said curiously: 'What's the matter with you, Monsieur Poirot? You seem very deep in thought.'

Poirot roused himself with a start.

'I reflect, that is all. I reflect.'

'Meditation on Death. Death, the Recurring Decimal, by Hercule Poirot. One of his well-known monographs.'

'Monsieur Ferguson,' said Poirot, 'you are a very impertinent young man.'

'You must excuse me. I like attacking established institutions.'

'And I am an established institution?'

'Precisely. What do you think of that girl?'

'Of Miss Robson?'

'Yes.'

'I think that she has a great deal of character.'

'You're right. She's got spirit. She looks meek, but she isn't.

She's got guts. She's – oh, damn it, I want that girl. It mightn't be a bad move if I tackled the old lady. If I could once get her thoroughly against me, it might cut some ice with Cornelia.'

He wheeled and went into the observation saloon. Miss Van Schuyler was seated in her usual corner. She looked even more arrogant than usual. She was knitting. Ferguson strode up to her. Hercule Poirot, entering unobtrusively, took a seat a discreet distance away and appeared to be absorbed in a magazine.

'Good-afternoon, Miss Van Schuyler.'

Miss Van Schuyler raised her eyes for a bare second, dropped them again and murmured frigidly, 'Er – good-afternoon.'

'Look here, Miss Van Schuyler, I want to talk to you about something pretty important. It's just this. I want to marry your cousin.'

Miss Van Schuyler's ball of wool dropped on to the ground and ran wildly across the saloon.

She said in a venomous tone: 'You must be out of your senses, young man.'

'Not at all. I'm determined to marry her. I've asked her to marry me!'

Miss Van Schuyler surveyed him coldly, with the kind of speculative interest she might have accorded to an odd sort of beetle.

'Indeed? And I presume she sent you about your business.'

'She refused me.'

'Naturally.'

'Not "naturally" at all. I'm going to go on asking her till she agrees.'

'I can assure you, sir, that I shall take steps to see that my young cousin is not subjected to any such persecution,' said Miss Van Schuyler in a biting tone.

'What have you got against me?'

Miss Van Schuyler merely raised her eyebrows and gave a vehement tug to her wool, preparatory to regaining it and closing the interview.

'Come now,' persisted Mr Ferguson, 'what have you got against me?'

'I should think that was quite obvious, Mr – er – I don't know your name.'

'Ferguson.'

'Mr Ferguson.' Miss Van Schuyler uttered the name with definite distaste. 'Any such idea is quite out of the question.'

'You mean,' said Ferguson, 'that I'm not good enough for her?'

965

'I should think that would have been obvious to you.'

'In what way am I not good enough?'

Miss Van Schuyler again did not answer.

'I've got two legs, two arms, good health, and quite reasonable brains. What's wrong with that?'

'There is such a thing as social position, Mr Ferguson.'

'Social position is bunk!'

The door swung open and Cornelia came in. She stopped dead on seeing her redoubtable Cousin Marie in conversation with her would-be suitor.

The outrageous Mr Ferguson turned his head, grinned broadly and called out: 'Come along, Cornelia. I'm asking for your hand in marriage in the best conventional manner.'

'Cornelia,' said Miss Van Schuyler, and her voice was truly awful in quality, *'have you encouraged this young man?'*

'I – no, of course not – at least – not exactly – I mean—'

'What do you mean?'

'She hasn't encouraged me,' said Mr Ferguson helpfully. 'I've done it all. She hasn't actually pushed me in the face, because she's got too kind a heart. Cornelia, your cousin says I'm not good enough for you. That, of course, is true, but not in the way she means it. My moral nature certainly doesn't equal yours, but her point is that I'm hopelessly below you socially.'

'That, I think, is equally obvious to Cornelia,' said Miss Van Schuyler.

'Is it?' Mr Ferguson looked at her searchingly. 'Is that why you won't marry me?'

'No it isn't.' Cornelia flushed. 'If – if I liked you, I'd marry you no matter who you were.'

'But you don't like me?'

'I – I think you're just outrageous. The way you say things. . . . the *things* you say . . . I – I've never met anyone the least like you. I—'

Tears threatened to overcome her. She rushed from the room.

'On the whole,' said Mr Ferguson, 'that's not too bad for a start.' He leaned back in his chair, gazed at the ceiling, whistled, crossed his disreputable knees and remarked: 'I'll be calling you Cousin yet.'

Miss Van Schuyler trembled with rage. 'Leave this room at once, sir, or I'll ring for the steward.'

'I've paid for my ticket,' said Mr Ferguson. 'They can't possibly turn me out of the public lounge. But I'll humour you.' He sang softly, 'Yo ho ho, and a bottle of rum.' Rising, he sauntered nonchalantly to the door and passed out.

Choking with anger Miss Van Schuyler struggled to her feet. Poirot, discreetly emerging from retirement behind his magazine, sprang up and retrieved the ball of wool.

'Thank you, Monsieur Poirot. If you would send Miss Bowers to me – I feel quite upset – that insolent young man.'

'Rather eccentric, I'm afraid,' said Poirot. 'Most of that family are. Spoilt, of course. Always inclined to tilt at windmills.' He added carelessly, 'You recognised him, I suppose?'

'Recognised him?'

'Calls himself Ferguson and won't use his title because of his advanced ideas.'

'His *title*?' Miss Van Schuyler's tone was sharp.

'Yes, that's young Lord Dawlish. Rolling in money, of course, but he became a communist when he was at Oxford.'

Miss Van Schuyler, her face a battleground of contradictory emotions, said: 'How long have you known this, Monsieur Poirot?'

Poirot shrugged his shoulders.

'There was a picture in one of these papers – I noticed the resemblance. Then I found a signet ring with a coat of arms on it. Oh there's no doubt about it, I assure you.'

He quite enjoyed reading the conflicting expressions that succeeded each other on Miss Van Schuyler's face. Finally, with a gracious inclination of the head, she said, 'I am very much obliged to you Monsieur Poirot.'

Poirot looked after her and smiled as she went out of the saloon. Then he sat down and his face grew grave once more. He was following out a train of thought in his mind. From time to time he nodded his head.

'*Mais oui,*' he said at last. 'It all fits in.'

—— 26 ——

Race found him still sitting there.

'Well, Poirot, what about it? Pennington's due in ten minutes. I'm leaving this in your hands.'

Poirot rose quickly to his feet. 'First, get hold of young Fanthorp.'

'Fanthorp?' Race looked surprised.

'Yes. Bring him to my cabin.'

Race nodded and went off. Poirot went along to his cabin. Race arrived with young Fanthorp a minute or two afterward.

Poirot indicated chairs and offered cigarettes.

'Now, Monsieur Fanthorp,' he said, 'to our business! I perceive that you wear the same tie that my friend Hastings wears.'

Jim Fanthorp looked down at his neckwear with some bewilderment.

'It's an O.E. tie,' he said.

'Exactly. You must understand that, though I am a foreigner, I know something of the English point of view. I know, for instance, that there are "things which are done" and "things which are not done." '

Jim Fanthorp grinned.

'We don't say that sort of thing much nowadays, sir.'

'Perhaps not, but the custom, it still remains. The Old School Tie is the Old School Tie, and there are certain things (I know this from experience) that the Old School Tie does not do! One of those things, Monsieur Fanthorp, is to butt into a private conversation unasked when one does not know the people who are conducting it.'

Fanthorp stared.

Poirot went on: 'But the other day, Monsieur Fanthorp, that is exactly what you did do. Certain persons were quietly transacting some private business in the observation saloon. You strolled near them, obviously in order to overhear what it was that was in progress, and presently you actually turned round and congratulated a lady – Madame Simon Doyle – on the soundness of her business methods.'

Jim Fanthorp's face got very red. Poirot swept on, not waiting for a comment.

'Now that, Monsieur Fanthorp, was not at all the behaviour of one who wears a tie similar to that worn by my friend Hastings! Hastings is all delicacy, would die of shame before he did such a thing! Therefore, taking that action of yours in conjunction with the fact that you are a very young man to be able to afford an expensive holiday, that you are a member of a country solicitor's firm, and therefore probably not extravagantly well off, and that you show no signs of recent illness such as might necessitate a prolonged visit abroad, I ask myself – and am now asking you – what is the reason for your presence on this boat?'

Jim Fanthorp jerked his head back.

'I decline to give you any information whatever, Monsieur Poirot. I really think you must be mad.'

'I am not mad. I am very, very sane. Where is your firm? In Northampton; that is not very far from Wode Hall. What conversation did you try to overhear? One concerning legal documents. What was the object of your remark – a remark which you uttered with obvious embarrassment and *malaise*? Your object was to prevent Madame Doyle from signing any document unread.'

He paused.

'On this boat we have had a murder, and following that murder two other murders in rapid succession. If I further give you the information that the weapon which killed Madame Otterbourne was a revolver owned by Monsieur Andrew Pennington, then perhaps you will realise that it is actually your duty to tell us all you can.'

Jim Fanthorp was silent for some minutes. At last he said: 'You have rather an odd way of going about things, Monsieur Poirot, but I appreciate the points you have made. The trouble is that I have no exact information to lay before you.'

'You mean that it is a case, merely, of suspicion.'

'Yes.'

'And therefore you think it injudicious to speak? That may be true, legally speaking. But this is not a court of law. Colonel Race and myself are endeavouring to track down a murderer. Anything that can help us to do so may be valuable.'

Again Jim Fanthorp reflected. Then he said: 'Very well. What is it you want to know?'

'Why did you come on this trip?'

'My uncle, Mr Carmichael, Mrs Doyle's English solicitor, sent me. He handled a good many of her affairs. In this way, he was often in correspondence with Mr Andrew Pennington, who was Mrs Doyle's American trustee. Several small incidents (I cannot enumerate them all) made my uncle suspicious that all was not quite as it should be.'

'In plain language,' said Race, 'your uncle suspected that Pennington was a crook?'

Jim Fanthorp nodded, a faint smile on his face.

'You put it rather more bluntly than I should, but the main idea is correct. Various excuses made by Pennington, certain plausible explanations of the disposal of funds, aroused my uncle's distrust.

'While these suspicions of his were still nebulous, Miss Ridgeway married unexpectedly and went off on her honeymoon to Egypt. Her marriage relieved my uncle's mind, as he knew that on her return to England the estate would have to be formally settled and handed over.

'However, in a letter she wrote him from Cairo, she mentioned casually that she had unexpectedly run across Andrew Pennington. My uncle's suspicions became acute. He felt sure that Pennington, perhaps by now in a desperate position, was going to try and obtain signatures from her which would cover his own defalcations. Since my uncle had no definite evidence to lay before her, he was in a most difficult position. The only thing he could think of was to send me out here, travelling by air, with instructions to discover what was in the wind. I was to keep my eyes open and act summarily if necessary – a most unpleasant mission, I can assure you. As a matter of fact, on the occasion you mention I had to behave more or less as a cad! It was awkward, but on the whole I was satisfied with the result.'

'You mean you put Madame Doyle on her guard?' asked Race.

'Not so much that, but I think I put the wind up Pennington. I felt convinced he wouldn't try any more funny business for some time, and by then I hoped to have got intimate enough with Mr and Mrs Doyle to convey some kind of a warning. As a matter of fact I hoped to do so through Doyle. Mrs Doyle was so attracted to Mr Pennington that it would have been a bit awkward to suggest things to her about him. It would have been easier for me to approach the husband.'

Race nodded.

Poirot asked: 'Will you give me a candid opinion on one point, Monsieur Fanthorp? If you were engaged in putting a swindle over, would you choose Madame Doyle or Monsieur Doyle as a victim?'

Fanthorp smiled faintly.

'Mr Doyle, every time. Linnet Doyle was very shrewd in business matters. Her husband, I should fancy, is one of those trustful fellows who know nothing of business and are always ready to "sign on the dotted line" as he himself put it.'

'I agree,' said Poirot. He looked at Race. 'And there's your motive.'

Jim Fanthorp said: 'But this is all pure conjecture. It isn't *evidence*.'

Poirot replied, easily: '*Ah, bah!* we will get evidence!'

'How?'

'Possibly from Mr Pennington himself.'

Fanthorp looked doubtful.

'I wonder. I very much wonder.'

Race glanced at his watch. 'He's about due now.'

Jim Fanthorp was quick to take the hint. He left them.

Two minutes later Andrew Pennington made his appearance. His manner was all smiling urbanity. Only the taut line of his jaw and the wariness of his eyes betrayed the fact that a thoroughly experienced fighter was on his guard.

'Well, gentlemen,' he said, 'here I am.'

He sat down and looked at them inquiringly.

'We asked you to come here, Monsieur Pennington,' began Poirot, 'because it is fairly obvious that you have a very special and immediate interest in the case.'

Pennington raised his eyebrows slightly.

'Is that so?'

Poirot said gently: 'Surely. You have known Linnet Ridgeway, I understand, since she was quite a child.'

'Oh! that—' His face altered, became less alert. 'I beg pardon, I didn't quite get you. Yes, as I told you this morning, I've known Linnet since she was a cute little thing in pinafores.'

'You were on terms of close intimacy with her father?'

'That's so. Melhuish Ridgeway and I were very close – very close.'

'You were so intimately associated that on his death he appointed you business guardian to his daughter and trustee to the vast fortune she inherited?'

'Why, roughtly, that is so.' The wariness was back again. The note was more cautious. 'I was not the only trustee, naturally; others were associated with me.'

'Who have since died?'

'Two of them are dead. The other, Mr Sterndale Rockford, is alive.'

'Your partner?'

'Yes.'

'Mademoiselle Ridgeway, I understand, was not yet of age when she married?'

'She would have been twenty-one next July.'

'And in the normal course of events she would have come into control of her fortune then?'

'Yes.'

'But her marraige precipitated matters?'

Pennington's jaw hardened. He shot out his chin at them aggressively.

'You'll pardon me, gentlemen, but what exact business is all this of yours?'

'If you dislike answering the question—'

'There's no dislike about it. I don't mind what you ask me. But I don't see the relevance of all this.'

'Oh, but surely, Monsieur Pennington' – Poirot leaned forward, his eyes green and catlike – 'there is the question of motive. In considering that, financial considerations must always be taken into account.'

Pennington said sullenly: 'By Ridgeway's will, Linnet got control of her dough when she was twenty-one or when she married.'

'No conditions of any kind?'

'No conditions.'

'And it is a matter, I am credibly assured, of millions.'

'Millions it is.'

Poirot said softly: 'Your responsibility, Mr Pennington, and that of your partner, has been a very grave one.'

Pennington said curtly: 'We're used to responsibility. Doesn't worry us any.'

'I wonder.'

Something in his tone flicked the other man on the raw. He asked angrily: 'What the devil do you mean?'

Poirot replied with an air of engaging frankness: 'I was wondering, Mr Pennington, whether Linnet Ridgeway's sudden marriage caused any – consternation, in your office?'

'Consternation?'

'That was the word I used.'

'What the hell are you driving at?'

'Something quite simple. Are Linnet Doyle's affairs in the perfect order they should be?'

Pennington rose to his feet.

'That's enough. I'm through.' He made for the door.

'But you will answer my question first?'

Pennington snapped: 'They're in perfect order.'

'You were not so alarmed when the news of Linnet Ridgeway's marriage reached you that you rushed over to Europe by the first boat and staged an apparently fortuitous meeting in Egypt?'

Pennington came back towards them. He had himself under control once more.

'What you are saying is absolute balderdash! I didn't even know that Linnet was married till I met her in Cairo. I was utterly astonished. Her letter must have missed me by a day in New York. It was forwarded and I got it about a week later.'

'You came over by the *Carmanic*, I think you said.'

'That's right.'

'And the letter reached New York after the *Carmanic* sailed?'

'How many times have I got to repeat it?'

'It is strange,' said Poirot.

'What's strange?'

'That on your luggage there are no labels of the *Carmanic*. The only recent labels of transatlantic sailing are the *Normandie*. The *Normandie*, I remember, sailed two days after the *Carmanic*.'

For a moment the other was at a loss. His eyes wavered. Colonel Race weighed in with telling effect.

'Come now, Mr Pennington,' he said. 'We've several reasons for believing that you came over on the *Normandie* and not by the *Carmanic*, as you said. In that case, you received Mrs Doyle's letter before you left New York. It's no good denying it, for it's the easiest thing in the world to check up the steamship companies.'

Andrew Pennington felt absent-mindedly for a chair and sat down. His face was impassive – a poker face. Behind that mask his agile brain looked ahead to the next move.

'I'll have to hand it to you, gentlemen. You've been too smart for me. But I had my reasons for acting as I did.'

'No doubt.' Race's tone was curt.

'If I give them to you, it must be understood I do so in confidence.'

'I think you can trust us to behave fittingly. Naturally I cannot give assurances blindly.'

'Well—' Pennington sighed. 'I'll come clean. There was some monkey business going on in England. It worried me. I couldn't do much about it by letter. The only thing was to to come over and see for myself.'

'What do you mean by monkey business?'

'I'd good reason to believe that Linnet was being swindled.'

'By whom?'

'Her British lawyer. Now that's not the kind of accusation you can fling around anyhow. I made up my mind to come over right away and see into matters myself.'

'That does great credit to your vigilance, I am sure. But why the little deception about not having received the letter?'

'Well, I ask you—' Pennington spread out his hands. 'You can't butt in on a honeymoon couple without more or less coming down to brass tacks and giving your reasons. I thought it best to make the meeting accidental. Besides, I didn't know anything about the husband. He might have been mixed up in the racket for all I knew.'

'In fact all your actions were actuated by pure disinterestedness,' said Colonel Race dryly.

'You've said it, Colonel.'

There was a pause. Race glanced at Poirot. The little man leant forward.

'Monsieur Pennington, we do not believe a word of your story.'

'The hell you don't! And what the hell do you believe?'

'We believe that Linnet Ridgeway's unexpected marriage put you in a financial quandary. That you came over post-haste to try and find some way out of the mess you were in – that is to say, someway of gaining time. That, with that end in view, you endeavoured to obtain Madame Doyle's signature to certain documents and failed. That on the journey up the Nile, when walking along the cliff top at Abu Simbel, you dislodged a boulder which fell and only very narrowly missed its object—'

'You're crazy.'

'We believe that the same kind of circumstances occurred on the return journey. That is to say, an opportunity presented itself of putting Madame Doyle out of the way at a moment when her death would be almost certainly ascribed to the action of another person. We not only believe, but *know*, that it was your revolver which killed a woman who was about to reveal to us the name of the person who she had reason to believe killed both Linnet Doyle and the maid Louise—'

'Hell!' The forcible ejaculation broke forth and interrupted Poirot's stream of eloquence. 'What are you getting at? Are you crazy? What motive had I to kill Linnet? I wouldn't get her money; that goes to her husband. Why don't you pick on him? *He's* the one to benefit – not me.'

Race said coldly: 'Doyle never left the lounge on the night of the tragedy till he was shot at and wounded in the leg. The impossibility of his walking a step after that is attested to by a doctor and a nurse – both independent and reliable witnesses. Simon Doyle could not have killed his wife. He could not have killed Louise Bourget. He most definitely did not kill Mrs Otterbourne. You know that as well as we do.'

'I know he didn't kill her.' Pennington sounded a little calmer. 'All I say is, why pick on me when I don't benefit by her death?'

'But my dear sir,' Poirot's voice came soft as a purring cat, 'that is rather a matter of opinion. Madame Doyle was a keen woman of business, fully conversant with her own affairs and very quick to spot any irregularity. As soon as she took up the control of her property, which she would have done on her return to England, her suspicions were bound to be aroused. But now that she is dead and that her husband, as you have pointed out, inherits, the whole thing is different. Simon Doyle knows nothing whatever of his wife's affairs except that she was a rich woman. He is of a simple, trusting disposition. You will find it easy to place complicated statements before him, to involve the real issue in a net of figures, and to delay settlement with pleas of legal formalities and the recent depression. I think that it makes a very considerable difference to you whether you deal with the husband or the wife.'

Penningotn shrugged his shoulders.

'Your ideas are – fantastic.'

'Time will show.'

'What did you say?'

'I said "Time will show!" This is a matter of three deaths – three murders. The law will demand the most searching investigation into the condition of Madame Doyle's estate.'

He saw the sudden sag in the other's shoulders and knew that he had won. Jim Fanthorp's suspicions were well founded.

Poirot went on: 'You've played – and lost. Useless to go on bluffing.'

'You don't understand,' Pennington muttered. 'It's all square enough really. It's been this damned slump – Wall Street's been crazy. But I'd staged a comeback. With luck everything will be O.K. by the middle of June.'

With shaking hands he took a cigarette, tried to light it, failed.

'I suppose,' mused Poirot, 'that the boulder was a sudden temptation. You thought nobody saw you.'

'That was an accident. I swear it was an accident!' The man leant forward, his face working, his eyes terrified. 'I stumbled and fell against it. I swear it was an accident. . . .'

The two men said nothing.

Pennington suddenly pulled himself together. He was still a wreck of a man, but his fighting spirit had returned in a certain measure. He moved towards the door.

'You can't pin that on me, gentlemen. It was an accident.

And it wasn't I who shot her. D'you hear? You can't pin that on me either – and you never will.'

He went out.

——— 27 ———

As the door closed behind him, Race gave a deep sigh.

'We got more than I thought we should. Admission of fraud. Admission of attempted murder. Further than that it's impossible to go. A man will confess, more or less, to attempted murder, but you won't get him to confess to the real thing.'

'Sometimes it can be done,' said Poirot. His eyes were dreamy – catlike.

Race looked at him curiously.

'Got a plan?'

Poirot nodded. Then he said, ticking off the items on his fingers: 'The garden at Assuan. Mr Allerton's statement. The two bottles of nail polish. My bottle of wine. The velvet stole. The bloodstained handkerchief. The pistol that was left on the scene of the crime. The death of Louise. The death of Madame Otterbourne. Yes, it's all there. Pennington didn't do it, Race!'

'What?' Race was startled.

'Pennington didn't do it. He had the motive, yes. He had the *will* to do it, yes. He got as far as *attempting* to do it. *Mais c'est tout.* For this crime, something was wanted that Pennington hadn't got! This is a crime that needed audacity, swift and faultless execution, courage, indifference to danger, and a resourceful, calculating brain. Pennington hasn't got those attributes. He couldn't do a crime unless he knew it to be safe. This crime wasn't safe! It hung on a razor edge. It needed boldness. Pennington isn't bold. He's only astute.'

Race looked at him with the respect one able man gives to another.

'You've got it all well taped,' he said.

'I think so, yes. There are one or two things – that telegram for instance, that Linnet Doyle read. I should like to get that cleared up.'

'By Jove, we forgot to ask Doyle. He was telling us when poor old Ma Otterbourne came along. We'll ask him again.'

'Presently. First, I have someone else to whom I wish to speak.'

'Who's that?'

'Tim Allerton.'

Race raised his eyebrows.

'Allerton? Well, we'll get him here.'

He pressed a bell and sent the steward with a message.

Tim Allerton entered with a questioning look.

'Steward said you wanted to see me?'

'That is right, Monsieur Allerton. Sit down.'

Tim sat. His face was attentive but very slightly bored.

'Anything I can do?' His tone was polite but not enthusiastic.

Poirot said: 'In a sense, perhaps. What I really require is for you to listen.'

Tim's eyebrows rose in polite surprise.

'Certainly. I'm the world's best listener. Can be relied on to say "Oo-er!" at the right moments.'

'That is very satisfactory. "Oo-er!" will be very expressive. *Eh bien*, let us commence. When I met you and your mother at Assuan, Monsieur Allerton, I was attracted to your company very strongly. To begin with, I thought your mother was one of the most charming people I had ever met—'

The weary face flickered for a moment; a shade of expression came into it.

'She is – unique,' he said.

'But the second thing that interested me was your mention of a certain lady.'

'Really?'

'Yes, a Mademoiselle Joanna Southwood. You see, I had recently been hearing that name.'

He paused and went on: 'For the last three years there have been certain jewel robberies that have been worrying Scotland Yard a good deal. They are what may be described as Society robberies. The method is usually the same – the substitution of an imitation piece of jewellery for an original. My friend, Chief Inspector Japp, came to the conclusion that the robberies were not the work of one person, but of two people working in with each other very cleverly. He was convinced, from the considerable inside knowledge displayed, that the robberies were the work of people in a good social position. And finally his attention became riveted on Mademoiselle Joanna Southwood.

'Every one of the victims had been either a friend or acquaintance of hers, and in each case she had either handled or been lent the piece of jewellery in question. Also, her style of living was far in excess of her income. On the other hand it was quite clear that the actual robbery – that is to say the substitution – had *not* been accomplished by her. In some cases she had been out of England during the period when the jewellery must have been replaced.

'So gradually a little picture grew up in Chief Inspector Japp's mind. Mademoiselle Southwood was at one time associated with a Guild of Modern Jewellery. He suspected that she handled the jewels in question, made accurate drawings of them, got them copied by some humble but dishonest working jeweller and that the third part of the operation was the successful substitution by another person – somebody who could have been proved never to have handled the jewels and never to have had anything to do with copies or imitations of precious stones. Of the identity of this other person Japp was ignorant.

'Certain things that fell from you in conversation interested me. A ring that disappeared when you were in Majorca, the fact that you had been in a house-party where one of these fake substitutions had occurred, your close association with Mademoiselle Southwood. There was also the fact that you obviously resented my presence and tried to get your mother to be less friendly towards me. That might, of course, have been just personal dislike, but I thought not. You were too anxious to try and hide your distaste under a genial manner.

'*Eh bien*! after the murder of Linnet Doyle, it is discovered that her pearls are missing. You comprehend, at once I think of you! But I am not quite satisfied. For if you are working, as I suspect, with Mademoiselle Southwood (who was an intimate friend of Madame Doyle's), then substitution would be the method employed – not barefaced theft. But then, the pearls quite unexpectedly are returned, and what do I discover? That they are not genuine, but imitation.

'I know then who the real thief is. It was the imitation string which was stolen and returned – an imitation which you had previously substituted for the real necklace.'

He looked at the young man in front of him. Tim was white under his tan. He was not so good a fighter as Pennington; his stamina was bad. He said, with an effort to sustain his mocking manner: 'Indeed? And if so, what did I do with them?'

'That I know also.'

The young man's face changed – broke up.

Poirot went on slowly: 'There is only one place where they

can be. I have reflected, and my reason tells me that that is so. Those pearls, Monsieur Allerton, are concealed in a rosary that hangs in your cabin. The beads of it are very elaborately carved. I think you had it made specially. Those beads unscrew, though you would never think so to look at them. Inside each is a pearl, stuck with Seccotine. Most police searchers respect religious symbols unless there is something obviously queer about them. You counted on that. I endeavoured to find out how Mademoiselle Southwood sent the imitation necklace out to you. She must have done so, since you came here from Majorca on hearing that Madame Doyle would be here for her honeymoon. My theory is that it was sent in a book – a square hole being cut out of the pages in the middle. A book goes with the ends open and is practically never opened in the post.'

There was a pause – a long pause. Then Tim said quietly: 'You win! It's been a good game, but it's over at last. There's nothing for it now, I suppose, but to take my medicine.'

Poirot nodded gently.

'Do you realise that you were seen that night?'

'Seen?' Tim started.

'Yes, on the night that Linnet Doyle died, someone saw you leave her cabin just after one in the morning.'

Tim said: 'Look here – you aren't thinking . . . It wasn't I who killed her! I'll swear that! I've been in the most awful stew. To have chosen that night of all others . . . God, it's been awful!'

Poirot said: 'Yes, you must have had uneasy moments. But, now that the truth has come out, you may be able to help us. Was Madame Doyle alive or dead when you stole the pearls?'

'I don't know,' Tim said hoarsely. 'Honest to God, Monsieur Poirot, I don't know! I'd found out where she put them at night – on the little table by the bed. I crept in, felt very softly on the table and grabbed 'em, put down the others and crept out again. I assumed, of course, that she was asleep.'

'Did you hear her breathing? Surely you would have listened for that?'

Tim thought earnestly.

'It was very still – very still indeed. No, I can't remember actually hearing her breathe.'

'Was there any smell of smoke lingering in the air, as there would have been if a firearm had been discharged recently?'

'I don't think so. I don't remember it.'

Poirot sighed.

'Then we are no further.'

Tim asked curiously, 'Who was it saw me?'

'Rosalie Otterbourne. She came round from the other side of the boat and saw you leave Linnet Doyle's cabin and go to your own.'

'So it was she who told you.'

Poirot said gently, 'Excuse me; she did not tell me.'

'But then, how do you know?'

'Because I am Hercule Poirot I do not need to be told. When I taxed her with it, do you know what she said? She said: "I saw nobody." And she lied.'

'But why?'

Poirot said in a detached voice: 'Perhaps because she thought the man she saw was the murderer. It looked like that, you know.'

'That seems to me all the more reason for telling you.'

Poirot shrugged his shoulders. 'She did not think so, it seems.'

Tim said, a queer note in his voice: 'She's an extraordinary sort of a girl. She must have been through a pretty rough time with that mother of hers.'

'Yes, life has not been easy for her.'

'Poor kid,' Tim muttered. Then he looked towards Race.

'Well, sir, where do we go from here? I admit taking the pearls from Linnet's cabin and you'll find them just where you say they are. I'm guilty all right. But as far as Miss Southwood is concerned, I'm not admitting anything. You've no evidence whatever against her. How I got hold of the fake necklace is my own business.'

Poirot murmured: 'A very correct attitude.'

Tim said with a flash of humour: 'Always the gentleman!' He added: 'Perhaps you can imagine how annoying it was to me to find my mother cottoning on to you! I'm not a sufficiently hardened criminal to enjoy sitting cheek by jowl with a successful detective just before bringing off a rather risky coup! Some people might get a kick out of it. I didn't. Frankly, it gave me cold feet.'

'But it did not deter you from making your attempt?'

Tim shrugged his shoulders.

'I couldn't funk it to that extent. The exchange had to be made sometime and I'd got a unique opportunity on this boat – a cabin only two doors off, and Linnet herself so preoccupied with her own troubles that she wasn't likely to detect the change.'

'I wonder if that was so—'

Tim looked up sharply. 'What do you mean?'

Poirot pressed the bell. 'I am going to ask Miss Ootterbourne if she will come here for a minute.'

Tim frowned but said nothing. A steward came, received the order and went away with the message.

Rosalie came after a few minutes. Her eyes, reddened with recent weeping, widened a little at seeing Tim, but her old attitude of suspicion and defiance seemed entirely absent. She sat down and with a new docility looked from Race to Poirot.

'We're very sorry to bother you, Miss Otterbourne,' said Race gently. He was slightly annoyed with Poirot.

'It doesn't matter,' the girl said in a low voice.

Poirot said: 'It is necessary to clear up one or two points. When I asked you whether you saw anyone on the starboard deck at one-ten this morning, your answer was that you saw nobody. Fortunately I have been able to arrive at the truth without your help. Monsieur Allerton has admitted that he was in Linnet Doyle's cabin last night.'

She flashed a swift glance at Tim. Tim, his face grim and set, gave a curt nod.

'The time is correct, Monsieur Allerton?'

Allerton replied, 'Quite correct.'

Rosalie was staring at him. Her lips trembled – fell apart.

. . .

'But you didn't – you didn't—'

He said quickly: 'No, I didn't kill her. I'm a thief, not a murderer. It's all going to come out, so you might as well know. I was after her pearls.'

Poirot said, 'Mr Allerton's story is that he went to her cabin last night and exchanged a string of fake pearls for the real ones.'

'Did you?' asked Rosalie. Her eyes, grave, sad, child-like, questioned his.

'Yes,' said Tim.

There was a pause. Colonel Race shifted restlessly.

Poirot said in a curious voice: 'That, as I say, is Monsieur Allerton's story, partially confirmed by your evidence. That is to say, there is evidence that he did visit Linnet Doyle's cabin last night, but there is no evidence to show why he did so.'

Tim stared at him. 'But you know!'

'What do I know?'

'Well – you know I've got the pearls.'

'*Mais oui – mais oui*! I know you have the pearls, but I do not know when you got them. It may have been *before* last night. . . . You said just now that Linnet Doyle would not have noticed the substitution. I am not so sure of that. Supposing she *did* notice it. . . . Supposing, even, she knew who did it. . . . Supposing that last night she threatened to expose the whole business, and that you knew she meant to do so . . . and supposing that you overheard the scene in the saloon between Jacqueline de Bellefort and Simon Doyle and, as soon as the saloon was empty, you slipped in and secured the pistol, and then, an hour later, when the boat had quieted down, you crept along to Linnet Doyle's cabin and made quite sure that no exposure would come. . . .'

'My God!' said Tim. Out of his ashen face, two tortured, agonised eyes gazed dumbly at Hercule Poirot.

The latter went on: 'But somebody else saw you – the girl Louise. The next day she came to you and blackmailed you. You must pay her handsomely or she would tell what she knew. You realised that to submit to blackmail would be the beginning of the end. You pretended to agree, made an appointment to come to her cabin just before lunch with the money. Then, when she was counting the notes, you stabbed her.

'But again luck was against you. Somebody saw you go to her cabin' – he half turned to Rosalie – 'your mother. Once again you had to act – dangerously, foolhardily – but it was the only chance. You had heard Pennington talk about his revolver. You rushed into his cabin, got hold of it, listened outside Dr Bessner's cabin door and shot Madame Otterbourne before she could reveal your name.'

'No-o!' cried Rosalie. 'He didn't! He didn't!'

'After that, you did the only thing you could do – rushed round the stern. And when I rushed after you, you had turned and pretended to be coming in the *opposite* direction. You had handled the revolver in gloves; those gloves were in your pocket when I asked for them. . . .'

Tim said, 'Before God, I swear it isn't true – not a word of it.' But his voice, ill-assured and trembling, failed to convince.

It was then that Rosalie Otterbourne surprised them.

'Of course it isn't true! And Monsieur Poirot knows it isn't! He's saying it for some reason of his own.'

Poirot looked at her. A faint smile came to his lips. He spread out his hands in token surrender.

'Mademoiselle is too clever. . . . But you agree – it was a good case?'

'What the devil—' Tim began with rising anger, but Poirot held up a hand.

'There is a very good case against you, Monsieur Allerton. I wanted you to realise that. Now I will tell you something more pleasant. I have not yet examined that rosary in your cabin. It may be that, when I do, I shall find nothing there. And then, since Mademoiselle Otterbourne sticks to it that she saw no one on the deck last night, *eh bien*! there is no case against you at all. The pearls were taken by a klepto-maniac who has since returned them. They are in a little box on the table by the door, if you would like to examine them with Mademoiselle.'

Tim got up. He stood for a moment unable to speak. When he did, his words seemed inadequate, but it is possible that they satisfied his listeners.

'Thanks!' he said. 'You won't have to give me another chance!'

He held the door open for the girl; she passed out and, picking up the little cardboard box, he followed her.

Side by side they went. Tim opened the box, took out the sham string of pearls and hurled it far from him into the Nile.

'There!' he said. 'That's gone. When I return the box to Poirot the real string will be in it. What a damned fool I've been!'

Rosalie said in a low voice: 'Why did you come to do it in the first place?'

'How did I come to start, do you mean? Oh, I don't know. Boredom – laziness – the fun of the thing. Such a much more attractive way of earning a living that just pegging away at a job. Sounds pretty sordid to you, I expect, but you know there was an attraction about it – mainly the risk, I suppose.'

'I think I understand.'

'Yes, but you wouldn't ever do it.'

Rosalie considered for a moment or two, her grave young head bent.

'No,' she said simply. 'I wouldn't.'

He said: 'Oh, my dear – you're so lovely . . . so utterly lovely. Why wouldn't you say you'd seen me last night?'

'I thought – they might suspect you,' Rosalie said.

'Did you suspect me?'

'No. I couldn't believe that you'd kill anyone.'

'No. I'm not the strong stuff murderers are made of. I'm only a miserable sneak-thief.'

She put out a timid hand and touched his arm.

'Don't say that.'

He caught her hand in his.

'Rosalie, would you – you know what I mean? Or would you always despise me and throw it in my teeth?'

She smiled faintly: 'There are things you could throw in my teeth, too. . . .'

'Rosalie – darling. . . .'

But she held back a minute longer.

'This – Joanna?'

Tim gave a sudden shout.

'Joanna? You're as bad as Mother. I don't care a damn about Joanna. She's got a face like a horse and a predatory eye. A most unattractive female.'

Presently Rosalie said: 'Your mother need never know about you.'

'I'm not sure,' Tim said thoughtfully. 'I think I shall tell her. Mother's got plenty of stuffing, you know. She can stand up to things. Yes, I think I shall shatter her maternal illusions about me. She'll be so relieved to know that my relations with Joanna were purely of a business nature that she'll forgive me everything else.'

They had come to Mrs Allerton's cabin and Tim knocked firmly on the door. It opened and Mrs Allerton stood on the threshold.

'Rosalie and I—' began Tim. He paused.

'Oh, my dears,' said Mrs Allerton. She folded Rosalie in her arms. 'My dear, dear child. I always hoped – but Tim was so tiresome – and pretended he didn't like you. But of course I saw through *that*!'

Rosalie said in a broken voice: 'You've been so sweet to me – always. I used to wish – to wish—'

She broke off and sobbed happily on Mrs Allerton's shoulder.

As the door closed behind Tim and Rosalie, Poirot looked somewhat apologetically at Colonel Race. The Colonel was looking rather grim.

'You will consent to my little arrangement, yes?' Poirot pleaded. 'It is irregular – I know it is irregular, yes – but I have a high regard for human happiness.'

'You've none for mine,' said Race.

'That *jeune fille*. I have a tenderness towards her, and she loves that young man. It will be an excellent match; she has the stiffening he needs; the mother likes her; everything is thoroughly suitable.'

'In fact the marriage has been arranged by heaven and Hercule Poirot. All I have to do is to compound a felony.'

'But, *mon ami*, I told you, it was all conjecture on my part.' Race grinned suddenly.

'It's all right by me,' he said. 'I'm not a damned policeman, thank God! I daresay the young fool will go straight enough now. The girl's straight all right. No, what I'm complaining of is your treatment of *me*! I'm a patient man, but there are limits to my patience! *Do* you know who committed the three murders on this boat or *don't* you?'

'I do.'

'Then why all this beating about the bush?'

'You think that I am just amusing myself with side issues? And it annoys you? But it is not that. Once I went professionally to an archaeological expedition – and I learnt something there. In the course of an excavation, when something comes up out of the ground, everything is cleared away very carefully all around it. You take away the loose earth, and you scrape here and there with a knife until finally your object is there, all alone, ready to be drawn and photographed with no extraneous matter confusing it. That is what I have been seeking to do – clear away the extraneous matter so that we can see the truth – the naked shining truth.'

'Good,' said Race. 'Let's have this naked shining truth. It wasn't Pennington. It wasn't young Allerton. I presume it wasn't Fleetwood. Let's hear who it was for a change.'

'My friend, I am just about to tell you.

There was a knock on the door. Race uttered a muffled

curse. It was Dr Bessner and Cornelia. The latter was looking upset.

'Oh, Colonel Race,' she exclaimed, 'Miss Bowers has just told me about Cousin Marie. It's been the most dreadful shock. She said she couldn't bear the responsibility all by herself any longer, and that I'd better know, as I was one of the family. I just couldn't believe it at first, but Dr Bessner here has been just wonderful.'

'No, no,' protested the doctor modestly.

'He's been so kind, explaining it all, and how people really can't help it. He's had kleptomaniacs in his clinic. And he's explained to me how it's very often due to a deep-seated neurosis.'

Cornelia repeated the words with awe.

'It's planted very deeply in the subconscious; sometimes it's just some little thing that happened when you were a child. And he's cured people by getting them to think back and remember what that little thing was.'

Cornelia paused, drew a deep breath, and started off again.

'But it's worrying me dreadfully in case it all gets out. It would be too, too terrible in New York. Why, all the tabloids would have it. Cousin Marie and Mother and everybody – they'd never hold up their heads again.'

Race sighed. 'That's all right,' he said. 'This is Hush Hush House.'

'I beg your pardon, Colonel Race?'

'What I was endeavouring to say was that anything short of murder is being hushed up.'

'Oh!' Cornelia clasped her hands. 'I'm *so* relieved. I've just been worrying and worrying.'

'You have the heart too tender,' said Dr Bessner, and patted her benevolently on the shoulder. He said to the others: 'She has a very sensitive and beautiful nature.'

'Oh, I haven't really. You're too kind.'

Poirot murmured, 'Have you seen any more of Mr Ferguson?'

Cornelia blushed.

'No – but Cousin Marie's been talking about him.'

'It seems the young man is highly born,' said Dr Bessner. 'I must confess he does not look it. His clothes are terrible. Not for a moment does he appear a well-bred man.'

'And what do you think, Mademoiselle?'

'I think he must be just plain crazy,' said Cornelia.

Poirot turned to the doctor. 'How is your patient?'

'Ach, he is going on splendidly. I have just reassured the
Fräulein de Bellefort. Would you believe it, I found her in
despair. Just because the fellow had a bit of a temperature
this afternoon! But what could be more natural? It is amazing
that he is not in a high fever now. But no, he is like some of
our peasants; he has a magnificent constitution, the constitution of an ox. I have seen them with deep wounds that they
hardly notice. It is the same with Mr Doyle. His pulse is steady,
his temperature only slightly above normal. I was able to pooh-
pooh the little lady's fears. All the same, it is ridiculous, *nicht
wahr*? One minute you shoot a man; the next you are in
hysterics in case he may not be doing well.'

Cornelia said: 'She loves him terribly, you see.'

'Ach! but it is not sensible, that. If *you* loved a man, would
you try and shoot him? No, you are sensible.'

'I don't like things that go off with bangs anyway,' said
Cornelia.

'Naturally you do not. You are very feminine.'

Race interrupted this scene of heavy approval. 'Since Doyle
is all right there's no reason I shouldn't come along and resume
our talk of this afternoon. He was just telling me about a telegram.'

Dr Bessner's bulk moved up and down appreciatively.

'Ho, ho, ho, it was very funny that! Doyle, he tells me about
it. It was a telegram all about vegetables – potatoes, artichokes,
leeks – Ach! pardon?'

With a stifled exclamation, Race had sat up in his chair.

'My God,' he said. 'So that's it! Richetti!'

He looked round on three uncomprehending faces.

'A new code – it was used in the South African rebellion.
Potatoes mean machine guns, artichokes are high explosives –
and so on. Richetti is no more an archaeologist than I am!
He's a very dangerous agitator, a man who's killed more than
once, and I'll swear that he's killed once again. Mrs Doyle
opened that telegram by mistake, you see. If she were ever to
repeat what was in it before me, he knew his goose would be
cooked!'

He turned to Poirot. 'Am I right?' he asked. 'Is Richetti the
man?'

'He is *your* man,' said Poirot 'I always thought there was
something wrong about him. He was almost too word-perfect
in his rôle; he was an archaeologist, not enough human being.'

He paused and then said: 'But it was not Richetti who
killed Linnet Doyle. For some time now I have known what

I may express as the "first half" of the murderer. Now I know the "second half" also. The picture is complete. But you understand that, although I know what must have happened, I have no proof that it happened. Intellectually the case is satisfying. Actually it is profoundly unsatisfactory. There is only one hope – a confession from the murderer.'

Dr Bessner raised his shoulders sceptically. 'Ah! but that – it would be a miracle.'

'I think not. Not under the circumstances.'

Cornelia cried out: 'But who is it? Aren't you going to tell us?'

Poirot's eyes ranged quietly over the three of them. Race, smiling sardonically, Bessner, still looking sceptical, Cornelia, her mouth hanging a little open, gazing at him with eager eyes.

'*Mais oui*,' he said. 'I like an audience, I must confess. I am vain, you see. I am puffed up with conceit. I like to say: "See how clever is Hercule Poirot!"'

Race shifted a little in his chair.

'Well,' he asked gently, 'just how clever *is* Hercule Poirot?'

Shaking his head sadly from side to side Poirot said: 'To begin with I was stupid – incredibly stupid. To me the stumbling block was the pistol – Jacqueline de Bellefort's pistol. Why had that pistol not been left on the scene of the crime? The idea of the murderer was quite plainly to incriminate her. Why then did the murderer take it away? I was so stupid that I thought of all sorts of fantastic reasons. The real one was very simple. The murderer took it away because he *had* to take it away – because he had no choice in the matter.'

—— 29 ——

'You and I, my friend,' Poirot leaned towards Race, 'started our investigation with a preconceived idea. That idea was that the crime was committed on the spur of the moment, without any preliminary planning. Somebody wished to remove Linnet Doyle and had seized their opportunity to do so at a moment when the crime would almost certainly be attributed to Jacqueline de Bellefort. It therefore followed that the person in question had overheard the scene between Jacqueline and

Simon Doyle and had obtained possession of the pistol after
the others had left the saloon.

'But, my friends, if that preconceived idea was wrong, the
whole aspect of the case altered. And it *was* wrong! This was
no spontaneous crime committed on the spur of the moment.
It was, on the contrary, very carefully planned and accurately
timed, with all the details meticulously worked out beforehand, to the drugging of Hercule Poirot's bottle of wine on the
night in question!

'But, yes, that is so! I was put to sleep so that there should
be no possibility of my participating in the events of the night.
It did just occur to me as a possibility. I drink wine; my two
companions at table drink whisky and mineral water respec-
tively. Nothing easier than to slip a dose of harmless narcotic
into my bottle of wine – the bottles stand on the table all day.
But I dismissed the thought. It had been a hot day; I had been
unusually tired; it was not really extraordinary that I should
for once have slept heavily instead of lightly as I usually do.

'You see, I was still in the grip of the preconceived idea. If
I had been drugged, that would have implied premeditation,
it would mean that before seven-thirty, when dinner is served,
the crime had already been decided upon; and that (always
from the point of view of the preconceived idea) was absurd.

'The first blow to the preconceived idea was when the pistol
was recovered from the Nile. To begin with, if we were right
in our assumptions, the pistol ought never to have been thrown
overboard at all. . . . And there was more to follow.'

Poirot turned to Dr Bessner.

'You, Dr Bessner, examined Linnet Doyle's body. You will
remember that the wound showed signs of scorching – that is
to say, that the pistol had been placed close against the head
before being fired.'

Bessner nodded. 'So. That is exact.'

'But when the pistol was found it was wrapped in a velvet
stole, and that velvet showed definite signs that a pistol had
been fired through its folds, presumably under the impression
that that would deaden the sound of the shot. But if the pistol
had been fired through the velvet, there would have been no
signs of burning on the victim's skin. Therefore, the shot fired
through the stole could not have been the shot that killed
Linnet Doyle. Could it have been the other shot – the one fired
by Jacqueline de Bellefort at Simon Doyle? Again no, for
there had been two witnesses of that shooting, and we knew
all about it. It appeared, therefore, as though a *third* shot had

been fired – one we knew nothing about. But only two shots had been fired from the pistol, and there was no hint or suggestion of another shot.

'Here we were face to face with a very curious unexplained circumstance. The next interesting point was the fact that in Linnet Doyle's cabin I found two bottles of coloured nail polish. Now ladies very often vary the colour of their nails, but so far Linnet Doyle's nails had always been the shade called Cardinal – a deep dark red. The other bottle was labelled Rose, which is a shade of pale pink, but the few drops remaining in the bottle were not pale pink but a bright red. I was sufficiently curious to take out the stopper and sniff. Instead of the usual strong odour of peardrops, the bottle smelt of vinegar! That is to say, it suggested that the drop or two of fluid in it was red ink. Now there is no reason why Madame Doyle should not have had a bottle of red ink, but it would have been more natural if she had had red ink in a red ink bottle and not in a nail-polish bottle. It suggested a link with the faintly stained handkerchief which had been wrapped round the pistol. Red ink washes out quickly but always leaves a pale pink stain.

'I should perhaps have arrived at the truth with these slender indications, but an event occurred which rendered all doubt superfluous. Louise Bourget was killed in circumstances which pointed unmistakably to the fact that she had been blackmailing the murderer. Not only was a fragment of a *mille* franc note still clasped in her hand, but I remember some very significant words she had used this morning.

'Listen carefully, for here is the crux of the whole matter. When I asked her if she had seen anything the previous night she gave this very curious answer: "Naturally, if I have been unable to sleep, if I had mounted the stairs, *then* perhaps I might have seen this assassin, this monster enter or leave Madame's cabin. . . ." Now what exactly did that tell us?'

Bessner, his nose wrinkling with intellectual interest, replied promptly: 'It told you that she *had* mounted the stairs.'

'No, no; you fail to see the point. Why should she have said that, to *us*?'

'To convey a hint.'

'But why *hint* to us? If she knows who the murderer is, there are two courses open to her – to tell us the truth, or to hold her tongue and demand money for her silence from the person concerned! But she does neither. She neither says promptly: "I saw nobody. I was asleep." Nor does she say:

"Yes, I saw someone, and it was so and so." Why use that significant indeterminate rigmarole of words? *Parbleu,* there can be only one reason! She is hinting to the murderer; therefore the murderer must have been present at the time. But, besides myself and Colonel Race, only two people were present – Simon Doyle and Dr Bessner.'

The doctor sprang up with a roar.

'Ach! what is that you say? You accuse me? Again? But it is ridiculous – beneath contempt.'

Poirot said sharply: 'Be quiet. I am telling you what I thought at the time. Let us remain impersonal.'

'He doesn't mean he thinks it's you now,' said Cornelia soothingly.

Poirot went on quickly: 'So it lay there – between Simon Doyle and Dr Bessner. But what reason has Bessner to kill Linnet Doyle? None, so far as I know. Simon Doyle, then? But that was impossible! There were plenty of witnesses who could swear that Doyle never left the saloon that evening until the quarrel broke out. After that he was wounded and it would then have been physically impossible for him to have done so. Had I good evidence on both those points? Yes, I had the evidence of Mademoiselle Robson, of Jim Fanthorp, and of Jacqueline de Bellefort as to the first, and I had the skilled testimony of Dr Bessner and of Mademoiselle Bowers as to the other. No doubt was possible.

'So Dr Bessner *must* be the guilty one. In favour of this theory there was the fact that the maid had been stabbed with a surgical knife. On the other hand Bessner had deliberately called attention to this fact.

'And then, my friends, a second perfectly indisputable fact became apparent to me. Louise Bourget's hint could not have been intended for Dr Bessner, because she could perfectly well have spoken to him in private at any time she liked. There was one person, *and one person only*, who corresponded to her necessity – Simon Doyle! Simon Doyle was wounded, was constantly attended by a doctor, was in that doctor's cabin. It was to him therefore that she risked saying those ambiguous words, in case she might not get another chance. And I remember how she had gone on, turning to him: "Monsieur, I implore you – you see how it is? What can I say?" And this answer: "My good girl, don't be a fool. Nobody thinks you saw or heard anything. You'll be quite all right. I'll look after you. Nobody's accusing you of anything." That was the assurance she wanted, and she got it!

Bessner uttered a colossal snort.

'Ach! it is foolish, that! Do you think a man with a fractured bone and a splint on his leg could go walking about the
boat and stabbing people? I tell you, it was *impossible* for
Simon Doyle to leave his cabin.'

Poirot said gently: 'I know. That is quite true. The thing
was impossible. It was impossible, but it was also true! There
could be only one logical meaning behind Louise Bourget's
words.'

'So I returned to the beginning and reviewed the crime in
the light of this new knowledge. Was it possible that in the
period preceding the quarrel Simon Doyle had left the saloon
and the others had forgotten or not noticed it? I could not
see that that was possible. Could the skilled testimony of Dr
Bessner and Mademoiselle Bowers be disregarded? Again I
felt sure it could not. But, I remembered, there was a gap
between the two. Simon Doyle had been alone in the saloon
for a period of five minutes, and the skilled testimony of Dr
Bessner only applied to the time after that period. For that
period we had only the evidence of visual appearance, and,
though apparently that was perfectly sound, it was no longer
certain. What had actually been *seen* – leaving assumption out
of the question?

'Mademoiselle Robson had seen Mademoiselle de Bellefort
fire her pistol, had seen Simon Doyle collapse on to a chair,
had seen him clasp a handkerchief to his leg and seen that
handkerchief gradually soak through red. What had Monsieur
Fanthorp heard and seen? He heard a shot, he found Doyle
with a red-stained handkerchief clasped to his leg. What had
happened then? Doyle had been very insistent that Mademoiselle de Bellefort should be got away, that she should not be
left alone. After that, he suggested that Fanthorp should get
hold of the doctor.

'Accordingly Mademoiselle Robson and Monsieur Fanthorp
got out with Mademoiselle de Bellefort and for the next five
minutes they are busy, on the port side of the deck. Mademoiselle Bowers', Dr Bessner's and Mademoiselle de Bellefort's
cabins are all on the port side. Two minutes are all that Simon
Doyle needs. He picks up the pistol from under the sofa, slips
out of his shoes, runs like a hare silently along the starboard
deck, enters his wife's cabin, creeps up to her as she lies asleep,
shoots her through the head, puts the bottle that has contained
the red ink on her washstand (it mustn't be found on him),
runs back, gets hold of Mademoiselle Van Schuyler's velvet

stole, which he has quietly stuffed down the side of a chair in readiness, muffles it round the pistol and fires a bullet into his leg. His chair into which he falls (in genuine agony this time) is by a window. He lifts the window and throws the pistol (wrapped up with the tell-tale handkerchief in the velvet stole) into the Nile.'

'Impossible!' said Race.

'No, my friend, not *impossible*. Remember the evidence of Tim Allerton. He heard a plop – *followed* by a splash. And he heard something else – the footsteps of a man running – a man running past his door. But nobody could have been running along the starboard side of the deck. What he heard was the stockinged feet of Simon Doyle running past his cabin.'

Race said: 'I still say it's impossible. No man could work out the whole caboodle like that in a flash – especially a chap like Doyle who is slow in his mental processes.'

'But very quick and deft in his physical actions!'

'That, yes. But he wouldn't be capable of thinking the whole thing out.'

'But he did not think it out himself, my friend. That is where we were all wrong. It looked like a crime committed on the spur of the moment, but it was *not* a crime committed on the spur of the moment. As I say, it was a very cleverly planned and well thought out piece of work. It could not be *chance* that Simon Doyle had a bottle of red ink in his pocket. No, it must be *design*. It was not *chance* that he had a plain unmarked handkerchief with him. It was not *chance* that Jacqueline de Bellefort's foot kicked the pistol under the settee, where it would be out of sight and unremembered until later.'

'Jacqueline?'

'Certainly. The two halves of the murder. What gave Simon his alibi? The shot fired by Jacqueline. What gave Jacqueline *her* alibi? The insistence of Simon which resulted in a hospital nurse remaining with her all night. There, between the two of them, you get all the qualities you require – the cool, resourceful, planning brain, Jacqueline de Bellefort's brain, and the man of action to carry it out with incredible swiftness and timing.'

'Look at it the right way, and it answers every question. Simon Doyle and Jacqueline had been lovers. Realise that they are still lovers, and it is all clear. Simon does away with his rich wife, inherits her money, and in due course will marry his old love. It was all very ingenious. The persecution of Madame Doyle by Jacqueline, all part of the plan. Simon's pretended rage. . . . And yet – there were lapses. He held forth to me about possessive women – held forth with real bitterness. It ought to have been clear to me that it was his wife he was thinking about – not Jacqueline. Then his manner to his wife in public. An ordinary, inarticulate Englishman, such as Simon Doyle, is very embarrassed at showing any affection. Simon was not a really good actor. He overdid the devoted manner. That conversation I had with Mademoiselle Jacqueline, too, when she pretended that somebody had overheard, *I* saw no one. And there *was* no one! But it was to be a useful red herring later. Then one night on this boat I thought I heard Simon and Linnet outside my cabin. He was saying, "We've got to go through with it now." It was Doyle all right, but it was to Jacqueline he was speaking.

'The final drama was perfectly planned and timed. There was a sleeping draught for me, in case I might put an inconvenient finger in the pie. There was the selection of Mademoiselle Robson as a witness – the working up of the scene, Mademoiselle de Bellefort's exaggerated remorse and hysterics. She made a good deal of noise in case the shot should be heard. *En vérité*, it was an extraordinary clever idea. Jacqueline says she has shot Doyle; Mademoiselle Robson says so; Fanthorp says so – and when Simon's leg is examined he *has* been shot. It looks unanswerable! For both of them there is a perfect alibi – at the cost, it is true, of a certain amount of pain and risk to Simon Doyle, but it is necessary that his wound should definitely disable him.

'And then the plan goes wrong. Louise Bourget has been wakeful. She has come up the stairway and she has seen Simon Doyle run along to his wife's cabin and come back. Easy enough to piece together what has happened the following day. And so she makes her greedy bid for hush money, and in so doing signs her death warrant.'

'But Mr Doyle couldn't have killed *her*?' Cornelia objected.

'No, the other partner did that murder. As soon as he can, Simon Doyle asks to see Jacqueline. He even asks me to leave them alone together. He tells her then of the new danger. They must act at once. He knows where Bessner's scalpels are kept. After the crime the scalpel is wiped and returned, and then, very late and rather out of breath, Jacqueline de Bellefort hurries in to lunch.

'And still all is not well, for Madame Otterbourne has seen Jacqueline go into Louise Bourget's cabin. And she comes hotfoot to tell Simon about it. Jacqueline is the murderess. Do you remember how Simon shouted at the poor woman? Nerves, we thought. But the door was open and he was trying to convey the danger to his accomplice. She heard and she acted – acted like lightning. She remembered Pennington had talked about a revolver. She got hold of it, crept up outside the door, listened and, at the critical moment, fired. She boasted once that she was a good shot, and her boast was not an idle one.

'I remarked after the third crime that there were three ways the murderer could have gone. I meant that he could have gone aft (in which case Tim Allerton was the criminal), he could have gone over the side (very improbable) or he could have gone into a cabin. Jacqueline's cabin was just two away from Dr Bessner's. She had only to throw down the revolver, bolt into the cabin, ruffle her hair and fling herself down on the bunk. It was risky, but it was the only possible chance.'

There was a silence, then Race asked: 'What happened to the first bullet fired at Doyle by the girl?'

'I think it went into the table. There is a recently made hole there. I think Doyle had time to dig it out with a penknife and fling it through the window. He had, of course, a spare cartridge, so that it would appear that only two shots had been fired.'

Cornelia sighed. 'They thought of everything,' she said. 'It's – horrible!'

Poirot was silent. But it was not a modest silence. His eyes seemed to be saying: 'You are wrong. They didn't allow for Hercule Poirot.'

Aloud he said, 'And now, Doctor, we will go and have a word with your patient.'

—— 30 ——

It was very much later that evening that Hercule Poirot came and knocked on the door of a cabin.

A voice said 'Come in' and he entered.

Jacqueline de Bellefort was sitting in a chair. In another chair, close against the wall, sat the big stewardess.

Jacqueline's eyes surveyed Poirot thoughtfully. She made a gesture towards the stewardess.

'Can she go?'

Poirot nodded to the woman and she went out. Poirot drew up her chair and sat down near Jacqueline. Neither of them spoke. Poirot's face was unhappy.

In the end it was the girl who spoke first.

'Well,' she said, 'it is all over! You were too clever for us, Monsieur Poirot.'

Poirot sighed. He spread out his hands. He seemed strangely dumb.

'All the same,' said Jacqueline reflectively, 'I can't really see that you had much proof. You were quite right, of course, but if we'd bluffed you out—'

'In no other way, Mademoiselle, could the thing have happened.'

'That's proof enough for a logical mind, but I don't believe it would have convinced a jury. Oh, well – it can't be helped. You sprang it all on Simon, and he went down like a ninepin. He just lost his head utterly, poor lamb, and admitted everything.' She shook her head. 'He's a bad loser.'

'But you, Mademoiselle, are a good loser.'

She laughed suddenly – a queer, gay, defiant little laugh.

'Oh, yes, I'm a good loser all right.' She looked at him.

She said suddenly and impulsively: 'Don't mind so much, Monsieur Poirot! About me, I mean. You do mind, don't you?'

'Yes, Mademoiselle.'

'But it wouldn't have occurred to you to let me off?'

Hercule Poirot said quietly, 'No.'

She nodded her head in quiet agreement.

'No, it's no use being sentimental. I might do it again. . . . I'm not a safe person any longer. I can feel that myself. . . .' She went on broodingly: 'It's so dreadfully easy – killing people. And you begin to feel that it doesn't matter . . . that it's only *you* that matters! It's dangerous – that.'

She paused, then said with a little smile: 'You did your best for me, you know. That night at Assuan – you told me not to open my heart to evil. . . . Did you realise then what was in my mind?'

He shook his head.

'I only knew that what I said was true.'

'It was true. I could have stopped, then, you know. I nearly did. . . . I could have told Simon that I wouldn't go on with it. . . . But then perhaps—'

She broke off. She said: 'Would you like to hear about it? From the beginning?'

'If you care to tell me, Mademoiselle.'

'I think I want to tell you. It was all very simple really. You see, Simon and I loved each other. . . .'

It was a matter-of-fact statement, yet, underneath the lightness of her tone, there were echoes. . . .

Poirot said simply: 'And for you love would have been enough, but not for him.'

'You might put it that way, perhaps. But you don't quite understand Simon. You see, he's always wanted money so dreadfully. He likes all the things you get with money – horses and yachts and sport – nice things all of them, things a man ought to be keen about. And he'd never ben able to have any of them. He's awfully simple, Simon is. He wants things just as a child wants them – you know – terribly.

'All the same he never tried to marry anybody rich and horrid. He wasn't that sort. And then we met – and – and that sort of settled things. Only we didn't see when we'd be able to marry. He'd had rather a decent job, but he'd lost it. In a way it was his own fault. He tried to do something smart over money, and got found out at once. I don't believe he really meant to be dishonest. He just thought it was the sort of thing people did in the City.'

A flicker passed over her listener's face, but he guarded his tongue.

'There we were, up against it; and then I thought of Linnet and her new country house, and I rushed off to her. You know, Monsieur Poirot, I loved Linnet, really I did. She was my best friend, and I never dreamed that anything would ever come between us. I just thought how lucky it was she was rich. It might make all the difference to me and Simon if she'd give him a job. And she was awfully sweet about it and told me to bring Simon down to see her. It was about then you saw us that night at Chez Ma Tante. We were making whoopee, although we couldn't really afford it.'

She paused, sighed, then went on: 'What I'm going to say now is quite true, Monsieur Poirot. Even though Linnet is dead, it doesn't alter the truth. That's why I'm not really sorry about her, even now. She went all out to get Simon away from me. That's the absolute truth! I don't think she even hesitated for more than about a minute. I was her friend, but she didn't care. She just went baldheaded for Simon. . . .'

'And Simon didn't care a damn about her! I talked a lot to you about glamour, but of course that wasn't true. He didn't want Linnet. He thought her good-looking but terribly bossy, and he hated bossy women! The whole thing embarrassed him frightfully. But he did like the thought of her money.'

'Of course I saw that . . . and at last I suggested to him that it might be a good thing if he – got rid of me and married Linnet. But he scouted the idea. He said, money or no money, it would be hell to be married to her. He said his idea of having money was to have it himself – not to have a rich wife holding the purse strings. "I'd be a kind of damned Prince Consort," he said to me. He said, too, that he didn't want anyone but me. . . .

'I think I know when the idea came into his head. He said one day: "If I'd any luck, I'd marry her and she'd die in about a year and leave me all the boodle." And then a queer startled look came into his eyes. That was when he first thought of it. . . .

'He talked about it a good deal, one way and another – about how convenient it would be if Linnet died. I said it was an awful idea, and then he shut up about it. Then, one day, I found him reading up all about arsenic. I taxed him with it then, and he laughed and said: "Nothing venture, nothing have! Its about the only time in my life I shall be near to touching a fat lot of money."

'After a bit I saw that he'd made up his mind. And I was terrified – simply terrified. Because, you see, I realised that he'd never pull it off. He's so childishly simple. He'd have no kind of subtlety about it – and he's got no imagination. He would probably have just bunged arsenic into her and assumed the doctor would say she'd died of gastritis. He always thought things would go right.

'So I had to come into it, too, to look after him. . . .'

She said it very simply but in complete good faith. Poirot had no doubt whatever that her motive had been exactly what she said it was. She herself had not coveted Linnet Ridgeway's money, but she had loved Simon Doyle, had loved him beyond reason and beyond rectitude and beyond pity.

'I thought and I thought – trying to work out a plan. It seemed to me that the basis of the idea ought to be a kind of two-handed alibi. You know – if Simon and I could somehow or other give evidence against each other, but actually that evidence would clear us of anything. It would be easy enough for me to pretend to hate Simon. It was quite a likely thing to happen under the circumstances. Then, if Linnet was killed, I should probably be suspected, so it would be better if I was suspected right away. We worked out details little by little. I wanted it to be so that, if anything went wrong, they'd get me and not Simon. But Simon was worried about me.

'The only thing I was glad about was that I hadn't got to do *it*. I simply couldn't have! Not go along in cold blood and kill her when she was asleep! You see, I hadn't forgiven her – I think I could have killed her face to face, but not the other way. . . .

'We worked everything out carefully. Even then, Simon went and wrote a J in blood which was a silly melodramatic thing to do. It's just the sort of thing he *would* think of! But it went off all right.'

Poirot nodded.

'Yes. It was not your fault that Louise Bourget could not sleep that night. . . . And afterwards, Mademoiselle?

She met his eyes squarely.

'Yes,' she said 'it's rather horrible isn't it? I can't believe that I – did that! I know now what you meant by opening your heart to evil. . . . You know pretty well how it happened. Louise made it clear to Simon that she knew. Simon got you to bring me to him. As soon as we were alone together he told me what had happened. He told me what I'd got to do. I wasn't even horrified. I was so afraid – so deadly afraid. . . . That's what murder does to you. Simon and I were safe – quite safe except for this miserable blackmailing French girl. I took her all the money we could get hold of. I pretended to grovel. And then, when she was counting the money, I – did it! It was quite easy. That's what's so horribly, horribly frightening about it. . . . It's so terribly easy. . . .

'And even then we weren't safe. Mrs Otterbourne had seen me. She came triumphantly along the deck looking for you and Colonel Race. I'd no time to think. I just acted like a flash. It was almost exciting. I knew it was touch or go that time. That seemed to make it better. . . .'

She stopped again.

'Do you remember when you came into my cabin afterwards? You said you were not sure why you had come. I was so miserable – so terrified. I thought Simon was going to die. . . .'

'And I – was hoping it,' said Poirot.

Jacqueline nodded.

'Yes, it would have been better for him that way.'

'That was not my thought.'

Jacqueline looked at the sternness of his face.

She said gently: 'Don't mind so much for me, Monsieur

999

Poirot. After all, I've lived hard always, you know. If we'd won out, I'd have been very happy and enjoyed things and probably should never have regretted anything. As it is – well, one goes through with it.'

She added: 'I suppose the stewardess is in attendance to see I don't hang myself or swallow a miraculous capsule of prussic acid as people do in books. You needn't be afraid! I shan't do that. It will be easier for Simon if I'm standing by.'

Poirot got up. Jacqueline rose also. She said with a sudden smile: 'Do you remember when I said I must follow my star? You said it might be a false star. And I said: "That very bad star, that star fall down." '

He went out on to the deck with her laughter ringing in his ears.

──── 31 ────

It was early dawn when they came into Shellâl. The rocks came down grimly to the water's edge.

Poirot murmured: *'Quel pays sauvage!'*

Race stood beside him. 'Well,' he said, 'we've done our job. I've arranged for Richetti to be taken ashore first. Glad we've got him. He's been a slippery customer, I can tell you. Given us the slip dozens of times.'

He went on: 'We must get hold of a stretcher for Doyle. Remarkable how he went to pieces.'

'Not really,' said Poirot. 'That boyish type of criminal is usually intensely vain. Once prick the bubble of their self-esteem and it is finished! They go to pieces like children.'

'Deserves to be hanged,' said Race. 'He's a cold-blooded scoundrel. I'm sorry for the girl – but there's nothing to be done about it,'

Poirot shook his head.

'People say love justifies everything, but that is not true. . . . Women who care for men as Jacqueline cares for Simon Doyle are very dangerous. It is what I said when I saw her first. "She cares too much, that little one!" It is true.'

Cornelia Robson came up beside him.

'Oh,' she said, 'we're nearly in.' She paused a minute or two, then added, 'I've been with her.'

'With Mademoiselle de Bellefort?'

'Yes. I felt it was kind of awful for her boxed up with that stewardess. Cousin Marie's very angry, though, I'm afraid.'

Miss Van Schuyler was progressing slowly down the deck towards them. Her eyes were venomous.

'Cornelia,' she snapped, 'you've behaved outrageously. I shall send you straight home.'

Cornelia took a deep breath. 'I'm sorry, Cousin Marie, but I'm not going home. I'm going to get married.'

'So you've seen sense at last,' snapped the old lady.

Ferguson came striding round the corner of the deck. He said: 'Cornelia, what's this I hear? It's not true!'

'It's quite true,' said Cornelia. 'I'm going to marry Dr Bessner. He asked me last night.'

'And why are you going to marry him?' asked Ferguson furiously. 'Simply because he's rich?'

'No, I'm not,' said Cornelia indignantly. 'I like him. He's kind, and he knows a lot. And I've always been interested in sick folks and clinics, and I shall have just a wonderful life with him.'

'Do you mean to say,' asked Mr Ferguson incredulously, 'that you'd rather marry that disgusting old man than Me?'

'Yes, I would. You're not reliable! You wouldn't be at all a comfortable sort of person to live with. And he's *not* old. He's not fifty yet.'

'He's got a stomach,' said Mr Ferguson venomously.

'Well, I've got round shoulders,' retorted Cornelia. 'What one looks like doesn't matter. He says I really could help him in his work, and he's going to teach me all about neurosis.'

She moved away.

Ferguson said to Poirot: 'Do you think she really means that?'

'Certainly.'

'She prefers that pompous old bore to me?'

'Undoubtedly.'

'The girl's mad,' declared Ferguson.

Poirot's eyes twinkled.

'She is a woman of an original mind,' he said. 'It is probably the first time you have met one.'

The boat drew in to the landing-stage. A cordon had been drawn round the passengers. They had been asked to wait before disembarking.

Richetti, dark-faced and sullen, was marched ashore by two engineers.

Then, after a certain amount of delay, a stretcher was brought. Simon Doyle was carried along the deck to the gangway.

He looked a different man – cringing, frightened, all his boyish insouciance vanished.

Jacqueline de Bellefort followed. A stewardess walked beside her. She was pale but otherwise looked much as usual. She came up to the stretcher.

'Hullo, Simon!' she said.

He looked up at her quickly. The old boyish look came back to his face for a moment.

'I messed it up,' he said. 'Lost my head and admitted everything! Sorry, Jackie. I've let you down.'

She smiled at him then. 'It's all right, Simon,' she said. 'A fool's game, and we've lost. That's all.'

She stood aside. The bearers picked up the handles of the stretcher. Jacqueline bent down and tied the lace of her shoe. Then her hand went to her stocking and she straightened up with something in her hand.

There was a sharp explosive 'pop.'

Simon Doyle gave one convulsed shudder and then lay still.

Jacqueline de Bellefort nodded. She stood for a moment, pistol in hand. She gave a fleeting smile at Poirot.

Then, as Race jumped forward, she turned the little glittering toy against her heart and pressed the trigger.

She sank down in a soft huddled heap.

Race shouted: 'Where the devil did she get that pistol?'

Poirot felt a hand on his arm. Mrs Allerton said softly, 'You – knew?'

He nodded. 'She had a pair of these pistols. I realised that when I heard that one had been found in Rosalie Otterbourne's handbag the day of the search. Jacqueline sat at the same table as they did. When she realised that there was going to be a search, she slipped it into the other girl's handbag. Later she went to Rosalie's cabin and got it back, after having distracted her attention with a comparison of lipsticks. As both she and her cabin had been searched yesterday, it wasn't thought necessary to do it again.

Mrs Allerton said: 'You wanted her to take that way out?'

'Yes. But she would not take it alone. That is why Simon Doyle has died an easier death than he deserved.'

Mrs Allerton shivered. 'Love can be a frightening thing.'

'That is why most great love stories are tragedies.'

Mrs Allerton's eyes rested upon Tim and Rosalie, standing side by side in the sunlight, and she said suddenly and passionately: 'But thank God, there is happiness in the world.'

'As you say, Madame, thank God for it.'

Presently the passengers went ashore.

Later the bodies of Louise Bourget and Mrs Otterbourne were carried off the *Karnak*.

Lastly the body of Linnet Doyle was brought ashore, and all over the world wires began to hum, telling the public that Linnet Doyle, who had been Linnet Ridgeway, the famous, the beautiful, the wealthy Linnet Doyle was dead.

Sir George Wode read about it in his London club, and Sterndale Rockford in New York, and Joanna Southwood in Switzerland, and it was discussed in the bar of the Three Crowns in Malton-under-Wode.

And Mr Burnaby said acutely: 'Well, it doesn't seem to have done her much good, poor lass.'

But after a while they stopped talking about her and discussed instead who was going to win the Grand National. For, as Mr Ferguson was staying at that minute in Luxor, it is not the past that matters but the future.

THE END